READER RESPONSES

Boman Desai has dramatized the story of the Schumanns and Brahms in the form of a novel, citing their original correspondence among his sources. He has researched this most romantic of stories thoroughly, but writes so compellingly that it is like discovering the story anew. The great composers of the age make appearances when their lives intersect those of the trio, and I was glad to see that Desai presents them to us, warts and all, with the deepest sympathy and understanding. It is perhaps his greatest achievement that they appear as fullbloodedly as if they might have been his neighbors.

Zubin Mehta (Music Director: Los Angeles Philharmonic, Israel Philharmonic, New York Philharmonic)

I finished your novel, *TRIO,* and found it compelling and illuminating. As a scholar and sometime singer, I fully appreciated the immense scholarship and empathy that went into it. Would that the American (or Canadian) reading public could appreciate such a story as well told. It's a story that Tolstoy might have told in similar terms, and I do hope that it eventually gets the recognition it deserves. It is surely a tour de force.

Vernon A. Howard, PhD (Former Co-Director, Philosophy of Education Research Centre, Harvard University, *Retired*)

I loved and admired this book.

Diana Athill (Author/Editor: *Instead of a Letter, Stet, Somewhere Towards the End*)

I loved your book. You completely transported me. I read it through at a gallop. The love & feeling you have for the subject comes through – you disappeared & they appeared on the page, in the flesh, & I could *hear* their music. Congratulations.

Sooni Taraporevala (Screenwriter/Photographer: *Salaam Bombay, Mississippi Masala, Parsis*)

I had the pleasure of reading *TRIO* during the past month and enjoyed it thoroughly.

Paul Pollei (Founder/Director: Gina Bachauer International Piano Competition)

In portraying the lives and loves of the Schumanns and Brahms in his novel, *TRIO*, Boman Desai accomplishes a remarkable feat. Exhaustively researched, charming and readable, I was loath to put the novel down. Desai is a gifted writer and one doesn't have to be a connoisseur of classical music to appreciate the drama that permeates the lives of these geniuses, as they intersect the lives of the other great men of that time. It is a massive achievement and I recommend *TRIO* wholeheartedly not only to music lovers but to all those who love to read.

Bapsi Sidhwa (Author: *The Crow Eaters, Cracking India, Water*)

Boman Desai approached his sprawling novel, *TRIO*, a dramatized history of the Schumanns and Brahms, as a biography for people who hate biographies and a novel for people who hate novels. Either way, it's a work for people who love Classical music. Other composers appear either as part of the central plot or in interpolative chapters: Mendelssohn, brilliant and graceful; Liszt, resplendent in Mephistophelean glory; Wagner, the villain one loves to hate. Desai does a wonderful job describing the music. The language of *TRIO* is so vivid it makes one want to explore the composers' repertoires which get some evocative descriptions. So do the performers themselves: Clara's meticulousness, Liszt's power and bravura, Brahms's perfection at the piano as a cocky young virtuoso and sloppiness as an old man, Mendelssohn's spot-on imitations of Liszt and Chopin. Like the music, the book is meant first and foremost to be enjoyed – and on this account, it does not fail.

Chris Speck, *Quarter Notes*

TRIO

ALSO BY Boman Desai

The Memory of Elephants
Dancing About Architecture; a Songwriter's Guide to the Lennon-McCartney Catalog

TRIO

(A Novel Biography of the Schumanns and Brahms)

Boman Desai

authorHOUSE®

Boman
DESAI

AuthorHouse™
1663 Liberty Drive
Bloomington, IN 47403
www.authorhouse.com
Phone: 1 (800) 839-8640

Published by AuthorHouse 06/26/2015

ISBN: 978-1-5049-1589-2 (sc)
ISBN: 978-1-5049-1590-8 (hc)
ISBN: 978-1-5049-1588-5 (e)

Library of Congress Control Number: 2015909228

Print information available on the last page.

FOREWORD

The beginning was simple, but took me by surprise. I love Brahms's music and when I came across Paul Holmes's pictorial biography on a weekend visit to Columbus, Ohio, I bought it out of curiosity – but returning home to Chicago, merging again with the straight line of my life, I shelved the book and forgot my purchase. It wasn't until a few years later, coming across Hans Gal's book on Brahms, that I was reminded of the Holmes. I am a writer, and turning the pages of the Gal I realized that if I bought the book it would be with the intention of writing a book on Brahms myself. I realized simultaneously that if I didn't buy the book then, I would be back for it at a later date.

The decision to write the book had been as unconscious as the preparation was not. I started by reading everything I could find on the man, devouring book after book until I could predict what I would read on the next page. I soon realized that the Schumanns were a large part of the story and they became subjects of the novel no less than Brahms, leading me to book after book on the Schumanns. There was no understanding Brahms without understanding his relationship with Clara (with whom he fell in love) and Robert (who became his mentor). No less could I avoid appearances by Mendelssohn, Chopin, Liszt, and Wagner among many others when their lives intersected – and no less historic events such as the Dresden uprising, the rise of Bismarck, and the emergence of Germany as a nation when they affected their lives. Ironically, Clara became the central character, threading the narrative from beginning to end more than either Robert or Brahms. I did not know what direction the book would take when I started, but I knew I did not want to write the kind of book that propelled fictitious events into the public consciousness by exploiting the celebrity of its characters. There was no need. The historical record was dramatic enough to require no embellishment.

To that end, I researched all extant materials as thoroughly as any biographer to combine the veracity of a biography with the dramatic impact of a novel, but nothing happens in the book that might not have happened historically. I took just one liberty with the historical record (the reader will know it in the fullness of time, but I won't spoil it by mentioning it here), but when the historical record was incomplete I felt free to extrapolate what might have happened. I have also taken liberties, for instance, with the bare facts in the interest of streamlining the narrative, condensing Robert's two sojourns with the Wiecks into one, likewise the many theories regarding his death. I would like to tender apologies to the memory of Wanda Landowska who once said, "You play Bach your way and I'll play him *his* way," a sentiment I found elegant enough to appropriate for Clara in an argument with Liszt: "Well, it appears, then, Herr Liszt, that you will play Mendelssohn your way, and I will play him Mendelssohn's way."

Some might call the book a nonfiction novel, but I prefer to call it a novel biography though it is neither wholly a novel nor a biography. It has the dramatic impact of a novel, but lacks a novel's concision – and, while it may be as inclusive as any biography, I have invented dialogues, streams of consciousness, and adopted other such novelistic techniques to tell the story. I could have left out any number of episodes to make the work more compact (for instance, Brahms's fear when he developed a catarrh of the ear that he was going deaf like Beethoven, or one or more of his fallings-out with his friends), but I would then have failed the biographical elements of the story. On the other hand, I have excluded footnotes and other such asides with which a biographer cannot dispense, but which would have been intrusive in a novel.

The book is aimed at a general reading public, not academics, not musicologists. I think of it as a book for the beach, the summer, the winter, a holiday, a holiday in itself, a book in which one may live for a while – a narrative of love, insanity, suicide, revolution, politics, war – and, of course, music.

I adopted the persona of a man who blames himself for the death of his sister in a plane crash as she flies to visit him. He finds solace in the music of Brahms leading to his interest in the life of Brahms. He becomes so obsessed that Brahms appears in his dreams, and finally one night in his apartment to provide the TRUE account of his life. My choice of Germanisms is admittedly subjective, but the format allowed me to incorporate a diction that commingled Brahms's century with the narrator's. It may occasionally appear arbitrary (for instance, I have used doctor and Dr. in the narrative voice, but Doktor in conversation, and Danke for Thank You, but not Bitte for Please), but there was no perfect solution to the problem. I needed to trust my instinct, knowing I was bound to fall into error at times, but I trust the reader will consider these to be minor and inevitable errors, especially in a work of this size.

I am indebted for the facts behind my story to more than a hundred biographies, correspondences, memoirs, and books regarding not only Brahms and the Schumanns, but also many other composers and their friends and acquaintances, not to mention books on history, music, travel, and fashion. I incorporated some of the letters into conversations on the assumption that conversation is more dramatic than correspondence; other letters I transformed into the very scenes they described for the same reason; and still other letters I edited for clarity, sometimes merging many into one in which case I doctored dates to fit the narrative. I like to think that what I have lost in absolute veracity (impossible in any case in a work of this nature) I have gained in dramatic impact. I wished to provide a credible account of the events and characterizations more than to cross every T and dot every I.

I am particularly indebted to Styra Avins for arguing convincingly that the Brahmses were not as impoverished as his biographers indicated – but that Brahms's father, Jakob Brahms, was instead a spendthrift, precipitating crises a more prudent man might have avoided. I do not agree with her conclusion that the boy Brahms never played piano in Hamburg's dockside bars, but I won't repeat the arguments here since we have dealt with our differences in two articles published in two issues of *19ʰ Century Music* (University of California/Davis): (1) "The Young Brahms: Biographical Data Reexamined" by Avins (Spring 2001, Volume XXIV, No. 3) and (2) "The Boy Brahms" by myself (Fall 2003, Volume XXVII, No. 2).

To readers interested in a strictly non-fictional account of the principals I would recommend Nancy Reich's book, *Clara Schumann, The Artist and the Woman*, Peter Ostwald's *Schumann, The Inner Voices of a Musical Genius*, and Jan Swafford's *Johannes Brahms*, each of which may arguably be counted definitive biographies of the trio.

For my Mom and Dad
Vera and Phiroz Desai

I am indebted to Arrand Parsons for entree to Northwestern University's excellent music library; Chicago's Newberry Library for its no less excellent collection; Francine Lahaye for translations; Sonny Berman for $10 dates; Valorie Fachs for Sonny Berman; Joanne Kellock and Linda Koptak (among the first readers); Daniel Platt for his exceptional Schumann website; Barry Birnbaum for Dvorak and the fly; Renate Nagarwalla and Tilman Ochs for reassurance on red hedghogs, black cats, cities of London, and general Germanisms; Colm Hennessy for the best jobs I ever had; Kevin Limbeck and Robin Blench for continually deepening and precious friendships; Zarine and Richard Weil for the reading and dinner; Lois and Ron Diller-Ernst for old time's sake; Frank Suerth for Thursday evenings; Susanna Ernst for Frank Suerth; Shirin and Giles Tata-Colchester, Vera and Farhad Choksey, and Pheroza and Jamshyd Godrej for neverending hospitality; Hedvika Miller for unexpected and generous support; the Dadabhoys for a home away from home; Wilma Steffes for late-night conversations and ice cream; Diana Athill for so much more than suggesting the title; and Ronnie for thoughtfulness without a second thought.

CONTENTS

PART TWO
ROBERT AND CLARA AND BRAHMS

PART THREE
CLARA AND BRAHMS

BOOK TWO / ... AND BRAHMS

PART FOUR
A MANIFESTO

PART FIVE
A GERMAN REQUIEM

PART SIX
THE C MINOR SYMPHONY

PART SEVEN
THE GLORY DECADE

PART EIGHT
CLARA AND BRAHMS

PROLOGUE

For months after my big sister, Mitzi, died, Brahms came to me in the night, inhabiting first my headphones, next my dreams, finally my apartment. In the first dream we went ice skating, the ice cracked, we fell in, made it back to the surface – but Brahms dove back into the diamondblue water, fish and ferns in his face, to recover a manuscript he had dropped. In another dream we had been vacationing, Mitzi and I, in an English country house – and Brahms, the landlord, served wiener schnitzel and sauerkraut. In yet another I dreamed he was in my apartment, standing by my bed, watching me sleep, before going to the piano, playing the first of the three intermezzi from his opus 117, what he had called a lullaby of his suffering, so private that even an audience of one would have been too many – and when I opened my eyes he was gone.

The apartment was in New York. I had arrived from Downers Grove (a Chicago suburb where I had grown up), following a dream – as had my Uncle Eustace, Mom's kid brother, thirty years earlier. After ten years in New York all I can say is I'm still a contender – as is my Uncle Eustace after almost forty of driving a hack and painting (abstracts, oils, huge canvases), still crazy though at 69 he's more than twice the age of Schubert when he died, almost twice the age of Mozart, Mendelssohn, Bizet, Chopin, Weber, and Schumann, older than Bach, Beethoven, and Brahms – still a contender, still a purist, still in the ring, still on his feet, and still slugging, spurning not only the family business, but magazine illustrations, cartoons, even a *New Yorker* cover.

I had followed in his footsteps, and tiretracks (I also drive a hack), but as a composer, and much to the disgust of my dad who calls us Solitaries in the City of Solitaries. In a family of bankers, brokers, mercantilists, and other such moneymen, we were pariahs – not to Mom and Mitzi, solicitous and proud of their kid brothers, but to just about everyone else. A hack hacking's what Uncle Eustace said about me when I published an article on Bartok in *Tutti*, but he spoke ironically. He understands better how I live and breathe than the rest of the family. I catch the sun when it rises as he catches the sun, sometimes in my windshield, sometimes in my window. Either way, I'm up most nights, sleeping when I can. Beer, coffee, TV, books, cigarettes, all entertain me, but most of all music, and most of all the music of Brahms.

Mitzi's was a different story, at thirty-five she was already a vice president at the Harris Bank – but flying to visit her impecunious brother in New York for a weekend her plane had crashed, and whether or not the family meant it I had felt myself the focus of their blame, made myself no less the focus of my own blame. More and more I listened to the music of Brahms, medicine for a healing heart. More and more I interested myself in his life, more and more the records and books I amassed about him crowded me out of the apartment, and more and more I looked forward nightly to dreaming about him – until one night in bed I imagined him standing in the room, glittering with moonlight, the man with the Moses beard, sprigs and twigs of white jutting from the jungle on his jaw, the jungle on his head swarming over his ears, fierce blue eyes narrow and penetrating. He wore a white shirt, black suspenders, black pants cut above his ankles (he had wielded the shears himself, protesting his tailor's efforts to civilize him), revealing drooping white socks, gleaming skin of his shins, dusty black walking shoes. I raised myself on one elbow. "Are you Herr Doktor Brahms?"

I could have called him just Brahms, but that felt disrespectful though his name is as much a metaphor now as Bach, Mozart, or Beethoven, and Mister didn't have the heft of Herr Doktor – but it was a stupid question and he stared as if I should have known it was a stupid question. He didn't have to say a word, his great forehead loomed like a mountain, clenched like a fist, and his eyes, icebergblue, amplified his thoughts: *Am I to be forEVer surrounded by IDI-yots?*

"Sorry. What I meant was thanks for the music."

He waved his hand in a charitable gesture. It's yours, he appeared to be saying.

I tried to explain. "It's cushioned my life, especially after …" Lips trembling, throat constricting, I couldn't finish. He nodded, mouth in a moue of commiseration, but eyes wandering. He was too much the stoic to dwell on what he couldn't change – but neither had I meant to focus so glaringly on myself and tried to deflect the focus. "And who knows how many other lives."

A smile began to glitter, but he turned his face away and when he looked at me again it was gone – but so was the fist in his forehead.

We were silent for a while, not an uncomfortable silence, but feeling the weight of my responsibility as host I goosed the conversation forward. "Any regrets?"

He twitched his lip, one cheek momentarily fatter, redder. "Ach! Regrets! Regrets are for old women."

He appeared to growl, but his voice was high, and I remembered he was often gruff to cover its pitch. I replied hurriedly. "I mean, what would you have done differently? What would you have changed?"

He answered without hesitation. "I would have gone to England. I would not have let a bad crossing stop me."

"Ah!" I took a deep breath. "That's what I thought. The English would have treated you like royalty. That was my regret too."

The fist mounted again in his forehead. "It is *not* a regret. If I had gone to England I would have missed Italy, or Switzerland, or Ischl, or Portschach, and in England they want you to wear a tie – even in the bathroom they want you to wear a tie, by government decree. Hah!"

2

He grinned. I smiled weakly. He had never visited England, not even when Cambridge had offered a doctorate, but not because of the bad crossings. "What about France?"

He twitched his lip again, so vigorously it twisted his face. "Ach! France!" He waved his hand again, enough said. The French were worse than the English, frivolous, given to frippery and finery – no less, you might argue, than the Viennese he loved so well, who loved him as well, but Vienna was the musician's Mecca, home to Haydn, Mozart, Beethoven, Schubert – also, of course, Strauss. Never mind that Vienna had treated them shabbily – all except Strauss (richest of composers). I remained silent.

"And I never wanted to be treated like royalty."

True, even after he could have afforded better, after he had consorted with royalty himself, he had maintained his humble lodgings at 4 Karlsgasse, humble fare at Zum roten Igel (just more of it), humble clothes despite the attempts of his tailor – but he had also been thrilled with the doctorate from the University of Breslau, the commemorative medal with his head embossed from the Friends of the City of Vienna, the Freedom of the City of Hamburg. *The distinction is a rare one,* he had written to Clara Schumann about the Hamburg honor. *I am number thirteen. The first were Blucher and Tennenborn, the last Bismarck and Molkte.* He couldn't help being flattered. True, he didn't like pomp, but the tales he had learned about the English and the French at his mother's knee couldn't have helped. Besides, though he had studied both languages in school he spoke them with a thick low-German accent and remained uncomfortable with etiquette, aware of his disease: foot in mouth. No London, no Paris, no wonder.

"And I would have missed Lichtenthal."

I imagined I heard a sigh. Clara had bought a house in Lichtenthal, near Baden-Baden, not far from Vienna, and the next question, the obvious question, the question on the minds of not just Brahmsians but musicologists the world over, popped into my head. Had they been lovers? I didn't ask, but his eyes grew tinier, beadier, his forehead crumpled, and I knew he had guessed what I was thinking. I prepared myself for one of his sarcasms, but surprisingly his forehead cleared again. He looked around for a place to sit, but the piano bench was too far, the couch too cluttered, and he sat on the bed, lowering his elbows to his knees, his head to his hands, and stared at the rug. I moved my legs under the covers to give him more room and heard another sigh, deeper than the last.

The wood of the floorboard showed through the rug, orange foam showed through the seat of the couch; Wagner, with his predilection for luxury, would have sneered; Liszt, more the gentleman, would have grimaced, however surreptitiously; Brahms did not care. "Some things you do not control." He turned his head, holding my eyes. "You know how it is."

I nodded, back in my puddle of shame and blame.

My eyes wandered; yes, I knew how it was, endless palpitations of the heart, of the head; but he caught my wandering eyes. "Mitzi?"

My smile was bright as the full moon; her name on his tongue.

He shrugged, returning my smile, ivory teeth, ruby lips, silver beard. "The same with Clara."

Strange enough I was speaking with Brahms in the box of my bedroom in the bowels of the night, but we were joined then by a thin darkhaired girl in pigtails who stood beside him, hand on his shoulder. I stared into her smiling face. "Clara?"

Brahms raised a hand to cover hers. "*My* Clara. You know what Goethe said?"

"What?"

"She played with the strength of six boys, this girl of twelve."

I nodded. Clara had been twelve when she had played for Goethe.

Brahms glared. "You want to know about us. *I* will tell you. People see what they want to see, nothing else. Academics are the worst, scholars and biographers, putting their snouts in other people's shitholes, piggybacking on the lives of their subjects because they have no lives of their own, leeches and parasites. They tell you more about themselves than about me. What they really want is to see themselves in their subjects. We destroyed letters, Clara and I, swore each other to secrecy, because there were still people alive who mattered, but all are now dead. No longer matters what people think. Listen. This is how it was."

Then began the blur: mists and streams, visions and images, coalescing into a hard bright knot of clarity; everything I had read, everything I had heard, everything he told me, all biographies, all stories, all snippets, rolled into one, roiled forward in a clear precise voice, providing words, pictures, music, reviving giants of the past, uncoiling this serpent of a tale.

BOOK ONE

THE SCHUMANNS...

The artist should beware of losing touch with society. Otherwise, he will be wrecked – as I am.

ROBERT SCHUMANN

PART ONE

ROBERT AND CLARA

Clara Josephine Wieck Schumann was not precocious, not as a composer, no Mozart, no Mendelssohn, but no less a prodigy as a performer, certainly more than Schumann, probably more than Brahms, perhaps even Beethoven, matching the men on their own turf, the only woman worth mention in the arena, among Kalkbrenner, Chopin, Liszt, Mendelssohn, and Thalberg, inflaming the imagination of all who heard, a girl to their eyes, a woman to their ears – indeed, a man to their ears.

She had eyes large as almonds, blue as midnight, and a nose sharp and narrow and full of command – the first things Robert Schumann noticed on meeting her at the house of Dr. Carus, a mutual friend of their fathers, she just nine, he eighteen. Their hostess, Agnes Carus, agog with Rousseau's theories of childrearing, noticed as well her thin lips, the sad triangle of her face, and upbraided her pappa for stealing from Clara her childhood for his own gain, even attempting to punish him by refusing him introductions for Clara's benefit in Paris. Friedrich Wieck had written to his wife, his second, the former Clementine Fechner, Clara's stepmother, not without pride, that their hostess had kept her introductions – and he had kept Clara.

That was in 1831, the year of the first Paris tour, but she had been established from the start (her first concert, in Leipzig, at the Gewandhaus, in 1828) though it had been almost a bad start. She was to play the treble in Kalkbrenner's Variations, with Emilie Reichold, another of her pappa's students, but she was so small of stature, so skinny, that she seemed lost in her blue evening dress. In the parlor mirror she looked like a puppet, curtseying to herself – but waiting for the brilliant glass coach of the Gewandhaus she imagined herself a princess, smiling through the window as they clopped through the streets, waving a motionless wave.

Her pappa was at the hall: there were always modifications to be made, regarding tickets, hand bills, refreshments, the instrument, all the logistics concerts entailed.

Her brothers played in the adjacent room, Alwin seven, Gustav five, Alwin beating Gustav as he was always beating Gustav with the advantage of his years. Her pappa beat Alwin more than he beat Gustav, but he never beat her. She had been the favorite since she had shown promise at the piano, beginning lessons shortly after her mamma had remarried and left for Berlin. She had been five, taking her mamma's place in her pappa's affection, prevailing over even his second wife. She was his creation, the advertisement for his Method, to be revealed for the first time in public that day.

"FRAULEIN CLARA!"

The call boomed from outside. Nanny came into the room. "Clara, it is time."

Clara swung from the mirror. "I am ready." She rushed down the stairs with Nanny to the street, prepared for anything except what she saw, a bus drawn by four nags, heads drooping, spines sagging, as if in former lives they might have borne Sancho Panzas and Falstaffs. Inside, two benches faced each other, their backs to the windows and street – wooden benches, without cushions, not even sheets, not to be compared with the glittering seat, soft and white and wide and upholstered, that she had been promised in the magical Gewandhaus coach. Worst of all, the bus was full of the commonest girls. They wore party dresses, but might as well have been wearing day clothes for the way they stared and pointed and giggled.

"Fraulein Clara?"

An older woman smiled from one of the benches.

"Yes."

"Come. Get in. Sit by me."

She must have looked as scared as she felt for the woman to have invited her to sit next to her.

Nanny squeezed her arms, pushing her gently. "Luck to you, little Clara. Auf Wiedersehen."

Clara nodded, pursed her lips to keep from crying, and got in without a word.

The driver flicked the reins. "GEE! HAW!"

Nanny waved as the bus jolted to a start, but Clara stared at the street between the heads of two girls across from her, conscious only of the low slow rumble of the wheels grinding the cobbles, reverberating around the second E flat below middle C.

She wasn't nervous, she had never been nervous when she played, not even for her pappa's friends in Dresden, once even with an orchestra (two violins, two violas, one cello, one flute, two horns), the Piano Concerto in E flat by Mozart, at a rehearsal for someone else's concert, about which she had written to her mamma in Berlin that she had made no mistakes – but the applause, roaring like a river, had frightened her.

"Whoa, Hans! Whoa, Bruno, Hilda, Greta! WHOA!"

The bus jolted to a stop.

"FRAULEIN ANTONIE!"

The door was opened, a new girl got in, dressed for a party, the older woman confirmed her name, "Fraulein Antonie?" and the bus was off again with another flick of the reins, another "GEE! HAW!" another jolt, and more desultory clopping along the cobbles. Clara couldn't imagine who the girls might be, but after the bus stopped again, picked up yet another girl, and showed no signs of picking up speed, she was afraid she would be late. She might yet have said nothing, but instead of turning down the Neumarkt and around the corner to the Gewandhaus the bus turned the other way. She turned to the older woman. "This is not the way to the Gewandhaus, is it?"

The woman's eyes opened as wide as Clara's. "To the Gewandhaus? Oh, no! We are going to Eutritzsch."

Clara said nothing, but her deep blue eyes grew larger as they grew blurrier.

The woman frowned with puzzlement. "What is it, Liebchen? Why do you cry?"

She remained dumb, the focus of all eyes. She was bad with words, better with notes. Her pappa had thought her stupid because she wouldn't talk, but notes had given her courage for words. She could pull notes from a piano as she couldn't pull words, and her pappa had encouraged her with words only after he had seen what she could do with notes. Nanny, with whom she had spent much of her babyhood while her mamma and pappa resolved their differences, was no better with words – but there had always been music in the house. Her mamma played, her pappa taught, which was how they had met.

She was saved by the drumming of hooves behind them. Girls and woman turned as one. The glass coach of the Gewandhaus swung around a corner into the street, the driver hailing them to stop. Clara filled with light and color to see her dream rise from the dead. Two horses, white and muscled, snorting and panting, glistening with exertion, rose on hind legs as the coachman pulled their reins.

Bus and coach screeched to a halt in clouds of dust. The door of the coach swung open. The porter's daughter, also named Clara, stepped out. The bus was headed for a country ball. Two Claras crossed paths, one tripping from coach to bus, the other floating from bus to coach. The ride to the Gewandhaus was not what she had expected, too fast for comfort, but in her anxiety – that she would be late, her pappa angry, the audience impatient – she no longer imagined herself a princess waving.

The Gewandhaus itself was unimpressive, the Clothiers Building, a converted warehouse, foursquare structure on the Neumarkt, without a formal approach, no portico, no column, no approach at all, a single step led off the street into the building, narrow wooden steps led to the narrow hall, bare walls, seats like pews, above the stage an inscription: *Res Severa est Verum Gaudium*, the Truest Joy Comes Through Seriousness.

She was afraid of what her pappa would say, but he approached with a papercone of sugarplums. "Clarchen, I forgot to tell you." He was smiling, her stern pappa who smiled only when he saw his advantage. "Performers are always taken to the wrong house the first time they play – always. It is the custom. Do not be afraid."

Seeing her pappa's lack of concern, she lost her own, matching him smile for smile. He patted her head, careful not to upset her bow, and handed her the cone, popping a plum into her mouth.

Onstage, both girls (even Emilie, though older, was hardly a woman) were graceful to watch – smiling, stately, never lifting eyes from notes, hands from keys – but their attack was as feral as their appearance was not, particularly Clara's, befitting the feral Variations. The discrepancy between what was seen and what was heard was startling, the performers still as madonnas, extensions of the piano, the music hard, brittle, brilliant, disquieting – and irresistible, the songfulness of the Variations being the essence of her pappa's Method.

Watching her one might have thought her concentration was absolute, but it wasn't that kind of work. The magic was mechanical, murder on her fingers more than her mind, and her fingers were trained too well to surrender however her mind turned, as it was turning then to how she would tell Alwin and Gustav her story, how they would laugh – and how she would tell Herr Schumann the next time she met him at Dr. Carus's house.

11

She was thinking also of the curtsey to follow, the descent from the bench, facing the sea of strange smiling faces, the staccato slap of hands more fearsome than the performance itself. Later she felt she had curtseyed too quickly, bobbed more than curtseyed, but it hardly detracted from her success.

The concert was reviewed the next morning in the *Allgemeine musikalische Zeitung*: *It was especially pleasing to hear the young, musically talented Clara Wiek* [sic], *just nine years old, perform to universal and well-earned applause Kalkbrenner's Variations on a March from Moses. We may entertain the greatest hopes for this child who has been trained under the direction of her experienced father, who understands the art of playing the piano so well and teaches with devotion and great skill.*

The experienced father, Friedrich Wieck, had drawn forth Clara's smile when she had needed it most, but as always it had been calculated. She was the principal proponent of his Method and he had needed her smile no less than she. He was an actor, a lawyer, a politician – not literally, but he used their techniques. He was a businessman, the prototypical professional, manufacturing smiles to his purpose, his face as plastic as a banker's, ugly as a robber baron's. His jaw, tapering under sunken cheeks to a narrow chin, was thrust forward, clamped by the thin, wide, concave, scowling vise of his mouth – arced like that of a shark. His eyes, narrow and piercing, glared over high cheekbones, heavy eyebrows plunging into the bridge of his commanding nose, the feature most visibly bequeathed to his daughter. His brow reached deep into his scalp, webs of white clouding his ears. Clara liked his hair best fanned by the wind, the romantic look, like a hero out of a poem by Lord Byron, but he preferred to adopt the latest fashion, wetting and combing it toward his temples like Napoleon, tucking his hand between the buttons of his coat

He maintained a piano dealership, sales and rentals, devices to aid the pedagogy of pianowork (silent keyboards, wrist guides, finger stretchers), and a music library. He corresponded and consorted with pianists and piano manufacturers in Vienna, had once visited Beethoven – but success was not his dream. Success was the bridge, money the tool; successful businessmen were common, industry made success of a monkey, but as a pedagogue he was unique, as a pedagogue he was divine, spreading his Method, teaching his students to make the piano sing. That was his achievement, and Clara his creation, his masterpiece and testament. It took two, he would have nodded vigorously, Clara was indispensable, but another pedagogue would not have mined her talent as effectively, another pedagogue would have lacked his Method, another pedagogue would have lacked the skill to encourage without making her complacent, to challenge without taxing her, to exploit without exceeding her limit – though her ability, Wieck marveled, appeared without limit and expanded continually with maturity. Watching her performances his smile was never mechanical, but winged with triumph more than tenderness as he pocketed the amazement of the audience: he had earned it, he owned it, and he prized it.

Clara was drawing to the end of the Bravura Variations by Herz in the drawing room of Dr. Ernst August Carus. Had their eyes been shut the audience might have sworn there were four hands at the piano. Even with eyes open Ludwig Berger imagined ventriloquism in her fingers. Bernhard Klein leaned forward, the better for his eyes to verify the evidence of his ears. Wieck was exultant to see everyone in the room, Wilhelm Taubert, Julius Knorr, Dr. Carus and his wife, Agnes, among others, splayed in the same incredulous attitude, enthralled by his accomplishment, all but young Robert Schumann, recently from Heidelberg, student of law, sometime poet, amateur pianist, dilettante supreme, lolling in an armchair, dandling a cigar between his fingers, eyes bright with intelligence, smile more tolerant than admiring, the only listener still possessing presence of mind. Their glances met: Robert rolled his eyes; Wieck raised an eyebrow at the impudence, but surrendered his glance.

Still a boy, barely twenty, yet to prove himself, Robert had all the pretensions to manhood apropos of his age. He thrust his mouth forward when puffing on the cigar to keep smoke from his eyes, squinting all the while and grimacing like a monkey. He was too soft, spoiled, indolent, fond of luxury, inclined to fat, for Wieck's pleasure, but Wieck had heard him discourse on music and found himself in sympathy with his views, found himself surprisingly affronted not to have won him to his Method as he had Berger, Klein, Taubert, and the rest – even including Robert's cohorts, the two Carls, Becker and Banck, and Ludwig Schunke, all mesmerized on the divan, eyes and ears for Clara alone – but Robert shifted restlessly, ready it seemed to sling a leg over the arm of his chair. He fingered the sconce on the table beside him, blowing gently to make the flame flicker, sipping cognac from a goblet, tapping his cigar over an ashtray, examining the tapestry behind him, the flame of the sconce through his cognac, and yawning – not that he was bored, of that Wieck was certain, but that he wished to appear a man of the world, not easily impressed. There was much of the poseur in Robert.

Clara struck the last chord. Applause surged into its wake laced with cries of Brava and Encore among other encomiums. Carl Banck applauded, getting to his feet. "Brava, Clara! Brava! Bravissima!" He was Robert's age, but taller, more muscular. His face was rounder, straight hair falling across his forehead which he tossed frequently to clear his eyes. There might have been no one else in the room for the way he stared at Clara.

Clara turned in her chair to acknowledge the applause. "Danke! Danke Schon!"

The cries still swept the room: Brava! Encore! but Agnes Carus rose. "I am very sorry, indeed, but the encores will have to come after the intermission. First we must replenish our plates and glasses." She opened her arms in invitation and smiled. "Come, please, all, I beg you."

Robert looked at her, raised his cognac, and nodded approval – whether of the cognac, of what she had said, or of Agnes herself, was a matter for conjecture. He watched her cross the room to the sideboard. A servant was lighting the candelabra, bringing cakes, currant bread, coffee, and cordials once more into view as the guests followed Agnes. Robert stayed in his chair, turning his attention from Agnes to Clara, speaking ironically. "Yes, little Clara, brava, indeed – and the next time you must try to finish more quickly yet. I find Herr Herz played best when he is played the quickest, do you not?"

Wieck, too, had stayed behind watching Banck watching Clara, Clara watching Robert, and Robert watching Agnes until he had turned his attention to Clara. There was a moment of silence, the closer heads turned toward Robert, the farther continued toward the sideboard. His tone was unmistakable, but he smiled to soften the irony. "And it follows as day follows night, does it not, that he is played best of all when he is played *not* at all – the quickest of all?"

Clara was too sure of herself to be intimidated, but she was surprised. If she had one fault it was that she played too quickly, a fault Herr Schumann had been quick to catch, no less to advertise – for which she could only be grateful since no one else would have said anything except her pappa, later – but on this occasion her pappa defended her, fixing his eyes on Robert. "A hundred musicians, Herr Schumann, often mean a hundred opinions – and what good is that?"

"All the good in the world, Herr Wieck, if every opinion is defended by a hundred reasons." Robert sat forward in his chair as he had not during Clara's performance. "The best of reasons must prevail – the best considered of all the reasons. It is most certainly legitimate to like Herz as much as Beethoven, but we must be clear that to like Herz is to admire the performer's skill, and to like Beethoven is to admire the performer's taste. It is one thing to pack as many notes as possible into every bar, and quite another to make them cohere logically and harmonically. If we do not make distinctions between the virtuous in music and mere virtuosity, we do not make strides – except backward. Might as well play the piano with your feet. It is not easy, but neither will it make you an artist."

Banck still stood, nodding agreement though looking at Clara for direction. Others in the room smiled, among them Agnes who had returned to shepherd the remainder of her guests to the sideboard, for whose benefit as much as for music itself Robert was staging his argument. He had fallen half in love with her hearing her sing, but he fell half in love with most women he met, more in love with the notion of love than with his lovers. She was married, eight years older (just five years younger than Schubert himself, now dead three years), but also the more romantic for being unavailable, Lotte to his Werther, and his yearning the more precious for being hopeless. He was more at ease playing fourhanded Schubert with her, accompanying her on the piano when she sang, than he would have been courting her, than he would have been had she been unmarried, but beyond his reach she became his Songstress, his Liedersangerin, his Maid of Holland, his Singing Swan, though he knew better than to address her so fancifully in public.

Agnes smiled. "Our Fridolin feels strongly about music, as you can see, Herr Wieck – and with just cause, though perhaps sometimes with too much feeling."

Her smile was too ingratiating for offence. Wieck noted she called him "Fridolin," the pure and guileless page from Schiller's ballad, a sweetheart without a sting. She had unearthed him from the unlikeliest town, Zwickau, where her husband's uncle and Robert's father had been friends, where she had first heard him perform his compositions, musical portraits of family and friends. She had lived then in Colditz, less than thirty miles north, where her husband had been medical director of the insane asylum. She had introduced Robert to Schubert lieder and chamber music (Haydn, Mozart, Beethoven) when she had asked him to accompany her at the piano in the home of her inlaws.

Wieck knew something about the Schumanns. Robert's older sister, Emilie, imagining herself ruined by an incurable ailment of the skin on her private parts, had drowned herself at the age of nineteen, not unusual among people who suffered from too much sensibility, the disease of the Romantic. The father had suffered attacks of the nerves, dying himself shortly after losing Emilie. Robert had suffered a similar attack on the death of his father, imagining himself destined for the asylum in Colditz; but Dr. Carus, being a psychiatrist, and Agnes (herself no less a doctor of the mind), had recognized his creativity, helped him recover, and Wieck liked him for speaking his mind – Wieck's mind as well though he cared less to voice it. If one minded one's business the rest fell in place, going against the grain one became troubled, like the Schumanns, but that was the way of artists – at least, of artistic sensibilities. No less an authority than Goethe himself had pronounced the Classical temperament healthy, the Romantic sick, though Goethe was, of course, of the old school. Wieck smiled, speaking gallantly. "Nevertheless, Frau Carus, there is something in what he says – but tell me, Herr Schumann, what, then, is the solution? The public wants virtuosity, the public wants to see you play the piano with your feet as you choose to phrase it, and if the public does not get what it wants it will not give us what we need. Is that not so?"

Robert crossed his arms. "If we give the public what it wants it will turn the mighty oak to ash. It is up to us which to choose, the oak or its ash."

Wieck grinned. "Of course, Herr Schumann – but there we are in agreement. Clara, what is the first rule I taught you about music? Will you repeat it, please, for the benefit of Herr Schumann?"

Clara looked from her pappa to Robert. She liked his straightforwardness, his lack of deference. Even so great a personage as Karl Gottlieb Reissiger, the new conductor of the Dresden Opera, who had replaced Carl Maria von Weber, was never so nervous as when he played before her, so he had said himself – but Robert saw her as she was, a gifted child, and admired her gift never forgetting she was a child. She liked as well that he was quiet – except in defense of music when even his rhetoric turned musical. She held up her chin as she recited:

> An artist must bend
> His skill to his end;
> But if skill be his end,
> Then art's not his friend.

The words poured so effortlessly she might have been reciting the alphabet, but Robert uncrossed his arms and jumped grinning from his chair. "Exactly! Skill needs will – but art," he thumped his chest, "needs heart – and mind, and soul. It is just what I have said. We must learn to distinguish between art and mere skill, between the virtuous and mere virtuosity."

Gotthold Fink, editor of the *Allgemeine musicalische Zeitung*, nodded slowly. "That is the responsibility of the critics, to distinguish the good from the bad. That is why we have newspapers and journals – and I assure you we have a wide readership."

"All the more reason for you to provide thoughtful and passionate reviews – but most of the time they are neither hot nor cold, nor up nor down, nor this nor that, nor here nor there – they use as many words as possible to say as little as possible, often to say nothing at all."

Fink faced Robert, shaking his chins at the impertinence, but Carl Banck spoke first. "Truer words were never spoken." He looked at Clara who looked at Robert. "I have said as much myself. The critics refuse to recognize genius as much as they refuse to oppose mediocrity. Above all, they value tolerance. 'Live and Let Live' is what they say."

Robert made a flourish with his hand. "And that, ladies and gentlemen is a good way to live your lives, but no damn good, this damnable German politeness, this damnable shrugging of the shoulders, no damn good at all for art."

"And that is especially true of lieder." Banck's face was smooth as a baby's. Clara wondered that he could see her at all for the veil of hair over his eyes, but he continued to gaze as if she held the philosopher's stone. "On the surface, it appears the easiest music in the world to compose, requiring no more than a verse around which to wrap a few notes, but the appearance is deceiving." He was a singer himself, a voice tutor, but Clara remained oblivious; he might not have spoken at all.

Ludwig Rellstab, editor of the *Iris im Gebiete der Tonkunst*, the same Ludwig Rellstab who had christened Beethoven's *Moonlight* Sonata, pursed his mouth in a frown, coming to Fink's rescue. "There is nothing the matter with politeness. We have all too little of it these days – as we have had all too little of it today. I cannot subscribe to your notion, sir, that a review should be a stream of bile and vomit from beginning to end. If you find the reviews neither hot nor cold you can be sure it is not that we are shrugging our shoulders, but that we prefer neither to provide hallelujahs nor to cast stones. We leave those activities to those who hear the call. We say only what needs to be said: whether a work is difficult or not, whether it is beautiful or not."

Robert got out of his chair, applauding slowly, facetiously. "Bravo, Herr Rellstab! Bravo! I salute you! That was well said, well said, indeed! No one can accuse you of being neither hot nor cold – *if* only half the bile in your reply were to find its way into your pen."

Agnes choked back a laugh. Clara turned her face to hide her smile. Rellstab shook his head vigorously, his round metalrimmed spectacles sliding down his nose. "Ach! This is nonsense! You are young, Herr Schumann. You have yet to learn how the world turns."

"But is it not because I am young, Herr Rellstab, that I see the world as it truly is instead of as everyone has learned to see it? Is it not because the old are afraid that the world is turning away from them, that they say the young have yet to learn how the world turns?"

Rellstab grimaced, pushing his spectacles back to the bridge of his nose with one finger. "You will learn the way of the world as it is, Herr Schumann, or not at all. If you do not, it will be at your own peril. These are not things to be explained, but to be learned. Soon, maybe too soon, you will see."

Robert turned his face away; his eyes drooped, losing their luster, blue turning to grey; his mouth trembled, drooping no less; he pushed his lips in and out, appearing suddenly admonished, penitent, and dejected. Clara remembered the stories about his family, sister and father, suicide and madness, and in that moment the stories

17

seemed to erupt around him in flames – but only for a moment. He focused his gaze again, bright and blue, on Rellstab. "But there is another reason, is there not, Herr Rellstab, that you wax neither hot nor cold in your reviews – and you, too, Herr Fink, is there not?"

Rellstab turned again to Robert, so did Fink.

"Is it not true that much of the music you review is published by the very publishers that publish your journals? Is it not true, Herr Fink, that your *Zeitung* is owned by Breitkopf and Hartel? And is it not true, Herr Rellstab, that your *Iris* is owned by Trautwein? And is not the *Cecilia* owned by Schott? and the *Frankfurt Anzeiger* by Fischer? Is it not true that your journalism is little more than advertising for your own publications? Is it not true that the sweat of your journalists provides no more than the grease required to slip your publications through the cracks in the doors of your readership – into their homes and onto their pianos?"

"True! Robert is right! This is all too true!" Carl Banck jerked his head, whipping the hair from his eyes. "Almost without exception the reviews call the pieces beautiful and easy to play – or, when they wish to be critical, not so beautiful and not so easy. No amateur pianist can resist the former, and only a fool would purchase the latter – but the reviews speak to the public alone, not to the music. They say nothing about the quality of the music itself."

Robert nodded acknowledgment; some of the party looked at Banck who still looked at Clara though Clara still looked at Robert. Rellstab's face turned red as a broiling lobster, Fink's mouth opened like that of a hooked fish, but neither said a word. Otto Hofmeister, another publisher, took up the gauntlet instead. "And, pray, Herr Schumann, what is the matter with that? As a businessman, I must count the favor of the public as everything – and that of the critic as nothing."

Robert replied without hesitation. "We do not write to make businessmen rich, Herr Hofmeister, but to honor artists."

Banck appeared not to hear them. "And sometimes what is not so easy – even what is very difficult – is also beautiful."

Hofmeister, wrinkling his nose, appeared neither to see nor hear Banck. "You are so very good with words, Herr Schumann. Maybe you will someday make a good lawyer."

Fink finally found his tongue. "Indeed, Herr Schumann, you are so good with words maybe you should publish your own journal."

Not even Clara missed the irony in his tone, but Robert smiled. "Maybe I shall."

Fink looked reproachful, shaking his head, blood receding from his face. "We must not blame youth for being young." Clara smiled, seeing he blamed Robert as much with his eyes as with his tongue.

Robert shrugged. "But no more must we blame the public – if critics and artists surrender the standards."

Agnes interrupted them. "Even critics and artists must eat. They must keep up their strength if they wish to continue our edification with their disagreements. Everyone, come now to table."

All smiled. Wieck got up first, flourishing his hand like a courtier. "By all means. After you, Herr Schumann, Herr Banck."

Banck nodded, stepping toward the sideboard; Robert got up, but moved not a step. "Danke, Herr Wieck, but I must defer to Herr Rellstab, Herr Fink. Sirs, after you."

Rellstab and Fink got up, but neither moved a step. Rellstab spoke without a smile. "After you, Fraulein Wieck."

Clara smiled. "Danke, Herr Rellstab." Many of the group followed her to the sideboard.

Fink lingered, inviting Robert and Rellstab to precede him, following with Wieck, Agnes ushering both ahead, hands gently on their backs. Fink looked at Wieck, barely aware of Agnes's touch. "I must compliment you on the job you have done with your daughter, Herr Wieck. So amazingly composed, she plays like a man, has the grace of a woman," he shrugged his shoulders in bewilderment, "and yet she is but a child."

"Danke, my dear Herr Fink, and I assure you it *is* a job – by which I mean that such deportment does not come naturally. One is not born with it. It must be nurtured. I treat her like an adult, and she responds like an adult. It is nothing to be amazed about, I assure you. I have simply put the theory to the test with the very amiable results you now perceive."

Agnes understood Fink differently, perceiving a melancholy about Clara's smile beyond her years which Fink and Wieck appeared to have missed. Clara appeared a child only when she looked at Robert. Her hand remained gently on Wieck's back. "But she is still a child, Herr Wieck. Should not children be treated as children?"

Wieck shook his head goodnaturedly. "The best way to spoil them, Frau Carus. Children need not to be spoiled but to be made aware of their responsibilities."

"But why have children if we must treat them like adults? how enjoy them as children if we must treat them like adults?"

Wieck grinned. "If it is enjoyment you seek, Frau Carus, I suggest you get a dog."

There was mirth among those who heard. Agnes herself smiled as she replied. "I can see my arguments lack the strength to withstand yours, Herr Wieck, but was it not Rousseau who said children need to be treated like children? They are not adults, he said, not even adults in embryo, but beings from whom we might learn what we have lost, from whom we stand to gain as much as they from us."

"Ah, Rousseau!" Wieck smiled. The name was ironic on his lips. "Let Rousseau be Rousseau, the eternal child – like all Frenchmen. If Bonaparte has proven anything it is that the French are barbarians. Children cannot help being children, but the French have not that excuse. The sooner children reach maturity the sooner they will reap the benefits of maturity – but the French, I fear, remain by their very nature beyond such benefit. You might even say that they are children – by nature!"

There was mirth again as they reached the sideboard. Clara had lingered, allowing Banck to move ahead, Robert to catch up; she cut a slice of strudel and shared it with Robert wishing she had worn her hair differently from the pigtails on which her pappa insisted. Whatever he said he preferred her to appear a child – the more she appeared childlike, the more she impressed her audiences. He even lied about her age to make miraculous what otherwise might appear merely amazing, but she said nothing. She wished to make a mature impression on Robert, felt she would do it best with her proximity, performance, and silence.

Robert stood by her side happily, accepting the strudel without thanks as if it were his due, addressing himself instead to Wieck. "And what of the benefits of childhood, Herr Wieck? Are those, then, to be reaped in maturity? or perhaps only in France?"

Agnes nodded, laughing again. "There is, perhaps, something to be said for the French after all."

Robert was smiling; he had offered the question rhetorically, but Wieck appeared to have anticipated him. "And what might those be, Herr Schumann? the benefits of childhood?"

"Why, no more than to dream, to build the castles of the imagination – which is, of course, also the work of the artist."

Wieck smiled. "I am a Kantian, Herr Schumann. I believe in the Categorical Imperative. German philosophy is best. The artist would do well to follow its precepts."

Rellstab grinned. "I must say, before we stray too far from the subject of Bonaparte, that I was never so glad as when I heard of what Blucher did at Waterloo."

Fink mirrored his grin. "Except when I heard of Bonaparte's death."

"Touche." Rellstab nudged Fink; both laughed; Wieck joined in.

Robert had lost his smile, but his tone remained level as he shook his head. "No one can defend Bonaparte. He might once have been a man of the people. Our own Beethoven dedicated his *Eroica* to the man – until he crowned himself Emperor and Beethoven tore up the dedication – but Bonaparte is not Rousseau, and all Frenchmen are not Bonaparte."

Fink frowned. "In 1810, all Frenchmen were Bonaparte. When he annexed Hanover, Bremen, Hamburg, Lauenburg, Lubeck, all Frenchmen were Bonaparte."

Rellstab nodded. "And they could all very well be again, especially when our very own German youth appear to defend them."

Robert's tone remained level. "My mamma has stories of Bonaparte's soldiers. It took two days for their ranks to pass through Zwickau on the way to Moscow, and on their return they looted, spread diseases – oh, and much worse. The stories do not bear repetition, not in these congenial surroundings, and not among such fair company, but this we must remember: All Frenchmen are not Bonaparte. Besides, I understand Herr Wieck wishes to show off our Clara in Paris."

Wieck nodded thoughtfully, cake in hand. "That is true. To conquer Paris, and then London, is to conquer the world. Clara can do what Blucher would not – or *could* not. A musician's power exceeds the soldier's."

Robert winked at Clara who smiled immediately, gratefully. "And our musician is but eleven years old!"

Wieck caught the wink and found himself wanting to impress young Robert as much as show him up for his arrogance. He turned to his daughter, cake still in hand. "Clara, I want you to change the second part of our program. Play the new variations instead."

"The new variations, Pappa?"

Wieck kept his eyes on Robert, a smile playing on his mouth as if he were playing a game. "Yes, you know the ones I mean."

"But, Pappa, do you mean the –"

"Yes, Clara! Hush! *Those* variations – but let us keep it a secret. The more we let them wonder the better they will remember the work." He spoke to Clara, but continued to look at Robert. "I think Herr Schumann might appreciate them a little better than he did the Herz." He took a bite of his cake.

"Oh, yes, Pappa. I think he might very well appreciate them better." She smiled broadly, found the game delicious, baiting Herr Schumann's curiosity, mocking his impatience.

WHEN SHE SAT AGAIN AT THE PIANO a hush descended upon the room. She lifted her hands slowly from her side and caressed the keys, raising a familiar melody, repeating it in different registers and figurations, providing a rumble in the bass, tremolos in the treble, as a prelude to a glittering staircase of notes spiraling from the highest keys, culminating in a crash, followed by explorations up and down the keyboard, before settling finally into a subdued rendition of the theme proper.

Robert's grin of recognition followed the first bar, almost the first note. Rellstab recognized the work as well from the beginning and nodded, but his grin was sour. Fink appeared more puzzled, whispering to Rellstab. "Mozart, *Don Giovanni*, but …"

"*Exactly*!" Rellstab huffed under his breath. "Mozart – But!"

Smiles of recognition lit many faces, followed by a shadow. They might all have been saying, "Mozart – But!" recognizing the composer but through a mist, the theme but not the variations. As the work progressed, Clara's mastery continued to amaze. A gallop of notes was followed by a canter, a flight by a rustle; there might have been hooves in her fingers, there might have been feathers. No one appeared to breathe during the performance, not even Robert, but the final cadence wrought a collective sigh from the audience, unceasing applause, Robert in the vanguard.

Rellstab was moved by the performance if not the music itself, and whispered to Fink. "Chopin, variations on the duet, 'La ci darem la mano' from *Don Giovanni* – between Zerlina and the Don."

Fink nodded. "Ah, Chopin! I understand he is all the rage in Paris at the moment."

Wieck smiled. "Indeed, he is. It will be perfect for Clara's Paris debut."

Robert clapped eyes on Clara as she approached. "Brava, little Clara! Brava! You have entirely outdone yourself."

Banck echoed Robert almost immediately. "Yes, brava, Clara. You were magnificent – indeed, just magnificent."

"Danke, Herr Schumann, Herr Banck." Clara smiled and sat near Robert.

Wieck smiled. "I see the work is not unknown to you, Herr Schumann."

"Most assuredly not, Herr Wieck. I have even written a review of it." He turned again to Fink. "I will send you my review, Herr Fink, and you will publish it in your *Zeitung*."

Fink opened his eyes wide again, his mouth again like a fish, managing finally to speak against the insolence. "You can send it to me – and I will read it. Beyond that, I cannot say."

Rellstab pushed his spectacles again to the bridge of his nose. "But Herr Schumann, is this not virtuosity, the same virtuosity you found so pernicious bare moments ago? Is this not among the most difficult works to be published today?"

Robert shook his head. "I have read your review in the *Iris*, Herr Rellstab. I know you find it difficult – but my complaint was not against difficulty as much as empty virtuosity, against virtuosity for the sake of virtuosity. When Chopin utilizes virtuosity in the service of the virtuous in music, it is our responsibility as critics only to praise him. Who are we to complain of difficulties when Chopin comes bearing gifts?"

Clara leaned forward in her chair. "Herr Schumann, may I make a request?"

"Of course, little Clara. Anything after your splendid performance."

Clara's eyes opened wide; all the candles in the room appeared reflected within. "Herr Schumann, may I read your review? It would pleasure me greatly to read your review."

Robert got up. He was to accompany Agnes next at the piano. "The pleasure will be mine. I will bring it to your house myself tomorrow."

Clara's eyes flickered. "Danke, Herr Schumann. That would mean a lot."

Robert clicked his heels and escorted Agnes to the piano.

Robert's face was full and oval. His thick brows and plump lips were the envy of women. Blue eyes and a dimpled chin heightened his charm. His hair (thick, brown, wavy) was parted on the left, swept in a pompadour, and fell in curls hiding his ears. He emulated the aristocrat as much in his ennui as in his appearance. During his student travels across the continent he had affected a moustache resembling nothing more than burnt wax; blackening his hair and sporting black shirts and red scarves, he himself had resembled nothing more than a highway robber; but he had since reformed, shaved the moustache, shed the clothes, let his hair regain its color, and disported himself in the garb and accouterments of a man of jurisprudence. Some said he looked soft, inclined to sloth; but to Clara, who didn't know any better, he looked a man of leisure.

He had studied law for two years, first at the University of Leipzig, then in Heidelberg, but liked it no better than when he had started, neither law nor Leipzig. No river ran by Leipzig like the Mulde by Zwickau where he had been born and raised, to which he had rushed when he pleased to lean over the bridge and lose himself in its undulations; no mountains loomed to match the sight of the Erzgebirge near Zwickau, no forests breathed and rustled, no valleys yawned.

Leipzig was a market-town, and he found odious its network of streets and alleys converging on the market square, rows of awnings, traffic of men, carts, animals, wheelbarrows, too much a metropolis though barely forty thousand strong. He lived with friends on the ground floor in the Jewish quarter among men with ringlets and strange beards, the wrangle and hawk of peddlers beneath his windows dogging his conversations.

He liked Heidelberg better than Leipzig, but Leipzigers had greater respect for music, they were more serious. Heidelbergers found in music more pleasure than beauty, more fun than profundity, but Leipzig's musical tradition was steeped in the holiest of holies: Bach. He studied law at his mamma's behest, but had planned his exit carefully, and Clara's invitation the night before couldn't have served his plan better. It was Wieck he wished to see, not Clara, but it was Clara's talent – more than talent, her genius – that had erased his last doubts.

He had chosen a blue coat in which to make his appeal, imagining himself more persuasive in broad lapels, a narrow waist, black velvet collar, and black satin scarf. He slid the fingers of one hand under his vest, showing his thumb, affecting Bonaparte's stance – not that Bonaparte was his model in all things, but there was something to be gained from his stance. Indeed, everyone, Wieck included, aped the stance. He cast a smile onto his mirror, twitching the corners of his mouth, keeping his dimple under control, imagining the low profile more manly – but so satisfied was he with his image that he almost jumped, clicking his heels. It was still early, but he wanted to catch Wieck before he left for his shop.

Closer to the Salzgasschen, sidewalks were paved, streets cobbled and swept. Houses gleamed, windows were shuttered. Streetlamps appeared at closer intervals, people at farther. No one shouted and jostled him for the right of way. He avoided puddles from the night before and the splash of oncoming carriages as he walked. Reaching 21 Grimmaische Gasse, he could hear piano music, a study from Czerny's School of Velocity, but played without Clara's authority, an F note being struck continually for an F sharp. He smiled, realizing it had to be one of Wieck's other pupils, implying Wieck was home. Lifting the iron ring of the knocker he rapped sharply twice.

Nanny opened the door. Clara stood behind. Robert provided his brightest smile. "Good morning, little Clara. How is it with you today?"

Clara couldn't stop smiling: a man was calling on her. "Very well, Herr Schumann, and with you?"

"Well enough, well enough. Hullo, Alwin, that was you, then, was it, that I heard on the piano?"

Clara had undone her pigtails from the night before and tied her hair in a pouf with a pink ribbon. Robert appeared not to have noticed, but Nanny had, not only her hair but the width of her smile.

Alwin grinned. "Yes, Herr Schumann. That was me!"

"Aha! And where is your teacher?"

Clara's smile widened if that were possible. "I am his teacher, Herr Schumann. Pappa says the best way to learn anything is to teach it. I started teaching Alwin just this year."

Robert frowned. "Ah! Is your pappa not home, then?"

Clara didn't understand the frown. "No, he has gone to the shop."

"A pity. I had reason to speak with him on a matter of some urgency."

Clara realized he had come to see her pappa, not her, making the review his excuse. She turned her head. "He will be back later."

Robert noted the diminuendo in her tone, the loss of her smile. "Ah, well, it is not *that* urgent. I have brought you the review, Clara, as I promised. I woke early this morning just to transcribe a copy for you."

"Just for me?" Clara's tone rose again. "You woke early? Oh, Herr Schumann, it was not necessary. I could have read your own copy and returned it."

Robert shook his head, smiling. "After your performance last night, Clara, I would gladly have labored over more than a piffling transcription."

Clara smiled again. Her stepmother called from within. "Clara, do not keep Herr Schumann standing in the hallway. Bring him up to the parlor."

Clara jumped. "Oh! Where is my head? Herr Schumann, let me take your coat."

Alwin stepped forward. "I will take it, Herr Schumann. I will hang it up, Herr Schumann."

Robert nodded. "All right, Alwin. You may take my coat."

Clara glared at Alwin. "Do not let it drag on the floor, Alwin! Do not get it dirty! Do you hear?"

"I hear! I hear!"

Clara's tone remained imperious. "Nanny, go with him. See that he is careful."

Nanny nodded, following Alwin.

Clara's tone sweetened as she turned again to Robert. "Shall we go up to the parlor, Herr Schumann? Would you like a cup of coffee or some chocolate?"

"No, I have just had breakfast."

"Are you quite sure?"

Robert smiled. "Quite sure – oh, damn!"

Clara giggled; he had tripped over the tabby, nuzzling his feet, scurrying now with a yowl. "Oh, Herr Schumann, Gretel likes you – and you kicked her!"

Robert noted her delight in his discomfort, also like a child. "I am sure I did not mean to kick her, but I think she meant to trip me up."

Clara giggled again. "No, she did not, Herr Schumann. Here, Gretel! Here, Puss! Herr Schumann did not mean it."

THE PARLOR WAS BARELY LARGE ENOUGH to hold the piano. Portraits of Wieck and his wife hung over the sofa. Bookshelves lined the walls. Alwin rejoined them as Robert sat in the sofa. There was room for another – but, not wishing to appear presumptuous, Clara sat in the nearest chair. They were also joined by Gustav, eight years old, younger than Alwin by two years, than Clara by four, rumpled with sleep. "Good morning, Gustav. Did you have a good sleep?"

"Yes, Robert. Good morning."

No one was more surprised than Robert by the change in Clara, springing from her chair, suddenly taller, eyes narrower, nose flaring, finger pointed at Gustav. "Gustav, apologize at once! How dare you be so familiar with Herr Schumann!"

Gustav frowned. "But he calls me Gustav, and he calls you Clara."

Alwin jumped too, grinning with excitement. "He calls you *lit*tle Clara."

Clara turned her finger on Alwin. "You, Alwin, mind your own business!"

Alwin lost his grin, shouting. "But it is true! He *does!*"

"That is his privilege! He is older! He has the right to address me as he pleases!" She turned again to Gustav. "Now, you, Gustav, apologize – at once."

Robert took a deep breath; he disliked hotheaded people.

Gustav frowned. "Herr Schumann, I am sorry."

Robert fluffed Gustav's hair. "It is all right, Guschen. It is all right."

Clementine Wieck stepped into the room. "Clara, what is going on? Why are you shouting? You *must* learn to hold your temper."

Clara said nothing, narrowing her eyes, her mouth a thin line.

Robert smiled, producing his deepest dimple. "It is all right, Frau Wieck. There was a misunderstanding, but it is now under control. I am sorry if we disturbed you."

"Good morning, Herr Schumann. You did not disturb me. I hope the children are not disturbing you."

"Of course not. Just a misunderstanding."

"I am glad to hear it. Would you like some coffee, Herr Schumann – or some chocolate?"

Clara spoke quickly. "I have already asked him, but he has just had his breakfast."

"I have, indeed, Frau Wieck. Clara has been most attentive."

Clara smiled again.

"Good. Alwin, Gustav, come along now. You must get ready. You are to spend the day with Boris and Heinz."

Alwin wailed. "But Mamma, there is still time."

"It is better not to keep your friends waiting. Go on, now. You know how long it takes you to get ready."

"But Mamma, we want to talk to Herr Schumann."

Gustav pleaded. "Yes, Mamma. We want to hear Herr Schumann play the piano."

Robert smiled. "I cannot understand why you would want to hear me, Guschen, when your sister plays so much better."

Alwin laughed. "You play funnier, Herr Schumann. Clara cannot play funny."

"I am sure I do not know what you mean."

Alwin shook his head, impatient to be understood. "You know! You know! Play something, Herr Schumann. Play anything. It is always funny."

Robert looked at Clara. "I am not sure that I like the sound of that."

Clara smiled. "What Alwin means to say, Herr Schumann, is that you are always witty."

Alwin jumped up and down. "What I mean to say is it makes me laugh. Please, Herr Schumann. Play something."

Robert shook his head resignedly, still smiling. "I am not sure that that is any better."

Gustav jumped like his brother. "Just plaaay, Herr Schumann. Pleeeaase! Just plaaaay!"

"Very well – but just one piece, and then you must get ready for Boris and Heinz."

The boys grinned, crowding with Clara around the piano. Clementine crossed her arms in the doorway. Robert seated himself, lifting hands dramatically to the keyboard, playing the Czerny study he had heard from the street – playing the same mistake, F for F sharp.

As soon as Alwin realized what Robert was doing he was on his back on the floor laughing, but soon stopped. Robert had incorporated the mistake into a different melody and was playing it as a theme, developing it so that the mistake sounded better than the original.

Clara clasped her hands under her chin when he was finished, simulating a lady she had seen in a picture. "That was beautiful, Herr Schumann. That was truly beautiful."

Alwin almost shouted. "Clara cannot do that! That is what I mean! Clara cannot do that!"

"I am sure she could if she wanted to."

"But she cannot. Just ask her."

"Come on, now, Alwin! Come on, Gustav! You have bothered Herr Schumann enough."

Alwin groaned, Gustav made a face, but they said goodbye, making Herr Schumann promise to come again soon, leaving the two alone.

"Clara?"

"Yes, Herr Schumann?"

"Do you know what is a doppelganger?"

Clara recited as if she were being tested. "A doppelganger is your exact double in the world. If you see him you will die."

Robert smiled. "Good. That is good. What would you say, Clara, if I were to tell you that I have found my doppelganger? In fact, I have found two of them."

Clara's eyes grew round, her hand rose to cover her mouth, open in horror. "Herr Schumann! How terrible! Do not tell me that!"

Robert raised his hand. "Do not trouble yourself, Clara. I have made them up. They are good to me. They have helped me to write my review of Chopin's Variations."

Clara's hand remained over her mouth. "But, Herr Schumann, is your … life in danger?"

Robert laughed. "No, my dear Clara, there is no cause for alarm – but I thank you for your concern."

Clara lowered her hand to her lap. "Oh, thank the good God, Herr Schumann. I was so scared. A doppelganger is nothing to joke about."

Robert shook his head. "I am not joking, Clara. I call them my doppelgangers, but they are not real. I have conjured them with my imagination. The first I call Eusebius, who is dreamy and quiet. The second I call Florestan, who is brash and outgoing. Both are extensions of myself, but each gives me a different perspective on the work, each contributes toward the whole."

Clara remained serious, her mouth contracting to a dot as she settled in a chair.

"I see you do not understand, but perhaps it will be clear if I read the review to you myself." He pulled three handwritten pages from his pocket, settled in the sofa, and began to read. "'One evening, not so very long ago, Eusebius dropped by, smiling as if he had a secret.'"

Clara closed her eyes as if she were listening to music.

"'I was with Florestan at the piano. He is good at anticipating trends in music, but this time he was surprised. Eusebius laid a piece of music before us. "Hats off, gentlemen," he said. "A genius!"'"

Robert paused to gauge his impact and Clara opened her eyes. "It is like a story."

He nodded. "'I turned the pages and the passages became clearer. I began to see Mozart's "La ci darem la mano" blended with a hundred chords, Leporello winking at me and Don Giovanni rushing by. Florestan spoke with wonder. "An opus 2! This is music, indeed! Who is this Chopin?"'"

Clara smiled, closing her eyes again.

"'Florestan was so affected that he talked that night in his sleep. "The first variation has the Don flirting with Zerlina. The second has him chasing her around the bush. The third has Zerlina's betrothed, Masetto, cursing the Don. In the fourth – but is it not as plain as it is charming? Zerlina's first kiss? on the D flat? And in the last variation, corks pop, glasses clink, the Don takes to his heels, but he has nowhere to run.""'"

Clara beamed. "It is amazing, Herr Schumann. I have played those variations so many times, but I never heard the corks pop and the glasses clink before – but, of course, that is just how it is."

Robert nodded. "That is the point of a review, to make you see what you might otherwise miss. Anyway, this is for you." He gave her the pages. "I shall have to see your pappa some other time."

Clara's face turned crimson with pleasure. "We could play the piano some more, Herr Schumann – if you would like?"

Robert said nothing right away, but seemed to be assessing her face. "Do you know, Clara, I believe you have just given me a melody."

Her face turned more crimson yet. "I, Herr Schumann? Just like that?"

"You must not be so surprised. It is not so very difficult when the subject is so very inspiring. Would you like to hear it?"

Her voice was hushed and serious. "I would be honored, Herr Schumann."

He seated himself again at the piano and played a hesitant waltz, leading first with his left hand, then with his right, the partners almost stepping on each other's toes.

Clara clapped her hands together when he was finished. "It sounded like somebody was waiting – somebody who did not mind waiting."

"It did, did it not? Would you say you are that kind of person, who does not mind waiting?"

"I cannot say that I like to wait – but I *do* feel that I am waiting. How did you guess, Herr Schumann?"

"I did not guess. It was what I felt from looking at you. For what do you think you are waiting?"

"To grow up, always to grow up. I feel like a woman in a girl's body. I do not have girlfriends. I do not go to school like other girls. Pappa gives me lessons in all the subjects, not only in music – and on my birthdays we invite mostly his friends – but they are also my friends, and Pappa is my best friend! And Cantor Weinlig gives me lessons in harmony and counterpoint and composition and fugue – and the rest of the time I practise. I have no time for girlfriends – but I do not mind. Girls my own age are like children and I cannot wait to grow up."

Robert could no more doubt Clara loved her pappa, loved music, loved the piano, loved to practise, than doubt the complaint in her tone – and that she was unaware that she complained. "I should say there will be time enough to be a woman when you are a woman, but you will never again be a girl."

"But I do not want to be a girl. I want to be a woman."

"But Alwin and Gustav have friends their own age. Why not you?"

"Because I play the piano."

"But so do they, do they not?"

"But not like me. No one plays like me."

"Of course not."

"And it is all because of Pappa's Method. He has sacrificed so much for me. I owe him everything. I am his favorite. He takes me everywhere, to all the concerts and ballets and operas. He never takes Alwin and Gustav – he hardly even takes Mamma! He says I should be very grateful to them all because he gives me time he should rightly give to them, he spends money on me that he should rightfully spend on them – and I am, of course, very grateful."

Robert didn't find her grateful; her smile was too smug; she might as well have been grateful for the air she breathed. "Do you think your pappa will be home at all this morning?"

Clara couldn't stifle her pique. "If you had wanted to see Pappa, Herr Schumann, you should have said so. Then he would have been here to see you."

Robert recognized the streak of caddishness she had uncovered and smiled, revealing again his dimple. "You are right, Clara. I wanted to meet your pappa – but it was because of something you did last night."

His smile began to take effect. "I? Really, Herr Schumann? What did I do?"

"Your performance. Listening to you, I knew I had to study music, not law – but I need your pappa's help to convince my mamma."

Clara lost her pique. "Oh, Herr Schumann, that would be wonderful. You have the gift, of that there can be no doubt. I can never get your opus 1 out of my head, your *ABEGG Variations*."

Robert smiled. He had met Meta Abegg at a ball in Mannheim and adopted the letters of her name for his theme. "Danke. I have absorbed something of the world in my travels. It is not to be taken at face value. In Coblenz I met an English girl – so beautiful a halo seemed to circle her head. To this day I think I want to marry an English girl. I wanted to sink to her feet and worship her like a madonna."

The worm of rapture lay in his reverie. Clara sighed, seeing the English girl on the wall at which he gazed, wishing her own nose were smaller, her face prettier, her aspect more full of grace, so men might sink to their feet and worship her like a madonna. "What happened, Herr Schumann?"

Robert pursed his lips. "We rowed in a boat, saying nothing the whole hour we were on the river, but we understood each other better for remaining silent – at least, that was what I thought, but then she said Jean Paul was a bad poet and the evening was spoiled. I could not believe my ears." He looked at Clara, acknowledging her for the first time since his reverie. "Can you believe it? She called Jean Paul a bad poet – a sentimentalist, she called him."

"Do you mean Jean Paul Richter – the novelist?"

Robert looked at her sternly. "There is no other. He has written novels, but his inspirations are as sublime as those of a poet." He shook his head. "I will not bother you with her name. She seemed a madonna, but she was a philistine. Things are not as they seem in the world, Clara. The homeliest women may have the greatest merit."

Clara wished no more for the beauty of a madonna, only for greater merit, wondering what her pappa might have in his library by Jean Paul. "I cannot wait to have travels of my own. I will be seeing Paris soon with Pappa, but I can hardly wait. Have you seen Paris, Herr Schumann?"

"I have not seen Paris, but I have seen something of France, also Switzerland and Italy – and, of course, Germany." He smiled, remembering finger games under the skirts of the girls, which had led to more games at the Hotel de Pologne right there in Leipzig with whores – but he frowned almost at once, recalling a rash, the same as his sister had discovered, precipitating her suicide. "I went with my friend, Gisbert. In La Scala it was as if God Himself stood before me and let me look into His face."

Clara sighed, running her fingers through her hair. "Herr Schumann, would you do me the honor of playing for me again, please?"

"The honor would be mine." His eyes remained unfocused, still dreaming of his travels, his voice turning bitter. "After all that, I had to come back to Heidelberg, back to the university, back to the study of law – dry, cold, lifeless, deathgiving: Law."

"Herr Schumann, will you play the *ABEGG Variations*?"

He shook his head. "No, I will play you a new composition. *Papillons*. Will that suit you?"

"I would be most honored, Herr Schumann!"

He started with a peroration of notes, searching it seemed for a key, before embarking on a melody, a ladder of music, eighth notes scurrying up a scale for a single measure before descending, hesitantly, in quarter notes. It was an easy melody to absorb and Clara looked forward to its development, but Robert continued instead with a new melody, more ingratiating than the first, followed by yet another, and so on, amazing Clara with his wealth of ideas more than his technique or development.

FIFTEEN MINUTES LATER, when he had concluded by returning to the ladder melody intermingled with one of the others, he was surprised by a slow clapping behind him. Wieck had returned and smiled as Robert turned. "For everything there is a reason. Had my trousers not been drenched by a passing carriage through a puddle I would not have returned to hear Herr Schumann in my parlor."

Robert noticed his pants were soaked, muddy prints on the black and tan tiles of the floor from his boots.

Wieck held up his hand. "Do not tell me. That was one of your compositions, was it not?"

Robert nodded, smiling. "Indeed, Herr Wieck. I am gratified you recognized my signature."

"You compose like no one else, Herr Schumann – and I know everyone's work."

Clara smiled broadly. "There are so many ideas, Herr Schumann. I must confess you lost me after the first five minutes – but I can hardly wait to hear it again. I can hardly wait to make a better acquaintance. Where do you get your ideas?"

"It is a depiction, in music, of the masquerade – the final chapter from Jean Paul's *Flegeljahre*. If you listen closely you will hear even the boot of the giant in F sharp minor."

Clara lost her smile again, determined that *Flegeljahre* would be the next book she read.

Wieck raised an admonitory finger. "That is very interesting, Herr Schumann, and the commentary might well enhance interest in the music, but commentary means nothing if the music itself is bad – which, happily, is not so."

"I could not have put it better myself, Herr Wieck."

Wieck spoke drily. "I am sure you could if you wished, but Clara makes a good point." His finger remained raised. "You have many ideas, Herr Schumann, but if I may say so that is your strength – and your weakness. There are ideas enough here for ten sonatas. Themes are plentiful – but development is negligible."

Robert shrugged. "I confess it freely, Herr Wieck. I have no understanding of harmony, counterpoint, thorough-bass, fugue – but we must not let the harsh paws of the lion of reason crush the tender hands of the Muse of inspiration."

Wieck grimaced. "I will not bandy words with you, Herr Schumann. I confess it freely myself. In matters rhetorical, in matters poetical, you are my master – but let me have my say and be done. I wish you only to consider that the lion of reason, to use your own phrase, need not crush the muse of inspiration. Indeed, the two might well support each other to a mutual benefit."

Robert was enjoying the conversation as he might a game. "And I wish you to consider this, Herr Wieck. A diamond must be allowed its sharp points, or we will pay a sharp price for rounding them off."

Wieck's smile remained ironic. "As I said, Herr Schumann, I will not bandy words with you – but tell me, who has been your teacher so far?"

"Herr Johann Gottfried Kuntsch of Zwickau. He is a schoolmaster and an organist."

"I know of Herr Kuntsch and I can tell you this. You have long absorbed all that you will from him. As a man he is harmless, but as a teacher not so. If you wish to grow, as a performer and as a composer, you must find another teacher."

"I am aware of that, Herr Wieck – but Mamma calls music the Breadless Art, and she became more concerned than ever after Pappa died. She wishes only my happiness – first to learn a dependable profession, then to do as I wish. I chose law for her sake, Herr Wieck – but I find myself at a crossroads. My whole life has been a struggle between poetry and prose, between music and law. Then, during one of my travels, in Frankfurt, I heard Paganini – and the choice was made."

Clara drew an audible breath and Robert amended what he had said. "But it was only last night, Herr Wieck, hearing Clara play, that I realized I wanted to be your student."

Clara smiled again. "I have played for Paganini myself. He told me I should not play so restlessly, with so much movement – but he moves like a dervish himself."

"If you have heard Paganini, then you will understand what a power it was that drove me from law to music."

Clara nodded. "He liked me so well he invited us to all his performances, he seated us onstage as his guests – he even invited us to rehearsals, even wrote in my autograph book: *almerito singulare di Madamigella Clara Wieck.*"

She stopped suddenly; her pappa was holding up his hand, looking stern. She understood it was unbecoming to talk about herself. Gaining her silence, Wieck turned to Robert. "And your mamma? What of her objections?"

"I have given it much thought, Herr Wieck. I shall write to her asking her to write to you. After that my fate will lie in your hands. I know that playing the piano is mere mechanism and execution – but it is nothing without guidance and there is no guidance to surpass yours. I know Mamma will be led willingly by you. She knows what everyone knows, what a marvel you have accomplished in Clara."

Wieck scratched his chin. "You present an intriguing proposition, Herr Schumann."

"And not without the gravest consideration, Herr Wieck. You are much like my own Pappa. He too was much interested in the arts – though his interest was more literary than musical. My mamma's pappa would not let them marry until Pappa had started his own grocery store, so he wrote seven novels, which brought him one thousand thaler with which he started the grocery store. I am cut from the same cloth as my pappa."

Wieck held up his hand again. "Herr Schumann, I hear you and understand what you say – but I am not convinced that you are not cut from lawyer's cloth. You thrust and parry words better than any musician I know."

Robert frowned. "That may be, Herr Wieck, but what is at stake is not the manner of my speech but its substance, not how I defend but what. The quality of my words is directly proportional to the quality of my cause – and there is no cause I would defend as I would the cause of music. I would even say it is the only cause I wish to defend."

Wieck watched the wrinkles multiply on Robert's brow, the frown deepen on his face. "I will accede to your request, Herr Schumann, on the following conditions."

"You have but to name them."

"Since you have said I am like your pappa, I will be even more like a pappa to you. You must not return to Heidelberg, but board with us instead –"

"That is no sooner said than it is done!"

"If your mamma writes to me for my opinion, I will tell her that I believe a virtuoso at the piano can make a living only if he gives lessons. People pay two to four thaler an hour for lessons in Berlin, Paris, Vienna, St. Petersburg – in London they pay six to eight thaler. Adding the income from your family to the equation, I believe you could live comfortably as a teacher."

"That is just what she will want to hear!"

"I will further stipulate that you must agree to an hour's lesson with me every day possible of the year – and on the days I am away, as I am bound to be occasionally on tour with Clara, you must promise to be assiduous, studying what you now call dry cold theory with Cantor Weinlig of the St. Thomas Church – as does my Clara."

Robert slapped his knee. "Done! It is no more than what I wish myself!"

Wieck looked at him sharply. "Herr Schumann, you must also understand that there is more to playing the piano than mere technique and execution. With so singular a view you will only hobble yourself before you have begun. If you believe technique and execution are all, they will indeed be all in your performance. Do you mean to say you see no more in Clara's performances than mere technique and execution?"

Robert shook his head. "Not at all! What I meant was simply this: What I do not know you can teach me, but what I know cannot be taught – you cannot sow in fallow ground, but I am fertile."

Wieck smiled again. "I can see that – and in more ways than I would care to enumerate."

Robert frowned, pondering Wieck's words.

Wieck continued, dropping his smile. "You must also agree to writing exercises in three and four part composition daily – as does my Clara – with Herr Heinrich Dorn. Do you say you will consent to be so industrious?"

"I do! and as proof I present the industry of my own pappa – who also translated Sir Walter Scott into German in his spare time."

Wieck nodded, held up his hand. "There is one more thing, Herr Schumann."

Robert nodded attentively.

"I hesitate to give voice to this objection because you will find it offensive. Do I have your permission?"

Robert nodded again, no less attentively.

"To my way of thinking, then, Herr Schumann, you are a soft, spoiled, lazy boy, in part because you have not needed to exert your finer qualities, because your family has had the resources to shelter you from the exigencies of the world – but I am not convinced that the exigencies of the world might not one day prove too great for you."

Robert still nodded, apparently unsurprised.

"I find you too inclined to cigars and champagne and the mindless endless conversation of students – as well as the mindless pursuit of sensual pleasures."

Robert's smile was sly. "Not so mindless, Herr Wieck – but if I have known some girls it is no more than the normal run for students."

Wieck held up his hand. "I mention it only to show that I know you, Herr Schumann – and while you are young enough to own your weaknesses with pride, I am old enough to own they are weaknesses. If you are to study with me, my word is to be law. There can be no other. Do I make myself clear?"

Robert nodded. "Clear as a pane of glass, Herr Wieck."

Wieck narrowed his eyes as if to read Robert's mind, finally raising his eyebrows. "Then, as long as we understand each other, as long as we are agreed on my conditions, I will pledge to your mamma to turn you within three years into a great pianist – and as proof of my pledge I shall present my own daughter, my Clara."

Robert grinned, almost jumping from the bench. "That is my fervent wish, Herr Wieck. I could not ask for more. I will write to Mamma at once."

Something was wrong, Wieck could not say what, but he had waited too long already. You could extend credit only so far – after which the longer you waited the larger grew the credit, and the larger the credit the more difficult it became to collect. He knew the Wagners, not well, but in Leipzig artists knew one another, and Klara Wagner, one of the daughters, took singing lessons from Herr Mieksch, who also taught his own Clara. That would be Klara he heard, singing "Practise Forever Faith and Loyalty." Practise also the piano, he would have said to Rosalie, the accompanist, the eldest daughter, who played as little like his Clara as a monkey.

A woman opened the door. Her face was round, like a flower, black hair in ringlets around, drooping like petals. "Yes?"

"Frau Wagner?"

"I am now Frau Geyer, but yes."

He touched his hat. "My deepest apologies. I had thought you might be the mother of young Richard Wagner."

"I am, but Herr Wagner died six months after Richard was born. He has kept his pappa's name. I have not."

Wieck nodded. "I am sorry. I am not making myself clear. My business is with your Richard – which is what led to my error. I am sorry. I have not even introduced myself. I am Friedrich Wieck, the teacher and father of Clara Wieck – of whom you have perhaps heard?"

"Yes, of course. Who in Leipzig has not?"

Wieck smiled his pleasure. "Frau Geyer, I am here, as I have said, for business with Richard. Is he here?"

She frowned. "Business? with my Richard? Does he expect you?"

"No, I have been unable to reach him. My communications have been left unanswered – for months now, and the payment keeps mounting. I thought it would be best to come myself before it got much higher."

"Payment? What kind of payment?" Her eyes widened.

"I own a library, Frau Geyer, in addition to my piano dealership – and some weeks ago … but I would prefer not to bother you with the details. May I not speak with young Richard?"

"He is not home."

"Ah!" Wieck frowned. "In that case – if I may take a moment of your time, Frau Geyer?"

"Of course."

She led him through a dark hallway, past the room with the piano where her daughters practiced, to a small parlor.

Wieck carried his hat in his hand. "Your Klara has a fine voice, Frau Geyer. I understand she takes lessons from Herr Mieksch."

"Yes, she does."

"So does my Clara, it helps develop a singing tone on the piano – but your Rosalie … I think I could help … bring out her finer qualities."

"I am sorry for your trouble, Herr Wieck. My Richard is not always reliable, I know that. Please sit down."

Frau Geyer appeared distracted, but Wieck couldn't tell whether or not (or what) she had heard. He unbuttoned his coat, taking an armchair, waving his hat in his hand. "I also have two boys. I know how it is."

Frau Geyer took an upright chair separated by a coffee table from Wieck, holding her hands tightly between her knees. "Girls are different. You only worry about who they will marry. Boys – you never know what they will do next, you never know if they will amount to anything."

Wieck nodded. "They need a strong hand."

Frau Geyer sighed. "Tell me, Herr Wieck. What is the matter? What has my Richard done now?"

Wieck put his hat on the arm of the chair, hands on his knees. "It is like this, Frau Geyer. Your Richard came to me almost ten months ago. He had written a play for the theater –"

Frau Geyer's knuckles whitened between her knees. "Not that again!"

"You know of it? *Leubald und Adelaide?*"

"We have all read it in the family. I thought we had got him off that hobby horse."

Wieck grinned. "I have not read it – but very imaginative, I thought, from what he said about it."

"Herr Wieck, the theater will be the end of this family. Already two daughters think they are actresses. They all want to be Wilhemine Schroder-Devrient. I beg your pardon, but if you have not read it you cannot begin to understand how feverish are Richard's fantasies, how bloodthirsty. Frankly, we are very much worried."

Still Wieck grinned. "Boys are like that, Frau Geyer, before they become men. They do not know what they want. I have written just recently to Frau Schumann in Zwickau about her son, Robert, who wishes to become a virtuoso of the piano. She wanted the benefit of my experience. I have undertaken his education in my own home. Your Richard is not dissimilar."

"I beg your pardon, Herr Wieck, but you must not encourage him. His mind is full of fantasies – unrealistic fantasies. They can do him no good."

Wieck nodded. Richard's play was, at best, grotesque, even from what little he knew of it. Leubald, informed by the ghost of his father of his father's murderers, proves himself no dithering Hamlet but an Othello in vengeance, murdering the entire offending family – only to fall in love with the last left alive, the daughter, Adelaide – but tormented by the spirits of the dead family he stabs Adelaide as well, and dies himself of his own torment in her arms, while she, too, bleeds to death. Wieck nodded. "Very juvenile, of course, but very Shakespearean, and the boy is yet young."

"Herr Wieck, he is not so very young as not to know better. He absented himself from school to write his big drama – and now he blames his teachers for his bad showing in the examination. You must not encourage his fantasies. You are right, he is mad for Shakespeare, but those who do not know Shakespeare say only that he is mad."

"Well, you know best, of course, Frau Geyer, as his mamma. It is, as I said, juvenile, and I told him so when he outlined his story to me – but his interest, when he came to me, was not theater, it was music. He wanted to write an overture to his *Leubald und Adelaide* along the lines of Beethoven's overture to *Egmont* –"

"So now it is music! What does he know about music, I should like to know." Frau Geyer rocked back and forth and side to side in her chair, hands still clasped between her knees, knuckles still white.

"He knows nothing. Of that he made no secret. He wanted me to recommend a book to teach him music."

"To learn music from a book! Might as well learn from the birds. What will he think of next! I hope you did not encourage him."

Wieck frowned. "What else was I to do? I own a library. He came to me to borrow a book."

Frau Geyer shook her head. "You should not have loaned it to him."

"Well, it is too late for that. I loaned him the book, Logier's *Method of Thorough-Bass*, the best book on the subject – but I did not give it to him. The price of the loan was two groschen a week. He has now kept the book for almost ten months –"

"Herr Wieck! You should not have let him keep it so long! He might as well have bought the book outright!"

"That is precisely my point, Frau Geyer – but if he cannot pay me now he will owe me more than the worth of the book itself, not to mention what he owes me for my trouble and my correspondence."

"Herr Wieck, what is the sum my son owes you?"

"Five thaler, Frau Geyer."

"Five thaler!"

"I am afraid so."

"Herr Wieck, you should be ashamed, taking advantage of a young boy's fancy."

Wieck frowned again. "Frau Geyer, I will have you remember that I am a businessman – but I am not without understanding. If you pay me the sum now it will bring an end to the matter – but next week you will owe me more than the cost of the book itself. We should not let the matter get to so ludicrous a stage."

"Indeed, not! It is too ludicrous already. You are, indeed, a businessman, Herr Wieck – and I daresay proud of your business acumen. You know exactly when the advantage ceases to acrue toward you, do you not?"

"It is, indeed, as you say, Frau Geyer. I am a businessman."

"I will bring you your money, Herr Wieck – but only on the understanding that you will do no more business with my son. Is that understood?"

"That is entirely up to your son, Frau Geyer. I am a businessman."

"I will repeat myself only once more, Herr Wieck. I will bring you your money – only on the understanding that you will do no more business with my son."

Wieck nodded, smiling politely.

In Paris everyone dressed French, even Germans – especially Germans, if they wanted to be taken seriously. Friedrich Wieck, the latest dandy on the boulevard, played and partied into the early hours of morning as best he could, whenever he could, hat in hand (a black topper), white neckerchief, yellow gloves, green frock-coat (velvet collar, brass buttons), black trousers, black boots, more bemused by his transformation than anyone else, more even than Clara, no less bemused herself, happily so, by her own, hair no longer in pigtails but parted down the middle, cinnamon tresses twined with a crimson ribbon and wrapped in a languid bow atop her head, contrasting sharply with her white gown, taffeta with gigot sleeves, a high waist, wide belt, and wide neck accentuating naked shoulders.

Eduard Fechner, Wieck's brother-in-law, an artist and man about Paris, got them rooms at the Hotel Bergere, rue de Bergere, Faubourg Montmartre, had them attired, sketched Clara to provide Wieck with engravings to peddle at her concerts, and familiarized them with Frenchisms, but Wieck despaired of mastering the nuances. The French thought differently, he could tell from the way they ate, drank, and walked – or, to put it in Wieck's own words to Clementine: *Child, you would not recognize your Friedrich. He looks half French, half German, and half in despair. In his ambitious new raiment he resembles a young oak in a Leipzig park more than a man.* He complained that in Paris, an ingenue such as Clara was expected to dress in white, always in white, and always in a new gown at each appearance, but no more was provided for cleanliness every week than a single small napkin, and no more than a single glass of water every morning for washing. Clara, of course, didn't mind, hating to wash as much as any girl her age, but Wieck insisted sternly: "We must show what is great about Germany, not absorb what is shameful about France."

The rule in Paris was to play first at soirees, and if and when the newspapers mentioned you to follow up with a concert. Eduard arranged for invitations to soirees and the first at which Clara played, the Princess Vandamore's, was notable as much for what happened as what did not. The chambers were upholstered, hung with tapestries and portraits, stuffed with porcelain, figurines, vases, cups, and stuffed animals and birds; dogs had the run of the rooms as did parrots and canaries – as, to Clara's delight, did a monkey, with whom she shook hands, though Wieck warned that she could not trust such an animal not to bite – alongside princes, ambassadors, and priests arrayed in their finest. Wieck shook his head in disbelief; the French were children pretending to be adults; how Bonaparte had conquered Europe he would never fathom.

A young man approached the piano for which he was glad, more comfortable listening to music than making conversation, particularly in French. The man was short, stooped, and frail, his eyes were heavylidded, and the long fair hair covering his ears was exquisitely combed, its sheen repeated in the sheen of his shoes. He smiled, appearing to enjoy himself, but looked beyond the walls and once he sat at the piano he appeared beyond the weal of the world himself. Wieck, more concerned with seating himself comfortably, paid little attention until the man began to play, one note in the high treble, so clear that Wieck became still. A configuration followed, more single notes, first descending, then ascending, but what a configuration! With an uncanny use of the pedal he had blended the individual notes into one great blooming undulating chord.

Clara gripped his wrist with a whisper. "Chopin."

It could have been no one else. Frederic Chopin had been expected. Wieck nodded, but hardly felt Clara's grip, staring and listening as if he were alone. Much of the music they heard in the salons and soirees was indifferent, but Chopin's excellence, presaged by that first note, only got fuller as he played. His fingers and hands were slender, tapered, but expanded over the keyboard when necessary like the jaws of a snake for its prey. Yet, despite the success of his Parisian debut just days earlier, so Wieck had heard, Chopin preferred the venue of salons and soirees to concert halls, the musical elite to the masses, and Wieck understood why. Chopin was more poetic than powerful; Clara, at twelve, could have matched his fortissimos, but there were so many gradations within his pianissimos that fortissimos seemed extraneous – and as fine as were Clara's pianissimos, as seamless as were her runs, they could not match Chopin's glissandos, a method he had developed, fingers and feet on keys and pedals, so songful it was the apotheosis of his own Method. The effect was particularly notable during the largo of his Concerto in F minor, the touch so delicate the trills might have been gossamer wafting and whirling in the wind, dust devils in dance and twirl, music of the spheres, sound without human agency.

Wieck had not heard the concerto, but felt young again recognizing patterns and configurations in the new music, new composers discovering new forms to carry the music, reminding him of Schumann doing no less in his own voice. The days were yet distant when Chopin would need to be carried up and down stairs like a baby in the arms of various hosts, but Wieck heard, even then, his struggle against the iron bones of the piano. His own experience with French pianos had not been good; and until Erard, a manufacturer with whom he had done business, had placed one of his pianos at Clara's disposal he had debated whether to tutor Clara differently for the French pianos.

Chopin appeared himself no less a listener than anyone in his audience, no less entranced by his own music, and finished by drawing his finger across the keys, punctuating the coda by ringing the tonic note like a bell, awakening himself from his own dream, both hypnotized and hypnotizer, spellbound and spellbinder, and looked at Felix Mendelssohn sitting nearby, his great friend of the moment, leading the applause with Ferdinand Hiller, third pillar of the triumvirate.

Wieck had rewritten Schumann's review of the La ci darem Variations, more soberly (maturely, he would have said) and presented it to his brother-in-law to present to his friend, Hiller, to present to his friend, Chopin, to edit, augment, translate, paraphrase, summarize, or otherwise doctor, before presenting it to Francois Joseph Fetis, critic of the *Revue Musicale*. He longed to show Chopin what Clara could do with his Variations, to know how he had received the review, but Chopin played the Variations next himself, and Wieck winced. Clara would have to play her second choice if she were not to appear impertinent or repetitive.

When he was finished, Chopin drew his finger across the keys as before, plinking the tonic again with the clarity of a bell, looking again at Mendelssohn before leaving the bench, acknowledging applause with the barest nod, the slightest smile, sitting again with Mendelssohn and Hiller, all outwardly serious but nudging one another and whispering like schoolboys, astonishing Clara, these men of flesh, blood, bone, sound, and spirit, whom she had known only in the abstract, names over compositions she had studied so diligently.

An Italian sang next with the clearest tone accompanied by Kalkbrenner on the piano, but cluttered her songs with the trills and scales and cadenzas and ritardandos Italians found so salubrious and Germans so painful. Wieck looked continually toward Chopin wanting to catch his eye, exchange a smile, wave congratulations, a prelude to introducing himself and Clara, but without luck. Chopin appeared to turn his head knowingly from Wieck, providing a fine outline of the famous nose, appearing too fragile, particularly beside burly Hiller, even to be sitting – and Wieck, too unsure of his French to approach Chopin directly, was sure he would fare better after Clara had performed.

In her turn after the Italian Clara played Herz's La Violetta, but when she was done, despite Bravas from all quarters led by Kalkbrenner, Chopin and his gang were nowhere to be seen. What neither Wieck nor Clara knew, what Eduard had found impossible to tell them, was Chopin's reaction to the review. "He says here, that the Don kisses Zerlina first on the D flat. Pray, tell me, my good Hiller, where do you suppose he found her D flat?" They had laughed at the imagination of "this German," and returned the review to Eduard saying they found it stupid. Despite Beethoven, Germany was no hotbed for musical appreciation, not like France; and Mozart, of course, was Austrian; not Berlin, not Hamburg, not Frankfurt, not Bonn, not Munich, not Leipzig, had the cachet of Paris – which was the very reason Wieck and his daughter had come to the Princess Vandamore's soiree. They might as well have appeared hat in hand on bended knee.

Clara got up from the bench, bowed and smiled as she had been schooled, seated herself again by her father, and the soiree moved into an intermission. Both father and daughter were so chagrinned by Chopin's departure that neither saw Kalkbrenner until he was standing before them, smiling – more accurately, cocooned in his smile – not a welcoming smile, not even showing teeth, but dimples at the corners, lips as soft as a child's – a wry, sly, insinuating smile. His curly hair parted like waves on one side and concluded in curlicues at his temples; mutton chops descended past his ears enclosing his head like a Roman legionnaire's helmet; an upturned collar cupped his chin; but as Heine had once remarked he looked like a bonbon picked from mud, his gestures infiltrated with gross Berlinisms. Clara was later to say that he looked as if he imagined the world thanked God for Kalkbrenner, an impression which began to congeal in that moment when he stood before her, clicking his heels, and kissing her cheeks. "A grand talent, grand, but such a pity, such a pity." He turned his attention to Wieck. "Germany will ruin her as a pianist."

Wieck had heard Kalkbrenner play and was flattered by his attention, but recognizing that his own reputation rather than Germany's was at stake replied in faltering French. "She will not be ruined, Monsieur. She is in my hands. I will not let her be ruined."

Kalkbrenner's smile glinted. "Admirable, my dear sir, an admirable sentiment – but the matter may not be in your hands at all. In Germany you all use but one method, the groping method, the Viennese school of Hopp and Hummel. Czerny, Ciblini, Pixis, Hiller, all came from Germany to Paris to rid themselves of the habit – and so, it appears, has your incomparable Mademoiselle Clara."

Wieck gathered himself, squaring his shoulders. "I really must beg you, Monsieur, to consider me the exception to the rule. I am acquainted with the method of John Field. It is his method I have developed for my daughter and my other pupils."

Field was the one influence Chopin readily admitted; Kalkbrenner had observed it and flattered Chopin with his observation; but beyond Field Chopin's inspiration remained unfathomable, his methodology beyond pedagogy, beyond ken and cognizance.

Kalkbrenner said nothing, but nodded, maintaining his smile, further enraging Wieck. "We played in many cities on our way to Paris, Monsieur – in Weimar, Erfut, Kassel, Gotha, Arnstadt, Frankfurt, Darmstadt, Mainz – and everywhere the newspapers could not praise Clara enough."

Kalkbrenner maintained his bumptious nod and smile. "All German towns, of course."

Wieck's eyes flashed. "I will have you know, Monsieur, that I have testimonials from Spohr – and from Goethe!"

Kalkbrenner raised his chin, smile implacably in place, and turned to the listeners. "As everyone knows, when Goethe was visited by Napoleon he sent his mistress to the door while he himself hid under the bed."

The audience chuckled. Wieck began to shake with rage, his voice to rise. "Bonaparte is long dead and buried, Monsieur, but Goethe still lives, and will continue to live after he is buried, remembered for his wisdom. Bonaparte will be remembered for his follies." He got up. "Come, Clara. True Germans know when they are not wanted." He spoke to Clara, but looked at Kalkbrenner as if to question his Germanness.

Clara's attention had been arrested by the monkey, seated on someone's shoulder, who smiled and raised his chin surveying the room – just like Kalkbrenner. She wanted to laugh, but Wieck's tone was too grim.

Kalkbrenner raised eyebrows in protest, as if he might have been the wronged party. "But my good sir, I only wish to help you and the incomparable Mademoiselle Clara."

Clara ignored him, looking again at the monkey which also raised its eyebrows, or what passed for its eyebrows.

"Such help we do not need, Monsieur. The incomparable Mademoiselle will shortly be accompanying Paganini. I daresay that is all the help she will need."

Kalkbrenner shrugged, still smiling. "As you wish."

A Spaniard, lying across two chairs, strummed a guitar, singing in Spanish, smiling and winking at women gathering round; his cape and sword trailed the carpet, and his broadbrimmed hat, plumed with ostrich feathers, sat like a mascot on a chair beside. Wieck found it unwise to let Clara play again, the room was emptying and he made his excuses, blaming the ossified bones of the French piano.

Driving home Clara told Wieck about the monkey. He was beginning to despair of Clara's chances, circumstances moved too slowly to win them the success he had expected, but he laughed. "The monkey had more brains than anyone in the room, but in a roomful of Frenchmen that is hardly a matter for wonder."

ii

"Herr Schumann, what is it? What is the matter? Do you not want me anymore? Is that it? Is it to be over before it has begun?"

Christel spoke urgently, but softly, conscious as ever of the ease of discovery. Robert occupied two rooms in Wieck's household, both hung and set with framed pictures of Jean Paul, Hoffmann, Paganini, Beethoven, and Goethe among others, the outer room with a desk, chairs, and shelves of books, the inner with a bed, dresser, and washbasin. Both were small, but the inner, rarely occupied by more than one, felt smaller yet for the presence of Christel who had visited him almost daily since Clara and Wieck had departed for Paris. Her own room was alongside Nanny's on the floor above among the other servants. The trysts were brief, hushed, hurried, delicious for their secrecy, and so frequent that Robert no longer dressed in the house, lolling all day instead in his robe. Clementine hadn't noticed, busy with the birth of her baby, Marie, Wieck's first child with her, halfsister to Clara and her brothers, and nursing the baby she remained oblivious through the days following the birth. If Nanny had noticed she had said nothing, and neither Robert nor Christel wished to give her reason. Robert shook his head. "It is not that. It is not that at all."

"Then what is it?"

"It is wrong. What we do is wrong."

Christel's round ruddy face turned pale, paler for the thick black frame of her hair. She was servant enough to know her cause with Herr Schumann was hopeless, but no less in the thrall of his compositions, and particularly in thrall since he had created a caricature of her in music which he had promised to incorporate into a larger work at a later date. That, if nothing else, she was sure, would gain her immortality, however anonymously, but now it seemed she was not to have even that. "Why is it wrong today? Yesterday it was not so wrong. Yesterday you said it could not be more right – you did, you know it, you said it."

"That was yesterday."

"How can it be wrong today what was so right yesterday?"

Robert shook his head again. "I am ashamed, so ashamed."

"Ashamed of what? You must tell me."

"I am ashamed to show you."

"Ashamed to show me what?"

"I am wounded. I have a wound."

"Let me see. Show me. You must."

Robert opened his robe, pulled down his undergarment, sat on the bed gently raising his flaccid pink penis from its pubic nest, pulling back the foreskin, manipulating the reddened head, squeezing the glans, opening the blind eye at its heart. "It is painful to touch. Do you see what I mean?"

Christel knelt before him and touched the head, but he flinched, covering himself with his hand. "I am sorry. Did I hurt you?"

"You must be very careful. It is a biting and devouring pain. Now do you understand?"

Along one side, the reddened head had hardened and darkened, seeming encrusted. She nodded. "I shall be very careful. May I touch it?"

"Carefully."

She nodded again, passing a finger like a breath over the encrustation, bringing a short sharp gasp from Robert. She looked up. "Did that hurt?"

He nodded.

She brought forward her feathery finger again. "It is scaly. Will you not show it to a doctor?"

"I have already. I have shown it to Glock."

Christian Glock was a cellist friend who had graduated of late from medical school. "What did he say?"

"He said … we should abstain."

"And that will make you well?"

"He also said that I should bathe it in Narcissus Water."

"And that will make you well?"

"We shall see."

Christel's face remained pale. "We are being punished."

Robert shook his head. "*I* am being punished. You have done nothing wrong and you suffer no consequences. It is *I* who am at fault for having pressed the issue upon you."

"If you are punished, then I too am punished. If you suffer pain, then so do I. I am sorry. I did not mean to cause you pain, but I have been a bad girl for you."

"Christel, no! On the contrary, you have been the best girl. You have inspired me."

Christel's smile was wan. "If I have inspired you, I have also wounded you. Where is the gain?"

"If you have wounded me, I too have wounded you. Have you not sometimes bled for me?"

She said nothing, but her eyes grew moist.

"You must believe me, Christel. You have been good for me – only good. Let me show you what I mean." He got up from the bed, fastening his robe, getting a brown book from the top drawer of his dresser. "This is my diary. Let me show you how good you have been for me." He was smiling. "Here we are. On 1 February: Christel in one minute."

He grinned, looking into her face; she turned her head, her smile more animated.

"And this. On 4 February: Christel came completely and was bleeding."

Again she said nothing, again her smile grew more animated.

He turned pages as he spoke. "And this. 6 February: Christel full of fire and flames. 7 February: Christel on the carpet. 11 February: Christel twice in one hour. 13 February: Christel four times today."

He stopped, grinning. "Do you see? I am being punished for my greed. There is nothing the matter with me that a little care will not set right – Glock was quite sure about that – but I must take heed. We must abstain for a little while. That is all."

Christel drew a deep breath. "If that is indeed all, Herr Schumann, then I am glad. I should hate it to be more than that. I should hate myself."

iii

They had arrived in Paris on 15 February, 1832. Wieck had imagined two months would make her fortune. He never doubted her talent, her genius, but their timing had been unfortunate. Chopin had made his debut on 26 February; Mendelssohn had performed the Paris premiere of Beethoven's Piano Concerto in G on 18 March; Liszt, Berlioz, and Paganini were all in their prime; Herz, Pixis, and Kalkbrenner, all in the running. He had placed much stock in her concert with Paganini, but the violinist had fallen ill and the concert had been canceled. Still, she had created enough of a sensation at various soirees to be scheduled finally in her own concert at the Hotel de Ville on 9 April – but a cholera epidemic coupled with a local insurrection had kept patrons away, the concert had been moved to the much smaller premises of Franz Stoepel's music school where she had already played on 19 March, and on 13 April they had left Paris, richer mainly for the experience and foothold on Clara's future. However he counted, she had proven less a treasure than he had anticipated.

Clara was hardly as disappointed as her pappa, hardly as interested in the pecuniaries of the enterprise. She had been feted and praised, in person and the papers, beyond her expectations; Giacomo Meyerbeer had given them tickets to his opera, *Robert le Diable*, then the rage of Paris; she had heard Chopin and Mendelssohn, met Kalkbrenner, Pixis, and Herz among other composers she had known only through their works; she had been praised by Spohr and Goethe; for a girl of twelve that was enough. She could hardly wait to tell Herr Schumann – who had written to say he missed her, whom she had hardly missed herself amid the excitement, but whom she now found herself longing most to see. She had kept his letter with her in the coach to Frankfurt and opened it again the moment Paris was behind them while her pappa fumed at the restrictions on smoking in the carriage, a restriction he had found surprisingly widespread in Paris. "What a country, France. They call themselves civilized, but think nothing of banning what most becomes civilization."

"Pappa, it is only out of respect for the ladies. There is no such respect for ladies in Germany."

"It is not a matter of respect. There is, of course, respect for ladies in Germany. You should be ashamed to say otherwise."

"Oh, Pappa!" Clara turned her attention to her letter.

Dear, honored Clara (she read, for the thirty-third time),

First, accept my best wishes for your great success. The world is a forgetful place, like a herd of cows gazing from its grazing for a moment when a light appears, only to continue grazing placidly when the light disappears. But some lights are like lightning flashes, too extraordinary to be ignored. Such lights were Schubert, Paganini, Chopin – and now Clara!

When I read of your performances, Variations by Herz, Hunten, Hummel – why do so many of their names begin with H, I wonder – a gentle smile comes to my lips, and I think of you no longer as a brother of a sister, nor as a friend of a friend, but rather as a pilgrim of a distant altar.

During your sojourn in Paris, I flew to Arabia in my mind's eye to learn more fairy tales for your pleasure. I have eight more stories of robbers, eleven of ghosts, and nineteen of doppelgangers, each guaranteed to chill the most modern Parisian. I tremble myself just to think of them. I also have one hundred and one new charades, fifty-two riddles, and twenty-six jokes.

Alwin has a new blue coat and a leather cap just like mine in which he looks quite dapper. Gustav has grown so much you will not recognize him. Both practice the violin with a devotion hardly matched by myself; but I have got to three-part fugues finally with our common nemesis – mine, I think, more than yours – Herr Heinrich Dorn. He imagines the world revolves around fugues! More important is my book of Papillons which is to be printed within a fortnight.

I could talk about the weather, I could ask you how things are with you, but I am tired of writing, writing, writing! I want to hear your stories directly, from your lips to my ears. And so this letter comes to an end, as all things come to an end, except the friendship with which I am Fraulein C.W.'s warmest admirer,

R. Schumann.

Clara sighed, put the letter back in her pocket, and looked out of the window.

Wieck heard her sigh. "Clara, is that Herr Schumann's letter again?"

Clara continued to gaze from the window. "Yes, Pappa."

Wieck's eyes narrowed. "Clara?"

"Yes, Pappa."

"You can never compensate me for what I am doing. You realize that, do you not?"

"Yes, Pappa."

"All the sacrifices I make – the sacrifices we all make, your brothers, your mamma, everything we do – it is all for you. For you, we all make sacrifices. You realize that, do you not?"

"Yes, Pappa."

"You realize that you are in their debt no less than mine?"

She turned momentarily from the window, rolling her eyes in disbelief. "Yes, Pappa! I realize!"

Wieck smiled. He had made his point. "Even for my long days and hours without tobacco – it is you who are responsible."

She couldn't share his mirth and turned again to the window, sighing again. "Yes, Pappa."

Wieck's eyes narrowed again. He pulled a letter from his own pocket; Clementine had given birth to their first child in his absence, but immersed in his cares about Clara in Paris he had given it little thought. He looked again at Clara, still staring out of the window, but she only sighed again.

"Clara?"

"Yes, Pappa."

"Have you finished transcribing all the letters I gave you?"

He gave her his business correspondence to transcribe into her diary, a diary he had begun himself for her when she was five, when they had started piano lessons, making the entries himself when she had been too young, referring to her in the first person, himself in the third. "No, Pappa. I have not."

"Why not?"

He undertook all business dealings regarding lodgings, halls, refreshments, pianos, programs, patrons, publicity, tickets, contacts, and gave her the correspondence to transcribe, to improve her hand, to improve her French. "What is the use now? We are leaving Paris. What does my French matter?"

"It is not just for your French. You would do better to transcribe what I have given you than to stare out of the window and sigh like a bellows. You would do better to apply your time profitably."

"Oh, Pappa."

"Come, now. Do as I say. Make use of your time."

"Yes, Pappa." She continued to stare out of the window, but drew notebooks from her bag, sighing yet again.

Leipzig choked the air from Robert, buildings surrounded him like enemies rendering the sky forever distant, the cobbled undergrowth a mockery of the plentiful patches of turf in Zwickau; but he took walks as much to get away from the town as from the Wiecks, particularly since the return of the old man and Clara from Paris. The old man appeared weaker, but no less arrogant; and Clara was prettier, taller, stronger, more confident, more woman than girl in her manner though not yet thirteen years old, but hardly more attractive for the change. She spoke German like a Parisian, but Leipzig would soon knock the Parisian out of her; she played the piano like a hussar, slayed his *Papillons* like a slavemaster, the consequence of playing too long on French pianos, so said her pappa, and Leipzig would just as soon knock the hussar out of her as the Parisian (if, indeed, there was a difference); but some things seemed changed forever. She wheedled what she wanted from the old man with the whimper of a child when the roar of a Leonora failed – and listened less to Clementine, newly risen in Robert's estimation being newly a mother, giving birth in the absence of her husband the less to trouble him, but she couldn't get Clara to come when she called, let alone do her bidding, reflecting badly on Clara who might easily have helped more with baby Marie.

Clementine was arbitrating a squabble between Alwin and Gustav in the kitchen. Robert hoped to escape without detection, buckling his shoes quietly, stepping as quietly from his room, descending to the hallway, and almost making his exit when Clara shouted from her room. "Herr Schumann, wait for me! I am coming with you!"

She had accompanied him once; no wonder she had been prepared. He minded less than he imagined, flattered by her attention in spite of himself, and the admiration for his compositions was even more welcome from one whose talent he greatly admired; he was glad also to have terminated the activity with Christel which would have been difficult to continue under her scrutiny; but he replied as one under duress. "Hurry! I am walking to Connewitz – and we must not be late for supper."

She was beside him in a minute in walking boots and bonnet. "We have plenty of time, Herr Schumann. It is only three o'clock. If we are late it will be only because you walk so slowly – with your head in the air."

Paris had also made her a joker. "I do not walk with my head in the air."

"Pardon me for disagreeing, Herr Schumann – but you do! By myself I can walk to Connewitz and back in one hour – but with you it takes almost three."

She was grinning, pleased with her whimsy – and so was he, but he kept his grin and his pleasure to himself, kept as well his silence as they left behind winding Leipzig streets, Clara skipping around him as they walked, taking twenty steps to his one, the funnel of a hurricane, Robert the eye, humming the third of his *Papillons*, her favorite, the most childish of the lot.

The road from Leipzig to Connewitz was bucolic, a beaten track through stands of pine and beech and oak, opening occasionally on meadows descending and disappearing into valleys, sward by sward and greener by the sward, brilliant as brooks in sunlight, appearing to Robert like fields of emeralds, and the movement of ducks and geese and cattle and sheep in the distance like a kaleidoscope, a jigsaw continually rearranging itself.

"Herr Schumann! Look out!" Clara tugged his sleeve, halting his step like a driver reining the horses of a carriage.

He stopped, bewildered. "What?"

"You almost stepped on that rock. Did I not say you walk with your head in the air?"

"I do not. I was going to walk around the rock."

"Oh, Yes! With your foot halfway in the air you were going to walk around it. OHH! OHH! OHH! OWCHHH!"

Robert turned. She had doubled back and in her continual hop, skip, step, and jump stumbled on the rock herself. His voice spilled over with triumph. "Ha! What were you saying? Who walks with his head in the air?"

She pretended to wipe tears, knuckles in her eyes, tracing her cheeks with her fingers. "Oh, Herr Schumann, I could have hurt myself. You were cruel to say that. I think, sometimes, there is a beast inside of you waiting to get out."

Satisfied she wasn't hurt, Robert laughed. "Yes, yes! I have never denied it! My doppelganger!"

"Yes, your doppelganger, waiting to spirit away your little Clarchen. Look out! There is another rock!"

He grinned, sidestepping the rock. It was a pleasure to watch her run and jump and skip around him like a child, yet care for his welfare like a woman.

"You know, Herr Schumann, you are not at all in your person as you are in your letters – and you have been even less like yourself since we came back from Paris." She stopped skipping for a moment, walking beside him, holding her head to one side.

"Who am I if I am not myself?"

"In your letters you say how you feel, but in person – you say nothing."

"Maybe because I have already said what I wanted in my letters?"

"Maybe, but I do not think so. I think you are angry with me."

"Why should I be angry with you?"

"I do not know. I wish you would tell me."

"I would tell you if I were angry – but I am not."

"I am glad to hear it – but you must promise to tell me if you are ever angry with me. I could not bear to have you angry with me and not even to know it."

"Why do you think I am angry?"

"I do not know – but you must promise."

He was silent.

"Are you angry, Herr Schumann?"

He shook his head. "No, Clarchen – but you are different since you came back from Paris. I am not so sure of you anymore. I do not know what to expect. That is all."

She smiled, happy he had called her Clarchen. It said better than anything that he liked her – and if he was less sure of her that only added to her mystery. She skipped around him again. "Oh, then I am happy! Oh, how happy I am, how happy!"

He grinned and walked ahead to hide his grin; she skipped behind him, singing to the tune of his third papillon. "Oh, oh, oh, oh, ohhh! O-o-o-oh! O-o-o-oh! Oh, oh, oh, oh, oh, oh, oh, oh, ohhh! How happy I am."

Robert was charmed, but not unembarrassed. "Oh, oh, oh, oh, oh, oh, oh, oh, ohhh! How happy you am!"

She tugged his sleeve again, upsetting his balance.

He dredged indignation into his voice. "Why did you do that? There was no rock."

She walked away. "You were making fun of me, Herr Schumann. That was not very nice."

Robert laughed. "I am sorry. I was just having fun."

She skipped back. "Then it is all right. It is all right to make fun of me – if you are having fun. I want you to have fun."

She took his hand, his right hand, but he disengaged himself and took her right in his left. She was curious, but too preoccupied to comment. They walked hand in hand in silence for a while, steering each other around incidental rocks, before she spoke again. "Herr Schumann, how am I different?"

"What?"

"You said I was different after I came back from Paris. How am I different?"

"You are bigger, taller."

"That is all?"

"You play the piano differently – like a valkyrie, like Brunnhilde."

She snatched her hand away. "Oh, but you are cruel, Herr Schumann. That is not a nice thing to say at all – and especially not to a pianist."

Robert held out his hand. "I am sorry, Clarchen. I was just having fun again."

She took his hand again. "I like it when you call me Clarchen, but you must not be cruel."

"I am sorry. I will try to be more thoughtful."

"But you are right. It was the French pianos. Pappa said they have iron bones and he is right. Only valkyries can play them. But your old Clarchen will soon be back. What else?"

"What else?"

"In what other ways am I different?"

Robert shook his head. "You ask so many questions. I am quite exhausted with your questions."

"But Herr Schumann, I have not even begun to ask you everything that is on my mind." She pulled his hand. "You must tell me. What else? In what other ways am I different?"

"Well, now, be quiet for a minute and let me think."

She said nothing; neither did he for a while, staring at the ground instead of the sky for a change, apparently lost in recollection.

"Well?"

He spoke more quietly. "You seem more thoughtful sometimes – but also more anxious, as if there is something on your mind."

"Oh, Herr Schumann, I can keep no secrets from you. You can read me like a sonata. It is true. I am not sure myself what it is, but something bothers me. I mean, it was wonderful, being in Paris, and meeting Paganini and Goethe and Spohr and everyone, and everything everyone had to say about me, and Pappa went to so much trouble – but what does it all mean? Fifteen minutes after we were home, what was I doing?"

She looked at Robert who shook his head. "I do not know what you mean."

"Fifteen minutes after we came back, what was I doing?"

"I do not know."

"I was cleaning knives in the kitchen, Herr Schumann! I was cleaning knives!"

He kept his eyes from hers, unsure what she meant.

"I felt like Cinderella, Herr Schumann. I had been to the ball, but I had nothing to look forward to. No prince was coming to get me. I had not left behind my glass slipper – and even if I had I did not know who my prince was, or even if there was a prince. I wish I knew what to make of it all. It was wonderful, but now it is over – and I do not know what is next, and I am afraid that whatever it is it will never be better than Paris. I am afraid my whole life is already over." She looked suddenly at Robert. "You understand me, Herr Schumann, do you not? You do not think I am just a silly girl, do you?"

Robert squeezed her hand more tightly. "No, Clarchen. No one who can play the piano like you can be just a silly girl."

She smiled. "Good. I do not care about the others, but I would hate for you to think I was just a silly girl."

Robert shook his head. "For you, Clarchen, the world is only beginning to open its doors. Already you are known in Paris. Soon you will be known in London, Vienna, Amsterdam, Copenhagen, Zurich, Moscow, St. Petersburg – who knows, maybe even New York."

Clara batted eyelashes, like butterflies, papillons, and took a deep breath. "Will you come with me, Herr Schumann? Will you come with me to London?"

"Of course."

"And to Russia?"

"Of course."

"Even to America?"

"Yes, yes, of course."

She exhaled slowly. "Oh, goody, then I am happy again." She sang. "Oh, oh, oh, oh, oh, oh, oh, oh, ohhh! How happy I am!"

Robert spoke sternly. "If you sing that one more time, I shall have to take back everything I have said. I shall have to think you are nothing but a silly girl."

She laughed, singing again. "Oh, but you cannot. You cannot take it back. It is too late. You have said it already."

"I can and I will. I will deny to anyone who will listen that I know you, that I ever knew you, that I ever wanted to know you."

"Oh, then I will not sing it again. I will never sing it again – just for you."

They walked farther, silent again, comfortable with the silence, until Clara looked again at Robert looking at the sky, and realized he was somewhere else again, perhaps even thinking of someone else. She spoke hesitantly, afraid to intrude. "Herr Schumann … you, too, are different. You are quieter. You have something on your mind as well, do you not?"

Robert sighed, still not looking at her. He might as well tell her what had happened; it was but a matter of time before everyone knew; he couldn't hide it forever. He stopped and held up his right hand, wiggling his fingers – except, curiously, for the ring finger which remained limp.

"Herr Schumann, you frighten me. What is the matter with your finger? Why does it not move?"

He sighed again, but put on a smile. "While you were away I did something foolish."

She stared in silence.

"I wanted to strengthen my fingers – you know what I mean, equalize them, make them independent of one another."

"But, Herr Schumann, why equalize them? Chopin says there should be as many different tones as there are fingers."

Robert lost his smile, even the pretence of a smile, curving his mouth downward like a sickle, afraid suddenly she was too young to understand his fear, afraid to reveal his fear to unsympathetic ears. She was more intent on reminding him she had met Chopin – and he had not – but he doubted she realized what she did. "Yes, of course. Chopin. He knows everything, does he not?"

His face scared her, she imagined he might cry; worse, he seemed to withdraw; blue eyes, receding in their sockets, became pinpricks peering through tunnels. She held his traumatized appendage with both hands. "I am sorry, Herr Schumann. Never mind what I said. I am so sorry. What does Chopin know? What does it matter what he thinks?"

Robert didn't look at her. "I put the finger in a sling for three days. I even slept with it in a sling, to strengthen it, to make it equal in strength with the other fingers. Instead, I damaged the tendon."

"Oh, Herr Schumann!"

"I wanted to get even tones with each finger – as you, the great Clara, get so easily. That was what I wanted, an even touch. I thought finger dexterity was in the main a matter of mechanical application. I was wrong."

"Oh, Herr Schumann! I am so sorry. Is there nothing you can do? Would not a doctor help?"

"I have been to see the doctor. He suggested cattle secretions."

"Cattle secretions?"

"To dip my finger in cattle secretions, swimming with raw meat, brandy, and herbs, or directly into the still warm belly of a freshly slaughtered pig, lamb, or a calf, directly from the butcher, directly into the entrails, blood, and feces – that was what the doctor suggested." He rolled his eyes. "Such a delightful prospect."

"And you did that?"

"I did – though I was afraid I would develop the characteristics of a cow myself."

She could say nothing and held his hand, stroking his finger tenderly, staring pitifully. "Oh, thank God, that will never happen!"

Her brow was so wrinkled he couldn't resist. "MOOOO!"

She dropped his hand. "Oh, Herr Schumann! You startled me. You must not do that, never do that, not even in fun –" She cut herself short, about to say he would turn into a real cow if he made fun. "What will you do?"

He surprised her with a smile. "It might be the best thing, after all. It will force me to concentrate on what is really important – for me."

"And what is that?"

"Composition! Composition, and nothing else! However much the finger might heal it will never be fit for the career of a virtuoso – but I can concentrate instead on what is truly important. You might say it is a sign from God. Your silly nine-fingered Herr Schumann was never meant to be a performer, but a composer."

"Oh, Herr Schumann, you take it much too lightly."

"How else should I take it? What else should I do?"

"Oh, I do not know, I do not know, but surely there is something."

"What?"

She shook her head helplessly.

"I must compose. That will be my salvation. Your pappa has said it himself. You know what he thinks of my *Papillons*."

"He says they are piquant and original – and he wants me to learn them all as soon as possible. He says they are like nothing that has come before."

"And Grillparzer has said almost the same thing. They cannot both be wrong."

Franz Grillparzer had called Robert a rarity of his age, acknowledged he stood on his own feet, neither with a crutch nor on the shoulders of others, drawing inspiration entirely from his own new and ideal world. Clara nodded. "And he should know! He is a poet!"

"And Dorn has said similar things – also about my Toccata, the *ABEGG Variations*, and the studies on which I am currently working derived from Paganini's Caprices. He says all my works are models of writing against the rules." He laughed, not unselfconsciously. "But he says he has had enough of my imagination. If I will not listen to him, he says he has nothing to teach me."

"Dorn is so bloody stupid!"

Robert raised his eyebrows, smiling. "But he is correct. I have Marpurg's *Musical Theory*, Bach's *Well-Tempered Clavier*. No one is more thorough than Bach – absolutely no one! They are all telling me what I have always known. I already have everything I need. All that is left now is to compose. That is all."

She stared into his eyes. "And there is nothing else?"

He stared back. "Nothing."

Her mouth drooped, her eyes dropped.

He imagined her chagrin stemmed from his misfortune, nothing else. "Actually, there is one other thing."

She looked up, a smile drawing her mouth again. "Yes?"

"A short time before your return from Paris we had got together, a group of us, and got to discussing the state of music in Germany. Just think about it, Clara. Rossini rules the stage, Herz and Hunten command the world of the piano – and yet it is only a few years since Beethoven and Weber and Schubert walked the earth. Mendelssohn and Chopin have come among us, it is true, and that is a blessing, but we decided we simply could not just look on and do nothing. We decided to establish a music journal that would not be afraid to draw clear distinctions between the good and the bad in music. If we do not dare to attack what is bad, how can we dare to defend what is good? Do you remember my review of the La ci darem Variations?"

"Yes, of course – with your doppelgangers, Florestan and Eusebius. I have a copy in my room of the *Allgemeine Musikalisch Zeitung* in which they were published."

Robert smiled. "Exactly, Florestan and Eusebius. I have a score more of such doppelgangers, and each has his own point of view which he is dying to express. They are all dying to do battle with the Philistines now dictating the music of the day. That is why I call them the Band of David, followers of King David, who will fight to defeat the musical Philistines. The journal is to be called the *Neue Zeitschrift fur Musik*."

Clara wished for something profound to say. "It is a perfect title, Herr Schumann! That is just what we need! I feel so proud! I had no idea!"

"I mean to write my heart out and so do the others. Knorr and Schunk have already committed themselves, and so have Ortlepp, Reuter, and Luhe. We have sent letters to Stephen Heller in Paris, Franz Otto in London, Joseph Fischhof in Vienna, and Richard Wagner in Dresden. I have also asked our venerable Herr Heinrich Dorn to join us. I would like to ask your pappa – I know he is a busy man, but he would not need to do a thing. The prestige of his name alone would add credibility to our enterprise. What do you think?"

"Herr Schumann! Words fail me! This is such a surprise – but such a wonderful surprise!"

"I did not want to say too much too soon, but Hofmeister has consented to be our publisher. The time for talk is past. It is time to show something for our gossip."

Clara beamed. "Oh, Herr Schumann! Pappa will be so proud. When will you tell him?"

"I was waiting for the right time, but maybe I am just procrastinating now. I have already found rooms for myself in the meantime."

"Rooms?"

"Yes, of course, rooms. I will need my own place if I am no longer boarding with you."

Clara's smile faded, her eyes wandered. "But why would you no longer board with us?"

"It would not be right, Clara, not if I were no longer taking lessons from your pappa. If I am to concentrate on composition there is little point in taking lessons. I will never be a virtuoso of the piano."

"But I do not want you to leave."

Her voice was smaller than before. Robert was surprised. "Why not?"

Clara turned her head from his. "Who would I walk with if you were to leave? Who would I talk to about how I feel?"

Robert remained silent, but when Clara said nothing more he became aware of the silence for once more than she. "We can still go walking, Clara – to Connewitz or wherever you wish – and I will not be so very far away that we cannot talk when we wish."

She kept her face from his, but took his hand again turning him around. "I think it is time we went back, do you not?"

THEY WALKED BACK in a comfortable silence, a comfort which expanded as they reentered the bustle of Leipzig. Clara insisted on holding Robert's right hand; as long as it didn't hurt she felt she might do some good, and so she did; it helped to know that his most crippled feature drew her greatest tenderness.

Approaching Grimmaische Gasse, mantled with comfort, they needed only to look at each other to smile; but raising the iron ring of the knocker Robert's smile was erased. They heard a yowl from within which resounded down the street: "YowoooOwoooOwoooOwoooOwooooo!"

Robert disengaged his hand as Nanny opened the door. They were greeted by a loud voice. "You wretch! Is this the pleasure a son gives his pappa? Is this the gratitude?"

In the parlor Wieck towered over Alwin, pulling him by his hair to his knees, throwing him to the floor before sitting down himself to still his own trembling, conserve his strength.

Clementine and Gustav stood in one corner; Robert and Clara might have been as invisible as servants as they entered.

Alwin crawled on his knees to the piano bench. "Please, Pappa, please! Please let me play! I will make you proud. I will play as well as Clara. Please, just let me play! I am sorry I have not practised. I will practise everyday. I will make you proud."

Wieck rose again. "No! That you will not! You are a blockhead of a boy who imagines his pappa speaks only for his own pleasure! You have forfeited your chance for today!" He pulled Alwin again by his hair, again to his knees, and pushed him again to the floor, staggering finally back to sink again in his chair, trembling with exertion and rage.

Robert was hardly unaware of Wieck's rages, but they always reduced him to a brooding silence.

"Clara!" It was the first sign that Wieck was aware of their presence.

"Yes, Pappa?"

"Play the sonata by Weber."

"Yes, Pappa."

Robert stared, amazed at her coolness, seating herself at the piano to play the sonata as comfortably as if nothing had happened – and flawlessly, beautifully. Wieck settled back in his chair, closing his eyes, his scowl banished. No one could soothe him like Clara, and no one moved until she had finished except Gretel washing herself in the window.

What Clara didn't know, what Robert couldn't confess, he could hardly believe himself. During his student years in Heidelberg and Leipzig, his peregrinations through Germany, Switzerland, and Italy, he had caught the disease of lovers, the same caught by Schubert, courting Countess Caroline Esterhazy, settling instead for her chambermaid, Pepi Pokelhofer, losing his hair in consequence, hiding his secret under a ratty wig, composing through the humiliation his string quintet, considered among the greatest chamberworks ever, also his greatest piano sonatas, all three of them in a single month, September 1828, almost within a month of his death, 19 November, composing to hours (perhaps minutes and seconds) before his death, scribbling imperishable work, redeeming himself, sad and funny and valiant to the end.

He had said nothing to Christel about his fears, imagining the disease might have surfaced as a consequence of their lovemaking, confessing the redness on his penis owed only to excessive friction. He had greased his sores with a brew of mercury mixed with pork fat, butter, vinegar, myrrh, sulphur, and turpentine – but he would never confess it to Clara. He never doubted she would be sympathetic, whether or not she understood, but whatever her ability at the piano she was a child, always first a child, finding paradise in a bowl of cherries, in strawberries and cream.

His pappa's death had provided an inheritance of eight thousand thaler to be administered by a guardian, Gottlob Rudel, a Zwickau merchant in iron and cloth, the kind of person who ruled the world – stiff in appearance as if he swallowed rulers. He had moved into his own rooms on the fourth floor at 21 Burgstrasse – and begun, finally, he liked to think, his adult life, precipitated by his misfortune. It was that simple: no misfortune, no life – at least, no life worth living, no life of any profundity.

He saw less of Clara than he planned, but he saw less of everyone except Christel whom he called to visit whenever she could get away. Besides, Clara toured continually with Wieck, further compounding his problems. Wieck, Ludwig Schunke, and Julius Knorr comprised the editorial board of the *Zeitschrift*, but with Wieck on tour, Schunke sickly, and Knorr uncommitted, the responsibility fell on Robert alone, a responsibility he welcomed, wanting from the start to make the journal his own, but he hated to remind writers and reviewers continually of deadlines and obligations.

The two rooms, small though they were, had become his office, and he had few enough articles of furniture, a bed alongside one wall of the inner room and a chest of drawers; a piano and desk in the front room and some chairs, but the apartment was flooded with paper: correspondence, manuscripts, newspapers, journals, files, books, on his desk, on the floor – and flooded no less with cigar smoke. He liked the panorama gained by his height of narrow streets, narrow buildings, narrow roofs, gabled windows and dormers clawing the skyline – also the extended daylight, more salubrious than lamps and candles. Best of all, the work progressed well, their first three issues had been received with respect – but without more cooperation the next would not be finished on time.

He had just written forty-three letters apologizing to subscribers for yet another delay in the publication of the forthcoming issue (thanks to the delinquency of their editor-in-chief, Julius Knorr), when he recognized Knorr's wheezing breath and shuffling step on the stairs, and took a deep breath preparing for the unpleasantness ahead.

Knorr scratched the door, too lazy it seemed even to knock. "Come in, Knorr."

Knorr shuffled in, a piano teacher, round of shoulder and stout, three years older than Robert, but his smooth cheeks and the long hair falling to his shoulders when he removed his cap belied his age, also his gender. "Good morning, Schumann." He spoke in a whisper, still panting from his climb, losing sound to his own breathlessness.

Robert stayed at his desk, barely looking at Knorr. "I do not know what is so very good about it, Knorr – unless you mean you have done a good morning's work."

Knorr laughed, getting back his breath, he-he-he-he-he, a soft laugh that seemed to trickle like drool from his mouth. "I have been out all morning, Schumann, listening to the birds. There is no music better. It is good for my illness. I am much the better for the morning – thank you so very much for asking. He-he-he-he-he."

"If I have not asked –"

"You have not!"

"– it is with reason."

Knorr rolled his eyes. "I have been sick, Schumann – sick with the ague, and you know it. I have been shaking with fever, alternating between hot and cold until I thought I would die – a malarial fever, the Herr Doktor said. My joints ache, my very bones. Paroxysms, Schumann. I have suffered paroxysms. I am told I am fortunate to be walking."

"And to be playing skat – and billiards. You were seen yesterday, Knorr. It is no use making excuses."

"Come on, man, Schumann. You cannot expect a man recuperating from the ague to sit immediately at a desk and churn out letters like a printing press, not even you. I have not been well. I am here now."

Robert got up from the desk. "Then pick up a pen and begin, Knorr." He cleared a corner of his desk, pointed to the pen, the ink well, the blotter. "I have completed the bulk of the correspondence. There are only twenty or so letters left to write. Why do you not begin, Knorr."

Knorr looked out of the window, pursing his lips. "I cannot. I must be home in an hour. I must rest."

"Then why did you come?"

"I came to visit Schunke. He too is sick, you know, always coughing. His mamma is staying with him."

Ludwig Schunke, Louis to his friends, occupied rooms on the ground floor. "I know. I saw him yesterday. He is in bed, like all sick men should be."

"But not like all recuperating men. I came to wish him well, and I thought I would wish you good morning while I was here – but, as you say there is nothing good about it, no good has come of it. I should have saved my breath. Climbing four flights of stairs for your benefit I have climbed for nothing."

Robert took a deep breath. "Perhaps not, Knorr. Perhaps not for nothing after all. Please, sit. Sit down. I have something to say."

He indicated a chair; Knorr sat.

Robert spoke, not looking at Knorr. He hated to say what he said, but the *Zeitschrift* was important. The best way, the easiest way for all, was a clean cut. "This is not the first time you have been sick, Knorr, as you say. I have talked it over with the others and we want you out. We *all* want you out. With Wieck on tour and Louis sick, I have done everything – writing, editing, proofreading – that you were contracted to do. Wieck, we understood from the beginning, would give us no more than the prestige of his name, but that is not the case with the rest of us. I had not meant to speak until Louis was well again – but if you refuse to help us when he is sick, there is no reason to wait until he is well. If I am to do your work, I would sooner do it without your interference. I am sorry to have to say this, Knorr, but we want you out, all of us, and the sooner the better."

Robert looked momentarily at Knorr; the fat face was whiter, the jaw lowered, the mouth open in a circle, his knuckles white clutching the arms of the chair. "This is your doing, Schumann. I cannot believe the others want me out."

"I will not lie to you. It is, indeed, my doing – and with good reason, as I have convinced the others. Whoever's doing it is, we all want you out."

"You cannot be rid of me so easily, not you. You are just an editor. I am the editor-in-chief. I have a contract with the journal which runs for three more years. You cannot simply order me to leave."

"You have signed the contract, it is true, but you have broken the contract yourself. It is no longer binding." He was prepared and pulled out the contract, turning the pages to the paragraph he wanted, setting the pages on the desk before Knorr, pointing. "This is the paragraph I wish you to consider." He read it aloud. "'Herr Knorr agrees to undertake the maintenance of records of correspondence, articles, and musical compositions, the responsibility for the finances of the paper, as well as for the first revision and proof-reading.'" Robert leaned back in his chair. "You have done none of these things as you have sworn. You have rendered the contract null and void yourself. It is not fair to me to have to continue along these lines. My own work suffers, my own health, and so does the work of the journal."

Knorr got up and shuffled to the door, turning before exiting, his face twitching. "I have not been well. I have suffered from the ague – but hardly as much as I have suffered here today, hardly as much as you have caused me to suffer today – you, my friend, Schumann." He paused, softening his face, blinking his eyes, but Robert just shook his head, not looking at him. Finally, Knorr drew himself to his full height, all sixty-four inches, and slammed the door behind him.

Robert jumped at the noise, shaking his head, picking up his pen again, but setting it down again a moment later, sighing and slumping in his chair. This was not what he had wanted, this was alien to his nature, however much Knorr had deserved his comeuppance. He remained slumped in his chair as twilight crept over the windowsill; much had happened, there was much to ponder.

Troubles with publishers were to be expected, but he remained aghast at people who attached their names to ventures meaning to undertake the ventures in name alone. When Hofmeister, their first publisher, had expressed doubt regarding the success of their project he had applied to his own brothers, Eduard in Zwickau and Karl in Schneeberg, both publishers like their pappa before them, and they had supported the venture until a new publisher, Hartmann, had declared an interest. He had not expected Wieck to be absent as much, Louis as sick, Knorr as undependable, the correspondence as numbing, the new compositions as secondrate – nor had he expected so many letters to write, manuscripts to judge, most of which he had managed himself. Wieck could no longer credibly say he found him soft, spoiled, lazy – but other forces were as well at work.

The matter of his disease still distressed him, the disease worse than death, as did his damaged finger – but there was also something else. His sister-in-law, Rosalie, wife of his Schneeberg brother, Karl, had died that year, as devoted to his music and enterprise as to her husband; she had been followed shortly to the grave by Julius, his third brother, recalling his sister Emilie, drowning herself at nineteen, supposedly insane, too overwhelmed by the malady of her skin to face the world, followed shortly by their pappa – so many dead, so young. His old fear had returned, of which the Caruses had disabused him when he had first met them, that he was destined for the asylum in Colditz, the daunting 15th century castle which had served already as a fortress, prison, poorhouse, hospital, and concentration camp.

There was more: Mendelssohn, Chopin, Liszt, were all his own age, but with reputations far outstripping his. They had never doubted their vocations, never sidetracked themselves, not with law nor anything else, but all were virtuosos, able to promote their works themselves, which led him back to the distress about his finger.

The *Zeitschrift* kept him from his real work, the Sonata in F sharp minor – and when his work suffered, he suffered. He recalled times as a boy, he had been no more than six, sitting at the piano in the middle of the night, when the family had found him playing progressions of chords, crying because he couldn't materialize the music in his head. Then he had been hampered by a lack of technique, now it was the *Zeitschrift* – but the *Zeitschrift* was no less important, for music in general if not for his own in particular, a service of which he was proud, a light to show the way, to show up the pretenders.

He remained slumped at his desk for hours before he recognized he had yet to light his lamp, but he couldn't get out of his chair. It wasn't until he heard a noise that he moved, a violin in his head, a yowling melody, like a cat, before he realized the sound came from the street, a live cat, and he got up to go to the window.

He was relieved to see a cat, relieved it wasn't in his head, even smiled looking down at the tabby, brindled and brilliant in the narrow street, nuzzling a lamppost.

A girl appeared from a doorway across with blond curls. "Lucy! You come here, you Lucy Cat!"

Robert continued to smile, but as the girl crossed the street the cat looked up and its eyes appeared to grow larger, greener, narrower.

The girl wagged her finger. "Bad cat! Bad Lucy Cat! Scaring us to death."

The girl disappeared with the cat, but the image of its eyes remained, Luciferian eyes, growing before his own eyes. He imagined himself toppling from the window, the street rising to meet him, spreadeagling him on its cobbles, head flattened, neck twisted, whites of eyes bulging and bleeding. Blood rose in his neck, choking him, rushing to his head, and he rushed from the window collapsing on his bed amid a haze of scarlet, then blackness. How long he lay there he couldn't have said, but when he regained consciousness he felt there was someone else in the room.

He lay on his back, afraid to betray himself with movement. Someone – or some thing – stood in the middle of the room, so large it seemed to carry the ceiling on hunched shoulders, arms wide holding apart the walls, a death's head masked in a black stocking watching him. The bed was wet; sweat congealed like a cocoon around him trickling past his temples, beading into his ears, tickling as it trickled, but he didn't dare brush it aside, unable to tell what was real from what was not. Had Emilie been subject to such visions? Was there a curse on the family claiming victims, now for insanity, now for death?

It was the thought of insanity that moved him, incarceration in the asylum in Colditz, any movement seemed preferable to none. He jumped from his bed avoiding the windows, afraid of what he might see on the street to tempt him to jump, and left his rooms, stumbling down the stairs, almost falling in his hurry in the dark, to Ludwig Schunke's rooms on the ground floor, throwing himself on the door, clawing and hammering with his fists. "Louis! Let me in! Louis!"

Someone answered him almost immediately, but it wasn't Louis. "Who is it? Who is it at such a time? Is it Robert?"

"Frau Schunke? Yes, it is me. Please let me in."

"If you will just wait a minute."

Louis's mamma, come to nurse her sick son, let him in. "What is it, Robert? What is upsetting you?"

"Is Louis awake?"

Frau Schunke was relieved to see Robert appeared all right but for his perturbation. "The whole house is awake, and if you do not come in and settle down the whole street will be awake."

"I am sorry, Frau Schunke. You are right. I am sorry – but I was so afraid."

"Come, come inside, Robert. Sit down. Will you have some coffee?"

"Yes, thank you. Is Louis awake?"

He was answered by a cough from the inner room, wrenched like a rattle from the throat of its host.

Frau Schunke lit a candle and the stove to boil water for coffee. "What was the matter that you had to come down in the middle of the night? What was the matter that you could not wait until morning? Go, go. Go inside. Talk to Louis. We can talk later. I will bring you coffee in a minute."

Robert nodded, walking into the bedroom. "Hullo, Louis."

Louis coughed again, long and hoarse; Robert heard the rattle again, carried a chair to the bedside, and sat down. "Robert?"

"Yes."

"What is ... matter?" Louis's voice was weak, drawing out the words slowly. "Over there ... candle. Let us ... light."

Robert lit the candle and brought it to the bed. Louis wore a white nightcap.

"Good, now I can see ... face." He coughed again. "What ... matter?"

Robert shook his head, not looking at Louis. "You are the one who is sick and you ask me what is the matter." He shrugged. "I do not know what is the matter, but it was horrible."

Louis spoke quietly, momentarily master of his throat. "What was horrible?"

"There was a cat outside the window in the evening."

"Yes, I heard it."

"Ah, so you saw the cat?"

"No, I heard it."

"Ah, but at least it was there."

"Yes."

"Good – at least, I did not imagine that."

Louis shook his head.

Robert took a deep breath. "I do not know how to explain it, Louis, but I was looking at the cat, and suddenly ... suddenly ..."

"Yes?"

"I wanted to jump, Louis. I wanted to jump into the street – for no reason."

Frau Schunke stood in the doorway. "Not for no reason, Robert. If you ask me, you have been working too hard. You must rest. It is no good driving yourself like an animal."

"But then who will do the work?"

"That is the most foolish question, but you men persist in asking it as if the whole world depends upon your work – but if you jump out of the window, then who will do the work?"

Robert said nothing.

Louis held out his hand from the bed. "We have not been good partners to you, Robert. I with my sickness, Wieck with his daughter, and Knorr ... oh, that Knorr!"

He had spoken too much; immediately the rattle was pulled again, up and down, abrading his throat.

"There is no more Knorr. I told him today what we decided about the matter."

Louis nodded.

Frau Schunke spoke from the next room. "He was here this morning. He said he was going to visit you."

Robert nodded. "He came."

"How did it go?"

"I told him. He said very little. I felt like an ogre. I have done no work since I told him. I wonder if we did the right thing after all. He was a friend."

Frau Schunke spoke gently. "That is business, Robert. That is how it is in business. You did the right thing."

"Thank you, Frau Schunke, but I am not cut out for business. I am a musician and a writer, not a manager."

"Still, you did the right thing, and that is what matters."

She brought the coffee. "Drink. Then sleep. Tomorrow you will feel better."

Robert took the cup. "Would it be all right if I stayed here for tonight?"

"Of course."

"I do not want to go near the window again."

"Of course."

"I could sleep on the floor."

"Sleep on the sofa. I will sleep on the chair. Now, drink, and then sleep. Do not talk so much."

ii

There was a chart on the wall of the doctor's office, the outline of a man, a map of the nervous system. He had come to the right place; with a map like that Robert was sure the doctor could trace his problem. He had understood that Frau Schunke was more worried than she appeared when she had suggested the next morning that he see a doctor if his distress continued; she had spoken lightly, she might have been recommending a walk, but he was glad for her concern; overwork had damaged his nerves, but they had medicine for damaged nerves, and Dr. Ohr, a friend of the Schunkes, was known for his skill, a skill now at his disposal.

The doctor was a small man with a large white beard, small brown eyes magnified by spectacles. "So, Herr Schumann! You are young Louis's friend. I have heard about you many good things. The Schunkes are old friends of mine. How is it with you this morning?"

Robert had not slept much of the night, but felt safe enough in the sofa not to disturb anyone; he had breakfasted with them before visiting the doctor. "I am a little tired. I did not sleep well last night."

"Ah, yes, of course. That is why you are here, and I am sorry to hear it, and we will discuss it in a moment – but let me say first how pleased I am to be making your acquaintance. My wife plays everything of yours she can find. She says you are among the finest of our budding composers." He winked. "And she is a discerning critic. You may want to consider her for your *Zeitschrift* – that is, if I may be so bold as to make such a suggestion."

Robert was proud the doctor knew the *Zeitschrift* and felt less tired already. "Danke, Herr Doktor. I am happy to hear it."

The doctor crossed his arms, leaned back in his chair, and spoke conversationally. They might have been old friends talking. "And what is your latest work, Herr Schumann? She is dying to know."

"I am writing a sonata, my first, in F sharp minor – but I have been so busy with the *Zeitschrift* I have made very little progress. Sometimes I think that affects my peace of mind."

"Of course, of course! What kind of composer can leave off composing without experiencing distress? I understand – I understand perfectly – but now, tell me, exactly, what were you feeling last night?"

In daylight his fears seemed silly, vain. "I think, after all, Frau Schunke may be right. I have been working too hard."

"No, no, no, no! I did not ask what you thought. I asked what you felt. I want to know *exact*ly what you felt last night."

Robert nodded, furrowing his brow, narrowing his eyes. "I think what started the trouble was –"

"No, Herr Schumann! No thinking! What did you *feel* last night."

Robert didn't hesitate. "Panic! I felt panic, Herr Doktor."

The doctor nodded. Robert might just as well have said he had felt great happiness. "Good! Panic. Now we can ask. Panic for what? What did you think was going to happen?"

"I thought I was going to lose my reason."

"Why did you think that?"

"It happened to Emilie – my sister."

"And where is your sister now?"

"She is dead. She drowned herself."

"And do you think about your sister much?"

"I have been thinking about her, recently – because my brother died – also Rosalie, my sister-in-law."

The doctor nodded. "Now we are getting somewhere. The next question. You must not be offended. It is necessary for me to know. Were you drinking anything?"

Robert shook his head. "Nothing. I had sat without moving for a long time. Before that I had been smoking cigars. That is all."

"Good. Now, you say you had been sitting without moving for a long time. What made you move?"

"I heard a cat outside. At first I thought it was a violin, a new melody in my head – but it was a cat. Louis heard it also, from downstairs."

"And then what did you do?"

"I went to the window."

"And what did you see?"

Robert told him about the little girl who had come for the cat and how he had felt. "I saw myself from the window, on the street, on my back, as if I had jumped. I was afraid I might actually jump. Is it not true that we try to make our visions come true?"

The doctor shook his head. "No, not always. It depends upon the vision, upon the person. Tell me what else has been troubling you."

"I have told you about my sister – and the others."

"What else?"

Robert mentioned his worries about the *Zeitschrift*, but nothing about his finger, nothing about his disease. When he was finished the doctor nodded again. "I might have guessed. It is not unusual. You have worries, emotional worries, financial worries, business worries. You are alone too much with your worries. It is understandable that your mind is playing tricks. It is your mind's way of telling you to relax."

"But the work has got to be done! And there is no one else to do it!"

"Of course! The work has got to be done! But there is always some work that is more important than other work. Do what is important. Leave the rest. When Louis is better it will get done. When you have found someone to replace Knorr it will get done even more quickly. In the meantime, answer only the important letters, read only as many compositions as you need to review. There is no need to harm yourself permanently to repair a temporary situation."

Robert nodded. "That is what I, too, have been thinking – but it helps to hear you say it out loud."

"Good. Now, listen to me. For your medicine I am going to order you to visit the Schunkes in the evening, every evening, for at least one hour. Is that understood?"

"Frau Schunke has already invited me to sup tonight."

"Good. Now, still, one more thing."

"Yes?"

The doctor smiled. "Medicine is of no use here, Herr Schumann. You must find for yourself a woman. A woman will cure you like no medicine can."

Robert smiled. He had been thinking the same thing. Women liked to pamper him, his mamma, Emilie through his boyhood, Agnes Carus, his sisters-in-law, Theresa, Rosalie, Pauline, even little Clara – and Christel though she was only a servant. "I will do my best."

"Good – and finish your sonata in F sharp minor. That will help more than anything else."

Robert nodded. "Danke, Herr Doktor. You are right about the sonata. I can think of nothing else sometimes. I am going to give myself a little holiday from letters and business."

"Good! My wife will be glad to hear it."

iii

Clara had a new friend, Ernestine von Fricken, three years older, seventeen to her fourteen when they met during a tour of Altenburg, Zwickau, Schneeberg, Plauen, Chemnitz, and Karlsbad, daughter of the Captain Baron Freiherr von Fricken and the Countess Franziska Ernestine von Zedwitz. Ernestine lived in Asch, but had attended the concert in Plauen with the Baron, an amateur flautist. Baron and daughter had been so impressed with Clara they had wanted lessons from Wieck who had arranged for Ernestine to board with them. Showing her friend to her room Clara talked about its previous occupant. "I cannot wait for you to meet Herr Schumann. I like him best of all our acquaintances." She clapped as she spoke and never stopped smiling.

Ernestine was a soft woman, a tender woman, an ingratiating woman, easily liked because she made herself likable, but felt it necessary to dampen her young friend's ardor. "I am glad to hear it, but I have a gentleman of my own in Asch. I do not think Herr Schumann would make me forget him because I like him very well indeed."

Her smile was private, excluding Clara, and Clara's own smile vanished. She looked away. "Do not be so quick to judge Herr Schumann, Ernestine. You have yet to meet him."

Her pique surprised Ernestine. "Oh, my dear Clara, I daresay you like your Herr Schumann splendidly, and with good reason, and I am glad for you, but I must beg to differ. I am sure my own gentleman satisfies me well enough not to care for your Herr Schumann."

Clara remained unsatisfied. "I am not your dear Clara, and I insist again that you must not be so quick to judge Herr Schumann." She left the room leaving Ernestine with her mouth dropped open.

Ernestine sighed; Clara was younger than she had imagined in the matter of men; but as a musician, and that was how she loved her best, she was older than them all. She followed her friend out. "Clara, I am sorry. I did not realize how important this was to you. I will look forward to meeting your Herr Schumann."

Clara paused in the hallway without turning. "It is all right. We sometimes go walking in the late afternoon, sometimes all the way to Connewitz. He may be here even today."

"I will look forward to meeting him then."

Clara smiled again. "I will call you when he comes."

"Good. Danke. I will look forward to the time."

It was a long time since Robert had visited, he had been busy with the *Zeitschrift*, but he had sent her a message, he meant to take more time for himself and wished again to visit; she had been half afraid he wouldn't appear, but he did.

They were at the piano in the parlor, but Clara recognized his touch, his rap of the iron ring, and announced him to Ernestine before Nanny opened the door. She beamed as she spoke. "Now, Ernestine, you will meet Herr Schumann."

Ernestine nodded, unable to stop smiling; a blind man could have seen through Clara's transparency; but Ernestine was no less excited herself, unable to imagine what might have inspired Clara's excitement. She expected someone who played the piano with Clara's exuberance and energy, with Clara's dark good looks. Instead, when Robert entered the parlor, he appeared more sober than any man she had known, old, tired, dreamy, moving so languidly he might have been spineless. His hair was fairer than Clara's, his eyes a paler blue, tired eyes, reflecting the worries of the world. "Hullo, Clara."

It had been a long while since Clara had seen him, but in her eagerness to introduce her friend she hardly noticed the difference. "Herr Schumann, I want you to meet my new friend, Ernestine von Fricken! She stays now in your old room. Ernestine, this is Herr Schumann."

Ernestine smiled, held out her hand. "How is it with you, Herr Schumann."

Robert took her hand, but without a smile, apparently sunk in thought. Ernestine had the head of a Madonna, the sensual dimensions of a shepherdess, the sky in her eyes, roses in her skin, a rainbow in her hair, flute in her throat. He looked at her as he spoke, but seemed to look through her. "'She doth teach the torches to burn bright. It seems she hangs upon the cheek of night as a rich jewel in an Ethiop's ear; beauty too rich for use, for earth too dear.'"

"What?"

"Shakespeare. When Romeo first met Juliet."

"I told you! I told you! Herr Schumann is a great reader! He knows everything! Even the motto for his *Zeitschrift* is from Shakespeare."

"'Only they that come to hear a merry bawdy play, a noise of targets, or to see a fellow in a long motley coat guarded with yellow, will be deceived.' It is from the Prologue to *Henry VIII.*"

Ernestine didn't understand what he said, but his manner was so soft, so poetic, that her hand flew to her mouth which had dropped suddenly open again. "Oh, but that is beautiful."

"Do you like to read?"

"Yes."

"What do you like to read?"

His expression remained the same, full of gravity, full of attention; his eyes seemed sad and dark despite their light blue color, his question delicate, curious but unaggressive. Ernestine found herself whispering. "I like Jean Paul Richter."

"Oh, that is one of Herr Schumann's favorite authors! He has composed music to go with Jean Paul's novel, *Flegeljahre!*"

The two heard Clara, but looked only at each other. "Did you, really?"

"I did, my *Papillons*. They have now been published for some time."

Clara looked from one of her friends to the other, neither of whom looked at her. "It is a beautiful novel, is it not, Herr Schumann? I have read it twice now."

Ernestine whispered again, staring at Robert. "I would love to hear them."

"I would love to play them for you, but Clara plays them better. I have hurt my finger too much to do them justice anymore."

"I will play them for you!"

Still they looked only at each other; Clara might have been a rug. Robert imagined Ernestine was the tonic the doctor had recommended; her timeliness could mean nothing else. "I once visited his widow in Bayreuth with a friend."

"Jean Paul's widow?"

"The same. She gave us his portrait. We also visited the tavern where he wrote *Flegeljahre*. We spoke with Frau Rollwenzel who owns the tavern. She told us the most amazing stories about him."

"That is so wonderful. I can hardly believe it."

Clara almost jumped. "Shall I play the *Papillons* now?"

Robert held up his lame finger. "I cannot play them. I am a nine-fingered man since my accident."

"I am so sorry." Ernestine's sorrow had less to do with Robert's accident than with a need to express herself in his behalf; her surprise was so great she didn't even ask about the accident. "That must have been terrible."

Robert didn't notice that she hadn't asked; it was more important just to keep talking. "On the contrary it has helped me to concentrate on what is important. Composition. My *Zeitschrift*."

"You do so much!"

"It is nothing."

Ernestine just stared.

"Shall we listen to little Clara?"

Clara played the *Papillons*; Robert explained how they followed *Flegeljahre*; they arranged a walk the next day, the three of them, to Connewitz.

When he left that day Clara spoke triumphantly. "There! What did I tell you? What do you think of Herr Schumann now? Is he not the finest of men?"

Ernestine remained bemused. "He has the silkiest hair."

Clara smiled, determined to look more closely at Robert's hair the next day.

iv

They walked to Connewitz the next day, and again the next, Clara delighted her friends were getting close, but sorry they appeared to find her almost bothersome; Robert still joked with her, but reserved serious conversation for Ernestine – who hardly spoke to her anymore, even at home.

Wieck was as delighted with the developments as Robert and Ernestine. He imagined Robert spent too much time with Clara, and after the injury to his finger did not rate his prospects highly, did not wish him attached to Clara. He sent Clara to Dresden to study voice, violin, theory, and composition, considering them integral to her finish as a pianist, throwing Robert and Ernestine together more than they might have managed by themselves.

But Clara wrote letters, and on the occasion of Robert's twenty-fourth birthday she wrote a letter which Robert kept all his life, reread many times, among the sweetest he had ever received, but to which he never replied.

Dresden, 8 June, 1834

My dear Herr Schumann,

Today is Sunday, 8 June, the day on which the good God let fall a spark from heaven and you were born, and here I sit, writing to you, though I have been invited to two places this afternoon.

I send you my good wishes – that you may not always be so contrary, that you may not drink so much Bavarian beer – that you compose with industry, that you write more for the Zeitschrift – and that you resolve to come to Dresden!

Do you mean to take so little notice of a friend, Herr Schumann, that you will not even write to her? Everytime the post comes I hope for a letter from a certain Herr Enthusiast, but ah! I am always disappointed.

Listen: If you do not know it already, Herr Richard Wagner has got ahead of you. His symphony was performed and is said to be just like Beethoven's in A major. But it is said he drives his symphony like a gig over stock and stone and falls into every ditch in the road — but still he gets to his destination though he arrives bruised black and blue!

I have been hearing the most flattering stories about you, that you forgot your linen in a carriage! What a pretty fellow you are! Did you get it back from the driver?

When you come to Dresden I will give you a piece of cake that I have saved for you — but first I shall have to bake it! I am also going to send you a contribution for your Zeitschrift, 8 pages long, and then you will have to pay me a lot of money.

When you write to me make sure your handwriting is not so very original that I cannot read it. This brilliant, unique, witty, intelligent letter comes to you from your friend,

Clara Wieck
Clara Wieck
Doppelganger

Wieck was onstage, trying to ignore the audience in the hall, six hundred strong, as he removed the keyboard from its bed to fix the sticking keys. Clara sat on the other side, surrounded by admirers, laughing as if the difficulty were his alone. He no longer knew what to do with her. He had interrupted her lessons in Dresden for a tour of Magdeburg, Brunswick, and Hanover, but she was no longer pliant, no longer the Clara of yesteryear, no longer willing to be guided in anything, not in her clothing, not in her practice, not in her schedule. She woke at nine in the morning, wasn't ready until eleven to receive visitors, dined with them at noon, and in the afternoon refused to practise, thinking only of the theater and the gentlemen she would meet – even on the days of her performances! Fortunately, her technique was so advanced she played flawlessly despite her distraction, even ignorant of what she was playing – but her distraction showed in her face, affecting the good wishes of those who saw her. Worst of all she complained about the quality of the pianos so loudly and so publicly that he was afraid she was ruining his business.

Her complaints were not without justification and her manner was typical, sitting across the stage from him, talking with Karl and Theodore Muller of the Muller String Quartet (also on the bill), and other musicians including Carl Banck (now her voice teacher, who never left her side, whom Wieck had invited on the tour the better for her to forget Schumann). She ignored her pappa, made him her lackey, and seemed to care nothing for his difficulty – as much her difficulty as his, but you wouldn't know it to look at her. The keys had begun to stick during the finale of the Chopin concerto and she had asked him to fix it during the intermission – she had demanded it – before taking herself to the other side of the stage and sitting prettily with her gentlemen.

Clara was too engrossed in the unfairness of her own situation to care about her pappa's. If she was spiteful, it was with reason. Herr Schumann had not written in so long she had given up expecting a letter. Instead, she smiled more sweetly at Herr Banck, fluttering eyelashes at whoever paid her court and writing to Herr Schumann of her triumphs onstage and off.

"Fraulein Wieck, is it permitted to ask if you are free to walk tomorrow afternoon?"

The speaker was Herr Guhr, a friend of the Muller brothers, an amateur violinist, handsome in a cloak with a cape and wide collar, top hat, high black cravat.

Clara smiled. "It is permitted –" she paused a moment, fluttering her lashes, "but it depends on who is doing the asking."

Herr Guhr laughed, as did the Muller brothers, but Banck frowned. Herr Guhr silenced them with a bow. "Your answer only renders my objective all the more desirable. It is I who do the asking."

Clara was delighted with the banter, with all her gentlemen. "And who is it –" pausing again, "that you ask for?"

Again there was mirth. Herr Guhr laughed again, bowing again. "I must confess it, since you ask it so pointedly, that I ask for no one but myself."

"Ah, it is good of you to confess it so boldly –" she paused again, "but, pardon me, it is so long since you have asked the question that I have forgotten it."

Again the laughter, except from Banck.

"I asked if it were permitted to ask you to go walking tomorrow?"

"Ah, yes, I recall it now, and I recall I have answered you already – that it depends upon who is doing the asking."

Again there was laughter. Herr Guhr closed his eyes. "I confess, Fraulein Wieck, you are quite as enjoyable as a county fair. You have ridden me around quite like a carousel."

Again the laughter, including, most loudly, Clara's.

Herr Guhr shook his head. "But I am too dizzy to continue this conversation. I shall simply leave my card instead – as perhaps I should have done from the start."

Clara responded with yet another wide smile. "Indeed."

Banck touched her arm. "Perhaps we should see how your pappa is getting on, Clara."

Clara drew herself away from the touch. "Well, then, yes, Herr Banck, perhaps you should."

Herr Guhr spoke amid the ensuing laughter. "Yes, indeed, Herr Banck, perhaps you should. You do not appear to have gained much merriment from the meat of our intercourse. Perhaps the bare bones of the piano will amuse you better."

Again the party laughed, Clara the loudest, Banck not at all. He turned instead on Guhr. "Perhaps, after all, it is you, Herr Guhr, who should visit the bones, since it has been made clear that your bones are not welcome for walking with Clara."

Banck meant to raise a laugh, but met not a chuckle; his tone had been too harsh. Guhr answered him seriously. "I do not think that was the inference Fraulein Wieck wished to make. She has consented to accept my card willingly enough."

Clara nodded. "I have – and I shall. I shall take it now if you have one upon you."

"I have not, but I will send one directly."

"Danke, Herr Guhr."

Clara smiled, full of the news she would send Herr Schumann – not that he cared, that much she understood, but to show that she cared nothing for his antics either; she had antics of her own, gentlemen vying for her company, gentlemen fighting over her.

"Clara!" Wieck called in an urgent whisper.

"Coming, Pappa!" She got up, smiling at her company. "If you will excuse me, gentlemen."

They parted to make way for her.

"Try it again, Clara. I think I have fixed the problem."

Clara ran through scales, arpeggios, an exercise. "It is fine, Pappa – except when I use the pedal." She pressed the pedal, releasing the damper, and the notes resonated clearly – but when she released the pedal, the damper remained clear of the strings. "It does not work, Pappa. The damper does not return."

"Damnation! There is not time to dismantle it again." He shook his head disbelievingly. "I shall return it manually myself while you play."

He stood by the piano for the rest of the recital, releasing the damper manually when and as Clara needed it, perhaps only a hundred times though it felt like a thousand, in full view of the audience, pretending no one could see, sharing in the end Clara's bravas and glory with a smile and bow, though Clara, smiling and bowing herself, never once met his gaze, never once took his extended hand.

When Schunke got better Robert moved into his rooms, wishing no more to live on the higher floor. Through Schunke he met Henriette, who studied music with Mendelssohn's teacher and was married to Karl Voigt, merchant by day in yarn and silk, aficianado by night in music. Both Voigts were older than Robert, Karl by five years, Henriette by two, both in thrall to his talent, both young and romantic enough to make of their home a trysting place for Robert and Ernestine, of which Robert and Ernestine took all possible advantage.

Word of their association had reached the Baron who had arrived in Leipzig to take Ernestine back to Asch, but he was a mild baron and the appearance of the twosome coupled with Wieck's assurances of the propriety of their friendship had mollified him enough to stay awhile in Leipzig. The day set for their return was a Sunday, also Clara's sixteenth birthday, and all had been invited, first to the Kuchengarten, then to lunch at noon in the Wieck household. Robert and Ernestine had elected to spend the morning alone together instead and join the company only for lunch, and the Baron had not objected.

Henriette shook her head. "I cannot believe he did not object after coming all the way from Asch to take you back."

They were sipping coffee, eating currant cake on the coffee table before them. Robert laughed, his face bright with excitement. "He did not object because the old man told him that while I was moody and stubborn and dreamy, I was also noble and majestic and energetic – also a genius of composition."

Ernestine slid her hand into his and they sat side by side on the couch, arms intertwined; a ring flashed on her finger, bright as her moist eyes and damp cheeks. "But you are, Robert, you are. The old man is right – but you are neither moody nor stubborn."

Robert smiled, squeezing her hand, turning again to Henriette. "He told the Baron that we were strongly attached to each other, but in no unworthy sense."

Ernestine smiled; her tears subsided; she appeared sly. "Again, the old man is right. Our attachment is in no sense unworthy."

Karl and Henriette were seated at opposite ends of the coffee table. He grinned at his wife. "That it is not, but perhaps the old man's definition of unworthiness might differ from ours."

Henriette returned her husband's grin. "I think it might. I think the old man's definition might very well be *very* different."

Robert caressed Ernestine's naked arm. "He told the Baron that no caress has passed between us. He said he could *prove* it!"

Ernestine snuggled close. "He said he could also prove no kisses had passed between us." She turned her head upward. "How did he know that, my Robert?" Her eyes had narrowed; she might have been reading his mind; she kissed him, tracing the line of his jaw with her lips to his mouth where she lingered, cupping his face with her free hand. Robert was first to break the kiss. "How did he know that, Robert? How did the old man know so much?" She giggled. "How did he know no kisses had passed between us?"

"I do not know, my love. I do not know. The old man knows everything."

Henriette laughed. "All right, you two. Enough! Finish your coffee. It is almost time to leave."

"Already?"

"You said the lunch was at noon."

Ernestine pouted. "Must we go?"

Robert nodded manfully. "For Clara's sake, we must – not for the old man's, but we must for Clara's sake."

"Little Clara?"

He nodded again.

"But when will we get another chance like this?"

"We will make the chance. Asch is not so very far away. We are now engaged."

"I know." She held up her hand with the ring, eyes threatening to burst as brightly again.

Robert took her hand, hiding the ring. "You must put it away, my love. They must not know, not yet. It is only for us."

Ernestine made a face.

"Only for a short while."

"I know, I know, my darling, but it feels already like forever – and we have not yet even parted!"

"We must be brave. You must keep in your memory all our beautiful walks, all our beautiful talks – yes, and all our beautiful silences. They will be our foundation for the future."

She nodded again, squeezing her eyes tight, shutting out tears. "You are so beautiful, my Robert, so beautiful."

ii

Felix Mendelssohn, more even than Mozart, is the wunderkind among composers; his Octet in E flat composed at sixteen, and his Midsummer Night's Dream Overture at seventeen, are finer than anything, by anyone, in any age, at a comparable age. He was also a great pianist, organist, and conductor, born to wealth, spoke five languages, read Homer in the Greek, played violin and viola, sketched masterfully – and unlike many composers of genius was a billygoat of a kid, nothing frail about the boy, his parents had provided a gymnastics teacher; he was as well a fine swimmer and dancer.

Even his name, Felix, meaning Happy, couldn't have been more apt. Many said then he had been too favored by the gods, and many say it now though he suffered from a form of narcolepsy, fell asleep standing, or midsentence, and his narcolepsy waned in inverse proportion to the ailment which finally killed him, the bane of the Mendelssohns, a cerebral hemorrhage, at thirty-eight, hardly fulfilling the promise of his childhood, easily outdistanced by Mozart, dead himself at thirty-six, but also by others, younger and older.

He was also handsome, wavy black hair cascading from a part on the left side of his head over a high wide brow, black almond eyes, aquiline nose, high cheekbones, a sense of humor in the curve of his mouth, and sideburns that framed his angular face as in a picture, narrowing almost to a point in his chin – also, at twenty-six, he was the youngest conductor to lead the Gewandhaus Orchestra and had come recently to reside in Leipzig. Clara had seen him in Paris at the Princess Vandamore's, but he had made good his escape then with Chopin and Hiller, concerned more with hijinx than discourse, much to her disappointment and Wieck's. His presence at the Kuchengarten for her birthday almost made up for Herr Schumann's absence – but the morning had proven successful mostly for Herr Schumann's gift.

A basket had been delivered in the morning and inside the basket a golden cylinder watch. The watch was from the Band of David as Herr Schumann called his writers, giving pseudonyms even to friends who did not write, including herself whom he called Zilia, Chiara, and Chiarina, as he pleased. Of course, there were Florestan and Eusebius, also Master Raro from ClaRA and RObert, Aspasia for Henriette, Eleonore or Estrella for Ernestine, Charitas for Christel, Felix Meritis for Felix Mendelssohn, and countless others. The basket (with a porcelain handle) came from Robert alone with a note saying that he and Ernestine would attend lunch, but not the party at the Kuchengarten. She was disappointed, but with so many friends at the Kuchengarten she couldn't be disappointed long. Their table had been set with an enormous bouquet and the rest of the Gang of David, including Carl Banck, had arrived wearing "burning love" (geraniums) in their lapels. She noted with satisfaction that Banck cast jealous glances whenever she spoke with Herr Mendelssohn and she raised the pitch of her smile a notch further as she spoke to him again. "How is it, Herr Mendelssohn, that you have been offered the conductorship of the Gewandhaus Orchestra at so tender an age? Herr Schumann is just your age and I cannot imagine him conducting a marching band, let alone an orchestra."

Ernst Pfund and Ernst Wenzel laughed loudly; so did redhaired Emilie List, her new best friend. Mendelssohn smiled like a father, knowing as always just what to say. "Perhaps because I am the son of a banker, Fraulein Wieck – which perhaps makes me older by far than a musician of the same years."

The two Ernsts laughed louder yet and Clara joined them. "You are too witty for me, Herr Mendelssohn."

Mendelssohn shook his head. "Hardly! If anything, you are simply too witty for yourself – you outwit yourself."

Clara wished to conduct herself with utmost maturity that day; turning her sixteenth year was different from the others and she wanted to appear more than a girl, but not annoyingly so. Despite his polish Mendelssohn appeared so boyish she was hardpressed not to pat his hair in place. "You are kind to say it, Herr Mendelssohn. Danke."

"If anyone is kind, Fraulein Wieck, it is you."

Clara wasn't sure he wasn't making fun of her. "You must not mock me, Herr Mendelssohn – and you must not say, 'If I mock you, it is only because you mock yourself.'"

Mendelssohn's smile broadened finally into a laugh. "Not at all, Fraulein, not at all. I do not mock you at all, but I am rather enjoying myself enormously."

He might still have been mocking her, but he appeared so devoid of malice she didn't care. Elsewhere, the Baron and her pappa had just clinked champagne glasses in a toast. Wieck grinned. "To fathers, everywhere."

"And to the fathers, especially, of daughters!"

Wieck laughed, delighted to be exchanging toasts with a baron in his own home. "To the fathers of daughters! I would have it no other way."

The Baron nodded, continuing their conversation. "Mark my words, Wieck. Bonaparte was the best thing to happen to Germany since the Reformation, but we will not realize it for the next generation or two."

Wieck kept his smile, surprising no one perhaps as much as himself. "If I may ask, Herr Baron, how exactly do you mean it?"

The Baron sipped champagne and looked into his glass. "How do I mean it? Come, Wieck. How else? He united us. Before Bonaparte, we were a grabbag of four hundred cities and states and principalities. We are now consolidated to less than forty, we have a German Confederation, we have better roads, we have customs houses, we have the Zollverein – all modeled on what we have witnessed in France, none of which we had before Bonaparte – all incidental benefits, I grant you, but benefits nonetheless – and without the wars we would still be muddling through the Middle Ages, fighting one another, German against German, instead of recognizing our might as a nation."

"Ah, yes, Herr Baron, and there is also of course the unity of money – our currency being standardized. No more dealing with florins here, thaler there, and gulden elsewhere."

"Of course, that is the only way to advance, what is good for business is good for the country. As our monies become one so will our various German states and cities and principalities. Baden, Bavaria, Saxony, Hanover, Prussia, Austria, all the others, all will be as one, all will recognize that the good of the other is the good of Germany where now they still recognize only what is good for themselves."

"You are right, Herr Baron. I have seen that coming."

"Of course, I am right – and you know, of course, about the new railway?"

"Of course. From Nuremberg to Furth?"

"Of course, our only railway. Well, I have traveled by the rails as they say – and what takes hours by coach, takes minutes by the rails. That will be a big boon to you as you travel around Germany – and around Europe, if you wish – with your Clara."

Wieck nodded, still smiling. "Do not think I do not know it, Herr Baron. My good friend, Friedrich List, the American consul here in Leipzig – that is his daughter, Emilie, with Clara – he is even now concerned with the construction of a railway from Leipzig to Dresden. Do not think I do not know it. We have the power to be industrial equals with France and England, to have our own colonies in Africa and South America, if only we unite as a country."

The Baron shook his head. "There is no 'if only' about it, Wieck. We *will* unite. There is nothing *but* to unite. Otherwise, we go backward, and that we will never do."

Robert and Ernestine were the last to arrive, Robert telegraphing volumes with his smile – at least, to Clara. "I am sorry we are so late. We lost track of the time."

Ernestine smiled, but said nothing standing beside Robert. Clara affected not to care, but her new friend Emilie would have said there was nothing else in the room that she noticed after Robert and Ernestine's arrival. She spoke without smiling. "Thank you so much for the watch, Herr Schumann. It will be very useful."

Mendelssohn noted Banck's frown and extended his hand. "Good morning, Herr Schumann – or should I say Good afternoon?"

Robert shook his hand. "Herr Mendelssohn, good afternoon, by all means. It is now past noon by almost thirty minutes."

The Baron acknowledged their presence with a single word, "Indeed!" before resuming his conversation with Wieck.

Robert apologized again, but the Baron no longer paid them attention and he turned again to Mendelssohn. "I have been reading the most amazing work, Herr Mendelssohn. Berlioz's *Symphonie Fantastique*. I have been writing about it for my *Zeitschrift*. Unfortunately, I have it in the transcription by Liszt for the piano. What is most amazing is that it is so orchestrally conceived I can hear the orchestra even while I read the transcription. I must get Clara to play it through for me sometime. She is my right hand, you know, since I have lost the use of my own."

Clara remained unsmiling. "Hardly even that. I am no more than his finger. He has no need of my hand."

Mendelssohn raised his eyebrows, but so imperceptibly they might have been raised inwardly. He didn't like the *Fantastique* and wondered how well he liked Robert. His sympathy lay with Clara.

Robert still smiled. "She is joking, of course. I can hardly take her finger without taking her hand."

Clara wanted to say he had taken everything: hands, head, heart. Emilie saw how she looked at him and spoke for her friend. "Her hands are all he wants, nothing else."

Clara looked gratefully at Emilie; no one else said a word; Robert turned to Mendelssohn, oblivious of the silence. "You know the work, of course, Herr Mendelssohn? Perhaps you have heard it performed?"

Mendelssohn found the instrumentation of the *Fantastique* so filthy he wanted to wash his hands after handling the score. It was disgraceful that a symphony might be created (or what passed for a symphony) out of blood and misery and mourning. He had said as much in private, but he couldn't bring such strong emotion to bear at such a gathering. Music, like politics and religion, was a private affair. Schumann should have known better than to ask, but Mendelssohn was politic enough to answer without answering. "Since you are such an enthusiast, Herr Schumann, let me tell you a story about Herr Berlioz I think might amuse you."

Robert looked at Mendelssohn, aware he was avoiding his question. "Yes?"

"He is very complimentary, you understand – very effusive in his judgments. If he likes you he likes no one else better, but if he does not care for your work he will not hesitate to tell the world."

"A Frenchman to his bones!" Clara smiled, pleased with her worldliness, her nose in the air. Robert had not yet been to Paris.

Mendelssohn nodded. "A Frenchman, as you say. No German would be so … feminine, you might say."

Robert spoke without smiling. "In what way was he complimentary to you?"

"He was apparently overwhelmed by some work of mine –"

"And what work was that – if I may ask?"

Mendelssohn smiled. "You may, of course – and if I were a Frenchman you would have had your answer already. I could not have held it back."

Robert smiled. "But you are German."

Mendelssohn nodded. "Exactly."

"What was it, then? What was it Berlioz said?"

"He wanted my baton, as a keepsake – and I agreed only if he would give me his in exchange. He said I would be getting copper for gold, but agreed, and sent me his baton with a note. Let me see if I can recall it." He held up his chin, presenting a charade of recollection as much as elocution. "'To Chief Mendelssohn: Hail, Great Chief! We have sworn to exchange batons. Mine is rough, yours is plain. Only squaws and palefaces have need of ornate weapons. Be my brother! And when the Great Spirit calls us to the hunting grounds, may the warriors of our tribes hang our tomahawks together over the entrance of the council wigwam!'"

Robert's brow furrowed. "Berlioz wrote that?"

Mendelssohn grinned. "He had been reading some novel by the American writer, James Fenimore Cooper."

Robert nodded. "Ah! That explains it."

Clara turned her worldly smile on Banck, mainly for Robert's benefit. "He speaks so like a Frenchman."

Robert spoke, oblivious of Banck. "Perhaps, but I find myself in harmony with his expressions."

Mendelssohn had read his review of Chopin's Variations. He had thought it had been Wieck's when Chopin had shown it to him in Paris, but had since read it in its published form by Robert. "I thought you might like the story."

"I do – but I must say I am disturbed by such casual talk of batons. An orchestra should function as a republic, surely, and not be subordinated to a higher authority. All rigidity should surely be avoided."

Mendelssohn, the first conductor to use a baton in Leipzig, had never rated writers highly, critics and journalists of music, failed musicians more than writers, which was how he saw Robert: first, a writer; then, if at all, a musician. He understood anew Clara's comment that she could not imagine Robert conducting a marching band, let alone an orchestra; he was a dilettante, not a professional; but, as always, Mendelssohn was urbane in disagreement. "Do you consider it a rigidity, Herr

Schumann, for all the instruments to be played together? Do you consider it a rigidity for the brass not to drown the woodwinds?"

"Of course not – but a baton is not the answer."

Nanny and Clementine began circulating, calling the company to dinner, and the dialogue remained unresolved. Clara took Banck by the hand to the table, seating him next to herself, and Mendelssohn on the other side at the same table with Wieck, Clementine, Emilie, and the Baron among others. Robert and Ernestine were at another table which included her brothers. The main dish had been prepared at Wieck's request to impress the Baron, a fried saddle of venison simmering in a red wine sauce with pears and potatoes, but one of Clara's favorites was also on the menu: pig's feet in aspic with dumplings. There was also a vegetable stew with crayfish tails and bits of veal – and a plum pudding to finish, heaped with cream, another of Clara's favorites.

Wieck pointed a fork at Mendelssohn. "I understand, Herr Mendelssohn, that you have heard Franz Liszt play. Is this so?"

"It is."

"And what did you think of him?"

Mendelssohn had reservations about Liszt as he had about Berlioz and found a similar path out of his difficulty, setting down his own fork for a moment. "Herr Wieck, let me tell you a story about Herr Liszt. I showed him once the manuscript of my G minor Concerto, which was barely legible – but he played it flawlessly, better than anyone else could have played it, without knowing it in the least to begin."

Clara gasped, mouth open; Wieck could not have been more attentive; at the next table, Robert and Ernestine were silent.

Smiling at the response, Mendelssohn continued. "But when I later told Hiller the story, he said he was not at all surprised – and not at all impressed. He said Liszt played most things best the first time – because the first time was the challenge. After that he added ornamentations of his own – which invariably spoiled the work." Mendelssohn chuckled.

There was an echoing chuckle from Wieck. The Baron let out the loudest laugh they had heard from him yet. Everyone was either laughing or grinning.

Mendelssohn picked up his fork again. "But having said that I must add that he plays with more technique than anyone else, more finger independence, more velocity – and a feeling for music which springs from his soul and pours from his fingers. Everyone who hears him is amazed, nonpianists are transported with joy – but most pianists are unbelievably depressed."

Ernestine raised her head. "Why are they depressed, Herr Mendelssohn?"

Clara rolled her eyes at the question, but Mendelssohn answered without condescension. "They realize immediately, Fraulein von Fricken, that he shines above them like the sun and remains just as far out of reach."

Clara couldn't help herself. "And you, Herr Mendelssohn? Are you also depressed?"

She wished immediately she had said nothing, felt she had pushed him in a corner, but he smiled. "I am not so unwise as to compare myself with Franz Liszt." He chuckled again. "But after dinner, if you wish, I will give you an impersonation."

AFTER DINNER Mendelssohn seated himself at the piano, putting on his gloves. They had moved again to the front room. Clara stroked Gretel in her lap. Mendelssohn smiled. "You must keep in mind that Liszt has straight long hair which reaches down to his shoulders." He stuck his chin in the air. "So when he shakes his head like this," he shook his head, "it blows like a veil in the wind." He touched the back of his head with gloved hands. "My hair, unfortunately, is too stiff. As you see, it does not move at all."

There was laughter: everyone was attentive.

Mendelssohn straightened his back and swept the room with a slow icy stare, a rude stare, silencing the laughter. Next he pulled the gloves from his hands, first the left, then the right, pulling with short, firm, measured tugs at the fingertips, tossing them with a languid flick of the wrist to the floor. Clara didn't know anymore whether or not to laugh; her hand froze in Gretel's fur. The others were no less unsure. Mendelssohn appeared vain but grand, arrogant but confident, mesmerizing but vexing. The impersonation was so profound that when he bowed his head over the keys Clara could imagine Franz Liszt's long hair falling like a veil, covering his eyes, his face, and when Mendelssohn shook his head the veil was brushed aside just as he had said.

Mendelssohn flung his head in the air, and staring over the piano directly at Clara raised his left hand above his head, swooping onto the lower regions of the piano in a sudden, sharp, loud, tremolo. His right hand joined the left almost immediately in scales taken at unbelievable speed, now ascending, now descending, and all the while he stared over the piano, apparently oblivious to what his hands were doing, encompassing the entire room before him in his gaze before focusing upon her alone.

There might have been no one else in the room; she felt he could have swiveled his head entirely around without missing a note, but when he stared at her, swaying like a dancer, his chin level with his nose, she felt he was willing her to smile, challenging her not to smile. The stare made her heart beat as if she were in love. No one had stared at her like that before and she giggled to cover her discomfort. She didn't know if she had been rude until Mendelssohn smiled and she knew he wished again for her comfort. There had been something in the impersonation, hands swooping like eagles, eyes glaring like a wolf's, more penetrating than when Mendelssohn played as himself.

The piece got progressively more difficult, until all ten fingers appeared to be employed continuously, while both hands appeared a foot above the keys, leapfrogging over each other, and the music was lost in the legerdemain – and still Mendelssohn kept his gaze, not on his hands, not on the keys, but on the audience. Clara was ready to applaud as the concluding cadences fell, but Mendelssohn slid immediately into another work. More surprisingly, his appearance changed, and his attitude: suddenly oblivious to the audience where before it had been all he saw; his hands hovered over the keys where before they had soared, caressed where before they had struck, skipped across octaves where before they had leapfrogged. Even the music changed, from a series of perorations to a discernible argument, special effects to melody, you heard the music where before you had heard mostly speed and power. Clara whispered, unknown to herself: "Chopin!" She recognized him from her time in Paris; there was a sound he evoked from the piano she had not understood, blending notes with the pedal where others, including herself, could only blur them, and Mendelssohn had evoked the specter perfectly.

The Baron was the loudest of the admirers when Mendelssohn was finished, which pleased Wieck more than it did Mendelssohn. Robert was the quietest, so struck he forgot to applaud, forgot even the cigar dangling dangerously from his lips.

The Baron rose to his feet, still applauding. "Will you oblige us with something by Herz next, Herr Mendelssohn, perhaps his Bravura Variations?"

Mendelssohn didn't like Herz, called him in private a gymnast, a rope dancer, a trickster. Again, he made a politic answer. "I beg your pardon, Herr Baron – if I may, I shall perform instead one of my personal favorites."

"By all means, Herr Mendelssohn, by all means. Play what you wish, but keep on playing – please."

Mendelssohn turned again to the piano, played a Bach fugue, and again his demeanor changed. As Liszt he had been a billboard announcing himself through his performance; as Chopin a poet lost in the music; as himself a classicist, separate from the music, using the pedal sparingly, every line of the music distinct yet adding to the whole. When he was finished, when the applause had died, he looked at Clara. "It is now your turn, Fraulein Wieck. May I ask you to oblige us for a change?"

The room turned to Clara, applauding again. She rose, dropping Gretel from her lap. "Of course, Herr Mendelssohn – though I doubt I can oblige everyone as well as you."

Mendelssohn smiled, his smile within a smile. "You are too modest, Fraulein. I for one would rather have you oblige us than myself anyday."

Clara couldn't stop smiling. "What shall I play?"

"Nothing by Herz!"

Everyone laughed at his suddenness – except Robert, who looked at Mendelssohn, but addressed Clara. "Clara, would you please play my new sonata – in F sharp minor? I would like Herr Mendelssohn to hear it. I would like to know what he thinks."

He spoke tentatively; she imagined he was unsure of her, but couldn't understand why. Whatever she thought of him, he knew how she loved his music. She had come to terms with her shortcomings, smiling at the irony, the maturity which allowed her to recognize Ernestine's maturity – but how she loved Robert still, as she loved no one else, and he wouldn't even look at her – revealing his immaturity, another irony not lost on her, but one which didn't make her smile. She didn't look at Robert either, hadn't looked at him more than she could help all afternoon, though Emilie was later to say she had looked at no one else; after more than a year of seeing him with Ernestine she still hated to see them together. "Of course, if that is what Herr Mendelssohn would like."

Mendelssohn smiled the same smile again. "Of course, but you must not ask me what I think. We should not be critics today. We should simply enjoy ourselves."

"I would still like you to hear it, Herr Mendelssohn."

"I would like to hear it – if Fraulein Wieck will oblige?"

"Of course."

Mendelssohn had heard Robert's work, found it amateurish, sweet tunes without continuity, unusual but undeveloped, pleasant but unmemorable, and settled himself for a few pleasant minutes. The sonata started as he might have expected, a motif of two notes, now rising, now falling, now maintaining the level of its pitch, played successively over a rumbling harmonic bass, but in a few moments it became evident the motif in its various guises was only a prelude, and the first movement proper began with a muscular theme, a masculine theme, a gallop in triplets, more satisfactory than anything he had heard yet by Robert, which developed generously and unpredictably. He found himself sitting up, listening intently.

Each movement was greeted with loud applause, the second an aria, the third a scherzo, the last a rondo. Mendelssohn requested her to play the scherzo again which she did. Robert could have found no criticism more generous.

So passed the afternoon, Mendelssohn and Clara played together one of his capriccios for two pianos, more Bach fugues, various other pieces, singly and together – but nothing by Herz! It was five o'clock when the Baron left with Ernestine, Ernestine tearful, Robert promising to visit the family in Asch with the Baron's blessing, taking a moment to whisper to his love. "Do not fear, dearest. You have my ring." The other guests left shortly after.

Chopin was to visit Leipzig returning from a visit to his parents in Karlsbad. Mendelssohn had warned the Wiecks he would stay no more than a day, but wanted to hear Clara, and Clara was no less eager to hear Chopin again. No less eager than Clara was Robert – and Wieck, though he nursed a grudge. Chopin had shunned him in Paris – after he had promoted him by featuring the La ci darem Variations continually on Clara's programs and written a review of the Variations himself for publication. Wieck shook his head when he learned Chopin would stay just a day. "He is lazy. He should give concerts. He should visit Dresden, Dessau, Chemnitz, Magdeburg. He should visit Berlin. He should visit Hamburg. He should perform everywhere while he can. Later it will be too late."

Mendelssohn nodded. "You are right, Herr Wieck. That is what he should do, but it tires him. His constitution is not like ours."

"All the more reason for him to do it while he is young."

"It tires him too much for composition. He can do only one or the other, but not both. It is not his fault. It is the fault of his constitution."

Wieck rolled his eyes. "Well, of course! His constitution must come first!"

"He is also a very private person. He does not like too much fuss. I shall bring him myself to your place in the afternoon after dinner – if that is to your liking."

Wieck frowned. "I may not be here. I may have business to attend to in the shop."

Mendelssohn hid a smile, but replied without hesitation. "He will not mind, I am sure. It is your daughter he wishes to hear."

Wieck nodded. "Yes, of course, of course. She will be here."

"Good. I will not be able to stay myself." Mendelssohn allowed himself his smile within a smile. "I, too, have business. I am sure you understand."

Wieck replied without humor. "Yes, of course."

On the day of Chopin's arrival one of Wieck's servants saw Mendelssohn, arm in arm with a gentleman in the street, approaching Grimmaische Gasse, and hurried to bring the news: "Chopin is coming!" Robert and Clara had gathered in the parlor with Alwin, Gustav, Clementine, and three of Wieck's pupils, Rackemann, Wenzel, and Ulex. Wieck himself retired to the inner chambers, growling he had business.

The iron ring of the knocker sounded twice. Nanny would normally have conducted the guest to the parlor, but Clara joined her at the door. Mendelssohn grinned broadly. "Here is Chopin!"

Chopin was as slim as Mendelssohn, but shorter, more grim, shoulders more rounded. He nodded, stooping in hat and coat on the top step. A cane might have completed the picture, but he carried instead a small bag.

Mendelssohn was older by a few months, but looked younger by a few years. Clara smiled, imagining Chopin tired after his ride and stepped back. "Herr Chopin, I am Clara Wieck. Please come in."

Mendelssohn tipped his hat. "You will pardon me. I cannot stay. You understand."

"Of course, Herr Mendelssohn."

Mendelssohn turned to Chopin. "You are in good hands with Fraulein Wieck, my friend – and I do mean good hands."

In a moment he was gone, laughing at his own joke. Chopin didn't smile, stepping into the sudden darkness of the hallway as the door was shut behind him.

Clara smiled. "If you will let me have your hat and coat, Herr Chopin? There is more light in the parlor and we have a few friends who are anxious to meet you."

Chopin grimaced, hoping there wouldn't be too many guests; but he had come to hear Clara and was prepared to be gracious. Setting his bag down he shrugged off his coat. Clara gave hat and coat to Nanny, offering to take his bag as well, but he preferred to keep it.

Clara led him up the stairs to the parlor. "I am so happy to welcome you to our home, Herr Chopin! We met once in Paris – at least, we saw each other. Perhaps you will remember?"

"I remember, Mademoiselle Wieck –" His hand went to his mouth, as if to snatch back the words. "I beg your pardon! I meant, *Frau*lein Wieck."

He spoke with the lilt of Paris. Clara replied with an answering lilt. "It is all right. I do not mind if you call me Mademoiselle. A change is always nice – and a habit is a very hard thing to break."

"Absolument! but I will try."

In the light of the parlor he appeared as Clara remembered him, fair hair parted on the left covering his ears, plastered to the side of his head by his hat; his eyes, deeply set, now grey, now blue, the lids so heavy he might have been roused from sleep; his nose crowning his face like the beak of a hawk; gaunt cheeks and thin mouth revealing not a trace of humor.

Clara introduced Clementine, Robert, Alwin, Gustav, and Wieck's students. Everyone said they were pleased to meet him though Chopin hardly looked at them. Robert smiled as did everyone except Chopin. "How was your journey from Karlsbad, Herr Chopin?"

Chopin didn't look at Robert. "It was very tiring. I hate to travel. It is an abomination – but, how do you say it, a necessary abomination?"

Robert raised his eyebrows. "But there is so much to see along the way."

Chopin still wouldn't look at him. "Not for me, not if I am to be jolted out of my body every two minutes like a Jack-in-the-box. My health is not the best. If I can get to where I am going without mishap, it is enough."

"I am flattered you made the journey to hear me, Herr Chopin."

"I have wanted to hear you for a very long time. It has been my great regret that we had to leave the Princess Vandamore's soiree just as you had begun to play. First, my deepest apologies –" He held up a hand to check Clara's protests. "I have had the best reports about you since then, that you are one of the few to do justice to my compositions – perhaps the only woman to do so."

Clara beamed. "Well, we shall see about that."

"And as I was with my parents in Karlsbad I would have been a fool to miss the chance. It is the closest I have been to Leipzig in a long while."

Clementine still smiled. "Herr Chopin, would you like some coffee, tea, some chocolate?"

"Coffee would be very good, merci, Madame Wieck."

Clementine had barely stepped out of the room before Nanny entered with the coffee on a tray, with gingerbread and almond cake – but when Clara offered to cut him a slice Chopin shook his head. "No. Only coffee. I have eaten dinner."

Not once did he smile; had he not been courtierly he might have been impolite; but he was Chopin, and Clara cared only that he was in her parlor, come to hear her play. More idle conversation followed while coffee was poured, about the healing salts of Karlsbad, the railways which would soon render coaches obsolete – which couldn't happen soon enough for Chopin, though he admitted it with no change in his demeanor – and Clara was soon preparing to play. She fussed at the piano getting comfortable. "Since you have said, Herr Chopin, that I am perhaps the only woman to do justice to your work, I shall begin with one of your own etudes."

"By all means."

She played the first etude in the set, the melody in the bass, fortissimo, mostly whole notes, a tramp of giant steps, accompanied by a filigree of butterfly notes, fluttering up and down the treble. To hear her she might have been pounding the keys in the bass, skipping over the keys in the treble; but to see her she might have been playing a lullaby, appearing hardly to move, fingers merely sliding off the keys. When she was finished Chopin betrayed no emotion, didn't applaud with the others, and spoke simply. "Please, you must play another."

She played another, number ten, which called for some velocity, during which she held herself back, she played too easily with too much velocity. When she was finished, she was pleased to see she had earned a smile from Chopin. "Brava, Fraulein." He spoke softly, clapped slowly, without excitement, almost without sound. "I often say to my pupils not to play my etudes unless I have shown them how – and often I show them how by requesting Liszt to play for them. I would like, myself, to play my own etudes as Liszt plays them, but I have not the force, I have not the health – but you, if I closed my eyes, you could be Liszt. I will tell him about you." Chopin appeared to reflect, his eyes turned inward, his smile turned ironic. "He will grant you a little kingdom in his empire."

Clara sensed bitterness, perhaps for his inability to play his own work as well as he might wish – but also, could this be so, bitterness against Liszt?

Chopin was reflecting on nothing else, his estrangement from Liszt. If asked, Liszt said no more than that their lady loves had quarreled, and as good cavaliers they were honorbound to stand by them – which was ungallant because it was untrue. Liszt had played a mazurka by Chopin at a soiree, embellishing it beyond recognition. Chopin had approached him in what Liszt called his English manner. "I beg you, my dear friend, if you choose to honor me by playing something of mine, then you must play it as it is written – or not at all. Only Chopin has the right to alter Chopin."

Liszt had risen from the piano. "Very well, then, play it yourself!"

"With pleasure!"

Chopin had sat at the piano and played the mazurka. Liszt congratulated him later. "You are right, my friend. The work of a genius should not be embellished. You are a true poet and I am only a mountebank."

Chopin replied without looking at Liszt. "We each have our genre." He was angrier than he had imagined, holding past grudges. When he had left Paris once for a while, Liszt had arranged a tryst in Chopin's rooms with his lady of the moment, incidentally the estranged wife of a friend of Chopin, and said nothing to Chopin, but Chopin could tell when his things had been disturbed, and he had soon learned by whom. Worse, the Countess Pauline Plater, a connoisseur of musicians, had let it be known that she would take Hiller for her man about the house, Chopin for her husband – and Liszt for her lover.

Liszt had avenged himself for Chopin's remark a week later at another soiree, arranging for the hostess to turn out the lamp again before Chopin played, and whispering to Chopin in the dark to let him take his place. Chopin, regretting his recent priggishness, had submitted to the trick, and Liszt had played the same mazurka, lighting candles on the piano when he was finished – to the consternation of his listeners who had expected to see Chopin. Liszt had whispered to Chopin: "What do you have to say now, my friend?"

Chopin had been as generous as he knew how. "I say what everyone says. I, too, thought it was Chopin."

Liszt had smiled, satisfied. "Ah, then, you see, Liszt can be Chopin when he wishes – but can Chopin be Liszt?"

Chopin's pores contracted, recognizing the game Liszt had played. He was not fit himself for concerts, lacking Liszt's force; crowds suffocated him, paralyzed him with their glare, struck him dumb with their dumb faces – but Liszt played best for audiences, the larger the better; if they resisted his artistry he overwhelmed them with sheer power; he was known to snap piano wires at performances, people came to see him break the pianos, after which he would bring a new piano onstage to renewed applause; at times he would break more than one, but never without a spare in reserve.

Clara imagined Herr Chopin was indeed a poet; he appeared as preoccupied as her own Herr Schumann. "A little kingdom, Herr Chopin? I do not understand."

Liszt enjoyed playing the Grand Seignior, the soul of generosity in word and deed, once he was convinced of his own superiority; when he was less sure, he was less grand, as he was with Sigismund Thalberg – but Chopin didn't explain. He focused again on the present. "Pardon, Mademoiselle Clara. You must not judge me too harshly. I am not myself. I have not been for a while. My mind is sometimes a hundred miles away. I beg a thousand pardons."

Clara smiled. "There is no need, Herr Chopin. Shall I play something else for you?"

"If you would be so kind."

Clara played the last movement of Chopin's F minor Concerto, which Chopin applauded, finally, unrestrainedly. "Brava, Fraulein Clara! I am in your debt – but now you must play me something by someone else, please."

"Certainement, Herr Chopin. What shall I play?"

Robert was hardly unaware of Clara's sudden affectation, but no less intent on impressing Chopin himself. "Play him my *Carnaval*, Clara. I think he will like that – if you know what I mean."

Carnaval was a series of scenes Schumann had built from the four letters, A, S (E flat in German), C, H (B in German), Ernestine's hometown, also the only letters in his own name lending themselves to the musical scale. The various scenes represented Paganini, Florestan, Eusebius, Clara, and Ernestine, among others, concluding with a parade of the Band of David against the Philistines – but Clara knew what he meant. One of the scenes was modeled on Chopin's nocturne style. She nodded. "I shall play for you *Carnaval*, Herr Chopin. It is Herr Schumann's latest composition."

Chopin would have preferred something by Bach, Mozart, even Kalkbrenner. He remembered Herr Schumann as the author of the odious review of his Variations, not as a musician, but he took another sip of coffee, settling himself instead for the ordeal, determined to get satisfaction from the Fraulein's artistry if not her program – and he wasn't disappointed. A series of nonmusical events were strung together with sublime artistry. Chopin beamed as she finished, applauding with everyone else. "Your tone is like a song. It is powerful, but not jarring – fluid, but not percussive. It is exactly what I say to my pupils, they must sing if they wish to play, they must listen to Italian opera. It is absolutely essential."

Clara was hardly less excited herself. "That is just what Pappa says – to make the piano sing." She knew her pappa would not recommend Italian opera, not anything Italian, nor French, not if there were a German equivalent, but that was an unnecessary detail, even irrelevant. "Pappa says not to strike the keys, only to touch them, to build strength by sliding the fingers along the keys before depressing them, to avoid the sound of the fingers on the keys. Everything is in the touch."

Chopin was glad that the pappa who had sent him the review was not present. "He is right."

"Herr Chopin, how did the nocturne strike you?"

Chopin knew he would have to say something to the hulking Herr Schumann, so intently awaiting his reaction. "It was very pretty, Herr Schumann – very pretty indeed."

"It was modeled on one of your nocturnes, Herr Chopin. That episode was meant to represent you. Did it seem that way to you?"

"It was very pretty, Herr Schumann."

Robert explained the significance of the various scenes, united by their variations on the notes, A-S-C-H, elaborating on his yearning for Ernestine – but again Chopin could think of nothing except how these Germans insisted on reading programs into their music as if the music itself were nothing. He spoke without conviction. "It was charming, Herr Schumann. The entire mise en scene was very charming indeed." He turned his attention rapidly to his bag. "Oh, I almost forgot. I have brought you a token of my appreciation."

"Oh, Herr Chopin, that was not necessary – but it is so good of you."

"I know." He remained so stoic pulling a booklet from his bag that they couldn't be sure he wasn't being ironic. "It is my newest publication, Four Mazurkas. I hope you will find them entertaining."

Clara beamed accepting the booklet. "For us, Herr Chopin? Oh, but I thank you so very much. This is so unexpected. I can hardly wait to play them."

"You may play them now if you wish."

Wilhelm Ulex interrupted. "Will you play them for us, Herr Chopin? Pardon me for being so importunate, but we may never see you again and I understand you do not give concerts."

"Not if I can help it. It is not good for my constitution – but I shall play for you – though your piano has a heavy touch. I can hardly refuse after the courtesies you have shown me – but I shall play just one piece, that is all, and not the mazurkas. Those I shall leave you to discover yourselves."

Robert's enthusiasm had remained unabated despite Chopin's faint praise for *Carnaval*. "I shall review them for my *Zeitschrift*."

Chopin grimaced; he had been afraid of that, but said nothing, taking his place at the piano. Everyone recognized the piece from the first note, even Clementine, the least musical of the listeners, the Nocturne in E flat, opus 9, number 2, Clara played it often, but never like Chopin.

Clara watched carefully: the base position of his hand was not c, d, e, f, g as she had been taught, but e, f sharp, g sharp, a sharp, b; his fingers seemed to multiply as he played, dropped trills like showers of pearls on a crystal salver; his runs were more fluid than percussive, almost harplike, a glissando on strings, not the hammer of wood on wire, recalling Mendelssohn's suave impersonation; his left hand was prim as a metronome, his right free as a hummingbird but reined by the leash of the left just when it seemed no longer possible. She noted as well, with pity, the phrases in fortissimo, played with a spasm of his body; the wrist, the elbow, the arm, none was enough by itself; he needed almost to get up on his feet, bring down the full weight of his being. Robert wrote something later, about the performance, comparing it with cannon lurking among flowers.

Herr Ernst Ferdinand Wenzel, then Wieck's pupil, subsequently Robert's pupil, and much later Grieg's professor at the Leipzig Conservatory, never forgot the evening he heard Chopin play. He strove continually until he died in 1880, almost fifty years later, to do justice to the performance, reducing himself to rapture, conjuring analogies with the choreography of fairies and flights of angels.

Nanny remembered the occasion best for another reason. She had rushed to the kitchen, locked herself in, and stuffed her mouth with a handkerchief to stifle her giggles. She had caught a glimpse of Wieck, Master of the House, seated in a chair in the hallway, holding the door ajar, eyes wide, mouth wider, listening intently, peeping into his own parlor like a schoolboy for a glimpse of Chopin.

On the evening she first played his Symphonic Etudes for him, Clara noticed Robert said little beyond commenting on her execution of the work. She would have sworn he looked at her while she played, but when she looked back his eyes reverted to the score, and when she asked what he was thinking he only corrected her interpretation of a passage. Ludwig Schunke, his friend and partner in the *Zeitschrift*, with whom he had shared rooms, had died of consumption. She did not expect him not to be affected, but the way he looked at her when he thought she wasn't looking, the way he opened his mouth and then closed it saying nothing, convinced her that Schunke was not solely the source of his distraction.

The work, Robert's most sumptuous yet, a series of variations on a theme by the Baron, perhaps Robert's way of ingratiating himself with his future father-in-law, featured harmonies she could scarcely grasp, among which the theme itself was periodically lost, like an old friend suddenly full of surprises – not unlike Robert himself. The Baron had visited Robert's relatives in Zwickau, Robert had visited Ernestine's in Asch, no one objected to the match – no one, that is, but the matchmaker herself. Her pappa was so confident of Robert and Ernestine he had encouraged her to learn Robert's new works. She was the one needing solace, not he, so close yet so far from his thoughts, but to look at them he was the one pining, not she. To her consternation he cut her off midphrase. "I should be leaving. It is late already."

It was much later than usual; she was surprised he had stayed so long, no less surprised by his suddenness, but didn't argue. She was glad for any time he spent with her. "I will get the lamp. I will see you down the stairs."

He said nothing, but waited while she got the lamp, following her down the stairs, waiting again when she opened the door for him, waiting so long she realized he wasn't leaving yet. "Herr Schumann, is something the matter?"

Robert sighed, sitting on a step. "My dear girl, I knew you would see it. I can keep nothing from you."

Clara remained standing, holding the lamp high.

"Put down the lamp, dear girl. There is something I must tell you."

Clara did as he bid, placing the lamp between them, sitting on a lower step.

He shaded his eyes with his hand from the lamp. "Put it away. I cannot speak with the light in my eyes. What I have to say can be said only in darkness."

Clara raised her eyebrows, but turned the lamp to a dim glow, placing it as far down the stairs as she could without getting up. Large shadows quivered on the walls and stairs around them.

Robert sighed again. "I do not know how to tell you gracefully, so let me be blunt. It is over. Between Ernestine and me, it is over. Everything is over."

Clara's mouth dropped; she covered it with her hand, glad of the lamp behind her though Robert appeared too absorbed in what he was saying to notice. "What are you saying, Herr Schumann? We have daily been expecting an announcement of your engagement. Pappa will be so disappointed."

"Nevertheless, it is so. Ernestine and I are not for each other."

Clara had difficulty commiserating; she could barely keep from smiling. Her eyes opened wide. "But why is this, Herr Schumann? What has changed?"

"I have received a letter." Robert swallowed. "It is from Ernestine. It seems that she is not what she claims to be. She is not what she appears."

Clara's big eyes got bigger. "She is not? What is she then?"

"She is not the natural child of the Baron. She was born to the Countess Zedwitz as she said, but her father is a gentleman by the name of Erdmann Lindauer, a manufacturer of something, I forget what, from Grun. Ernestine was born herself in Neuberg, near Grun, in Bohemia. She has lived with the Baron all this while as his daughter, and he means next month to adopt her formally – but she is not his daughter, she is not what she has claimed all along."

Clara found herself breathless, afraid to imagine the implications of his story; her mouth opened again, but her hand remained in her lap; she was glad of the darkness, it covered her face, but the air was too thin to cover the fortissimo beat of her heart.

Robert looked at her. He didn't want to say it, hardly admitted it even to himself, that he had assumed Ernestine rich, in the market perhaps to aid an indigent musician, but he had learned she was to inherit nothing, he would be obliged to work for their living, perhaps as a laborer, at the cost of his music. He shook his head. "If she has deceived me on this matter I cannot imagine what else I am to believe of what she has said. She might never have loved me; she might have accepted me for no more than my respectability; but I cannot allow myself to be used thus. Can you understand that, dear Clara?"

She nodded.

"The good thing about this is that I am finally clear about what I want."

He leaned forward, elbows on knees. Clara closed her eyes.

"Ernestine had to come in order that we might be united." He gripped her arm. "You and I, Clarchen. So it was ever meant to be."

She drew a sharp breath. "How can you say that, Herr Schumann? How can that be? Does Ernestine know anything of what you say?"

"Ernestine knows. She is in full agreement. She always maintained, she even wrote to me, that she believed I could love no one but you. She knows she drove you first from my heart, she knows how I loved you before I met her. She saw more clearly than I. I was blind, but I can see it now."

Not once had he said anything about her feelings for him, not once had he asked. "But, Herr Schumann, how can that be? You always treated me like a joke. You always laughed at me – yes, you did, do not say it is not so – and so did Ernestine, on so many of our walks – and now that I see you turn so cavalierly from her to me, how am I to know you will not turn as cavalierly from me to someone else?"

Robert released her arm as if it were too hot to touch. "How can you say that, Clarchen? How can you say we laughed at you? Give me an instance, if you can – just one instance."

"What about the time we went to the Wasserschenke?"

"Yes?"

"And you ordered the duck?"

"Yes?"

"And I did not know if a duck was a goose or a swan – and you said a duck was a duck?"

"Yes?"

"I remember you both thought I was very foolish for not knowing."

"Yes – and you were!"

"But how was I to know? I was thinking of the story, in which the ugly duckling became a swan. It was not a gosling that became the swan. It was not a … a swanling. It was a duckling. How was I to know?"

Robert laughed.

"Herr Schumann, you are *still* laughing at me!"

Robert controlled himself. "I am sorry – but if you make a joke you must expect me to laugh. I never heard of a swanling. A baby swan is a cygnet – and, of course, in the story it is a mistake. A cygnet becomes mixed up with the ducklings. The ugly duckling was never a duck. It was always a swan. No, no, dear Clara! This does not count. You will have to give me another instance."

Clara turned her head to one side. "What about the time we were at the menagerie?"

"Yes?"

"And I was afraid of the panther?"

"Yes?"

"And you said I was silly, then, and so did Ernestine."

"Yes?"

"But I was afraid the panther might escape. It would not have been so funny then."

"But he was in a cage. How was he going to escape?"

"Animals have escaped from the menagerie before. It could happen again."

"Clarchen, Clarchen, I am sorry. You are right. I should have been more considerate. I did not realize those times meant so much to you. You are right. I have been inconsiderate. I am sorry."

Clara's head was still turned to one side. "Herr Schumann, you know I have not been to school or to the university. You know Pappa has always educated me in the house. I am not so smart as you who have studied in universities, studying literature and law and so much more. Sometimes, I feel not so smart when you talk – but I am not stupid – and I do have feelings."

Robert nodded again, almost hanging his head. "You are right. I am the stupid one for not noticing. I am sorry. Can you ever forgive me, Clarchen, my Clara?"

She straightened her head again, smiling. "Well, then, if you are truly sorry, then it is all right – but you should remember I am not without feelings. I was very hurt when you both first ignored me. You were my best friends – and when I first told Ernestine about you she said she had a gentleman in Asch of whom she was very fond, but after you met she wanted to be called everytime you visited – and no sooner had I called her than I was forgotten. Herr Schumann, you must not misunderstand. I was glad she liked you, I wanted her to like you, but I lost both my friends. You no longer talked to me except to make a joke, and she became very ... little-syllabled."

"Little-syllabled?"

"She hardly spoke to me at all."

Robert smiled, but stopped himself laughing. "Ah!"

She waited for him to elaborate, but he didn't. "What was I to think? I had been betrayed by my two very best friends. What was I to think?"

"Ah, poor Clarchen. It was nothing like that. Ernestine thinks the world of you, I swear it. If you would read her letters you would believe it too."

"It did not seem that way – and when you visited you talked only with her. With me you only played childish games. What was I to think? I consoled myself daily – and nightly I cried myself to sleep. I told myself that you had always had me, that she was older, she was more sophisticated – but I was hurt, and I did not know what to do about it."

"I am sorry, Clarchen. You must believe I am sorry. If I had only known."

She shook her head. "Even now I do not know what to believe. If you say, as you do, that I was for you from the start, why did you pay court to Ernestine at all? Was I not always here? Was I not always available?"

Robert nodded, sober again. "True, my Clarchen. That is all too true – but it is a longer story than you know." He patted the stair beside him. "Come, sit by me. Put your head on my shoulder. I shall tell you the whole story."

She shook her head. "I would like to hear the story from where I am."

Robert nodded again. "As you wish. I will tell my story. You be the judge."

He told her, graphically, of the night he had seen the cat on the street from his window. "Such was my state when I heard of Rosalie's death, following so soon upon Julius's, that I was visited with the most terrible thought possible – that I would lose my reason, that I would no longer have the power to think for myself. I cannot tell you, my dear Clara, how heavily the thought fell upon me. So great was my anguish that night, so deep was my despair, I cannot say I would not have laid hands on myself. I was a statue – all of that day I was a statue. How things would be if not for Louis and his mamma I do not know, I cannot say – and now Louis, too, is gone."

Clara nodded, eyes wizening in commiseration, squeezing his hand.

"The next morning I went to the Herr Doktor. I told him everything, of all the symptoms from which I was suffering, how my breath stopped at the thought of what I might do, how I sat sometimes for hours doing nothing – but he said that medicine was of no use to me. He said I should find myself a wife, and in haste. The love of a good woman would cure me like no medicine could. That was what he said."

Clara nodded again, squeezing again his hand.

"You were the first girl I thought of – but you were only fourteen."

"Fourteen and a half!"

"Fourteen and a half."

"And then came Ernestine, as good a girl as any man might wish. She would save me, of that I was sure, and I clung to her with all my force. I became better. I saw that. She loved me. You know what came next. That, I swear, my dear Clara, is the whole story."

Clara squeezed his hand yet again, sitting next to him on the stair, putting her head on his shoulder. He put an arm around her. They sat in silence for a while. "My poor Herr Schumann."

"And you, Clarchen?"

"Me? What about me?"

"From your letters, on your tours, you said you had gentlemen paying you court."

"Oh, those!"

"Those."

"It is true, what I said. There were many gentlemen."

"And what about them?"

"I never cared for them. I never cared for any – but you. Never!"

"Not even Carl Banck?"

"He is the worst of them all. He is a coward."

"Why do you say that?"

"He left because Pappa told him to leave. I sent him a message with Nanny, not to heed Pappa if he was to have me – but he refused even to see her. He would not talk with Nanny, so afraid was he of Pappa. I do not know what Pappa might have said, but Carl Banck behaved like no gentleman – indeed, he behaved like no man at all but a craven."

Robert squeezed her shoulders. "I think I understand. I think, sometimes, that your pappa has chosen me for you. I know how he feels about my music. I am sure he was looking out for our interests."

"I am not so sure, Herr Schumann –"

"I think, dear Clara, that you should call me Robert. We have known each long enough, and after what we have just said to each other …"

"Robert? I may call you Robert?"

"That is the very least you must call me now."

"Robert! Robert, Robert, Robert, Robert-Robert-Robert-Robert!"

He laughed. "Yes? Yes? Yes? Yes?"

She was serious again. He was surprised how quickly she changed. "Robert, if you care about me you must not listen to Pappa. If you are afraid of him, as Banck was afraid of him, I could no more care for you than I do for him."

"I am not afraid, Clarchen, but I think you are wrong. I think your pappa is our ally."

"I hope you are right."

"We must tell him."

"Must we?"

"Why not?"

"I would like it to be just our secret for a little while. I would like us to enjoy it alone – just for a little while."

Robert smiled. "My Clarchen, of course!"

"My Robert!" She smiled, viewed him askance, head tilted.

They stayed awhile in silence on the stairs, almost an hour, mewling, caressing, Robert with his arm around her, Clara nuzzling against him. "Robert?"

"Yes?"

"What are you thinking?"

"I should be going home."

She sighed; it was not what she wanted to hear. "I suppose you are right. It is late."

"I hate to leave, but Willy will be wondering what has happened." Robert now shared rooms on the ground floor with Wilhelm Ulex, also once Wieck's student and now a writer for the *Zeitschrift*.

"Does he worry about you a lot?"

"I think so, sometimes too much."

"Good. Someone should worry about you all the time."

If he understood what she was saying he gave no sign; she picked up the lamp; they descended the stairs arm in arm, but he lingered before the door, his brow in a knot of thoughts left unsaid. "I like your dress."

"What about it?"

"It is blue."

"Is that all?"

For answer he turned to her, holding up her chin with his hand.

She turned her face away. "You are sure Ernestine will not mind?" She cared less that Ernestine would mind than that the change had been too sudden. She wanted time, and the Rubicon lay ahead.

"Quite sure."

"How can you be so sure?"

"She is engaged to be married to someone else."

It was a lie, but he didn't care; he would write to Ernestine later.

"Oh, my goodness, I am always the last to know everything! Then, of course, it is all right."

He drew her to himself, lips to her brow – but when she shut her eyes, raised her face, rose on her toes, fitted her length to his, garlanded him with her arms, and grazed his lips, he gathered her like a braid of gold and lifted her in a full body hug off the floor.

It was a moment she had long awaited, a moment she had realized only in dreams, overwhelming in the flesh. Her heart sped like a toy newly wound, and she dropped the lamp extinguishing its meager light – but she'd been lost in her dream before she'd lost the light, fluttering the tips of her toes, dancing like a fairy in the clouds, listening to the flap of invisible wings. Had she not been secure in Robert's arms, she would have fallen in a faint.

Nothing was said by either Robert or Clara, but there is no secret worse kept than one that will not be kept. Wieck wasn't blind; words were plain in their gestures, looks, laughs, smiles, touches, and caresses, which might as well have been speeches, testaments, and proclamations. Robert gave Clara a pearl necklace for Christmas; Clementine, taking her cue from Wieck, said pearls meant tears; Robert and Clara, beaming, hardly heard; while they busily kept their secret Wieck heard them more clearly than they heard themselves, making plans while they basked in each other's arms and glowed in each other's auras. Wieck had once called Robert a second Beethoven, but he was just beginning to realize the dividends from his investment in Clara. Her triumphs were his own, her skills, her talents, her reviews, even her compositions, were his own. She recompensed his ego as much as his purse. He would not have yielded her to even the first Beethoven. Composers made no money, not even the greatest. One evening, in the darkened parlor, coming upon them, Robert leaning against Clara, both in the armchair, her arms around his shoulders, her chin on his head, he chose his moment. "Clara, you do not hold Herr Schumann as one might a friend. I must ask you to be more prudent."

Wieck brightened the lamp on the piano. Robert and Clara didn't move, but smiled, though not at each other, not at Wieck, smiled for the light, finally, suddenly, on their embrace. Robert whispered to Clara, but not so softly that Wieck could not hear; it was too small a room. "What do you think, Clarchen? We have kept our secret long enough?"

"No, but maybe there is no help for it."

"Maybe."

"Then shall I tell Pappa?"

"As you wish."

"Tell me what?"

"Pappa, if I do not hold Robert as I might a friend it is not because I am not prudent. It is because we have chosen to be more than friends."

Wieck stood over them, so close it was impossible for them to disentangle without touching him. "*You* have chosen! And, pray, who are *you* to have chosen such a thing?"

It was their first intimation that Robert could not have been more wrong in his estimate of Wieck. "It is not Clara alone, Herr Wieck. We have both chosen."

Wieck took a step back. "First, I want Herr Schumann to sit over there." He pointed to a chair separated from the armchair by a couch. Robert did as he was told. Wieck addressed Clara alone. "Next, you, Mademoiselle Clara, I wish you to understand something."

"Herr Wieck –"

Wieck turned on Robert. "Silence! When I am ready to speak with you, you will have your chance. For now, silence!"

Robert's eyes were so wide they appeared white, but he remained silent.

"Now, you, Clara. As I said, I wish you to understand something, and I wish you to understand clearly. I shall repeat myself as often as necessary, but I trust you will understand the first time, because if I have to repeat myself even once I shall be very angry indeed."

Clara appeared less astonished, crossing her legs, crossing her wrists in her lap. "What is it, Pappa?"

"It must be understood, Clara, that I make the decisions in this house. You will choose when and how and whom I tell you to choose. Choices are to be earned; they are not yours for the taking; and you have much to learn before you will have earned your share. Is this clear?"

"But Pappa –"

"Is it clear!"

"Pappa, you are not fair!"

"Clara! I asked you a question! Am I clear?"

"Pappa, you do not listen –"

"I am not here to listen to you, Clara. I am here to tell you what to do. That is my duty as your pappa. That is my responsibility. Now, do you hear me? I asked you a question. Was I clear?"

"Pappa –"

"CLARA!"

"Yes, Pappa, since you put it that way! It is clear!"

"Good, now go to your room."

Clara got up, looking sternly at Robert, willing him to be firm.

"Goodnight, Clara."

"Goodnight, Robert."

Wieck turned to the window as Clara left, raising his hands to his hips, turning to Robert. "Now, Herr Schumann, I must say I am surprised. How do you explain yourself?"

Robert leaned forward. "Herr Wieck, first of all, Clara is blameless in this. We should never have hidden our feelings, we should never have hidden our thoughts. It was my idea to say nothing to anyone – but only at first. We were waiting only for the right time to tell you."

"And what is it you wish to tell me?"

"Herr Wieck, I have known Clara for a long while. I have known her since she was no higher than my hip. She was then like a sister to me, replacing my own Emilie, taken so early – but of that I do not need to say more."

"And what of Ernestine? Are you not to be engaged?"

"Between Ernestine and me it is over. Clara knows."

"Does Ernestine know? Does the Baron know?"

"Ernestine knows!"

Robert had hesitated, just a moment, but the moment confirmed what Wieck suspected. "Ernestine knows?"

"It is as I have said." Robert wanted to turn the focus from Ernestine. "Herr Wieck, I have watched your daughter grow, as a friend, as an artist, and most recently as a woman. She is now of a ripe age. Is it not natural for a woman of her propensity at the piano and a man of my propensity at composition to blend their propensities – and with their propensities other aspects of their lives? Is it not inevitable?"

"You would more appropriately have said a *girl* of her propensities, Herr Schumann. She is but a *girl* of sixteen – and you a *boy* of twenty ..."

"Twenty-five, sir – a *man* of twenty-five."

Wieck waved his hand. "Whatever. Twenty-five, but no man. A man would be better able to support a woman than you – and were you a man you would know I am right."

"I have my own income, sir, and the *Zeitschrift*. I do well enough for a man."

Wieck laughed. "Your *Zeitschrift*, my dear Schumann, can hardly keep you in cigarettes and beer. I must have better than that for my Clara."

Robert flinched; Wieck's laugh, no less than his sentiment, was like the crack of a whip.

"I opened my home to you, Schumann. I fed you, I taught you. Is this how you repay my hospitality?"

"Herr Wieck, to what exactly do you object? What exactly is my transgression? Of what do you accuse me?"

"Of what do I accuse you? Have I not said already? You reach too high, Schumann. You could not keep Clara in spit. Your *Zeitschrift* is the product of a smallminded man. A man who is industrious in small pursuits remains a small man however successful the pursuit."

Robert recoiled as if he had been slapped. His mouth dropped, but he remained speechless as if a gorgon had materialized in the room.

Wieck smiled, suddenly changing his tone. "Now, Robert, you must not be distressed. If I have said more than I wished it is because you have wrenched it from me. You are a good boy, as I have said, and a good composer – but you are not the man for Clara."

Still Robert said nothing.

"Now, then, I think I have been as clear as you have any right to expect – clearer than I wished perhaps for my own sake, but I hope clear enough at least for yours. There should be no misunderstanding between us. Clara is *not* for you. Now, if you have something to say, I am willing to hear it. If not, I wish you to leave, never to communicate again with my daughter."

Robert got up. "I can comply easily with your first wish, Herr Wieck – but, as to your second, I believe we have surprised you too greatly. I can account in no other way for your unwelcome remarks – and I call them unwelcome only out of my great respect for you and your daughter. We will speak again when you have had time to digest what we have said."

"There, Herr Schumann, you are mistaken. We will not speak of it again, not *ev*er. We will have no need. You will *not* approach Clara again – not *ev*er. I forbid it. Is that understood?"

"I understand that is what you wish, Herr Wieck. Beyond that I cannot say what I understand."

Wieck's eyes narrowed to slits. "You will understand what I *mean*, Herr Schumann – and you will abide by what you understand!"

Robert left the room, trembling with anger, afraid of what he might say if he stayed; Clara stood outside and kissed his cheek, her own cheek hot and wet against his face, and slipped a note into his hand. "Read this later, my darling – but for now, goodnight."

He pocketed the note; Wieck followed him out. Just an hour earlier he and Clara could not have been closer; now he was being shoved and yanked and driven from her house. He read the note by a streetlamp, a few houses down. *Dearest Robert, do not doubt I love you. I will send you news with Nanny. Have courage. Everything depends on us – and on us alone. No one else can defeat us. Your loving Clara.*

ii

Wieck had planned a tour with Clara of Dresden, Gorlitz, and Breslau, from February to April; arrangements had long been made, but the first note Nanny brought informed Robert that he had changed plans, they were leaving Leipzig the very next day instead, mid-January, ostensibly to remove Clara from his influence. They would stay with friends who, incidentally, admired Robert's music, and might prove sympathetic to their plight. She also mentioned her pappa would be away from Dresden on business for four days. Robert sent word back: he would be in Dresden, he had associates of the *Zeitschrift* with whom he could stay.

The Kaskels, with whom the Wiecks stayed, offered to let Robert stay with them during Wieck's absence. Clara declined, wishing not to create a wedge between them and her pappa, but their solidarity put the blush back in her cheek, the light in her eyes, and her mouth widened with hope. If Nanny, the Kaskels, Robert's *Zeitschrift* associates, all wished to help, the justice of her cause swelled, her guilt diminished.

Waiting for Robert at the coach house she thought she would faint; her breath fogged the air and she shivered, but whether from the cold or anticipation she couldn't have said – but seeing him again, head bent, hair uncombed, eyes bleary, face sallow, shoulders slumped, shuffling one foot ahead of the other, recalling the depressions to which he was prone, of which her pappa reminded her unceasingly, her face shrank again. He put down his bag, embraced her without the tiniest smile, appeared hardly to see her. "Robert, my darling, are you not happy to see me?"

He shook his head. "It is something else."

"What?"

"I cannot talk about it."

She found herself helpless, unable to console him. "Robert, you must tell me. I am on your side. Do you not understand that?"

"It is not you, Clarchen. It is something else. I cannot talk about it yet."

The hollow tone belied the sweetness of his words. In the cab to Boll's, where Robert was to stay, she wouldn't let go his limp hand. They were silent until he began to squirm, then to whisper, but she couldn't decipher the words. "What, my darling? What? Tell me."

"Mamma is dead."

He stopped squirming and she stared, still as Robert herself. When he began to squirm again she put her arms around him. "Oh, my dearest Robert, I am so sorry. I am so sorry."

She hadn't meant to display herself in public with Robert more than she could help, hadn't meant to put the Kaskels to more trouble should someone recognize her, but she kept her arms around him, kissed his face repeatedly, combed his hair with her fingers, and caressed his chest, careless of who might see them, until he nestled snugly against her.

She had been five when separated from her own mamma, once Marianne Tromlitz, then Marianne Wieck, finally Marianne Bargiel. Her mamma had preceded her as a pupil of her pappa, preceded her also with a performance at the Gewandhaus before she married Adolf Bargiel, another of Wieck's students, with whom Wieck had accused her of having an affair, driving her into Bargiel's arms after the divorce. In the eyes of the law children became the property of the father under such circumstances. A tearful time it had been, visitations only when her pappa permitted – and after the Bargiels moved to Berlin, after Clara's lessons began in earnest, after her pappa remarried, there had been no time for visits. In the eyes of the law no need, a divorced woman being suspect by definition. Her mamma still wrote when she could, but she had also started a new family, bearing Bargiel four children, and while Bargiel was a better musician than Wieck he lacked his business sense, he was less robust, and Marianne was forced to give lessons cutting further into her time.

Robert's friend, Gustav Boll, understood they needed time alone and made himself scarce when they arrived. Robert refreshed himself while Clara made coffee, but he wanted beer. "It is the only thing that has kept me going, Clarchen – beer, and my image of you, your darling head like an angel's peering from every corner."

She imagined he might at least look at her when he voiced such sweet sentiments, but he seemed instead in a trance. She noticed also he hardly touched his beer, but never released his stein. She sat with him at the table, shaking her head disbelievingly, mugful of coffee in hand, plateful of pastries before them, courtesy of Boll. "When … did it happen?"

"On the fourth."

"The fourth!" It was now the seventh. "And when was the funeral?"

"I did not go – I could not go."

She bit her lip. "You could not?"

"Do not judge me, Clara. You do not know how I am affected. After Emilie's funeral my nerves were like the strings of a violin strung on a cello. You cannot imagine the thoughts that went through my head. She was only nineteen and so pretty. I wanted to follow in her footsteps, drown myself as she had done, and I was but sixteen then. And then Pappa died – and then Rosalie and Julius – and then Ludwig – and now Mamma – and all in ten years. Enough of death, enough of funerals! They make me ill. They make me wish I were dead myself. I am afraid for myself at funerals. I cannot explain it any other way."

He had run as well from the other funerals, all after Emilie's. She took his hand. "Poor Robert! It is all right. Everything is going to be all right. It is for the best. It is always for the best." His lips twisted, and she recognized immediately the banality of her sentiment. "I am sorry, Robert. I wish I could help."

He took her hand. "You do help, Clarchen. Just sitting with my hand in yours, that helps – sharing a meal with you, that helps."

She didn't smile, but squeezed his hand. She had met Robert's mamma, his entire family, on the occasions of her visits to Zwickau, her tours. "I remember your mamma well, Robert. She said to me once that you were her Lichter Punkt, her bright spot, little point of light."

"Yes, that is from my name. 'Robert' means a light, the light of glory, of fame."

"Does it, indeed? Did you know that 'Clara' also means a kind of light, the light of clarity?"

"Ah, yes, indeed, it does!"

Clara's mind raced: perhaps she was meant to bring clarity to his compositions, present them to the public, her clarity to bring him fame. "Do you know what else she said, Robert?"

"What?"

"I was not quite fifteen then. We were at the window of your parlor, watching you come up the street. You had not seen us. I was about to wave, but she drew me aside. She said something that stayed my hand."

"Yes?"

"She said, and I remember this exactly. She said: 'One day, you must marry my Robert.'"

Robert sighed, shaking his head again. "Dear Mamma, she knew. Even then, she knew."

"She told me you had written her a letter about our walks to Connewitz, holding you back from the stones by your sleeve – and falling over the same stones myself." Robert almost smiled at the memory as did Clara. "She said that was a lovely story. She said it was meant to be developed further."

"Mamma knew!" He almost jumped from the chair, slapping the table with his palm, the most animation he had shown since his arrival. "She *knew* about Ernestine, but even knowing she could say such a thing. She *knew* we were destined. She is with us, even now, I know it!"

Clara wished to ask more questions about Ernestine; her pappa had fostered the doubts; but this was not the time. Instead she caressed his hand, his arm, his face, wiping his tears. He held the back of her hand to his warm wet cheek before drawing it to his mouth, kissing the back of her hand, her palm, putting a finger in his mouth and sucking. She didn't understand, but he closed his eyes, appearing to derive comfort from her finger; she wanted to remove her finger, wipe it dry, but cupped his face instead with her free hand, giving him more fingers for his mouth, drawing herself close, kissing and licking his face, tasting the salt of his neverending tears.

He clutched her then, burying his head in her breasts. For a long moment she held back, hands in the air, but he held her more tightly around her waist kissing her more fiercely, and she cuddled his head to her bosom like a kitten, kissing and caressing his hair, calming his pitiful whimpers and moans with a new and profound motherliness.

iii

Wieck called the Kaskels into their own drawingroom and seated them in their own chairs, calling as well Clara and seating her. Paul Kaskel, co-owner of a cannon foundry founded by his father-in-law, was surprised at Wieck's surliness, but awaited an explanation. He and his wife, Martha, music lovers both, had attended Clara's concerts in Dresden and befriended the Wiecks. Clara and their daughter Sophie had been good company for each other and the Kaskels had offered to host the Wiecks.

Clara was not surprised, neither at what her pappa was doing, nor that he had learned of Robert's visit. He had associates in the city, Robert had not cared to keep his visit a secret, and she had not cared to fight him – but she was surprised at her pappa's manner. He appeared angry as well at the Kaskels, his mouth a thin straight line, his narrow eyes ferreting around.

Paul Kaskel was bewildered and no less annoyed. "Herr Wieck, this is most unusual. I trust you have some explanation for this most extraordinary behavior."

Wieck remained standing, conducting proceedings like a Master of Ceremonies. "Herr Kaskel, I might say the same for you. I trust *you* have some explanation for *your* most extraordinary behavior."

Kaskel shook his head. "I have not the slightest idea what you are talking about. Pray, be more specific."

"Very well, then, since you insist on being secretive I will come to the point. I know Herr Schumann visited Dresden in my absence. I know he had commerce with my daughter during that time. I would like to know why you did nothing to prevent it."

The Kaskels looked at one another and at Clara who looked blankly ahead.

Wieck crossed his arms. "I know Clara was to be at the theater last Saturday, but I have learned that Sophie," Wieck glared at Sophie, "taking the boa, went in her stead – leaving her with Schumann."

Paul Kaskel shook his head, beginning to take hold of himself, addressing Wieck firmly. "Herr Wieck, first, it is not I who insist on being secretive, but you, certainly, who insist on being very mysterious indeed. Second, I am your host, not your daughter's keeper. Third, it is presumptuous of you, indeed, to have had my daughter followed and her manner of dress reported upon. If there is an explanation forthcoming, I think it should be coming from you. And fourth, I must insist that

100

you sit down. Sit, Herr Wieck, I pray you. Take a seat. It is unseemly of you to hover over us like an invigilator."

Wieck walked to Kaskel and stood over him. "Herr Kaskel, what do you know of Schumann?"

"Herr Wieck – first, take a seat, I pray you, that we may discuss this as civilized beings. Otherwise, this interview is over."

Wieck sat in the closest empty chair. "Herr Kaskel, I repeat: What do you know of Schumann?!"

"Herr Wieck, I must ask you also not to shout. We are not in the street. We are in a drawingroom. We are among women and children. My hearing is quite proficient. Am I understood?"

Wieck lowered his tone to a whisper, a slow sibilant sinister whisper. "Herr Kaskel, I repeat once more: What do you know of the Schumann?"

Frau Kaskel's eyes were wide, Sophie and Clara exchanged looks. Kaskel leaned back in his chair. "About Herr Schumann, I am not aware of any reason fit to prevent his commerce with your daughter. If there is any such, it is up to you to enlighten us, not to assume that we are privy to all the machinations in your head. What is the substance of your complaint, Herr Wieck?"

"You have not yet answered my question, sir. What do you know of the Schumann?"

Kaskel took a deep breath. "What I know of Schumann is what all Leipzig knows, what all of Germany will soon know. He is one of our most original living composers. I have heard you say it yourself. I would have considered him more than an ideal companion for your daughter. I am surprised only that you seem unable to see what is so evident to everyone else."

Clara smiled, Sophie returned her smile; Frau Kaskel caught the exchange, still bewildered, still alarmed.

Wieck caught the smile as well and gripping the arms of his chair rose from his seat. "Herr Kaskel, you know nothing. This Schumann is a profligate and a craven. He lived in my house, ate my food, profited from my lessons before his own stupidity rendered his finger useless – and he repaid me by seducing my daughter. That is the Schumann I know, whom no one else knows. That is the Schumann I excoriate. That is the Schumann with whom I accuse you of leaving my daughter."

Clara's face turned white. She refused to look at Wieck. "Pappa! His mamma has just died. He came seeking comfort from our old friendship. That is all."

Kaskel rose himself from his chair and put a hand on Wieck's shoulder. "Herr Wieck, these are sore charges you make. I understand you believe you have reason for your grievances, but you must not slander Herr Schumann in his absence."

"Believe me, Kaskel, I would slander him with far greater pleasure in his presence."

"That is not what I mean, Wieck. I mean you must not slander him on the strength of hearsay."

"Hearsay! Is he not a profligate for running to Clara before his poor dead mother's body has even turned cold? Is he not a craven for sneaking into Dresden during my absence? No, Herr Kaskel, believe me! Were he in my presence today, I would spit in his face with the greatest pleasure!"

"Pappa!"

"Do not dare to use that tone with me, Clara! I know whereof I speak. I have been in touch with the Baron about Ernestine. She had full expectation of an engagement from the Schumann before he wrote to her breaking his promise, offering no reason whatsoever for his change of heart."

Clara took a deep breath and stiffened; Frau Kaskel and Sophie thought she might faint. Kaskel turned his attention from Wieck. "Clara, are you all right?"

She nodded, not looking at him. Her face remained white.

"Would you like some water?"

She shook her head.

Wieck's face turned as white as Clara's. "This is the proof! This is the proof of her iniquity with the Schumann! Do you not believe me yet?"

Kaskel was grim, looking at Wieck. "I do not know yet what to believe, Herr Wieck." He turned to Clara. "Clara, tell me – tell us yourself what you know of this matter."

Clara's oceanblue eyes filled. "I will say what I know – that I love Robert – with all my heart, I love Robert. That is all I know. That is all I will say for now." She dabbed a handkerchief at her eyes and sniffed.

"Ah, a moment ago you were friends, you consoled him from an old friendship. Now you say you love him! I ask you, Kaskel, do you not believe me yet?"

Clara got up. "Please, I wish to be excused."

"*Sit, Down, Girl!* You will leave when you are excused, not before."

Clara walked from the room in a trance, eyes on the carpet.

"Clara! Come back! You will leave when I tell you to leave! Do you hear me?"

Kaskel put his hand on Wieck's arm. "Let her go, Herr Wieck. Let her go. She is troubled."

"And well she *should* be! If he sees Clara again I will *shoot* him!" He shouted. "DO YOU HEAR ME, CLARA! IF YOU *SEE* THE SCHUMANN AGAIN, AS GOD IS MY WITNESS, I WILL *SHOOT* HIM!"

Kaskel flinched. "Sir! I must ask you not to speak with such violence in the presence of my wife and daughter."

"And what would you do, *Sir*, if a scoundrel were to make a harlot of your daughter, *Sir*? Answer me that, *Sir*, and I shall allow myself to be schooled by you – *Sir!*"

"I must repeat, first, Herr Wieck, that you are not to speak so freely in front of my wife and daughter. If you insist on speaking with such violence you will no longer be welcome in my house. It is only my regard for Clara that allows me to keep you even now. Is that understood?"

"Tell me, *Sir*, what you would do, *Sir*, in my place – and I shall be schooled by you – *Sir!*"

"First, Herr Wieck, I would be sure of my facts. I would then reveal them in a measured and restrained manner to the party in question. I would give them a chance to defend themselves. That is what I would do."

"Well, it seems we each have our own ways."

"That we do, indeed, Herr Wieck – and in my house it is my ways that must prevail."

iv

Clara received two letters shortly, the first from Robert within a week, the second from Ernestine in response to her own within a month.

ROBERT TO CLARA   *From the Coach House in Zwickau*
                                                      Past ten at night
                                                      13ᵗʰ Feb. '36

Dearest Clara,

My eyes are full of sleep. I have waited two hours for the Flying Coach, but the roads are so bad I may not get away before 2 o'clock. My darling, darling Clara, I see you so clearly I could touch you. I had no difficulty once saying what I felt, but words elude me now. I could not tell you how I felt if you did not know already. Love me, always, will you? I ask much because I give much.

This has been a difficult day, dealing with my mother's will, hearing accounts of her death, but your image shines behind the darkness, and I can bear the rest.

I must say also that my future is better assured. I shall not be able to sit with my hands in my lap, and I have much work ahead before I can win for myself what you see everytime you pass a mirror, but I know you wish to remain an artist yourself, not to retire like Henriette Sontag at the height of her career to become a Countess Rossi. I know you will want to share my load, my joys, my sorrows. Write to me about this.

What remains is to take care of my external affairs in Leipzig. You have already taken good care of my internal affairs. But I trust all will be well now that we are reconciled. I trust even your pappa will understand once he has weighed the good against the bad. I will explain these things more clearly when we meet again, and perhaps my hand prevents you from reading even what I have written. For now, know this: I love you more than I can say.

The room grows dark, passengers sleep around me, the snow falls heavily outside, but I will tuck myself in a corner with a cushion and think of nothing but you in your little red hat.

Farewell, my Clara.

Your Robert

ERNESTINE TO CLARA   *Asch*
                                                      25ᵗʰ Feb.

My Dear Clara,

I cannot say how glad I was to hear from you in my sorrow. I have felt often that I was to blame for your own sorrow about Sch. No good can come of this, not for me, except perhaps for me to unburden myself.

Sch. has sunk in my estimation, but it was my own fault for holding him up so high. Oh, if only I had never known him! I loved him beyond words, I would have given my life for him, I could think of nothing but him, his words, his portrait from which he smiles so roguishly. Indeed, you know his smile. Oh, it is so enchanting!

There is nothing I want from life so much now as to be out of it. There is nothing in this life for me now but anxieties, torments, and cares. He wrote that I should save myself while there was time, that was all he said, apart from this he gave no reason. Save myself from what??? But I did not want to involve myself in long questions – no, nor him. I love him, and I set him free – at once, I set him free.

He is wholly to blame for my misfortune, he and no one else. I am wholly abandoned and miserable, and I never want to see him again – but still I wish him everything good, and if ever I could be of service to him I would be so joyfully.

He is yours. I saw it – indeed, I told him so, but he assured me differently. He said you were too young. Well, you are not so young anymore, and I wish you, as I wish him, only the joy of love.

Ernestine

Returning to Leipzig in May, Clara and her pappa found a published manuscript by Robert awaiting them, the Sonata in F sharp minor, which she had played for Mendelssohn on her birthday, with the inscription:

SONATA FOR PIANO
DEDICATED TO CLARA
BY FLORESTAN AND EUSEBIUS
OPUS 11

In response her pappa told her to return to Robert all his letters and to ask for her own back, which she did. She was too tired and depressed to think further. Robert had turned to Ernestine to soothe himself when Rosalie and Julius had died, then turned to her when his mamma had died with no apparent regard for Ernestine. Indeed, his regard for Ernestine appeared to have fluctuated with his regard for her inheritance, his fear of being wed to a Countess Rossi. They both knew she could make more money in a month of concerts than he in a year of composition. She immersed herself in the piano, learned new works, more difficult works, developing dexterity beyond even her pappa's expectations.

She walked away from Robert when she saw him in the street, drew back her hand when he touched her, remained silent when he spoke, but he followed her once determined to have his say. "Clara, I have received a letter from your pappa. He calls me a thief, a craven, a profligate, all kinds of names I do not deserve – but I bear them all proudly for your sake. He says he will shoot me if I talk to you again. Well, here I am, talking to you. Let him shoot me. I care for nothing if you will not talk to me."

She remained silent, walking ahead, afraid for Robert, afraid who might see them, afraid of her pappa, afraid he would realize his threat. "If you will not talk to me, Clara, I will shoot myself." His face twitched, his hands trembled. "Do you *hear* me, Clara? I will *save* your pap*pa* the *trou*ble." Robert was shouting. She stared blankly ahead, heads were turning. She was afraid again, of what he was saying, who might hear, what might reach her pappa. "But first I will shoot you – before I shoot myself I will shoot you! Do you *HEAR* me?"

She looked quickly back at him. His eyes were wild, his hair uncombed, scaring her further, but as she stared his eyes shrank, his voice became a whisper. "I am sorry, Clara. I did not mean that. I am not myself. Will you not say something? anything?" She saw in his trembling mouth the roguish smile which had deceived Ernestine, and walked on; it was the beginning of a silence that was to last more than a year.

In 1837 the Princess Belgiojoso lived in Paris, exiled for her support of rebels, so-called because they fought for the unification of her native Italy, but reduced to refugees for their patriotism. The Congress of Vienna had divided Italy into three regions, among the Hapsburgs of Austria in the north, the papacy in the middle, and the Bourbons of Spain in the south. Ironically, Bonaparte had sown the seeds of unification in Italy as in Germany. The Princess was aiding his efforts, no less ironically, raising funds in Paris. She was to be arrested later, again no less ironically, for reasons unrelated to her political activities – but more about that later.

Her salon, the rooms in which she held her soirees, was as tightly sealed and padded as a womb. Door curtains, flush with wall fabrics, flush with carpets, were silk and plush and twill. Walls and floors of marble, stone, and wood were concealed by Persian rugs, velvet curtains, and Greek tapestries, all doubly draped and layered. Among the various bibelots stood Chinese porcelain, funerary urns, decorative plates, and gold candelabra. A tiger skin swooped over the fireplace. The ceiling was invisible behind ferns and flowers. Windows, the mantelpiece, and even the piano, were clouded with cushions, fabrics, and pads, all colorful, bright, and soft. The rooms were crowded as well with chairs, scattered at random, chaise longues, ottomans, pouffes, and sofas. At one end a table had been set with cakes and petit fours and sandwiches of mutton and beef.

The occasion, for which the guests (plumed in capes, cloaks, cravats, caps, caftans, and collars) had paid forty francs apiece, had been announced in the *Gazette musicale*: "Two titans of talent, balanced as precariously as Carthage and Rome, will appear simultaneously at the salon of the Princess Belgiojoso, on 31 March, the MM. Litzt [sic] and Thalberg." The French never got Liszt's name right, but varied it inventively: List, Lizt, Litst, Littz, Lits, Ltilz, Ltis, Tzlits, Slitz. The rooms resounded with hum and hubbub, reeked of perfume and perspiration.

Franz Liszt, first in Paris in 1823 at twelve, had been hailed a second Mozart: "His arms barely span the piano, his feet barely touch the pedals – but he is the first pianist in Europe!" He had already toured Hungary, Austria, and Germany; now he toured England, Ireland, and France; but by the time he was sixteen, after seven years in the limelight, he was exhausted, taking a sea cure in Boulogne, when his father, his manager and traveling companion, weakened by their travels, dying of typhoid fever, had issued a caution: "I fear for you, Franz, my son. I fear what women will do to you."

There were many women; they shrieked, fainted, and threw jewelry onstage; one choked on the stub of a cigar he had smoked, another framed the seat cover on which he had sat, others fought over the gloves he tossed carelessly into the audience, anything he might have touched, remnants of his dinners, his drinks. Finally he absconded to Switzerland with the Countess Marie d'Agoult, six years older, twenty-eight when they met and married to a man twenty years older (though estranged from her husband). She was to become the mother of his children, the three he acknowledged, and to provide the final polish to his persona, the touch of the aristocrat.

Critics were reduced to ecstacies no less than women and spoke of him elementally: "[he] worked up a storm, runs like rain, trills like hail, arpeggios like lightning, chords like thunder." One even berated him for drawing accolades for behavior which would have drawn the sternest censure for anyone else: destroying pianos, snapping strings, breaking hammers. Mendelssohn criticized his taste and sensationalism, so did Chopin, Schumann, and Moscheles, but not his pianism which was irreproachable, transcendant.

Of course, he was beautiful, tall and slim – but so was Sigismond Thalberg, the Swiss virtuoso, beautiful, tall and slim, the blueblood bastard son of Count von Dietrichstein and Baroness von Wetzlar, named Thal (valley) for his childhood, Berg (mountain) for adulthood, by his mother. Women loved him no less than they loved Liszt, but he was gentler, less histrionic; Liszt had swooned once into the arms of his pageturner, only to return to the stage revived in moments to collective sighs from the audience; Thalberg would never have conceived such a stratagem, never have pounded the keys, never have broken pianos, but with no surrender of force. He could be loud without being noisy, make the piano sing if not spit – for which Liszt had called him the only man who could play the violin on the piano – and, as with Liszt, everyone expressed praises and reservations, Mendelssohn, Chopin, Schumann, Moscheles – and again, as with Liszt, Thalberg had patrons, generous beyond understanding, one presented him with an estate, another a mansion in Vienna, and so on.

Thalberg arrived in Paris in 1836, while Liszt was in Switzerland with the Countess d'Agoult, and began to eclipse him from the minds of Parisians. Liszt hurried back to reclaim his precedence, but Thalberg had left the city. Liszt gave two concerts, consolidating his reputation. Reviewing Thalberg's compositions in the *Gazete musicale*, he had shut himself up for an afternoon to study the works, only to find them dull, empty, and windbaggy. When Thalberg returned Liszt suggested a double bill on two pianos, but Thalberg declined, saying politely that he did not like to be accompanied, following with a concert at the conservatory, selling out 400 seats. Liszt responded with a concert at the opera house, selling out 3,000, leading to the Princess's invitation to both pianists to play a benefit for the refugees.

No other duel had generated such a furor, not between Mozart and Clementi, nor between Beethoven and Steibelt. Chopin, Herz, Pixis, Czerny attended, among others. Many artists provided the prelude to the main event, but we need not consider them. Liszt insisted on performing last; Thalberg was too gentlemanly to refuse. Each chose to play the piece just performed at the conservatory and opera house,

Thalberg his "Fantasy on Themes from Rossini's *Moses,*" Liszt his "Grand Fantasy on Pacini's *Niobe.*"

Thalberg's face was gentler, his eyes dreamier, his mouth more delicate, high cheekbones, fair angelic curls, the semblance of a part on the left side of his head, trim sideburns framing a perfect jaw and commanding nose. He held his head high, cradled in a stiff white collar, girded by a white cravat, dark coat, velvet lapels, grey waistcoat, betraying no emotion, nodding to wellwishers, barely smiling, eyes on the piano, his best friend in the room. His one concession to the moment were the studs glittering with diamonds in his collar. Seated he was still as a buttoned soldier; it was said he practised with a Turkish pipe before him, just long enough to maintain his posture, one of the tricks for which he was known, producing volumes of sound, waves that would have done an ocean proud, without appearing to move, beginning mildly, like the dawn, working himself to high noon.

A hush descended as Thalberg sat before the piano, his movements so small the audience would have missed his hands settling on the keys had they blinked; they would also have missed the first ripples of his Fantasy, so inobtrusively did they steal into the room; they would not have noticed anyone was playing, so naturally did the ripples blend with the air, until the first rising chords sliced the room a minute into the work, an upward run like breakers crashing supported by an undertow of deep chords – but just as they settled into the new decibel level the dynamic returned to the ripples – but in a different direction, a varied melody.

Thalberg's merits were immediately apparent, boneless hands, velvet fingers, singing melodies. He used Chopin's methods, Chopin's effects, but Chopin was rooting for Liszt – no surprise since asked once about Chopin's concertos Thalberg had praised the tuttis. Chopin envied Thalberg, taking tenths as easily as he took eighths, but criticized him as well for using the pedal more than his hands.

The second melody accelerated and swelled, ripples emanating from ripples, the room aswirl, until the final melody announced itself, momentum building from peroration to peroration, revealing another of the tricks for which Thalberg was known: a threehanded performance, the melody holding the center of the keyboard while runs spanned the entire length. He played the melody with his thumbs leaving his fingers free to travel easily in either direction.

All the while, uncannily, however exalted the sound, Thalberg remained expressionless, still except for his hands rolling over the keyboard, fingers turning like waterwheels, concluding with the specter of a smile, pleased with his performance, but no less pleased that it was over. The applause came in waves and breakers no less tumultuous than the ones Thalberg had just released, but Liszt cut them short, striding to the piano, a small clap in his hands, tendentious flick of his head, flipping hair from his face.

The number of Liszt's cravats was a matter of much speculation, it was said he had one for each day of the year, but he had chosen to wear none of them, not even a collar. He wore a black coat, red waistcoat, yellow shirt, and removed green gloves revealing on his forefinger a gold ring, a silver death's head. His hair was so lank and long it covered his face like a mop when he bowed. His face was awash with lines and angles, aquiline nose, thin mouth, sharp chin, straight eyebrows, fair hair pouring like a waterfall.

His frame was slight, the only thing about him that was slight, but hardly apparent from the way he swayed even before playing, as mobile as Thalberg had been still, as much the focus of everyone's eyes as their ears when he struck the first chord, opening with a martial theme, almost a march, a quick march, establishing tone, theme, rhythm, from the beginning, followed shortly by two thrilling runs descending the length of the keyboard. Gentle phrases followed, sandwiched between the louder, but never so they took precedence. Thalberg was subtle, storming his audience when they weren't looking; Liszt hit them in the face with runs like rockets and volleys like bullets.

Beethoven had been the first thunderer, sweeping arms like windmills, preferring the catharsis of expression over the taste of the moment, but he differed from Liszt in one important aspect: the accuracy of his notes may sometimes have been in doubt, but never his emotion; Liszt's notes were never in doubt, but his emotion was always suspect. His hands appeared to multiply, now above the piano, now to one side, now to the other; his fingers multiplied no less, separating from his hands like so many lizard tails, scurrying across the keyboard.

A quieter middle episode followed, but the velocity of the pianissimo runs and trills scarcely diminished, and soon the march returned, ominous as a firing squad. Amazingly, with all the activity, Liszt appeared never to look at his hands, the keys, or the piano, focusing instead on his audience, measuring his effects to their susceptibilities, singling individuals for attention as if he played for no one else. With the last resounding chord he raised his arms in a V, jumping from his chair, flipping his hair once more from his face, holding his chin high, triumphant in his finish as a gladiator.

The histrionics gave Liszt the edge, but with so much incomparable pianism on display, so much to feed so many appetites, only vulgar sensibilities would have demanded a winner, all others would have been offended: spectators, performers, winner, and loser. Wieck, hearing both later, declared both inspired, Thalberg in his vacuity, Liszt in his affectation. Mendelssohn, more measured, declared the two represented the highest pianism of the day between them. The Princess's announcement showed her breeding: "Thalberg is the first pianist in the world. Liszt is the only."

The Princess, not above fainting herself at the opera when she wished, was soon to be arrested, not for political activities as I have said, but for concealing the embalmed corpse of an old lover in her closet.

Wieck was amazed; Clara continually exceeded expectations, all benchmarks were ephemeral, raised with successive performances; he was no longer her arbiter, she knew her strengths, and her weaknesses became apparent only when he heard them overcome; he had never exacted more than three hours of practice daily, believing fatigue brought its own problems, but she pushed herself to four hours, five, six, thirds for half an hour, sixths for another half, octaves next, with no sign of fatigue – but with a sacrifice.

The public at large, which noticed only brilliance in technique, which came only for brilliance, for the works of Herz, Pixis, Kalkbrenner, and Thalberg, were delighted with her brilliance – but the private audiences, the connoisseurs, who demanded Bach, Beethoven, Mozart, Chopin, and Schumann, works of greater profundity, who made greater demands as well on the performer, were less delighted. She had lost her vanity, her vivacity, her pride, without which a musician was no more than a machine, and Wieck knew the cause. He meant to take her again to Paris, but before that to Vienna, and before that to Berlin, to make of Berlin her training ground, trusting the presence of her mamma to reinvigorate her pride.

He delivered Clara to Marianne Bargiel with impudence. "Here, madam, I bring you your daughter." Frau Bargiel's face was a palimpsest for Clara's; her head was larger, but dominated as was Clara's by a commanding nose, firm mouth, and determined chin. She wore a faded blue dress; her hair fell in streamers around her head. She said nothing, but her face dissolved: her mouth softened, her chin retreated, her brow flattened, her eyes enlarged; even her nose appeared all but invisible. Clara dashed into her open arms. "Mamma!"

Wieck smiled, crossing his arms, watching the women embrace on the Bargiel doorstep. Marianne drew away first, holding Clara at armslength, drinking her with her eyes; Clara smiled, bobbing in her mamma's hands, bouncing from foot to foot. Finally, Marianne took Clara's hand, looking at Wieck. "Will you not come inside?"

Wieck shook his head, keeping his smile, bowing like a courtier. "Not I, madam. I am but the queen's lackey. I have much yet to prepare for her concerts."

"Is there nothing I can do? I would be happy to help with arrangments for the concert. I know something about how Berlin works. I know some people."

Wieck shook his head; Marianne had not changed, still wanting to wrest his control, meddle in what did not concern her. "No, madam, I know what I am about.

Berlin can hardly be as difficult as Paris. Just see that she is returned to the hotel by five o'clock this evening."

"Yes, yes, of course, as you wish." Marianne hardly looked at Wieck; she had offered help for Clara's sake, not his, but she was glad he had refused; she had never seen Clara without him since her move to Berlin, never seen her as a young woman, and taking her hand led her indoors.

"Goodbye, Pappa!"

Wieck grunted; Clara was smiling as she had not in a while; he had made the right calculation.

Within the door a number of heads bobbed, Clara had met them all at different times, her stepbrothers and sister, Ludwig, Carl, Woldemar, and Greta, and behind them all Adolf Bargiel, her mamma's husband, who had once managed the Logier Institute, a piano school for which they had moved to Berlin in 1826 – but a cholera epidemic in 1830 had closed the school, students had left the city, Bargiel had been further incapacitated by a stroke. Clara said hullo, hugging them all. Bargiel shook her hand, smiling kindly at Clara, but she could see even with her tender years how she might use such a smile to her advantage, a smile that spoke too soon, unlike her pappa's which appeared only for his advantage, which said nothing at all. "How goes it with you, Clara?"

"It goes well, Herr Bargiel. Danke."

He nodded, still smiling. "It is good to have you among us again."

"Danke."

"Clara, will you have coffee? We can talk in the parlor. Would you like coffee or chocolate?"

"That sounds lovely."

"What? Coffee? Chocolate?"

"It does not matter – just to talk, I meant."

"Good. I have heard such wonderful things about my little girl – not so little anymore. I will join you in the parlor in a few minutes – as soon as I have prepared the coffee."

The parlor was smaller than her own, upholstery was frayed, wallpaper torn. Marianne and Greta brought coffee and pastries in chipped cups and plates. Marianne chased the other Bargiels from the room and soon they were sipping coffee, nibbling pastry, just the two of them, Clara with a book in her lap, scraps her mamma had collected, reminders of her babyhood, brown hairs in an envelope, outlines of tiny feet – also letters, all the letters she had ever written, including notes from Wieck regarding her care. *Madam!* said one of the earliest, accompanying one of Clara's visitations, *I am sending you my most prized possession, with the caveat that you say nothing of what has happened – or, if you must, that you express yourself in such a manner as not to arouse the suspicions of a guiltless and natural child. Furthermore, you must not spoil her with pastries, nor condone any naughtiness, nor allow her to rush through her practice. If my wishes are not exactly fulfilled, my anger will be incurred,* which meant Marianne might not see Clara again for as long as he pleased, such were the laws of the state governing divorced women.

Clara picked a pastry. "Oh, Mamma! And pappa specifically said you were not to spoil me!"

Marianne didn't even smile. "I do not care what your pappa says. I know better what is best. You help yourself to as many pastries as you wish."

Clara also read her own first letter, written when she was eight, listing birthday gifts, a beautiful dress, a plum cake, a lovely knitting bag – listing also a problem she was having with a chromatic scale. A later letter gave an account of her first concert at the Gewandhaus, when she had taken the wrong coach.

"Clara, darling, what is the matter?"

Clara looked at her mamma. "Why do you ask?"

"I do not know, but you look sad."

Immediately, Clara's eyes welled with tears. "I am not sad, Mamma. I am not sad. I am happy to be here with you. I do not know why I am crying." Her hand shook, spilling coffee on one of the letters. "Oh, I am sorry." She put down the cup, put the book aside, bowed her head, wiped tears from her cheeks, but they streamed faster than she could clear them.

Marianne's eyes too had swelled, her cheeks too glistened. She too put down her cup, put her arm around Clara. Clara sobbed on her breast, great heaving sobs, while Marianne held her, her cheek on Clara's head, rocking her, kissing her, saying nothing. "I am sorry, Mamma. I do not mean to be difficult."

Marianne shook her head. "Never say that, child. You are never difficult. I do not wish to say anything about your pappa; you know him better than I do perhaps after all these years; but some things I understand without knowing. I know how he was." She brushed Clara's hair behind her ears. "Clara, I want you to know I have always been proud of you – long before everyone else, long before your talent blossomed, I was proud of you – when you were just a baby, even when I had to leave you because of differences with your pappa, I was proud of you – because you were my child. There have been times I have wondered about you, hoping you were happy, wishing I could be with you – but it was not to be."

Clara looked up; her mamma continued to brush her hair, wipe her cheeks.

"When you were a child it was difficult to explain. It is no less difficult now, but I think you might understand things better now without explanations."

Clara stared, saying nothing.

"Do you understand that you can count on me for anything I can do? Do you understand that you are not alone?"

Clara nodded slowly. "I do, Mamma. Danke."

"And can I count on you to let me know if there is anything I can do for you?"

Again she nodded, more quickly. "Yes, Mamma. Sometimes all I want is someone to talk with. I have no one to talk with."

Marianne smiled. "Like we are talking now?"

Clara smiled back, almost shy, nodding yet again.

"Oh, my dear, that should be the easiest thing – and yet sometimes it is the most difficult. Is there something you wish to talk about now?"

"Yes, Mamma."

"More coffee first?"

Clara smiled, eyes drying fast. "Yes, please. Danke."

She told her mamma about Robert. Marianne listened without interruption, and when she was finished spoke without hesitation. "Oh, but my dear Clara, the solution appears so very plain to me."

"It does?"

"Indeed. I would tell you to follow your heart, but if your heart is unsure it is plain you should do nothing. You are but seventeen. There is no hurry. If Robert loves you he will wait until you are sure. If not, you will find out and the decision will be made for you."

"That is what I have been doing, Mamma. I have been waiting for a sign – but I hate to keep Robert guessing. It does not feel right."

"Far better to keep him guessing than to make the wrong decision. Far better to keep him guessing than to tell him what he wants to hear – when it just might not be true. Do you not think so?"

"Yes, Mamma – but what about Pappa? Should I not worry about what he might do, whatever I may think or feel?"

"Your pappa is a practical man. He will say and do whatever he needs to get what he wants – but he will not do anything to hurt himself. If he were to carry out his threat against Robert it would ruin his reputation. I do not think he would want to risk that, do you?"

Clara nodded. "I could not believe what he said. I cannot believe, even now, that he believes it himself."

"But he got what he wanted, did he not? He scared you into believing he meant what he said."

"That he did."

"It is no wonder your pappa is such a good businessman, Clara. He knows how to make an argument. It is a pity, though, that he deals with his friends and his family as if they too were no more than pianos for barter."

Clara laughed.

Marianne smiled. "Sometimes I think it a rare man, indeed, who knows the difference between pianos and people. There are those who, like your pappa, treat people like pianos – but there are others who treat pianos like people. I am not sure which is better."

Again Clara laughed. "That is my Robert. Such a softhearted man you never saw."

Clara's Berlin debut was a greater success than even Wieck might have imagined. He complained incessantly – of the censors who scrutinized his advertisements five times before passing them, of the number of complimentary tickets mandated by custom, of the supporting musicians, the bureaucracy, the servants, the cost of food, of postage – but he raved just as incessantly about Clara's triumphs, *his* triumphs, *he* had routed the enemy, crushed the critics, destroyed the cabals, become the talk of the town, reduced all other artists to despair; not even Paganini had been as honored as Clara in Berlin, thanks to *his* tutelage, *his* guidance.

Miss Anna Robena Laidlaw was as English as her complexion implied, milky and suffused with the pink of roses; her nose had not the regality of Clara's, but was perfectly straight; her auburn hair, streaked with the colors of autumn, was so thick it settled on her head like a hat. She had studied piano with Robert Muller in Konigsberg where her parents had settled, in London with Heinrich Herz, and in Berlin with Ludwig Berger, Mendelssohn's teacher. She had played concerts in Konigsberg, London, Berlin, Riga, Warsaw, been appointed court pianist to Frederica, Duchess of Cumberland, and come that summer to Leipzig to make Robert's acquaintance. He had interested himself in her concerts and reviewed them in the *Zeitschrift*; she interested herself in his compositions and played them at her concerts.

Robert had read of Clara's triumphs, first in Berlin, then Hamburg, finally Bremen, but with no less despair than pride. Robena was hardly Clara's peer (no woman was), but she was prettier, and a good enough pianist to make him forget. Even their names, Robert and Robena, seemed serendipitous.

He liked her best as she appeared now, asleep under the covers, hair spread like a mantle on the pillow, mouth parted in a crescent. The weather enhanced the coziness, dark rain when the sun might have been rising, cold though it was late summer. He held his hand to her mouth, felt her warm wet breath, got out of bed, put on his robe, went to the next room, and stared out of the window wishing he might have seen a park, a single tree, birds, squirrels, instead of the street, curtained windows across, shadows of clouds over the shadows of buildings, but Leipzig was not a city of parks, and the patter of rain on the cobbles provided a blanket of sound, extending the silence of the night. Two persons passed, holding umbrellas; shroud of clouds, shroud of buildings, shroud of umbrellas; seven o'clock, and the world was shrouded in rain and sleep.

Wilhelm Ulex, with whom he shared his rooms, could not have been more considerate. He knew of Robert's troubles, and when he had learned of Robena's visit had made plans to visit his parents. Even so, things were not as Robert wished; even at their most intimate a face divided him from Robena, a radiant face with a smile Robena couldn't begin to approximate. He sighed, moving from window to piano. He had composed a series of pieces, alternating Eusebius's dreaminess with Florestan's rowdiness, the first of which he called "Of the Evenings" though it seemed to mirror better the dark early morning.

The melody had a long breath and dripped from his fingers in slow, soft, single, sinuous, even beats, descending, then ascending, then descending again, echoed insistently by the same note on the offbeat, with minimal harmony, coiling and uncoiling, quietly mesmerizing the listener to stillness until the listener was enraptured and wrapped in its cocoon.

Robena entered the room while he played, eyes soft with sleep, and slid her hands into his robe from behind when he finished. "Robert, my Schumann, you never cease to amaze me. Your ideas are so plentiful it is all I can do just to follow them. I must learn that for my next concert."

He held her arms and leaned against her as her hands explored his chest and stomach, her fingers scratching his lower belly. "It is yours, my Clara. It was written for no one but you."

The first he knew something was wrong was when her hands stiffened under the robe. "What did you say?"

"I said it was written for you."

"That is not what you said."

"What did I say?"

"You called me Clara – again."

"No. No. No. No."

"But you did."

"Benchen, I am sorry. I am so sorry."

Of course, he was sorry. What else could he say? But it was no less true for his apology, no less true that his thoughts were not with her, might never have been. She removed her hands from his robe. "This is not right. I must go."

"Not now, Robena, Benchen! Not now, you cannot go! I have said I am sorry! What more can I do?"

"But that is just it. There is nothing to be done. It is so obvious you do not think about me that it is humiliating. I must go."

Robert got up so suddenly the bench fell over with a crash. "No! I forbid you! Do you hear me? I forbid you!"

She stared in disbelief: he was glaring like a madman, but if she let him have his way she would lose her own. She gripped his shoulders. "Robert, listen to me. This is not the first time. Last night you called her name – more than once you called her name – even after I told you, you called her name. It is not right. I should not be here."

Robert shrugged her hands from his shoulders. "It is impossible what you say. I have no recollection of what you say. Between Clara and me, it is over. *Over!*"

Robena shook her head. "I do not believe it. I believe you wish it to be over. I believe you might even believe yourself that it is over. But *I* do not believe it is over – and you would not be so illtempered with me if it were indeed over."

"I have said I am sorry! If there were some other way to show you I would take it. What you say has neither head nor foot!"

He was shouting. Robena lowered her voice, hoping to lower his. "You may be right, Robert – but it is how I feel. I cannot argue with the way I feel. If I stay I risk shaming myself."

"And if you leave, you risk shaming me! I refuse to let you go! I cannot let you go! You will need to remove me bodily if you wish to leave! Do you hear me?"

Robena spoke more sternly. "Yes, Robert, I hear you – I and everyone else in the house! I beg you to lower your voice – or you will create a scene."

"If that is what it will take to get you to stay then that is what I will do!" He was shouting, striding around the room, pushing chairs around. "If you will not listen to reason then I will make you listen to unreason! Do you hear me? I will make you listen to *un*reason!"

115

He was beyond understanding. Robena realized nothing she said would make a difference – not then, but perhaps later. "All right, then, Robert. Since you leave me no choice, I shall stay – though against my will. Now, will you please be quiet?"

He stopped midstride, smiling, lowering his voice immediately. "It is only right, Benchen." He held out his arms. "Come."

She didn't know what she would have done then had someone not knocked on the door.

"Herr Schumann!"

Robert lost his smile. "It is Frau Devrient, my landlady."

Robena merely nodded.

"Herr Schumann! Open this door!"

Robert smiled again, and Robena understood the charm that had seduced her aside from his talent. He put his finger to his lips, cautioning silence, and she nodded. "In a minute, Frau Devrient!"

He pulled his robe closer, motioning her to do the same, and opening the door. "Good morning, Frau Devrient! What seems to be the matter?"

Frau Devrient was a large woman in her early fifties. She had not thought much about Robert when he had appeared with his friend looking for rooms, but she had learned since that he was more than he appeared. Herr Mendelssohn paid him visits and many other musicians, once even Herr Chopin. She had a nephew who taught piano and understood that musicians made bad tenants; Beethoven had moved constantly in Vienna, more than a score of residences in as many years; but she had never rented rooms herself to a musician and was sorry she had taken a chance on Herr Schumann though she hadn't known he was a musician until they had installed the piano. "Herr Schumann, I am asking you the same question. I was awakened just now by a loud crash – and then all this shouting. It is I who must ask you the question. What is the matter?"

Robert never stopped smiling. "Ah, Frau Devrient, I am sorry. I bumped into the bench, and when I jumped to catch it I pushed over the chair. That is all. I am sorry to have awakened you."

"There was also much shouting, Herr Schumann. There must not be so much shouting – not at any time, but definitely not so very early in the morning."

"Ah, Frau Devrient, again I am sorry. We have had a difference, my friend and I – you have met her, I believe – at least, I am sure you have heard of her – Miss Anna Robena Laidlaw, here from England to give concerts. We had a disagreement, but it is over. There will be no more noise. We shall be as quiet as mice in cotton."

Neither Frau Devrient nor Robena looked at each other. "I am sorry, Herr Schumann, but that is not good enough. This is not the first time I have had to come to you. My other tenants are complaining and I have to think about them. They too have rights. I am sorry, but I must ask you to leave."

He knew what she was talking about, two parties he had hosted, celebrating Clara's successes, except he had drunk so much beer and champagne he couldn't have said whether he was celebrating Clara or burying her. Each time the neighbors had complained; each time Frau Devrient had interrupted. Robert bowed his head, suddenly too tired to fight. "You are right, Frau Devrient. I am a monster and you are an angel to put up with me. I will leave as soon as I have found another lodging."

Frau Devrient's eyes widened. She hadn't expected capitulation, not so soon, and found herself suddenly full of pity. Herr Schumann wasn't well; his exhaustion was more than physical; it was mental or spiritual or something intangible like that; something was wrong with his life; his skeleton lacked the finer bones; there was too much phlegm in his composition, too much black bile. "Thank you for understanding my position, Herr Schumann. I am sorry it has come to this."

Robert merely nodded, closing the door softly behind her, turning to Robena. "I beg your forgiveness, Robena. I have behaved abominably. I am not myself. If you wish to leave, I will not stop you."

Robena shook her head, her eyes wet, her conclusions not dissimilar from Frau Devrient's. "My dear Robert, there is nothing to forgive. If I could help I would stay. You know that, do you not? But that is not the help you need. You know that, do you not?"

She needed reassurance and Robert gave it gladly. "You are right in everything you say – to the littlest detail, you are right, Robena, and I am wrong."

"I am so sorry." She kissed his cheek before leaving.

He sighed, sitting again at the piano. Willy wouldn't be back until late in the evening and he was faced with the prospect of the long day ahead. Christel would come if he called, but it would not be right, no one would be right anymore but Clara. Besides, with Christel he had experienced the friction, the encrustation on his penis, but with no one else, and he no longer wished to risk such a recurrence. He had work to do on the *Zeitschrift*, the *Fantasiestucke* he was writing for Robena, but he sat at the piano instead, doing nothing – or so it appeared, but something was spinning in his head that he needed to let out and he could let it out only on the piano.

He couldn't explain how it worked: had he not pined for Clara there would have been nothing to release; had he not sat motionless at the piano there would have been no conduit for release. He couldn't have said how long it had been, but something had congealed in the time, the red blood, the hard bone, of the new composition, a strident melody, roiling harmony, interspersed with tender interludes, pulled from the collision of the thunder outside, the purr of the rain, and the noise in his head. He held his hands over the keys and under them the landscape of his nerves, blood, and bones sprang to life, little kingdoms growing under his fingers.

Willy was amazed, seeing that evening what Robert had written, not only by the work, but the speed with which he had written it. He fixed Robert with his gaze. "This is not for Robena. I cannot see her in it."

"No!" Robert was smiling. "It is not for Robena. That much is clear."

Willy nodded. "Something in it throbs, like the pulsation of the heart, ripples from a bloodstream."

"You have hit upon it. That is just what it is – a lament. I am glad you see it so clearly."

Willy did not have to ask who was lamented, but he was glad to see Robert jubilant again – and amazed again at the music he appeared to write so effortlessly. "Shall we try it?"

"In a minute. I shall be right back."

He rushed up the stairs to Frau Devrient's door. She was as surprised as Willy to see him so joyful. "Frau Devrient – first, I must apologize again for my contretemps this morning. I was not myself. I have not been myself for a while. I think you have seen that, and you have been most patient, for which I am most grateful – but I am here to beg your patience further yet. I know I said I would leave, but it would be wrong. I see it now. A lucky star led me to your house and nothing short of violence will persuade me to give up my rooms."

His words seemed violent, but he smiled guilelessly, and Frau Devrient was amazed anew at the changeableness of musicians. He had burst upon her with the familiarity of a son, accosting her so cheerfully, so relentlessly, with his arguments, words pouring like rain from his lips, that her resistance failed – and even as he won her to his arguments he gave her no opportunity to respond.

He spoke and smiled nonstop. "In short, my dear Frau Devrient, you must blame the weather for my troubles, you must blame my circumstances, blame the world, but you must not blame me for my troubles – nor must you take your care away from me, my dear Frau Devrient. I rely too much on it already."

Whatever she thought, whatever she felt, Frau Devrient refused to smile. "Herr Schumann, I have a regard for you. I understand you are a great composer – but I cannot let you inconvenience my other boarders. I cannot afford to lose my other boarders on your account."

"That will never happen, Frau Devrient – never! I will not let it happen. I have regained my balance. One more chance is all I ask. You will not be sorry."

Frau Devrient crossed her arms. "I do not know, Herr Schumann. This is already the third time."

"You will not have to ask me again, Frau Devrient. If I am again troublesome I will boot myself out. You will not have to do a thing."

Frau Devrient shook her head disbelievingly. "Well, all right. I will give you just one more chance."

"That is all I ask." Robert bent quickly, kissing her cheek. "You will see, Frau Devrient. Your patience will not go unrewarded. But I still have a request to make."

"What?"

Robert smiled. "Would you do me the honor of listening to my new sonata? It is just the first movement, and it is still the first draft, but I would consider it a great honor if you would come."

Frau Devrient shook her head again. "As God is my witness, I will never understand musicians."

"But you will come?"

She sighed. "Yes, yes, I will come."

iii

Clara, back in Leipzig, had much to consider. She continued to read Robert's reviews in the *Zeitschrift* of concerts by visiting artists, works by new composers, and reviews of his own works in other journals. She had seen Robert from her window across the street more than once, staring at the house, reducing her spine immediately to ribbons, rendering her helpless to sit, stand, walk, talk, eat, read, listen; the only help then was to play one of his works at the piano, hoping he would hear. She found herself peering through the curtains, afraid when she saw him, disappointed when she didn't, afraid of being seen by him, but also by her pappa.

An understanding began to dawn of why Carl Banck had disappeared so suddenly from her life. Might not her pappa have theatened him as he had Robert? as he might anyone who showed an interest? If she let Robert go, despite how she felt, what right did she have to take someone whom she could love no better? who could love her no better? Her pappa still allowed her to play Robert's works at private performances, and that seemed the place from which to initiate a probe. She was to play again at the Gewandhaus on 3 August, and wanted to play the sonata Robert had dedicated to her. Her pappa was cordial, his rage against Robert had cooled through the months, now more than a year, but he still disagreed. "I do not think that is a good idea, Clara."

"But why not, Pappa? It has always been well received when I have played it at the Reissigers, or the Kragens, or the Kaskels. Why should I not play it at the Gewandhaus?"

Wieck shook his head. "Robert's work is not like that, Clara. I thought you understood. It is not the work for a crowd. They want their music hard and furious, so brilliant it glitters. They want to be dazzled. Variations are just the thing for them, a theme from an opera with which they are familiar, followed by variations they can follow easily themselves. It makes them imagine they are connoisseurs."

Clara had marshaled a number of arguments to be capped by a journal she held in reserve, which she kept aside for the moment. "But Pappa, if artists never speak to them except in the old ways how will their understanding ever improve? Is it not up to artists to show the way rather than to be led."

"You are right, Clara. That is the responsibility of artists, and they fulfill them – as you have yours at the Reissigers and the Caruses and so many others – but those who know no better, the crowds at the concerts, would be disenchanted, they would feel foolish, they would feel cheated – and I think you will agree that the responsibility of the artist is to edify, not to insult the audience."

"But Pappa, we insult them all the time by assuming they are incapable of understanding anything new – by not challenging them we only pander to them."

"Clara, life provides enough challenges. When they go to a concert they want to be catered to – pandered, if you wish – but that is what they want, and that is what they pay for, and for an artist to give them less than they pay for is unworthy of the artist."

"But, Pappa, for an artist to give them more?" She opened the journal in her hand to a place she had held with her finger. "Pappa, I do not wish to be difficult, but I would like to read you something to make my point."

Wieck frowned, but nodded.

"It is from the *Paris Revue et gazette musicale*, a review by Liszt about Robert's sonatas. This is was Liszt says: *We direct the eyes of musicians everywhere to the works of a young composer, Robert Schumann of Germany. No connoisseur can fail to appreciate their high merit and rare beauty. Among all recent compositions of which we are aware – excepting those of Chopin – these contain the most individuality, novelty, and technique. He reveals passion indirectly, but in depth. His appeal is to contemplative minds, who plunge past the surface into the deepest waters, there to uncover hidden pearls.*" She looked up. "There is more, but my point is surely made. If Liszt is willing to promote Robert, why should not we?"

Wieck knew of Liszt's reputation though neither he nor Clara had heard him. Robert's reputation was no mystery to him, but still he shook his head. "It is all right for Liszt, Clara. He can afford to take chances, but your reputation is hardly as secure."

"Well, then, Pappa, I will not play Robert's Sonata, but his Symphonic Etudes. They are variations on a theme. Would that not be well, since the public is so very fond of variations?"

Wieck shook his head. "We cannot risk it, Clara. With Robert, even variations become difficult to follow. He does not even bother to call them variations, he calls them etudes –"

"Because they *are* etudes as much as they are variations!"

Wieck raised his hand. "Do not raise your voice at me, Clara. I know full well what they are. It takes a trained mind to follow these variations. I confess even myself at a loss sometimes to follow this work."

"Well, then, Pappa, I will play only three of the Etudes. I will play the simplest of them all so that even the simplest in the audience will be able to follow them. What say you to that?"

Wieck realized that he would have to acquiesce to her wishes at some time; Robert was developing a reputation no respectable pianist could ignore. The Etudes averaged less than two minutes apiece. He could afford to give Robert six minutes out of a program of almost two hours. "Very well, Clara. You may have your wish – but only if I am to choose which Etudes you play."

Clara smiled. "Of course, Pappa. I will play whichever you choose."

iv

Clara performed the Etudes so well she almost defeated her purpose – to say in public what she could not in private, let Robert know she still thought of him – but Robert couldn't imagine she could play his work with such mastery unless her personal regard had dwindled, so very professional a performance demanded an objectivity he did not wish in Clara, not in relation to his work. Sunk in new despair at the end of the concert he didn't notice Ernst Adolf Becker's approach through the throng in the Gewandhaus until he spoke – whispered, rather. "Robert, I bear a message from Clara."

Becker was a mutual friend, Robert's and Clara's – and Wieck's. The change in Robert's expression was comical, tragedy turning itself upside down, a smile so incredulous it was cretinous, a half moon of a mouth, but Becker did not laugh. "From Clara? Did you say from Clara?"

"Yes."

"What is it?"

Becker smiled. "She says she would like you to return your letters to her– which she was forced to return to you so many months ago."

Robert's smile became more normal. "She does, does she?"

"She does, indeed!"

Robert almost laughed with relief, almost shouting his answer. "Well, she shall not have them – but she shall have new ones if she wishes."

Becker still smiled. "I am sure she will like that even better."

"Shall I send them with you?"

"I would be glad to be your messenger."

"Becker, I could kiss you."

"Robert, not in public. We do not want Wieck to know yet the source of your happiness."

Heads were turning; friends were approaching; Robert was immediately sober. "Let us get away, Becker. Let us get away as fast as we can – or I will explode with all my questions."

Soon they were headed down a narrow street, Robert leading the way, not caring where they headed. Robert squeezed Becker's arm. "You have saved my life, Becker. When she played my Etudes, and played them so powerfully, I was convinced she no longer cared for me. Now I see she is able to control her emotions rather better than I imagined – she is a braver woman than I imagined."

"A brave woman, indeed!"

"Braver than a man – and I was convinced she had substituted my Etudes for myself."

"Believe me, my friend, that is as far from being the case as is the moon. I do not understand the old man any better than you. He must know your heart as I do, and I cannot imagine whom I would rather have for my daughter, particularly as a musician, than a man who can write such Etudes. Wieck should have no difficulty recognizing their majesty and grandeur."

Robert nodded. "Whatever Wieck may think, I thank you for your intercession."

"No intercession, none necessary. Clara approached me. She wishes this reconciliation more than anyone."

"Except me! But now you are our intermediary, and for that I cannot thank you enough. I shall have a letter for her tomorrow."

"I am glad to be of help."

v

Robert enclosed his letter in an envelope and enclosed the envelope with a note in yet another envelope. Clara read the note first as intended: *After many months of silence and despair, I hope these lines will be received with the love of old. If it no longer exists, I beg you to return the letter to me unopened.*

She opened the letter, dated 13 August, 1837: *Are you still firm and true? As devoted as I am to you, even the stoutest heart wavers when absolutely nothing is heard from the one that is dearest in the world, as you are to me. I have thought about it all a thousand times, and always come to the same answer: It <u>must</u> come to pass, if we will it, and we act. Write me a simple "Yes" if you will give your pappa a letter from me on your next birthday, less than a month away.*

Say nothing to anyone about this. It may yet come to ruin if it is announced too early and too freely.

Above all, give me the Yes. I must have that assurance before I can think of anything further.

I mean what I say from the bottom of my soul, and I sign what I say with my name. Robert Schumann

Clara found the letter cold and grave – and beautiful beyond measure. Her reply was dated 15 August: *A simple "Yes." Is that all you ask? Such a small word, and yet how important. I say it, "Yes," and from the bottom of my soul I whisper it to you eternally.*

Shall I tell you how I have suffered, how many tears I have shed? No, not yet! It will be timelier when next we meet, and meet again we shall.

Your plan seems to me dangerous, but a loving heart cares not for danger, so once again I say "Yes." God would not make my eighteenth birthday a day of sorrow. That would be too cruel. I too have long felt that it <u>must</u> be. Nothing in the world will now turn me aside. I will show Pappa that a young heart can also be firm. In great haste, Your Clara

More letters were exchanged, some through Becker, some through Nanny, during which time Clara read and approved the letter Robert wrote to her pappa. They also exchanged rings. On the 13th of September, Wieck received the letter and shut himself with Clementine in his study to read.

Honored Sir,

What I have to say is simple, yet words will fail me. A trembling hand cannot firmly grip a pen. Therefore, if here and there I fall short of the perfectest expression, I beg you to excuse me. Even under the best circumstances my hand is not good.

Today is Clara's birthday, the day on which the dearest being in the world for you as for me first saw light, the day on which I have always taken account of my own life. I have never contemplated my future as calmly as I do today. I am secured against want – as far as it is possible to foresee the future. I have a fine head, a young heart, a willingness to work, a magical sphere of activity, and I am still in hopes of securing all my ambitions, still in hopes of realizing my powers to their fullest. In addition, I am honored and well received by many friends. Is this not enough? Painfully, I submit, it is not! It means nothing if I am to be parted from the one who strives as truly for me as I for her. Seek the truth in her own eyes if you believe not me.

For eighteen months you have put me to the test as not even fate would have done. Put me again to the test if you wish for as long again a time, and if you do not demand the impossible I shall perhaps win back your confidence. If then you find me manly and true, bless our union, for nothing but your sanction is wanting for our highest happiness. It is no little excitement of the moment, no ephemeral passion, nothing merely external, that binds me to Clara, but the deepest conviction that our union was fated – and it is this admirable exalted girl herself who provides surety of the happiness of all in her sphere. If you can accept these convictions as your own give me only the promise that you will decide nothing immediately about Clara's future, and I promise you on my honor not to speak to her against your wish. I will ask one boon only, that you allow us to write to each other when you are on long journeys.

I lay my future in your hands. My position, talent, and character deserve a considerate and complete answer. It would be best if we spoke to each other. These will be terrible moments before I have your answer, and I beseech you, with the utmost earnestness, to be gracious to us, once more a friend to one of your oldest friends, and the best father to the best child!

Robert Schumann

vi

Wieck had expected something like the letter from Robert, particularly after Clara had performed his Etudes. Robert could not be ignored as a composer, nor as Clara's suitor, and Wieck had allowed the performance so he could control what was to follow. Opening his doors he became privy to their plans, maximizing his advantage; keeping them shut he shut himself off, minimizing his advantage; if a snake entered one's house, it behooved him to know of its presence – so he could kill it while it slumbered.

Robert smiled, entering Wieck's study, ushered by Nanny. Of all the rooms in the house he had visited the study least during his stay, a small room with a large desk, shelves along one wall, laden with books, ledgers, manuscripts, windows along another, curtains drawn. He had been brought directly to the study, seen no one in the hallway, nor been offered refreshment, nor a cigar though Wieck was smoking, nor a handshake, nor had his coat been taken, nor his hat. Wieck appeared engrossed in his thoughts, barely nodding when Robert wished him Good Morning, until Nanny left the study closing the door behind her. Still he said nothing, but indicated the chair in which Robert was to sit across the desk from him; he remained almost hidden himself in a black waistcoat against the paneled wall behind, clouds of hair mingling with clouds of cigar smoke.

Robert removed his hat and coat, folding the coat over his arm, sitting where he had been told, draping his coat over his lap, holding the hat in his hand. "I cannot say how pleased I am to be talking with you again, Herr Wieck, despite all the troubles we have both undergone in the interim."

Wieck grunted, appearing to observe Robert for an advantage, a gladiator in the arena.

"Herr Wieck, I submit that I am to blame for much of the trouble between us. I should never have approached Clara without your permission. You had every right to be angry. I was wrong and I apologize again. I ask you only to consider the circumstances. My mamma had just died. I was in no reasonable state. I beg you to consider that in your judgment."

Robert saw he was not to set the agenda. Wieck made no response, but stared as if he meant to pierce him, maintaining a silence no less deadly, but finally speaking. "I have received your letter, Herr Schumann, which is why I have summoned you. You have things to say and so do I, and what I have to say is mainly this. I will grant that you are a splendid man, I will grant that you have promise as a composer, and I will grant that many fathers would gladly adopt you for a son-in-law – but not this one. You are not the man for Clara. That is my firm conviction! Nothing will move me! Of course, she is a pianist, and you are a composer, and that is an intercourse I do not wish to prevent, not as a father, nor as her teacher – but that is as much as I will allow. Now, if you have something to say, this is the time."

Robert's mouth dropped; so implacable a stand he had not expected. He took a deep breath. "Herr Wieck, I do not understand. You grant freely that I am a splendid man – but assert in the same breath that I am not for Clara?"

"As I have said, Herr Schumann, you are a splendid man – but there are others more splendid."

"Herr Wieck, do you not believe that Clara and I should be the happiest people together?"

"I believe that *you* believe it, and I will grant that I do not entirely *dis*believe it, but more importantly I also believe that you would need more than you think."

"What would we need more than we have?"

"I speak of *mo*ney, Herr Schumann. I realize that as a poet and composer you find pecuniary considerations ignominious – but as the best father to the best child, as you so eloquently phrased it," Wieck permitted himself a smile, "I have first to consider Clara. I cannot permit myself the luxury of your grand contempt for money."

"Herr Wieck, I hope I have displayed no such contempt, grand or otherwise. I realize the value of money and can offer Clara as much as hundreds of the best families. I cannot imagine Clara would need more."

Wieck put down the cigar, pursing his lips so hard he might have been gnashing his teeth. "There, Herr Schumann, I believe you are wrong. I believe I know Clara a little better than you. She would weep in secret and in silence, but weep she would, and copiously, were she unable to host the grandest receptions. As a pianist of the grandest manner she will wish to live in the grandest style. Anything less will only gnaw at her bones. It will devour her in the end like a cancer."

Robert crossed his arms under the coat in his lap. "Herr Wieck, what sum would you find satisfactory for Clara?"

Wieck tapped fingers on the desk, piercing Robert again with his stare, smiling like a fox. "I think, to meet all Clara's needs, a man would have to provide surety for at least three thousand thaler per annum. Do you think you could manage that, Herr Schumann?"

Wieck's smile appeared so wide it threatened to split his face. Robert saw finally how Wieck meant to fight him. He could offer no more than a quarter of the sum. His hope lay only in Clara's ability to resist her pappa. "Herr Wieck, Clara is but eighteen. We are both young and have much to accomplish. I ask only, as I did in my letter, that you decide nothing immediately about her future – and I promise in return not to speak to her against your wishes."

Wieck shrugged. "There, Herr Schumann, we are in agreement. I do not know what I shall do with Clara – so it is fitting that I do nothing immediately. We are soon to be in Vienna for some months, as perhaps you know, and I wish you to be of help to us during our tour."

"Anything, Herr Wieck – anything I can do."

"I will send you articles and reviews from Vienna of our progress. I would like you to publish them in the *Zeitschrift*. I believe they will be of help to Clara."

"Of course, Herr Wieck. I shall do so with pleasure." He began to understand Wieck better; he cared less for Clara than for what Clara represented, an extension of himself. The interview was hardly going as well as he might have wished, but if nothing else he wanted a clear understanding and that was forthcoming. "Herr Wieck …"

"Yes?"

"I believe I understand you well – but I would like to clarify for myself two more points – to be sure I know what is permitted – to prevent future misunderstandings."

"Yes?"

"Are we permitted to meet, Clara and I?"

"You are permitted – but only in the presence of others."

Robert nodded. "And may we correspond for the months you are in Vienna?"

"You may – but I will read all the correspondence. I will decide what is suitable between you and what is not."

"Then I believe, Herr Wieck, we have come at least to a perfect understanding – if not a perfect accord."

Wieck nodded. "It is as you say, Herr Schumann. I bid you good day."

Robert saw no one on his way out as he had seen no one on his way in, but put his thoughts immediately to paper in a letter to Clara.

ROBERT TO CLARA   *18ᵗʰ Sept. 1837*

My Dearest Clara,

My interview with your pappa has depressed me horribly. He is so cold, illwilled, contradictory, confusing that he drives both blade and haft into your heart. What comes next I cannot say. I do not know. I will be guided by you. Tell me what to do if you can. Reason does not prevail against him, emotion even less – but I trust you with all my heart and that gives me courage. He said "Nothing will move me." Be on your guard at all times, fear him in all things. What he cannot get by force he will get by cunning.

I feel so dead, so degraded, I can think of no way out. I cannot even envision you, not even your eyes. It makes me sick to think of you in Vienna with our affairs in such disarray. He treated me like dirt under his feet. We are not to see each other – except among others, like a spectacle at which the world may gawk.

I search in vain to explain his behavior. I have always considered him noble and humane, but I find nothing noble or humane in his continual refusals. He does not fear that you will suffer as an artist were you to marry too early, that you are too young for marriage even otherwise. Such parental concerns are not his considerations. I believe he would sell you to the first suitor with money and titles enough. Beyond this he has no ideals. Music, travel, concerts, these are merely his means to that one god: Mammon – and his handmaidens, power and prestige. He said you would need 3,000 thaler per annum to be truly happy, that you would weep if we could not regularly host large parties in society. Clara, can this be true, or do you find it as laughable as I do? He could not forward one objection with any foundation in reason.

Ah, but I look at your ring and it brings me a measure of peace again, though just for a moment. If he drives us to extremes, if in another year and a half or two he still refuses to be reasonable, we must seek our rights in the courts. We have reason on our side. Heaven forbid it should come to this, but if necessary the authorities can marry us.

But perhaps it is not so bad; now that we know the worst we can work with it. Nothing is lost, I believe. We have perhaps even won a little. We are permitted to see each other, even if only among others – and we are permitted to write to each other, even if he will read our letters. At least, there, thanks to Becker and Nanny, we have the advantage over him. We must proceed slowly. I am convinced even now that eventually he will accept the idea of losing you. His obstinacy cannot prevail against our love.

I shudder at the thought of what might happen were he to prevail instead. Only swear, by your salvation, that you have the courage to stand by the trials that loom so ominously ahead. Lift up the two fingers of your right hand in token, as I do now, and take the oath: I will never forsake you; you can rely upon me.

Return this letter to me with your answer. God help us both. I remain forever Your Robert

CLARA TO ROBERT   *25 September, 1837*

My dear Robert,

Do you still doubt me? I forgive you, for I am after all a weak girl. Yes, I am weak, but my soul is strong. I am firm and unalterable. Suppress every doubt.

I have taken the oath as you wished. Oh, never was an oath more fervently taken. We are committed, dear Robert, forever together. All that remains are the details.

Write always directly to Pappa, not to Mamma. She is not to be trusted, whatever she says. It grieves me to say this – but she has warned me not to trust you! She says you are false, that your heart is no more constant than the moon.

I have promised Pappa to be cheerful and to live for some years more for art and the world. Next month, you know, we plan to be in Vienna. You will hear many things about me, Robert, and many a doubt may arise in your mind, but you must say to yourself when the doubts arise: She does it all for me! Do you still doubt me, Robert? If you do – well, you will break a heart that loves but once.

Send back this letter now with your reply, and do it soon for my peace of mind.
Clara

ROBERT TO CLARA *Leipzig, September 1837*
Dearest Clara,
    I could not possibly return such heavenly words. I, too, am determined. Now, not another word about the past, but let us fix our eyes firmly on the future.
    Your Robert

The wide marble stairway was carpeted along the middle and appeared gold in the gaslight; lamps rested on wide posts along the balustrade under the high vaulted ceiling; the mezzanine provided an array of romanesque arches leading into the concert hall. Men in black tails and women gloved in white to their elbows thronged the auditorium, six hundred strong; chandeliers on long spindles burned above with the white heat and milky sweep of nebulas. Onstage, a young woman, barely a woman, tiny and alone, in a white dress, pink camellia in her dark hair, shoulders bare and silver, curtsied and smiled, seated herself at the piano, and silenced the audience with a single note. Her frown might have indicated that she played with the deepest concentration, but her mind was on a letter she had yet to write, words she was formulating even as her fingers danced over the keys.

CLARA TO ROBERT   *Vienna, November 1837*
Dear Robert,

Why have you been so silent? Why have I heard nothing from you in four weeks? Why have you not answered Pappa's letter – which he wrote without my knowledge? Nanny told me about it later. Pappa trusts her, but she loves me too well not to tell me everything. What will you say to him? I do not care myself what you say – but you must tell me what you think, and whether you tell Pappa everything or only what you think prudent for the moment. Address your letters to Herr Julius Krause at the post office. Nanny will know how to pick them up from there. To be doubly safe, it might be better to have the address written by Doktor Reuter since Pappa knows your hand.

My concert in Prague went well, a good sign of what was to come. The public was intelligent and educated in music. We had no advance subscriptions, no orchestra, and only one other soloist, but they gave me the most enthusiastic applause. I was recalled 12 times! Among other things I played my concerto and Henselt's Variations.

The soirees and my first concert in Vienna went even better. The audiences here are so appreciative one never wants to go north again where the men have hearts of stone (you, of course, my darling, are the exception). Even when they speak German it sounds like Italian or some other such language in which words and music mingle more freely. Just think! My portrait is everywhere! And they serve "torte a la Wieck" in the inns! It was advertised in the Theaterzeitung that the dessert is so light it flies into the mouth of the eater. I could not stop laughing to think of all my enthusiasts eating the cakes.

But I must say I can no more stand these adorers of mine than I understand them. I believe you love me because you have known me so long and because I love you. But these others? I do nothing to encourage them, I am not pretty (that much I know) and my art cannot count for much. My suitors know even less of art than they know of me! It is all most mysterious, but a mystery that benefits me. And my vanity! So I will let it be!

Dear Robert, I begin to understand why Pappa has been so afraid to lose me. This is what I was born for, what is happening in Vienna. He is afraid that if we were to marry, you would not be able to support me in the way an artist should live. That is why he wrote the letter. (Tell me what he said.) That is why he says I should forget you. He is thinking about me, nothing else – but forget you?!! Might as well forget Pappa, might as well forget myself! But I understand him better, and for his sake, and for all our sakes, you must forgive him the pain he has caused. You are not the only one wronged, Robert. All three of us. He says you have not written because you recognize the same difficulties. Well, I do not know what you recognize because I do not know what Pappa has written, but this I know. If in two years, when I stand before Pappa and say to him that we have done it his way, and still he refuses us, I know what I shall do then.

But in the meantime you must write as soon as possible. It has been too long already.
Your Faithful Clara

ROBERT TO CLARA   *Leipzig, November 1837*
Dear Clara,

For a child you are as demanding as a Leonore. Why is this? Why is that? Do this! Do that! Do it now! Why have I not written in so long? I might ask you the same. You knew how to send me your news, but I knew not how to send mine, not until you wrote, not so your pappa would not know. Why did I not write to him? Well, you do not know what he wrote to me – but since you have asked I will tell you. He said that rather than condemn two such fine artists as ourselves to a wretched existence he would marry you off to someone else. He said that if we were to marry he would disown you forever, even on his deathbed. These are confusing statements, but their sentiment is clear. Whatever he thinks of my art, it is not what he thinks of my person. I would be wanting in dignity if I were to reply to such a letter. You say all three of us suffer the consequences of our misunderstandings, but you seem well to me from your letter and so does your pappa – but you do not know how I have suffered these past weeks and days.

There was more. He taxed me as well with being unmanly, unfaithful, and a spendthrift. That was the thrust of his accusations; the exact names I will not repeat out of respect for his daughter. Let it suffice that they bear neither repetition nor response. He is just testing me, I say – but after 18 months of silence between us I would have imagined further tests unnecessary.

Hearing about your concerts is a mixed blessing. I am joyous for you and sorrowful for myself that I am so far away. Is it always by your own wish, Clara, that you play your concerto at the concerts? There are stars of thought in the first movement – but it leaves also an impression of incompleteness. Of course, it is different when you play it. Then the performance overwhelms any structural defects.

My life is not much changed – except for your absence. I awaken before six every morning and work on my compositions. I would say more, but that would lack modesty.

I will send you the pieces with my letter to Fraulein Clara Wieck so that your pappa's suspicions will not be aroused. I am thinking also of writing quartets. I am amazed at the ideas that will not stop. And there is of course the Zeitschrift. In the evenings I go to Poppe's, but do not stay as late as once was my wont because I prefer to be up again early the next morning. I sleep with images of you and our life together. We live in a nice house near the town, a dreamy darkness in one room, flowers in a vase by the window, another room in pale blue with the piano, also some engravings. We guide each other, correct each other, praise each other. You love Bach in me, I Bellini in you. We play duets. You see, we would not want for much, not if you chose to play for pleasure rather than profit, for the chosen few who would appreciate you best – but if you wish to play for the world we could leave home for three months a year, I could not be away longer from the Zeitschrift. You would play in the German towns – or in Paris and London, and we would return laden with treasure. And were you to tire of such a life I would whisper that I had composed symphonies and other masterworks and was dying to hear them performed in lands strange and far. We would both win crowns and laurels and garlands then, my Clara, I for composition, you for performances – but I think of your pappa then and my dreams shatter, my hopes sink, and the pale blue room turns black.

Ah, my Clara, how will this masque play itself out? Sometimes, when the night is at its blackest, I am no less black with despair and all that keeps me going is the thought of you, a letter from you. Write to me and at length. I need to hear from you if I am to keep my hopes from sinking. Tell me about your dreams and adventures. I live for them – and for the day you return again to the arms of

Your Robert

ii

Clara and her pappa were driven through the grounds of Schönbrunn Palace in a carriage past the Neptune Fountain, past statuary, topiary, a zoo at which the Viennese had seen their first giraffe, an aviary that sprang from the ground like a giant birdcage, and the crown and glory of the garden, the Gloriette, an enormous loggia, Roman arches mounted by the Habsburg eagle.

The Palace had been modeled on Versailles, but despite 1,200 rooms and a balustrade running the length of the roof, in late evening with a cloud of swallows further obscuring the light, Clara thought the yellow wash and tiled roof gave it an appearance not unlike a row of terraced houses, but she was impressed with herself, and so was Wieck, to be on neighborly terms with the Emperor, and no less impressed, both of them, by the red and gold military uniforms, the velvet and gold decor, rooms large enough to hold their Leipzig house, windows which could accommodate horses, and the array of crystal chandeliers, gilded scrolls, frescoed ceilings, and oriental miniatures.

The Emperor, in a velvet cape fastened with gold and satin braids, an overlapping shoulder cape in white flecked with violet, and a white satin shirt filigreed with gold thread, smiled whenever he caught Clara's eye. His head, shaped like a pear, seemed to wobble, tilt on the stem of his neck, eyes to wilt, cheeks to fall in jowls, nose so long and thin it divided his face in two.

CLARA TO ROBERT *Vienna, December 1837*

Dear Robert,

As great was my joy when I received your letter, so was my sorrow when I learned I had still to earn your trust, that my steadfastness through all our trials meant nothing. Are you still so very afraid, Robert, that I can be blinded by trinkets? That you will read of my engagement in the newspapers to the Earl of Pearls or the Duke of Diamonds? Perhaps you are afraid I will obey Pappa out of fear of what he might do to you as I feared not so long ago, but you must not be afraid, my Robert. I will never again be afraid of Pappa. He will never again bend me to what I do not wish for myself. You must be clear on that and press me no more to repeat it.

You are so industrious you make my mind reel. You want to write quartets! One question, though – and you must not laugh. Do you know string instruments well enough? I am sorry if that sounds rough, but I have a bone to pick with you, my Robert. It is sweet when you call me "child," but not when you think of me as a child. Forgive me, but it is you who are very much the child when you talk about returning home laden with treasure. What are you thinking? It is not so easy. You have no idea what needs to be done before one can return home with even just a few thaler! When you are sitting at Poppe's at 10 o'clock in the evening or idling your way home after beers and cigars and Leipzig talk, I, poor thing, am just arriving at a party, where I have to play for just compliments and a cup of warm water. I get home at 11 or 12 o'clock, tired as a dog, drink another draught of water, lie down, and wonder if an artist is, after all, more than a beggar.

But tired as I get, I am never unappreciative of my gift. How exquisite is the ability to clothe one's feelings in music, to give hours of happiness to people through art, and to know that I have given my life to this pursuit. And how amazing that an ordinary girl like me gets to talk with the Emperor and the Empress because of this art! They say Emperor Ferdinand is Emperor in name only, and that Prince Metternich rules the country. They say also it is for the best because the Emperor is an epileptic, and some say he is also an idiot, but the people love him because he is very kind. He is sometimes called Ferdinand the Kind. They said I was not to be afraid of him when I played. I was not afraid, how could I be afraid of someone everybody loved, and when I saw him I understood. He did not say very much, but he looked so confused I wanted to do my best to please him, I wanted him to like me. He is like everyone's unmarried uncle, who seems always a little sad – except he is married, and the Empress Marianna looks at him so lovingly – which reminded me again, my Robert, of you. If we can be so loving, when we are so old, we shall have done something right. I played for him today at the Schloss Schönbrunn. Mozart played there once when he was six for Maria Therese and jumped into her lap - and asked for a kiss! Afterward, the Emperor asked how long I had been playing and did I not enjoy it immensely. He was smiling, and I was so happy to have made him smile I almost fell in my rush to curtsey and answer. I could not say if he heard me, but the Empress smiled and asked how I liked Vienna. I was able to say honestly that I had never had so much fun in my life. I told her about the 'torte a la Wieck!' And she said she would try it herself! But Robert, you must not think I would not rather have been talking with you than with the Emperor and the Empress. I am like you when you talk about mixed blessings. I too wish you could share Vienna with me. It is with such a jumble of thoughts, then, that I lay myself down, finally, happy and contented.

Robert, I too have been giving some thought to the future, in particular after the great success of my second concert. During the first I played only the bravura pieces, I wanted to win the confidence of the public before I challenged them, but the last time I played a Bach fugue – and was asked to repeat it! It was unusual for a fugue to be played, but unprecedented for it to be repeated. But of all the items in the program it was my concerto that had the best reception. You ask if I played it always by my own wish. Of course, I do! It has been well received everywhere, by the connoisseurs and the public. Do you suppose I do not know its faults? Of course, I do! But the public does not – and it need not! Indeed, the music has been so well liked that I was presented with the autograph of Schubert's "Erlkonig."

Also, as you know, Schubert left behind a great many works, among them a Duo for Four Hands only just published by Diabelli – which Diabelli dedicated to me! I am so affected by this, Robert, that I am easily upset these days. Sometimes I think I am too sentimental. Pappa, too, was sentimental! There were tears in his eyes! Real tears! I had never seen them before. He looked at me as if to say: This is what I wanted for you, Clarchen, and now that we are within reach of our goal you would throw it all away for Schumann. He did not say it. He did not have to say it. I understood for the first time how much I mean to him, how much he has done for me, how much I need for myself. I must say, Robert, that I cannot be yours until circumstances are completely altered. You must ask yourself if you are in a position to offer me a life free from care. I do not want horses or jewels, and love is all very beautiful, but if I have to worry about my daily bread my art will suffer. I have never wanted anything except to make music in my life. And am I now to bury my art?

Please do not be angry with me. Ah, God! I wish I could be more clear, but I write in haste. I do not have even the luxury of privacy. Pappa goes into a rage if he finds my door locked. Instead I write standing, my sheet of paper on a chest of drawers, running to the next room everytime I need to dip my pen. If I brought the inkstand to my room Pappa would know I was writing to you. Nanny stands guard so I may store pen and paper hurriedly into the top drawer if he should come. Write soon – and write clearly! Nanny says my eyes get bleary from poring over your letters for two hours on end to understand what they say. See of what you are guilty! My tea is ice cold, the room gets colder, but she grows warmer who writes this letter thinking of you,

    Your Clara

ROBERT TO CLARA   *Leipzig, January 1838*
Dear Clara,

    This is the heart of your letter: You can never be mine unless circumstances are completely altered. Ah, I see your pappa standing by you while you wrote that – but you have written it and you are right to think of your external happiness. I am only troubled that you make the objection for the first time now, which you should have made when I first explained my circumstances to you. Otherwise, I would never have written the letter to your pappa.

What I wrote then, first to you, then to your pappa, holds good now. My income is not overpowering, but many a girl, even a pretty girl and a good one, would give me her hand on it, saying it might be difficult, but we could make it work to our benefit. At the time, you were the same. Now you are different. My mind reels!

You say nothing of my Kinderszenen or my Kreisleriana. I had hoped to hear how they appealed to you. There is something wild in my Kreisleriana, of your life and mine, and of some of your looks. The Kinderszenen are different, more tranquil, you will have to forget you are a virtuoso to play them, they express my child – by which I do not mean you as much as the child in myself. You are right, Clara. I am sometimes a child. Ah, but this is no good. I am avoiding the issue.

Well, then, unless a fortune falls from heaven I do not know how I can increase my income soon. You know the kind of work I do. It is intellectual, it cannot be carried on like manual labor. I have shown I can persevere and it goes without saying that I would like to expand my income, and in this I shall not fail, but it will not be soon, and it may never amount to what you might wish, or even as much as you have now – but in about two years, I can say with a clear conscience, I will be able to support a wife without anxiety, though not without continuing to work.

I may of course work harder to make more money, but it would be superficial and mediocre work. The power of creation sets its own limits. One cannot force one's best powers at will; one can only stand ready to open the door when the powers knock. I have so much music in my head, Clara – not just sonatas but quartets (do I know string instruments well enough? you ask. Of course, I do! That goes without saying. What are you thinking, my Clara?) – yes, quartets, and symphonies too. But only I know what is in my head, and only I know when it is ready to appear. I cannot expect anyone else to understand, not even you, only to have faith that I understand myself, a faith that transcends reason – and, dear Clara, your letter has brought me down to earth to wallow among the toads of reason. You might have expressed yourself more romantically – but as I said I see your pappa standing by your side, holding your pen. There is coldness in the words, something murderous. I dreamed I was walking by a deep pool into which I cast your ring, but found myself filled next with a passionate longing to throw myself after it. Can the ring you wear mean so very little to you after all, given you by

Your Robert?

CLARA TO ROBERT   *Vienna, February 1838*

Dear Robert,

The ring? You set stock by the ring? Did not Ernestine also wear a ring? Did she not also have your sworn promise? Think not of the ring. It is but an external, a symbol, nothing more. But I should not have written as I did. It was the impression of a dark hour. I can hardly believe it, but I allowed Reason to rule my Heart. But could you so wound me as well, my own Robert, draw from me such bitter tears? Could my Robert have read so ugly a meaning in my words? Yes, I know there must be many a good and beautiful girl at your disposal – and yes, they would make better housewives than any artist has any right to be. This I know, but it is not well that you saw fit to remind me, nor that such a thought even came to you – not if you loved me. I want but two things, my Robert: your heart and your happiness.

You have misunderstood me and Pappa as well. Whatever you may think of him you cannot argue with what he has made of me – he and he alone, no other. The third concert was the greatest success of all. 800 attended in a crush, and every concert now brings a clear profit of more than 1,000 florins. Papa showed me a letter he wrote to Mamma to say she is to find more capacious lodgings for us all, I am to have my own room, Marie and Cacilie are to have rugs on the floor to keep them warm – but Alwin and Gustav, since they have turned out badly, are to be turned out into the world. Alwin is to be shipped off during the first week of the fair or else he is to be apprenticed to the instrument maker in Pressburg. Gustav is to be fitted with a suitcase and apprenticed to a maker of pianos. If they try to get out of it he says he will send them to prison. Keeping ungrateful boys at home only makes them more ungrateful.

You see, Robert, he does it all for me, and I would be no less ungrateful than Alwin and Gustav were I not to recognize it. In addition to these successes I have been made an honorary member of the Gesellschaft der Musikfreund – <u>and</u> I am to be nominated Royal and Imperial Chamber Virtuosa by the Emperor, an honor that places me among only seven others, among them Paganini and Thalberg. There were three counts against me: I was too young, I was a foreigner, and I was a Protestant, but the Emperor himself said that if it was agreeable to me (agreeable to me!), and if I seriously desired it (I had not even imagined it!), he would make an exception. It is not for nothing he is called Ferdinand the Kind! So now I am to be an Austrian subject as well, assured special protection and the support of the Austrian ambassador in every country, and I am to be as well a Viennese citizen with the right to remain as long as I wish!

Pappa also says the old saying is true: "Much honor, many enemies." The opposition is rising against me and he is now too old for the battlefield, too old to be traveling from country to country like a Turk, best now for him to retreat in victory – but my fortune is made, and he has made it for me. The rest, after our next visit to Paris, will be up to me, but his work as both father and teacher is mostly done. He even wrote to Mamma that she was to hold kisses on ice for his return. Had you any notion that he could be so very romantic? I did not think so.

He also sent Mamma my reviews for you to print in the Zeitschrift alongside a sketch of my life which he wishes you to write. He asks for fifty copies of the Zeitschrift to distribute at my concerts. He says he wonders that you have not thought of it yourself, and reminds me that I do more for your cause, playing your pieces for the Viennese elite, than you do for mine – and, my dear Robert, I do think he is right to make such a request. I do think it is very little to ask after he has accomplished so very much for me – <u>and</u> for you! He said you were to be welcomed again as a friend of the house – and when I assured him that I could nevermore think of you as just a friend, that I could never love another, he consented – IF WE WERE TO RESETTLE IN VIENNA.

Robert, I want you to consider it seriously. If we stay in Leipzig we will always suffer in comparison to the way Mendelssohn and David live – so, at least, says Pappa, and maybe he understands these things better than us – but in Vienna I am appreciated by the highest aristocracy, loved at court, also by the public. I can give a concert every winter that would easily bring me 1,000 thaler; I could bring in another 1,000 thaler through lessons; and then you have 1,000 thaler of your own. What more could we want?

This is my suggestion, that you come to Vienna on your own and speak to Diabelli about publishing the Zeitschrift in Vienna. Your work will be paid as well here as in Leipzig, you are certain to be more respected and recognized, and life is lived more cheaply in Vienna than in Leipzig. Pappa says if you do not wish to stay here without me, he will stay in Vienna himself for our benefit. Now tell me if he is not after all the best father to the best daughter. Do not be so illwilled toward him. You see, he means the best for us both, after all.

Your Clara

ROBERT TO CLARA   *Leipzig, February 1838*
Dear Clara,

Everything is changed! Life opens again, options multiply. Your letter raised me like a ladder from joy to joy, like an angel leading the first man through creation, from height to height, each successive vista lost to another yet more beautiful, and at last the angel said: "All this shall be yours." Did you not know, Clara, that it is one of my oldest, most cherished wishes, to live some day in the holiest of cities, the womb of music, where Beethoven and Schubert lived? Let us shake hands, our minds are made, I have considered what you have said seriously, and my most intense desire, our goal, is Vienna. We shall leave behind our native land, Leipzig – which is not a bad place, after all – our relations, our home, our soil, I am a Saxon, body and soul, so are you, who will have to separate from your pappa and brothers – but it is decided. We go!

I must submit I am astonished by your pappa again, but for the better. When I consider what he has said in the past, what he has written me, I cannot help but wonder sometimes if I have given him cause. When things are said about you enough you begin to wonder if there is not some truth to what is said. Am I so base, I asked myself, that he treats me as he does? I know I am spoiled, accustomed to getting my way, overcoming difficulties easily, but I had been slandered, insulted, discarded – hated – and for no reason that I could perceive – but I see more clearly now. His concern was always first for you, the best father to the best daughter, and I hope now the best father to myself as well, who will try to be the best son.

One more thing, dear Clara, and you must not be angry, but after what has passed I would be very foolish indeed to give up my life in Leipzig without a word from your pappa's own pen that he has changed his sentiment. Forgive my suspicion, but I need his assurance that I might be certain of you. Write me some words about what I am to expect, how I am to behave.

Oh, my dearest Clara, if all is indeed as it appears, my room becomes a chapel, my piano an organ, your picture my altarpiece, and Bach my daily bread, to the grave and after.

Your Robert

iii

When Liszt first played for Clara she recalled immediately Mendelssohn's suave impersonation on her birthday, hands swooping like eagles, sound pounding like cannon, while he held her captive with his eyes over the piano. When Mendelssohn played she had giggled to cover her discomfort; but in Liszt's presence she could only hold her breath, and when she ran out of breath she dissolved into sobs. Mendelssohn was a handsome man; but Liszt, in a green satin formfitting waistcoat, green kid gloves, black coat spangled with decorations, was handsomer. She was flattered that he held her with his gaze while performing work too devilish for Lucifer – that so amazing a man, so handsome, so talented, so loved across the continent, genius of the keyboard, idol of men, even more of women, paid her the least attention. Liszt was the touchstone, the final measure for not only pianists but all men and women – and since none but Liszt could be Liszt all vied for the great man's presence, his blessing, his smile.

They stayed at the same hotel, zur Stadt Frankfurt, and played as much as they could together after dinner, her pappa and friends in attendance. Clara always dreaded the moment she would be called upon to play. After Liszt she felt like a beginner, but he was so unfailingly generous with praise and attention that he comforted her enough to perform. He was playing something by Herz, but under his hands Herz sounded as divine as Beethoven, both transmuted by Liszt into Liszt; it mattered little who or what he played, only that he played.

Liszt finished with a sweep of his hands across the keyboard, gathering and spreading the notes in a final flourish before striking the last chord fortissimo, raising high his hands in the air, dropping them with a slap to his lap, turning to acknowledge the applause of the room, but acknowledging only Clara with his gaze. "Mademoiselle Wieck?"

Still breathless, Clara didn't dare speak, barely dared smile, but took her place at the piano suddenly eager to play; it was easier than matching Liszt's grace and gentility; his gestures were as eloquent as speech, his speech as graceful as a gesture. She had elected to play *Carnaval*, but even as she played she was more aware of the slender man staring at her than of the music in her head, his long sleek hair spread like a hood, rendered more serpentine by his movements, swaying in his chair to currents of music as birds to currents of air, as fish to currents of water. He appeared to hold the room even while she played, attaching praise to himself for honoring her with his appreciation.

CLARA TO ROBERT   *Vienna, April 1838*
Dear Robert,

You see, Pappa wants riches for me and I love you when you forgive him – but maybe you are right when you say he should give you a sign himself. He is too busy to write to you, so perhaps we should leave it until we return to Leipzig which will not be long now. Oh, I could cry or laugh to think of seeing you again. I do not know what to say, but refuse to worry about it now when everything is going so well.

You did not know, did you, that your Clara is a shepherd child? Well, I will tell you a secret! I did not know it either, but the poet, Grillparzer, has found it out. At my last concert I played Beethoven's Sonata in F minor, which had never been played on the concert stage before in Vienna, where Beethoven himself walked the streets, because it was considered too advanced for the public – but they loved it and the poet has written a poem about how the work was given to them by a shepherd child – me, your Clara! He wrote in his poem that Beethoven, the Magus, had wearied of the world, and locked his magic in a receptacle of pearls, and cast the key into the ocean – and that a shepherd child (my little self) had slipped her hand in the water and drawn out the key again!

Oh, but I will hate to leave Vienna, indeed. Something is always happening. A few days ago, Liszt came to Vienna – and flung his card in our window. He is staying at our hotel, so we have seen quite a lot of him. He is an artist one must both see and hear. He cannot sit still when he plays – not even when he listens! If he were to play behind a screen half his poetry would be lost. I played him your Carnaval, but there was a sound continually as I played of shells rustling and rattling in the wind, and I had to look over my shoulder. Liszt was writhing in his chair as if he were playing the music himself. His decorations made the noise. You would get along with him well, Robert. He rates your compositions extraordinarily high. "What a mind!" he said when I played him your Carnaval. "That is one of the greatest works I know." Liszt said that, Robert, about your work. But I am not surprised. I only wish the rest of the world were not so ignorant of it.

We have played duets together, he played Weber's Konzertstuck (and broke 3 brass strings). He beats everything to pieces, but his playing is so full of genius my own playing feels dull. After him I feel like a schoolgirl. He also played my Soirees, directly from the notes, and to hear him you would think he had played them all his life – and if that is not enough he says he will dedicate his new Etudes to me!

Pappa says he uses the pedal too much, making the sounds jangle, but he plays with such fire that only an old woman would complain. Still, Pappa says if he could have taught Liszt ten years ago he would have been the foremost pianist in the world. I like Thalberg better myself, but I can do what he can do. Liszt makes me uncomfortable, he is so wild – but there is something there, something I do not have, but also something I am not sure I want. It is perhaps in the way he looks at you when he plays, as if he is playing for no one but you, as if he cares about no one but you – but that has nothing to do with musicianship. It is a cult of personality which distracts one from the music. I am not so sure it is the best thing for the music. It hypnotizes one so that one is unable to tell the good from the bad.

Now, my dear Robert, I cannot wait to see you again – and yet I am afraid. Will we know what to say to each other? – but I am not worried. Oh, my Robert, to love is not to be worried in the presence of the lover, is it not? I am not worried. Your little shepherdess,
Clara

The knock was so loud and arrogant Robert could not have prepared himself even had he expected a visit. He looked up from a manuscript he was reading for the *Zeitschrift*. "Come in! The door is open!"

The door opened, Wieck stepped in, slamming the door behind him, saying nothing, but his eyes might have emitted icicles; Robert felt his face freeze, pins pricking his arms.

A voice yelled from the other room. "Who is the madman, knocking so shamelessly on a Sunday morning?"

Robert's voice was guarded. "Quiet, Willy! It is Herr Wieck!" He turned to Wieck, rising from his chair by the window. "Good morning, Herr Wieck."

"Do not get up." Wieck held up his hand, palm forward, and Robert felt pushed back into his chair. Wieck had spoken softly; Robert would have said he had hissed.

Willy came into the room. "Herr Wieck! I am sorry! I thought it was just one of our stupid friends making a stupid joke."

Wieck barely glanced at him. "Good morning, Herr Ulex."

Willy was flustered and recognized he had said the wrong thing yet again. "Herr Wieck, I am truly sorry."

Wieck's eyes remained fixed on Robert. "It is of no consequence to me what you say, Herr Ulex, if that is of any consolation to you. I am here to speak to Herr Schumann!"

"Of course! I will leave if you wish?"

"It does not matter to me. It is up to Herr Schumann."

Willy looked at Robert, whose eyes remained wide, appearing more tired than just a minute ago. He found himself whispering. "If you would give us a moment, Willy."

Willy picked up his coat, winking at Robert to wish him luck – but Robert, caught in Wieck's glare, didn't notice, and got up again from his chair after Willy left. "I am sorry. My manners seem to have deserted me. Will you not please sit down, Herr Wieck?"

Again Wieck held out his hand, and again Robert sank back into his chair. "I prefer to stand."

"Of course. Whatever you wish."

Wieck's face was twisted in a sneer, nostrils dilated, eyes black as coal, face grey as stone. Robert took a deep breath. Clara had warned him to give Wieck no excuse to oppose them. "My congratulations, Herr Wieck, on your success in Vienna."

Wieck looked down his nose. "What do you know of my success?"

"Only what Clara has written me – and what Frau Wieck has told me of your wishes."

"You did not carry them out, Herr Schumann! You did not carry out my wishes."

If he had carried out all Wieck's wishes he would have turned the *Zeitschrift* into a journal for the benefit of Clara's enthusiasts and nothing else, but he didn't think Wieck would understand; nor did he want Wieck to think he would carry out his agenda just to curry his favor. "Where did I not, Herr Wieck? Where did I not carry out your wishes?"

Wieck stared, making no answer.

"Are you quite certain, sir, that you will not sit? Will you not have something to drink?"

Wieck grunted, remained standing, remained staring; he might have been reading Robert.

"Perhaps you know, Herr Wieck, I am planning to visit Vienna myself, in accordance with your suggestion. I am considering removing the *Zeitschrift* to Vienna. The ground now burns under my feet everywhere else."

Wieck had made the suggestion only because he had not imagined Robert would leave Leipzig. "If the ground burns under your feet, Herr Schumann, I suggest you learn to walk on water. There is no other way I will bequeath Clara to you. That is what I have to say. You may see her in public, you are welcome as I have said as a friend of the house – but otherwise she is not for you. That is my final word."

The room seemed so cold Robert shivered. "I beg your pardon, Herr Wieck, but why do you say that? Your concern until now has been financial. You have said you wanted Clara assured of at least three thousand thaler per annum. Clara has explained that between the two of us we can be assured of such a sum."

"Clara has explained? Where has Clara explained it?"

In his consternation, his wish to please, Robert had blurted out more than he wished, revealed what he wasn't to have known; Clara had mentioned the sum in a private letter, one Wieck had not read. "She mentioned it to Moritz. Moritz told me."

Dr. Moritz Reuter was a mutual friend, Wieck's and Robert's, but sympathetic to Robert and Clara. "Since when has Doktor Reuter become a confidante? Why would he bring such news?"

"It just happened, Herr Wieck. It was not planned. Clara said she could make a thousand thaler in concerts, another thousand teaching, and a thousand thaler per annum is within my reach. Between the two of us we would make up the sum you wished for her with ease."

Wieck raised his hand again, a headmaster commanding silence. "Herr Schumann, let me ascertain one last time that we understand each other explicitly. It is true that I have discussed the matter of money with you and with Clara; and it is true that the sum mentioned in each instance was, at the very least, three thousand thaler – but at no point in the discussions did I suggest that Clara might supply two-thirds of the sum. She is to have no concerns, Herr Schumann, except her music. When you are in a position to provide for her, you may apply for her again. Do I make myself clear?"

Robert took a deep breath. "It is money, then, is it not? It all comes down to money, does it not? Is that not all that is the matter?"

"That is a naive response, Herr Schumann, and another reason I find you unsuitable. Money is indeed all. It is everything in such matters. No money, no matrimony, is the soundest motto. It would save innumerable heartaches if only the young people realized this early rather than late – but that is not the way of the young."

"Herr Wieck, I make enough money for many a girl. If Clara wishes for more she does not lack the means to provide it – but, more importantly, we have a surpassing affection for each other. Does that not count for something? You have said it yourself, you do not doubt we could be happy together, you merely say we would need more than we imagine. Is it not our right to find that out for ourselves?"

"Not with my daughter, it is not your right, never with a daughter like Clara who is one in a thousand – I might even say, without exaggeration, one in a million. She is fit for a king. She has consorted already with royalty. You are a writer and a composer, Herr Schuman. You are not of the same circles. If you love Clara, you will let her go."

"It is because I love Clara, Herr Wieck, and because she loves me, that I do not, and I cannot, and I will not let her go." He saw it was hopeless to attempt to appease Wieck, might as well attempt to appease a wild animal. He had not meant to say more, but found Wieck too insulting and needed to take a stand as much for Clara's sake as for his own. "With the greatest respect, sir, we have our plans. I mean to go to Vienna and see how I might accommodate my *Zeitschrift*, regardless of what you might wish, and then we will decide how to proceed next."

Wieck crossed his arms, his nose predatory as a beak, eyebrows springing from his forehead like wings. "You may go to Vienna, if you wish, Herr Schumann. That is not my concern, but it will not be under my auspices. I will write to my contacts to say that you do not come with my blessing. I warn you here, now and forever, I will fight you with fire and sword, Herr Schumann. I will fight you until one or the other of us is damned. Do you understand? You bring this upon yourself."

Robert took a deep breath. "I do not see how, Herr Wieck. I do not see how I bring it upon myself."

Blood rose in Wieck's face like mercury in a thermometer. "Herr Schumann, you are a scoundrel, a drunkard, and a fornicator."

Robert wondered what Wieck might have heard, but rallied. "You do me an injustice, Herr Wieck. I have done nothing with Clara against her sanction."

"Do not be coy, Herr Schumann. You are lower than a worm to bandy words with me. I know what such a sanction means. I know of your congress with Ernestine. I have her admission in writing. I know of your congress with Robena Laidlaw. Herr Rackemann has told me. I know of the drunken revels you have conducted in these very rooms. You disturb your neighbors more than you think. Do not think you are the only one with connections, and do not think I will not use everything I know, in every way I can, to bend you to my will. If it is a fight you want it is a fight you will get such as you never thought possible – such as a womanish man like yourself could never win." His mouth twisted as if he were gnashing teeth and he spat in Robert's face.

A thick wad of saliva hit Robert's forehead, clung to his eyebrows, fell to his cheeks, and trickled to his mouth and chin. The contact paralyzed him; he made no movement, his eyes glazed. Wieck turned and left without a backward glance.

When Willy returned an hour later he found Robert in much the same position he had left him, a statue in the chair, face and forehead bright, gazing at air. He shook him from his stone prison, but could get no explanation, no response except in monosyllables.

ii

Clara had never found Dr. Moritz Reuter handsome, he cut his hair so short his ears seemed too large, and he wore such tiny spectacles his eyes seemed like buttons, but she didn't know what they would have done without him, and without Ernst Becker, the Voigts, and the others who assisted in conveying messages between her and Robert. Astonishingly, seeing Moritz down the stairs to the door, she found herself admiring the shape of his head, cut of his jaw, neat handlebar moustache, even his ears seemed smaller; when he winked she found him dashing; an ugly duckling became a swan through service. She was congratulating herself on her insight when Wieck called and she hurried back. "Yes, Pappa?"

"Come into the parlor!" He was staring down the stairs.

"Yes, Pappa."

He kept his eyes on her as she came up the stairs, leaning into the door to let her pass, following her into the parlor. Nanny watched from the hallway, Clementine from the parlor. Clara turned to face them all. "Yes, Pappa?"

"Empty your pockets, Clara."

"My pockets? But why, Pappa?"

"Do as I say."

She knew what he was doing. He no longer trusted Moritz and wanted to be sure Robert hadn't sent a message. She removed a handkerchief, some change, a red ribbon, two blue buttons, a comb, and three wrapped sweets from her pockets. "That is all I have, Pappa."

"Clementine, search her properly. Search her dress, her underthings."

"Pappa, no! I will not allow it!"

"Clementine!"

Clementine approached Clara, but Clara stood against her. Clementine took Clara's hand, but Clara shook her off with a twist of her wrist.

"Clara, you only make things more difficult for yourself. Let your mamma do as I say."

"She is not my mamma!"

"Child! Do as I say!"

"No!"

141

"Clara, you *will* do as I say. Whether you do it voluntarily or not is up to you – but you *will* do as I say. Do you understand? Now, do not resist your mamma anymore."

Clara held her chin in the air. "I refuse to do as you say. You have not the right to violate me like a criminal."

"You are mistaken, Clara. In this instance, it is you who have no rights. Children have no rights over their pappas. Now, will you do as I say?"

"No!"

"Very well, then. You force me to be rough."

He held her by her shoulders, digging his fingers so deep she cried. "Pappa! No! You are hurting me!"

"Clementine!"

Clara squirmed to get out of her pappa's grip, but couldn't; she kicked at Clementine reaching to search her, but Wieck twisted her arm, hoisting her to her toes, leaving her without leverage to kick. Clara screamed, but her pappa only twisted her arm further, drawing a gasp, followed by breathlessness, and Clementine's fingers finally burrowed into her dress, her sleeves, her drawers.

They found nothing, but when Wieck released her she couldn't stop crying from the humiliation of the search and stamped her foot with indignation. "How could you! How could you dare!"

Wieck glared without sympathy. "I dare because I am your pappa. Enough of your sniveling! It is over. You have not been hurt. It is only your pride that makes you weep – and a false pride it is. *Enough*, I say!"

Clementine adjusted her own clothing, patting her hair; she might have been no more than an observer, she might just have been to the theater.

"Clara!"

Clara barely acknowledged her pappa with a nod.

"You know we have made preparations already for Paris this coming winter."

Again the barely perceptible nod.

"If you do not give up Schumann we will not go. I will not accompany you to Paris."

Her face was shrunk with tears, a large teardrop itself, but she looked at her pappa purposefully. "I will never give him up!"

Wieck hissed, so sudden was the intake of breath through his teeth. "Go then. Go alone to Paris. Go to the city of the shameless. Go as the harlot of a fornicator. See how you prosper on your own. Ungrateful daughters die daily in the streets of Paris – but I warn you. If you go, I will wash my hands of your affairs permanently." He turned, jerking open the door to leave, and was startled to find Nanny waiting outside. "What are you doing, Nanny?"

Nanny was no less startled; a sheath of fear flattened her features. "I thought you called, sir."

"Nonsense! I never called."

"I thought you did, sir. I swear it. I thought you called."

She retreated immediately toward the kitchen, but Wieck followed her with eyes hardening once more to coals.

Clara became calmer. She had had a narrow escape. Moritz might easily have brought her a note; instead, on this occasion, she had given him a note for Robert. They would have to be yet more careful in the future. She took a seat by the window, petting Gretel in her lap, not moving for an hour.

iii

Robert read once more the note given him by Moritz: *Be at our window on 10 June, at EXACTLY 9. If I signal with a white cloth, walk slowly toward the old Neumarkt. I will catch up with you, since I have to fetch Mamma at her mamma's. IF I DO NOT SIGNAL, SHE HAS NOT GONE.*

It was 10 June, nine o'clock, and he was across the street from her window. When a white cloth flashed his heart beat faster and he walked slowly as he had been instructed. He sensed her behind him though nothing was said and walked toward an alley. In the past month they had trodden all the alleys in Leipzig. She took his hand from behind, but he shook it off after a quick squeeze. "I hate this, Clara, this plotting and planning and stealing of a few minutes – and for what? We are not criminals to be hiding in the shadows. I would rather not meet at all than like this. I want a wife, not a girl for secret meetings and kisses. It is not the way of lovers who have nothing to hide."

Clara walked alongside, careful not to touch him. "That is what I want too, Robert – but what are we to do? I grow more fearful daily of Pappa. I grow fearful of my own feelings for him."

"What has he done now?"

She didn't want to tell him about her search, afraid of what he might do. "We will have to be more careful, Robert. He suspects Moritz – and, oh, Robert, he has dismissed Nanny."

For the first time, Robert looked at her. "Nanny?"

Clara stared ahead, but he could see she had been crying. "She has been with me since childhood, Robert. Pappa trusted her – but no more. He suspects we corresponded behind his back from Vienna, and blames Nanny for our success – and rightly so, but …"

The alley got narrower, more encrusted with mud. "My God, Robert! Where are we going? What a horrible smell! Mamma will know I went somewhere just from the smell. It will cling to my dress."

"This is cruel, indeed."

"What?"

"About Nanny."

"Oh, yes."

"Through no fault of her own – indeed, through our fault!"

"Robert – look out!" She pushed him to one side so hard he stumbled.

"What?" He looked at her, perplexed. "Why did you push me?"

She grinned. "Look what you almost stepped into, what some dog left behind. Once again I have saved you. We might as well be on the road to Connewitz again."

143

He looked behind. "That? That is just fertilizer. It makes the earth rich."

"Yes, too bad it will not make you rich to step into it. Pappa would love you then!"

He refused to smile.

She took his arm, refusing to be shaken. "Oh, Robert, I am afraid I begin to hate Pappa. I owe everything to him, and yet when he ridicules you, when he calls you names, I feel I could be happy never to see him again – but he is my pappa!"

Robert no more wanted to reveal the outcome of Wieck's visit than she the outcome of Moritz's. "That is the crux of it. He is your pappa and you are attached to him – as you should be, and I respect you for it – but he poisons our lives, he tramples all we hold sacred, and he worships only gold. Forgive me, Clara, for speaking my mind, but I am sick when I think you might give me up on his account. My blood turns to ice. He even haunts my dreams!"

She squeezed his arm. "Oh, Robert, that will never be! I shall never give you up! Do not fear. He said he would not come with me to Paris if I did not give you up – he means to show me I cannot do without him – and I told him so then, I told him I would never give you up. He does not believe I will go without him, but I am determined – whatever happens, I am determined to show him what I can do. I will go – with or without him, I will go."

He clasped her hand on his arm, walking faster. "Clara, we can expect nothing from him. He takes with one hand what he gives with the other. We must act for ourselves. I will go to Vienna and you must go to Paris – but why do we not set a date for our union? If we settle on Easter of 1840, almost two years hence, you will have fulfilled your filial responsibility. You will have no need to reproach yourself after that time, not even if you should have to tear yourself from him violently – and there will be no question anymore of putting our love to the test, there will be no question of our constancy."

Clara squeezed his arm. "Yes, Robert! Yes! That is a good plan. That is what we must do."

He glanced at her, saw she was smiling. "Then it is settled. On Easter of 1840 we are to be wed."

"We are to be wed! Oh, Robert! It sounds like a dream!"

"A dream that is in our power to realize."

"Yes, it is! And, Robert, how lovely if Therese could be with us the first weeks of our marriage. She could show me things I cannot learn at home."

"What kind of things do you mean?"

Clara laughed, looking ahead; Robert could tell she was embarrassed. "Household things. Pappa never wants to see me anywhere except at the piano. I know nothing of the things housewives do."

"Oh, for a surety, Therese will show you whatever you wish. She will be happy to show you. She has shown herself already invaluable to me, she has provided the best comfort during all the months I have been without you. I do not understand how Eduard spares her at all. He is the best of brothers for sharing her so generously."

"Good! Then it is settled. You will go to Vienna and I to Paris – and then shall we be wed!"

Robert spoke almost to himself. "Yes. Then shall we be wed."

"You do not appear to like the idea very much."

Robert shook his head. "I would be happier if we could be wed tomorrow. When I leave for Vienna we will again be parted for a long while. You might be in Paris before I return. That does not make me happy."

"Oh, I had not thought about that."

"But it must be done."

"It must be done – and we have come so far already."

"That we have. We cannot go back now."

"I must go, Robert. Mamma is waiting for me. We have already walked too far."

Robert shook his head. "This is what I hate, Clara. We have barely met before we are parted. This is what is most difficult – much easier not to have met at all."

"But we have settled our plan, Robert. We had to meet for that, did we not?"

"We did, but I hate it no less for that."

"I will come to your rooms when I can, Robert. Then we will have all the time and privacy we need."

Robert shook his head again. "No, Clara. It is too dangerous. If you are seen we might lose all we have gained at once."

"Oh, but I *must* see you. If I cannot see you I will have lost anyway."

"Then we will meet whenever you can get away."

"I will send you word."

"I will look for it."

"Robert, do not trust Herr Rackemann. He carries stories about you to Pappa."

"I know. I do not speak to him."

"And do not leave my notes lying around. They might fall into the wrong hands."

"Do not worry. I am careful."

"I have a new friend, Robert. Her name is Pauline Garcia. She is a singer touring with her mamma and brother-in-law. She accompanies herself at the piano and she can play anything by ear. I think we might have a confidante in her. I will let you know how things develop."

Robert nodded, but he wasn't listening anymore; the days were always empty immediately after their meetings.

"Robert, I love you!"

"My Clarchen."

"Goodbye, my Robert! Goodbye, my love!"

"Goodbye, Clarchen."

She kissed him; he pushed her away, still afraid to be seen, afraid to give Wieck more ammunition against him, but she pressed him and he found courage to return her kiss as fervently as she gave it, kissing her as long as she allowed.

"I am so glad to see so many parks, so many trees. We have nothing like this in Leipzig – just buildings and streets, and then more buildings and streets."

Robert was in a carriage with Joseph Fischhof, the Vienna correspondent for the *Zeitschrift*, also a professor of the piano at the conservatory, with whom he was staying. They were to visit Count Joseph Sedlnitzky, Chief of Police, head of the censorship bureau and right hand of Prince Metternich, in his Town Hall office. On the seat between them lay a folder thick with manuscripts, Robert's hand on them to prevent them sliding to the floor. Fischhof smiled. "The closer to nature, the closer to God. That is what the Viennese believe – or would like to believe." The smile was ironic; Robert was more of an innocent than he had expected, his general enthusiasm more childlike.

Robert missed the smile, staring from the window. "A motto with which I could live comfortably – and if all goes well a motto with which I *will* live, I and my Clara."

Fischhof chuckled, following Robert's gaze to the point of its appreciation. "Aye, if you can keep your eyes off the girls."

Robert laughed too, glancing at Fischhof. "They are the prettiest. We do not have such pretty girls in Leipzig – but Clara understands. I may have eyes for a beautiful face, but my heart is only for Clara." He grinned, looking more directly at Fischhof. "She says the only reason I stay with you is that you have a pretty sister. Do you see what I mean, how modern she is? She trusts me."

Fischhof laughed. "Ah, well, then, that is all right, if she is so modern. That is good. I am sure my sister will be glad to hear it – also of Clara's trust."

Robert looked out of the window again, sighing. "And they are so gay, they smile all the while – they smile at me, a stranger. In Leipzig we would find them shameless, in all of Germany – but here, in Vienna, they are refreshing, more openhearted than our German girls."

Fischhof narrowed his eyes. "It is cultivated, you know, Herr Schumann, this openheartedness. Metternich knows we need no more bloodshed. It is an uneasy stability we hold. Students need little to incite them to revolt – and now that we contend with power looms and steam engines and the like there are major upheavals in the way people live. Most of all the economy must be expanded. Everything else is subjugated to that need. Sedlnitzky is instrumental in ensuring that there is no unrest. It is for no other reason that he has banned Grillparzer's work. He corrected even Goethe's *Faust* before he would let it be published."

"He censored Goethe!"

"For the good of the people, for the common good."

"But surely the common good should be dictated by those for whom it is provided."

Fischhof raised a warning finger. "I would not repeat that, Herr Schumann, not to anyone – and least of all to Sedlnitzky."

"But that is censorship!"

Fischhof frowned. "Censorship is his business. The point is to keep the citizens happy enough not to want too much – happy enough to forget the revolution until the royalists are firmly back in power in France. Give the people enough cotton and they will allow their rulers to wear silk. That is the thrust of the policies."

"But that is seditious!"

"No, Herr Schumann!" Fischhof was grim. "It is seditious only to *say* it is seditious! You would do well not to forget it if you would seek Sedlnitzky's aid."

"Clara said he was one of her patrons."

"So he was, and remains her great admirer – but he has great responsibilities, and great power to meet his responsibilities."

"Clara said he could rule out anything he liked, and leave in anything he liked – and that he reads everything, every word, before it is printed."

"That is correct. That is why I say you would do well not to offend him."

"I do not wish to offend him. I merely wish to state my views."

"Those can be conflicting statements – and if you wish to publish the *Zeitschrift* in Vienna, you would do well not to offend Sedlnitzky."

"I thought you said Grillparzer was banned, but he published a poem about Beethoven and Clara – and that was not banned."

"Only through Sedlnitzky's edict, Herr Schumann. I cannot impress this upon you enough. Listen to me."

Robert nodded, appearing attentive.

"Grillparzer once wrote that it is better to live in the danger of democracy than to have the noblest human needs sacrificed to a system of stability. That is all very well for him – but stability is Sedlnitzky's responsibility, not Grillparzer's – and he must do what he can to ensure it. Do not misunderstand. We have liberty – but also enough satisfaction not to wish to exercise it unnecessarily. That is all. Every country must guaranty, first, its survival – and relative to survival freedom is a luxury. We have been through a difficult period, Herr Schumann, but we have survived. Freedom will come. That is Sedlnitzky's wish as much as anyone's, and he must follow his conscience regarding its attainment."

Robert turned to the window again, silent.

"You must not misunderstand. Sedlnitzky wants progress. He encourages the study of science and technology, all positive technology – but anyone can philosophize and criticize as the spirit moves him. It means little and causes much harm."

Robert looked again at Fischhof. "I am a critic, Herr Fischhof, and so are you, and I would like to think our philosophizing means more than a little."

Fischhof raised his eyebrows. "I am sorry, Herr Schumann. I am merely attempting to explain the prevailing ethos. It is how things are in Vienna, how they must be for a while. Otherwise, there would be no Vienna."

The carriage passed St. Stephen's Church. Robert indicated the church with a jerk of his head. "Do you see that church, Herr Fischhof, before which Haydn raised his head – and the Danube which Mozart traced with his eyes – and the Alps in the distance upon which Beethoven gazed – that is what comprises Vienna. That is its portrait. That will remain, whatever Sedlnitzky does."

"That is fair to say – for an outsider."

Robert wasn't listening anymore. "And everything neatly arranged – like battalions. Everywhere, little flower gardens – hollyhocks, sunflowers. Even the trees, so formal, those cypresses, like soldiers, guarding an empire – but they are trees."

"Yes, indeed! They are trees, not soldiers – but what do I know, Herr Schumann? You are the poet."

Robert said little after that except to acknowledge the sights Fischhof indicated. The carriage stopped and they got out. Fischhof led Robert up a wide stone staircase into the Town Hall, through a vast entrance hall, up five flights of stairs, and along a long hallway to Sedlnitzky's office. They were expected, and Fischhof nodded to the many officials and guards who returned his greeting.

They waited a few minutes first in an outer office, next in a small room with a large table, a window overlooking Schönbrunn Park. Neither spoke, Fischhof sat at the table, Robert stared from the window. Sedlnitzky was not long in coming, a short man who reminded Robert of Wieck, the same beaky nose, craggy eyebrows, eyes like slits, erect shoulders, proud chin, hair like clouds over his ears. He smiled, holding out his hand first to Fischhof. "Gentlemen, I am happy to see you."

Fischhof shook his hand. "Thank you for your time, your Excellency."

"Not at all – and this must be the Robert Schumann of whom I have heard so much."

Robert smiled, unnaturally, unaccustomed to smiling to order. Sedlnitzky's grip too was like Wieck's, like a vise. "Indeed. I am pleased to meet you myself –" Fischhof was frowning at him over Sedlnitzky's shoulder, "your ... your Excellency."

"Not at all. It is the least I can do for the estimable Fraulein Wieck."

"Clara said you would be most helpful."

"I will do what I can. How is she, the charming Fraulein Clara?"

"She is well. She is planning a tour of Paris early in the new year."

"Ah, yes, in Paris, she will reap more laurels yet, a musician nonpareil – and how is her triumphant pappa?"

Robert imagined he heard mockery in his tone, but couldn't be sure. "Herr Wieck is fine."

"A very forceful gentleman."

"That he is."

"And charming."

Robert's smile had deserted him; now his gaze turned from Sedlnitzky as well. "Of course."

"Please, please be seated – no standing on ceremony among friends."

Fischhof and Robert sat at the table; Sedlnitzky across from them.

"Now, what can I do for you?"

Robert turned his gaze again on Sedlnitzky. "Well, your Excellency, let me be concise. I know your time is valuable."

"*In*valuable – but no matter."

"Well, then, I wish to move to Vienna – with Clara. We plan to marry and live in Vienna –"

"Marry! Fischhof said nothing to me about marriage!"

Fischhof shrugged. "It is a private matter still."

"No one knows, your Excellency. We want to be sure of our prospects first – to explore the possibilities."

"Well, then, may I at least offer my congratulations, or is it too early yet even for that?"

Robert blushed. "By all means, your Excellency. Danke schön."

"A perfect match, a musician and a composer! What could be better. I love music."

"Do you?" Robert's eyes became more animated. "That is another reason I wish to move – to Vienna, the home of Beethoven and Schubert. I can hardly believe I am breathing the air they breathed. That is a pleasure in itself."

"Ah, yes, of course, Beethoven, he is all very well for musicians – but a little too intellectual for me. Myself? I love a good waltz, Lanner or Strauss – or a good Fantasy, the way Thalberg plays the Rossini themes – or even the way your excellent Clara played them."

Robert's voice turned frosty. "She also played the Beethoven Sonata in F minor. Grillparzer wrote a poem about it."

Sedlnitzky's smile froze, just a little. "Of course, when your Clara plays, it matters little what she plays. It is Clara we listen to then, not Beethoven."

Robert's smile was dry. "She will be glad to hear it."

His irony was not lost on Sedlnitzky. "In Vienna, we encourage music – also the theater. We have been through difficult times recently, as you know – and the evenings are the times most susceptible to trouble – so we have music and dance and the theater to keep the public satisfied."

Robert spoke unhappily, against his own judgment. "But that is a fraudulent use of music. It should instead uplift the soul. That is the goal of the artist."

"Yes, of course, of course, but let me also tell you something, Herr Schumann. We have in Vienna a population of almost three hundred and thirty thousand people, many of them only recently come from the countryside – but we do not have facilities for these numbers. We are crowded in among the walls of the city. We have room to build only upward, which leaves little light and air for the lower quarters – as you must have seen. There is dust from the roads, mud on the streets, slums proliferate. All of this is unavoidable. We have only to look to Paris to see what such overpopulation does. Already we have typhus, dysentery, and tuberculosis in numbers beyond expectation. This leads to misery, starvation, corruption. Revolution! We have already restricted the number of marriage permits to be issued to newcomers – but, of course, this would not apply to you. I would see to that personally as a friend of Fraulein Wieck. For a while we had banned the construction of new factories. As far as we can, we wish to control the growth of the population – for the good of all concerned, you understand?"

Robert appeared noncommittal, pursing his lips, but nodding.

"Good. Now, what I say is that if music can help avert some of the unrest we should welcome it – and if Strauss can help better than Beethoven, we should take Strauss. Do you follow me?"

"Yes, of course … your Excellency – when you put it like that."

"That is how I put it."

Fischhof's face had flattened, all expression ironed out. "Herr Schumann is a great composer himself, your Excellency. It is only to be expected that he would defend Beethoven against all other composers."

Sedlnitzky smiled. "Of course! I am not so very provincial as not to understand that! So, tell me, Herr Schumann. What can I do for you?"

Robert held up his folder of manuscripts. "I am currently the chief editor of a music journal in Leipzig … your Excellency. Perhaps you have heard of it, the *Neue Zeitschrift fur Musik*?"

Sedlnitzky shook his head. "I have too much to read right here in Vienna. I cannot keep up with all the journals that are published."

Robert nodded. "That is only to be expected. Clara said that you have power over everything that is printed – that you read every word before it is printed."

Sedlnitzky smiled again. "It would seem that your Clara has eyes and ears everywhere as much as the Chief of Police."

Robert smiled, though without apprehending the irony. "As I have said, we wish to move to Vienna, and I wish to apply for a license to publish the *Zeitschrift* in Vienna. I have brought the manuscripts for our next issue. Perhaps you will do me the kindness of reading them?"

Sedlnitzky held out his hand. "Give them to me." Robert got up, but Sedlnitzky stopped him. "Just slide them across." He looked through the manuscripts. "When do you need these back?"

"If I may say so … as soon as possible. My friend, Oswald Lorenz, is managing the *Zeitschrift* in my absence in Leipzig, but I would not want to impose on him more than necessary. I would like to publish the first Viennese issue in January of the new year. It is now the end of October – so shall we say by the end of November … Excellency?"

"I think that is workable. I shall let you know. Where can I reach you?"

"I am staying with Herr Fischhof."

"One more question, Herr Schumann."

"Yes?"

"Why do you think we need this publication in Vienna? Do you not think we have enough journals already?"

"Not like this one! Most journals publicize their own publications. That is their sole reason for existence. The *Zeitschrift* is beholden to no one – and to no publication. That is why it is trusted."

"And you think that is a good thing?"

"The truth, Herr Sedlnitzky – er, your Excellency – properly expressed, can offend no one – not even the censor."

Sedlnitzky laughed, appraising Robert through his slitted eyes. "You know, Herr Schumann, I cannot make up my mind if you are a very clever man – or a very stupid one."

If Robert recognized an affront he didn't show it, but replied directly. "I am neither, Excellency – merely an honest one."

"Hmmm!" Sedlnitzky smiled. "Then I still do not have my answer."

ii

ROBERT TO CLARA *Vienna, February 1839*

Dearest Clara,

Thank you for your letters and your news. I am so proud of my Clara, so young and alone and determined in Paris – so brave – and all on my account. Sometimes at night, when I wake to the wind and rain beating against my window, I think of you huddled in the coach, forging through fields and ditches thick with snow, and I am shamed from my fears – and inspired to do in days what would otherwise take weeks. You must not concern yourself about money, my darling. I have set aside a fund of 1,000 thaler for your benefit to be drawn from the bank in Leipzig anytime you need it.

I am afraid, though, that Vienna is not the place for us after all. Here is the city in which Beethoven lived and died, and yet there is perhaps no city in the world in which Beethoven is less played – or even mentioned. Everything new is feared, everything old revered. Rossini and Strauss are the big favorites and musicians wallow in their works like flies in buttermilk. In theaters more handclapping is heard than music. Serious people are little sought, little understood, people who care about Shakespeare and Jean Paul. In Leipzig people carry books in the street; here they carry food.

It is true the people are more humorous, they have more gaiety than in Germany, and the women are more sensuous by far (now, Clarchen, you must not be jealous if I happen to admire a beautiful face or two now and again) – but I sometimes wonder if their good humor has any more depth than their agreeable faces.

The woods are beautiful, and the mountains and the river. It is a pity beautiful scenery does not nourish the body as it does the soul. If that were the case I would say Vienna has everything – but we have to think about other things. I have not yet received my license for the Zeitschrift – and I do not think it is forthcoming. It appears I would need Viennese citizenship, or I would need to turn ownership over to a Viennese citizen – which, of course, I shall not do. But that is not all.

Sedlnitzky could have secured all for me that I needed had he been willing, but he is not, for reasons impossible to discover. There is far more intrigue in Vienna than might be gleaned from the surface. One official in Sedlnitzky's council warned me that another publisher, Haslinger, has offered bribes to keep the Zeitschrift out of Vienna because he fears competition. I think I would need more of the serpent in my makeup, dear Clarchen, than I possess – or care to possess – to establish myself here. As Metternich's right hand man, Sedlnitzky clamps all free expression. It is no surprise they do not want the Zeitschrift here. Leipzig is a haven of liberty by comparison.

Do not misunderstand me. There is much here that is good for music, by which I mean there is much opportunity for good music. There are concerts and operas daily. There is also the theater, and they are all well attended, but there is no strong organizing principle, no distinction between the bad and the good. What a crying need for a Mendelssohn to lead the way as he leads the Gewandhaus!

But the visit has been more than worthwhile if only for my discovery of Schubert's C major Symphony. The more I study it the more I am entranced. It has a heavenly length. It is finer than anything by anyone besides Beethoven, even by Mendelssohn. It is fit to stand even by Beethoven's 9th – but Beethoven was past fifty years when he wrote his 9th. Schubert had barely passed his thirtieth year, a time at which Beethoven had barely delivered his First Symphony, and the C major far surpasses Beethoven's 1st. Grillparzer's epitaph for Schubert could not be more appropriate: Music buried here a precious treasure, and an even more precious promise. Mendelssohn will be producing the symphony sometime in March. It promises to be as significant an event as when he produced the Bach Passion.

I have been working like a dog on some new works in the meantime, my love, and can hardly wait to hear you play them yourself, among them a Carnival of Vienna and a Humoreske I think you will like.

I have one more piece of good news to share that I have saved for the last. You know I had applied for a doctorate from the University of Jena. I had planned to write a thesis on Shakespeare, but I have been informed that I am to be granted an honorary doctorate for my work as a composer, critic, and editor. Are you not proud?

Courage, my Clara – of which you have shown much already – and the battle is all but won. When you return from Paris your glory will be complete. There will be a Herr Doktor in Leipzig who will ache until he is in your arms again,

Your Robert

He said nothing to Clara about paying the University of Jena for the doctorate, nothing about the University of Leipzig turning him down (he wished to match the title conferred upon her by the Viennese Emperor: Royal and Imperial Chamber Virtuosa), nothing either about his dealings with Breitkopf and Hartel in the behalf of Ferdinand Schubert, brother of the famous Franz, who had relinquished unpublished manuscripts to Robert imagining he would be more fair than publishers who had cheated him in all their dealings. Anxious himself about money, Robert had promised the publishers the symphony at a bargain rate if they consented to include two of his own works in the price, leaving for Ferdinand the paltry sum of 180 florins, hardly more than he might have secured himself, but of this too he said nothing, hardly admitting it even to himself.

Clara marveled again at Paris, but less at Paris than its sameness after eight years. The soirees of which people spoke with such envy in Germany were the same boring affairs, fifty silly women huddled for hours in a tiny room coquetting around the same ironboned pianos, but she marveled as well at the quality of the artists; no other city in the world harbored so dense a concentration of great pianists. She surveyed Erard's salon with a twist of her lip, no longer impressed by its luxury, giltedged portraits, porcelain vases, Persian carpets, Peruvian tapestries, chandeliers like clusters of stars. Erard called it a salon, but it was large enough to hold four hundred. Erard had sent her one of his pianos for practice, but so had Pleyel. She preferred the touch of the Pleyel, but couldn't refuse Erard after he had been so kind. Her pappa would have secured Pleyel's piano without upsetting Erard, but she was less gifted in such matters and had accepted both pianos, cluttering their rooms, rationalizing that the tougher the bones of her piano the finer would be her final performance.

Someone had just performed the Henselt Variations. Henriette Reichmann, standing beside Clara, whispered in her ear. "You are as good as he, Clara – better – but it must take great courage to play in so feverish an atmosphere."

Henriette, with dark hair and dark eyes, was much like Clara, the same age and height, but her awe was distinctly more profound. Clara laughed. "He is good, Henriette – but I am not currently at my best. I must not play until I am confident of playing my best, especially on these French pianos."

"Of course, but … are you not the least bit afraid?"

"Of course – but what has that got to do with it?"

Henriette shook her head in admiration, but Clara was looking elsewhere. Henriette followed her gaze to a man with a head like a tulip: thin chin and thin nose swelling to a wide brow and hair swept like an umbrella on his head, eyes and mouth cast to the ground.

Clara edged toward him, whispering to Henriette as she pulled her along. "He looks so sad, but I have heard him mention my Robert's name more than once."

The man was talking with two others, all of whom appeared the same age, around forty, but Clara was more intent on what he said than to whom it was said. "I believe he lives in Leipzig – at least, that is where his *Zeitschrift* is published."

One of the other men nodded enthusiastically. "I believe he is a composer himself. I have heard Liszt speak well of his work. Indeed, he published a review of some of his sonatas."

Clara plucked courage to interrupt them. "Pardon, Monsieur, but I could not help overhearing you speak so very highly of Robert Schumann. I am his friend and wondered who you might be that I might convey to him your regard."

The man turned slowly to Clara; even drawn to his full height he remained a small man; his mouth trembled as if expecting a blow. "I am Hector Berlioz – and who is it that I have the pleasure of addressing?"

Clara almost squealed. "Herr – Monsieur Berlioz! Robert Schumann is your great admirer. The longest article he has ever written for his *Zeitschrift* was about your *Symphonie Fantastique* – but, of course, you must know that."

Berlioz's smile was almost comical to watch, the fear in his mouth turning immediately to joy, spreading to his eyes. "But of course!" He bent to kiss Clara's hand.

The two other men smiled at each other. Both wore moustaches, but there the resemblance ended; one was fat and dark with a twig of hair spiraling from lower lip to chin; the other might have been an Indian maharajah perfectly educated in Calcutta. Clara did not know, she was never to know, the first was Alexandre Dumas, the second Eugene Delacroix. Seeing Clara they decided to give Berlioz his chance with her. His new opera, *Benvenuto Cellini*, had been a failure. The attentions of a young girl would cheer him more than any felicitations they might forward.

Having kissed her hand Berlioz appeared to be at a loss, looking around, surprised to find his friends departed.

Clara suddenly remembered her manners. "I beg your pardon. I am so glad to have met you I have forgotten to introduce myself. I am Clara Wieck – Robert Schumann's betrothed." She turned her head away, unable to stop smiling, unable to stop blushing.

"His betrothed! I did not know he had a betrothed!"

She hadn't meant to confess it, but Berlioz's discomfort, prodding her own, had compelled her. "It is not known yet. I would not want it announced here, please?"

Berlioz felt further complimented by the confidence. "Of course, of course, I understand perfectly. Is he here himself, then, the great Schumann? I would be honored to shake his hand."

She felt taller and larger, hearing what he said. "No, he is not."

"No? Then who are you with?"

She stepped aside, pulling forward a reluctant Henriette. "I am with my friend, Henriette Reichmann."

Berlioz bowed, kissing her hand, proclaiming himself charmed. "Ah, and no one else? Just you two?"

Clara and Henriette exchanged glances, almost giggled, and spoke simultaneously. "Yes."

Berlioz looked from one to the other. His narrow eyes widened momentarily. "Are you not, then, Clara Wieck, the pianist?"

"Yes, I am."

"Aha! Then we will be hearing you tonight, I hope?"

"Not tonight, but I hope soon. That is my purpose in coming to Paris."

"Ah, yes, then let me warn you to be careful what you say to me. I will be on the lookout for your concerts. I will be your reviewer."

Clara laughed. "I am not afraid. When I am ready, I will play for you with pleasure." She turned to Henriette. "Robert has written that Herr Berlioz does not care either to be pleasing or to be elegant. What he hates he seizes by the hair, and what he loves he crushes to his chest – and so it is with his reviews."

Henriette joined her hands. "My God! One almost does not know whether one would prefer to be loved or hated, does one?"

Berlioz smiled from Clara to Henriette and back, a smile beginning again to falter. Clara groped for something else to say when someone tapped her shoulder.

"The very gracious Mademoiselle Clara Wieck – but how can it be?"

Clara turned. A redheaded girl, Clara's age, smiled back. "Emilie!"

The girls hugged each other; when they parted Berlioz still stood beside them, more diffident by the moment. "Herr – Monsieur Berlioz, this is Emilie List, my old friend from Leipzig. Emilie, this is Monsieur Berlioz – and this is my friend, Henriette Reichmann. Oh, but my dear Emilie, this is such a wonderful surprise!"

Berlioz's smile became more distant yet. He bowed, almost clicking his heels. "I must take my leave, but I will look forward to seeing you again. I will look for your concerts. It will be my pleasure."

"Thank you, Monsieur Berlioz, but the pleasure will be mine."

Berlioz nodded to all the girls, leaving without a smile.

Emilie whispered fiercely. "Did I hear you say you were Robert Schumann's betrothed?"

"Were you listening?"

"Of course, I was listening. I always knew it. I always knew it would be so." She looked at Henriette. "On her sixteenth birthday, there she was with all her presents, with *Men*delssohn playing the piano – and she had eyes only for her Robert – who had eyes only for his Ernestine. It was all so very amusing."

Clara whacked Emilie's arm. "It was anything *but* amusing. It was the worst birthday I ever had – except for the next, when I did not get to see my Robert at all. My carriage overturned on the way to a concert, and I had to play with my hands bruised."

Emilie took Clara's hands in her own, "I am sorry to hear that," before turning to Henriette, "but I can tell you with the greatest confidence, even though I was not there, that she did not miss a note."

Clara smiled. "It is true. I did not even feel the pain until the next day."

Emilie turned again to Henriette. "You must pardon us, but we have not seen each other in a long while. We have much to catch up." Henriette smiled and shrugged. Emilie turned again to Clara. "How is your fine Robert? How did you ever convince him to do the right thing? I thought he was engaged to Ernestine."

"Oh, it is hardly settled. It is a long story and I am very afraid there is a longer yet to come. Pappa has yet to be won."

"I thought your pappa called him the second Beethoven?"

"He did."

"Also the German Chopin, and the German Bach." Emilie snickered. "One would have thought that Bach was Japanese from the way that he said it."

Clara laughed against her will. "Yes, he said that also."

"So what is it that bothers him now?"

Clara shrugged.

"Where is he?"

"In Leipzig."

"He sent you alone?"

"Did you not overhear us just now with Berlioz?"

"I cannot believe he sent you alone!"

Clara looked past her friend. "He has business to attend. I am convinced he will follow later."

"You are convinced? You do not know?"

Clara shrugged again, still looking past her friend. "I do not."

Emilie saw the pinch in her eyes. "Oh, Clara, I am here with my pappa. If there is anything we can do …"

"Oh, Emilie, I do not know how I would have survived without Henriette. We met just last month in Stuttgart. I was hoping Nanny would come to see me off – but Pappa has dismissed her and she did not come because of Pappa, but Pappa did not come to see me off either, and Mamma does nothing without Pappa's approval."

"Do you mean to say there was no one with you?"

"No one but an old Frenchwoman Pappa sent to chaperone me, but I was more afraid of her than anything. We rode together for three days to Nuremberg, over fields and ditches so deep with snow I thought it was the end. I was never more afraid than the first night we slept together."

"Oh, my poor dear Clara!"

"Fortunately, my concerts in Nuremberg were a success. The mayor of Ansbach heard me there and insisted I play as well in Ansbach. That gave me the courage to go on next to Stuttgart – which is where I met Henriette – who wanted to travel with me to Paris after she heard me play, to learn from me. She said she could not be happy if I were not happy – and I felt I could not be such a bad girl, after all, if so many were so fond of me in Stuttgart. The Queen herself gave me a jeweled pendant."

Emilie nodded sympathetically, listening intently.

"Then we went to Karlsruhe – where again we were given a good reception."

Henriette laughed. "And then we came to Paris – and dismissed the old Frenchwoman!"

Clara grinned. "Yes! We dismissed the old Frenchwoman. I felt so grown up."

They laughed, but Emilie responded almost immediately. "But how do you manage?"

"It is not easy – but the Frenchwoman did nothing. She stayed out all day. Besides, her purpose was served. Pappa did not want me to be alone. I was no longer alone. I had Henriette."

"And Clara knows everything she needs to do."

"I learned from Pappa. He made me copy his letters to practise my French the last time we were in Paris – but he has always made me copy his letters, even before that, just for my handwriting. I copied all his business letters. It was the best way to learn the business."

˙ "And she has a friend at the hotel."

"Another friend?"

Clara laughed. "Pauline Garcia – she is a singer. We met last year, she was on tour in Leipzig, and now she is in Paris, staying at the same hotel, with her mamma and brother-in-law, Charles de Beriot, who is a violinist. We have talked about giving a concert together, all three of us."

"Which hotel?"

"The Hotel Michadiere at 7 rue de Michadiere."

Henriette smiled. "Just follow the sound of the music. She is always practising or giving lessons. You cannot miss it."

ii

Robert was called from Vienna by a letter from his sister-in-law, Therese; his brother, Eduard, was ill, not expected to survive. Having accomplished his purpose, he did not regret leaving Vienna; it was not the city for the *Zeitschrift*, not for him and Clara; they would need to develop new plans, but later – Eduard had died while he had dithered in Vienna, his oldest brother, third of his four siblings to die – first Emilie, then Julius, now Eduard.

He stayed with Therese for a while, as much to comfort as to be comforted, but Therese was less comforted than he imagined. Something ailed the Schumanns, the entire clan, a nervous condition; she mothered them, doctored them, understood them, but Robert appeared so unaware of her own suffering she began to lose patience. He was in Zwickau for her comfort, but never let her forget his fears about Clara – who was, at least, alive, healthy, and unfailingly faithful whatever her pappa did – but he was selfish even with Clara.

When she wrote, distraught about her pappa's silence, his fear was not for her comfort but his own – just as his thought every morning was for his own comfort, not hers, expecting her to bring him breakfast, bring him coffee, whatever he wished, while he luxuriated in his sorrow. Her sympathy dried as she watched him at the table, cup in one hand, letter in the other. "My poor Clara – can you believe it, Therese? My letters were held from her at the post office for eight weeks because she did not have her passport. She has asked me to send her letters to Emilie List." He shook his head. "It is a wonder anything works at all in Paris. We have no such problems in Leipzig – not even here in Zwickau."

"Different countries have different customs."

"I suppose so." Robert nodded, reading further, but she couldn't be sure he had even heard her.

Therese raised her voice. "Paris is not a metropolis for nothing. There is no city in Germany to compare with Paris."

Therese didn't believe what she said, but spoke to disagree with him – and again he didn't notice. "You are right, of course. It is just as I said. It is a wonder anything works at all in Paris. But I cannot believe my Clarchen still worries about how it will be after we are married. She and her pappa are like children. He scolds, she cries, and it is always the same. She refuses to choose between us and stick with her choice. I am so sick to death of it all."

"What can you expect, Robert? He is her pappa."

Robert looked up from his letter for the first time, puffing himself to his full size. "Does he treat her like a pappa? Does he treat me with the respect I deserve? Does he not constantly prove himself unworthy? Do I not constantly prove myself worthy?"

"I beg your pardon, Robert, but you do *not!* You confuse her as much as her pappa – but you are *not* her pappa. You do not have the right. Feelings for a pappa do not disappear just because the pappa abuses his trust – not if they meant anything in the first place. If she could forget her pappa as easily as you wish, she could forget you as easily after you are married."

Robert's mouth opened, his lips moved, but no words came. He watched Therese pour herself a cup of coffee before he looked away, nodding. "What you say has head and foot. One does not forget one's pappa in a moment – not even in a year – but … how do I confuse her? I strive always for the best clarity between us, do I not?"

"*No*, Robert, you do *not!* Not from what you have said, not even just this morning from the letter you say you plan to write."

He was not accustomed to disagreement from Therese. She was upset, Eduard was dead, but that was an upset they shared; she would not use it against him, and yet that was how it appeared. "What did I say?"

"You have contradicted yourself, as you have often contradicted yourself."

"How have I contradicted myself?"

"You have said on the one hand that wives must cook for their husbands. You have said they must keep house properly if they wish to have contented husbands."

He recalled his conversations with Clara, her wish that Therese might live with them after their marriage until she had learned the best way to be a wife, and wondered if Therese resented their presumption. "Therese, you do not have to show her how to keep a house if it is against your wish. I will gladly show her myself."

"That is not it, Robert. It is not against my wish. If anything, it is something I would gladly wish myself – but just listen to me for a little."

She was more stern than he had seen her yet. He nodded, saying nothing.

"Danke. Now, as I was saying, you wish her to keep house for you as if she had nothing else to do. You tell her also that she is not to undertake great journeys after you are married because they would interfere with her duties as your wife."

"Yes, they would, and I stand by what I have said. I see nothing contradictory about it."

Therese looked at him again and he dropped his eyes. "And yet you tell her not to leave Paris until she has gained a great triumph. You tell her not to go to London until she is secure first of Paris."

"Yes, that is true. I have said so. If her reputation in Paris precedes her to London, she will have an easier time of it in London."

"Just think about what you have said, Robert. You wish her to be a devoted wife, which I know she is only too happy to be – but you also wish her to be a great artist.

These are not compatible demands – or if they are both to be met they will require more understanding than you appear to possess at this moment."

"She will be a wife first. The wife stands higher than the artist. For the first year of our marriage she will think only of herself, her house, and her husband. If I achieve nothing but to make her forget the artist in the first year I will have achieved much."

"Oh, Robert, you do not listen, not even to yourself. You forget that for which she has trained all her life, and you expect her to forget it as easily. You are a composer and she is an artist. Is it any fairer to ask her to give up her art than to ask you to give up yours?"

"Of course, it is! I am the man – and men are above women in all things!"

"Ah, Robert! You lose me completely when you talk like that. You both have reputations, but hers outruns yours by leagues – and you would have her give it up just because she is a woman? How can you be so stupid?"

Robert's jaw dropped. He had never seen her so unlike herself. Losing her he lost part of himself. "Therese, stay true to me. I have lost yet another brother."

"I have lost a *hus*band, Robert! You are not the only one who suffers." It would have been too easy to hold him as he wished, pat his head and straighten his hair as she had done before, but he was a man of twenty-eight, no boy, and no matter the Schumann ailment. She hoped Clara was aware of the worm in their constitution. "You are a man, Robert. Show some manliness."

iii

Clara's and Henriette's bedroom in the Hotel Michadiere was small and bare, two beds and dressers. They needed no more, but Emilie had spent the night with them and the room was now full of their things. Clara liked it, the sense of life reflected in their belongings, the sense of hominess. Henriette had left to collect their letters, and Emilie lay on the bed reading a booklet as Clara walked in from the kitchen. "I have washed all the dishes. They sparkle now like mirrors. My Robert would be so proud – and he thinks I do not know what it is to be a housewife."

Emilie stretched. "They should give you a medal. I will give you a recommendation. I will say: Clara Wieck is a Cook Extraordinaire, Queen of the Dishrag, and Empress of the Kitchen! I will write to your precious Robert myself."

"See that you do. That was an excellent breakfast – and you know it."

"Did I deny it? It was excellent – and nothing was burned, not even your precious pianoplaying fingers."

Clara threw a pillow at her. "Of course not, you silly goose. There is no trick to preparing a breakfast."

Emilie mimicked Clara, "Of course not, you silly goose," and Clara attacked her again with the pillow. Emilie laughed, warding her off with her arm. "You are the goose, Clara, for ever thinking there was." She threw the booklet she was reading at Clara.

Clara picked it up from the floor. "Careful! I have not read my new booklet yet."

"And a good thing too. *My Love Is Pepper-Hot Paprika!* Indeed!"

"Ooooh la la!" Clara laughed. "It was either that or *Cardinals in Love* – or *The Queen and Her Revolutionary.*"

The booklets were available in the street for a sou from vendors who shouted the titles in the evening. Emilie laughed as well. "You should have got *Cardinals in Love.* I do like birds."

"Birds? What have birds got to do with it?"

"Why, Clara, do you not know? A cardinal is an American bird, and – no, no, no, no, do not distress yourself – I know he is not talking about birds. It was just a joke!"

"Well, pardonnez moi, my well traveled friend – but I am just a little German girl who has never been to America."

"A little German goose, you mean."

"A little German goose who tries very hard to improve her French despite her very distracting American friend."

"Oh, yes, that is the way to improve your French, reading *My Love Is Pepper-Hot Paprika.* I am sure your Robert would approve."

Clara laughed. "My Robert has had his share of pepper-hot paprika. He has traveled to Italy and Switzerland. Even now he likes to look at girls and he says I am not to be jealous. I am not jealous, I know my Robert – and I know he would not begrudge me my harmless amusements."

"Aha! so your Robert is not to be trusted – and what would your pappa have to say?"

Emilie was prepared to fend off another pillow, but Clara looked wan, tired, suddenly a lost child. "I wish he would say something, anything at all. He has not written a word, not in all these weeks, not one word."

Emilie remained silent. They had done much together in the past weeks, visited Notre Dame, the Pantheon, Tuileries, Invalides, Palais Royal, the stock exchange, attended the opera, ballet, concerts; but in the midst of her gayest moments Clara's face would turn blank and she could tell she was no longer among them.

"I have written to him three times now, telling him everything I have done. I thought he would be so proud, but he has written nothing. I thought he would follow me once he had finished his business, but now I am not so sure. I do not think he cares about me and he will not change, not as long as I care about Robert – but on Robert I am fixed."

"Oh, my poor Clara."

Clara sighed. "Do you know what I long for?"

"What?"

"One lesson from Pappa. There is nothing in the world so right for me as a lesson from Pappa. I rely on him to tell me my faults. I am too absorbed in the music myself to hear the bad notes – but I can trust him to tell me. Oh, how gladly would I listen to his faultfinding."

"But Clara, you do not need him anymore. The reviews have been uniformly splendid. You do not hear the bad notes because you do not play any bad notes."

"Berlioz was not so kind."

"Berlioz praises your pianism to the heavens. It was your Scherzo with which he found fault – but you say it yourself that you are no composer."

"Still, I am not accustomed to hostile criticism."

"It was not hostile – and the rest of the time it is not even the least bit adverse. Besides, Clara, there is nothing so good for an artist as to accept hostile criticism. It can only improve him if he listens."

Clara wasn't listening. "Of course, you are right – as in everything."

Henriette came through the front door and Clara jumped, leaving the bedroom. "What kept you so long, Henriette? Do you have anything for me?"

Henriette smiled. "If you are the Royal and Imperial Chamber Virtuosa, Clara Wieck – then I do."

Clara grinned immediately. Robert addressed all his letters the same way. "Yes, that is me, I do declare." She held out her hand like a countess.

Henriette gave her a letter, but held another back. Clara's eyebrows rose. "Did you get a letter as well?"

Henriette held the letter as if she were unsure what to do with it. "It is for Emilie."

Emilie entered from the bedroom. "Well, then, give it to me. Here I am."

Henriette gave her the letter. "It is from Clara's pappa."

"To me?"

"That is what it says."

"But why would he write to me?"

Clara shrugged. "It must be for me. I asked him to send letters through you because I was not sure when they would clear up the problem with my passport."

Emilie looked at the letter. "But it is addressed to me. It does not mention your name."

"Open it."

Emilie opened the letter, looking at Clara. "He addresses only me, but you may read it. I am sure it is for you."

Clara shook her head. "No. If Pappa wrote to you I am sure he means you to read it."

"I would rather you read it."

"No, please, you must."

Emilie read the letter; Clara and Henriette watched, Clara holding Robert's letter in her hand. Emilie finally looked up. "He is very concerned about you. He does not wish you to marry Robert, but his concern is for your happiness – but if you absolutely must marry Robert he says he would wish Robert to gather a small capital for you both first – and I must say that I do not find that unreasonable."

Emilie did not mention the threats Wieck had made in the letter to deprive Clara not only of her inheritance but of the money she had earned, held for her in trust until she was of age; she did not mention that he had threatened them both as well with a lawsuit if they married; but she gave Clara the letter to read herself.

iv

The law in Saxony required consent from both sets of parents for a marriage. When Robert and Clara wrote to Marianne Bargiel she replied to Robert in Zwickau saying she had heard much about him from Clara and was not disinclined, but wanted first to make his acquaintance. Robert left immediately for Berlin, fortified with pictures of himself and Clara, copies of the *Zeitschrift*, and his compositions. Marianne welcomed him, introducing him to the family, but Robert was disappointed she didn't know his compositions better and let Marianne know how he felt. "I am surprised you do not know them. I am surprised Clara does not play them for you when she visits."

Marianne never doubted Clara, but she knew Wieck better than Robert, better than Clara, understood Robert's own doubt better, and wanted to help the lovers, be a mother to Clara as she had not been able before, for Clara's sake and Robert's – but also for her own, her final defiance of Wieck, her retribution as much as her fulfillment. "She has played your work, but she does not visit often. It is not possible with her schedule – and when she was here last we had not met in so long we wanted more than anything just to talk. There was simply not time enough for everything."

Robert nodded, but resolved to take it up with Clara later. Marianne appeared sympathetic, enthusiastic, and he needed a confidante, no one better than Clara's mamma, the previous claimant on Clara's affection against Wieck. He sighed. "I still worry. When we are together there is no doubt how we feel, what we must – what we *will* do. We *will* marry. But when we are apart, as we have now been for almost nine months – I in Vienna and she in Paris – when we are apart the smallest doubts magnify as under a glass and I see things I would otherwise ignore."

They were in the same room she had shared with Clara over a year ago, before them the same chipped cups of coffee, the same plates of pastries. Marianne nodded, happy to let Robert ventilate his doubts, reveal himself in his true colors.

He sighed again. "She loves her pappa and I am glad that she does – one has only one pappa – but she does not see how he leads her to his own purpose, not to hers. He would rather have her fail in Paris than succeed without him – but she does not see that. She has done well, but not as well as she had hoped. She is too laden with cares. I know how much she does, she sent me her daily schedule – up every morning at seven, plays from nine till noon, lunches till one. In the afternoon she runs errands – which can take three hours or more because Paris is so large. She comes home tired, but still she studies French with Emilie, gives lessons to Henriette and to others. Then she sups. Then there are letters to be written, details to be considered, tickets, halls, piano tuners and movers, everything. Her friends are helpful, but they cannot do what her pappa can do – and she has written to him for help. She wants to tour with him – Belgium, Holland, then England – before going back to Leipzig. But she does not think she can do it without his help – which is *just* what he wants her to think. It will tie her to him forever."

Marianne could see Robert's words had been bottled too long, needing only sympathetic ears to vault from a troubled heart, and spoke soothingly. "That need not be a concern. I know Friedrich. He will want her to admit a complete failure before he will help, but he will succeed only in turning the knife upon himself. I would counsel you, Robert, only to hold your breath – be patient as you have been for so long already. Time is on your side. Friedrich will not help her until she humbles herself, and Clara will not humble herself, not as he would wish."

Robert nodded, but hardly listened, still too full of words himself. "I am glad to hear it, but I wish I could be sure."

"There is nothing else but to wait. She will appreciate your patience as she will nothing else."

Robert nodded again. "It is good to have your counsel, Frau Bargiel, but I am afraid to wait too long. He has threatened us with a lawsuit if we marry – and she has written to me to suggest that we wait a little longer yet. She is afraid the lawsuit will delay the marriage, perhaps even by a year, but imagines we will all be happy if we meet his conditions – but she does not realize that if we meet one set of conditions he will only supply another."

"What are his conditions?"

"He wishes me to show that I can offer her a life free from care, to show that I can acquire a fixed income, a security of two thousand thaler per annum."

"And what can you do?"

"I can do all that he wishes, and more. It is an unfortunate circumstance that allows me to meet his conditions, the death of my brother, but meet them I can – and handsomely." Robert paused. "Clara knew my brother well – and his wife, Therese. She wishes Therese to teach her how to be a housewife."

Marianne remained silent.

"My yearly income, from my *Zeitschrift* and my publishers, is about a thousand thaler. This is, of course, not a fixed income – an artist's income can never be fixed – at least, not that of a creative artist – but I have as well, from government bonds, from my brother Karl's business, and from what was left me from my brother Eduard's business, a sum of fourteen hundred thaler. I have some reputation already as a composer and a great ambition to increase it."

Marianne sighed deeply. "I would say your problems are solved."

Robert shook his head. "One would think so, but what bothers me is that we have had this discussion before, when Clara was in Vienna, and once more this was not my Clara speaking, once more her pappa was guiding her pen. Everytime I think we have overcome a problem, another looms – and I am afraid the longer we wait, the more unattainable becomes our goal."

"Does Clara know of your income?"

"No, I have said nothing."

Marianne smiled for the first time in the interview. "I would say you have only to tell her. If Friedrich still objects, if he raises new conditions, he will show his hand, and she will see through him. It is more than ever a time to be patient – and firm."

Robert felt himself expand with relief. He would be well if he let himself be well. Clara had addressed her letters to Herr Doktor Schumann, signed herself Frau Clara Schumann, the first time she had called herself by his name.

Marianne squeezed his hand. "Tomorrow, we will go to the new museum – well, it is almost ten years old now but we are still so proud of it here in Berlin. There are eighteen columns at the entrance, quite majestic – but I think you will like best the rotunda at the heart of the building. When you sing a note, even quite softly, it resounds from the roof as from a thousand voices. It is quite enchanting. It is modeled, they say, on the Pantheon in Rome, but the echo is the jewel of the rotunda, and if the Pantheon is without the echo I would rather be without the Pantheon."

v

Clara received the letters from Robert and her pappa under dramatic circumstances. No sooner had she returned from the post office with Henriette and turned on rue de Michadiere than two horsemen galloped past, shouting: "The revolution has come! The revolution has come!" The girls ran into their hotel and up the stairs to the window. Drums sounded, calling the National Guard. Much of what happened they learned later, but from three in the afternoon until midnight they heard shots continually everyday. During the brief state of siege it was said the Tuilleries looked like a fort, the palace had been surrounded by troops, and almost a hundred people had been killed; a woman and child had been murdered on rue de Michadiere itself. Clara and Henriette watched from the window when they dared, soldiers in blue with red epaulettes, swords and muskets, cavalrymen thundering over the cobbled street, a dead horse dragged from sight, fires in the distance, even once a cannon being drawn past the hotel.

Peace was soon restored, the Dukes of Orleans and Nemours rode the streets composing the Parisians, the King was agitated, the Queen trembled, and Clara realized she had lost her chance to play again at the court. It was amid this chaos that she contemplated her letters, from Robert and her pappa. Robert's letter came with two enclosures, the first a copy of a letter for her approval renewing his suit that he planned to send her pappa:

Honored Sir:

Once more we come before you, Clara and I, to beg your consent to our marriage next Easter. Two years have passed since my first proposal. You doubted then we would remain true to each other, but we have done so and nothing can make us waver.

What I wrote to you then about my income was entirely true and circumstances have proven me even more fortunate in money matters than I had imagined. I beg you to heed the fate we follow and not to drive us to extremes. In a few days Clara will be twenty years old. Give us our answer on that day. Make it a happy day. Say Yes.

Your long since, and ever attached and confiding
R. Schumann

The second enclosure was addressed to the High Court: *We, the undersigned, have long cherished a heartfelt wish to be united to each other in matrimony. There has been one obstacle in our course and it is with the deepest pain that we seek to remove it in this manner. The father of the co-signatory, Clara Wieck, refuses his consent despite courteous and repeated appeals. The grounds of his refusal remain unclear; we are conscious of no faults; our circumstances are such as might ensure a secure union. The cause preventing his consent can only be animosity toward the other co-signatory, who has fulfilled every duty due the father of the one whom he has chosen for his companion through life. However that may be, we are not willing to surrender our carefully determined plans, and wish to approach the High Court with a most humble request:*

That your worships give Herr Wieck occasion to give us his consent or see fit to give us your consent for his. We would not make such a request unless we were convinced of its urgency and we remain hopeful that time will heal the painful division it precipitates.

Leipzig, September 1839   Robert Schumann

Clara Wieck

(presently in Paris)

These are cold enclosures, Robert wrote, *but we cannot help that. If your pappa refuses his consent we must send the brief to the High Court. We must act and we must continue to act. Please write and tell me what you think. If you approve, sign the brief and send it to me with your letter. Dear Clarchen, it is a beautiful world that holds you in it. Remember me to Emilie and Henriette. Write soon, my love.*

Your Robert.

Her pappa's letter was long, so insulting to both her and Robert that she hated to think he could have written it, but at its heart he demanded that she sign five conditions under which he would consent to the marriage:

1. That Robert and Clara not live in Saxony, but that the *Zeitschrift* earn as much as if they did.
2. That Clara renounce the 7,000 thaler she had earned in the last five years, of which Wieck would give her the interest of 4%.
3. That Robert have the statement of his income audited by an accountant chosen by Wieck.
4. That Robert make no attempt to contact Wieck, not by word of mouth, nor by letter, until Wieck professed himself ready.
5. That Clara renounce all claim to her inheritance.

Clara still wished to believe her pappa wanted only her happiness, but after deliberation realized he had laid down conditions she could not meet without losing dignity; these were not conditions but sentences of punishment. Finally, she reopened Robert's letter, signed the brief, posted it, and wrote as well a short letter to her pappa in which she said among other things: *I have not signed your conditions and I tell you I shall never sign them. I have too much pride. You cannot be serious, and if you are you will never bring me to sign a document that slanders the man I love.*

Robert wrote one more letter to Wieck, looking for one last accommodation of their differences, but received a letter written by Clementine saying *Wieck will have no communication with Schumann.*

vi

Clara met Robert on her return from Paris in Zwickau, staying with Therese, planning to delay her return to Leipzig for a few days, knowing she would lack the luxury there of time and space. They visited neighboring towns, met with Robert's old friends, played the piano, picnicked and walked. Robert wanted to show her off, show off his childhood haunts; she couldn't stop smiling. "Oh, my Robert, it is so good to be with you again, but with all the troubles in Paris I still hated to leave Emilie – and I hated to leave Henriette in Stuttgart. I was so lonely in the coach. A Frenchwoman sat next to me reeking of perfume. It was horrible. But now I feel I could never be lonely again."

It was no longer early morning, but nightcaps still bobbed in some windows and streets were still bare except for streetcleaners emptying buckets of water on the grey cobblestones. Robert held Clara close, avoiding the swirling pools. "You know, Clarchen, I think sometimes that there is something wrong with growing up. When I was a boy I would jump into those puddles. Now I worry about my shoes. I worry about pneumonia."

Clara rubbed against him. "You must – for my sake if not for your own. I would not want you with pneumonia. I would not want you even with wet shoes. I want you well and dry for the rest of your life – for the rest of our lives!"

"And so do I – but here, back in Zwickau, among my boyhood haunts, I am tempted to play the fool again. Everything brings back memories."

"You must share them with me. I want to know everything about you."

Robert wore a hat, Clara a bonnet, carried also an umbrella. They were headed for the Mount Bridge from which he had stared often and long at the Mulde flowing underfoot. Robert spoke proudly. "Zwickau has grown. Herr Schiffer's house was once the last. Now it takes another whole minute to get out of town."

Clara laughed again. "Oh, you are so silly." She slapped his arm.

Robert grinned and she was glad; their long separation had rendered him less cheerful, more easily distracted, prone to longer silences; the feud with her pappa was marking them both, but she bore it better because she loved her pappa better and forgave in him what she would have denounced in anyone else, even in Robert, for what she owed him.

They walked in silence, Robert no longer grinning, but smiling again when he caught her looking at him. She raised her eyebrows. "What are you thinking?"

"Nothing."

"If it is nothing, then it should be nothing to tell me."

He grinned. "Well, then, it is something."

"Robert, do not be coy. It does not become you. If it is something, then you must tell me what it is."

He squeezed her arm. "I will tell you, but you must promise not to be angry. It is something that puzzles me."

"What is it?"

"Promise?"

"I cannot promise if I do not know what it is that I promise – but you must tell me. You must *trust* me."

"Well, then, you are right." He lost his grin. "It struck me first when I visited your mamma. No one in the household knew my work. Your mamma said you had not seen each other in so long you had too much to say – but then I realized you do not play my work much even in your concerts. I wondered why that might be so."

"But, Robert, I *do* play your work. I play it for the connoisseurs. I play it as much as I play Beethoven and Bach. I hate to play it for people who diminish you through their ignorance. Your melodies and figures so cross one another that more sophistication is required than is possessed by the general public – but you know that, do you not, my Robert? I hate to play your work if it does not get the appreciation it deserves."

"But how is it to get the appreciation if it is not heard?"

"But you *are* heard by those who matter." She was distressed; he accused her of the same offenses that she had accused her pappa, and she found herself using the same defenses her pappa had used. "Oh, Robert, why do you not compose something brilliant and easy to understand, without many directions, not too long and not too short, which holds together easily? I would love to have something like that from you, suitable for the general public – and I know you could do it."

His arm stiffened in hers. "You would have me prostitute myself?"

"No, that is not it – that is not what I am saying. It would just be bending to the will of the public for once, that is all, giving them what they want. Do you mean to say that everyone is a prostitute who does not write as you write?"

He pulled his arm from hers, walking to one side, staring ahead. "Yes, if they can compose as I can compose, then yes – but if they cannot, then no. They are only required to do the best they can."

"Robert, I understand you very well – but I must insist on not being misunderstood myself. You know Liszt has said the same thing, that your work is not destined for popular success – but that no fine intelligence can fail to see its beauty."

Robert looked ahead, walking silently.

"You wish to please the public, do you not? And you could do it very well, and so very easily – and sometimes I wish that you would."

Robert pushed his lips in and out. "I do wish to please the public – but on my terms, not theirs. If I submit my art to the public demand we all become losers – and the best works are never composed, let alone heard."

Still he wouldn't look at her, still he kept his distance, and she relented, not wanting a quarrel so soon after their reunion. She took his arm again. "Perhaps you are right. I am sorry. I wish only for your success. I wish the public to love you as I do. I hate to get a bad reception for your work – but you are right. If they do not hear you they cannot appreciate you."

He said nothing, but let himself be held.

"While we are on the subject, Robert, I have something to ask as well."

His attention was diverted to a stand of beeches ahead and he followed it to a finger of the Mulde visible through the trees. They could hear the water gurgling, ducks quacking. "Yes?"

"Why is it that you do not mention me more in the *Zeitschrift*?"

He smiled at the reversal of their roles. "That is simple. I do not wish your pappa to think I curry his favor. That is not the reason to write. I must maintain the integrity of the *Zeitschrift*. That is why I prefer to let the others write about you."

"Well, that I can accept – but not what they write sometimes."

"What do they write?"

"Well, when Becker criticized my concerto he wrote that there could be no question of real criticism since he had to deal with the work of a lady. That is not right, Robert. It is the work that is to be dealt with, not my sex."

Robert stared once more ahead, silent for so long Clara thought he wouldn't speak, but at length he did. "You are right. That was clumsily done. I shall not let that happen again."

She smiled. "Well, then, we are even – and I will strive to include more of your work in my concerts."

They kissed once, quickly, she snuggled closer, they walked as one body the short distance to the bridge, and watched the river standing at the rail. He was silent again, gazing into the depths; she imagined he relived his boyhood and said nothing, comfortable with the new silence, watching the bobbing ducks, until he spoke again himself. "Clara?"

"Yes, my darling?"

"You do realize, now that we have signed and mailed the brief, that we will have to face your pappa in court? that you will need to be there?"

He was looking at her, but she gazed into the Mulde herself instead. "I realize it."

"And how do you feel about it?"

She took a deep breath. "I hate to think of it, but he has left us no choice."

He stroked her hand on the rail. "That is just it. I hate to put you through this, but he has left us no choice."

Clara turned her palm upward, clasping his hand. "Oh, Robert, even now, if Pappa were to relent, if he were conciliatory, I would want it more than anything. If he gives us an inch I am ready to give him a mile, but he gives us nothing. Do not concern yourself on my behalf. If ever I was infirm I am no longer so, but firmly set on our purpose."

Robert stood behind her, enclosing her with a hand on either side on the rail. "My brave Clärchen."

She turned in the enclosure, circling his neck with her arms. "If I am brave it is you who make it possible."

He gathered her in his arms. "Whatever happens, Clärchen, remember we have options. He might turn you out – as he has turned out Alwin and Gustav – but we have options. We have money, you can stay with your mamma in Berlin. Do not forget. We are not children to be told what to do. We must stand for what we know is right – otherwise, we have no right to happiness, to each other."

She rubbed herself against him. "I know, my Robert. I know. Let us not talk about it. I love you. That is all. I love you."

Clara wondered if Robert was right, knew her pappa better than she; he had warned he might turn her from the house as he had turned Alwin and Gustav, and so he had, with none of her belongings, not her clothes, her music, her piano, not even her diary. When she had sent for her winter coat she had received his reply from the mouth of her servant: "Who is Mademoiselle Wieck? I know only two Fraulein Wiecks, my own two little daughters, Marie and Cacilie, who reside with me. I know no others."

She was to stay with her mamma in Berlin until she was to wed Robert – but her pappa had sent word on the eve of her departure from Leipzig, he wanted to see her again, and against Robert's inclination, against the recommendation of their counsellor, Wilhelm Einert, she wanted to see what reconciliation he might yet offer. They had consented to let her go only when she had consented not to make any promises without first consulting them.

Approaching the house she was momentarily overcome with sentiment; she harbored no hate for her pappa, she owed him too much; he thought he acted in her interest, but he was wrong, he was cruel, and she couldn't allow him to rule her; most of all she found him sad, and herself sad when she linked her fortunes to his – but sad as well when she didn't. She was overcome as well with trepidation and more sadness that she couldn't trust her own pappa.

Seeing him again in the parlor her sadness deepened. His eyes were downcast, shoulders slumped, no longer the proud pappa, strong and ambitious for his daughter. His hair was flatter, not in clouds about his ears as before, his head reflected more light, his eyes were dusty, his wrinkles deeper. He motioned her to join him on the couch; she would have been more comfortable sitting apart, but couldn't disappoint him in so small a matter and joined him despite her discomfort. "Clarchen, how is it that we have grown so far apart?"

Even now the name turned her to liquid. "Pappa, I wish it were not so! How I wish it were not so!"

"We speak through lawyers, Clarchen. We are to settle private matters in court like common people. We sacrifice our dignity. And for what? I for one do not wish it."

"I do not wish it either, Pappa. Neither does –"

Wieck interrupted her, he might not have heard her. "We have allowed a mountebank to come between us, Clarchen, a man of no principles and less talent."

Clara's head turned immediately, she might have been slapped. "No, Pappa! You must not talk like that about the man I love. Otherwise, we will have no more to say to each other."

Wieck looked at her, gauging the damage, momentarily silent. When he spoke he was soft again, placating. "I cannot change my mind about the man, Clara. He has disappointed me hugely and that is putting it as diplomatically as I know how – but because I wish a reconciliation with you, because I do not wish to lose my daughter, my most prized possession, I am willing to change my previous conditions for new ones. Since I cannot protect you from a life with Schumann, I wish at least to safeguard your interests from him."

"I am willing to listen, Pappa. I too would like a reconciliation. I would like to hear the new conditions."

"Very well, then. We shall disregard the previous five conditions. We will discuss only these new ones."

Clara nodded, daring to hope from his even tone and rational discourse that they might meet the new conditions more easily than the old.

Wieck opened a folder on the coffee table and pulled out a sheet. "If you find these conditions agreeable you may sign the document before you leave – and our relations will once more be on the mend. We will need no lawyers, no courts, no one to tell us what is right and what is wrong."

Clara said nothing.

"I will read it as it stands so that there is no misunderstanding. You know, of course, that the language of the law is not the language of your pappa. It is merely the law. It is merely the way such documents are written."

Clara nodded.

"First, then … that I, Clara Wieck, the undersigned, renounce the seven thousand thaler I have earned in the last five years, held in trust by my pappa, which is to be given to my brothers, Alwin and Gustav, for their great sacrifices on the behalf of my talent, including the sacrifice of their pappa."

Clara closed her eyes, gripping her knees on the couch so her fingernails whitened. Wieck kept his focus on his page.

"Second … that I am to receive back my belongings, including my piano, for the sum of another thousand thaler, also to be given to my brothers, Alwin and Gustav.

"Third … that Robert Schumann, my husband-to-be, shall settle eight thousand thaler of his capital on me, the interest of which shall also be mine, and in the case of a separation that I alone shall have power to dispose of the capital.

"Fourth … that Robert Schumann, my husband-to-be, shall make me his sole legatee."

Clara rocked back and forth in the couch. The new conditions were no improvement over the old, only the cover was new. She could never sign such a document except to show the greatest mistrust of her husband-to-be.

Wieck placed the sheet on the table before them. "Now, as you can see, it is quite different from the first. Before it was I who reaped the benefit of the money, now it is your brothers – to whom you owe a great deal considering that I dedicated all the time to you that they deserved equally, being equally my children."

Clara shook her head as if she might never stop, but Wieck continued as if he had not seen.

"And as for the last two conditions, they are designed to protect you, no one else. If Robert loves you as he says I see no impediment to his agreeing to these terms."

"Pappa, I cannot sign the document. It is not right. Do not ask me to do this."

He looked at her sharply. "Why not? What is not right about it?"

"Everything, Pappa! Everything!"

"Can you not be more specific? Are not Alwin and Gustav turned to the wolves through my consideration for you? Are they not now in greater need than you? Do they not now lead lives like gypsies and Jews, wandering where their employment takes them?"

"But Pappa, it is because of you that Alwin and Gustav are like gypsies and Jews. It is you who have turned them out of the house – as you turned me! How can you blame me for your own deeds?"

"I do not blame you. I merely indicate how circumstances have developed."

"But you *do* blame me. If you wish me to make reparations, you *do* blame me. I would be glad to help Alwin and Gustav, and I *will* help them – but of my own will, not as the consequence of a declaration of guilt. That is not right – and nor is it right to punish Robert for marrying me."

"How do we punish Schumann?"

"He is to give me eight thousand thaler? That is two thirds of his capital! Is not this unworthy of a man? It is the man's business to control his wife's money, not the other way around – and even otherwise there is the matter of trust. It would appear as if I did not trust him."

"That is the very hub of the matter. I do not trust him – and I do not trust him for your sake. I look out for you alone, your benefit, not mine. Surely that is clear. What do I stand to gain from this document?"

"I do not know, Pappa – and I do not care. I cannot sign it." She got up. "I see it is meaningless to stay. We cannot have a meeting of minds after all."

"Clarchen, wait!"

Something in his tone made her stop.

"If this is not to your liking, I will put it away for the present – but sit down. Do not go yet. I have more to say."

He put the sheet back in the folder, patting the seat beside him. She sat again.

"I want to make you an offer – but first another condition –"

"Pappa, no more conditions. What kind of man marries a woman on conditions? What kind of woman submits to such a marriage?"

"Just one small condition, Clarchen. Listen to me."

She was silent.

"Just this, that you wait at least until after your twenty-first birthday. Is that too much to ask?"

He was asking for an extension of less than six months from the date they had chosen for Easter of the coming year. She shook her head. "No, that is not too much to ask, but why? What purpose would it serve?"

171

"It would allow us to come to a better understanding, Clarchen. It would allow us to become father and daughter again. I would like to propose a tour, just you and I, for three months. We can discuss where we shall go, back to Paris, London if you wish, St. Petersburg – but wherever we go, whatever we decide, I will guaranty a fixed sum of six thousand thaler. Is that not fair? You will be older and in a far better position to judge the wisdom of your undertaking. Is that so very much to ask?"

Clara saw in his face a new expression, she was never to see it again, mouth parted, eyes wide; he stood, hands open in appeal; she had never seen him in such want, never so vulnerable, but it was too late. She understood it was a ruse, a tactic for time, to ward off the wedding, perhaps he even believed what he said – but she understood as well that she had to defy him for her own sake more even than Robert's. She got up again. She knew she would have done better in Paris with his help, but she hadn't done badly on her own. She knew he needed her as much as she needed him, perhaps more, but she had to learn to do without him. Whatever he said, whatever he believed, he could no longer help her, his help was a closet hindrance; she had to help herself. "I am sorry, Pappa, but it is too late. You must let me go – and you must let me go with your blessing. Otherwise, we can never again be as father and daughter."

She turned, she would have left the house, but he stamped his foot; the vase on the coffee table clattered, the geraniums shook, two fell out, a freestanding lamp rocked. Clara froze. "Child! You will go when I tell you to go – not before!"

She understood how Alwin and Gustav must have felt, often the objects of his anger, but never she, the queen, always pampered. His mouth was a thin line again, his eyes as thin, glazed like glass. He sat again.

"Sit down, Clara!"

She hesitated.

"I said, sit, Clara: Sit! I have one more thing yet to show you."

She sat again. He picked up the folder again.

"Now, just so we are clear. I have offered you this document to sign – but you have refused it. I have offered you a tour, I have guaranteed six thousand thaler – but again you have refused me. You leave me no choice." He pulled a sheaf of about ten pages from the same folder and waved it in her face. "This is a Declaration that I shall read out loud at the hearing. It is a complete record – or as complete as I can make it – of all Schumann's vices – the stupidity with which he damaged his finger, the lies about his income with which he has demoralized a fresh young girl so that he might live off her earnings as an artist – and turning her against her pappa, a sin in itself. Also that he may turn her into a housewife though she has been bred only for her art, and that as an artist she has special needs for which he is unable to provide. I have categorized as well the lies with which he has demoralized other young girls, among them one Ernestine von Fricken, upon whose testimony I shall rely – also that he drinks to excess, that he creates havoc in his rooms, for which testimony his landlady, Frau Devrient, will provide –"

Clara got up again, Robert was right, there could be no coming to terms, her pappa did not want it, he brought the judgment upon himself.

Wieck slammed his fist on the coffee table, the vase fell to the carpet, and he jumped up as suddenly as Clara. "CLARA, *SIT* YOU DOWN! I AM *NOT* FINISHED! I WILL *YET* MAKE YOU REGRET WHAT YOU DO!"

Clara ran from the room afraid she had driven him mad; blinded by tears, moving by intuition more than sight, she dashed past Clementine, past Marie and Cacilie, down the stairs and out of the house. She didn't stop running until she had put two streets between them, but couldn't rid herself of the voice ringing in her ears: COME BACK, POOR FOOLISH WRETCHED DEMORALIZED GIRL! COME BACK BEFORE YOU ARE FOREVER LOST!

Leipzig was a hub of industry, birthplace of Bach the solid citizen, with wife and continually swelling brood, who had been newly revitalized via his *St. Matthew Passion* discovered by Mendelssohn, himself no less a solid citizen, with wife and continually swelling brood, whose family was rooted in banking – not surprisingly a more favored son of Leipzig (though born in Hamburg and raised in Berlin) than Wagner, also Leipzigborn, but no solid citizen – but more about him later. The Gewandhaus was a bastion of respectability, standard bearer for Classicism, lacking patience for the frivolity of Vienna where people came to be entertained at concerts, or Paris where they came to be seen. Leipzigers came to hear the music, not sound effects, and if they could hear the music over the sound effects they asked nothing more. They were smalltowners, upholders of thrift and purity, suspicious of scandals following artists such as Liszt, and while they listened willingly to all they were won by performances, not reputations.

1811, the year of the Great Comet, Liszt was born in Raiding, Hungary, not far from the Esterhazy estate where his pappa had worked and walked with Haydn, where Haydn had invented the symphony and string quartet; 1813, as soon as he could sit, he learned the piano from his pappa, so went the legend; 1820, he gave his first concert at the Esterhazy court; 1821, he went with his pappa to Vienna to study with Salieri (Mozart's nemesis, Beethoven's contemporary, Schubert's teacher), and Czerny (Beethoven's greatest pupil); 1822, he met Beethoven, met Schubert; 1823, he toured Munich, Stuttgart, and Strasbourg; 1824, he played London, for George IV at Carlton House; 1825, his opera, *Don Sanche*, was produced in Paris (a failure, he never wrote another, but he had been just 14!); 1827, his pappa died, he retired from concerts, brought his mamma to Paris, gave lessons, endured a time of introspection, which turned to depression when he was surprised one midnight in the arms of his first love (the daughter of a nobleman to whom he gave piano lessons) and turned from the house like a servant stealing silver, not for the seduction, but the presumption (seduction was welcome, but not from a music teacher); 1830, the July Revolution revived his spirits.

Three influences were to set his style forever: hearing Berlioz, he wanted to expand the palette of his piano to that of the orchestra; hearing Paganini, he wanted to drive his listeners to the same paroxysms of frenzy; and hearing Chopin, he wanted to develop feathers in his fingers as he had already developed hammers. Playing into the night at a small party at Chopin's, for Heine, Delacroix, Rossini, Meyerbeer, and George Sand, he met Marie d'Agoult, six years his elder, who abandoned her husband, twenty years older, and two daughters, to abscond with Liszt to Switzerland, which didn't help his reputation with the solid citizens of Leipzig – who nevertheless flooded the Gewandhaus. They came to hear the music, to hear the great man, to hear for themselves.

Liszt's first selection was unfortunate, his transcription of the Scherzo and Finale of Beethoven's *Pastoral* Symphony for the piano; the prevailing wisdom dictated that anyone playing a transcription played for himself, not for the symphony, serving himself, not the composer, dazzling with his ability, not his interpretation – and even Robert, sympathetic though he was to Liszt's cause, subscribed to the wisdom. In a smaller hall the transcription might have succeeded, but at the Gewandhaus the piano revealed itself a distant cousin to the orchestra. You saw the blood and bones of the work, the toil that went into resuscitation, but never the rosy flesh, the breast swelling with breath; you heard hammers on wires, a mechanistic tour de force, the bass rumble, the treble trill, but the giant never walked, the birds never flew.

His second selection was more successful, the "Grand Fantasy on Pacini's *Niobe*" with which he had vanquished Thalberg, though again he relied on execution more than music; the third, a Chopin etude, the most tender of the selections for the evening, was the best received; but Liszt concluded with his signature tune, the *Grand Gallope Chromatique*, and encored with the *Grand Valse de Bravura*, works whose titles said as much as their music.

The applause was accompanied by hisses; for Liszt, it was unbelievable, intolerable; he canceled the concert scheduled for the next day and took to his sick bed, too exhausted and indisposed to perform. Even Robert, writing for the *Zeitschrift*, said they had seen the lion shake his mane, but Liszt would have served himself better by understating his case than by matching his piano against their orchestra.

ii

So long was the boy's hair, so frail his physique, so wan the expression of Liszt's favorite pupil of the moment (also his manager and traveling companion though barely eighteen years old), that he might have been mistaken for a girl. Mendelssohn remained expressionless as the door opened into Liszt's hotel suite; Robert smiled from the plush red hallway. "Good morning, Herr Puzzi."

The boy scowled, shifting his weight to one leg. "My name, Monsieur Schumann, is Hermann Cohen."

Robert's eyes widened. "I am sorry. I was informed differently."

Mendelssohn bowed his head. "Is Herr Liszt well enough to receive us?"

Cohen bowed. "If you would like to wait for a moment, Monsieur Mendelssohn, and you, Monsieur Schumann, I will ask him."

"Of course."

Cohen led them through a room with a desk at which sat a secretary, into a waiting room furnished in the Queen Anne style, upholstered in red, filled with flowers, wreaths, scarves, cravats, and other gifts from admirers, also a piano. Robert was drawn to two crossed daggers on the wall set with sapphires and pearls, a jeweled sword, a goblet of gold. Mendelssohn, more accustomed to extravagance, sat patiently waiting.

Cohen was back almost at once. "If you will follow me, messieurs, Monsieur Liszt will see you now."

They were conducted through a hallway, past three more rooms, all luxuriously furnished and decorated. Mendelssohn looked neither left nor right, but Robert spied at least two more pianos. There was a piano as well in the bedchamber, but the middle of the room was taken by a fourposter bed looming like a yacht in full sail, nets of silk billowing from the canopy, mahogany hull gleaming, satin bedclothes aswirl, Liszt almost hidden in a blue nightshirt under blue covers. Robert was the first to speak. "Good morning, Herr Liszt. How are you feeling today?"

Liszt's dark blond hair was fanned on his pillow like a halo. "My good Doktor Schumann, I wish I could say I was entirely well, but I am not – but I am better, am I not, Hermann?"

Cohen was dragging chairs alongside the bed, Robert helped him, Mendelssohn stood by the bed. "I am glad to hear it, Herr Liszt."

"Thank you, Herr Mendelssohn. Your very visit is a tonic. It is good of you both to have come. I am glad of your company. Pray, be seated."

They had met the day before, all three, and talked about music, Vienna, Clara, but briefly, nothing of consequence, time had been dear, the concert pressing. Mendelssohn sat closer to Liszt. "Herr Liszt, I know I speak for all Leipzig when I say we wish you a speedy recovery. If there is anything at all that you need …"

Liszt smiled. "Thank you, Herr Mendelssohn, but as you can see I am well taken care of. I could not ask for more devotion than I get from Hermann – nor, indeed, from the hotel staff. Everyone is, indeed, most considerate."

Mendelssohn remained expressionless. "I am glad to hear it. I had hoped we might speak in private – about a matter of some urgency."

Liszt raised his chin in the air. "Hermann is my manager. You may speak freely."

Robert looked at Cohen standing by the door; Mendelssohn hesitated. "It is, I am afraid, Herr Liszt, a very urgent matter, indeed – and a very private one."

Liszt stared a moment, then nodded. "Very well, Hermann, please see that we are not disturbed."

Cohen bowed and left the room.

Mendelssohn nodded. "Danke, Herr Liszt. I shall be very frank. The concert last night was a success, but not the success expected of the great Liszt."

Liszt turned his head on the pillow. "That does not bother me. I am in Leipzig, a city of merchants. I played at the Gewandhaus, once a linen factory. It is to be expected. There are no princesses here, no countesses, no duchesses – not like in Dresden. There is no aristocracy, no culture, not even a sense of fashion. I understand – and I assure you, my dear friend, I do not let it bother me, not a jot."

Robert frowned, but said nothing. Mendelssohn shook his head. "I beg your pardon, Herr Liszt, but I must submit that you have misunderstood the Leipzigers. They are good people, hardworking, and have little respect for those who are less so than themselves. Their aristocracy is of the merchant class. It was not the music that failed us last night, nor yet the Leipzigers, but something else."

Liszt turned his head from the pillow, eyebrows rising like hooks. "Pray, tell, Herr Mendelssohn, I beg you. What failed us?"

"Do not take this amiss, Herr Liszt. I speak with all due respect – but, truth be told, the cause of the failure lies at the door of the management."

"My management? Hermann? I assure you, not! I have said: he is devoted to me."

"It is not his devotion that is in doubt, Herr Liszt, but he is perhaps unaware of how business is conducted in Leipzig. May I be more explicit?"

"Please."

"Well, then, I will make my points as briefly as I can. You see, there were too many changes made last night at the very last minute, which discommoded even our generally placid Leipzigers. Your manager, er …"

"Hermann Cohen – Puzzi." Liszt grinned. "George Sand gave him the name. He hates it."

"Him, your manager, Herr Cohen, he raised the price of tickets from sixteen groschen to a thaler – now, I do not say it is not worth the money. No one says that. A thaler is a pittance to pay to hear the great Liszt, and they know it – but the Leipzigers like to eat their meals before they pay for them. They knew you, of course, but by your reputation, not your ability, and were unhappy about paying the highest rates – on hearsay, so to speak."

"It is a question of money, then, is it? That is why they are displeased?"

"They are not displeased, no one could be displeased by the great Liszt, not even on his worst day – but perhaps they were not as pleased as they might have been had the circumstances been less onerous."

"There were other circumstances?"

"Many. For example, we are in the habit of issuing a list of complimentary tickets for every concert – but Herr Cohen insisted we suspend the list. There were many who were outraged, they found it highhanded, but they had no recourse but to submit to the demands – Herr Cohen's demands, but they hold you responsible –"

"Again, then, it is a question of money – but that is to be expected, I would think, in a city of merchants."

Again, Mendelssohn shook his head; he might have been addressing a child. "Herr Liszt, I beg you to consider. What are managers but the merchants of artists? I beg your pardon, but I speak with all respect. Managers and agents and their kind are viewed here like parasites. It is a new phenomenon, and people still prefer to deal directly with artists. I daresay we will grow accustomed to managers in time as we grow accustomed to all manner of pestilence, but I believe, firmly, that both you and the Leipzigers have been led astray through the inexperience of your manager, Herr Cohen – which is to be regretted because I believe neither you nor the Leipzigers care as much about money as the other would believe.

"There were also differences regarding publicity and programming which I am sure contributed to the disappointment of the evening more even than the money matters. I believe also that you have more in common with the Leipzigers than you imagine. Believe me, there are none more serious about good music in all Europe.

If anything, you might accuse them of being too serious. I hope I can make you see that. We must do what we can to mend the breach." He paused, taking a breath. "I beg your pardon. I do not generally speak at such length, but this is important."

Liszt sank sighing back in bed, staring up at the canopy, writhing as if he heard music. Mendelssohn confused him: impeccable musicianship juxtaposed with bourgeois piety; a true artist, but shackled, and willingly, to a wife who cared little about music, and to children; gifted, intelligent, brilliant, multilingual, but as regimented as an accountant; out of sympathy with the music of Berlioz, even of Chopin, Schumann, and his own, but their champion onstage; generous with time, but miserly with praise; other composers would have gloated at his failure, but he wanted to help. "Not another apology, my good Herr Mendelssohn. I, too, would like to mend the breach. What would you suggest?"

"I would like you to consider a soiree for about four hundred at the Gewandhaus. I will take care of the arrangements. All I need is your consent. If you are agreeable I shall commence work on the details immediately. I shall fix the program, find the artists, and keep you apprised of all developments."

Liszt remained on his back, staring again at the canopy, stretching his arms to the sides, writhing again under the bedclothes, smiling finally, looking at neither Robert nor Mendelssohn. "I am agreeable. You may discuss the details with Hermann."

Mendelssohn remained seated.

"It is all right, Herr Mendelssohn. Do not fear. I will talk to him. He is a good man, no more interested in money than I am. He was merely looking out for my best interest, that is all – but I will make it clear to him that he is to follow your lead in all things. It will be all right, but if there are any problems I trust you will bring them directly to me."

Mendelssohn rose, extending his hand. "I am glad to hear it. I will take my leave, but you will be hearing from me. You can count on it."

Liszt took his hand. "Good. I shall look forward to it."

Robert had remained not only quiet through the exchange, but strangely disinterested, staring at the wall, frowning. It became clear what had distracted him when he spoke again, still frowning. "Herr Liszt, we have our own aristocracy in Leipzig! One hundred and fifty bookshops, fifty print shops, thirty newspapers – we have publishing houses, cultural journals – the university. You would do well to remember that. There is no such aristocracy in Dresden."

Liszt's mouth fell open, but eased into a smile. Schumann astonished him, but very differently from Mendelssohn; he could never tell what he was thinking; so obsessed had he been with Liszt's denigration of Leipzig culture that he seemed to have heard nothing of what had passed between Mendelsshon and himself. "But of course, my dear Herr Schumann. You are right. What was I thinking?"

Robert nodded, easing his frown, but remaining seated.

Mendelssohn caught Robert's eyes. "Will you come, Herr Schumann, or will you stay?"

Robert smiled suddenly. "I will stay – that is, if Herr Liszt does not feel too unwell."

"I feel better already knowing you will stay. We have much to talk about."

Mendelssohn nodded. "I will take my leave, then."

Liszt waved from the bed. "Adieu, Herr Mendelssohn. My deepest thanks for your courtesy."

"It is nothing."

Robert nodded goodbye.

Liszt turned to Robert as Mendelssohn left, but Robert was staring again at the wall, seemingly oblivious to his presence; Liszt, unaccustomed to disinterest, was puzzled by the man. He knew his *Zeitschrift*, his compositions which he admired more than Mendelssohn's; they relied less on the models of the past, they were more original, but for that very reason would take longer to penetrate the public; but he appeared so passive, so sensitive, it was amazing he got anything done, unlike Mendelssohn who would move heaven and earth for his purpose. Liszt shook his head: unless he said something it seemed Robert would be happy just staring at the wall. "And how is the incomparable Clara Wieck, my friend, and her charming pappa?"

Robert turned suddenly from the wall. "Charming? You find the old man so very charming? He has turned his own daughter from her home. He has cast her adrift without a groschen to her name. You find that charming?"

Liszt's eyes widened. "I did not know that, my friend. I am sorry to hear it. I understand you are to be married?"

"Maybe before we die. We still have obstacles to overcome that most couples do not endure in a lifetime of marriage. He will not give her permission to marry me. He will not give her money she has earned. He will not even give her her own clothes, her piano – not even her diary. We are obliged to go to court to get what is rightfully ours, and the court obliges us to delay indefinitely the day of our marriage. In the meantime he slanders me and vilifies her – his own daughter. Do you find that so very charming?"

Liszt shook his head. "I am sorry, indeed, to hear it. You have my deepest sympathy. If there is anything I can do …"

Robert shook his head. "Danke, Herr Liszt. Your friendship is enough. Your friendship means much."

"That was yours when I heard your *Carnaval* in Vienna, played by your Clara. She also played some of my own music, so very precisely, and with such great energy, and the deepest understanding. That is a rare phenomenon. She is a true artist."

"It is kind of you to say it. She will be most glad to know what you have said."

"I do not pronounce the words idly. Kindness is easy, but your Clara makes it as easy to be truthful as to be kind."

Robert nodded.

"I am sorry I will not get to shake her hand. You said last night she now resides in Berlin?"

"With her mamma – but she is touring now, also with her mamma, the northern towns: Stettin, Stargardt, Hamburg, Bremen, and Lubeck. She does not want to be a burden. She does not want to begin her marriage by impoverishing her husband. I have told her I am not so easily impoverished. I have enough for two, and she is a frugal girl – but she wants at least to provide for her own dowry."

Clara had earned almost a thousand thaler in five weeks, half of which needed to be deducted for purchases for her mamma, herself, the household, and travel expenses. It was still a most satisfactory showing, but he wished she might have been less intent on the recompense, as if his own earnings were inadequate.

Liszt sat up in the bed. "Ah, but she is admirable! What an enchanting creature! You must give her my warmest regards when you write – even better, I will write her a postscript myself to your next letter, if I may."

"Nothing would delight her more – nor, indeed, myself."

"Good, then it is settled. I would visit Berlin myself, but it is too important a city to visit on a whim. I would be obliged to perform at least three or four concerts and my time is too short – but you must persuade her to come to Leipzig in time for my last concert. Her tour will then be finished, will it not?"

Robert grinned. "I will command her – as her husband-to-be and master."

"Good – and her pappa, from me, from this moment on, he gets nothing – no complimentary tickets, no comments, no attention at all. He is not a person, not in my life, not any longer."

Robert nodded. "I begin to think he is not even human to treat a daughter as he does. He thinks only of himself – and money!" He allowed himself another grin. "Herr Allesgold, that is what I call him."

"A true merchant, I see."

"But not a true pappa!"

"I see that too – but speaking as a pappa myself, let me say how well my daughters love your *Kinderszenen*. I have to play it for them everytime we are together. Otherwise, they will give me no peace. They are, in fact, learning it themselves."

Robert grinned. "My Clara finds me a child sometimes, she says. That was why I wrote them, to show her what her child can do."

Liszt nodded, raising himself in bed. "My friend, if your time is not pressing I would like to play something for you."

"I would be honored."

Liszt got out of bed, donned velvet slippers, a satin robe with a sable trim, and led Robert into the hallway, into another room, swaying as he walked, stooping a little, gesturing him seated, walking to the door. "Hermann, we are not to be disturbed, si vous plais."

Liszt's eyes never left Robert; he sat at the piano, shaking his elbows, wrists, hips, waggling his satin sleeves, wiggling his tapering fingers. His head bobbed on the gimbals of his neck. Robert would not have been surprised to see him touch his toes or jump in the air.

He recognized the piece from the first note, his deep lament for Clara, during the affair with Robena, which he had played first for Willy and his landlady, Frau Devrient, the day she had asked him to leave, his Fantasie in C major. *Something in it throbs*, Willy had said, *like a pulsation of the heart, ripples from a bloodstream*, and Liszt replicated every tremor – but Robert had never heard it played with such grandeur. The piano seemed to glow, sparks to crackle between Liszt's fingers and the keys.

He listened in silence, watching Liszt's hands, slender as a woman's, fingers with twice the number of joints as others, so flexible they curled like ribbons, stretched like rubber, multiplied over the keys. He swayed, eyes closed; Robert remembered what Mendelssohn had said, his soul seeped through his fingers when he played – but when he looked again Liszt's mouth was curved upward, minutely at the corners, and his eyes were open; he had been watching Robert, aware of his power, and Robert, breathless, looked quickly away, momentarily unnerved, dizzy, recalling how Clara had been affected, mesmerized by Liszt's personality more than his pianism, more in the thrall of the man than the music, as if he were being seduced.

As the last reverberation of the first movement died, Liszt, still swaying in his seat, still hearing the music, turned to Robert, hands hidden in his mandarin sleeves, but Robert said nothing, didn't even move. When he realized Liszt was waiting he spoke simply. "Play the March first. Then I will tell you what I think."

Liszt turned back to the piano, disappointed, but no less determined to win Robert, and resumed his sway, charmed already by the music he was about to play. The March was among Robert's more triumphant passages, and more triumphant yet played by Liszt. He watched Robert as before, as if to hypnotize him, and at the end of the movement Robert could no longer sit still; he jumped from his chair, face bright, eyes wide, cheeks gleaming, as animated as he had been still before, as noisy as silent before. "My God, Herr Liszt, but we think identically. That is just how I heard it in my head, but never dreamed I would hear out loud. You have brought it out of my head with your fingers – like a Merlin."

Liszt grinned, swaying back, swinging his arms, his conquest complete. "I beg pardon for my presumption, but I feel I have known you for twenty years. Hearing about your troubles with the bad pappa and playing your music back to you, I feel that we are comrades. I feel I have understood the music anew."

Robert had not known the feeling before, lightness in his step, breast full of air; he stared at Liszt. "I would like to dedicate it to you, Herr Liszt, if I may. You have made me understand, as if for the first time, my own music."

Liszt returned the wild stare with silence.

Robert repeated himself. "If I may."

Liszt bowed his head. "My friend, I would be honored."

"Good, then it is settled. I will tell my publishers."

Liszt clapped his hands. "This calls for a celebration, indeed. Shall we have champagne?"

Robert grinned. "Again, my friend, you have read my mind."

iii

"Clara, the carriage is here. Are you ready?"

"Yes, Mamma." Her voice was soft; she felt giddy standing up, almost too weak to raise her arms. Her hand hurt to write, let alone practice, let alone perform, but she had conserved her strength, and meant to stomach the pain. She couldn't disappoint her admirers and the Hamburg concert had long been sold out.

"Are you sure you are all right, Clara?"

"I will be all right, Mamma. Just get me there. I will know what to do then."

Her mamma knew Clara felt badly, knew why she felt badly, but not how badly she felt. Wieck had sent the Declaration against Robert to be circulated by his acquaintances in the cities they visited. Clara hated to think that people who didn't know her, who had never met her, judged her on the merit of her pappa's correspondence – but not all were inclined to believe him. Herr Stadtrat Behrens, one of her pappa's customers, had supplied her with the piano, one of her pappa's own, one of her favorites, a piano by Andreas Stein of Vienna. He had shown her as well a note he had received from her pappa: *This is to warn you that the pianist, my former daughter, Clara Wieck, consorts among you without my consent. We have been estranged from each other through the machinations of her paramour, Robert Schumann, a thorough scoundrel, who has thoroughly demoralized a once thoroughly innocent girl. Be warned, she comes to you with the glowing cheeks of a cherub, but with carrion in her heart. I write to warn you not to entrust your instruments to her hands. She is now accustomed to the stiff French mechanisms and breaks all other pianos. It is also my hope that the Noble King of Prussia will not allow her to perform in his dominions since she does so against the express wish of her pappa.*

Behrens had given her the note to warn her of what she might expect. She had thanked him, shown the note to her mamma, and kept it in her pocket.

Jolts from the carriage shot like bolts up her arms, scurried like needles in her face. Clara closed her eyes, recalling the last time she had visited Hamburg, with her pappa, and how different it had been, but found herself wishing now to share it only with Robert, the Alster by dawn, its fleets of swans, the Jungfernstieg. An admirer had sent her the freshest oysters and she had commissioned a small barrel to be sent to Robert. He had written about his friendship with Liszt for which she was glad: Robert thrived on affection, needed friends more than most, and one as powerful as Liszt would do him good in her absence, but she had been surprised that Liszt had added an immensely flattering postscript.

Backstage she rehearsed her program in her head, the Beethoven *Archduke* Trio, Henselt's Etude in E flat minor, Liszt's transcription of Schubert's "Ave Maria," a sonata by Scarlatti, Mendelssohn's Prelude in E minor, and her own Variations on a Theme by Bellini. She wore a white dress; her mamma tucked a pink geranium in her hair and kissed her cheek; she drank a glass of champagne, then another, and walked onstage, her mamma praying in the wings.

The public was a monster, a roaring monster, a sea of clapping hands, silent as she sat at the piano and started the Beethoven, the cantabile introduction, joined shortly by violin and cello, followed by bursts of thunder interrupting the pastoral. She no longer prayed for a great performance, only that she wouldn't faint; too often the keys appeared black before her, her hands shook, she was sure she had missed notes, but next morning, Rellstab, the eternal carp, said only that she had played the Scarlatti too fast, the only performance with which she had been entirely happy.

Her hands had agonized throughout the concert, her face been paralyzed in part, but the "Noble King of Prussia" himself had been present, applauding wildly with the audience. She took the note from her pocket, ripped it three times in half, and threw away the pieces.

iv

Schubert's song, "The King of the Elves," his first opus, is an ominous work: the Erlkonig, the Elf King, is a killer, chasing a father and son on horseback, the son aware of their pursuer, the father telling him it's the wind; the wind blows past, the father rides on, but his son is dead in his arms. The original poem is by Goethe; Schubert's genius had been to discover the musical context for the words, Liszt's to discover that Schubert had rendered the words extraneous. Incorporating the melody into the rhythm, Liszt had provided one of the earliest instances of a tone poem.

A single note sounds insistently in triplets like a drumming in the head and driving runs thread the rhythm in a minor scale. The triplets conjure hooves and rain, the runs mist and night. Goethe was too much of a fossil to appreciate how Schubert had immortalized his poem, but Beethoven had been less obtuse: "Truly the divine spark resides in Schubert."

Liszt had chosen to play his transcription for the soiree because Mendelssohn had chosen to open with Schubert's Ninth which Liszt had not heard, which had yet to be published, which Robert had uncovered during his stay in Vienna, the symphony of heavenly length, dubbed the Great C major to distinguish it from his other C major, now the little C major, and Schubert, little Franzl, known best as a songwriter, whirled suddenly into Beethoven's orbit, while his Unfinished Symphony remained still undisclosed, still twenty-five years from production.

Mendelssohn's calculation proved successful. The audience hurled Bravos onstage for Schubert as much as Liszt who closed the first part of the program with a fantasy on Donizetti's *Lucia di Lammermoor.*

Mendelssohn had organized the soiree as promised for four hundred of the Leipzig elite at the Gewandhaus. He had charged no admission, plied the guests with mulled wine and cake, followed the intermission with his overture, A Calm Sea and a Prosperous Voyage, three choruses from his oratorio, *St. Paul*, and concluded with Bach's Concerto for Three Pianos in D minor, for which he was joined by Liszt and Ferdinand Hiller, thus rehabilitating Liszt's Leipzig reputation.

v

"I am so glad you have come."

"Did you think I would not? after my Lord-and-Master so commanded?"

"I have the best news!"

"So have I!"

Clara had barely alighted from the coach and could not remember when she had seen Robert so exuberant. "Willy will take your things home. I told the Freges we would walk."

She was to stay with the Freges, her friends, and thanked Willy as he and Robert transferred her portmanteau from the coach to the Freges's carriage. Willy smiled, not without irony, winking at Robert. "It is my pleasure to honor a prophet in his own country."

Clara raised her eyebrows. "A prophet? My Robert?"

She looked at Robert, who stared at Willy, who laughed.

"I will tell you about it after he leaves. Otherwise, he will keep laughing like the fool he is. Go on, Willy – leave us. Your work is done. Go before you make a still bigger fool of yourself."

Willy waved. "Welcome back, Clara. It is good to see you again."

"Thank you, Willy. It is good to see you."

"Go on, Ulex. Go on home. You have outlived your usefulness."

Willy laughed as the carriage pulled away; Robert grinned.

Clara smiled. "If I could always see you so glad, I would stay away more – just so I could come back more."

"Just so long as you came back, my Clarchen."

"But what is your big news? I am dying to know. Why did Ulex call you a prophet?"

He took her hand and they walked along the road from the Coach House. "He was talking about what happened after Liszt's concert. I wrote to you about Mendelssohn's soiree for Liszt, which could not have had a better success – but Liszt gave his second concert alone, just one man, on that huge stage, the whole evening. He played Weber's *Konzertstuck*, some Schubert, and he played as only Liszt can – but you will read about that in the *Zeitschrift*. I want to tell you what happened *after* the concert."

Clara squeezed his hand, still smiling to see him so excited.

"Hiller hosted a dinner for Liszt – the mayor was there, councilmen, many others – and Liszt toasted Mendelssohn and Hiller, both of whom had performed the Bach Concerto with him as I wrote to you – but he saved the most flattering toast for me. He praised me not for my qualities as a writer, not as an editor, though these he said were considerable, but as an artist and an original composer, as a prophet without honor in his own country – and, Clarchen, everyone's eyes were upon me."

"Oh, Robert, I wish I could have been there!"

"He said some words in French because he said some things can be expressed only in French. I could think of nothing to say. I daresay my face was the color of the sun when it rises – and just as hot – but it felt grand. I feel I carry a new weight, people look at me differently."

"But that is so generous of him – not that it was not deserved, but so few artists are generous with praise for other artists. They think only of themselves."

"Liszt is not like that – and he is generous as well with his earnings. He was not so obliged, but he said he had been so honored by his reception in Leipzig that he would undertake a third concert – of which the proceeds were to benefit any charity we chose."

"Oh, that is good. That is, indeed, noble of him."

"And in addition to his own *Hexameron* he will play Mendelssohn's D minor Concerto for the Piano – which he has not yet even seen!"

"Oh, that is the very definition of Liszt. He plays at sight what we toil over and get nowhere with in the end."

"I see you know him, but to finish what I was saying, he means to honor each of us – Mendelssohn, Hiller, and myself – all Leipzigers, in his concert. He plans as well to play two etudes by Hiller and parts of my *Carnaval*."

"Oh, my dear Robert, that is, indeed, thoughtful of him."

"It is – but do you know what pleases me most about him, Clara?"

"What is that, my darling?"

"It is his confidence – in his ten good fingers. At his first concert he played on a Hartel piano – which he had never seen, and he did not care to see! Can you believe that?"

"That is Liszt – I will believe anything of Liszt."

"You see, he can well afford to be generous – because he knows what everyone knows – that he is the first pianist in the land."

Clara could not prevent a sigh. "Ah, yes, I suppose he is." She sighed again, but he remained ignorant of what she felt.

"Clara, he has offered even to help us in court against your pappa, if we would so wish, to testify in my behalf."

He looked at her for the first time since they had begun walking, but now she turned from him. "Why would he go so far?"

"We have become fast friends, Clara. You wrote to me yourself from Vienna that we would get along well – you were right! Our understanding is identical. We are even rude to each other – in fun, of course. Our friendship allows it. He played my *Fantasie* as I heard it in my head, as I could never write it on paper – and my *Novelletten*."

Clara shook her head, disbelievingly, frowning. "Now it is clear. I read Pappa's letter in the paper about Liszt. It was wrong of Liszt not to send him a ticket. Pappa has been good to him. For years he has loaned him pianos at more loss than profit to himself – when you think of how many pianos Liszt has broken, playing them so roughly. When I played the *Konzertstuck* with him myself in Vienna we had to stop three times – because he broke the strings three times."

Robert stared, aware for the first time something was the matter. "He does it out of friendship for us, Clara."

She disengaged her hand from his, reaching for her handkerchief. "And what of his friendship for Pappa. Must everyone forevermore choose between us? It was not right of you, Robert, to encourage him to torment Pappa."

"I did not encourage him, Clarchen. He said it of his own volition. I am sorry if it causes you distress."

Clara dabbed her eyes with her handkerchief. "It does – indeed, it does – it makes me bitter."

"Clara, I am sorry to hear it, but you must not forget the circumstances. You know of the Declaration your pappa has circulated about me. You know we are forced to the court to obtain what is rightfully ours. You know of the anonymous letter he sent you about me – and who knows to who else. You realize there are laws of honor as binding as the laws of love. You cannot expect me to entertain any thought of reconciliation between us. He is shaking the fruit from our trees like a madman. You realize this, do you not?"

"I do! I realize he has gone too far with you – but not with Liszt! Why must Liszt choose? Pappa has lost me already. Why must he lose his friends as well when he has all the greater need of them?"

Robert sighed. "Liszt meant it as a gesture of friendship, Clara. That is all. Should I tell him how you feel?"

He reached for her hand, but she would not give it to him. "It is too late. Pappa knows what Liszt thinks. He has already been refused the ticket."

Robert's shoulders slumped. "Clara, I am sorry. Believe me, if it were in my power I would change it."

vi

The days with Liszt had been days of dinners, champagne, music, and parties – but this peace, this calm, this comfort, this walking once more to Connewitz with Robert, was what pleased her best, this solace left in Liszt's wake. His carriage, drawn by four white horses, large as a gypsy caravan, with a bed and drawingroom, rich with velvets, perfumes, tapestries, like the rooms of a pasha, had departed in the morning like a ship being launched, Liszt himself in full sail as he boarded, catching the wind in his billowing sleeves and the cape of his coat as he waved, cravat rippling like surf, plumes from his hat like spume, swaying himself as one on deck, Leipzig in the dock, the mayor, merchants, musicians, Mendelssohn and the rest like shells on his shore, pebbles and grains of sand. Clara recalled what Chopin had said: He will grant you a little kingdom in his empire.

Liszt had silenced all, carpers, grumblers, growlers, with his vivacity, his sheer verve; the concert had raised almost six hundred and fifty thaler for the Pension of Aged and Ailing Musicians; but Clara was glad to see him go, glad to regain her life; not all his gifts overcame the trembling he induced, the imperative to match his gaiety, thrive on his terms or not at all. He was not Liszt as much as he played at being Liszt; he did not flatter as much as he appeared to flatter. He complimented her first on her technique, twice as large as his own he said, her hands being twice as small, but proceeded immediately with a demonstration of a perfect chromatic glissando, pitting his technique against hers – but she didn't need a chromatic glissando to play Robert's *Carnaval*, and she knew she played it better because she played it as it was, without ornamentation, but she was also jealous: Liszt appeared to have supplanted her in Robert's imagination as a person and performer.

"Robert?"

"Yes, Clarchen?"

"What are you thinking?"

"About Liszt, of course."

"Of course. So was I. What about Liszt?"

"Do you know, it might surprise you to hear this, but I must say I am worn out with all the excitement of the last few days. When he is around I can get no work done – and as much as I admire his pianism I realize his world is not mine. Art should have an intimacy, my Clara, a charm which is absent in Liszt, but it is in your work when you play, and in mine when I compose. For all his splendor I find there is too much tinsel in Liszt's work."

Clara nodded vigorously. "You do not surprise me. That is what I was thinking. When I first heard him in Vienna he so overwhelmed me that I sobbed out loud, but last night he played less freely than I might have wished. It was distracting to see him looking at the notes all the time."

"That was because he was so little prepared."

"But he *should* prepare. It is his responsibility to his public – though I am aware his public rarely complains. If they knew how little he prepares they would be even more amazed – but I think Hiller is right. He plays everything best the first time, after which he embellishes the work to challenge himself – but he is not so good at embellishing as he is at playing."

"That is the very heart of it. He loses the rosy thread of the melody in his embellishments. It is like reading a dictionary instead of a novel. The words are all there, but their form is all wrong."

Clara laughed. "You always know the right thing to say – also, I think too often his enthusiasts have more on their minds than music and I believe he encourages them, but does he not have a girl – a countess, no less – waiting for him in Paris?"

Robert stared a moment before laughing. "The Countess Marie d'Agoult, it is no secret – but he is a man of the world. That is to be expected."

"Even when she abandoned a husband and two daughters to be with him? Even when he has three children of his own with her? and perhaps others by others of whom he does not even know?"

Robert shrugged.

"And you, Robert? If you defend him, do you not agree with him?"

"I am done with all that, Clara. I am in love now with just one girl. For me there can be no other. Liszt is not so lucky."

She smiled, squeezing his hand. He returned the squeeze and they walked on silent and smiling.

The courtroom was set like a church, two columns of wooden benches like pews, a wooden rail separating the columns from the arena. Wieck arrived first and sat in the front row, heading one of the columns of benches, speaking to no one and looking at no one. Clara, Robert, and their counsellor, Wilhelm Einert, sat at the head of the other column. Wieck was alone, appearing more alone for his cravat askew, hair awry, coat a dusty grey, face like ash. He smiled, seeing Clara (her pappa who never smiled except for his advantage), but appeared to those who didn't know him to snarl, twisting his face in a grimace. Clara froze, wanting to speak to him, but Einert discouraged her, not wishing to jeopardize their case, and she knew he was right. Whatever happened, she had lost her pappa.

Einert had recommended conservative dress: musicians had unsavory reputations; Wieck would try to impress the court with their immorality; they would need to impress the court with their respectability; the burden of proof lay upon Wieck, but they could help themselves by presenting a solid front. Spectators filled the room, staring and pointing; Clara wondered who they were, what their interest might be in something that concerned them not at all, shrinking to think they would hear her innermost trials.

The President of the Court presided from his desk, raised on a dais across the arena, not unlike a minister at his pulpit – but, unlike the minister whose business was to forgive, the President's was to judge and sentence. He appeared from a chamber behind the dais, old for his powdered peruke and judicial robes, but young for his smooth face and quick walk. The court stood, sitting again after he had taken his place.

He looked at no one, opening a folder handed to him by a court attendant, taking spectacles from his pocket, and narrowing his eyes as he read. "This court is convened to examine the merit of the plea forwarded by Herr Counsellor Wilhelm Einert, on behalf of his clients, Herr Doktor Robert Alexander Schumann, the composer and writer, and Fraulein Clara Josephine Wieck, the pianist, to convince the father of the said Fraulein Wieck to consent to their marriage, or, in the absence of the said consent, to grant the consent itself. Is that correct?" He looked up. "Herr Counsellor?"

Einert nodded. "That is correct, Herr President."

"And are all parties concerned represented here today?"

"Yes, Herr President. You see my clients before you, Doktor Schumann and Fraulein Wieck, sitting by my side. I believe Herr Wieck intends to represent himself."

The President looked at Wieck. "Is that correct, Herr Wieck?"

Wieck got up. "Yes, Herr President, that is correct."

"Please be seated, Herr Wieck. There is no need to stand until the court calls on you for your testimony. This is a civic case, a domestic case. We are all friends here. I hope we can resolve this soon to the satisfaction of both parties."

Someone snickered; Wieck looked around, unsure of his ground. Clara wished again she could talk to him, hold his hand, but nailed to her seat she could hardly look at him, hardly even move; Robert was no less a statue. Wieck faced the President again, nodding, and sat. "Danke, Herr President."

The President pursed his lips. "I find these cases very sad. The state does not like to come between families to resolve their difficulties, a father and his daughter as in this instance. These are private matters, best settled privately. I had wished the individuals concerned to come to a reconciliation among themselves – but I understand the wish has proven futile. Is that correct, Herr Einert?"

"I regret to say, Herr President, that it is so."

"Herr Wieck?"

"That is correct, Herr President – but a reconciliation implies meaningful offers from both sides, and all my offers were rejected, and I was offered nothing in –"

"Herr Wieck, you will get the chance to air all your grievances in good time. Please be patient."

Wieck pursed his lips, holding his head high.

"Herr Counsellor, we shall hear your story first. How was the reconciliation attempted?"

Einert stood. "Thank you, Herr President. I visited Herr Wieck myself, according to the wishes of the court, to learn the substance of his dissatisfaction. He revealed nothing to me of reasons, but listed a series of conditions – which, if met, would make him consent to the marriage. Unfortunately, the conditions were the same as he had demanded of his daughter, Fraulein Clara, on a previous occasion, which she had already refused. They are such as no man might accept if he wished to maintain the respect of his peers. One might even say they were designed to be refused –"

Wieck shot up, gripping the rail before him. "Herr President, that is not so. I meant the conditions in all sincerity, and I still do. If the … person to whom they are addressed refuses them I cannot help but question his intentions. To me he appears dishonorable. To me he appears still the gadabout and rogue I have always suspected."

There was a murmur behind him; Wieck turned again, glaring at the spectators through narrowed eyes, sweeping the court with his gaze before returning his glare to the President – who spoke quietly. "Herr Wieck, be seated! I have said already that you will have your chance later. You may refute the charges then, but for now you must be guided by the rules of the court. Am I clear?"

Wieck sat, grumbling under his breath.

"Herr Wieck, I asked if I was clear?"

"Yes, Herr President. You were clear."

"Herr Counsellor, please continue."

"Thank you, Herr President." He took a deep breath. "As I was saying, then, the conditions demanded by Herr Wieck were preposterous. He did not appear desirous of a reconciliation. I appealed to him next as a father, to consider his daughter, a brilliant pianist with a brilliant career ahead – and as a musician himself to consider Doktor Schumann, a much respected composer with the promise of much success ahead, both of whom have suffered greatly against his obduracy, but to no avail. Herr Wieck would not be moved. Schumann would not have his daughter, he said, not if it brought about the suffering of thirty."

An uproar burst from the court, in tutti, followed by murmurings, like a door opened on a busy street; all eyes were again on Wieck – except Einert's on the President, and Clara's closed – but Wieck was no longer discommoded by the attention.

"Herr Wieck, is it as Counsellor Einert has said?"

Wieck remained seated, gripping the rail again, knuckles white. "I submit that I might have said it, Herr President, in a moment of anger."

"This a court of law, Herr Wieck. We do not deal in probabilites. Is it, or is it not, as the Herr Counsellor has said."

Wieck spoke in a monotone. "It is as he has said – but I would like it to be known that I spoke under duress. I was about to lose my daughter, my most prized possession –" his voice rose in a sudden crescendo, "to a *scoun*drel."

Again the uproar; again Wieck ignored it; again the President addressed him. "That she is your daughter, Herr Wieck, we know; that she is your most prized possession I am willing to believe; but that Doktor Schumann is a scoundrel has yet to be proved – and until it is proved I must caution you that you leave yourself open to charges of slander."

Wieck continued to grip the rail, speaking in a quiet but trembling tone. "Is it a slander, Herr President, to defend your own daughter against a villain and a mountebank? Is it a slander to protect what is rightfully yours?"

The last uproar, never completely stilled, rose again. Clara stared at Robert staring at her pappa, whitefaced by the slurs but bearing them for her sake – for their sake. The President rapped his gavel continually for order. "I must warn the court to maintain order – or I will be forced to clear the court." As the noise died he turned again to Wieck. "Herr Wieck, once more I urge you to think about what you say and be guided by the rules of the court – or else you leave yourself open to grave charges, indeed."

Wieck struggled, gripping the rail against the urge to stand again. "I do not care. In my daughter's defense I am willing to brave the gravest consequences."

"Herr Wieck, I strongly advise you to care. You do not help your daughter with your demeanor and you greatly harm your own case. Again, I advise you to be patient. Your turn will come. Counsellor Einert?"

"Herr President, there is nothing I can say that would better illustrate our problem with Herr Wieck than his own behavior. You see the difficulty we have in coming to terms. He accepts only his own. His primary concern appears to be Doktor Schumann's ability to care for his daughter financially – but this is an ability Doktor Schumann has more than convincingly demonstrated this past year, when Herr

Wieck himself turned his daughter from his door – he turned from the door his most prized possession, for whom he now says he would brave the gravest consequences. In addition, he spits on Doktor Schumann's cloak in the marketplace, in full view of passersby, continually –"

Again the uproar, again Wieck's indifference, again the President's question of Wieck to corroborate the accusation. "Herr Wieck, is it as the Herr Counsellor says?"

"If your daughter were on fire, Herr President, would you not spit on the flames?"

The President rapped continually with his gavel; after peace had been restored again and the President had warned the court one more time, Einert continued his story, concluding with Wieck's conditions. Wieck remained quiet during the rest of the testimony, the courtroom swelled occasionally with murmurs, but waited mainly for Wieck's rebuttal.

When his turn came Wieck stood tall, holding a folder in his hand, extracting a sheaf of pages; Clara closed her eyes again, knowing what to expect; the pages were more voluminous even than when he had begun to read them to her during their interview. Wieck held them up. "Herr President, these pages hold the essence of my complaints against Schumann. I call it my Declaration. With your permission I would like to read it to the court."

The President nodded. "You may proceed, Herr Wieck."

"Danke, Herr President. I will begin with a complete list of my grievances against Schumann – after which I will provide the proofs of my grievances."

"Please proceed, Herr Wieck."

"I intend to prove, Herr President, that Schumann is no composer and no writer as he pretends. I intend to prove that his music is unclear, mediocre, impossible to perform – and that his writing is as eccentric as his hand is illegible and his speech unintelligible.

"My Clara is still young, unfit and untrained to be a housewife. I shudder to think of her with the perambulator. She was meant for better things, but that is how Schumann would dispose of her. It is beyond dispute that she is a musician of the highest rank, as a pianist and composer, but her expectations of the support Schumann can provide are not realistic. Her career would come to nothing if she were to travel with this incompetent, childish, unmanly person –"

The President had to rap his gavel again for order. "Herr Wieck, once more I must warn you. You go too far. Be more prudent with your words – or supply the proofs."

"I will supply the proofs, Herr President. That is my whole intent. That is what I wish more than anything – for everyone to know what I know."

The President nodded. "As long as you understand, you may proceed."

"One direct proof, Herr President, is the stupidity with which he ruined his own career, paralyzing his finger in an attempt to circumvent the hard but necessary hours of practice at the piano, using a mechanical device – but that is perhaps to be expected of someone as lazy, unreliable, conceited –"

"Herr Wieck!"

Wieck stopped and smiled though he appeared again to snarl. "I beg your pardon, Herr President." He started again, calm again. "In addition, Herr President, he is an alcoholic. He has been in the habit of drinking since his youth and is seen almost every night in beer gardens and wine houses – often by himself, drinking alone. This I can prove. I have witnesses.

"I do not believe he loves my daughter. He has too mystical and dreamy a personality to understand what it means to love. My daughter, unfortunately, believes she can change him. She does not understand that he will change her instead, he will make a housewife out of an artist, he will destroy in months what I have spent years developing.

"To be fair to Schumann, I submit it is not his fault. He has been badly brought up, he lacks social grace, he is spoiled beyond understanding – but I submit as well that that cannot excuse his behavior, cannot excuse his turning a fresh young girl against her pappa with lies – as he has turned other young girls against their pappas with lies." The pace of Wieck's delivery mounted, his voice rose to a roar. "And that in addition to being a liar he is a sot, a fop, a fool, a cad, a parvenu, and a charlatan – that he has jumped to prominence on the back and shoulders of my daughter."

The uproar behind him drowned his voice; the President rapped continually with his gavel for silence. "Herr Wieck, I say this for your own protection. I fear you open yourself constantly, and increasingly more widely, to charges of slander. For your own protection, I will ask you to give me your Declaration to read. I will make the determination in private whether you have grounds for complaint."

Wieck betrayed no emotion. "Herr President, I would like to read my Declaration out loud myself – but to lay your fears to rest I will show you a letter first. You may then decide whether I open myself to slander or not and I will be guided by you." He took a letter from his pocket which the attendant carried to the President. "It is a letter from one Ernestine von Fricken, now Ernestine von Zedtwitz, residing in Asch, now happily married, but once the paramour of Schumann. She was once like a young plant, residing with me, one of my pupils, until she was scorched by Schumann. If I had spit on him earlier I might have saved young Ernestine as well."

There was a brief murmur. Robert and Clara exchanged glances, she squeezing his hand. The President rapped the gavel briefly before turning to the letter. His eyebrows danced as his eyes widened and narrowed. "Herr Wieck, it seems to me this letter does not make your case at all – but rather the case against you."

Wieck stared, saying nothing, seeming bewildered, shaking his head in a nervous twitch.

The President adjusted his spectacles. "I shall read a few lines, which sum the letter in essence."

Still Wieck said nothing, appearing still incredulous, his face still twitching.

"Ernestine von Fricken, a friend it would appear of the Wiecks and Doktor Schumann, writes as follows: *How is my good Clara? I read much about her in the papers, much that gives me and my parents pleasure. She will never be happy without her Schumann. She has assured me repeatedly that she loves him beyond words.*"

He looked at Wieck. "Herr Wieck, these do not seem to me the words of a woman scorned – or scorched, as you would have it."

The murmur of the court turned to laughter, Wieck seemed not to hear, seemed not to hear even the President. "She is hardly the only one, Herr President. This vile

Schumann has consorted with many a helpless girl, among them one of my servants, one Christel."

"And where is this servant, Herr Wieck? Where is this Christel?"

"She would not come, Herr President. I tried to force upon her the import of doing right by the courts, but she would not come. She is a silly girl, a servant, with little understanding of right and wrong, but this I know: the Schumann has had his way with her, many times and more."

"And how do you know this, Herr Wieck?"

"She has as much as spoken to me to that effect, Herr President. She said she loves him too well to speak ill of him."

Laughter swelled again in the court. The President took a deep breath. "That, Herr Wieck, would seem once more to make the case against you rather than for you – but even so I cannot allow such evidence. It is hearsay – and, as such, inadmissable – and, again, slanderous. I shall not warn you again, Herr Wieck."

Laughter rose like a storm. The President rapped his gavel again, but the spectators paid little attention until Wieck himself rose to face them. "Hyenas! All of you, Hyenas! You laugh when a man is threatened to be parted from his daughter by a shit-eating, turd-swallowing toad –"

The roar from the court more than the President's gavel or words cut him off. Only Robert remained still and white in the frenzy that followed, Clara's hand squeezing his hand, her large eyes darting deerlike between him and Wieck, neither of whom spared her a glance. After silence had once more been restored the President addressed him again. "Herr Wieck, I can see you are a man beside himself with anger – which, no doubt, you imagine is justified – but the disrespect you show Doktor Schumann reflects no less as disrespect on the court. Hence, I must disallow all further communications from you to this court. I will look to your Declaration instead to make your case for you."

Wieck rose again.

"Sit down, Herr Wieck. You are no longer at liberty to address the court. You have abused the privilege once too often."

Wieck remained standing. "Herr President, it is not about the Schumann I wish to speak."

The President frowned. "What is it, then?"

"I will be brief. For myself I can bear the truth, I am accustomed to hardship – but it is a sad day for Germany when the courts themselves laugh at the truth. It is for Germany that I ache, Herr President, and you that I blame for the partiality shown today. That is all I wish to say."

The noise swelled in the court, but subsided almost immediately as Wieck sat in expectation of the President's response. Wieck appeared beaten, shoulders bent, looking at the rail before him, hands in his lap, appearing older by far than fifty-four years warranted, so alone Clara shut her eyes to hold back tears. She wished she might save him, go to his side, hold his hand, hide him from the cruel glances, but she squeezed Robert's hand instead, hiding her face in his shoulder. Robert drew a deep breath. Wieck appeared to have defeated himself with his demeanor as much as Ernestine's letter, too obsessed with the matter to sort what was in his favor from what was not.

The President spoke calmly. "Herr Wieck, Germany wishes to discover the truth, whether or not it agrees with your version. If you disagree with the verdict of this court you are free to appeal to a higher court. I will read your Declaration as I have said and you will be informed of the Court's decision. Until then, there will be nothing more for you to do. Herr Counsellor, do you have any further questions?"

"No questions, Herr President, but a statement and a request. Herren Mendelssohn, David, Verhulst, Friese, Count Reuss, Doctor Reuter, and many others of Leipzig's eminent citizens have professed themselves willing to testify if necessary in Doktor Schumann's behalf. I request a copy of Herr Wieck's Declaration – so that we may refute it point by point in the name of what is fair."

"Of course, Herr Counsellor. That was understood."

Einert bowed his head.

ii

The judgment of the court was never in doubt to anyone present, particularly not with the support of Mendelssohn and other Leipzig luminaries strongly behind Robert, who married his Clara at ten o'clock on 12 September, 1840, one day before Clara's twenty-first birthday, and they moved into small but cozy rooms on 5 Inselstrasse, but perhaps a brief note of explanation is necessary regarding Wieck's obduracy. He would have said without hesitation that his greatest joys in life were meeting Beethoven – and Clara; the rest was fodder. He lost everything, his business suffered, and he moved to Dresden, but Robert still sued for slander, for Clara's money, for her belongings, and the court made him pay everything he owed, even making him spend eighteen days in jail – perhaps no more than he deserved, but he had lost, as he imagined, his dearest possession.

He had been the youngest son in a merchant family with little interest in music and declining fortunes, less than thirty miles from Leipzig in Pretzsch, a sickly boy ordained for the ministry. He never practised but became a private tutor in the homes of aristocrats and taught himself music, developing his own pedagogy, borrowing money for a piano dealership, marrying well, tending his daughter like a hothouse orchid, and dreaming of a duke for a son-in-law, at least a baron – never a musician.

His interview with Beethoven is recorded in the Master's Conversation Books. Wieck had pretended to be an ear doctor; Beethoven had asked so many questions he had needed to scribble like a madman. They had drunk red wine, talked like old friends about the Gewandhaus, piano techniques, Bonaparte, democracy, Italian versus German opera; Beethoven had talked also about his deafness, troubles with his brothers, with the Viennese, all mad for Rossini; Beethoven had rolled his eyes and torn his hair, but Rossini had been kinder to Beethoven than the Viennese. Visiting in 1822, appalled by the squalor in which the great man lived (chamberpot under his piano, unemptied for days), he had attempted to raise a subscription for him, but in vain.

He is a dog, the Viennese said, a wild man, a troublemaker; he cannot keep friends; we stay away from him – true, all true, but he was also Beethoven, as much a pure child as a wild man, isolated by genius even more than deafness, his loneliness was legion, and as he had once told Prince Lichnowski there had always been, and would always be, a thousand princes – but there was only one, and could only be, one Beethoven. He said it without exaggeration, without immodesty, and he said it once refusing to perform for guests of the prince among whom were numbered Napoleon's officers, rushing into pouring rain to escape the prince, forfeiting his annual compensation of six hundred florins in the bargain, preferring to lose his remittance than his self-respect. He had also been given the freedom of the city, but arrested for vagrancy, unable to convince the authorities of his own identity.

They had talked as well about Beethoven's servants who laughed behind his back. It was Beethoven's habit, while composing, to pour pitchersful of water over his naked self, howling scales to the walls, before scurrying back to his score, unaware of what he was doing until the paper got too soggy, or tenants howled below about water leaking through the floor. It was considered a curative then, immersions in water, but you can understand the dilemma of his thirtyplus landlords; there is hardly a street in Vienna that was not once inhabited by Beethoven.

Lastly, Beethoven had improvised on the piano. Wieck had left the house drunk, drunk with talk, drunk with music, drunk with rapture even more than wine, a thousand songs in his heart. He had never been so happy, was never again so happy, except during Clara's Viennese success.

They made it up later, father and daughter, but it could never be the same. Wieck had ignored Clara's card sent on his fifty-fifth birthday and Robert's announcement shortly after of the birth of Marie, his first grandchild, but he wrote finally to Robert: *Tempora mutantor et nos mutamur in eis*: Times change, changing us. *For Clara's sake, and for what people think, we should no longer remain strangers. You are also now a father. What need is there for long explanations?*

We were always of one mind where Art was concerned – I was even your teacher – it was my word that got you started in music. You do not need my assurance of sympathy with your talent and noble aspirations.

There awaits you, joyfully, in Dresden,
Your father, Fr. Wieck.

Robert wasn't willing, not right away; when Clara had accepted an invitation to play in Copenhagen and Robert had stayed in Leipzig with the baby, Wieck had spread the rumor that they had been separated; but with the birth of Elise, the second granddaughter, Robert was glad for the reconciliation, less for himself than for Clara.

PART TWO

ROBERT AND CLARA AND BRAHMS

Christiane Brahms sighed, hemming a dress, looking for her husband from their window. In ten years of marriage they had moved seven times. First from a cheap flat because Jakob had found it too hot, next on money she had earned sewing, a third time to a bigger flat when his earnings had improved, a fourth time closer to his employment in St. Pauli where his earnings were better still, a fifth time again for more space (they had stored the new sofa and table in the attic of the first St. Pauli flat for six weeks), a sixth time back to Hamburg when he tired of the lewd atmosphere of St. Pauli, and finally to Ullricusstrasse next to her aunt who owned a shop.

Needless to say she was sick of the moves, costly in themselves, and costly for the elegance he demanded to impress visitors. When they had married he had been less conscious of appearances – or so he had said, and she had been desperate enough to believe him, a dashing young man of twenty-four wishing to marry an old maid of forty-one. Additionally, he never tired of buying whatever caught his fancy: furniture, sheet music, instruments (he had bought a horn for a hundred marks which he used barely once a year), and so much else. Once, when she had surprised him with three hundred marks she had saved from sewing linen, expecting at least humility if not gratitude, he had gambled a hundred marks in the Number lottery and she no longer remembered on what he had spent the rest, only that it had been wasted. She soon learned the kind of man she had married: he lived to spend where others spent to live. For such a man the problem was not earning, but keeping what he earned; he was poor not through lack of money, but through spinning it in a widening spiral, never letting it rest enough to do any good.

Their circumstances were no longer desperate, even with three children (Elise now nine years old, Hannes seven, and Fritz five), but she never knew what extravagance might seize him next, and was careful herself with the household allowance, lighting not even a tallow candle to sew by daylight when she could sit next to the window – but her own comfort always counted for less than the family's, and she kept the rooms bright with white curtains, red geraniums, and embroidery on the walls.

Jakob was out much of the day, a member of the Town Guard, hornist with the band; all citizens between twenty and forty-five had to serve and he was proud to be a citizen, prouder than she who had been born and raised in Hamburg. He also played the double bass with the sextet at the Alster Pavilion. They might have lived happy secure lives, but his eyes were always one size too large for his pocket, and when she attempted to hold him to their budget he grew defiant, insisting he did everything for her, to satisfy the gentlewoman he had married – but she understood him better than he understood himself. He was a peasant from the country, she a burgher of the city, and the longer they were married the more he wished to make up a difference he could never admit.

"Mamma?"

"Ja, Hannchen?"

"In France … are the people very bad?"

Hannes was playing with lead soldiers on the floor. Everything about him was pale, hair of white gold, eyebrows barely visible, eyes flecked blue like ice, and skin colorless as air, but his clothes gave him color, a blue smock and blue socks knitted by his mamma. Christiane looked up from her needlework. "Why do you ask, Hannchen?"

"Pappa and Herr Goetsch were talking yesterday. I heard them."

Fritz, sitting at his mamma's feet, playing with colored beans, looked up momentarily. "Mamma, I also heard."

Turning onto his belly on the floor, lining up his beans, Fritz had already lost interest in the conversation. Elise, sleeping off another of her continual headaches, breathed audibly in the adjoining bedroom. Christiane looked at Hannes. "What did you hear?"

"Herr Goetsch was saying … in France … are bad people."

Fritz nodded, speaking to himself. "Bad … very bad!"

Christiane nodded. "He is right. They are very bad – and the English are the same. They are always fighting with each other – and with everyone else, everywhere in the world. Germans are the best people. They mind their own business."

"But Pappa said they were not so very bad!"

"Your pappa does not know everything. He was only just born when the French came to Hamburg in the year of our Lord, 1806 – and he was born in Heide. In Heide no one knows anything if it does not happen in his backyard. If he had been in Hamburg he would know what they did."

"What did they do, Mamma?"

There had been bitterness between them when she had recognized their differences: she saw the future in the past, understood that deeds had consequences; Jakob focused only on the present. She had been living with her sister and brother-in-law, the Detmerings; he had been their boarder with his friend, Fritz Becker, musicians from Heide, trained at zur Stadt Pfeiferei, certified "Full of Faithfulness, Desirous of Learning, Obedient, and Industrious," and between the two of them played all instruments. His pappa was an innkeeper, also a grocer, still in Heide; his brother a pawnbroker, also a dealer in antiques; the family had wanted him to join the businesses, but he had wanted to be a musician. Musicians were wanderers, no better than gypsies, never settling, no good for families, but he had listened to the fiddlers in the dance halls, at weddings, harvests, and inns, and wanted only to be a musician. He had defended himself: his grandpappa was a wheelwright, a carpenter, and a joiner, who had come from Hanover to Brunsbuttel; his pappa had gone from Brunsbuttel to Wohrden, from Wohrden to Heide; everyone who was here went there, everyone who was there came here, but because he wanted to be a musician he was a gypsy. After the second time he ran away from home, working on a farm for his keep at zur Stadt Pfeiferei, his pappa had relented and let him become a musician. He had come next to Hamburg, a musician's prospects being negligible in Heide, scrabbling for work in the taverns, the streets, and the Alster Pavilion (whenever their regulars were sick). Christiane kept her eyes on the dress she was hemming. "I was seventeen when the French came – and I was in Hamburg. What your pappa does not see with his own eyes he does not believe – but I saw, and I know what they did."

Jakob had proposed after just a week, but if not for their differences they might never have married. She had braided her hair in a poignant effort to appear girlish and hide the first grey from a man seventeen years younger. He had a handsome haughty face, cheeks like apples, chin in the air, and walked like Napoleon – and, if that wasn't enough, he *wanted* her, which alone would have been enough. She had resisted for the sake of modesty, she was old enough to be his mother, but Jakob had said he didn't care about appearances – and won her heart. She had not expected such generosity from a peasant, descended herself from a twig of German aristocracy traceable to the fourteenth century – but her ancestors had given her one leg shorter than the other and a nose that met her chin. She had realized too late that he just couldn't afford better. Her Uncle Detmering had said this would be her last chance, life was short, shorter for her than for him, and she had considered it Destiny. They had wanted the same thing – but, as always, for different reasons: she had looked to the past (no one else had asked her to marry), and to the future (no one appeared likely); he had looked to the present (wanted a wife, she was available and amenable, cooked and sewed).

Hannes looked up from his soldiers, hair framing his face, but his features were so pale they were lost in the frame – except his eyes, so blue they seemed to hover even in the absence of a face, like the smile of the Cheshire Cat. "But Mamma, what did they do?"

"First it was not so very bad. Hamburg became a part of the French empire. They gave us the benefits of a great city, all the benefits of Paris. Then the Russians liberated us – but in just two months the French came back and everything was changed."

"How was it changed, Mamma?"

"They made the city a fortress. They saw how the walls were built, how no one could come in except from the gate, and they wanted a place for their soldiers to rest, where they would be safe for a little while, for a siege, until they could get help."

"What is a siege, Mamma?"

"A siege, Fritzchen, is when you need enough food to stay for a long while without going out. If there is an enemy outside your house, then you must have everything you need inside your house – because you cannot go outside."

"What will happen if you go outside, Mamma?"

"They will kill you. The French would have killed us."

Fritz returned to his beans, but Hannes's eyes widened. "But why, Mamma? Why would they kill you?"

"Because they wanted something that was ours – and we would not give it to them. They were just like you and Elise. If you take her dolly she will fight you to get it back, will she not? It is just like that. If Elise takes your soldiers you will fight her to get them back, will you not?"

Hannes nodded, but his forehead wrinkled.

"It was just like that with the French. They wanted to take Prussia, they wanted to take Austria, they wanted to take Italy, they wanted to take Russia – all the countries they could take they wanted to take."

"But why? Did they not have their own country?"

"Ja, they had France, but they wanted more."

"But why?"

"When people are unhappy they think having more things will make them happy. The people of France were so unhappy they killed their king and their queen and all the rich people who had been taking things from the poor people. Then Napoleon Bonaparte came and instead of taking things from only the rich people they took things also from other countries – and the English are the same, stealing from defenseless countries. It is a pity the world cannot all be like Germans. It would be so much more peaceable in the world."

Hannes nodded, forehead still wrinkled. "Were you in the siege, Mamma?"

"Ja, but I was one of the lucky ones. By the end of the year everyone had to have enough food to last for six months. Otherwise they had to leave the city. Thousands of people were turned away from their own homes. Hundreds of people died."

Hannes's eyes grew so large the blues swam like fish.

"Do not look so worried, Hannchen. You can see it has all turned out all right. By the next year the French had too many problems. Napoleon was defeated and the control of the city came back to the council, but so much damage was done in just months. People wanted only to carry on, but they never forgot – and that is only right. They must never forget what happened – we must never forget. Otherwise, it will happen again."

"That was what Herr Goetsch said – not to forget."

Christiane got up, putting down the sleeve. Jakob had appeared down the street lugging his horn case. "He should know. He was also in Hamburg. He is also older than your pappa." Dragging her leg she crossed the room to the kitchen. It was time to heat supper.

JAKOB WAS NOT A LARGE MAN and lugging the horn was not a problem, but sometimes trundling his double bass he took the space of two; had the stairs been narrower he would have had to hoist it through the window; but he was large in other ways, so boisterous he seemed in two places at once, his smile threatening to fly off his face – but at home, standing next to his wife, he shrank. It wasn't the difference in their ages, but their temperaments: she wished he would stay home more, pay more attention to her than to his double bass; he wished she would accompany him to the Alster, show more interest in his music; but Hannes united them. She smiled serving dinner, showing approval of his plan to take Hannes to the Herr Professor after the meal. The dinner harked to the days of their courtship, eel stew with vegetables in a thin white gravy, black bread, and Rote Grutze (a creamy pudding thick with large juicy berries). She had even put a new cloth on the table.

He recalled why he had asked her to marry him; she had a kind smile, she had always been a good cook, even in the days when he had boarded with her in-laws. You took the chance and made the best of it; otherwise, no one would marry – like Becker, still a bachelor after so many years. "Everything is delicious, Christiane, just like I remember."

"That was what I wanted."

Becker had been with them on the night of the meal, they had sung love songs, he and Becker accompanying on the double bass and horn: "A Merry Soldier Spread His Mantle Wide upon the Meadow Grass," "O Mother, I Want Something," "In Silent Night," "And When the Moon Her Face Does Cover." He had never seen Christiane so gay, and was rarely to see her so again, but that was the night he had proposed.

When Hannes was four he had hummed "A Merry Soldier Spread His Mantle Wide," amazing them with the perfection of his pitch, humming even a Christmas song from the previous season when he had been just three. Jakob never forgot the day, resolving to teach his son music, only to learn he had already fashioned a musical language of his own, scrawling black notes on parallel lines in a book they had given him for Christmas, explaining that when the music went up he drew ascending notes, when it came down descending, and ascribing a numerical value of his own to the notes. "How did you know to write this, Hannes?"

"I made it up, Pappa. I wanted to remember."

Jakob had slapped his knee. "Hah! The boy is a genius! Elise still cannot carry a tune, not even in a carriage – but Hannes…. Hahahah!"

Elise had clapped her hands over her ears. "My head hurts, Mamma. There is too much noise."

For once Christiane had taken Jakob's side against Elise. "In a carriage, of course, she can carry a tune. In a carriage anyone can carry a tune – but Hannes can carry a tune in a thimble!"

Jakob had slapped his knee again. "Hah! Ja, in a thimble! He can carry a tune in a thimble! I must tell Becker!"

Elise had stared at her mamma, eyes turning to glass, hands still covering her ears, and run to the bedroom with her usual complaint: "My head hurts!"

With Christiane's blessing Jakob had begun to teach Hannes the violin, but now he wanted to learn the piano; hence the interview with the Herr Professor.

A cockroach scurried across the table. Jakob smashed it with the flat of his hand, swept it off the table, and wiped his hand on his shirt.

"Jakob! Why do you do that? You know I do not like it. It is not polite."

"What should I do? I should maybe wish him Good Morning first? I should maybe feed him from my plate?"

Hannes and Fritz laughed, Elise wailed from the bedroom, Christiane's face stiffened.

THE CITY OF HAMBURG (from "Ham," an old Saxon word for a bank or shore) sports more canals than Venice, more than London, also more bridges, almost three times as many, two thousand and something; wherries glutted the canals, buildings

203

loomed on either side, mostly grey in the enclosed spaces near the Gangviertal, warehousing tea, coffee, sugar, tobacco, and rice; even the roofs, capping tenements, capping slums, tall, tiled, and narrow, appeared more grey than red. Jakob observed everything as he walked with Hannes, proud of the distance he had traveled since arriving in the city from Heide.

At Hannes's birth they had lived at 24 Specksgang, a gabled tenement in the Gangviertal, not even on the main road but around a tiny court, the Schluterhof, approached through a damp unlit passage. Wooden shoes were a blessing, especially at night, inhabitants hurrying to avoid whatever might crawl, scurry, or slither across their feet. Two centuries ago the lanes around the court had been garden paths, but lack of space within the walls of the city had packed rows of tall skinny rickety houses together of brick and timber and loam. They no longer suffered the smells of sausages, onions, and sauerkraut in their hallways; nor odors in the alleys of fish, rubbish, piss, and shit concentrated by the narrowness of the passages; nor rats large as rabbits scurrying between their feet by night – but Christiane appreciated nothing. Neighborhoods, like people, came in all shapes and sizes: mazes of narrow alleys fanned into wide streets, ancient woodframe houses grew into sturdy buildings of brick and plaster, and people in patched clothes and shabby hats gave way to carriages, gentlemen in collars and cravats carrying walking sticks, and ladies in silk hats carrying parasols. "Very nice, na, Hannes?"

Hannes wore a brown cap, wooden shoes painted red and green, and carried his little violin in its black case. He was too distracted to look at his pappa, the outcome of the interview was too important. "Ja, Pappa."

"We are here – Steindamm, number seven." Jakob understood his nervousness. "Look, Hannes, on the board. The Herr Professor's name is Otto Friedrich Willibald Cossel – hah! but to his mamma he is still Otto – maybe even Ottchen, hey? What do you think?"

Hannes's brow furrowed in thought. "Maybe ... maybe Ottlieb?"

His smile was tentative, but brought a hearty laugh from his pappa. "Hahahah! Ottlieb! That is good! Ja, maybe!"

A servant answered his knock and led them into a room with two black pianos side by side. Hannes stared as at treasures; his eyes fixed as gravity even when Cossel entered the room. "Good morning, Herr Brahms. How is it with you?"

Cossel appeared taller than Jakob because he was thinner; he was cleanshaven with a high forehead and wide mouth; his hair was wet and flat against his head except on one side where it flared into a fan, looking as if he had been awakened from sleep but it was just the style.

"Good, Herr Professor. How goes it with you?"

"Well. It goes well."

Jakob stood, hat in hand. "I know you are a busy man, Herr Professor. I will come to the point. I know you from the Musikverein. We are both members of the union. We even met at one of the meetings."

He paused. Cossel showed no sign of recognition, but gestured to a chair. "Will you not be seated?"

Jakob sat with Hannes (still gazing at the pianos), Cossel across from them. "I come for my son, Johannes, Herr Professor. He is a musician like his pappa – but he wants to learn the piano. I have taught him already, the horn, the flute, the violin – then at least he can play in a band or an orchestra. Take myself, I am now the bassist in the sextet at the Alster Pavilion – after old Oskar died. There is a living in it, but the boy is stubborn" (he laughed) "just like his pappa. He wants to learn the piano, a rich man's instrument. What he will do with it I do not know, but he is set on the piano."

Cossel had once set himself on a career as a virtuoso, but found he lacked the fire, the health, the confidence – also the interest to repeat ad nauseum the pieces the public demanded; the finer work was beyond their ken. He preferred to teach, showing his pupils how to distinguish the good from the bad. "One has to practise that much harder on the piano. One has to be that much better, but there is money to be made, lots of money – if one is a Liszt or a Thalberg or a Clara Wieck."

"Of course, Herr Professor – but not everyone can be Liszt."

"True. Not even Liszt can always be Liszt." Cossel looked unsmilingly down at Hannes, but with pianos in his eyes Hannes remained oblivious. "How old is your Johannes?"

"Seven – almost eight, he is."

"And why does he want to play the piano? Why not the other instruments you are already teaching him?"

Jakob turned his hat in his hand. "He tells me, after he hears me at the Alster, that the bass by itself is nothing – but in concert with the other instruments it is beautiful. So I tell him that is how it is with the organ in the church, all the harmony from one instrument – but it is the piano which affects him, not the organ, after he sees it at the Musikverein. After that, there is no talking to him. It is an expensive instrument, I tell him, not like these other instruments his pappa can teach him – but he is set on the piano."

"That is true. It can be expensive. Are you prepared for the cost?"

Jakob looked at the carpet. "I had heard, Herr Professor, that you do not always … that is, you do not always …" He looked to one side, groping with his hands for the elusive words.

Cossel frowned. "Only when the pupil shows promise. What can you show me?"

Jakob gestured to Hannes. "Hannes, take it out. Take out the violin. Play 'A Merry Soldier Spread His Mantle.'"

Hannes wrenched his gaze from the pianos, jerked his head to shake the hair from his face, tucked the violin under his chin, and drew the bow confidently across, rocking boisterously as befitted the tune, occasionally double stopping for harmony. Jakob rocked along, smiling and looking from Hannes to Cossel and back. Cossel remained still, unsmiling.

Hannes finished with a triple stop. Cossel scratched his chin. "Not bad – for a seven-year-old boy – but that is not a suitable song for a child."

Jakob smiled. "It is a courting song, Herr Professor, with which I courted my wife."

Cossel didn't look at him, but nodded. "What is more important is he plays with feeling – more important to play with feeling than to hit all the right notes, to express with your fingers what you feel in your heart. That is the essence of what I teach."

Jakob, still smiling, pulled a manuscript from his coat and handed it to Cossel. "Also, he composes. He has made up his own notation, see? He wrote the notes himself, his own invention."

Cossel smiled for the first time looking at the manuscript. "That is unusual, that he would invent his own notation."

"He has written more. Let me show you."

Jakob dug further into his coat, but Cossel gave him back the first holding up his hand. "No, all children like to compose like all children like to paint – but first he must learn the basics. If I undertake his lessons I will teach him, first, exercises, the three C's – Czerny, Cramer, Clementi. First we must free his fingers and his hands – then he can compose. Composition comes last. Otherwise, he will forget everything else. How good is his ear?"

Jakob sat upright in the chair. "He hears better than other people see. As easily as you can tell a squirrel from a tree he can tell a C from a C sharp." He grinned. "Why do you not give him a little test?"

Cossel went to one of the pianos and lifted the lid. "Johannes, I want you to turn to the window."

Hannes's eyes had swung back to the pianos as soon as he had finished the song, and now grew larger, straining to see the keys, but he turned his back on Cossel to stare from the window. A woman with a hat and parasol was climbing into a coach; he had never seen so tall a hat and wondered how it would fit in the carriage.

Cossel struck a note.

The woman wore the hat well and climbed smoothly into the coach. "Middle C."

Cossel struck another note, much lower.

The driver walked around and took his seat. "The second B flat below middle C."

Cossel struck two notes at once.

The driver lifted the reins and started the coach. "B flat and F around middle C."

Cossel tried other combinations – in the treble, in the bass, three and four notes together, notes following one another – and each time Hannes responded without hesitation, following all the while the activity in the street. Cossel smiled finally more widely even than Jakob. "You may turn around, Johannes."

Cossel could not stop smiling, and the smile told Hannes everything he wished to hear, but he had eyes again only for the pianos. Cossel spoke to Jakob, his eyes still on the boy, his smile widening further. "The boy has perfect pitch."

Jakob nodded. "I know it."

"I shall undertake to teach him –"

"Good! His mamma will be pleased –"

Cossel held up a finger of caution – "on one condition."

"What condition?"

"Too many times it happens, Herr Brahms. Parents withdraw my best pupils just as they begin to develop, and my teaching is wasted. If I undertake to teach your Johannes you must give me your word that his musical instruction will be left entirely up to me. *I* shall say when he is ready, and for what, and what he is to do next. Are you willing to leave his musical instruction up to me until he knows everything I know?"

"Everything you know, Herr Professor? Of course, I am willing. Then he will know enough."

"I do not say this lightly, Herr Brahms. You know that I still take lessons myself from Doktor Marxsen?"

"Herr Doktor Eduard Marxsen of Altona – ja, Herr Professor, of course, I know. All musicians know of the great Marxsen – but what about his fees?"

"No fees."

"Then he is yours. Keep him until he plays good as yourself." The condition meant little to Jakob; if Hannes played well enough for the taverns and restaurants, for parties in the big houses of Hamburg, he would be assured of an income; as a pappa, Jakob was satisfied.

"Good, now, does he have a piano to practise?"

"No."

"He can use mine. He can stay longer after the lesson, or he can come when it is convenient, but practise he must."

"Of course! You hear, Hannes? Practise, you must!"

Hannes smiled, seemingly to himself. "Herr Cossel. May I look at the piano?"

Cossel nodded, patting his shoulder. Hannes went to the piano and stared at the keys.

"When will you send him?"

"After school he can come. Will that be all right?"

"After school will be all right, twice a week – with practice everyday."

Hannes played a D minor chord followed with a B flat and stared again at the keys.

Cossel watched him. "What are you thinking, Hannes?"

Hannes didn't look up from the keyboard. "If I can really get everything out of it that I want."

"You will get out of it what you put into it."

"That I can do. I can put everything into it – but can I bring it out again?"

Cossel's eyes narrowed with thought; it was the most the boy had said. "That will depend on what is in you to begin. That will depend on what you put into it. That is what we must find out."

There were angels in the frescoes on the ceiling, maybe a hundred cupids and madonnas, swathed in white in a haze of pink and hovering on the wings of finches and eagles. The vault of the ceiling rested on eight columns almost hidden by the drapes adorning the walls of the salon. The columns were fluted and bordered with Egyptian patterns, ibises among reeds, cats and queens with slender necks and eyes like fish. An ocean of faces flooded the room, women and nobility seated in rows, men standing in a crush behind, bearded and balding, decorations flashing, all eyes riveted to the figure at the piano.

The room was silent except for notes cascading from the piano and occasional gasps from women staring like flies caught in a web. A man in the doorway edged forward, poking and prodding through the crush, phased by nothing, not threats in his ears, not elbows in his ribs, not gorgon looks, and standing among the men in the front row seemed less to listen than to glare at the pianist.

His coat shone from one wash too many, but his shoes had lost their shine, almost their soles. In his hands he held a blue beret which too had seen better days. He sported no moustache, no goatee, but his sideburns met under his jaw framing his face. His hair was brown and short and straight, parted on the left, his mouth a scar, his nose a fist, his brow a dome; his eyes, greyish blue, glared with such intensity his thoughts seemed audible.

He knew about Liszt, all about Liszt, kissed by Beethoven, darling of women, envy of men, toast of Vienna, Paris, London, all Europe, boy wonder, man of the world, friend of Berlioz, Paganini, Chopin – but if he practised twenty-five hours a day, as did Liszt, he too could perform like Liszt, so could a monkey trained to push digits one over the other. Where was the magic in such manipulation? being no more than mechanical? prestidigitation? sleight-of-finger?

Beethoven's greatness lay in exploration, mapping what had never been mapped, never been known, never imagined. Ironically, shamefully, a Frenchman, Francois Habeneck, had introduced him to the glory of the Ninth, conducting it as he had heard no German, this final utterance in music, this cul-de-sac of symphony.

He had himself composed a symphony, derived from Beethoven's A major, not bad as derivations went, but nevertheless a derivation; after Beethoven there could be no more than derivations of Beethoven, and he wanted to be more, to pick up instead the baton Beethoven had dropped, wedding the orchestra to the voice, not as in opera, with the orchestra a handmaiden, but an equal partner, orchestra and voice, bride and groom – as Schumann was doing with lieder, making the piano an equal partner with the voice, making them carry equal shares of the melody, drama, and development.

His purpose was as clear as it was royal, but in escaping from creditors in Leipzig, Wurzburg, Magdeburg, Konigsberg, and Riga, the damned rabble of Jew tradesmen, he had found new creditors in Paris, and found himself again at the mercy of Jews, tradesmen upon whom he depended for necessities, and impresarios like Giacomo Meyerbeer, Paris's reigning god of opera, whose *Robert le Diable* had played in almost 2,000 theaters in Europe through the 1830s, whose gargantuan effects, both visual and orchestral, had sent even Rossini into retirement.

Tracing the path that had led him to Liszt the man wrung his beret like a washerwoman. Meyerbeer had seen promise in his *Rienzi* – but been powerless to secure a production, *if* you could believe a man in his position might be so powerless. Meyerbeer was a Jew, like Mendelssohn a Berlin Jew, and like Mendelssohn from a family of bankers, rich even before *Robert le Diable* – and Mendelssohn, like Meyerbeer sabotaging his *Rienzi*, had sabotaged his symphony, withholding comment and racing through it at the Gewandhaus like a greyhound. The Jews had no country, but their cabals permeated the soil, the water, the very air of Europe – but at least with the Jews there was no question of a debt, not even of gratitude; a Jew, by definition, was owed nothing.

Liszt passed for German in Germany and French in France, but was no less Hungarian for passing, and no less a gypsy for his wanderings – and no Jew, perhaps, but just as rich. Two concerts were sufficient to keep him in clover for a year while he, the new Beethoven, the new Meyerbeer, once a conductor, now no more than a copyist, knowing his superiority, gazed with envy and prepared to importune the great man's favor.

Soon he was applauding and disgusted with himself for applauding, following the lead of the audience, tucking his beret under his arm, too preoccupied even to remember what he had heard, glaring at Liszt as if to draw his attention. Everything disgusted the man with the blue beret: infatuated ladies with wide eyes, wider smiles, and legs widest of all; gentlemen no less fatuous, no less silent, showing off with questions to impress the ladies; Liszt himself, basking in adoration, swaying like a sapling in the wind, a reed in a current, his chin in the air, whipping hair from his face, waving hands as he spoke, showing long tapered fingers.

They talked about his last Hungarian concert, Italian refugees, flood relief, Liszt the hero of each episode, center of all attention, savior of all who applied, speaking French as impeccably as a Frenchman. The man glared as if to shout with his eyes, gripping his beret as if he might tear it apart. Would Liszt never cease talking about himself? As if in answer to his question Liszt paused in his speech. "Monsieur, is there something I can do for you?"

The man with the beret spoke hesitantly, uncomfortable in French. "Oh, ah, I wish only to make the acquaintance of the great Herr Liszt – ach, I mean, Monsieur Liszt."

Liszt bowed his head. "And you are?"

"Ah, ah, I am Richard Wagner."

"And you are a musician?"

"Ach, no! I am a com*po*ser."

Liszt smiled; so he had imagined, guessing the man needed help – money. "What might we have heard of yours, Monsieur Wagner?"

Wagner twitched as he spoke. "I have composed an opera, *Rienzi*. It has not yet found a producer, but Meyerbeer has seen it and approves."

Liszt bowed his head again. "If it has found Meyerbeer already you may be sure it will not be long before it has found a production. Let me be the first to congratulate you."

Wagner nodded, almost bowing his head, almost scowling, hating himself for his subservience. "I thank you, Herr Liszt, from the bottom of my heart."

Liszt saw and understood the conflict between the man's words and expression. "In the meantime, I will send you a ticket for my next matinee, if you wish."

Again Wagner nodded. "Oh, ah, Herr Liszt, I thank you again. You are very kind."

Liszt nodded, saying nothing, but keeping his gaze on Wagner as did others.

A silence followed, incumbent now upon Wagner to fill, the need for light conversation which he hated most of all. "Are you familiar, Herr Liszt, with Loewe's setting of 'Erlkonig'?"

"No."

"Ah, just Schubert's?"

"Just Schubert's."

"Och, but that is fine, that is well. Schubert's is better."

Liszt nodded; Wagner fumed at his clumsiness. "I have to leave, Herr Liszt. Where should I leave my address for your ticket?"

"You may leave it with my secretary, Monsieur Cohen."

A man in the audience raised his hand.

Wagner nodded. "Ah, I thank you again, Herr Liszt. Auf Wiedersehen."

"Au revoir, Monsieur Wagner."

Wagner attended Liszt's matinee with his wife, Minna, during which Liszt played his Fantasy on themes from *Robert le Diable*. He might have stayed and thanked Liszt for the tickets as Minna wanted, but Wagner grimaced. "What a vain, misguided, presumptuous, supercilious, selfaggrandizing woman of a man – a mere performing monkey who imagines he is god. He is unfit to tie Beethoven's shoelaces, but he could buy and sell a hundred Beethovens."

Minna was unable to dissuade her husband from his beliefs, unable to dissuade him from proclaiming them to the world at large, unable to dissuade him from publishing an article calling Meyerbeer a pickpocket and Liszt a buffoon – but Wagner was clever enough to publish the article anonymously, hiding behind the initials of a conductor whose work he hated, referring to Meyerbeer as no more than "M," tarring both conductor and Meyerbeer with a single stroke.

Clara was in the kitchen with two servants arranging oysters on a plate, keeping the trout warm, troubled by thoughts of Liszt. He was a child, and untroubled like a child by the consequences of his actions, whether he kept a party waiting (as he had kept them waiting almost two hours) or blazed a trail of abandoned women and children. He had returned a favor, playing in her concert as she had in his, but promising to attend her postconcert dinner, the first she had hosted at home, he had vanished – with two women who appeared to have possessed him after the concert.

She faulted the women, not Liszt, for courting him so brazenly, kissing his hands, caressing his sleeve – but no one mentioned the women. There was no doubt he should more vigorously have discouraged them, but he was too much the gentleman, and she understood how he had been spoiled since childhood by the adulation of Europe, particularly the adulation of women. He was a father – three times a father at the very least, more likely many times more, but had not married even the mother of the three. She was now a mother herself and understood the difficulties, planning to perform in Bremen and Hamburg early the following year, traveling with Robert, leaving their baby Marie with Robert's brother Karl in Schneeberg – but Liszt made opportunities of the absence of his children and the absence of the mother of his children.

"Clarchen?"

Robert was at the door. "Yes?"

"Are the oysters ready?"

"They have long been ready. Where is Liszt?"

"No one knows."

"I do not think we should wait much longer."

"I agree – another half hour. Then we eat."

She said nothing. He refilled her champagne glass. "To your good health, Clarchen, and your magical performance tonight."

How soothing he was, her Robert, how different from Liszt, who would never have given her a moment of peace, always kept her wondering where he was, what he did, with whom, why. As a man, a husband, a father, a composer, in every way, Robert was the finer of the two. A kind word from him banished her anxieties, a kind word from Liszt would only have made her wonder what it concealed. She lifted her glass, beaming. "Thank you, my darling."

"Come. We must not keep our guests waiting."

"I will come – soon. I am almost finished."

"Good."

Robert left. She couldn't have asked for more tumultuous applause than they had received that night, filling the Gewandhaus, 900 strong, repeating parts of their program for the insistent audience, she and Liszt – but she had been uncomfortable, too long without practice, and Robert's works, his "Overture, Scherzo, and Finale" and Second Symphony (in D minor), had been overshadowed, less well performed, less well received, in deference to the excitement over Liszt. There had been other vexations: their carriage had been late, music forgotten, her piano bench unsteady.

They had played a duet, Variations on a Theme from Bellini's *I Puritani*, commissioned by the Princess Belgiojoso (more relief for Italian refugees), who had requested a variation each from Liszt, Thalberg, Pixis, Herz, Czerny, and Chopin. Liszt had linked the variations, provided an introduction and finale, and called it *Hexameron* (collaboration of the six), but only Chopin's contribution had transcended mere virtuosity. Worst of all had been Liszt's histrionics, not merely swaying as he played, but standing, smiling, waving, acknowledging applause, milking applause, smiling at her, appearing her benefactor while competing like a woman, stealing the approbation of the audience while she worried about missing notes. Once more she recalled Chopin's warning, *Liszt will endow you with a little kingdom in his empire*, and understood better the frail man's pique. Those Liszt couldn't conquer with musicianship he conquered with charm, but what passed for charm in a man appeared vulgar in a woman, coquettish at best, and though she was no coquette she could see how a coquette might succeed where a mere artist would fail. Coquetry was a weapon and sometimes she wished herself a greater coquette, seizing victory with a hollow pose, an idle gesture, an insincere smile, like a flatterer, an actor, a Liszt.

Robert had drawn her into the intricacies of Bach fugues, pointing out passages where the theme continually recurred, and she was no longer satisfied with the glories of mere virtuosity, mere excitement, wanted as well the glories of the mind, the heart, the soul, which Bach provided, and Beethoven, but not Liszt. Bach was difficult, but in the service of music, and in the service of music she welcomed difficulties – but in Liszt's work, as in the work of the virtuosos, the difficulties lay in fingerwork, rhetoric, intrepid displays to rouse the audience, and such difficulties she found increasingly unwelcome.

"Clara?"

Livia Frege was at the door. "Yes, Livia?"

"Liszt is here – finally!"

"Finally!" She wiped her hands on a towel. "Ulla, bring the oysters."

"Yes, madam."

"Elena, the kitchen is in your hands."

"Do not worry, madam. I know what to do."

A circle had congregated around Liszt who bowed when he saw her. "Ah, Madame Schumann, my humble apologies for the delay – but you of all people must know how it stands between an artist and his admirers. They never leave you alone."

He was so gracious, smiling so widely, gazing so unwaveringly, almost worshipfully, she almost left his statement unchallenged. "I wonder that they do not. Not one of my admirers holds me for more than fifteen minutes if I do not wish it."

He raised his eyebrows. "You are most fortunate. I wish I might say the same."

The corners of his mouth twitched, but she refused to smile. Raimund Hartel laughed out loud, Ferdinand David followed, so did others, even Robert smiled, but not she. Mendelssohn watched with interest as she recalled her responsibilities. "Well, whatever the reason – your presence honors us."

"Thank you, but the honor is mine."

Hartel's voice lacked conviction. "Yes, yes, of course. The honor is yours, the honor is hers, the honor is everyone's – but who gives a damn? Everyone is honored and everyone is hungry. Let us eat."

David winked at Liszt. "Herr Hartel's wife does not feed him. He lives from one dinner invitation to the next."

Hartel looked at Liszt as well, lowering his voice, speaking with gravity. "He can say this now, while my wife and the other fraus are in the next room with the little one, but I will tell you something."

He called Liszt closer, Liszt bent his head forward – everyone listened more closely.

Instead of speaking in an undertone as Hartel had led them to believe he might, Hartel shouted. "He is right!" The company laughed, Liszt as loudly as the rest. "He is right! My wife is no housewife, but she has no reason not to be a housewife, not like Clara – who adds to her husband's coffers. My wife's sole talent is spending money – *my* money."

Clara did not laugh with the others, but looked at Robert who avoided her look; he imagined himself, stupidly, less a man for his inability to earn more than her; he had ingested her pappa's poison more deeply than he would admit.

Hartel grinned. "Anyway, to get back to the subject, I could eat a whale."

Clara smiled finally. "I am sorry, but all we have is trout." It was a feeble joke, but she was relieved that the party had finally commenced.

Robert carried a bottle of champagne, refilling glasses for the guests, when Liszt clapped him on the back. "Ah, Monsieur Schumann, you have planned it just right. You compose and your wife performs your compositions. I have to do everything myself. You must not be selfish with the talents of your accomplished wife." He smiled at Clara. "I, too, need an interpreter."

Clara could no longer be angry; Liszt was too much the courtier; when so many vied for his attention, his mere glance was flattering. She laughed. "Only Liszt can interpret Liszt. You forget that we others were born with just five fingers to a hand."

"It has been said, Madame Schumann, that I often use my elbows, my nose, my chin, and whatever other appendage I might find to my purpose."

"So *that* is your secret."

"No, my secret is not that I *know* what my fingers are doing – but that I have not a clue. They each have minds of their own. If I knew what they did I could not make them do a thing."

Johann Barth spoke with gravity. "You prove, then, that where music is concerned, Aristotle was wrong. A equals nonA."

Liszt smiled. "I do not know about that, but I do know that there is more wisdom in a glass of champagne than in a river of philosophy." He held out his glass; Robert was quick with a refill.

Mendelssohn's tone was ironic. "If that is your secret, Herr Liszt, merely that your fingers know not what they do, then I must confess myself disappointed. It is said that Paganini murdered his wife for his effects and fashioned the G string of his violin from her intestines. I had hoped your secret might have been at least as provocative."

Clara slapped his wrist. "Oh, Herr Mendelssohn, that is a terrible thing to say."

Mendelssohn shrugged. "I do not make it up. I merely repeat what is commonly known."

Liszt nodded. "Of course. We have all heard the stories. At twilight, with the glow of sunset behind him, it was said you could see the devil at Paganini's elbow."

David nodded agreement. "And who knows now, if he is not with the devil still." Paganini had died the previous year.

Robert spoke somberly. "I saw Paganini, and no one can deny he was the greatest of virtuosos – but Schubert, the greater composer by far, lay dying while the public was mad about wearing gloves a la Paganini."

Liszt echoed the somber tone. "Ah, yes, but Paganini too was overshadowed. He had to cancel a concert once because a newly acquired giraffe at the zoo had drawn his audience."

Mendelssohn's smile was sly. "Maybe, at twilight, with the glow of sunset behind it, we might have seen the devil at the giraffe's elbow – or at whatever passes for a giraffe's elbow."

Not even Clara could resist laughing out loud and picked the moment to call them to dinner. "Come along, everyone. Dinner is served – finally."

The wives were called from baby Marie's room, Clara seated the company at the table in the diningroom, pleased her dinner promised a success after the awkward beginning. Liszt watched Cecile Mendelssohn with interest, a pretty woman, blond hair, violet eyes, but quiet, a banker's wife more than a musician's, not interested in her husband's work, not in the Gewandhaus, not in his composition, not in his conservatory; he knew women well enough to define her from her movements, exchange of glances, the quintessential Biedermeier housewife, happy with house and children; that she was Mendelssohn's wife said more about Mendelssohn than about her.

Clara puzzled him still, not unlike Cecile, but more outspoken – and, of course, the finest woman pianist of their time, which made her more interesting yet. He grinned again. "I am reminded of another Paganini story – actually, about Rossini, but related to Paganini. Rossini, it is said, has cried but three times in his life: first, when he heard Paganini play; next, when his first opera failed; and finally – when, accidentally, he dropped a turkey stuffed with truffles overboard during a boatride."

Rossini's epicureanism was wellknown. After the laughter had settled and guests were serving themselves Barth spoke again. "What is Rossini doing now? Why have we heard nothing new from him in so long?"

Liszt shrugged. "He does not wish it. He has retired. He wishes to make way for the new composers – Meyerbeer, Wagner. Has anyone heard Wagner's *Rienzi*? I was most impressed. I believe Wagner is himself from these parts, from Leipzig."

Clara nodded. "We know Wagner. As a boy he borrowed books from my pappa's library." She looked at Robert. "Robert knows his work better."

Robert shook his head. "Wagner has shown me drafts of *Rienzi*." He shrugged. "I thought it had too much spectacle. I found it an assault on sight and sound – too Meyerbeerish. It is no surprise Meyerbeer found a theater to produce the work."

Liszt sipped champagne. "My dear friend, pardon me for disagreeing, but how can there be such a thing as too much spectacle? The greater the spectacle the better. Spectacle is the essence of opera."

"But not of music. For spectacle you need a cannon, not an orchestra. Meyerbeer's *Huguenots* belongs in Franconi's circus. Music should win your heart, but Meyerbeer succeeds only in nailing it down."

"But again … perhaps."

Robert shook his head. "There is no perhaps about it. There we must disagree."

Liszt just nodded. "Then, with the best intentions, indeed, let us disagree."

ii

Robert's first impulse, hearing the carriage outside, was to hide the empty bottles – but there were too many, he had lost count, he had been sitting motionless too long to move easily, even to lift the bottle in his hand, and hearing Clara laugh (someone from the court must have accompanied her back to the inn) he chose to leave them on the table where anyone might see, make of them what they might, shame her for abandoning him.

This was what he had feared, what he despised about his situation; she was less the wife of Robert Schumann than he the husband of Clara; he had not taken from her the name of Wieck, but she had taken the name of Schumann, she was now the first Schumann in Germany. In Bremen he had been content, the concert was billed as "the Schumanns," his First Symphony complementing her program – but here, in Oldenburg, a wretched side trip they had undertaken at the last minute before the conclusion of their tour in Hamburg, she had been invited to play at court, and he had not – and she had accepted the invitation, leaving him in this dingy room at the inn. The insult was insupportable, but he had made the adjustment to accommodate her – he had allowed her to abuse his kindheartedness.

He sat at the table, unmoving, bottle in hand, candle on the table, watching the night sky as she came in. A streetlamp cast large shadows of the bottles in a row on the wall. Clara noticed nothing at first, accustoming her eyes to the darkness. "Robert?"

He said nothing.

She put her purse on the table, hands on his shoulders. "I had an absolutely wonderful time, my Robert." She rubbed his neck and shoulders. "The best thing about these provincial towns is they are so starved for music that even mediocre talents are appreciated like geniuses – not that I consider myself mediocre, of course!"

She bent to nuzzle her cheek against his head, but drew back smelling the beer. "Robert, are you all right?"

He didn't turn around, but his voice was thick. "Do I not make enough money that you must force me into these humiliating circumstances?"

Clara turned away, taking off her coat, loosening her hair, getting a better look at the bottles. She spoke quietly. "These are not new subjects, Robert. We have discussed them before. I thought we had settled the matter."

"We settled nothing. We identified the problem. That is all. Either I neglect my talent to escort you on trips, or you neglect yours because I am chained to the piano and the *Zeitschrift*. Is that not a fair description of our dilemma?"

"It is fair, and I have submitted my talent to yours for more than a year. I have not practised because then you cannot compose. I have copied manuscripts for you when you needed my help, transcribed your orchestrations. It is now my turn." He still had not moved. "Robert, you must be fair."

"I am *try*ing to be fair – but what is fair to you is worse than unfair to me. It makes me appear womanish in the eyes of the world, a man led by his wife, a man subordinated to the earnings of his wife."

Clara sighed. "It is only so because you make it so. If you are led by what people think you will be oppressed, always, by their good opinion – but if you are led by your own thoughts you will mold their opinion. I thought we had settled that."

He turned finally from the window. His voice remained slurred, but was newly hesitant. She thought he might cry. "It is one thing to say it, Clarchen, but it is quite another to live it."

She still melted when he called her Clarchen, particularly so hesitantly, but if she let him rule her in this now she would hurt them both later. "But we must, Robert. Otherwise, we are lost. We made a plan, we must stick with it. How are we going to go to America for two years if we cannot get through three weeks in Germany without squabbling?"

They had discussed an American tour. European artists were paid almost a thousand thaler per concert in New York, Boston, Philadelphia, Charleston, New Orleans – plus expenses including a staff of secretary, servants, and a carriage. Robert had calculated that two years in America would allow them to retire in Germany – but she wondered how they would manage in America when they squabbled so easily over a subject already discussed.

When he remained silent she forwarded her argument again. "I still say we should go first to Russia. We should see first what comes of that, a tour of four or five months, before we talk anymore about America."

"I was willing, Clara, last winter – but it was not meant to be. I am willing this winter – but you will not go because Liszt is touring."

There had been no question of touring during their first winter as man and wife, a cholera epidemic in Russia had scuttled discussions the second winter, and a tour by Liszt the third. "I will not compete with Liszt. He does not play with you, but against you. He will be your best friend – but only on his terms, and only after he has bested you. I will not give him that satisfaction."

Robert said nothing.

"Robert, this is my time now, while I am young, before I am burdened with children and bad health. This is my first tour in a year and half, time enough to lose ten reputations. New pianists are everywhere nipping at my heels, waiting to take my place. The public looks constantly for new faces. It is difficult enough to keep their interest, but would you have me simply lie down and die? You have heard of Rubinstein, just eleven years old and already they call him the second Liszt. If I rest, Robert, I rust – I die. Can you not understand that? I am a pianist. You knew that when you married me. I thought it was even part of the reason you married me. I must play the piano or I am finished, I am lost, I do not survive. It is not a matter of money, nothing so sordid. It is a matter of who I am and what I am. If I do not perform, I am not Clara Schumann – there *is* no Clara Schumann. That is my gift. If I do not use it I abuse God himself. Can you not see that, you, a composer, who must compose himself to feel alive?"

Robert remained silent, turning again away from her.

She turned away herself, sighing. "I am sorry. I know you think the housewife is greater than the pianist, but then you should not have married me. I have not deceived you in this matter."

Still he remained silent.

"I have one more thing to say."

He looked up.

"I have been invited to Copenhagen to play at the court and I have accepted. From Hamburg I will go directly to Denmark."

He slammed his fist on the table, one of the bottles fell, another rocked. "That is impossible. I cannot leave the *Zeitschrift* with Lorenz any longer. I cannot escort you everywhere you are invited – and a woman alone cannot travel as she wishes. It is unseemly. It is impossible."

Clara remained firm; she was accustomed to worse scenes with her pappa. "You do not need to escort me. There is a woman from Bremen who wishes to accompany me. You may return to the *Zeitschrift* – and to baby Marie. That appears to me the best solution. We will each then have what we wish."

He stared, losing all rage, wondering what she meant, afraid of what she implied. "Clarchen, we have never been separated. Since the day we were married, we have always been together. What do you mean?"

"I mean exactly what I have said, Robert. I do not understand what objection you might have to that."

"But ... what will people think? What will the world say?"

"They will say I am a wife who earns nothing at home, who is gaining her mite for her husband. Why should anyone think ill of me for that, or of my husband for going home to his child and his business?"

"They will not say that, Clarchen. You know how the world is. They will say we are separated, and we will have given them food for gossip."

"But why should we worry about what they say. Do we not know what is true? Is that not what matters most?"

He sighed, knowing she was right. Therese had made the same arguments long before they had married. Besides, counting the baby and the prospect of more children ahead, money mattered more than they liked to think. "I understand, Clarchen – but that does not make it less difficult."

She smiled, knowing she had won, but won for them both; it was what he wanted as well when he didn't let his pride get in the way; she kissed his cheek. "I know, and I am grateful that you understand. It is necessary. You will see. I will make you proud."

"I am already proud."

"I will make you prouder."

"I do not wish to be prouder."

"You will see. It is necessary." She kissed him again.

Mendelssohn was accustomed to luxury and high society, but felt anxious, even dwarfed, waiting in the great room. The room was cool, shielded by blinds from the July sun, but he shivered less from the temperature than anticipation. He had not imagined to what his dinner with the Prussian Ambassador to England might lead, nor his dinner with the Bishop of Chichester where he had played for the company after they had eaten. Apparently, both hosts had praised him highly as a musician and gentleman and the ultimate invitation had been extended.

The room was thickly carpeted, large enough for an auditorium, flanked by columns nestling benches among them built into the walls, and almost empty but for paintings over the benches. He was staring at the organ beside him, wondering about its touch and the music on the stand, when a door opened behind the organ, hidden behind a column, and the Prince appeared, accompanied by the secretary who had led Mendelssohn to the room and now presented him to the Prince.

The Prince's hair was short, curled over his ears, displaying soft highlights; his whiskers were but a whisper on his lip, trailing to his chin. He nodded. "Mr. Mendelssohn?"

Mendelssohn bowed. "Your Highness."

Mendelssohn had barely straightened before the Queen came through the same door; had he not been expecting her he would not have recognized her, girlish in a morning dress, her hair loose behind. He had forgotten; Queen and Prince were each just twenty-two years. He kept his head bent, waiting to be presented again, but a draft from the open doorway blew the music from the organ, sending pages flying to the floor. The Queen's eyebrows rose, "Oh, my goodness!" and she kneeled to gather the scattered sheets. The Prince joined her immediately – and so did Mendelssohn.

When the pages had been collected he dusted his knees and stood up again, smiling. The Prince, too, was smiling, and so was the Queen. The accident had punctured their formality. The Queen was no beauty, shy and smiling more than he had expected, but standing beside him, as vulnerable as any young woman, as informally dressed, and having just shared the floor with him on her knees, she appeared charming – and ravishing when she spoke. "We must apologize for our appearance, Mr. Mendelssohn, but we leave for Claremont this very afternoon – London is simply too hot in the summer – and we shall not have time to change afterward into a traveling dress."

Mendelssohn bowed his head. "I understand, Your Majesty, perfectly. I am delighted simply to make Your Majesty's acquaintance."

"It is only just. We have long been most happily acquainted with your music. It brings us exceeding pleasure."

"The pleasure is mine entirely. I have heard that Your Majesty sings, and that Your Highness plays the organ?"

The Prince was modest. "Only rudimentarily, I am afraid. I am sure your understanding of organs is outstanding Mr. Mendelssohn, but perhaps I can interest you in some of the features of this particular organ."

"Certainly."

The Prince showed Mendelssohn the stops, while the Queen appraised them together. They were not unalike, both serious, but Albert's hair was shorter and thicker, his complexion paler, his face moustachioed with a wisp of hair under his lower lip. Mendelssohn, unlike any musicians they had met, was a family man, without French habits, who did not drink or run with singers. Wellbehaved, welldressed, he seemed conscious of his position, what he owed them no less than what he owed himself.

Unaware of the Queen's scrutiny, Mendelssohn attended to what the Prince showed him until the Queen spoke again. "Will you play something for us, Mr. Mendelssohn?"

"Of course."

He took his seat before the organ and played a chorus from his oratorio, *St. Paul*. Before he had reached the end of the first verse both Queen and Prince were singing along, the Prince also managing the stops, swelling perfectly into the forte, dwindling into the piano.

They applauded when he was finished; the Queen appeared so friendly, so courteous, as did the Prince, that Mendelssohn felt comfortable making a request. "Your Highness, would you do me the honor of playing something for me?"

The Prince raised his eyebrows. "You wish me to play something for you?"

Mendelssohn smiled. "It would give me something to boast about in Germany, Your Highness."

The Prince smiled. "Ah, as you wish, then." He sat at the organ and played clearly, a chorale without benefit of music, not without charm, and using the pedals. The Queen sat by his side, smiling.

When he was finished Mendelssohn clapped softly, only his fingers. "Thank you, Your Highness. Thank you very much indeed. Many an organist could learn much from you."

The Prince nodded acknowledgment. They had been joined in the meantime by the Prince and Princess of Gotha and Mendelssohn was introduced. The Queen led the conversation. "Have you composed any new songs, Mr. Mendelssohn? We do so love to sing the ones that have been published."

The Prince looked at the Queen. "You ought to sing one for him. It will give him something else to boast about in Germany."

Mendelssohn laughed; the Prince and Princess of Gotha looked bemused, unaware of the joke; the Queen smiled, but appeared less sure. "Well, perhaps the Spring Song."

The Prince pursed his lips. "Ah, that would be very well if it were only here, but the music has already been packed for Claremont."

Mendelssohn spoke too quickly. "Oh, but perhaps it could be unpacked."

The Queen looked at him, unsmiling, and he wondered if he had been presumptuous, but she nodded. "We must send for Lady Nelson."

The bell was rung, servants were dispatched for the music, and the Queen once more led the conversation. "In the meantime, let us take tea."

The party relocated through galleries and corridors to a sittingroom dominated by an enormous rocking horse and two large birdcages; paintings of animals by Paul Potter adorned the walls; books, gorgeously bound, lay on tables and filled bookshelves; stacks of music were piled on the piano. The Duchess of Kent joined them as well for tea. After they had settled themselves, after tea had been poured, the Prince of Gotha resumed the conversation. "Where do you get your ideas, Mr. Mendelssohn?"

"Ideas are everywhere, Your Highness, in nature, in people, in paintings – but, with Her Majesty's permission, I would like to recite some verses I wrote when I was seventeen answering that very question."

The Queen smiled. "Please."

Mendelssohn raised his head in recollection and recited slowly.

> If the composer is grave
> He only depresses us;
> But if he is not
> He hardly impresses us.
>
> If he goes on too long
> He puts us to sleep;
> But if he does not
> He cannot be deep.
>
> If he is too clear,
> He cannot be clever;
> But if he is not
> He will lose his endeavor.
>
> All who wield composers' pens
> Succumb to this disease,
> Until they learn this lesson:
> They've but themselves to please.

He looked again at the company, taking a sip of tea; the Prince was smiling, the Queen clapping, softly, fluttering palms together like the wings of a dove. "Very clever, Mr. Mendelssohn."

The Duchess also clapped and smiled. "Delightful."

The Princess of Gotha put her hands in her lap. "And now that my husband has the answer to his question he has no more excuses for not creating musical works to match yours, Mr. Mendelssohn."

The company laughed, the Prince of Gotha the loudest. "None whatsoever, I am afraid."

A message was brought; Lady Nelson had already left for Claremont with the Queen's effects. The Queen pursed her lips, wrinkled her brows, looking at Mendelssohn. "This is most unseemly, indeed. I must say I am quite displeased."

Mendelssohn pursed his lips. "I pray, Your Majesty, that this does not mean you will not sing something else."

The Queen looked at the Prince who shrugged. "Perhaps something by Gluck that you know by heart."

The Duchess went through the stacks of music on the piano. "Let us see what we have here."

Mendelssohn joined her and finding his earliest set of published songs, his opus 8, held it up. "I think this means Your Majesty would prefer *not* to sing Gluck after all."

The Queen laughed, coming to the piano; Mendelssohn sat on the bench, hands ready, but the Queen touched his shoulder. "Wait. The parrot must go out. He screams louder than I do."

The Prince of Gotha picked up the cage with the bird, but Mendelssohn stopped him. "Your Highness, permit me."

The Prince gave him the cage which he took to a servant outside the room before reseating himself at the piano. The Queen had chosen "Schoner und schoner" and sang with a small voice, but clearly, expressively, and almost perfectly in tune. Twice, when he led her to a D, she followed to a D sharp – but the last time, when she should have stopped at the D sharp, she stopped short at D. On the other hand, her German was better than he had expected, but he remembered the Prince was German, from Thuringia.

The Queen clasped her hands at her breast when they finished. "If only I were not so nervous. Otherwise, I have a really long breath."

He had not thought it his place to compliment her, but her confession encouraged him. "I thought Your Majesty took the long G at the close beautifully, all in the same breath with the three notes next to it. I seldom hear it sung so effectively."

The Queen nodded acknowledgment.

"But I have a confession to make, Your Majesty. I must ask you to choose another song. You see, the one you chose was composed by my sister, Fanny Hensel."

"Ah!" The Princess of Gotha and the Duchess exclaimed in unison.

The Prince of Gotha echoed the sentiment. "Aha!"

The Queen raised her eyebrows. "Indeed? Then why was it printed as yours?"

"Our parents did not think it becoming for a girl to put her talents on display."

222

The Prince appeared thoughtful. "Would that be the Fanny Hensel married to Wilhelm Hensel, the painter?"

"Yes, Your Highness. It would, indeed."

The Queen looked at the Prince. "Do you know the lady?"

"We have a painting by her husband, *Miriam*. You have seen it."

"Oh, yes, I remember. My goodness, it *is* a small world – but now I would like to sing one of your songs, Mr. Mendelssohn. You must differentiate them for me from your sister's so I do not choose one of hers again."

Mendelssohn obliged; they sang more songs, the Queen, the Prince, the Prince and Princess of Gotha, the Duchess, singly and in combination; the Prince asked Mendelssohn to improvise on the theme he had played earlier on the organ and a song he had just sung, and Mendelssohn obliged incorporating as well "Rule Brittania" and "Gaudeamus igitur," after which there was much applause. The Queen shook his hand, bidding goodbye. "I do hope you will visit us again soon in England, Mr. Mendelssohn."

Mendelssohn couldn't stop smiling. "With a great deal of pleasure, Your Majesty. Whenever I am in England I am in a constant state of dry intoxication."

The Queen laughed; she and her party took their leave, all but the Prince who led Mendelssohn by the arm. "Let us sit a while longer. Where will you be going next?"

Mendelssohn talked enthusiastically about Leipzig, his "artistic kingdom," where he conducted the Gewandhaus, where he had initiated the conservatory, and about the tasks entrusted him by the new King of Prussia, Friedrich Wilhelm IV.

The Prince listened attentively, rising finally to give Mendelssohn a small jewel box he drew from his pocket. "She asks you to accept this gift from her – as a memento."

Inside was a gold ring, engraved *Victoria Regina 1842*. When Mendelssohn looked up again the Prince was gone; in his place stood the secretary who had led him to the great room with the organ, who bowed, leading him again through galleries, through corridors, past paintings, past footmen, to the door.

Mendelssohn passed a dozen chaises in the courtyard waiting to take the Royal couple and its entourage to Claremont, scarlet postillions, ostrich plumes, crests of lion and unicorn, on the way to his own hansom, waiting to drive him back to Cecile. There was fanfare, the flag on the palace roof was lowered. Next day the court calendar noted: "Her Majesty left the palace at thirty minutes past three."

He dismissed his hansom, too exhilarated to sit still, and walked home instead. A light rain had commenced, but so great was his bliss it protected him like an aura; not a drop touched him all the way home.

Hannes's subscription concert had sold out, thanks in part to his pappa's friends from the Musikverein who had accompanied him through the evening on Mozart's G minor Piano Quartet and Beethoven's Quintet for Piano and Winds; he had aso played an etude by Herz among other works. His pappa had rented the hall of Zum alten Raben (the Inn of the Old Raven), organizing the concert for the "benefit of the continuing musical education of Johannes Brahms." He had ignored the whispers when making his introductory bows: "he cannot be more than seven," "he appears so delicate," "he is so pretty." Herr Cossel had said to let nothing distract him, and he hadn't; he hated to appear younger than his ten years, but his pappa said that only added to the wonder of the American, the impresario in the audience, now consulting with them, his pappa, his mamma, and Herr Cossel, in the tiny office of the inn.

The American, arrayed in a black cloak, black cape, black top hat, high black cravat, and wide white collar, sported a walking stick with a handle of pearl, and had been as visible in the audience as Hannes had been onstage. He showed all his teeth when he smiled, speaking with a narrow nasal voice, appearing not to move his lips. Hannes had looked at him, but he had looked back only once, smiling suddenly his broadest smile before turning as suddenly away, addressing his pappa. "Mr. Brams, I fail to see the difficulty. I can assure you he'll make more in a month in America than he could in a year in Germany. There's a kinda hunger in New York, and Boston, and Philadelphia, for the kinda culture that's second nature to your Hanis."

He never stopped smiling, not even in the office, not even talking, apparently upset by nothing, but the more he smiled the more Herr Cossel frowned and glared – and the larger his pappa's face grew, the smaller his mamma's. Christiane pursed her lips, in conflict about what to do. Jakob's extravagance had sprouted new dimensions: in addition to the costs of moving and furniture and other acquisitions he had decided to go to America, selling all their things, but deciding after all not to go and buying everything back – of course, at a loss. Her aunt had sold the shop for a song to Jakob when her husband had died; he had also bought a dog, rabbits, chickens which he had fenced, doves and a dovecote, for all of which he had paid in merchandise from the shop until the shop was no longer viable and what remained had to be sold – again, of course, at a loss. She spoke hesitantly. "But he is still so young. He is still but a child. That is a difficulty."

Cossel gave her an approving nod, but Jakob shook his head. The American turned his broadest smile on Christiane. "That ain't no difficulty, Mrs. Brams. That's the key to his success. He's so young – but he plays like a grown man. Next year he'll be too old. He's a Moe Zart, Mrs. Brams. He's better'n a Moe Zart."

Cossel almost jumped. "How do you know? How do you know he is better than Mozart? Have you ever heard Mozart?"

The American shrugged, turning to Cossel, still with the smile. "Who in America has heard Moe Zart? But if we tell 'em enough times they'll believe it. They'll believe anythin' if we tell 'em enough times. That's entertainment. Facts're the raw material, and it's my business to shape 'em into commodities."

"Into a fraud! That is what you mean. That is what you are. A fraud!"

Still the American smiled. "How's it a fraud if the public's satisfied? How's it a fraud if the public gets its money's worth?"

Cossel turned to Jakob. "Do you not hear what the man is saying? Do you not see what he is doing?"

Jakob shook his head. "Herr Professor, he is telling the truth. Hannes can make us a lot of money in America. We can use the money. We have two others. What is wrong? Where is the harm?"

Cossel's face turned red. "*Where is the harm?* Our Hannes shows promise of becoming a great pianist, maybe even someday to match Liszt" (he grimaced, pointing at the American), "but this man here, what do you think he sees in Hannes? What? He sees a fountain of gold, nothing more. A fountain of gold – and *you!* You are the same!"

Jakob held his hands open in question. "A fountain of gold – and we should turn away?"

"Herr Brahms, Hannes is your son. He is not a money pump. If you let this man take him away he will put him in one catchpenny Wild West show after another. He will put him between a wild Indian who will dance with his tomahawk and a gunslinger who will shoot holes in cards, he will put him on display between a bearded lady and a midget – like a freak. Is that what you want for our Hannes?"

Hannes's eyebrows rose. He had never left Hamburg; America was no more exotic than Bremen in his experience, but he had read the novels of James Fenimore Cooper, and sometimes lined up his lead soldiers as cowboys and Indians.

Christiane's frown deepened. She understood why her husband was persistent. They had moved yet again from Ulricusstrasse to Dammthorwall, their rent rising from 90 marks to 300. They had enrolled the children in a private school; there was no reason for children to suffer a bad education because the pappa was a spendthrift, and Jakob had agreed though he argued he had survived his own lack of education very well, thank you, if anyone wanted to know; but she wondered if the hunger for gold shrouded all fatherly concern, and voiced her own concern to the American. "Is this true, sir. Is this what happens?"

The American turned to her, losing not a beat, not a sliver of his smile. "He's exaggeratin', Mrs. Brams. He's exaggeratin' everythin'. He's got a good imagination, he has, but he's been readin' too many novels. It ain't like that at all. It ain't nothin' like that. I cain't understand why he's bein' so difficult."

Cossel turned to the American, turning redder, louder. "I shall tell you why. It is because I care about our Hannes. I care about him like I would care about my own son. I taught him for nothing because I saw his promise from the start – and I am not going to let my teaching go for nothing, not now. There is too much at stake."

The American laughed, wiping spit from his cheek. "Ah, Mr. Cossel! I see it now. You should've said somethin' from the start. You'll be paid for your trouble. Of course! You *must* be paid. Without you there wouldn't be no Hanis. There'll be enough money for everyone."

Cossel took a deep breath between his teeth; Hannes thought he would spit again – this time, intentionally. "Money! I care nothing about the money – only about Hannes! You can keep your money. I am not for sale," he turned to Jakob, "and neither is Hannes! Tell him, Herr Brahms! Tell him yourself! Tell him what I should not have to tell you to tell him."

Jakob was getting bolder; Herr Cossel did not need the money like he did. "I do not see what is the harm. It is only right that Hannes should help in every way that he can. We are all family. I do not see the harm."

Cossel became suddenly thoughtful. "Herr Brahms, think for a minute. Mozart came to a sad end because his pappa milked him for money like a machine. He did not know better, but we do. If you do not see the harm, you should see something else. When I agreed to teach Hannes – for nothing, as you begged me then – I made the condition that he was to stay with me until *I* said he was ready to leave, did I not?"

Jakob nodded unwillingly. "Ja, you said."

"And you agreed, did you not?"

"Ja."

"Then would you not be breaking your word if you took Hannes away now?"

Jakob was impatient. "Ja, ja – but who can predict the future? Who could have said what a chance Hannes would get?"

"Only God. That is in God's hands – but in our hands is to keep our word. You must keep your word."

Jakob shook his head, grimacing, avoiding the American, but turning finally back to Cossel with a smile. "Herr Professor, what I said was he should stay until he plays good as you. Hannes is good now. He plays as good as you."

Cossel stared, but just for a moment, before nodding vigorously. "Yes, he does, he plays as good as me – but I also said he should stay with me until he knows what I know, and to know what I know he must learn from Marxsen. I say he is ready now. Next we must ask Marxsen himself."

Jakob hesitated. Eduard Marxsen had studied first with Johann Clasing, who had studied with Schwenke, who had studied with Philip Emmanuel Bach, the son of Johann Sebastien himself. He had studied next with Ignaz von Seyfried, who had studied with Mozart. Seyfried had also been the pupil of Johann Albrechtsberger, who had taught Beethoven. He had been a friend of Beethoven in Vienna. He took a deep breath himself, dropping his smile. "If Marxsen accepts – but what about his fees? Always it comes down to money. Who will pay his fees?"

"Money? He can always make money. He can play in Hamburg. He can play like you play – in restaurants and at parties. He can teach. He can write arrangements for publishers. Money you can always make."

"Not like in America, you cain't."

Cossel turned again to the American. "We are not in America. We are in Germany – and thank God!"

The American looked at Jakob.

Jakob looked apologetic and spoke softly. "First we talk to Marxsen."

"Time's runnin' out, Mr. Brams. That's all I gotta say. Time's runnin' out. Next year your Hanis'll be too old. He's almost too old already."

Jakob spoke more firmly. "First we talk to Marxsen."

ii

The young girl walked in a daze across the street, tilting her head as if she were listening for something, nodding finally and walking slowly into the piano warehouse, BAUMGARTEN & HEINZ. Her walk remained tentative past innumerable pianos, some crated and ready for shipment, approaching the source of her curiosity, the introduction to Beethoven's *Waldstein*, insistent bass, tinkling treble, repeated until an ascending bass met a descending treble in a thunderous embrace. She had heard it before and other works, some familiar, others not, passing the warehouse, wondering who was playing, but hadn't found the courage to follow her curiosity before, trepidatious even now until she saw the performer, a boy of no more than eight, lower lip thrust forward in concentration, pretty blond hair falling across his face.

She backed out of the field of his vision, not wishing to disturb him. When he had completed the first movement she waited to see if he would continue with the second; instead he played the first again, and the second time he finished she stepped forward, applauding and smiling. Listening had given her courage as had the age of the performer.

Hannes looked up, eyes wide, bewildered. A girl was walking toward him through the dim light, dark hair piled on her head in the French fashion in puffs and curls. She wore a white dress and a shawl across her shoulders fastened by a cameo brooch. He frowned. "Who is it?"

The girl smiled. "I am Louise Japha. I am sorry to interrupt, but I had to see who was playing. I hope you do not mind."

Hannes looked at her, still frowning, but shaking his head. "I do not mind."

He appeared older for his expression and the way he played. "And what is your name, if I may ask?"

"Hannes."

Still he frowned, making her feel stupid, prompting her to fill the silence quickly. "You were playing something the other day that I have not heard – a sonata I think it was. Do you know the one I am talking about?"

He shook his head, looking at the keys, raising his hands, bringing them down hard on the thumbs, tracing a theme, developing it with a harmony that made her wince into a key that seemed too distant to resolve until the final cadence appeared more naturally than she would have imagined. "That?"

"Yes. Could you play it a little more?"

227

Hannes played a few more bars, developing briefly a second theme, stopping before the cadence. "Enough?"

She would have been unsettled by the belligerence if not for the girlish voice, but she didn't want him to play against his will. "No, but if you do not want to play ..."

"I do not mind, but it is meant for two pianos. Do you play?"

"Who is the composer?"

"Who do you think?"

"You?"

He stared, making her feel stupid again. "Do you play?"

"Yes, a little bit. I take lessons on the piano with Herr Fritz Wahrendorf and lessons in composition and theory with Herr Wilhelm Grund."

Hannes's eyebrows rose again. Grund was the conductor of the Hamburg Philharmonic. "You take lessons in theory?"

"Yes."

Hannes's lip curled. "You would like to compose?"

She was aware of the prejudice against women composers. "I *do* compose."

Her indignation curled Hannes's lip further. "Will you play something you have composed?"

She wished she had more confidence in her music. "I would rather listen to you."

"Will you play it with me, the second part? I want to hear how it sounds."

"Are you sure it will be all right?"

"Why should it not be all right?"

"I mean, here, in the warehouse?"

"I have permission from Herr Heinz. I do not have a piano at home. I played for Herr Heinz once and he said I could practise here – when there are no customers. I practise anywhere I can, also at Herr Cossel's – he was my first teacher."

"Who is your teacher now?"

"Doktor Marxsen. He is the best teacher in Germany."

He was so sure of himself, his smile, his pronouncements, brooking no disagreement, that Louise wished to reprimand him, but didn't, wanting to hear more of his music. "No, he is not. All of Germany is a big place, but I think the best teacher is Schumann for composition, and his wife for the piano. Someday I will take lessons from them both."

"Schumann?" Hannes laughed. "Robert Schumann?"

The more they talked, the more indignant Louise became. "Yes, Robert Schumann! There is no other. What is so very funny?"

Hannes shook his head, brooking no disagreement, his smile smug in one so young and set in his beliefs. "Marxsen does not think much of him. He is too much of a romantic – too much of a modernist."

"Ah, well, I know your Marxsen. He loves no one after Beethoven. He thinks all the good composers are dead."

"No, he thinks Mendelssohn is a great composer."

"Mendelssohn is good, but Schumann is just as good – better, I think. What have you heard by Schumann?"

"*Carnaval.*"

"Do you not like it?"

"It is tuneful, there are some nice things, but they are all little pieces. There is nothing solid. One sonata by Beethoven, one movement by Beethoven – even just a few bars – and you forget all about *Carnaval*."

Louise could no longer restrain herself. "For a little boy you are very opinionated."

Hannes frowned immediately and she could tell he was not often contradicted, not in matters of music; neither could he have liked the reference to his size. "For a girl, you talk," he hesitated, just long enough to rouse her curiosity – "you talk just like a girl."

He laughed so loudly he astonished her, more pleased with himself for his joke it seemed than his music. She smiled herself. He was, after all, just a boy. "What do you know about Schumann – as a man, I mean, not a musician?"

"Nothing."

"If you knew more about him you might appreciate his music better. Do you know the story about his hand?"

"His hand? What about his hand?"

"He was already in his twenties when he started taking lessons from his wife's pappa. He used a machine to strengthen his fingers to save time, but instead he lost the use of one of his fingers."

Hannes laughed. "Hahah! Such a stupid man!"

Louise almost shouted. "You must not be so … thoughtless. If you laugh at the misfortunes of others you are not very sympathetic yourself." She would not have spoken presumptuously, not to a stranger – but he was a boy, she did it for his own good, and he belittled Schumann whose work had so enriched her life. "As it is it has turned to everyone's benefit. He realized his true calling was composition. Fortunately, he is married to one of the best pianists in the world. His wife, Clara, it is said, plays like a man, but still fulfills her responsibility as wife and mother."

Hannes appeared suddenly chastened and looked away. "Can you not be both, a good pianist and a composer?"

"Of course, think of Mozart, Beethoven, Chopin."

"Mendelssohn!"

"Yes! Mendelssohn!"

He looked at her again. "Shall we try my sonata?"

"I should like that."

They sat next to each other, playing and talking for three hours, discussing technique, composers, and pianos, arranging finally to meet again the next day.

iii

In the rondo from Weber's Piano Sonata in C, opus 20, a harmonic line burrows continuously through the movement for more than four minutes, semiquavers without end. Marxsen had followed it carefully through with Hannes, asking him to practise it for the next lesson, and watched as Hannes flawlessly performed the piece.

He rarely taught children, however precocious, finding them fundamentally uninteresting; technical mastery could be mechanically developed, but not musical mastery, not new solutions to old problems. As a child, a composing child, only Mendelssohn, not even Mozart, had proven interesting, and not even Mendelssohn, not before he was sixteen, with the Octet in E flat. Cossel's recommendation would have meant nothing, nor Hannes's technique, if not for his interest in composition.

Composition was a seductive art, too easily accomplished by too many bad composers, too many of them too young to know better, too often encouraged by adults too uninformed, too doting, to know better – but in Hannes's work he had seen an unwillingness to accept conventional solutions – an exploration instead, sometimes awkward, sometimes successful, toward something different, something new.

Hannes finished, turning to Marxsen. "I have also practised it another way."

"Yes?"

Hannes said nothing, but began to play again. Marxsen marveled; he had transposed the entire harmony from the right to the left hand and played it through again without error. When he was finished he spoke again before Marxsen could say anything. "I have also transcribed it into the keys of E and A flat. I can play them in both keys if you wish."

Marxsen placed a hand on Hannes's back. "Play it in E." He knew he could expect yet another flawless performance, but was no less thrilled for knowing what to expect.

Robert pointed to a brown stain on the white pillowsham. "Look at this, Clara! The next time you want to tour – Russia or Germany or England or America – just think about this!" He was in bed, frowning under four blankets, holding up the pillow for Clara's inspection, pushing his lips in and out. "While you are off enjoying yourself I have to sleep in dirty beds. The wife wears pretty hats, red and blue and green and purple, while the husband lays his face down on dirty brown pillows."

Zur Stadt London in Dorpat was as bad as zur Stadt London in Riga, the room was tiny leaving barely space to stand, but Clara would not be bullied. Three months into the marriage she had learned: Robert was never entirely well, never had been and never would be; he was merely better sometimes than others, that was the best he could do, that was Robert, but she would not be bullied. "Robert, why must you remember every little discomfort? You said it yourself. We spend more than we earn. We are doing what we have to do. Do you think it is easier for me than for you? In addition to the hardships of which you complain I have to give concerts, three hours long, all by myself – and sometimes the halls are so cold it is all I can do to hit the right notes – but this is our life and it is not so bad."

She was reminding him again, he didn't make enough money, he was the husband of Clara Schumann and they now had two daughters. "Yes, I said that, and it was true, we spent more than we earned, but that was a year ago, before I found I have a flair for conducting. That is a talent on which I can build, but instead here I am again squiring you through this savage country where the wind cuts like a knife, heedless of the danger to my health – and to my work."

He mentioned conducting rather than the course he taught at Mendelssohn's Conservatory, "Piano Playing and Composition," to emphasize their difference: she too taught, starting after the birth of Elise, their second child, but only he conducted, the preserve of the man – but his conductorship was no security. He had made his debut late the previous year with his oratorio, *Paradise and the Peri*, and been greeted with a laurel wreath at the podium, but her friend, Livia Frege, who had sung the Peri to much acclaim, suggested later: "If you could only persuade your dear husband to scold a little, to demand greater attention, all would go well at once." She had watched him from the piano; he beat time conscientiously, but never gave the musicians their cues, rarely gave instructions, and then so softly that no one heard. She had attended the rehearsals, explained to the musicians what he expected, and provided cues from the piano. She shook her head now. "We must not count on what is not secure, Robert, and we have long planned this tour. It is what we have to do, what we have always had to do – if for no reason other than to learn it was the wrong thing."

He had resisted her to the end, but she had secured Mendelssohn's help with their itinerary, she had written to Liszt to set his mind at rest about the difficulties of the journey, and he had relented, imagining he would compose a new oratorio, *Faust*, reading continually the play, mapping scenes, but the constant movement, huddles under furs and rugs, his illnesses, the indignity again of his position (a baron had pressed 150 rubles into his palm at a soiree as if he were a servant, Clara had motioned him to keep quiet), all conspired against him. "I cannot help it, Clara. My situation is unmanly, and your conduct is not womanly."

She knew he referred to what he ironically called his "tip" and understood his frustration. He needed routine and familiar surroundings to compose – but what about her own frustration? She could no more give up performing than he could composing; they needed the money. Why could he not understand that? She might long have lost respect for him but for his music. She shook her head, but knew not what to say.

He continued the movement of his lips, in and out, in and out. "This cannot go on, Clara – nor this." He held up again the stained pillow.

She took a deep breath. "Robert, I do not know what to say except what I have always said. I need to perform like you need to compose. I have often surrendered my need to yours, but I cannot always. I do not have the answers any more than you, but I know what I need to do as surely as do you. Why not think about the good that is to come of this tour? Your music gets better known, my reputation grows, and we have more money to show for our pains than we ever did in Leipzig. I cannot believe this means nothing to you. Do not say it is not so."

A strain in her voice, like a scold, made him look up. She wasn't looking at him though it was the longest she had spoken about her feelings, and she was right in everything she said. He had conducted his First Symphony in Konigsberg, would again in St. Petersburg, she had organized players for his Quintet, and performed his *Kreisleriana*, all his works had been well received, and complimented on their "Slavic" breadth. Often he had slept while she had packed half the night following a performance, only to rise at four the next morning, travel all day, and perform the same evening. She sat at the table, resting her elbows, head in her hands, eyes closed, breathing deeply, more tired than he could remember, and he was scared. "Clarchen, I am sorry. I am being selfish, am I not?"

Since their departure from Berlin in the comfortable Flying Coach they had passed through Konigsberg, Tilsit, Tauroggen, Riga, Mitau, in less than a month, and were now in Dorpat, but their greatest challenges lay ahead: St. Petersburg, and Moscow. The last ten miles before St. Petersburg were the roughest and the language turned strictly Russian. Clara shook her head. "You are not well, Robert. It is not your fault, but I cannot help wondering how we will get through three more months together."

"The problem is not serious, Clarchen – just cumbersome enough to make me selfish."

She looked at him again. The problem was hemorrhoids though he had complained as well of rheumatism and dizziness. "The doctor said Napoleon lost Waterloo for the same problem."

He smiled. "He also lost Moscow. You must conquer Moscow – and you will."

She was too tired to smile, but sat by his side in bed, holding his hand to her cheek. "Thank you, Robert, my darling. It does me good to hear you say it."

"If we could only get some decent food it would make all the difference."

She said nothing, squeezing his hand. There was a knock on the door. He looked at her. She shrugged.

"Who is it?"

"We have a special delivery for Frau Schumann from the Countess Sievers."

He raised his eyebrows, looking at her for an explanation.

"She was at the soiree this afternoon. She was most sympathetic." She kissed his hand, opening the door.

"Frau Schumann?"

Two servants stood outside, flanking a cart of two tiers on wheels holding pots, tureens, canisters, decanters, some steaming, some chilled, suffusing the dim hallway with welcome aromas.

"I am Frau Schumann. Yes?"

"The Countess begs you to accept her bounty with her compliments." He lifted the lid from the largest canister, revealing two roasted partridges.

Clara stared so long Robert called from behind. "Clara, what is it?"

The other containers held meat dumplings in a tomato sauce, salmon and mushroom pie, blini and caviar, cabbage pastry, black bread, cold borscht, stewed fruit, jellies, pickles, and wine. There were also dishes, knives, forks, serviettes – candles. An hour and a half later arrived two feather pillows, two sets of bedding, a counterpane large enough to cover the room – also eau de cologne, lavender soaps, sachets.

The two smiled at each other. For the next five days, until he felt well enough to travel to St. Petersburg, Clara's many new admirers continued sending meals and other amenities, and for at least a while Robert was filled again with the excitement with which he had begun the tour.

ii

In winter the frozen Duna became a village, bearing a market where the summer had borne a river; vendors in rows sold timber, carriages, and sleighs, people shoved and drivers yelled as if they were on a thoroughfare. Staring from the window of the sleigh, her muffs on display (a gift from Cecile Mendelssohn when leaving Berlin), Clara clutched the door handle, afraid the ice might crack beneath them, but soon let go laughing at herself: they were no more than straw on the river. Robert slumped under a large yellow furcoat, eyes closed, clutching a fur blanket, footwarmers in place, hiding his face.

The people wore huge furcoats and furcaps covering their faces, peepholes for noses; the poorer people wore sheepskins turning the wool surface inside, bare white leather out, legs and feet swathed in rags tied with string, tramping on wooden soles; many lived in tiny wooden sheds, children in the doorway, some barefoot, clad in no more than a chemise.

As the evening deepened they left the timber market behind. She had never been so far north, never seen the sky shimmer more brightly with stars. She was too excited to sleep all night, but Robert shivered and slumbered.

There were wolves in the forest on either side; she had heard they sometimes appeared by the highway; she could hear them howl and wished she could see them, yellow eyes flickering in the night like fireflies, and offered the driver a bonus if he found one, but it was below freezing, too cold even for wolves.

The sleigh stuck often in the snow through the night; there were stations everywhere, for rest if they wanted or sleep, but it was far enough to St. Petersburg, farther yet to Moscow, and a night on the road saved time and money.

Next morning the sunrise was pink through a gauze of snow, silver over a tangle of giant white birches. She shook Robert, sleeping enough for two, but failing to wake him let him sleep, smiling alone at the wonder of the morning.

THE WINTER PALACE IN ST. PETERSBURG was big enough for a town, and kept growing, gaining extensions, from the Old Hermitage to the New to the Large, so stately the blue of the facade seemed grey, colonnades white, edged with gilt, a gallery running its length mounted with statuary of Roman legionnaires – Roman gods keeping watch.

Clara was led up stairwells of polished marble, past tables of malachite, cabinets with settings of silver, goblets of gold, decorations of jasper, porphyry, lapis lazuli, through a room full of Rembrandts, a garden of exotic plants, goldfish large as trout, birds of paradise, to the family room, a small assembled circle: Nicholas I, his Tsarina, Alexandra, the Tsarevnas, Olga, Marie, and Alexandrine, and Prince Friedrich von Hessen-Kassel, some whom she knew from concerts they had attended in Germany. She played for two hours, among other pieces Mendelssohn's Spring Song, three times by special request, dedicated just recently to herself in Berlin. The Tsarina sat beside her all evening, occasionally interrupted by the Tsarevna, Marie, who also played.

She told Robert everything, talking into the night over a bottle of champagne, showing him the jeweled bracelet given her by the Tsarina; she wished he would visit friends in her absence, admirers of his music, but if he couldn't be with her he preferred to be alone; she wished he might have been happier for her, but he couldn't see beyond what he called his disgraceful situation. She shouldn't have brought the champagne, the bottles lining the window told her what she needed to know. He picked one of the empty bottles as she talked and blew over the top sounding a note. "Can you tell me what note that is?"

The row of bottles was not a new sight; he had not been invited again; he was no more again, he would have said, than Mr. Clara Schumann, she had taken his last name only to give him her first, but she wanted no arguments, not after her triumph.

The note was F sharp; if she guessed correctly he would be angry, but if she didn't he wouldn't believe her, he would accuse her of patronizing him. "Robert, please, I do not want to play games."

He put the bottle in his mouth, puckered his lips, and blew again.

She got up. "Robert, please, I wish you would not do that. It frightens me."

He blew the note again. "What is the note?"

"F."

He slammed the bottle on the table. "F sharp."

She was relieved to see him smile, imagining he had proved himself her better; he was not going to argue, but she hated to think how it might end another time.

MORE THAN ANYTHING Robert enjoyed the Kremlin, visiting almost everyday during their month in Moscow, writing a poem many pages long about the birthpains of its Tsar Bell, largest in the world, 200 tons, Big Ben times fifteen, likening its tongue to the tongue of a poet tolling the presence of the Almighty – another poem about the star, the spark, the inferno that was Moscow, greeting Napoleon's French, and three more poems, all mailed to Wieck. He wrote as well about the Tsar Cannon (forty tons, twenty feet, never fired) and a benison of churches, but most of all about the onion domes emblazoned by the sun, turbans on towers renowned the world over, the touch of the orient, nights of Arabia, minarets of Constantinople, ringed by crenelated walls, crowning the hill on which they held court, watching the city, crowned themselves by crosses.

Crowns shone as well in the Treasury, with swords, scepters, and thrones, bejeweled and blinding, a bowl by Cellini in mother-of-pearl, a saddle studded with diamonds, pearls the size of a baby's fist, just one of which, Clara said, would have covered all their expenses.

In a confectionary, Pedolli's, Robert sat frowning with newspapers and beer; Clara sat smiling with ice cream and cake, scribbling on paper, drawing his contempt. He put the newspaper aside. "Such a child you are, Clara. Ice cream?" He shook his head. "What are you doing?"

She was totting up their own treasure and smiled, slipping a piece of paper across the table:

Gross Profit:	5,600 thaler
Total cost of preparation:	<u>804</u> thaler
Net Profit:	4,796 thaler

It was an amazing sum to have made in four months; it would have taken him five years, but he refused to give her the satisfaction of even a smile and looked away. "My head hurts."

She did not believe him. "What do you mean?"

"I am dizzy. The room spins. I cannot see clearly."

Still she did not believe him. "But you look all right."

"I am not all right. I tell you I am not all right."

She got up. "Do you want to go home?"

He said nothing, but got up, stumbling from his chair, steadying himself against the table.

She came hurriedly to his side. "Robert, what is the matter?"

He puckered, unpuckered, puckered; she stopped his mouth with her hand. "Robert, talk to me. Tell me what is wrong."

He supported himself, arms around her shoulders, holding her so close she almost suffocated, leaning on her so heavily she almost fell. The proprietor joined them, helping her seat him again, nodding sagely. "It happens sometimes with our Moscow beer. It can knock you out if you are not accustomed to it."

Robert sat, head lolling to his shoulder, eyes closed, face blanched, Clara stooping beside him, face tiny with worry, circling him with her arm, steadying his head, the proprietor hurrying for water, a customer fanning his face with a menu. "Robert, please say something. Can you hear me?"

Robert slowly opened his eyes and turned his head in the narrow circle of her arms, color returning to his face, but he appeared to register nothing. The proprietor returned with water and held the glass forward, but Robert appeared to look through it. "Clara?"

"I am right here, darling. I am right beside you."

His face turned white again. "Clara?"

"Yes, I am right here."

"I cannot see you."

"Robert, I am right here – by your side."

He just shook his head.

Clara's face turned white. "Do not tire yourself, my darling. You will be all right. Drink some water."

"Yes, water."

She held the glass while he drank. Slowly, the color came back. He smiled. "I am all right now. I thought I could not see for a moment – but I am all right now."

"Oh, thank goodness, Robert. You scared me so."

iii

"Robert?"

"Yes?"

"Doktor Helbig is here."

Robert grunted, but he might not have heard, staring out of the window from his bed. Dr. Helbig entered the bedroom behind Clara. "How are you feeling today, Herr Schumann?"

Robert grunted again, still staring from the window.

"He is still not sleeping well, Herr Doktor. He sees pictures in the night – horrible pictures, he says." She spoke hesitantly, afraid what the doctor might think.

The doctor spoke calmly. "Doktor Schumann, is this so?"

Robert nodded.

"What do you see?"

Robert said nothing.

Clara clenched her fists. "He sees wolves, Herr Doktor. They chase him through the forest all night. In the morning he wakes up tired and crying."

The doctor remained calm. "Is it so, Doktor Schumann? Is it wolves that you see?"

Robert nodded again.

"Can you tell me what you see – exactly, in your own words?"

"Wolves, all through the night, in the forest, chasing me."

"And where do they come from?"

Robert stared at Clara. "Russia."

The doctor felt he blamed his wife for the pictures; he had felt the same during his last visit. He looked at Clara who smiled in apology, but whether for Robert's fears or to exonerate herself he could not say.

"I do not understand, Doktor Schumann. Can you tell me more clearly?"

Robert turned to the doctor. "There were wolves in the forests when we were driving past. Any moment they could have come out, we had so many breakdowns, and it would have been the end. As it is, I thwart them. Every night I have to thwart them – but it is not without great effort. I do not know how much longer I can keep it up. In the end, they will catch me."

He was breathing heavily, staring wildly, tired apparently from just talking. Clara wanted to hold him, reassure him, but was afraid of a rebuff, afraid he blamed her for the wolves, afraid the doctor blamed her, and remained expressionless. "Every morning he is tired, Herr Doktor, out of breath from running from the wolves – and from crying, his pillow is soaked through."

Despite her stoicism her concern was not lost on the doctor; there was a catch in her voice she couldn't conceal, an involuntary sudden intake of breath. "It appears, then, that something in Russia has started this problem. Do you think you could be more specific?"

Clara shook her head. "We were back from Russia by the end of May – and until August he was all right. When things began to go wrong we were already back from Russia a long time." She didn't mention it, but in June she had become pregnant with their third child; she was now in her fourth month. Clara feared he blamed her for the child, adding to his worries when he was already ailing.

Robert shook his head vigorously. "No, from the beginning, just after Russia, I was sick. I was able to control it better then."

The doctor looked again at Clara for clarification. She nodded. "It is true, he could not work from the beginning. He tried to finish his *Faust*, but then he got started on his *Corsair*, which also he did not finish. He does not usually work like this. When he starts something he finishes it before starting something new. Usually he is tired after finishing a work – but now he is tired because he cannot finish."

"I have done nothing since we came back – nothing. It is making me sick."

He stared at her again; she knew he blamed her and smiled again for the doctor, a painful smile, almost an admission of guilt. "In Russia his routine was disturbed. He lost his focus. He does not know how to get it back." She didn't mention what had happened in August, didn't want to embarrass him, but Mendelssohn had undertaken new responsibilities in Berlin for the King of Prussia and the conductorship of the Gewandhaus had been offered to Gade of Denmark, a friend she had met during her tour. Robert had wanted the conductorship, a post for which he imagined himself the natural successor, Gade was not even German – but he had been elected, the humiliation had to be borne, and Robert had borne it badly.

The doctor's brow furrowed. "I wonder, Doktor Schumann, if that might not be in fact the problem."

"What?"

"You must understand that I say this as one who admires your work tremendously. I play many of your works myself with the greatest pleasure, particularly your *Novelletten*."

"Yes? Do you, really, Herr Doktor? Go on."

"I have known others – accountants, for example – who work at one thing to the exclusion of all others, who pay a price for their dedication. I wonder if your problem is not similar. If you could find something else to absorb you – just for a little while – you might do for yourself what all the medicine in the world cannot."

Robert's lip curled. "What do you suggest, Herr Doktor? That I take up fencing?" Clara laughed, showing solidarity, but her smile remained apologetic.

Robert was a troublesome patient and had resisted the doctor's suggestions before, refusing medicine for fear of poison, refusing to eat off metal plates, but consenting finally to hydrotherapy, immersions in baths, in rivers, which helped, though not enough. The doctor grinned. "Nothing so strenuous, Doktor Schumann, though exercise is always good. I meant a study of physics, or philosophy, or whatever appeals to you."

Clara's eyes widened; she might have said something, but restrained herself; too often Robert refused suggestions just because she found them appealing.

Robert nodded, not looking at the doctor.

"And you must keep up the water treatments."

Again he nodded.

"And walks in the early morning."

Again he nodded.

The doctor spoke to Clara as she saw him to the door, out of Robert's earshot. "The main thing, Frau Schumann, is to keep him comfortable. Artists are different from others, more sensitive. They see things we mere mortals cannot, but they pay the price for their sensitivity. There is nothing to do but to wait out the malady."

"He is better, Herr Doktor – from last month he is much better. Last month he could not cross the room. He tired so easily. You know how he was. Sometimes he thought he was blind."

The doctor nodded; the Schumanns had visited first the Harz Mountains to distract Robert, then Karlsbad for the salts, and finally, now, Dresden, for the change, fresh people, fresh surroundings. Robert liked it well enough to suggest moving from Leipzig permanently. The slight from the Gewandhaus had not helped, but neither did the absence of Mendelssohn who had tirelessly promoted his work and found professorships for him and Clara in the Conservatory. "It is difficult for ordinary people to understand the workings of artists. We take their labor for granted, but have no consideration of the suffering that goes into creativity. Your husband is fortunate to have a wife who is a musician herself, who understands what others can only guess at."

Clara nodded, hardly imagining herself as considerate as the doctor believed. She had the healthy person's skepticism for mysterious ailments, but pondered as well, constantly, the source of his creativity. "Danke, Herr Doktor, for explaining it to me. I will be more considerate yet."

"Good. That is all you can do. I trust your own condition is well?"

She was glad he had asked. "I am well. There is no more morning sickness."

She went back to Robert after the doctor had gone, now sitting up in bed, nodding approval. "He is a good Herr Doktor. I like him."

Clara nodded. "I too like him."

"He understands. If we had not gone to Russia I would not be like this. We should never have gone, but you would not let the matter rest."

She was glad he spoke more freely when alone with her, but resented the implication that the doctor understood him better than she did; despite what the doctor had said she hated the injustice of her position. Russia had been her triumph – *and* his. A wife's triumphs were no less her husband's. "Robert, that is not fair. We agreed upon this even before we married."

Robert might not have heard. "My nerves, they are ribbons – slashed like my face in the Russian wind. We should never have gone."

"Robert, I do not understand how you can say that."

"Look at me. You do not understand? Just look at me."

She looked away. "We needed the money, Robert. You know that we did."

"The money would have come. I was conducting. I was composing. I was teaching. I had the *Zeitschrift*. The money would have come."

"But you are now giving up the *Zeitschrift* – and if we move to Dresden you will give up teaching as well."

"I have to compose. I have lost too much time already – in Russia. Never again, I tell you, not for that length of time, will I let myself be drawn from my work, not for any reason."

Clara would have defended herself, but remembered what the doctor had said; she would be careful in future choosing which arguments to win. "I will never again attempt to compel you against your will, Robert, not in anything."

Robert nodded, but wasn't finished. "My humiliations were bad enough, but your conduct made them worse."

"My conduct?"

"You do not say what is on your mind, Clara, but you write it down – and I read what you write."

"Robert, what are you talking about?"

"In our Russian diary, for the day in the confectionary, when I could not see – do you not remember what you wrote?"

She shook her head. "It was too long ago, Robert. I cannot remember what I wrote so very long ago."

"But I remember it all too well. You wrote that we could not explain my blindness until someone said later that it was the effect of the Moscow beer. Others had experienced the same effect as the beer had on me – on 'Robert's *strong* body.' That was what you wrote."

"But what is wrong with that?"

"I am not impervious to irony, Clara, but since you insist on playing games I will explain. *My* strong body succumbed, but *your* supposedly weaker one did not – and later, when I was seasick during the storm, do you remember what you wrote?"

They had taken a steamship for the return, from Kronstadt through the Gulf of Finland to Stettin in Poland. She shook her head. "I do not. It was too long ago."

"But *I* do. You wrote that almost all of us crowded on the small pavilion on deck – but a few of us, including Robert, *with admirable repose,*" he glared at her, "fled to the lower room of the ship. There are many other such incidents that you have recorded, Clara, but I rest my case. You humor me, but you do not believe me. You mock me while appearing to love me – and this is what hurts the most."

Clara stared; she had meant no disrespect, but understood why he might think so, and wondered if she might not after all have hidden her resentment as he believed. "Robert, if I have not believed you it has been against my will. I am sorry. I begin to understand new things about you and about myself everyday. Believe me, I do – and if I should forget myself again I shall count on you to remind me of it."

Robert stared at her so long she imagined he did not believe her, but finally he looked away, shaking his head, his voice devoid of bluster, his face of anger. "It is not you, Clarchen, it is me. I do not say what is on my mind. It is my own fault." Tears rolled down his cheeks. "You support me, you are always the truest wife, and I always let you down. I am sorry. You deserve better."

She ran to him, cradling his head. "Oh, my Robert, no, my darling, never. You never let me down – but sometimes I am so afraid. I do not always understand what happens to you – but as long as we say what we mean we shall be all right. I love you, my darling Robert."

He snuggled under her arm, curling on his side, resting his head on her breasts, caressing tenderly her belly. "And I you, my Clarchen. That is for always. Even when I am angry that is never in question. You know that, do you not?"

"Of course, Robert! Of course! There was never any question of that!"

iv

His appearance belied his talent, but the boy with the thick dark wavy hair falling over his ears, narrow eyes, wide nose, plump cheeks, thick lips, and the confident, even arrogant, thrust of his jaw, was destined to be the greatest violinist of the nineteenth century, to study with Mendelssohn and Liszt, to popularize the Beethoven and Mendelssohn and Brahms violin concertos, even to be the dedicatee of the Brahms.

The boy smiled continually at Robert and finally Robert nodded, beer in hand, cigar wagging in his mouth. He had torn himself from the party, seeking a little time alone. Once they had decided to move to Dresden they had become busier, happier, convinced they had made the right decision, needing a change, nothing more. Clara had concert engagements in Halle to which Robert had accompanied her gladly, and engagements in Leipzig which he had attended as gladly. Innumerable farewell parties had followed. Leipzig was Clara's birthplace and had been his home for a long time, but both were convinced it was time to leave.

The nod was all the boy needed; he approached Robert holding a glass of punch. "I would like to wish you great good luck in Dresden, Doktor Schumann, though I know you are irreplaceable in Leipzig – you and Frau Schumann."

Robert nodded, smiling in his best party manner, no longer as difficult as less than a month ago. The boy was young, perhaps thirteen, and appeared to know him, but he couldn't place him. "Danke, young man – and who might you be?"

The boy looked scared. "I beg your pardon, Doktor Schumann. I am Joseph Joachim. We were introduced last year – but I apologize. It was presumptuous of me to assume you would remember."

"Pray, do not concern yourself about that. It is I who should beg your pardon. I am not always myself these days. Where was it that we met?"

"You were very busy at the time, Doktor Schumann – staging your *Paradise and the Peri*."

"That is no excuse. I beg your pardon. I shall not forget again."

Ferdinand David, Konzertmeister of the Gewandhaus, joined them. "Indeed, you will not, because today you will hear young Joachim play. Believe me, there has been no such violinist since Paganini."

Robert grinned. "Aha! So he is your pupil. Careful, my boy. David likes to get his pupils young. If he can get them into bad habits at an early age they belong to him for life – but you must remember, always, a good teacher teaches independence."

David grinned. "You are too clever for yourself, Schumann. Master Joachim was considerate enough to get rid of his bad habits before he came to me. I have Herr Bohm of Vienna to thank for that."

"Indeed? Joseph Bohm? You are from Vienna, then?"

The boy seemed no longer scared, but spoke with great seriousness. "Yes, but first from Pesth, where I studied with Herr Stanislaus Serwaczynski. He was the konzertmeister of the opera."

"I know his reputation, the best violinist in Pesth."

"Yes, that was his reputation."

Robert frowned. "Do you not think it was deserved?"

"Oh, yes, absolutely, among all I heard."

"And would it have been deserved in Vienna?"

"Oh, yes! He would still be the best violinist in Pesth."

The boy blushed, unaccustomed apparently to speaking lightly, but appeared pleased with himself when Robert laughed. "And then you came to Leipzig?"

"Herr Bohm thought Herr Mendelssohn might be able to give me the best direction."

"Bohm is a wise man – and Mendelssohn sent you to David?"

"Yes, Doktor Schumann."

David shook his head. "Not exactly. Master Joachim is already beyond the stage where he might benefit from the teachings of another. He merely shows me what he does on his own and I give him the benefit of my counsel – but I find myself the beneficiary in the bargain."

The boy smiled. "Herr David is very kind." Joachim had been nervous auditioning Bach solos for Mendelssohn and remembered Mendelssohn's words exactly: "Smile, man, you have much reason." Mendelssohn had suggested further that they play together every Sunday morning as far as possible, also that he take lessons in harmony, counterpoint, and theory with Moritz Hauptmann at the Conservatory – and in Latin, geography, history, literature, and divinity with Magister Hering. A child prodigy was not to be blamed, neither for being a child nor a prodigy; the parents were invariably at fault, too excited to think clearly, sending their children far distances for long periods of time, often alone to the detriment of the rest of the child's education, and Mendelssohn had seen the ravages in Joachim already at eleven, the serious expression, emotional immaturity, absorption in nothing but the violin, lack of sophistication in all matters except music, hunger not just for music but the admiration it generated, the performer's counterfeit for love. Joachim imagined he was loved not for himself, but his prodigality with the violin.

Their hostess, Minna Hartel, waved from the other room where two grand pianos stood back to back, the curves fitted in an S, the backs raised like large black wings. Clara and Mendelssohn were ready to begin the entertainment, the Scherzo and Wedding March from *A Midsummer Night's Dream*; the Scherzo, scored to open with flutes, perfectly evoking the flutter of fairy wings and tapdance of pixie toes; the effect wasn't the same on pianos, but Mendelssohn compensated by accelerating the tempo while keeping his touch light. Clara, less familiar with the work, followed as far as she could, as fast as she could, but finally raised her hands in frustration and started a Bach fugue.

Mendelssohn stopped and looked across the pianos while Clara finished the fugue. The guests applauded, enjoying the apparent prank. Mendelssohn smiled, applauding himself. "That is funny – thoroughly enjoyable, but I do not remember writing it."

Clara laughed. "You were galloping along at such a pace, that I lost my place. I did not know where I was and the best way for me to find myself is through a fugue, always – by Bach."

The guests laughed, including Robert, but he noted she didn't mind when Mendelssohn showed her up as she minded Liszt.

The Wedding March followed without mishap, Mendelssohn sharpening his attack to match the brass in the score and Clara applying her singing tone to match the strings.

The piece de resistance was the boy Joachim's turn with Mendelssohn, performing the *Kreutzer*. The first yowl of the violin, leaping an octave, turned the guests to statues. The rib of the violin protruded from his chin like a third shoulder, its tone issued like a second voice. His fingers, now strangling, now caressing, spread like a cat's cradle along the neck of the violin, bending and stretching like rubber. The pores of the instrument seemed to breathe no less than the pores of his skin, the tip of the bow, stabbing and receding, focusing the attention of the room.

Livia Frege was next to sing, Clara to play, and Mendelssohn. Robert chose his moment, calling the boy to the verandah with a smile, holding a finger to his lips. He sat with him in silence for a while, still smiling, while Mendelssohn played, finally squeezing his knee, pointing to the nightsky, his face no less bright than the stars. "Do you know, Herr Joachim, that there are creatures out there among the stars who could amaze us with their beauty – but I do not think they would be any less amazed to have heard a boy right here on earth tonight perform Beethoven's *Kreutzer* with Mendelssohn."

Joachim gave him one of his rare smiles; only Mendelssohn's praise meant as much.

Christiane Brahms watched the retreating figures of her husband and Hannes from her window, not without misgiving. Being a gentlewoman she had never frequented the seedier Hamburg locales – indeed, she had been warned against them – but Jakob's first money in Hamburg, even during the time of their courtship, had been earned in the dance halls, giving him a perspective she would never understand. When she voiced resistance he said it was just people being people; it was not their fault if they were not as fortunate as she; they did what they knew best and who was she to sit in judgment? She was no longer a Nissen, but a Brahms, no matter what she might imagine or pretend – and Hannes no longer a boy, but a man, in need of the understanding that came with being a man, such as he himself had received in the locales with no harm to himself. Indeed, it was a necessary part of every man's education. A man should know all kinds of people, the kind no gentlewoman should know, which placed her neatly outside the argument. She knew exactly the kind of people he meant, but it was difficult for a gentlewoman to acknowledge them. The widow living next to Marxsen rented rooms to girls to improve her income – as did a resident in their own new and improved neighborhood on the Dammthorwall.

After the American impressario had returned to America, Jakob had insisted Hannes was old enough to go out in the world. *Out in the world! A boy of ten!* She had screamed her disbelief. It had been an ugly night, she and the children crying, Elise choking so badly she had sent Hannes for the doctor in the middle of the night, greeting his return with freshly brewed coffee. It had ended well, the doctor giving Elise an emetic, Jakob relenting amid the chaos – but never forgetting, and she had relented at length herself to an alternative when Hannes had turned thirteen. If he was not to go out in the world, and if he was not to be a burden to his parents, he could still earn his mite. He played already for merchant families on the Reichsstrasse and transcribed popular operas for the piano (Marxsen had introduced him to the publishers), but he wished to do all he could – and she had sighed, swelling with pride, finally giving her consent.

HANNES DESCENDED THE STAIRS behind his pappa to Zur schwarzen Katze. The basement tavern seemed much different from the afternoon before, not just darker as might be expected in the evening, not just more crowded, but with a different focus, a different purpose. In the afternoon he had played for Herr Grummer, who had barely listened, barely even looked, a sick and sleepy and tired man with sad eyes and sallow cheeks. Music had loomed large in the conversation between him and his pappa and Hannes had felt important, but the evening light had reduced him to an accessory.

A girl sat in a man's lap, giggling as he whispered in her ear, their faces curtained by her hair. Two men argued at another table, one slamming his fist on the tabletop, rattling his stein, spilling beer, the other laughing. In the afternoon there had been no one else, daylight had filled the basement windows; now the room was choked with smoke, amber with lamps and candles – but walking behind his pappa, threading the tables along the length of the bar (almost the length of the room), Hannes felt eyes clamped to his face and back. "Where is Herr Grummer?"

There was a woman behind the bar wearing a white band around her head, her hair hovering in webs. Even Hannes could see she was untidy but not unattractive, fleshy but not without shape, her shoulders soft and round, plump red chest bulging with a slight white meniscus where it strained against a lacy white bodice. "What do you want?" Her voice was sharp, accustomed to obedience.

"I am looking for Herr Grummer."

"Herr Grummer is not well. I am his sister. You can tell me what you want."

"I want nothing. I am Jakob Brahms and I am here for my son, Hannes. He is to play the piano."

Frau Grummer looked at Hannes, still without a smile. "He looks very young."

"He is thirteen."

"He looks younger."

"Herr Grummer said nothing about that. He heard him play yesterday. That was enough for him."

Frau Grummer continued to look at Hannes, saying nothing. Hannes looked at the floor, his head cold, knees like ribbons.

Jakob's voice got sharper. "I cannot stay all evening. I have got an engagement at the Alster. How he looks is nothing to do with how he plays. When he plays he is older even than you look."

Frau Grummer frowned. "He is your son?"

"What am I saying? Have I not said already?"

Frau Grummer lifted her chin. "If it is nothing to you, it is nothing to me. Let him play."

Jakob nodded. "Hannes, go. Play the piano."

Hannes spoke softly, his voice rising so high it almost disappeared. "What shall I play?"

Frau Grummer's voice softened. "It does not matter as long as it is loud – and lively." Hannes saw her eyes were green, staring with more interest.

"I have got to go." Jakob's voice softened as well. "Hannes can play anything – loud, lively, anything – but you will keep an eye on him, na, Frau Grummer? He is just a boy."

Frau Grummer smiled. "Except when he plays."

"Ja – except then – but he is just a boy."

"I shall keep an eye on him. Do not be concerned."

Jakob smiled. "Thank you, Frau Grummer. I am not concerned, not for myself, but his mamma worries. You know how it is."

Frau Grummer held her smile. "I know how it is."

Jakob turned to Hannes. "Hannes, if you have any questions, if anyone gives you any trouble, you go to Frau Grummer, you understand?"

"Ja, Pappa."

He hated to see his pappa leave, and wanted to smile to show his courage, but couldn't. His mamma hadn't wanted him to come, but his pappa had insisted; his mamma said he was just a boy, but his pappa said he was becoming a man, it was nothing to worry about, he was not going to America, just to play the piano; he had played himself in such places before joining the Town Guard and the sextet at the Alster Pavilion; it was good practice, a place to start, and Hannes had nodded, longing to get started. He threaded his way through the tables again, around the narrow space in the middle for dancing (about ten feet square), to the piano wedged under a window, the better to beckon customers from the street. He saw a woman bent over a table passing out steins from her tray, smiling at a man whose hand was under her skirt, but he turned his head, focusing instead on the piano. He hated its jangle, breadcrumbs wedged between its keys, bits of wood among the strings, loose change, its uneven tone, stiff action, but no one cared; the bench rocked, so high it kept him from reaching the pedals easily, but again no one cared.

Zur schwarzen Katze was a tavern, dance hall, some said worse, among the more crowded, more popular, establishments of its kind because of its proximity to the docks, in the Ehebrechergang, Adulterer's Walk, first refuge of sailors pent too long at sea, absent too long from the beds of women, crazy with their dreams. Outside it was cool, but inside it was hot with smoke and sweat, the crush of bodies, and Hannes perspired as well from anxiety.

The ceiling was invisible for the smoke and it was difficult to tell the size of the room. He hated to interrupt the noise and draw attention to himself, but he looked across the dark smoky room at Frau Grummer who nodded and began to play loudly, a waltz, a sweet tune, chords shifting from tonic to dominant to tonic again, the usual progression for such tunes, occasionally varied with a simple modulation, a sally into the subdominant. When he was finished he segued into another tune, another waltz; it was easier than stopping and facing the room again.

As he continued from tune to tune he became aware of feet marking the rhythm of the music, thumping the wooden floor, someone humming out of tune but merry, and gained courage enough finally to stop and face his applauding audience, raucously calling requests – and to start again making a medley of the requests he knew. A girl brought him a stein of beer, placed it on the piano, and whispered while he played. "You play like the devil, but drink up! You have to make it worth your while."

He grinned, understanding what she meant. He was to be paid two thaler an evening, plus all the beer he could drink. His pappa had laughed when the deal had been struck, but he hadn't drunk much beer, just what his pappa let him sip when his mamma wasn't looking. "Danke."

Pleased with his success Hannes felt himself part of the jigsaw of the room, just another piece in place, no longer a matter of curiosity, stopping when he felt comfortable, lifting the stein, starting again. The girl returned to refill his stein and stare; he stared back, noting her round smiling face, red hair in a bow behind, shoulders white under the straps of her dress. She puckered her red mouth blowing him a slow kiss, a low sucking sound terminated with a sudden intake of breath, no longer smiling; his palms were sweaty, but his temples froze, and he felt something was expected but couldn't imagine what.

He nodded his thanks without a smile, but when he stopped again he was as afraid to see her again as not to see her. Peeking from the corner of his eye he saw her giggling at a table, avoiding the embrace of a man with a heavy black beard. When she came again, pitcher in hand, he gulped the beer, and started to play again. She whispered, staring at the stein. "What? You have finished?"

He didn't look at her, pretending to be engrossed in the music, but following her every move. She put down the pitcher after she had refilled the stein and whispered again. "I am called Helga. I want to talk to you … Monsieur. Wait for me the next time you stop."

He felt she mocked him, calling him Monsieur, and continued to play, not looking at her, but nodding. She smiled, adjusting her bodice, saying she would be back when he stopped – but when he didn't stop for a while she came back. "When are you going to stop, Monsieur? Did you not hear me? I said I wanted to talk to you."

She was grinning, shaking her head disbelievingly; he stopped at the next cadence, staring at her, saying nothing. She crossed her arms huddling her breasts, waggling her shoulders, leaning her elbows on the piano. "Do you like me?" Her voice was low and smoky, almost a whisper.

"Ja."

She smiled. "Do you think I am pretty?"

He could see the dark tunnel between her white breasts as she leaned forward, but hardly dared look. "Ja."

"Would you like to touch me?"

The temperature in the room had risen fifty degrees in fifteen seconds; he was hot already from the beer and smoke, sweating from the constant fortissimo on the piano and stretching for the pedal, and swayed on the high bench, barely able to breathe. "Ja."

She removed her elbows from the piano, arms still crossed, dropping her smile, saying nothing until Hannes raised his hands again to the piano, but he held back his hands when she spoke again. "How old are you anyway?"

She seemed angry; he didn't understand his discomfort, didn't like the way she made him feel. "How old do you think?"

She smiled again. "Ten?"

He scowled, hating his size, not yet five feet. "I am fifteen years old."

She laughed. "Of course."

His scowl was not the scowl of a ten year old; she stopped laughing. "Do not be so angry, little man. I should have known. You do not play like a ten year old."

"I could play like this when I was ten."

"Oh, really?"

247

"Really – and I can play even better today. I have given concerts. My teacher is Marxsen of Altona. I can play Bach and Beethoven – but *you* would not be able to appreciate that."

She lost her smile. "Oh, really?"

"Really."

She lifted her chin. "I thought you liked me, but I can see you are really a snob. You think you are too good for me."

"I am just telling the truth."

"Maybe, but you are still a snob – and that is also the truth."

He shrugged, not caring; she was smiling again.

"What is your name, Monsieur?"

"Hannes."

"Monsieur Hannes, do you still want to touch me?"

"Ja."

"Do you have any money?"

He shook his head.

"Then you will have to earn it. Do not look now, but did you see that sailor I was with just now, with the black beard?"

Hannes didn't have to look; he had seen the man with Helga, the beard was unmistakable; he nodded.

"He is very rich – but he is a miser."

"He doesn't look like a rich man."

She giggled. "He is rich tonight. That is all that matters. If you do as I say, he will give me a lot of money, and I will let you touch me. Do you agree?"

Hannes nodded again.

"When you see me sitting at his table again, come to me. Then, if you do exactly as I say, I will let you touch me. Do you understand?"

"But I have to stay at the piano."

"You have to go outside, do you not, or what kind of bladder have you got? Go outside, and when you come back I will be at the table. On your way you must stop at the table. Do you understand?"

Hannes nodded. "All right."

He was glad she had suggested it; he had wanted to go for a while but felt glued to the bench, safe while he played, the piano his protector, though he had soon realized no one seemed to care what anyone did. He saw a sailor lying on his back on a table, another pouring beer into his mouth, others clapping. Occasionally, one of the girls smiled or winked and blood rushed in his head turning him hot and cold again. He was unsteady dismounting from the high bench and stumbled, almost falling as he walked slowly, steadying himself against chairs and tables on his way out.

The cool air refreshed him and he walked more steadily on his return, past the table with Helga and the blackbearded man, keeping his eyes on the piano. "Hannes!"

He looked at her. "Ja."

She patted her lap. "Come here."

He stepped to her side, but she pulled him off balance and strapped him in her lap like a child within her arms. He squirmed, more from surprise than resistance, until she slapped his knee. "Hannes, be still!"

He thought of the spectacle, but no one was watching, he was lightheaded with beer and liked the smell of her perfumed sweat, her arms around his torso, breasts against his back, and stopped struggling.

The man with the black beard smiled, a thin tall man wearing a dirty white cap, a dirty white undershirt, his beard damp with beer and spit, grimy creases appearing in the corners of his eyes as they narrowed with questions.

Helga giggled; her voice purred in Hannes's ear, but she wasn't talking to him. "All right, you, pay attention now. These are the rates."

The man lifted his stein, brushing his mouth with the back of his hand, smiling all the while.

Hannes couldn't see Helga, but heard the smile in her voice. "This is what you get for two thaler." She held Hannes tight, brushing the hair from his ears with her chin, pressing her cheek against his. He felt her hot breath in his ear and began to squirm again, but settled down when she held him tightly, sucking his lobe, putting her tongue in his ear. The sound of her lapping aroused him, amplified like the ocean in a shell, but she held him tightly again when he squirmed, whispering "Be still, Hannes!" and he remained still.

The blackbearded man leaned forward, elbows on the table. "Look, the little bastard is shaking like a rabbit."

Hannes was surprised; the large man had a girlish voice. He didn't understand the discomfort in his pants, the forking prong hidden under the clasp of Helga's hands – and though grateful for the cover he wondered if Helga was aware of what she hid.

"This is what you get for five thaler." Helga unclasped her hands, rubbing the prong under his pants with quick hard strokes – and he panicked, no longer master of his secret, unable to understand what was happening.

The bearded man's laugh, no less surprisingly high than his voice, was loud in his ears. "For a little fucker he has got a big pencil."

Helga laughed, holding him with greater difficulty. "And full of lead."

"Like a rabbit!"

The man's laugh was continuous and breathless, like a long hacking cough; Helga's was no less loud in his ear as she continued to stroke him. Hannes's hips stiffened, bucking of their own accord, and he exploded out of her arms.

"Like a fucking rabbit!"

The pit of his stomach felt warm and seemed to rise and climb his gullet to spray from his mouth a grey liquid, specks of clotted matter, the sour gravy of his glands.

He was on his hands and knees on the floor, shaking with rage, confusion, and frustration, when he became aware of Frau Grummer stroking his back, helping him to his feet, walking him out of the back door, where she let him fall again to his knees to the ground and brought him a basin of cold water.

ii

The next time he played with a glass of water on the piano (Frau Grummer's orders) and a book on the stand, *Kater Murr*, by E. T. A. Hoffmann. Herr Grummer was well again and behind the bar, but his eyes were still sad, his cheeks still sallow; Frau Grummer was nowhere to be seen, but she had met him when he came, told him to come to her rooms in the back before he left. She was glad he had come back, sorry about what had happened, everyone liked the way he had played the piano. He had said nothing; he had come back for Helga, but looked for her in vain. Another girl approached him, prettier than Helga, less round in her face, smiling as she placed a stein on the piano. "From Grummer."

"I am drinking water."

Her smile twisted. "I see." She picked up the stein.

"But let it be. If I change my mind …"

She set the stein down again and turned to leave.

"Where is Helga?"

"It is her day off. I am called Lena. If you want something tell me."

"Will Helga be here on Tuesday?" He played Tuesdays and Thursdays.

"Maybe. What is it to you?"

Hannes shook his head. "Nothing. I was just wondering."

Lena smiled her twisted smile. "Do you want to see her again?"

Hannes shook his head again. "I was just wondering."

"People are never *just* wondering. They are always wondering for a reason – but you do not have to tell me you are sweet on her if you do not want to."

"I am not sweet on her."

"Ah!"

"Tchah!" He turned back to the piano, playing more loudly.

Lena leaned on the piano. "It is no shame to be sweet on a girl, you know – not even a girl like Helga."

Hannes continued to play. "I tell you I am not sweet on her."

"She could teach you a lot, you know." She arched her eyebrows. "I could teach you a lot – if you are willing to learn."

Hannes's head began again to freeze and burn, freeze and burn. There was something he didn't understand that everyone else seemed to know. He pounded the piano more fiercely. "I am not sweet on her."

"Do not be so sure. She told me what happened on Tuesday."

"Nothing happened. I had too much beer. That is all."

"That is not what I heard."

Hannes swept from a waltz to a quick march. "I do not know what you heard – but I was here."

"Why are you getting angry, Hannchen? I am only telling you what I heard."

Her smile infuriated him further; he said nothing, playing more furiously, pretending to read his book.

Lena stopped smiling. "Are you playing from the book?"

Hannes smiled himself, a twisted smile to mock hers. "I am reading the book."

"How can you read and play music at the same time?"

"This is not serious music. This is dance music. I can play it while eating dinner, I can play it in my sleep." He lifted the stein she had brought, drinking while keeping up both rhythm and melody with his left hand.

Lena crossed her arms. "Helga was right. You are a snob."

Again Hannes said nothing, but his heart sped like a metronome too quick for its melody. He didn't like to boast, but couldn't help himself, wanting Lena's admiration as he had wanted Helga's – but if music was not the way he did not know what was.

Lena saw his eyes widen, the fear of a small animal, and nodded, smiling again her twisted smile. "Drink the beer. It will give you courage – little baby."

He was sorry to see her go, but also relieved, not understanding her hostility. He thumped the piano again, inserting his own melodic lines within the lines of the dance tunes, sympathizing with the crazy musician, Johannes Kreisler, in the book he read, seeking refuge in music from the world.

"I say, boy!"

A fat unshaven man sat by the piano, leaning back, resting hands on his belly, an anchor tattooed along one forearm, a cigar clamped between the fingers of one hand, ash dropping on his pants, his grin revealing gaps in teeth yellowed by tobacco.

Hannes looked at the man, but said nothing.

"I heard that you can play anything, boy. Is this true?"

Lena stood nearby, watching and grinning. Hannes's belly contracted, but he nodded.

"Can you play 'Ding Dong Danke Dong'?"

He shook his head. "I do not know it – but if you can hum it I can play it."

The fat man spoke slowly. "I can do better than that. I can sing it."

Hannes nodded.

The fat man put a hand on each knee, stomped his left foot, then his right, establishing a rhythm, keeping time as he sang a simple melody in a pleasant gravelly voice, rocking between two notes, a fourth apart.

> Ding Dong Danke Dong.
> Ding Dong Danke Dang.
> All your love, for a song.
> Look at me, I'm singing.

Hannes accompanied him from the first line, guessing the melody as it progressed. The fat man raised his eyebrows, continuing without interruption.

> Ding Dong Danke Dong.
> Ding Dong Danke Dang.
> You are short, and I am long.
> Look at me, I'm singing.

He cupped his crotch at the third line. Someone laughed at another table; Hannes didn't understand, didn't care; they were enjoying themselves. Someone at the second table took up the song.

> Ding Dong Danke Dong.
> Ding Dong Danke Dang.
> You're all right, and I'm all wrong.
> Look at me, I'm singing.

Hannes added trills, scales, arpeggios, appoggiaturas, as they progressed, new verses being constantly invented, finally inventing one of his own.

> Ding Dong Danke Dong.
> Ding Dong Danke Dang.
> You're so old, and I'm so yong.
> Look at me, I'm singing.

The rhyme wasn't perfect, but that only made it better, funnier, cleverer, more daring; he finished with a flourish, a fanfare spanning the keyboard. The fat man slapped his knees, laughing. "You look like a little fellow, but you play like a giant."

The second table also applauded and Hannes ignored Lena in his triumph, but she was not to be ignored. "You mean he looks like a little girl. Look at his hair. His name should be Hanna."

Hannes felt again the contraction in his belly, heat in his head. He felt he had won a victory, but couldn't explain why. Looking at her he found her staring, eyes wide, at a face in the window above the piano, a hatless head, lank brown hair, handlebar moustache, thread of beard, but most memorable for the pale slivers of his lips silently mouthing her name and the tunnels of his eyes. The face disappeared as soon as he had seen it, but Lena's reverent whisper, "Heinrich!" confirmed what he had seen.

Coming into the bar Heinrich took long strides, slow but deliberate, appearing to walk a straight line through people and furniture toward Lena who seemed rooted, a statue, directing him like a beacon. Hannes wished he might affect her the same way, wished he might affect anyone that way. Neither said a word but when he reached her he picked her up, sat her on the table, kneeled before her, and buried his face in her lap; she moaned, gripping his hair in her fists.

The fat man who had watched the charade with no less astonishment jumped out of his chair with a growl, a speed Hannes wouldn't have imagined possible, and grabbed Heinrich by the neck pulling him from Lena.

Heinrich sprang to his feet, pushing himself backward into the fat man loosening his grip, jabbing an elbow into the fat man's ribs.

The fat man howled, but grabbed Heinrich in a bear hug and began exerting pressure on his spine.

Heinrich raised his feet off the floor, wrapping his legs around the fat man, pulling them both down, sending a chair crashing. Suddenly, sad sallow Herr

Grummer was standing over them, yelling to Hannes to continue playing while he and two others separated the men.

Hannes hammered the keys, howling the melody, kicking the piano in his excitement, making as much noise himself as he could to keep from getting lost in the noise, producing one variation after the other of "Ding Dong Danke Dong."

FRAU GRUMMER HAD TWO TINY ROOMS in the back, but so dimly lit when Hannes came to see her that they seemed large, one lamp turned so low it might have been extinguished, one candle blazing in a candelabra for three. The bed filled almost the entire room, and with a chair and dresser left him little space to stand without touching her, but he didn't mind. He liked her smell of lemons, but wondered what she wanted to talk about. "Herr Grummer was very happy with you today, Hannes. He said you did very well during our little … crisis."

Hannes sat on the bed; Frau Grummer stood at the dresser, pouring from a bottle. The candle on the dresser threw her shadow on the wall, tints of gold on her hands. The lamp, hanging from a corner of the room barely above her head, cast a sheen on her dark hair, on the white band holding it in place, making both hair and band appear silky. Hannes grinned, pleased. "It was nothing, Frau Grummer. It was easy."

"Good. I am, indeed, glad you came back. I was afraid you would not after what happened the first time."

Hannes laughed; he was tired, he had been up early, been to school, to Baumgarten's to practise, walked everywhere, but he was happy with the evening; after what had happened the first time it was a triumph. "That was not your fault."

"But it was. I told your pappa I would keep an eye on you." Frau Grummer turned, holding out a glass. "Take it. You will like it. It will help you to relax."

Hannes hesitated.

"Are you all right?"

"Ja, I am all right. I drank only a little beer."

"Then take it. It is only a sherry, a woman's drink. It will make you feel good."

Hannes took the glass.

They clinked glasses. "Salud, Hannes!"

"Salud, Frau Grummer!" He sipped, feeling better yet – not only for the sherry but the moment with Frau Grummer, the independence of the thirteen year old, the maturity.

Frau Grummer put her glass back on the dresser. "How do you like it?"

She pulled down the straps of her dress; her naked breasts tumbled free. Hannes opened his mouth to answer, but his mouth made no sound. In the spotlight of the candle her breasts appeared red and round and gold, filling his vision. She pushed her dress over her hips and let it slide to the floor, stepping out completely naked. He turned his head; maybe she thought it was too dark to see. "You may look if you wish, Hannes. I would like you to look."

He looked, but still said nothing.

She removed the band of cloth from her head, shaking her hair free, shaking her breasts. "You still did not answer my question, Hannes."

"Ja?"

She bent in front of him to open one of the dresser drawers, showing buttocks as red and round and gold as her breasts. "How do you like it, Hannes?"

His mouth dropped open, but he could say nothing.

She pulled a robe from the dresser. "The sherry, Hannes? How do you like it?"

"The sherry! I like it!"

She saw his eyes wide open and smiled, slipping into the robe. "Hannes, there is nothing to be afraid of."

"I am not afraid."

"Good. I want you to listen to me carefully."

Hannes nodded, more attentive than he had been all evening.

"If you want to work here successfully you must know what happens between a man and a woman. That is one reason your pappa brought you here. Do you know what I am talking about?"

He frowned. "Making money? You are going to give me my money?"

She stared a moment herself, frowning herself with thought before she laughed. "Yes, Hannes, this is about making money, but I am not going to give you your money. I am going to give you something else, if you want it, instead of money. I will keep your money in exchange for what I am going to give you – *if* that is what you want."

She sat by the bed and he shivered. "What are you going to give me?"

"Hannes, to be a man means to be able to protect yourself – means to be prepared – means knowing about the world. I cannot show you everything, but I can show you some things."

His hand was shaking; he got up, put the sherry on the dresser, and did not sit down again.

"If I do something you do not want, you must tell me – and I will stop. Do you understand?"

His voice was a whisper. "Ja."

She took his hand and slipped it under her robe, cupping it around one breast, sighing long and deep. "Ah, Hannes, that feels good. Do you like it?"

He put his other hand forward. "Ja."

She opened her robe again. "Come."

He knelt before her, burying his head in the soft warm cavern she had created with her body and robe, his face in her breasts and belly.

Wagner put down the manuscript on the small round table before him, lifting his wine and swirling it in his mouth before swallowing, his tongue dry from reading – declaiming, rather – for almost two hours, the entire manuscript of his new opera, *Lohengrin*. His cap, yellow with a fringe of green, peeped from the pocket of his jacket, also yellow but with a red and blue braid. He looked around, but the company remained silent. They were the Engels Klub, named for the restaurant at which they met, on the Postplatz every Thursday where they reserved their own special room, for bread, wine, and conversation. The group was puzzled. Rudolf Hubner frowned, knitting heavy brows. "It reads like a play more than a libretto, Herr Wagner. I do not see how it can be set to music."

Hubner was a painter, so was his brother-in-law, Eduard Bendemann, also present, a good friend of the Schumanns, who had just completed a set of frescoes at the Royal Palace; both taught at the Art Institute. "That is precisely my difficulty. There are no quatrains, no couplets, no triplets."

Robert had grown heavier in Dresden and appeared in profile like a penguin. He nodded, sucking on his cigar, sharing Bendemann's difficulty; he had contemplated setting the story of Lohengrin in an opera himself, but had settled instead on the story of Genoveva.

Gottfried Semper, architect of the Court Theater, thumped the table with his fist. "I, too, have the same question. This is an opera, not a symphony; the phrases need more symmetry."

Wagner turned to Semper with a grin. "Ach, my good friends, that is just my point. Why cannot a verbal phrase be molded like a musical phrase? Why cannot an opera be constructed like a symphony? Why not?"

Ernst Rietschel looked like a crow, stooped over his table, black eyebrows arching forward, craggy cheekbones protruding. "It sounds well in theory – but can it be done?"

"Can it be done? I will do it! Then ask me if it can be done."

Rietschel admitted grudgingly. "You read it very well. It is almost scary how well you read it."

Wagner scowled. "If you are scared now, do not bother to listen to the opera. It might frighten you to death. I have a precise musical intention for every passage."

Robert nodded; something moved inside his head like a pulse, a tiny beat of drums. "It will be worth hearing – if it can be done as you say."

Hubner nodded. "Indeed, that is the key – if it can be done. Even a symphony is bound by its time signature. Whatever its subject, whatever its length, the conductor holds it together with his baton."

Wagner grimaced. "Ach, yes, but even that must change. A symphony must be held together, of course, of course – but it must also be allowed to breathe, to grow. Unfortunately, Mendelssohn has taught everyone that a symphony can be packed into a box like a score – but it is not so, it is not so – not if it is done properly."

Ferdinand Hiller was a year younger than Robert, a penguin no less in profile, but his head emerged from his thinning hair like a rock where Robert's remained submerged under thick waves. He raised his eyebrows; he had disagreed recently with Wagner regarding a performance of Beethoven's Eighth, taking the minuet too quickly to suit Wagner. "And I suppose you are the one to show us how it is done. Is that not so, Herr Wagner?"

Wagner seized a breadknife for answer. "Since you are all so skeptical, I will show you exactly what I mean." He bore down with the knife. "This is how Herr Mendelssohn conducts." The "Herr" was ironic, becoming more obvious as he continued, simulating a tremolo, the opening bars of the Ninth, "Nnnnnnnnnnnnnnnn," downbeat, upbeat, down, up, interrupted, "ta-da" falling a fifth, "ta-da" falling a fourth, "ta-da" falling another fifth. His tone was no less regular than his tempo, a steady mezzoforte.

Bendemann and Hubner got out of the way. Wagner slashed the knife briskly through the air, presto, down, presto, up, down and up, down and up, clean regular strokes, reducing the theme to a march. Robert grimaced, the pulse tightened in his head like a drum being tightened, but only Bendemann noticed; he knew of Robert's headaches and visits to the doctor.

Hiller blew smoke from his cigar, shaking his head. "I beg your pardon, Herr Wagner, but that is much too fast. Mendelssohn would not set such a pace, not for the Ninth."

Wagner stopped, pointing the knife at Hiller. "Ach, do not tell me what Mendelssohn would not do. I know what he did! I know! I conducted his Philharmonic Society once in London. I was allowed only one rehearsal, there was no time to wean the orchestra from its bad habits, habits inculcated by Mendelssohn – that is how I became acquainted with his methods. Every allegro became a presto – there was never a genuine forte, never a genuine piano, always mezzoforte." He waved the knife punctuating each expostulation. "When I remonstrated he said to me – och, this is what he said, this is what Mendelssohn said, this is *exactly* what Mendelssohn said. I do not embroider his words, not a tittle nor a jot. He said a slow tempo is the devil to play, a good performance is always a rarity, and with a little care you can gloss over the difficulties by covering the ground at a good stiff pace. That is what your great Herr Mendelssohn said. He picked a detail here, a detail there, and he polished it till it shone, doing great service to the detail – but what I did not understand, what I still do not understand, what I will *never* understand, is why he did not render the same service to *all* the details – unless it was that he cared for an expedient performance more than a good one." He shrugged, flicking the knife again in consequence.

Bendemann touched Wagner's sleeve. "Wagner, I beg your pardon – but please, man, put down that knife."

Wagner stared, turning from Hiller to Bendemann. "But why? Do you not trust me?"

Bendemann nodded. "It is not a matter of trust, but of safety."

Robert put down his cigar. "Bendemann speaks for me. Ever since Doktor Helbig hypnotized me with his key I have had a fear of metals. He says it is psychosomatic, a passing phobia, I will get over it, but in the meantime ... all metals," he shook his head, "they give me a headache."

Wagner put the knife back on the table. "Everything bothers you, Schumann. It is a shame, but I did not mean to upset you."

Robert nodded again, sucking again on his cigar. "But there is something in what you say. I once said something similar to Mendelssohn. An orchestra is a republic, not a subject – but a baton forces rigidity, it regulates what should flow naturally, from the soul of the orchestra."

Wagner shook his head violently. "But there you, too, are wrong. How can I explain it to you people? The response is rigid only if the conductor is rigid. The composer can give only indications, but the tempos which define the work must come from the conductor. What I say is that quick tempos must be taken even more quickly –"

Hiller interrupted. "But is that not just what you accuse Mendelssohn of doing?"

Wagner glared. "If you had only let me finish, Herr Hiller, you would have saved yourself the bother of your question. That is not what I accuse him of doing, not at all. As far as he goes, I commend him – but I accuse him of doing nothing else, I accuse him of doing nothing more. He should also take the slow tempos more slowly. He would then discover the infinite range of tempos in between – which would allow him to announce the entrance of a theme with a ritardando, or the return of a theme, or the introduction of any significant phrase. Ach, why can you people not see what is so very clear to me? Otherwise, it is all over before it is begun and the audience is beaten into submission when it should have been wooed."

The drum in Robert's head tightened whenever Wagner raised his voice.

Wagner pointed his finger at Hiller. "Listen, and I will show you how it is done." He kept his gaze on Hiller, raised his hand, and recommenced the tremolo, "Nnnnnnnnnnnnnnnnnnnnnnnnnnnnnn," downbeat, upbeat, down, up, "ta-da" dropping a fifth, "ta-da" dropping a fourth, "ta-da" dropping another fifth, but more slowly than before, less regularly, and continuing, slowing before each part of the principal theme, the subordinate theme, all the motives they encompassed, now raising, now lowering, his voice, his entire body, for the right effect. The company stared, amazed; had he been less solemn they might have laughed. He had begun the development before they realized he meant perhaps to conduct the entire symphony, certainly the entire movement, humming all the parts himself, all the instruments. Hubner interrupted again. "Yes, Wagner, yes, man, of course. We quite see what you mean, quite."

The others agreed, applauding just in case Wagner had missed their point, all except Robert, who scowled. "I see what you mean, but then the whole work becomes trivial, not to say unbearably long, if it is reduced to one ritardando after the other – but, doubtless, you exaggerate to make your point."

"On the contrary, my dear Schumann, I do not exaggerate at all. That is e*xactly* how it must be played. That is how Beethoven meant it to be played."

Bendemann took a deep breath. "Well, as to that, no one can say. As you said yourself, the composer provides but indications. Beethoven also provided indications for the metronome – but you see fit to ignore those?"

"Ach, no! I do not ignore them. I use them as a guide. I always come back to them, but I never let them weigh me down."

Again Robert nodded. "That is what Chopin says about rubatos – also about ritards – but it has to be heard to be believed. Only Chopin can show perfectly how it is done."

"I have never heard Chopin. What I know I have learned from Liszt. I have listened closely to Liszt."

"But Liszt learned from Chopin. It is perfectly understandable. You seek to do for the orchestra what Chopin did for the piano. It is a good idea, but I do not know that it will work. The palette of the orchestra is too large for such precise control."

"All the more need then for a firm hand. You say only Chopin can play like Chopin, and I say only Wagner can conduct like Wagner. It will take a little while, but my orchestra is beginning finally to understand what I want, and the beginning is always the most difficult."

Wagner was Conductor of the Royal Opera; Robert was sure he would achieve his goal, but whether they merited achievement he couldn't say; there was something in the work he couldn't understand. Reading the score of *Tannhauser* he had found it turbid, full of fifths and octaves, indeterminable tonalities, but hearing it he had been profoundly, surprisingly, moved – disturbed, actually, because he couldn't understand why he had been moved. Hubner echoed what was on everyone's mind. "You are a strange man, Herr Wagner. For someone who professes the symphony dead after Beethoven you appear to have given it a lot of thought."

Wagner smiled, waving a benevolent arm. "With apologies to my good friend, Schumann, and to Mendelssohn, the truth proclaims itself – always, and in every sphere, the truth proclaims itself. There is no way to follow the Ninth without failing – without falling from the height, the pinnacle of symphonic achievement. The symphony is dead. Whoever believes differently deceives himself."

Robert scowled again. "We do not seek to surpass Beethoven, Herr Wagner. I know that I do not, and I am sure I speak for Mendelssohn as well. What we seek is to express what is most profound in ourselves in the best language we know. That, surely, is an objective worth pursuing."

"Perhaps for yourselves – but why should others have to listen when they might listen instead once more to the Ninth? Ach, I shall repeat myself over and over and over as long as it takes to get it into your heads. Beethoven has rendered the symphony obsolete. After Beethoven, there is no symphony. You follow him at your peril, you scurry in his shadow, you creep like worms."

Hubner sipped his wine. "But you profess yourself to be a follower of Beethoven, do you not, Herr Wagner? Have you not said that he influences you more than – say, Meyerbeer – even though you and Meyerbeer both write operas and Beethoven wrote symphonies?"

Robert had written about Meyerbeer's influence on Wagner – the spectacles in sight and sound, drums, organs, horses, guns, tubas, cannons, naked women, even the first gaslight illuminations onstage – which had infuriated Wagner, but many saw Meyerbeer in Wagner, no one Beethoven. Meyerbeer had found a producer for *Rienzi* in Dresden, for *The Flying Dutchman* in Berlin, after which Wagner had found a producer himself for *Tannhauser*. From Paris, Wagner had written to Robert not to let others malign Meyerbeer's name, he owed him everything, including the great fame he was soon to achieve – but arriving in Dresden, achieving fame, he had been quick to disown the help and influence of Meyerbeer – who was, after all, a Jew.

Robert expected an outburst, but Wagner surprised everyone, turning to him from Hubner with a smile. "I see it confuses everyone here. Let me give you an example of what I mean."

Robert said nothing, raising an eyebrow in question.

"As you know, Schumann, we have both put Heine's poem, 'The Two Grenadiers,' to music, have we not?"

Robert nodded.

"And we have both incorporated the *Marseilleise* into our songs, have we not?"

Again Robert nodded.

"But you have incorporated it into the melody of the song, and I have incorporated it into the harmony. Is it not so?"

Again Robert nodded.

Wagner's grin broadened. "Meyerbeer would have put the *Marseilleise* in the lyric, as you did – but Beethoven would have put it in the orchestra – as I did!"

Meyerbeer's fame and riches surpassed that of much of Europe's royalty, but no musician wished to be coupled with him, no pure musician, and few were as pure as Robert. The wine trembled in his glass, ash fell from his cigar to the floor. His voice was soft with anger. "You are hardly the first to have incorporated ideas into the accompaniment instead of the lyric, Herr Wagner. It has even been said that I was the first to have done so in my lieder – and you should know that."

Still Wagner smiled. "I know it, I know it! Of course, I know it! We understand each other perfectly, then, do we not?"

Robert said nothing, unsure of what Wagner meant.

"I have one more point to make."

Robert didn't want to hear more, but remained silent.

"I have heard your A minor Concerto for the Piano, which has been so well received, both here and in Leipzig – and deservedly so, if I may say so."

He bowed his head in Robert's direction; Robert nodded acknowledgment.

"My dear Schumann, you have done with your concerto what I did with 'The Two Grenadiers.' The piano is not merely a virtuosic vehicle but an equal partner with the orchestra. Your concerto, if I may say so, is a symphony with a piano obbligato – and I wish to do something similar with my operas – to create symphonies, if you wish, with vocal obbligatos – and that is why I say my model is Beethoven, and not Meyerbeer, nor any other composer of opera."

Wagner still smiled, staring with expectation, but Robert remained silent. He had planned his concerto as a cross between a symphony, a concerto, and a large sonata; Wagner's perception gratified him; the pulse in his head slowed to a dull heavy beat.

Wagner's smile congealed; Schumann was impossible even to compliment. "Then you understand me, my dear Schumann. We have no quarrel. Your intellect is merely a stranger to your instinct."

Robert marveled that Wagner could be disagreeable even when he wished to be agreeable. He looked around. "Does no one else hear drums?"

There was a hush, no one said anything, even Wagner stared.

Robert rubbed his temples with his fingertips – "and trumpets?"

Still no one spoke.

"In C major? Trumpets in C major – and drums?" His voice grew tinier, close to breaking. "Does no one else hear them?"

Bendemann spoke softly. "No, my friend. It must be as Doktor Helbig said – hallucinatory."

Robert rubbed his eyes and laughed to everyone's relief. "Hah, yes, hallucinatory." He looked at the company, the focus of six pairs of eyes. "That is what Doktor Helbig says. It is hallucinatory, psychosomatic – and doctors are always right, are they not?"

Bendemann saw Robert home soon after and told Clara what had happened, but Robert smiled, saying he heard no more drums, no more trumpets, and Clara said no more about it. He spoke lightly of the evening later. "Wagner has some mad ideas, does he not?"

"Foolish ideas, entirely, if you ask me."

"But he has the courage to see them through – and his *Tannhauser* is altogether a hundred times better than his earlier operas."

"I do not know about that. I will grant you his technique and instrumentation is more masterly than before – but this is not music at all to me."

Robert shrugged, nodded. "True, there is much that is trivial – but also much that is deep and original."

Clara stared, wondering how far to carry her argument. *Tannhauser* disturbed her; she found it lascivious, sensual, music and drama to inflame more than soothe the passions; as a good wife and mother she found it impossible to condone, but felt its power no less for her reservations. "I do not know about that. I can see he has dramatic power – but I think I had better hold my tongue about Wagner. I cannot speak against my convictions and I do not feel a single spark of sympathy for his work."

The girls were asleep, four-year-old Marie and Elise almost three, both to be taken on tour to Vienna the next month, but Julie, not yet a year, would be left behind – and Clara expected her fourth child within three months.

Robert had been healthier during the year in Dresden than the last in Leipzig, composing again, but both were disappointed with Dresden. With twice the population of Leipzig it was a center for drama and painting, but Leipzig was the center for music and literature; Dresden was a court city, Leipzig a commercial, Dresden the Florence of Germany, Leipzig a little Paris, Dresden a small big town, Leipzig a big small, Dresden aristocratic, Leipzig democratic, Dresden had palaces, Leipzig a university. Dresden was embraced by hills, verdant with gardens, paved with promenades, resplendent with villas, host to the Elbe, a pretty city, untouched by industry, immortalized in paintings by Canaletto, and even the famous china was manufactured in nearby Meissen leaving the city itself untouched by the factory squalor; Leipzig was choked with smoke, alleys, factories, and flats upon flats – but, as Robert liked to say, the powdered pigtail still hung mightily down people's backs in Dresden, petty princes framed the music programs, and Beethoven was presented once a year so prettified he wouldn't have recognized himself. Clara had met resistance in starting subscription concerts because they might have hurt the turnout for Palm Sunday, they might have hurt the pension fund. She had found refuge in concerts elsewhere, the journey by train, four hours to Leipzig, but Robert had found nothing else. His studies of philosophy and physics had come to nothing, boring him before they had begun. She wished he had maintained the *Zeitschrift*; it would have kept him engaged, allowed him to express in words what he couldn't in music, but he had sold it to Franz Brendel, for a mere five hundred thaler.

Perhaps Vienna would prove a more salubrious city, the seat of her greatest success, the title from the Emperor, the poem by Grillparzer, the torte a la Wieck!

ii

Eduard Hanslick, the music critic, had been twenty-one when he had first heard Clara that winter in Vienna, a concert he remembered for the integrity of its program and performance, with never a deviation from the composer's intent, never a concession to popular taste, the first time he had encountered so uncompromising an approach. He wasn't deaf to her shortcomings, limited by her sex in strength, surpassed by others in virtuosity, but no other pianist stood as squarely at the nexus of so many directions. He was to write later, as lucid as he was respectful, that she neither overpowered nor transported with her personality, nor did she cultivate worshippers, that was not her style, but cultivated instead the clearest expression of each work, penetrated deeply its character. Unfortunately, as she had discovered, the Viennese preferred personalities.

He had met her backstage after her first and second concerts, spoken as adoringly as any worshipper, extolling her mastery of Beethoven, Chopin, Scarlatti, and Schumann, whose works she had just performed; for the second concert she had been joined by seventeen year old Anton Rubinstein on Schumann's Andante and Variations for Two Pianos; but her disappointment was palpable, the audiences had been cool, receipts had dwindled, and the third concert, the most daring, consisting of only Schumann's works, the Piano Concerto in A minor and *Spring* Symphony, had followed the same pattern.

"They are coming."

They were in a tiny room off the wings of the stage; Joseph Fischhof, who still taught piano at the Vienna Conservatory as when Robert had been his guest a decade ago, caught Hanslick's eye. Hanslick nodded. Both stood almost at attention.

Clara entered, stopping when she saw the two men, and sat in silence in her chair. Hanslick thought she looked lovely, the silk evening dress of blue and white stripes contrasting alluringly with her bare white shoulders, her chin held high, blue eyes black with passion, and her masculine stride. Robert followed, looking at the men looking at Clara for direction, and when she remained silent refusing to acknowledge even him he followed her lead, but walked delicately, small steps, sitting not far from her as did Hanslick and Fischhof, staring from Robert to Clara and back, staring at each other; Robert stared at Clara, who stared at the floor, all without a word.

Both Hanslick and Fischhof knew what was wrong, but not what to do. Clara was paying the price for her choice. It didn't help that Robert had no stage presence; he knew how to compose, but had never learned how to acknowledge an audience, not even how to bow; he started in one direction, turned before he had completed the bow, perhaps to include the entire hall in a single bow, but appeared instead to be searching for something as if he were a puppet, a toy made of wood, spurred by clockwork.

Clara faced a reckoning, her reception had been more kind than enthusiastic, the second concert had barely covered expenses, and the third, this last, had lost money, almost a hundred florins, too embarrassing to mention for an artist of her stature. She finally broke the silence. "I cannot believe it. I cannot believe how ungrateful they are – how bloody ungrateful."

Hanslick spoke soothingly. "It was splendid, Frau Schumann, a splendid performance."

There was much she could complain about, bills hadn't been placed, tickets hadn't gone out, a singer had canceled – but none of that should have made a difference, her name should have been enough, but it wasn't. She feared as well for Robert, playing Herr Clara Schumann again. "They liked you, Robert. It was not you. They called you back several times."

Hanslick would have said the applause had all been for Clara, but understood her husband was unaccustomed to the stage, unaccustomed to audiences, unaccustomed even to conducting, and said nothing.

Clara shrugged, raising hands in helplessness. "I do not know what else I could have done. I simply cannot think. It is too unjust for words."

Fischhof cleared his throat. "My dear Frau Schumann, if I may make an observation?"

She looked at him. "Yes?"

"What has happened is in no way a reflection of your performance, not even of the quality of the program – which is of the highest merit – but of the taste of our foolish funloving Viennese audiences. They want the bravura pieces, they want virtuosic warhorses, particularly around the holiday season – and when they do not get what they want they are like children. Your program was too good for them, and when you cast pearls before swine…." He shrugged.

"But I have played Beethoven for them before. I introduced them to the Sonata in F minor. Grillparzer wrote the poem. You know about all that."

"Yes, of course, but that was when you were eighteen years old. That was a novelty in itself. And you played the Sonata among other pieces with which they were familiar. Your current programs have, how shall I say it … too much integrity. They do not yield."

Clara's eyes darkened. "I beg your pardon, Herr Fischhof, but I must submit I have never heard such damned rubbish. I gave them the best work I know, and I gave it to them as best I knew how. Do you dare to suggest I should instead have patronized them?"

"My dear Frau Schumann, I am your friend, you know that, and your great admirer. I do not suggest anything. I only make an observation, and only because I wish to help."

It was the first Christmas she had been unable to give Robert anything, they had lit a tree, given Marie and Elise some things, hardly what they had wished, but it was not Fischhof's fault. She was angry most of all at herself; she had received a letter from her friend, Emilie List, with the name of a musician of some influence who could have helped with publicity, but she had been too arrogant, written to Emilie that her reputation, especially in Vienna where she was loved better than in Germany, was all she would need – and she had been wrong. Her pappa had managed the details then, she had been new, eighteen, girlish, vibrant, piquant, but no more, though her technique had never been more formidable. She made fists of her hands and looked away. "I am sorry, Herr Fischhof. You are a true friend, indeed, I know. It is just that … you must understand I am not myself."

Fischhof nodded. "Of course. Yours is the dilemma of all great artists. You patronize them when you pander to their taste, but otherwise you risk appearing too good for them, too much of a snob. It is ever the dilemma of all who know more than others – poor Beethoven, not least of all."

She just nodded, sorry she had embroiled Robert in the concert business; it was his responsibility to compose, hers to perform his compositions, but also to provide the rest, climate, freedom from anxiety he needed, but she had only made it worse, raising his hopes needlessly – but she had wanted to make him proud. She was scheduled for a fourth concert, but doubted the wisdom of seeing it through, afraid for the first time that they would lose more money than they could afford. She rose from her chair, hands still clenched, almost shouting. "Oh, this is all so bloody ridiculous, this is all so bloody stupid. I wish I knew what to do next."

Robert had not seen her so helpless since the days she had overcome her pappa's influence; he spoke quietly, motionless in his chair. "Clara, my dear, calm yourself. In ten years this will all have changed."

Hanslick spoke soothingly. "He is right, Frau Schumann. Timing is everything. Christmas is the season for nostalgia and reminiscence, people want to hear what they know, but the concerto has already taken hold in Dresden and in Leipzig, and I am convinced it is only a matter of time before it will take hold in Vienna."

"That makes it no less a disgrace!"

A new voice had entered the discourse; all four looked to the door; only Clara spoke.

"Jenny!"

"My dear Clara, it was an astonishing concert, excellence piled upon excellence. I was ashamed to be part of so unresponsive an audience."

"My dear good Jenny, I thank you for saying it. It is good to hear. I must confess myself at the end of my rope. I do not know what more I could have done."

Jenny Lind, the Swedish Nightingale, was a year younger than Clara, making her own name in Europe, not a beautiful woman, thick features, round face, piggy eyes, potato nose, sallow skin, she was the first to admit her flaws, but when she sang you fell in love. Hers was not a big voice, but even her softest notes carried easily, always mellifluous, into the farthest reaches of any hall. Robert and Clara had met her earlier in the year, traveling to Leipzig for a concert. Wieck had persuaded them, as he persuaded all his students, wishing them to appropriate the straight line of the Lind's singing into their performances on the piano.

"You did everything. There was nothing more to be done – except by the audience. Oh, their stupidity makes me so angry!" Jenny congratulated Robert on the concerto – and the symphony which she had heard before; Clara introduced her to Fischhof and Hanslick. She turned then to face Clara again. "First things first. When is your next concert?"

Clara looked away. "It is scheduled for the tenth – but I am not sure it should not be canceled. The Viennese appear to have changed their minds about me."

"That is bloody nonsense, Clara! You *will* perform, and you *will* let me perform with you."

Clara raised her eyebrows. "But that would not be fair to you."

"I beg your pardon, but that is again bloody nonsense. You have done no less for me already."

Clara knew what she meant; Mendelssohn, slated to perform at Jenny's concert in Leipzig, had dropped out at the last moment, substituting Clara in his place. Clara smiled. "Well, then, since you put it that way, I thank you from the bottom of my heart."

"I *do* put it that way. There is no other way I *could* put it. There is absolutely no need for thanks."

The fourth concert sold out. The Schumanns more than recouped their losses and had more than three hundred thaler to show for their tour – but Clara reflected in her diary: *I could not get over the bitter feeling that two songs by Jenny accomplished what I, with all my sweat and skill, could not.*

Hannes waited for Helga as she had asked in a doorway by a streetlamp, down the street from Zur schwarzen Katze, keeping an eye on the door, huddling to keep warm, hands deep in his pockets, hat pulled over his ears. The streets were cold at two in the morning, particularly near the docks. He swayed from one foot to the other, teeth chattering like castanets.

The streetlamp was dim, made dimmer by the mist coiling and uncoiling like serpents in the night, but he set his eyes, peeled for her hat, on the lantern of Zur schwarzen Katze. She had avoided him before, even after she had asked him to wait, and he worried even as he waited that she might slip out of the back door again.

The night was noisy, people still going home, but he wasn't distracted until a couple emerged from the mist, approaching him, the woman breaking away from the man. "Hannes?"

It was Helga – but she was with a man. "Ja."

"Hannes, listen. I cannot help it, but I am with a friend. I told him I had a date tonight, but he would not listen. I will only be a few minutes. Will you wait?"

Hannes took a deep slow breath; he didn't want to wait, but knew he had no choice, not if he wanted to be with her. "I have been waiting – just like you said. What are you telling me?"

"Hannes, if you are going to argue, it is over – now. What was I to do? I did not call him. I was not expecting him."

"Tell him to go. Tell him you already have a date. Tell him to wait. Why can you not tell him to wait?"

"I cannot tell him that. He is willing to pay much more than you."

"How much more?"

"Never mind how much more."

"How much more?"

"It is out of your range, Hannes."

"I have a right to know. How much?"

"Fifteen thaler."

They had agreed on five; he had been saving from his tips. He shook his head. "It is not right. I was first."

She put her hands on her hips. "If you are going to be such a baby you can just forget about it. Will you wait or no?"

She was beginning to shout. He looked at the ground. "Where shall I wait?"

"That is better. We are going to my place. I will be only a few minutes. You can wait outside if you want."

"Only a few minutes?"

She lifted her chin. "What did I say?"

"I will wait outside your window – but only a few minutes. After that, it will be too late."

She smiled. "Of course. Now do not follow too closely. You know where I live."

"Ja, I know where you live."

He lost sight of them in the mist, keeping track of their tramp on the cobbles. He knew her window, long and narrow, eight panes, and waited for her to light a candle, but the window remained dark. He sat slumped on a doorstep from which he watched her window; the ground was wet, mudpuddles left by boots, a cockroach clambered over his shoe; he hugged his knees, drew his feet close, buried his face in his arms, and shut his eyes; he had been awake since five in the morning.

Frau Grummer had never invited him back to her rooms and he had never asked. It was understood, her work was done. He was depressed, but he was on his own. He had never been so alone, unable to tell anyone what he wanted, unable to get it – except when he could afford it, subject even then to the whims of girls like Helga. A song he had been playing that evening ran incessantly through his head:

> Fat Cheeks, White Cheeks
> Like you never seen
> Fat Cheeks, White Cheeks
> You know what I mean
> Fat Cheeks, White Cheeks
> Rosy bud between
> Fat Cheeks, White Cheeks
> My fat brownholed queen

He tucked himself more tightly into the doorway; a clock chimed three. The next thing he knew he was being shaken, addressed by a strange voice. "Go on, little cock. It is your turn."

He didn't recognize the man shaking him, unshaven and grinning – Helga's friend, he could have been no one else. The man touched his cap in a mock salute, kissing the tips of his fingers, leaving before Hannes could say a word.

The street was deserted as Hannes crossed; trudging up the cracked narrow wooden stairs he wanted only to sleep, but he had come too far and the itch would return as soon as he was with Helga. He felt in his pocket for the money; she wouldn't let him touch her without his money on her dresser; he felt his other pocket. He came quickly awake; he had been surprised that the man had awakened him; now he understood what had happened.

He sat on steps made concave by the steady tramp of feet, his face in his hands, moaning like a girl. He couldn't have said how long he sat, but the clock chiming four alerted him to his situation. He got up, wiping his face, taking off his shoes, scurrying quietly away, hugging the wall on the street so he couldn't be seen from above. If he left unseen he would deprive Helga of the satisfaction of knowing he had waited. He escaped without detection, but his weariness caught up with him; he almost fell walking, but steadied himself from tree to tree, sitting down finally on a bench to rest falling asleep until sunrise.

ii

Bridges divide the Alster into the inner and the outer, Binnen und Aussenalster. The Pavilion, a cafe on the bank where the Sextet played, Jakob on the double bass, provided a princely view of the Binnenalster ballooning into the Aussen, flotillas of sails and swans, and the vast shore lined with rhododendrons, rosebushes, willows, and poplars. Shining mansions and villas graced the hinterland, nestled behind exquisite gardens. A boat on the Aussen provided a fine panorama of the skyline, steeples and spires, churches and Rathaus.

The Pavilion served many purposes for Jakob, putting food on the table, providing food as well for his soul, a home away from home more luxurious than his home, and hobnobs with the Hamburg elite, one in particular, not even of Hamburg, Herr Adolph Giesemann of Winsen (a nearby townlet), owner of a paper mill, also of a farm, who liked to sing, play guitar, listen to the occasional movement by Haydn, Mozart, and Beethoven, provided by the Sextet, whom Jakob now approached at his table, hat in hand. "Herr Giesemann?"

Giesemann looked up from his company, pipe in hand. "Yes, Jakob?"

Jakob touched his hair, his smile too wide for sincerity. "Herr Giesemann, excuse, please, one word, please – in private?"

Giesemann raised eyebrows blond as his skin and nodded, excusing himself from the table, walking along the bank a short distance with Jakob. "Yes, Jakob? What is on your mind?"

"Herr Gieseman, it is about my Hannes. I have told you about him, some say he plays the piano like Mozart, some say better. He takes lessons from Marxsen. He has given concerts."

Giesemann nodded. "Yes, Jakob, you have spoken about him."

"I worry about him, Herr Giesemann. I am worried. He is not well. He is now fourteen, but so small, still so small, he could be eleven, and he is always tired. He works so hard – so very very hard."

Giesemann puffed on his pipe.

"He is up early – that is when he composes, when it is quiet. His best ideas come when he blacks his boots – he says it himself. Then he goes to school, then two days in the week he goes to Marxsen, then he is practising, or he is doing homework, or transcriptions. Then he plays piano – you know, for money. He is a good boy. I want to give him a holiday – now, in the summer, while the school is out."

He looked at Giesemann, hoping he would understand, but Giesemann said nothing, continuing to listen.

"The other day he comes home after sunrise. It was so late when he left the dance place, he was so tired, he sat down in a doorway, just to rest, just for a minute, but he fell asleep, he did not wake till the sun came up. You see how it is."

Still Giesemann puffed, nodding and listening, nothing more.

"He needs more air, he needs more light. He has never been outside of Hamburg. He needs to get out. He needs to see more of the country."

Giesemann raised his head, taking the pipe from his mouth, beginning to understand what Jakob was saying. "Do you mean he should come for some time to Winsen? Is that your meaning?"

Jakob smiled. "You have a daughter, na, Herr Giesemann? Her name is Lieschen, na, you said? You said, na, also, you want her to learn the piano? My Hannes, he could teach her. He could accompany you, when you play guitar, if you want. He could work on the farm – whatever you want. It would be good for everyone, na?"

"Ah, yes, Lieschen is now thirteen – a good age to learn the piano."

"Ja, any age is a good age."

"Yes, I think we might arrange it. I am agreeable and I think I may speak as well for my wife."

Jakob grinned, his sincerity no longer in doubt. "Hah, ja, I will tell Hannes tonight, I will tell my wife. They will be very happy. It is very good of you, sir, Herr Giesemann – thank you, sir, and I speak also for my wife. Hah, no sir, you will not be sorry."

iii

Lieschen Giesemann wore her hair in two blond pigtails, twined with red and blue ribbons. She was younger than Hannes by a year, but no smaller. They looked well together, similar, like brother and sister, Hansel and Gretal, which pleased her, she had always wanted a brother and she liked Hannes, but she hated lessons, hated the piano, preferred to sing, loved the ABC song he had written for the way it swelled from a small introduction to a mighty finale: first he used just the letters of the alphabet for the text, then letters grouped in twos, then small words like in a spelling competition, and finally, in a full chorus, fortissimo and lento: WINSEN: EIGHTEEN HUNDRED, SEVEN AND FORTY! Everyone loved it, everyone in Winsen was amazed, particularly to see Hannes standing on a table conducting the men's chorus – but best of all she liked the days in the countryside when they bathed in the Luhe, found birdnests, picked flowers, fished, and read.

In Hamburg Hannes had bought books from the barrows of peddlers, but in Winsen they borrowed them from Frau Lowenherz's lending library, striking a deal with her son, Aaron, Lieschen's classmate, to get books at halfprice, for a groschen apiece. The loans were secret; Aaron made the profit.

She carried a picnic lunch in a knapsack to meet Hannes who had already been out for hours with his silent clavier, his notebook, needing nothing else. He said he got drunk on the outdoors – a strange expression, her pappa had said, coming from a fourteen-year-old, exchanging a glance with her mamma, but he had smiled, refilling Hannes's empty milk glass, no sooner filled than drained. She enjoyed no less the streams, rustic paths, leafy canopies, but took them for granted; they had always been hers – never his.

Approaching their rendezvous she heard shouts. "Give it back! It is not yours!" Willi Schultz held Hannes's arms behind his back, Heinz Muller tore the clavier from his hands, Gunther Mann his notebook, also the book just borrowed from Aaron. A wild kick from Hannes struck Gunther's knee; Gunther threw the books immediately aside, punching Hannes twice in his ribs and stomach. Willi was older than Hannes, Heinz and Gunther were both younger, but all were bigger.

Lieschen ran forward shouting. "You! Willi Schultz! You big bully! Let him go! Let him alone!"

The activity stopped, but Willi still held Hannes.

"Let him go, Willi, I am warning you – or I will tell my pappa."

Gunther mimicked. "I will tell my pappa."

Willi pushed Hannes at Heinz. "Sissy!"

"How dare you!" Lieschen struck his chest. "He is our guest!"

Heinz pushed Hannes at Gunther. "He is a sissy! He is a mamma's boy. He likes to play with girls."

Hannes looked at Gunther. "Where is my notebook? Give me back my notebook."

"Such a crybaby – Hannes from Hamburg. Nobody wants your notebook. There it is. Get it yourself."

The notebook lay behind a bush where Gunther had tossed both books.

Gunther shouted. "Look at him crying like a girl. We did not even do anything."

Hannes was crying, outraged, helpless, embarrassed, striding past Heinz to collect the books and clavier. Heinz yanked his hair as he passed. "Look! Even his hair is like a girl's."

Hannes screamed; Lieschen jumped at Heinz; but Heinz let Hannes go, avoiding Lieschen.

Willi laughed. "Give him your ribbon, Lieschen. He will look so pretty with a ribbon."

Gunther also laughed. "He will look prettier than Lieschen."

The boys left. Hannes couldn't look at his protector, refusing her hand as they walked to their favorite spot, a fallen tree, limbs and junctions of which provided seats, armrests, footstools. "I will tell Pappa. They will be sorry."

"No, you must not! It will only get worse."

"But they will only do it again!"

"Let us see – but you must not tell."

"All right – but if they do it again, I will."

"Let us see."

They were out of sight of the road. Underfoot the ground was soft, a carpet of mosses, lichens, and leaves; mushrooms and berries grew in clusters; daffodils, daisies, and buttercups bobbed like an audience; overhead the wind sighed through cherry trees and hawthorns, brilliant with color; in the distance they could hear the babble of the Luhe.

He was silent again; the underbrush throbbed with the sound of scurrying things: hares, beaver, partridge. They had seen boars and deer, but nothing stirred him until Lieschen tapped his arm, pointing to a crane rising fifteen yards ahead of them in a cloud of white feathers with a wingspan of five feet. Neither said a word, but he smiled again, nodding satisfaction, and so did she.

He showed her the book Aaron had loaned him, Ludwig Tieck's *Wondrous Romance of the Fair Magelone and Count Peter of Provence*. She brought out the food, sausages and cheese, sandwiched between thick buttered crusts of bread, to be chased by bottles of milk and water.

After they had eaten Lieschen settled herself in a crook of the tree; Hannes sat at her feet, legs crossed, the book in his lap, reading aloud. She had taken off her shoes, wagging bare feet not far from his face. From the corner of his eye they seemed like flapping wings; her calves swelling from thick white ankles; her knees were covered by her dress, blue squares on a lemon backdrop; one hand rested on one knee, the arm bare to the elbow, encased there in a puffy white sleeve to her shoulder. She listened intently, chewing on one pigtail. Three squirrels chased one another in the canopy of leaves overhead, sparrows chirped.

Hannes got up, covering the hand on her knee with his own. The Giesemanns had been kind beyond expectations, bought tickets once for him and Lieschen to see the great violinist, Joseph Joachim, just two years older than himself, in Hamburg. "Lieschen."

"What is it, Hannes?"

"Nothing."

Another time Herr Giesemann had bought tickets for Mozart's *Figaro*. Hannes had never known such happiness. Her hand trembled under his; she was prettier than his sister, Elise – pretty as the girls at Zur schwarzen Katze, but not as old, not as round.

"Lieschen, do you like me?"

She searched his face. He stared back, unblinking. "Hannes, what *is* it?"

"Nothing, Lieschen. I just like you."

She smiled. "I like you too, Hannes."

"I like you very much, Lieschen."

Her smile became pastier. He leaned forward; she thought he might kiss her cheek, even her mouth, and leaned forward herself, but he kneeled instead, suddenly thrusting both hands under her dress, gripping her thighs, burying his face in her lap and lower belly, covering her dress with kisses.

"Hannes!" She screamed, pushing his head, and when he wouldn't budge beating her fists against the back of his head. "Let me *go*, Hannes! LET ME GO!"

He looked up, eyes as wide with horror as her own. She jumped from her seat, running from him, crying. He followed. "Lieschen, I am sorry! I am sorry! Please, do not cry."

She tripped, falling on her face, lying where she had fallen, still crying. He knelt by her side, afraid now to touch her. "Lieschen, please do not cry. Are you hurt? I am sorry."

She asked no questions, but refused to look at him; she could still feel the pressure of his fingers on her thighs, on her buttocks.

"Lieschen, I like you. You said you liked me. That is what a boy and a girl do when they like each other."

Her breath still came in gasps, she still spoke with lungs full of air, cheeks streaming with tears. "I have never seen anyone do that before – never!"

Hannes shook his head; his voice shook no less than hers. "I have, Lieschen – many times – but maybe I was wrong."

She was finally able to look at him. "Hannes, you must never do that again – not ever!"

Still he shook his head, disbelievingly. "Never, I will never, never ever again, never, I swear – never. I am sorry. I really like you, Lieschen – really."

She said nothing, but wouldn't look at him.

He wondered suddenly if it were a matter of money. "Is it because I am poor and you are rich?"

"Oh, Hannes, no! It is nothing to do with that! That is nothing!"

He said nothing.

"Hannes, it has nothing to do with money. I do not understand you."

"Then it is all right?"

She took a deep breath. "No, you must never do it again."

"I will not – I swear."

He touched her hand in friendship, but she pulled it away and he retrieved his own, dumb and confused.

The party had gathered for almost two hours, a small group of musicians, painters, professors, friends of the Schumanns, in a circle in the sittingroom; from the plates and punch, half empty, you would have imagined the party well begun, but all were pretending all was well, all except Robert who said nothing, all awaiting the guest of honor: Liszt. She should have known he would be late, dallying with yet more admirers, not for Liszt the rules that governed others, not if they interfered with his pleasure.

Ernst Grabau spoke to fill the silence. "I understand congratulations are due, Doktor Schumann. I understand you are to succeed Herr Hiller as Direktor of the Men's Choral Society."

Robert looked at Grabau without a smile, barely even a nod.

Clara hurried to maintain the thread of the conversation. "We will be sorry to lose Hiller. He is a good friend, but who can blame him for leaving. One goes where there are opportunities, and it is nothing to laugh about, to be Direktor of Musik at Dusseldorf."

"Of course not."

"He recommended Robert himself for the Choral Society. It will be Robert's first elected situation."

Robert looked at her; to the rest his face was a blank, but she knew better; she had meant to praise him, but he had felt rebuked again – his first *paid* situation was the implication, and she spoke again to dilute the implication. "I think there are almost seventy members in the Society, and Robert plans as well to start a mixed choir."

Robert turned to the company, ignoring her. "It is almost too much to bear. All our friends leave."

She knew what he meant, everyone knew, but she explained anyway; the company had been rendered too silent by the long wait, what appeared to be a rebuff, but resentment against Liszt was not to be voiced. "He means Mendelssohn. He was our great friend. In music there was none greater."

Frau Bendemann commiserated. "Of course. We understand." Robert had been at the Bendemanns when he had heard of Mendelssohn's stroke and gone to Leipzig for the funeral.

"His children were playing with dolls when I went to the house." Robert spoke in hushed tones; he might have been recalling the image. "His face was even more noble in death than in life, twenty years older he looked – like a warrior he looked, with a smile upon his face. Even in death he might have been merely asleep, having a little joke, like a conqueror. Two veins crossed his temples, so engorged with blood they looked like wreaths, like palms."

The company nodded sorrowfully; they had heard the story before.

"You were there, Herr Professor." He nodded to Bendemann. "You know how it was – and you, David. You bore the coffin on the left with Hauptmann and Rietz. I was on the right with Moscheles and Gade. The funeral procession was too long to be seen all at once."

Bendemann nodded; David nodded; the tragedy was profound, Mendelssohn had been just thirty-eight, but Robert grieved as much for himself, not just the loss of a friend, Mendelssohn the man, but a standard bearer, the loss of an era.

"He was unconscious, but it is said he died like Mozart – trying to make orchestral sounds."

He looked around at the company as if there were a lesson in what he said. Clara despaired of his mood; more than Mendelssohn they had lost a son, Emil, barely sixteen months, in the past year, to tuberculosis.

"It is said that after Fanny died – his sister – he did not much care to live himself. He did not survive her long, not even by six months – and they all died the same way, all the Mendelssohns, the father, the mother, Fanny – of cerebral hemorrhages."

He looked again at Clara: of his own family only he and his brother, Karl, in Schneeberg, survived – and Karl was unwell. The others were dead: father, mother, sister Emilie, brothers Eduard and Julius. There had also been good news: a weeklong festival in Zwickau, entire programs of just his works, his old music teacher, Kuntsch, proudly parading his prodigy; even more significant, *Paradise and the Peri* had been performed in New York; but for Robert the bad covered the good like a shroud.

Clara got up. "It is ever like this with Liszt. He is ever later than expected."

Frau Hubner smiled at her husband. "We must remember, if ever we invite Herr Liszt, to invite everyone else hours later."

Clara was relieved by the laughter, however feeble. "I would have done it myself – but he was the one to request this party." She had received a note from Liszt saying he would be in Dresden for a day and wanted to hear Robert's D minor Piano Trio. She had scurried to find musicians and prepare dinner at the shortest notice, and he was now late by more than two hours. "Why do we not play something while we wait?"

Becker nodded. "I second that."

Eckert clapped once joining hands. "A capital idea."

They chose to play Beethoven's D major Trio, the *Ghost*, the *Geister*. David and Grabau drew their instruments from their cases, violin and cello, Clara took her place at the piano.

Almost thirty minutes later, as they sped through the final page of the final movement to the final ascent, strings chased presto up a ladder of octaves by the piano to the final cadence, Liszt made his appearance, striding into the sittingroom, applauding and shouting. "Brava, Madame Schumann! Bravo, all!" Wagner followed, seconding Liszt, aping Liszt. "Brava, indeed, Madame Schumann! Bravo, all!"

The company was distracted between their appreciation for the performance and the boisterous new guests. Liszt wore a light skyblue swallowtail coat and a shirt of black velvet, Wagner a pink jacket, with puffy white sleeves; both grinned, clapping louder than anyone else, drawing attention from the performers. "You were wise, my dear Madame Schumann, not to wait. My business with Wagner took longer than I expected. I hope I was not too presumptuous for inviting him to join us."

He had not apologized, not even appeared sorry, but for all his trespasses remained winsome, a boy wellpleased with himself and slender still as a boy, while Robert ballooned to almost twice Liszt's girth. Clara understood the appeal, the smile as if no one else mattered, which could as soon be turned off as on, as soon given to one person as another. Still, she was his hostess and he was Liszt. "Of course not, Herr Liszt. Herr Wagner is no stranger to our house."

"Splendid, then! It is wonderful to see you again, I must say – and you too, of course, my good Herr Schumann."

Robert managed a smile. "Always a pleasure, Herr Liszt."

Wagner knew everyone; Liszt knew some and spread his charm like a mantle over the company as Clara introduced him to the rest.

Frau Hubner smiled. "Is it true what we have heard, Herr Liszt, that you plan to stop giving concerts?"

Liszt gave her the benefit of his full attention, eyes boring into hers; the news had long been heralded all over Europe, the end of his years of Glanzzeit, his glamorous tours if not his travels; these were people to be suffered, but never gladly; trust the Schumanns to surround themselves with Leipzigers, even in Dresden, with the bourgeoisie in a city known for its aristocracy. "It is *not* true, Frau Hubner, that I plan to stop." She gasped, smiling her pleasure, but he smiled back, pausing to bait her with his smile before netting her in his trap. "I have stopped already. My last concert is already in my past by eight months, October last, at Elizabetgrad – just as it said in the newspapers."

Frau Hubner blushed; his mere presence had reduced her to the babble of a schoolgirl. "Ah, you know how it is, Herr Liszt. One simply cannot trust the newspapers. It is so much better to get the information from the lion's mouth."

Liszt nodded, still smiling. "To beard the lion in someone else's den, so to speak?" His smile widened; Wagner laughed loudly as did others though more politely.

Clara attempted to keep the peace. "But why now, Herr Liszt? Has something happened of significance of which we are not aware?"

"Why now?" Liszt looked at Wagner, who said nothing, but grinned. Clara felt they had come to some agreement and wasn't far wrong. Wagner had approached Liszt for suggestions regarding funding; his salary, fifteen hundred thaler, becoming a Royal Kapellmeister, bountiful by the standards of the bourgeoisie, was insufficient for Wagner, deep in debt, living as always on anticipated earnings, borrowed securities; Liszt had connections, ideas for productions of Wagner's works. Liszt shrugged, turning to Clara. "There is no place left to go. In the last ten years I have circled Europe, from Lisbon, Cadiz, and Gibralter, to Constantinople, to Moscow, St. Petersburg, Edinburgh, Glasgow, Limerick, Cork –"

Wagner interrupted. "Ach, yes, and a hundred and one points in between."

Clara didn't blame him, aware of the perils of travel, rails in their infancy, roads hardly mature – and, despite the renowned comfort of his coach, travel remained at the mercy of the elements. Liszt acknowledged Wagner with a nod. "Quite so, but there is also a more compelling reason."

Frau Bendemann braved another smile. "And what is that, Herr Liszt?"

"With all my travels I have no time to do what I want most, to compose. My friends all outstrip me: over here, Herr Wagner; over there, Doktor Schumann; and everywhere, Chopin. It is my new life – and if I am to amount to anything as a composer I must devote myself to it one hundred percent."

Liszt had been appointed Kapellmeister-at-large to the Grand Duke at Weimar in 1842, six years ago, but wanted no longer to be at large. Court duties were minimal, leaving not only time for composition but an orchestra at his disposal. "I also want to make Weimar a center for new music. In Paris they are interested only in opera and in Leipzig only in the music of the past. I want to look ahead, to follow new paths."

Robert looked up, sharper than Clara had seen him all evening. "The music of the past has not been so very bad, Herr Liszt. It is not the easiest thing to leave Bach and Beethoven behind. It is not even a necessary thing. They are relevant to all generations, past and future."

Liszt shook his head. "That is not what I am saying. Bach and Beethoven have no need of my humble services to propagate their music. What I want is to make the world more aware of the music of Robert Schumann and of Richard Wagner and of whoever else is worth hearing. I want to make the world more receptive to the new."

He smiled at Robert, his special smile. Robert nodded, almost smiling himself. "That is music to my ears, indeed."

Clara was less convinced. "Of course, we must make the world more receptive to new music, and I am the first to play my Robert's music when I can – but surely the difference should not be between the old and the new as much as the good and the bad. There is much that is old that is not heard that is good, and much that is new that is heard that is bad."

Liszt shrugged, finding pious all talk of good and bad music; he could play it all, making even bad music sound good, and prided himself on his ability. "Of course, and it is up to us as artists to make the choice – but the public is a monster. If you do not give it what it wants, what it has heard a thousand times, what makes it comfortable, it will ignore you. That is the way of the world."

Clara shook her head. "But if you give the monster what it wants it will swallow you whole. It will allow you to do nothing else, play no other music." She had in mind her failure in Vienna which remained a cloud, but had not deterred her from playing the music she liked.

Robert spoke sagely. "It will kill the goose that lays the golden eggs."

Liszt shrugged again; talk was cheap, arguments were academic, introspection for idle minds. "Precisement!" His calendar was full and getting fuller. He had said nothing of the Princess Carolyne von Sayn-Wittgenstein awaiting him in Weimar, whom he had met in Russia, who had attracted his attention by donating a hundred roubles anonymously to his favorite charity and prostrating her brow to his feet when he had tracked her to her home in Woronince, the twenty-eight year old daughter of a Polish landowner, in possession of his vast fortune, maintained by more than thirty thousand peasants, and of the title from her husband, Prince Nicholas von Sayn-Wittgenstein, a German aristocrat, serving in the Tsar's army, from whom she was now separated and awaiting a divorce – so she could marry Liszt.

He said nothing about her because of the questions, spoken and silent, that would follow, the concerns of the bourgeoisie, about Marie, the Countess d'Agoult with whom the split was irrevocable, particularly since she had written a 'novel' about their affair – and about their children, Blandine, Cosima, and Daniel, residing with his mother in Paris, to whom he wrote, but rarely saw. "But I have taken up too much time already with idle chatter. Why do we not get on with the entertainment of the evening? I am ready for your trio, Doktor Schumann, if everyone else is."

The trio, Clara's gift from Robert for her last birthday, an immediate favorite, found favor as well with Liszt, swaying and smiling through the performance, applauding when appropriate. Wagner, Clara noted, as did others, not without surprise, took his cues from Liszt, but his face appeared to twitch more than usual and his feet almost to stamp in protest, accustomed as he was to being always the center of attention.

Robert's quintet followed the trio and Liszt reacted no less favorably, rising to his feet, smiling and applauding, but with a sly comment. "An excellent work, Schumann, but perhaps just a trifle Leipzigerish, do you not think?"

Robert replied immediately. "I am sure I do not know what you mean. It has not proven too … Leipzigerish for Moscow, nor for St. Petersburg."

Clara noted again his sharpness. "No, it has not. I can vouch for that for I have played it – nor for Denmark, nor Austria."

Liszt recoiled; he might have been surprised, but he might as easily have been acting. "No, that is not what I mean. You misunderstand me. I mean it is, perhaps – just a trifle – too regular, too conservative, too foursquare?"

Karl Eckert leaned forward. "What about Bach, Herr Liszt? Would you discount him as well for being too regular and conservative and foursquare?"

"Bach is the original Leipziger, of course. I would not say I would discount him – but I think we have learned from him all we have to learn. He has nothing new to offer us."

Ernst Becker shook his head. "On the contrary, Herr Liszt, I find the study of Bach a lifelong occupation. He has always something new to offer."

Wagner grinned and almost yelled, finally unable to endure his own silence. "Ach, I would say not. I would say Bach is to Beethoven as the Egyptian Sphinx is to Greek sculpture."

Eckert raised his eyebrows. "I beg your pardon, Herr Wagner?"

"I mean just what I say, Herr Eckert. Just as the Sphinx strives to free its human head from its animal body, so Bach strove to free his face from his wig."

Everyone stared, including Liszt; everyone incredulous, shaking heads, rolling eyes, except Liszt, who just grinned.

Eckert's eyebrows remained raised in consternation. "But how do you know, Herr Wagner, that the Sphinx strives to free its head from its body. The Sphinx is the Sphinx. That is what makes it the Sphinx."

"Ach, but would you not wish to free your head from your body – Herr Eckert – if you were the Sphinx?"

"Of course, but that is because I am not the sphinx. I am myself. Were I the Sphinx, Herr Wagner, I might very well wish to remain a Sphinx. Does a lion wish to free his face from his mane and become a man?"

Grabau laughed. "I do not know about that – but I know many a man who might wish to be a lion!"

Wagner turned his eyes to Grabau. "Ach, I think you misunderstand me, Herr Grabau."

"If that is the case, I beg your pardon, Herr Wagner – but I have tried very hard, as has everyone here, to understand you."

"Then let me put it another way. I do not deride your Herr Bach as you appear to think. What I mean is that Bach is to music what Sanskrit is to language: estimable, and incomparable, and complete – but defunct."

Robert's voice trembled. "There you go too far, Herr Wagner. Bach cannot be defunct. He is, by definition, the essence of music. Take away Bach, and you take away everything. Without Bach, there is nothing – not even your *Tannhauser*."

Wagner opened his mouth, but Clara interrupted. "Herr Liszt, will you not play something for us? I think we might be talking too much."

Liszt touched his forehead in a mock salute. "Your wish is my command, Madame Schumann – but I must say I find the talk refreshing."

Clara turned her head away. "We can refresh ourselves later over dinner. Please, Herr Liszt, will you not play something?"

The focus of the room shifted as Liszt seated himself at the piano, launching into a Bach fugue, but playing so it was scarcely recognizable, stretching each measure almost in two, utilizing a rubato too daring even for Chopin. He grinned, turning again to the company when he was finished. "I thought Herr Wagner might appreciate old Bach better played this way."

Wagner had grinned through the performance, seeing through Liszt's prank. He laughed when Liszt was finished. "Bravo! That was quite definitely not Leipzigerish. I would never have imagined Bach could be made to sound like Chopin."

Liszt rocked in his chair. "You see, my dear Wagner, even old Bach has something new to offer after all. The old pianos could not do what today's pianos can do, they did not have the power, they did not have the pedal – but a little rubato can bend even a fugue into a waltz."

Eckert smiled. "One might as well argue, Herr Liszt, that a little rubato can break the backbone of a fugue as dependably as on a rack."

Liszt raised his chin. "I would put it another way, Herr Eckert. A little rubato can make a Viennese out of a Leipziger."

Wagner laughed aloud, but no one else.

Liszt returned to the piano, playing something else, with no less disdain than he had shown for the fugue, blurring tempos until the pieces were unrecognizable. The

Jacobis left during the performance. Clara wanted to leave herself; the evening was a disaster, but Liszt continued to play and Wagner to applaud. Robert lapsed again into silence, pushing his lips in and out, glaring at his outspoken guests.

"Do you see what I mean, Doktor Schumann, how a little rubato leavens the heaviest performance? The Gewandhaus has been too indoctrinated by Mendelssohn. He has infected all of Leipzig with his influence – but, fortunately, all bad habits can be broken."

Clara could remain silent no longer. "Mendelssohn had no bad habits, Herr Liszt, not when it came to playing the piano. He had the cleanest, the most precise, touch."

Liszt spoke more sharply, though still smiling. "I beg your pardon, Madame Schumann, but I do not refer only to his playing. I played, once, his G minor Concerto, from the manuscript, and finding it just a little too simple I broadened it with my own ideas – but Mendelssohn could never take a hint. He refused to accept any suggestions. He was a refined pianist, but no virtuoso. He could never play my works to any great effect, but rather than take a lesson from me he preferred to withhold the effects from his own work."

"You have misunderstood him, Herr Liszt. I heard him more than once talk about the time you played his G minor Concerto from the manuscript – in Paris, was it not? He was always full of admiration for your performance – as is everyone." It is your taste we question, she wanted to add, but didn't.

Mendelssohn had once drawn a picture of Liszt on a blackboard at a soiree playing his G minor Concerto, but with hammers attached to his hands instead of fingers, an exquisite cartoon. Liszt had never expunged the image, nor its corollary: jealous Mendelssohn, propitiating himself by vilifying Liszt. He shook his head. "I do not dispute it, Madame Schumann. My performance was never in question – but my ideas?"

Mendelssohn was not the only person to dislike Liszt's ideas, but no one dared tell Liszt anything, not even Mendelssohn, who had voiced his complaint elsewhere: Liszt's performance was exemplary – for a first reading, but if he had granted Mendelssohn the courtesy of a rehearsal he would have avoided the mistakes he had covered with improvisations, what he called his ideas. Clara raised her chin. "Well, it appears, then, Herr Liszt, that you will play Mendelssohn your way, and I will play him Mendelssohn's way."

Liszt grinned, but tired of arguments, tired of Mendelssohn, found the evening ripe for mischief. "Well said, Madame Schumann! Well said, indeed! But the Mendelssohnians would do well to consider the internationalism of Meyerbeer. Just think, he is a German, a Jew to boot, just like Mendelssohn, but writes operas in French, in the Italian style. That is the true musician of the future, the internationalist, with the flavor of nations in his music rather than of just one town or city, be it Leipzig or Paris – a true European."

Robert sat up straight. "You cannot be serious. Meyerbeer is the essence of effects without causes. The raison d'etre of his music comes from the reactions it provokes, not from the music at all."

"Ah, perhaps, but see how the world receives him. One could fill a library with just what is borrowed from his works, pieces arranged from the airs of his operas. *Robert le Diable* played in almost two thousand European theaters during the Thirties. In London it played in four theaters at once – and you could hear the music as easily in taverns as in churches, in parades as in concerts, in cottages as in palaces." He grinned, knowing how Robert felt about Meyerbeer, familiar with articles in the *Zeitschrift*.

Robert turned red. "It is also well known that he carried the critics of Paris in his pockets, he paid them annual pensions, hundreds of thousands of francs. He could have popularized leprosy had he so wished. He was rich enough."

"But so was Mendelssohn, my friend – so was Mendelssohn – both from banking families, you know."

"Yes, I know, but Mendelssohn had talent, he did not need claqueurs for applause – and he had integrity, in his music as in his life. One cannot say the same about Meyerbeer."

"Everyone employs claqueurs, Schumann. You know that. I will say it again: It is the way of the world, and if we do not accept it –" he shrugged again, "why, then, it will not accept us."

"Do you, Herr Liszt? Do you employ claqueurs?"

Liszt grinned. "I do not need them. I am my own best claqueur."

Robert remained silent, resuming the fishlike movement with his lips.

The silence made Liszt more patronizing. "Of course, Mendelssohn had talent and integrity. That is not in doubt – but he lacked daring. Had he taken but one page from Meyerbeer's book –"

Robert got up suddenly and seized Liszt by the collar. "Who are you to talk so freely about Mendelssohn? His music will live in the world, not just in Leipzig. Meyerbeer is a pygmy next to Mendelssohn – and you, sir, had better watch what you say."

Wagner got up, stationing himself behind Robert; others intervened; but Robert drew his hands from Liszt as he might have drawn them from filth, his face twisted in a grimace, and he left the room.

There was silence; Clara had nothing to say, but stared at Liszt who stared silently back.

Professor Hubner broke the silence. "I beg your pardon, Herr Liszt, but whatever you think of Mendelssohn, he was a good friend of our hosts, he is only recently dead, he is much respected by all present. Professor Bendemann was called to his funeral to sketch and model his face."

Becker spoke next. "And begging your pardon again, Herr Liszt, but was it not Mendelssohn who made a success of your debut in Leipzig? Was it not Mendelssohn who arranged a soiree to win back the regard of the Leipzigers?"

Liszt did not like the reminder. He had neither forgotten Mendelssohn's help nor forgiven him for it. Ignoring Becker and Hubner, he kept his gaze on Clara. He had consorted on his own terms with royalty – refused to play for Isabella II of Spain because court etiquette forbade her to receive him personally; kept Ludwig I of Bavaria from his concerts because both were rivals for Lola Montez, the Spanish dancer; stopped playing when Nicholas I had talked through one of his concerts, saying "Music herself should be silent when Nicholas speaks," silencing the Tsar himself for the rest of the performance – but found himself now upbraided by the dullest people. When Clara remained mute he spoke. "I see how it is and offer my regrets for the evening. Please tell your husband that there is only one person in the world from whom I would take such words as he has given me."

He had not apologized, merely offered regrets. Clara refused to look as he and Wagner took their leave, shaking her head as the door closed behind them. "That wound is too deep for Robert to forget. I am finished with Liszt forever."

Outside, Wagner grinned. "They are very serious people, are they not?"

Liszt returned his grin. "Madame Schumann is not the kind of girl upon whom one makes advances, is she?"

Wagner laughed, shaking his head. "She is the kind who wishes for advances – only so she may spurn them."

ii

ROBERT TO LISZT   *Dresden, April 1849*

My dear Herr Liszt,

I have received your communication through Reinecke and would like to thank you for your very gracious request. Would I be satisfied if my Faust were to be performed for the Goethe Centenary celebrations in Weimar? I would, most certainly, and I would be happy to send it to you – but do you not think it might be just a trifle too Leipzigerish? There is, after all, the scene in Auerbach's Cellar, set in Leipzig, in which Mephistopheles says of Leipzig that it is a little Paris.

But all jokes aside, I would like to take this opportunity to clear any misunderstanding that might remain between us from your last visit. I was at fault for responding so roughly. I was, after all, your host – but let me have my say.

I would not have expected so sweeping a generalization from a man such as yourself, who knows so many of my works. If you study them carefully you will find a great variety. I always attempt to bring out something different in each composition, and I do not mean in form alone. Besides, surely the Leipzig crowd was not so bad – Mendelssohn, Hiller, Bennett, etc. – we can surely hold our heads high against Parisians, Viennese, and Berliners. If there are similarities in some of our works, which you might call Philistinism or whatever you wish, you will find such similarities in any artistic era. You will find them in Bach, Handel, and Gluck – and Haydn, Mozart, and Beethoven are similar enough to be mistaken for one another in a 100 places (I except the last works of Beethoven – but these point right back to Bach, the first Leipziger). Nobody is entirely original. So much for your remark, which was unjust and insulting. For the rest, let us forget the evening – a word is not an arrow – and the main thing is to move on.

As for myself, I am well, except that sometimes every noise turns to music in my head. Perhaps as a musician yourself you will understand this better than others, but sometimes there is too much music in my head to get on paper at once and my head aches for every note I lose. To add to my pain, my last brother, Karl, died just recently. I am the only one left of my generation. I feel sometimes my own time is running out, but I still have work to do. My opera, Genoveva, on which I have been laboring for almost the last two years, is finally to premiere early next year in Leipzig. Perhaps, dear friend, you will come. If you like I will tell you the exact day when I know it myself.

Awaiting your response with much eagerness, I remain yours,
Robert Sch.

LISZT TO ROBERT   *Weimar, April 1849*

My dear Doktor Schumann,

Before all else, let me repeat what you should have known long ago, that no one honors and admires you more than my humble self. Surely we can occasionally differ in a friendly way about the importance of a work, of a man, or even of a town.

I am delighted, indeed, that we shall have your Faust for the Goethe celebrations, and I thank you from the bottom of my heart.

I am very sorry to hear about your brother. I learned early, as did you, what it means to lose one that is dear. I was sixteen when my pappa died, as I know were you. But I am happy, indeed, to hear about your Genoveva. Do keep me informed about the date, my friend, and I will be there. Your most ardent claqueur of the evening will be

Frz Liszt

iii

Chopin wished it might have been different, but the piano in Dr. Lyschinski's den was across the room from the fireplace. If he played he was cold, if he stayed warm he couldn't play. The choices appeared reflected as well in his hosts, the doctor and his wife. He had accepted invitations from friends in England and Scotland to visit and perform, even canceling his last concert in Paris, the February revolution rendering music impossible, the interest on the continent being all politics.

Dr. Lyschinski had met him at the Edinburgh station, greeted him in Polish and taken him to his hotel, but he had hated the hotel, taken a liking to the doctor, and said he couldn't do without him. The doctor had invited him to stay with him and his wife instead, sending his children to a friend's house, converting the nursery into a bedroom, and prepared the adjoining bedroom for his manservant. He had recognized as well the last stages of consumptiveness in Chopin's fatigue, explaining it to his wife who sympathized but resented the changes in their lives to accommodate him.

The hospitality of the English was unlimited; he had at his disposal a Broadwood, a Pleyel, and an Erard, but not the energy for any; he was dragged from one duke to the next, one lord to another, from picture galleries to libraries, hunts were arranged, with horses, dogs, and dinners. His imagination was constantly stimulated by visits to parks, precipices, and ruined castles – but you needed a robust constitution to enjoy England and Scotland and his was too sensitive (the constitution of the artist – worse, of the consumptive) to take advantage of the pleasures. It was all he could do to accommodate his concert dates. The rest of the time he rested.

The doctor was kind enough to carry him up and down the stairs, but the wife delighted in teasing him, stretching his nerves like the high string of a violin on a double bass. He was glad he would soon be again with Jane Stirling, who had visited Paris as his pupil and invited him in return, a slender pretty woman with the smallest mouth and the bearing of a dancer, the most perfect antidote for George Sand, but he was no longer in shape to appreciate even her kindness in full. "Madame Lyschinski, I would like you to sing for me."

Mrs. Lyschinski looked at Chopin stuffed in her armchair, clad even indoors in cravat and coat, hooded eyes, limp hair, knees crossed, hands in his lap also crossed, looking into the fire as if making his request he had only to wait for its fulfillment. For all his genius he was a comical person, rising late in the day, expecting soup in his room in the morning, and his hair curled daily by his manservant, more vain in his dress than a woman and strictly forbidding maidservants in his room. She understood that he was unwell, that he was continental, that he was Chopin – but she was an Englishwoman, unaccustomed to obeying orders. "I am sorry, Mr. Chopin, but I am afraid I do not feel very much like singing."

Chopin's eyes widened with disbelief and he turned to the doctor when she refused to meet his glare. "Dr. Lychinski, would you take it amiss if I were to force your wife to sing?"

Dr. Lyschinski laughed. "I am afraid that would be impossible. Nothing short of a revolution can make her change her mind – and perhaps not even that."

His wife found Chopin's astonishment astonishing, but also amusing. "Why do we not have a nice long talk instead, Mr. Chopin? There is really nothing so salubrious after dinner as a good conversation, do you not agree?"

Chopin wouldn't look at her. "What shall we talk about?"

Mrs. Lyschinski smiled. "I would like very much to talk about you, Mr. Chopin. I find you fascinating, I find you so very gallant, but I find – oh, dear, but you must not take this amiss – I find you have no heart."

Chopin's face was stern, turning finally toward her. "I do not understand you."

"I mean that you have no particular friends among the ladies. That is what I mean."

"It is true, what you say. I have no particular friends among the ladies. I give to them all an equal share of attention."

"But that is just what I mean. That is heartless – but perhaps I am wrong. Perhaps Miss Sterling is one such friend of yours and you are too gallant to admit it without her consent."

Chopin's face remained stern. "It is true again, what you say, they have married us already in the gossip columns – but you see how I am. They might as well have married her to Death."

"Oh, Mr. Chopin, you do so exaggerate your circumstances, but you tell me nothing. Am I to believe that not even George Sand is a particular friend of yours?"

"My dear Madame Lyschinski, it has been a long time since George Sand was a particular friend of mine. We no longer visit each other, and if by chance we meet she calls me her dearest cadaver." He got up, ready for bed, still a young man, just turned forty, but burdened with age, trembling as much with anger as weakness – a sprig, a specter, a willow, a wand, of a man. He spread his hands, his face remaining stern. "Look at me, madame! Look at me closely! I am not long for this world!"

Robert would have stayed with Clara when the knock sounded again on their door, but Clara was wiser. She told him to stay in the bedroom, told Henriette to answer the door, and went herself to the sittingroom where Marie and Elise played the piano, Julie with dolls; Ludwig was asleep in his crib in their bedroom.

"Yes, madam."

Henriette, never entirely responsive, was getting worse, and didn't look at Clara as she went to the door. Something was bothering her, but Clara wished she had chosen a less difficult time to be difficult. Additionally, she was pregnant, in the seventh month of her seventh time (including her miscarriage and the death of Emil, both three years ago).

"It is the guard again, madam. They want to see Doktor Schumann."

"Tell them to wait. I will be there soon."

"Yes, madam."

Clara met the guard at the door; Marie, Elise, and Julie, seven, six, and four, trailing, Julie clutching her dress, all eyes wide, faces blank with apprehension. Clara wanted to impress the girls and her pregnancy on the men; homes with children and pregnant women had different needs from homes without. Henriette waited behind, and behind her their cook, Mathilde.

The two men were not the same as had come an hour earlier, but as young, younger than Clara, both with long knives in sheaths in their belts, one carried a staff, the other a rifle. "Gentlemen, yes?"

The man with the rifle spoke. "Frau Schumann?"

"Yes?"

"You know, of course, what is happening?"

A cry rose from an inner room. Clara turned, afraid Robert would comfort the baby, afraid they would hear. "Henriette, go see to the baby."

Henriette appeared not to hear her.

"Henriette, I said Go! At once!" Henriette's eyelids drooped; she might have been medicated for the way she moved, but she left.

Clara turned back to the guard. "Yes, of course, I know what is happening. I walked yesterday with my husband in the streets. We could hardly believe it."

Two days ago, 3 May, returning from dinner at a new restaurant they had heard the thud of drums, clangor of bells from the towers, howl and hubbub of the mob, the crack, whistle, and pock of rifles. Discontent had simmered for months, everyone read the newspapers; the King of France, Louis-Phillippe, the Citizen-King, had been overthrown in Paris, Metternich had resigned in Vienna, disturbances threatened Lombardy, Switzerland, Hungary, all Europe; a thousand Berliners had been killed fighting Prussian soldiers, all for freedoms which should have been taken for granted – of the press, of the people to determine their future. Of course, the monarchy and aristocrats resisted – but so did many of their friends, imagining themselves on par with the nobility. Robert had had a discussion with Bendemann not unlike a quarrel, and she with Frau Hubner – all because they believed they knew better than the working class what was best for them. The trouble had begun in Dresden when the King of Saxony, bolstered by assurance of military aid from the King of Prussia, had dissolved both houses of the Saxon Parliament and rejected the constitution of the Frankfurt Parliament proposing a national government, royal lineage, and legislature limiting the power of the King.

A crowd had removed the poles from the King's carriage and attempted to gain his arsenal from which they had drawn fire. Fourteen citizens had been killed and displayed to the Dresdeners in the court of the hospital on 4 May, limbs and heads at impossible angles, to indict the King. They had seen the corpses and heard the gasps and wails of citizens coming unexpectedly on the sight. Barricades had been erected in the night from the paving stones of the streets, and were defended by men with scythes. Robert had been calm, absorbing everything, saying nothing – so calm, in fact, she imagined he denied what he saw, or saw it as a dream or nightmare – and had remained calm after they had returned, but so remote she was anxious.

The man with the rifle had a sharp voice. "You know the King has escaped?"

Clara's eyes widened. "No, I did not know."

"He got away in the night – to Konigstein, it is believed – but his soldiers are still camped in front of his castle – with cannons. The citizens are in the town hall even now, choosing a temporary government."

The baby had stopped crying; Clara closed her eyes, momentarily relieved, shaking her head. "I cannot believe what is happening. It is terrible – but all men are equal and must be treated so."

The guard nodded. "You know how we feel. The students are with us, and many citizens, but we need to be organized, and we need every man we can get. I am sure you understand. We know Doktor Schumann is sympathetic to our cause. He has always professed himself a Republican. Will he come with us?"

"Of course. He is out at the moment – but he will be back soon."

The man peered into her eyes. "We will be back. If your husband is not here we will search the house. We do not fight just for ourselves, you know, but for everyone, for you and your husband as well – not just for Dresden, but for Germany."

Clara held his gaze. "I know. My husband will be back soon."

The man saluted. "Long live the Republic." The second followed him silently without another look at Clara and the girls.

As soon as she had shut the door Clara rushed to the bedroom. "Robert, they will be back. We must leave at once. There is no other way."

Henriette stood by the crib; Robert sat on the bed looking at the wall, as remote as she had left him; it had been just a week since his last brother, Karl, had died.

"Robert, there is no time to waste. Get your shoes on, get your coat!"

"Where will we go?" His voice was hollow, childish.

"We have to get out of here. We will find a safe place."

"What about the children?"

"The children are safe. It is not the children they want. It is you. Hurry, Robert!"

She was busy with her own shoes, it took longer with her big belly, shodding herself sideways; Robert roused himself. "We cannot leave the children."

"We will take Marie. We will come back for the others when we have found a place. They will be all right with Henriette."

Elise clung to Clara's arm. "Please, Mamma. Take me also! Please take me with you!"

Robert got up finally. "No! The fewer we are the better."

"Pappa is right, Elise. With too many it will be too dangerous. It will look as if we are running away."

"We will be back soon – most likely by the evening."

"You will be safer here with Henriette and Mathilde."

They escaped through the garden in the back. Clara led, chin up, belly extended, holding Marie's hand; Marie held her dark head low, expecting bullets; Robert followed, looking around like a tourist, stumbling on the rubble. Clara detoured twice around barricades, heading for the Bohemian Station, keeping an eye on Robert as they walked. They were met along the way by another guard, three armed men, two holding scythes, one a rifle. The man with the rifle stopped them. "Halt!"

They stopped. Clara spoke. "Yes, sir?"

"Where are you going?"

Robert did not seem to hear, not even to see what was happening. "We are expected at a friend's, in Maxen. We are taking the train."

"Are you armed?"

Clara smiled. "You can see what I am carrying." She put her hands on her belly. "I have no room for anything else."

The man seemed embarrassed and let her pass with Marie. Robert was searched, yielding amiably, smiling.

"It is all right. They are unarmed."

The first man spoke again. "The King is at Konigstein. We go to make one more effort to get his concession. Will you come with us?"

Clara's smile pleaded for understanding. "We would if we were not expected – and if we did not have the child. We are Republicans – but our friends would wonder, they would worry. You know how it is."

She presented a charming picture, twenty-nine years, holding her daughter's hand, her belly round with life. The man nodded. "Let them go. They are not armed." He turned back to Clara. "Be careful. They say the King has sent for the Prussians. The guard is apt to shoot first and ask questions afterward. Anything can happen."

"Thank you. We will be careful." When they were out of earshot she turned to Robert. "It might be a good idea to go to Maxen, Robert. What do you think? We could stay with Major Serre until we see how it is."

Major Serre and his wife, whom Clara had known since childhood, on whose estate she had holidayed with her pappa, where she had stayed when she played in Dresden, would welcome them to their villa. Robert did not look at her, but nodded.

ii

7 May, three o'clock in the morning, fog descending on the fields, a carriage stopped outside Dresden. Clara stepped into the night. There was another woman in the carriage, Frau von Berg, whose hands flew to her mouth as she looked out of the window. "Oh, my God! Look! The city is burning!"

Clara looked; across the field, through the fog, an orange glow permeated the blackness like a giant lantern. She took a deep breath. "That will be the opera house. It was the last news at the villa yesterday. They were going to burn it to protect Semper's barricade from a surprise attack – so easy to burn, they said, so full of wood and canvas."

Frau von Berg looked at Clara. "You are sure you want to go? You can come with me to Strehla, you know. We can come back when we know it is safe."

Clara shook her head. "I am sure. When it is safe it might be too late – if it is not too late already. The fire will light my way like a beacon. Otherwise, in the night, I might get lost."

"You are a brave woman, Frau Schumann. Across the field is the Reitbahngasse. I shall be back here after sunrise. Good luck to you."

"Thank you, Frau von Berg. Good luck also to you."

The carriage took off down the road; Clara stepped into the field; the ground was soft with dew, and her feet and the hem of her dress became immediately damp, bathed in grass.

The cannonfire had been so constant she would have imagined something wrong had it stopped. The shots were audible in Maxen, but now she imagined she heard as well, following the roar of each explosion, the whistle of the ball through the air, the crack of contact. She walked unsteadily, holding her full belly before her, praying for courage, questioning the sanity of men – but never the rationale of what she did. She had listened too long already to the cannonfire, the whole day past, doing nothing, while Elise and Julie and Ludwig remained stranded and imperiled, but there was no one to go with her. By the reports, all men who could were compelled to pick up rifles; she would be safer than Robert, safer without him; and when Frau von Berg, getting her things from Strehla, had offered to drive her, she had seized her chance.

The air resonated between each blow from the cannon, each whistle, each crack, with a silence more pure, numbness beyond noise, like a stoppage of time during which time she floated, blessings like wings on her back, bolstering her courage, providing a sense of invincibility, until the next blow of the cannon – and the next step again into the empyrean. Approaching the Reitbahngasse she could see the black silhouettes of buildings against the glow, the trees in the foreground, movement below, a traffic of heads bobbing in the dark. Whether the fog had thinned, whether there had been nothing before to see, or whether she was finally close enough, she couldn't have said, but a group of men appeared, perhaps forty, staring and silent, advancing with scythes in hand.

It was too late already to sidestep the men, too late to retreat. Clara held up her chin, folding her hands under her belly, turning her head neither to left nor right, walking on, her face expressionless, eyes glazed – and the men parted, letting her pass, one staying with her as she entered the city, escorting her safely home.

The streets were cluttered with rubble, the air pungent with gunpowder, thick with dust and smoke – and hot when the wind blew her way. Her mouth was dry, gritty; she found it hard to breathe, also to see, but some streetlights burned, a glow was everpresent over the city, her eyes grew accustomed to the dark, she rolled her tongue in her mouth and spat continually, covering her nose with a handkerchief. Looking up she saw an unmade bed, table by its side, lamp on the table, picture on the wall; she looked again, the side of a wall had been blown away; above and below flats were similarly exposed, a cuckoo clock, rocking cradle, dog barking in silence, public views of private rooms like sections of giant dollhouses; she didn't look again. She heard a moan close on her left, but did not stop; and the silence which had seemed so pure until then between blows from the cannon was flooded with the moans she had taken before for silence.

The windows had been smashed, outer walls pocked with bullet holes, but the front door was secure. The children were asleep; she tore them from their beds, dressed them, packed some things, warned Elise and Julie to hold onto her dress, to look at nothing whatever they heard, whatever moved in the corner of their eyes. She picked Ludwig in her arms, slung a bag over her shoulder, another over Elise's, both too sleepy or stunned to cry, and was soon across the streets, crossing the field again. Henriette had taken no notice, sleeping when she had entered, sleeping through the visit, sleeping when they had left; Clara, immersed in her task, telling Mathilde what to do, noticed only her uselessness. Later they learned she had smallpox.

Back in the carriage with Frau von Berg, back on the road to Maxen, Clara heard the Marseillaise. The rising sun revealed a column of soldiers by the Reitbahngasse, a glint of rifles in a row; and emerging from the mountains, the Erzgebirgler, mountain people, miners, to reinforce the Saxons in the city, brandishing scythes and staffs.

Rumors had been stirring before she had left Maxen of support from the Saxons. She was thrilled by the courage of the villagers, the worst brought out the best – but rumors had also been stirring of the King, safe in his fortress in Konigstein, expecting reinforcements, Prussians from Berlin.

iii

Liszt had scheduled a performance of *Tannhauser* in Weimar during the second week of May, the first to be held outside Dresden, and had invited Wagner, but heard at last count that he could not obtain a leave of absence from the Royal Opera – the greater his surprise, then, when Hermann Cohen announced Wagner at the door to his rooms at the Erbprinz Hotel. He advanced on his friend, smiling broadly, appearing more to float than walk, feet in clouds, arms open in greeting. "My friend, what a surprise! I did not expect you – which only increases my joy."

Wagner almost bound into his arms. Liszt was more than his friend, his savior. Already, he had transcribed for piano the *Tannhauser* Overture, transcribed also extracts, and written an article publicizing the opera in Paris. "Ach, Liszt, I am pleased to see you! Pleased, indeed! Oh, you cannot imagine, you cannot imagine!"

Liszt drew back, grasping Wagner's hands. "And your timing could not have been better, my friend. *Tannhauser* is scheduled for a rehearsal within the hour – and I have so many questions regarding the execution."

Wagner's appearance was in stark contrast to Liszt, hair uncombed, face unshaven, clothes wrinkled, eyes wild, feet leaden, voice whispering and trembling. "Och, Liszt! We have got to talk! We have got to talk!"

He appeared more agitated than usual, but Liszt imagined he wanted to discuss the finer points of the score. "Of course, but after the rehearsal."

"No – not after! At once. It is important!"

"Of course, it is important – but there is time yet."

Wagner's voice rose. "Ach! No, I tell you! How am I to make you understand? Do you not see, man, how I am? Do you not hear me? We do not have time. We must talk at once!"

Liszt dropped his smile and put a hand on Wagner's shoulder. "What is the matter, my friend?"

Wagner rolled his eyes at Cohen, whispering again. "In private!"

Liszt would have said he trusted Cohen, but Wagner's eyes lost focus, his head swiveled on a gimbals, he might have imagined enemies in the drapes, the drapes themselves alive and inimical. "Hermann, please leave us. See that we are not disturbed."

Cohen nodded, but even before he had closed the door behind him Wagner had begun talking. "Liszt, there is a warrant for my arrest. There are bills posted in Dresden with my face, like a common criminal. The Saxon police are hounding me. I need money, I need asylum, I need your help!"

Liszt led him to a couch and seated him. "My friend, what are you saying? Tell me from the beginning what has happened."

Wagner told him, sentences rolling from his mouth, tumbling one over the other, the story of his part in the battle of Dresden. "Ach, Liszt, but this is the end. The Prussians have the upper hand. The barbarians have won the day. Twenty-six students were found hiding in a room and shot in broad daylight. People are being thrown from the third and fourth storeys of buildings into the streets. I was lucky to escape, Liszt, but my deeds are known. I never made a secret of my sympathies. You know how I am – not one to fit my words to the fashion, not against my convictions. I speak the truth, always, whatever the consequences – but you know that about me."

Wagner told Liszt of the speeches he had made from the town hall, the strategies he had planned with the rebels, the grenades he had ordered of which there were records, the barricades he had constructed. He didn't mention his overestimation of the strength of the rebels which had led in part to their defeat, nor his erroneous reports of the movements of the Saxon and Prussian troops.

He had escaped purely by chance, rooming at a different inn from the other rebels he had planned to meet, Bakunin and Hubner and Semper, all of whom had been seized in their sleep from the inn and imprisoned in the Frauenkirche with five hundred others, charged with treason, and now awaiting death, while Prussians swarmed the city and camped in the Altmarkt, the lords of Dresden. He had escaped from the inn to his sister's house in a suburb, where he had already installed his wife, dog, and parrot – from where his brother-in-law had helped him escape by night in a post-chaise to Weimar.

Liszt was not unaware of the political climate elsewhere. The revolution had spread to Weimar the year before, demonstrations in the marketplace before the palace, but the Grand Duke, Karl Friedrich, had responded more cagily than Friedrich of Saxony, granting amnesty to political prisoners, approving cosmetic changes in his own constitution, giving an inch, gaining yards. It was another twenty years before Bismarck's victories finally incorporated all of Germany.

His problems were also more personal. His newest and greatest love, Princess Carolyne Sayn-Wittgenstein, lived on the outskirts of Weimar in a mansion, the Altenburg, named after the hill on which it stood. Her husband was the adjutant to Nicholas I of Russia, whose sister, Marie Paulovna, was the Grand Duchess of Weimar, wife of the Grand Duke, Liszt's employer – and the Tsar was already voicing objections to his sister regarding the Princess's plans to marry Liszt. Adultery was a crime punishable by imprisonment in Weimar, but Liszt planned to join her in the Altenburg sooner rather than later. He was Liszt, not subject to common laws, but neither did he wish to be indebted to the Duke for protection.

Liszt stood again, hands knotted in fists, looking no longer at Wagner, speaking almost to himself, but aloud. "How stupid they are! How selfish! They mind everyone's business but their own – no one thinks of anyone but himself. I am sick, sick of it all."

Wagner stared, unaccustomed to such emotion from Liszt. "You are right, absolutely right. People are stupid and selfish. I, too, am sick of it. If you and I ruled the world we could show them. We could give pleasure to the people. It is love that matters, good Christian love, and music – German music – but what are we to do? This is the world and it is not our world. It is not in our power."

Liszt stared at Wagner. "Do you know something, my friend?"

"What is it, my friend?"

"Just the other day someone was telling me how moved she had been by a performance of the Marseillaise on the Paris stage." He shook his head. "Can you tell me, my friend, how it is possible? Is it not rather a folly, is it not rather a criminal act, a sin, to sing the Marseillaise today? What have the revolutions of today to do with that one of the last century? What has this bloodthirsty hymn to do with us now, during this time of social upheaval, whose basic principal is love, and whose single solution is only possible through love?"

Wagner nodded. "Ach, yes, love! That is the only solution, the only solution – the *Chris*tian solution!"

Liszt unclenched his fists and held out his hands, palm open. "I would be the first to answer the call to arms – you know that, my friend. I would be the first to shed my blood, even to face the guillotine, if that is what it would take to bring peace and happiness to the world – but what is required today is ideas, to bring about the right social changes."

"I am with you, my friend. I, too, would be first to the guillotine – if it would bring peace to the world – and happiness. I would follow you."

Liszt nodded, sitting again with his friend. "But it is as you say. This is the world and we have no power over it."

Wagner nodded. "It is as you say. This is the world and it has got me in trouble through no fault of my own."

Liszt sighed. "I will do what I can, my friend, to help you. In the meantime, you must keep out of sight."

"Ach, but yes, so it must be. I understand perfectly."

Within the next twelve days Liszt outfitted Wagner with money, a false passport, and safe passage to Zurich. Wagner would be Professor Werder from Berlin with a Swabian accent to accord with the passport.

"It is the most curious thing about Hamburgers. They are an appreciative, but silent audience." Clara was at the piano in their hotel room with Jenny Lind and Robert, ready to rehearse for their evening concert in Altona. Robert had written to Jenny to say they wished to visit her in Berlin on their return from the Hamburg tour, but she had shown up herself instead in Hamburg and offered to join Clara on the bill. She had been gladly received, but Clara was hardly in need of rescue as she had been in Vienna. "Our receipts are good, our reviews are good, and backstage they are not too shy to tell us how they feel – but they rarely show it. Their faces remain like stone even when their words could not be sweeter."

Jenny stood by the window, resting a hand on the sill, staring at the Alster. "My dear Frau Schumann, you must not let it trouble you. It is just their way, you know. They are the same with everyone. It is said that Hamburg is the most English of German towns – perhaps an extension of what is known in England as the stiff upper lip."

Robert spoke quietly, expressionless himself. "Someone said yesterday – one of the staff – that when it rains in London, Hamburgers unfurl their umbrellas."

Clara laughed, but without mirth, and spoke not without edge. "Their appreciation is the same, like a shower, no sooner begun than ended."

Jenny had noticed the change in her friends, their immediate circumstances much improved since Vienna, their concerts a success, but they appeared bitter, Robert bulkier, face in shadow, surprised when addressed, otherwise distracted, walking like an old man but not yet forty; and Clara, barely thirty, no less at ease, eyes with rings, anticipating trouble, smiling with difficulty, even her nose appeared sharper. They had always been highstrung, that was the way with pure artists and none were purer than the Schumanns; the three years since she had seen them might have been ten. The uprising must have affected them in ways she couldn't fathom. "But it is also beautiful, is it not, Frau Schumann? the Alster, the Jungfernstieg?"

"Oh, you are right, of course. My dissatisfaction is but of the moment. There is such life, such wealth, in Hamburg, and especially along the Jungfernstieg – the promenaders, the shops – I could stand and watch them forever – and the people are so kind. We could almost think of settling here."

Jenny turned from the window. "Really? In Hamburg? Do you not like it in Dresden anymore?"

Clara shook her head. "We never did, not really. It is a good city, but not for music. One has to fight to get a concert produced. One has to fight for anything not sanctioned directly by the Court – and after the uprising it has only become worse. Artists in general, but musicians in particular, are viewed with suspicion."

Robert nodded, still expressionless, almost toneless. "When Mendelssohn died I requested the use of the Frauenkirche for a memorial service, but they would not allow it. When Chopin died, it was the same. They have no understanding of the good in music, the importance of such men." He had requested as well complimentary seats at the opera, due their status as artists, as they had received in Leipzig, but been told without apology that such seats were only for musicians who wrote for the stage. He had written nothing yet for the stage, but he had been writing *Genoveva*, his first opera, which made him more anxious yet to attend, but he had been refused again, even more rudely.

Clara spoke again, drumming her fingers on the piano. "Robert has composed more and published more in the past year than in almost any other year, but most of it remains unheard. The clods in Dresden have no appreciation for what is in their very midst, no enthusiasm for anything, no blood in their veins, no life in their shriveled faces. They are like blocks of wood." Clara clenched her fists in her lap. "I am sorry if I appear ungrateful, but so it is."

Robert said nothing, but noted how she had changed; hardships hardened you, her tone had turned imperious; true, she defended him, and he loved her for it, but the once proud Republican now mocked the clods of Dresden for their stupidity, allied herself with aristocrats, for which he blamed himself, unable to shield her from the hardships.

Jenny left the window, coming toward Clara, beginning to understand the change in her. "You do not appear ungrateful to me, not if what you say is true, and never have you given me reason to doubt you."

"It is most definitely so." Clara had been amazed by Robert's output in the wake of the uprising; all that time he had been quiet, almost comatose, he had been processing events, what he had seen, what he had heard, transmuting the violence and despair to music, hunting songs featuring horns, marches, motets, cantatas, a requiem, many more scenes from *Faust*, the finishing touches to *Genoveva* – she had lost track. Her eyes narrowed, her voice thickened. "It *is* stupid, do you not think, to stay where you are ignored?"

Jenny spoke softly. "Indeed, but not so stupid as the people who ignore you."

Clara sighed; there was another reason of which she said nothing. She had hoped for a greater reconciliation with her pappa in Dresden, to be again his daughter, even occasionally his pupil, but he was now dedicated to her stepsister, Marie, and a new pupil, Minna Schultz, whom he called his daughter, neither of whom could match Clara at the piano. "You are kind to say it, Fraulein Lind, a true friend. Thank you." She nodded, looking at Robert. "We do plan to leave."

"Oh, my dear Frau Schumann, then I am happy for you. For me such decisions are easily made, where to go, what to do, because I am but one. Give me herrings and potatoes, a clean wooden chair, a wooden spoon for milk soup, and I will skip like a child with joy – but for you, with your darling children, the decisions must be made so much more difficult. Do you know where you plan to go?"

"We have received an offer from Dusseldorf, from our friend, Hiller, who has been offered a conductorship in Cologne and offers us the one he will vacate. We are thinking of accepting it." The salary was just seven hundred thaler; Liszt received a thousand in Weimar, board and lodging at the Altenburg was paid by the Duke; Wagner had received fifteen hundred right there in Dresden, another situation for which Robert hadn't been considered; but it was a guaranteed income, they would have an orchestra at their disposal, Robert's duties would be light (ten secular concerts a year, four sacred) leaving time for composition, the Hamburg tour had already raised eight hundred thaler, and other tours could do the same if necessary in the future.

Robert lit a cigar and spoke again, still without conviction. "It will be a great advantage to have my own orchestra." He said nothing about his fears, his ability to lead an orchestra, to communicate what he wanted. Hiller had said the orchestra was well rehearsed in the classics, nothing more.

Jenny was seized with a cough and waved smoke from her face with her hands.

Clara looked at Robert, frowning; they both knew how she cared for her throat, neither drinking (not wine, not tea, not coffee), nor abiding smoke – not even dancing; she hated celebrity and parties and was the first to leave when she was obliged to attend; she shut out noises when she slept with stoppers of wool, and was plagued no less than Robert with headaches and rheumatism at an age far less advanced – which perhaps accounted for the sympathy between them. Robert put out the cigar.

Jenny bowed her head. "Thank you, Doktor Schumann. My throat, I am afraid, is much too sensitive, but it is all I have."

Robert nodded. "And we are most grateful to have a share of your treasure. I beg your pardon. I merely forgot for a moment."

"Ah, but Frau Schumann, I still wish you would let me increase your own treasures with mine."

She had wanted to raise the price of tickets, but Clara had been firm, wanting to remain within reach of as many as wanted to attend. She shook her head. "You do enough. It is enough that we will be together."

It was good of Clara, but Jenny was more canny, less democratic, never mixed her ideals with business. She said nothing about her forthcoming trip to America, sponsored by P. T. Barnum, for which she was to receive a hundred and fifty thousand thaler for a hundred and fifty concerts, paid in advance to a bank in London, plus the cost of horses, carriages, servants, a secretary, a companion, whatever she wished.

There was a knock on the door. Clara looked up. "Come in."

A liveried servant entered, a large envelope in his hand. "This was delivered for Doktor Schumann by hand to the concierge."

Robert and Clara exchanged glances. Robert held out his hand. "I am Doktor Schumann."

The servant gave him the envelope. He frowned reading the name on the envelope. "Johannes Brahms? I do not know any Johannes Brahms."

"He is from Hamburg, Doktor Schumann. He plays the piano in the dance halls. The concierge has seen him before."

Robert weighed the envelope in his hand, still frowning.

Clara's eyes hardened, also her tone. "What is it, Robert? More manuscripts?"

Robert nodded. "I am sure of it."

Clara maintained her stoniness; Robert spent too much time on unpromising manuscripts from unpromising musicians. "Send it back. There is no point even in opening it. Send it back as it is."

"Perhaps you are right, perhaps it is for the best." He looked at Jenny. "Some people think we have nothing better to do than look at any old manuscript they choose to send us."

Jenny nodded, smiling. "That is how it is with me, too. They are constantly sending me songs to sing."

"What do you do with them?"

"I send them back – unopened – just like your dear wife has suggested."

Robert nodded. "That is wise, I am sure." He returned the package to the attendant. "Please return this with our regrets to your young piano player."

After the attendant had gone Clara shook her head. "What a fool the man must be! He plays the piano in dance halls – and sends manuscripts to Robert Schumann! What a world it is we live in!"

ii

Robert was paralyzed, unsure which of the entrances to take, but the longer he waited the more the walls spun, and the dizzier he grew. The applause, ever rising, never even dipped, from the roar of hands to a chorus of Bravos and calls for SCHU-MANN! SCHU-MANN! SCHU-MANN! SCHU-MANN! Blood thickened in his head, calcifying his face, stopping his breath. The last major event of their years in Dresden was taking place in Leipzig, the first performance of *Genoveva*, and he couldn't have asked for better attendance. Joachim, Gade, David, Hiller, Spohr, Moscheles, among others, had arrived from Bremen, Hamburg, Konigsberg, Dresden, so had Wieck, Clara's mamma from Berlin, Kuntsch from Zwickau, in-laws from Schneeberg, Liszt from Weimar, and all called for him from the hall. First, he had rushed, but lost himself in the labyrinth of passages leading to the stage – and the longer he hesitated, the more he was deafened by the applause, the quicker beat his heart, the slower grew his step.

He had worn a frockcoat and striped pants; not anticipating so volatile a reaction he had left his dress-suit in Dresden; and might have hidden himself had Clara not appeared suddenly behind him. "Robert, why do you keep everybody waiting?"

She giggled. He had not heard her giggle in a long while and smiled, but remained rooted until she pushed him toward the correct entrance and he stumbled onstage. He would have fallen had one of the performers not caught him and came to a standstill as soon as he found his balance, staring at the audience, eyes of glass, mouth of plastic, body of stone; he might have been staring at a monster.

Clara shouted from the wings. "Bow, Robert! Take a bow! BOW!"

He looked like a sweet fat boy, bobbing his head like a woodpecker, popping lips like a fish; shying like a horse when someone threw a wreath onstage – which one of the sopranos picked up and placed on his bobbing head like a crown.

Clara imagined she had never seen him more lovable, neither as a man nor an artist, and almost wept to see him so simple and unassuming. She had never doubted him, always defended him, but found herself tiring, wishing the world could see him as she saw him, he was not the kind to make the efforts demanded by the world; unlike Liszt, unlike other virtuosos, unlike even herself, his work meant more to him than its approbation, but approbation was gratifying when it came, all the more for not having been courted.

The following day Liszt played with Clara, the Overture to *Genoveva*, playing always with aplomb and daring, throwing down scarf and gloves before seating himself, flinging his hair about, mocking his own stage manner, breaking a bass string, muttering gravely, shaking his head in wonder, "I beg your pardon, but such a thing has never happened to me before," eliciting laughter from the select company, including Robert, but the laughter remained hollow, polite, unspontaneous, despite everyone's effort to regain the old camaraderie.

The critics had been less ingratiating than the audience, complaining that the orchestra overpowered the voices, the opera lacked drama – and the Schumanns, realizing their success had been less than they had imagined, remained too unsure of themselves and their future to trust Liszt or anyone who disagreed with them.

iii

In September 1850, an article, "Judaism in Music," was published pseudonymously in the *Zeitschrift* by Karl Friegedank (Free Thought); its argument, much abridged and sanitized, was as follows. (1) The language of the Jew, Hebrew, was a dead language, (2) the Jew spoke in borrowed tongues, the languages of Europe; ergo (3), he could never speak as a native, never from his soul, never colloquially, never authoritatively, but always as an outsider, always superficially. (4) It was impossible to create in a borrowed tongue; ergo (5), the Jew could only imitate, never create, neither a poem nor any genuine work of art. (6) The arts of the Jew were usury and cunning; ergo (7), he bought his way into society, and (8) baptised himself into a Christian, but (9) his relationships depended upon money and duplicity, and (10) money and duplicity never thickened bonds between men; ergo (11), the Jew remained alone, uncomfortable in borrowed robes. (12) Native speech is unavailable to the Jew, (13) song is speech impassioned by music; ergo (14), music is unavailable to the Jew, and (15) any musical effort by the Jew was infected by his own emptiness, and (16) infected all who heard it, infected the pure Teutonic body politic, the Germanity, of Germany. One such Jew was Felix Mendelssohn-Bartholdy, who showed how a Jew could possess culture, talent, honor, and still lack profundity, who could mimic the forms of music and still lack content. Another such Jew, Giacomo Meyerbeer, wrote operas, disguising his lack of content with a form too blinding for clarity, disguising what was foolish with what appeared modern, producing them in Paris, and sending them around the world, a dependable way for the nonartist to appear an artist. Such Jews polluted the purity of Germany and had to be eliminated, the question was whether through ejection or assimilation.

The transgressions of logic are glaring, but need perhaps to be enunciated for the occasional idiot who imagines he's found a palimpsest to fit the warp in his own head. Let me get you started: (1) A masterpiece is, by definition, universal, not national, not German, but Beyond German; (2) your native language is the one you use, not the one your long dead ancestors used; (3) outsiders are not, by definition, superficial; (4) usury and cunning are no more prevalent among Jews than among nonJews; (5) you cannot have culture, talent, honor, without profundity; (6) Mendelssohn wrote the Overture to "A Midsummer Night's Dream" when he was seventeen; the Overture is a masterpiece; and (7) Mendelssohn was a Jew; ergo (8), a Jew may create a masterpiece of music; and (9) all prior assumptions must be false. You get the picture, you fill in #s (10), (11), (12), (13), ad infinitum – especially you there with the warp in your head.

The editor of the *Zeitschrift*, Franz Brendel, also the new owner, also a Professor of Musical History at the Leipzig Conservatory founded by Mendelssohn, provided a disclaimer: (1) The above essay had been published in the interests of intellectual freedom, a preeminent claim of the new Germany, particularly in the scientific field; and (2) the views may be disputed, but not the breadth of the author.

Brendel's disclaimer tarred him with the same brush; many recognized the style of the article, but it was twenty years before Wagner felt secure enough to claim authorship; in the meantime a petition was signed by other professors of the Conservatory, among them Joachim, Moscheles, Hauptmann, Rietz, David, requesting Brendel's removal from the staff, but he was retained, not even censured.

"Who is the composer?"

"Never mind that. What did you think of the theme?"

"It is you, Hannes, is it not? You are the composer?"

"What do you think? After all this time you still have to ask?"

"Why do you always answer my questions with a question?"

"Why should I have to answer a question when the answer is obvious?"

"Because maybe it is not so very obvious to everyone else."

"Ja, ja, maybe not to some people, but never mind. What did you think of the theme?"

The implication that some people were stupid, she among them, wasn't lost on Louise – but his charmlessness was compensated by his talent, she would have said genius, a boy of eighteen writing sonatas Schumann might have envied, muscular beyond anything by Mozart, anything by Haydn; like his personality they were charmless, but compensated by strength, modeled on Beethoven, intertwining so many voices they needed two pianos, sounding discordant until a closer acquaintance revealed the vast, various, intricate, individual pleasures. "Which theme do you mean?"

They were again in the piano warehouse, BAUMGARTEN & HEINZ, where they practised. Hannes shook his head. "Which theme? Which do you think? What have we been playing?" He brought his hands down with a crash on the piano, exaggerating the theme they had been playing, letting his derision seep into his music. "We have only been playing it for the last fifteen minutes!"

It was unnerving to see this child with flaxen hair play like a savage, no less unnerving to hear him scold her with his birdy voice; she had learned to accept it, but found herself often uncomfortable in his presence. "I thought it was very … passionate!"

"Passionate?"

"Yes, passionate."

"You did not find it a little bit … ordinary?"

"Well, since you put it that way, I will say it is not one of your best themes."

"Ach, then why did you not tell me what you thought? Why did you tell me it was … passionate? Why did I have to say it first? I want to know what you think. I already know what I think."

Louise took a deep breath; if she said nothing she would only fester, cry later as she had done before – but she couldn't let him treat her like a child when he was barely more than a child himself. "Hannes, you are impossible!"

"I am impossible? How am I impossible? I ask a question. Should I not expect an answer? Why is that impossible?"

"You are rude – but not just to me. You are rude to everyone."

"Then you should not take it personally."

"I do not take it personally – but it is difficult to be your friend when you insist on being so disagreeable."

"How am I disagreeable?"

Louise shook her head. Hannes rarely said anything unless he wanted something; even she was no more than a sounding board for his compositions; he was selfish, but she was glad to befriend him for his gifts. "Sometimes I think it will not be difficult to leave you behind, Hannes. You are a very difficult friend – sometimes hardly a friend at all." She and her sister were going to Dusseldorf, she to study with the Schumanns, Minna to attend the Academy of Art.

"Tchah! What you say has neither head nor foot. You are talking about that Schumann again. He is no good. You should stay in Hamburg. You should study with Marxsen. He knows everything."

"About Bach and Beethoven, maybe – but nothing about Schumann – but I do not want to talk about this, Hannes. We have been through this before."

"And as before, you are still pigheaded."

She almost screamed. "*I* am pigheaded? *Me?* Hannes, you may know everything about music, but you know nothing about people. I am not the one who is pigheaded." She got up, buttoning her coat, picking up her purse. "*You* are the one who is still angry because Schumann returned your manuscripts. *You* are the one who will not see the good in Schumann because he was too busy to look at your manuscripts."

Hannes had been angry, but not even Louise knew how angry. He had smashed his favorite lead soldier, but said nothing to anyone. "He should have looked! He should have taken the time, at least, to look. It was your idea to send him the work. Otherwise, I would never have sent it."

"It was a good idea to send it. If he was not too busy he would have looked. He has a reputation for helping new artists. You can see from his articles in the *Zeitschrift* how carefully he reads everything. If he returned your work it does not mean he did not like it, only that he was too busy. If he had returned it opened, that would have been a different story – but I do not wish to argue. When you find out who is being pigheaded, then you can come and apologize. Otherwise, you can leave me alone!"

Hannes's eyes opened; he might have been seeing her for the first time. "But why are you so angry?"

"Why am I so angry? Hannes …" She shook her head. "I do not believe you."

"What do you mean?"

"I do not understand how you can be so dense."

He grinned. "Now who is being rude? Who is calling who stupid?"

"I am trying to make you see yourself as you appear to other people. That is what I am trying to do. That is *all* I am trying to do."

Still he grinned; he had learned about people from the ladies of Zur schwarzen Katze, but never talked about them; Louise would never understand such women, but she played the piano well – for a girl. He patted the space she had vacated on the bench. "Louise, do not go away angry. Stay."

She remained still; she understood he was rude to hide his discomfort, but at least he talked with her; with others he was rude through silence.

Still he grinned. "Sometimes I think I am composed like Kapellmeister Johannes Kreisler from the book by Hoffman, *Kater Murr* – too little phlegm and too much distemper. That is my personality – too little phlegm and too much distemper – but you must not let it trouble you."

It was as close as she would get to an apology; at another time she might have laughed, but now she shook her head. "You know what your trouble is, Hannes. You have to get out of Hamburg. You know it. There is nothing for you here. You are bored."

It was true; he had given more concerts and received mostly good notices, but never caught fire; politics was changing the face the world; the pulse of independence, emanating from Paris, had swept countries like dominoes, Hungary the last, discarding the dominion of Austria – and squeezed between Austria and Russia, Hungary filtered refugees into Europe, filling the hotels of Hamburg, pushing music low in the pantheon of priorities, his own music the lowest. He was without direction, bored without knowing he was bored, angry without knowing the source of his anger, helpless without recognizing his helplessness. "Maybe you are right. Will you play the sonata with me one more time?"

She sat again beside him, unbuttoning her coat, sighing. "Hannes, I wish I could make you see."

ii

The face, chubby and smooth, shaped like an egg, and the tonsure, shorn and thinning, belonged to a bank clerk, but the stance and smirk belonged to a musician and revolutionary, which Eduard Remenyi emphatically was, also an extraordinary fiddler – also a refugee from Hungary present at the crucial battle, the last battle, the lost battle, of Vilagos, wanted still by the Austrians, the dangerous violinist agitator, as were so many others, hiding in various parts of Germany, some on their way to France, England, and America. Hamburg, a free city, a Hanseatic city, had proven hospitable before to refugees, and proven itself again to Remenyi, living comfortably by his violin, his services always in demand. There was a knock on the door.

He strode to the door, violin in hand; his engagement was at seven, there was little time. He opened the door. "Herr Brahms, is it?"

"Ja. Herr Remenyi?"

"Yes, yes. Who else? Come in."

Remenyi shut the door behind him. "Sit down. Why do you wait? Play something. Show me what you can do."

Hannes looked for the piano; it was five o'clock, twilight of a January evening; the room was small, but cluttered, covered with music, clothes, newspapers, smoke hovering in the middle like a shroud, still and thick as a mantle. "Where is the piano?"

Remenyi laughed, looking more closely. "Eh, eh, what have they sent me? I asked for an accompanist. They have sent me a maid."

The reference was to his voice, to his hair. In the sudden rush of anger Hannes found it even more difficult to control his voice. "I am to be your accompanist. Herr Bohm said you were in a hurry. I came as soon as I could."

Remenyi put down his violin and lit a candle. "Yes, yes, of course. Now do not waste more of my time. Sit. Show me what you can do. There is the piano. Look, na, have you not eyes?"

The piano was alongside one wall; Hannes sat and played the rondo from Weber's Piano Sonata in C major, playing it with the left hand as he had transcribed it for Marxsen, playing it flawlessly.

Remenyi was momentarily paralyzed, staring at Hannes's tiny fingers, blurred and scurrying up and down the keys, nodding when he was finished. "Very good, but do you always start with your best work?"

"That is not my best. I do not know what is my best."

"Play something else."

Hannes played the *Waldstein*, thundering left hand, glittering right, colliding in the middle, until Remenyi tapped him hard on his shoulder with his bow. He flinched, but said nothing. "Eh, eh, Beethoven! Herr Brahms, I take off my hat to you. Can you play the *Kreutzer*?"

"Ja."

"Good, we can do that. I see you are a serious musician, but can you play the popular songs? That is what people want to hear."

"I can play anything – if I can read it I can play it, if I can hear it I can play it. If I cannot read it or hear it, I can make it up."

"Good, good." He put some music on the stand. "Herr Brahms, have you traveled by the railway train?"

"Na."

"Have you seen a steam engine?"

"Ja."

"I want to hear you play that," he tapped the music with his bow, "and I want you to make believe you are a steam engine – I want to hear you play it as fast as you can – and powerfully, full of zest. This is a czardas – which means you must play it like you are running for your life, full of pep, peppy. Do you get what I mean?"

"I get." The piece was in cut time, a dotted rhythm, heavy downbeat, followed by a melody that spanned an octave and a half in less than a measure, rising and falling in fourths and fifths. Hannes played without difficulty, but was interrupted again by Remenyi's bow tapping his shoulder. "Slow down there, Herr Brahms – where it says to slow down, you must slow down. Can you not read?"

Hannes scowled. "Ja, I can read – but you said to play it peppy, like a steam engine, full of zesty."

"Yes, but there," he marked the page with his bow, "where it says to go slow, there you must go slow. Otherwise, why would they have the direction?"

"I can play it like it is written, and I can play it like you ask. Just tell me which you want."

Remenyi stared at Hannes. "Play it like it is written – but when the direction says Fast play it as fast as you can, and when it says Slow play it as slow as you can. That way, when you build up the speed from slow to fast the effect will be like a blow in the face. Do you see?"

Hannes grunted.

"I am going to play it with you. Let us see how we fare together."

Remenyi was an idiosyncratic player, changing the tempo to please himself, but with flair and drama, bobbing his head, grimacing to the music as he played. Hannes followed him easily, enjoying the rhythm of the work, following his own habit of humming the melody as he played.

He tapped Hannes's shoulder again with his bow when they were finished. "So, Herr Brahms, what do you think? How do you like playing the czardas? or is it not serious enough for you?"

Hannes scowled. "Herr Remenyi, do not hit me again. I can hear without being hit. You can tell me what you want without hitting me."

Remenyi grinned. "Eh, eh, it is just a friendship tap. I mean nothing by it."

"I do not like it."

The boy would make a good accompanist; Remenyi nodded. "So, are you going to answer my question, or did you not hear it?"

Hannes still scowled. "I liked it. I liked the rhythm."

"Eh, eh, good! I think you will do." He had received a letter from his accompanist the same day, too sick for the evening soiree, and enquired at Bohm's music establishment across the street for another accompanist. He was thinking already of using Hannes permanently, but something puzzled him. "What I do not understand, Herr Brahms, is why you are here. You should be giving concerts, you should be touring. Instead, I hear you give lessons and you play in dance halls, at the soirees – that is what I hear."

Hannes was surprised to hear the personal note, but not sorry. It was a subject on which he wanted guidance. "I have given concerts. I do not know what to do next. The times are not good for music."

"You must not let that stop you. I mean to make my way around the world with my violin. You must do the same."

"I would do it if I knew what I should do, but I do not know what is expected – but I do not mind. I compose – so I do not waste my time."

Everyone composed, everyone imagined he was a genius. "Eh, eh, you will decompose if you do not do something else. What is there to know? You must tour, make yourself known, make your music known. You make a little money, you go somewhere else. You make a little more money, you go somewhere else again. I have been to America, I have been to Paris. It is the same everywhere. It is the only way – and it is a fine way."

Hannes nodded.

"Look at me. I have traveled far already, and I am only twenty-two years. How old are you?"

"Nineteen."

"And what have you done?"

Hannes shrugged.

"Now, look at me. I have a plan. I want to make the acquaintance of Liszt. He is a Hungarian, like me. I am sure he will help me if I can only get an introduction to him – and do you know how I am going to do that?"

"How?"

"I know another violinist, who is a friend of Liszt. He was his konzertmeister in Weimar, but he has since settled in Hanover. He is the konzertmeister for the Hanoverian court. I am sure he will give me an introduction. When this winter season is over I will go to him. His name is Joseph Joachim."

"Joachim?"

"You know him?"

"Who does not? I heard him play the Beethoven Violin Concerto when he was in Hamburg. He is your friend?"

"We were together at the Vienna Conservatory. We had the same teacher."

"He is your friend? Joachim is your friend?"

"Yes, yes, I know him."

"He is the best."

"He is all right."

Robert talked with Julius Tausch, his assistant, and showed him his baton, tied to his wrist with string; he had lost his grip before, sending the baton sailing into the orchestra, striking a bassoonist; another time a violinist had caught it sailing past. Robert smiled, pleased with himself as a schoolboy. Tausch nodded, but shook his head at Robert's retreating back.

Clara, seated at the piano, did not like Tausch; they had known him in Leipzig; he had taken lessons, first briefly with Robert, later with Mendelssohn who had helped him gain the post in Dusseldorf, and she was sure he wanted Robert's position for himself.

The hall filled with chatter like a schoolroom, choristers and musicians mulling around laughing as if they were at a party, but they were gathered to rehearse Handel's *Messiah*. Robert tapped the lectern with his baton, requesting attention. Some ambled to their places, almost unwillingly, others ignored him. He spoke like a mouse, she was the first to admit it – but the players weren't children, it was their responsibility to mind him.

She found Dusseldorfers neither as serious about music as Leipzigers, nor abstemious as Dresdeners; they were instead informal, breezy, gay, influenced by the French before they had been annexed by Prussia in 1815, bound (unbound, rather) by the Napoleonic Code, permissive by German standards, in marriage and social affairs. Even the lower classes imagined themselves their equals, the women worse than the men, flirting without shame – behaving, as they did now, like children, disrespecting her husband. Robert, embarrassed, looked at her, begging help with his eyes.

She would have said Dusseldorf was Dresden squeezed into Leipzig, of ducal origin but small, at the confluence of the Rhine and Dusel, at the foot of a fledgling mountain range, in repute already for painting and sculpture, wanting next to build a reputation for music. They had been greeted at the station by the concert committee, including Hiller, the departing director, escorted to the Breidenbach Hotel, rooms redolent with flowers, laurel bushes at the entrance, choir serenade outside their window, but the pleasantries had subsided almost immediately. The hotel cost sixty thaler a week, exceeding their entire travel allowance from the Music Society. Accommodation was expensive and unsatisfactory: gardenless houses with flat brick walls abutted the street, windows so large you felt like a goldfish in a bowl, but when their furniture arrived a week later they had been forced to take what was available.

The first concert had gone well, drawn an audience from Elberfeld, Krefeld, and Munster. They had both been announced by flourishes of trumpets, but Hiller, who had come from Cologne and stayed for the postconcert celebration, had carelessly proposed a toast only to Clara, not to Robert, reawakening his insecurity, prompting a protest: a credit to his wife was no credit to him. Worse, she had been sent a basket of flowers from the Music Society for her participation and written an indignant letter: she was not Robert's assistant, nor some busker from the Altstadt, nor was her participation a separate matter; she was an artist in her own right and expected to be paid. She could not live on flowers.

She understood the mistake; she had long subjugated her career to Robert's, playing neighboring towns but no longer touring; family made it impossible (three girls, two boys, when they had arrived; a fourth girl in the first year); so did Robert, however unconsciously, needing her, resenting his need, punishing her for his need. She had drawn instead a colony of students to herself from all over Germany, her reputation allowing her to choose the best, but she recognized her conflict: to support Robert, build his confidence, while appearing to do neither; be the man of the house while appearing to be the woman. He had never resolved his own conflict: admiring her virtuosity while deploring his place in her shadow; but the composer outranked the virtuoso, and her reverence for his music made all things possible – except when he expected her help though she knew he would resent it later. At the last rehearsal the orchestra had ignored his request to play pianissimo until she had shouted from the piano: "My *hus*band said pia*nis*simo!"

These were the moments when Robert should have said something, Tausch should have said something, players who professed themselves friends should have said something, but all remained mute, looking at Clara, and she rose, shouting again from the piano against her better judgment. "*Ev*eryone, *si*lence! Take your places! We are about to begin!"

There was silence immediately, but the women pouted, glaring as they took their places, muttering under their breaths; she ignored them, sitting again, waiting for Robert's cue, but he spoke instead, looking away, loud in the sudden silence. "Tausch, you should accompany us today. The drumming on the piano will surely tire my wife. It is more suitable for a man."

Tausch had a reputation: best pianist in Dusseldorf, also the best teacher, but Clara's arrival made him a distant second. She understood his pique, but he wasn't her responsibility. Tausch approached with a smile, pretending sympathy. Everyone stared, a woman snickered, a snip of a girl. Clara's head ballooned with blood, her face crawled with worms, but she got up and left without a word, not even a backward glance.

Robert nodded vague approval, imagining he had established rapport with the chorus, and lifted his baton commencing with a downstroke, focusing all eyes. Tausch provided the introduction, sopranos soared, colored by altos and tenors, grounded by basses, "And the glory of the Lord shall be revealed." The rehearsal seemed to progress well, but Robert frowned. He called a halt, but said nothing, and indicated with his baton that they were to start over.

Tausch sighed, shaking his head; it was Schumann's way to start over when he was displeased, but to say nothing about what displeased him. He rarely acknowledged you unless he needed something, and rarely spoke, mumbling in his thick foggy colorless voice when he did. His wife was able to convey his wishes, but without her they were reduced to conjecture. Friends who had known him long appeared better able to understand him, but a conductor's responsibility was to make himself understood, not to depend on his friends. The best conductors heard every performance three times: first, in their heads, reading the score, the raw material; next, still in their heads, their interpretations, which they communicated to the orchestra; finally, with their ears, as everyone else heard it. Most of the time Schumann appeared to hear nothing but the interpretation in his head, and nothing else disturbed him; and when it did he couldn't say what it was, making the orchestra repeat itself arbitrarily until he chose to continue.

During the repetition the sopranos were too high and the effect was ludicrous, but the baton never wavered, not even when the sopranos ceased, not even when the altos, tenors, and basses all fell silent. Robert continued to beat time, stiff jagged movements, a clockwork conductor, though no one sang. Not until Tausch stopped playing did Robert put down his baton to call him to the lectern. Tausch sighed again, anticipating a reproof.

The musicians stared, some shaking their heads, no one saying a word, Robert ignoring everyone but Tausch, smiling, putting a hand on his shoulder, indicating a passage in the score. "Look, is this bar not beautiful?"

Tausch just stared; the man appeared to subsist in a different world.

ii

Clara hated to act behind Robert's back, but otherwise he blamed her for what went wrong – as he had never ceased blaming her for the Russian tour. She had fooled him before to both their advantages, also of their children, feeling circumstances made it inevitable, even necessary, and wrote again to Wilhelm Joseph von Wasielewski, a violinist and friend, now settled in Bonn, with whom she had played soirees and concerts in Leipzig and Dresden among other places.

My dear J. v. Wasielewski,

I have one more question for you, dear friend, of which Robert must know nothing. Please choose your words with care so that your answer will appear as an inquiry from you rather than a response to one from me. If your answer is not to my wish, then do not bother to answer at all. I will know what you mean.

My inquiry is about another concert in Bonn. It would give me the pleasure of playing with you and Reimers again (I am thinking, naturally, of Robert's Quintet), and whatever small income there might be forthcoming would also not be unwelcome. There

*is not much here, as you know, and our household requires very much! This is between
us, dear J. v. Wasielewski, is it not?*

*Please excuse my terrible handwriting. I am trembling violently at yet another insult
that Robert has had to sustain – but you must say nothing about this to anyone. He must
not know that I have written to you.*

Clara Schumann

iii

Sunlight streaked the Rhine with spears of silver. The broad back of the river turned
in Robert's imagination into the broad scaly glittering back of the dragon guarding
the Rhinegold. The Lorelei held court underwater, slender as reeds, breathing water
like air, gills in their noses, webs in their hands and feet and armpits and between
their legs, skin glittering with bejeweled scales, hair of gold, subsisting on algae, ferns,
and fish. He had suggested once to Wagner that there was an opera in their story.

Walking cleared his mind, alongside the Rhine, along the promenade, reminding
him of walks in Dresden alongside the Elbe with Wagner who also walked to clear
his mind, accompanied by Peps, his spaniel, darting around their ankles. They had
made a strange pair, the one raging to say everything he thought, the other raging for
silence, the one not caring who heard, the other not caring to hear anyone.

The Dresden years had been difficult relative to the Leipzig, but he had composed
some of his best works, the Piano Concerto and the *Peri*, but despite its tumultuous
reception in Leipzig *Genoveva* had not been the success he had wished – nor anything
during the Dusseldorf years though accounting for almost a third of his output,
not the Cello Concerto, not the *Rhenish Symphony*, not the later chamberwork, not
the pianowork, but the pressure for a great success grew less bearable as you grew
older, his reputation demanded it publicly, his family privately. Neither would have
mattered had he satisfied himself, but the quality had fallen as the quantity had
risen. Whatever Clara said, whatever anyone said, he remained the best judge of his
work, and the best of his work was behind him, receding as the family advanced,
resources subsiding as responsibilities grew. He had failed, betrayed his promise,
devoted himself to husbandry before music, depended on his wife before himself,
shown himself unmanly, unworthy of his wife, the more wife she the less husband
he, the more courageous she the less he, if he hadn't known it when they had married
he had learned it during the Dresden uprising, and if he hadn't learned it then it
mattered even less.

He had paid the toll with his health though the doctors never divined the matter,
suggesting mineral water, health pills, leeches, all of which helped momentarily,
before the tug of responsibilities shattered him again. Immersions in the Rhine
had followed, disrobing in a cabin on the bank, a cold plunge daily, before news of
Clara's pregnancy had undone the benefit of eleven consecutive days. They had visited
Scheveningen in Holland with Marie, their oldest, now eleven, for seabaths, a cold
water establishment, Clara too participating – resulting in a miscarriage, Clara in
bed as one dead, he wringing his hands and crying aloud, scaring Marie when she

needed comfort, failing her as he had failed Clara, failing as pappa as he had failed as husband.

Neither had his pronouncements on new composers amounted to much; Wagner and Liszt had hijacked the honors, declaring themselves Beethoven's heirs, spawn of his symphonies, and they had declared it in the *Zeitschrift*, born of his blood, now Franz Brendel's *Zeitschrift*, home of the New German Music, Music of the Future, trumpeting the death of the symphony, casting him aside before he had died – but he would have said what Schiller said: He served the future best who best served the present.

He heard as well the howl of the public, a letter following the end of his first season in the *Dusseldorfer Zeitung*, saying he was too vague and retiring to be a conductor, calling him incompetent. The letter had been anonymous, but surely from someone he knew, making his private affairs public. The reception to the premiere of his Overture to The Bride of Messina had been worse, greeted with a roar of silence, leaving him the only person in a hallful of people, the only being in Dusseldorf, desolate as a man on the moon.

He stared into the Rhine from the bridge as he had stared into the Mulde as a boy, watching the shadow of his head, black circle over the black edge of the rail, floating disembodied on the river, projecting beyond reach on the water where it was quiet, unlike his home with the noise of the street, barrel organs, rumble of carts on the cobbles, the English family in the adjacent flat, their piano against his wall, young children, new construction on the other side – but under the water it was cool and shadowy, sprawling with the Lorelei calling him, tugging his sleeves, a seductive world where you caught your food on the fly, slept where you swam. He leaned forward over the rail, spots orbiting his eyes, the heat of the sun a clamp on his neck pushing him down, black circles multiplying beside his own on the water, bobbing like balloons over the black edge of the rail, tiny hands tugging at his sleeves, and he surrendered. The Lorelei appeared like girls, dressed like Dusseldorfers. "Hello, you dear little people."

"Oh, Pappa, you are so funny!"

Marie smiled, the most cheerful of his daughters, pliant, domestic, practical. "We have only been calling you for a whole minute."

"What were you thinking, Pappa, staring like that into the river?" Julie was eight, the youngest of the three, the smallest, the thinnest, also the prettiest with high cheekbones and a serious face, a fairy, the most likely Lorelei. She took his hand and he squeezed back.

"I was looking for you, my Lorelei, under the water. You were singing to me. I heard you calling."

"Oh, Pappa, we were calling you, but not from under the water. What *were* you thinking?" Elise was blond, ten, the most spirited, stubborn, and disobedient, with the best sense of humor, the least imagination, most often requiring the switch.

"So, what are my lovely Lorelei doing here?"

"Pappa! We are *not* Lorelei!"

"Pappa, we *al*ways promenade here at this time."

"Pappa, what are *you* doing here?"

"Nothing." Robert said nothing else, but walked home smiling, three fledglings fighting to nestle under his arms.

Ludwig and Ferdinand, five and four, met them at the door, Ferdinand wanted to hear the "Bear Dance," one of Robert's recent works for the piano, for children little and big, but played by his pappa, not his mamma, she couldn't play it like he did, curling his hands like paws on the piano, the drone and rumble of a bear in his left hand, a tinkling Turkish tune in his right.

Clara stood by smiling, holding baby Eugenie, recalling how he had played with her and her brothers so long ago by setting a lantern on the floor to enlarge his shadow on the wall and entering with his furcoat like a bear on the loose, recalling stories of doppelgangers and caricatures on the piano. She wished everyone could see him now, the pappa playing with the children, so they could know him as she knew him.

She tried to catch his eye to let him know that she was happy, that he made her happy; he frightened her sometimes how tired he looked, but he was too busy tumbling on the floor to look at her. She put Eugenie down and got on her hands and knees, joining the huddle on the floor, grabbing his hand and smiling as she scratched his palm; it was their code, an invitation to bed, it had been a long while.

He stared at her, ignoring Ludwig and Ferdinand fighting for his attention. She smiled, noticing his pupils dilated almost to the size of his eyes, but he snatched back his hand, tottering on his knees, taking a deep breath, holding his neck as if he were choking.

Clara stared only a moment, kneeling beside him, putting an arm around him, caressing his face. "My darling, what is it? What is the matter?"

He resisted her effort to raise him to the sofa, falling on his side on the carpet, lying stiff and curled. His brow was damp with sweat, eyes showing only whites. When she leaned over him on the floor he straightened without warning, knocking her down, knocking down a coffee table. He laughed, but with an unrecognizable voice, hollow and metallic. The children were huddled to one side, eyes wide. Clara got up. "Marie, get Doktor Hasenclever at once, do you hear? Elise, bring me some water. Julie, take the others away – at once! Do not dawdle."

The group scattered. Marie remembered her pappa in Scheveningen, crying without end; her mamma had been sick then, now it was the turn of her pappa; but she was less afraid with her mamma in charge.

iv

"It is strange how wrong one can be." Robert shook his head. "I thought it would sound truly magical, but I could not hear it at all." He referred to a passage for solo horn in Joachim's Hamlet Overture. Behind him the orchestra grumbled. "I looked forward to it, Herr Joachim, I cannot tell you how much. In my mind it was beautiful."

Joachim spoke with gravity; in his experience all musicians, but particularly composers, were eccentric, all except Mendelssohn. He wondered how he appeared himself to others. He had been eight when he had left his family for Vienna to study the violin, then for Leipzig under Mendelssohn's tutelage, finally for Weimar after Mendelssohn's death to be Liszt's konzertmeister – where he had befriended Hans von Bulow, Joachim Raff, Liszt himself, and found himself for the first time among peers, no longer alone – but philosophically at odds, uncomfortable with their disregard, their derision of Mendelssohn, uncomfortable no less with Liszt's music.

He had tried to hide his distaste for Liszt's music, but in vain. Liszt had said himself, in sorrow more than anger, "I see my writings give you no pleasure." He could not have been more gracious and had given Joachim his blessing when George V, the blind king of the Court of Hanover, had offered a konzertmeistership – but Joachim was not without regret, and found none of the camaraderie of the Weimarites in the kapellmeister at Hanover, Heinrich Marschner, composer of *The Vampire* and *Templar and Jewess*, music for a bygone era, none of the glee of the Weimarites in their work, and turned instead inward, to composition, to Hamlet, surrogate for himself, prince of procrastination and peripateticism, dull, dark, and depressed.

"Actually, Master, what has happened is quite understandable. You see, the horn player never actually came in with his solo."

Robert's eyes widened. "Is that so? Well, that would explain why I did not hear him. We must try it again." He turned back to the orchestra, speaking sternly to the hornist but with glazed eyes as if he were addressing air. "Did you hear that? You must pay closer attention. You must not miss your count in the preceding rest."

Joachim might have suggested giving the hornist his cue at the appropriate time, Robert had ignored mountains of notes from the beginning and did little more than mark time, but Joachim didn't dare, nobody dared, the Master wasn't well, and the result was no different the second time.

Robert turned again to Joachim, large blue eyes filling with tears, baton trembling in his hand. "It is no good, it is no good. I did not hear it that time either."

The grumble swelled within the orchestra, but Robert didn't hear. Joachim's voice was soft with sympathy. "Master, would you like me to try it?"

Robert smiled, relieved. "Yes, Herr Joachim, please. It is your overture." He disengaged the baton from his wrist, but Joachim held up his own. Mendelssohn's five batons had been distributed among his four children when he had died, the fifth presented to Joachim.

With Joachim at the helm the hornist made a perfect entrance, but Joachim refused to raise his baton for the concert itself at the Rhine Festival, where he was also to perform the Beethoven Violin Concerto (Robert conducting), much as the orchestra pleaded. His regard for Robert was too great – but the rehearsal proved sufficient. The concert, which included Robert's *Spring* Symphony and Piano Concerto with Clara, was a success, particularly the Beethoven, the orchestra taking cues from Joachim playing first violin while Robert, swinging the baton, kept his head in the score. The reviewers raved of a French frenzy, an Italian idolatry, within a German audience.

Joachim was convinced there was a well of music in Robert's head, whether he liked it or not, whether he heard it or not, from which he could draw at will; when he could filter the notes from his head to his hand he was happy, but when he couldn't he was sick and could do nothing else.

Clara glowed when she heard Joachim play the Beethoven Violin; he played so effortlessly that everything went forward and upward as naturally as the sun rising, drawing so little attention to himself that the audience remained undistracted by the performance, keeping the focus on Beethoven rather than on himself, on the forest rather than a few tall trees. Best of all, he was in sympathy with Robert and his music.

Robert was no less complimentary, saying he had seen the Master himself during the performance, lionmaned and beetlebrowed, showing all his teeth, hovering over the orchestra.

v

The maid, Bertha, conducted Herr Wasielewski into the Schumanns' new sittingroom. Clara had not expected him, but received him with pleasure. "Dear Herr Wasielewski, how good to see you, but why did you not send word you were coming to Dusseldorf? We could have arranged a soiree."

"I am sorry, Frau Schumann, but I received scant notification myself."

"Nevertheless, it is good to see you. I am glad you have come to see us."

"Of course, I came. I could not come to Dusseldorf and not see your husband. How is he?"

The program of concerts they had planned in Bonn had been successful. Robert had gone against his will, putting up with life at the Golden Star Hotel, but he had been exhausted and suffered a collapse. The doctors had counseled rest, they always counseled rest, some called his condition rheumatism, some paralysis, some sciatica, but all counseled rest, and returning to Dusseldorf he had improved. Robert had said nothing about it, but now she blamed herself: she had deceived him, taken him to Bonn, and she was afraid Wasielewski blamed her as well. "He is better. Our new house makes a difference. He has his own space in which to compose or play or read or whatever he wishes. He spends so much time in the room now that I call it his cage."

She laughed; Wasielewski knew she meant to set him at ease, but didn't smile, merely nodded. "It is a nice house – a nice large house."

"It was absolutely necessary. I think it has made all the difference. Now I can practise without disturbing him, I can teach, I can do many things – for him, for the family – that I could not do before."

"May I see him?"

"Of course!"

She led him to a room in the back, smiling as she gestured him to wait in the hall, poking her head in the room. "Robert, you have a visitor."

Robert, reading on a sofa by the window, looked up as Wasielewski entered.

"How are you, Doktor Schumann?"

He remained seated, eyes half closed. "Wasielewski."

It was a small room, but cozy, lined with books and pictures. Clara smiled. "I am sorry, but I must leave. I have much to do."

Wasielewski bowed his head and turned to Robert who was reading again. "What is it you are reading, Doktor Schumann?"

"Wasielewski, do you know about table-tapping?"

Wasielewski smiled, raising his eyebrows. "Table-tapping? Well!"

Robert's eyes opened wide; he jumped from the sofa. "It is held in great repute everywhere – in America, England, France, Turkey, even in China."

Wasielewski drew back, speaking softly. "Of course! I do not doubt it, but I do not know very much about it."

Robert nodded, drawing down his eyelids again, looking at the coffee-table as if it were listening, speaking in a spectral tone. "The table knows all."

Wasielewski's mouth opened in pity, but he spoke finally, still staring. "I am sure."

"Would you like a demonstration?"

"A demonstration?"

Robert held his finger to his lips for silence, drawing the curtains, pulling the table away from the sofa, adjusting its cover. "Now, Wasielewski, you will see. We are, all of us, all of the time, surrounded by wonders, magnetic wonders."

Wasielewski said nothing, hardly daring to move. Robert leaned on the table, gripping its sides, closing his eyes, speaking in his new deep spectral tone. "Dear table, once again we come to thee. Will you give us, please, the first two measures of Beethoven's C minor Symphony?"

Robert's eyes remained closed while they waited. Wasielewski shut his in pity, recalling a time in Leipzig he was never to forget: Robert improvising at the piano, calling forth unique tones and tunes, unheard combinations, a fairyland of sound, chords that brought to mind harps, lights, stairways to heaven; he had felt he might dissolve into the music. In the magic of that moment he would have served Robert in any capacity, konzertmeister, secretary, servant. What a price men paid for their visions!

There were four taps, the table's leg on the floor, slow taps, much too slow for the opening of the C minor. Robert spoke again. "But the time is faster, surely, dear table, is it not?"

There were four taps again, quicker than before. Robert smiled, opening his eyes. "Does it not fill you with wonder? There are magnetic fields everywhere."

"Indeed." Wasielewski managed a weak smile.

"I plan to get the table a new dress. This one appears too tattered, do you not think, Wasielewski? What color do you think it would like?"

Wasielewski lost his smile. "I could not presume to say, Doktor Schumann. I am sure whatever color you choose will be fine." He did not stay much longer. Robert did not take it amiss that he had stayed so short a while, settling again with his book by the window.

Clara was surprised to see Wasielewski again so soon. "Do you not think he is better? He is much happier, is he not? Do you not think so?"

Wasielewski didn't know how to disappoint her; she wasn't well herself, wanting so badly to believe Robert was well. "You know about his table-tapping, do you not?"

"Of course!" She smiled; it might have been no more than a boy's prank. "Is it not wonderful? It appears to have settled him so well."

"Frau Schumann, it is not scientific. The table cannot tap itself, it is the experimenter who taps it – however unconsciously. There is an English scientist, Michael Faraday, who has proven this – and the experimenters, once they realize it is they who cause the table to tap lose their ability, they lose their ... I beg your pardon, Frau Schumann, but I must say it – they lose their delusions."

Clara lost her smile. "I have heard of Michael Faraday. I do not believe he has demonstrated yet how a symphony is composed, has he?"

"He can help your husband, Frau Schumann. He can cure his delusion."

Clara no longer looked at him. "If his delusions keep him happy, they are the best medicine. He does no one any harm."

"Except himself."

"I do not see that. He is much better. All he needs is rest." She looked at him again, eyes flashing. "Yes, and the encouragement of his friends."

Wasielewski looked at the floor. Friends didn't encourage delusions, but he couldn't tell her that; he never doubted her love, but Robert's illness was taking a toll on her as well.

Joachim owed Mendelssohn much, his nonmusical more than his musical education, and continued the education during his annual leave of absence, five months of summer in Gottingen, studying history, philosophy, whatever he pleased at the university. He had barely returned from the Rhine Festival before he was ready to leave again, but was met in his rooms on Princes Street by someone professing to be an old friend. He looked twice before recognizing the eggshaped head, and frowned. "Was not your name then Hoffmann?"

Remenyi punched his arm. "Yes, yes, it was, but I am Hungarian, I wanted a Hungarian name. This way, when I am with Jews, like you, I can be a Jew; when I am with Brahms I can be a German; and when I am with Hungarians, like Liszt, I can be Hungarian. He is my model in all things."

Joachim understood immediately why Remenyi had sought him out.

"You know what I mean, Joachim. In Paris, Liszt is a Frenchman; in Weimar, he is a German; but he never stops being a Hungarian. He is a true European, a true internationalist, that is Liszt. Wherever he is, and whatever he becomes, he is always Liszt – and Liszt belongs everywhere. There is no one like him."

"You plan to visit Liszt?"

"We plan everything that is possible. First, we visit you – then, maybe, with your blessing, we visit Liszt, I and my accompanist, Herr Johannes Brahms, Capital Musician and Pianist, from Hamburg. He composes too, like you never heard before – like Beethoven."

Brahms didn't look at Joachim, scowling instead at Remenyi, wishing he might muzzle him. Joachim might then take them seriously.

Remenyi slapped Joachim's back. "He is your greatest admirer, Joachim. He has heard you play." He turned down the corners of his mouth – "but he does not have the same admiration for me."

Brahms ignored the rebuke. "I saw you once perform the Beethoven Violin, Herr Joachim, in Hamburg. It was a happy day."

Joachim nodded seriously. He didn't like Remenyi and didn't know what to make of his friend.

"I did not have money for a program. I thought you had written it yourself."

Joachim nodded again, permitting himself a smile. "You do me too much honor, Herr Brahms. There is only one Beethoven."

Brahms nodded, grinning. "My teacher, Doktor Marxsen – he told me afterward who had written the concerto."

"Marxsen is your teacher?"

"Ja, you know him?"

Joachim nodded. "I know of him. He was in Vienna before me, but I knew people who knew him. He knew my teacher, Joseph Bohm. He was well regarded."

Brahms nodded, glad to have discovered a point of contact. "With good reason."

"How came you to study with him?"

"He was the teacher of my first teacher, Herr Cossel."

"Aha! That is how it was with me too!" Joachim turned to Remenyi. "You will recall, Herr Remenyi, that Bohm was the teacher of my first teacher, Stanislaus Serwaczynski?"

"I recall, I recall very well. What do you hear from old Bohm these days?"

Brahms didn't interrupt, letting them catch up on old times, observing the room, portraits on the wall of Beethoven, Mendelssohn, Liszt, Schumann, a painting of the siege of Vienna by the Turks; he noted as well Joachim's satin robe of many colors, red fez worn even indoors, water pipe on the table. He rolled his eyes but not so anyone could see; Remenyi was telling war stories again, primping and pimping his stature.

The stories were not uninteresting, but he spoke as if no one else had stories to tell. Joachim listened in silence, turning finally back to Brahms. "And how came you two to meet?"

Brahms opened his mouth, but Remenyi spoke first. "In Hamburg I needed an accompanist. He was sent to me – and after the music season he was doing nothing. He knows nothing and there is no one to show him in Hamburg. I said to myself I will show him, I will take him on a tour. I had to get him out of Hamburg, you see."

Brahms interrupted. "I have friends in Winsen. They had heard of Remenyi, and when I said I had played with him they wanted to hear – so we did a concert."

Remenyi took over again. "We played in Winsen, and the judge heard us, and he said he had a son in Luneburg, and he would arrange for a concert for us there – the same with Celle. It was in Celle that Brahms truly showed his mettle." He looked at Brahms.

Brahms shook his head. "It was nothing."

"Nothing, he says. He is too modest. This is no way for a virtuoso to behave, my little friend."

Brahms scowled.

"We had one program we played everywhere. We started everywhere with the Beethoven Violin Sonata in C minor, then I played violin solos, then we did the Vieuxtemps Concerto, the Elegie by Ernst, some Hungarian music – but it was the Beethoven we were having trouble with." He looked again at Brahms, but Brahms looked at the floor, at a pattern of crescents on a Turkish rug. "You are fortunate, indeed, Brahms, that I am willing to do your bragging for you." He turned back to Joachim. "The piano was terrible, flat by half a tone – but Brahms transposed from memory as we played. We never carried music, we had always played it in C minor as it is written, but he played it in C sharp minor, just like that, like magic, without the music, without one mistake. Eh, eh, Joachim. Now what do you think, hey?"

Joachim looked at Brahms who just shrugged. "After that we went to Hildesheim. Then we came here."

"Eh, eh, eh! Then we came here, I and my little Beethoven."

Brahms scowled again, gritting his teeth. "Do not say it, Remenyi." He turned to Joachim. "I am no Beethoven."

Joachim nodded, still serious. "Who among us is or can be?"

Remenyi laughed. "I do not say it. I only repeat what others say."

"You must not repeat it."

Remenyi waved Brahms down with his hand. "He is so modest it is a shame, it is a sin."

"It is hardly modesty to say one is no Beethoven!"

"But it is arrogance not to allow others to say it."

"It is not. It is merely prudence."

"Ah, yes, yes, indeed, Herr Brahms is most prudent. In Celle, Frau Blume, the judge's wife, she wanted to give us a party, and Brahms says, 'Will there be girls?'" Remenyi mimicked Brahms's high earnest voice. "Frau Blume says, 'Would you object?' and Brahms says, 'It is so much nicer without them, do you not think?'" He nudged Brahms hard. "Eh, eh, so nice, do you not think, little Hannchen?"

Brahms couldn't explain it. He was comfortable with Louise, musician first, girl second; and with Lieschen, a sister after the misunderstanding in the forest; but with others, he became a statue, his mouth a plaster. He knew what he wanted, and the girls of Zur schwarzen Katze gave it to him as long as he had money, but he couldn't understand what the other girls might want if they didn't want money, and that made him uncomfortable. "It is nothing to talk about." He glared, but Remenyi remained oblivious, grinning.

Joachim looked at Brahms, registering the contrast between his guests, not just the appearance (Hannes with the golden locks of a milkmaid, the sweet voice, even in anger), but the demeanor. "What have you composed?"

"Everything, he has composed everything – sonatas for the piano, violin sonatas, trios, quartets, songs – everything."

"Is this true?"

Brahms looked directly at Joachim for the first time. "It is better to show what one can do, do you not think?"

Joachim nodded. "Of course, by all means, show me."

A change was apparent as soon as Brahms seated himself at the piano. He no longer appeared unfocused, no longer bored, brought his hands down with confidence from a great height above the piano, opened with a fortissimo chord, without apology, a rhythm immediately identifiable from Beethoven's *Hammerclavier*, just the first four measures, before branching into an idiom as yet unknown to Joachim, powerful but personal, hands propelling notes like projectiles from the piano, the left moving south, the right north, culminating in a series of crashing chords, one more when least expected, and another for good measure, before the hands came together again in the middle, developing the theme, pianissimo, introducing the second theme.

Joachim said nothing, not even after he had finished the first movement.

Remenyi took out his violin. "We will play a czardas next."

Joachim shook his head. "I should like to hear the complete sonata first."

Remenyi raised his eyebrows, Brahms continued; the second movement comprised a set of variations on an old folk melody, recognized by Joachim, "The Moon Steals Upward," which softened the mood to a hush, moonlight in a midnight blue, followed by a scherzo and a freeform rondo, both characterized by barrages of notes, beaten like hammers on the strings, savage in their assault, but clear in their outlines as a new suit. Hard as a diamond, Joachim was later to say, and soft as snow.

He was smaller than Liszt, more serious, but otherwise in their appearance at the piano they were not unalike: blond hair and fingers flying, arms and legs throbbing to the music, swaying in their seats, as had Beethoven. Liszt was the greater pianist, the greatest, calculating every effect, aware of every sigh in his audience, every breathless individual, while Brahms knew only what the music told him – but this boy, barely twenty, had already composed a sonata greater than anything by Liszt. The comparisons with Beethoven were inevitable, but Joachim wisely said nothing about it when Brahms finished, said nothing at all about the work, asked instead for another, and Brahms smiled. Joachim had paid him the greatest compliment.

Remenyi suggested the violin sonata and Brahms nodded. Joachim settled himself to listen to the sonata, as thunderous a work as the last, but more melodic in the violin, the last movement with a Hungarian rhythm, played with much swagger by Remenyi.

Joachim noted as well how little he heard of Chopin in the work, how little of Schumann, or any other contemporary composer; he discerned Beethoven, some Bach, but both filtered through a bold, original, individual vision, already more Brahms than anything else. He would do what he could for Brahms, a concert at the Hanoverian Court, the introduction to Liszt they wished, write as well to Schumann. He wished he might watch the amazement of his friends as they listened to his work, wished he didn't have to leave for Gottingen, wished to be better acquainted with Brahms's work himself immediately, but consoled himself instead: deferred pleasures were sweeter.

ii

The Villa Altenburg, named for the hill on which it stood, on the outskirts of Weimar, was spacious, doublestoreyed, thirtyroomed, but architecturally unprepossessing, a block of a house, a box with windows, flatfaced and hiproofed with dormers and chimneys. Steps had been carved into the hill by the hundreds alongside an iron rail, the first reason for breathlessness; the view from the top the second reason, the River Ilm at the foot of the hill, woodlands all around, the panorama of the city, Rathaus, Stadtkirch, Ducal Palace; third the treasures of the Altenburg, from Liszt's years in Paris, keepsakes also of his Glanzzeit, oriental rugs, Turkish trays, mother of pearl tables, exotic water pipes (Brahms understood where Joachim got his taste), portraits of great composers, including two lifesized of Liszt, swords of honor (including a jeweled saber) from Hungary, Russia, and Turkey, books autographed by Hugo, Lamartine, Sainte-Beuve, scores by Mozart, Beethoven, Chopin, Rossini, Berlioz, Schumann, Wagner, medallions of the same, also of Clara Schumann, medallions also of gold from the crowned heads of Europe; also, everywhere, pianos, representing every maker, Erard, Streicher, Bechstein, Boisselot, Bosendorfer, the Hungarian Beregszaszy, also Beethoven's Broadwood, Mozart's spinet, also a custommade piano-organ sporting three keyboards, eight registers, a pedal board, and stops for winds – and, for Brahms the most glorious treasure, the death mask of Beethoven.

They had saved some money, Brahms and Remenyi, from concerts, the last in Hanover for George V, during which Remenyi, Hungarian refugee, agitator at large, brought to the attention of the Chief of Police, had been arrested, but released to the cognizance of Joachim, and given hours to leave town. In Weimar they roomed at the Hotel de Russie, but when Liszt learned from Remenyi through Joachim Raff, his copyist cum instrumentalist, that their money was low, he had invited them to stay in the rooms of Hans von Bulow, then on his first tour of Europe. Remenyi had bought a new coat and tonsured himself, but not Brahms, still in his patched coat, cracked boots, drawing stares, drawing remarks in the drawingroom from guests on the evening they were to meet Liszt.

Brahms was overwhelmed and sought refuge even more than usual in silence. Barely six months ago he had barely left Hamburg, but the week before he had played in the court of a king – blind, but a king – and now found himself sharing a house with a princess, Carolyne, like no princess he had imagined, blue eyes, brown hair, sallow skin, always in black, gown, jacket, bonnet, features manlier than his own, nose dominating her face, who walked like a goose, head constantly in a cloud of thick aromatic smoke from her cigars (dipped, it was said, in iron filings for double strength), speaking idiosyncratic German, more often French, both with Slavic overtones. Over her bed, it was said, hung a huge wooden crucifix; in her drawingroom a painting, *The Three Magi*, the magus in the middle resembling Liszt, a resemblance difficult to miss among the fourteen busts of Liszt standing around in the smoky blue haze.

Raff was their guide, walking them around with the somber face and measured steps of a headmaster, not without pride, the Altenburg his school, introducing them to inhabitants and visitors, Peter Cornelius and William Mason among others, indicating Liszt's quarters, a special wing built into the back of the house overlooking the garden, including his Blue Room dressed in blue-white drapes, blue-gold wall coverings, and blue floral upholstery, where he breakfasted with the Princess who busied herself through the morning with correspondence as did he with composition.

Raff led them down yet another flight of stairs, talking all the while. "A long time ago, 1845 it was, when I was twenty-three, just another poor music student, just another admirer of the Master, I walked through a thunderstorm from Basel to Zurich to hear him – but when I arrived there were no seats. His secretary saw me, wet as a rat in the sewer, and took my story to Liszt – who had me brought onstage, seated beside himself among his admirers. He played his Reminiscences of Meyerbeer's *Robert le Diable* while I dripped water like a landed trout forming a pool around my chair – but I could think of nothing except that I was watching

Liszt, hearing Liszt, with Liszt – and that was the beginning of my good fortune. He needed an orchestrater, I knew something about orchestration."

Remenyi could not talk enough and spoke with no less reverence, even greater enthusiasm. "That is my story, exactly. I am now twenty-three, I have knocked about the world enough, I have been in the wars, I have been to America, but all I want now is to play the violin and dedicate myself to Liszt, to his genius, to show him all my devotion – that is all I care about now – for me, there is nothing else, nothing!"

Brahms grimaced, not knowing he grimaced.

Raff nodded, approval in his tone. "That is of course in the Master's hands."

"Yes, yes, of course, in the Master's hands, where I wish to be. I wish to put myself in the Master's hands." He slapped Brahms on the back, draped his arm around his shoulders. "Eh, eh, eh, and so does Brahms, is it not so, Herr Brahms?"

Brahms scowled and would have shrugged off Remenyi's arm had he not been overwhelmed by his surroundings.

Again Raff nodded. "You will soon have your chance. Our guests are gathering even as we speak."

He led them into a large music room, windows and doors draped in red velvet, chandeliers and candelabra lit to a rosy glow; the guests, about thirty men and women, sitting and standing, talking animatedly, drinking champagne, smoking cigars, spared a glance for Raff as he entered, and cast quizzical looks at Brahms as Raff led him with Remenyi to the piano in the middle of the room.

Brahms felt goosebumps bulge like marbles from his skin, his cigar turn to ash between his fingers, eyes like claws on his wrinkled cotton shirt (not quite blue anymore, discolored by the sun), on his gray waistcoat (discolored no less than his shirt), and on his boots, meant for muddy roads and fields of grass, falling like lead on the carpet, each thud calling attention gingerly though he stepped. He had played in elegant homes in Hamburg and met elegant people, but always on their terms, and was now, though a musician among musicians, even less comfortable; something was expected that he knew he didn't have, the happy talk that possessed Remenyi, the easy insincerity. There were also too many women in the room laughing too loudly and easily, the chief offender the princess, the loudest and no less voluble for her idiosyncratic German, her French disfigured by Slavic accents.

Raff held up a finger in warning to Brahms. "Be prepared. The Master might expect you to play. He has read Joachim's letter of introduction, and your music is on the piano – or he might play something of his own, or by someone else. I have written a new work myself." He picked pages from the piano, showing them to Remenyi who held them so Brahms too could see them and read the title page. Raff spoke with reverence. "It is as yet but a sketch for the piano, but I intend to develop it into a symphony for Germany to be called: *To my Fatherland*. I have fully outlined the program."

Brahms read the program along with Remenyi:

First Movement: Allegro. A Portrait of the German Character: the power to soar to the skies; a tendency for introspection; courage and compassion as contrasts that impact and interpenetrate; a passion to be pensive.

Second Movement: Allegro molto vivace. In the Open Air: winding through the forests of the Fatherland, horns winding through the fields and streams with the music of the folk.

Third Movement: Larghetto. At the Hearth: metamorphosis through the muses and love.

Fourth Movement: Allegro drammatico. Foiled from laying the foundation for solidarity in the Fatherland.

Fifth Movement: Larghetto – allegro trionfale. Rededicated, renewed, soaring again.

Remenyi put down the pages. "This is beautiful work, Herr Raff, such sublime sentiments. I cannot wait to hear it – eh, Brahms, what do you think?"

Brahms only blinked, wishing Remenyi would turn to the music itself, but Remenyi returned the pages and Raff placed them again on the piano as if they were a Bible.

There were footsteps in the hallway. Raff straightened the music on the piano. "The Master comes."

All eyes turned to the door, a line had formed not unlike a greeting line though Liszt was the host. A sigh rent the room as he entered, everyone rose to face their host, Brahms last of all.

Liszt wore a green satin shirt open at the neck, gold scarf, high collar, black waistcoat, and fawn trousers. Brahms saw a slender man, not much taller than himself, long blond hair brushed straight back, not unlike his own, shoulders erect, chin in the air, looking down his hawknose at everyone, who gave his hand for men to shake and women to kiss, a slender hand extended like an ornament, fingers so tapered they might have been tentacles, or webbed, more than five to a hand. He might have been taking inventory glancing around the room, uninterested in seeing anyone except from a higher plane.

Brahms was struck that the women kissed his hand and not he theirs; his own heart pounded as if Liszt were a woman. He had barely reached them before Remenyi sank to one knee; Brahms had never seen his smile wider. "Your servant, Master – your servant, if you will have me."

Liszt stopped, looking at Remenyi, speaking kindly in French. "Ah, Monsieur Brahms. Welcome. You come well recommended, indeed, by our good friend, Joachim."

Remenyi's voice flattened. "I beg your pardon, Master, but I am not Brahms. I am Eduard Remenyi. Brahms is with me." He got up, looking at Brahms.

Liszt's eyebrows rose. "Ah, but Monsieur Remenyi, it is I who must beg your pardon. Of course, I have heard of you and looked forward to our meeting. Joachim said you would be accompanying Monsieur Brahms. I humbly apologize."

Remenyi bowed his head, but couldn't hide his frown; Brahms was accompanying him, not he Brahms. "It is most gracious of you, Master, but not necessary. Anyone could have made such a mistake."

Liszt nodded, turning to Brahms. "Monsieur Brahms?"

Brahms stood, feet apart, right hand tightly gripping his left, brow furrowed, eyes narrowed, nodding, afraid to speak, imagining he would have no voice – worse, his girlish voice grew more girlish when he was nervous.

Liszt smiled and his voice softened. "Our friend, Joachim, is most complimentary about your work, Monsieur Brahms. I have never heard him so enthusiastic about a new composer. He absolutely raves. We are ready to hear your compositions whenever you are ready to oblige us."

Brahms gripped his upper lip with his lower, his right hand a claw over his left; he would not play, he could not, not in such company, whether more intimidated by the finery or contemptuous of the obeisance of the audience he couldn't have said. Not trusting himself to speak, he shook his head. Remenyi nudged him. "Are you crazy, Brahms? Go on, play at least the Scherzo."

Liszt saw Brahms's clothes, his whitening knuckles, understood his trepidation – and, bowing lightly, still smiling, spoke as softly as before. "Very well, then. I shall play it – unless you have some objection."

Again Brahms shook his head.

Liszt went to the piano; the room waited until he had seated himself before sitting and remained quiet as he riffled through the music on the piano making his selection. "A Scherzo in E flat minor by Johannes Brahms." He nodded in Brahms's direction.

Brahms stared back, not daring to move. The scherzo was scribbled so no one could read it except himself, a hen might have walked across the page; Liszt couldn't possibly do it justice; he wished he were elsewhere, invisible, wished he had never left Joachim.

The scherzo began with a phrase, four rhythmic unaccompanied notes, so quick and light it was gone before you realized the scherzo had begun, a wisp of a phrase like a butterfly, but repeated in different configurations so frequently you heard nothing else, hands echoing each other, tossing the phrase back and forth, multiplying the image of the butterfly, until a march emerged from the bass, resisted by a waspish three note phrase in the treble, while the original phrase continued to dart between the two, dance and chase, butterfly and wasp.

Liszt kept his eye on Brahms as he played, nodding and smiling, raising his eyebrows when a particular development pleased or surprised him, and commenting all the while, but Brahms was too amazed by Liszt's skill to hear what he said, his ability not only to read the indecipherable notes but play them as if for the hundredth time. When he finished to much applause, Liszt turned to Brahms who was also applauding, grinning as he couldn't before, but Liszt turned again to the music, raising his hands, and a hush fell again over the room. "We must do that again." When he was finished the second time, he turned again to Brahms. "Our friend, Joachim, was right, as always, astute in his musical judgment."

One of the men spoke, smiling. "The performance is everything, Master."

A woman clasped her hands in adoration. "Indeed, to have read so clearly from so unclear a manuscript."

Raff's admiration was no less grudging. "There is something of Chopin in the work. It is not unlike one of his scherzos, the initial phrase."

Brahms lost his grin, shaking his head. "I know little of Chopin."

Someone laughed; Brahms felt again their eyes on his shirt and boots.

Liszt riffled again through the manuscript. "Let us try something else. I see you have written two sonatas. Which should I play?"

Brahms shrugged. Remenyi spoke breathlessly. "The C major would be better, Master."

Liszt placed the untidy pages again on the stand before him. "The C major it shall be."

He played as impeccably as before, reading scribbles as easily as print, the introductory bars harking prominently to Beethoven's *Hammerclavier* with which he was familiar, but the technical demands were greater. Brahms did not restrict himself to two voices when moving in double counterpoint or contrary motion, often adding a third, a fifth, or an octave, simultaneously adding a pedalpoint two octaves below, a combination of ancient counterpoint and modern technique that was new in his experience.

Brahms marveled again. Liszt seemed to know his mind as well as his own, following his development as easily, commenting like a critic as he played; more intrepid even than the performance was the legerdemain of juggling his reading with his performance and his commentary.

There were again raptures when he finished, encomiums to the performance more than the work, though Liszt had kept Brahms in the spotlight and addressed him directly with a smile. "You are welcome to stay with us as long as you wish, Monsieur Brahms – and, of course, your friend, Monsieur Remenyi."

Brahms nodded; Remenyi appeared ready to descend again to his knee. "Master, again we thank you. Your grace and your bounty are indeed without limit."

Liszt smiled; he never actually stopped smiling, but varied his meaning continually with the tiniest gradations of movement, saying more with a twitch than a word.

One of the men spoke. "Will not the Master honor us next with his own sonata?"

Another: "I am sure Monsieur Brahms has not heard it."

A woman spoke: "He has been deprived too long, indeed – no Chopin, no Liszt, no wonder he remains silent."

A murmur of merriment hovered over the assembly; Brahms scowled, keeping his eyes on the carpet. Liszt smiled. "Very well, then, of course, for Monsieur Brahms."

He turned back to the piano, drawing all eyes, closing his own, sitting erect, hands on his knees, chin in the air, in an attitude of prayer held for almost a minute; the room was silent. He raised both hands slowly, touched three G's in the bass, pianissimo of pianissimos and held the notes, letting the sonority permeate the room. He repeated the performance, following with a descent, still slow, still pianissimo, into a cellar, a well, down the scale to darkness, returning to the G's, repeating the descent in a different configuration, before erupting into fortissimo, a concatenation of the themes bringing the introduction to a boil.

Brahms listened closely, absorbing themes and development; surprised by the eruption, he continued to listen closely, awaiting its rationale; instead, much rhetoric followed, a headlong pace, washes of color, dramatic chords, but while the original theme, the descent, continued to appear, much of the work was obscured by passagework. He frowned; he could have developed the theme better himself.

Liszt appeared to play everything with his eyes closed, oblivious to everything but the rise and fall of the music, swaying to its current, imprisoned by rhapsody, communing with spirits, but occasionally his eyelids cracked, encompassing the room as a sweep of his head accompanied a sweep of the keyboard – and his mouth, curling at the corners in the specter of a smile, betrayed his awareness. He had hooked his audience like a fish on a grapple and closed his eyes again, confident of victory. Many of his listeners knew little about music, heard with their eyes more than their ears, least of all with their minds, his appearance and reputation louder in their heads than his music, and he never disappointed them, enjoying the show as much as the music himself – but something happened that evening that had never happened before and was never to happen again.

For a moment Liszt's mouth thinned, almost disappearing into his face. His performance suffered the barest hesitation. His gaze had fallen on Brahms, slumped in his chair, shoulders fallen, hands limp in his lap, chin in his collar, hair in his face, eyes closed, chest gently rising, gently falling.

When he was finished Liszt shut the piano and left the room, acknowledging no applause – which turned quickly to silence as bewildered faces turned to one another, alighting as had Liszt's on Brahms. The Princess was the first to rally, announcing truffles and ices in the next room; Liszt, she said, would join them later.

Brahms stuck to Remenyi, seeking reassurance after his great gracelessness, but Remenyi pushed him away, whispering fiercely as the audience filtered into the next room. "Stay away from me. I am no longer with you. You and me, it is finished, it is over."

"Remenyi, what are you saying? What have I done?"

Remenyi pulled him to one side, out of earshot of the others. "What have you done? You do not know what you have done?"

Brahms spoke defiantly. "I was tired."

"You were tired? You were not too tired when he was gracious enough to play your scherzo and your sonata – after you sat like a sulking child – and from such an impossible manuscript."

Brahms grimaced, speaking insistently. "I just closed my eyes for a minute."

"While Liszt was playing you closed your eyes? You closed your eyes for a minute while *Liszt* was playing?"

"I was listening. I do not need my eyes to listen. I did not like the sonata."

"Brahms, are you crazy? He was kissed by Beethoven, do you not know that? Liszt was kissed by Beethoven. He is the anointed – and after he has been so gracious –"

"What has grace got to do with music? Liszt is gracious, but that was not a good sonata. If that is all he can do, then Liszt is not a good composer."

"Well, there it is. There we part company. I cannot agree with you. I say Liszt is a great composer."

"Remenyi, what you think is up to you – but what has that to do with us?"

"It has everything. It is over, Brahms. You have the best chance in the world, other musicians would die for such a chance, for an audience with Liszt, and you throw it away. I will no longer drag myself from town to town with you. I want to stay here if the Master will have me – but you cannot stay. I will not stay with you."

"All right, all right, if that is what you want. Tomorrow I will go."

"Good!"

Brahms was in conflict, his grand tour ending in a crash leaving nothing to show anyone for his time, and asperity rose like mercury over a flame. "But let me tell you something!"

"What?"

"When Beethoven kissed Liszt – *if* it is true that he kissed him –"

"What are you saying? Liszt would not lie about something like that."

"Why not? It harms no one, and it helps him – but let me make my point. What I am saying is Beethoven was deaf when he kissed Liszt. It did not matter who he kissed, Liszt or a lizard or a block of wood. It is all the same to a man who is deaf. If he cannot hear, he will anoint anything. Why should he care?"

Brahms might have been a lizard himself for the way Remenyi looked at him. "Ach, you are talking like a madman now. I am glad I found you out early."

Brahms sneered. "I may be a madman – but I do not get on my belly like a worm to lick anyone's boots."

Had they been elsewhere Remenyi might have spit, he might have struck Brahms; instead, he turned violently away. "Tchhah, Brahms! You are a fool!!"

iii

Joachim's chin, cupped in the chinrest of his violin, lengthened his face; eyebrows rising into his red fez made his face longer yet. Brahms had written a serenade for a string trio, "Hymn to the Veneration of the Great Joachim," for his twenty-second birthday, which he played with Otto Brinkman and Arnold Weber, fellow students in Gottingen, with all the solemnity demanded by the title, veneration pasted like a mask on their faces – easily the worst of Brahms's compositions, but Joachim couldn't tell him so.

He was surprised; the hymn was unusual for Johannes whose work was full of thunder more than rain. He was no less surprised at the other students in the tavern, solemn and silent as the hymn was played despite the empty steins before them; even their applause was muted. Brahms got up and bowed as Joachim lowered his violin. "Dear and Revered Royal Court and State Violinist" (he looked at the floor), "our very own Jussuf" (he appeared overcome with emotion), "it is my honor ... and my great and glorious privilege" (he continued looking at the floor, but peeked sideways as he spoke) "to serve you this humble address" (shoulders were shaking around them, faces breaking into grins) "on the occasion of the twenty-second year of your sojourn on our great and glorious planet ... Earth ... which has ... one sun ... one moon ... and ... oh, so very many stars, the foremost of which ... is none other than ... your bright and glorious self."

Suddenly Brahms burst into his girlish giggle, the students into raucous laughter, and Joachim understood the joke he had been too humorless to recognize. During his first visit to London he had been billed the Hungarian Boy at Drury Lane Theatre between two acts of a popular play, *The Bohemian Girl*. Mendelssohn had never let him forget his pique, calling him forevermore his Hungarian Boy. Joachim pointed a stiff finger at Brahms. "You, Johannes! You dog, you donkey! I am going to get you, man, for this." Brahms eluded his grasp around the table and the chase was on.

A cheer rang through the tavern as the two circled the table, but Brahms was laughing too hard to run and stopped so suddenly Joachim almost bumped into him. "Sorry! Sorry! I shall never do it again!"

Joachim glowered. "Well, then, I suppose it is all right – but see that you don't – or I shall give you such a hiding."

Brahms leaned on his elbows over the table, laughing so hard he might have fallen to the floor. He was careful to place the table between them before speaking again. "Hah! You, Jussuf, and what regiment of violinists."

They called him Jussuf for his Turkish affectations, the fez, water pipe, and upturned slippers adopted during his tenure with Liszt. Joachim swung around the table too quickly for escape. "You swine! I shall not need even a regiment of worms to handle the likes of you." He caught up with him as Brahms, helpless with laughter, fell to the floor dragging Joachim down with him.

Brahms giggled more than Joachim could remember; he had been giggling more himself since his arrival, shucking his Hamlet mask. Growing up among elders, protected in all quarters, he was revered by all who heard him; even Magister Hering, whom he had visited for studies arranged by Mendelssohn, had carefully aired his room of cigar smoke before his arrival, burning pastilles in his stove for their fragrance – but Brahms had introduced him to cigars making him sick in the attempt, pulled him into taverns to ply him with beer (even in the mornings), and he enjoyed the camaraderie, hardly realizing Brahms needed a friend no less, his peer, his age. They shared as well a conflict regarding Liszt.

On the morning of Brahms's departure Liszt had professed admiration for his work, presented him with an inscribed leather cigarette case, extended an open invitation to the Altenburg, and offered to write to Hartel, publishers in Leipzig, recommending his compositions. Brahms had thanked him and written to Joachim to second the offer recommending his compositions to Hartel; he couldn't go back to Hamburg, not without something to show for his travels. Joachim had invited him again to Gottingen, to share his flat and attend lectures, and he had accepted, everything except the lectures, preferring to read books on his own. He had explained his antipathy: "Liszt will offer you champagne, but you must drink it from his slipper. I could not stay. I would have had to lie if I had stayed."

Joachim had not been surprised, no less in conflict himself between Liszt's kindness and his compositions, the man and the music.

Brahms had complained: "A genius is proclaimed everyday in Weimar as if by a pope – but the Altenburg is not the Vatican."

Joachim hadn't laughed; his eyes had clouded. "That is so, and that is the reason I am no longer in Weimar myself, but there is also the other side of Liszt, and you know it. I traveled with him once from Vienna to Prague – a cold night's journey we had for which I was unprepared – but Liszt brought me hot grog in the coupe and covered me with rugs and wraps. He was as kind to me as my own mother. That is how he is. He confuses me completely."

Brahms had nodded. "But there is always a price to be paid. He wants you to join the New German School – *his* New German School, *his* Music of the Future – as if there were no other."

Joachim had been relieved to unburden himself, he had been Liszt's konzertmeister for more than two years before he had realized he didn't belong, unable to conform to Liszt's musical ideals. "When he plays, of course, there is nothing to criticize. His fingers do not play as much as conjure images from the piano. We played Mendelssohn's Violin Concerto once, he and I – and he played the entire finale with a lighted cigar between the fingers of his right hand."

Brahms's eyes had widened. "Ja, there he has the advantage. We others have only our ten fingers."

Joachim had nodded. "He is a showman, there is no doubt, but I had to ask myself if he did not also show some contempt for Mendelssohn – and this is the difference between them. I once played Mendelssohn's D minor Trio with Hancock and Mendelssohn. We had only the violin and cello parts. Of course, Mendelssohn knew his part, but rather than appear superior he had another book of music placed on his stand. Liszt, on the other hand, with all his grace, never allows you to forget his superiority."

Brinkman thrust another stein in his hand, but Joachim declined. "I have to attend a lecture in thirty minutes."

Weber almost shouted. "You are going to the lecture today of all days?"

"Why not? It is always good to imbibe – wisdom as well as beer."

Brahms stood beside him, stein in hand. "Books and beer, that is my motto too." He raised his stein, chugging it dry, wiping his mouth with his sleeve. "And I will escort you personally to your lecture today in honor of your birthday."

There was a raising of steins all around, cheers of "Books and beer!"

A few minutes later the two new friends stepped into the street. Brahms had been in Gottingen for a month, but still wondered at his luck, drawing all the benefits of student life, none of the drawbacks. The market square was as busy with students as a children's playground, halftimbered houses ranging in rows, Gothic spires towering overhead, the square diverging into narrow streets from the fountain in the middle, the Old Town Hall standing across – all conjuring vistas from the Brothers Grimm who lived in Gottingen and nearby Kassel. Joachim put his arm around Brahms's shoulders, singing:

> Oh, submerge, oh, submerge, all your sorrow, my sweet
> In the sea, in the deep blue sea.

Brahms had put the words to music, a poem by Robert Reinick. It was hard to say whether he found the melodies or the melodies found him: if he read a poem slowly, and if he liked the poem, the melody followed so inevitably that he could never again consider the poem without the melody. Joachim loved the song, it gave voice to his Hamletmania which Brahms found his least agreeable feature. The song continued: "A rock will remain on the ocean floor, but sorrow will rise to the top," but Brahms drowned Joachim's voice with his own, substituting new words.

> Tied to a rock, it will sink like a stone
> And be killed like a rat or a mouse.

Joachim laughed, pushed Brahms away. "Always, you are the clown."

Brahms spoke solemnly. "I am Johannes Kreisler, Jr. Do you not know it yet?"

Joachim shook his head, pulling a note from his pocket. "Well, Junior, I have written a letter to your Senior and your mamma, telling them how you have been wasting your time and my money." He unfolded the note and gave it to Brahms. "Tell me what you think."

His mamma and pappa, elated by his constant good news, his triumphs in Winsen, Celle, Luneberg, Hildesheim, his friendship with Joachim, the greatest violinist in the world, his meeting with Liszt, the greatest pianist, had expressed concern when he had parted from Remenyi, moving to Gottingen where he lived off Joachim's largesse, surely injuring his good will, their relations, everything he had built. "She is amazing, my mamma. I made her promise, before I left Hamburg, that she would write to me once a week, three pages, no matter what – so what does she do?" He shrugged. "She copies pages out of the newspaper. She is no philosopher. She runs out of things to say."

Joachim smiled; he didn't doubt the affection of his own relatives, but the family was too large, he had been away a long time, he was lucky to hear from them once a month. "She must be a very caring and loving mamma."

"Ja." Brahms read Joachim's letter as they walked:

Dear and Honored Sir and Madame:

I am not known to you, but you must allow me to write and say that it is I whom am more blessed in the company of your Johannes than he is in mine. He has stimulated my own work beyond all my hopes and provided me with the spur that all creative artists must have, without which indeed we poor musicians would experience only the thorns of our toil and never the roses of appreciation. His purity, independence, and intellect have already found sympathetic utterances in his music and bring joy to all who have had the good fortune to hear it. It goes without saying that I am glad to be of service, my friendship is always at his disposal, and I pray you will bless our new friendship with your approval.

Truly yours,
Joseph Joachim

Brahms pursed his lips. "Ah, best of Jussufs, this will make her very happy. I am in your debt."

"No more than I am in yours. Your music makes *me* very happy – but have you thought about what we discussed?"

Joachim had accepted an invitation from Liszt to attend a music festival in Karlsruhe, from where they planned to visit Wagner still exiled in Zurich; he planned as well to visit Schumann along the way. Brahms needed to plan himself what he wished to do next. "Ja, I want to travel along the Rhine Valley. I have read so much about it. I would like to make more contacts along the way. This will be helpful, do you not think, for publications?"

"If you are going along the Rhine you must see Schumann, you absolutely must see Schumann. He will be able to help you like no one else, and he will do it willingly. I will tell him about you when I see him." He had written already to Robert about Johannes, but Johannes had appeared diffident from the start; he couldn't understand why.

"Ja, Schumann – but is there no one else? Must it be Schumann?"

"Why not Schumann? Have you not heard his music?"

"Some."

"What?"

"*Papillons, Carnaval.*"

"What else?"

"Some other things. I do not remember now."

"You did not like them?"

Brahms grimaced and shrugged. "They are so small, they are finished before they are begun. They do not have ..." he gestured with his hands, "you know ... breadth."

"Schumann is different. You must look for different things. If you look for Mozart or Beethoven or Schubert you will be disappointed, but if you look at what is there you will be amazed. His inspiration seems to come from nowhere, and then he is hardpressed to find a form to fit his inspiration – but he finds it, and if you are willing to listen you will hear it – if you search, you will find."

Brahms sighed, saying nothing, not wishing to tell him that Schumann had once returned his manuscripts, knowing Schumann was his friend.

"He is not unlike you in some ways, he uses internal voices much as you do."

"Schumann?" Brahms looked at Joachim, recalling how Louise, now studying with the Schumanns in Dusseldorf, had talked. "You may be right. I still have to think about it."

"Think, think all you want – and then go to Schumann. You will not be sorry. In the meantime, what will you do for money?"

Brahms looked at the ground as they walked. "That is a good question."

"For which I have a good answer. We shall give a concert. That will give you enough for your Rhine journey. Would you find that agreeable?"

"Agreeable? More than agreeable, I find it providential."

The brick building was symmetrical, two storeys tall, whitewalled and redroofed; six sixpaned windows lined the upper storeys; the entrance from the street was wide, an arched wooden door flanked by columns, two windows on either side. Brahms didn't understand his trepidation, the house was large but no Altenburg, well situated but no landmark, peopled with strangers but no princesses. He had met one of the inhabitants the day before, a girl, perhaps twelve, Schumann's daughter, to whom he had given Joachim's introduction; Schumann had been out on his daily walk, and he had been invited to return the next day, an hour earlier at eleven o'clock. He had arrived at ten and paced the street until a bell tolled eleven, there were heartbeats within his heartbeats, but he stepped finally to the door, passed through the foyer into the courtyard, and rang Schumann's bell.

A tall hulking man with a serious face opened the door, his body about to spill out of his robe, feet in felt slippers, lips puckered as if he were whistling. The hair covering his ears was wavy and fair, but darker than his own; the eyes were blue, but again darker than his own. "Yes?"

The seed had long been planted; Louise had suggested four years ago that he make Schumann's acquaintance, but he had resisted; Louise was a girl, ruled more by fancy than fact, too sentimental to take seriously, but he couldn't say the same about Joachim. Still he had resisted, walking along the Rhine, staff in hand, knapsack on back, from Mainz to Coblenz to Bonn, presenting his card and Joachim's introduction to Wasielewski (once Schumann's konzertmeister in Dusseldorf), who had played with him and advised him to visit Schumann. He had visited the Deichmanns in Mehlem, friends of Wasielewski and Joachim, for whom he had played, with whom he had stayed, who were also admirers of Schumann with a library of his publications, where he had familiarized himself with the works, among them the *Kreisleriana*, supposedly the compositions of Johannes Kreisler, Jr. He had met Reinecke (Schumann's pupil), Hiller (Schumann's friend), and taken finally a train to Dusseldorf. Whatever transpired, it was ordained that he meet Schumann.

Brahms removed his hat. "Herr Doktor Schumann?"

"Yes?"

"I am Johannes Brahms. Here is my card."

Robert remained silent, pulling spectacles from his pocket, looking long at his visitor, absorbing the short grey alpaca summer coat, dusty shoes, hat in hand, shapeless with age, discolored by the sun, surprised most by his girlish face, blond hair to his shoulders.

Brahms stared back, digging his nails into his hat. "I am a friend of Joachim."

Robert shook his head as if waking himself from a trance, pushing the spectacles up the bridge of his nose. "Of course, forgive me. He has written to me about you."

He unpuckered his mouth to speak, but remained barely audible; his expression did not change, but he held the door wider, stepping to one side to let Brahms in.

"The sittingroom is ahead of you."

Brahms walked through a hallway past a staircase into a sittingroom, potted plants on the sills and hanging from the ceiling, portraits on the walls, books alongside, a piano the centerpiece, sheet music everywhere. He was relieved most that the house was a home, not a showcase, no jeweled sabers on the walls, no oriental tapestries, no gold medallions; he was comfortable as he had not been in the Altenburg.

"Joachim would like me to hear your compositions. Would you like to play for me now?"

Brahms jumped. Robert stood right behind him, still without a change of expression; had he not spoken he might have seemed unaware of Brahms. "Ja, I am ready." He sat at the piano.

Robert stood behind him holding an elbow in one hand, pushing his puckered lips with the other, spectacles on his nose, eyes heavylidded.

Brahms began with the Sonata in C major as he had begun for Joachim, bringing down his hands from a height, hammering the mighty multifingered chords, but he had played barely eight measures before Robert stopped him with a hand on his head. "Wait a minute." Brahms stopped; Robert ruffled his hair, caressing his ear with his thumb. "My wife must hear this."

He lumbered out of the room, dragging his slippers, appearing to have no bones in his body, shouting in the hallway as if he were unaccustomed to shouting, unaware what volume might be required. "Clara, come at once." Brahms jumped again.

Brahms heard a muffled response before Robert returned, silent again but smiling as he wouldn't have thought possible moments ago. Short quick footsteps pattered down the stairs, through the hallway, into the sittingroom. "What is the matter, Robert?"

A woman appeared in the doorway, her face white, whiter for her dark hair parted down the middle, drawn over her ears, and braided in a knot behind, as he had seen Queen Guinevere's in an illustration in Herr Giesemann's copy of the Knights of the Round Table – so white she might have been in shock, as indeed she had been to hear Robert shout, but she regained color seeing their visitor, seeing Robert smile, lead her to a chair, and sit her down. He seemed unable to stop grinning. "You must hear this, my dear, music such as you never heard." He turned, standing behind Brahms, slapping his shoulders. "Now, young man, begin again."

Brahms's heartbeats multiplied again, his blood ran on rollers; the presence of a pianist increased the pressure, and not only a pianist of renown but of youth, younger than her husband, younger than the Princess of the Altenburg, more slender and more gracious – or did she too smoke cigars like a man and shout her opinions? Her husband had not even introduced them yet. He raised high his hands again, dropping them accurately, eight fingers, each on target, each following a path apparently independent of the others, pounding out magisterial chords.

Clara heard echoes in the preliminary phrases of the *Hammerclavier*, of Schubert's *Wanderer*, but she had heard nothing before like the development, spun it seemed from deep solitude, the heart of a mountain, the bed of the ocean. She looked at Robert, but he was too absorbed by what he heard and saw to look away, following Brahms's fingers. She joined him, standing to one side, following as well the fingers – and the face lost in the spell of his music, no less transfigured by the work himself than Robert, bowing his head to the keys, pulling away and humming as he played, surmounting the greatest difficulties with the greatest ease – though not always the greatest elegance. He made his work more difficult than necessary, the most beautiful solutions were always the simplest, but solutions were easily found, ideas could only be intuited.

Brahms hesitated after completing the first movement, but only a moment; Robert gripped his shoulders. "Play on, Herr Brahms. Play the entire sonata." Brahms brought his hands back to the keyboard and completed the sonata before lacing his fingers in his lap.

Robert gripped his shoulders again, smiling as Clara had not seen in a long while; she picked his card, left face down on the piano by Robert. "Johannes Kreisler, Jr.?" She smiled. "You?"

Brahms had scribbled the pseudonym on the backs of his cards. "It is a joke among my friends. I am called Johannes Kreisler, Jr."

She couldn't stop smiling. "I cannot see it in your face, but I can hear it in your sonata."

Brahms said nothing; his heart was beating more furiously than when he played, in counterpoint, more beats within beats; playing was easier than talking.

Robert shook him by the shoulders. "What else can you play for us, Herr Brahms?"

"I have composed another sonata, in F sharp minor."

Robert released his shoulders and stepped back. "We are all ears." Clara left the card again on the piano, face down as before, and Brahms played the entire sonata, no less explosive than the C major. He was a beautiful boy, the kind poets wrote about, dreamy as a poet himself, silky blond hair, azure blue sky in his eyes, Hellenic beauty in his hands. She felt a glow in her breast, a well rising in her head, breath coming more quickly. When he was finished, he put his hands in his lap again. "If you wish to make any suggestions or comments, Herr Doktor, I would be honored to hear them."

Robert couldn't stop smiling and shook his head. "Herr Brahms, it is I who am honored. There is nothing I would add, nothing I would subtract! These are not sonatas but symphonies waiting to be born – so many voices still singing to me, a whole chorus, an orchestra."

Clara took Robert's arm, looking at Brahms. "Herr Brahms, if I may say a word?"

Brahms was surprised; she appeared to contradict her husband. "Yes?"

"My husband is right. I, too, hear orchestras in your sonatas. These are grand works, full of passion, the most profound thoughts."

Brahms looked at the floor.

She was unsure how much to say; he played like a composer more than a virtuoso, too immersed in the music to care about the fingering, giving the music a rough texture a virtuoso could finesse with ease; but she needed first to win his confidence, test how much she might say without losing him. "I beg your pardon, Herr Brahms, if I am presumptuous, but that last movement, for instance seemed less … how shall I say it … less heartfelt than the others."

He looked up. "I do not understand."

"Oh, I am not good at this. My husband is so much better. He is the critic in the family. It seemed more … fantastical. It seemed less … structured, without the resolution of the other movements."

Brahms's lower lip protruded. "That was intentional. I meant it to express … unsatisfied longings."

"Ah, well, then there is no more to be said. You follow your instinct as any good composer must. I hope you will not take it amiss what I have said – that I have presumed to criticize what appears almost beyond criticism."

Brahms shook his head, but still wouldn't look at her.

She had noticed as well in the very beginning of the C major sonata that his strength was also sometimes his weakness, the theme was announced, uncompromising and arresting, first in C major, then in B flat, but as he expanded the theme, hands moving in contrary motion, a void opened between them, and the sound from his hands failed the sound in his head, he needed another two hands to fill the void, needed an orchestra, as Robert had realized though he had voiced it differently, and she didn't want to voice it differently herself, not for the present. Instead, she made a request. "May I try the C major?"

Brahms's eyebrows rose. "You would do me a great honor." He was curious about her ability; despite her fame she was still a woman. He got up, setting the pages for her.

She looked over the first page, squinting.

Brahms grinned. "No one can read my writing." He wanted to add, Except Liszt, but didn't, didn't want to trumpet his peccadillo more than he could help.

She smiled. "I think I can manage."

Her performance made her a different woman. The counterpoint of beats within Brahms's heart multiplied. Had he closed his eyes he would have sworn he was listening to a man – but with an elegance he would not have thought possible. She played more smoothly than himself, more smoothly than Liszt though not as flawlessly, making observations similar to Liszt's as she played, particularly about fingering, gauging his response with her eyes as she spoke. She used a configuration of her fingers he had not imagined. "What do you think when I play the phrase this way?"

"I would like to try it."

"Of course."

He sat beside her, within the warmth of her body. She covered his hand with hers, fingers over his fingers, to show him what she meant. His skin expanded and contracted where their hands met as if there were breath in her touch. She was set apart from girls he had known by her age no less than her ability, at once less intimidating and more, less for her unavailability, but more for the fascination she exerted, less for her interest in his work, and more for the same reason – you couldn't separate the work from the man.

Brahms followed her suggestion, playing the phrase five times to his satisfaction. "It is much easier this way."

She said nothing, but couldn't stop smiling, dimples indelible as beauty spots in her cheeks.

"Madam, dinner is ready." Bertha stood with two girls popping their heads in the door, one of whom he recognized from the day before.

Clara turned immediately to Brahms and put a hand on his knee; with anyone else she might have seemed forward, but Brahms was just boyish enough to pass for her son. "Herr Brahms, will you not stay for dinner? Do say that you will – and in the afternoon we can study the entire sonata. It would give us great pleasure."

"Indeed, it would." Robert folded his glasses into his pocket and put his hands again on Brahms's shoulders.

Brahms nodded, feeling he had been adopted; the warmth of Clara's hand on his knee, Robert's on his shoulders. "Thank you. Ja, I will stay."

"Good! Then it is settled. I must warn you, though. We have six children." Still she smiled, gay for their discovery, gay for the effect on Robert.

Brahms nodded again, saying nothing, getting up from the piano, staring at the floor, smiling all the while. Robert also smiled, slapping his back. "We two understand each other, Herr Brahms."

ii

His room, in a boarding house in the Altstadt alongside the Rhine frequented by laborers, fishermen, and dockworkers, was tiny, dark, and dingy. Going to bed that night, he couldn't help imagining Clara (he called her Clara) still in his company, unbraiding her hair, imagining the creak of the bed as she lay down, dark hair spread like a fan on the white pillow, nightdress flaring, providing a glimpse of a white thigh, her smile, dimples in her cheek, one arm by her side, languid, open in invitation, the other no less languid, hand resting on her belly, his own hand caressing the exposed inner thigh, parting the nightdress farther, as he bent to kiss, to lick, to knead the soft flesh with his lips, to sniff her womanly scent – but she was not the woman, she could not be, she was no Helga, no Lena, no Frau Grummer, nor any of the others, you did not do that, not with a lady, not with a woman of genuine accomplishment, not with an extraordinary artist, not with a married woman, not with the mother of six – and certainly not with the wife of Robert Schumann, no less kind himself, of even greater gifts and accomplishment than his wife.

They had invited him back the next day, but after an early breakfast he had set off for a walk through Dusseldorf. He had heard of the French influence, that Dusseldorfers were the greatest of dandies in Germany, caring more about their appearance than other Germans. The city was lovelier than most he had recently visited, resplendent with long broad straight streets, solid brick houses, wellheeled inhabitants, and he wished to plan where he might go next while admiring the city.

He walked through the Altstadt and back along the Konigsallee lined with cafes, pastry shops, chestnut trees, a canal down the middle bearing ducks and swans, careful not to cross Bilkerstrasse even by accident where the Schumanns lived. He couldn't go back to Hamburg emptyhanded, nor could he go back to Joachim, but he had learned to make his own way, he could be the itinerant musician, Johannes Kreisler, Jr. – finally, in actuality – until he had harvested a greater crop of compositions, which he could exhibit with greater confidence than the current, but the argument rang hollow. He was satisfied with his current crop, particularly the new sonata which had been percolating in his head since he had begun his Rhine journey, which percolated further even as he walked – but he knew he couldn't go back to the Schumanns, and he didn't know where else to go.

By late afternoon he was no closer to a decision, but returned to the boarding house knowing only that he had to leave; the farther from Dusseldorf the better. A fisherman repaired his boat, a dog peed against a wooden bench, a boy turned cartwheels. "Herr Brahms?"

He turned. "Frau Schumann!"

"Oh, Herr Brahms! Thank God I have found you."

She wore a dark blue walking dress, darker at the rim with mud, and a bright red bonnet; her face was white, searching his own for clues, but could hardly have been whiter than his own; the face of the boarding house was discolored behind her, a smell of fish hung in the air, a dog barked.

"I have searched for you all day, Herr Brahms. You would not believe the places I have visited – every inn, every hotel, every boarding house, every tavern, restaurant, snack bar, wine cellar, in the Altstadt. I asked everyone, everywhere, about you."

He raised his eyebrows, imagining how close he must have been to discovery all morning. Despite her labor there was no sign of displeasure in her face; her eyes, her smile, were as bright as a lover's as she took both his hands in hers. He thought she might embrace him, so relieved did she seem, so happy.

"I was so afraid, when you did not come, that we had offended you – that *I* had offended you. That would have been unforgivable, indeed. I am so glad to have found you at last. My husband would have been so upset had I not. You are like a tonic for him – and for me, too. You have made us both so very happy. We cannot thank you enough."

Brahms imagined all eyes upon them and his hands squirmed in hers. She let go as if she had read his mind and took a step backward. "Look, I have muddied my dress, I have muddied my shoes." She lifted her dress so he could see the mud on her black walking pumps. "But I do not mind, now that I have found you."

Dimples highlighted her cheeks, no longer white, pink as a baby's, many teeth in her smile. He could only mumble. "You did not offend."

"I beg your pardon."

He spoke more loudly, keeping eyes on the ground. "You did not offend. You could not offend."

"I am so glad to hear it. Will you come with me, then, back to our home for dinner? My husband will be so happy to see you again."

Brahms remained mute.

"Is something the matter? Will you not come?"

"I beg your pardon, Frau Schumann ..."

"Yes? What is it?"

He shook his head, mumbling again. "I do not belong."

Clara looked around, lowering her voice. "On the contrary, Herr Brahms, it is here that you do not belong. These are common people. You are of the elect."

Brahms did not know how to answer without offending her, but she offended him without knowing it. He spoke with new confidence. "They may be common, Frau Schumann, but they are like me. I am no more of the elect than they."

Clara saw she had misunderstood him and searched his face again for clues, but still he looked at the ground. She spoke softly. "But there is no one quite like you, Herr Brahms. You misunderstand me. What I mean is we share a passport, you and I and my husband – and so many of our friends, as musicians, as you will see if you will only give them a chance – even better, we are musicians with similar sympathies, we are in perfect harmony."

Brahms shook his head again. "I do not belong."

She saw finally how it was; he wore the same alpaca jacket, the dusty black walking shoes; she saw the grime in his face, and she knew what to say. "You are right, Herr Brahms, to value yourself so highly – but you will have difficulty finding peers anywhere. You will always have to settle for less – but this I can guarantee: nowhere will you find others who will better value your gifts, who will appreciate you better, than will my husband and I."

He smiled at last. "Na – it is not like that, nothing like that. I value myself – but not like that."

"Then come with me. No explanation is necessary. We wish only for you to be among us."

iii

Returning to Hanover from Karlsruhe, Joachim stopped in Dusseldorf where the Schumanns surprised him with a party. Among the guests, some of whom he had met before, were Rosalie Leser (an older woman, a blind neighbor for whom Clara sometimes played), Elise Junge (her companion), Albert Dietrich (one of Schumann's students), Louise Japha (Brahms's Hamburg friend, now Clara's pupil) – and Brahms, more sleek and content than Joachim had seen him yet, Clara holding his arm, smiling. "I know you were the one to send him to us, Herr Joachim, and we thank you for your service from the bottom of our hearts, but he is now Robert's Johannes. Indeed, we cannot do without him, none of us."

Joachim smiled. "I am glad to hear it, Frau Schumann. I like him too well to be jealous of him."

335

Robert moved more quickly than Joachim could remember. "Clara does not speak lightly, Herr Joachim. Let me show you what she means." He opened a book. "Let me read you a few entries from my diary since we have met Herr Brahms." He led with his finger as he read. "30 September: Herr Brahms from Hamburg." He looked from Joachim to the rest. "That was the first day he visited – but Clara and I were out walking, so Marie told him to come back the next day." He frowned at Marie. "You should have asked him to wait, Marie. That was naughty of you."

"Oh, Pappa!"

Elise jumped, blond pigtails bouncing. "That is what Pappa says now, Herr Joachim, but if Marie had asked Herr Brahms to wait, he would have sent her to bed without pudding."

Her pappa smiled. "Mind what you say, Elise, or you know who will go to bed without pudding tonight."

"Who, Pappa?"

Robert looked at Joachim, shaking his head as if to say *You see how she is!* He read quickly. "1 October: Visit from Brahms (a genius). 2 October: Scherzo by Brahms. 3 October: Hungarian Dances by Brahms. 4 October: Music at home, Fantasy by Brahms. 5 October: Songs by Brahms and Sonata for Violin and Piano. 7 October: String Quartet by Brahms. 8 October: Clara played my F minor Sonata for Brahms. 9 October –" He stopped suddenly, looking up from the diary; on the ninth he had started an article on Brahms he wished to publish, but didn't wish to make public yet. "I will not bore you with the entries for each day, and I see I am embarrassing our guest – and it is time anyway for our big surprise."

"What? Another surprise?"

Clara hadn't stopped smiling in days despite their other problems; it was the most Robert had spoken, the merriest she had seen him, in a long while.

Julie entered the room, wearing a rustic outfit and straw bonnet, carrying a basket of roses and carnations which she handed to Joachim with a curtsey.

Joachim was glad to be within the Schumann circle again. The festival in Karlsruhe had been a success, he had played Bach's Chaconne and his own concerto and enjoyed meeting his old friends again – Raff, Bulow, Cornelius – Weimarites with whom he had consorted daily when he had been Liszt's konzertmeister, but other developments had been less enjoyable. The company had traveled to Zurich to see Wagner, and he had shown Bulow his own music to be sure that Wagner, the author of "Judaism in Music," wouldn't find it too Jewish. Wagner had appeared not to notice, or not to care, and read his poem, the Nibelungenlied aloud. Under the spell of Wagner's dramatic recitation Joachim had offered his services as konzertmeister though the music had yet to be written, but later regretted his weakness; his old conflict had also resurfaced, reconciling Liszt, the man with the composer.

He took the basket, smelling the flowers, caressing Julie's cheek. "Thank you, little Julie. You look so pretty in your little peasant dress."

Julie blushed, playing with her long dark plaits.

Robert chuckled. "You are not very perceptive today, Joachim. There is something for you under the flowers."

Joachim looked, pulled out a rolled manuscript and opened it, crinkling his brow as he read: "F.A.E.?"

Brahms almost shouted. "Read on, Jussuf! Read on!"

Joachim read the entire title of the scroll.

F. A. E.
In Expectation of the Arrival of their Friend
JOSEPH JOACHIM
This sonata was written by
Robert Schumann, Johannes Brahms, Albert Dietrich

Joachim still looked puzzled. "But what is F. A. E.?"

Brahms shook his head in wonder. "The man is a great violinist, but no riddler. F. A. E., best of Jussufs. Your motto: Frei Aber Einsam."

"Ah!" His motto was known: "Free but Lonely." He made no secret of his life.

Robert raised his hand, smiling and speaking clearly. "We have used the notes F-A-E as a theme for a sonata for the violin and piano. We three have written movements for the sonata which you and Clara must play – and you must guess the authors of each movement."

"Aha! Now I understand! Well, what are we waiting for? Let us strike up the band!"

Clara jumped to the piano and Joachim pulled out his violin. He had no trouble identifying the authors, Dietrich had composed the first movement, Robert the second and fourth, Brahms the scherzo.

Champagne and refreshments were served, cigars lit, and the guests mingled, Joachim with Brahms and Dietrich. "Johannes, it is good to see you looking so well."

Brahms blew smoke and grinned. "Thanks to you, Jussuf – all thanks to you. Have a cigar."

Joachim took the cigar, looking at Dietrich. "Johannes taught me how to smoke, and now he wants to be sure I have not forgotten."

Dietrich smiled, shaking his head. "He is full of bad habits. Every morning he rushes up my stairs, bangs on my door with both fists, and dashes in without waiting for an answer. If I did not know better I would swear he was a Prussian."

"Hahah! If not for me you would be late for breakfast every morning." He turned to Joachim. "We breakfast in the Hofgarten – in the open air. You must join us tomorrow."

"With pleasure."

"Just remember to get up early – or Brahms will scare the devil out of you with his banging."

Joachim laughed. "I thank you for the warning."

"How was the festival in Karlsruhe?"

Joachim didn't want to dwell on his misgivings in Karlsruhe. "It went well. How was your Rhine journey?"

Brahms seemed unaware Joachim had dodged his question. "I never dreamed it could be so … hah, so like a dream! I walked past so many ruined castles I felt I was walking through history – but the most dramatic was the Lorelei Rock. I swear to you, man, Jussuf, I heard the Lorelei sing – and so beautifully. If I had been the captain of a ship I would gladly have abandoned it to the Rhine – ship, life, love, everything, for the Lorelei!"

So the legend went: the Lorelei, sirens, last seen where the Rhine was narrowest, the rock face steepest, lured ships to their ruin with their songs.

Joachim spoke with authority. "You know what it is, do you not? There are deep hollows in the river bed which cause the currents to swirl dangerously around the rocks. That is the true hazard to the ships."

Brahms shook his head. "That is what you think, my friend, but I was there. I was walking along the bank, staring up the black face of the rock, when – what do you think I saw?"

"Lorelei!"

"Ja, but only the hair, and their song was an echo in the valley – but this is the mystery, this is what people do not know. They think the hair is blond – but it is not, it is many colors, rainbow hair. You tell me, who would not abandon his ship for girls with rainbow hair? It is not the song, it is the rainbow hair that lures the sailors and fishermen."

Fraulein Leser lifted her sightless face in their direction. "Herr Brahms is a wonder." She spoke ironically. "When he plays the piano it is wonderful enough – but when he talks like that it is enough to cause the blind to see – yes, and also the deaf to hear, I am sure."

Clara laughed. "He is changed since we met. He would look at no one then, only at the piano."

Brahms had never felt so appreciated before, never so carefree, speaking so fancifully with not a hint of irony, but sometimes the attention overwhelmed him and he extricated himself from the circle, shouting for his friend. "Louise, let us choose another book. We are almost finished with *Robinson Crusoe*."

Fraulein Leser nodded satisfaction; blindness forced her to play games with herself, gauging someone's height from a handshake, character from intonation. Heading for Robert's library with Louise, Brahms had confirmed her suspicion that he was a reader.

iv

Clara would have been glad to see Dr. Hasenclever, their friend and family doctor, also a member of the Music Society, responsible for hiring Robert at Hiller's recommendation, a frequent guest to dinner, also a poet and collaborator with Robert on a choral ballad, *The Luck of Edenhall*, but she was warned by his expression, thoughtful and sympathetic, also of his companions, both of them advocates, Herren Iling and Herz, that this was no social call. All were older men, Hasenclever's head still full of hair but white, Iling's hair still dark (what little was left), Herz leaning on his pearlhandled walking stick. She smiled, greeting them as Bertha led them to the sittingroom. The three nodded in return, grim and polite, but avoiding her eyes as they seated themselves, except Hasenclever whom she knew best. "We would like to speak with your husband, Frau Schumann, if possible."

"He is taking a walk. He always takes a walk at this time – for his health – but you are welcome to wait if you wish – or if there is something I can do …"

Iling and Herz nodded at Hasenclever. Hasenclever turned to Clara. "We have a message for your husband. Perhaps you will convey it for us."

Clara's eyes widened as if she were keeping watch on all three at once. "Yes?"

Hasenclever spoke slowly. "It is regarding his health, Frau Schumann. We are all most concerned as you know. We wish to make things easier for him if we can."

She spoke quickly, eyes darting from one to the other. "He has not been well – but he has been much better now for a while."

"We are glad to hear it, indeed, Frau Schumann." At a recent mass Robert had continued to conduct after the priest had begun to intone the service – even otherwise, the mass had been badly conducted, the congregation had found it disrespectful, some had found it blasphemous. The reviews after the Rhine Music Festival had stated the obvious: Robert Schumann was a great composer, but Hiller was the better conductor. "We wish for his continued health – and to help in every way we can."

"You are already doing everything you can, Doktor Hasenclever." She meant what she said; Hasenclever had proven an ally on more than one occasion. Robert had received a letter signed by three members of the Music Society requesting his resignation; an Anti-Music Society, dedicated to stamping out bad and badly performed music, had singled him out for ridicule; and each time Hasenclever had secured an apology for Robert – but she was still afraid of what he might say and talked to keep him at bay as much as to comfort herself. "We are most grateful. Robert is most grateful."

Hasenclever nodded, the others still said nothing, but looked sympathetic. During the time of Robert's sickness Tausch had substituted to the satisfaction of audiences and musicians; Robert's return had been icily received; Tausch, too, had complained. Robert wished him to rehearse the orchestra, but conducted the final performances himself; when all went well he reaped the benefit of Tausch's work – but when it didn't, owing to Robert's own incompetence, he blamed Tausch. "What we wish to suggest, Frau Schumann … and this is only until your husband is entirely well again … is that he should conduct only his own works. Tausch will conduct the rest. We have discussed the matter among ourselves and find it the best solution – of course, only until your husband is well again."

Clara saw Tausch's hand in the suggestion; he had already suggested that Robert conduct the large works and he the smaller; she knew what he wanted, understood what he was doing, worming his way into the grace of the audience, stealing Robert's authority and position – but she had been waiting for just such an attack and the wait had stretched her nerves. "I am sorry, Doktor Hasenclever, but what you suggest is unthinkable. You should have known better than to suggest it. I could never make such a suggestion to my husband – and it is better you say nothing to him about it either. He is better than he has been in a long while, as I have said, and such a suggestion would only make him worse. I must say I am surprised. I thought you were his friend."

Hasenclever blinked and continued to speak regretfully. "I am your friend, Frau Schumann. That is why I am here. Better you should hear this from a friend."

Iling spoke, as regretful as Hasenclever, touching the wisps of hair escaping over his ear. "It is only because we are so very concerned about your husband, Frau Schumann, that we presume to make such a suggestion."

Clara almost rose from her seat, trembling as she spoke. "If you were so very concerned about my husband as you say, you would defend him as I do. You would rebuke those who disobey him and criticize him and work against him. It is their insubordination that threatens his health, nothing else. He needs your encouragement, he needs your confidence, he needs your faith. He does not need to have his work taken away. He does not need you to suggest he is incapable of fulfilling his responsibilities."

Herz grimaced, tapping his finger on the pearl handle of his stick, speaking in calm measured tones, no less sympathetic than Hasenclever and Iling. "Frau Schumann, no one is suggesting that he is incapable of fulfilling his responsibilities. We merely wish to make it easier for him to do so."

Clara stared at him, but said nothing; it was the first thing he had said, she might have forgotten he was there.

Hasenclever spoke again; he was convinced part of the difficulty lay with Clara building a buffer when she needed to build a bridge, protective of Robert when he needed to be among others; the more he depended on her, the less on himself when he needed more independence himself. "Frau Schumann, let me say I am the first to admire the courage and strength with which you defend your husband. I think I speak for us all when I say he is a great composer and the finest of men – but I think it is perhaps also the case that he needs to communicate more directly with the musicians. It is this lack of communication that leads to so many of the difficulties we face."

Clara was sensitive to the subject and understood what he meant, but refused to acknowledge it. "On the contrary, Doktor Hasenclever, if more of his friends defended him the way I do he would be better yet. He does not fail his friends; it is they who fail him."

Hasenclever's eyes twitched; he took a deep breath; his sympathy never wavered. "It may not seem that way to you at present, Frau Schumann, but his friends do their best, even as we speak, not to fail him. They have only the greatest respect for him – I know I speak for everyone here."

Iling nodded slowly. "Absolutely, Frau Schumann. I wish we could convince you of our sincerity."

A new voice sounded almost like a tap on the shoulder. "Gentlemen?"

All faces turned. Robert stood in the doorway. Clara wondered how long he had been waiting.

"Gentlemen, I will not have you disturbing my wife."

"Robert!" Clara went to his side, coming back on his arm.

The others rose. Dr. Hasenclever spoke. "We do not mean to disturb your wife, Doktor Schumann. I am sorry if that is how it appears."

Having announced himself Robert appeared to have nothing more to say, but stood with Clara on his arm, lips pursed.

"Doktor Schumann, we have come from the committee to make a suggestion –"

Clara stiffened on his arm. "A vulgar suggestion – not to be considered." She wished Brahms might have stayed, his presence alone gave Robert strength, but he had stayed in Dusseldorf more than a month, visiting them almost everyday, and chosen finally to return with Joachim to Hanover, though not before he had played them yet another sonata, stronger than the first two, longer and more difficult yet, from memory, not yet written, already more mature, no wild wingflapping as Robert liked to say of beginner's works, which he had fermented in his head during his Rhine journey and stay in Dusseldorf.

"Frau Schumann, I beg your pardon, but I am required, nevertheless, by the committee to make the suggestion to their Musik Direktor." When Clara and Robert remained silent he continued.

When Robert understood what was proposed his eyes lost focus. "That is impossible! It would undermine my authority."

Clara tightened her grip on his arm. "It is no suggestion at all."

Robert covered her hand with his. "It is also a breach of contract. As your Musik Direktor, I am contracted for ten concerts and four church music services annually, and weekly rehearsals of the Choral Club, but your suggestions make it impossible for me to fulfill my responsibilities. If you persist I will sue you for breach of contract."

Iling was quick to respond, but still spoke quietly. "It is not a breach of contract, Doktor Schumann – merely a suggestion. We are all concerned about your health. That is our primary consideration."

"Your suggestion would make it impossible for me to carry out my responsibilities."

Hasenclever pursed his lips. "I am sorry you see it that way, Doktor Schumann. I hope that will not be your last word – but perhaps you need time to think about what we have said."

"I have thought about it as much as I ever will and serve you my notice now. I will not be conducting the November concerts. You have rendered my service impossible. My wife and I have been invited to Holland for the month after, as you know. I must conserve my energies for the tour, I must go where I am appreciated."

"I am truly sorry you feel that way, Doktor Schumann. I do hope you will reconsider. The Committee has the greatest respect for your abilities."

Clara raised her chin. "They do not show it."

Robert nodded. "My mind is made up."

Hasenclever shook his head. "I wish we could change your mind, Doktor Schumann, and begging your pardon – I do not mean to be presumptuous – but I would like to assure you that we will wait as long as we can for your answer."

"That is entirely up to you. As far as I am concerned you have it already."

Clara's eyes were steel; it was difficult standing on principle when you had six children, and she was two months pregnant, but they would find a way.

"Schumann wishes you to present your works to Breitkopf and Hartel in Leipzig for publication – in person. He urges me to use all my powers of persuasion to influence you." Joachim looked up from his letter smiling. "I am afraid he misjudges my powers."

Brahms sat across the breakfast table from his friend, also reading a letter from Schumann, frowning. "I do not know what to say. Schumann is in such a hurry to get me published my head spins. I have never desired to visit Leipzig. It is no more than a giant counting-house from what I have heard, but he has written to Breitkopf and Hartel already to expect my first works in the next six days. That gives me too much to think about and too little time."

"But what is there to think about? Is this not what you want?"

"Ja – but I was thinking one work, two works, of which I was sure. Schumann has in mind six opuses already. Look." He passed Joachim his letter. "He has even suggested his own program. What do you think?"

Joachim looked at the letter. Robert had listed songs, sonatas, a scherzo, a trio, in no apparent order, identifying selections with opus numbers.

"I am satisfied with only the scherzo, but Schumann thinks I should start with the weaker works – and he is right. I should either start with them or leave them out altogether and try not to fall so low again – but I cannot make up my mind whether to publish them at all."

"What you publish is up to you, Johannes. Schumann is only making suggestions."

"Ja, I know. Less than two months ago I would have been happy with one publication, any publication. Now it is a problem choosing among my works." He grinned. "It is not such a bad problem. I only want to make the right choice. What do you think?"

"Well, what I think is that you are too modest, but since you ask I will say that you cannot make a wrong choice. It is immaterial which work you choose to begin. A vision is a vision, even when it begins with a big toe – but if you wish to begin with your brow you may choose both sonatas, the C major and the F sharp minor, for your first opus."

"Ah, hah! and then I can show my ears and nose and mouth and who knows what else until I run out of body parts. Jussuf, you have a priceless way with words. You should be a poet – or a jester."

Uncomfortable with irony Joachim didn't laugh. "You know what I mean."

"My dear Jussuf, it was only a joke. You must not take everything I say so seriously."

"I thought in this matter you would want me to be serious. Did you not ask my opinion?"

Brahms shrugged; some things he couldn't explain; some things Joachim would never understand. "Ja, that is true – so, what do you think?"

"Well, then, I will make my own list – but whatever I think, I would defer to Schumann – and I am in complete agreement with him when he says Hartel should bring out three works simultaneously. It will show you are serious from the start – but here is something I think you should read while I am making up your list."

Brahms raised his eyebrows; Joachim was smiling, leafing through the pages of the *Zeitschrift*.

Joachim handed him the journal. "It is an article by Schumann." Brahms took the journal, leaning back in his chair and lifting his coffee – but putting it down again, leaning forward again, unaware he continued to hold the cup as he read.

NEW PATHS

Years have passed – ten, to be precise – since I have chosen to appear again in this venue. I have been tempted often, many talents have appeared, each bringing fresh musical energy (among them, Joseph Joachim, Theodor Kirchner, Albert Dietrich, Niels Gade, and Robert Franz), though their works are known to mostly a limited circle.

Watching their paths, I was convinced that they but prepared us for the arrival of one who would appear suddenly to provide the ideal form, the highest expression, of our age, who would not present his mastery in gradual stages, but spring forth like Minerva fully armed from the head of Jupiter.

He is now among us, a young blood at whose cradle graces and heroes stood watch. He is Johannes Brahms from Hamburg where he has been initiated into the most arcane and difficult tenets of the art by Eduard Marxsen, a distinguished and inspiring teacher, and more lately he was sent to me by the esteemed and eminent master, Joseph Joachim.

He bears all the signs of the elect. Sitting at the piano he revealed to us regions of wonder and drew us into circles of enchantment. His playing, too, is full of genius, transforming the piano into an orchestra of wailing and joyous voices. There were sonatas like veiled symphonies; songs whose music proclaimed their meaning as completely as their words; pieces for the piano, demonic and angelic; sonatas for violin and piano; quartets for strings; each so different it might have flowed from a separate source, but all of which he has united into a single thunderous river pursuing a single glorious waterfall, past the arch of a rainbow, over turbulent waves, to be met ashore by fluttering butterflies and the song of nightingales.

Once he waves his magic wand over choruses and orchestras he will provide glimpses into spiritual worlds. May the highest genius guide him, which is entirely possible since another genius, modesty, also resides within him. His friends greet his first steps into the world with joy. He will undoubtedly meet with slings and arrows, but also laurels and palms. We welcome him as a champion.

A secret bond holds all kindred spirits. You who belong to the circle keep it tight so that the truth of art may shine and spread its blessings throughout the world.

    R. S.

It had not taken Joachim long to make up his list, after which he had watched Brahms, smiling – but Brahms had turned white. He had set his cup down and let one hand slide limp to his side; the other hand, no less limp, let the *Zeitschrift* fall on the table.

Joachim still smiled, but spoke seriously. "Well, what do you think?"

Brahms continued to speak under his breath. "My God! Ah, Jussuf, Schumann means well, but this …" He shook his head.

Joachim frowned. "What are you saying, Johannes? This is only the beginning – and you could not ask for a greater introduction."

Brahms stared at Joachim. "That is just the point of it! Who can live up to such an introduction?" His voice began to regain strength. "If I were a musician who had been toiling long and hard to no avail, and if I were then to read this about someone new, I would be well disposed – indeed, very well disposed – to hate such a person – at least, to dislike him intensely. Do you not see that?"

Joachim shook his head. "I do not – well, perhaps, but my disposition would change, I am sure, once I had familiarized myself with his work."

"But everyone will not feel as Schumann does. He flatters me, but he does not tell the truth about me. He exaggerates every detail."

"Well, if that is how you feel you must not blame Schumann. I helped him, you see."

"You? How?"

"He wanted to know what I thought – I was your friend – and I told him he could not have done better – and I am convinced we are right. I do not feel he has exaggerated the matter at all."

"You do not? You do not think he was wrong to name so many names as he did?"

"He named my name, did he not? But you see how I feel."

"But you are a friend – a selfless friend. That is why you feel as you do."

"Johannes, you are indeed too modest. I am the friend of many. I am Liszt's friend, I am Berlioz's friend, I am Dietrich's friend – but I do not feel about their music as I feel about yours. Friendship has nothing to do with it. You must have greater faith in your work."

Brahms narrowed his eyes and straightened his back. "I have faith in my work. But I prefer to let it speak for itself. I prefer not to build expectations beforehand – which might appear false. I prefer to keep expectations low. Then, I cannot lose."

Joachim's frown deepened. "You are far too modest, Johannes. Besides, there is nothing to be done about it now. If I were you I would go to Leipzig and meet with Hartel as Schumann has recommended – and publish whatever you wish."

Brahms said nothing.

"I would also write a letter of gratitude to Schumann. He has done you a great service though you may not see it yet."

Still he said nothing.

Joachim smiled again. "It is part of your allure, Johannes, that you do not recognize your own great merit. Schumann has recognized it, your genius, your modesty – and so will others, even those predisposed to dislike your work – but you must learn to recognize it yourself, you must not let it get in your way."

"It is not modesty. It is caution. I do not wish to make a false step from the very start."

"Then you must watch where you step. That is all."

Brahms nodded. There was no going back. Whatever he thought, Schumann had acted with the greatest generosity; it was up to him not to betray his trust. "Perhaps you are right. Let me look at your list."

Joachim had listed the same works as Robert in a different order, adding as well a quartet. Brahms spoke with determination. "At least, I do not have to think anymore about what to publish. After such an article I can show only my best features." He drew thick lines across the fantasy, the violin sonata, and the quartet.

ii

The primary theme in the last movement of Brahms's Sonata in C major brings a herd of stallions into the concert hall at full gallop, a drumbeat of hooves thundering across prairies, the earth moves and the listener is caught in his seat between a gasp and a grin, and Brahms was beginning to recognize its power, his own power over the Gewandhaus audience when he played.

He had found himself a celebrity on his first day in Leipzig, snatched from his hotel by Heinrich von Sahr, a friend of Dietrich, who had insisted he stay with him – and shown him around Leipzig, introducing him to the musical lights, Hartel, Julius Rietz (Kapellmeister of the Gewandhaus), Ferdinand David (Konzertmeister), Ignaz Moscheles (who had known Beethoven), Friedrich and Marie Wieck (Clara's pappa and halfsister on a visit), and Julius Otto Grimm (a musician, twenty-six, von Sahr's neighbor), among others.

All were in the audience; so was Berlioz, come to Leipzig to conduct his works; so was Liszt, come to hear Berlioz, with other Weimarites, among them Raff and Remenyi; so was Hedwig Salamon, younger daughter of a wealthy household, long a friend of the Mendelssohns and Schumanns, who had known Joachim as a boy.

When Brahms concluded with a series of chords leaping across the keys, hurtling to a cadence, the applause was immediate, audience on its feet, rows of teeth sparkling from every tier like pearls. Jussuf had been right, so had Schumann, his presence vanquished whatever animosity the article might have raised. Hedwig Salamon understood his appeal best: Schumann's article led you to expect no less than a warrior, ready to battle you for preeminence; instead you got little Hannes, a boy's voice, a girl's delicacy, a child's face you could kiss without shame, with the guile of a lamb, and you could no more take arms against him than against a puppy.

345

Brahms remained seated at the piano, staring at the crowd, apparently unaware he was expected to smile, stand, and bow; but as the applause continued he stood, bobbing his head, raising his hand, wondering whether to wave, when someone from the audience mounted the stage.

It was Berlioz, hair bobbing like a cloud on his head, arms swinging like the vanes of a windmill, who caught Brahms by his shoulders and smothered him against his breast, held him again at armslength and smothered him again. The applause continued, unabated, until Berlioz began to speak. "Schumann was right. This is new music – and you will suffer for it – but you will triumph – if you only have faith in your music you will triumph. You show yourself already a diffident man – but an audacious musician. I salute you."

The congratulations had only begun; every moment brought a new smiling face into his circle, a new hand thrust forward, a pat on the back, an introduction.

Liszt met him in the lobby with his entourage and bowed low. "Herr Brahms, we meet again – to my great pleasure."

The honor was overwhelming, a nod from Liszt in public. "The pleasure is mine, Herr Liszt. I thank you for coming."

The corners of Liszt's mouth curled. "I hope, Herr Brahms, that your New Paths will soon lead you back to the Altenburg. Your place among the New Germans was never in doubt."

The irony didn't escape Brahms, but he was too flushed with the success of the evening, the presence of the great man at his occasion, to mind. "Thank you, Herr Liszt. I will remember."

Liszt bowed again, as did Raff and others in their company, following Liszt out of the lobby, including Remenyi who barely looked at Brahms.

iii

Jakob rushed up three flights of stairs calling his friend's name. "Fritz! Fritz!" He thumped once on the door with both hands before throwing it open, dashing in, through a tiny parlor, and into a darkened bedroom. "Fritz! Look! Look what I have got!"

It was still early morning, a Saturday, Fritz in bed, nightcap on his head; he and Jakob had returned late the day before, but Jakob's news couldn't wait; he had almost rushed to Fritz's rooms the night before, but Christiane had stopped him. "Who is it? Who is it?"

"Ach, who do you think?"

"Ach, Jakob, I should have known. It is not good manners, do you not know, to burst into someone's house so early, when they are still sleeping?" He turned on his side, away from Jakob, pulling the covers closer.

"Hah! Look who is talking about good manners, a horn player from Heide. Just look what I have got, na?"

"I am not interested."

Jakob reached into the bed, pulled the covers in a single tug, and threw them on the floor. Fritz sprang out of bed immediately. "Jakob! You go too far. This is not your home. Who do you think you are? The Pasha of Turkey?"

"Look, Fritzi, look, na! Just look what I have got."

"What? What can be so very important?"

Jakob held up a letter.

"What? Is that all? Another letter from that lying urchin son of yours?"

"No, not from him!"

"What is it now? Has he met Beethoven at last? Has he met Mendelssohn? Is he communing now with Mozart? Or has he finally come to his senses?"

Jakob couldn't talk enough about Hannes's adventures with Joachim, Liszt, and Schumann; but his friends did not entirely believe him. "You are not listening, Fritzi! I said it was not from him."

"Then who is it from?"

"It is from Schumann! Look! He says my Hannes is a great artist. He will become a second Beethoven!"

"Beethoven? There is only one Beethoven! You should be ashamed, Johann Jakob, even to suggest it."

"I do not say it. Schumann says it. Look!"

"Schumann?"

"Ja, look!"

He thrust the letter in Fritz's face, but Fritz pushed it aside, bending to pick the covers from the floor. "Why would Schumann write to you, Johann Jakob? He is a great composer and you are just a bass player. He is the mountain, you are the gutter."

Jakob stared at Fritz so fiercely he might have hit him and Fritz altered his tone.

"Do not get so excited, Jakob. I was just using a figure of speech. It is not for nothing that I am the son of a schoolteacher. Do not get excited over nothing."

Jakob thrust the letter out again. "Read it, na? Read it, what it says. Then talk."

Fritz sat on the bed, shaking his head, finally holding out his hand. "All right, give it to me." He read the letter slowly, looking at the address. "Ja, it says it is from Schumann – but who can tell? I have not seen Schumann's hand and neither have you." He handed the letter back. "Someone is having a joke at your expense, Johann Jakob. If you are smart you will disregard such a letter."

"Ach, Fritzi, you are a dumbkopf! When Hannes comes you will see what a dumbkopf you are. We will all see!"

"Ja, ja, when Hannes comes, when Hannes comes. Always, when Hannes comes, but never a word about when he will come. Listen to me, Jakob. Your boy is lost. He has come to no good. That is why he writes so much nonsense. Your poor Hannes has lost his mind."

"He is coming. He is coming for Christmas. He will be here soon."

"Ja, he is coming. We shall see, then, na? We will know the truth then – *if* he comes."

iv

Clara laughed to see Robert running down the street ahead of her; he cut a comical figure, grown so bulky he waddled more than ran, but that was not why she laughed; she laughed for joy to see him run at all, to hear him giggle, to see him continually mobile and noisy again, and ran after him down the street and up the stairs to Joachim's door. It was amazing the change their recent successes had made, first in Holland, now in Hanover. She had been concerned at first in Holland when he had been haunted by a tone, a distant trumpet, an "A" lodged like a leech on his brain, but their first success had vanquished the tone.

Brahms, behind Clara, heard bells in her laugh, saw arabesques in her every step, but hadn't known the Schumanns long enough to note the change in Robert. Behind him came Julius Otto Grimm humming a tune, his new friend from Leipzig who had come with him to Hanover for the month of January, Brahms to work on a piano trio, Grimm to rest before beginning a new position in Gottingen.

Joachim, at the rear of the company, was the most sober of all. He was glad Robert appeared to enjoy himself, but afraid he appeared to enjoy himself with too much mania. He couldn't forget Robert's recent letter: *My dear Comrade-in-Arms, I have fired several twenty pound charges into the enemy camp bringing a lull in the battle, but I expect a mine very soon to detonate under my feet – and I am very much looking forward to the fun!* Joachim knew there was trouble with the Music Society, but not the details; and he had arranged the concerts at the Hanoverian Court knowing the King liked Robert's music, and wanting to score another success for the Master.

Robert rang the doorbell, his hand fluttering like a pigeon; Joachim hurried forward with the key, explaining as he opened the door, "Gustav will have gone home." Robert strode into the rooms behind Joachim, familiar enough with the place to shrug off his coat and find a chair in the dark while Joachim lit a lamp. Clara picked up the coat from the floor and hung it on the tree. Brahms marveled once more at her multiple capacities: great artist, loving wife, fecund mother, pregnant again. Grimm still hummed the tune unbuttoning his coat. "Doktor Schumann, I simply cannot get your D minor out of my head –"

Robert interrupted him fingers beating a tattoo on his own lips. "My dear Ise, tonight, please, we shall have no formalities. Tonight we shall be as young Kreisler has christened us. I am Dominus, my wife is Domina, you are Ise, and Joachim is Jussuf."

Brahms had written to Robert, dubbing him Mynheer Dominus and Clara Domina for their conquest of Holland, dubbing Grimm after the wolf, Ise Grimm, in the fable, less for the slight beard ringing his clear face than for his nature – anything but wolfish.

Grimm grinned, bowing his head. "Well, then, Mynheer Dominus, at the risk of repeating myself I must tell you once more how much I have enjoyed your D minor Symphony."

Robert waved his arms in a facsimile of merriment – conducting, prestissimo, an invisible orchestra. "No risk, dear Ise, no risk at all. You can never tell an artist enough how much you appreciate him."

Clara sat by Robert's feet drumming a tattoo on the floor. "That is indeed true. They could not tell us enough in Holland how much they appreciated us – and I cannot tell you how much we appreciated their appreciation." She laughed. "In Utrecht they would not stop calling for him, 'Doktor! Doktor!' until he appeared for a bow."

Robert placed his hands across his belly, but couldn't keep his fingers still, first lacing them, then steepling, then lacing again. "But best of all was Rotterdam."

"Oh, yes! Without a doubt, that was the best!"

Robert lit a cigar with movement enough to light two. "After the concert a choir gathered outside our hotel, a hundred voices it must have been, with an orchestra. They brought their own torches and serenaded us with my choruses – for almost an hour."

Clara got up to bring him an ash tray.

Robert drew on his cigar. "They did not leave us until midnight."

Clara settled again by his drumming feet. "I was freezing. Those Dutchmen do not know what it is to be cold – but we did not mind. Their sentiments kept us warm for days." She saw Robert's hyperactivity as clearly as Joachim, but saw it instead as a sign of health after his long melancholy and fell in easily with his mood. "My dearest Robert, it is only what you deserve."

Robert grinned. "Thank you – but you, too, Domina – you, too, must call me Dominus tonight."

She pushed against his knees vibrating with the motion of his feet. "Oh, my Dominus, forgive me."

He giggled, waving his hand again like a pope conferring benediction. "Forgiven, forgiven, all is forgiven!"

Clara turned to the others who had seated themselves, loosening their cravats, lighting cigars – but Joachim, realizing he was out of champagne, was buttoning his coat again. "I will be back shortly."

Clara's voice turned sour with disappointment, wishing to keep Joachim's company for Robert. "But where are you going?"

"Just to my landlady. I must get her key – for emergencies. I shall be back in just a little while."

"To your landlady?"

"I shall be back very soon."

He was gone before she could press him further. She turned, bewildered, to Brahms. "Did you understand him?"

Brahms shrugged. "Jussuf is like that – a very mysterious man."

"Sometimes a little too mysterious. Whatever could have possessed him to get a key. He was not to be locked out this very minute – nor even this night. Could he not have waited until the morning?"

Brahms shrugged again, looking away.

Robert lost his smile, speaking sharply, momentarily ceasing all motion. "Do not worry yourself, Domina! Jussuf knows what he has to do!"

"Of course!" She smiled immediately, not wishing to contradict him, turning again to Brahms and Grimm. "As I was saying, it is only the attention he deserves after all these years – and after Robert – I mean, after Dominus had given a few words of thanks, a deputation appeared from the Dutch Musical Society with yet more words of appreciation!"

"But you should have heard my Domina the next day in Amsterdam. I conducted my Second Symphony and she played the Beethoven E flat Concerto – even better than today."

Praise from Robert meant more than her own, as had once praise from her pappa. She played for Robert now as she had played for her pappa, became his instrument as she had been her pappa's, lived for his praise as she had lived for her pappa's. "How could I not play well? I was transported to see how they respected my husband – as a composer *and* as a conductor. The Dutch are more cultured by far than the Rhinelanders."

Brahms drew on his cigar, saying nothing; he had attended Robert's concerts in Dusseldorf and knew his faults. Robert smiled, speaking with pleasure. "I needed only to mark time. The compositions had been well prepared. The Dutch orchestras know my works better than I myself."

Grimm had only heard Robert in Hanover conducting an orchestra prepared by Joachim, and drew on his cigar with Robert and Brahms. "I wish I might have heard you conduct your other works as well. I so enjoyed the D minor and the Fantasy tonight."

Robert giggled again, drumming his feet again on the floor. "For that you might have to go to Holland. It seems I am better appreciated there."

"It is true, a prophet is least appreciated in his own country."

"It has ever been thus."

Clara smiled, happy with the conversation. "But you cannot say about the royal family what you can about the citizens. Dominus, tell them what the Prince said."

Robert grinned. "Prince Friederich came up to me." Robert stood up mimicking the Prince's steps, bouncing on the balls of his feet, nodding his head politely, mincing his tones. "'Are you, too, musical, Herr Schumann?' That was what he said."

Clara laughed; it was the kind of question which had caused Robert humiliation almost ten years ago in Russia – but no more. He was much changed, much better.

"I wanted to say, 'Do you not read your own newspapers, Herr Prince?' but of course I could not – not unless I wanted to start a war." Robert cackled like a xylophone. "And when I answered in the affirmative he asked, 'And what instrument do you play?'"

Again Clara laughed. "He wished to make a bigger fool of himself than he had already."

"I wanted to say, 'I play them all, I play the orchestra,' but of course, I did not."

"Oh, he was too amusing by far. We had such a good laugh about it afterward – and the very next day, at The Hague, after Dominus had conducted his Second Symphony, he was crowned with a laurel wreath."

Robert shook his head, opening and closing his hands in a spiral of fingers. "I do not remember that."

"He never even noticed it, not even the garlands, he was in such a state – but I remember thinking as I watched, 'This is as it should be.' I thought that to myself over and over the whole evening." Her voice grew soft with nostalgia. "We plan to go again next winter."

Robert nodded vigorously, head bobbing as if on a spring. "We have had enough of Rhinelanders. We are thinking of leaving next year, either for Berlin or Vienna – I think Vienna, most likely. It will depend on what is available. I have heard some things – but only third hand so far."

Grimm was the only one surprised. "You are leaving Dusseldorf? Is that for a certainty?"

"Yes, but we have told no one yet – except Jussuf and young Kreisler." He turned to Brahms. "I told them I could not conduct under the terms they wished. I think Jussuf might have said something to you about my letter?"

Brahms nodded.

"I wrote to Tausch that I would consider him ill disposed toward me if he conducted in my place."

Clara nodded approval. "And, let me tell you, it was not a letter he would consider framing."

"No, that it was not – but, at any rate, he conducted the concert – and the one after."

Grimm tapped ash into a tray he shared with Brahms. "What may we expect from you next, Dominus – I mean, in terms of compositions?"

Robert shook his head. "No music for a while – next, I have two books in mind."

"What kind of books?"

"The first will be a collection of my essays from the *Zeitschrift*."

"That would be very useful – to have them all in one place."

Robert nodded. "And the other will be a collection of quotations on music from all the great books – Plato, Aristotle, Shakespeare, the Bible, Goethe, Schiller, Jean Paul, Hoffmann."

"That will take very long, will it not?"

"I have started already. I have long been making notes."

Clara noticed again Brahms's silence, almost disinterest, and wondered what new music pivoted through his head, imagining he lived in a private world much like Robert – but so had Joachim been silent that evening. Grimm, whom they knew least, usually the quietest, talked the most. "What do you suppose has happened to Jussuf?"

Brahms looked up. "I am sure he will back soon."

Clara fixed her eyes on Brahms. "We talk too much about ourselves, do we not? We have read so much about young Kreisler – but he does not say very much himself about his successes."

Brahms noted again, the dimples in her cheeks, how like a girl she could be, her pupils large in the artificial light, turning her blue eyes black, her hand the color of the sun next to the lamp. He preferred not to talk about his triumphs; audiences had raved uniformly, reviewers less so; some had praised performances, others compositions; more surprisingly, they had compared his profile to Schiller's, his head to Raphael's heads, the sheen in his hair to the halo of John the Baptist, his eyes to forget-me-nots. "Young Kreisler can say only that he has accomplished all that he has accomplished through the benediction of Dominus."

Robert smiled. "Young Kreisler is modest – but that is perhaps wise." He had awaited Brahms's letter of thanks with anticipation, sensing ambivalence in the delay, but had read it often enough since to commit it to memory:

Honored Friend:

I am taking the liberty of sending you your first foster children (they owe you their passports into the world), still doubtful they deserve your indulgence and affection, so extraordinarily high have you raised the pitch of my own expectations. In their new clothes they appear almost too prim, even embarrassed. I cannot get used to seeing my innocent children in such smart new clothes.

I look forward with the greatest pleasure to seeing you again in Hanover, to tell you that my parents and I owe you and Joachim the most blissful time of our lives. We are, all of us, gloriously happy, including my teachers and all of our friends.

I beg you to convey the most cordial greetings to Frau Schumann and your children from Johannes Brahms

It had pleased Brahms enormously to place copies of his publications under the Christmas trees of friends, see Onkel Becker goggleeyed, gogglemouthed, his pappa's satisfaction. He had sent them money, two hundred thaler, the first payments on his publications. His pappa, too, had met with fortune, promoted to double bassist for the Hamburg Theater Orchestra, and the family had moved to more spacious quarters again in Lilienstrasse.

Clara heard a noise at the door. "Here is Jussuf – finally!"

Joachim walked in with a smile, a bouquet of champagne bottles in his arms.

Clara grinned, getting up to help Joachim unload the bottles on a table. "You must introduce us to your landlady, Jussuf. I see her keys unlock more than doors."

Robert slapped both knees, clapping his hands. "These are the keys that unlock sparks – mental sparks, divine sparks."

Brahms punched Joachim's arm. "It is a key wine, indeed. C major, would you not say? Not the least bit flat, and not the least bit sharp?"

Grimm joined in the fun. "But she modulates into so many keys. Your landlady must be a fine lady."

Joachim grinned unstoppably himself. "That she is – she is a key lady."

v

ROBERT TO JOACHIM   *D'dorf, 6 February, 1854*
My dear Joachim,

It is now a week since we left. We might not appear to have written to you in this time, but I have often written in invisible ink, and between these lines there is also invisible writing which will some day be visible.

I have dreamed of you, dear Joachim. We were together for three days. You held heron's feathers in your hands from which flowed champagne – how prosaic, but how true!

We have often thought of the past days; may many more such be in store. The gracious royal family, the excellent orchestra, and Brahms and yourself hurtling to and fro like two young demons – we shall not forget it. Music is silent just now – outwardly, at least. In Holland we sounded the tonic; in Hanover we sounded the third; and that is our situation now, but we count on Brahms and yourself to supply the fifth. The virtuoso caterpillar disappears by degrees, reappearing as the butterfly composer.

I must conclude now. It is already getting dark. How is it with you? Write to me soon – in words, and also in notes.

My wife sends kind regards. Remember me also to Herr Grimm. It seems to me he does not at all resemble his namesake, Ise.

R. Sch.

Bertha interrupted Clara giving Marie a piano lesson. "Madam, there is someone here to see you." She appeared unsure how much to say and looked to one side; the family had enough troubles; she hated to announce more.

"Does he say who he is?"

"A Herr Schultz. He says he is the manager of Dauch's restaurant."

Robert visited Dauch's in the evening as part of his routine: work in the morning, their walk together at eleven, dinner with the family at midday, work again till six, visit to Dauch's for beer and newspapers, back home for supper at eight.

"Has my husband seen him?"

"No, madam." Bertha's round face appeared angular, her eyes to lose focus. "He asked for you – specifically. He does not wish to bother Doktor Schumann."

Robert had busied himself with his book of musical quotations since their return from Hanover, visiting occasionally the library, but relying greatly on his own extensive collection. "Is my husband still in his study?"

"Yes, madam."

"Good. I will come at once. Please ask Herr Schultz to wait a minute."

"Yes, madam."

Clara took a deep breath and told Marie to continue with her practice, saying she would be back soon, hoping to resolve the problem without disturbing Robert.

Herr Schultz bowed when she entered. "Frau Schumann, I thank you for your consideration. I am Schultz."

She didn't invite him in, not wishing to take more time than necessary. "Not at all, Herr Schultz. How can I help you?"

Her urgency communicated itself at once to Schultz. He had noticed her deep hollow eyes, even the eyes of the maid; no one in the household appeared to get much sleep. "I will not take more of your time than I can help, Frau Schumann. The matter is about your husband."

"Yes?"

"I am the manager of Dauch's. Your husband visits us daily, as you know, of course – but for a week now … for a week now he has not been paying his bill."

Clara merely stared, not certain she understood.

"Do not misunderstand, Frau Schumann. I know he means to pay – but he appears to have much on his mind … and I do not wish to disturb him if it is not necessary."

"Please be specific, Herr Schultz. Does he refuse to pay? Is that what you wish to tell me?"

"Na, na, Frau Schumann, that is not it at all – rather, he appears to forget."

"Do you not ask him to pay?"

"Ja – but the first time he asked the waiter from what country he came. Well, he is from Germany, right here in Dusseldorf, and that is what he said – but Doktor Schumann did not pay him even then. He asked instead if he knew anything about music."

Clara's eyes grew misty and her focus shifted from Schultz to a point behind him.

"The waiter said he had a sister who played the piano, but that was all, and Doktor Schumann asked him if he did not hear music sometimes – specifically, an 'A,' in trumpets. Of course, Wolfgang, that is his name, said he did not – and Doktor Schumann merely nodded and went on reading his newspaper. I told Wolfgang not to bother him again because I knew he would come again the next day. I thought maybe for one day he had forgotten to bring money. It happens – he would pay us the next day."

Clara's face turned white; Schultz wondered how much he should say.

"But the next day was the same. Doktor Schumann forgot to pay his bill. He just left it behind."

"Did you not ask him again to pay?"

"Not until the day after that – I asked him this time myself – but this time Doktor Schumann asked me if I smoked." He shrugged. "I said ja, I did, I thought he was going to offer me a cigar – but he forgot what he said and started reading again, the newspaper – and when I asked him again he asked me again if I smoked – and again he read the paper." He shrugged. "I left him alone. He did not seem well. He put down the paper after a while – frowning, as if it were difficult to concentrate. I went to him again to ask if he was all right and he asked me if I heard an 'A.'"

Clara shifted her weight from one foot to the other.

"I could hear nothing, and told him so – but he said it was too loud even to read the newspaper." Schultz saw Clara rub her hands against her sides, roll her head, and spoke hurriedly. "Frau Schumann, your husband is always welcome at Dauch's – but I did not want to bother him. He seemed a little bit ill. I thought I would settle his bill with you instead. That is all."

Clara took possession of herself at once. "You did well not to bother my husband, Herr Schultz. He is, indeed, not as well as he might be. He has been working too hard. How much do we owe you?"

Schultz told her, she paid him, and told him not to bother Robert. She would continue to pay him weekly.

ii

Robert lay on his back in the dark, staring at the ceiling; Clara lay by his side, cradling his head, resting it on her belly, growing once more (the tenth time) with their baby. Her eyes were closed, but not in sleep; she had slept, but only in starts, for almost three hours, Robert not at all. She dreaded going to bed, couldn't recall their last peaceful night. The "A" note had turned into a chord and the chord was incessant; every sound became a note, every note part of a chord, every chord part of a melody, the music became continuous, the last reverberations of each cadence sowed the seeds for what followed, and his mind knew no rest. Dr. Hasenclever had recommended an associate, Dr. Boger, more experienced in matters of the mind, but he too had been helpless.

"Clara?"

His voice had grown thicker and slurred. "Yes, my love?"

"It grows – still, it grows. Can you not hear it yet?"

"Oh, Robert, I wish I could hear it, I wish I could share it with you. Together I know we could resist it – but I cannot."

"It is painful ... Clara ... but an exquisite suffering."

She held him closer, caressing his face. "I do not care how exquisite, not when I see how it hurts you, my darling."

"I wish you could hear it ... even for a moment. It is a full orchestra ... no, it is better. It has instruments I have heard in no orchestra. You have never heard such music, Clara. The instrumentation is so finely colored, but I wish it would let me rest – but there can be no suffering more wonderful."

"Oh, Robert – can you not sleep, even for a little while?"

"It will give me no rest, Clara. It will give me no rest." She felt him tremble in her arms, his brow moisten with sweat. "Oh, Clara, if it does not stop – if it does not stop ... I am afraid ... I am afraid it will take my reason."

Clara held him closer. "Will it not let you rest, Robert, if you ask it to stop?"

Robert seemed not to hear. "Look, Clara! Look at the ceiling!"

Clara was afraid to look upward, afraid of what she might see, afraid she might not see what he saw, but she saw nothing, just the ceiling. "What is it, Robert? What do you see?"

"Do you not see the clouds? Do you not see the light streaming, as from a sun, from behind?"

Clara trembled, but tried to maintain the conversation as if it were nothing unusual. "I see the ceiling, Robert – but nothing else. It is a white ceiling. Perhaps that is why you imagine they are clouds."

Robert's lips puckered. "They *are* clouds, Clara, as plain as if we were outside. This is how it must be, after we shuffle off the mortal coil."

"But we have not done so, Robert. We are alive, both of us, still very much alive."

"It is but a taste, my dear Clara – but a taste of what is to come."

Clara feared to encourage him, feared no less to upset him with discouragement – wished to welcome his confidence, but not his delusion. She caressed his face again. "Well, there is a long time yet for that. Do you not think we should try to sleep?"

His eyes remained wide open, locked on the ceiling, appearing hardly to blink. "I do not think it will be as long as you think, Clara. They are calling already to welcome us. They say we will be with them, both of us, together, before the year is out."

Clara felt her face turn cold; Robert was turning into a stranger. He tried to get up, but she held him more tightly, speaking urgently. "There is no one, Robert. There is no one there."

"But there is – there are many of them – calling me – but it is nothing to be afraid of."

Still Robert tried to get up, still Clara held him back, but he gathered strength as he struggled and she let him go, not wishing to excite him further. "Who is calling you, Robert? I see no one there."

Robert smiled. "They are angels, Clara. There are angels hovering all around us. We are blessed by angels. The music is their heavenly choir. I am listening to their orisons. They love us, both of us. Everything is all right."

He got out of bed, fumbling with a lamp. "Robert, what is it? Where are you going?"

"I am not going anywhere – but I have to write down what they say."

Clara stared, unsure what to say. "Do they speak German?"

He shook his head. "They speak the universal language: music. They are singing to me, a theme."

He was grinning, suddenly intensely excited, searching feverishly for a pen and paper. "A theme? What kind of a theme?"

"A theme! They say it is sent by Schubert! The spirit of Schubert sends us a theme!"

She watched in silence as he scribbled, unable to comprehend anything. He was finished in barely a minute. "May I see it?"

He smiled, giving it to her. "Of course!"

It was a short theme, but an old theme, one he had composed himself, the slow movement of his Violin Concerto, written at Joachim's request – but she said nothing. "And what will you do with this theme?"

Still he smiled. "They wish me to write variations on the theme – but they say I may write them tomorrow if I wish. They are very kind. They have waited a long while and they can wait a little while longer."

"They will let you sleep?"

"They will let me go to bed."

"Then let us go to bed, let us go to bed at once – and tomorrow you can write the variations if you wish."

Still he smiled. "It is not I who wish it, dear Clara, but they."

"As you say. Come to bed, Robert. I am tired."

He joined her again in bed, lying on his back, more peaceful though he still heard music; Clara, within the crook of his arm, fell asleep almost immediately, hands crossed over her enlarged belly, but he remained awake, staring at the ceiling, listening to the music, harmonies in brass, so faint they might have come from afar, watching the clouds in the ceiling, the light, the angels. He would be well if he let the music wash over him, but sleep wouldn't come and the light from the clouds grew brighter yet.

He couldn't have said how long he lay in bed, but gradually he imagined heads bobbing in the descending light, and wings, some tiny and fluttering, others large and flapping, and he strained his eyes for a clearer vision of the angels, imagining some of them fatcheeked like babies, some tiny as insects, some curlyhaired, muscled like gods, wings large enough to furl around them like cocoons or caskets.

The light remained at first too bright for him to distinguish more than faint outlines, but as the cloud of angels descended the music built to a crescendo and details became clearer. Two angels appeared to lead the rest, but angels such as he had never imagined, eyes blazing beams of orange, mouths red as blood, fangs bared, saliva dripping, furry faces striped like tigers and drawn in snarls, men with the savagery of beasts poised to pounce.

The music turned simultaneously loud, harsh, and dissonant, trombones rending the orchestral cloth in a roar, strings descending like a frigid haze, a cackle of trumpets, screaming clarinets, the steady leaden boot of bass drums. He had been fooled; these were no angels, but demons, come for a reckoning, for a judgment. The first demon alighted on one side of the bed, sitting on its haunches and leering like a gargoyle, batwings veined like the roots of ancient trees, speaking in a voice like earth cracking, pointing a gnarled clawed scaly finger.

SINNER! REPENT!

SCHUMANN, REPENT!

The second demon, eyes beaming red, alighted on the other side, webbing unfolding under the Grendal arm pointed in accusation.

TOO LATE FOR REPENTANCE!

YOURS IS THE FATE OF HELLFIRE!

TO BE BURNED BY THE FIRE THAT BURNS WITHOUT END!

The first demon spit in Robert's face.

GODLESS MAN!

SINNER!

The second demon leaped upon him, gripping him in leathery hands, his face so close his fangs seemed to grow into tusks. His breath smelled of rotting meat. Robert leaped from the bed and stumbled to the floor, screaming and flailing.

Suddenly the demons vanished, the room filled with people, Aschenbach, their landlord, Hasenclever, Boger, all holding him down, Clara staring, a streak of blood down the left side of her face. Aschenbach and Hasenclever held his arms from behind; Boger sat on his legs, speaking calmly. "Doktor Schumann, it is all right. You are among friends. There are no demons here. It is all right."

He looked around, it was morning, the room showed signs of struggle, scattered papers, an overturned chair, a broken lamp, the bed askew, bedclothes on the floor, a felt slipper on the bed. His body was tense, reinforced it seemed by steel wires, stiff as a block of concrete. Clara stood to one side, eyes wide, face whiter for her large dark eyes, for the streak of blood down her cheek. "Did I do that?"

She shook her head, unable to speak, but he knew he was responsible. "I am sorry, my dearest Clara."

She rushed to hold him, eyes glistening. "There is nothing to be sorry about, my darling. You have nothing to be sorry about, my Robert, my darling."

He went limp like a puppet at her touch. "My dearest Clara, I did not mean to hurt you."

She shook her head, holding him more tightly, unable to speak, shivering with tears; he seemed to be turning to air even as he spoke.

The doctors helped them up and put Robert in bed where he was finally able to sleep a few hours, but he was awake again in the afternoon, revising his Cello Concerto, explaining to Clara: "It gives me relief from the infernal voices. Work gives me relief."

THE NEXT MORNING he spent at his desk, staring apparently at nothing, paper, pen, ink, before him, writing occasionally a few notes, staring again as before, eyes round, smile wide. He kept also beside him a Bible. Clara understood he was listening to the angels, copying their songs. "May I see what you are writing, Robert?"

He showed her the page, variations on the theme he imagined sent by Schubert. She spoke softly, covering his hand with hers. "Robert, you know you are sick, do you not?"

He nodded, but his eyes remained round, his smile wide, as if he were hearing someone else, seeing someone else.

"The doctors say it has to do with your cranial nerves. They are overstimulated. You must rest. You must not work so hard."

The smile vanished, he seemed to see her again; his face seemed to shrink, wrinkle, and collapse as if it lacked the muscles to hold it in place. "You do not think I would tell you untruths, do you, Clara? You do not think I would tell you lies about the demons, do you?"

She held his hand tight, relieved he was listening. "No, Robert, of course not – but it is all in your head. It happens sometimes to creative people who have too much imagination – and there is no one as creative as you, my dearest Robert – but there are no demons. You work too hard, you need rest."

He pulled his hand away, his lower lip quivering. "No, Clara. I am a sinner. I must repent. That is why I am being punished." He put his hand on the Bible.

She wondered if he had been confused when he had searched the Bible for musical quotations; his religious imagery implied no less. "Robert, we are all sinners, but you are no more a sinner than anyone else, no more than I. You need to rest, that is all."

He frowned. "You are confusing me, Clara. You are trying to trap me. I know what I have seen. I know what I hear. No one can understand."

She took his hand again, eyes filling with tears. "I am not trying to confuse you, my dear Robert. I am trying to see things clearly myself. I am trying very hard to understand you. I want to help you, my Robert. I love you. You know that, do you not?"

He pulled his hand away again. "My head hurts. The room is spinning." She put an arm around him to lead him again to the bed, but he brushed her aside. "I do not need your help." He went to the bed and lay down without removing his slippers, pulling the covers over himself.

It was nine-thirty in the evening a week later, when he stood up at the dining table. "I want my clothes." Dietrich had visited, Robert had played so exuberantly for him he had been sweating; he had eaten a large meal, a late supper, sausages in aspic, quickly but with apparent enjoyment.

He had been under constant vigilance; either Clara or Bertha or Marie or Fraulein Junge always by his side. Clara gave thanks continually for their friends, Becker, Dietrich, Hasenclever among others, who accompanied Robert everywhere, the library, restaurants, walking. Dietrich looked at Clara who stared at Robert. She appeared the sicker of the two, more haggard for her vigil, dark wells under eyes hollowed by sleeplessness, days and nights by his side (or in the next room when he wished her away, until she could return without upsetting him) – but Robert appeared normal – until he mentioned the theme sent by Schubert, the theme yet to be sent by Mendelssohn.

There had been no discernible improvement, but if he wasn't getting worse Clara liked to think he was getting better; now she dreaded the worst. "Why do you want your clothes, Robert?"

He smiled, shaking his head. "I have to go, just for a little while."

"Where do you have to go?"

He displayed a confidence Clara lacked, his mind was set. "I have to go to the insane asylum."

Clara took a deep breath; it could only mean he was well if he recognized his sickness. "But why, Robert? Why do you want to go there?"

"It is not what I want, Clara. It is what I have to do."

"But why do you have to go?"

"I have thought for a long time, Clara, that I need my own professional attendant. You know it, I have said it before. It is the only way I will get well."

"But, Robert, do you not see? If you are well enough to recognize you are sick you cannot be as sick as you think."

Robert frowned, shaking his head, leaving the dining table, heading for the bedroom.

Dietrich spoke softly. "Frau Schumann, shall I get the doctor?"

"Please, Herr Dietrich. That would be a big help. I will try to hold him until you return."

Clara asked Bertha also to get the landlord, Aschenbach, before she followed Robert into the bedroom. There were objects on the bed – his watch, wallet, music paper, pens, cigars – which he wished to take with him. He paid no attention to Clara, but continued to lay objects in an orderly manner on the bed.

"Robert, please tell me why you have to go. Do I not make you happy? Have I not always placed you first? Have I failed you in some way?"

He shook his head again, refusing to look at her. "I am not able to control myself, Clara. I cannot answer for what I might do. I am a danger to everyone around me." He laid his clothes on the bed; she might no longer have been in the room.

"Robert, what about your wife and children? Will you abandon them?"

"Yes, but not for long. I will come back soon – cured. I am not well. You have said it yourself."

"But, Robert, you are not … insane. You are just a little sick. You have been working too hard. That is what Doktor Boger says."

Robert brought out a traveling bag. "I am a danger to you, Clara. I do not know what I might do in the middle of the night. I might cause you harm. I am not in control of my actions. It is for the best that we separate for a little while."

"But Robert, you are better already than you were a week ago. All you need is rest – and the care of those who love you. Do you think there are others who will care for you better?"

"Yes … because they are trained to care for people like me."

She was afraid she would be unable to hold him and kept talking to distract him until the doctor stood outside the door. "Frau Schumann?"

She sighed. "Doktor Boger, please come in. Please."

Dr. Boger stepped into the bedroom, nodding to Clara, addressing Robert. "May I ask where you are going, Doktor Schumann?"

"You may. I am going to the insane asylum. They will be able to help me."

"The insane asylum?"

"Yes. Do not try to stop me. My mind is made up."

"That is not my intention, Doktor Schumann – but I think I might save you some trouble."

Robert looked up from packing for the first time. "Oh?"

"Yes, you see I have taken the liberty of bringing with me a nurse. He is a trained specialist. He can stay right here with you. It would be simpler for everyone, do you not think?"

Robert smiled. "You have brought him with you? You have brought a nurse with you?"

"He is waiting outside."

Robert stepped into the sittingroom where a young man waited with Bertha, Dietrich, and Aschenbach. He held out his hand. "Doktor Schumann?"

"Yes, yes, and you?"

"I am Boris Bremer. I am to be your nurse – if that is your wish."

Robert was shy, he might have been meeting a lover, and looked the man over carefully, replying slowly. "It is, indeed, my wish, Herr Bremer. I thank you for coming."

"You are quite welcome, Doktor Schumann."

Robert turned to rush back to the bedroom, excited as a boy at Christmas to thank Dr. Boger, but Clara and the doctor had followed him out. "Doktor Boger, Herr Bremer is highly suitable. I find him most acceptable. I thank you for bringing him to me."

The doctor nodded. "I am glad you find him acceptable, Doktor Schumann. If there is anything else we can do, you know where I can be reached." He turned to Clara. "Doktor Hasenclever asked me to let you know he will pay a call tomorrow morning – but of course you can call me as well if you need me."

Clara's eyes shone. "Danke, Herr Doktor."

361

Dietrich took his leave with the doctor, promising to return the next day in case she needed him, leaving only Robert and Clara and Herr Bremer. "Do you not think we should go to bed, Robert? It is much later than usual."

Robert still smiled and Clara wondered if the nurse might be all he needed. "No, not yet. I wish Herr Bremer to read the newspapers to me. I have not read them yet today. Herr Bremer, will you read to me?"

"Of course."

"In the bedroom. Will you read me to sleep? I would like you to stay with me in the bedroom tonight to watch over me."

Herr Bremer spoke softly, looking at Clara who looked at Robert who looked at Herr Bremer. "It will be all right. He will be all right with me – if that is all right with you."

Clara's face flattened, losing contours, losing expression; they had not slept apart, not since they had been married, not as long as they had been under the same roof; but she forced herself to speak. "Of course. Goodnight."

Herr Bremer nodded, but Robert ignored her. She left the room, but hovered in Robert's study outside the bedroom, listening to Herr Bremer read until she could hear Robert snoring. She wished she might have put him to sleep as easily, but was glad he was able to sleep, with or without her.

His snoring deepened with the night, but Clara lay awake in a sofa in the study wondering how it would end. A wind had gathered all evening, rattling through the trees, but Clara was unaware of the storm until she was awakened by thunder beating the earth, lightning blazing the sky. It was five o'clock; she got up, unable to sleep, and listened by the bedroom. Robert still slept. She sat at his desk, staring out of the window until she heard him wake, but didn't interrupt his privacy with Herr Bremer.

The morning remained dark and wet, seeming to affect Robert; gone was the excitement of the night before, gone his appetite. He wanted no breakfast but Clara brought him a tray in the bedroom, also one for Herr Bremer, coffee, black bread, butter, softboiled eggs, oranges. She knew how he liked his bread and butter, thickly sliced, thickly dabbed, and proceeded to slice and dab, but he pushed the plate aside; he accepted the eggs from a spoon like a baby, oranges from her hand, but appeared little aware of what she did, little aware of Herr Bremer's presence; coffee, too, he accepted from her hand, but wouldn't drink it himself nor acknowledge her service. His eyes, barely open, turned inward again, giving no sign, neither of recognition nor appreciation, but he seemed anxious to get started again on his variations; he meant to finish them that morning.

Herr Bremer offered to return in the evening if they wished; Robert said nothing, Clara thanked him and said she would call if they needed him.

Herr Bremer wished him goodbye, but Robert barely nodded. Clara turned her attention fully on him. "Did you sleep well last night, Robert?"

He said nothing.

"Robert?"

Still he seemed not to hear. She remembered how he had been when they had first met, wavyhaired, pinkcheeked, sharpeyed, confident, handsome; he had always been round of face, but in his present despondence he seemed more haunted, cheeks hollowing before her eyes, expressionless, unaware and uncaring of his appearance. She caressed his cheek. "Robert?"

She might have slapped him for the way he jerked his face away.

"Robert?"

He turned away. "Oh, Clara, I am not worthy of your love."

"Robert? You? How can you say such a thing? I revere you as I revere no one. Tell me what to do and I will do it – anything to convince you of my love. Robert?"

He shook his head, wouldn't look at her. "I am a sinner, Clara. I do not deserve you. You are too good for me. You deserve the best of men."

"But Robert, you *are* the best of men. There can be no one else for me – no one – whatever has happened, whatever happens."

"Mamma!"

Marie stood outside. "Yes?"

"Herr Dietrich and Doktor Hasenclever are here to see you."

"Will you come to see them, Robert?"

He shook his head.

She caressed his arm. "I will be back soon."

Marie waited in the study. Clara spoke in a confidential tone. "Marie, please be attentive – if Pappa needs anything. I will not be long."

"Yes, Mamma."

Marie heard her pappa shuffling in the bedroom and seated herself at his desk to await her mamma's return, the open Bible before her and her pappa's new variations; she liked the rain, especially rainy mornings, waking in a warm bed, snuggling under covers, listening to its patter on the window and the street. Sensing she was no longer alone she turned to see her pappa staring from the doorway in a green robe and yellow felt slippers, but without recognition, as if she were a stranger.

"My God!" He covered his face with his hands.

He said nothing else, but turned back to the bedroom, closing the door, leaving her staring. She couldn't have said how long she waited, but heard her pappa sighing, then sobbing, then silent. Needing to reassure herself she called softly, "Pappa?" and when there was no answer, more loudly. "Pappa! Pappa!"

The bedroom was empty, the adjacent door open to the hallway, the door beyond open to the courtyard, rain entering the hallway, her pappa nowhere in sight. She ran to her mamma in the sittingroom with Dietrich and Dr. Hasenclever. "Mamma! Pappa has gone!"

Clara felt herself turn to stone, the hammer of her heart was sick and seemed to stick like a fly to paper. "What do you mean he has gone?"

Marie, breathless with fear and anxiety, told them the story, unable to hold back tears. "I did not think he would leave the bedroom, not in his robe and slippers."

Dr. Hasenclever was the first to respond. "Let us search first, worry afterward."

Bertha was called, the children were told to stay in their rooms, Hasenclever and Dietrich searched the house, Clara sent Marie to tell Fraulein Leser what had happened. Marie dressed hurriedly, grabbed an umbrella, and dashed into the courtyard, the rainladen street. It was the pre-Lent season, carnival time, revelers frequenting the street even in the rain, a noisy procession approaching ahead of her.

She thought little of it until she realized her pappa was being returned home, two strangers holding him under his arms, robed as before, but barefoot, bareheaded, drenched, and covering his face in shame with his hands, the procession led by a dancing witch, sprigs of hair sprouting from her chin.

Marie screamed and ran sobbing to Fraulein Leser's house.

iv

Robert sat on his bed, his face in his hands, deep sighs turning to sobs; his own daughter, twelve years old, had been left to mind him; but this had been only the last in a series of humiliations he had heaped upon himself. It was not Marie's fault, not Clara's, no one's but his own, and the last he would allow. He had written Clara a short note and slipped through the hallway into the courtyard, onto the street.

The rain was a blessing, hiding his tears; so were the revelers in the rain, paraders of the carnival: Harlequin flecked with diamonds, hoisting his wooden sword; Columbine by his side, polka dots on her cheeks; Pierrot in whiteface and white costume; Pantalone, the skinny old goat, in spectacles, slippers, and stockings; all hardly unlike himself, bulky and doddering, the green robe and yellow slippers giving him cover. The irony loomed like the final joke: his last sights were to be of characters he had portrayed in one of his earliest works, *Carnaval*.

It was a short walk from Bilkerstrasse to the Rhine; Robert could barely see for the rain, his tears, and the gloom of the morning, but he made his way easily to the bridge, the tollgate, where he was stopped. He searched his pockets, upset anew with himself, he should have brought money, but he couldn't go back, a failure to the end. He smiled, holding up his hand for time, and pulled a silk handkerchief from his pocket. Handing the handkerchief to the tollkeeper in lieu of the toll, he rushed onto the bridge. The song of the angels began again, but this time he imagined it was the Lorelei singing. He flung his ring into the river, clawed the rail slippery with rain, lost his grip, missed his step, hit his face against the rail, but managed to haul himself up – and over.

The rush of air and slap of the water took his breath; the first gulp filled his mouth, throat, and lungs, with the Rhine; the river swallowed first his slippers, bounced him in its icy jaws, and sucked him into its belly. Music filled the water, a grand keening, the knell of the orchestra. He struggled, he couldn't have said for how long, before a boat appeared with fishermen who pulled him out against his will, and he found himself too weak to resist, a failure in his greatest enterprise. He crouched in the boat covering his face, a blanket over his shoulders – only to rise without warning, rocking the boat, keeling himself toward the water, stepping wildly left and right – but his chance was past, he lost his balance, fell within the boat, was easily subdued, and brought again to land. A crowd had gathered, he was recognized, found his arms around the corded shoulders of fishermen, and hefted back to Bilkerstrasse, covering his face, dreading more than ever to see Clara and Marie and the others again.

Dr. Hasenclever received him from the procession, seeming to understand his fear. He saw neither Clara nor the children, but Herr Bremer again, and another nurse, Herr Strauss, who cared for him the whole day round.

v

"We could not believe it, what we read in the newspaper, not after we had just seen him so happy and healthy in Hanover."

Brahms liked Fraulein Leser's home; a blind person had different requirements; the room was stark, nothing stood that couldn't be nailed down, but the textures were richer, tapestries along the wall, satin upholstery, the smell of roses from pots hung from the ceiling – but he could hardly believe the change in Clara, sitting on the sofa beside Fraulein Leser, less aware than the blind woman what happened around her, eyes large and running like eggs, cheeks shiny and soft, hair long and loose, handkerchief twisted around her hand.

Fraulein Junge sat on another chair by their side, her hair drawn tightly in a bun. He wondered at the wisdom of saying more, but continued to talk. "Joachim wrote to Dietrich for confirmation, but I did not want to wait if I could do something. You have only to say what you want. If you wish me to play for you, provide music, mind the children, go to the market, anything, that is why I am here."

It was impossible to tell what she heard, head bowed, dabbing constantly at her eyes, but he spoke again. "They would not let me see the Master. It would excite him too much, they said – and excitement is not good."

"Herr Brahms …" Clara spoke without changing her position, without turning her head, her tone husky as if she were unaccustomed to talking. "I thank you for coming. I am glad you are among us. I know Robert will be glad to hear it."

"I have taken a room in the Altstadt. I am here as long as you need me."

She nodded, but barely. Fraulein Junge looked at Brahms, nodding vehemently, encouraging him to talk further.

"Joachim has engagements, but he will be here on Sunday morning, the day after tomorrow. He will take the night coach directly after his concert. He has engagements again on Monday, but I have none – and after the Master returns I wish to dedicate myself entirely to him – to his health."

Brahms looked suddenly at Fraulein Junge, wondering how much Clara knew, afraid he might have said too much, but Fraulein Junge nodded reassuringly. "We got the letter from Doktor Richarz only today to say they are ready to receive him. It should be for only a short while. Doktor Hasenclever is taking him to Endenich tomorrow himself."

Suddenly Clara looked at the ceiling, drawing a sigh that might have been dredged from the center of the earth. "Him! My glorious Robert! In an institution! How can I bear it?"

Fraulein Leser's arm was immediately around Clara's trembling shoulders, steadying her as she bowed her head again, covering her face, and wiping her eyes.

Fraulein Junge spoke gently. "It is what he wanted, Frau Schumann. It is what the doctors recommended. Some things are not in our hands."

"I know it! They are in His hands. That is why I say he needs a preacher, not a doctor. He said it himself that he was a sinner. A preacher understands these matters best – a stern preacher, someone who will be firm with him, show him the way to repent."

Fraulein Leser spoke no less gently than Fraulein Junge. "My dear Frau Schumann, that is not what your dear husband wants. More important, it is not what the doctors recommend. Besides, we have to think about you as well. Too much excitement, in your condition, is no better for you than for him."

Fraulein Leser referred to her pregnancy, now in its sixth month. Clara appeared again not to have heard, but looked at Brahms, speaking without passion, explaining her outburst. "Herr Brahms, I saw them bring him back – but I was not allowed to see him. It was still morning, the sun was coming out again after the rain, but I could see nothing, the world only grew darker. In my heart it was night. I was sent here to Fraulein Leser's home because I was not to excite him – but I could not have stayed in the same house with him if I was not to see him – and here I have stayed since that terrible hour." She remembered the note she had found, too personal to mention to anyone: *Dear Clara, I shall cast my wedding ring into the Rhine. Do you the same. Then shall we two be as one.* She didn't know exactly what had happened at the bridge, no one had told her, and she hadn't asked, but she had guessed from the note. Her voice broke suddenly into tiny fragments. "Herr Brahms … have pity … on me. I have not … touched him in all this time. I am not even to see him before he is taken to Endenich. How am I to bear … such a trial? Tell me, please, if you know. Oh, my God!"

Brahms held her hand wishing to provide a conduit for her sorrow, drain her tears and absorb her shock; his own eyes were bright and no less watery. "Your friends will help you, Frau Schumann. I am here now to stay. Joachim will be here soon. Grimm will be here on Wednesday. Our services are yours to command."

Fraulein Junge nodded. "And your mamma is here from Berlin, looking after the children with Bertha. You have received so many letters from wellwishers, many of whom have seen you only on the stage. All their blessings are with you."

Clara took a deep breath. "Herr Brahms, he shows no anxiety about me – no, nor about the children. He does not miss me. He knows where I am and he is glad." Her tone accelerated, having begun she appeared unable to stop. "He asks nothing about me, but I receive reports hourly of his doings. On the first day he wrote innumerable letters, he made also a transcription of the variations which have so consumed him, and he sent them to me with the admonition that I play them for Fraulein Leser – which I have done."

Fraulein Leser nodded, squeezing Clara's shoulders.

"I sent him a pot of violets, and some oranges, and he sent me news that he was getting on very well, indeed – but I was told later he became violently excited the same day, and was confined to his bed. No one is to see him anymore, no one who might excite him, no one who is near and dear to him – no one to whom he is himself so near and dear. Oh, my dear Herr Brahms, I think sometimes I could bear anything if I could only hold him once more in my arms – if I could only clasp him to my breast. That is what hurts the most, that he is happy enough with his nurses not to ask about anyone who cares for him more deeply. He seems to wish nothing as much as to be with nurses for the rest of his life, as if they might care for him better than I. I am not even to return until he has left the house tomorrow. I have no notion even of when I may see him again."

Brahms held her hand so tightly she felt her blood might stop, but in the matter of a moment she found herself held even more tightly by the expression on his face, so full of yearning she imagined she saw Robert – the young handsome dashing Robert with whom she had fallen in love; she imagined she could very easily find herself comfortable in his care and loosened her hand only to grip his arm more fiercely herself, drawing herself toward him until her head rested on his shoulder.

vi

It was sunny, the morning of Saturday, 4 March, 1854. The carriage was brought into the courtyard from the street to shield Robert from curious eyes. He had dressed hurriedly, entered the carriage without a backward glance, and without an inquiry about his wife and children. The children watched with Bertha from an upstairs window; Bertha said he would be back soon, but she cried uncontrollably. Their mamma was with Fraulein Leser, so was their grandmamma. Dr. Hasenclever gave him a bouquet Clara had picked, not divulging the source; Robert smiled, pressing his hand. The doctor followed him into the carriage, so did Herr Bremer and Herr Strauss. The ride to Bonn was eight hours; Endenich was a suburb of Bonn. Robert wanted to know within the first hour, "Will we be arriving soon?" He looked out of the window, smiled a lot, smelled the flowers, and distributed them among the others in the carriage.

Clara drove home with her mamma at six in the evening to be joined by Brahms and Dietrich, also later by the Frauleins Leser and Junge. She was grateful though she imagined she would have preferred a free rein for her unfathomable grief in *his* room. Late that night Herr Strauss returned, saying Robert had arrived safely.

Joachim arrived the next morning and talked with her till midday about Robert, playing Robert's music with her through the afternoon and evening; she was comforted while she played, but the tears flowed again the moment she stopped, wishing she could touch his hand and tell him how inspiring she found his work.

The next day, Monday, Clara began again to give lessons; she had seven children, another on the way, Robert's hospital bills soon to arrive, and her income was insecure despite gifts from friends, among them a draft of four thousand thaler from Mendelssohn's younger brother; she returned all monetary gifts, not wishing others to think Schumann had left his wife destitute, but replied to Paul Mendelssohn saying she would hold the draft in case she needed the money in deference to the delicacy of his letter: he had said his dead brother, Felix, had urged him to offer the money, and she was not to thank him, but he her, for helping fulfill his dead brother's wish.

PART THREE

CLARA AND BRAHMS

There was music everyday through the following weeks, often at Fraulein Leser's house, all of it Robert's; it was all she could do to listen, play, cry, awaiting the doctor's letters, face shrunk with care, eyes a paler blue for the constant tears, lashes matted, cheeks glistening, mouth in a constant gummy grimace, but she was grateful for her friends, a constant round of Brahms, Dietrich, Joachim, Grimm, the Frauleins Leser and Junge, continual visits and letters of condolence from others more distant, friends and admirers.

Her mamma had returned to Berlin, but not before Clara had persuaded her to visit Endenich for a personal report; the hospital was small, accommodating no more than fourteen patients, a number of small buildings rather than one large, on an estate of seven acres, the main building two storeys tall; Robert had a suite of rooms and access to a piano in a nearby waiting room; he had been sedated during the first month to curb his occasional manic episodes, but ate and slept well, talked with the doctors during lucid moments, and in April had visited the garden, begun walks, twice daily, even as far as Bonn, attended by the nurse – but Clara was not to see him, not even to write, not until he had shaken the hallucinations for an extended period of time; she might otherwise excite him too much.

The doctor's news was welcome, but not what she had wished; he had asked nothing about her, nothing about the children, nothing about anyone, only about violets he wanted to pick in the garden; sometimes he recalled Dusseldorf, places he had visited – and sometimes, pacing his room, he dropped to his knees, wrung his hands, and covered his face as if he were being admonished, but he was otherwise gentle, smiling and apologizing for the inconvenience he caused, even making a joke for his attendant on April Fool's Day.

For Clara, the nights were the worst; Fraulein Leser had been kind enough to sacrifice her companion every night, and Fraulein Junge kind enough to abandon her customary bed, but sleep was impossible. She lay in a twilight world, between dreams and darkness, horrific images mingled with images of Robert. She fought the images by tracing Robert's works in her mind, the *Carnaval, Symphonic Etudes, Kreisleriana, Fantasy in C*, but these awakened memories now no less painful. Her main solace was a new work by Brahms, a piano trio, the first work she had heard not by Robert since his incarceration, a grand work, more spacious than any of Robert's trios, or Mendelssohn's, more spacious than their symphonies, as spacious as Beethoven's *Archduke*, and as fine in the last three movements, the more astounding for its origin in this overgrown boy, this undergrown man, the scherzo bounding on a locomotive pulse, the adagio sinking into space, the finale flowing steadily from a stream into a river – but the first movement troubled her.

It began with a soaring melody in the piano, reinforced by the cello, but the violin entered with a song of its own, fragmenting the development into a series of episodes. Besides, he had played so whimsically she had been unable to follow him that morning, even with the score in her hand, but this was the work that had finally wrenched her thoughts from Robert; she wanted to learn it, but wondered how much she dared say about her reservations. "Herr Brahms, I cannot get accustomed to these constant changes in tempo. Are they all necessary?"

There was silence. Grimm and Dietrich stopped playing; Brahms had been scornful, narrowing his eyes when they had been unable to follow him earlier, saying they were to play the score as he had written it or not at all. "Do not be upset, Herr Brahms. I only wish to understand your intention clearly."

Still he said nothing. He appeared to have no defense against criticism except sarcasm or silence; like many North Germans, particularly Hamburgers, he could be blunt and he could be silent, but rarely diplomatic. Finally, he leaned over the piano. "My intention is clear on the page, Frau Schumann. I would not have thought a pianist of your reputation would have difficulty with the work of a beginner."

Clara could almost feel Fraulein Leser stiffen with disapproval behind her. She had warned her not to be careless about her dignity around Brahms, not to make herself cheap around someone so young, not to allow him to speak indiscriminately, but while Clara valued her counsel she couldn't make her understand: Brahms knew her worth, of that she was sure; and if he was sometimes overbearing he was not to be judged as other men, an artist was judged less by his age than by his work, and in the presence of his work she was the student, his work the only joy she allowed herself in her time of trial; besides, she might have been an invalid for the way everyone else spoke to her, but unlike the others Brahms never patronized her. "I beg your pardon, Herr Brahms, but some of the changes are so irregular that I ask only to reassure myself. Are they all necessary?"

Brahms cursed himself for a fool; he had meant to be ironic, even to provoke a laugh, but he had sounded only sarcastic, even to himself. Under the circumstances it was perhaps impossible to laugh, and even before the tragedy he had noted Clara had a fragile sense of humor, too much delicacy, as if dignity were all she had left and she feared its loss when she had already been robbed of so much else, but he tried again, grinning to relieve the tension. "Hah! You shall have the answer to your question, Frau Schumann, when I have it myself."

BRAHMS REMAINED WITH HER after the others had left, all but Fraulein Junge who prepared herself for the night in an adjacent room. He had settled temporarily in Dusseldorf, taking rooms in the same house on Bilkerstrasse, making himself available for music anytime she wished – and he had proven himself indispensable as well in more mundane ways, helping Bertha with the children, taking charge of finances, rent, expenses, schoolfees, servants' wages, the entire household; she couldn't thank him enough, couldn't believe sometimes he was there, so timely was his presence – and so unbelievable sometimes his actions. That morning he had performed gymnastics on the banisters, supposedly for the children, but no less she felt for herself, swinging finally into the midst of the group gathered at the foot of the stairs to watch, glancing at her with a big smile as if to say: Look, Mamma, see what I can do! She had returned a smile as big herself; he was almost young enough to be her son, but she was reminded as well of Robert playing among the children, and was suddenly in tears again.

He remained silently on the sofa beside her; such moments came without warning; he wished he could deflect them, but felt privileged to share them, proud of her trust, the implied intimacy, bearing witness to her sorrow. She dabbed her eyes, mistress once more of herself. "I am sorry, Herr Brahms. Sometimes I feel I defeat your best efforts to cheer me up."

He shook his head. "Na, Frau Schumann. You defeat me only when you are sorry. I want only your comfort, and if it comforts you to cry then cry you must – without being sorry."

"You *do* comfort me, Herr Brahms. I cannot say how much. The worst of it is I no longer know what to expect. I wish to be useful again, but I have no idea when that might be. I wish to perform again, to be onstage, to tour." She didn't wish to speak of her financial problems, but Endenich cost fifty thaler a month in addition to her regular expenses; she didn't wish to sell any of Robert's investments, but since the incarceration there had been no income. "I am an artist, Herr Brahms. When I do not perform, I waste." She understood the surprise in his eyes easily. "Do not imagine it is my condition that keeps me from following my wish. I have performed to within days of giving birth. It is not that at all – but you know what it is."

He looked away as her tears flowed again, but she watched him as she dried her eyes. He appeared sensitive beyond his years; she began to understand his rudeness as well, recalling his pride when she had fetched him from the Altstadt, his identification with the commonest people; she would never understand how his sublime inspirations could germinate in such desolate places, but no more would she question her circumstances. God sent comfort with every grief if only one recognized it; such a comfort was he, revering Robert as she did, sharing her sorrow. She liked talking about Robert best with him because in the end Robert had liked him best and he had proven Robert's affection well spent – but she had heard nothing from Robert since he had left, not even that he had asked about her, and imagined he no longer cared, blaming herself for pushing him away, submerging herself in guilt. He had clearly been unfit for the directorship, perhaps even recognized it himself, but she had defended him against the world, and in the end perhaps against himself, shielding him when she might instead have swallowed her pride, listened to Dr. Hasenclever, admitted the problem, helped her husband. "Herr Brahms, what will you do after the baby is born?"

He turned toward her immediately. "I will stay as long as you need me, Frau Schumann – as long as you wish. I have no commitments, as you know."

"Yes, that I know, but I cannot imagine – that is, I cannot expect you to make such a sacrifice. You have your own life – and such a glorious life it promises to be. That would be too much to ask, that you cut it in half for my sake."

"But you do not ask it. It is my own wish."

"But it is too much!"

"But it is what I wish."

"But my company must prove such a trial these days. I am never in good spirits, and I do not imagine I ever will be again until my Robert is returned to me whole – and it is impossible to say when that will be."

Brahms shook his head vehemently. "You do me too much justice, Frau Schumann – and yourself too little. I can never repay what you and your husband have done for me. If you knew me better – my life, my family – you would understand better."

She wanted to know him better, understand him better, as an artist, as a man. "But what we did, Herr Brahms, it was not charity, it was merited – and more than merited. You not only earned our admiration, but you provided Robert with his happiest days toward the end. You have long repaid any debt you might imagine."

Again he shook his head. "I am what I have always been – but until your husband recognized it, until he told the world who I was, the world remained oblivious – but it is more than merely a matter of recognition, it is a matter of understanding. I felt no one had understood me as deeply, as beautifully, and as fully, as did your husband – and your good self – not even my mamma and pappa. That is a debt I will hold unpaid forever. My music existed as if in a vacuum before your husband gave it air and allowed it to breathe."

Clara remained silent; he had rarely spoken as much before, and never about himself.

"It is the obvious thing, for me to devote myself to you and your husband. When I wrote to my mamma what had happened – directly, she sent me money. It made them so sorry your husband was so ill after he had been so good to me. They will never forget the letter he sent. That was a kindness to which he was never obliged, by which he made two good people very happy. She said I was right to do as I had done." Again he shook his head. "What you call sacrifice I call consecration. You and your husband have given my life a meaning I never suspected. I live for the time when we three shall be together again. Joachim, Grimm, Dietrich, all the others, all have other responsibilities, but not I. What could I do better than what I do now?" He did not mention his relief that his next steps had been so unmistakably taken for him; Robert's prophecy still oppressed him, a reputation easily won was a reputation easily lost; he despaired of deserving it and welcomed a brief hibernation, time to define and meet the challenges on his own terms; it was one thing to be proclaimed a Messiah, another to be one.

Clara touched his hand; his face was earnest as a boy's; even his voice, highpitched, was a blessing; she could touch him as easily as she might a boy though his comfort was the comfort of a man. "Herr Brahms, I thank you, and I know my husband would thank you if he knew what you have done. What you say comforts me more than you know, more than I can say. I had no idea so deep a consciousness could reside in one so very young. You are most often so silent."

Brahms smiled. He might in that moment have put his arms around her, he did not think she would have minded, but he restrained himself. "Much is too sweet to be thought, but more is too sweet to be spoken."

She squeezed his hand. "That is profound, indeed."

"It is by Novalis. He knows just how to say things that might otherwise never be said."

"You surprise me continually, Herr Brahms. I believe I am only beginning to know you."

Her voice trembled; she was crying again, and this time he put his arms around her. She yielded to his comfort, snuggling her face against his neck, tears burning his flesh; he kissed the top of her head; she neither kissed him back nor resisted, pressing herself instead more firmly against him, heat from her body irradiating his own.

Brahms held her delicately, like a treasure, this pregnant mother, wife of Robert Schumann, and greatest woman pianist in the world, scarcely believing their intimacy, never doubting her innocence, never doubting even his own, while blood gushed like rivers in his veins where one breast was squeezed against his arm. Slowly, gently, he tightened his embrace, while Clara clung to him like one drowning.

Fraulein Junge stood suddenly in the doorway. "Frau Schumann, I shall see you to bed if you like."

Clara withdrew from Brahms like one coming out of a dream. "Yes, I think I would like that." She looked at Fraulein Junge as if to get her bearings and took the hand she held out, rising bellyfirst to her feet. "Good night, Herr Brahms. I shall see you in the morning."

"Indeed. Good night, Frau Schumann."

ii

Brahms sat in the waiting room, unsure whether he had acted precipitately. He had arrived in Endenich at half past four in the afternoon barely knowing what to expect, and been kept waiting now almost thirty minutes for Dr. Richarz by Fraulein Reumont, Robert's nurse.

It was more than two months since Clara had given birth, a son, to be named Felix after Mendelssohn, and after her convalescence was now in Ostend with Frauleins Leser and Junge. She had encouraged him to holiday as well, visit the Black Forest as he had wished for a while. He had seen too little of the world, but the deep dark forest of dreams and nightmares had held little pleasure for him, any part of the world away from the Schumanns held little pleasure. He had recognized his loss of independence only when he had found himself again on his own. Tubingen, Lichtenstein, Schaffhausen, so adventurous to consider, he had found colorless, as he found everything unassociated with the Schumanns. Young women no longer attracted him; he imagined they carried merely the seeds of heaven, but Clara bore its fruit. A more unusual woman he would never find, more accomplished, more energetic, who would understand him better and share equally his deepest passion, who could be teacher, mother, lover, all in one.

He had written to her about his longing to see her, but also that she was to take full advantage of her holiday and not hurry back. She had replied full of recrimination: people who didn't know her found her highstrung, but did he join them in thinking she needed a holiday so desperately? How poorly she had repaid him. Had she felt less shame before the others, before herself, she would have returned to Dusseldorf herself, but she had performed a couple of times in Ostend and that had helped best of all.

Could he have afforded it he would have journeyed to Ostend himself, but more than the cost of the journey he had been defeated by the cost of life at the resort. Instead, he had journeyed no farther than Ulm before returning. He was anchored in Dusseldorf, now hallowed with memories, but along the way he had stopped at Bonn and walked to Endenich, hoping to bring news of Robert to Clara.

Robert had still not mentioned Clara, but picked roses and carnations from the garden, and when Fraulein Reumont had asked for whom he had smiled. "Oh, you know very well." The flowers had been sent, Clara had danced around the room, but the doctors still forbade correspondence; they wanted him first to mention her by name.

A man entered the room. "Herr Brahms?"

Brahms got up, held out his hand. "Ja, Doktor Richarz?"

Richarz nodded, shook his hand, a stout man, but not unhandsome, in his early forties, shorthaired, cleanshaven, with sad round eyes, bags underneath like crescents. His face was fat, the face of a man who had been pinched but dared not say Owch! dared not draw ridicule. He spoke in even tones, emphasizing his humorlessness. "I have heard of you, of course, Herr Brahms. I am pleased to meet you."

Dr. Hasenclever had mentioned Brahms to Richarz for which Brahms was relieved, hating explanations. "I would like to see him, Herr Doktor. If I could but give a report of him to his wife she would be so relieved. She needs no less attention in this matter as you know, she is no less a patient herself – in a different way, of course, but sometimes not knowing is worse than knowing the worst."

Richarz nodded, gazing at the floor, revealing not a gleam of what he thought. Robert had mentioned his fear, a recurrence of the disease of lovers, for which he had long ago applied mercury treatments among other things to his sores – tertiary syphilis, from which he suspected Robert was ailing. He spoke again, evenly. "That is true, Herr Brahms, and your thoughtfulness is to be commended. Good friendship is rare – but my first allegiance is to my patient, and I must be at least as good a doctor to him as you appear a friend. I would be remiss in my obligation, you see, if I were to bow to the desire of even the best of his friends. You know the reports, do you not? You have seen the weekly reports?"

Brahms nodded; a fortnight might pass with no evidence of psychosis, no fears, delusions, or confusion, but trailed by a hallucination. The prevailing diagnosis was discouraging: *There is no certain prospect of a favorable issue to the illness, and it is impossible to look for recovery until the patient has continued in a favorable mood for some weeks at a stretch.* When Clara had received the report she had locked herself in her room, locked out even Brahms for the day, locked out conversation, company, music, everything, emerging late for something to drink. They had listened outside her door, in case of an emergency, and heard her cry until too tired to cry. "Ja, I have seen the weekly reports, but you have not seen the effect of the weekly reports. Frau Schumann needs more than weekly reports. She needs to know he is thinking about her. She needs to know he loves her. That is what she needs, that is what she lives for, not weekly reports."

Again Richarz nodded, gazing thoughtfully at the floor. "Believe me, Herr Brahms, I understand your dilemma and I sympathize – but the Schumann you know and the Schumann I know are not the same. You know him as he was, your friend, but I know him as he is, my patient. You see, it would not help Frau Schumann to see him as he is, and I know it would not help Doktor Schumann himself."

Brahms said nothing, but stared unconvinced.

Richarz raised his finger, making a point. "Just last week he displayed a new symptom – actually, a form of paranoia. He was talking quite lucidly about a Beethoven sonata when he suddenly poured the wine from his glass onto the floor. When I asked why he had done so he remained calm, but he said the wine was poisoned." Richarz shook his head. "You see, we must wait until such irrational behavior is eradicated – at least, wait until it has been absent for a long while. That would give us some hope of recovery."

Brahms said nothing, but couldn't hold Richarz's eyes.

"The other strange matter is that he has not yet asked about his wife, not even once, which leads me to believe it might excite him too much to hear from her – unless he asks about her first."

"There I think I can be of some assistance, Herr Doktor. Doktor Schumann is not a demanding man. Anyone who knows him will tell you that. It does not mean that he does not care, but it is not his nature. If he is not told that his wife asks about him, he will assume she does not wish to ask about him. He will never ask himself first. That is not the way he is – but if you tell him she thinks of no one else, and nothing else but to be with him again, both will benefit."

Richarz gazed again at the floor. "Herr Brahms, I can see you care deeply about them both, and they are fortunate to have a friend such as you, but I must be the final judge in these matters. You must understand I work for his benefit, and I bring to his benefit years of study and training. It is the only reason I am here." He looked up again.

Brahms said nothing, but again couldn't hold Richarz's eyes.

Richarz could see he didn't wish to leave without a more substantial report. "I cannot let you meet him, Herr Brahms, but I can let you see him, I can let you hear him. Maybe that will be of some help to you and Frau Schumann."

Brahms looked up, still saying nothing, but nodded.

BRAHMS HID AS HE WAS TOLD behind curtains by a garden window. Richarz had indicated a path between two flowerbeds down which he would bring Robert. Across the garden and beyond stood clusters of trees: apple, pear, apricot, and peach. One other patient walked in the distance with an attendant. He felt vile for spying on his friend, reducing him to a fly under glass, but there was no alternative, and soon Richarz brought him into the garden leading him gradually to Brahms's window.

Robert peered at the flowerbeds holding a lorgnette in one hand, a cigar in the other, smoking in his usual manner, pushing his lips out as far as he could, squinting to avoid the smoke. He wore dark clothes though the day was warm, but so did Clara in constant mourning. The sun was sinking, and Robert's long shadow reached into the room falling partly on the curtain. Richarz stopped at the window and so did Robert with him. "We had many flowers in our home, Herr Doktor, in Dusseldorf. I find them lovely, do you not? They bring nature right into our homes."

Richarz looked at Robert. "Indeed, but tell me, Doktor Schumann, what else do you remember about your home in Dusseldorf?"

Robert frowned, staring into a flowerbed, appearing buried in thought. Suddenly, he looked at Richarz, and pointed past the asylum gate. "That is not Bonn, you know, Herr Doktor, that town that we see in the distance."

Brahms's eyes widened, but Richarz showed no surprise. "But, Doktor Schumann, those are the towers of the Bonn Cathedral, are they not?"

Robert nodded, raising his chin, triumph in his face. "Exactly! I know very well that the Beethoven monument is next to the Cathedral – but you do not see the monument, do you?"

Richarz nodded, speaking mildly. "But do you not think, Doktor Schumann, that we might be too far to see the monument itself?"

Robert frowned again, shaking his head. He put away the lorgnette and brought out his handkerchief, dabbing his mouth as if it were bleeding. "Herr Doktor, may I ask you a question?"

"Of course, Doktor Schumann."

"It is about my wife."

Behind the curtain Brahms gritted his teeth, holding his breath. Richarz still showed no surprise. "Of course, Doktor Schumann. What about your wife?"

Robert shook his head. "I hate to trouble you, Herr Doktor … but I have not had a letter from her in so long … and sometimes I wonder … I cannot help but wonder … if she is dead."

Richarz spoke as if they were discussing breakfast. "She is not dead, Doktor Schumann. I shall let her know you wish to hear from her – if that is what you wish."

Robert's face was suddenly aglow. "Most fervently, that is what I wish."

Behind the curtain, Brahms's face was no less aglow, eyes turning misty. Robert walked farther into the garden, waving his handkerchief as if he were waving goodbye, as if he knew someone were watching; the setting sun framed him like a halo as they left the garden.

iii

CLARA TO ROBERT   *Dusseldorf, 12 September, 1854*

My Dearest Robert,

I am overjoyed that our first communication in so long will be on the 12th – our 14th wedding anniversary, my darling, as if you needed reminding, followed by my 35th birthday!

The best news first! We have a new son, my love. I have named him Felix, after the dear one. I thought you might like that best. He was born on 11th June, only three days after his pappa's birthday. Just imagine, for a little while I thought you might even share a birthday. He is a dear healthy boy, with his pappa's lovely ears and mouth.

The other children too are well. The good Brahms taught Marie and Elise how to play two of your Scenes from the East. They quite surprised me how well they played together – and I had been so busy with my lessons I had no idea they had even been practising.

I am proud also to tell you, my darling, that a complete collection of your works has recently been published – the Concerto for Cello, the Violin Fantasy you composed for Joachim, the Introduction and Allegro in D minor which you wished to dedicate to Brahms. I hope this pleases you.

Brahms has settled in Dusseldorf. He is a dear fellow whom I have come to rely upon and to love as a son. He spares no effort for my comfort and for that of the children.

Robert, my darling, the doctors continue to give me news of you, and I am never so glad as when I hear you are well.

With deepest love, always and ever, I remain
Your Clara

Richarz had sent Clara specific instructions regarding her letter. She was to write two letters, one including a reference to the anniversary and birthday, the other not; if Robert showed that the dates were important he would receive the letter in which they were mentioned. She was to write only a few lines, not to excite him, to see what impression her letter would make. She found it distressing to write so little after being so obediently silent for six months, but she was obedient again.

On the fifteenth of the month, at midday, a parcel arrived from the doctors. Brahms handed it to Clara praying they were not returning her letters for whatever reason. She held her breath opening the parcel, joining her prayers with Brahms's, but staring next at Brahms, stammering, "From my husband," before sitting again, crying for joy.

ROBERT TO CLARA   *End/14 September*

My Dear Clarchen,

My deepest thanks for remembering to write on the day of our wedding anniversary, and for sending your love and the children's love. The good news about our newborn son is the best of all, and the dearest of names which you have given him. Kiss all the little ones for me. If only I could see and talk to all of you, but the distance is too great.

I am glad Marie and Elise are making progress. Do they still sing? Are you getting along well? Do you still perform as magnificently as always? Do you still have the Klems piano I got you on your last birthday? Do you still keep my letters of love from Vienna to Paris? Are my compositions safe, and my autograph collection of Goethe, Jean Paul, Mozart, Beethoven, and Weber?

Was it a dream that last winter we were in Holland, and that you were received so brilliantly everywhere, but most of all in Rotterdam where they gave us a torchlight procession, and how magnificently you performed the E flat Concerto and the sonatas in C major and F minor by Beethoven, Chopin's Etudes, Mendelssohn's Songs Without Words, and also my new Concerto in D minor?

I am so glad to hear that Brahms has settled in Dusseldorf. What has he been composing now, and the other dear one, Joachim? Please remember me to him when you write to him next.

I do not like to trouble the doctor, but would you send me something interesting to read, maybe the poems by Scherenberg, some early volumes of my Zeitschrift, and my Musical Rules for the Home and for Life? Would you also send me some of your own compositions and portraits of us both? Do you remember the theme in E flat I heard in the night for which I later wrote variations? Could you please send them to me as well? I also need music paper very badly, since sometimes I have much to write and no paper.

You will think I have nothing but questions and requests. I wish I could come to you to discuss them at length. I am much stronger again, and look younger than I did in Dusseldorf. Do you still give lessons? Who are your pupils, and which are the best? Do you not find it tiring, dearest Clara?

8 pm. I have just got back from Bonn where I go often to visit the Beethoven memorial, which always makes me happy. Will you also please send Doktor Richarz some money for me to give to the beggars when I go to Bonn. I feel so sad when I have nothing to give them. My life is not so eventful now, not like it used to be. Everything was so different then.

Your Robert

Walking down the streets with Clara, Brahms found Hamburg at once more brilliant and more squalid, brilliant because of Clara, squalid because it couldn't be brilliant enough, not for Clara. His mamma had written: how lovely that he was coming, they'd had no time to talk the Christmas before, now he should stay a long while to make up for lost time; and how lovely that Frau Schumann was coming, how happy they would be to meet her; but Brahms would know best if they should offer to put her up – it looked better than before, the old kitchen range no longer stood in the sittingroom, Elise was no longer ill, and if dear God spared them all illness they would enjoy it all the more, but he would know best.

Brahms had forgotten the sheer bustle of his family life, always two to three people in a room, someone running in and out, four or five others conversing about his new coat while he struggled to write a letter. Privacy had come to mean more to him since he had left. He couldn't ask Clara to live with them, not until she had at least met the family, but in his anxiety to see her again he had rushed to Harburg, the next town, and entered Hamburg with her, escorting her now to lunch with his family, indicating his childhood haunts as they walked, the road to Cossel's, to Altona and Marxsen, to BAUMGARTEN & HEINZ where he still practised, and homes where he had played.

They didn't touch, but their smiles were linked; you couldn't tell who smiled more widely, who glanced more at the other as they walked. "I must tell you, Herr Brahms, how much easier my concerts have been because I knew you were thinking of me – as I have been thinking of you." She had written nothing to Robert about the tour afraid he might be distressed, imagining she needed money.

"I did, indeed! I thought of you constantly. I filled the air with prayers for your comfort. I worried about you particularly in Weimar, among Liszt's apostles and his princess, surrounded by philistines. How distasteful that must have been."

Her concerts had all been successful, but sometimes, listening in her box to other parts of the program, she had burst into tears. "Liszt tries to be kind, Herr Brahms. You know that."

Brahms nodded. Liszt had sent her the manuscript of his Sonata in B minor with a dedication to Robert, perhaps wishing her to add it to her repertoire. Brahms had played it for her, but Clara disliked the work as she disliked much of Liszt's music, finding it noisy and cluttered, without clear harmonic progression – but worst of all she found herself beholden to Liszt for the dedication and had chosen to pay her respects and her debts with a concert.

"We played Robert's Concerto together as you know, and he conducted Robert's Fourth Symphony, and we were well received, but I was invited as well to a soiree at the home of some Hungarian countess." She grimaced. "The rooms were small and crowded and the ladies stood around fanning themselves – and melting with heat in their crinolines." She laughed suddenly. "On my word of honor, Herr Brahms, their wigs made their heads twice the size God intended." Brahms smiled, but she shook her head. "For such company anything would have been good enough and I cried to think of my work going unappreciated – but Liszt played the fine gentleman as always. When I complained that my pieces were unsuitable he said, 'Why do you not play some bad pieces by Liszt?'" She laughed again. "He can be quite charming as you know, but I am afraid I was not very polite. I said he was right, but that was not something I could do."

Brahms laughed, less for what she said than that she was with him again, that they laughed easily in each other's presence whether or not they had occasion. "It seems to me, Frau Schumann, that you have had quite an adventure."

She had been lonely despite her companion, Fraulein Schonerstedt, lonely most of all for Brahms, no one else sympathized as deeply. "Liszt means well, but I simply do not know what to do about him. He honors Robert because he respects his music – which obliges me to respect him – but I cannot respect his music. Still, I have paid my respects and need do no more." She seemed to be talking to herself. "He knows the performer belongs to the hour and the composer to eternity and wishes now to follow in Chopin's footsteps – but one does not compose on a whim, one does not set aside so many years for performing and so many years for composition. One has to be prepared constantly for inspiration, as my Robert was – as you are, Herr Brahms – but one does not decide all of a sudden to be a composer. I know. I have composed, but I am no composer. I know the technique, but I have not the inspiration, and neither does he."

Brahms shook his head. "Frau Schumann, you do yourself an injustice –"

"No!" She looked at him sharply. "I know my worth, and it is not as a composer – but that is no blow to my own gift which is that of the interpreter, of which I find myself newly proud. I know my place, and it is elevated, though not as high as that of the composer."

Brahms didn't argue. "Let me thank you, then, for your interpretations of my work."

She had played movements from his sonatas. His works had already been performed in public, ironically by Hans von Bulow, Liszt's star pupil, the first movement of his C major Sonata, earlier the same year in Hamburg; and the B major Trio had been premiered in New York, ironically again by another of Liszt's disciples, William Mason, an American staying at the Altenburg during his visit; but this was the first time Clara had performed them in public. His work was more difficult than Robert's, would take longer to find an audience, but she was determined to keep them on her programs. She smiled. "I wish I could do more, Herr Brahms."

"JAKOB, remember to behave yourself! Watch what you say. She is a lady coming to our home."

Christiane wore a new dress, black, ruffled, highnecked, longsleeved, sewn by herself; so did Elise, sewn also by Christiane, brown, white lace collar, gigot sleeves. Jakob growled; he hated the cravat, but wanted to make an impression for Hannes's sake, and also wore a high collar and waistcoat. "Tchhahh! She has a head, na? two legs, two arms, na, just like everyone else? She eats and drinks, na? Ja, and she smells, too, na, like everyone else? If she is a lady, then what are you?"

Fritz Becker stared from his friend to his friend's wife. He wore his collar and cravat with no less distaste than Jakob, but less resentment.

Christiane remained disappointed with Jakob; she had thought once she might change him, but he had remained a peasant. "What am I? I am your most unfortunate wife! That is what I am! How can I be a lady, the wife of a musician?"

"And what is our Hannes if not a musician? And what is Frau Schumann if not a musician? And is she not also the wife of a musician?"

"She is a lady first, Jakob! And our Hannes is a composer first – just like Doktor Schumann. Now, hush, I hear them coming. Fritz, do not just sit there! Talk to Jakob!"

"What should I say?"

"I do not care what you say, but do not just sit there like a blockhead! We do not want Frau Schumann to feel she is on exhibition."

"Tchhahh, Christiane, listen to yourself! We are not five years old – not even Elise."

Elise was twenty-three, her face plump, hair parted down the middle, cut like a bowl around her ears. "Elise, you too! Look busy!"

Elise scowled; the rooms had long been dusted, swept, and scrubbed; she had sat in her dress all morning, not allowed to move, not even to help with the cooking in case she spilled something on her clothes. Even the windows had been left open, despite the cold, so the rooms would not be humid from cooking, drenched with smells. "What should I do?"

"I do not care! Close the window! Smile!"

Elise deepened her scowl. "I cannot smile to order. I am not an actress."

"Then think happy thoughts!" Christiane smiled. "You will soon be seeing someone famous in your own home."

Elise dropped her head; a smile began to appear. There was a loud knock on the door, a shout from Brahms. "We are here!"

Christiane looked at the others, her brow suddenly shriveled with anxiety, suddenly whispering. "They are here."

Jakob opened the door. Brahms stood smiling with Clara on the landing. Jakob stepped aside. "Please, come in." Brahms entered, leading Clara by the hand.

The family and Fritz stood silently in an arc, four around the two. Brahms began by introducing the family, but Fritz interrupted before he was finished. "I am Hannes's Onkel Fritz."

Brahms grinned. "Ja, this is my Onkel Fritz – my favorite onkel."

Fritz grinned widely himself, finally finding courage to look Clara in the face. Clara smiled. "I am most pleased to meet you, Herr Brahms."

"Na!" Fritz took a step backward, looked at Brahms. "Tell her. I am not Brahms."

"His name is Becker – but he is my pappa's friend, his oldest friend. They came to Hamburg together, running from Heide."

"Oh, my apologies, Herr Becker."

Fritz kept grinning and stealing glances.

Suddenly, Christiane almost shouted. "Elise, take Frau Schumann's hat and coat. Put it on our bed – carefully."

Elise smiled, taking the hat and coat. Christiane noted with approval Clara's black dress though the sleeves were short and the collar lower than she would have allowed Elise – but she was a musician, and she lived in Dusseldorf. She noted also the gold ring Clara still wore.

Clara smiled. "Danke, Elise. Your brother has told me so much about you – about all of you – that I almost feel like I know you."

Jakob, also like Christiane, almost shouted. "We have heard also about you, Frau Schumann – many good things – our deepest regrets for your good husband's misfortune."

"Indeed, yes! We were so sorry when we heard – and after he had been so good to our Hannes. May the dear God bless him with a speedy recovery."

Clara's face lost its composure for a moment, but regained it focusing on Elise returning with a smile from the other room. "My other brother, Fritz, would also have liked to have met you – but he is now in Leipzig, teaching the children of the Countess Ida von Hohenthal.

Brahms had found his brother the position; it had been Grimm's before he had moved to Gottingen. "So I have heard."

"But he would have liked to have met you."

"I would have liked to have met him too. Maybe another time."

Elise couldn't stop smiling, no less in awe of Clara than the rest. "Doktor Marxsen says he heard you play in a concert. He says you play with the strength of a man, but the delicacy of a lady. He says there is no one like you."

"Elise, enough!" Jakob stared at her. "Frau Schumann does not need to hear from you about herself – that she is like a man. You must not be so rude."

Elise scowled, but magically her smile reappeared almost instantaneously.

Brahms looked at Clara. "We will go to meet Doktor Marxsen, maybe tomorrow. He would like to meet you."

"I would like to meet him too."

"And Cossel – you must meet him. Without him, I would be nothing."

"Then he is important to me also."

Christiane smiled selfconsciously at Clara. "You must excuse me for just a moment, Frau Schumann. I have to see to the cooking. Lunch will be ready in a few minutes."

Clara had known Brahms's mamma was seventeen years older than his pappa, but she was still surprised to see her age, her cheeks hollow, her long chin and nose, her hobble across the room, and wondered if she had long to live, if she Clara were fated to take the mamma's place in Brahms's life. She returned Christiane's smile. "What is the smell? It is like heaven."

"Hahah! What have I always said? My wife's eel is like going to heaven. Just wait until you have tasted it."

Christiane smiled, but shook her head. "Jakob is easy to please, but I hope you will also like it."

"If it tastes like it smells it is a hope already realized."

Christiane couldn't stop smiling. "I have also made the thick oatmeal cakes. My Hannes always liked them from when he was a baby. He likes them also in thick slices."

Clara was reminded momentarily again of Robert who also liked his bread thickly cut, thickly buttered, but Brahms distracted her touching her hand. "Mammas know everything – but I want to show you something. Come." He stood up.

Clara looked around, not wishing to be so rude as to leave her hosts.

Brahms nodded impatiently. "Come. Do not worry about them. It will only take a minute."

Jakob nodded without a notion of what Brahms wished to show her. "Go, go, Frau Schumann. Our home is your home. Go with Hannes."

Fritz, too, grinned, Hannes's official onkel for the day, encouraging Clara though he had no idea what Brahms intended. "Ja, Frau Schumann. Our home is your home. Go with Hannes. He will show you something."

Clara followed him into the bedroom, smaller with a single window, and sat on the bed. Brahms went to the dresser, removed a cardboard box from the top drawer, and spread the contents on the bed, grinning all the while. "Another of Johannes Kreisler, Jr.'s treasures."

From his grin she might have imagined he had spread the treasure of Ali Baba before her. Instead she saw toy soldiers, more than fifty pieces, infantrymen, cavalrymen, Prussians, Turks, sultans, cannon, towers, tents, palms, firs. His smile was wider than she could remember. "When I was a boy I spent hours setting my battalions in order – almost as much time as I spent on music."

Again Clara thought she might some day replace his mamma; she understood his music better, she was younger; his were good simple folk, but she wondered how his genius had flowered amid such surroundings. She smiled. "Thank you, Herr Brahms, for revealing your treasures to me."

Brahms grimaced. "There is one more thing, Frau Schumann – just one more thing I must ask you."

"Yes?"

"I wish you would not call me Herr Brahms. I wish you would call me by my name. It would mean so much."

Her eyebrows rose and her smile faltered, but only momentarily. "Of course … Jo-hannes."

ii

Brahms didn't know what to expect, but when Clara opened the door and stood before him he felt as if he had regained his sight. It had been two days since he had seen her; he had accompanied her on the steamer to Emmerich just short of the Dutch border, after which she had gone ahead with Fraulein Schonerstedt for her tour of Holland and he had returned to Dusseldorf – but a Dusseldorf that seemed continually a blur. His face burned, sharp pains shot through his chest, he could neither play the piano nor read, and he took the next steamer to Rotterdam. It was the first time he had left Germany, but the world remained a blur until he had asked directions to the Rijn Hotel. Staring at the ground, he had noticed brightly painted clogs, and rushing toward his destination he had become aware of windows of flowers, porcelain, slabs of cheese, stalls smelling of herring and onions, but he had lost his appetite though he hadn't eaten in a while. Besides, he had spent his last thaler reaching Rotterdam.

"Johannes!"

Clara took a step back and he imagined for a moment she was sorry to see him. Her eyes blinked repeatedly in fear and her hand rushed to her mouth suddenly stiff.

"Johannes, why are you here?"

He was unable to speak and didn't dare touch her, but he couldn't stop grinning.

A glow began to form around her, emblazoning her in a halo. "Well, then, since you are here I must confess I am glad to see you. Will you not come in?"

The room was long and narrow, a carpet down the middle of the wooden floor, a sofa alongside, a coffee pot on a table, a tall window at the end, a door by the sofa leading to the bedroom. He set his knapsack on the floor, still without a word; she shut the door behind him.

"Say something, Johannes. I still cannot believe you are here."

His smile faltered; her face still showed bewilderment, even fear, though her eyes had grown more steady, her mouth more soft. "I shall go back if you would rather."

"Oh, no! No, indeed! That is not what I meant. That is not what I meant at all. You do not have to explain. I am glad you are here, but I am simply amazed. I have been so lonely for a friend. I wished you might be here and here you are like the answer to a prayer – like a vision."

He couldn't help himself, taking her in his arms, and when she didn't resist, when she put her arms around him, he covered her hair, her face, her neck, with kisses. The pains in his chest ceased, his arms bulged with blood. "Clara! Oh, my God! Clara! Clara!"

He lifted her off the floor, kissing her lips. She returned his kiss her own arms throbbing no less with blood, floating on air. She had blamed herself too long for Robert's incarceration, imagining he had found her ugly, overbearing, domineering, mannish; with Johannes she felt restored to youth, beauty, womanhood, to imagine that one such as he might want her. She had felt it for a while and longed to feel loved again as he loved her; but she suddenly pushed him back. "Johannes, no! We cannot! What are you doing? What are you thinking?"

He put her down at once, staring at the floor. "I am sorry. I do not know what has come over me. I am no longer master of myself. I am no longer responsible for what I say and do. I am like a man under a spell, Clara. I can think of no one but you. I can do nothing without your sanction. What is happening to me, Clara? Will you not tell me?"

She breathed heavily, holding his face in her hands, kissing his forehead, eyes, cheeks, and chin. "It is the same with me, Johannes. I am lost without you. When I am at my lowest ebb, I think of you and I am restored. I thank God daily that he has seen fit to send you to me. It is so sweet to be with you like this, to be held by you."

He couldn't hold her close enough though they stood as one person in the circle of their arms. "Clara, I cannot help it. I must say it. I love you. I know it is wrong, but it is not of my volition. It is even against my volition, but I love you as I have never loved another, and I do not know what to do about it. There, I have said it."

Her face was flushed with the dark red of autumn, suffused with tenderness. "Oh, my Johannes, my sweet darling!"

They held each other for a long while, swaying on their feet, not daring to do more. "What is to be done, Clara? I shall be guided by you, whatever you say."

It had been a year since her triumphant concert in Rotterdam with Robert, the serenade at their window with the choir despite the cold, late into the night. His most recent letter had voiced the fear that he might never see her or the children again, his demons wouldn't allow it. "Dear Johannes, we must remember who we are. If we forget we shall be forever lost."

His eyes were closed. "I know, my Clara, I know."

"I cannot see that it is wrong to love. It is perhaps the best thing we can do for each other, to love each other. We must not deny our love, it is too precious to be denied, but we must not forget that the noblest part of love is the denial of the self. If we can deny ourselves without denying love, surely it cannot be wrong then to love?"

"I do not see that it can."

"Then that is what we must do, is it not?"

It was not the answer he might have wished; he didn't know what he might have wished, but it was how knights had loved maids during the Middle Ages, courtly love was the purest love. Besides, it provided resolution, and that was more than he had hoped. "I will make it my motto. I have made it so already."

They held each other for a long while before Clara broke away. "I shall tell Fraulein Schonerstedt that you will be traveling with us for a while. Will that be all right?"

"I could not ask for more."

"Good. Do you have money?"

"I spent my last thaler on the steamer ticket. I have not eaten in almost a day."

Her face softened again. "Oh, Johannes, you must not be so silly. You must take better care of yourself – for my sake, you must take better care of yourself. They serve a good breakfast downstairs. I think we should eat first, do you not?"

"I was not hungry before, but now I could eat for ten."

They were joined for breakfast by Fraulein Schonerstedt who looked at them both strangely, but the two had eyes for only each other.

iii

"Doktor Schumann, here is someone to see you."

Robert looked over his shoulder from his desk and gasped to see who accompanied Richarz. His mouth trembled, but otherwise he looked as well as when Brahms had seen him last, walking into the sunset. His hand went to his mouth the way Brahms remembered to steady his lips, and his voice was as soft and hushed. "Jo-han-nes? Can it be?"

Brahms smiled, noting he had called him by his first name. "Master! At last!"

Robert moved quickly to embrace Brahms, kissing his cheeks, holding him as if he might disappear. "My dear, dear Johannes!"

The room was almost spartan; bed, desk, dresser, blue curtains on the window, mountains in the distance. Brahms held him a long while, trembling himself, his voice reedier. "I prayed my turn would come next, after Joachim was allowed to see you. I knew it would not be long."

Robert released Brahms, still holding him at armslength. "How is it with Joachim, and with *her*, and the children?"

There had been more letters back and forth; Clara had written, so had Joachim and Brahms, and Robert had written back. Joachim had visited Endenich over Christmas and been allowed to see Robert – and now Brahms, but not yet Clara who might still excite him too much.

Brahms nodded. "Everyone is well. You know she is touring again. She plays now with a power I never knew before."

"Ah, yes, she plays magnificently. I wish I could hear her again. I wish I could see the children. How are they?"

"Felix has just got his first tooth."

Robert's eyes glazed. "Felix? His first tooth already?" His breath came in shallow gasps. Brahms couldn't tell if he was laughing or crying, but he finally sat on the bed smiling. "Poor little Felix! That can be painful."

Richarz cleared his throat. "Herr Brahms, I have to go. You must not excite him too much, you know."

Brahms looked back, surprised Richarz would talk about Robert as if he were not there. He hadn't smiled all the time he had waited. "Yes, Herr Doktor! Yes, I know!"

Richarz nodded, leaving them alone, but Brahms was aware they might peer through the peephole whenever they wished. "I have brought some things you wanted. If you wish for anything else you must ask." Brahms opened his bag, bringing out cigars, an inkstand, a portrait of Clara, another of Robert.

Robert held Clara's portrait in his lap, gazing into her eyes, shaking his head, his breath reduced again to gasps. "Oh, how long have I wished for this!" He stood it on the desk, hands trembling, never removing his eyes from Clara's. "My dear Johannes, I have often wished for your portrait as well, the one under the mirror in my room. Do you know the one I mean?"

"Ja, I know it."

"Will you bring it the next time?"

"Of course." He rummaged further in the bag, drawing out a necktie. "Hah! This is an item for which I must take responsibility. Since your wife is in Holland I had to decide. You do not think it is too flashy?"

Robert took the necktie, but put it aside. "Clara is in Holland?"

"Ja! And next she goes to Danzig, Berlin, and Pomerania. Everywhere she goes, wherever she can, she plays Bach, Beethoven – and Schumann."

Robert smiled, "I like that program," but his smile quickly disappeared, his eyes grew large, his lips pursed. "Does she stay in the same rooms?"

Brahms shook his head. "Na, that she cannot do. You will understand, I am sure." He had stayed in Rotterdam just two days, returning to give lessons to a Miss Thomas and a Fraulein Wittgenstein. "I visited her for a little while myself – but she went with Fraulein Schonerstedt."

Robert sighed, looking away from Brahms. "How is Fraulein Schonerstedt, and the others – Leser and Junge and my good Bertha?"

"They are all well. They all ask about you and think about the time you will return."

Again Robert sighed. "I wish I could have been with you over the Christmas season. Joachim told me some things. Tell me how it was for you."

Brahms sat beside him on the bed. "Your wife is most thoughtful. It was my first Christmas away from my own family. She had met them just recently, as you know, when she played in Hamburg, and she felt badly about keeping me from them for the season, about robbing me from them as she wrote to my mamma. She sent them also my portrait. She could not deny herself the pleasure, she said, to send what would serve as a remembrance of herself and her husband as well as of me." She had added as well a reassurance that she and her husband would stand by her Hannes all his life, gladdening his mamma's heart despite his absence.

Robert's voice got softer yet, steeped in memory. "That is my Clarchen. A more considerate and devoted wife a man could not ask for."

"Indeed! Joachim joined us in the evening – after he had visited you. She was glad for his news – we were all glad, and my hope, as I said, was immediately that my own chance was near, but we could see her heart was no longer with us. Marie and Joachim played your A minor Sonata, Elise played your *Kinderszenen* – your wife will be writing soon, I am sure, to tell you how well they played – but we could tell she was gay only for our benefit, her heart was elsewhere."

Robert's voice remained in the past. "She sent me new issues of the *Zeitschrift* as I had asked, but it is so full of gossip and nonsense now I no longer care to read it. Would you do me the favor of sending me some issues of the *Signale* instead?"

"Of course. Is there anything else you wish?"

"I cannot think of anything."

"Do you not wish to write to her more often? She is never happier than when she hears from you."

"I should love to, always and always, but I have not paper – and I do not like to ask the doctors. I do not like to ask them for anything. They are all so very busy with so many other patients."

"They are not so very busy that they cannot do what they are here for. They are here to make things better for you. You must ask them for anything you wish."

Robert sat upright, frowning and pushing his lips back and forth. "I should love to write, but I have not paper."

Brahms got up. "That I think we can easily manage. If you will pardon me for a moment." He was back, almost at once. Robert had not moved in the time he was gone. "See?" He held out writing paper. "If you do not tell the doctors what you want they will not know. You must tell them."

Robert frowned. "These pages are too large."

Brahms's eyebrows rose. "We can cut them to whatever size you wish." He folded a sheet in two and tore it down the fold.

Robert shook his head, still frowning. "That is not the way. The size should be right, from the beginning. You should not have to cut the paper. You must not change the size of the paper. That is not right." He crossed his arms. "Clara would know what I mean."

Brahms stared momentarily, tidying the pages, arranging them in a corner of the desk. "I will consult her about the paper – before talking again to the doctors."

"See that you do. It is very important that the paper is the right size."

Brahms was tempted again to stare, but tidied other items on the desk. "Doktor Schumann, I shall ask your wife about the paper the next time I see her, but will you not write something for her, just a little something? I am sure she will not mind the size of the paper in the least, and she will be so very happy to read anything you might write."

Robert's eyes brightened like a child's at the mention of a toy. He sat at the desk and picked up his pen, but pushed away the pages. "I am too excited. I will write tomorrow." He smiled, perhaps in apology for his contrariness. "Clara sent me your magnificent Variations, Herr Brahms. I recognized at once your presence. Here and there the theme bobs up very mysteriously, then more passionately, then intimately, only to disappear again completely. It is a most splendid work indeed."

Brahms nodded, acknowledging Robert's attempt at reconciliation, though none was necessary. He had been more puzzled than offended. "I received my inspiration from your own Symphonic Etudes, Doktor Schumann. If not for the allusions to your other works my Variations would never have existed."

"You are too modest, Herr Brahms. You provide so much more than mere allusions to my work – but best of all you honor both my wife and myself, developing my theme and dedicating it to my wife. You have done the same with the transcription of my Piano Quintet."

Clara had mentioned once that Robert had long wished for a piano transcription of his Quintet, and he had made one for Clara, for four hands, for Christmas. "You are most welcome, Doktor Schumann. I wish I could do more."

"I wish I could hear it. I would love to hear it."

"We could play it ourselves, the two of us, if you wish."

"Do we have time?"

"Plenty of time."

It was a warm day for January, the Endenich Road deserted except for Brahms and Robert and the attendant in their wake. They had used the piano in the waiting room; Brahms had played his Variations, his ballades, the Quintet with Robert. A change had encased Robert, wonderful to watch, as he had listened; his mouth relaxed first, no longer puckering and unpuckering, followed by his eyes, no longer glazed, no longer unfocused, followed by the rest of his face, no longer as lined. Robert had wished to accompany him to the station; on the pretext of fetching his hat and coat Brahms had requested the doctor's permission, heavy doors had been unbolted and they had set off at a brisk pace, Brahms careful not to look at his watch, noting Robert kept up with him better than Clara when they walked.

"Does my Clara still walk everyday?"

"She does not like walking alone, but I take her whenever she is in Dusseldorf."

"That I can readily believe. In the old days we always took our walks together." He smiled. "My dear Johannes, wherever did you get that hat? I must say you look quite the gypsy."

The hat was brown, with a narrow brim, a braided band, interlinked metal rings, and a white feather. "Hah! I was wondering when you would notice."

"How could I not notice?"

"My Hungarian hat. Joachim jokes about it. He is Hungarian, but wears a fez. I am German, but this is my favorite hat."

"It looks well on you."

"Danke. That gives me ammunition against Joachim if ever he dares speak against it again."

Robert laughed; Brahms's grin stretched off his face; but almost at once Robert's face contracted again, stamped anew with worry lines. "Johannes?"

Brahms swallowed his grin. "Yes, my friend?"

"My demons tell me I am not to get too excited. Am I too excited?"

Brahms noted he had confused his demons with his doctors. "Na, not at all. Joy is good for you."

"Ah, I thought so – but the doctors …" He shook his head, shaking a memory. He looked again at Brahms, filled now with nostalgia, realizing their time was getting short. "My God, Johannes, but we have not seen each other since Hanover – not in a whole year."

"It will not be so long again."

"Those were happy days, were they not?"

"Indeed – and they will come again." He shook his head, wishing to clear his doubts, unable to clear his own. "My dear Master, until I met you and your wife I did not know what happiness was, and since I have settled in Dusseldorf I have come to love you both more and more. I have so accustomed myself to your wife's society this past summer, and learned to love and admire her so well, that I live for the time we three shall live together, and it will be as it once was. Without you and your wife in the world, everything turns grey."

Robert nodded, still serious, mouth puckering again. "I wish I could be with you, but my demons will not let me. I think sometimes they are jealous demons – but I cannot ignore them. They can make things very difficult."

Brahms grimaced, turning his head, feeling his eyes get full. Robert had written to Clara: a terrible danger stood before him, he quailed at the thought that he might never see her or the children again; but Clara had said nothing to the doctor, against Brahms's counsel, wishing to conceal Robert's groundless fears, worrying they might otherwise incarcerate him longer.

They were silent the rest of the way to the station. Robert took Brahms's hand. "Do not forget what I have said, my friend. You must write symphonies next. Your ballades are already too demonic to be contained by the piano alone."

Brahms felt his breath grow shorter; he was beginning to recognize the solution to his problem: in order to love Clara as he did, he had to love Robert no less, encompassing both in his love, he could not love one without the other. "My dear Master, I will come to see you again as often as I can."

Robert held him, kissing his cheeks. "My dear Johannes." He was crying, trickling tears down Brahms's face, which Brahms left unimpeded to mingle with his own.

He wrote to Clara the same evening relating precisely what had passed between him and Robert in the four hours they had been together, mentioning everything, from the joy with which he had received news about her and their children, the lucidity with which he remembered music, to his specificity regarding paper and his confusion of the doctors with his demons. He had offered to be installed himself as Robert's nurse so that he might write about him everyday to her and talk about her to him, but the doctors thought it might excite him too much.

He mentioned that Eugenie had a cold, but the boys were well. They were learning the alphabet with difficulty though he bribed them with sugar and sweets, but they had no difficulty learning to wrestle and somersault which he had undertaken to teach them as well. The older girls would be visiting from school the following Sunday for a lunch of potato salad.

He implored her also to write however busy her concert schedule kept her, a friendly greeting to say she would be back in 14, 13, 12, 11, 10, 9, 8, 7, 6, 5, 4, 3, 2, 1 days! That was not too much to ask for someone over whom she had cast a spell, who could do nothing but think of her, to whom her presence had become indispensable, who sometimes saw her as if she were standing in the flesh before him.

iv

Four stagehands stood in the wings watching the woman in black deliver the last thunderous chords of Beethoven's E flat Concerto, followed by applause no less thunderous. The woman rose from the piano, bowed, and swept like a ship of state from the stage only to collapse like a sack in a chair out of sight of her audience. She made no attempt to hide her streaming eyes and shining cheeks, but held her hands to her throat as if she were choking, shoulders jerking, breath coming in long rattles and clicks.

The stagehands looked at one another, one ran to get a glass of water, but the woman never noticed; she stroked her throat downward continually with both hands to her breastbone until her breath was regular again; she wiped her face with a lace handkerchief, rose from the chair, adjusted her black satin gown, and sailed back toward the stage to continue her program.

Entering the sittingroom Brahms could tell something was afoot: the door to the diningroom was closed; Elise and Julie giggled in a corner; and Eugenie wore her blue party dress, a flower basket swinging from her wrist. Her back was to Brahms who couldn't resist scooping up the three-year-old without warning. "Ah-hahahahah, little girl! At last you are mine!"

"Aaaaaaaheeeeeee!" Eugenie pedaled her legs in the air, but held onto her basket. Elise and Julie couldn't stop giggling and Brahms narrowed his eyes, but before he could say another word the door to the diningroom was flung open.

"HAPPY BIRTHDAY, DEAR JOHANNES!"

Clara stood in the doorway with Joachim, Grimm, and Dietrich. He was twenty-two that day. The diningroom was festooned with ribbons, streamers, and balloons. Clara stepped forward, dressed as always now in black, and kissed his cheeks. "My dear friend! Happy Birthday!"

Brahms looked around; Marie, Ludwig, and Ferdinand had gathered, and Bertha with Felix in her arms. "My God! This is a complete surprise! Jussuf, I thought you were in Hanover!"

Joachim embraced his friend, kissing his cheeks. "I was, but how could I resist when Frau Schumann called me?"

Brahms grinned, still looking around. "Grimm, Dietrich, I am so glad to see you."

Eugenie presented her flower basket; Marie, Elise, and Julie recited a poem they had written; Ludwig and Ferdinand turned somersaults until Clara stopped them; Grimm played a Polka composed from the musical letters of Brahms's name; Dietrich gave him books, Joachim the complete Jean Paul, Clara the manuscript and dedication of a Romance she had composed for the occasion, also photographs of his mother and sister – and from Robert, received that very morning, the manuscript of his overture, The Bride of Messina; Robert's gift had been accompanied by a note to Clara, the only shadow marring the occasion:

My dear Clara,

On 1 May I sent you a gay messenger of spring, but the following days were much disturbed. You will hear more about them in a letter to follow the day after tomorrow. A shadow falls across it, my darling, but the rest of its contents will give you pleasure. I had forgotten our loved one's birthday, and so I put on wings to send you The Bride of Messina in time.

  Farewell, my beloved.
  Your Robert

They had settled in the sittingroom, the children dismissed with Bertha until dinner. Clara shook her head. "I no longer know what to expect. I no longer know what to do. I am afraid to do nothing, but I am also afraid to do anything at all. I am afraid of everything."

Brahms knew to what she referred. They had visited Hamburg again in April to attend performances of Robert's music and stayed with his family; his mamma had suggested, as had others, that Robert be brought home, that he would improve among loved ones, but Clara feared to be responsible again for his wellbeing, feared she had been responsible for his collapse, feared she couldn't support the family with Robert to care for, feared to stop touring again, feared to disrupt once more the newly even keel of her life – feared, in brief, to lose more control of her life than she had already. Marie and Elise were in a Leipzig boarding school, Julie in Berlin with Clara's mamma, the rest she could manage with the help of Bertha and Brahms and the other servants, but not if Robert were back needing special attention. She wanted him back, but *her* Robert, the man she had known, not the man he had become – but that was not something she could easily explain.

Brahms suspected all these fears, but there was one she feared to suspect herself, that Robert no longer loved her, that he blamed her for his misfortune. His letters rained endearments, but asked more about Brahms and Joachim, their lives and compositions – never asked to see her, but welcomed visits from Brahms and Joachim. The doctors never suggested a visit and she feared to suggest it herself, feared what they suspected, feared he would reject her, feared to see him herself.

Joachim frowned. "I do not think we should accept the doctors' word as an oracle. Richarz says he would rather promise too little than too much, but I have heard about cures by electrical stimulation for such disorders – galvanization, I believe it is called. I have heard of hydrotherapeutic cures. I think we should consider all these options – perhaps even different doctors and a different institution."

Clara shook her head. "I have considered these matters hundreds upon hundreds of times, but however I consider them the end is always the same – always horrible."

Brahms squeezed her hand. "We must not make it worse than it is. We do not know what is in the letter to which he refers. We only make matters worse with speculation."

Clara shook her head again, shaking off cares. "You are right. Today, at least, will be a day of joy. We shall will it so – for your birthday. Does anyone not have any good news for a change?"

Joachim leaned back in his chair, stretched and crossed his legs before him, his smile contented. "I do."

The company turned its collective gaze on him.

Joachim's smile spread. "It is still a private matter, so I will request my friends to keep it among themselves – but next month I am to be baptised a Christian."

He looked around; faces greeted him with varying shades of surprise. Clara was the first to break the silence. "Aaaah! Herr Joachim, you are only about six months too late! But why now?"

He knew what she meant; she had delayed Felix's baptism, hoping Robert might be well enough to attend, but finally given in on the first day of the year, asking Brahms and Joachim to be his godparents, but Joachim had been unable, being a Jew. "Well, I have always had to struggle against the many disadvantages of my faith – and, of course, Mendelssohn too had been baptised ..."

"But what decided you now?"

Joachim raised his hand for patience. "Some of you know that I have had my differences at the court with the King, and to such a degree that I had decided to leave his employment."

Clara's eyes widened, her tone was injured. "You had decided to leave the employ of the King, Herr Joachim, and you never said a word about it to me?"

"I beg your pardon, Frau Schumann, but you had troubles enough of your own. I did not wish to add to them."

"You would have done no such thing, not if I could have been of help, nor if I could have commiserated with you. I should have been glad of an opportunity to be useful – especially after you have proven so staunch a friend."

"Then it is my fault alone – and I apologize. I should have known better, and in future I shall – but, to my surprise, when I approached the King regarding the matter he could not have been more distressed. He said he did not know how he and the Queen would manage without me. In fact, he asked me for a list of my grievances, and redressed them all, even as I listed them. I am now, in fact, the final authority on what I may or may not do, when I may take time off for composition, or to visit my family, or for any other venture I please." He grinned, looking at Brahms. "I had never expected him to grant me so free a hand."

"My congratulations, Jussuf, but what has this to do with your baptism?"

"Well, we came next to discuss music, and Bach – which led the King to ask me how it was that I appreciated him so well being born in a Catholic country – which was when I told him of my Israelitish origin. Then he wanted to know what had prevented me, with my Christian nature, from conversion – to which I confessed my chief reason, my dislike of outward demonstrations regarding spiritual matters – to which the King asked if he might not be my godfather himself."

"The King himself?"

"None other!"

"He must hold you in high esteeem, indeed!"

Joachim shrugged. "He has arranged himself for a most discreet ceremony. He will take a walk with the Queen as is their habit at midday, when they will enter the church – where I shall be waiting with the clergyman."

"How could you refuse?"

Joachim grinned. "How, indeed, and to what end? I felt I had shaken my bitterness for the first time, the weight of my Judaism, against which I had become more inimical the more I had had to conquer its disadvantages. All of my life I have had to labor under its yoke, at first unconsciously, then less so. I will never forget Frau

Bohm, the wife of my teacher in Vienna, with whom I lived, how she would say to me: 'I say, Peperl' – as a youngster, they called me Pepi – 'I say, Peperl, I had such a sermon again today for housing a heathen like you, but never mind. Practise like a good boy and we will answer to God for the rest!' Of course, she was joking, but I felt it then, I had felt it before, and I never stopped feeling that I was fundamentally unsound – but no more. It is such a relief – but there was also a plus side to what she said. I took her at her word as well about the practice. I never stopped practising – but I never stopped feeling fundamentally unsound."

Brahms saw his opening. "That is what you think, but your friends know better. You may *feel* you are unsound – Pe*perl* – but your friends *know* it. Haaah!"

Joachim picked up a cushion. "That is just what I am talking about, that is just what I have always to guard against." Brahms rushed around the room, Joachim in his wake beating him with the pillow; Grimm and Dietrich called after the two running around the room, encouraging first one, then the other; Clara collapsed laughing on the sofa, following Brahms with a look of indulgence. He could make her feel giddy on the worst of days; his childishness only made him seem unselfconscious, it was his inheritance from his family – even his rudeness was a function of this naturalness, not of malice, easily understood and easily forgiven – but she worried about him. He appeared to have no concerns about money or reputation, joked about "coming a cropper," but she worried as much as his mamma. During her last visit to Hamburg she had overheard his mamma say it was good of him to do what he did, but he had to think of his future, seize the moment which Schumann had given him, which he was losing by babysitting in Dusseldorf. He disliked teaching, but couldn't live on what he published; he had to give concerts; only men of money were respected.

It was true, money was important, but Brahms had dedicated himself instead to her cause when he might instead have been touring himself. She had given him her pupils, but that was little money, times were more difficult than usual, business was at a halt, publishers had no money, prices had doubled. The Crimean War was to blame, begun by Nicholas I – who had been so friendly when she had met him, his Tsarina, and their three Tsarevnas, for two hours in the Golden Room of the Winter Palace during her triumphant Russian tour.

At first she had believed Brahms meant what he had said, consecrating his life to her and Robert, but while she never disbelieved him she suspected he had another motive: he disliked performing in public. She was determined to persuade him with Joachim's help to mount the stage, perhaps on a triple bill with the two of them before launching him on his own.

Her next challenge was England, which she had meant to include in her last tour, but she had allowed Joachim to deter her. The English thought too much about money he had said, sacrificing beauty for gain, making of music an industry, pandering to pleasure seekers, seeking the greatest living in the shortest time, and she was currently secure from want, too tender to thrive under such conditions, not dutybound to do more, and owed it to herself and Robert to stay strong for the time she could visit under *his* protection, when he would preserve for her the fineness of her nature. She had said nothing to Joachim, but she had never relied on Robert's protection more than her own; the ability to make money and provide for her family was its own protection. She thought less of the time Robert would return, more of how she would continue to manage without him.

Joachim was young, as was Brahms, neither understood the worth of money, neither had dependent families; but on a deeper level she performed for love, not money – and on the deepest, not even for love, it was just what she did, what she was born to do, she knew nothing else, it defied rationale – but she enjoyed their adulation, also of Dietrich and Grimm, felt younger herself in their company, and yielded to Joachim's counsel, agreeing instead to perform soirees with him again in Berlin that winter as they had the last, though never surrendering her determination to visit England.

Meanwhile, Brahms lived upstairs from her, Joachim roomed nearby for the summer, they met daily for dinner and walks, weekend excursions with the children, and the Rhine Festival loomed during which she would meet again her old friend, Jenny Lind, now Jenny Lind-Goldschmidt – after which she had planned a Rhine excursion with Brahms and Bertha from Coblenz to Mainz, and farther to Frankfurt, Heidelberg, Karlsruhe, and Baden-Baden.

ii

CLARA TO BRAHMS   *Detmold, 16 June, 1855*

My dearest Johannes,

Was it really just yesterday that I saw you last? It seems like a month already, but my fortnight in Detmold has only just begun. How hard it was, my friend, to say goodbye, how hard not to show it too clearly to Frl. Wittgenstein who must have thought it very strange indeed, how quiet I was the whole way, but I no longer care what people think. What we feel and do is correct. The rest matters not. I cling to you with all my heart, and feel it terribly when we have to part.

I had so looked forward to spending more lazy days with you and dear Joachim through the summer, but I begin to think the meeting with the princesses at the Rhine Festival was destined. At first, as you know, I did not take their offer seriously. Royalty is so often affected and unmusical, and just as often the last to admit it, but the princesses were not to be denied, not after they asked me to name my own terms, not if I were to be faithful to my responsibilities, and my responsibilities are greater than those of many another.

I feel better today. Though it is dreadfully cold and uncomfortable for this time of the year, I see that it is also possible to spend a very pleasant time here. The neighborhood is pretty, my rooms are comfortable, and the daily intercourse with my hosts promises to be salutary indeed. They have proven themselves artistic and grateful already in our intercourse.

In addition to giving lessons to the Princess, I am expected to play every afternoon when the ladies and gentlemen will come to my rooms. Next week, there is to be a soiree at the Palace at which I shall play Beethoven's E flat major Concerto. Prince Leopold has recently augmented the number of the orchestra from thirty-three to forty-five. They are under the conductorship of Herr Kiel, who is a pupil of Spohr. Best of all, they have invited Joachim to play with me. I pray he will be able to oblige us. I shall then, at least, not be entirely without a friendly face.

Dearest Johannes, you must not be angry if I remind you once more, but you must think about what we have spoken. You must think seriously about performing on the stage in the fall. I shall never forget the many services you have rendered me in Dusseldorf, but I shall feel much remiss myself as a friend if I take too much advantage of your goodness, while encouraging you not at all toward what I know would long have been your goal if not for my own misfortunes. I know you do not like playing to audiences who are unable to appreciate your worth, but you need not compromise your standards. You must play only what you deem worthy. That is the only way to enjoy what you do. Promise me that you will consider what we have discussed, and that you will continue to think of me with kindness,

Your Clara

BRAHMS TO CLARA *Dusseldorf, 25 June*
My Beloved Clara,

You must have received my letters of the 16th, 18th, 20th, 21st, and 23rd – as I have received yours of the 16th, 18th, 21st, and 23rd. If you have not written again already, you will owe me at least two letters to make up for the one I am writing today. It is strange sometimes when our letters cross, but also delicious, to have answered questions before they have been asked, to have anticipated what the other might wish before the wish is made ink.

Thank you for the little nosegay, the stalks of which look like silk. They have found their home in the long blue vase in the sittingroom, and each of the flowerheads recall yours to me.

I share your indignation to a great extent about the abominable weather. I am so sick of the icy damp air that I have already got up a dozen times to make sure that all the windows are fastened. As you know, that is not something I often do.

Early this morning Ferdinand showed me a piece of paper on which he had scratched Bertha's name. I always kiss them for you, but more than anything I would like to give you back their kisses.

Yesterday, Frl. Leser sent me a large cake for St. John's Day. I was deeply touched since this has never happened to me before on my name day. The boys and I had a feast. We finished the whole cake in less than an hour even over Bertha's objections.

I am always sorry when I cannot send you news from Endenich, but the usual news from the doctor should come today or tomorrow. If I could have had the slightest hope of seeing or speaking to the dear man I would have gone there in any case, but you know how the doctor is about these things.

I wish I had learned to play the violin instead of the piano. I might then have been invited to play with you instead of Joachim, but it is he who is the lucky devil who left for Detmold this morning.

I have acquired Liszt's transcription for two pianos of Beethoven's 9th. This is what he does so marvelously well, unlike his composing. I cannot wait to try it out with you.

And now farewell. Please go on loving me as I shall go on loving you always and forever.

Wholly your
Johannes

iii

Brahms and Otten looked at each other from their places at the piano and podium, Brahms nodding, Otten raising his baton, the Hamburg Philharmonic Orchestra obliging with a crashing E flat chord, Brahms following with a run commanding the key and keyboard like a general surveying the lay of the land, leading to a second crashing chord from the orchestra, in the dominant, a second exploration of the keyboard, one more time in a minor key, before the orchestra explicated the themes of the Beethoven concerto, and Brahms put his hands momentarily in his lap.

He had performed already with an orchestra in Bremen, Schumann's Piano Concerto, which he had practised in the hall itself the night before following Clara's counsel. He had liked performing with the orchestra and despite the colorless tone of the piano had performed well enough to entertain hopes of performing with greater confidence yet.

His latest debut, on the Danzig concert stage, had been less promising though he had shared the bill with Clara and Joachim (uncomfortable with the touch of the piano he had stopped in the middle of a performance and started again on another piano), but he had begun to understand the need to make the stage his own: days of concerts saved him from months of teaching.

A second alternative had also presented itself. Princess Friederike had followed Clara to Dusseldorf to continue lessons and offered him a position at the Court of Detmold which he wished to contemplate.

From Danzig they had headed for Berlin, where he had left his friends for Hamburg, remembering still the sweet goodbyes from his train window, little Julchen, just ten years old, promising already to be the prettiest of the Schumann daughters, her sleepy eyes, Clara's sad face, Jussuf's tired. Clara had finally met with Richarz to discuss the possibilities suggested by Joachim of hydrotherapy and galvanization, but Richarz said Robert was not to be moved, his auditory hallucinations and insomnia had returned, correspondence had been curtailed, and visits restricted.

Otten glanced again at Brahms, heralding the close of the orchestral tutti, and the reentry of the piano. He would have sworn Brahms's head was anywhere but with the music, he had played deferentially during rehearsal fearing the orchestra – which was understandable since he had little experience, and Otten had suggested he play as well a canon by Schumann, a march by Schubert, so the audience could hear him undaunted by an orchestra.

When his moment came Brahms tore into the symphonic fabric with a chromatic scale, but Otten's reservation was borne out in a review the next day in the *Hamburger Nachrichten:The solo part of the concerto was performed with youthful modesty by Herr Brahms who kept it subordinate to the symphonic work as a whole. We think that he carried his reticence to the extreme. He could well have exhibited more virtuosity without damaging the spirit of the composition. That he possesses such virtuosity was proven by his performance of a canon by Schumann and a march for four hands by Schubert arranged by himself for two.*

Brahms agreed more closely with a review in the *Signale*: *Many artists could have exhibited greater technical skill, but not the gift of so completely interpreting the composer's intentions, or of understanding, as Herr Brahms does, the workings of Beethoven's genius and of discovering its magnificence. Besides, the young artist, who thinks more of the work he happens to be interpreting than of selfdisplay, has already won many friends in the art world with his compositions.*

iv

In Endenich, too, a man played the piano, the flotsam of a man, emaciated and spasmodic, a machine with broken springs, clockwork running down. When he stopped he spat repeatedly on the floor, complaining there was shit in his mouth.

Clara had not written, sent no word, no one visited, the doctors said little. She could not love him and he could not blame her; she had loved him long and he had long been unworthy. He was tired of the same life, the same view of Bonn.

The fault was in him, not in her, not in the doctors, that he was ill. There was nothing anyone could do, not the doctors, not his friends, not Clara, not even himself, but to let go, his only alternative, to desist, cease, forever.

Lady Overstone's home was as comfortable and plush as any of the aristocratic homes and courts Clara had visited in Germany, Vienna, Paris, and Prague: seats were upholstered in velvet; lamps, chandeliers, and portrait frames were gilded; and rugs, draperies, and tapestries softened the interior; but lapdogs yapped, roaming freely, and the company talked while she played Robert's Symphonic Etudes.

Joachim was right, the English made themselves stupid for money. Sterndale Bennett, Robert's old friend and correspondent for the *Zeitschrift*, was a good man, but no conductor, lacking in vigor, and no wonder: he gave lessons from seven in the morning to nine at night, or composed, or read scores preparing for concerts; his only chance to learn new music was in the carriage from one lesson to the next, but the fever for wealth was everywhere in England: Manchester, Liverpool – even Dublin had been contaminated – as if music were to be dispensed like so much tea, or silk, or sugar, measured by the return on its outlay. A rehearsal meant no more than playing once through a work without attention to the details, and when she expressed her dissatisfaction they laughed.

She relied more than ever on Johannes; the last parting had been the most painful, the rainy night following, the lonely hours, and miserable crossing. He had tried to dissuade her: in the first three months of the new year she had toured Prague, Vienna, Budapest, Leipzig, and Hanover; she would wear herself to ribbons in London; friends in Leipzig had organized an annual subscription, eight hundred thaler for Robert's maintenance, not a gift, not charity, not even for her, but for Robert, an offering of love to a respected composer; it was her obligation to accept, a matter of generosity to Robert's wellwishers – but she had refused, unable to explain to him any more than to Joachim. She had added five thousand thaler to Robert's capital in the two years since his incarceration, more than his salary for four, but her drive was toward her destiny more than money; she was a pianist, did what every pianist did, and she had avoided London too long already. She had written to ask Bennett if the time was favorable, but her letter had crossed one of his inviting her to England, clinching her decision; she had scheduled twenty-six concerts for two and a half months.

It struck her that she was now differently received; in Vienna, where she had once needed Jenny Lind to fill the hall, she had been recalled fifteen times, even scheduled an extra concert to accommodate everyone; Robert might have been dead the way his music was received; whether they hailed her for his music or her interpretation of his music she couldn't have said, but she had introduced as well, successfully, Johannes's music to Vienna, which the *Wiener Zeitung* called "pieces of special beauty, which confirm the impression of the young composer's exceptional talent."

Brahms's first letter arrived the day before her first performance advising her to break her engagements and return to Germany, but she had long resigned herself to Robert's fate. Richarz had written baldly, Robert was incurably insane, suffered disorders as well of taste and smell, her presence could be of no help, it had taken her long enough to get to England, and she had to get on with her life.

She had neither been able to practise a note all day, nor sleep at night, her pillows wet with weeping, her hosts, two kindly sisters, the Misses Busley, no less teary watching her. How she managed the first concert she would never know, her fingers Myrmidons, her mind a Merlin, but she played flawlessly, Beethoven's E flat major Concerto, to enthusiastic applause. London was won in an evening, audience, critics, and musicians – and gradually she was won by the English. She found them cold and difficult to approach, but once they were warmed they were warm forever, giving their respect they gave it forever, and she had won the respect of many.

Lady Overstone was surely no different. Clara had played barely a third of the Etudes when she put her hands in her lap. She would do Robert a disservice, not to mention herself, her audience, and Lady Overstone, if she continued to play while they talked. Lady Overstone came to the piano, addressing her politely. "Mrs. Schumann, why is it that you do not continue to play?"

Clara replied no less politely. "I am not accustomed to playing while people are talking."

Lady Overstone looked at her guests all of whom stared back. "There is no one talking any longer."

"There are still dogs barking."

The dogs were turned from the room. Clara nodded, "Thank you," and started again from the beginning.

The next day she received a polite apology from Lady Overstone, added the note to her correspondence file, and wrote to Brahms about the incident, another long letter. The hours spent writing were her most bearable, and the hours reading.

She read again as well his first fateful letter.

BRAHMS TO CLARA   *Bonn, April 1856*

My dearest beloved Clara,

I wish I could talk to you about only agreeable things. I wish I could send you only the fairest news. I regret every word I write to you which does not speak of love. You have taught me, and you teach me better everyday, how to recognize and how to marvel at the nature of love, this sweet mixture of affection and self-denial. I should like to call you endearing names all day long and pay you compliments even without hope of a return. I should like to put you under glass or set you in gold. If you have any pretty ribbons from your hats please do not throw them away. I would like them very much to tie around your letters or for a bookmarker. I wish you could read directly what is in my heart. I shall never be able to transcribe it into words and yet I must be the bearer of terrible news about the dearest man, your husband and my friend.

I spoke with Doktor Richarz about transferring him to a hydrotherapeutic institution, but he says it is too late. He is much too weak to be transferred anywhere. The best we can hope is it will not be too long a wait and not too painful for him.

I have moved myself to the Deutsches Haus in Bonn and I plan to stay as long as necessary. I have saved quite a bit of money from my concerts and lessons. I visited Robert again yesterday. He had asked for an atlas and I took him the largest I could find, the Kosmos Atlas, beautifully bound, with 83 gargantuan maps. I wish there were some way to say this without alarming you, my lovely Clara, but there is not. He pored over the atlas, made lists in alphabetical order of cities whose names might be transcribed to music, but he took little notice of me. I do not think he understood me when I talked, and when he spoke I could discern the words – Beethoven, Mozart, Marie, Julie, Berlin, Vienna, Joachim – but not the meaning. He has lost much weight because he refuses to eat. The staff has to insert a tube up his mouth or his nose to feed him. He subsists now on wine, milk, consomme, meat extracts, and saltwater. He is confined to his bed because his feet are swollen with edema. You must consider breaking your English engagements. Surely even the cold Englishman will understand your circumstances are special.

Ah, my Clara! What kind of words are these to write to the one I love! Think of me with kindness, dearest beloved, as I do of you all the time, and with so much more than kindness.

Your Johannes

ii

Clara looked neither left nor right as she walked, but in the hinterland of her sight the institution looked drearier than she had imagined though hardly drearier than she might have expected – courtyard, building, and anteroom, bricks showing through cracked walls, a dirty red roof, two sooty chimneys, a sooty cupola mounted by a sooty cross, shuttered windows worn and smudged, threadbare carpets, musty air, dusty floors, barren rooms, emptiness everywhere.

She had returned from England on 4 July, Brahms had met her at Antwerp, he had often visited Robert who was rapidly deteriorating, but Brahms wished to shield her from the nightmarish sight and she had been easy to dissuade, they had visited Ostend instead, both glad for the brief reprieve together.

On 14 July she had received a letter from Richarz, Robert had less than a year to live, she had visited Bonn, visited Endenich, been dissuaded again, by Richarz and Brahms: Robert was horrible to see, she had a duty to her children not to upset herself, and she had returned to Dusseldorf.

On 23 July she had received a telegram from Richarz: *If you wish to see your husband alive, come at once.* She had gone at once, but the crisis had been averted, and it was 27 July, six o'clock in the evening, before all were finally in agreement that she should see him, whatever the cost.

Richarz looked through the peephole, turning to Brahms and Clara. "He is asleep."

Clara nodded, her heart too full for breath, and Richarz opened the door leading them in. At the bed he stepped aside, allowing Clara an unrestricted view, watching her for signs of weakness. Brahms stood ready in case she fainted.

Clara stared first without comprehension; the man lying on his back in the bed, bedclothes to his chin, one arm outside, was not her husband, too skeletal, cheeks too gaunt, chin too bony, fingers like sticks, a declivity between the bones of his forearm, but gradually recognition dawned, and the image of her husband, the curve of his temple, eyes in sleep, hair like a mop, small mouth, settled over the palimpsest before her.

She put her hat to one side, sank slowly to her knees, joined her hands, rested elbows on the bed, eyes riveted to the face of the man she loved; she didn't know it but her shoulders shook, her eyes were wet, her face twisted in a grimace, and she couldn't break the grip of his face on her eyes. She was silent, breath caught in her throat, and appeared to be choking when Robert opened his eyes. She stopped shaking as their eyes locked, but her voice trembled. "Robert?"

He stared a long while with no sign of recognition, then parted his lips though with difficulty, as if they were glued together. "A-ba-ba."

"Robert, my darling."

"A-ba-ba-da …"

"Oh, my Robert, do you not know me?"

His eyes narrowed, his lips pushed in and out in the familiar movement, the nervous reaction. She put her hands on his face, stroking his lips with her fingers, steadying the movement, and was rewarded with a smile. He had recognized her, there could be no doubt.

He struggled to get up, but couldn't. Richarz, on the other side of the bed, helped him sit. He struggled next to raise his arm; Clara helped gingerly; he seemed so fragile, bones brittle as dry twigs, until his arm was around her shoulders, light as straw.

"Ma-ma-my …"

He could not finish his sentence, but smiled, eyes moist, and Clara understood. "Yes, my Robert. Your Clara. I am your Clara – always your Clara."

His arm spasmed around her shoulders. She put her arms around him, wanting to hold him in a tight embrace, but afraid she might hurt him.

Brahms watched, choking himself, digging nails into his palms, the holy sight, a pieta, never would he be privileged to love more purely, to love a purer person, his ideal forever, Robert – and never would he be fated, he hoped, to revisit such a tragedy, share such suffering.

Robert tried again to speak. "Ah-a, I … know … ah, ah …" Again his smile conveyed what his words could not. Clara didn't care what he said; he had recognized her, understood she loved him.

Robert's head lolled back then, and Richarz supported it from behind. "A-ba-ba, ba-ba-ba, da-da." He lost his smile, looking no longer at Clara, appearing to be conversing with someone behind Richarz, but there was no one there.

Richarz was grim nodding to Clara not to be alarmed; he understood what was happening. Robert frowned, apparently disagreeing with someone, and with

Brahms's and Richarz's help she lay him on his back again, covered him with the sheet and caressed his face, but his limbs twitched like the limbs of puppets, and his head swung convulsively, alarmingly, on the narrow stem of his neck. He began to shout. "AH-BAY-BAY-DOH! GARABOHLADEH! BOR!" Clara was afraid he would hurt himself.

An attendant joined them, helping Richarz and the others to hold him until he was still again, and Richarz gave him an injection "to help him sleep."

Richarz explained when they were outside again. "He argues constantly with his voices. He believes they doubt the worth of his work and defends himself constantly. He says they get angry when he talks to others, such as yourselves – or any visitors – and he tries to pacify them. He believes that they believe that we wish to take him away from them – which, of course, in a sense, we do."

"Oh, my poor Robert."

"There is nothing more to be done, but to hope that the end comes soon."

They talked a while; Clara determined to stay in Bonn at the Deutsches Haus where Brahms too was staying; that night they wrote to Joachim.

Clara: *I saw him today. Let me be silent about my own despair, but I did perceive some loving glances and his embrace is something I shall treasure for the rest of my life. I pray for a quick and merciful end. I shall not leave him again. Oh, Joachim, what grief it is to see him like this, but I would not forego the sight of him for anything in the world.*

Brahms: *I am writing in case you wish to see him once more, but you must think it over carefully. It is a pitiful and horrifying sight. He is very thin, almost unrecognizable, and there can be no question of conversation, nor even surety of consciousness.*

iii

"I am glad you have come, Jussuf."

"I came as soon as I got your telegram. I came by the first train."

"Danke, Herr Joachim. I cannot tell you how happy I am to see you. Robert is blessed, indeed, in his friends – and so am I. I shall always be indebted to you and Johannes for this."

The Endenich Road was alive with summer under the blanket of the sun: picnickers at play, lambs in the meadows, chestnut trees in full blaze.

"How is he now?"

"Ah, but there is no comforting answer to that question. He is in an impossible state, neither in our hands nor yet in God's. I pray hourly for his release. There can be no other escape."

"He was asleep when we left him, less than two hours past."

"I think he might rest a long while this evening. He rested hardly at all yesterday – and all day today until we left. We have watched him mainly through the window. He is too violent in his speech and in his actions for company. He can neither appreciate it nor benefit in any way."

Brahms marveled with what control Clara spoke. "But he recognized Clara yesterday and the day before – almost as soon as he saw her. Yesterday, he accepted food from her hand though he refuses it from anyone else."

Clara's smile was joyless, but not without satisfaction. She spoke almost dreamily, her eyes unfocused. "I fed him some jelly and wine. He licked my fingers for the wine and sucked with great haste. Ah, he knew – he knew who it was that fed him. His expression was the happiest we had seen yet. He had not eaten as much, nor as willingly, in a long while."

"The trouble is he eats little, but his delusions tire him endlessly. He is constantly fighting imaginary foes, talking to the walls – mostly without coherence."

"His speech is often vehement."

"It is violent!"

"And his limbs twitch –"

"His limbs are racked with convulsions – his whole body. They are like seizures of the lungs – but Richarz insists he is in no pain –"

"But I do not believe him. I do not believe these doctors know as much about mental illness as they say. I am convinced now I should have been allowed to see him from the start. He needed to know I loved him, but they did not wish to excite him – but what have they accomplished instead? He could hardly have been worse off with my attention." She glared at Joachim, daring him to disagree.

Joachim turned his head. "I am sure they do what they think best."

"Oh, I am sure they do – but I am no less sure that they have no understanding whatsoever of what, indeed, is best. They never asked me a thing about him – I who know him better than anyone. They never asked even to see me. The one time I spoke with Richarz I was the one to seek him, but he should have sought my counsel from the start, and even then we met not in Endenich, not even in Bonn, but in Bruehl – and even then he said he knew what was best – nothing else. I am angry most of all at myself that I listened to him – but I am done listening. It is too late, but I shall never leave him again."

Joachim said nothing, frowning and shaking his head.

"And no more did they listen to your suggestions, Herr Joachim, nor to Johannes's. It is an arrogance with which I have no more patience." She turned to Brahms. "I am convinced your mamma is right about mental illness. The doctors are as helpless as anyone. The patient is best served among those he loves best, those who love him best. Never once have I heard of a patient being cured in an institution, merely cared for – and that is best done at home – and isolating him from everyone only aggravates his condition."

Brahms nodded, saying nothing; his mamma had suggested they bring Robert home, care for him with the help of an attendant, but Clara had then been too fearful of the responsibility – no less fearful, he had felt, of the restrictions on her own movements, her career burgeoning anew, but he had said nothing, too in love with her himself, without answers himself like everyone else. He said nothing either of the premonitions of disaster in Robert's letters that she had withheld from the doctors, fearing that in their ignorance the doctors would construe the worst possible meaning, but refusing to enlighten them herself about his past and clarify the correspondence. In difficult times everyone blamed everyone else though no one was without a share of blame – if, indeed, anyone was to blame. He never doubted Clara's love for Robert, but neither did he doubt her fear of the unknown, her first long deep paralysis, her need for reassurance.

They walked the rest of the way in silence arriving at half past four. Brahms gave Joachim a warning glance as they entered the house, but Joachim had been long prepared. He nodded to Richarz and followed Clara to Robert's rooms, Brahms following behind.

Robert appeared still asleep, forehead so pale it might have been transparent, more arched than Joachim remembered, the consequence of his long enervation, but his face was gentler than he had expected, grave but calm, pure as few others he had seen.

Clara stood by the bed; he was more still than before; her understanding was gradual. She knelt by his side, giving thanks he was finally free, her beautiful husband, and felt already his eyes watching over her, his presence hovering above, her tears of sorrow mingling with tears of relief.

ROBERT WAS BURIED two days later, 31 July, in a Bonn churchyard, at seven o'clock in the evening. The coffin was borne from Endenich by the Dusseldorf choir which had serenaded the Schumanns outside their hotel window on their arrival, followed by Brahms, Joachim, and Dietrich, each bearing wreaths, followed by the pastor, the mayors of Dusseldorf and Bonn, and by Clara, almost a straggler. The pastor delivered an address, the choir sang a partsong, Hiller had been called from Cologne to deliver the eulogy – but no one else; Clara had not wanted it, Robert would not have wanted it, it wasn't his way to call attention to himself; friends threw earth on the coffin, all was soon over.

Richarz's autopsy was vague, a series of random observations: distended blood vessels, ossification of the brain, concretion and degeneration of the inner coverings of the brain, atrophy of the whole brain, which meant little without more detail. Some have speculated syphilis was the cause of death, contracted during his student years, early Italian travels, some have speculated schizophrenia, but the most credible thesis appears to be starvation – or rather, too sudden a nourishment for too chronically starved a body, when he had so eagerly sucked wine and jelly from Clara's fingers, delivering too severe a shock to his physiology. Disclosures of suicide by starvation at Endenich came much later when case histories, including Robert's, had somehow been lost.

In 1885, almost thirty years after his death, Robert's head was removed from his body for study, the fate of geniuses – but has since been lost.

For Clara a new life began, but happiness she insisted was in the past. Brahms and Joachim returned with her to Dusseldorf to help manage Robert's papers, also her grief.

CLARA TO BRAHMS'S MOTHER   *Dusseldorf, 6 August, 1856*

Dear Frau Brahms,

Johannes should arrive on Friday, and return with Elise on Monday. We should all arrive in Gersau on 14 August and be back in Dusseldorf in a month. We shall try to visit the country around there and also spend a few days in Heidelberg before we return, but whatever we do we shall not hurry.

I am writing to make some suggestions for Elise. Do not let her take too many things. Too much luggage only makes a journey inconvenient. If she wears two chemises a week, let her bring six. If she wears just one, let her bring four. Stockings, six pairs. She will need two changes of dress. Do not send the nice blue one; it would be a pity if it were spoiled in the packing. A black petticoat would be best for traveling if she has one, and one white underskirt in case she wears a light dress – but she will not need it if she wears only dark dresses. I am not taking one myself. She will need only one hat, a dark straw would be best. She will also need a warm shawl. Do not buy gloves. I have some she can use.

Ludwig and Ferdinand are very excited. By all reports the resort is beautiful – Lake Lucerne in front and the mountains of Rigi behind. Our chalet should be quite private, but the village is nearby if we should need anything. We could not ask for better walks, nor healthier air. I will be so happy if Elise benefits from this holiday. You know how heavy my heart is. I do not want to talk of it; my heart bleeds at once. Johannes is my true friend and protector. How wise of him to make such a suggestion. What a blessing I have in him! I wish you and all your dear ones well. With all my heart,

Cl. Sch.

ii

"I can hardly believe it, but my head has not ached once since we arrived."

"Hah! That is, I am sure, the best recommendation for any resort. Come to Gersau! We guarantee your head will not ache!"

Elise scowled. "Well, it is true. Everything is beautiful. The lake is so blue it could be a painting, and the mountaintops are so tall and white I have only to open my eyes and my head is full of light."

Clara smiled. "Do not let Johannes upset you, my dear. Brothers are like that. I should know, I have two myself – both younger, just as you do."

Elise's face cleared in a moment, her scowl no more than a passing shadow, grateful that the wonderful Clara Schumann, whom she couldn't praise enough, had found a point of similarity between them, the glamorous pianist and the homely seamstress. It was unkind of Hannes to laugh at her afflictions, but Frau Schumann understood. She smiled, her round face dumb with delight and attention, and played with her hair, her loveliest feature, thick, lightbrown, and grown to great length in the hope of attracting a man.

Brahms grinned. It was early evening, the sun still high on the horizon; they sat in the verandah of the chalet, tea and pastries before them, Brahms drawing on a cigar, stein by his side. Lake Lucerne was indeed as blue as a painting reflecting the paler blue of the mountains behind. The path to the village passed near the house, flanked by trees of chestnut, laurel, and fig; country smells of bark and grass reached the verandah, and country sounds of woodbirds and animals in the brush.

A crash from the sittingroom interrupted the reverie. Clara was instantly on her feet. "Ludwig! Now what have you done?"

She darted into the next room. Brahms grimaced, anticipating what followed, Ludwig loudly smacked, loudly scolded, how could he be so careless when she worked so hard for them all? was it too much to ask that he please her for a change? why could he not be more like Ferdinand who never gave her a moment's anxiety? He imagined how they looked: sturdy Ludwig, thatch of black hair covering his forehead, his mamma's colorless complexion, the large darkbrown eyes of a deer, less afraid of the smacks than of disappointing his mamma; Ferdinand more slender, also with black hair but the deepblue eyes of his mamma, fine white skin of his pappa, sitting amiably by; and Clara gripping Ludwig's shoulder with one hand, the other raised in anger, eyes flashing, face steaming with blood, too immersed still in her own tragedy to recognize Ludwig's sweetness, his wish to please her, his deep disappointment when he couldn't, too hurt herself to remember he was just a boy, just eight years old.

Ludwig had knocked over a wine bottle; he was more prone to accidents than anyone Brahms knew – but his expression was so poignant, mouth open with disbelief, eyes wide with sorrow, that Brahms forgave him easily, but not Clara returning with the two boys to the verandah. "You will sit where I can see you. It is most tiresome of you, Ludwig. You are the older brother and should really be setting an example for Ferdinand. You should really be ashamed of yourself."

The boys sat quietly by the railing, Ludwig staring at the wood floor avoiding everyone's looks, Ferdinand smiling seeking them out. "Will you tell us the story again, Fraulein Brahms, of Wilhelm Tell?"

They had filled knapsacks with lunch two days before and climbed the mountains to the shrine of Wilhelm Tell where the famous Swiss had landed after jumping Gessler's boat. Elise had been awestruck, momentarily fused with history, and recounted the story to the boys of Tell's refusal to bow to Gessler's cap on the pole, the apple shot off the head of his son, his capture and escape; she had lost count already of the number of times she had recounted the tale, but they had yet to tire of hearing it, and she of recounting it to the most rapt audience she had ever entertained. "I am sure your mamma is tired of hearing the story, but maybe I could tell you if we went for a walk?" She looked at Clara.

Clara looked back and Elise looked away. "Ferdinand may go, but not Ludwig. He has got to learn his lesson."

"Tchhah, Clara! Let them go! Let them both go! He did not do it on purpose – and after all, we are on holiday, are we not?"

Clara stared at Brahms who stared back; she wondered if he were making an opportunity for the two of them to be alone. "Very well. Ludwig also can go – but you must behave yourself, Ludwig, do you hear me? You must not give Fraulein Brahms trouble when she is so kind as to take you for a walk when you have been so careless."

Ludwig looked gratefully between Elise and Brahms, mumbling his response. "Yes, Mamma." Ferdinand grinned. Hats and coats were donned. Clara and Brahms waved from the verandah watching the trio disappear.

Settling in her chair Clara looked at Brahms, already distant, hardly the Johannes to whom she was accustomed, no longer his attention without end, apparently with more will of his own, and the will to exercise it against her. If he had wanted them to be alone he wasn't going to make conversation any easier. "Why do you defend Ludwig, Johannes, when you know how he is? How is he to improve if you undermine what I say?"

Brahms stared resolutely down the road, shaking his head impatiently – again a different Johannes; he was often impatient, but she suspected it provided a mask for his true feelings. "Clara, he broke a bottle of wine. You can afford a hundred bottles. It is nothing to smack him for."

"I do not smack him for nothing. You should have seen how Pappa used the switch on Alwin and Gustav – and they have still wound up good for nothing. I do not want that for my Ludwig."

Brahms wanted to say there was maybe a lesson in what had happened to Alwin and Gustav, but didn't. "It was an accident, Clara. There was no malice."

"You are right, but it is not just the bottle. He is lazy. Ferdinand is the younger by a year, but he is not so careless. He is more aware of my difficulties than Ludwig, he does everything better than Ludwig, he even reads better – and he is the younger!"

"Yes, yes, but Ludwig tries harder. He is not lazy. Things come to him more difficult – but no one is more upset than himself when he disappoints you, not even you. He is hurt when you are hurt, and the most hurt when he perceives it is he who has caused the hurt. You can see it in his eyes. He is not eight years old then. He is a baby of one. You would not slap a baby, would you?"

Clara narrowed her eyes. "Still, why do you defend him? He is not your son."

Brahms shook his head impatiently again, but this time Clara had identified a problem he had yet to resolve himself. "He has no one else. No one understands him."

"And you do, better than his own mamma?"

"Only because I have nothing to gain or lose – but for you there is more at stake."

Clara shook her head, staring down the road with Brahms. "Perhaps, after all, you are right. Boys need fathers and mine are all fatherless. It is a heavier burden than I would wish on anyone." She glanced at him; her sons knew him better than they had known their own pappa.

Brahms avoided her glance. Yes, and motherless too, he wanted to say, and sisterless and brotherless: Marie and Elise lived in Leipzig with her friends, Julie in

Berlin with Clara's mamma, Ludwig and Ferdinand were soon to be sent to boarding school, Eugenie and Felix remained with Bertha only because they were still young. She was constantly on tour, soon to leave for Copenhagen, making plans already for another tour of England the following year, also her first of Switzerland. "They need to see you more, all of them, all your children. They do not see you enough. It is not right."

Clara was unaccustomed to being told what to do, particularly since her new independence, and resented the change in Johannes when she needed most the Johannes of old, his tenderness now that Robert was truly gone – or had all the words been mere expressions of sentiment, extensions of his ego? She knew for sure only that he had withdrawn from her and his withdrawal was a knife in her back. Robert had provided the glue between them, and without him they danced like bodies without purpose, feathers in the wind. She took a deep breath, sitting straight in her chair, speaking more stiffly. "And what do you propose I do, Johannes? My needs grow daily. They do not recede. I have seven who depend upon me. What do you propose I do with them?"

"We have discussed it, Clara. You can give lessons, you can teach in the university, you can find a sinecure somewhere in a court – maybe Detmold. With your reputation it would not be difficult. You would have money – and you would have time for everyone." She could marry, he wanted to say, but Robert was still too recently buried – but he had touched again the problem he had yet to resolve. With Robert gone she was newly available, but availability had changed their relations. When she had been unavailable he had expressed himself without reservation, and without consideration – but now he felt trapped by considerations. When they had denied themselves for Robert they had been united by a common purpose, a noble aim, but without the need for denial their words continued to hang between them though their passion had long been spent in denial – at least, so it was with him – but he remained beholden to his speeches and letters, a prisoner of his own words.

Her stiffness remained. "We have indeed discussed the matter, and still you do not understand. I intend to do all the things you suggest, but I do not understand why I should not perform as well. I do not perform for my health. I wonder that you cannot see it still. I perform because it is what I do best. It is what I was born to do."

At the expense of your children, he wanted to say, but didn't; she toured at the expense of everything, and everyone, including himself, but he didn't want to say it, and were they to be married it would be the same, as it had been with Robert. "Indeed, we must indeed do what we were born to do, what we do best. That is not a point with which I take issue." He wanted to say more, but didn't – couldn't. He couldn't tell her he didn't wish to encumber himself with conflicting responsibilities as she had, however unconsciously.

She caught his note of resignation, but couldn't catch his eyes staring down the road. With Robert gone he was the dearest man in her life – he had been so even during the last months of Robert's life. She had realized later she had lost Robert long before he had died, she had lost him when he had stopped asking about her, she had mourned him while he was still alive; his death had released her no less than himself. Whatever had been fated, whatever she liked to believe, whatever she said, she had felt betrayed. She had sacrificed her career for his, defended him in health as she had defended not even herself, but her love had not transcended the illness, she could not love without return, and during his illness only Johannes had returned her love, not without sacrifices of his own, his own career for her comfort. He had made it his choice, called it consecration, and he had paid the price. All choices came with a price; the choice was the price you were willing to pay. He was still young to the eye, but old to the ear, old in his heart, but even his face showed wear, not in lines but in expressions, a weariness she had not noticed before, too absorbed in her own difficulties, a constant look of resignation, even shock, as if he had been struck and awaited another blow. She spoke more tenderly. "Johannes?"

"Yes?"

"What will you do now?"

It was the question he had asked himself often. When she had been Robert's wife he had made of his yearning his joy, loved her purely as she had loved him; despite the dissatisfactions, it was a love with which he had grown comfortable – more comfortable than with the love now expected of him. He leaned forward, taking her hand. "That will depend upon you."

She frowned. "Upon me? But why?"

Her hand lay limp in his, but he had taken it only as a gesture. "I do not know."

He appeared to be asking her to take the lead, make up his mind for him. "Johannes, do you not know what you want?"

"No, I do not."

The kindest interpretation she could derive from his response was that he wished to salve her pride: he knew what he wanted, and it wasn't her. She took back her hand. They stared at each other, finally aware that the final obstacle had proven an illusion, obscuring the other obstacles. She understood he wished her to give up touring not for the children, but for himself; he wanted a wife no different from Robert, one who would mind him first, herself second, but she wanted no more that kind of life herself; he might even want children, but she wanted no more herself; she knew his composition would come first, as had Robert's, but could no more come second herself. Besides, she was thirty-seven, and a large part of her life was behind her; he was twenty-three and though he had shared a great part of her life, the greater part lay ahead. She had found as well a new purpose for herself, to proselytize for Robert's music, and had gained notoriety already as the widow of a living composer.

Brahms's sigh seemed to rise from the pit of his stomach. He had composed nothing of consequence in a long while, nothing complete: a sonata in D minor for two pianos, rearranged as a symphony, rearranged again as a piano concerto, which remained a torso; a piano quartet in C sharp minor which remained no less a torso. Both had been efforts to resolve in music what he could not in life, Robert's tragedy in the concerto, unrequited love for Clara in the quartet. He needed peace and quiet for his work of which he'd had too little for too long, but with others dependent upon him he would have even less. "Ah, Clara, why cannot things remain the same?"

Clara leaned forward speaking again with tenderness. "You cannot mean that, Johannes. Things cannot remain the same. Time is relentless. If we do not grow with time, we only grow old."

"Yes, but sometimes we need time to think, to consolidate what has passed, to make room for what is to come – but time does not allow us the luxury. Time demands only that we act – or grow old."

She began to understand his dilemma. "But thinking is acting – if we think toward a form of action. We grow old only when our actions fall behind our thoughts."

He sighed again: he had perhaps thought too much, but action came less easily. His commitment to Clara appeared at odds with his commitment to music; he wanted her still, but had nothing more to offer; time would solve the problem, time away from her, but he didn't know how to break it to her. "Yes, but we grow no younger when we act without first thinking."

She understood him better. He had acted from his heart, without thinking, found consecration in a love now faced with consummation, found purity in a denial no longer necessary, and himself adrift with inaction. Much as it pained her, whatever she wanted for herself, she wanted him to have his way. "If it is time you want, it is time you shall have. I am thinking of moving to Berlin myself. I have nothing in Dusseldorf now but memories – but my mamma and her family are in Berlin. That should give you all the time you wish."

He stuck his lower lip over his upper. It was what he wanted, but not how he wanted it. He had sacrificed, dedicated, consecrated (the words did not matter) almost three years of his life, formative years, to the Schumanns; he had done it voluntarily and his motives hadn't been entirely selfless, but now that he needed his independence she had seized the initiative, taken herself out of his reach, conferred time upon him like a gift, forcing her terms. His tone was no longer weary, but piqued. "You must do it for yourself, not for me. For myself I shall take all the time that I wish."

She was no less piqued; he should have understood she did it for them both. "I *do* do it for myself. I have long wished to leave Dusseldorf, but my circumstances bound me fast – but they bind me no longer. I am my own agent."

"That you are, indeed." Brahms replied quickly, wishing it might have been different, wishing he might be her agent; his circumstances barely allowed him to be his own agent, even less an agent for her and seven others, but no less did that release him from his guilt.

She felt no less guilt herself for taking years from his young life – but with the goal at hand, for which they had sacrificed so long and so patiently, he no longer seemed to want it. She was willing to give him what he wanted, but not to guess at it. "And so shall I always be. If I have learned one thing in all these years it is to depend upon no one before myself."

iii

Walking hand in hand with Clara alongside the train at the Dusseldorf station Brahms felt himself shrivel, imagining himself nothing without her. Joachim was back in Hanover, Grimm in Gottingen, Dietrich in Bonn, each holding positions with orchestras, Clara would be in Berlin within a year, and he was returning finally to Hamburg. They had not spoken again of the conversation in Gersau, but with time shrinking the conversation seemed misconceived: they had misunderstood each other, meant nothing of what they had said, needed not time but each other, they belonged together, the rest would follow. He stopped, squeezing her hand, putting down his bag. "Clara!"

She was in his arms, hands clutching his back, breasts smashed against his chest, lips moist on his own, heartbeat synchronized with his whirring like hummingbird wings. The train alongside, people rushing around, porters, vendors, families, all turned to a blur, all sounds to silence, everything to nothing except Clara in his arms.

The whistle blew, she pulled back. "Oh, my Johannes, my beloved friend. Always be my friend, always!"

"Always, my dearest darling Clara. Always!"

"I want to see everything you write. I want to be the first."

"You will. Always, in all things, you will be first."

The whistle blew again. "You will miss your train, my love."

There would always be another train; it was his choice, his last chance, but he said nothing, and she understood he had said all he wished. She shook her head, eyes full; she tried to speak, but her mouth was dry; she pushed him away instead and the relief in his face was like a needle in her chest.

He kissed her again. "Goodbye, my Clara, my dearest."

"Goodbye, my darling."

Boarding the train he felt elastic, boneless, stretched. His destination was Hamburg, but his destiny seemed to pull him still, like an undertow, back to Clara. The carriage was a blur; he bumped into people without apology, without realizing he bumped into anyone, focusing his eyes to a point beyond anything visible to anyone else while his cheeks burned and gleamed.

She didn't realize until the train was past that her own tears fell in sheets, staining the front of her dress; she couldn't stop shaking and left the station as she might have another funeral.

END OF BOOK ONE

BOOK TWO

...AND BRAHMS

I have no friends. If anyone says he is a friend of mine, don't believe it.

JOHANNES BRAHMS

PART FOUR

A MANIFESTO

Brahms had clinched his appointment at the Court of Detmold, performing Schubert's Trout Quintet and Beethoven's G major Piano Concerto with the court orchestra. August Kiel, the Kapellmeister, jealous of his sinecure, had joined the applause but without enthusiasm. He had the soft boyish face of an academic, thinning gray hair parted low over his left temple waving raffishly over his right temple, and wore spectacles over a large fleshy nose. He had approached Brahms with a frown of inquiry. "Herr Brahms, I am in the habit of putting scripture to music, but sometimes I am puzzled by scriptural expressions. I am presently setting one of the Psalms to music. I wonder if you could tell me what is a *gittith*?"

Karl von Meysenbug, nephew of Laura von Meysenbug, sister of the Hofmarschall of the Court of Detmold, once Clara's pupil, had signaled Brahms to ignore Kiel, but too late. Brahms had frowned, nodded, and replied as seriously. "Actually, I do, having a fondness for scripture myself. To my best understanding a *gittith* is a very beautiful Jewish girl."

Invited to play at the Court through Clara's patronage and retained as Court Pianist, Brahms had maintained his brown study as Kiel had stared over the rim of his spectacles, but Meysenbug had barely been able to control his mirth and later introduced Brahms to a less buttoned audience. The night had deepened and disappeared into wine and pastries until Brahms had expressed a wish to see the sunrise from the Grotenburg and only Meysenbug had remained lively enough to accompany him. They had left the castle in great spirits and tramped along the path to the Teutoberger Wald by moonlight – but a picnic table and benches, hemmed by trellises strung with ivy, couched within the arbor of an inn, had proven irresistible. They had missed the dawn, sunrise, early morning light, and would have missed more had Brahms not been awakened by something wet and cold, floppy jowls and whiskers tickling his cheeks, a furry sniffing face peering from above. Recoiling from the sour breath, he fell off his bench. The spaniel, too, recoiled, sniffing next his boots, still on his feet. Raising himself on his elbows, Brahms blinked continually, shaking sleep from his eyes.

Karl grinned, rising from an adjacent bench. "If you could only see yourself!" His young face was stubbled and frowsy with sleep, cheek creased from a crack in his bench, hair tousled and limp with the night air, boots as dusty as Brahms's, dressclothes as wrinkled. "Too late for the sunrise." He pulled a watch from his pocket – "and too late to get back unnoticed."

Brahms returned his grin, sitting up straight, wiping his face, brushing limp blond hair behind his ears, accentuating the widow's peak evident at just twenty-four years. "Do I still have a position, do you think?"

"That depends. Am I not still the son of the Hofmarschall?"

Brahms grinned, saying nothing, his complexion and hair so pale he might have disappeared in a bright light, his eyes a blue no less pale, his face distinguished for the moment by a single red line, creased like Meysenbug's, by the bench on which he had spent the night.

"And can you not still play the Beethoven Sonata for Piano in C sharp minor?"

"Yes."

"And is it not the favorite composition of the Hofmarschall?"

Brahms got up, lightly kicking Meysenbug's foot. "And will you not stop asking questions? And should we not be getting back? And are you not hungry? And did you not sleep well last night?"

"Not so well as you until you woke up with that dog in your face. Did you think it was a *gittith*?"

People were stirring at the inn. A woman called from a window. "Herr von Meysenbug, would you and your friend like coffee?"

Meysenbug looked at Brahms who nodded. "Yes, please, Katerina, and quickly. We have little enough time."

Brahms shook his head. "I think you had better give it up. Our little excursion is sure to be discovered. We might as well enjoy our breakfast at leisure."

"Maybe you are right, but why take a chance? You saw how they were last night."

Brahms knew what he meant. The court retained etiquette from the days of perukes and powder. When in doubt you bowed, when not in doubt … you still bowed."

Katerina brought them black coffee, black bread, and butter. They ate hurriedly and were soon scurrying down the hill, forested with beeches, back to town. These were historic hills, inhabited once by Arminius, subsequently Hermann to the Germans, whose tribe had vanquished the legions of Publius Quintilius Varus in 9 A.D. driving the Romans forever from the Rhineland, who had been murdered in 21 A.D. by his in-laws, forgotten until the nineteenth century, and hailed continually since by some as the first man to envision a united Germany.

With the forest behind them, they continued to run along a beaten track flanked by rolling fields, but had barely reached the town gate when Meysenbug stopped – so suddenly Brahms bumped into him, almost knocking them both to the ground, but through a tornado of arms and legs they managed to keep their balance, laughing all the while. "Hey, man, Meysenbug! You must give a fellow some warning if you are going to stop like that!"

Meysenbug looked straight ahead and whispered. "All is lost! Aunt Ursula approaches, out for her morning constitutional."

"What?" He followed Meysenbug's gaze beyond the town gate. A woman was walking toward them wearing a black hat, veil fluttering behind like a sail. "Oh, I see her now. Do you think she has seen us?"

"I have no doubt. She has the eyes of a ferret – even without her spectacles."

"Ah!"

"She is an old crosspatch – like almost everyone else in Detmold. You will see."

They met the aunt at the gate. Meysenbug smiled. "Good morning, Aunty."

Brahms bowed. "Good morning, Fraulein von Meysenbug."

The aunt said nothing but surveyed them thoroughly, peering over her spectacles, absorbing their crushed hats, wrinkled dressclothes, loosened neckties, dusty shoes. "Pray, young Karl, what is the meaning of this?"

"It is nothing so very extraordinary as it appears, Aunty. Herr Brahms had a wish to see the sunrise from the Grotenburg. I merely did what any host would do to oblige an honored guest."

The aunt sighed so deeply, her bodice was so tight, that Brahms was afraid her buttons, running up to her neck, might snap. "Young Karl, do you not realize what a scandal you invite by appearing so dishevelled in the town for the perusal of any young maiden who happens to stand in her window?"

"I am sorry, dear Aunty, but our plans went awry. We did not plan to return so late. We planned to be indoors again before anyone knew we were gone – and the sooner we return the sooner we escape scandals we never meant to invite in the first place."

Brahms grinned; he could not imagine a more polite way to excuse themselves, but the aunt was clearly undaunted by a sight that might have daunted younger maidens and appeared unwilling to let them go easily. "I can understand Herr Brahms's wish, coming from Hamburg, unacquainted with our customs – but I cannot understand how you, young Karl, could have been so smallbrained as to expose him to such calumny, to stain his reputation even before it is made. He is too ideal an artist to commit such an extravagance so wilfully on his own." She turned to Brahms. "I apologize, Herr Brahms, for my nephew's indiscretion. He should have known better."

Brahms bowed his head. "It is kind of you, Fraulein von Meysenbug, to be concerned for my wellbeing, but you must not condemn Herr von Meysenbug. There is no musician who would not be proud to stain his reputation in such a manner."

The aunt frowned. "Explain yourself, Herr Brahms."

Brahms bowed his head again. "What I mean to say, Fraulein von Meysenbug, is that no less ideal a musician than Beethoven was given to wandering in the Wiener Wald. They say it is where he found his muse most often, and they say he was found there often himself in the most unbuttoned state."

The aunt tilted her head, the brim of her hat, and adjusted her spectacles, apparently the better to look at Brahms. He had appalled the court already once appearing sans collar, sans cravat. Apparently, he had forgotten to complete his dress, but appeared no less ready to compromise his already sorry reputation. "My dear Herr Brahms. Surely you understand we cannot all be Beethoven."

Brahms dropped his head, contrite. "No, of course not, Fraulein von Meysenbug, but maybe the closest we can come is to emulate his dress."

Meysenbug broke into a cough that would not stop. The aunt said nothing for a moment, but kept her hand on her spectacles, her eyes on Brahms. "Herr Brahms, some of us think Beethoven was a great composer, some of us disagree – but all of us are agreed that his dress was certainly not to be emulated. If we cannot emulate what was best in Beethoven, we must certainly not emulate what was worst."

Brahms kept his head bowed.

"Now hurry on back to your dwellings and prepare yourselves for the day. I am not sure what the Hofmarschall will have to say about this, but I will of course have to tell him."

Brahms and Meysenbug walked soberly into the town, breaking into giggles around the first corner, running down the street past the good burghers of Detmold in their nightcaps opening their windows, until they came to the house of Karl Bargheer, Konzertmeister of the Court Orchestra, once Joachim's pupil, with whom they shared their adventure.

Bargheer warned him. "You will have to get accustomed to a lot of that. The 'revered' court still resides in the eighteenth century."

Brahms did not mind; he had weighed his advantages carefully; he liked Detmold: large halftimbered houses interspersed with buildings of stone, turrets of the medieval castle overrun with ivy, moats overgrown with grass, the Teutoberger Wald within easy reach, friends like Meysenbug, Bargheer, and Julius Schmidt (the court cellist). His duties were minimal for the three months he had been hired – to conduct the choral society, tutor Princess Friederike on the piano, and perform for the court. Board and lodging, including meals and wine and a piano in his rooms at the best inn, zur Stadt Frankfurt across from the enclosure of the castle, were paid for. The great rooms among which he walked in the castle were hung with damask and Gobelin tapestries and lit by Murano glass chandeliers. He had access to the court orchestra and received almost six hundred thaler for the three months, enough to last him a year, allowing him time as well to compose, practise, travel, even give lessons to make more money if he wished from the countless ladies of the court, all of whom took piano lessons.

The year he had spent in Hamburg, giving concerts and lessons, visiting Clara (first in Dusseldorf, then in Berlin), had proven unsatisfactory, so had living again with his family (too crowded and noisy for serious work). Robert's incarceration had preoccupied them for so long that his death had found them in a state of unpreparedness – all except Clara who found greater purpose in his death than his life, spreading the gospel of Schumann across the continent. The Detmold appointment had resolved his problems. Mornings he worked, noon he dined with Bargheer at zur Stadt Frankfurt, afternoons hiked with friends through the Teutoberger Wald, evenings read, wrote letters, played music with friends late into the night; Sundays they picnicked all day. Suffering small minds was a small price to pay.

ii

Hans von Bulow, Liszt's favorite student, was an insect of a man, limbs like sticks, eyes bursting their sockets like bulbs, head no less a bulb though gaunt as a skull – but in his best humor, as he was now, he appeared almost handsome, his hair thicker, eyes less bulbous, face filling with a smile; even his canary yellow waistcoat reflected his cheer. He drew deeply on his cigar and exhaled a perfect plume of smoke. "Do you recall, dear Master, what you said to my mamma not even ten years past?"

Liszt's smile was ironic as he blew his own plume of smoke to entwine with Bulow's overhead and sipped coffee laced with cognac. His shoulders swayed as he put down his cup and fixed Bulow with his eyes. "My dear Hans, how could I forget?"

The diningroom of the Altenburg, draped and upholstered in red velvet, carpeted in burgundy, was cozy in the muted light of late afternoon; the Princess's silverware adorned shelves on the walls. Bulow shook his head. "I will never forget. It has made all the difference in my life, as you know."

Bulow and his mamma had attended a concert in Weimar conducted by Liszt in August 1850. Bulow, then twenty, torn between studying music to satisfy himself and law to satisfy his mamma, had studied both, music with Friedrich Wieck when the family had lived in Dresden, law at the University of Leipzig. Frau Bulow had been divorced the year before, Liszt had met them after the concert, pressed Frau Bulow's hand, embraced Bulow in farewell, and spoken fondly to his mamma. "I am very attached to this boy. I regard myself his father – and in ten years it will be the same."

Liszt had known the Bulows since the early Forties and accepted invitations to their home whenever he played in Dresden. Hans, a sickly child, had shown little interest in music until his ninth year, during a convalescence, when he had studied scores by Bach and Beethoven, the Old and New Testaments of music as he called them still, and had begun lessons. He had also studied law until he had renewed his friendship with Liszt during a visit to the Altenburg in 1848 and won him to his cause with his talent. Liszt had arranged for Bulow to visit Wagner in Zurich where he had apprenticed as a conductor for two seasons before returning to the Altenburg to resume studies at the piano with Liszt. Bulow liked to say that the B, L, and W in his name henceforth stood for Berlioz, Liszt, and Wagner, leaders of the New German School – though Berlioz was French, Liszt Hungarian, and Wagner exiled from Germany. "And now you are indeed my pappa in more ways than anyone might have guessed."

Liszt loved Hans as a son, as his musical heir, but less as a son-in-law, too familiar with his moods – but however accidentally he had only himself to blame for the nuptials. He had kept his daughters from the influence of their mamma, Marie d'Agoult, who had written a novel about their affair – false as all novels were false, falser for masquerading as truth – housed them instead in Paris with his own mamma and Princess Carolyne's old French governess, brought out of retirement from Russia for the purpose. The presence of the governess emphasized the importance of the Princess in his life, and not coincidentally in theirs, more than that of their mamma. He had forbidden contact with Marie, forbidden even her mention in his presence – but not even Liszt could guard against fate. His mamma and Carolyne's governess grew old, the daughters were brought first to Weimar for a visit, but returned to Berlin instead of Paris to stay with Frau Bulow, where they were taught the piano by her son. Bulow was ecstatic with his charges, the daughters of Liszt, but especially with Cosima; Blandine, the elder, clearly the prettier of the two, had many suitors, but Bulow saw service in marrying the younger plainer daughter, in giving the bastard child of the Master the prestige of his name, descended as he was from Count

Friedrich Bulow of Dennewitz, the composer-hero of Waterloo. Liszt spoke delicately. "Indeed, who could have known at the advent of this year that its close would see both my daughters wed?"

Liszt swayed as always to inaudible currents of music though less than Bulow remembered – but perhaps he appeared less restless only because he felt more rested himself. Most of Liszt's acquaintances complained of the influence of the Princess, but she had managed more than anyone to create the environment in which he had composed his major works; and Bulow imagined Cosima might do the same for him. He drew on his cigar, shaking his head, still smiling in wonder. "For me Cosima is greater than all women, not only because she bears your name but because she mirrors so closely your personality."

Liszt smiled, but not with his eyes. It was not the reason he would have wished someone to marry his daughter, but after Cosima consented there was little he could do, no paragon himself of marriage. Cosima was not unlike him in appearance either, their noses in particular, two sizes too large for their faces, stamping them father and daughter; but while his nose was perhaps his least perfect feature it was hardly Cosima's. At forty-six Liszt, in a black formfitting waistcoat, silk shirt, puffy white sleeves, remained slender as a youth, hawknose and high cheekbones giving him the aspect of an American Indian, as did the thick luxurious hair framing his face, but Cosima would never be lovely. Her sister Blandine called her the Stork – and not without reason, the resemblance was compelling, though Bulow saw in her only Liszt. "Even in her playing I recognize the *ipsissimum Lisztum*. She has much talent yet to be tapped."

Liszt's eyes narrowed as he held Bulow in their glare; his hair flared as he shook his head. "Her mamma saw in her the makings of a second Clara Schumann, but I disagreed –"

Bulow interrupted, losing momentarily his smile. "So do I! Madame Schumann plays like a woman – too much sentimentality – but Cosima plays like a man. It will be a revelation to see how she develops."

Liszt shook his head again. "That might be so, I do not deny it, but that was not the point of my disagreement. The life of a virtuoso is too strenuous, not the life for a woman – not the life I would wish for Cosima."

Bulow leaned back in his chair, blowing another plume of smoke, smiling again. "Of course, my dear sir. I merely meant her talent is strong enough to best Madame Schumann if she wished – but you are right. It is not the life for a woman." He laughed. "Mamma finds it too strenuous even for me."

Bulow had conducted the premiere in Berlin of Wagner's Tannhauser Overture and Venusberg music. His mamma had been in the audience, also Blandine and Cosima, Liszt had come from Weimar, Bulow had conducted magnificently, Wagner had trained him well – but he had been booed off the stage and fainted in the wings. He was criticized for making more of the score than it deserved, but Bulow recognized he might more fairly have been criticized for giving the score its due, for resisting the public's desire for merry melodies. Liszt and some supporters had stayed, the three women had returned home, Cosima had insisted they stay awake until he returned, but by the time Liszt pushed him through the front door it was two in the morning, only Cosima still awake, Blandine and Bulow's mamma having retired at midnight. Cosima and Hans had talked until dawn; he found her indispensable; she professed love. Liszt smiled, ironic again. "More importantly, women tend to be bound by tradition, they wish to conserve, men to explore. Madame Schumann is a good example. She always gives an exemplary performance, but it is always the same. I call that laziness – tradition is laziness. I have been accused of laziness myself because I do not always practise a work beforehand – but I do not practise because I do not wish to be tied to a single interpretation. I wish each performance to uncover something new, I wish each performance to be fresh."

Bulow nodded; he was familiar with what Liszt called the Pilate Offence, washing your hands of interpretation as if every pianist were an oarsman rather than a helmsman, and every conductor no more than a windmill. Inspiration was not to be communicated through words, too much reverence for old composers inhibited the growth of the new, and Liszt preferred instead to search beyond the letter of the composer's indications to the spirit. Beethoven had criticized Mozart on the same score – not for his musicality (that was beyond question), but his pianism. Mozart was more concerned with taste than expression, the first an eighteenth century concern, the second a nineteenth. Beethoven found Mozart's touch neat and clean, but flat, empty, and antiquated – in short, oldfashioned, but the oldfashioned way was good enough for his students. Beethoven could transcend the occasional false note himself with the force of his ideas and emotions, but not his students, and he advised them instead to do as he said, not as he did. "Of course, of course! I am the same as you, but Madame Schumann is like a statue for which our old friend Joachim has made himself the pedestal. I am afraid he and I will have a hard time recognizing each other when next we meet. We are moving in completely different directions."

Liszt nodded again patiently. Clara's joint concerts with Joachim in Berlin the past two winters had diminished prospects for all others, including Bulow. "I still hope to win him to our cause. Among violinists he has no peer, and his compositions would credit our cause no less."

"But he has made his choice – in all but name."

Liszt smiled. "Yes, in all but name he has made his choice – but his work belies his words. He does not write sonatas and symphonies and chamber works in four movements. He does not write absolute music like the old masters. His overtures – Hamlet, Henry IV, Demetrius – are symphonic poems no less than my own. They are New German works. You would think actions spoke louder than words – but he listens only to his words, not even to his own music."

Bulow's wide brow was corrugated with wrinkles. "I remember what Rubinstein said, and he is right. Joachim and his friend, Brahms, are indeed the high priests of virtue – purists – and Rubinstein's word is to be respected. He has tested his arms and attained a higher stage than Brahms. What is Brahms doing, brooding and hiding in Detmold, writing songs and conducting choirs in the forest? If that is the best he can do Schumann's prophecy has come to nothing after all, has it not?"

Anton Rubinstein, making a name for himself as a pianist second only to Liszt, had written devastatingly about Brahms to Liszt: *For the drawingroom Brahms is not graceful enough, for the concert hall not fiery enough, for the country not simple enough, for the town not cultured enough. I have little faith in such natures.* From what he had seen of Brahms onstage Liszt had concurred with Rubinstein's assessment. Brahms lacked the desire to please an audience, in both his programs and his performances (not a virtue in a virtuoso), but he had always been more interested in Brahms the composer than the performer. "It matters little to me what Brahms does, but I cannot say the same about Joachim. I wish he would not make such a stranger of himself. He was once of our family."

"Schumann's tragedy has bonded those three, but he might yet come to his senses."

Liszt shrugged. "Maybe, but I have better things to do than watch the sands run through their hourglass. I was happy indeed to hear Wagner is progressing well with his huge work."

Bulow leaned back again in his chair, smiling again. "Wagner could not have been happier. He said our visit was the most pleasant event of the autumn for him." Bulow and Cosima had been married in Berlin on 18 August, 1857, returned with Liszt to Weimar the same day, continued their honeymoon in Baden-Baden, Lausanne, and Zurich (where they had been Wagner's guests for a month in the Asyl, a house on the estate of the Wesendoncks, Wagner's patrons), after which they had returned to Weimar making brief stops along the way. Bulow had remained in Weimar, and Cosima returned to Berlin to set up their new home. "I could only cry in wonder at everything he showed me. I played *Rheingold* and *Walkure* from the transcriptions, and the first two acts of *Siegfried* from the pencil sketches, and I was reduced to the gibberish of a schoolgirl. 'Colossal!' and 'Unique!' and 'Heavenly!' I could say nothing else."

Liszt smiled. "I am not surprised to hear it. I cannot wait until the work is complete. I hope to convince the Duke to hold the premiere in Weimar. I told him Solomon was wrong. There *is* something new under the sun – but he talks about expenses." Liszt arched his eyebrows and sighed.

Bulow shook his head in sympathy. "Wagner also read to us daily from *Tristan*, and Cosima took his manuscript to bed every night to reread what he had read that day. She was so disturbed she was almost always in tears! She was much reserved with Wagner after that."

Liszt's mind appeared elsewhere. "One can forgive Wagner almost anything for the work he has undertaken."

Poor Bulow was not to know until later, nor was Liszt, but Cosima had recognized her mistake almost at once, her incompatibility with Bulow, and fallen immediately into an affair with his good friend, Karl Ritter. Bulow would have much to forgive Wagner, beginning with the honeymoon in Zurich when Cosima had prostrated herself before the composer, washing his feet with her tears, but it was more than he or Liszt or any rational being might then have guessed.

iii

"Jussuf! Happy New Year!"

The two friends embraced on the platform at Hanover as the train chugged away. "Happy New Year, Johannes! Detmold has been good to you, I see. That is a new coat you are wearing, is it not?"

"Indeed! I am rich, man, Jussuf, rich! It is a sin what they pay me for what I do."

Joachim wagged his finger. "Do not deprecate what a musician does, my friend. It is rare enough for most of us to find any work at all, let alone enough for a living."

Brahms picked up his bags. "Oh, believe me, I do not deprecate what we do. I count my blessings instead, man – groschen by groschen."

Joachim laughed, surprising himself. "Hah! Men have lost their souls for such blessings."

"Hah, yourself! It is, then, too late for me already."

Joachim grinned, glad for the company of his friend for however brief a time before he boarded the train for Hamburg. He took one of Brahms's bags from him. "Two bags! Since when have you become such a heavy traveler, my friend?"

"Since it is the holiday season. Since I am going home."

Joachim understood. They had already exchanged presents through the post, a music encyclopedia for Brahms, a pouch of tobacco for Joachim. "Shall we take a cab?"

"Why do we not walk? I am tired of sitting – and I am not yet done with sitting for the day."

"Very well, if that is your wish. The air is just bracing enough for a nip, but not for a bite."

"Well, I do not know that it is any advantage to be nipped than to be bitten, but there is nothing I like better than a good long walk – except a good long talk."

"You shall have both – we shall both have both. When do you have to be back?"

"One o'clock. We have plenty of time."

They left the station, each carrying a bag, Brahms setting a brisk pace, turning to his friend. "What do you hear from Clara? How is it with her?"

"Have you not heard from her?"

Brahms longed for news of Clara, but preferred to get it from friends, afraid too direct an inquiry might say more than he wished. Since their parting at Gersau he had blamed himself for leaving her – while crediting himself no less for his good sense. He hardly understood his feeling, wishing her well, but not if she could be well without him – and not if she could be well with him either. "Yes, but I wondered if you had heard anything different. She is always depressed when she writes to me – and, besides, you have toured with her recently."

Joachim pursed his lips, a moue of regret. "I wish I could say it was different. She is happiest when she is performing. She is then with her husband again – most assuredly when she plays his work. You see it as soon as she mounts the stage when she is so heartily welcomed, when she strikes her first notes her face turns radiant – and with her last bow she reverts back to her melancholy, like Cinderella. I noticed it during the last season, when we played in Dresden and Leipzig – but she continued by herself, as you know, from Augsburg through Munich. She was recently in Switzerland again and plans to be in London again this year. I know of no one who works as hard as she does."

Brahms shook his head. He often doubted he had done right by Clara, but never acted on the doubt. "It is a shame. I do not see that she needs to do it. You will never find me in that land of fog everlasting."

"Ah, do not be so certain of that, my friend. There is much in England to commend. After London every other place seems provincial and small, everything must be scaled back a little. It is a great city – and a more musical city than is generally credited."

"Yes, yes, Clara never tires of commending the city to me. I could live comfortably for a month she says on two hundred thaler – but I can live on less, and more comfortably, anywhere in Germany. Besides, I see quite enough of Englishmen in Germany, and I am not so very sure that I like what I see. Just because their empire spans the globe they imagine there are no better people in the world than Englishmen. They imagine they are overlords as well in Germany. No, thank you, my friend. I am not for England and England is not for me."

Joachim raised his eyebrows. "I did not know you felt so strongly."

Brahms had meant to speak humorously, but recognized the seep of his bitterness. Four years had passed since Robert's prophecy and he had yet to make it his own. Detmold had brought him time, shielded him from the glare of the world, but not from his own. "Jussuf, I do not know sometimes if I was meant to be a composer after all. My choir rehearsals in Detmold make me aware of my limitations. I lack practicality. My understanding of orchestration is frightful. I cannot imagine Mozart or Beethoven floundering under such a predicament."

Joachim frowned. "If everyone compared himself with Mozart and Beethoven we would nevermore have new music. That is foolish talk."

Brahms shrugged. "But I am not good enough even for Brahms – or, at least, for what I imagine Brahms to be, and I do not know if I will ever be good enough. I have spent too much time already on the D minor, and it is still – after almost four years – still so very unsatisfactory. I should wait, I should be patient, but waiting brings its own evils – and I would not have got even so far without your help."

Joachim was careful what he said; he had been a midwife no less than his friend to the Piano Concerto in D minor, but he had helped only with orchestration in which Johannes had neither training nor experience. The entire edifice had been constructed, foundation to turrets, by Johannes, all themes, all developments. "Not to me – it is not unsatisfactory to me. It is more satisfactory to me than the work of any other living composer. When I see what you are doing with your D minor, and when I see what Liszt has done with his E flat, I am never in doubt about the future of music. Could the concerto be better? Yes, absolutely, of course – but so could the first concertos of Mozart and Beethoven. Everything will come out if only you do not succumb."

Brahms respected Joachim's opinion, but said nothing.

"Johannes, you know of the problems I have with my own D minor – but do you know what is my biggest problem?"

He had been writing a concerto for the violin. "What?"

"I ask myself continually: what is the point of composing when there is a Brahms in the world? That is my biggest problem."

Brahms laughed.

"Yes, yes, you can laugh, my friend, but to me it is not so very funny. I tell myself to concentrate on performing instead and to leave the composing to Brahms. What do you say to that?"

"What do *I* say? I say you are too modest. That is what I say."

"*I* am too modest! *Brahms* says Jo*ach*im is too modest! That is rich! That is rich, indeed! We are like two little old ladies, giving each other the palm. We cannot even acknowledge our own excellences."

"But it is true. You need no help with orchestration. You are, yourself, the compleat composer. I am only half."

Joachim shook his head. "That is a halftruth itself. What I know I learned because Mendelssohn insisted I play with the Gewandhaus during my apprenticeship – and as Liszt's konzertmeister I had still more exposure to the orchestra. Besides, remember, Liszt had his own concerto orchestrated by Raff – but that, too, is not of consequence. Orchestration is no more than paint, a mask – it can be used to enhance the meaning of a work, but also to hide meaninglessness. Liszt's weapons are virtuosity and ornamentation, yours are logic and harmony. He is better able to gloss his difficulties than you are able at present to meet yours – but when you succeed, and succeed you will, you will show them what can be done with a concerto for the piano. I know whereof I speak, man. If nothing else, that much I know."

Brahms was silent again. Joachim put a hand on his shoulder. "Let me tell you something else, about my own concerto. You see, what I wished more than anything else was clarity – and soon after I was finished I felt a certain passage was too long – so what do you think I did?"

"You recast it."

Joachim pushed his friend playfully. "*Exact*ly – to make it clearer, but it came out longer than before! Do you know what I said then?"

Brahms pushed him back. "What?"

Joachim pushed him again. "I said Brahms would know how to fix this – but unfortunately I am no Brahms!"

Brahms pushed him back again. "Hah! Everyone should be so fortunate!"

Joachim pushed back. "Hah, yourself! And if you push me one more time I will leave your bag on the road."

Brahms pushed. "And I will tell everyone they have no presents because Joachim left my bag on the road."

Joachim laughed and kept the bag. "They will never believe you. Your good mamma loves me too well. Frau Schumann keeps a portrait of me in her sittingroom that your mamma sent."

"That she does, but they will believe what I say. They do not love you better than they love me."

"Maybe not yet!"

They put down the bags, overcome with laughter. Finally, Brahms put his arm around his friend and they walked on. "So tell me what else has been affecting you of late?"

Joachim became more serious. "I received another letter from Liszt."

"Another? What does he say, the old swindler?"

Joachim plucked a letter from his breast pocket and handed it to Brahms. "Read it yourself."

Brahms unfolded the letter with one hand and read as they walked:

My Dear Joachim,

What a long time it has been since I heard from you! I hear you have been in the Tyrol, in Venice, in Heidelberg, and God knows where else! I saw your pappa in Pesth and several other of your acquaintances, who gave me the news. How much better it would have been had I received the news directly from you, but a wall of dense mist appears to have come between us. Let it not be too long before the sun shines again. We have not seen as much of each other as we were once accustomed, my dear friend, but let us always remain comrades as befits two fellows such as ourselves. Others more intimate with you may attempt to make you doubt my friendship, but let their trouble be in vain.

Your viola pieces are magnificent. They soothe and refresh me. I wish I might have written them myself, but I am happier yet that they are by you. I have saluted heartily the innumerable kings of Hanover who roam through their landscapes.

Hartel will have sent you my things – or, rather, my "nothings." Even if you do not care for them, let them not place an apple of disunity between us. No less a man than Goethe once said: "It is a grave fault when a man rates himself either higher or lower than his worth." I wish to avoid this fault, which accounts for the objectivity of my survey of my own accomplishments, and the objectivity with which I would hope any man might take the measure of your old friend,

F. Liszt

"It is a kind letter."

"It is, is it not? You see my predicament, do you not? My friends know how I feel about his music, Liszt knows himself, but the world thinks I am his acolyte, one of his New Germans. I am nothing of the kind, and yet Liszt has been nothing if not kind to me – and, yet again, I feel false in his company. If I meet him again I will have to tell him what I think, that I find he has a greater regard for the effect of his music than for its depth, that I find him cunning – and yet again, no one was kinder to me when Mendelssohn died. He gave me a home among musicians I esteemed, who became my friends – but who now follow paths that are alien to my beliefs. Ach, it is enough to drive a man mad."

Brahms returned the letter. "I would like Liszt better without his acolytes – but he must have his chorus of yeasayers around him."

"That is not what bothers me. I was one of his yeasayers, and gladly so – but I can yeasay his music no more, nor his crimping and cringing for effect on the stage. He is so restless in everything he does. I wish I could change him, but I do not have that kind of strength. He has too strong a personality for me to speak my mind in his presence. I would feel presumptuous."

Brahms nodded; his own feelings about Liszt remained far from untangled. "Clara feels not unlike yourself."

Joachim nodded. Clara had refused to perform a concerto at the Mozart Centenery Festival in Vienna because Liszt was conducting. He needed to make a similar public gesture. "Frau Schumann has at least made her feelings known. I must do the same – in the right time."

> I *hear* my sweet*heart*
> He's *swing*ing his *ham*mer
> It *thun*ders, it *cla*mors,
> Its *sound* travels *far*
> Like *bells* from a*far*
> *Wheeen* he *works* at his *art.*

Joachim had likened Agathe von Siebold's voice to the clear steady tone of an Amati violin. Brahms grinned in her wake, knapsack on his back holding her sketchbook, his notebook, a picnic lunch, and blanket, playing an imaginary keyboard with his fingers, voicing the part he had written for the piano to "The Blacksmith," accenting the beats. "Tink *tunk*-tink, tunk *tink*-tunk, tink *tunk*-tink, tunk *tink*-tunk, tink *tunk*-tunk, tunk *tink*-tunk, tink-*tunk!*"

They walked along a narrow path on a hillside, shaded by cypresses, beeches, chestnuts, firs, showing the plumage of late summer. Agathe turned briefly, giving him a breathless laugh before returning to the path and the second verse – and he continued his accompaniment. Her waist was impossible to discern swaddled in her dress, but her laugh was a compliment considering her serious demeanor, and he was full of appreciation for the swell of her hips and the heels of her tiny black shoes peeking rhythmically from the bell of her dress.

> He *sits* among *sparks*
> My *hard*working *dar*ling
> As *black* as a *star*ling
> But *if* I go *past*
> His *bel*lows blow *fast*
> *Aaand* he's *bright* in the *dark.*

"Tink *tunk*-tink, tunk *tink*-tunk, tink *tunk*-tink, tunk *tink*-tunk, tink *tunk*-tink, tunk *tink*-tunk, tink-*tuuuunk!*" He had exchanged his piano for a hammer and anvil and grinned as he reached the cadence. The path widened and she laughed, falling back in line with him. "Oh, Johannes, that was so much fun!"

He loved her voice, she his songs – and was that not a kind of marriage? even a prelude to the other? She had a pretty face, but resisted prettification, refused to powder her face, crimp her hair, or blacken her lashes. She parted her long black hair in the middle and pulled it behind her ears in a bun – unlike her stout sister, Josephine, who braided her hair in coils over her ears, and wore dresses with double flounces and tripletiered sleeves. He smiled, taking her hand, saying nothing.

She returned the smile. "We are almost there, Johannes – my valley is around the next bend. Then you will see what I mean."

His return to Hamburg had been disappointing. The family, supplemented by his income, had moved to 74 Hohe Fuhlentwiete, an old narrow street, spacious rooms, the parlor large enough to hold an open fireplace flanked by hobs, his own room to hold a desk, bookcase, washstand, piano mounted with a bust of Beethoven, sofa doubling as a bed, prints on the wall, one of da Vinci's Last Supper, and the apartment itself to hold two additional boarders – but privacy remained elusive in so inhabited a dwelling.

He had visited Clara during April in Berlin, enjoyed the art galleries, music they had played, but they had also quarreled. He had said that she admired his work too indiscriminately, she that he should find himself a nice young wife. He wondered sometimes if he goaded her to say such things, unsure whether he needed forgiveness for leaving without warning or permission to court another.

He had returned again to Hamburg, almost with relief, to find an invitation to Gottingen for the summer from Grimm, recently married: *If it would please you to have a few good voices lodged in some very lovely young girls, they will be pleased to be at your disposal. You will have time for composition and we will have performances of your work – if that is your wish. Come quickly!* He had left almost immediately; Clara was to follow later with all her girls and Felix, so was Joachim from England, but in the meantime he had met Agathe, Grimm's student in harmony, a professor's daughter, and would not have minded seeing no one else.

The path widened and as they turned the bend he understood what she had meant. The colors of autumn glittered along the hillside, red and brown and rust and sienna, mixed with the still lingering greens of summer. "It is like a quilt, is it not, Johannes, a patchwork of many colors?"

"Like Joseph's cloak, yes, you are right."

"Yes, that is a nice way to see it – but here is the point I wish to make. Do you remember the house I showed you before we left Gottingen?"

"Yes?"

"Do you not see how the patchwork on the hillside resembles the facade of the house?"

Flowers had overflowed their troughs from the windows of the house: roses, carnations, camellias, crysanthemums, and sunflowers had painted the walls in squares and rectangles of color; ivy had provided the wash. He squeezed her hand. "They are both like quilts!"

She returned the squeeze, bouncing on her toes. "Ah, I *knew* you would see it! I *knew* you would see it!"

Brahms removed his knapsack. "They are like a theme and variations."

"You are a musician, indeed, Johannes. That is e*xact*ly what I wished you to see. It is this harmony in nature I find so meaningful – a harmony I attempt to sketch and that you compose so well."

"No! What you mean is that I attempt to compose, and that *you* sketch so well."

"No, Johannes, it is as *I* say!"

"No, it is not! You are too modest!"

"No, I am not, no more modest than yourself!"

He was smiling again, facing her. "Well, now, that I can accept – that we are modest in each other's behalf."

Agathe was still, no longer bouncing, not even smiling, but she still held his hand and stood closer than before. "That I like, that we are modest in each other's behalf. That I like very much."

Her eyelids descended, narrowing her dark eyes; her lashes, fine and long, fluttered; her fragrance was strong between them. Brahms dropped her hand, put his arms around her, held her tight, and kissed her lips before whispering in her ear. "Gathe, it is so sweet to feel the way I do when I am with you. I think I might just evaporate like a chord and float into the atmosphere."

She held his head like a grail, hands gentle on his ears, brushing his hair, marveling at its paleness, so perfectly matching the paleness of his eyes. "And what chord would that be?"

"It would have to be a minor chord."

"Oh, but that is too sad. Why would it have to be a minor chord?"

"Because I would then no longer be with you."

She laughed. "Oh, you are a flatterer, but you must be a major chord. There is no reason you should not be a major chord with me. You must always be a major chord."

"I will be. I will be a C major chord!"

"Ah, that is how I like to hear you talk."

Brahms's voice softened, his smile disappeared. "I love you, Gathe."

Agathe could hardly believe the evidence of her eyes and ears: a genius (for that was what everyone said) was in love with her – handsome as a hero in a drama by Schiller – but this it seemed was her destiny. She closed her eyes, gave him her lips, and they kissed again, more slowly. She did not want to let him go after the kiss and nestled her head against his, resting her chin on his shoulder, holding him close.

Brahms was no less in the thrall of destiny. This was the meaning of life, his head overflowing with music, his arms around a pretty girl. The time in Detmold and walks through the Teutoberger Wald had focused him on what was important; life was simple, meant to be lived simply; looking too deeply you lost yourself, feeling too much you hurt yourself, and thinking too much you only grew old. Kissing Gathe was its own meaning, its own reward. If you looked too far you missed what was in front of your face. He spoke without moving. "Shall we eat?"

"No. I want to stand here with you for just a little while longer, just as we are."

They remained standing, arms around each other.

Agathe was the first then to break the silence. "Herr Grimm has given me an exercise in composition. I hate to do it because I am not very good and he always scolds me when I make mistakes."

"Ach! Grimm? Grimm scolds you? He dares!"

Agathe smiled. "He is my teacher first, Johannes. Should he pat me on the back when I make a mistake?"

Brahms grinned. "Ha! I have an idea. We will surprise him. I will do your exercise for you. Then let us see what he says."

"But do you not think he will know that I have not done the exercise myself?"

"Not if I am careful to make some mistakes."

"But then he will scold me in any case."

"Tchhah! He will not dare!"

ii

Not wishing to make Agathe jealous Brahms had warned her that he would need to spend time alone with Clara – but he resented the sacrifice more than Agathe, recognizing Clara's incongruity within the group, at thirty-nine the oldest by far, Grimm was next in age at thirty-one, then Philippine his wife, Joachim, Brahms, Agathe – and Clara's children: Marie (seventeen), Elise (fifteen), Julie (thirteen), Eugenie (six), and Felix (four). Ludwig and Ferdinand (ten and nine) had been placed in a boarding school in Herchenbach and sequestered for the summer for their disappointing scholastic performance, a punishment Brahms was convinced benefitted Clara more than either of the boys. At twenty-five, Brahms was closer in age to the girls than to the mamma, but arriving in a white muslin dress with black sprigs and a black sash Clara appeared almost as slim as her daughters, even shorter than her oldest, only her expression so solemn, her smile so dutiful, her conviviality so restrained, separated her from the others – her aspect more than her age.

In Dusseldorf the difference had not mattered, nor anywhere else, but their time apart had exposed the contrivances that had bound them: the rapture with which the Schumanns had welcomed him; their recognition of his talent; their celebrity and worldliness; his innocence and susceptibility; and, overshadowing everything, tragedy too romantic and profound to be borne. He regretted nothing, but understood too well how his perceptions and responses had been bloated out of proportion by events too large for his young mind: a genius had attempted suicide, incarcerated himself in an asylum, and died two and a half years later, his young widow spreading the gospel of his music; and he, little Hannes from Hamburg, had ferried messages from husband to wife and wife to husband, loving both wife and husband, unable to come to terms with either, making all decisions in one long ecstatic swoon, reaching for the sky, legs paddling air.

How much simpler was his love for Gathe, devoid of torment, of considerations other than their own contentment. He never denied culpability in his relations with Clara, it was no fault of hers that he had stayed in Dusseldorf, nor that he had fallen in love, nor even that they had gone separate ways after Gersau, but he had finally found his ground. The high spirits of the students in Gottingen, Gathe's quiet ministrations, Clara's dour presence, all indicated he had made the right decision, but he would always feel indebted to Clara and always resentful of the debt.

Without realizing it, he found himself retracing steps with Clara he had recently traced with Agathe, past the street of the house overflowing with flowers, along the path leading to the valley, the hillside patchwork of autumnal colors.

"Will you go back to Detmold in October?"

She had asked the question directly, but her gaze seemed directed elsewhere. "Yes, but as late as I possibly can. I hate to leave Gottingen. This has been my happiest summer – ever."

They were outside the town, no one in sight. She took his hand in both of hers and squeezed. He had changed before her eyes, her angelfaced boy, to a young man. He remained serious, as she wished, but more at peace, confident of his place in the world as a man as he had not been as a boy. He remained long in the face, but his mouth curved at the corners, seeming to harbor unspoken riddles. He had always been handsome, but the puppyfat of boyhood was yielding to the chiseled features of a man. "You are right. It is nice, indeed, to be, all of us, together again, in such improved circumstances. It was good of Grimm to invite us all, was it not?"

Brahms left his hand limp in Clara's. That was not what he had meant, but whether she had intentionally misunderstood he could not say. She had surprised him with her smile and he recalled how pretty she was, prettier than Gathe, her face less round, more thoughtful, her gaze more grave even when she smiled. The sun gave a sheen to her straight dark hair, parted down the middle like Gathe's, over her ears in a bun behind, framing her brow like a black scarf, a black ribbon her only nod to vanity. He wished to tell her about Gathe, but found himself saying what was of no consequence to cover what was. "Indeed, Ise could not have done better."

If she had not known before she knew it now. When he refused to look at her, when his hand remained limp, she knew what it was he could not say. "She is a nice girl, is she not?"

She felt his hand stiffen, but his voice betrayed nothing, his eyes remained focused ahead. "Gathe? Yes, she is. I am exceedingly fond of her."

"And she of you?"

"I would like to think so."

"She has a lovely voice. That is certainly an asset."

Brahms found courage. "More than that, she has all a man could want in a wife."

"Ah, yes, of course, how comforting to be ordinary and have so ordinary and easy a life. A large family that loves you, a large house in which to dwell, to learn how to sketch, and music, as if they were no more than handicrafts with which to amuse a husband – or children – and, of course, the luxury of learning how to cook and maintain a household for your husband, who will take care of everything else – a professor like her pappa, or a lawyer or a merchant or someone who makes at least as much money. Such an enviable life, do you not think so?"

She was right, but he resented her speaking so freely when he had not asked her opinion. He took his hand away. "Not necessarily – her husband would not necessarily have to make as much money. Gathe is not so very materialistic."

Clara was surprised herself how freely she spoke and recognized that she carried bitterness in her skin, but not that it was unseemly. "Of course, she is not – she has never had to think about it. It is so much more romantic to imagine you can live on love and roses and picnics, but she will soon tire of that – and what about children?"

Brahms laughed. "Clara, you get too far ahead of yourself. No one is thinking about children, not even about marriage."

She looked at him without mirth. "Well, it seems to me that if no one is thinking about it, someone *should* be thinking about what someone is doing – or people will get the wrong impression."

"Aah, Clara, you are so suspicious. Nobody is getting the wrong impression. We are merely enjoying what is given to us, letting nature take its course – and you should do the same."

"I would if I could, I am sure – if I knew what it was that was given to me – but life holds little enough in store for me now."

He grimaced. "Tchhah, Clara! That is stupid thinking. You must learn to keep your melancholy within bounds. Life is good, but if you abandon yourself to the bad times you will miss the good times when they stare you in the face. The more you learn to greet your bad times with calm the more you will enjoy the good times that inevitably follow."

She was accused often of melancholy and solemnity and sobriety as if they were crimes; even her pappa had encouraged her to court the affection of the public; but she was no coquette. She had felt Johannes understood her better, sharing so intimately her loss of Robert, but however much he and Robert might have loved each other it paled before the love she had shared with her husband, and he knew nothing of her earlier losses, her mamma to divorce before she was five, the nurse of her childhood years in her teens, her pappa to the madness of ambition, her first son Emil to an infant death, her two miscarriages. She had borne everything through dedication to art: indeed, she relieved her soul when she played as if she cried herself out. "That is easy for you to say. You do not know what I feel. I wish only to see my children settled – and my friends happy. Beyond that, what does anything matter?"

Brahms laughed again. "That is too dramatic, Clara. Your friends will be happy if you are happy. Believe what I say. Such passions as you feel are not natural. They are always the exception. The ideal man is calm, both in joy and sorrow, but when passions burst their limits they boil the blood like a sickness and their victim would do well to seek a cure. That is what I have learned from our past."

"Oh, Johannes, these are cold words indeed, especially coming from you. It has been said that ours is the Romantic age, and that the Romantic seeks to burst all limits. What is the good of limits if they keep us from our true selves?"

"But they do not! It is one thing to be a Romantic in your work, but quite another to be a Romantic in your life. I am willing to push hard my musical limits, but if I push too hard at the limits of my life I will only lose myself. I will never accomplish anything." He shook his head, exasperated; she was not looking at him. "It is not I who say these things, Clara. It was Goethe. When he called the Classical age healthy and the Romantic diseased, he was not talking about the destruction of art, but of human lives. He was talking about people like Rousseau and Hoffmann and Shelley and Byron and Poe, who lived their lives too intensely for their own comfort." He could have mentioned Robert, but left her to draw her own conclusion.

It was easier to lose your sanity than to regain it – but that was not a subject for discussion like a Christmas goose or a Whitsuntide festival. "Goethe wrote about it best in *The Sorrows of Young Werther* – but, of course, you know the book."

He could not tell her he had once been Werther to her Lotte, the married woman for whose unrequited love Werther had killed himself. He could not tell her about his String Quartet in C sharp minor, begun in part to exorcise his feeling for her, which he had left incomplete. He could not tell her he wished to avoid the fate of the Romantics. He could not tell her he wished *her* to avoid their fate.

She remained silent and he felt her silence like a rebuke, tightening the guilt in his temples. "Clara, you must not be unhappy. You must find the things that make you happy and you must pursue them. You must make the resolution every morning when you wake that you will be happy. That is all I am saying – and I say it because I wish you to be happy."

She faced him triumphantly then. "I *do* pursue the things that make me happy. Your music makes me happy, but when I have told you about it you have chastised me – and that makes me unhappy."

She was referring to their quarrel when he had visited her in Berlin. "Tchhah, Clara! Do not bring that up again. That is behind us. Let us not quarrel about that again."

She shook her head, holding up her hands in exasperation. "I do not wish to quarrel with you, Johannes, but I *do* wish to understand. Do you not believe me when I tell you your music makes me happy? Do you not believe how happy I am to make others aware of your work? Do you not believe that it is no blind enthusiasm that fires me with these feelings? When I have disagreed with this or that about your work have I not made my disagreement known? I simply cannot understand why you deny me this one great pleasure I have left. This I know, I feel it in my bones, that you are one upon whom heaven has poured its greatest gifts, but more and more I realize that even with regard to music I am to fetter myself – and *that* I find more painful than anything."

Brahms had been shaking his head all the while she spoke; the hillside dissolved to nothing, the plumage of late summer in the valley to a faded quilt. "If that is what you think, Clara, you misunderstand me completely. Of course, I value the pleasure of my friends, and you know only too well whose pleasure I value the most, but what I wish is that people who might resist my work at first would be compelled upon hearing it again to succumb. That would ensure a more lasting victory than if you were to attempt to arouse in others an enthusiasm to match your own. Art is a republic. You cannot expect others to agree with you when you place one artist above another. The work must win its own champions."

The warmth of the autumn and colors of the sun were no less lost on Clara than on Brahms. Hearing him speak she had shaken her head no less than he had shaken his listening to her. "Johannes, I do not know anymore who misunderstands whom. I wish you would interpret my feelings with a little more generosity and not see fit to smother my enjoyment with such cold philosophizing. Anyone would think I was too emotional a person to be believed, who worshipped you like a god, and that is surely more presumptuous of you than it is for me to share my enthusiasm with others – and to accuse me of en*thu*siasm, as if it were a crime!" She walked quickly as if she wished to get away. "You know I only express myself freely with people I think will like your work. I do not tell them what to think, I only ask them to listen – and if I am not to share my enthusiasm with my friends what is the point of it, of my enthusiasm, of my friends? Should I share it with my enemies? Should I nevermore be enthusiastic about anything? And if that were not enough you say now that I should *will* myself to be happy? I do not understand you at all."

He bent his head, watching his feet as they walked, unable to say what he wished. He did not resent enthusiasm, not from anyone else, but her enthusiasm shackled him, kept him from moving ahead, dragged him back to Dusseldorf, tied him securely to the past, to a time when he had needed from her something other than enthusiasm and not known it himself. If she meant to pay him back for his years of sacrifice with no more than enthusiasm he wanted none of it. Enthusiasm he could get anywhere he wished, but what more she could have done he could not say; his resentment of her enthusiasm was resentment against himself – a resentment he was still unable to explain.

Her voice broke when she realized he was not going to say anything. "Oh, I am so sick of this bickering between two who would pass for friends – and over what? That I love your music too much, my friend's music? Why you wish to destroy the beautiful confidence which enables me to tell you everything I simply cannot understand." She shook her head in disbelief. "I have been studying your concerto now and find myself in raptures over it, but I am afraid I will be rebuked for liking something so estimable. I do not understand you at all. I always imagined I understood you, you who are so difficult to understand, and I imagined you gained some comfort from my understanding, but I was wrong. I do not understand you at all. I imagined I recognized your worth in music as did few others, that my recognition brought you some comfort, but again I was wrong. I understand nothing, and my enthusiasm is no more than a wedge between us, an impediment to our friendship – or for what passes for friendship." She made no attempt to dry her cheeks, shook her head in bewilderment. "I confess I am lost, completely lost. I give it all up, all claim to your friendship, to understanding you or your work – if that is what you wish. Tell me if that is what you wish."

"That is not what I wish."

She waited, but he said nothing more, appeared entirely unsympathetic, looked past her, retired into silence, and she felt sorrier for herself, afraid she would lose him forever. "Johannes?"

"Yes?"

"I have not been well, you know. You know of my recent troubles."

She meant her bouts of rheumatism, first in Munich, inflammation brought on by exertion, also a chill, which had immobilized her for more than a week, canceled concerts, the pain like red hot irons tearing the bones from the left side of her body, for which she had been given opium, but had remained exhausted, constantly on the brink of fainting; next, in Geneva, her right side, the same problem. She had written to him and he had been sympathetic, but not anymore, afraid where sympathy might lead, unconvinced her tears were not for his benefit. "Yes, I know."

"Do you know – well, since you have quoted Goethe, so can I. Goethe said as well that the only reality, and that which begets further realities, is the pleasure, joy, and sympathy we find in things. Everything else is vain and merely destructive."

Brahms nodded, still looking away. "I do not disagree. I merely advise moderation, recognizing the limits."

He spoke so soberly she almost screamed. "You advise joy within limits? I do not understand what that means. If joy is good, then surely a boundless joy is a boundless good – and just as surely a joy with boundaries is no joy at all. I do not understand you, Johannes. I feel as if you resent my very presence and I do not understand it."

He took a deep breath. "If you do not understand it, I cannot explain it further. I do not understand it myself." He had given the matter more thought than she imagined, but said nothing more because it made no more sense to him than to her. Away from her he was happy, but he could not be away from her long. With Gathe he was happy, but it was a puppypure happiness, and puppyprofound. In Clara he had invested his blood, but she seemed no longer constituted for happiness. Gathe would allow him Clara's friendship, she would insist upon it, she would even be the happier for it – but Clara's friendship would then be impossible. Clara would allow him Gathe's friendship no less – but if he could be sure of Clara, Gathe's friendship would not matter. Perhaps Gathe mattered only because he could not be sure of Clara; perhaps, even, Gathe's love mattered less than Clara's friendship – but to be sure of Clara he would have to change himself, reconstitute himself, possibly to the detriment of his work, her needs would have to be counted sometimes before his, the needs of her children – but with Gathe his needs would always come first – but he would need to provide for Gathe as he would never need to provide for Clara. Clara could provide better for him than he ever could for her, as she had provided for Robert.

The valley spread its patchwork before them, the numberless shades of autumn, but Clara's vision was too blurred to see even daisies along their path. "Shall we go back?"

"Maybe we should."

They walked back in silence, their picnic lunch uneaten, but as they reached Gottingen Brahms spoke again. "Clara?"

"Yes?"

"You say you do not understand me, but that is not your fault. I hardly understand myself. Everyone I know, and you more than anyone, thinks me different from what I am. I am never quite as happy as I appear. I fluctuate constantly myself between contentment and depression, but because I hate to speak of it people imagine I am different from what I am. No one is better aware than myself of how much I lack genius, even mere skill, and when I am praised exorbitantly, even if you might think it justifiable, I am only made the more uncomfortable – but when I am pleased that others like my work, most of all yourself, then people imagine I am confident and smug – which, in fact, is one more misunderstanding about me. I am not so very sure of my powers, but I hate to talk about it. Can you understand that? Does that make a difference for you? More than this I cannot say."

Clara smiled and squeezed his hand again, happier with the consolation of his attempt than the words, the compassion in his face and voice. "My dearest Johannes, of course, it does. I thank you for telling me. I wish you would talk more to me as you have just done. It makes everything easier to bear. It softens my poor heart again."

He nodded; it also tightened the bond between them, made more complex what he wished to simplify, but he said nothing, left his hand limp in hers, wishing he had said nothing after all. All attempts at understanding became fetters to a past he wished to transcend.

CLARA STAYED IN THE SAME HOUSE as Grimm. When they returned, both Agathe and Grimm greeted them, smiles for Clara, glares for Brahms. Agathe clapped her hands in his face as if she were shooing a goose.

Brahms understood what had happened and laughed. "What? Why are you hitting at me? What is the matter?"

"You – you prankster! You know very well what is the matter! Do not pretend you do not! You will only make it worse for yourself!"

"Ah, well, then, I confess – to what I do not know, but I will confess."

Clara looked at Grimm for an explanation. He was laughing himself. "Johannes has played a joke on us both."

Agathe turned to Clara. "I told Johannes that I was having difficulty with an exercise in composition that Herr Grimm had set for me – and he said he would do the exercise himself, he said we would astonish Herr Grimm."

"And astonish me he did. It is the most terrible composition I have ever seen – one of the finest examples of bad composition it has ever been my privilege to witness – and I said as much to Gathe."

Clara smiled in spite of herself.

Agathe turned to Clara. "Well, I was so embarrassed I was speechless, but Herr Grimm was so angry that finally I had to say something."

"And she said, in just such a voice –" Grimm mimicked Agathe, "'but what if Johannes had written it?'" He looked at Agathe. "At first, of course, neither of us realized what the rogue had done."

Agathe turned to Clara. "You should have heard Herr Grimm then." She mimicked Grimm, a deeper voice, hands clutched in fists by her side, rocking on her feet. "'Then it would be all the worse!'"

Grimm and Agathe stared at each other; Grimm turned again to Clara. "Then, of course, we realized Johannes had been fooling us both."

Still Clara smiled; Agathe raised her hands to clap them again in Brahms's face but he was outside already, running to the house he shared with Joachim, his laughter faint as he ran down the street.

iii

Clara could not have said what she had expected, but the holiday was turning into no holiday. She was not shy to admit her jealousy of Johannes, but jealousy she could bear if he paid her the respect she deserved. Agathe was welcome to his attention, but not at the cost of attention to herself. Even that she could have borne, she wielded no rights, no ties to bind them, but he paid more attention to everyone, even to the servants.

She had looked forward to a parade of gay days among friends, but he had spoiled it as he now spoiled everything. His experience with the orchestra in Detmold had interested him in composing for instruments other than the piano; the party had just returned from an afternoon performance of his nonet (flute, bassoon, horn, two clarinets, four strings), everyone plying suggestions. She had as much to say as anyone, but said nothing, sure that he cared for neither her suggestions nor herself. He never solicited her opinion, never looked her way; for all their former intimacy she was now a stranger – worse, a stick of furniture – worse, yet, a pillar of salt, too much a reminder of the past. He gloried in the circle of his friends, but looked at her as if she were air. "I am thinking of enlarging the strings, maybe three each of first and second violins, two each of violas, cellos, and basses – or maybe four and three. What do you think, Jussuf?"

"I would advise as many strings as you can get – at least four firsts and seconds."

They sat in the sittingroom, Philippine and Agathe poured beer and wine and passed plates of pastries, the children played blindman's buff in the next room. Grimm was thoughtful; he had always been thoughtful, but marriage had added gravitas; his large forehead and the hair ringing his face gave him the appearance ever more of a prophet though his eyes remained gentle. He spoke deferentially as always. "Have you considered, Johannes, that it might be an advantage to add other instruments as well – maybe an oboe, or another horn?"

Brahms's inexperience with the orchestra prevented him from adding instruments indiscriminately, but these were matters he had confessed only to Joachim and Clara. "Actually, yes, I have thought about it – but I do not wish to add more instruments unless I am convinced they are necessary, and I am not convinced that they are. I cannot even say yet whether this should remain a chamber work or become an orchestral."

Agathe sat by his feet on the floor, snug against his leg, her head on his knee, arms twining his calf. She looked into his face, her smile beatific. "It is a beautiful work, Johannes! An amazing work!"

Brahms squeezed her shoulder, not caring what Clara saw. Gathe knew only that the great Clara Schumann was his good friend, more than that he had not said wishing to keep their relations simple. He squeezed her shoulder for Clara's benefit as much as his own and Gathe's, to outline their relations in the thickest black ink. If they were to remain friends Clara would have to accept the worst, and better sooner than later. "Do you really think so, Gathe?"

"Indeed, I do."

Philippine's clearcut features, tidy hair, firm mouth, sharp eyes, contrasted sharply with her husband's. "It is the pastoral character I like best. I close my eyes and there are birds around my head, there is a brook at my feet."

Brahms nodded, his hand still on Agathe's shoulder. "That too constitutes a problem. The woodwinds bear out what you say, but then the question becomes whether this is merely a woodland serenade or something more substantial." He laughed. "I am thinking of calling it a symphonic serenade – but then it seems as if I myself do not know whether it is a symphony or a serenade."

Clara gained courage; he had touched on the subject foremost in her mind. She was like Agathe in her approbation, but more considered where Agathe was blind. He might resent her for her words as much as her person, but if so she wanted to know him as he was, not as she wished him to be. "That is just what I was thinking. The development and transitional passages are worked out seriously enough for a symphony, but the dances and the repetitions and the scoring for woodwinds suggest very much a serenade. Haydn or Mozart come to mind."

Joachim nodded. "Frau Schumann is exactly right. I hear Haydn, but with advanced harmonies – which perhaps should be developed in a larger framework rather than a smaller – more strings, more woodwinds, and then we will see how it sounds."

Clara, glad for Joachim's support, smiled finally, her first time since the concert. "May I make one more observation?"

"Of course!" Brahms nodded without looking at her.

"It is also the first of your works, Johannes, that is clearly not written for the piano – even your concerto is essentially pianistic – but the symphony, or serenade, or whatever you choose to call it, is essentially orchestral."

Joachim nodded again. "Again, I think Frau Schumann has touched the heart of the problem. Orchestral it is, but whether symphony or serenade is for you to decide – and to develop accordingly. The concerto is more profound, more worthy of symphonic development – but this nonet is more orchestral."

Philippine spoke firmly. "It is a serenade, not a symphony. Does no one else hear my birds and my brook?"

Brahms laughed. "Frau Pine is right. It is a serenade. It would be a sorry excuse, indeed, for a symphony. I will give her even more birds and brooks if she wishes."

"Oh, but does no one else hear them besides myself?"

Grimm took his wife's hand. "*I* hear them – and I hear as well, with the expanded instrumentation, the thrum of bagpipes in the basses, and of fifes in the flutes – but it would be a mistake, would it not, to imagine too distinct a program in the music. Twenty people might hear the same piece of music and draw twenty different inferences – one might hear birds, another brooks, and yet another ladybugs and dragonflies, all in the same music."

Clara spoke so suddenly the company was startled. "That is what my Robert used to say. Show me first that you can compose beautiful music, and then I will also like your program."

"Ach, but that is not how it is for the so-called New Germans." Joachim had received another letter from Liszt, an invitation to the jubilee of Carl August of Weimar, patron and friend of Goethe and Schiller, stirring anew his irresolutions about Liszt. "For them a run of notes is an animal scurrying, a roll of tympani is thunder, woodwinds are birds, music is always something other than itself. Without a story there is no music. That is what Liszt means by a symphonic poem – not that you need words, but a story expressed in music: a program."

Philippine frowned. "I beg your pardon, Herr Joachim, but may one not say the same about your overtures to Hamlet and Henry IV and the others? Are you not painting portraits as well in music?"

"Frau Pine, you are right. I see I must either clarify myself or eat my words. The difference is that my Hamlet might as easily be called Brutus, the two characters have much in common – but what matters is the music, not what it portrays. It is as Schumann said: if you like the music it matters little whether you like the program – and it is as Beethoven said of his *Pastoral* Symphony: it is an expression of feeling more than painting – but a symphonic poem about Hamlet would follow the story, detail by detail, from the ghost on the battlements to Polonius behind the arras to the final tragedy. Musical themes would become subordinate to the themes of the story – but that kind of story is better told in words or in images than in notes. My Hamlet, if I may say so, is not like that. It portrays a feeling, not a story."

Brahms clapped. "That is well and clearly stated." He squeezed Agathe's shoulders; she squeezed his hands on her shoulders; Clara pretended not to notice. He ran one hand through Agathe's hair; the other Agathe held, nestling it against her cheek; and Clara felt her face turn to ice. She carried, it seemed, something dead in her breast. It was a strange turnaround: when she had been jealous of Robert with Ernestine she had been too young to hold Robert's interest; with Brahms she was not too old, but she was beginning to realize they were yoked by a past too complex to match the simplicity of his bond with Agathe. For all his protestations of love, all the profound experiences they had shared, he now left her alone, transferring his affections all too easily to a girl with a pretty voice and an even disposition.

LATER THE SAME EVENING Joachim took the opportunity of Liszt's invitation to write the letter he had long promised himself:

JOACHIM TO LISZT   *Gottingen, 27 August 1858*
Dear and Honored Master,

Your continual goodness in including me in the community of your friends makes me ashamed of my own lack of candor – a shame I do not experience for the first time, and one that would deeply embarrass me were I not convinced that it is rooted not in cowardice, but in my best feelings.

It was presumptuous of me to imagine that I had the power to turn into a thorn with which you might be wounded, but that was how I felt – and my genuine affection for you found itself in direct conflict with my no less genuine affection for what I perceive is the truth.

What is the use of hesitating any longer to say plainly what I feel? Accustomed as you are to meet with enthusiasm, my passive attitude toward your music must have revealed it to you already. I will no longer remain silent on a subject which, I confess, your manly spirit has long deserved to have clarified.

Your music is entirely antagonistic to me. It contradicts the spirit of the great masters with which I have been nourished since my earliest youth. Should the unthinkable come to pass, and I be deprived of all that I love and honor in their creations, all that I believe music can offer, your strains would not fill one corner of the vast wasteland in their wake. How, then, can I feel myself united in aim with those who, under the banner of your name, under the belief that they must join forces against the artists of old for the justification of their contemporaries, make it their life's work to propagate your works by every means in their power? Rather must I separate myself from them and work for that which I know to be good.

I can be of no assistance to you and I can no longer allow you to think that your aims and the aims of your pupils coincide with mine. I must, therefore, refuse your last kind invitation to partake in the festival at Weimar in honor of Carl August. I have too much respect for you, and for the memory of the Prince who lived with Goethe and Schiller and is now buried with them, to act hypocritically, or to be present out of curiosity.

Forgive me if I have saddened you for a moment during your preparations for the festival, but I had to do it. Your immense industry and the number of your followers will soon console you, but when you think of this letter always believe this: that I will never cease in my heart to carry a grateful pupil's deep and faithful memory of all that you once were to me, of the often undeserved praise you bestowed on me at Weimar, and your divine gifts from which I strove to profit.

Joseph Joachim

EARLY THE NEXT DAY, Clara left Gottingen for Berlin, taking the girls and Felix, without warning, without explanation, disappointing and astonishing Grimm. "Does anyone know why?"

Brahms frowned, but said nothing; what had happened was inevitable, better now than later.

iv

The tympani barked like an attack dog, announcing the opening bars of Brahms's concerto. He sat at the piano on the Gewandhaus stage, hands idle in his lap. Next came a whirlwind of trills in the strings, springing from measure to measure, parading the fury bound in its giant coils, while the attack dog of the tympani crescendoed into the sounds of cannon.

He had wanted to work longer on the piece, but had lost all objectivity. There came a time when you had to let go. Joachim had arranged a rehearsal in Hanover five days earlier. Brahms had been so pleased he had played the entire third movement prestissimo, but the premiere had been received with indifference.

The orchestral whirlwind subsided, but Brahms remained idle at the piano, staring at his hands in his lap. The second theme was gentle, soaring violins providing a brief lull before the orchestra returned to the theme of the whirlwind, brass echoing strings in the second appearance.

He had much to ponder. His second term in Detmold, the last three months again of the year, had been one long swoon, daily letters to his shamrock of Gottingen as he called Gathe, her face in the foliage of the Teutoberger Wald, her hair in the trees, her voice in the wind, her eyes in the stars. He had written more songs, an Ave Maria, worked on his serenade and concerto, but now found little pleasure in the company of Meysenbug and Bargheer. He had rushed on the day of his release to Gathe in Gottingen to exchange rings, rushed next to Hanover for the premiere of the Piano Concerto, rushed finally to Leipzig where he had received a letter from Grimm: *It would be tactful in a town the size of Gottingen, for Gathe's sake, to make your intentions public.*

He wondered as he waited whether the long delay before the entrance of the piano had accounted for the reception in Hanover. The custom was to introduce the piano early and milk its virtuosity from the start – but he had composed the longest orchestral introduction yet for a concerto. The custom was to state the themes in the orchestra, state them again on the piano, and develop a dialogue between orchestra and piano – but he had introduced so many themes in the orchestra that he had chosen to develop them directly on the piano without stating them again. He had given the most dramatic theme to the orchestra, not the piano, reducing the piano from soloist to a member of the choir – but this was not what audiences expected.

He made his entrance finally with a long dreamy passage, developing themes already stated, before leading the piano back to the theme of the whirlwind. The impatience of the audience was palpable through the long movement, longer than the whole of Liszt's concertos – but its conclusion was met with silence, a hush so loud it rendered him numb. He lowered his gaze to his hands again in his lap, not daring to look at the audience, podium, or musicians.

The first movement had been set in motion by Robert's anguish when he had jumped from the bridge. The second, another long movement, a requiem for Robert, proceeded like a voyage into space, solemn as a dirge, pristine as a hymn, but was met again with silence. The third opened directly with a vibrant theme ascending the piano, a massive movement to complement the others, concluding with a resounding tutti – only to be greeted with the glare of a single unblinking cyclopean eye.

Three pairs of hands rose in applause – to be silenced immediately by the hiss of a large snake in the room. He might have been in a village square, his head in the stocks, an adulterer or worse, for the way he felt – but he shook off his paralysis, bowed hurriedly, nodded to the podium, and left the stage.

He made light of the fiasco, convinced the concerto would succeed after he had streamlined it further, but his regret was plain in a letter to Joachim: *The concerto was a brilliant and indisputable … failure! But failure is a good thing. It forces you to confront your weaknesses. But the hissing was maybe too much of a good thing.*

The critic of the *Leipziger Signale* echoed the response of the audience: *A new composition was borne to the grave at the Gewandhaus, a thoroughly disconsolate work, wasteful and dreary. The solo part was thoroughly unpleasant and the orchestral no more than a series of slashing chords. For almost an hour one was forced to endure a rooting and a rummaging, a dragging and a drawing, a tearing and a patching of phrases and flourishes, all served with the shrillest dissonances, the most unpleasant sounds. Herr Brahms has deliberately made the piano part as uninteresting as possible, and wherever something appeared which gave promise of effect it was immediately crushed and suffocated by a thick crust of orchestral accompaniment.*

Breitkopf and Hartel refused to publish the concerto, making Brahms fearful. He had staked his happiness with Gathe on the concerto. Recalling the materialism against which Clara had warned, the expectation of any bourgeois wife, a house and children and more, so easily provided by a professor or lawyer or merchant – but not by a composer – he wrote to Agathe in a panic: *I love you! I must see you again! But I cannot wear fetters. Write to me whether I am to take you in my arms again, to kiss you and tell you that I love you.*

He regretted his lack of tact, but not the outcome, though Agathe understood him better than he imagined. She wrote to say he was not to come if that was how he felt. Three years later, unable to put the matter behind her, she took a position as governess to an English family in Ireland. Ten years later she married, apparently happily, but toward the end of her life published an autobiographical novel concluding that she could never have fulfilled a man like Brahms, indicating a depth of awareness possessed by neither Brahms nor Clara: geniuses belonged to humanity more than to a particular time, place, or person.

Navigating the wide squares and narrow streets and canals of Hamburg, Brahms and Clara looked like family, the more so for not touching each other though they might have been walking hand in hand for the breadth of their smiles. They were bound for Eppendorf, a northern suburb, for what Brahms called a Brahmaho. It was a thirty-minute walk. They were going to be late, but did not hurry. The massive brick warehouses seemed less ominous to Clara when she walked with Brahms, the tall halftimbered tenements less forlorn, the promenaders like neighbors. Brahms pointed to the barrow of a secondhand bookdealer under one of the bridges. "That is how I built up my collection. You can find things there you will find nowhere else – and cheap!"

Clara liked learning about him. "It is good to be walking with you again, Johannes." He smiled, holding his hat in his hands behind him, his head forward, striding forcefully to pull her into his gait, but she swung her arms idly pulling him into hers. "I cannot recall when I last saw you look so well. Surely it cannot be because you no longer reside at home?"

His cheeks deepened into dimples as he grinned, combing fingers through his hair, pushing it behind his ears, back from its widow's peak. "That could be. I have been much spoiled since I left home. I cannot work if there is noise. I wish I could be like Schubert or Mozart – in the middle of an evening with friends, while talking as we are now, they could scribble masterpieces – but I need quiet before I can even think about work, and at Fuhlentwiete there is no quiet."

She would understand that his home was too crowded, but he said nothing about what bothered him most, the quarrels between his parents, his mamma constantly sick wanting attention, his pappa constantly wanting to practise the bass, audition for the Hamburg Philharmonic, waiting for his chance – for someone to die, as he enjoyed telling people. His mamma complained that his pappa was never home, but when he was home she complained about everything else. Elise, also constantly sick, sided with their mamma; Fritz, when he visited, with their pappa; and Brahms was caught in the middle.

"Tomorrow, when you see my place, you will understand." He had rented a room with a balcony overlooking a garden in Hamm, an eastern suburb. "I sleep to the song of nightingales and wake to trees outside my window. That is the reason I feel so well – at least, part of the reason."

Robert, too, had needed quiet to compose; it had been a source of deep disagreement between them because she could not practise quietly; she would have had the same problem with Johannes, but she smiled and kept the thought to herself. "And the other part?"

"That you know already – my girls! I now have forty of them."

Clara wore black as always, but appeared cheerier than usual. "Forty girls!" She danced ahead. "Oh, Johannes, of what use then is your poor old Clara?"

"My poor old Clara has enough vigor to match any of them. I think she will be much amused."

"With forty girls, Johannes, you will have forty ways in which to lose your heart!"

Forty were safer than one, he wanted to say, and the cure for losing one girl was gaining forty, but he did not. Clara had been right: he should never have raised Gathe's hopes, but he found it difficult even now not to think of her. Had he followed his heart he would have been with her still – but talent, conscience, ambition, all pointed in another direction, and whatever Clara said he felt sure a union with Gathe would have risked a permanent rift with her; she would have found him ordinary for marrying an ordinary girl. "Hah! It is too late for that."

"What do you mean? Do you have a sweetheart?"

He laughed. "No, it is nothing so complicated. I am in love with all my girls. It is as simple as that – and though I say it myself I have become quite a cult among them."

She laughed. "A cult? Why? Do they think that you are Liszt?"

He laughed again. "They are but forty. If I were Liszt they would be four hundred!"

She laughed, but lost her smile immediately, as did he. They walked in silence for a while, Clara the first to speak again. "I came to the conclusion not long after I came to know Liszt that he was no more to be trusted in his life than in his music."

Brahms pursed his lips. "What he does with his life is his own damn business, but what he does with music is a damn shame. His influence with the young is something to be feared. There are times when I have felt compelled to do something before the plague of his music spreads much further and the ears of the public are stretched forever like a donkey's."

Clara spoke quickly, afraid she might otherwise lose courage. "I, for one, wish somebody *would* do something before it is too late. His music has already taken root in Prague. In so many of the places I have performed there is a great enthusiasm for his so-called symphonic poems."

Brahms nodded slowly. "Otten has introduced them in Hamburg as well."

Clara shook her head, amazed at the idiocy of the world. "Otten, of all people, should know better. It annoys me, Johannes, that you remain on good terms with him. Is it not incumbent upon us and those who think like us to speak our minds? What right do we have otherwise to complain? My fear is that we condemn ourselves with our silence and we will be judged before we have had our say."

Brahms had performed with Otten, a conductor of subscription concerts, of Hamburg's musical elite, a group he wished to cultivate. He was beginning to envision a career for himself among the city's musical faculty, after which he might pursue Gathes of the future with more ease. He did not want to jeopardize his chances by telling Otten how to program his concerts, but did not wish to admit it to Clara. "It is a subject to which I have given much thought. If Joachim and I and other likeminded musicians were to step forward with some kind of declaration professing the truth as we see it, it might do some good, do you not think? But I am not yet decided about how to proceed."

Clara spoke with determination. "I think that is a capital idea."

"But Liszt's influence is so vast that a challenge from such as myself and Joachim would only look foolish. Joachim knows the Weimarites. They are too sophistical, too skilled in rhetoric and stratagems to be outdone. Liszt knows only too well how to arouse enthusiasm and how to exploit it for his own ends. An honest debate is almost impossible."

"All the more reason to swell your ranks. The more the musicians that support you the more credibly you will be received. You have me already – and Joachim and Grimm and Dietrich – and those are just off the top of my head. We will never know how many others share our views until we try. It is mainly a matter of organization."

"I would like to give it more thought yet."

Clara made fists of her hands. "Oh, these are the times I wish I were a man. It would count for more – what I say, what I do."

They had reached the country, on one side flowed the Elbe, willows along its banks. It was midevening and their shadows, long and slender as the willows, became one though they continued to walk separately.

Clara smiled again. "But to return to what you were saying – why do you imagine you have become a cult?"

Brahms, too, smiled, spinning his hat on his finger. "I do not imagine it. It is so!"

"Ah, Johannes, your modesty is overwhelming! Why do you say it is so?"

"Well, for one thing, they ask continually at the music shops, my dear singing girls, for my publications. One or another of them is always in Jowien's or Schuberth's or Brunner's or Niemeyer's – until they have set up quite a demand for my work. They call it a Brahmanen run, their attempt to persuade the dealers to keep my works on hand."

"And what is it you pay them for such sterling service?"

"I conduct them in the choir, that is all. Is it not a fine exchange?"

He had played the organ once at a wedding in the Church of St. Michael and liked the acoustics so well he had wished for a performance of his "Ave Maria" in the same space. One of his pupils, Friedchen Wagner, had organized a choir for him of twenty-eight girls, subsequently increased to forty. A performance at the church had proven so successful they had continued to meet weekly to rehearse and perform his music. Karl Gradener, from whose singing school the girls had been recruited, like Otten, was of the Hamburg elite: composer, conductor, and cellist – and, like Otten, a friend.

"I have arranged them into three choirs, actually – like a funnel. First, there is the full choir of forty girls. Then a smaller one of twelve, for whom I compose three-part folksongs – and then the smallest, of four, for whom I have written quartets and songs for solo voices. Our motto is 'All or nothing at all' – and the girls live up to it completely."

"How do they compare with your chorus in Detmold?"

"In Detmold? Hah!"

Brahms raised his head to the sky, Clara her eyebrows. "Hah?"

Brahms laughed. "I wanted to perform oratorios and cantatas by Bach and Handel – which needed a larger number of singers than could be made up by the princesses and their ladies-in-waiting. The Prince gave me permission to recruit singers from the townsfolk – but I am afraid the townsfolk did not enjoy it very much."

Clara, familiar with Detmold, laughed as well.

"They were not allowed even to bow to their Serene Highnesses – indeed, they hardly dared even lift their eyes from the music in their presence. The music, surprisingly, did not suffer – but I wish I might say the same for the townsfolk."

"And yet you plan to go back?"

Brahms nodded. "I wish to have more practice in conducting. I think the Prince might allow me occasionally to share the podium with Kiel."

Clara understood again. Friedrich Grund, conductor of the Hamburg Philharmonic, was soon to retire. Brahms was waiting, as his pappa would have said, for old Grund to die. "You plan to stay in Hamburg then?"

"Why not, if I have the means? Hamburg is as dear to me as my old mamma."

She sensed his prickliness. She had attempted to draw him into a tour, written from Vienna, London, Basel, Berne – the Swiss were more openhanded than Germans, generous beyond expectation with fees, halls and orchestras provided gratis – but she sensed his unwillingness to perform. He performed from necessity, not desire, unlike herself and Joachim. She understood him better than he understood himself when he continually persuaded her to give up touring herself. She no longer complained about arthritis, memory lapses, and other infirmities. They only gave him a whip.

Sensing from her silence that he had been too stern he spoke more gently. "But what about you? Will you be touring again this year?"

She had toured already, Vienna, Prague, London, in the first half of the year. "Yes, but only Cologne, Bonn, Bremen, and Dusseldorf. I do not plan to leave Germany again this year."

He nodded, keeping his eyes on the path ahead, saying nothing.

She sensed not disapproval, but the difficulty he had approving. "They could not get enough of your Hungarian Dances in Vienna, Johannes – but I have refrained from telling you because I was afraid you would say something unkind."

"Ah, Clara, that is stupid of you, indeed. Have I not sent you my new songs as you wished? Do you not know how much I wish to know what you think?"

She flinched. It was his way to be brusque, she had seen it in his pappa, she knew he meant no harm, but could not reconcile herself to rudeness. "I do, but I sometimes prefer to say nothing. I enjoy your work too much to let you spoil it with your customary remarks. I have learned my lesson. If I let you spoil your own work for me, it will not be your fault."

Brahms knew he had offended her again and blamed her again: plainspeaking was no fault. He said nothing, but strode briskly ahead, hat still in hand behind him, head and lower lip thrust forward, as Beethoven was said to have walked.

"YOU ARE LATE, HERR BRAHMS!"

"And you are very perceptive, Fraulein Marie."

"Frau Schumann, welcome!"

"Welcome to our Brahmaho!"

"Frau Schumann, I heard you once at Wormer's Hall. You were wonderful."

"Danke. That is always good to hear."

"I was there, too, Frau Schumann. You were, indeed, wonderful – heavenly."

"Aaahh, do you see, Clara? Do you see how they love to chatter, like chimpanzees? You will forgive me if I do not introduce you to each one of them – or they will eat up your brains."

It was all Clara could do to nod and smile, overwhelmed by the sheer numbers. There were men as well, friends, sweethearts, family members, but all of them onlookers from the distance they kept.

Brahms studied Latin with Dr. Emil Hallier whose daughters, Julie and Marie, were members of the Hamburg Frauenchor, designated by a badge each of them wore, HFC in the three leaves of a clover hovering over a large B. It was past seven o'clock when they arrived, to be escorted immediately around the house, sounds of festivity swelling as they approached the garden in the back.

Brahms had described the idyll, but Clara was unprepared for what she saw: a hothouse, furnished with benches, streaming with vines, thick vegetation, exotic flowers; a little farther a pond stuffed with goldfish, fountains of gods and nymphs; farther yet, grapevines clinging like gossamer to the hillside. Most astonishing, girls converged upon them in clusters from all points of the compass. Brahms held up his hands. "Girls, please, this is not a zoo, this not a circus. You will give our guest the most unfortunate impression of our choir!" No one backed away, and whatever Brahms said he appeared to enjoy the crush. He could not have said whether he was prouder to present the Frauenchor to Clara or Clara to the Frauenchor.

"She is not merely our guest, Herr Brahms! Today she becomes an honorary member of the Frauenchor!"

"That is Fraulein Marie Reuter, Clara – who is shouting at us so rudely." Brahms grinned. "She is one of the four."

Clara understood, she was a member of the quartet, taken from the choir of twelve, taken from the ensemble of forty. She smiled. "I am deeply honored, Fraulein Reuter, to be considered a member."

Marie Reuter had a plump square face and wore a dark blue dress with a red bonnet. She nodded to Clara. "The honor is ours, Frau Schumann." She turned next to Brahms, taking a deep breath. "I am not being rude, Herr Brahms – I am not the one calling everyone a chattering chimpanzee."

The girls laughed; so did Brahms, shaking his head at Clara. "Do you see what I mean? They have no respect for their kapellmeister."

"But, Herr Brahms, you are the one who is late today, not us. We had respect enough for Frau Schumann not to be late ourselves."

"And that is Fraulein Betty Volckers – and that is her sister, Fraulein Marie. They are two more of the four."

The sisters were similarly dressed, plaid dresses, blue and red, blue bonnets, Betty holding hers in her hand; both were slender, Betty with a smile, the prettier and more mischievous of the two. Both nodded for Clara.

"And where is the last of the four, our prize soprano? Where is Fraulein Laura? Do not tell me she is late today of all days."

"I am right here." Laura Garbe raised a hand, smiling at Clara. She had a large nose, a dress with a satin hem though of a less colorful print than the Volckers sisters.

"Ah, there she is, our nightingale – but it is too bad that she knows it. She thinks nothing of keeping us waiting. It is too bad she knows that we cannot do without her."

"Aaaah, but that is not fair, Herr Brahms! You are the one who has kept us waiting today, not I!"

Brahms looked at Clara. "They are not usually refractory, but today they just want to show off to you."

A new voice spoke, clear and unapologetic. "Will you conduct us again today from a tree, Herr Brahms?"

"Hah!" Brahms's pale blue eyes grew deeper as he faced his latest interrogator. "Clara, I would like you to meet our resident foreigner, from Vienna, Fraulein Berta Porubsky."

Berta's smile was in her eyes, one shut slightly more than the other, giving her a sleepy look, but her gaze was direct, her mouth a thin straight line. "Frau Schumann, how is it with you?"

Clara nodded. "I am very glad to meet you."

Berta's hair, light brown, was tied with a yellow ribbon, pulled less tightly than the others, like a coronet around her head. Her blouse was velvet; the neckline, deep and square, of lace; a gold locket hung from a black band emphasizing the length and complexion of her neck. "Herr Brahms conducted us from a tree the last time – like a monkey from India."

The girls laughed. Brahms drew himself to his full height. "A monkey would not conduct so well."

"Perhaps not – but he would look better in a tree."

Again the girls laughed; Brahms turned to Clara. "I keep Fraulein Berta to test myself. She sings the wrong notes deliberately – just to see if I can hear them."

Berta laughed.

Clara noticed Brahms became more flushed and flustered as Berta spoke. He thrust his lower lip forward. "Shall we begin?"

Soon the air filled with the strains of Brahms's "Ave Maria," melody rising like a leaf or feather, borne gently, lifted rhythmically, one line after the other, streams of gossamer, filaments in the wind, before returning, as gently, as rhythmically, to the ground.

Two hours later they were still singing, gathered around an apple tree, Brahms at the hub, the garden flooded with moonlight, pond aglow with paper lanterns. The pauses between songs were filled by firecrackers; the show, lanterns and crackers, had been staged for Clara, smiling continually through the evening, enchanted by the ambience, but even more by the performances. The singers appeared to understand easily what Brahms wished, a simple "Good!" meant they had performed exceedingly well. They could neither have been more dedicated nor have had more fun. Nightingales echoed the cadences of the songs, the girls echoed the nightingales, frogs and crickets accompanied the echoes.

"Careful, Fraulein Seebohm, your A flat was a little too flat that time."

"But Herr Brahms, I was meant to sing second soprano, not first."

"Yes, yes, of course, of course. That is why you need me. If not for me you would all be singing second soprano. There would be no altos, no sopranos – but I know you can do it."

Marie Reuter almost jumped in her place. "But Herr Brahms, even Herr Grund says you should not write so high."

Clara, sitting by Brahms's feet, could hear his interest sharpen. "Herr Grund? When did he say that?"

"Last week, when he came to our home for breakfast. I sang him some of Schumann's songs," she nodded to Clara, "and I showed him my notebook. He said it was a mistake to write so high, but he said that you were a pleasant little fellow."

The girls tittered. Brahms paused, conscious of Grund's condescension. It was Grund he wished to replace, Grund who would have a voice in the nomination of his successor. He hoped the families of the Frauenchor, so influential in Hamburg, might add their voices to his nomination. "It is no wonder he would say such a thing. Grund is getting too old to hear the high notes anymore."

Again the girls tittered. Clara made a suggestion she had been contemplating since she had heard the choir. "Indeed, the next time I perform in Hamburg, I would be honored if the Frauenchor would join my program. We could sing the songs with the highest notes. That would surprise him, indeed, would it not, not to be able to hear anything at all?"

The girls were almost too astonished to laugh.

"Oh, Frau Schumann, but that would be wonderful!"

"The honor would be ours – entirely ours!"

"But can you be serious, Frau Schumann?"

"I cannot believe it!"

Brahms smiled. "I think it is a splendid idea – perhaps at your next concert?"

"My very thought!"

Clara had not been as delighted with an evening in a long while. The walk back to Hamburg was almost an hour, but they sang the whole way, dropping members one by one, thinking nothing of walking into strange gardens, waking people with their singing, all of whom seemed entranced by the magical choir in the night.

ii

Berta Porubsky sighed. "It is sad, Herr Brahms, to be parting from a circle in which I have been so happy."

Brahms, wishing to see her once more, had asked her to walk with him. In the deepening twilight she appeared more approachable, in her sadness more lovely, more sensual for one eye more closed than the other. "I prefer to think of what lies ahead. The past, after all, is the past." He spoke with more conviction than he felt. He was returning to Detmold again the next week, already his past more than his future, and she to Vienna.

Berta sighed again. "It is different for men. They have their work. We poor women," she sighed yet again, "we have only romance."

Her tone was ironic. Brahms looked at her, but turned when he saw she was looking back and lost his grin. "But will you not be visiting Frau Brandt again next summer?"

Berta had spent the summer with her aunt in Hamburg. "I might." Herr Brahms puzzled her: a man apparently reluctant against his own will. He seemed to like her, appearing often at her elbow, often to be staring, but gave her nothing, neither word nor touch. He appeared glad to be near her, but she needed a declaration of his intentions. "And then again, I might get married."

If she had not been watching she would have missed his misstep, eyes widening momentarily to marbles, brief intake of breath, descent of the corners of his mouth. Why had he imagined she would wait until his circumstances ripened, until he might court her as she deserved? He spoke quickly, covering his discomfort. "Is there someone you wish to marry?"

Berta smiled, keeping her eyes on him. "I do not know – but I would like to marry."

Brahms smiled and sighed. "Ah, yes, I, too, would like to marry."

"Who would you like to marry? You know you have your pick of the Frauenchor, do you not?"

Brahms walked with his mouth open, unable to say what he wished, wishing she could read his mind. Words always got in the way of what he wished, particularly when he did not know what he wished himself. "They have been so very thoughtful, all of my girls." His voice rose in pitch. "And you, Frau Berta, you have been perhaps the most thoughtful of them all."

"I?" She walked closer to him. "Why do you say so?"

He liked her scent of jasmine, the brush of her elbow, brook warbling in her throat, but there was a challenge in her question he could not answer. It was easier to make a joke of the situation. "Hah! Was it not your aunt who selected my gift?" For their last meeting the Frauenchor had worn black and presented him with a silver inkstand hidden under a bouquet.

Berta was not offended, but responded without mirth. "Why, yes, so it was." When people joked about serious matters they were less serious than they liked to think, less sure of themselves.

Brahms felt her withdraw as clearly as if she had whisked a welcome mat from under his feet, in her tone suddenly flat and the distance she placed between them again as they walked, but he clung to his argument like a dog to a bone. "I cannot get it out of my head. I have done so very little to deserve it."

"You have deserved it ten times over and more, Herr Brahms. It is the perfect gift for a composer – but you have not answered my question."

"I am sorry. I have forgotten. What question was that?"

Berta smiled. "The same as your question to me. Is there someone you wish to marry?"

"Hah! My answer is the same, too. I do not know any more than you – but I, too, would like to marry – I think."

"You think?"

"It is surely not something to be undertaken without thinking?"

"Oh, but it is just as surely not something to be undertaken with no spur other than thinking?"

"No, that it is not. It is to be undertaken with something more than thinking."

"Aha – and what might that something be?"

Brahms, pursing his lips, spoke more slowly. "That ... I cannot say – but there has got to be something else – or it is merely a marriage of minds, not hearts."

Berta spoke more quickly, to get him to respond as quickly, without thinking. "And what kind of marriage is that?"

"Why, no marriage at all, but a merger – and maybe something worse."

"And what, then, is a marriage of hearts?"

"Why, I suppose, a marriage of love?"

"You say it as if you are not quite sure what it means."

"I am not. I confess it freely."

"And what do you think it means?"

"I cannot say. It is a feeling ... too fluid to be expressed."

"Ah, Herr Brahms, you phrase it so well, but you avoid the issue."

He could not tell her what he thought because his thoughts were unclear to himself. It had been less than nine months since his message to Gathe. He mourned her still, but could not be sure it was not Clara he mourned, could not be sure it was not Clara he sought even in Berta, Clara he sought in everyone but Clara. There was no one, there could never be anyone, to compare with Clara – but with Clara he had let his chance slip, and as long as she remained unattached he could attach himself to no one else. He could not even be sure whether it was Clara he missed or the way he had felt when he had been with her, Clara or the piquancy of her situation, Clara or his deep immersion in her tragedy, love or the denial of love when she had been attached and unavailable. He was not sure he could separate one from the other, Clara from her tragedy, love from its denial, but he could give up neither one nor the other. They had been like Werther and Lotte and Albert, he and Clara and Robert, but he had not succumbed like Werther. They had been like Lancelot and Guinevere and Arthur, but he had not transgressed like Lancelot. Gathe and Berta were clear streams, bubbling babbling brooks, offering all the pleasures of domesticity; Clara was the deep dark uncharted ocean, harboring currents and tides, specters from the past. A simple love could no longer hold him. Domesticity, much as he yearned for its comfort, would shackle him, but not domesticity with Clara – but domesticity with Clara seemed a contradiction in terms, which only made her more enigmatic, more alluring – more elusive. "If I avoid the issue – and I do not say that I do not – it is because I have no answer. What do you think it means?"

"I think it means just what it says in the marriage vows, to give oneself to one's love fully, for rich or poor, in sickness and in health, with every thought for what he – or she – wants and needs, and only then for oneself. Would you not agree with that?"

Brahms laughed. "That is exactly what I would say about music! I will forever be writing love songs to music."

She began to understand better. She had heard his serenade at Wormer's Hall and been more disappointed for him than he had appeared himself. She knew of the hostility toward his immense piano concerto. His was an unusual destiny, deserving unusual sympathy, always the case with men of creativity, and some said Herr Brahms was a man of genius. From what she knew of his work she did not doubt it, but men of genius had different priorities, and could be accommodated perhaps only by women of genius like Clara Schumann, with similar propensities and priorities. She recalled lines by Goethe with which her aunt had warned her when she had sensed Herr Brahms's interest:

> One does not crave to own the stars,
> But one loves their glorious light.

Brahms was laughing, perhaps expecting her to laugh as well at his observation; instead, she spoke soberly. "Well, then, we are perhaps not so very different. We agree in our definitions, but differ in the objects of our affections."

He was immediately sober. "But do you not care about music?"

"Not more than about people."

It was perhaps the wrong thing to say; he sighed, looking at his feet as they walked, holding his hands behind him, shoulders bent, appearing more burdened; but she felt unburdened herself, something had been settled – perhaps also for him, though not to his satisfaction.

She began to sing softly, a melody which rocked slowly like a cradle.

> You think perhaps, you dream perhaps,
> That love will yield to force.
> But love, the gentlest love, can bend
> The mightiest river's course.

He looked up again sideways, watching as she sang. A smile spread slowly across his face. "That is beautiful, Fraulein Berta – another Viennese folksong, is it not?"

"Yes. Why is it you have never visited Vienna, Herr Brahms?"

Brahms sighed. "It is farther than I have ever traveled."

Berta laughed. "To listen to you one would think Vienna was in Africa – or Australia. It is not so very far – and with the trains now it is so much more comfortable and quick. You must come, Herr Brahms, and you will not lack for friends. I will see to that myself. I will introduce you to everyone I know." She added, her insight quickening: "I will introduce you to everyone who might help with your music. I am well connected in Vienna."

"Be careful what you say. I might hold you to it."

"I wish you would. You must visit me after I return. It is so different from Germany – all of Austria is different."

"How is it different?"

Berta danced around him in a 3-step. "It is so much gayer. There is music every night of the week – and dancing. Pairs of ladies and gentlemen spin like tops waltzing across a hall, crossing one another's paths, passing one another by, the women covered with flowers and diamonds, the men decorated with medals. It is intoxicating to watch – and even more intoxicating to waltz yourself."

"Do you waltz?"

"You cannot be Viennese and not waltz, Herr Brahms."

"I must say you make it sound almost unreal."

"Even the songs are gay – not about death and loss, as in Germany, but about love. They would laugh in Vienna at some of the poems you have chosen to set to music."

"Indeed? And what might those be, that they would laugh at?"

Berta laughed. "You must not be angry with me, Herr Brahms. I only tell you what is so. Listen to the words of your Harfenlieder. 'My loves and delight are dead, My life is over,' says one – and another: 'I still turn over my garden and sing, but soon I will be digging my grave.'"

Brahms raised his eyebrows, quoted himself from another: "'Not a flower, not a flower sweet / On my black coffin let there be strown. / Not a friend, not a friend greet / My poor corpse where my bones shall be thrown.'"

He grinned as if he had made a joke, but she almost jumped in acknowledgment. "There! You know exactly what I mean! You make my case yourself! It is very romantic, and it is very sad, and it is very pretty – but in Vienna they would laugh. They are serious only about enjoying themselves."

"But those lines, my dear Fraulein Berta, were written by Shakespeare."

Berta pushed him gently. "Yes, but Shakespeare puts the lines in a play, where they are voiced by a character – and you choose those very lines, and others like them, to set to music. When they are presented out of context, their meaning alters entirely."

Brahms recalled what Clara had said about Austrians, they had fire like a flash in the pan, but she wanted the fire that burned long and deep. "Well, then, you may be right – but Bach and Handel also chose such texts for their music."

"Of course, they did! They could not help it! They were Germans, poor fellows!"

He laughed. "But is not death also a part of life?"

Berta laughed, pushing him again. "Of course, but not exclusively. Had Bach and Handel been Austrian they would have written nothing but dance music."

He pushed her back gently. "They wrote that, too."

"But not enough!"

He pushed her again, saying nothing, smiling, enjoying the push.

"Ah, Herr Brahms, but you are flirting with me, are you not?"

"Is it not how they are in Vienna?"

"But we are not in Vienna!"

"But I only wish to make you feel at home."

"Ah, it is as I feared. You are a dreadful flirt, Herr Brahms. You do not mean a word of what you say."

Brahms's room was in a ferment of paper. You could not see his desk for the magazines, correspondence, and music journals. He tapped the letter from Julius Rietz that he had just read out loud to Joachim. "This is the key, Jussuf, would you not say?"

Joachim sat by the window, leafing through pages of the *Berlin Echo*. "We have waited so long. Three more weeks will not matter."

"Hah! Do not let your joy overwhelm you, Jussuf. We are finally doing something – after months of sitting on our hands we are finally doing something. It feels good, does it not?"

Joachim turned a page, looking out of the window, watching two squirrels chase each other along the branches of an elm. "I would like it very much to be over, Johannes. I dislike the anticipation. It is not my way to be confrontational. You know that about me."

Brahms had been disappointed with his last stay in Detmold. He had been more in demand among the ladies of the court, as performer and teacher, but remained without access to the orchestra. The Prince had been unwilling to offend his kapellmeister, the old man who composed songs about *gittiths*. Tired as well of the formalities and frivolities of the court, Brahms was determined not to return, determined no less to build a reputation in Hamburg, determined finally to take up the gauntlet thrown down by the so-called Musicians of the Future. "Tchhah, Jussuf, such an old woman you are! This is not Bonaparte we are confronting. It is not pistols and muskets. Where is your manliness?"

Joachim's eyes grew wide as saucers, but he said nothing. He forgave his friend his carelessness with words, but each time the words drove a wedge more deeply between them.

"Dammit, Jussuf! Do not look at me like that. You are worse than an old woman. You are an old goose. What is the matter with you? This is the right thing that we are doing. You surely do not question that, do you?"

"I am not so sure about that. The way to fight bad music is with good music, not with words – but what do I know?"

"Jussuf, you are too fainthearted for your own good. They use words all the time, you know that, do you not?"

"Yes."

"Then why is it different for us? Why should we not fight words with words?"

Joachim shook his head. "It is different for me than for you, Johannes – it will always be different for me. You know that."

Joachim still felt deeply an obligation to Liszt, if no allegiance, and wanted to make it public. Clara, long annoyed by questions regarding Liszt, had long wished to declare herself. The impetus had come for Brahms when the *Zeitschrift* had declared that all musicians of importance saluted the flag of the New Germans – including the North Germans. "Yes, I know that. We have talked about it forever – but it is still the right thing that we do."

There had been other provocations: the *Zeitschrift*, Robert's magazine, had celebrated its Silver Jubilee the year before, but invited none of the founder's closest friends, not Joachim, not Brahms, not even Clara, only the Musicians of the Future. The New Germans also planned to attend a Schumann Festival to be celebrated in Zwickau, Robert's hometown, claiming him for their own, making it uncomfortable even for Clara to attend.

Brahms and Joachim had drafted what they called their Manifesto, their declaration against the Music of the Future, and sent copies to musicians they imagined sympathetic to their cause appealing for signatories. Clara and Joachim had wanted to name names, Wagner and Berlioz in addition to Liszt, but Brahms's differences were with Liszt alone, and they had agreed finally to exclude all names.

The response had been invigorating. Of the musicians they had contacted Julius Schaeffer, Robert Volkmann, Gustav Flugel, and Robert Franz had refused, but Max Bruch, Niels Gade, Karl Gradener, Theodor Kirchner, Franz Wullner, Karl Reinecke, Ernst Naumann, Woldemar Bargiel, Dietrich, Grimm, and Clara had agreed. Vincenz Lachner, Moritz Hauptmann, and Ferdinand Hiller had agreed to sign if Julius Rietz signed, and Julius Rietz, in the letter Brahms held, had written to say he wished to sign – but not for another three weeks, after the close of the Schumann Festival in Zwickau which he felt sure would provide a fresh provocation, a topical pretext for their protest. Some signatories had found the Manifesto too mild and suggested toughening the language, allowing no confusion about where they stood. Three weeks would give them time to sharpen their declaration.

Joachim ignored Brahms, suddenly too engrossed in what he was reading. "We are doing the right thing, Jussuf. Can you not see it? We should not have waited even this long."

Joachim took a deep breath, looking up from the journal, his mouth as round with surprise as his eyes, his face as white. "Johannes, look at this."

Brahms looked where he pointed:

The undersigned have long followed with concern the proceedings of a certain party whose mouthpiece is Brendel's Zeitschrift fur Musik.

The said Zeitschrift continually asserts that all musicians of consequence today accept the theories espoused by this party, recognize artistic merit in the compositions of its leaders, and agree that the controversy for and against the so-called "Music of the Future" has been settled, especially in North Germany, in their favor.

The undersigned consider it their duty to protest such a distortion of facts, and declare that they do not recognize any such settlement. They find the productions of the adherents of this party contrary to the innermost heart of music, and strongly to be deplored and condemned.

> *Johannes Brahms*
> *Joseph Joachim*
> *Julius Otto Grimm*
> *Bernhard Scholz*

Brahms's mouth and eyes were no less round than Joachim's, his face was no less white. "Who could have done this? How could they have got our Manifesto?"

Joachim shrugged. "Anyone could have given it to them. There were some who disagreed with us – maybe, even, some agreed with us just to throw us off the scent."

Brahms took a deep breath. Against such established figures as Liszt and Berlioz and Wagner their only chance had been the number of their signatories, but with just four they would be a laughingstock. His only major work for orchestra had been hissed; Joachim's reputation was primarily that of a violinist, not a composer; Grimm was even less known – and Scholz, the Court Conductor at Hanover, two years younger even than Brahms, still less. He had hoped to show himself a man of substance, organizing the Manifesto, a worthy successor to old Grund, but shown himself instead an innocent, merely naive. He had foreseen the possibility, but not the probability, of the scoop.

"This is not the end of it, you know, Johannes. The Weimarites will waste no time answering us, and they will not debate the merit of our argument but attempt only to make us look foolish."

Brahms nodded, still in a trance. Less than a week later the *Zeitschrift* published the response Joachim had anticipated.

PUBLIC PROTEST

The undersigned would like just once to play first violin, and for that very reason would like to protest everything that comes in the way of their much deserved rise in the world – particularly against the musical direction provided by what Doktor Brendel has designated the New German School. After the destruction of this barricade, the undersigned would like to hold in its place an immediate prospect for likeminded and welldisposed people of a Brotherhood for the Advancement of Monotonous and Tiresome Music.

> *Hans Newpaths*
> *John Fiddler*
> *Tom*
> *Dick*
> *Harry*

You could not tell Clara's mood from her clothes, she was too much the professional widow. Liszt called her the perpetual priestess; it was her persona now as much as her mystique. People came to see the Widow play her dead husband's work in the greyest greys, the blackest blacks. She had worn a widow's garb even with Robert alive, incarcerated in the asylum; but in the carriage with Brahms from Wormer's Hall to zur Stadt St. Petersburg she wore a dark blue bonnet, the brim trimmed with cherries and lace, and her hair in a bun trailing a blue ribbon. She had begun to imagine a new future.

A fog had descended on the night rendering the streets invisible from lamp to lamp, but in the carriage, sharing a seat with Clara, listening to the steady clop of hooves on the cobbles, protected from the night and fog, Brahms could not have been cozier, particularly when the carriage swerved sliding them together on the upholstery. Clara did not resist the pressure of his thigh against hers – indeed, she returned it and held his hand in her lap. "Oh, Johannes, you will never understand the power you have over me. I am so bewitched at times by your melodies that I cannot get them out of my head – I cannot get *you* out of my head. It was ever thus with me and my Robert."

She had fulfilled her promise that night, shared her program with the Frauenchor, Brahms conducting his girls in a set of his songs. She had been gayer all evening, her face softening when she looked at him, speaking to him without words. He felt the heat of her body, her breast against his arm, her head on his shoulder. The evening could not have been more successful, nor his girls more delightful, nor Clara more receptive, nor he more congenial, nor the present more promising. He recalled the day, 17 January, 1855, now six years gone, when he had followed her to Rotterdam, more in her thrall than he had ever been, surprising her with a declaration of love, and she had accepted his declaration – but with Robert committed to Endenich they could find fulfillment only in denial. He recalled it now as an orgy of denial, a love with no recourse at the time but to invert itself, but in their new glow of affection he began to wonder what might not be possible after all.

A swerve of the carriage dislodged her bonnet to the floor. He gripped her knee through the thick gown and undergarments, bending to pick it up, but Clara held him tightly, shaking her head. "Let it be. It is only a bonnet. It does not break a bone by falling." She laughed at her own silliness. "I was talking about your songs. Did you not hear what I said?"

He leaned back in the seat, massaging her knee. "I heard, I heard – but they are your songs no less than they are mine. They exist by your decree."

"Ah, you are a flatterer, Johannes. You are the composer. They exist by *your* decree alone."

"No. When I have written a song – or any composition – I ask myself first whether it is worthy of you. If it is not, then into the fire it goes."

She slapped his arm. "That is not good of you, Johannes. You must show them to me first. God knows what gems you have destroyed on my account. I will not be held responsible for your delinquencies."

He grinned. "It is too late for that. You have made me delinquent in more ways than one."

She caressed his arm where she had slapped him and snuggled closer until he put his arm around her. "I am almost afraid to ask what you mean by that."

He kissed her cheek. "I think you know."

"Do I?" She caressed his cheek, combing his hair with her fingers, brushing it behind his ear. "Your hair is so soft, Johannes, like satin, like ribbons – but you don't care about it. You should care about your appearance, really. A man is known to the world by his appearance – also to women."

"To women? Have you not met my Frauenchor? Do you not think they are women enough for me?"

He had always been her senior in music, a lad of twenty (looking like ten) when they had met, she a mother of seven (fourteen years his senior). In the eyes of the world he had been among the slowest to shed his boyhood, the last to lose the voice of a child, the last to reach the height of a man – but short as he remained and high as his voice, there was no doubting his manhood, the sheer handsomeness of a man trumping the prettiness of a boy (though his wardrobe seemed cobbled still by commoners: walking shoes and flannel shirts and badly fitted trousers). She would not have admitted it then, but she had been jealous of the affection between him and Agathe and was jealous now of the affection between him and the Frauenchor. She might have said more, but the carriage came to a halt.

"STADT ST. PETERSBURG!"

Neither moved.

"I hate to say goodbye, Johannes. I am so cozy."

His head spun with the fragrance in her hair and he tightened his arm around her shoulders as he murmured into her ear. "I, too, am very cozy."

She did not resist, nuzzling her cheek instead against his. "I feel I could talk with you all night, Johannes. I always feel we have so much to discuss."

"I feel the same, Clara … Clarchen."

"STADT ST. PETERSBURG!"

Clara laughed. "Do you think he is trying to tell us something?"

Brahms did not move. "Maybe we should ask him to drive us around a little?"

She had a better idea. "That would be an unnecessary expense, Johannes, but you could come to my rooms for a little? We could have coffee and talk as long as we wished. Would you like that?"

The question was a formality. "Yes, I think I would. I would like that very much."

HER SUITE WAS SMALL, two rooms, economical and comfortable: in front a loveseat, armchairs, coffeetable, sideboard, and a cuckoo clock recessed in the wall; in the back a cupboard and bed, pale blue wallpaper, a floral pattern, barely visible in the dim light from three candles in a sconce on the wall. They had left the lamp unlit. Clara poured coffee; Brahms sat in an armchair. "It is my boys I worry about, Ludwig and Ferdinand. The poor fellows have no homelife of any sort. I think sometimes of keeping them in Berlin with me after the autumn, but I am not sure it is the best thing. I am told that Ludwig wants strengthening and cannot be sent to an ordinary school anymore. I am advised to send him to a clergyman in the country, but I do not wish him to think Ferdinand is taking his place." She handed Brahms his cup. "The girls weigh so much less heavily on my mind. With them I know what to do, but the boys need a man, they need a pappa. There is only so much that I can do."

Brahms took the cup; the mood of the evening had changed already from what he had anticipated. The family remained scattered across the country. Marie, now her secretary and seamstress, often her traveling companion, and Elise, both lived with her in Berlin; Julie stayed with friends in Nice, too delicate in health for Berlin; Ludwig and Ferdinand in boarding school most of the year; Eugenie and Felix, also in Berlin, in the same building but on another floor with Elisabeth Werner, their governess, because she and Marie were rarely home and Elise was barely eighteen. Clara had come to Hamburg after concerts in Barmen and Cologne, and was to leave the next day for Altona, Hanover, Osnabruck, Detmold, and Dusseldorf, all within the space of a month, followed immediately by a tour of Belgium. They had talked about it before, and this was not the time to revisit their points of difference, better to keep the conversation idle. "Will you go to England again this year?"

He had changed the subject, but she might have expected it. It was not a new subject – but she was beginning to perceive it as he did and wished confirmation that he had not changed. She was convinced that Robert would have approved, even wished it himself. She poured a cup for herself, sat in the loveseat, her knee nudging his. "I have not yet come to a decision about England. It will depend upon whether I can find quarters in a private house where my expenses will not be too great." She shrugged. "Even so, I might just take what I can find."

Her look as she shrugged, her accompanying smile, told him she had changed, she was more willing to listen. "Clara, if you would only work no more than you were obliged, if you would give no more concerts than you absolutely needed – if you would choose a place and settle, spare your health for your family and your friends …"

Still she smiled, holding his glance. "I have given it much thought, dearest Johannes. I have been thinking I might have been rash for refusing Joachim's offer."

Joachim's employer, the blind King of Hanover, had doubled his salary for his birthday while adding no responsibilities. Clara had said, only half in jest, that she might be tempted to cease her wandering life if he could contrive a similar situation for her. Joachim had responded with an offer from the Queen: she would match Joachim's salary, two thousand thaler yearly, provide free residence, if Clara undertook piano lessons for the princesses for half the year. She would be expected as well to play at royal soirees, but she could also expect leave, three days at a time, to perform in nearby towns if she wished. Clara had been tempted, but refused, still feeling the power to play before the public, and wishing to maintain her autonomy. Brahms was surprised at her admission, knowing no one as stubborn as Clara. "Have you, really? Jussuf will be so pleased."

"I am thinking about it. I sometimes feel the need for a quieter life. I sometimes believe that I might recover a measure of peace if I settled in the same town – with a dear friend – though it could never be the same, of course, as it was with my Robert."

Brahms's eyebrows rose in surprise, but he nodded his approval. "Of course, but I think it is promising that you begin to see it."

"Maybe, after all, you are right about that."

She had put down her cup, leaned forward, elbows on her knees, fingers caressing Brahms's knees, hair luminous in the candlelight. Brahms smiled, finished his coffee in a gulp, and closed the distance between their lips.

She had begun to close her eyes as he drew near, but his lips were so sudden, so hard against her own, she drew back, opened her eyes wide, and when she drew back he almost fell on top of her. She put her hands between them, pushing against his chest, "Johannes, wait!" but he pushed back against her hands with his chest, pushing her lips again with his, and she slid down the loveseat onto her back. The table was thrust aside. A coffee cup, fortunately empty, fell on its side.

His mouth slid from hers, between her breasts, to her belly. He was on his knees burying his face between her legs, gripping her buttocks so hard they hurt, pulling her toward him. Robert had never been so wild. Johannes handled her like a doll, something he had bought. She pushed him away, but had to beat his head to make him stop, almost to scream. "Johannes, wait! What do you think you are doing?"

He stopped as suddenly as he had started and spoke in a burst. "What is it? What is the matter?"

His voice had risen to a squeak. His face appeared so bewildered, like a child expecting a slap, she had to smile again. "Johannes, have you never taken a woman before?"

He backed into his chair again. Lines multiplied on his forehead, his face shrank with anxiety. "Why do you ask?"

She pulled herself up in the loveseat, unable to face him. "You are much too wild. You must be more gentle. We are not animals."

Brahms said nothing, shrinking further in his chair.

She reached behind her, pulling loose her ribbon, letting fall her hair, holding out her hand. "Come, let me show you what I mean."

AN HOUR LATER they emerged from the bedroom, Brahms frowning as before, in streetclothes again, Clara frowning no less than Brahms in a robe, each avoiding the other's eyes. Brahms clutched the doorknob as if he might leave without a word, but turned his head unexpectedly. "Clara?"

"Yes?"

"I wish I could meet you again – as if for the first time. I could then fall in love with you all over again. I would not then have this ... trouble."

Clara said nothing, and Brahms continued to stand with his hand on the knob. They were like an old married couple, but with a singular difference: they had never had a honeymoon, never a wedding night, and they could not force things in reverse, they could not force things at all – if nothing else, that was clear from the night.

"It will go more easily the next time, Clara."

She shook her head. Robert had never had such trouble. They had had relations right to the end, three and four and five times a week without discomfort or trouble. It was the easiest thing they had done together toward the end – but she had been the younger then and Brahms was the younger now. He could not make her feel better, could not make her feel less ugly, not with words. She did not blame him, it was not his fault, a fault of nature if of anything – but neither did she wish to complicate her life further. He perhaps needed someone younger, someone prettier. She had problems enough with her children, she had had problems enough in her life not to add more. "No."

"No?"

She was afraid of what life with him might mean. She had imagined him healthy in the ways a man was healthy no less than she had imagined Robert, but she had been wrong about Robert and she could no longer afford to take chances. She was getting old. "I do not think there should be a next time, Johannes. I think we should take this as a sign – from him – that it was not meant to be. I can think of no other explanation for this … this trouble."

He knew whom she meant, but could neither agree nor refute her, could only imagine she found him unmanly and remained silent.

She spoke more gently. "I do not think it would be wise, Johannes, but you must not feel badly. I see it now, I can have no husband after Robert. My course is set – but *if* I were to choose a husband I would want no one but you – and after you there is no one at all."

He wanted to argue, but was too ashamed. Had she not checked his first mad rush he might have been all right, but he felt himself constantly foiled by the gamesmanship of gentlewomen, the pretence that they needed to be won, not taken like a woman with his money on her dresser or an animal by the side of a barn. He had never understood what the hard horny act had to do with the rules and etiquette of courtship. The mingling of the two worked to the benefit of neither.

She caressed his cheek. "Johannes, I do not wish you to see me again as if for the first time, by no means, nor for you to fall in love with me all over again. All our current advantages would then vanish. I wish only that you love me now as you have loved me all along. I think that would be the best of all. I think that is what he would want, do you not?"

She was wrong to invoke her husband's name like a weapon, but it disarmed him like nothing else. He looked away, striding across the room, slamming the door, running down stairs, wishing to put as much distance between them as quickly as possible. She was now a habit he wished never to break, but he was afraid he had lost her forever. He could have taken a cab, but strode home instead through the cold fog-infested January night, the better to compose his frustration, recalling nights striding home from Zur schwarzen Katze – and Helga and Lena and Frau Grummer

469

among others who had taunted him for his youth and size, knowing he was neither too young nor too small to be titillated. They would give him what he wanted for money, but without money it seemed something else was required of which he knew nothing. It was a riddle: his pappa had said that was how the world worked, but what he had learned about women from sailors in the taverns and peasants like his own pappa did not seem to have currency in the world at large. His pappa had played the same taverns and successfully courted his mamma, but he seemed cut from a different cloth. These were hardly conscious thoughts, but when they glimmered his veins froze and his head settled on his shoulders like a block of ice, enveloping him in a deep freeze independent of the frost in the air.

PART FIVE

A GERMAN REQUIEM

Residences in Vienna were not as in Hamburg. Joseph Epstein's dwelling was in the vicinity of St. Stephen's (Old Steffel from the thirteenth century) on Domgasse, among the shorter narrower streets in the first district, also called the first city, old city, inner city, Innerestadt, innermost ring of the ring city, circumscribed by the Ringstrasse, now the major thoroughfare, fifty-seven meters wide with separate paths for horsemen and pedestrians, replacing the thick walls once surrounding and fortifying the city.

Brahms entered a small lobby under an arched doorway, watched from his left by the concierge through the round window in her front door, an old woman with the eyes of a lizard, one part guarddog, the other headmistress. This was the house in which Mozart had written *Figaro*. Such were the thrills a musician experienced in Vienna: he drank wine where Beethoven had drunk wine, and buying some of Schubert's unpublished manuscripts had met people who had met Schubert.

The city was in a ferment of reconstruction and liberalization: the first brick of the fortress walls had been broken just four years earlier; bankers and chiefs of industry built lavish homes alongside the Ringstrasse; the old city gate where police officials examined papers of arriving visitors had been demolished; the dark days of Metternich and Sedlnitzky were no longer in evidence; medical services had been reorganized, roads classified – and, among other things, regulations introduced prohibiting cruelty to animals. The Emperor's change of policy toward Hungary liberalized the government, benefiting the city as much as the country. The economy benefited from free trade, agriculture from the abolition of forced labor, and the middleclass from the end of the wars against Italy and Germany. The population swelled a hundredfold within twenty years, and banks and joint stock companies multiplied, giving rise to a boom, the Austrian midcentury miracle.

The Viennese, too, were different, not only from the stolid Hamburgers, but from all Germans, even the gayer Rhinelanders. Grand houses dotted the districts no less than in Germany, but butchers, bakers, tailors, tradesmen, people of the humblest origin, lived on the landings, neck and shoulder with the nobility, accounting for the peculiarly Viennese ambience called *Gemutlichkeit*, translated most nearly as coziness, a mix of comfort and familiarity.

Clara and Joachim had long advised his visit to this holy city of musicians, so had Berta Porubsky, now Berta Faber, married to Artur Faber, a Viennese industrialist – but he had learned the lesson of the Manifesto. You won respect with work, not words; you fought bad music by ignoring it, you wrote according to your conscience, the rest followed – and he had worked during the last two years, composed two piano quartets, two sets of variations, honed to his own satisfaction, before he had taken their advice.

The last movement of his first quartet was a rondo to be played presto, but he had added an unusual suffix, alla zingarese, in the gypsy style, part of the influence of his days with Remenyi, launching the movement with a heavy downbeat. Epstein was barely a year older than Brahms, a professor at the Conservatory, among the busier pianists and teachers in the city, and Brahms had waited almost a month before they had met, introducing himself simply: "I am Brahms." Seeing the quartets, Epstein had wasted no time arranging for a tryout in the rooms of his friend, Joseph Hellmesberger, teacher, conductor, violinist, leader of his own quartet, and Director of the Conservatory.

The rooms were deep and dark as a cavern, furniture no less dark, solid mahogany and teak, ornamented with scrolls and arabesques, curtains of lace fluttered from draped and shuttered windows. Epstein smiled, nodding approval, rubbing the bald spot on his chin where he had parted his beard in the the fashion of the men of the city, modeled on the beard of the Emperor, Franz Joseph, and watched Brahms lead the trio of fiddlers into an episode of perpetual motion punctuated by pizzicato strings.

Hellmesberger heard continually about new talent and was habitually cynical. It seemed he had never not known about Brahms, first through Schumann's article, then from Clara and Joachim when they had visited Vienna, now from Epstein, but he had never heard his work, never cared to hear it after what he had heard about him, no one could be that good, and Epstein enjoyed his expression the better for his earlier cynicism, eyes large as eggs following the score, the widening O of his mouth, movement by movement: four staggered notes erupting into the beanstalk of the first movement; the gently rocking relentless intermezzo of the second; the heroic rhythm of the third emerging from an andante; the finale, ala zingarese, culminating in a thunderclap.

Hellmesberger's dark hair was combed back without a part, the domes of his forehead endowed his face with the shape of a heart, cracked in the middle by a dark drooping moustache, but even the moustache appeared to smile as his head snapped back with the last crashing chord, his chair thumped the carpet, and he shot from his seat to embrace Brahms.

"Mark my words, Epstein! Mark my words!" He kissed Brahms's cheek. "This is Beethoven's heir!" Brahms jerked his face away with a grimace, surprised again how freely Austrians expressed themselves.

Epstein, noting the grimace, realized Brahms would never be his own best clacquer – but stroking his beard he laughed in his resounding adagio. "Ha! Ha! Ha! No, Hellmesberger, it is you who must mark my words. Who was it that called you here? Who was it that said to me: 'This had better be good'?"

The other players tapped their bows in appreciation. Brahms nodded acknowledgment; he had chosen to write piano quartets to avoid direct comparison with Beethoven who had written all four of his piano quartets during his earliest years, but he recognized the implications of Hellmesberger's comment. Even Wagner, exclaiming there could be no symphony after Beethoven, had turned to opera – but his task was to find a way. He hated to think about it, but he had committed himself. There was nothing else for him but to test the limits of his powers.

Hellmesberger grinned broadly and kissed Brahms again. "Look, he even shoots out his lip like Beethoven when he was vexed!"

Brahms turned red. "Herr Hellmesberger, I am not Beethoven. I have said: I am Brahms."

Epstein laughed. No piano quartet had been written with more breadth, more variety, not by Schumann, not Mendelssohn, not Beethoven, not Mozart – and Brahms had written another no less powerful, even more lyrical. He spoke quietly. "Well, then, Hellmesberger, we must take care not to vex him further, must we not?"

ii

The Hauptallee cutting across the grounds of the Prater was a drive fit for kings, giant horsechestnuts on either side standing like guardians and sentinels, clubheaded leaves in clusters leavening the grounds. Brahms's favorite section was the Volksprater where wine, beer, coffee, tea, lemonade, and pastries were hawked from stalls, and barkers called you to shooting galleries, bowling alleys, coconut shies, comic revues, puppet shows, caricaturists, and roundabouts. Hat in hand he nudged Karl Tausig, at twenty-one his junior by eight years, wunderkind contender in the piano sweepstakes, pupil first of his pappa, then of Thalberg, finally of Liszt himself at Weimar. It was said he had shed Liszt's eccentricities, transcended the sturm and drang, noise and rhetoric, emerged not only as a virtuoso of the highest rank but also an accomplished musician. If Bulow was Liszt's dearest pupil, Tausig was his best, his fingers accredited steel by Liszt himself, his technique infallible, some said ineffable – but he seemed less so, standing with Brahms, both staring and giggling at the approach of Eduard Hanslick and Gustav Nottebohm, each bearing a cone of refreshment in each hand.

They made an odd foursome: Tausig, with a shock of thick dark glossy hair flopping over his forehead, his moustache no less thick and dark and glossy flopping over his mouth, could have passed for a brigand on an eighteenth century highway; Brahms's haberdashery remained as ragtag as a gypsy's and his hair long and straight and pretty as a girl's, but his eye was more hawkish, his step more firm, his cheeks fleshier; Hanslick, the most esteemed critic in Vienna, friend of the Schumanns, eight years Brahms's senior, had a chiseled face and handlebar moustache and was bald to the dome of his head; Nottebohm, eight years Hanslick's senior, friend of Mendelssohn and the Schumanns, tiniest of the four, with large eyes made larger by spectacles (black with oval frames), balding head, whitening beard ringing his face, was best known for his Beethoven scholarship, the insight he provided into Beethoven's mind from his sketchbooks, the progression of his works from seeds to worlds of sound.

Posters announced sword swallowers and fire eaters; jugglers and stiltwalkers roamed the crowds; a roundabout hummed on their left; the air was scented with

475

cordite, lit with flowers of fireworks; a czardas band threaded the air with strains from accordions and guitars, couples danced in gardens. Brahms had found the Viennese needed little stimulus to dance. He slapped his knee and yelled. "Hanslick! Behind you! Look out! If you lose my chestnuts I will want my money back."

Hanslick, looking over his shoulder, saw a dancing bear standing on his hindlegs, sniffing the air, staring at the cones in his hands – leashed and muzzled, but Hanslick stepped adroitly away grinning as he approached. He had made his reputation in the Fifties with a book, *On the Beautiful in Music*, arguing that music, unlike literature and painting, was fundamentally abstract, notes were unable to depict the images so easily realized by words and pigments, one man's inferno was another's waterfall, one's thunder was another's galloping steed, which put him squarely in the line of fire of the New Germans who sought to synthesize music and literature in their symphonic poems.

Brahms preferred Hanslick's company to his criticism, found his book incomprehensible as he found most writing about music, but Hanslick had attended each of his concerts in Vienna arranged by Epstein, both quartets had received a hearing, also his Handel Variations, and both serenades were scheduled for performances. He had performed as well Bach, Beethoven, and Schumann, gaining a reputation for pianism more than composition and Hanslick's guarded approval: *It is still too early to pass judgment.* Brahms could not agree with Hanslick regarding earlier composers, Palestrina, Bach, Gluck, all of whom Hanslick found dispensable, but at least Hanslick admitted his prejudices without defending them.

Hanslick handed Brahms his cone of roast chestnuts. "Herr Brahms! You do not know me very well. It would take more than a bear to bear away my refreshment."

Tausig took his cone from Nottebohm. "A bear will bear it away. Hah! He is ever the writer! Pray, leave your pen alone for a moment, Herr Hanslick. Enjoy what is before you."

Hanslick had accused Tausig in a recent review of jabbing the keys even during cantilenas, chopping frozen notes out of ice, but admitted the concert had not lacked for applause. "If I do not enjoy what is before me, Herr Tausig, it is news to me indeed."

Brahms was grinning, ignoring Tausig and Hanslick, gazing at Nottebohm who smiled happily consuming his chestnuts. The plot unfolded gradually. "What is it, Herr Nottebohm? You look as if you have seen a ghost."

Nottebohm stared at the cone in which the chestnuts were wrapped and stared momentarily at Brahms before throwing away the rest of his chestnuts and opening the paper cone. A musical score was handwritten on the page which he held up, still mute, for the others to see.

"What is it, Nottebohm? What is all the excitement?"

"This is Beethoven's handwriting! I would swear to it!"

Brahms raised his eyebrows. "No! It cannot be!"

Tausig looked at the score. "Are you sure? Can it be? After all these years?"

Hanslick smiled, saying nothing.

"But what is it? What is the score? Is it a quartet? an orchestra? What?"

"It is just a sketch, Herr Brahms. It might be for an ensemble – but that is his hand! I would swear to it that that is Beethoven's hand!"

"Maybe we should check the other cones? Maybe we shall find more sketches?"

"Do you think so?"

"It would be logical, would it not?"

"That it would – indeed, it would. I will go at once."

Brahms could no longer contain himself; his laugh was loud and rude, AAAAHAHAHAHAHA-HAHA! followed by Tausig's, no less loud and rude. Nottebohm's huge eyes blinked behind his lenses, his face shrank almost entirely into his nose.

Hanslick shook his head, popping chestnuts into his mouth, twirling his moustache, reappraising Brahms one more time, not as shy as he seemed, appearing in his music like Cordelia preferring to conceal her finest feelings to heaving her heart into her mouth – but this same Brahms had forged the page Nottebohm now held and bribed the hawker to use the page. It was a good joke – cruel, and the laughter more cruel, but Hanslick could not resist a smile. Nottebohm was the most fustian of men and the fussiest.

iii

Beyond the Hauptallee and Wurstelprater lay the Grunerprater, rolling meadows bearing stands of oaks, pines, beeches, flanked by the Danube canal, some distance from the city, hardly as peopled as the rest of the grounds, perfect for reflection. Walking alone, Brahms could imagine himself in a forest far from human habitation. It seemed there was no such thing as an unalloyed joy. The Viennese were more appreciative than Hamburgers and applauded him onstage like friends in a parlor, but he could not tell whether they liked the work or the performance. The first clarinetist of the Vienna Philharmonic had refused in the name of a body of the musicians to play his A major Serenade, saying it was too difficult; but order had been restored when the kapellmeister, konzertmeister, and first flautist, had threatened to resign unless the serenade were played, which it was, and successfully. Hanslick had stated in his review: "If any of our younger composers has the right not to be ignored it is Brahms." The *Zeitschrift*, which had published the parody of the Manifesto, had proclaimed recently in a series of articles on his works that he might yet do for music what Goethe had done for poetry. Hanslick had contrasted his sextet favorably with excerpts from Wagner's *Ring* and *Tristan*, understandably since he had heard the two concerts on the same day, but Brahms wanted to be judged on his own, not relative to Wagner, nor to anyone else. Hanslick had also contrasted their personalities, mentioning his modesty, his reluctance to acknowledge applause, the haste with which he had returned to his seat, pleasing him still less. His modesty was not on display, and no more a matter for judgment than Wagner's arrogance, and no one's business but his own. Hanslick had made him a pawn in his own differences with Wagner, but Brahms welcomed the publicity.

These were minor and temporary annoyances, to be expected, even welcomed, to be got behind him, if he wished to advance, and he accepted them, but Ave-Lallemant's letter from Hamburg was more than an annoyance, a setback – worse, hemlock mixed with honey as he had written to Clara. Ave had asked before he had left if he would accept the conductorship of the Hamburg Philharmonic, giving him reason to believe it was his for the asking, but had given the conductorship instead to Julius Stockhausen.

Brahms leaned against the grey trunk of a beech. The canal hummed before him, a couple strolled along the bank, white and yellow blooms colored the boughs overhead, a nuthatch called tuit-tuit-tuit-tuit, a spotted woodpecker beat a tattoo, a flycatcher disappeared into a tree. A man with as few ties as himself could disappear as easily. Without a post he was without prospects, without prospects he was no prospect himself. He wanted nothing more than to settle, and nothing would have inclined him to settle more than a post in the town of his birth, his Hamburg, to lead a normal life, like a normal man – instead of the nomadic life of a musician. Brahms held Ave responsible for the rejection, not Stockhausen, whom he liked, with whom he worked well and planned to work again.

Clara, giving concerts in Hamburg, had spoken with Ave. Ave had said there was much spadework to be done with the orchestra, unsuitable for a musician of Brahms's caliber. Clara had added in her letter to Brahms that he was still young, and with a loving wife a man found heaven in every town – but, however unknowingly, she had only underscored her own unavailability, exacerbating his feeling.

Joachim had written to Ave: he respected Stockhausen's talent; among singers he was perhaps the best musician, but relative to Brahms his limitations were flagrantly evident. The Committee deserved punishment, which Joachim would gladly administer. Ave had written that some of the Committee members could not forget Brahms's seedy past, his birth in the Gangviertel, Bacon Alley, and his history with the dance halls and taverns among the denizens of Ehebrechergang, Adulterer's Walk. His character was less than desirable to the elders.

The hypocrisy was hardly surprising and no different in Vienna than elsewhere: young women supposedly suffered no desires, but governesses accompanied them everywhere, inspected every book they read, kept them ever diverted with music and dance, lessons and games, art and literature and languages; and young men supposedly suffered no desires until they were in their midtwenties, mature enough to provide for a family – but Brahms was almost thirty and he knew better. Women had the coarsest desires and men matured sexually long before they matured socially.

Men in his situation had affairs with bored titled married women if they were lucky, as was said of the young Mendelssohn, or with servants and shopgirls and widows and waitresses who were never to be taken seriously, or with dancers and actresses and other such artistes, amphibious creatures living in constant twilight, merwomen straddling respectability and the underworld – but Brahms never understood what they expected and found himself turning to butter in their presence, found himself milkier with the Helgas and Lenas and Frau Grummers of the world who expected only money. It seemed more honest – but honesty, in this respect, made them disrespectable – even dishonest to genteel minds.

HIS SHADOW LENGTHENED BEFORE HIM as he returned to the city, across the Danube canal, across the Landstrasse, the third district, across the Stadtpark, back to the heart of the metropolis, struck again by the variety of the Viennese: Bohemians, Magyars, Slavs, Latins, Swiss, Teutons, from bordering countries, all comprising the Austrian character.

The streets narrowed to alleyways as he walked, lamps spaced farther apart, evening shadows deepened into night. He hated what he did, where he was going, not for what he did, but the subterfuge, the anonymity, the pretence of normalcy. Women appeared in lit windows: one in a red evening gown; another plumping her breasts over a corset; a third with a shoulder strap of her chemise dangling over her arm; a fourth showing a silvery calf, bloomers yellow in the artificial light, painting her toenails, her foot on the sill; others dressed like nuns or ballet dancers, or men in bowlers and top hats brandishing canes.

He saw women as well in the doorways advertising shows, music, dances, refreshment, heard waltzes tinkled on pianos, folk tunes, dance tunes, popular tunes, not unlike tunes he had played himself, at establishments not unlike the establishments around him, and found himself more at home than in some of the fancier salons he had visited, the clientele seemlier than the sailors he had known, mostly single men like himself flicking their attention from window to window, doorway to doorway, none of whom looked you in the eye, and disappeared finally into one of the doorways, or to unknown destinations with women on their arms. None of the women wore the more cumbersome accouterments, no bustles, no crinolines, the quicker to be ready, but for a price they would have worn them as willingly.

"Would the gentleman be looking for a lady?"

The voice was soft, almost a child's, the smile as appealing for the lipstick skewed to one side. Brahms would have smiled at the euphemisms, but was not in a humorous mood. "He might be, if she is the lady he is looking for."

The girl wore a pink and dingy cotton dress, white imitation roses at her breast, pink shawl and black hat. Her hair was too red to be natural, her smile too bold behind the soft voice, her eyes too steady. "She would be that lady, sir, if she were the lady he was looking for last month."

Brahms smiled. "It is Cheri, then, is it?"

"If you wish, sir, or Sara, or Gertrude, or Anastasia – whatever you wish."

"I wish for Clara."

"Clara it is, sir."

"May I see your book again?"

"Of course, sir."

Brahms owed Epstein a debt for volunteering some brotherly advice. One man in ten in Vienna fell victim to disease, one house in ten displayed the plaque on its door: *Specialist for Skin and Venereal Disease.* Prostitutes were taxed on their earnings, issued books by the police, certificates to practise, which recorded as well the results of fortnightly visits to a doctor – but the legalization was a fiction, instituted for the benefit of the men, not the women, who had no recourse to the law if their clients later refused to pay the agreed price.

Brahms held his finger to his lips cautioning Joachim's servant to silence, padding past him through the hallway and peeking into the sittingroom. Joachim sat on the sofa reading a newspaper waiting for Gustav to announce their visitor, but Brahms's attention was drawn to a woman sitting at a desk writing a letter, blond hair piled like a helmet on her head, plump white flesh seeming riper than her twenty-three years, skin whiter yet for the dark blue of her bodice. He sighed involuntarily. Joachim saw him first. "Johannes! God in heaven, what a surprise! Why did you not send word you were coming?"

"I did not want you to go to any trouble at a time like this."

The friends embraced. When they parted Joachim could not have been smiling more broadly. "Well, then, allow me to introduce –"

Brahms interrupted, turning to the woman. "Say no more! He is engaged! Yes, yes, yes! Thrice blessed word!"

He was echoing his friend's words from a letter. The woman rose so quickly her chair toppled. Her laugh as she righted the chair was loud, vivacious, and unapologetic. Her eyes were blue, grained with black like a mosaic, and she smiled with all her teeth. "Herr Brahms – *finally*, we meet! My Joseph cannot stop talking about you. I cannot tell you what a pleasure it is *finally* to make your acquaintance."

Brahms took her hand, bowing exaggeratedly. "Your pleasure is my enchantment."

The woman giggled without embarrassment. "You should be careful what you say to me, Herr Brahms. You are almost as handsome as my Joseph."

Brahms still swam in the glory he had gained in Vienna. There was no trace anymore of the Hamburg boy, and the Viennese man who emerged had learned to smile with his eyes though his mouth remained still. His jaw was fixed like an anvil, his face planed like crystal, his widow's peak sharp and tidy – but hair fell in waves about his ears. He wished he might have been taller, his voice deeper, but that seemed not to have mattered to the ladies of Vienna. In that gay city all things were permitted. He kissed her hand and did not let go. "The snowwhite hand of a snowwhite lady!" The pun was on the lady's name: Amalie Schneeweiss.

Joachim's voice was dry. "It seems Vienna has made a courtier of you, Johannes."

Seeing wrinkles multiply in his friend's brow, Brahms smiled. "Yes, kissing pretty hands is something I have learned to perfection in Vienna – and I understand your fiancee has much experience of the Viennese stage."

Joachim took Amalie's hand from Brahms, gently but deliberately. "My Ursi has been on the stage since she was sixteen, but that is not to say you are to believe all the stories you hear about life in operatic circles, particularly not in Viennese operatic circles – and most particularly not about my Ursi. She is giving up the stage for me."

Brahms noted that he called her not only Ursi after her middle name, Ursula, but Myursi, as if it were a single word. "I am ready to believe whatever you wish about your Ursi, Jussuf – but why does she give up her profession if she is as good as you say?"

"My Ursi does not give up her profession, Johannes. Her voice is too expressive and her talent too dramatic to waste. She merely gives up opera. She continues to perform, but not in opera. Her farewell performance is for the Queen's birthday tomorrow in *Orpheus*. You will be there, will you not?"

"Of course – and if she is as good as you say I will write songs for her to sing."

"That is just what I wish for my Ursi, to be a songstress and perform in recitals and oratorios."

"And what has Mademoiselle Schneeweiss to say about this?"

Amalie had sobered at mention of the stage, but smiled again with all her teeth, bringing dimples to the corners of her mouth, focusing attention on the snowwhite babysoft skin of her cheeks, the shallow cleft in her jaw. "It is as my Joseph says. My plan is to give up both of my names, Weiss and Schneeweiss, when I take his."

Weiss had been her stage name. Brahms took a deep breath. "That you would give up Weiss I can understand. It is a common enough name – but Schneeweiss? That is a name out of a fairytale, full of magic. I cannot understand why you would give that up."

"It is for *me* that she gives it up, Johannes. Do you imagine Schneeweiss suits her better than Joachim?"

Joachim had spoken contentiously, making Brahms smile. "Ah, Jussuf, do not make faces at me. I was only joking. Can you not see that – you, a child of Vienna yourself?"

Amalie took Joachim's hand and spoke seriously. "*I* see it, Herr Brahms, even if my husband-to-be does not. He is too serious a man for jokes and for that I love him deeply, but –"

Joachim took his hand away from Amalie. "I am not so very serious a man as all that. When I applied to Mendelssohn he made certain I studied subjects other than music. He taught me also how to appreciate a joke. I owe him much, more than will ever be known."

Amalie took Joachim's hand again, smiling at Brahms. "And what Mendelssohn didn't finish, I will. It is good for friends to joke with one another and I wish nothing to change on my account between my Joseph and his friends. I have told him already he is to continue as if nothing has changed. I have written to Frau Schumann about it – and I wish it to be the same with you. You must continue as you have always been." Giving way again to merriment, she dropped his hand and stamped her foot: "And *that* is an *or*der!"

Joachim saw no jest in her pantomime. Clara had met Amalie on a visit and Amalie had maintained a hushed admiration in the presence of the legendary Clara

Schumann, but Joachim's smile was now carved in wood. "As to that, I can vouch. She has written to Frau Schumann – but do you know she would not let me read what she wrote? It appears not even her husband is to be privy to all her thoughts." The wrinkles gathered again on his brow as he stared at her like a headmaster over his spectacles. "She never allows me to read what she writes. Is that not unkind of her? And now I will be scolded for complaining."

Brahms knew Joachim as everyone knew Joachim for his seriousness without end, his dignity stiff as cardboard, his resort to Mendelssohn as a talisman, but even he was surprised by the knot of resentment in his brow, the pique of a child in his glare, and slapped his arm. "And you will have deserved it, my idiotic friend – but it seems to me that you are the one doing the scolding. An independent woman is the very best to counsel a husband judiciously and the way I see it you have plucked the fairest apple from the tree. If anyone has reason to complain it is me, not you. I am eaten with envy and I admit it freely."

Joachim smiled again, as did Amalie though her voice was firm. "He must have his friends, Herr Brahms, and I must have mine. That is what I wrote to Frau Schumann. I believe it provides a firm foundation for a good marriage, do you not, that we should maintain independent friends?"

"Of course – but what I believe most of all is that Jussuf is a lucky dog. My heartiest congratulations! I could not wish you more happiness than if I were wishing myself!"

Joachim grinned again. "It will be your turn next, Johannes, and our turn to be happy for you."

Brahms shook his head, suddenly unable to look at his friends. "Ach, that would be well, but maybe it is not meant to be. The whole time I was in Vienna – and especially after getting your news – I never ceased to wonder whether … well, whether I had better not experience and enjoy everything – with that one exception … or whether I should make sure of that one thing, go home, and let the rest slide…." He turned away as if he had spoken against his will and wished to retract his words.

Joachim frowned. "Johannes, I can make neither head nor foot of what you say. Whatever the devil do you mean?"

Amalie's laugh was loud, but not malicious. "I think what Herr Brahms is trying to say is that he, too, would like to be married."

"Hahahahah! Is that what I am trying to say?"

"That is *exact*ly what you are trying to say, Herr Brahms."

Brahms stopped laughing. "I think I would agree except for one thing."

"And what is that?"

"Simply that I could never marry any girl who would choose a man like me!" He laughed again, a hollow laugh, but Joachim and Amalie smiled, Amalie more tenderly, and he felt obliged to explain further. "It is like this, you see. Every respectable man should have a home and a family, but you see –" he laughed yet again, "I am not a respectable man, and that is that."

He joked about his respectability only to hide a truth too troublesome to reveal, but the night with Clara at zur Stadt St. Petersburg had confirmed for him his lack of respectability, and he was more uncomfortable with the subject of marriage than he would admit even to himself. He envied Joachim more than he could say, longed for explanations but had no one to ask. He was not good enough for women such as Clara and bound to disappoint all such respectable women.

Amalie and Joachim exchanged glances. Joachim imagined the rejection from Hamburg was responsible for Brahms's bitterness – but he had also been offered another post. "Johannes, will you not accept the offer from the Singakademie?"

The Vienna Singakademie, an oratorio society, had offered him the directorship of its next season. He pursed his lips. "I am considering it."

"Then it seems congratulations are in order for all of us! It seems champagne is in order!"

Amalie smiled. "Congratulations, Herr Brahms! Vienna holds many memories for my Joseph and me, and the good always outweigh the bad."

Amalie was Austrian, born in Styria, to the Imperial Counsellor and his wife, her pappa played violin, her mamma sang, but she had been orphaned in her eighteenth and nineteenth years, first by her pappa, then her mamma and sister, and found herself in Vienna (part of an opera troupe whose manager had absconded with the box office proceeds), where she had been discovered by Bernhard Scholz, the Hanoverian court conductor, who had introduced her to Joachim – and, as Joachim imagined, back to respectability.

Baden-Baden, casino town and health resort, separated from the suburb of Lichtenthal by a gurgling ribbon of water, the River Oos, readily forded by a footbridge, was home during summer to royalty and the upper registers of society from all points of the European compass for the weather as much as the roulette ball. When Hermann Levi, the twenty-three year old conductor of the Karlsruhe Opera House, crossed the bridge with his St. Bernard, Schufterle, named for the black spots raccoonlike around his eyes, he became a different man, lost his erect bearing, his manly stride, and slouched instead, loping like an adolescent. He looked the son of his father, the rabbi, thick black beard coming to a point under his chin, but the hair on his head was shorter, barely touching his ears, and the head itself was almost too small for his slender frame. Most prominent, particularly in profile, was his thin sharp nose, sporting an imposing knuckle on its bridge. Even Schufterle changed crossing the bridge, bounding by Levi's side.

The first time Levi had visited the Schumann household at 14 Lichtenthaler Allee he had peered through the trees from his cab at the box of their cottage. Unable to imagine it could house Clara's large brood he had shaken his head at the driver. "This cannot be number fourteen. I am looking for Frau Schumann's house." There had followed giggles from the hedges from which Eugenie and Felix had emerged. Eleven-year-old Eugenie had smiled and spoken shyly. "Herr Levi, this *is* Frau Schumann's house." Nine-year-old Felix had grinned. "We call it our doghouse, Herr Levi."

The facade was deceptive: chimneys at each end and two gabled windows gave an impression of length to the width of the rambling house. Two long rooms, living and dining, extended on the ground floor into Clara's bedroom in the back, opening onto a verandah overrun with ivy, overlooking rolling hills of pine forests. A narrow kitchen beside a narrow hallway holding a narrow staircase filled the rest of the floor. The upstairs held a room with a window for each of the four girls and Felix, also a general room on the landing for closets and clothes. The house also held three grand pianos, all provided by the manufacturers.

Despite Schufterle by his side, a bear gamboling like a lamb, the house remained quiet. It was almost four in the afternoon, still the time for napping, knitting, and needlework. Levi carried a bottle of champagne in a bag, whistled the fairy scherzo from Mendelssohn's *Midsummer Night's Dream*, the melody of zigzagging flutes with which he always announced himself, and rapped on the door, a tattoo in the rhythm of the melody.

Julie opened the door, wearing a white dress with tripletiered sleeves and a tiny white bow at the collar. Her blond hair, woven with red camellias, gathered loosely in a clip, gave her an angelic appearance. Levi understood Brahms's attraction easily, but not his qualms: his major objection, the difference in their ages (she was eighteen, he thirty) left him unconvinced. You had to be eighteen to enter the casino, and Brahms to his embarrassment had been turned away for appearing too young – but Brahms was either unwilling or unable to be more frank.

"Hallo, Herr Levi. Hallo, Schufterle. How is it with you today?" She bent to stroke Schufterle, almost falling over backward when he rose to greet her. Elise and Eugenie called from their board game at the table.

"Hallo, Herr Levi!"

"Hallo, Herr Levi!"

Elise, two years older than Julie, blond hair in braids, face angular, mouth thin, ears long, also dressed in white, large brass buttons leading to a high collar with a black band, turned blue eyes on Levi. Eugenie, the youngest daughter, looked schoolgirlish in a blue dress with black buttons leading to an open white collar, her hair in a blue ribbon.

"Hallo, Frauleins! HALLO, FRAU SCHUMANN!"

"HOOF! HOOF! HOOF! HOOF!"

Clara called from within. "You are early, Herr Levi, but come on in – but, please, must you shout so? It is not quite evening yet."

"I did not want to be late. I did not want to wait any longer."

"HOOF! WHOOF! WHOOOOF! WHOOOOOF!"

Clara entered with Felix. "Schufterle! Quiet! Sit!"

Schufterle, large enough to unsettle the room with a bound, his wagging tail disruptive as a gale, paid no attention, until Levi roared: "SCHUFTERLE, SIT!" He sat then, but stood again on his hind legs when Felix put his arms around his neck, towering over the boy. He was almost taller than Felix while still on all fours.

"Felix, if you want to play with him take him outside – in the back."

"Okay, Mamma!"

Felix had asked permission to skip practice that day. She had let him off, but not without disappointment. Her own pappa had kept her from the piano to punish her, but Felix liked nothing better than to be let off practice. Of all the children he looked most like Robert, but none showed any musical promise, and only Elise showed even an interest in performing onstage.

"What would you like to drink, Herr Levi? Coffee? Chocolate?"

Levi held up his bag. "How about some champagne?"

"Champagne? But it is only four o'clock – and what are we celebrating?"

"Frau Schumann, only philistines need an excuse to celebrate. Champagne is its own celebration, is it not?"

"Oh, very well, but I will hold my share for later during supper. It is still too early for me."

Julie turned to Clara. "What will you have, Mamma? What will everyone have? I will be in charge of the refreshments."

Clara wanted coffee, Elise chocolate. Eugenie took the bottle from Levi to open in the kitchen where Marie was preparing supper. Julie followed.

Levi sat at the piano, pursing his mouth, cracking his knuckles, looking at Clara and Elise. "I think it is time to set the mood for the evening, do you not?"

The women looked at each other. Clara extended her palm graciously. "Of course, Herr Levi. What would you suggest?"

For an answer Levi raised both hands with grace, brought them down gently on the keyboard, and played the first shimmering bars of "The Blue Danube," everyone's favorite, but he played it in two keys at once, B and C.

Clara jumped up holding her ears and left the room. Elise went to his side, also holding her ears. "Herr Levi, why do you torture us like this?"

Levi continued to play. "Because torture is the best instruction, Fraulein Elise. Do you not know that yet?"

"You are talking nonsense, Herr Levi. By your argument, then, the worst players would give us the best instruction."

"You are right, of course, if you mean that their worst is no better than their best – but you are wrong if you mean that they play their worst by design. It is more difficult to play badly by design, would you not agree, than to play badly because you are unable to play well? And if that is so, does it not follow that only the best players can play the worst music?"

Elise laughed. "I cannot argue with your logic, Herr Levi – but I am afraid I cannot agree with it either. I am afraid of where such logic leads."

Levi never stopped playing as he talked; Julie could neither stop laughing nor coughing. Clara tapped Levi's shoulder, a glass of champagne in her hand. "Herr Levi, please stop. If you make Julie laugh too much she coughs, and she is not to be excited."

Levi stopped and took the glass of champagne from Clara. "Of course, Frau Schumann. I am sorry, Fraulein Julie."

Julie, still coughing, waved her hand to indicate no apology was necessary. She had been isolated from the family since she was two for her health, first with Clara's mamma in Berlin, later in warmer Mediterannean climes with her mamma's friends, but remained prone to coughs – worse, to cataleptic fits every two months which rendered her motionless for hours. Her cough concerned Clara, but the doctors assured her it was nerves and anemia which accounted for her fits, not her chest and lungs which were sound.

BRAHMS MOUNTED THE STAIRS HEAVILY. He boarded at the Bar Inn down the road, but moved so easily among the Schumanns, supping with them almost everyday, his place set at Clara's right, that he might as well have had two residences. There had been no one in the sittingroom when he had let himself in and he had gone upstairs imagining he heard Levi among the girls, but instead of Levi he found Elise, Julie, and Eugenie, all staring at him.

His head turned slowly to stone as it did in Julie's presence. He scowled, lowering his voice, almost growling to cover his consternation. "Where is he?"

Elise raised her eyebrows. "Who do you mean, Herr Brahms?"

Brahms looked around, careful to avoid looking at Julie. "I mean the devil himself – Levi, of course. Is he not here?"

"Levi? Should he be here?"

"I thought I heard him."

"Why should you think that?"

"Is that not Schufterle barking?"

"Schufterle is downstairs. Maybe Levi is too."

Brahms frowned. "I must have made a mistake." He turned to go downstairs again, but a voice sounded from one of Clara's trunks by the wall. "O, Freunde!"

Brahms stopped. The girls giggled as the trunk opened and Levi emerged singing. "Freunde, schoner Gotterfunken, Tochter aus Elysiam."

"Levi! You dog!" Brahms sprang to the trunk attempting to stuff Levi back, but he was too late and found himself struggling with Levi instead. He gave up the struggle, turning instead on the girls. "What the devil were you girls doing with Levi anyway? It is a good thing I came before your reputations were completely in tatters."

Levi grinned. "With all respect, Herr Brahms, but what we were doing must remain our secret."

Brahms was not upset, the friends often pulled pranks on each other, but he wished to assert himself in Julie's presence. "Secrets be damned! What were you doing?"

Elise and Julie remained quiet and grinning, but the shouting upset Eugenie. "Herr Brahms, we were only showing Herr Levi Julie's new dress. That is all."

Brahms grinned. "Oh, if that is all then why not show it to me?"

The three girls and Levi exchanged glances. Elise faced him finally, answering for all. "But Herr Brahms, you do not care about such things, do you?"

"Why should you think such a thing, Fraulein Elise?"

Again the four exchanged glances. Brahms wore a bright red shirt without a collar, a patched alpaca coat, sleeves and waistcoat smudged with cigar ash, trousers an inch too short, and the hat in his hand was frayed.

Julie focused her blue eyes on Brahms. "Herr Brahms, you must not bully my sister. We simply do not think you care about such things – and there is an end to the matter."

Brahms nodded, sputtering an answer. "Aha! I know what it is you mean to say, Fraulein Julie, but I dress to please myself – and who is it that you please to dress?"

Elise grinned. "She pleases to dress no one, Herr Brahms, and you should be ashamed for suggesting that she does – but she always dresses pleasingly."

The girls giggled again and Levi laughed as Brahms turned red. "Tchhah! You know what I mean. You must not put words in my mouth."

Levi grinned. "We might put words in your mouth, Herr Brahms – but we are not to be blamed if you follow them with your foot."

Brahms glared, putting on a show, wishing to be clever for Julie, but his brain turned to ice, his tongue to fur. "Has anyone told you, Levi, that you laugh like a sheep? You do not laugh, but bleat!"

Levi laughed again, bleating more loudly yet. "Yes, of course, it is no secret among my friends – but you would be surprised to learn how many goats love to tell me that I laugh like a sheep."

The girls giggled again until Julie began again to cough.

CLARA SAT AT THE HEAD OF THE TABLE, Brahms on her right, Levi her left, Schufterle on the floor between Clara and Levi; Eugenie and Elise sat next to Brahms, Felix and Julie next to Levi; Marie faced Clara across the table. Brahms chewed thoughtfully. "Mmmm, Fraulein Marie, the baked pork is delicious. Where did you get the recipe?"

Marie, black hair in a bun, stringy from the heat of the kitchen, turned grey eyes on Brahms. "Danke, Herr Brahms. The recipe is from Frau Vera's book on cookery."

Brahms continued to chew. "Hmmm, it is delicious, indeed, but something is definitely missing. Now what the devil could it be?"

"Herr Brahms, you are always teasing me."

"Hmmm, now, where do you keep Frau Vera's book on cookery? I should like to confirm something for myself." He pushed his chair roughly back, wiping the back of his hand against his mouth, his hands on his waistcoat. "I will be right back. Now where is the book, Fraulein Marie?"

"Johannes, please sit down. You can confirm what you want later."

"No. If I do not confirm it while I have the taste in my mouth I will not be able later."

Marie shrugged at Clara. It was impossible to tell Herr Brahms what to do once he had made up his mind. "It is on the cupboard, Herr Brahms. The recipe is on page seventeen."

Brahms returned from the kitchen, his nose in the book. "Hmmm, now, let me see. Peas, carrots, asparagus, yes, yes, everything is there – and bratwurst, yes, and pork, yes, of course, yes."

Clara suddenly slapped her forehead with her palm. "Levi! Levi! What are you doing? Oh, mein Gott, Levi! Noooo! He will break the glass! Oh, Levi, how could you?"

Levi had lowered his champagne glass to Schufterle who held it firmly between his paws, licking it clean with his thick large tongue.

"Onions! That is what I am missing! Fraulein Marie has left out the onions!"

Marie laughed. "I am sorry, Herr Brahms. We were out of onions."

"No more champagne for you, Schufterle – and not for you either, Levi – not if you insist on giving it to poor Schufterle."

"I can assure you, Frau Schumann, that he appreciates the champagne at least as much as you and I. His taste buds are more finely developed than ours – just like his sense of smell."

Clara groaned, could hardly believe the regard with which these men, now cavorting like clowns, esteemed each other, but just days ago they had each taken her separately into their confidences, Brahms to say of Levi that his eyes were fixed on the brightest star in the firmament, and Levi of Brahms that he soared to heights he could follow only with his eyes.

Marie and Elise grinned, shaking their heads at the pandemonium; Eugenie and Felix rocked with laughter in their chairs; Julie made faces to keep from laughing too hard.

"BUYING THIS HOUSE was among my greater inspirations, Johannes." Clara laughed. "It is so beautiful outside that if I wanted to take a walk all I have to do is to look out of my window."

Levi had left after supper. Sometimes the children joined them on their walk, but this time they were alone. Brahms laughed, walking by her side, but he laughed ironically, nervous, unsure how to say what he wished. "Why did we not just stay in the house, then, and look out of the window?"

Clara frowned. Pink and red and yellow azaleas blossomed around them; lilacs scented the air; the steep hillside to their left threw firs like spikes into the sky. When the children joined them, Clara warned them continually to mind the precipices. "Johannes, must you make fun of everything I say? It is very annoying, especially when you know exactly what I mean."

Brahms grinned, getting further from his subject. "Yes, of course, I know what you mean, but do you not find it funny? Just as we are taking a walk you say we should have just looked outside the window."

"No, I do not find it funny, not at all, not when you mock everything I say, not when it emerges as a *pat*tern of mockery."

"But I do not mock everything."

"Oh, but you do! And do not say that you do not. I do not wish to argue with you further."

Brahms still grinned, but remained silent, wishing no more argument himself.

Clara spoke more placatingly. "I have all the advantages in Lichtenthal, not only of nature, but of society, privacy – and the girls, too, have wellpaying pupils – and the children can all be together."

Brahms nodded, but remained silent, hands behind him, holding his hat. Their shadows grew longer, soon to be recast by gaslight, vanish into the night. Clara grew defensive, understanding he was thinking about her boys.

"I chose to leave Ferdinand in Berlin because he is getting along well there – and Ludwig is very industrious. I always knew he had more to him than met the eye and I am so glad to be proven right."

Brahms said nothing. Both boys had pleaded to be with the family in Lichtenthal, but Clara had insisted they would serve themselves better where they were. They had been orphaned as much by her lifestyle as by Robert's death, but he had never been able to convince her differently and no longer wished to discuss it. At least, Ludwig, apprenticed to a bookseller in Karlsruhe, was not too far to visit.

Clara changed the subject. "I am so very glad you have accepted the post in Vienna, Johannes. There is no city in Germany where you would find recognition so easily as in Vienna. I knew that once you had tasted the life of Vienna, Hamburg would lose its appeal. I am sure even your poor mamma will come to find some pleasure in it despite the distance."

Brahms had visited his family after leaving Joachim and Amalie. Stockhausen, who had gained the post he had coveted, had appointed his pappa to the Hamburg Philharmonic. The old man could not have been more excited and practised daily for hours – but his wife, now seventy-four years old, was less pleased, and condemned her husband, just fifty-seven, to the attic for practices, pleading headaches. She wished to sit with her hands in her lap, let others care for her, but he was still too robust to retire, certainly to do her bidding at home. Brahms sympathized with both, but he had disregarded his mamma's plea not to go to so far a place as Vienna. "I hope so. She has little enough joy left in her life now – but I must confess I am more than a little shy at making my first attempt in this line in Vienna of all places."

"But it is not your first attempt, Johannes. You have done similar things in Detmold."

"But not on this scale, not with this responsibility."

"You will surprise yourself – and you will surprise them all. I am sure of it."

"I hope you are right. I must say that if not for Dietrich I would feel much less sure of myself."

Albert Dietrich was now choirmaster in Oldenburg and Brahms had visited him between Hamburg and Lichtenthal to pepper him with his doubts, ideas, and questions.

They walked in silence again for a while. Brahms thrust his lower lip forward, Clara inhaled deeply, a bouquet of grass, roses, and daisies. Her days started with family counsels at breakfast, in the garden if the weather permitted, letters were read, plans laid for the day. Mornings held practises, visits from Frauleins Leser and Junge who had proven so helpful during the difficult years with Robert, who were also in Lichtenthal for the summer. Each of the girls had responsibilities: Marie cooked and sewed; Elise gave lessons to Eugenie and Felix; Julie cleaned the house. Clara gave lessons as did the older girls to the wellheeled clientele of Baden-Baden: foreigners, nobility, offspring of local and visiting Croesuses. From their house was a view of the broad avenue along which notables promenaded: painters, writers, musicians, not excluding the King and Queen of Prussia. Among the artistes was an Italian tenor who had taken a house across the street. After dinner, when Clara opened the diningroom window and the girls sat watching the promenaders on the street, the tenor would appear on his balcony to watch them. They had not known how to deal with the annoyance until Julie had appeared at the window and curtsied deeply – before thumbing her nose and sticking out her tongue at the tenor. The man was nevermore seen on the balcony. Clara laughed suddenly at the memory.

Brahms became more preoccupied after she had explained her laughter, recognizing his opportunity though Clara appeared not to notice. "What did you do then?"

Clara smiled. "Oh, I scolded her, of course. What else could I do being her mamma? They are not to behave rudely to strangers – but they knew my heart was not in it. They knew how wholeheartedly I approved. Julchen may be the most loving of all my children."

Brahms nodded. Julchen was the only one of her children to whom he had dedicated a composition, a series of variations on her pappa's last theme, a theme Robert insisted Schubert had sent from the grave. "There is, indeed, something very special about … our Julchen." He spoke breathlessly. "It is difficult to think of her without emotion."

When Clara smiled she appeared girlish and he imagined he saw mother and daughter in each other. In his imagination she was now always Julchen, never Fraulein Schumann, never even Fraulein Julie, or just Julie. He looked at Clara, but her attention seemed to have wandered. "Johannes, why is it you no longer send me your things as and when you write them. Why do I have to learn about them from other people?"

He frowned; she accused him of silence, but when he spoke of Julchen she did not listen. He pursed his lips, wanting to stamp his feet or hit something to shake understanding into her, most of all to clarify what he meant, but he could be no more specific. He twisted his mouth as he spoke. "I would send them to you if what you said was helpful – but all you say is to make this longer, or that is too short. You say I should work it out, but you do not say what needs to be worked out, or how, or why. What is the use of that? Any mincing little pedant can say what you say."

Their shadows moved around them as they passed a lamp. Clara's hand went to her breast as if to slow her beating heart. This was what she could never get used to in Johannes. He could be as dutiful and loving as a son in one moment and as hateful as ten devils in the next. No one else addressed her with such disrespect – but she wondered if it were true, as Fraulein Leser had suggested, that it was her own fault for letting him go too far so very long ago. He continued walking, but she stopped. "A mincing little pedant? Is that what you think of me?"

He turned to face her, stopping only because she had stopped. "What? I never said so."

"You did! You just did! Not one minute past you called me a mincing little pedant!"

"I did not. I said any mincing little pedant could have said what you said. I did not say you were a mincing little pedant."

"I do not see a difference."

"There is a difference, whether you can see it or not."

She couldn't say what was more insulting, what he said or his rationalization of what he said. She shook her head. "Johannes, I swear, sometimes I think you will make me say something hateful against my best will."

He shrugged, seeming more disrespectful yet, as if he were forgiving her instead of she forgiving him. "It is all right, Clara. I have learned to do without you. I used to think I could never do without you, but I have learned differently since."

Clara took a deep breath. "Johannes, I simply cannot believe how very unkind you can be sometimes – and with no apparent provocation. First I am to tell you everything I think, but when I do I am to be rapped over the knuckles – and worse. I am sorry I am no musical scholar, but I have done my very best for you – and you know it. You accused me once of being too enthusiastic and now you say I am too pedantic, but you cannot have it both ways."

Brahms grimaced. He had overstated his case, venting his frustration about Julchen. "Ach, Clara! I did not mean it that way."

"I do not see what other way you could have meant it that could be satisfactory."

"Simply that I have developed greater confidence in my own judgment. I do not need the same encouragement. That is all."

"That sounds to me a very facile explanation."

"It is not, and I am sorry if you think so, but it is the best that I can do."

ii

Brahms was sorry to see the season come to an end just as he felt he was beginning to make progress, but in matters of the heart you only hurt yourself when you hurried, and he was convinced Julchen at least suspected his intentions. He had not been so very subtle, and she was not so very stupid as not to understand. Passing the house he chose to make a visit – or perhaps he had chosen to visit on the pretext of passing the house. It did not matter as long as he made his visit. He had impressed Clara less favorably of late and if nothing else he might at least improve the impression.

He walked around the house; Marie practised a Beethoven sonata in one corner of the house, Elise her pappa's *Papillons* in another, Eugenie and Felix waved from a tree behind the house, each with a book in hand; Clara was nowhere to be seen, possibly in her room; Julie was in the kitchen, looking through the larder, making a list of things they needed. He let himself in. "Julchen, hallo!"

Julie swung her head around, hair of gold sweeping her shoulder, pencil falling from her hand. "Herr Brahms! You startled me!"

Brahms hurried to pick up the pencil, glad for something to do. "Who? Me? Do you not know who I am?"

"I did not mean that. I meant I was not expecting anyone."

"But I have visited before without being expected, have I not? I am in the habit, am I not? Your mamma – she does not mind, does she?"

"No, Herr Brahms, of course she does not. I meant only that you startled me."

He heard reproof in her words, his head began slowly to anesthetize again, his smile to grow pasty. "Ah, yes, well, I am sorry. I did not mean …"

Julie smiled. "I know, Herr Brahms. It is all right. Would you like coffee?"

"If it is not any trouble."

"Do not be silly, Herr Brahms. You are family and you should know it. Please, sit down."

He grinned, always pleased when she spoke informally with him though it only made him more formal himself. He had to force himself to be lighthearted. He laughed. "Well, then, I think I will sit – but where is the old woman?"

Julie did not laugh. "Who do you mean, Herr Brahms?"

Brahms laughed again, but more selfconsciously. "I mean your dear sweet mamma, the old woman – who else?"

Julie set about making coffee without looking at him; he was afraid he had spoken more lightheadedly than lightheartedly. "She is visiting Herr Kirchner."

"Ah, she is visiting Herr Kirchner." Theodor Kirchner had once been Robert's student and was now the organist in Winterthur. "Why does she go there?"

"To play the piano."

"Ah, of course, to play the piano – but why does he not come here?"

"Sometimes he does."

"But why not today?"

"Why do you not ask her, Herr Brahms? I am sure I do not know the reason." Brahms's smile turned plastic again. "Ha! Of course! And why should you?"

"Why, indeed?"

"Indeed!"

"Herr Brahms, why do you always repeat what I say?"

"Ha! Why do I always repeat what you say? Do I, indeed?"

"You have just done it again."

"Yes, indeed – but I am sure I do not know the reason."

Julie, climbing a stool to get coffee cups from a shelf, raised her eyebrows at Brahms over her shoulder. "Herr Brahms, sometimes it is very strange being with you."

"Ah, yes, I have felt it, too – very strange, being with me. It is stranger, is it not, that I am closer in age to you than to your mamma?"

Julie climbed down again and spoke without looking at him. "I have never given that any thought, Herr Brahms. To me you have always been an onkel. You have been with us so much that you have become our pappa almost more than our own pappa."

Brahms stared at the wall, appearing not to have heard, continuing his original thought. "It is like that in my family. My mamma is seventeen years older than my pappa – but age matters so very little when there is love, do you not think?"

"I am sure you are right, Herr Brahms. I am sure I do not know what to think myself."

"Between you and me there are only twelve years – but between your mamma and me there are fourteen. Now do you not find that strange? Do you not find it something to think about?"

Julie was quiet: Herr Brahms was fond of a joke and had joked before about marrying her, also about marrying Eugenie – even about marrying Dietrich's daughter, still a baby – but the joke, if it was still a joke, made her uncomfortable, especially for the way he looked at her, his eyes heavylidded, lashes fluttering – and his own discomfort made her more uncomfortable yet. She was glad for Elise's appearance in the kitchen.

Elise grinned. "Ah, Julchen, I am glad to see you are all right. Eugenie said she saw Herr Brahms spying on the house."

Brahms jumped up, acknowledging Elise, relieved to see her. "Spying? Me? I came in broad daylight!"

THEODOR KIRCHNER WAS FOUR YEARS YOUNGER THAN CLARA, among the first of Robert's students at the Leipzig Conservatory, cleanshaven, a fine pianist, organist, and conductor, in appearance not unlike Robert though his brow was more creased at a younger age and Clara had never seen in his face the brazen smile of the young

Robert. More even than Robert he was a dreamer – a virtue in an artist, but a vice if he had not the strength to visualize his dreams, and Clara feared that Kirchner had been too long lost in his dreams to recover, not only the artist but the man lacked backbone. For all his talent he had never accomplished much – but criticizing his Preludes she had thrown him into a depression, and in helping him out had mired herself more deeply. Kirchner revered Robert and had asked for a lock of his hair, she had complied, and from such interests other interests had developed. If the Russian novelist, Turgenev, among Baden-Baden's notable visitors, and her friend, Pauline Viardot, the contralto, could conduct their liaison publicly, she found it not unseemly to conduct her own privately. Besides, she hated to see so musical a spirit lose itself in shadows and imagined she might help him yet to his best nature.

Seeing him again in the deep afternoon, his untidy bachelor apartment, crumpled jacket and tie, she felt her ribcage tighten – but his smile, however tentative, loosened it again. "Clara, it is good to see you. I have much to show you since we last talked."

"Indeed?"

He would have gone straight to the piano, but she held him in a long embrace, initiated a kiss, and felt his confidence soar. His smile was wider and more confident when they parted. "Indeed!"

She smiled. "Then show me, Theodor. You must not keep a lady waiting."

"Ah, indeed not." He sat at the piano so quickly she was sorry again. "You were right, Clara, entirely right about what you said – about my Preludes."

She had said that though they contained much beauty the harmonies were farfetched and flowed unnaturally, and the forms were too trivial for the ideas. She stood behind him as he played, smiling; the Preludes were much improved, even charming, but they remained small exercises; next she would advise work on a larger scale. She put her hands on his shoulders, slid them around to his chest, loosened his tie, and kissed the top of his head. "They are enchanting now, Theodor, quite enchanting."

Brahms felt a familiar paralysis in his head. Elisabet von Stockhausen was not conventionally beautiful, her neck was too thick, her forehead too low, but her appearance was luminous, sunlight in her hair, moonlight in her skin. Her eyes were sometimes green, sometimes brown, sometimes in between, but most bewitching of all she appeared always to be smiling – in harmony it seemed, even at the tender age of sixteen, with a cosmic joke he wished he might share. She had a slight stoop, but appeared to be stooping in sympathy, all the better to listen. Epstein had sent her to him for lessons, warning that no man who set eyes on her could keep from falling in love, and seeing her at the piano in his rooms at 7 Singerstrasse Brahms knew what he meant. The room polarized itself around her smile. His voice rose an octave, words became whispers. "Fraulein von Stockhausen, why are you smiling?"

Her smiled widened. "Should I frown, Herr Brahms? Should I be so very displeased to be here?"

He longed to caress her neck, white as the lace of her wide collar, whiter for its black band and pendant, a black cameo. "No, that is not what I meant. I was only wondering – I mean, I do not understand why you are smiling."

Her eyes were catlike for more than their color. "Perhaps I am smiling because I am Austrian, Herr Brahms – and we Austrians never expect you Germans to understand us?"

Brahms's smile flattened to paste. She was no relation to her namesake now directing the Hamburg Philharmonic, but the daughter of the Hanoverian Ambassador to Vienna, a music lover himself who had taken lessons from Chopin during his previous assignment in Paris where Elisabet had been born and lived the first six years of her life. "Perhaps – and perhaps also it is because you are more Parisian than Viennese?"

He could not have said what he meant except that anything French was suspect, but he could not break the spell of her smile. "Perhaps – and perhaps you imagine I am more Parisian than Viennese because you are more Hamburger than German?"

She was alluding to the independence of the Hamburger, citizen of the free city, bestowing on him the benefit of the doubt, but he lacked the wit to continue. "Perhaps – and perhaps it is only because I am too much of a goat to imagine one needs a reason at all to smile?"

"Oh, no, Herr Brahms, you are too clever for me – but you will not get me to call you a goat."

"Hah! It is you who are too clever for me by far– but maybe you are right. I know what the members of the Academy say – and maybe you do too?"

Still she smiled, raising her chin. "I have heard what they say."

The first two concerts of the Singakademie were over, the first a success, the second less so. The main criticism of the first had been that all the composers, among them Bach, Beethoven, and Schumann, were dead, but for the second he had chosen composers even longer dead, among them again Bach and Beethoven, but also Gabrieli, Eccard, Schutz, and Rovetta, of whom few had heard and fewer cared. Among the works he had chosen were Bach's cantatas, "I Had Much Grief" and "Dearest God, When Shall I Die?" and Schumann's and Cherubini's Requiems. Hanslick had written that the Viennese enjoyed serious music, but not for the purpose of attending their own funerals, first Protestant, then Catholic – and Hanslick's had been among the kinder reviews. Brahms's smile remained pasty. "It is no secret. My choristers say it to my face. When Brahms is in good spirits, they say, he gets them to sing 'The Grave Is My Joy.'"

Still she smiled, not unsympathetically. "Indeed, it is no secret, Herr Brahms, but not being a Viennese you are handicapped in your choices. On the other hand, being a Viennese myself – or a Parisian, if that suits you better, who has lived in Vienna for most of her life – I understand their complaints perfectly."

Brahms recalled what Berta Porubsky, now Berta Faber, had said of his choices for the Frauenchor programs. "But I think I have learned my lesson. I think I am beginning to understand what it means to be a Viennese and I have prepared an agreeable surprise for the next concert."

"Oh, yes?"

He grinned. "I will begin with a completely different cantata: 'Death Is My Delight.'"

He was rewarded with a laugh and comfortable for the first time during their conversation, but he had decided already to discontinue the lessons before he made a fool of himself – as he had the Christmas before, proposing to Ottilie von Hauer, a girl with glossy black hair who loved his songs – which had given him the courage to approach her – that, the Christmas spirit, and a fortification of champagne. She had laughed so gaily when she had understood him that he had not been offended, grinning instead himself, asking without selfconsciousness: "Do you find it so very funny, then?"

"I beg your pardon, Herr Brahms, but I do not laugh at you. I laugh at the situation."

"The situation? What is the situation?"

"I would, of course, marry you happily, my dear Herr Brahms, but I have just this hour consented to marry another. I am to be the wife of Herr Doktor Ebner in the new year."

"Ah-hahah! That is funny, indeed – but otherwise you would have been my wife?"

Ottilie had been coy. "Maybe."

"Ah, and maybe, if you had not consented to be the bride of another, I might not have asked you."

She had laughed, and he had imagined he had conducted himself in the manner of the gayest Viennese gallant, but he had left her presence sober – and relieved. His prospects remained too uncertain for marriage, but it was a wonder what an idiot he became in the presence of a pretty face and voice and he felt no less idiotic in the presence of Fraulein von Stockhausen. If he saw much of her he was sure he would propose again, perhaps without the good fortune of being too late. She was a baroness; he could scarcely believe she had climbed seven narrow flights of stairs to his tiny rooms on the fourth floor, but he could not imagine her within the circle of his family where Clara had so easily found a niche during her first visit. She was not as fine a pianist as Clara, no woman was, but she had a finer musical memory, could reproduce symphonies on the piano after just a couple of hearings, and read scores more easily. She was also younger than Clara, younger than himself (at sixteen almost half his age), but age had less to do with his ambivalence than her upbringing. Clara shared her money woes without embarrassment, woes he imagined the Baroness could never understand – at least, he told himself, such was the rationale a responsible bachelor was forced to entertain.

ii

The twenty-second of Brahms's variations on a theme by Handel tinkles like a music box, a fairytale told by a glockenspiel. It provides a lullaby before the final bounding galloping variations which culminate in a massive fugue. Individual variations were expected to have individuality, but he had broken precedent. Whereas variations of the past had been discrete, Brahms's twenty-five gained from their context, each more important for the variation it followed and preceded than for itself, each link in the chain stronger for its predecessor, the concluding fugue the strongest of the set, four voices rising, circling, echoing, blending finally into a single indestructible edifice. This was his manifesto, his flag unfurled, the mandate of his music, not the sorry declaration he and the others had signed against the New Germans in their moment of hubris. A long silence followed the conclusion of the set. Looking up from the piano he saw the eyes of the company drift toward Wagner.

Wagner had long envied the facility of pianists. He had come to music on the heels of half a dozen other aspirations at the advanced age of fifteen, hearing Beethoven's Ninth. Mesmerized, he had declared it the final utterance of the symphony and made it his springboard into music drama (as he preferred to call his operas) – but however well he might compose he would never be a pianist. It mattered little: he was the greatest of composers. Such facility as Brahms showed on the piano was a boon to composition, he could have exploited it to the fullest, but it had to be developed in the egg, in puling children sucking their thumbs. He had come too late to the recognition and was condemned instead to rely on the Liszts of the world, and the Bulows and Tausigs and Corneliuses to transcribe and play back to him what he had been granted the power to compose – and the Brahmses, though the young man had acquitted himself no less fairly as a composer, however antiquated his inspiration. He had also been good enough to help Tausig and Cornelius and Weissheimer with copywork for *Meistersinger*, leading the older composer to attend a solo recital by the younger of his Piano Sonata in F major, and later to extend an invitation to play. The silence in the room seemed suddenly to bark, its eyes settled on him like lead, and he leaped to his feet, applauding wildly. "Bravo, Herr Brahms! Bravo, indeed! One sees what may yet be done with the old forms in the hands of one who knows what to do with them. We can see that you are no joker."

Others followed suit, standing and applauding with Wagner, ceasing when he ceased, eyes continually on his lavish form. Wagner's wardrobe was a subject of ridicule in Vienna, but seeing him earlier Brahms had been too dumbstruck to think, let alone laugh. His host wore matching black satin pants, jacket, slippers, a white silk shirt, pink silk tie, and a black velvet cape lined with fur. Even in slippers he was taller than Brahms, though barely. Brahms nodded. "Danke, Herr Wagner. If I may return the compliment, I consider myself the best of Wagnerians."

Wagner almost stepped forward in his puzzlement. He had expected little from an author of the misbegotten manifesto, but Brahms had surprised him on more than one occasion. "You do, do you?"

Brahms nodded again. "I do. Indeed, I do. There is no one who understands your music better."

Wagner's smile under the eagle nose and brow more closely resembled a snarl. Just fifty-one, he looked older, distracted, hair graying at the sides, but suddenly he laughed and raising his arms took a step forward, ready it seemed to skip across the room as he addressed the party, a company of about thirty. "We would like to thank Herr Brahms for his performance today as well as his timely aid. He has been good enough to help us in our efforts to raise funds when he is himself already a musician with a sufficient reputation not to have bothered."

Wagner's fortunes had been at an ebb: *Tannhauser* had been disrupted in Paris for political reasons, *Tristan* forsaken in Vienna for financial (after fifty-seven rehearsals); and Wagner wished to replenish his coffers performing orchestral excerpts from the *Meistersinger* and *Ring*. Tausig had approached him, and for his efforts Brahms had been invited to meet and perform for Wagner in Penzing, an affluent Vienna suburb, where Wagner occupied the upper storey of a baron's mansion, including the garden and servants. "Herr Brahms, please avail yourself of our hospitality. There is wine, champagne, food. Please consider yourself a member of the household."

Brahms nodded again. "Danke, Herr Wagner. I will take your words to heart."

Wagner smiled again his snarl of a smile. "Nothing would please us better." He turned to Peter Cornelius, a thin smiling man with thinning hair, a floppy moustache, neck like a chicken, and started a conversation, the sign for others to talk among themselves.

A group formed around Brahms, congratulating him, among them Wendelin Weissheimer and Tausig. Weissheimer smiled. "Herr Brahms, so you, too, are now a Wagnerian."

Brahms understood the taunt. At one of Wagner's concerts Weissheimer had applauded unendingly until Brahms had told him to be careful he did not wear out his brand new white kid gloves. "It would seem that way, would it not, Herr Weissheimer?"

"Then you admit it?"

"Well, it seems in Vienna one must be either a Wagnerian or an antiWagnerian. There is no such thing as a nonWagnerian – and the antiWagnerians speak so frivolously of Wagner that I am forced to confess myself an … anti-antiWagnerian."

Brahms allowed himself a smile at his wit, pleased with the laughter that followed, but Weissheimer turned grim. "Well, then, that would still make you a Wagnerian, would it not?"

"So it would seem."

Luise Dustmann-Meyer, Isolde for the recently abandoned *Tristan*, had a distinctive laugh. It rippled in arpeggios through three octaves, catching everyone's attention. "Whatever Herr Brahms professes, Herr Weissheimer makes it clear from his interrogation that he wishes he had been a man of jurisprudence himself rather than music."

The group chuckled. Most of them knew Weissheimer to be a generous man with a generous allowance from a wealthy father, which was why Wagner indulged his limited musical talent. Weissheimer's grin stiffened – as did Brahms's. Luise had a figure to tempt Paris, a voice to charm the deaf. Brahms had met her at the Cologne festival the previous year, the second Viennese woman he had met (after Berta Porubsky), and the second woman to call him to Vienna. The Viennese were more vivacious than Germans, certainly than Hamburgers, but Luise was also a member of the opera, where Gemutlichkeit was taken to extremes. He had not called on her since his arrival in Vienna though they had maintained a correspondence, and found himself suddenly afraid of what she might say (in her letters she had called him Hansi). "Frau Dustmann, how is it with you?"

Luise's hair had the gloss of a raven's wings and danced with the least movement, an effect of which she was well aware, bouncing lightly on tiptoe as she spoke. "It is good of you to ask, Herr Brahms, but it would have been even better if you had done so before the question was pressed upon you, would it not?"

Brahms forced a smile. "I am sorry, Frau Dustmann. If it were up to me I would have left my card with you upon my very first day, but my obligations seemed to grow by the hour once I arrived in Vienna."

Luise's smile was mischievous. "Well, then, if it is such an obligation to visit me, consider yourself released, Herr Brahms."

Brahms's face turned red, his smile again to paste. "It is no obligation, Frau Dustmann."

"Well, then, if it is no obligation, perhaps it is too far a distance to come to Hietzing? Perhaps the badness of the times is no help either?"

Hietzing was a suburb, but not far, with trains running hourly.

Brahms was speechless. She was clearly not angry, but enjoying herself too well to quit. "I am sorely in need of a tuning, Herr Brahms. Did you not know that?"

Brahms's mouth dropped. "I did not even know you played."

Her laughter spanned the octaves again. "I did not say my piano needed tuning, Herr Brahms – but maybe your ear is not so good after all?"

Brahms was again speechless. He knew what to do when a barmaid winked and smiled, but not a lady – who should have known better.

Luise winked as if she had read his mind. "But you have shown yourself an excellent tunesmith, indeed, tonight on the piano."

Luise was a married woman – but considered herself free. Tausig intervened. "I am sure he will be visiting you soon, Frau Dustmann – and I would be very surprised indeed if he did not bring his tuning fork with him."

Brahms's laugh was high and thin, joined by Luise and the guests. He might have said something, but found himself rescued by a scream like that of a young eagle from the other side of the room – and the group dispersed to congregate around Wagner. Luise whispered in his ear with a smile. "You have drawn too many to your side, Hansi, but now the monster must be fed."

BRAHMS SAID LITTLE THE REST OF THE EVENING; Wagner, more even than Liszt, demanded that all roads led to him. He might have remained silent even in the carriage returning home with Tausig had Tausig not opened the conversation. "You did not seem to enjoy yourself very much."

"It is not that I did not enjoy myself, but I was amazed. Did you not say that Wagner's fortunes were at an ebb?"

"Yes, so it is."

"Well, then, I must be even more stupid than I had thought, but I cannot see it. If his fortunes are at an ebb, mine are as dry as a desert. I could live for years on what he spends on clothes alone."

"Ah, yes, that, but you see his skin is very sensitive. He has erysipelas. He has to be very particular about the clothes he wears – for his health."

Brahms shook his head. "It is not just his clothes, Tausig. I felt I was smothered – like I was inside a very grand pillow, all silk and satin – and the smell everywhere, so sickening, so sweet. I thought I was going to suffocate while I was playing."

The air in the rooms had been saturated with lavender and roses, walls covered by yellow satin hangings; poufs, carpets, cushions, upholstery, all in violet and red, had been everywhere soft, deep, and heavy; pink satin drapes adorned with artificial roses had been hung from the windows, and the ceiling festooned with white satin, the center a pink satin rosette. Tausig shrugged. "He can only compose when he is surrounded by luxury. Otherwise, he cannot compose. That is Wagner."

Brahms snorted. "Hah – and all this time I had thought that he was a revolutionary."

"He is – when it suits his purpose. Wagner can be all things to all men, and always with the greatest sincerity – when it suits his purpose."

"And who pays for all this?"

"Nobody! It is not paid for, except with optimism – and debts. Wagner loves to play the grand seigneur – but always with other people's money. What is more amazing is that so many of them let him get away with it – because he is a genius, of course."

Brahms's tone was dry. "Of course."

"He believes so intensely he does them a favor by taking their money that they believe it themselves – some of them." He laughed. "From the others he is always on the run."

Again Brahms shook his head.

"He is not like other men, Johannes. When his need is great, when most men would think of exercising caution, recouping their losses, he thinks nothing of making his need greater." He slapped Brahms's arm. "Let me tell you: I was with him and Bulow recently in his hotel room. We had never seen him so disconsolate. He had accepted that *Tristan* was not to be given after all in Vienna, but he had long squandered his advance on dinners for friends and performers until his hotelkeeper now held a bill against him for two months of food and lodging. He was pacing the room, moaning about his condition. We were sitting on the sofa, listening sympathetically. Suddenly he stopped, ran to the door, rang for room service, and ordered two bottles of champagne on ice. We were no less astonished than the waiter, but Wagner spoke very seriously." Tausig shrugged. "He said only champagne could help us in such a state – and he is doing it again, spending what he does not have. Soon either someone will give him money, or he will leave everything – decorations, clothes, house, women, wine cellar, everything – and be on the run again. That is the kind of person he is. Is there not something magnificent about it?"

Brahms's eyebrows rose, but he said nothing.

Brahms and Clara nursed steins of beer, cozy behind a trellis of vines and daisies, in the arbor of zum Raben, about a mile from her house in Lichtenthaler Allee. The waitress brought pancakes, hot and freckled, gleaming with butter and smothered in sugar, recommended by Clara. She cut hers into neat mouthfuls, he tore his to pieces. She smiled, watching him gulp his food. He had never learned how to eat, never learned the ways of gentlefolk, and she had long stopped prompting him. "How do you like them, Johannes?"

Brahms barely looked up. "Too small."

"Too small!" The pancakes flopped over the sides of their plates. "I swear there is no pleasing you, Johannes. To make pancakes this big they must use a pan as big as a roundabout – at least, as big as your head."

He grinned. "I was only joking, Clara, but I forget you have no sense of humor."

She flushed, aware of her failing. "And you, Johannes, have never learned to eat properly."

"Tchhah! What is it to anyone how I eat? I eat to please myself, no one else."

She remained flushed. "It is strange that you should say that, Johannes. It seems to me that you eat as well to please the table and the bench." She pointed to spilled beer, wedges of pancake, also on the ground. "Yes, and to please the ground as well, it seems – and the ants and squirrels and whoever else may wish a share of your meal. It seems to me you eat to please just about everyone and everything in your vicinity."

Brahms continued to eat quickly and carelessly.

She remained flushed, abashed further by his silence. "Johannes, I was only joking. Who is the one without a sense of humor now?"

Still he said nothing.

"Why do you not answer me?"

He looked at her. "Yes, indeed, you are very funny. Hahah!"

She looked away. "Something is the matter. I wish you would just tell me what it is instead of being so very prickly, like a hedghog."

He spoke as he chewed. "It is nothing to talk about. It is the same thing again. I am again at a crossroads. I have that feeling again of being neither pushed nor pulled. Why is it so difficult to know what must be done when nothing is expected?"

"It is your own fault, Johannes. I, for one, am sorry you are leaving the Singakademie. I must confess I am at a loss to understand. I was sure you would keep the post. I was sure you would settle in Vienna. It is the best place for you."

Brahms chewed more slowly, fixing her finally with a look like an animal fixing its prey. "Clara, you know, if you were to settle in Vienna – sooner or later – I would consider it myself. It would be easier for me to make up my mind."

Clara did not look at him, shaking her head, appearing unaware her answer meant much. "You must not make your plans contingent upon mine. That is the reason I will never again marry. I am too fond of my freedom. I do not wish to make plans contingent upon anyone else's – nor do I wish anyone to make plans contingent upon mine – but it is different for you."

"How is it different?"

"I already have a family, Johannes, but you have never married. You must think about it more seriously."

Brahms shook his head. "I may not be married, but a family I have got – and of late it appears to have become larger."

The tensions between his parents had separated them. His pappa had moved into two tiny rooms, and Brahms had helped his mamma and sister move into rooms more suitable for their needs alone, undertaking the additional expense. His brother had his own place and was earning well, but refused to help, pleading his own expenses while dressing like a Parisian – as was expected, so he said, in the homes of his pupils, the Hamburg elite. Brahms understood his disaffection: his reputation rested on being the lesser Brahms, though he liked to say he was the taller. He was known everywhere as the wrong Brahms. He sighed again. "I have written to my pappa to visit them – at least, for meals – or to help with moving things – or give them money if they ask, and I will pay him back – whatever they wish, to give it to them and I will pay him back. I have asked him to settle some of my accounts with Mamma – the cost of sending my music to Vienna – just to get them to talk, but my hopes are not high."

She could see he was doing all he could, subtly as he could, to keep them together. "On this subject I can give no opinion about who is right or wrong, Johannes, but I do think most of the time it is the woman who should bend. It is the man, after all, who bears responsibility for the family – but if the man is unfaithful, or if he gambles or drinks, then, of course, no one can blame the woman if she leaves – but there is no question of this in your father's case. I long to hear the truth of the matter."

"It is no big mystery, Clara. My mamma is old and my pappa is not. She wants to do nothing, he cannot stay in one place. She needs silence, he needs to practise. Maybe it is not a good thing for the woman to be so much older than the man. A woman tends to a man's spiritual needs and the man to the woman's material needs – but it is not possible if the woman is so much older – when her spiritual needs become greater than her material needs."

"Maybe they will still get together again. After all, they have been married a long time."

"Thirty-four years."

"And that is maybe more significant than that she is so much older than him."

"I am beginning to think not. I am beginning to think it is good, after all, for the man to be older. I think now, after all, I would want a younger wife myself."

She could no longer miss the significance of what he said. "Well, perhaps you are right, but again first you must settle – which makes me wonder again why you have chosen to leave the Singakademie. A man needs security to marry, but you have thrown yours away."

"Tchhah, Clara, I have thrown away nothing. I took the position to prove to myself that I could do it, and I have done it – but I did not like it. The music part I can manage, that is the part I like – but for the rest I felt like a ringmaster in a circus, always keeping an eye on everyone and everything, always on the lookout for cheap soloists and novelties and suchlike for the programs."

"But, Johannes, everything cannot always be as you want. My Robert was the same, he did not wish to be bothered with the day-to-day cares of the orchestra – but he did not give it up just for that. You cannot have it all at once."

"But I do not want it all. I never wanted it all. I wanted to try it – and now I have tried it."

"I must say you surprise me. If you had been elected to the Hamburg Philharmonic as you had wished, would you have given it up so easily as well?"

Brahms frowned, stabbing his pancake with his fork. "No! That I would not have given up! That was my due! That is still my due! That much they owe me!"

"In that case, I confess I do not understand you at all. You could not do better than to command an orchestra in Vienna, certainly not in Hamburg, but you appear to be of a different mind."

"It is not so difficult to understand, Clara. I am not like you. I am not a wanderer. I cannot help it if I like my native town best." He was always sorry to hear from her in foreign locales; she appeared then least like the woman he wanted; but early every year she toured outside the country (France, England, Russia, Switzerland, Holland, Belgium); in the summer she was in Lichtenthal; otherwise in various parts of Germany as opportunities arose. "I cannot be like you, scattering your children like seeds in the wind so you can roam from country to country like a gypsy."

Clara straightened her back and stiffened her lip. "Johannes, you are always presumptuous when you assume you know better than me what is best for my children. Let us not talk about it again. We have discussed it before, it never changes anything – and it makes me very angry."

"Clara, listen to me. If you settled in Vienna – and I settled in Vienna – can you not see how good it would be? You could give concerts, you could teach, you could do what you wanted, you know how it is in Vienna – and the children would have their mamma with them instead of being like orphans for half of the year and more."

"Johannes, no more! I will not listen to you! What you say is nothing for me to consider!"

"Tchhah! That is how it is with you, always! You know best about everything! Always!"

Clara said nothing. They finished their pancakes in silence; Brahms ordered his fourth stein, she her second. He had sent her the draft of the first movement of a symphony from Vienna – his apology, she was sure, for calling her a mincing little pedant that summer; he was more comfortable with gestures than words. She had been excited enough to quote the first bars for Joachim in England, who had requested to premiere the work when it was complete – but Johannes refused to talk about the symphony, refused even to reply to Joachim's letters. When she had interceded for Joachim, who continued to popularize his sextet and quartets in England, he had just laughed. "Johannes, please let us not argue. It makes me so unhappy when we do."

"I do not wish to argue, only to make you see head and foot. In Vienna one lives better without a regular position. There are libraries, there are picture galleries – there is the Burgtheater –"

"Johannes, let it be. What is head and foot to you is not always head and foot to me. Let us agree to let it be."

He grunted. "I only meant to say that I am going back again to Vienna for the winter – but I mean to make my living from concerts alone, and what I can make from my compositions."

She spoke more tenderly. "I am glad to hear it, Johannes. I am sure you will be a success, whatever you do."

He grunted again, looking past her head again.

She changed the subject. "What do you think about what is happening?"

He knew what she meant; it was almost all anyone talked about anymore. Schleswig-Holstein, northernmost of the German states, southernmost of the Danish, was again being contested. The last time Prussia had marched on the duchies had been in 1848, the year of revolutions: Britain, Russia, and Sweden had threatened to interfere, and Prussia had desisted – but in 1863, Denmark had claimed a common constitution with Schleswig and lost the support of the European countries. Bismarck had forged an alliance with Austria against Denmark, and late in 1864 Schleswig-Holstein was ceded to Austria and Prussia. "What is there to think? Time will tell. We will see if Bismarck knows what he is doing."

"But in the meantime people are dying."

"People are dying all the time. What matters is what they are dying for. My pappa was from Heide, you know. If Bismarck's idea is to unite Germany, that is not a bad thing."

Heide was in Holstein. "But Holstein now belongs to both Prussia and Austria. How is this to be resolved? It cannot last. One cannot serve two masters."

"That is why I say we will see if Bismarck knows what he is doing. It is too early to tell."

Clara finished her beer. "Ah, I am afraid it is too much for my poor woman's brain. Men like to fight, women only want to keep the peace. I cannot see it your way. I am afraid Bismarck might be another Bonaparte, he appears so eager for war – but I hope I am wrong."

"Time will tell." They spoke gently again. Brahms lifted his stein, stealing a glance. "How is Julchen?"

Julie had left Lichtenthal early that summer. "She gets better and she gets worse. I am thinking of spending a month with her in St. Moritz. I think it might help her."

"She looks more like you, you know, than any of the other girls."

"Do you think so? I am told she is the most beautiful of my girls."

"Aha, and do you think so?"

"Yes, I think there might be some truth in it – but they all have different excellences. I could not do without my Marie who does everything for me as you know – but I am no less proud of my Elise's independence. My Julie, as you have said, is very beautiful – and Eugenie is still young, but shows promise of being very selfwilled – just like Elise, unfortunately." She smiled.

Brahms noted she had said nothing about the boys, and said nothing himself.

ii

Clara had known Joachim too long to be impressed with the way he looked, but seeing him in tie and tails again for Elise's debut she appeared to see him anew, dark curly hair, clear eyes, high cheekbones, hardly the boy she had known so long ago, now with a wife and baby boy of his own, but he remained childish, easily surprised.

She saw everything anew that night, a night of firsts centered around Elise, her second daughter, but the first to appear onstage, the first to leave home settling in Frankfurt to teach music. She had worn a yellow gown complementing her hair, drawn in ringlets and twined with red camellias, softening the lines of her angular face. She had shown no fear, making Clara yet more fearful though she had been careful to hide her own fear.

Joachim smiled broadly approaching her in the artists' waiting room after the performance. "Well, Fraulein Elise, was it not delightful to play with your mamma in public?"

Elise's head snapped up from where she sat. "Never again!"

Clara watched, amused as Joachim's smile dropped like lead. "No?"

"I have never been so scared in my life, Herr Joachim. I was trembling like a straw in a windstorm. Could you not see it?"

Joachim shook his head. "Actually, no."

Clara smiled. "Elise, I was no less scared than you – and for you even more than for myself, but you hid it well – and that is the mark of the artist. You channeled your fear into your performance."

"Perhaps, but I still say: Never Again!"

Clara could not stop smiling. "If that is what you say I will certainly respect it, but I am so glad that you found the courage, even just this once, to do it. I cannot recall when I was last filled with such tenderness. I had the feeling while we were playing that *he* was watching and smiling and blessing us with his eyes. Even if it never happens again, my dearest Elise, this once will always be beautiful."

Joachim and Clara had opened with the *Kreutzer*, Clara had followed with a piano transcription of the variations from Brahms's Sextet in B flat major, and concluded in a duet with Elise of Robert's Variations for Two Pianos after which they had received four curtain calls.

Whatever Elise said Clara could see she was pleased with herself; she spoke with too little reserve not to be pleased with herself. "I imagine the introduction to the *Kreutzer* is very difficult, Herr Joachim?"

Joachim smiled again. "It is, indeed, but why do you focus on just the introduction? The entire sonata is difficult."

"But it is only the introduction that you play out of tune."

Again Joachim's smile fell. "Do I, really? I will have to be more careful about that."

Clara might once have been surprised that a performer of Joachim's stature would take the criticism of a child to heart, some would have said he should not allow it, but her children were too accustomed to the presence of artists of the highest caliber to be intimidated, and spoke as easily to Johannes and Levi and the others, more easily than she herself with less reason. Joachim's nature made him the most susceptible of all. She recalled also what Stockhausen had said about him as a conductor: successful in every tempo, possibly the foremost conductor of his time, if only he would lead with a smile, a joke, an inspiring glance, as Mendelssohn had done, but baton in hand he was always grave.

Still, next to Johannes he was her greatest friend, a man of principle of whom there were all too few, especially among musicians, and she regretted only that she could not see him more often. Except when they were in England their schedules clashed and with his new family he was busier yet, particularly since he had left the service of the King – another matter of honor for which she admired him. He had resigned his position to protest an injustice to a peer: Herr Grun, engaged by Joachim on the promise of promotions when they became available, had been repeatedly overlooked because he was a Jew. The politics had turned ugly: Joachim, taking his suit to the King, had been accused in the newspapers of converting to Christianity to protect his own position, and had resigned finally declaring he could not be a Christian in good conscience when others of his race were humiliated.

He had become more the itinerant musician, more like herself, spending almost six months of the year in England and France proselytizing for German music. Johannes detested what he called this worship of Mammon and Joachim feared that Johannes detested him, but she understood her friends better than they understood each other: Johannes was afraid to lose Joachim to England, but Joachim now had a family.

"Do you think Elise will be all right?"

"I am sure of it. She is a sensible girl. Of all my children she is perhaps the best prepared to be on her own – but I hate to think I will no longer have her with me when I please."

"It must, indeed, be difficult – but it is no less a pleasure for me to see how she has grown and developed. I have known you long enough to remember when she was just a baby girl."

These were the times Clara liked best, past the cares of the concert, relaxing with a friend. She had taken the precaution of ordering a lettuce salad beforehand to her hotel rooms. Joachim had joined her at her table nursing a glass of wine. "Ah, Joseph, it is lovely to talk with you like this, so freely and so comfortably." She picked a cucumber from her salad. "Did I tell you that as a child I used to refresh myself during practices with pickled cucumbers?"

"Did you really?"

"I kept a bottle by the piano and took a bite to reward myself after each set of exercises."

Joachim smiled. "It is amazing, is it not – how the simplest pleasure can lead to the greatest work?"

"Indeed! Had cucumbers become a scarcity I might never have become a pianist." She laughed. "My other great pleasure was our cat, Gretal, and her kittens. Then, between exercises, I would take them in my lap and pet them – and sometimes my blood would be on the keys from their tiny little scratches – but I did not mind."

Joachim nodded. "With me it was the fiddle, always the fiddle, and nothing but the fiddle – until I applied to Mendelssohn, and he made it a condition of his sponsorship that I study other subjects – and he was right. I think I fiddle better for having studied subjects other than the fiddle."

Clara crunched lettuce as she spoke. "Mendelssohn knew something about everything. He was at home in the best society and the worst, he could paint and conduct and converse upon any subject – and I have not known a man to this day to match his touch at the piano."

"Neither have I. It is too bad Johannes never met him. I think they might have become good friends."

Clara grimaced, shaking her head. "Do you think so? I am inclined to doubt it. I think Mendelssohn might have found him … too rough – in fact, I know it – though, of course, he would have recognized his genius and done everything for him that he could – as he did for everyone."

"Maybe you are right. You know Johannes better than I do. I do not know anymore where I stand with him. I think I have offended him. I had thought at one time to represent his symphony, but he never said a word – and now, of course, without an orchestra myself, I am of no more use to him."

His mouth drooped, and Clara squeezed his hand. "Ah, dear Joseph, no. How can you think that of Johannes? You know, of course, he can think of nothing but his mamma for the present?"

Joachim nodded, hanging his head. "Yes, of course."

"He has written to you about her, has he not?"

"He has."

Clara had received the same letter. Brahms's mamma had been returning from a concert. She had been in good spirits, even made a joke to Fritz getting out of the carriage, but as soon as he had driven away she had complained to her daughter about her tongue. Elise saw her mamma's mouth drawn to one side, her tongue swollen and protruding. She had called the doctor at once, Fritz had telegraphed Brahms in Vienna, but he had arrived too late.

Joachim pursed his lips. "He has such a healthy constitution that I envy him. His letter was entirely philosophical. You might have thought he never cared about his mamma – but, of course, that is not so."

"But it is the best way, do you not think, to be philosophical?" Brahms had written to them both: a sensible man regretted nothing. It was a matter of keeping your head above water and keeping on. For his mamma, estranged from his pappa, things could only have become worse. He had played the *Goldberg Variations* when he had received the telegram, Bach provided balm for the deepest trouble. He would have sounded facile had Clara not experienced the balm of music herself in her trouble, had she not known he had fetched as well his estranged pappa, stood with him over his mamma's body, held his pappa's hand over his mamma's, weeping all the while – had he not written as well that he knew the deepest sorrow was yet to come, after the shock of her death. She shook her head. "After my Robert ... I know, there is no other way but to be philosophical."

"But even before that, I was not sure of him. He seemed to be moving away from me. When I invited him to tour with me he scolded me for moneymindedness. It is all very well for him. He has no family depending upon him."

"Actually, he does. There is still his sister. She is but a seamstress and cannot live on her earnings – but you are right. It is not the same as having one's own family to support – but I sometimes wonder if that might not very well be his trouble."

"What do you mean?"

"He wrote to me that now that he has no mamma he has to marry. I think he might envy you, after all, more than you think. If he could only find someone like your Ursi it might rid him of his black moods forever."

"Do you think so? He does, indeed, appear to like my Ursi. He never failed to secure her services for the Singakademie when he could, when he was still director, and she was no less grateful for the honor, not to mention the publicity – but, of course, that was strictly in a professional capacity."

"Yes, but I wonder if that might not be the problem. He seems interested in women only in a professional capacity – because less is then expected of him – but I think he would like to do more though he knows not how."

"I wonder if you may not be right, that he appears to care too little because he fears to care too much."

"That is how the North Germans are, especially Hamburgers – you know how it is, even with their applause. It takes a hundred Hamburgers to show the appreciation of one Viennese."

Joachim grinned. "You are only too right about the Hamburgers. His pappa once told me a story about him. Before his first visit to Vienna he said very seriously to his pappa that music was always a great solace, and should his pappa find himself in trouble he was to turn to his copy of Handel's *Saul* on the bookshelf. After he had gone, his pappa turned to the manuscript out of curiosity – only to find it was stuffed with banknotes."

Clara returned his grin. "Yes, his pappa told me the same story. You see, it is not so at all that he does not care."

"I am sure you are right – but that does not make him easier to deal with, constantly to have to remind oneself that he means well."

Clara lost her grin, understanding Joachim's complaint entirely. "I know what you mean. I have broken many a lance for him in my concerts, but I receive scant thanks for my efforts." When she had first played his *Handel Variations* to much applause after barely a month's practice he had said nothing except that he no longer wished to hear them – but she had played them at his own request! She continued to perform his concerto for which she received little enough appreciation even from her audiences, but still less from him.

"He is the same with me. I wish he might have seen the letter I wrote to Ave when they chose Stockhausen over him – but I wonder if it would make a difference. If it were not for his music I would no more put up with him than I do with Liszt – but Liszt is always gracious, even in his disagreements."

Clara scraped her salad plate. "Johannes, too, has moments of grace. He was considerate enough to send me a photograph of my house in Lichtenthal – for no reason at all other than that he thought I would like it."

"Yes, and he wrote a cradle song for my own Johannes." The Joachims had named their first son after Brahms. "He even showed more kindness than usual."

Clara nodded, smiling. "Sometimes, he is no better than a child, and looks to us as a child looks to its parents to meet its needs – and howls like a child when its needs are not met. I wonder if maybe we have let ourselves be taken too easily for granted – but is that not what friends are for?"

"Yes, but friends are sometimes lost for the same reason."

Clara lost her smile. "I am afraid you are right. There is nothing he can do or say to change how I feel about his music, but I do think twice about what I say to him. I no longer speak as freely as I once did. I constantly edit myself. I no longer trust him as I did – not as a man."

Joachim sighed. "I am the same. My trust, too, is eroded. I will never cease to break lances for his music, but as a man he has grown too harsh – with his friends, in particular."

iii

"Fraulein Marie, you have forgotten the onions again – but even otherwise the baked pork is not as good as usual. It needs more salt." Brahms grinned looking around the supper table, but no one found him as amusing as he seemed to find himself.

Marie passed him the saltceller without a smile. "Here is salt if you want it, Herr Brahms."

"And I suppose you have a little onion-celler somewhere as well. You know how well I like onions."

Brahms looked around again, but again no one smiled. Instead, he had snuffed out what had been left of their merriment. Clara, on his left, only stared wishing she had the gaiety to smooth their differences without injury to anyone, but it was not her way. She hated confrontations, but found them easier than the light touch which might render them unnecessary. In particular, she hated confrontations with Johannes before her children.

Eugenie and Felix stared silently from Brahms and Marie to their mamma; Julie was upstairs in bed; but Elise, seated on Clara's left, could not hold her peace. "Herr Brahms, you should thank Marie that she has left out the onions. You would otherwise only have spilled more food on yourself – but I suppose no one would notice an extra onion or two on your shirt."

No one laughed, but everyone beamed, everyone except Brahms, even Clara though her voice became stern. "Elise! That is no way to speak to Herr Brahms. Apologize at once! Do you hear me?"

"I will apologize if he will apologize to Marie."

"Elise!"

"But, Mamma, he is so rude."

"He is our guest, Elise, and he is no more rude than you have just been. You will apologize."

"But, Mamma, he was rude first. He is here everyday. He is always our guest. Does that mean he has the right to be rude whenever he wishes?"

Clara was no longer beaming. "Elise! Apologize! At once!"

Elise spoke quickly, barely whispering, without looking at Brahms. "I apologize, Herr Brahms."

Brahms was no less startled than anyone else with the developments and did not acknowledge Elise's apology, wiping his mouth with the back of his hand and wiping his hand on his brindled shirt. "You are a fine one to talk about my clothes, Fraulein Elise, wearing your reds and your blues and your stripes and dots and flowers from England. For me, German clothes are good enough, thank you." He referred to Clara's habit of bringing yards of material for dresses back from England. "And if my food gets on my clothes, at least I do not dress like your Felix, with his jackets and trousers trimmed with braids – like a girl."

Marie made the dresses, trimming the boys' clothes with braids. "With all respect, Herr Brahms, I must say that my family at least cares enough about my clothes – and my cooking – not to spill it upon themselves. With yourself, I can never be sure whether it is my food you dislike or your own clothes."

"Marie!"

"But Mamma, he is wrong! If we let him get away with it he will only do it again and again and again – as he has already done so many times – and then it will be our own fault for saying nothing. We must say something for his sake as much as our own!"

Clara was silenced. Marie was right. The altercation was not the first, but she found herself paralyzed with indecision between her children and Johannes.

When she remained silent, Brahms spoke. "I see how it is. The mamma is no less thoughtless than the children."

She wondered if he knew about Kirchner: the affair had been briefly happy, but collapsed from within when she had realized that he had been a fully mature man when they had met – not clay to be molded, just clay. "Johannes, I do not know what you are talking about. If you have something on your mind I wish you would simply say what it is. I cannot believe we are arguing about onions and soup and clothes. What is the matter with you that you make things so disagreeable between me and my children?"

He knew about Kirchner, but was hardly as bothered as he might once have been. He imagined it cleared his path toward Julchen and wished to charm the family into accepting him as a suitor, but in his confusion succeeded only in offending them. "The matter with me? I was only making a little joke and everyone becomes disagreeable. I was only making a joke."

"Your jokes are not funny, Johannes. Whatever you say there is always something else the matter. Perhaps even you do not know what it is, but there is more to it than just a joke. Of that I am certain. I do wish you would consider what you say with more care."

"Well, I suppose it is my fault, then, if my jokes are not funny. I suppose it is all my fault, is it not? God forbid that Clara Schumann should ever be at fault."

"But it *is* your fault. We are never so disagreeable among ourselves. It is only when you are among us."

"Ah, yes, of course, I should have known. The great Clara Schumann is the highpriestess not only of music but of breeding as well. She is an oracle and the rest of us are mere swine. Is that not so?"

Clara shook her head in disbelief. Elise took her hand. "Herr Brahms, you must not speak that way to our mamma."

Clara recalled a letter she had received not long ago, *Dearest Clara, How glad I am that I can write so gladly thus: Dearest Clara...*, and recalled her joy at the letter, recalling as well his comfort in her hour of need – her *years* of need, when it seemed God Himself had deserted her – for which reason he aroused such confused and conflicting emotions.

Eugenie, seated next to Brahms, rushed to stand by her mamma. So did Felix, standing between Clara and Brahms. Elise still held her hand and Marie smiled in defiance. Brahms rose, wiping his hands on his shirt. "Tchhah! This is not a good time. I will come back when you are all in a better mood."

The Schumanns remained silent, watching him as he got his patched grey alpaca coat and let himself out the door.

Dr. Theodor Billroth was a big and burly man, thin of hair but blond and bushy of beard making his head appear larger yet. His gestures were so emphatic, his speech so eloquent, and his blue eyes so narrow, that he appeared magnified yet one more time, easily the focus of any group. He was also among the leading surgeons of his time.

Anesthesia and asepsis were already staples of surgery, allowing the abdomen to be entered more safely than before – but without xrays, transfusions, and penicillin there remained a need for surgeons of confidence and courage. Billroth was the first to successfully remove the stomach for carcinoma of the pylorus and the first to remove the larynx. He broadened the fields of abdominal surgery and gynecology. Patients and doctors, peasants and kings, all sought his services. His textbook on surgery was translated into nine languages including Japanese.

He wrote as well a book on music, a collection of essays, *Who Is Musical?* of which only the first two of seven chapters were complete when he died. Weeks before his death he sent the manuscript to Hanslick, who edited and published the book. It ran through three printings in four years. During his first semester at the university he had studied only music, playing creditably the piano and viola, believing that art and love outlived science. Just thirty-six years in age he had already been Professor of Surgery for four years at the University of Zurich.

His large sittingroom showed signs of his practices, medical and musical, tomes and scores on the cluttered bookshelves lining one wall, barely a harbinger of the collection in his library. Still lifes of instruments and sections of the body were juxtaposed on the other walls alongside photographs of family members and romantic landscapes modeled on those of Casper David Friedrich. Classical statuary was spread around the room behind glass and on pedestals. A table by the window held platters of meats, breads, cheeses, steins of beer. A servant girl stood by periodically replenishing the plates. The cathedral tower chimed seven. "If everyone is ready, let us begin."

Brahms at the piano nodded to Dr. Joseph Gansbacher straddling his cello, peering at the sheet music on the stand, a doctor of law, soon to change his vocation to music. Despite his heavy black beard, heavy head of hair, his advantage of three years, despite Brahms's girlish complexion, Gansbacher appeared the novice behind his instrument, earnest as a boy. Brahms gave Gansbacher a sharp nod and they began, a melody with a long breath emerging from the deepest tones of the cello, accompanied by chords plucked from the piano, lyrical but subdued. When the piano took the lead Gansbacher was already in trouble, sharping and flatting his notes, losing his place, and as the themes developed his trouble deepened. Brahms grimaced, playing loudly, until Gansbacher stopped. "Herr Brahms, you are playing so loudly I cannot hear myself."

Brahms played more loudly yet, shouting to make himself heard. "THEN YOU ARE THE LUCKY ONE!"

Gansbacher was a good friend. He had secured Brahms the position with the Singakademie, secured as well for him the autograph of Schubert's *Wanderer* for just thirty-two florins – but his enthusiasm was unmatched by his ability.

Amid the laughter Gansbacher surrendered his cello to one of the other musicians. Brahms spoke sternly. "Do not be alarmed, Gansbacher, but ..." He frowned, letting the suspense build, searching apparently for a euphemism. Gansbacher's eyes grew large, his face more earnest, his mouth trembled, before Brahms grinned: "... but, dog that you are, I am going to dedicate this sonata to you – on the condition that you never again play it for me."

Billroth noted Brahms's satisfaction with Gansbacher's alarm and delight, how he had preyed on his uncertainty, playing cat and mouse with his words, and was not without trepidation himself. Next on the program was the new Sextet in G major for which Billroth was to play the viola.

THIRTY MINUTES LATER Billroth's face was no less red than Gansbacher's, a victim of the sextet no less than Gansbacher of the sonata. "Herr Brahms, I practised this. I swear it. I cannot say it with greater sincerity. This, I practised."

"Well, then, Herr Doktor, it is a good thing you still have your surgery, is it not?"

Billroth wanted to blame the heat, Zurich in the summer, his trials in the operating theater the day before, but shook his massive head instead. "I have learned one thing today, Herr Brahms – never to play anything in the presence of the composer." As one of the other musicians took his place Billroth broke suddenly into a grin. "Does this mean, Herr Brahms, that you will be dedicating the sextet to me?"

Brahms's grin matched Billroth's. "Herr Doktor, you must not be so hard upon yourself. You did not play *that* badly."

After the musicians left Brahms stayed to consult the doctor. Their friendship astonished and delighted him: both were alike in some respects, both Protestants, North Germans, Billroth from Bergen on the island of Rugen, alike even to their blond hair and blue eyes; but the doctor was a patrician, man of culture and education; and Brahms, not to his chagrin, a man of many corners. He had played a concert in Zurich including his first serenade, inducing Billroth and other prominent Swiss citizens to organize a private concert programing his other orchestral works, the D minor Concerto and the second serenade. They had hired an orchestra and telegraphed friends across Switzerland about the event.

Since then he had been invited to try any new works in Billroth's house – and so he had, the sextet, the cello sonata, a horn trio, and segments of his *Requiem* transcribed for two pianos – all of which made him comfortable enough to approach Billroth about his problem.

"Well, Herr Brahms, what is it? How can I be of service to you?"

"We are quite alone?"

"My wife is abed as you know, and so are my girls. Other than them, it is just you and me."

There was also the servant girl clearing the table, but Billroth discounted her. Brahms said nothing, but jerked his head in her direction.

"Well, then, why do we not go to my study?"

Brahms followed Billroth to a smaller room with more cluttered bookshelves, a dark cherrywood desk, and deep upholstered sofa. Billroth shut the door behind them and lit just one candle: confidences came more easily in the dark.

"Now, Herr Brahms, I can assure you we are quite alone."

Brahms sat on the sofa, unable to meet Billroth's eyes. His voice was a whisper. "It might be nothing at all, Herr Doktor, but I am not sure how to say it."

Billroth saw his discomfort. "Herr Brahms, whatever you say stays within these walls – and all that is in my power is at your service. You have my word on it."

Brahms nodded, grateful for the reassurance. "Well, then, since you are straight with me I will be straight with you. I have some reason, you see, to be afraid … of women." He shook his head, gritting his teeth. "Ach! It is not easy to explain."

They talked into the night, aware of only each other's faces in the light of the candle, Brahms revealing, haltingly, the story of his life, not without sorrow, not without difficulty, love for his mamma and pappa, the Gangviertal, Ehebrechergang, Zur schwarzen Katze, Helga, Lena, Frau Grummer, and the others, his love for Robert and Clara, nurtured by Clara's distress, terminated by Robert's death – his subsequent difficulties with Gathe, Berta, Elisabet, and so many others, his head filling with ice while blood boiled in his veins, the price of love proving more than he could afford except with money.

Billroth listened patiently, probing delicately when a detail remained unclear, speaking finally sympathetically. "Herr Brahms, you must not imagine there is anything wrong with you. It would be more astonishing, under the circumstances, if you were *not* afraid of women."

Brahms's voice rose. "But what is to be done? How is it to be changed?"

Billroth spoke more calmly, appearing more sympathetic. "In such matters, Herr Brahms, it is easier to say what is *not* to be done. It is hardly as uncommon a problem as you might think. Unfortunately, in psychological matters, it is always difficult to predict cures – but the worst thing you could do would be to allow yourself to become a victim of your moods. There is nothing worse than moods in these matters – but you know already what you must do when they strike." He nodded, eyes narrowing, boring into Brahms. "Get to work and the moods will vanish – and if your difficulty remains, your character at least remains unblemished – and that is an accomplishment."

"But where there is an identifiable wrong, should there not be an identifiable way to make it right? Should there not be a way to undo what has been done?"

The irony of the dilemma was deepened by Brahms's high cheekbones, bright eyes, hopefulness. He was a small man, but a handsome man, a man of genius. "Not necessarily, my dear Brahms. We are hardly as advanced as that. What we can identify is not what is wrong, but an etiology, a causation. It is not a matter of right and wrong but cause and effect – and you must guard against thinking about it. To paraphrase Shakespeare: there is nothing that is right or wrong but thinking makes it so. You must remember that, Herr Brahms, and guard against it."

Brahms was silent, frowning, appearing to be chewing.

Billroth spoke more gently. "My dear friend, I cannot impress this upon you enough. You are a composer, a creative artist, a pianist, and you must know, especially in the wake of your experience with Schumann, how closely related are genius and idiocy, inspiration and eccentricity, art and fantasy. You must practise your scales and your counterpoint, you must not grab past the correct note. That is all. That is your responsibility. The rest is His."

Brahms understood: he had incorporated Agathe's name into the notes of his new sextet, purging himself of the residue of her memory; he had written the adagio of his Horn Trio for his mamma; he had begun his *Requiem* after Robert's death, laying it aside but returning to it when his mamma died. The piano quartet with which he had tried to purge himself of Clara remained incomplete, but he meant yet to finish it. He wished he could resolve the matter as had his pappa who had written to him: *Life, as I am now living, contains so little that is agreeable, that I have decided to make a change. I believe this will be for my happiness. It is easily understood that I, who for 34 years had lived with my family, if not very happily, must find it hard to accustom myself to the life I have led for the past two years. Therefore, if you think it over, you will not hold it against me if I tell you that I am thinking of marrying again, especially as my choice has fallen on a woman, who, though she will not make you forget your mamma, has every right to your respect. She suits me and I am sure I have not made an unbecoming choice. She is a widow, a homely body, 41 years of age. It would make me particularly happy if this should be another reason for you to visit us. I hope, therefore, my dear Johannes, that we will see each other soon, and I hope until then that you will think kindly of my intention, even it if surprises you.*

When he remained silent Billroth spoke again. "You must indulge yourself, Brahms, with the entertainments you most enjoy. Tomorrow is flower-market day. There will be baskets of blossoms on the steps of the library: lilacs, narcissi, violets, lilies-of-the-valley –"

Brahms interrupted. "Consider the lilies, et cetera."

His voice had turned sepulchral. Billroth's brow wrinkled. "What?"

"From the Bible: Consider the lilies…."

He did not want to or could not finish the quote. His voice seemed to splinter. Billroth saw his face, a travesty of melancholy, flat and pale as paper in the dim light, eyes downcast, mouth like a sickle. "Yes, of course, the Bible – charity, resignation, good works, generosity of spirit, all contribute toward the cure." It was cold comfort and Billroth knew it. "Brahms, I wish I could do more, but since you like so much to be out in the country I will draw up an itinerary for you. I would advise you to take up the stretch of Interlaken, Lauterbrunnen, Wengern Alp, Grindelwald, Scheideck, Rosenlaui. Do not miss staying in Giessbach for at least one night. The illumination of the falls is beautiful. If you have any questions, never hesitate to ask my opinion. Consider me at your disposal day and night."

Brahms nodded. The chimes struck midnight.

"Herr Brahms, one more thing?"

"Yes?"

"This, too, is in confidence."

"Yes?"

Billroth leaned forward. "You know, marriage is not always so very wonderful, but as with everything, those who have it wish to break their chains – and those who do not, want it more than anything."

His voice trembled, eyes moistened, face flattened. He might have been confessing a failure. The great surgeon had been unable to help his own son, born deaf, dumb, autistic, who had died that very year. Brahms had heard his marriage was troubled and recognized his own expression in the doctor's face. He was proud of the confidence of a man of consequence, respectful of their mutual respect. He was rarely at ease among the elite, too selfconscious of his learning among those for whom it was natural as breath, but Billroth never condescended, never spoke with anything but respect. Not even Clara saw the fine line he trod, his peasant elegance, the code of the outsider, at once careless of his appearance and proud of his carelessness, resentful of his difference and disdainful of the herd, at once mocking and wanting their indulgence. "Danke, Herr Doktor. Kindness alone is a big help in matters of this nature – and you have been very kind. What you have suggested is what I had concluded myself, especially what you said about … what you said about Schumann – but if there were something else to be done I wanted to know. You have done me a great service."

Billroth shook his head, frowned. "Ach! I have done nothing but for myself. I want nothing but to keep you composing."

JOACHIM TO HIS WIFE   *Basel, Nov '66*

My dearest Ursi,

I must tell you a hilarious story. After our concert in Aarau, Brahms and I went to a tavern called the Stork Inn for supper. Brahms was in a good mood. We had opened a few bottles of a fine Swiss vintage, the "vin mousseux" of Lausanne. The manager brought us the box office receipts in a little chest. It looked like a pirate's chest and when Brahms opened it and saw the coins and notes he said: "What have we here? Doubloons?" We began to divide the money there and then, each of us picking in turn, coin by coin, note by note, until there was just one twenty franc piece left. It was my turn and I was about to pick it up when Brahms shouted: "Hold, thou varlet. That piece is MINE!" Well, and I can hardly believe it myself, but we argued over that piece – quite noisily, I might add – until Brahms seized an alpenstock nearby and thrust another in my hands, saying, "There is nothing to do but fight for it." Of course, we were just having fun, we are always in high spirits when a concert goes well, but the poor manager rushed away imagining he had a real brawl on his hands and came back with change.

As you can imagine, we are having a splendid time. Brahms is in the best spirits – something to do with his Requiem, I am sure. The work makes me want to retract all the petty little complaints I have ever voiced about him. It stamps him as a great man – and yet he can engage his friends in fights over doubloons!

He has taken the train to Mulhausen ahead of me – to practise, he says, believe it who may! That is his daily resolution. The other day in Schaffhausen, his playing got freer and finer with every piece, but you will never hear Brahms at his best in the concert hall. He is never as comfortable as when he plays at home among friends.

But in spite of Brahms I would rather be with you. If only I were a bird, or better yet an electric spark, so I could flash across a wire to you in the matter of a moment. Instead, after Mulhausen, we will be going to Mannheim, after which Brahms will return to Vienna and I will continue to Paris.

About your request, my dear child: of course, you are at liberty to stay in Hamburg as long as you see fit to study with Stockhausen. He has proven to be of much use, but you must not tire your dear voice and chest. I have heard that Stockhausen is inclined to tax the voice beyond its limit. The fault I have sometimes found with your singing is that it does not always have enough rhythmic precision, that you linger too long sometimes on a note or syllable, not from choice, but because you cannot help it. Most violinists do the same in bowing, so that their rendering of a phrase is determined by their technical skill *more than their intellectual conception. I imagine your faulty pronunciation is due to this too. Otherwise, no one has more feeling for declamation than my Ursi. Your notices have delighted me. They prove what an impression you must have made.*

Alas, my dear Ursi, this life apart is not what we anticipated when we married, but the advance of Prussia has shown us better than anything that nothing is to be taken for granted. If I had not resigned when I did my resignation would only have been delayed until Prussia had annexed Hanover – but it is better to have resigned as I did, on a matter of principle, than to have been forced from office as I would then have been. Still, in spite of my differences with the King, I feel sorry for him and his Queen. All they have left are memories. What is left for a King to do when his kingdom has been seized? The news from Vienna is that the Queen has adjusted to her circumstances with much grace and nobility, but the King's bitterness against Bismarck grows daily.

Give a kiss each from their pappa to little Johannes and to little Hermann, and keep one for yourself, my dearest child, from your loving
Jo

BRAHMS TO JOACHIM   *Vienna, September 1867*
My dear Joseph,
You know what a character my pappa can be. He plays bass in the Hamburg Philharmonic, but he tells his Herr Kapellmeister that he is not to bother him! A pure note on the bass is pure chance! It is his bass and he will play it as loudly as he wants!

I recently experienced a delightful lifting of spirits through a little trip we made together. I can hardly remember when I have seen him so happy as now in his new marriage. The story of his courtship alone brings a smile to my face. His new wife, Frau Karoline nee Schnack, was proprietress of the restaurant where he took his midday meal. He likes to say she worked her way from his belly to his heart. She was just 41 years, the same as my mamma when they met – but he was 17 years younger than my mamma, and he is 20 years older than Frau Schnack – and my mamma had not been married when they met, and Frau Schnack is two times a widow. He never thought she would have him, but one day he said to her: "Frau Schnack, I am just a muddleheaded old fool and I need your advice." He gave her a piece of paper with four names, asking which she thought he should marry – and she marked an X next to her own name. Is that not a charming story? She also has a son named Fritz, so I now have two brothers by that name, and I am glad to welcome both mother and son into our family.

Since his new marriage my pappa had shown some interest in traveling. He revisited Heide, where he was born, and other parts thereabouts, which led me to invite him to Vienna to share a holiday in parts hereabouts. I advised him to come soon as travel only becomes more difficult as one gets older and summers in Vienna only get hotter. I sent him a railway timetable, marking all the convenient trains from Hamburg to Vienna, and I said there is nothing more comfortable than a journey by night in a train with a glass of grog warming your belly.

Where did we not go? What did we not see? From Vienna we took the train through Styria, Carinthia, to the Salzkammergut. Along the way we stopped at Murzzuschlag, Mariazell, Wilalpen, Bad Ausee, Bad Ischl, and of course we made a Mozart pilgrimage to Salzburg, and later excursions to Berchtesgaden and Konigsse. In Vienna we saw the emperor with the Turkish Pasha, and in Salzburg we saw two emperors together, Franz Joseph and Napoleon III.

At the top of the Schafberg, I was amazed once more by the snowy peaks like giant crystal chandeliers, but he said to me: "Look here, my boy! Promise me you will never do this to me again!" This from a man who had never before seen a mountain in his life! I think the climb must have taxed him overmuch, but he wrote to me later in a letter: "You cannot imagine how people envy me. Of course, I exaggerate properly. I tell them I climbed right to the top of the Schafberg, all 5,400 feet, but I do not tell them that I rode a donkey three quarters of the way."

After we returned home I sent him, for a souvenir, a map of the country marked with a blue pencil to show the places we had visited. Now I am in Vienna again, and here I will quietly stay for a while, but my soul is as refreshed as a body after a bath. My dear pappa has no idea how much good he did me. I almost went back with him to Hamburg.

Always your
Johannes

ii

Brahms and Joachim were met by Freiherr Bodo Albrecht von Stockhausen at seven o'clock on the steps of the King's mansion in Hietzing, a Viennese suburb – the exKing, rather, and von Stockhausen was the exambassador of the exprincipality of Hanover. "His Majesty will be delighted you have chosen to come, Herr Brahms, and I would like to add my thanks in his behalf for your trouble."

Brahms grimaced, stuffed in his coat and trussed by his tie. "It is nothing."

Von Stockhausen led them up a flight of wide marble stairs carpeted in red plush, through hallways lined with gilded portraits of Hanoverian royalty, past bas reliefs of the doubleheaded eagle of the Habsburgs. Joachim spoke under his breath. "Have you told him of my decision?"

The exambassador shook his head. "I have not had the courage. After tonight you will understand. I would advise you not to say very much yourself – at least, not until you see how the matter lies."

Joachim steepled his brows and nodded; Brahms followed, silent. He had come at Joachim's special request, also out of respect for von Stockhausen, whose kinship was clear in his face to his daughter, Elisabet (sunlit hair, moonlit skin, green eyes), to whom he had briefly given lessons in Vienna before giving her up, afraid to make a fool of himself over her.

The room into which von Stockhausen led them was so large it appeared empty at first. Their hosts sat in tall chairs in a corner, their backs to the doorway, but as they padded across the hall, as von Stockhausen made their presence known, the King and Queen rose. The Queen smiled, but waited for her husband to speak first. The blind King appeared more blind for the strange surroundings, hardly as all-seeing as in Hanover. He appeared also to have aged ten years in the two since Joachim had seen him, thinner, whiter for his longer hair and beard, and more frail despite the wealth of medals and decorations on his chest. "My dear Joachim, we are very glad you have come. We had feared never again to be with you."

Joachim bowed, not unaware of his debt despite his resignation. "A fear that will ever be groundless, Your Majesty, as long as you wish to see me." His face remained impassive, but his stomach shriveled as the King felt his chest for the Guelphic Order. He had expected it and written to his Ursi to send him the Order, wishing to avoid disrespect to the King in his difficult time, but it had not arrived, and he had fastened a simple blue ribbon in its stead despairing of getting his Ursi ever to do his bidding except on her own terms.

The King turned next to Brahms who remained wooden while he was felt in turn. "Herr Brahms, we are glad that you too have come."

Brahms bowed lightly and spoke almost in a whisper. "Majesty."

The Queen appeared no less wan for her trials, but more charming for her smile. "We recall your music with great pleasure, Herr Brahms. We hear it even more here in Vienna."

Again Brahms bowed. "Danke, Majesty."

The Queen turned her full smile on Joachim. "Herr Joachim, it is always a pleasure to see you."

Joachim bowed again. "Your Majesty is too kind. The pleasure is mine."

They sat in an arc, King and Queen beside each other, Joachim to the King's right, Brahms to Joachim's right, von Stockhausen to the Queen's left. The corner was gloomy, barely lit, drapes covered the windows, plush furnishings blanketed sounds. Brahms squirmed, settling in his seat for a boring couple of hours.

The King spoke first. "We are all friends here. Let us not stand on ceremony. That would be something of a farce under the current circumstances. Joachim, Brahms, make yourselves comfortable. Smoke if you wish. Herr von Stockhausen has made arrangements for potations. As you can see, we have started the evening already." He raised a goblet. The Queen smiled, wine at her side.

Brahms wasted no time pulling a cigar from his coat and both friends made a selection from the cart of wines offered by von Stockhausen.

"We apologize for our meager hospitality, dear Joachim. It is much constrained owing to the circumstances, as you know – but we wish also to make it clear that we do not hold Wilhelm responsible for the state of affairs as much as that man. Wilhelm could have done nothing without that man."

The King's expression did not change, but no one misunderstood his bitterness, his refusal to name "that man," the architect of his defeat.

"We were brought up in Berlin. We know Berliners well enough not to expect any good of them – but Wilhelm was always an honest and wellmeaning man. It is that man's counsel that has corrupted him."

Joachim understood why von Stockhausen had cautioned against mentioning his plans to settle in Berlin. Brahms squirmed again. He never traveled without Bismarck's speeches in his bag, confident he would yet unify Germany. Not for nothing was he called the Iron Chancellor. Prussia and Austria had jointly administered Schleswig-Holstein since they had routed the Danes – but instigating a diplomatic crisis Bismarck had splintered the alliance and marched into Holstein, precipitating the Seven Weeks' War. The German states had sided mostly with Austria, but provided only token support. Bismarck's chief of staff, Count von Moltke, had administered the coup de grace to the Austrians under General von Benedek at the Battle of Koniggratz, annexed Hanover, Hesse, and Saxony, excluded Austria from German affairs, and offered military alliances and a customs union to the southern German states, Bavaria, Baden, Hesse-Darmstadt, Wurttemberg, all now isolated and wary of France.

"You know, of course, do you not, dear Joachim, how this man planned everything from the start? He instigated points of difference among the parties concerned. You know that, do you not? He manufactured ruses to start the battles. Wilhelm would never have done it alone, but this man was never interested in peaceful settlement. His thrust was clear from the beginning – a Prussian empire."

Joachim nodded. "Yes, Your Majesty, of course. There is no one who is unaware of … the stratagems." He had almost mentioned Bismarck by name.

"He was very clever, this man. He isolated Austria from the beginning. He bought the support of Russia when he helped the Tsar subdue the Polish insurrection, and he bought the support of Italy by promising them Venetia, and he bought a promise of neutrality from Napoleon who is too involved himself with Mexico at present to bother with European powers – but Napoleon will himself be a target some day, and who knows who else. Mind what I am saying, Joachim. This man will not rest until he dominates Europe."

Joachim nodded again, turning gloomier by the moment.

The Queen spoke, perhaps noting his discomfort. "We are mostly homesick, Herr Joachim. We are comfortable here, but we belong in Hanover. It is difficult to become accustomed to the differences under the circumstances."

Brahms was less sympathetic than Joachim. He was too much a republican and too little a monarchist even for the benign rule of Franz Joseph of Austria whose portrait stared at him from the wall, barely visible for his dark clothes in the gloom though his medals shone brightly. Beside him gleamed his wife, the Empress Elizabeth, more resplendent in white, whiter yet for the Russian wolfhound seated at her feet.

The King looked toward Joachim. "God will not permit this injustice to continue. We will bear a short separation from our beloved Hanover with courage. If not for the new weaponry he would never have won. Our time will come again."

Joachim murmured, nodding again, lost for words. The new weaponry was impressive – breechloading, quickfiring rifles – but the King had ordered his soldiers into the Battle of Langensalza knowing they could not win, driven them into a slaughter, lost the support of his people for being blind in more ways than one. He spoke quickly as the silence grew. "God recognizes His faithful servants by the firmness of their trust in Him in their misfortune!"

The Queen rescued him again during the moment of silence that followed. "Herr Joachim, how is your wife? We understand she has been suffering from bouts of rheumatism?"

"It is true, Your Majesty – but she is much better. She will be glad to know you have asked about her."

"And do you see anything of Frau Schumann? We wonder sometimes how the princesses might have fared had she been free to give them lessons on the piano as we had wished."

"Herr Brahms has seen Frau Schumann more recently than I have. I am sure he could give you a better account."

Brahms gave an account of Clara in Lichtenthal, her house, her family, her company.

"And how is it with you, Herr Brahms? We hear you have written a quite splendid requiem?"

Brahms nodded. He could never be sure whether the Queen meant herself alone or included the King. "I have written a requiem – but how splendid it is I cannot say. Three movements were hissed in Vienna last –"

Joachim interrupted. "Herr Brahms was called to acknowledge the applause."

Brahms looked at Joachim. "I debated whether to acknowledge the applause because nothing could drown the hissing. I might almost have been acknowledging the hissing."

Von Stockhausen smiled. "Herr Brahms is exceedingly modest, Your Majesty. There are musical factions in Vienna just as there are political which accounted for the hissing – but Herr Hanslick, our most respected critic, said the hissing was a requiem for civility and decorum in Vienna –"

Brahms interrupted. "But in one respect they were right. It was my own fault it was hissed – but I have made the adjustments. The tympani were too loud in the third movement. The dynamic markings were unclear. Hanslick mentioned that too. He compared it with a train in a tunnel."

Von Stockhausen smiled. "Herr Brahms is indeed modest. From my reports the *Requiem* was much admired."

"I am not being modest. This was but a dress rehearsal for the entire *Requiem*. It is not to be premiered in its entirety until Good Friday, next year, at St. Peter's Cathedral in Bremen."

Von Stockhausen kept his smile for the Queen. "Another reason for the hissing, if Herr Brahms will permit me, might also have been that this is a Protestant requiem, and the audience was primarily Catholic."

The Queen leaned forward. "That interests me greatly, Herr Brahms, that you have chosen your own words for your *Requiem*. What made you do it? Did you not find the Latin text good enough?"

Brahms took a deep breath; he would have preferred to let the *Requiem* speak for itself. "It is not that I did not find it good enough – but that it was not what I wanted. I have called it a *German Requiem* because I have extracted the text from Luther's Bible – but I would as soon have called it a Human Requiem." He had deliberately avoided texts naming the Christ; his concern was less with salvation for the dead than comfort for the living; but more he did not want to say.

IT WAS TEN O'CLOCK when Brahms and Joachim were in a carriage again headed back to their hotel. "Well, Jussuf, that was a fine waste of time – and not even to offer us anything to eat. I am starving."

The carriage cost fourteen gulden, the late dinner at the hotel would cost more. Joachim nodded. "The King is now too poor, he cannot even send us a carriage – but I am told there are still sixty horses in his stables."

"Tchhah! Kings! Thank God for Bismarck."

"Careful, Johannes! You never know who might hear you. We are still in Vienna, you know. Besides, he was not a bad king. He treated me very well. I wish my Ursi had sent me the Guelphic Order as I had asked. I knew he was going to feel for it. He must think he has lost his authority entirely."

"He has! We only visited him out of courtesy. There is nothing he can do for anyone anymore."

Joachim frowned. "Civility matters – even more in times of war."

"Why did your Ursi not send the medal?"

Joachim spoke through his teeth, making fists of his hands. "I am sure she did, but not right away. I will receive it tomorrow, or the day after when I will have no more need of it. I do not know what is the matter with her. She acts as if she is married to herself. She does not seem to realize we now have children to care for."

Brahms raised his eyebrows. "What are you saying, Jussuf?"

"It is true. She has received offers to appear again on the stage – and she is thinking again of performing – even when she knows how set I am against it. I cannot believe her."

"You do not trust your own wife?"

"You do not understand. It is not a matter of trust. The Opera House in Paris asked me to play six times in their next season. I was told this has not happened since Paganini's time – but I did not accept because I did not wish to give up my few quiet days with her. Instead, she now says she wants to go on the stage."

"It still sounds to me like you do not trust her."

"I trust her! It is those around her I do not trust, her so-called friends. The world of opera is a world of fleshpots – but you know that, Johannes. In the theater my Ursi is but a butterfly among wasps."

"Tchhah, Jussuf! You will make yourself crazy with suspicion. You see wasps sometimes where there are only butterflies."

"I cannot help it. I love her too well to risk losing her."

"But if you do not trust her – that is the best way to lose her."

"Well, I do not know about that. I am doing what I think is right."

"Yes, yes, of course. Everyone always does what he thinks is right. It is always the other person who is wrong."

Joachim frowned. "You do not understand. You do not know my Ursi."

Brahms laughed. "I do not need to know your Ursi, Jussuf. I know you."

"No, I mean, she can be very playful – you know that about her – but it is too easy for others to misunderstand her playfulness. One New Year's party she went under the table with a hatpin – just high spirits, you understand – but the others at the table only think the worst."

"On New Year's everybody goes under the table – or on top of the table – but if it was so very important to you why did you not order her out? As her husband you surely had the right. It was even your duty to safeguard her reputation."

"I would have, but she would not have listened – and then it would have been worse for both of us. People would say she does not listen to her husband – and that would be worse than going under the table with a hatpin."

Brahms grunted, saying nothing, imagining Joachim at the table, stiff as a statue, his face carved with Olympian disapproval.

BRAHMS TO CLARA   *Hamburg, Jan 68*

My dear Clara,

I spent Christmas with Berta and Artur Faber and I have visited Bremen to adjust the tympanist's part with Reinthaler who is preparing the orchestra for me to conduct on Good Friday. In the meantime, I plan to play with Stockhausen in Berlin, Dresden, Kiel, and some other nearby cities, perhaps even going up to Copenhagen.

You have perhaps heard that Stockhausen has resigned from the Hamburg Philharmonic, and they have offered the appointment to Julius von Bernuth. I do not know much about him, and I do not care to know more. The appointment was mine – even before it was Stockhausen's it was mine – but I see how it goes in Hamburg. I am forever to be discounted in my native city and I am done with wishful thinking. I am sorely tempted now to find an unfurnished apartment for myself in Vienna. How much it would help, dearest Clara, if I were to know that you too were thinking of moving there sooner or later. Your unsettled way of life must come to an end in time, and next year the time will be ripe. There is only one thing to consider, and it applies to everybody, to me as well, and that is whether it is necessary for you to continue to earn money in this way. No other consideration should have any weight with you or with anyone else. Think upon what I say so we can discuss it when we meet next, maybe when you come for the Requiem in Bremen.

I have enclosed the piano score for the Requiem as I promised. It seems almost unnecessary to send it to you since you say you are afraid of scores, but I had promised it and here it is.

Other than that there is little to say – except that you and Joachim belong here in Germany, especially now when so much is happening, and not in England, regardless of the amount of money you can make.

Your Johannes

CLARA TO BRAHMS   *17 Half Moon Street*
Piccadilly, London
10 February, 1868

My dear Johannes,

It is a good thing I know better than to give too much consideration to what you say. I know you do not mean to be hurtful, but that does not lessen the hurt. I am sorry if I have given you a wrong impression. It is not true that I am afraid of scores, but I am aware of my incompetence in reading a complicated score. If I had more leisure I would find someone to teach me to do it properly. I hope I will find the time to follow the score of your Requiem, but it hurts me deeply when you say you find it unnecessary to send it. That was not warranted, but as I say it is a good thing I know you better than to care too much about what you say.

And so you are really going to settle in Vienna? I do not think that is such a bad thing. I too should like to live there if I could only find what I wanted. You seem to imagine that I have made enough money and that I am now traveling for my own amusement, but one does not exert oneself to such an extent just for pleasure. It is not merely a matter of money. If that were the case I would be in America. Jenny Lind and Rubinstein have both made more money in a single American journey than I might make in three in Germany, but I do not go precisely because in America the cult is for the personality of the performer more than for the music, and that is not what I wish to cultivate.

Besides, my powers are at their zenith and I am at my most successful. It is hardly the time for me to withdraw into private life. During the past year I have been received everywhere with such warmth, and with few exceptions played so well that I cannot see why I should stop just at this moment. As far as music is concerned I feel as strong as ever – nay, I often think that I play many things with greater mastery than I have in years – in both the spiritual and technical sense. For instance, I played Robert's concerto in Brussels, which had been a failure there before, to an audience of 3,000 people, and with such success as I have seldom had. This was not only a joy to me but fresh proof that there is life in the old mare yet. As a matter of fact I can easily claim that public appreciation for my playing has greatly increased in the last few years.

But what I do not understand is why you have chosen to say such things to me at a time when I am in England and most in need of all my powers. It was inconsiderate of you, to say the least, and unkind to include Joachim in your condemnation, especially since he and I have both broken many lances for you – but he too understands, as do I, that you do not mean the things that you say. It is merely a reflex action. You speak your mind, which we both find admirable, but sometimes it appears your mind is not much engaged. Be careful, dear Johannes, that you do not say the wrong thing some day to the wrong person, who will be less inclined to understand you as are your friends – and do <u>not</u> take what I say amiss. You <u>know</u> I mean well by you.

I have said this before, and I will say it again. You must find some well-to-do girl in Vienna whom you can love – and you will become more cheerful. You will still have cares, but you will also experience new joys and you will embrace life with a fresh zest. The time is ripe, dear Johannes, and Joachim joins me in urging you to think about it.

Something else I must think about are my children. We received such bad news about Julie between Christmas and New Year's that I sent Marie at once to Divonne to see for herself how bad she was. The doctors say it is only a matter of nerves, but is that not bad enough? She is taking a coldwater cure and I am afraid she has been rather overdoing it. She insists on taking two plunge baths a day despite my earnest entreaties. I suppose she imagines that an intensive regimen will cure her more quickly, but it appears only to have debilitated her further. She is barely able now to walk and needs to be carried from the bed to the sofa.

I would have gone with Marie but for a production of Genoveva by Levi in Karlsruhe. My Robert's opera is all too seldom performed for me to have missed such an opportunity. Besides, I was shortly to leave for Brussels before coming to England, so there was nothing else for me to do but hope for the best.

Ludwig, unfortunately, has once more lost his post through unpunctuality, and Felix's lungs show signs of deterioration which is a particularly bad sign in one so young. He is but thirteen. So you see, my troubles are many, and they eat very quickly into my allotment. Besides, I do not know how many years I have yet been given to live myself, and surely you can understand I must prepare for the time when I will no longer be able to perform in public.

Let me hear from you soon.

Your old Clara

BRAHMS TO CLARA   *Hamburg, March 68*

My dear Clara,

You say you want to hear from me soon, but you also say you do not pay much attention to what I say. That is hardly an incentive for me to write – but I write precisely because your other friends are too nice to tell you what I will tell you freely – and I include Joachim among these friends. We have talked about it, how our Joachim is. He is the first to tell you what is pleasant, but holds what is unpleasant until it is too late. You must think of us as complementary friends. We both tell you the truth, but because we have different natures we tell different truths – and the truth is people only come to see you now out of curiosity, to see the widow play her husband's music. They come out of pity because you press your husband's music upon them. At your age you must beware of selfdeception. What you say about your powers is no doubt what you believe – but only out of habit. You are not as yet accustomed to recognizing yourself as an older woman, and that is the truth about yourself you must accept, and sooner rather than later, before you are driven to make a fool of yourself. The mark of a great artist is one who knows when his peak is past, who does not merely bask in past glory. You must think about it, dear Clara. What other friend would dare to tell you such a truth? I am in all likelihood the only one who will speak to you about this matter and that is why I implore you to bear the inevitable in mind. Take an example from others in your situation and do not believe yourself to be an exception. Even Liszt, as you know, stopped a long time ago. We must talk about it soon, but in the meantime remember that I say this only because it is impossible for me to harbor the smallest unsympathetic or unfriendly thought about you.

I was so sorry to get the news about Julchen. She is so delicate, and yet when one thinks of her all thoughts of illness are banished. I feel about her as I might about one of my own family. I would never have thought you would have left her alone during Christmas so far away and so ill, but I do understand your family worries. I have a new one of my own. You know, of course, that since my mamma died my sister Elise has been living with the family of my old teacher, Cossel, since she feels she can no longer live with my pappa after what happened between him and our mamma. Unfortunately, she threatens to give me further serious trouble for she has got a most unsuitable marriage in mind, to a watchmaker by the name of Friedrich Grund, a widower with six children twenty years older than her. We Brahmses seem to have a propensity for marriages with the widest age differences. I only hope that this bitter cup will pass from me. Is it not enough that I have refrained from putting the sweet draught to my own lips on her account?

    Your loving Johannes

CLARA TO BRAHMS   *Piccadilly, 19 March, 1868*

Dear Johannes,

    You never fail to astonish me. I am now convinced that I should expect from you only the unexpected. The better I think I know you the more you surprise me. How you could imagine yourself a friend when you wrote what you wrote I cannot fathom. You have ever been at pains to stop me from touring. I do not understand your motive and I do not much feel like speculating, but I believe strongly that whatever your reasons they can only be selfish. There can be no other answer.

    I do not feel like saying very much, but this much I wish to impress upon your stubborn and inconsiderate nature. The whole of the past year I have been received enthusiastically everywhere, all my concerts have been packed, and people hardly pay to go to concerts out of pity. You have not even heard me recently in concert. All artists who have heard me have assured me, without my asking, that they have never heard me play better or show more spiritual and technical mastery over the works I produce than I am doing now – and these were people who had absolutely no ulterior motive for saying so and who spoke from their hearts. Your reproach is so unjustified that I hardly feel inclined to defend myself against it further.

    I will add only that I press Robert's works on nobody – but I know of no greater joy than to be able to do as much for their popularity as everybody insists upon my doing now.

    I had so looked forward to seeing you again and hearing your glorious Requiem in Bremen, but you have spoiled it all. I am now in two minds about whether I wish to see you anytime soon at all. I appear to have much to think about where you are concerned.

    Your Clara

BRAHMS TO CLARA   *April 1868*

My dear Clara,

    What am I to say? I am not good with words. The more I say the worse it gets. You are right about me in a hundred and one things. I do sometimes say what is on my mind before I have considered it thoroughly. You warned me about it recently and it was a warning I did not heed – much to my disgrace – but I will tell you about that when we meet – and meet we must, dear Clara. I am a musician and speak best through my music. If you come to hear me on Good Friday you will understand me best. Indeed, your presence would be half the performance for me. If it goes as I hope, you will indeed have reason to rejoice, but I am not a man who succeeds in getting more than people wish to give him of their own accord – and since that is always very little I am resigning myself to the thought that this time, as in Vienna, it will go fast, too fast and too sketchily. But do come!!

    Let me hear from you soon and hold out some hope that you will be present on the 10th of April. I am anxious not only that you should listen but also that you should see.

    Your loving Johannes

Klaus Groth was a poet who wrote in the Low German dialect of Heide, his place of birth, and a professor of literature at the university in Kiel where he had moved. A chinking sound awakened him from sleep. In the first blur of consciousness, the halflife of diminishing dreams, he imagined the King's Treasurer in the garden, hedges of money, waterfalls of coins. The darkness exaggerated sounds, imagination exaggerated them further, but consciousness gave them focus and made them clear. The chink was accompanied by footfalls, the clink of buckled shoes: someone was pacing the garden. He looked at his watch: it was not yet five o'clock.

"Who is it?"

Groth recognized Herr Graebner's voice on the ground floor.

"I am looking for Klaus Groth."

"He is asleep. Come back in the morning."

"I have to see him now."

"You are waking everybody up. Now go away."

The voice whispered. "I am sorry, but I have to see him now."

The voice was familiar: Groth was still shaking sleep from his eyes when he opened the window. "I am Klaus Groth. Who is it?"

"Groth, you sleepyhead! As if you do not know! Let me in!"

"Brahms! What are you doing at this hour, waking up everybody?"

Brahms slapped his trousers. His pockets, bulging like sacks, jingled and chinked. His traveling bag stood to one side. "I have made a pile of money, Groth! Be quick and let me in!"

Graebner was still at his window. "Ssshh! Have you no consideration at all?"

"Groth, will you let me in or not?"

"Be quiet, Brahms. I am coming. I am coming."

He closed the window and descended the stairs to open the door. He had met Brahms at the Rhine Festival in the year of Robert's death, their families had been acquainted in Heide, and Brahms had set some of his poems to music. It was less than a week since Groth had last seen him, bound for Denmark with Stockhausen, the last lap of their tour, but he had not expected them back for another week.

He led Brahms up the stairs, lit the kitchen lamp, and made coffee, remembering his guest liked it black and strong. Brahms, emptying coins from his pockets on the kitchen table, seemed unable to stop talking about his triumphs with Stockhausen in Denmark and sightseeing in Copenhagen, and unable to stop smiling – but his smile was hard and hardened further through Groth's continued silence. "Well, what do you think, Groth? Why do you not say something?"

Groth, fourteen years older than Brahms, with the bushy moustache and beard of a billygoat, bushier yet from sleep, knew he was not getting the whole story. "Brahms, put away your money. Tell me what has happened."

Still Brahms smiled. "I am telling you. I have made a lot of money. See?"

Groth served steaming coffee. "Where is Stockhausen? Why do you show up in the middle of the night? Why do you make such a show of your money? If I did not know you I would say you have robbed somebody – or, God preserve us, killed somebody."

"Aaah! Groth, you should have lived in the olden days. You would have made a good jester."

"I am not jesting, Brahms. Tell me what has happened and I will help you if I can."

Brahms shrugged. "Well, then, since you insist. It is a silly thing, just a misunderstanding – so silly you will hardly believe it, but it will make you laugh."

Groth remained silent, sipping coffee, fixing Brahms with his eyes.

Brahms took a sip and shrugged again. "It is really much ado about nothing. You know the Thorwaldsen Museum in Copenhagen?"

"Yes, I have seen it."

Brahms rubbed his forehead and spoke ironically. "Yes, yes, everyone sees it who goes to Copenhagen, the great Thorwaldsen."

Albert Bertel Thorwaldsen was Denmark's foremost sculptor, known for massive neoclassical works. His museum, constructed largely with his own funds, exhibited a large collection of his sculptures.

"Gade gave a reception for me and Stockhausen after one of our concerts. All the leading musicians were there – so we might all meet one another."

Niels Gade, composer and violinist, Mendelssohn's successor as conductor of the Gewandhaus concerts, now Director of the Copenhagen Conservatory, had supported Brahms's Manifesto with Joachim and remained his friend through the years.

"Somebody asked me if I had seen the Thorwaldsen Museum. I said I had seen it, and yes it was extraordinary – but I said it was a shame it did not stand in Berlin."

Groth grimaced. "Brahms, you said that? How could you say that? In a company of Danes, you said that, after what Bismarck has done?"

Brahms's grin again stretched his mouth. "Yes, I said that. So what?"

"So what! Are you crazy? Do you think they have made a gift to us of Schleswig-Holstein? Do you think they have forgotten that we took it from them?"

"We did not take it! They lost it!"

"Brahms, I will not argue with you. That is not the point, whether we took it or they lost it – but how could you say such a thing?" He shook his head. "They could not see it as you do. Whatever you thought, that much you should have known. How could you be so stupid?"

Brahms lost his grin. "I meant it as a compliment. I meant it would be better if so many beautiful objects were in a great center where many people could see them – I meant Berlin would be proud to boast such a collection. That was all I meant."

"But did you not think that the Danes would not put up with such a remark? Do you not know how they feel about Prussians and Bismarck? Could you possibly be a more complete idiot, Brahms?"

Brahms shook his head. "It did not occur to me, Groth – but I could hardly believe the reaction. It was in the newspapers. People were returning tickets. I saw how it was going. It was me they did not want, but Stockhausen they still wanted to see. He has called Joachim. They will continue without me." His grin stiffened his face again. "I was advised to leave right away – but I have earned so much money it is a matter of indifference to me. I will not want more for a long time."

"Brahms, you should know better than that. It is not a matter of indifference to you and you should not say that it is. I cannot believe you. First you say you have behaved in a most atrocious manner, and then you say it is a matter of indifference to you. You were an ambassador for Germany and you have behaved shamefully – and you continue to behave shamefully."

Brahms knew Groth was right: he had behaved shamefully, he had behaved stupidly, but the Danes had been no less stupid. It was not his fault they were thinskinned. "I cannot think about this now, Groth. I have to think about my *Requiem*. It will be no easy task. I cannot do important work if I am expected also to live up to everyone's expectations."

"Tchhah! Brahms, you are talking like a fool. You can do what you want. I am going back to sleep. Maybe in the morning you will come to your senses."

iii

Brahms's *Requiem* begins with a slow steady throb, a pulse sounding deep within the ocean: a melodic phrase rises above the throb in a dotted rhythm, falls in a steady drumbeat, rises again in another register, falls again to the drumbeat, rises one more time, falls, lies low gathering strength, and, joined by a choir, "Blessed are they that mourn, for they shall be comforted," rises one more time, bursting the surface: "They that sow in tears shall reap in joy." Phrases vault into the firmanent, streamers of melody, crisscrossing beams of light.

Brahms, at the podium, could not have been more pleased: Reinthaler had prepared the choir and orchestra well; every nuance, every detail, had been attended; he needed barely to mark time; but most astonishing had been the response. St. Peter's Cathedral had opened its doors at six o'clock and filled to capacity within the hour, two thousand strong, bursting the doors, including his closest friends, the Joachims, Dietrichs, Grimms, his pappa, members of the Frauenchor, other friends and admirers from Hamburg, Vienna, Belgium, Holland, Switzerland, England, composers, critics, artists. Clara had caused the only anxiety, almost the last to appear with Marie, and he had led them with no less relief than pride to sit beside his pappa.

The second movement was already fourteen years old, begun during the months following Robert's plunge into the Rhine, once part of a sonata he had played with Clara for two pianos – now, in the last of many incarnations, a funerary march in triple time, tympani thudding in triplets, a deepthroated choir echoed by rising brass, monolithic in cast: "For all flesh is as grass, and all the glory of man as the flower of grass, but the word of the Lord endureth forever."

Watching Brahms at the podium Clara recalled Robert's prophecy: *Once he waves his magic wand over choruses and orchestras he will provide glimpses into spiritual worlds.* He had known then of Johannes's power, heard the *Requiem* in the early sonatas. She had almost not come, but was glad Marie and Fraulein Leser had finally persuaded her, and wished Robert might have been with them, forgiving Johannes everything with every bar: creators abided by different rules. Through all their disagreeable moments he had been carrying these gigantic melodies and harmonies in his head. Her breath came in short gasps, her lungs constricted, her eyes grew misty.

Brahms echoed the motif from the first movement – rise, fall, transcendance – in different forms in all seven movements, adding musical unity to arias of Consolation, Patience, Hope, Joy, Grief, Trust, and Redemption, while displaying not only mastery of harmony, counterpoint, and orchestration, in solo, choral, and instrumental episodes, not only a synthesis of musical forms from the Renaissance to Schumann, but in employing the form of an oratorio to express personal emotions he had infused Classical modes with Romantic sensibilities, fused past and present and projected them into the future, using old forms to purposes heretofore unconceived and inconceivable.

AFTER THE PERFORMANCE a hundred guests squeezed into a nearby rathskeller for a celebratory supper. Lamps burnished the enclosure: low ceiling, wooden floor, wooden beams, wooden tables and benches, halftimbered walls, kegs of beer to one side. Plates of sausages were passed around, plates of bread and cheese, frothing and sparkling steins. Clara sat on Brahms's right with Marie, Joachim on his left with Amalie, his pappa and Stockhausen among the others at his table. Conversation hummed in crosscurrents through the air, congratulations flew continually until Reinthaler rose at his table tapping his stein with his fork for attention. "Ladies and Gentlemen!"

Guests scurried, refilling steins, returning to their seats. Reinthaler waited, continually tapping his stein, a rhythm soon taken up by others. "Ladies and Gentlemen!" Someone continued to pour beer, someone burped followed by someone else, but the room was soon quiet.

"Ladies and Gentlemen, it is with great pleasure and pride that I greet this distinguished assemblage of visitors, some of them gathered to perform, others to hear, the new work of the composer who is in our midst."

Applause broke immediately, directed toward Brahms's table.

"Bravo! BRAVO! For Brahms and Germany!"

Reinthaler joined the applause before continuing. "That it has been performed for the first time here in Bremen gives me particular happiness. It is a great and beautiful – one may say it is an epoch-making work, which has filled all of us who have heard it today with pride, since it has inspired in us the conviction that German art has not died out, but begins to stir again and will thrive as gloriously as of old – when our last dear master was carried to the grave."

Another burst of applause broke. The room, including Brahms, directed a collective glance at Clara, but refrained from comment. Clara wished she might have been less of a woman, but could not help trembling, bowing her head, choking with each breath. Her eyes, barely dry all evening, poured in sheets down her cheeks. Brahms steadied her, his arm around her shoulders, and Reinthaler continued.

"It had almost seemed as though music had entered its twilight, but today we are reassured. In the *German Requiem* we believe that we have a sequel worthy of the achievements of the great masters of the past."

Again there was applause, and again Reinthaler waited. "You will all certainly rejoice with me that the creator of this glorious work is present among us and will joyfully raise your glasses to the health of the composer – our Brahms!"

The applause reached its zenith, steins were raised, healths proclaimed, patriotism reaffirmed, but for Brahms the moment was no less splendid than dreaded. He got to his feet, but would rather have delivered ten more requiems than a single speech. Clara squeezed his hand, eyes deep blue and glistening. "Johannes, my dearest, I am so very proud, so very proud, and so would *he* have been, so very proud, indeed!" She squeezed his hand so tightly it was bloodless when she let go.

"Ladies and Gentlemen."

His voice was small, almost cracked. "I must begin by saying that oratory is not one of my gifts." He pursed his lips, almost as breathless as Clara, making fists of his hands. "There are, however, many I wish to thank – friends who have been good and kind, chief among them my friend Reinthaler who has sacrificed much of his time and effort for my *Requiem*. I place my collective thanks, therefore, upon his head – or at his feet, if you prefer – and call three cheers for Reinthaler. Hip-hip!"

The speech had been so short the response came slowly, "HURRAH!" but the exuberance mounted with each successive "Hurrah."

There were not many dry eyes among the audience, but Brahms liked best the response made by his pappa. Asked if he were not proud of his son, Jakob had calmly taken a pinch of snuff, betrayed no emotion, and held his questioner in suspense before replying: "It was not bad."

THE *REQUIEM* WAS THE BEGINNING of Brahms's Big Fame, played again in Bremen the same month, shortly in Leipzig, Basel (twice), Zurich (twice), Karlsruhe (twice), Munster, Cologne, Hamburg, Weimar, Dessau, Chemnitz (twice), Barmen, Magdeburg, Jena, Cologne (twice), Vienna (again), and within a couple of years in London, Berlin, Munich, St. Petersburg, Utrecht, and Paris (1875). Despite the clamor of the Musicians of the Future, Brahms was among the leading composers of his age, more direct a descendant of Bach and Beethoven than the New Germans, showing himself not their acolyte, not their twin, but their sibling – their younger sibling, more threatening for his youth.

He was not rich, but able now to live as he wished on royalties from published works, and proud to display the original manuscript of the *Requiem* on pages of various shapes and sizes because through the years he had been unable to afford much paper at a time, revealing incidentally its long gestation, twelve years from the time of Robert Schumann's death.

His speeches rarely grew to be more inspired than his speech in the Rathskeller. During a banquet in Vienna after an early performance of his First Symphony, he stumbled through a similar circumstance: "Ladies and gentlemen, composing is very difficult. Yes, indeed, it is very difficult, indeed. Copying is far easier. Yes, indeed, copying is easier by far – but on that subject my friend, Popper, is a much greater authority, and can give you a great deal more information."

He had sat, yielding the stage to David Popper, a cellist and friend, who rose to the occasion with a smile. "Ladies and gentlemen, my good friend Brahms has just told you that I know all about copying. Well, about that I do not know, maybe he is right, but this I know. If I were to copy anyone there is only one man I would consider, and that is Beethoven – but no one knows more about copying Beethoven than Brahms."

Popper sat down amid much laughter – including, to his credit, Brahms's, much as he hated the comparison. Beethoven loved practical jokes no less than Brahms, but unlike Brahms not when they backfired.

PART SIX

THE C MINOR SYMPHONY

It was dark when Brahms let himself into the wicket gate at 14 Lichtenthaler Allee clutching a manuscript in his hand. He did not bother to knock, but let himself into the house, looking among the Schumanns in the sittingroom to see if Clara was among them. "Where is your mamma?"

Elise was at the piano, Eugenie and Felix were reading curled at opposite ends of a sofa. He could hear sounds in the kitchen. Staring at Eugenie his eyes narrowed, his forehead wrinkled. Elise might have continued playing – but his tone, almost an accusation, made her stop.

Eugenie said nothing, too surprised by his suddenness – Felix, too, merely stared. Marie entered from the kitchen. No one spoke, but in the silence he could hear Clara at her piano and stalked into the passage leading to her bedroom. Marie called after him: "Wait, Herr Brahms! I will let Mamma know you are here."

Elise shouted. "Herr Brahms, you must not burst in upon Mamma like that!"

Brahms appeared not to hear them. The passage leading to Clara's bedroom was dark, a descent of three steps so uneven Clara occasionally still stumbled over them.

Eugenie shouted behind him. "Mamma! Herr Brahms is here!"

Brahms lost his balance on a step, struck his shoulder against the wall, dropped his manuscript, dropped to one knee, and swore fiercely retrieving the pages. He did not bother to knock on Clara's door either, but kicked it open still swearing at the step, shuffling pages in his hands. The girls and Felix stared through the passage until he slammed the door shut behind him, and when it bounced open slammed it shut again.

During the day Clara's room was bright; sunlight entered through three windows along the long wall which overlooked a verandah covered with vines. Beyond the verandah the garden appeared, and beyond the garden the River Oos flanked by oaks and chestnuts. A grand piano stood across from the windows. Clara and Marie had selected grey wallpaper, flecked with gold, to offset two prints of a mountainscape and river valley. An Apollo stood in one corner, a Venus de Milo in another. The sofa, alongside a short wall, was topped by a lifesize portrait of Clara. Folding doors in the other short wall led to a smaller room, her bedchamber. Clara got up from the piano as Brahms entered, but he waved her violently down again seating himself in the sofa.

Clara sat, but her voice was breathless. "Johannes, what is the matter?"

Brahms spoke in staccato phrases. "That – my dear Clara – is what I – should be asking – you."

He refused to look at her, eyes turned inward so they appeared almost white, his face locked, his lower lip clamped over the upper. His red plaid shirt was dusted as usual with cigar ash, but she had long stopped brushing it off. He only did it more purposefully, even burning a hole in his shirt once in response to her nannying while laughing at her consternation. "Johannes, I will not stoop to playing guessing games with you. If you have something on your mind, you must tell me what it is."

"As if you do not know!"

"Aaaah, Johannes! It is always thus with you. You assume I can read your mind and I never know what you are talking about. It is only days since you were here last – and without a trace of this ugly mood you bring with you today. I have absolutely no idea what could have upset you since then."

It was less than a week since he had last visited, breakfasting at the Schumann house following the wedding in the Lichtenthaler Catholic Church of Julchen to Count Victor Radicati di Marmorito whom she had met in Turin. It amazed him that she could refer to it so nonchalantly. His tone lost its edge, his eyes gazed through Clara, beyond her. "You must hate me, Clara. Why do you hate me so?"

Clara's voice rose, almost to compensate for his own, suddenly listless. "*I hate you?* Johannes, you never cease to amaze me! It is *you* who are disagreeable with your moods – not just now and then, as among friends, but constantly, day after day, week after week. You give so little thought to making your visits pleasant to me or to my children that it is a wonder we stand by you at all."

Brahms shook his head. "My moods are not to be disputed. Each of us has an opinion and insists on being right. I too have reason to complain. It seems there is no end of obstacles to overcome if I am to gain any sympathy in your house. I cannot help thinking it is all because of my letter to you. What a very long time ago it was and yet it remains a wall between us and I continue to batter my head against it in vain. It has made you hate me, maybe even against your will. I cannot see it any other way."

"Aaaah, Johannes, do not bring that up again. That is forgotten – that is long forgotten. Have I not proven it? Did I not come to you in Bremen, fatigued though I was from my English tour? Do you not know how unobliged I felt to hear your *Requiem* after all you had written in your letter – and, yet, did I not come? and why do you suppose that was if not to please you? I have put the letter on the shelf long ago, I have thrown it away with the rubbish – but you are the one who insists on retrieving it and reading it constantly." She shook her head. "The letter is nothing, there is no wall between us – except the one you build with your own evil moods. I confess my children are angry when they see how I suffer from your unfriendliness, when they see me pass many an hour sadly that you might have made so happy. You have only to show a little friendliness, dear Johannes, a little more control of your moods. That is all. That is the wall of which you speak, not the letter."

Brahms did not move, his voice did not change. "I see how it is now. You are to insist on talking about my moods while I am to insist they are only a matter of differing opinions. You must hate me so very much, dearest Clara."

"Ohhhh, Johannes! I swear you will *make* me hate you *against* my will – but I do *not* hate you! I have no place for hurtful feelings in my heart, and I hope you will never give me cause to find it!"

"Clara, what I wish you to consider is this: what I wrote about you I have neither written nor spoken to another soul, only as a friend, to your good self to prevent you from making a fool of yourself before it was too –" She rose, opening her mouth, but he raised his hand. "No, Clara – let me have my say. Then you can say what you will."

She sat again, taking deep breaths.

"Danke. Now, as I was saying, what I wrote about you is no more than what I have heard you say so many times about others – about your friends, Schroder-Devrient, Lind-Goldschmidt, Garcia-Viardot. We are all human. Our powers must fail, and fade – and how much more glorious is he who makes his last bow before it is forced upon him. I have heard you say it yourself. You cannot deny it. If I made a mistake it was not in what I said but in the time I chose to speak. Had I spoken in the autumn instead of the spring I might have been forgiven. Were I to speak in 1878 instead of 1868 I might have been forgiven. If it is not true of you now, it will be true of you sooner or later – but it would always have been a difficult thing to say, and it is better to have it said too early than too late. So you see, it is only in the matter of the time that I am in error, and the mistake about the year does not seem to me to be so very serious. Can you not grant me at least that? Is not a good friend allowed to say things for which an outsider would be turned away? I am to be forgiven not so much for telling the truth, not even for an overdose of the truth, but for choosing the wrong time. Is that not so?"

Clara had wanted constantly to interrupt while Brahms spoke, but now that he was silent she was calmer herself. "Am I now to speak?"

"I have had my say, yes."

She sighed. "Johannes, I see I have nothing to say after all. You make me so very angry, but I can see that nothing I say will make a difference. You are not concerned with listening to what I have to say, only with hearing what you wish to hear, and that I cannot tell you. I will say only that the enthusiasm with which I am received, particularly in England, continues to rise. The last time a gentleman in the front row seized a wooden footstool and beat it on the floor. I am greeted with such furious applause that it is a long time before I can even begin my concerts, and when I appear with Joachim it seems sometimes as if we might never begin – besides which, I am never allowed to leave without encores." She sighed again. "There is so much more I could say, but I do not wish to dignify this conversation by defending myself further." She shook her head, looking pityingly at Brahms. "No, dear Johannes, the answer to your problem is simplicity itself. You must marry. I have heard Rieter-Biedermann's daughter is partial to you. She is charming, she is pretty, and she is rich – which for a composer is very necessary. Have you never thought about her? In my opinion it is high time that you did. There are so many reasons you should not be alone any longer. That is what I feel."

Rieter-Biedermann was one of his publishers. "Rieter-Biedermann's daughter? Do you imagine this is about Rieter-Biedermann's daughter? Ah, Clara, you understand me even less than I thought. You understand me not at all."

"Why, Johannes, whatever can you mean?"

"I wished to marry – but not Rieter-Biedermann's daughter."

Clara stared uncomprehendingly.

"You have said it a number of times, Clara – and I understand entirely your interest in my art, in my music – but do you not see how willingly I would do without this kind of interest. I speak through my music, it is true, but the problem … the problem … is … that a poor musician such as myself … would like to believe that he is a better man than he is a musician."

Still Clara remained silent.

"That is the satisfaction I wish, Clara. That is the satisfaction you have continually denied me. First you have denied me your own self, and now …"

"Johannes, I am sorry. I do not understand. I simply do not understand. And now – what?"

"Why was I not told?"

"Told what?"

"About Julchen's engagement."

"Julchen's engagement? But you were – you were the first to know."

"Yes, I was, but only after all the arrangements had been made, after the Count had already embarked upon his … Countess. You must have known about it long before you told me."

Levi had told her, Johannes was in love with Julie. She had never believed it, he had said nothing himself, shown no regret presenting her with her wedding present, a large photograph of Clara that Julie had wished, also a daguerreotype, also of Clara – and Julie had shown no reciprocal inclination, but she recalled how his face had shrunk when she had told him, how seldom he had visited afterward, how monosyllabically he had spoken. Her voice softened. "Johannes, I said nothing because I was unsure of the match myself. The man is a Count, he lives in Italy, he is a Catholic, he is so very rich, he speaks little German and she little Italian, he has children from a former marriage to whom she would become a mother – but I know all too well from my own experience that love is not to be frightened. I mentioned the difficulties to her for my own satisfaction more than hers, to be sure she was aware of what she undertook. My heart bled, Johannes – even as I wrote my consent to the Count my heart bled, that she would be so far away from us, in a foreign land, but what else was I to do? They were in love. My consent was but a formality – but why did you never speak for yourself, not even to me?"

"Ah, Clara, you know how it was between you and me. It was difficult to say anything – and for me, words are always difficult." He held the manuscript toward her.

She took it, looking through the pages. The words were by Goethe, culled from his *Harzreise im Winter*. She was familiar with the poem, Goethe's use of the Harz Wald as a backdrop for the fruitful lives of hunters and foresters – and of the solitary misanthrope who lived apart. Brahms had selected three verses for his purpose, arranged in three strophes, a recitative, an aria, and a chorale, to be sung with an orchestra, but arranged on the manuscript for the piano. "Do you want me to play it?"

"What do you think?"

The sarcasm was back, but she recognized the hurt it covered and seated herself at the piano, imagining how it might sound with an orchestra.

The attack with which the work began was so sharp it seemed to jump at you, deep trembling strings meandered through the nether regions of the orchestral register punctuated by shudders of hornblasts until the alto entered with a recitative no less desolate, music suiting the words:

> Who is that lonesome wanderer whose tracks lose themselves in the bushes? The branches close behind him, the grass springs up again, the desert swallows him whole.

The aria sprang directly from the recitative, smoothing the lament, woodwinds alternating with strings now in a higher register – and the mood lifted, however slightly, with the music:

> Who can heal the pain of one who finds poison in balsam, who has drunk hate from the cup of love?
> Once scorned, now scorning, he wastes himself in search of himself.

Finally, a male chorus girded the alto, pizzicato strings underpinned the work like harpstrings, and the melody soared, as did the words, finally, with hope:

> If there is in your Cup, dear Father of Love, one tone to soothe his fears, to revive his heart, then turn your thousand springs upon this soul thirsting in the desert.

When she had struck the last note Clara put her hands in her lap, bent her head, and remained silent, until Brahms approached the piano, picking up the pages from the stand. "I keep this under my pillow when I sleep. It is dearest to me of all that I have composed. I will be sending it to Simrock soon for publication – but it will be with rage, with an anger I cannot explain, for it is something with which I would not easily be parted. Now do you understand?"

Still Clara said nothing, wishing he would speak directly, express himself as tenderly as he did in music. She had had no idea he felt this way, he had said not a word; but she recognized also it was not his way to speak, something prevented him. Without music to release him she felt he might explode.

Brahms saw her face was wet and left the room abruptly, almost falling again on the steps, leaving the house saying nothing to the others who stared as he crossed the room.

Walking home the tears came, his shoulders shook, his heart compressed and decompressed. He walked off the road, almost off a precipice, and sat against a tree, burying his face in his hat, his tears thick, milky, curdled. The darkness and solitude did some good. It was almost an hour before he walked on to Frau Becker's house where he had rented two small uncarpeted attic rooms for the summer, still crying though more silently.

Late into the night he moaned into his pillow, wet with tears, and kissed his manuscript no less wet with tears – but he knew even then it was not Julie he mourned, it was himself, all the women he had known, all the women he would know, there was no difference. Cause and effect, right and wrong, it mattered little how Billroth analyzed it, rationalized it, if the consequence was the same. Deep within himself he would never lose the notion that he could never be the man for the women he loved. Billroth had been right only about the work; work was a blessing; without his work he was nothing.

Hermann Levi walked to 14 Lichtenthaler Allee wearing a top hat, adding height to his small slender frame, also to his thin trim face, longer for his narrow beard, broader for his smile. Whistling the scherzo from Mendelssohn's *Midsummer Night's Dream*, he knocked on the door.

Clara opened the door, beaming when she saw who it was. "Levi! Oh, you must pardon my woman's heart, but it does me *so* much good to see you! You will not believe what we have all suffered these past few weeks." She held his face, kissed his cheeks, embraced him. "Oh, Levi! Is it not wonderful? Is it not the best news we could have?"

"It is, indeed, Frau Schumann, and I have come to ask if the Schumanns would grant me the honor of their company on a day trip to a Strasbourg – German again after almost two hundred years."

When the war had begun the entire nation had appeared to flee, confusion reigning at the station. Clara had almost left herself, Lichtenthal was too close to the fighting, but she had chosen to stay when she had learned empty houses would be the first billeted by soldiers. For weeks Lichtenthal had been a city of the dead, but when the King of Prussia had sent a telegram, news of a great victory at Metz, bells had been rung, the orchestra called, trumpets flourished, and she had run a flag up the side of the house. Marie, Eugenie, and Felix crowded around.

"Oh, Mamma, please, let us go!"

"It would be such a treat!"

"Please, Mamma!"

"But, Levi, is it safe? Do you think it is safe?"

"I would not ask you if I thought it was not."

"Oh, Mamma!"

"Of course, then. That would be grand."

The battle for Strasbourg had been the last. Napoleon III had already surrendered, and nightly the Schumanns had slept shuddering in their beds, cannonade thundering in their ears, reverberations shaking their house. They had walked once to the old castle in Yberg overlooking the Rhine Valley, and watched the spire of Strasbourg Cathedral, fires in the neighborhood, dust of skirmishes. They had been paralyzed by the first sound of the guns: Felix, seventeen, had stood up straight; Eugenie, twenty, had blanched; Clara and Marie had held hands.

"Frau Schumann, what news have you of Ferdinand?"

"He is at Metz – but thanks be to God, he is safe. We have sent him woollen shirts – chocolate."

"And tea!"

"We were given to understand these are of great comfort to soldiers!"

"We have been making woollen bandages to send to the camps!"

"It is almost all we have been doing, Herr Levi."

"Oh, Levi, it makes me want to laugh just to see you again. We are all so glad of company we cannot even stop talking – as you can tell. We have been so afraid."

"We hid our things in the cellar, Herr Levi, even some wine, just in case – but if the Turcos came we would have left immediately."

The Turcos were a French regiment of Algerians, renowned for savagery. "We planned to go to St. Moritz if we were forced from Lichtenthal – but it was said that the Swiss sympathized with the French!"

"Herr Levi, Julie has had a baby boy!"

"Has she, really! That is good news indeed! And how is she?"

"She is well, thank God! In the midst of all this turmoil we have been blessed with a little countling in the family. I am now a grandmother!"

"Congratulations, Frau Schumann! I am indeed glad to hear it." He did not ask about Ludwig, now incarcerated in the Colditz asylum. "What have you heard from our friends?"

"Stockhausen wrote to me, bless his heart, to invite us all to Cannstadt where he was sure everything would be quiet – but we did not want to leave our house to the soldiers – and Joachim has written, asking about Ferdinand."

"And what about Brahms?"

"He is with Joachim in Salzberg. He, too, wrote to us, but I must say he has disappointed us sorely. He promised to join us in Lichtenthal, and we expected him daily for a week, thinking it so kind of him to join us in our hardship – but he wrote to say the trains were all being deployed by the army and he could find no way to reach us."

"But he is right. You must not blame him. It is one of the reasons we have won the war so quickly, and with so little loss of life. Bismarck had been ready for the war before it was declared. The trains were deployed to mobilize three armies in less than three weeks. In such matters, readiness is all."

"Still, we were disappointed. I wished he might have found a way." She felt he could have found at least a carriage coming to Lichtenthal if he had tried, but she feared he no longer cared enough, perhaps even he had been afraid to put himself in danger.

"Surely, Herr Levi, Bismarck could have spared him one train?"

"Perhaps he would have, Fraulein Eugenie, if you had written him a letter?"

Bismarck had taunted the French into declaring war: when Queen Isabella II of Spain had been expelled from the throne the Spanish council of ministers had sought Prince Leopold of Hohenzollern, a relative of King Wilhelm I of Prussia, for her successor. France had protested German sovereignty in Spain, accused Prussia of attempting to upset the balance of power, and Prince Leopold had withdrawn his candidacy – but France had demanded as well a declaration that no Hohenzollern's candidacy would ever be renewed. The King had declined, despatched a telegram for Bismarck to send to the French, but Bismarck had edited the telegram – worded it so strongly, some said, that he had left the French no alternative but to declare war.

"Bismarck appears to have known all along what he was doing, does he not?"

Three wars, all engineered by Bismarck, had given Germany preeminence among European nations in a little over six years: first, the alliance with Austria against Denmark, to gain Schleswig-Holstein; next, against Austria to nullify her interference in German affairs; finally, against France.

"Yes, Frau Schumann, but the King has acquitted himself no less splendidly. Just imagine, a man of over seventy years, on the battlefield, behaving like a hero."

"Oh, yes, of course. It makes one so proud to be a German. I can hardly wait for the celebrations. Everything has been so well planned and everything has gone like clockwork."

She had been amazed at the courage of soldiers: braving enemy fire from above while scaling hillsides without firing a shot; running in plain sight of the enemy, bags of powder on their backs, to the sites they wished to explode.

"Herr Levi, where is Schufterle?"

"Ah, Fraulein Eugenie, he will be glad you asked about him. I asked him if he would like to join us, but he said it was of little consequence to him whether Strasbourg belonged to France or Germany."

Eugenie laughed. "He did not!"

"Well, you are right. What he actually said was quite different. It went something like this." Levi raised his head, cupped his hands in front of his mouth, and closed his eyes. "OwooWowooWowooWowoo! Whooof-woof-woof! OwooWowoo!"

THE SCHUMANNS AND LEVI had visited Strasbourg before, but Clara was reminded of nothing as much as Dresden during the revolution of 1848, streets of rubble, sections of buildings showing through the walls. An image flashed through her mind: unmade bed, bedside table, lamp on the table, picture on the wall, cuckoo clock, cradle rocking, dog silently barking, all visible through a broken wall two storeys high. She had then been pregnant with Ferdinand, who was now with the garrison at Metz. She could never reconcile the ugliness of war with its necessity, her hatred for Napoleon III with pity for his humiliation, pride for Germany with sorrow for French soldiers and their mothers. The contrasts were no less stark in Strasbourg: boisterous Germans by the hundreds among the remaining frightened French; narrow medieval streets of the old city cluttered with debris alongside willows brushing the River Ill. Many of the visitors were too young to know better, but she wished she might have been more excited herself, and was grateful for Levi who delighted in everything, even the houses built so close together, roofs growing from roofs, beaver-tailed tiles known for their shape. They visited the fortifications where they were warned about shells (exploded and unexploded), walked through the Cathedral which Clara was glad had survived, and finally found an inn.

La Table Alsace provided round white tables sheltered by large bright umbrellas towering like trees. People drank white wine from greenstemmed glasses and ate nuts dropping shells on the floor. Splotches of geraniums painted the dusty landscape.

Levi ordered a bottle of Riesling, another of Pinot. Clara's mood improved once the fruity sparkling liquid went to her head. The day could not have been better (bright and hot), nor the food, commencing with a quiche Lorraine, followed by a smoked shoulder of pork in a horseradish sauce, another dish of sauerkraut with various meats, concluded with plum tarts laden with vanilla cream and Munster cheese.

When the last train was ready to leave the crowd was so large that people climbed onto the roofs of the carriages – and, when they were ordered off, climbed off and climbed on again. The trains were finally given the signal to depart, returning to Baden-Baden with singing, shouting, stomping revelers overhead.

ii

Eugenie laughed, leaning upon the flat wide parapet. Three Englishwomen appeared in profile on the street below, each erect with an extended bustle, walking it seemed in formation, appearing like nothing as much as a trio of geese, but she stifled her laughter. "Mamma, it is so vast you almost cannot see the park for the trees."

Clara smiled, standing behind her in the verandah. "I have always maintained that England is a country of gardens. I am glad you think so too."

Marie sneezed in the sittingroom.

"God bless you, my dear." Miss Alice Burnand faced the verandah. "Perhaps you had both better come inside, my dear Mrs. Schumann. It is still cold for April, and I would so hate for any of you to catch influenza during your stay."

Clara had never imagined she could like foreigners so well, but hospitality such as the Burnands offered was not to be found in Germany. Not only had they invited Eugenie to join her and Marie on their tour, but they had asked Marie for her preference in beds. Since they had asked, Marie had said she was in the habit of sleeping on a spring mattress. The Burnands had appropriated spring mattresses for all three and Clara slept better than she had ever slept before in England. They had also undertaken to show London to Eugenie.

Joachim, also in the sittingroom, sipping tea, smiled ironically. "I wish, my dear Miss Burnand, you might have said that to my Ursi before she had succumbed to her cold."

Amalie was in bed in their hotel room. "I wish I might have too, Mr. Joachim. It is too easy to catch your death of cold in England in the spring. I say it to all our visitors. Just ask my brother."

Her brother, Arthur Burnand, laughed. "Indeed, she does – but it is easier yet in Scotland. You can catch your death of cold there even in August. The air is always damp."

His friend, Harry Clumly, smiled. "Indeed, it is. It reaches into your nose like a finger, it tickles your lungs, and it lodges in your esophagus like an icicle. You might say Scotland is a country of lakes – or lochs as they prefer to call them." He winked at Clara. "They are just too damn stupid to speak the language correctly, you know."

Clara liked neither smile nor wink. She had been assured by the Burnands that his bark was worse than his bite, and she excused him for their sake, but she could

548

not say she much liked his bark either. She closed the verandah door behind her ignoring Clumly. "Maybe we will take a walk in the park tomorrow, Eugenie, if the sun comes out."

"I would like that, Mamma. I have heard so much about Hyde Park I almost feel I have been there already."

"Well, then, why on earth would you wish to go again?"

"Because, Herr – er, Mr. Clumly, I have not actually been there at all."

"Hmphh! Well, that is all very well, but I warn you, take my word for it, a park's a park for all that. There is none among us so very large that needs a park so very large for our entertainment."

Mr. Burnand laughed. "I think, my dear Miss Eugenie, that you have quite succeeded in tying Clumly's tongue in knots – and his mind, in the bargain."

Eugenie smiled, seating herself far from Clumly, as did Clara.

Mr. Burnand turned to Joachim. "Do you imagine, Mr. Joachim, that you might persuade your friend, Mr. Brahms, to come with you on your next visit? It would be such a pleasure to meet him considering how well we have come to love his work."

Miss Burnand's eyes widened. "Oh, yes, Mr. Joachim, it would be *such* a pleasure to meet him. His music tells me he cannot be anything but a pleasure to meet."

Joachim exchanged ironic glances with Clara. "He is very selfwilled, Miss Burnand, and I would say he is quite lazy – except where composition is concerned. He does not really care to conduct or perform – except his own work – and even then I think he prefers to hear it performed by others than to perform it himself. Would you not agree, Frau Schumann?"

Miss Burnand turned to Clara. "Mrs. Schumann, do you have any influence you might add to Mr. Joachim's to persuade Mr. Brahms? You know, of course, he would be treated as well if not better than in Germany."

"I do not doubt it, Miss Burnand, but I am afraid Joachim is right. Brahms does nothing anymore unless he wants to, or unless it is necessary – and since his *Requiem* has made him so well known it is no longer necessary for him to do anything except what he wishes."

"Do you suppose, Mrs. Schumann, he might at least send us an autographed photograph of himself if you were to ask him?"

"That I think he might – but I cannot guarantee it."

"But do ask him, will you not, Mrs. Schumann?"

"Of course."

"Did I not read recently that Brahms has composed some jingoistic piece in honor of the recent atrocities that he has dedicated to the Kaiser himself? I understand he –"

Miss Burnand interrupted. "Oh, Mrs. Schumann, Mr. Clumly speaks much too freely. I give you my word of honor I should not allow him within a hundred paces of Mr. Brahms should you be able to persuade him to visit."

Joachim put his cup down. "It is called the *Triumphlied* – and it is far more than just a jingoistic piece as you put it, Mr. Clumly. It celebrates the victory of a great man and a great country. Long live Bismarck – and Germany!"

Clara clenched fists in her lap. Much as she liked the Burnands it was a difficult time to be in England, perhaps anywhere but in Germany, as Clumly soon made clear. "Oh, the man ran a fine campaign, and his assistant – what's his name, Moult something –"

"Moltke! Count Helmut von Moltke!"

"Exactly, the Count, he has proven himself a faultless tactician – but all that hoohah, a coronation no less, and at Versailles – that was a bit much – and the terms! When a dog is beaten a gentleman lets him go – but not Bismarck. Bismarck breaks his leg. He has a few things yet to learn about realpolitik. The French will want revenge, and it will come – sooner, I am afraid, rather than later. They will not rest until Alsace and Lorraine are French again."

Clara sat up straight. King Wilhelm IV of Prussia had been declared not Emperor of Germany, but a German Emperor, titled Kaiser Wilhelm I, at Versailles – but this was the nonsense they heard repeatedly in England, that Bismarck should not have laid siege to Paris, that his terms for peace were too severe, including a war-indemnity of 5,000 million francs and the annexation of Alsace and Lorraine. Already Parisians insisted they had been conquered not by Prussians, but by hunger. She had swallowed much such talk, silence was best, especially for a woman in questions of politics, but it made her wish herself back in Germany instead of England, even as a guest of the Burnands.

Joachim spoke stiffly. "The French would have wanted revenge however generous we might have been. Were we to be more generous we would only allow them to revenge themselves sooner. As it is it will take them a considerable time, if ever."

Mr. Burnand spoke calmly. "Gentlemen, gentlemen, there are no French here, and neither are we here to fight their battles. Mr. Joachim, I assure you Clumly has a greater sympathy with argumentation than with the French. Take my word for it. Had you been French he would have argued that they deserved all that they got for their stupidity."

Clumly smiled. "That they did, of course."

Joachim nodded. "Ah, the English appetite for debate?"

"Precisely, the appetite for debate – a hunger for clarity."

Clara was not convinced the English were not jealous of a great new power in Europe, but German friends in England had argued vehemently that it was not jealousy but compassion for the underdog that fueled their arguments.

London, Feb 73

My dear Johannes,

We have been out of touch too long, dear friend, and I am ashamed that I have taken up my pen again only to ask a favor, but it is a favor I think you might grant with some pleasure. Admirers of our old friend, Schumann, in Bonn, formed a Committee to organize a Schumann Festival sometime this summer. I am to be the Herr Direktor and the proceeds will go toward the erection of a memorial at his grave. I have been asked to conduct and organize the programs.

I spoke with Frau Schumann yesterday and she was very excited. The Festival means even more to her in the wake of her recent tragedies. You know about poor Julie. Not even the climate of Turin, nor all the wealth of her husband could save her from her tuberculosis – and she just twenty-seven years of age. You know also about poor Ludwig shut up in Colditz just like his father was in Endenich. But you may not know as yet about Felix's new trouble. His asthma is so severe he cannot climb stairs without help. It is ironic, but thank God our Ferdinand, the one most in danger during the war, has returned safely. He is doing well as a clerk in a Berlin bank and soon to be married. Frau Schumann is selling the house in Lichtenthal and resettling in Berlin as you know. It is more central to all the places she visits and she would like to cut down on traveling as much as possible.

That is a long preamble to the point of this letter. As I said, I am to be the Herr Direktor of the Festival, and the Committee wishes me to ask whether you would be disposed to compose a new work for the occasion? Frau Schumann will, of course, be performing her husband's Concerto, but she had expressed the hope herself that we might count on something from you as well since her husband had long singled you out as the man upon whom our highest hopes lay for the future. Anything from you would be most welcome.

Your Joseph

Vienna, March

My dear Joseph,

Many thanks for your letter. I will look forward to attending the Festival, of course, but I cannot find a text suitable for a new composition – but neither do I find any necessity to speak when one who speaks my language better is available. In short, use something by Schumann.

Your Johannes

JOACHIM TO BRAHMS   *London, 31 March*

My dear Johannes,

Thank you for your letter. The days for the Schumann Festival have been set for 17-19 September. I have suggested to the Committee that we might perform your Requiem on the first day along with Schumann's C major Symphony. They still imagine you will compose something new in time for the Festival though I have tried to disabuse them of the notion.

What do you think? Which of us do you think should conduct the Requiem? Any ideas you might wish to contribute would of course be most welcome.

Your Joseph

BRAHMS TO JOACHIM   *Vienna, May*

My dear Joseph,

I will be in Tutzing for the summer working on some things. I need the peace and quiet that comes only to a stranger on holiday. Levi will not be far, in Munich, where he is now court conductor. I will be glad to receive him and whoever else cares to visit. He sends me librettos for operas so incessantly that I wonder if he means me to succumb to their quantity regardless of their quality.

As to your wanting to put on my Requiem – yes, of course, you may, because, indeed, I cannot tell you my reasons against it – and so on and so forth. I would be agreeable to whatever you wish.

Your Johannes

ii

The rain beat like hail against Brahms's window. Midday had turned to midnight in minutes, blue skies to indigo; thunder rapped the earth, lightning cracked the sky. He had rushed to the latticed window, watched the deep blue lake turn black, green along its shore, luminous when the lightning flashed, luminous also the snowcapped peaks of mountains, disembodied by the darkness, hovering over the hinterland like flying carpets. "Rina! Come quick! You must see this!"

He spoke without turning from the window. A squeaky voice rose. "No, Herr Brahms! I hate the thunder. It scares me. Please, will you not come back to bed?"

"It is too beautiful to miss, Rina. I would never forgive myself. Come quick, see for yourself."

"I have seen it all of my life, Herr Brahms. I have never been anywhere but in Tutzing. One thunderstorm is much like another. I *hate* it. I *hate* the thunder."

Tutzing was a village on the Starnbergersee. Brahms had rented rooms for the summer. Levi was his most frequent visitor. He might have laughed at Rina's vehemence, but mesmerized by the landscape said nothing, not even turning his head, but remained by the window until her hands caressed his flanks, her lips and breasts grazed his shoulder blades, her belly warmed his back, and pubic hair brushed his buttocks. Her hands slipped under his arms to scratch his belly and comb his own pubic hair into wings. Already he was tumescent though he had been with her just minutes ago. When the thunder cracked again she pretended fright, gripping the base of his penis, loosening his interest in the storm.

She was no taller than himself, her voice squeakier, her hair long and black, not unlike Gathe's, her face round, brown like a berry from the sun, plump cheeks, plump breasts, plump limbs, plump belly. He lifted her in his arms and would have dropped her in the bed had she not clung to him, arms around his neck, legs around his waist, pulling him down with her. "These are not spring beds, Herr Brahms. You almost broke my back before. You must be more gentle."

He pounced, straddling her hips, clutching her shoulders. "You want gentleness, go to a gentleman. I am a musician!"

Rina giggled. "It is said you are a famous musician, Herr Brahms – like Mozart. It is whispered everywhere in Tutzing. It is said you are known all over Europe. Can it be?"

Brahms spoke seriously, whispering in her ear. "That would be very nice, would it not, for a musician to be known all over Europe?"

She kissed his ear. "Is it so, Herr Brahms?"

He could have told her of his appointment to the Gesellschaft der Musikfreund. He could have told her he commanded hundreds with a baton in Vienna. He could have told her about the quartets he was composing, the variations on a theme by Haydn. She would have been in awe but she would not have understood. "Yes, yes, I call myself a musician – but compared to Bach I am an organ grinder. He is the musician. We others – we do what we can and we hope it passes."

"You do not mean Herr Anselm Bach who lives on the Grunnerstrasse, do you?"

Brahms raised himself on his arms. "Oh, no, I do not mean that Bach. I do not know that Bach."

Rina smiled. "Good! I am glad to hear it. I did not think he was much of a musician. I sang for him once and he was unkind to me."

Brahms leaned on one elbow and pinched her nipple. "Really? I did not know that you sang."

She squealed, cupping his hand on her breast. "It is just for myself. I enjoy it and my mamma says I have a beautiful voice – but my sister only laughs. Would you like to hear me?"

"Do you mean now?"

"Why not?"

"Over the thunder and the rain?"

"Why not?"

"All right."

She sat up, her back against the headboard, and crossed her legs, tossing her hair from her shoulders with a shake of her head. "This is a song about a soldier who spread his mantle out on a meadow." She closed her eyes, singing more squeakily than she spoke.

> A soldier spread his mantle upon the meadow grass.
> Here rest, my bonny maiden. Wet not thy hair, my lass,
> Upon the meadow grass.

It was the song with which his pappa had courted his mamma, one of the first he had learned himself, the tune he had played on the violin for Herr Cossel, his teacher, when they had first met, but he said nothing about that. He understood Anselm Bach's distress and grimaced.

Why should I lie for you, my lord? I've neither goods nor gold.
My eyes and hair so black, my lord, are all that make me bold.
Besides, the grass is cold.

My lover climbed into my room. I was afraid he'd fall.
I never called him, Mother, but he's my one and all.
He came without my call.

She opened her eyes, tossing her hair again, raising her eyebrows in question.

Brahms raised his eyebrows, speaking without a smile. "I should tell you something."

Rina said nothing, but her mouth remained open, a redrimmed O.

Brahms nodded, still without a smile. "You have a real gift."

Her smile was spontaneous, her hands cupped his face, but withdrew immediately, followed by a frown. "Really?"

"Yes. Not many people can sing in more than one key at the same time as you do."

"Really? I do not know what that means, but I cannot wait to tell my sister."

"Na, that you must not do. When a gift is so special you must be modest. You must sing only for yourself – and for your mamma, since she has expressed her admiration – but for no one else. It is too precious a gift for others to understand. Not many people can sing like that."

"Herr Brahms, you are making fun of me."

"Do you think so?"

She was not sure what to make of him. She had met him when he had offered to cut vegetables in the kitchen of the inn where he ate, where she was the maid. She held his face, drawing him near. "Yes, I do, I think you are making fun of me, but I do not mind – because you are not unkind, not like Herr Bach."

Brahms marveled at the simplicity of his passion for Rina – for servants, waitresses, whores, women of little education, imagination, talent, curiosity, unequal in all ways but one. He pulled her from the headboard until she was on her back again, suspending himself over her in the bed. "Rina, you have a kind and forgiving soul – and you have another talent which I much admire."

She giggled, submitting again, responding again, to his overtures, accustomed to their violence.

BRAHMS TO JOACHIM   *Tutzing, June*

Dear Joachim,

I read in the newspapers that my Requiem is not to be performed at Bonn, but I was more annoyed to read that you had justified its exclusion on the grounds of a letter from me in which I was unclear about whether a performance would suit me. If I had indeed been unclear I would have preferred you to ask me again instead of assuming what you did because I think my letter was quite plain.

It is easy to attribute any motive you wish to a man such as myself who prefers not to explain more than is absolutely necessary – so you say I wrote <u>diplomatically</u>? It would have been more accurate to say I said <u>nothing</u>, but that was not diplomacy, merely my dislike of explanations. What I wished was to put all doubts and misunderstandings aside so as to cast no shadow on the memory of that excellent man and artist, but I write too impatiently and reluctantly to say even the most important things – and for this very reason it is unlikely that I would have written a diplomatic letter.

But I do think I am clearheaded enough to know what I <u>did</u> write, and for that reason alone I would be very annoyed if a letter of mine were not read as I wrote it – as I <u>meant</u> it. Moreover, I do not think it needed a particularly friendly eye to read it that way.

If you had simply considered the matter you would have known how completely and inevitably the Requiem belonged to Schumann – so much so that in my heart of hearts it seemed to me a matter of course that it would be sung for him. The Committee requested a new work for the occasion, but they should have realized – <u>you</u> should have realized – no work could have been more appropriate than the Requiem which owes its existence to no one as much as to Schumann.

I must not write any more. You must believe me when I say I had meant to write a cheerful letter to the effect that I had never believed the performance would come off. I believe the <u>Committee</u> did not wish it, still awaiting a new composition from me, and the <u>Herr Direktor</u> was too polite to disagree. I am sorry if that offends you, but that is what I believe.

Yours,

J. Brahms

JOACHIM TO BRAHMS   *Berlin, 7 July 1873*

Dear Brahms,

You write that I have justified myself for giving up your Requiem on the grounds of a letter from you, but I have also <u>expressly</u> stated that after a careful consideration of the works by Schumann which are to be performed, it seemed to me impossible to cram a work which needs so much study into the two rehearsals of the Festival. I would rather give up my pet scheme than give a faulty performance. It was very difficult to know what you meant because your letters were short enough to fit on postcards, and indifferent enough to mean whatever you wished – but let us be quite frank.

For the last few years, whenever we have met, I have felt that your manner toward me was not what it used to be – though I gladly credit you with making the effort several times to make it so. There may be fifty reasons for this and I am very far from saying that I *may not be partly at fault. No doubt I have disappointed your hopes for me as a composer, and been more indolent than you wished in many respects, and more sparing than was necessary with proof of my affection for you – but, mein Gott, what accusations will an honest man not make against himself! I know you would prefer me to be a more diligent composer, but – I have said it before and I will say it again – what is the point of another composer when there is a Brahms in the world? I know you think I spend too much time in England making money, but you have never been there and possess no yardstick with which to take such a measure of myself.*

    What could be more natural than for me to imagine that our old intimacy owed only to our relation to Schumann, something you now found embarrassing rather than desirable, but that you could not bring yourself to say it? You require so much energy for your work that I can understand your letting things take their course, and not always making your feelings clear – but in this matter I considered it my duty not to deceive myself, and so the enthusiasm with which I originally intended to put the work through evaporated.

    Always yours sincerely
    Joseph J.

CLARA TO JOACHIM   *Baden, 11 July, 1873*
My dear Joachim,
    The Brahms affair is very distressing! I fancy he would have liked to conduct and was offended because he was not definitely invited to do so <u>by the Committee</u>, and I think he is justified in this.

    I am extremely sorry that matters have turned out so that he is to take no part whatever in the Festival. I wonder if he will come. If he stays away he will be blamed, but if he comes I am afraid he will be in a bad temper. He is in an awkward position and it might have been so different, but there is nothing to be done now.

    It goes without saying, dear Joachim, that not a day passes when I do not think of you with gratitude for your many exertions in behalf of my husband. The thought of the Festival, that I and the children are to enjoy it <u>together</u>, and that I am to have the joy of taking part in it as a performer (in ten years this will not be possible), and many other reflections besides, have exalted me and filled my heart with happiness I have not known in a long while.

    Clara Schm.

iv

Brahms and Clara faced each other across the winged sixlegged black beast (two grand pianos back to back, curves fitted like a jigsaw, lids raised) in Joachim's suite in Bonn, playing the Haydn Variations Brahms had brought from Tutzing. Scattered across the room were the Joachims, Stockhausens, Reinthaler, Levi, Hiller, Bargheer, Max Bruch, and more Schumanns, chief among them Ferdinand and his bride, Antonie Deutsch, now Antonie Schumann, on their honeymoon, all gathered for a toast before the first day of the Festival.

The focus had been on the newlyweds, but Brahms had approached Joachim with a glare, handing him two manuscripts. "Since you esteem my music so very well, I have brought you some more." His tone had been no less ironic than his words and Joachim had been too uncomfortable to say more than Danke, but he had scanned the pages within the hour. The two string quartets excited him more than the Festival, as did the Variations resounding through the suite, but he couldn't shake his gloom.

He had sent Johannes's offending letters to Clara by way of explanation when she had asked about the problem. She had shown them to Levi, and Levi had taken him aside to say that he could not find Johannes as cold, unkind, and inconsiderate as Joachim had said. He had been laconic, he had been unclear – but it had never been his way to express himself fully. Either he had been unworthy of friendship twenty years ago, or he was unworthy of it now – but Joachim could not have it both ways.

The theme of the Haydn Variations was distinguished by five-bar phrases alternated with four. Eight variations followed the theme, each distinct in character, but the crown was the finale, a passacaglia. A five-bar progression in the bass formed the infrastructure while the superstructure eddied above: variations multiplied within variations like living organisms.

Brahms recognized Clara's look when they finished, a mother's mingled with a lover's which no new work of his failed to evoke, but he turned away to acknowledge the applause of the room instead though she stared and smiled without end.

Joachim tried to catch his eye, also without success. Around him the room filled again with chatter, Amalie refilling wineglasses and encouraging guests to refreshments, but Levi's words blanketed everything. He should have pressed Johannes for clarity; he should never have let him discover from the newspapers that the *Requiem* had been excluded; but the tug of his responsibilities – to family, to concert engagements, more recently to the Hochschule fur Musik (the new Berlin Conservatory of which he had been appointed director by Kaiser Wilhelm himself), most recently to the Festival (negotiations with the Committee, concert halls, artistes, managers, Johannes, not to mention programming, invitations, publicity, rehearsals) – had snapped his tolerance. He had allowed personal differences to get in the way of professional and hoped for more help from Johannes, at least for no hindrance – but Johannes had been engaged on his variations and quartets. Joachim had overcommitted himself, but Johannes's commitment never faltered where it mattered most.

Clara watched them across the pianos, Joachim pursuant, Brahms recedent, nonchalant, noncommittal. Levi stood by Clara, cigar in hand, smiling as the two finally left the room, nodding to Clara. "Now it will be all right. They only needed to talk."

Clara joined them fifteen minutes later to call them out again – but they shut her out, busy discussing the new quartets.

Ten years had made little difference to Elisabet von Stockhausen's appearance, her skin still glimmered with moonlight as at sixteen, her hair still radiated the sun, but she was now married, and for Brahms the marriage made all the difference. She wore a jacket of blue velvet and their forearms brushed as they played his fourhanded Liebeslieder Waltzes, but he could bear it now with pleasure, not the least discomfort, lovely white hands and wrists undulating next to his own, red and leathery in contrast. He was reminded again of his strangeness: discomfort with Berta Porubsky until she had become Berta Faber, discomfort with Elisabet von Stockhausen until she had become Elisabet von Herzogenberg. No man can resist her who has once laid eyes on her, so Epstein had said when he had sent her to Brahms for lessons – but unable to bear her availability, afraid he might propose to her without his own consent, he had sent her back to Epstein.

Clara, Amalie, Joachim, and Freiherr Heinrich Aloysius von Herzogenberg hummed and sang around them, swaying to the rhythm of the waltzes, the lilting melodies, beating time with their hands, conducting the air. Applause followed the last cadence, joined by Elisabet before she put her hands in her lap and turned smiling to Brahms. "It seems I was wrong after all, Herr Brahms. It seems a North German *can* understand a Viennese after all."

He knew what she meant, remembered how she had laughed at his choices for the Singakademie in Vienna, following "I Had Much Grief" with "Dearest God, When Shall I Die?" and "Death Is My Delight," so different from the waltzes they had just played. He grinned. "Vienna allows one to be shallow without shame."

Her husband was a thin man. His beard, thick and layered, resembled a Christmas tree. His moustache had the wingspan of a swallow, and thick lenses made his earnest eyes more earnest. "But Herr Brahms, if you will allow me, there is a great deal of difference between what is shallow and what is merely light. I would maintain that a great composer cannot compose anything shallow – and when he composes something light he becomes a god at play. The contrast only adds profundity to his other works, do you not think?"

Herzogenberg was founder and president of the Bachverein in Leipzig and had organized a Brahms Festival of four days at the Gewandhaus, inviting Brahms who had accepted not without irony: he had been absent from the Leipzig stage since his piano concerto had been hissed almost fifteen years ago; Clara had played the same concerto at the Gewandhaus with scarcely more success, nor had the *Requiem* been received in Leipzig as enthusiastically as elsewhere. Brahms respected Herzogenberg's musicology, but hated earnest discussions of music. "For an answer to your question, Herr Herzogenberg, you would have to ask a great composer and the great composers are all playing skittles with the gods: Bach, Mozart, Palestrina, Beethoven."

Elisabet smiled, her face so bright there might have been a circus in her head. "But Herr Brahms, you are now a certified great composer, are you not? It is now official, is it not?"

Amalie smiled no less brightly, no less ironically. She was to sing the *Alto Rhapsody* at the Festival. "That is right, Herr Brahms. It cannot mean nothing that you have been made a Knight of the Order of Maximilian!"

Clara almost bounced in her seat. She was to perform the Schumann Variations with Brahms. "To be appointed by King Ludwig himself."

Joachim grinned. He was to conduct the Haydn Variations, Brahms's first work for the orchestra since the D minor Concerto. "Ludwig must surely know a great composer when he sees one, would you not agree, Johannes? After all, he is *the* great admirer of Wagner."

Brahms groaned. Joachim had long disliked Wagner, but for personal reasons. Wagner had written in a recent essay that Joachim had accepted the directorship of the Hochschule fur Musik because he had failed as conductor and composer, and even as a violinist was not to Wagner's taste. He waved his hand deprecating himself. "Ach! A strip of ribbon and a wedge of metal do not a composer make."

Heinrich smiled. "Yes, but some need it more than others. Wagner does not need the Order to trumpet to the world that he is a great composer. No one blows his trumpet louder than himself."

Brahms was aware of the antipathy against Wagner in his circles, also that being their champion meant no more than being their prod against Wagner. He, more than anyone, recognized Wagner's huge merit – but also that in return for the prod he was provided a platform, and accepted the platform, the role of champion, even while he defended Wagner himself. "Yes, yes, but it behooves us to listen to that trumpet. The man has something to say – not like the monkeys who imitate his every sneeze and fart."

Elisabet took her husband's hand. He and Joachim had once listened to an act of *Siegfried*, saying Gute Nacht as a joke each time they heard a diminished ninth – but she liked Herr Brahms better for his generosity to Wagner. Too many were shipwrecked by fame, but not her Herr Brahms. He did not display the halo of infallibility like Wagner, but appeared sure of what he wanted and how to get it. Best of all, his discomfort around her had disappeared, but his veneration remained, leaving her more than a little delighted, more than a little flattered. "Heinrich is exactly right, Herr Brahms, and since you refuse to trumpet your virtues others must do it for you – and the Order of Maximilian is a loud trumpet, indeed."

Elisabet spoke sensibly: she might have been ordering a pound of mutton. Clara's eyes widened with respect. She liked her better for everything she said, liked her husband as well, quiet but dependable, both staunchly in support of Johannes, more endeared himself of late. Felix, the most creative of her children, had written poems which she had sent to Johannes for his opinion. His only criticism had been to send three of them back, set to music, returned in time for Christmas. The conclusion of one of the songs led so fluidly into its beginning that she had played it with Joachim like a loop until Felix had asked if there were words to the song. She could not have found him a finer present for Christmas.

Brahms smiled ironically, recognizing he had been patronized. He might once have been reproved for talking about Wagner's farts, but no one contradicted him now. A great man only endeared himself with a lack of civility, like a pet doing tricks.

ii

Tendrils of hair escaped the blond helmet on Amalie's head, framing her snowwhite face and seablue eyes in a halo. Her voice rose as she spoke, breathless with indignation. "For me, marriage has turned into bondage – a benign bondage if you wish, but a bondage no less."

Stockhausen stroked his luxurious beard and brushed back the slick wavy hair on his head, smoke rising from his cigar. "A benign bondage? One might almost wish for such a state – much better, would you not say, than – let us say, a sinister freedom?"

Fritz Simrock, host of the party, also stroked his beard, like a beehive, kinkier than Stockhausen's, but the hair on his head was thinner and flatter. "I do not understand why it must be a question of one or the other. Surely, that only obfuscates the issue. Why must one oppose a benign bondage with a sinister freedom, as you say? Why not say simply that bondage is bondage, not to be desired under any circumstances?"

Amalie twirled her champagne glass. "Danke, Herr Simrock. That is what I say. Bondage is bondage – and you, Herr Stockhausen, of all people, should defend me in this matter, not forward sophistical arguments in *his* defense. He has for*bid*den me, sir! He has for*bid*den me to sing with you. What is that if not a kind of bondage?" Her lip quivered, her hands clenched, the cleft in her jaw became pronounced, so did the dimples in her snowwhite cheeks.

Simrock's sittingroom was large enough for guests to sort themselves into pockets, but Amalie's voice continued to rise and Clara was afraid she would say something she would later regret. "Amalie, my dear, have a care for your husband. He is not here to defend himself, and surely these are matters best sorted in the privacy of one's home."

"Ah, Frau Schumann, but that is e*xact*ly the problem. If my husband were home more we might never have reached so advanced a stage in our difficulties, but the Hochschule is of more importance to him than even his family, and I am expected to be home minding our children while he is permitted to go wherever his heart leads. Tell me, Frau Schumann. Is that not something like bondage? Have I no rights as a wife to pursue a career?"

"Of course, you do. I am the best example of a wife with a career, and you must insist upon your rights – but you must not make of your differences a matter of public discourse."

"But it is not *I* who make it public, Frau Schumann. It is *he!* It is *he* who does not trust me. He for*bids* me to sing with Herr Stockhausen – but what are people to believe if we should stop singing together except that the allegations are true? Is this how a husband safeguards his wife's reputation?"

The matter was becoming increasingly a scandal. Joachim had accused Amalie of an affair with Stockhausen. No one believed the accusation who knew the pair, who knew Stockhausen's wife, a treasure, so Clara had written to Brahms, naturally cheerful but who entered into everything seriously, and Stockhausen was entirely aware of his fortune – but Joachim, convinced that the affair had sprung from singing lessons with Stockhausen, had forbidden her to sing with him. "I do not contest that you have grounds for complaint, Amalie – but I fear that you harm yourself as much as your husband by complaining with so little control, and in so public a manner. You only give power to his enemies. I beg you to govern yourself better."

Simrock spoke calmly. "We are all friends here, Frau Schumann. What is spoken here is spoken in confidence. Frau Joachim relieves herself of her frustrations only among friends – as should anyone among friends. What is the good of having friends if one cannot speak freely among them?"

"I do not say that she should not speak freely, Herr Simrock. To speak freely is one thing, and all to the good – but to speak without control is another thing, and not to anyone's good, least of all her own."

Stockhausen removed the cigar from his mouth. "But Frau Schumann, Frau Joachim does not speak without control – at least, I would not say so. Would you, Simrock?"

"I am inclined to agree with Stockhausen. I think Frau Joachim has always conducted herself most properly."

"Frau Schumann, I understand my husband only too well. He has played the fiddle since his earliest childhood. He has done almost nothing else – though he will tell you differently. He will tell you Mendelssohn saw to it that his education was suitably finished, that he was tutored in the fine arts and sciences and social niceties, he never tires of telling me that – but I am convinced Mendelssohn came too late into his life. He would not otherwise feel compelled to tell the story so many times. I am sure Mendelssohn made a difference, but not enough of a difference. He imagines the worst of anyone who has been connected with opera – and he never lets me forget that I was once with the opera myself. He thinks he has saved me from a life of dissolution through our marriage – but the worst of it is that he sees dissolution where there *is* none! It is said that a busy man is a faithful man, but apparently one who loses faith in his wife."

Simrock nodded, observing Clara's frown. "You must say what is in your heart, Frau Joachim. If you keep it choked, it will choke you in the end."

Amalie ignored Simrock, also observing Clara's frown. "I do not mean to complain, Frau Schumann, but he made me promise before we married that I would give up opera, and now he forbids me even to sing with Herr Stockhausen. If I am to agree – without having given him cause – I do not know where it will end. If anything, I wish to reverse our direction. I wish to go back to the opera as well as to sing with whomever I please – and with or without his consent I swear that that is what I will do. I will do as I wish."

Clara shook her head. Amalie had developed no small reputation of her own performing with Joachim and Stockhausen through Germany, Austria, and England. Her singing was always beautiful, and she herself cheerful and easy to satisfy. "It was a mistake – to forbid you to sing with anyone would be a mistake, a man should trust his wife above all others – but it is a mistake of his nature, Amalie, not of malice – and from what you have just said it would appear no one understands him better than yourself – and since you have identified the problem so conscientiously I would beg of you to seek the solution no less conscientiously. What Joachim seeks, at bottom, is the same as what you seek. It is only in the details that you differ."

Amalie's respect for Frau Schumann made her quiet. She recalled her excitement when Joachim had been appointed director of the Hochschule for life, his full salary to be retained even should he become unable to work, two thousand thaler, more than which they would not need. She recalled the zest with which he had pursued his appointment, searching for the best teachers, the letters in which he had "nabbed" De Ahna, Muller, Hausmann, Stockhausen, Dorn, Haupt, Hartel, Kiel, to teach violin, cello, voice, piano, counterpoint, theory. The Hochschule had started with nineteen pupils, in three years the number had swelled to a hundred plus. She was proud of her Joseph, she loved their three children, but if she did not stand up for her rights she deserved to lose them. "I made it plain from the beginning, Frau Schumann, that he was to maintain his friends and I was to maintain mine. I even wrote to you about it."

Clara nodded patiently.

"He does not understand me. He does not understand that a woman is a person in her own right first, and a wife second – but he thinks first of his Hochschule, even before his family. He thinks of the family only in terms of economics – and there it is true we have nothing to complain about – but there is more to life than economics."

Joachim had been persistent in persuading Clara and Brahms to join the Hochschule, but both had declined, Clara believing she had some years left yet to perform, Brahms unable to commit to anything besides his work though he had later confided to Clara that he could not be too long in close quarters with Joachim anymore. She was even gladder now that she had declined, imagining how small the Hochschule appeared with Stockhausen in Joachim's employ. Johannes had declined posts as well in Cologne and Dusseldorf among other places, but accepted the post at the Gesellschaft shortly after: his pappa's death had severed his last ties with Hamburg and he had taken two rooms on the third floor at 4 Karlsgasse in Vienna, an annuity of three thousand gulden had proven no deterrent.

"Frau Schumann, how did you do it? How did you maintain your career alongside your husband's?"

Clara recalled the fictions she had maintained to keep Robert happy, her collusions with Wasielewski for concerts behind Robert's back, and remained convinced the subterfuges had corroded trust between them contributing to the final cataclysm. She could not face Amalie. "It was not easy."

Wagner leaned on his knuckles on the back of a black leather sofa, one of four in the huge drawingroom. His pink satin robe was tufted at the shoulders with an ermine trim running the length of the robe down the back. His hair was flat, limp, grey, uncombed under the purple velvet beret he wore even indoors. His cheeks were sunken, skin slack under his jaw edged by a growth not quite full enough for a beard. His face seemed hard as stone, more eroded than chiseled. His eyes, one narrower than the other, mesmerized his guest. "Will you tell me, my dear Herr Doktor Nietzsche, how long you plan to leave that *thing* on my piano?"

The piano stood in the middle of the room. The *thing* was an edition of Brahms's *Triumphlied*, celebrating the German victory over France, dedicated to the Kaiser. Wagner wished an alliance with the new power in Germany and had composed a Kaisermarch celebrating the same victory, but received scant attention. He was not to know that having appropriated King Ludwig's kingdom Bismarck did not care to appropriate his composer as well, much as Wagner might have wished it. Realpolitik demanded diplomacy, and Bismarck wanted to win Ludwig and all the petty princelings to the cause of the Kaiser.

His guest was a small man sporting a moustache two sizes too large, like a mop over his mouth, though the fine wavy hair of his head was neatly combed. He wore a white shirt, grey coat, and sat as if he were being interviewed, observing Wagner like an organism under a microscope. Wagner spoke loudly as always, as if there were a wall between him and everyone else, but sounds were muted in the room, walls and doors draped with heavy pink silk curtains, the floor covered with two carpets. The room itself appeared smaller for the plants and busts of Wagner and Cosima and characters from his operas. The Bayreuth project was much in debt, but at no peril to Wagner's home. Nietzsche spoke quietly, as if he were talking to a child. "I heard it performed in June at the Basel Cathedral, Master. It was a magnificent performance such as you would have appreciated. I wanted to share it with you."

Nietzsche was not yet thirty years, Wagner was sixty plus, and angrier that the puppy attempted still to bait him. His knuckles whitened. The funnel of his voicebox, always wide, widened further as he spoke. "Do not think, little man, that I do not see through your game. Do not think for a moment that I do not know what you are about! I know e*xact*ly what you are about!"

Outside the room dogs barked, a chorus of yelps and howls, sparked by their master's voice: a spitz, three Newfoundlands, and a clutch of terriers. Nietzsche did not know that Cosima had dissuaded Wagner from returning his Order of Maximilian after Ludwig had awarded it as well to Brahms. He did not know that Mathilde Wesendonck, Wagner's inamorata for Isolde, had subsequently applied to Brahms, writing him adoring letters, sending him poems to set to music, offering him the use of the house in which Wagner had composed *Tristan*. He did not know that Bulow, who had premiered *Tristan* and *Meistersinger*, had set before him the piano transcription of Brahms's *Alto Rhapsody* much as he had set the *Triumphlied*, both attempting to say that here was another composer of merit – both, in Wagner's imagination, attempting only to taunt him.

In the dawn of their friendship, fueled by their mutual admiration and their admiration no less for Schopenhauer, they had held discussions into the dawn regarding the primacy of the instinct, of Dionysus over Apollo, of music over the other arts, the most instinctive of the arts, not a reproduction of images, not a shadow, but the idea itself, the essence in abstract, able to alter you as could no painting or work of literature. Wagner had sent Schopenhauer a copy of the libretto of the *Ring*, but received no reply. "He should have hailed me as joyously as Schumann did Brahms," he had told Nietzsche, "but that seems to happen only among donkeys." Nietzsche had shared Wagner's outrage against Schopenhauer, against so many others, but never had the rage been turned against himself. Blood rose in his head, creases appeared in his brow, his eyes widened, but he spoke so clinically his voice seemed disembodied, providing merely a bridge to his next observation. "Master, whatever can you mean?"

Wagner raised fists in the air and slammed them onto the sofa. "You *sit* there, my dear Nietzsche! You *sit* there – like a wellbehaved jack-o-lantern! The professors of our esteemed universities know very well how to talk about Dionysus, the supremacy of the instinct, but their lives are mushy – like pumpkins. Do not imagine I have not seen you look at my wife. You have not the *nerve* even to raise your eyebrows at her, nor even to *think* what you would like – but do not imagine that *I* do not know what you would like to think. You have not the *bree*ding to conceal your thoughts. You are too callow, a puling boy still tied to his mamma's apron strings."

Cosima was older than Nietzsche by seven years, no less a stork in her appearance for her years, but notoriety had added luster to her charms, her desertion of Bulow, her public cohabitation with Wagner, her scorn of bourgeois values, her will to pursue her instinct, had all captivated him, reduced him to her errand boy, but he respected her no less than he did Wagner. Constrained by responsibilities to the university, personal studies, obligations, he still shopped for her at Christmas, buying toys for her children which he discussed with Basel salesgirls, he still proofread chapters of Wagner's autobiography. He had soon learned his value to the Wagners: he was Professor in Ordinary of Classical Philology, awarded the title by the university faculty and the Swiss government, and the Wagners had made him their propagandist for the respect that he commanded – but he had propagandized to his peril and dismay. When the Wagners had professed disappointment with his *Birth of Tragedy* he had revised it for the second edition, included a long epilogue praising Wagner and *Tristan* – for which he had been pilloried by the intellectual community, called

Wagner's lackey, and no students had registered for his classes. "Master, I have the greatest respect for Frau Wagner. I am only surprised that you do not know it."

"Ach, do not patronize me, my dear boy. I know it. I know it very well. That is, in fact, your greatest problem – your great respect for all things!"

"Do you not, then, like the work, dear Master?"

The *Triumphlied*, bound in red leather, appeared to wag in Wagner's eyes like a red rag in the eyes of a bull. "Do I not like the work?" Wagner stepped over the back of the sofa onto the seat and jumped screaming, fists in the air, to land with a thump almost on Nietzsche's feet. He gripped the arms of Nietzsche's chair caging his guest, fixing him with his bulging brow and eagle eyes. Wagner was a small man, no bigger than Nietzsche, but could fill the largest room with a single step. "Mein Gott! I would give a hundred thousand marks to have such *splen*did manners as this Nietzsche, this *sta*tue of a man, always wellbred, always distinguished. It is a tre*men*dous advantage in the world."

Under the overhang of his moustache Nietzsche parted his lips, but said nothing. Wagner was the statue he had put on a pedestal, but he had to be on guard the statue did not crush him when it toppled. The higher the pedestal the greater the fall, and the greater the danger to himself.

Wagner leaped to the piano, grabbing the offending publication. "Do I not like the work?" He flung the *Triumphlied* at Nietzsche, striking his face. "Handel, Mendelssohn, and Schumann swaddled in leather! What is there to like? Why do you throw these stupid questions at me? You, who profess to be my friend, the great Herr Doktor of Philosophy and Philology, do you not know me yet? I am not like others. I have finer nerves. The world owes me what I want. Have I not proven it? Do I not command kings?"

The *Triumphlied* lay where it had fallen on the floor, pages askew like the wings of something dead, but Nietzsche couldn't tear his eyes from Wagner. One king the man commanded, a boy king, some said a mad king, whom he governed by holding from him his music, like a ransom – or a toy. Some believed Wagner was no less mad himself, and his jealousy, out of proportion with the provocation, put teeth in their belief. Many believed he had sacrificed his humanity for his great success as a composer.

Wagner gripped the arms of Nietzsche's chair again, thrusting his face within inches of his guest. A blue vein throbbed in the craggy brow, a delta of capillaries coursed the beak of his nose, the thin red line of his mouth wriggled like an earthworm. "You can be most tiresome, my little friend, with your gentle superior ways. Do you know that?"

Nietzsche remained silent. Wagner's breath heated his face (coated now with a patina of saliva), but caged within Wagner's arms he dared not move.

Unexpectedly, Wagner smiled, his voice dropped, turning almost tender. "You do not know it. I can see that you do not know it. But I know what is the matter with you, my good Doktor Nietzsche. I wonder if you can guess what it is."

Wagner removed the shackle of his arms, but Nietzsche did not move, not even to wipe the spit from his face.

His smile broadening, Wagner placed the *Triumphlied* in Nietzsche's lap and skipped across the room, waving as if he were dancing. "Well, since you insist on silence, my dear friend, I will have to tell you." He turned to face Nietzsche to gauge the effect of his words. "You need a woman, that is all. You have been accustomed too long to the satisfaction of your own hand – but it is that simple. You need a woman! I should know better than to be angry with you, you dear little boy."

The clamor of the dogs had subsided, but not for Nietzsche, nor the echoes of Wagner's jeers. He got up and left the room, but his trials were not over. Walking with his head in the air, his face frozen, his mind numb, through a hallway paved with marble, he stepped into something soft and wet. He walked past the bust of King Ludwig in the garden, along the path lined with white poplar trees, into the street, unaware of the shit stuck to the sole of his shoe. Not for nothing was Wagner's house called Wahnfried: Illusive Peace.

ii

Everything about the man at the piano was neat: clothes well fitted, beard trimmed and combed, dark hair parted down the middle so flat it might have been pressed to his head. The narrow beard accentuated the length of his face, as did high cheekbones, narrow eyes, and the small bow of his mouth. He looked over his shoulder. "You understand, Nicolai Gregorievich, it is the mechanics which worry me, not the structure."

They were in a classroom in the Moscow Conservatory. Nicolai Gregorievich Rubinstein sat at one of the benches, thin fair wavy hair brushed straight back without a part, fat fair moustache wriggling over his upper lip, jaw thick and cleanshaven, hairline in retreat. A thin black bow, barely thicker than his moustache, graced his collar. His clothes fell without lines, without fit, like a nightshirt on his frame. From his scowl he appeared disinterested, impatient, even angry, saying nothing, spinning his forefinger to indicate they should get on with the business.

The man at the piano froze momentarily, hairs on the back of his neck tickling him like a premonition. He should have asked someone else for help, but it was too late. Rubinstein was Professor of the Piano at the Conservatory, the best pianist in Moscow, a musician of distinction, and would have been offended had he chosen someone else – but he had also written the concerto with Rubinstein in mind, made him the dedicatee, hoping he would premiere the work. They had known each other awhile, Rubinstein had offered him the position in the Conservatory, Professor of Composition, which he had accepted, accepting also board and lodging at his home for six years – but their personalities differed too much for a close accord. Rubinstein was gregarious – and, wishing to introduce Tchaikovsky to others who might help, entertained a variety of people in his home – but Tchaikovsky wished for quiet, solitude, and time to compose.

Stretching fingers over the keys, Tchaikovsky opened with four descending notes to be met by a crashing chord. The four notes descended again to be met again by the chord, but found with the third descent a net of chords – if only for a moment. Massive chords followed, ascending to counter the earlier descents, striding the keyboard in heels and spurs – so massive the pianist may have been slamming fists into the piano. The chords were slammed repeatedly while the melody swam underneath, rising finally to the surface, tranquilizing the chords.

Rubinstein's scowl communicated itself to Tchaikovsky who held his neatly manicured hands like claws, ploughing the keys, dredging the keyboard, concluding the movement with a final series of savage chords. In the resounding silence following the finale, hands in his lap, Tchaikovsky turned again to Rubinstein, but receiving no acknowledgment turned again to the piano. He felt foolish, placing a dish before a so-called friend, cooked with his own hands, only to have the meal ignored. He had wanted help, not disapproval, but silence meant only that the work was beyond help. A single word would have made a difference, even a disagreeable word if constructive, but Rubinstein remained silent.

The first movement was the greater part of the concerto, longer than the last two together. He lifted hands again to the keys though his intent was no longer to win Rubinstein, only to conclude the punishment. The second movement showcased a reverent melody, a procession with candles. The third was a rondo, melody bounding like a stallion released from long confinement, concluding with a series of tumultuous chords.

Tchaikovsky sat with his hands in his lap, refusing to turn to Rubinstein – and when Rubinstein remained silent he rose from the piano, still refusing to face his companion. "Well?"

Rubinstein still scowled, holding Tchaikovsky with his gaze. "Piotr Ilych?"

"Yes?"

"I cannot tell you how disappointed I am. When you asked for my help –"

"Just regarding the mechanics, Nicolai Gregorievich. I want to know how I might improve it technically. You know I am not a pianist."

"I do – of course, I do, but hear me out. You asked for my opinion and I am going to give it to you. I cannot comment upon the mechanics without commenting upon the structure. One is a part of the other. Where should I begin? Maybe the passagework is the most obvious place – so manufactured and clumsy it is beyond help – but, here, let me show you." He pushed past Tchaikovsky, sat at the piano, played a few measures, rattling his hands up and down the keyboard, caricaturing the concerto, mocking its magnificent violence. "I ask you, what is that?" He played another passage. "And that? Really, now, Piotr Ilych, you should be ashamed. A professor of composition should know better."

Tchaikovsky sat on the bench. He should have known better than to show Nicolai Gregorievich anything, he should have heeded his premonition, but even so he had been surprised by his companion's virulence.

Rubinstein spoke sharply to capture Tchaikovsky's attention, but Tchaikovsky didn't wish to hear him and said nothing, refusing still to look at him – causing Rubinstein to speak more sharply yet. "The composition is commonplace, trivial, a bad piece of work altogether. Mark my words: it will do your reputation no good."

As a composer Tchaikovsky's reputation soared above Rubinstein's, but as a pianist Rubinstein excelled, with a reputation almost parallel to that of his brother, Anton, one of the few favorably compared to Liszt.

"This is worthless, absolutely worthless! Unplayable! What were you thinking, Piotr Ilych? Answer me!"

Still he said nothing, still he looked away.

"All right, if you will not talk to me, at least look at what I am showing you. I am trying to help you, can you not see that? Here, look at this phrase." He played a few measures. "Does it not sound like Balakirev? Where is your originality? And listen to this." He played more measures. "That is from Mussorgsky – and this is from Rimsky. It is a hodgepodge, Piotr Ilych – all of it, a hodgepodge. Why bother composing when you have no ideas left of your own, hunh? Answer me that!"

Still Tchaikovsky said nothing. He had approached Rubinstein, colleague to colleague, friend to friend, but he might have been a student who had bungled his homework, an idiot showing doodles to a great man.

"There are maybe two or three good pages here, Piotr Ilych. The rest cannot be salvaged. You should throw it away – or remodel it completely – but I would advise against it. Better to give it up as a bad job. Start afresh, something new, something different –"

Tchaikovsky got up, picked up his manuscript, and left the room without a word.

Rubinstein's head twisted suddenly, eyes latching on Tchaikovsky's retreating back, recognizing finally the effect of his words. "Piotr Ilych, where are you…." He remained seated, but noted that Tchaikovsky had taken a staircase leading up rather than down and out.

It was Christmas Eve, the Conservatory was deserted, he and Tchaikovsky were expected shortly at a party. Much as he liked the man and admired his work he had never understood him. Just five years older, he had practically adopted him, bought him clothes, taken him to dinner, premiered his work (including the two symphonies), but despite their long acquaintance, despite his favors and hospitality, his almost paternal affection, Tchaikovsky remained aloof, and when he had chosen to leave Rubinstein's roof the host had felt betrayed, a proud pappa unwilling to let go. He traced Tchaikovsky's steps to another classroom on the upper floor and found him sitting at one of the benches. "Pyotr Ilych, why did you run away like that without a word? I was not finished talking."

Tchaikovsky stared at Rubinstein. He had been crying. His lip trembled. "I wanted an evaluation of the mechanics of my work, that was all, because you know how limited is my knowledge of the piano. I wanted friendly advice and criticism, such as I will always need. I asked for the benefit of your opinion as a virtuoso – as a comrade, as a colleague – and what did I …." His lip continued to tremble, his mouth to stay open, but no words issued.

Rubinstein sat on the bench adjacent to Tchaikovsky, nodding as if he understood. "My dear Piotr Ilych, you are taking this much too hard. If I spoke too freely it is only because we have known each other a long time. I care about your work as I care about myself – surely you know that. What else can it be? I have said it before: you are needed by us. You are needed by Russia! Do you not believe me when I say that?"

He spoke softly, tenderly, but Tchaikovsky looked away, keeping his mouth shut. His lip still trembled, and he didn't trust himself to speak.

Rubinstein touched his hand. "Come, let me see the manuscript again. We will go over it together. I will show you what needs to be changed – and if you can make the changes in a month or so I will bring it out at my next concert. Now will that not be good? Will you not like that, my friend?"

Tchaikovsky appeared not to hear him at first, but laying the manuscript between them he crossed out the dedication and put in its place the name of Hans von Bulow who had played in Moscow the year before, who had also conducted his works. He got up to leave the room. "No, that will be no good at all. I refuse to change a single note. I will publish the concerto just as it is. See if I do not."

Rubinstein stared again at his retreating back, stiff and proud.

iii

A servant offered to take Brahms's traveling bag as he alighted with Levi from the carriage, but Brahms shook his head, following Levi into the house. "Where are Stan and Lila?"

Levi led him through the hallway. "I had to let them go."

"Let them go? Why?"

"They left me no choice. I left my box of cigars on the table and noticed some were missing. So I left a note in the box: *Is the theft of cigars no theft?*" Levi turned to Brahms, selfrighteous in his smile. "The next day the man confessed and begged me to take his notice."

"And you took it?"

Levi shrugged. "What else?"

"But they had been with you for years, was it not?"

Levi shrugged again. "That was not my concern. The man was a thief."

Brahms followed Levi into the guestroom and set his bag on the bed. "He was a poor man whom you led into temptation. For years he has been faithful, and now you ruin him over some cigars you could have given him ten times over?"

Levi pursed his lips. He had anticipated trouble, but not immediately. Their differences had little to do with Stan and Lila. "I did not ruin him. He ruined himself. The rest is not my concern."

Brahms shook his head. "Tchhah, Levi! It is not my concern either, but where are they to go now, an old man and his old wife, both of them out of work? Could you not have given him another chance? Could you not have bought him a box of cigars and be done with it? Did they not deserve better after so many years of service?"

"Believe me, my friend, there was nothing else to do. You are too goodhearted to see it differently, but a leopard does not change its spots. Did I not tell you how you would feel about the Gesellschaft, and was I not right? In some things I know you better than you know yourself."

Brahms had resigned the directorship of the Gesellschaft. Levi had counseled against the assignment from the start saying Brahms was best employed with creative work, not the man to hurdle the hundred and one obstacles of a bureacratic post, and with the return of the original director, Johann Herbeck, he had resigned and invited himself to visit Levi in Munich. "There you were right. I am not the man to wrangle and intrigue and you know how Herbeck is. It was a question of resigning now or of waiting until he had eased me out – and I did not want that either." Brahms spoke without bitterness, he had proven he could do the job and preferred to leave of his own volition than fight for what he wanted so little in the long run.

"Well, then, man, it is for the best. We should celebrate your newfound freedom. What do you say to some champagne?"

Brahms nodded, but remained dumb.

Levi clapped for the servant to bring a tray to the parlor before turning to Brahms again with a laugh. "Now you will have time for that for which you were born – your symphony and your opera."

Brahms narrowed his eyes, mistrustful of Levi's motive, reminded again of how much his laugh resembled the bleat of a sheep. Since Levi had become Court Conductor in Munich, Wagner's stronghold, he had plagued him with librettos – taunting him, it seemed, to cross swords with Wagner on Wagner's territory. He said nothing. It was no less a joke to talk about his opera as to talk about the symphony on which he had been working since Schumann's death. After the fiasco of his piano concerto he had determined to take no chances. In the meantime, he prepared continually for the symphony. His chamberwork had strengthened his understanding of structure, the Haydn Variations had done the same for orchestration. He could not explain how he felt, following in the footsteps of the giant. Wagner had sidestepped the problem, pronouncing the symphony dead after Beethoven (the Ninth pointing the way to the future from its choral movement to Opera), and crowning himself Beethoven's successor, a mantle to which Brahms would have said no one could make a credible claim (though there were donkeys in Vienna who made it even for him).

"Well, my friend, you are silent – and I could have predicted as much – but it must come, your symphony must come – and come, it will. Come, shall we go to the parlor?"

A vein throbbed in Brahms's brow so violently he imagined it bulged like a twig and rubbed it down. "Yes."

The servant had brought a tray holding a bottle and glasses and Levi poured for them both. "I have visited Bayreuth, as you know – and I must tell you, what Wagner is doing is going to cause a radical upheaval in our artistic life. It is going to be a festival like no other – ever!"

Five years ago Nietzsche had heard Levi conduct a performance of *Meistersinger* in Karlsruhe and reported his delight to Wagner who had invited Levi to visit him in Munich, which had led to his appointment with the Court Opera. To friends who had warned him against stepping into Wagner's stronghold he had said only that he would have a larger sphere in which to exercise his influence. Besides, his own strength lay in opera and no conductor of opera could avoid Wagner in Germany. The entire country was talking about what he was accomplishing in Bayreuth – but

Brahms had brought a boxful of new compositions to Munich about which Levi had shown not the least curiosity. "I remember how you used to talk about Wagner, Levi – and that is what leads me to suspect your new enthusiasm. I do not understand what has changed to make you talk this way."

Levi had anticipated the conversation. He had conducted the premieres of his friend's *Schicksalslied* and *Triumphlied*, staged a private premiere of the *Alto Rhapsody*, secured a new triumph with the *Requiem*, secured the first unqualified success of his Piano Concerto, but all in Karlsruhe. His performances of the same concerto, the new Haydn Variations, and the Hungarian Dances had met with silence in Wagner's stronghold, and he had begun to lose interest himself in the work of his friend. "Brahms, you know better than that – or you should. There can be no doubt how much I admire your work – and your self, my good friend. You do not doubt my word on that, do you?"

Brahms's mouth twisted, his irony not in doubt. "I confess, my *friend*, that I do not always find it easy to match your words with your actions. Your enthusiasms appear to go against the grain of what you once professed. Perhaps it is my fault for being too stupid to understand, but it seems to me that your present inclinations do not grow naturally from your past. Something has got twisted along the way. Either you were true then – or you are true now. You cannot have it both ways."

Levi sighed. "Brahms, I am sorry. I have misjudged you. I took you for your better. This is about Wagner, is it not? If I spoke too enthusiastically it was but to compliment your generosity, the greatness of your spirit. I did not think it would affect you adversely, but I see that I was wrong."

Levi seemed unaware of his own irony, but Brahms could not be sure. "So now I lack generosity – but you miss the point, Levi. This is *not* about Wagner. It is about you. You are the turncoat, not Wagner. With Wagner, at least, one knows where one stands – but with you one knows only which way the wind blows –"

Levi interrupted sharply. "Brahms, please, not another word! Let me first have my say. It is clear you do not understand me at all."

Brahms leaned back in his chair, staring at Levi, eyes cold as icebergs, extending his palm.

Levi took another deep breath. "My views may appear paradoxical, Brahms, but you wrong me to call me a turncoat. It is like this. One can argue about Wagner no more than about religion." His face burned as brightly as any apostle's. "People resist Wagner because he forces them to change – he forces them to understand music on a different and more difficult level, and this is what they resist as they resist all change, but if they do not resist – if *you* do not resist him, Brahms, you will feel the joy of the change, and it will make all your pain worthwhile. Do you understand me?"

The bleat in Levi's laugh had turned as well to a bleat in his eyes. "Levi, you talk like a crazy man. You talk like a man crazed."

It was how Levi had once talked about him, but now he only smiled. "I will not argue, Brahms. I am crazed by his music – and I am comforted – but let me put it more matter-of-factly. You would agree, would you not, that it is easy to establish the difference between a dramatist and a musician?"

The constant attacks of Wagnerians in the press and at his concerts had made Brahms mistrustful. He found it hard to believe a champion for Wagner could champion his own works with the same fervor. He said nothing, but held Levi's gaze, the twig bulging in his brow throbbing into a branch.

"As a musician I would say you stand as high over Wagner as Mozart over Gluck – but does not Gluck hold a place at least after Mozart just the same? Wagner does not consider himself a musician in the classical sense; his instrumental compositions are dull and paltry; if any pupil of mine were to bring me his *Albumblatt* I would show him to the door – but when he uses music as the servant of the drama he produces effects such as none before him – and since he is so different from anyone before him or next to him, and since he is neither able nor willing to create just music, but is attempting instead to establish a German drama, I do not understand why an honest admiration of his work is incompatible with an honest admiration of your work. I do not think any less of your G major Sextet and your *Schicksalslied* because I consider *Tristan* a great work of art. Why must it be one or the other? Have you not professed admiration yourself for his work on more than one occasion? Have you not said yourself that it is the *mis*understood Wagner who creates all the problems? Have you not called yourself the best of the Wagnerians because you understand him better than his most ardent followers?"

Still Brahms stared. Wagner had never ceased belittling his work, calling him tedious, calling him St. Johannes after his *Requiem* had proven a greater success in Vienna than excerpts from the *Ring* – but he did not wish to focus on himself. "I was talking about Wagner the musician. I understand his importance as a musician as well as you, but as a man he is not so easily *mis*understood – but, again, the question is not about Wagner, but about you – not about my admiration, but about your disloyalty – and not just to me, but to the Schumanns as well. You know what he says about them, and you know what he has written about them as well."

Wagner had called Schumann's music vulgar, turgid, hollow, crude, bad, had accused him of overextending his talent, failing to produce a single melody, diluting German music with Jewish influences, had called him a silly man, even suggested he had been driven mad for envy of Wagner. Cosima had laughed at the Schumannians, called them bigots, scoffed at Robert's unworldliness, Clara's unstylishness, in her performances, in her appearance – but Levi had continued to perform Schumann and Brahms regularly. "There, I will grant you, he is wrong, Wagner is wrong – but if he is wrong, surely he has the right to be wrong?"

"*If* he is wrong?"

"Brahms, Wagner is the finest and noblest of men. It is natural that the world misunderstands and calumniates him. Men always blacken everything that shines – but posterity will acknowledge he was as great a man as an artist, as do those who are close to him even today – and I will say it again. If he is wrong, surely he has that right?"

Brahms might have excused Wagner's transgressions; a great artist was allowed great transgressions; he was not without transgressions himself; but he could not agree with Levi's estimate of Wagner the man. He said again: "*If* he is wrong?"

"It is his right!"

"It is surely not his right to be insulting."

"That is true, but there he does himself an injustice, not Schumann, not you – and not his music either."

"And what of the injustices to yourself, to all of the Jews – or do you willingly sacrifice your honor on the altar of his music?"

Wagner's antiSemitism dated at least twenty-five years, when he had assumed the pseudonym of Karl Friegedank to publish *Judaism in Music*, but he had republished the essay, giving it the cachet of his newly respectable name, adding new arguments to the old, glossing the dust. He had also suggested that Levi convert to Christianity – but Levi's father was the chief rabbi of Giessen and he respected his father too well. "I know what he is supposed to have said, but he has always treated me well, and surely that says more about what he thinks about my people than rumors circulated by those who hardly know him?"

Brahms clenched his fist. He could feel Levi slipping away. "Levi, you are either a greater fool than I imagined, or you imagine me a greater fool than I am. He treats you well because he has need of you. When he has no more need of you he will cast you aside as he has done so many others. It has ever been Wagner's way, anyone will tell you that who has known him."

"But *you* do not know him. *You* cannot say that."

"*Him* I know – but it seems to me, my friend, that I have never known you – but I know you now. What I took for your enthusiasm was no more than a lack of spine, a want of principle, but I know you now – indeed, I do."

Brahms was showing his roots, his peasant stock. Levi had known him long enough to know he could be abrupt. He recalled the times Clara had complained of his boorishness and recalled what he had told her: If Brahms did not succeed in snatching his better self from his worse he would suffer as both man and musician. Only a bottomless love could create great works of art – but he recognized the flaw in his own argument. He overlooked the same shortcomings in Wagner, never reconciling the man with the musician, never doubting his worth as a musician, forgiving the man for the music. "Does it mean nothing to you, Brahms, that I shun even the most distant intercourse with the Wagnerians? Does it mean nothing to you that I am thoroughly hated by them? They see me first as a Jew, and only then as a musician – but Wagner sees me first as a musician, as I do him. Should that not make you reconsider your judgment?"

"But you do not shun them, Levi. You advance their cause. You have become their champion!"

"But against their wishes!"

"So much the worse for you!"

"But if I am their champion, I am no less yours. Give me your symphony. Give me your opera. I am longing to perform them. Nothing would give me more pleasure."

"Tchhah, Levi! This is just talk. At least, do me the courtesy of not taking me for a fool."

"But I do not! I do no such thing."

"A fool, a dupe, a donkey – I can see that I have been all of these things where you are concerned – but I am not, and I will never be, a lying doubledealing traitor." He got up. "I cannot stay, Levi – not while you persist in this duplicity."

"Brahms, think, man, what you say. That is the champagne talking, not you."

Brahms snatched breath between his teeth and glared at Levi. The branch in his head had burst into a tree, veins popped like roots and vines. "You do not listen well, Levi. That was not the champagne talking. That was me." He hurled his glass at the wall. "*That* is the champagne talking." He left the room without a backward glance.

HEINRICH VON HERZOGENBERG TO BRAHMS   *Aussee, 23 July, 1876*
My dear Herr Brahms,

I trust I am not intruding too strenuously on your holiday, but I am sending what I believe are the first variations ever to be written on a Brahms theme. When you open my roll of music, you will think for a moment that you see one of your own – though strangely unfamiliar – compositions! My publisher obviously accepted the piece with the sole malicious intent of frightening your publisher out of his wits with the title-page. Of course, it sells all the better to the shortsighted buyers who lose their heads completely at the sight of JOHANNES BRAHMS, printed large. The little notice underneath quite escapes their attention. It amuses me, of course, and my publisher, so please take it as a joke yourself – but on reflecting that you will probably glance inside I cease to be amused – while for you the fun, quite possibly, begins?

With this grave query let me close, throwing myself upon your mercy.

Yours very sincerely,
Heinrich Herzogenberg

ELISABET VON HERZOGENBERG TO BRAHMS   *Aussee, 23 July, 1876*
Dear Herr Brahms,

I have been assured by a mutual friend that you have expressed a wish to see Heinrich's Variations on a Theme by Brahms – even on your holiday! I am only too delighted because Heinrich did not want to bother you with the variations, imagining you must be glad to hear nothing but the roar of the ocean and the lapping of waves, and that printed music would be unwelcome in your retreat. But your kind wish alters everything. I hope you will not entirely disapprove of the piece, but should it have the misfortune of displeasing you, do not hesitate to say so.

Do you ever think of visiting Leipzig again? You did not have such a bad time of it as I recall the last time, and you know how many devoted friends you have made here in spite of all the philistines – bother them!

In the event of your returning, I have a favor to ask: that you should stop at the Herzogenbergs' instead of Hotel Hauffe. I promise you a bed at least as good, much better coffee, no very large room but two of a decent size, a silk bedcover, all the ashtrays anyone could desire, and above all peace and quiet. Your rooms would be situated so you could easily refuse to receive not only strangers should their visits be inopportune, but also ourselves – though we beg you will not use this privilege too freely with regard to the latter. To compensate for all the gilt and stucco and glories of the Hauffe establishment we would make you cozy, refrain from worrying you, and make you realize only the great pleasure you would be giving us. If nothing else you will be quieter in our well-guarded house than in any of the hotels. Do think it over!

    Goodbye, dear Herr Brahms. Give a kindly thought once in a while to
Elisabet Herzogenberg

ii

Georg Henschel followed Brahms from the town across the moor. They had made their way past rose bushes, thatched cottages, and white houses, but as the town receded the country was barren even of people – rugged, but with undulations revealing patches of grass, sedge, and heather. Billroth had recommended the island of Rugen, land of his birth, off the northern coast of Germany, for a holiday. The peacefulness and privacy could not have suited Brahms better, working on the final drafts of his symphony. He had taken two rooms with balconies, windows overlooking the sea, the village straggling up the hill to his left, and cornfields in front providing the murmur of waves by night. He had arrived before Henschel, and on the night of Henschel's arrival, despite a storm, despite the midnight hour, he had waited for his friend, and they had talked into the night in the coffee room.

The weather was mild by morning, the wind ran fingers through their hair, but showed not a trace of the storm which had delayed Henschel's diligence the night before. Henschel had visited Rugen before, but crossing the island to Sassnitz in the peninsula of Jasmund he was struck again by the variety of the landscape, from flatland in the southwest (the point of entry from the mainland), to beech forests extending to the sea, and massive chalk cliffs in the northeast; in sunlight the cliffs gleamed like icebergs; the heartland displayed airy forests, picturesque villages, avenues of lime and chestnut, and seas of cornfields blowing like surf in the wind – all contained on an island comprising less than four hundred square miles.

Henschel remained quiet as Brahms listened intently to a chorus of bullfrogs and shook his head. "No, that is not my pond either."

Henschel did not believe it was possible to locate a spot by the sound of its bullfrogs, but Brahms was no less sure of himself though they had walked a long while – aimlessly, Henschel would have said.

"There! That! Do you hear that?"

Henschel concentrated on the croaking chorus. "I hear it, Master, but it is surely no different from the others we have heard."

"Aaah, Henschel! Listen carefully! Listen to them in isolation – that one first, a diminished third, descending from E flat to C sharp, such a small sad compass – like the small mouth of a henpecked husband. Do you not hear the one I mean?"

Henschel listened. "I think I do."

"Na, that is not good enough – not from you. Listen again."

Henschel listened again. "From E flat to C sharp. Yes, I hear it."

"Good! Now listen to the other. The compass is still further diminished, a minor second, from C to B. Do you hear it?"

Henschel listened again. "Yes, I do."

"Good! Now put them together – and see if you can add some of the others."

Henschel laughed. "It is not very harmonious, is it?"

"No, but it is distinctive. It does not sound like the others. Come, this is my pond. I recognize it now."

Henschel followed Brahms over a low promontory to a small carpet of green enclosed with a pool as in a garden. Bullfrogs scampered as they descended, diving into the pool, scattering tiny fish. Some remained on the rocks, inflating and deflating like balloons, but silent. "There! Is it not beautiful, my grotto? Sit – that stone over there is quite comfortable and you can lean against the slope."

Henschel sat on the stone leaning as Brahms had indicated. He had the eyes of a deer and cheeks of a child. Not even his black untrained beard, his hair piled like a fortress on his head, could counter the sweetness. "Indeed, this is most comfortable."

Brahms laughed, opening his calabash filled with champagne. "Shall we drink to the day?" It was the sixth anniversary of the French declaration of war.

Henschel opened his own calabash. "By all means."

"To Bismarck and the Fatherland!"

Henschel raised his calabash with Brahms. "To Bismarck and the Fatherland!"

Brahms wiped his mouth with the back of his hand, lit two cigarettes, passed one to Henschel, drew deeply on his own, and leaned on one elbow on a mattress of grass. "Listen, there he is again, the mournful prince with his mournful diminished third. This is where fairytales begin, Henschel, do you not think?"

Henschel said nothing, leaning back. They listened in silence to the bullfrog concert, smoking cigarettes. Not even the wind could touch them in their grassy hollow. Finishing his cigarette, Brahms dipped his hand in the pool and with a sudden twist raised it again with a laugh. He had caught two baby frogs. "Look, Henschel! Are they not sweet?"

Henschel grinned. Brahms placed the frogs on a stone from which they jumped back into the water, from which he fished one out again to hold against his chest, stroking its head before setting it free again. Henschel noted again his ruddy outdoor face, broad chest, dense burly muscular body, thick straight hair browned by the sun, sprinkled with grey, hanging to his shoulders, also his stature, short and stout. He was seventeen years younger, more slender, and a couple of inches taller. They had met at the 1874 Rhine Festival in Cologne, when Brahms had invited him to perform for the Gesellschaft concerts in Vienna, Bach's *St. Matthew* and Bruch's *Odysseus*. The Master had been more slender then himself, his jaw more visible, now swallowed in the growing thickness of his face – but no less unmistakable was the growing confidence of his gaze, his stance, his stride.

Setting the last frog free, Brahms dried his hands on his pants. "Come, Henschel, you have been very patient. Shall we look at your songs?"

An hour later they were walking home again. "Never forget, Henschel, by perfecting one piece you gain and learn more than by starting on a dozen. Let it rest, let it rest, and go back, always go back, to work it over and over and over again, until it is a finished work of art, until there is not one note too many nor too few, not one bar you could improve upon. Whether it is beautiful is an entirely different matter, but perfect it must be. You see, I am quite lazy, but I never cool down over a work, once begun, until it is perfect. In that respect, it must be – and it *can* be – beyond criticism."

"Thank you, Master. I am forever in your debt." Henschel nodded, brows furrowed in thought. They walked a while in silence before he spoke again. "Master, have you thought about going to the inauguration performances of the *Ring* next month in Bayreuth?"

Brahms knew Henschel planned to attend, knew Henschel had sung the role of Hans Sachs in Leipzig's *Meistersinger*. He shook his head. "I am afraid at three hundred marks for four evenings it is too expensive for me – especially when one takes into account the travel and the cost of the stay – and I must confess also some fear of the Wagnerians." He grimaced. "I am set up so often as the enemy that it could get quite unpleasant. They are capable of ruining my enjoyment of even the best of Wagner. It is not worth the trouble."

"That is a pity."

Brahms shrugged. "I have seen *Rheingold* and *Walkure*, and I have read the scores of *Siegfried* and *Gotterdammerung*. I do not care much for *Rheingold* and *Siegfried*, but I must confess the other two interest me enormously, and Wagner's energy and ambition are to be admired whatever the quality of the work – what he is accomplishing is nothing short of miraculous – but ..." He shrugged again.

Henschel nodded. "I understand, but it is still a pity – but why is it, Master, that you have never attempted an opera yourself?"

"Partly because I have never found a libretto that satisfied me." The Russian novelist, Ivan Turgenev, had offered him a libretto in Lichtenthal; his Swiss friend, the poet, Viktor Widmann, had suggested various librettos, as had many of his friends, but however much interest he showed initially it always turned to air. "But also, in opera, especially the way Wagner sees it, the drama dictates the music. A theme is not a theme, but a character – not to be developed, but repeated everytime the character appears. The drama dictates the music, not the music the drama, and that is where I lose interest – at least, in the music. For me music is the queen – but in opera the queen becomes the subject of the drama."

"There is much to what you say. Opera is about drama at least as much as about music. It would be difficult, indeed, to save an undramatic libretto with even the greatest music."

Brahms nodded. "You do understand. I think Wagner's finest opera is *Der Fliegende Hollander*. I like the setpieces. I like the construction of *Don Giovanni*, and *Fidelio*, single numbers bound by recitatives. Wagner's declamation is no different from recitative reined to a snailpace – but after Wagner it is very difficult to get back to basics. I am not the man to renew the classical opera. I will leave that to someone else. If I succeed in writing my symphony, that will be enough. I feel about opera as I do about marriage."

"And how is that?"

Brahms grinned. "If I do it once, I will want to do it again – but it is probably too late."

"Too late – for marriage?"

Brahms nodded. "I should have had a little boy by now, about ten years old – like Leopold Mozart. I would have taught him everything I know, and then the world would have seen a real genius – but when I was the right age for marriage I lacked the position, and now …" He sighed, Henschel's sympathy made him sentimental. "Now it is too late."

HENSCHEL WATCHED BRAHMS as their diligence jostled across the moor. It was barely past five o'clock in the morning, just beginning to turn light, but a storm threatened. The wind whistled and licked the windows, rocking the diligence as did the terrain; rain spattered the roof and trickled down the sides.

Henschel was leaving for Bayreuth and Brahms had risen early, not just to see him off but to ride with him out of Sassnitz though he had no way of returning except afoot. Neither said a word; Henschel would have spoken, but the Master seemed sad, deep in thought, and he did not wish to intrude even when the Master occasionally caught his eye and smiled. They had spent the rest of his stay walking, playing and discussing music, talking while sharing a hammock, diving for coins and pebbles in the sea, swimming naked in the coldest water (the Master pronounced anything warm above twenty degrees Celsius), and the night before had provided the guests of the Fahrnberg with an impromptu concert.

Brahms let down the window, rapping the diligence on its side, stopping the carriage. He held out his hand to Henschel. "This is far enough. I will get out here."

Henschel wanted to hug the Master and thank him for all he had done, but realized he would only make him uncomfortable. He gripped his hand tightly instead. "It is raining."

"Then I will get wet."

"You could come with me and take another diligence back."

"It is not far – only about three miles back. I have been in the rain before."

Henschel could think of nothing to say. "I cannot thank you enough, dear Master. You have given so much."

Brahms grimaced and shook his head. "It is nothing."

Henschel still held his hand. "Goodbye, then – for now."

Brahms smiled, but looked away. "Yes – for now." He alighted and the diligence continued.

Henschel's backward gaze was rewarded with brush and moor and cloud – and Brahms, rugged as the landscape and fixed as a rock, returning his gaze as he shrank and became enveloped in mist.

Walking back to Sassnitz, Brahms was at home with the wind and rain, earth and sky, gloomier than the landscape, lonelier than Lear upon the heath, no fool for company but himself, and the music of his symphony in his head.

iii

BRAHMS TO THE HERZOGENBERGS   *Sassnitz, 13 August, 1876*

My dear Friends,

    It appears to me that you really must talk to each other more. Imagine my surprise when I received not one, but two copies of your Variations – sent separately on the same day by each of you!

    Let me say how sincerely I thank you for your gift, I might even say your advertisement, of the Variations. It is most gratifying to find a song of one's own absorbing another person's thoughts so effectively. You must have some affection for the theme, I take it, and in your case the affection is multiplied by two.

    But you must forgive me if my remarks end sooner than you would like. How can I be disinterested when, as I open the duet and play it in my imagination, I am haunted by a distinct vision of a slender lady with golden hair in blue velvet sitting on my right? If I say more I will probably offend one or the other of you.

    What I will say without hesitation is that I will make a point of <u>playing</u> the variations. There is nothing worse than merely reading a duet when the music is at all complicated. Then, when I have the pleasure of chatting with you again, if I should have anything but praise to bestow, I will let you have my opinion.

    Kindest remembrances to you both.

    I remain, most sincerely yours,

    Joh. Brahms

The swimming machine consisted of a twenty-foot iron pole mounted on a threewheeled trolley. The Rhinemaidens ascended a ladder to be strapped into slings at the top. Three men operated the machine, raising or lowering the slings, propelling them forward or back, leaving the maidens free to move their limbs in natatory motion in the air.

When Lilli Lehmann had first seen the contraption she had been recovering from a sickness and refused to climb the ladder, but Wagner persuaded her and she found the freedom of movement exhilarating. Listening to the deep persistent rumble of the E flat chord held for a hundred and thirty-six bars, she could hardly wait to burst into her lines.

The audience was no less expectant. The E flat chord reverberated on so low a frequency that it seemed primordial, less to begin than to rise into audition, to grow in the belly, blood, and bone no less than the brain. Currents of water rose continually in a dotted rhythm, proclaiming the theme in different registers, one leapfrogging the other, until they rose finally in concert – and Lilli, now Woglinde the Rhinemaiden, emerged through jets of steam colored by gaslight to wrench the key into A flat. "Weia! Waga! Waft us gently on your waves, oh, waters, like a cradle on your crests! Wagalaweia! Wallala weiala weia!"

The stage appeared like a bright screen. The auditorium had been plunged into darkness, the orchestra sunk into a pit, and boxes and balconies banished to blanket distractions. Seats had been tiered in a fantail to focus attention on the stage. Singers had been instructed to address only other singers, not the audience, and during monologues to look up or down, not at the audience, again to focus attention on the stage. The Rhinemaidens, wearing beads, flowers, feathers, and lace, languidly flapped bare white arms swimming in the Rhine, while Alberich, the misshapen Nibelung, crawled from the riverbed, feasting goggleeyed on the Rhinemaidens.

FOUR THOUSAND PILGRIMS had descended on tiny Bayreuth, among them the Kaiser, the Emperor and Empress of Brazil, a Grand Duke from Russia, and assorted German princes and dukes. Sixty newspapers were represented from across the world, the new transatlantic cable allowing stories to be flashed to America. Among the musicians were Tchaikovsky, Saint-Saens, Gounod, Grieg, and Liszt. Begun during Wagner's years of exile in Zurich and developed in stages through twenty-five years, the *Ring* was to have three complete performances, each of four consecutive days. Wagner had done everything, raised the money, built the theater, found the players – composed the *Ring*. Watching Wagner's luxurious carriage following the Kaiser's, Tchaikovsky reported what many thought: "What a welter of emotions must have welled in the heart of the little man who had overcome apparently insurmountable odds to realize his artistic vision." Those who wished to see him were told he no longer saw anyone. King Ludwig, his benefactor, declared him god and man and infallible. Wagnerians, who believed he was Shakespeare and Beethoven reborn as one, threatened violence to those who disagreed. People rose in his presence with cries of "Hoch!" Wagner's triumph was complete.

The strings hurled a streamer of light through the sky, followed by a second, a third, a fourth, until the firmament shimmered with multiple bolts of satin in the sun. Brass provided a rhythm for horses, long whinnies sounded in the strings, until the valkyries gathered through the shimmer in winged helmets, bearing long spears and shields, metal cups encasing their breasts, and bracelets wound like asps around their forearms. They stared into the distance, anticipating Brunnhilde bearing Siegfried astride her winged steed, Grane, fleeing Wotan.

IN THE LAST SCENE Brunnhilde sets Siegfried's pyre aflame. Bearing the ring she leaps onto Grane and into the fire. The music surges ever higher, as do her vocals, each captive to the other, girded by triplets in brass and tympani. When one appears to reach a plateau the other urges it higher yet, and as the flames envelope the stage the Rhine floods its banks pouring into the flames.

Hagen, son of Alberich (who had first stolen the ring), materializes to grab the ring back from Brunnhilde but the Rhinemaidens are quicker. Strings descend in long cascades as they pirouette with glee in the water, undulating with the music, the ring back in rightful hands. The music turns fluid and merges with the cataclysm until sight and sound engulf each other.

Wagner felt not unlike Brunnhilde: despondent, betrayed, afraid he would be remembered for his energy more than his art. For Bayreuth, for the world, the Festival was a success; it had made him the most discussed man in the world; but the *Ring* showed a deficit of 150,000 marks. He had been dissatisfied as well with Hans Richter's formulaic approach to the music, his foursquare beat, he missed Bulow's flexible baton – but Bulow was lost forever. The first performance had been sold out, but despite enthusiasm rows of empty seats had greeted the second and third. The newspapers had emphasized technical malfunctions, high prices. The dragon's hunchback had provoked giggles (its separate parts had been mailed from England, the neck by accident to Beirut, forcing them to do without).

There had been impatience with the declamations, the extended arias, the interminable scenes. Endless melody became merely endless, stretched too far it snapped. Not for nothing had Rossini said of Wagner: brilliant moments, boring quarter-hours. Rossini had invited a Wagnerian critic once to dinner and served him fish without sauce (to complement his taste for music without melody).

Writing to his brother, Tchaikovsky had said he had felt released by the last chords of *Gotterdammerung* as if from a prison, but hindsight had ripened his review: the *Ring* possessed passages of extraordinary symphonic beauty, remarkable since Wagner's intention had not been to write a symphony – and despite many dull, incomprehensible, and vague passages he planned to make a continuing study of this work, unparalleled in the evolution of symphonic art.

At the tail end of Wagner's great year Brahms made a smaller splash, but generated ripples still regenerating. He wrote to Otto Dessoff, Levi's successor in Karlsruhe: *It was always my desire to hear the symphony first in a small town which possessed a good friend, a good conductor, and a good orchestra.*

The response to the production in Karlsruhe was more respectful than enthusiastic. Subsequent performances followed in Mannheim, Munich, Vienna, and Breslau with the same respectful response. In Leipzig, Brahms prepared to conduct the symphony himself, not without apprehension though his friends had gathered to regale him before the performance in the artist's room of the Gewandhaus: Schumanns, Joachims, Stockhausens, Grimms, and Herzogenbergs among others, all of whom had seen or heard something of the symphony through the years. He joked to soothe his nerves: "Times like these drive a composer to thoughts of suicide. I have been sweating three days thinking about this concert."

Elisabet squeezed his hand. "You have nothing to fear, Herr Brahms – especially not today. You are among friends. Just look around you."

Brahms's face turned radiant. Clara watched, not unaware of Elisabet's charms. From what she had heard of the symphony in the piano transcription it lacked melody. She had confessed her disappointment to her diary, but wanted to reserve judgment until she had heard it played by an orchestra. She took his other hand and pressed it to her breast. "My dear Johannes, Frau Herzogenberg is right. Today you are, indeed, among friends."

Brahms's method at the podium was similar to Mendelssohn's, his baton brisk and energetic, infecting more than leading the orchestra. The musicians felt what he felt more than did what he bid. More difficult than conducting was taking his bow on taking the stage. He stooped, dangling arms and baton like a puppet, shaking his head as he straightened again like a diver shaking water from his hair, but the first savage bar of the symphony banished all thoughts of humor.

Strings tore upward, winds downward, and tympani tolled like sacrificial drums. Brahms stabbed the air with his baton to mark the end of the introduction and the battle was joined. Brass blared and strings surged, snarling triplets swiped and slashed. The music swelled and shrank and swelled again, the first movement subsiding rather than concluding, retreating to tents to rest for the night, restorative for the day to come.

The middle movements provided respite, nightslumber and dawndreams. The finale awoke with an orchestral yawn and sigh, a shudder of tympani recalling the unfinished business of the day before. Gloomy winds and strings led hopelessly to another shudder of tympani bringing the proceedings to a halt. Clara wondered how Johannes would find his way out of the impasse when a call on the horns made her gasp. He had sent her the call on a card for one of her birthdays: *Thus blew the shepherd's horn*, a call he had heard on a hillside eight years ago, the year of the *Requiem*, now leading the movement from dark to light, caves to valleys, C minor to C major.

The horns were echoed by flutes and developed in a hush of orchestration. The darkness had been dispersed, but the horns seemed to await reinforcements. Another impasse seemed imminent, another retreat, when a chorale emerged in the strings and melody poured like a river, a hymn in the wilderness. The earlier phrases returned to the fray, resurrecting the gloom of the caves, damming the river of the chorale, but with horns and hymn at hand the triumph was assured.

The response at the Gewandhaus was the greatest he had received yet for the symphony, but amid congratulations after the concert, before the party had adjourned to the Hotel Hauffe for a celebration, a bearded man approached him. "It is remarkable, is it not, my dear Herr Brahms, that there is such a resemblance to the Beethoven symphony?"

Brahms remembered the man, a critic who had called his D minor Piano Concerto a rooting and a rummaging, a dragging and a drawing, a tearing and a patching of phrases and flourishes. Aside from moving from conflict to triumph as had Beethoven in his Fifth, Brahms had also alluded in his hymn to the Ode to Joy – but he had done a great deal more than parrot Beethoven and seized the chance for some truthtelling. "It is even more remarkable, is it not, my dear Herr Critic, that every jackass can see that?"

The critic's smile froze as Brahms led his friends out, Elisabet smiling at his side chiding him for his Prater manners.

The reviews were mixed, but Simrock paid fifteen thousand marks for the honor of publishing the symphony, the largest sum yet for an orchestral work, but the response longest to be remembered came from Hans von Bulow, recently returned from America, less recently Wagner's foremost champion.

Only since my acquaintance with the Tenth *Symphony, alias the* First *Symphony of Johannes Brahms, have I become so intolerant toward pieces by all others. I believe it is not without the intelligence of chance that Bach, Beethoven, and Brahms are in alliteration. The imagination of Bach seems to be dominated by the organ, that of Beethoven by the orchestra, that of Brahms by both.*

PART SEVEN

THE GLORY DECADE

BRAHMS TO THE HERZOGENBERGS   *Vienna, 13 Dec 1878*

My very dear Friends,

I will be coming to Leipzig late in December and staying at Hartel's, or Engelmann's, or the Hotel Hauffe. I will allow myself to be guided by the stars (with which Baedeker decorates so many places in Leipzig).

I send you both my best remembrances and request the honor of inviting you personally to the premiere of my violin concerto. Joachim will do the honors – who would doubtless have been a better choice as well for the conducting honors – which have fallen to me. I shall also be playing my concerto for the piano.

Most sincerely yours,
J. Brahms

THE HERZOGENBERGS TO BRAHMS   *Leipzig, 15 December, 1878*

My very dear Friend,

I confess I expected something different when I received your note, and was as delighted as a child to think that you were coming to see us. Instead of which – Hartel's, Engelmann's, the Hotel Hauffe, and the stars of Baedeker's!!! Now you must admit it would have been much friendlier to say: "I am coming to you late in December. See that you have good coffee, and fresh – not boiled – cream this time, since you have at last realized I prefer it. Do not starve me either, but give me a decent lunch – which, in my case, must be twice as decent as for any ordinary man. If these conditions are fulfilled, I will play you my new concerto at once."

Yes, that is how any nice comfortable person would have written, but your letter only made me sad. You see, I knew long ago that you were coming with a new concerto in your bag – but I forced myself to write nothing, out of modesty, imagining that Brahms would write and invite himself if he wanted to come. And this is my reward! Modesty be hanged, I say!

If you really want to be quite free and go to Hauffe (who has added a new storey, and grows more splendid everyday), you might have broken the news to me differently – but no, your letter was horrid. You cannot go to the Hartels because they are in Italy; nor can you go to the Engelmanns because they have too many guests already – and Frau Emma Engelmann, the lucky woman! is expecting a baby.

So, if you are not intent on going to Hauffe, write and tell your devoted friends
Elisabet Herzogenberg
Heinrich von Herzogenberg

Vienna, 22 Dec

Dear Lady,

    Modesty is the most impractical garb anyone can wear. Are you only teasing me, or did you not see the insinuating way in which my letter pulled your beard? I mean, of course, the beautiful one adorning your husband's face?

    Your general information, by the way, is superfluous – and, moreover, untrustworthy. It is true the Hartels are in Italy, but the good storks will not be returning to the Engelmanns for yet another couple of months.

    You may expect me, then, on 31 December.

    With kindest regards, yours in great haste,

    J. Br.

Leipzig, 26 December, 1878

My dear Friend,

    You are right – I was a goose about the storks! Much as I like Frau Engelmann I cannot help but envy her. She can do so much, play so incomparably with those tiny white hands, laugh like a bird, bewitch everybody, and bring children into the world, which is surely the best and most wonderful thing a woman can do – but do we others not also merit consideration? Thank you for coming back to us. If you went to Hauffe I would be as sad as, say, Simrock, if you published your concerto with someone else.

    Your rooms will be ready from the 28ᵗʰ, and you will be so good as to come directly to us. Once you are here I will seat you at the piano, and then depart lest you feel shy. After all, who better than someone who knows what you like in puddings, pastries, and pianos?

    Your Devoted Wife of Herzogenberg

ii

On the day of the concert Joachim was unwell, his performance less than ideal – but Brahms unwittingly distracted attention from the performance. He had forgotten his suspenders and the necktie he had tied around his waist to hold up his grey trousers had loosened, revealing a larger expanse of his shirt with each movement, and fascination with the slipping trousers overwhelmed interest in the concerto itself.

    Unaware of his predicament, Brahms swung with the rhythm, arms ablaze, eyes glazed, loosening the tie further, amazed as always to hear finally with his ear what he had heard so long in his head. He had followed the Symphony in C minor within a year with a second in D major, the rugged landscape of Rugen with the idyll of Portschach (in Carinthia, on the Worthersee), where he had stayed on his return from Italy with Billroth, the differing landscapes seeming reflected in the differing symphonies. Billroth had said of Portschach, *It is all rippling streams, blue skies, sunshine, and cool green shadows*, and the same might have been said of the symphony.

    Brahms phrased it differently: so many melodies flew about Portschach that one had to be careful not to tread upon them. He had returned the following summer, to the same "seven beds," the large house he had rented for privacy, most of which he kept locked, to pick up more melodies for his Violin Concerto, whose tone and waltz rhythms in the first movement made it a sister to the Second Symphony. The melody of the second movement soared through the solo violin like a glowing ball through inky space, moving so slowly space seemed to expand around it only to swallow it finally in a blaze of light, the burst of strings announcing the third movement.

The years had settled into a routine: from January to April he toured, mostly Germany, Switzerland, and Holland, as conductor and pianist, performing mostly his own works; in the spring he holidayed, most recently in Italy; summer he worked, though not in Vienna, most recently in Portschach; autumn he consolidated, finalized, and printed his work; winter he planned premieres and concerts. Except for the holidays he lived no more lavishly than before, covering his expenses and those of his sister, stepmother, and stepbrother, with tours. Royalties from publications were gravy, pouring directly into the bank and securities. Life was cozy.

Elisabet had noticed a change in him, the contentment that came with confidence, but also the cockiness that came with being spoiled, and Brahms was being spoiled like never before. His Second Symphony was more popular than his First, both were constantly performed, and he himself, whether praised or censured, was constantly news. Strange women gazed with adoration, grew breathless, and squealed when he passed – which explained, but did not excuse, his rudeness though it was warranted: when an admirer asked where he got inspiration for his divine adagios, he said, "my publishers demand it"; but when another admirer presented him with a portrait she had drawn of him, he had torn it to ribbons in her face. "They cared nothing when I was nothing," he said to Elisabet, "and most of them still know nothing about me, only what the world makes of me – and why should I care about that?" She had rationalized that great men earned the right to be selfish because only they knew what they had yet to accomplish. One loved them as children, for themselves, at the cost of inconvenience to oneself.

When the concerto concluded she noted his hand clutching his waist – even when he yielded the stage to Joachim, to whom the concerto was dedicated, his hand remained on his waist, his bows less energetic than usual, and she smiled, nudging her husband as they applauded. "It is only my big lunch that has saved Herr Brahms's dignity today."

The critics were hardly uniform: Tchaikovsky said Brahms had created a magnificent pedestal, but instead of mounting it with a statue had provided another pedestal; Hellmesberger, who conducted the Viennese premiere, said Bruch had composed a concerto *for* the violin, but Brahms had composed a concerto *against* the violin – to which another critic had rejoined that it was a composition *for* the violin *against* the orchestra – "and the violin *wins!*"

iii

ELISABET VON HERZOGENBERG TO BRAHMS   *Leipzig, 10 February, 79*

My dear Friend,

I absolutely must write and tell you with what delight we look back to those early days of the year. The beloved concerto haunts us awake or asleep, and we do not know how to thank you enough for happiness such as seldom comes our way – but I am also compelled to write for another reason. I am going to quarrel with you! I hope we are on a footing which permits of an occasional word in earnest as well as in jest, and you must take it meekly from one of the most assiduous of your crowd of incense-burners. On this cheerful assumption I venture to proceed.

You were so sweet and good on your visit, and I cannot tell you how much I enjoyed the logic of your arguments – but then the name of that worm, Goupy, cropped up, and sure enough you gave us the old story of his praise for Heinrich's quartet – and his dismissal of yours with contempt – all this with a complacent irony, as if you were to say: Of course, the man has made a fool of himself for all time.

Now, it was no impartial third person of whom you were speaking, but Heinrich, the first man to laugh at such an ignoramus; no puffed-up creature whose opinion of himself needed modification, but one who does not think himself worthy to unlace your boots. I cannot understand how you – you who ought to be quite indifferent to such incidents – could be guilty of such ungenerosity (I can only call it that), and it hurts me even more on your account than on Heinrich's, sad as it is that you should so misjudge him.

I was ready to pick this quarrel with you last year, but I could not find a suitable occasion. I was also a little afraid of being suppressed by some cool witticism though I would not fear that now. Let me tell you straight out that it was neither kind nor just of you, and therefore so unlike you, that I can only hope it was a drop of alien blood which you may now get rid of by opening that particular small vein without the least danger of bleeding to death!

It is I who suffer most in this case and I assure you my Heinrich knows nothing of this audacious letter, but goes to sleep with a good conscience, assured that it will all come out right with sunrise. His wife is a bit of a firebrand, however, and cannot resist flaring up in your face. You deserve it this time, too, but I feel sad as well as angry because nothing upsets me more than to bear a grudge against him upon whom I should like to heap kindness without reserve, respect without measure.

I know you do not <u>mean</u> to be cruel at such times, but there is a kind of imp (no intimate acquaintance, thank Heaven!) on your shoulder who prompts these words, so deadly in their power to wound others. If you knew how deadly you would give them up – for you are, at bottom, a kind person, and would never consciously throw scorn on true affection.

So do pull out this weed in your garden, and above all do not hate me for this abominable letter. Women can never be brief, you know.

My profound respects to Johannes Brahms, and – a hearty shake of his hand.

Elisabet Herzogenberg

BRAHMS TO ELISABET VON HERZOGENBERG   *Vienna, 13 Feb*

My dear Friend,

You were so right to do as you did. I confess your letter was a real blessing, for I had feared you were out of sorts with me. Now this is not so, is it? And since you say yourself that I must be a kind fellow, I can assure you quite solemnly it is so. We encounter few enough good persons and good things in the brief and rapid course of life. The things I say are things of the moment. Though I do not deserve such consideration, you must not take them amiss – nay, you must not consider them at all. Otherwise, you would never cease to be hurt. Would it not be better not to begin at all?

Yours

J. Br.

ELISABET VON HERZOGENBERG TO BRAHMS   *Leipzig, 20 February, 1879*

My dear Friend,

Thank you for your letter. It does, indeed, reassure me of my original estimate of Johannes Brahms, the man. Well, since you say it yourself, in future I will take no notice of your most cutting remarks. It would, however, be better if you reformed a little. As you know, my Heinrich has long sent you his setting of Psalm 94, but though you have written to him more than once since, he has yet to hear a single word about his music. And it would mean so much to him.

Goodbye, you kind person. Do <u>really</u> reform. It would be well worthwhile.

Elisabet Herzogenberg

BRAHMS TO ELISABET VON HERZOGENBERG   *March 79*

My dear Friend,

Nobody can receive and examine your husband's pieces with more zeal and affection than I do, but please do not ask me to go into greater detail. The words of this psalm do not inspire me. They bring to mind a bloody religious war, the kind of thing one does not set to music.

As for the music itself, let me put it this way. Your husband is more like Brahms than Brahms himself, but that is a greater compliment to Brahms than it is to Herzogenberg – which makes it no less difficult for me to praise him than to praise myself, and you know how little I would be justified in doing that.

You see, I have no way of winning such an argument. After all, there is such a thing as being too clever for oneself.

In his behavior, thank God, your husband is nothing like Brahms – and is that not something for which to be grateful?

J. Br.

ELISABET VON HERZOGENBERG TO BRAHMS   *Leipzig, 13 April 1879*
My very dear Friend

Thank you so much for your letter, but it is almost tragic to think of you writing from Venice, Florence, Siena, Orvieto, Rome, Naples, Palermo – anywhere, in short, where you are so far out of reach. Must it really be the middle of May before you return? I envy Nottebohm and Billroth for being in your company, but as you say they have their uses, Nottebohm for analyzing Beethoven, and Billroth for amputating legs – if, Heaven preserve us, it should come to that!!

We thought of you particularly at yesterday's concert. Bulow interpreted Beethoven, but aimed all the while at special effects, both as pianist and conductor. Once he was sure of himself he was fine, but before that I felt as if I were attending an anatomy lesson, as if he were stripping the loveliest flesh and forcing us to worship the workings of muscle and bone: his affected little pauses before every new phrase, every notable change in harmony, sometimes even coming to full stops. He turned to the audience at these times as if to say: "See? That is how it is done."

Much rather would we have seen and heard you conduct with your swinging beat and the expressive movements of your arms – which always respond to an impulse from within and not some desire to produce deliberately planned special effects.

Take care of yourself, especially in Sicily, for everyone catches cold there.

Your devoted Herzogenbergs

BILLROTH TO HIS WIFE   *Rome, 1 May, 1879*
My dearest wife,

You will tire of hearing this, but my greatest delight on this trip is Brahms's delight in Italy. He is already more at home than last year, and however many times I have been to Italy I enjoy it better through his eyes. My pleasure is doubled because he is charmed with everything. I am astonished how well prepared he is, especially in the arts and historical and cultural affairs – but he also has the desire, as does every newcomer, to become familiar with everything Italian, and eats the most ugly big beast of the sea rather than the most beautiful roast beef!

We do almost everything on foot and find ourselves in splendid shape though we make rather a peculiar threeleafed clover, seldom together on the street. Brahms, the youngest, is always ahead, always jolly, looking into all the stores, amused with everything. I follow ten to fifteen paces behind, somewhat more slowly, and Nottebohm follows thirty to fifty paces behind me, more slowly yet! We meet on corners to discuss the map of the city. Brahms bubbles with the desire to speak Italian, and has studied the grammar for months and learned all the irregular verbs, but he seldom finds what he needs for the moment and looks surprised when I throw all varieties of words at him.

Even here, in my hotel room, he gives me no rest, but calls me to the balcony again and again! He says if he had a wife he would write to her too, but as it is to whom can he talk?

Speaking of wives, I trust mine is well. My love to her and all my girls.
Affectionately,
T

CLARA TO BRAHMS   *Berlin, 7 May, 1879*
My dear Johannes,

Marie and Eugenie join me in wishing you a very happy 46ᵗʰ birthday! What a lovely present you have given yourself – I mean, of course, Italy!

Please be careful about typhoid fever. The climate is dangerous for foreigners who want to see as much as possible in the shortest possible time, and often come to harm, particularly in the cold galleries. This is all twice as dangerous for you as for anybody else because you have not been ill a day in your life and never think anything can harm you.

Your letter from Rome gave me a special pleasure. Let me tell you why. I am currently going through my husband's letters for publication, as you know, with Herzogenberg who has come with his wife to help me make the selection objectively, and though I have known them but a short while I feel I could trust them with my life – and with Robert's letters! At this point, though, we are looking through only the very early letters during his student days, when he was in Heidelberg, and France – and Italy! Yours in its joyous enthusiasm reminded me of his.

The Herzogenbergs are both so charming that one does not know which to like best. Every morning we play Bach concertos, Brahms variations, the Ninth, etc. etc. on two pianos. It is a real joy to play with Frau Herzogenberg. How gifted she is and how much she knows! How well she reads and with what enthusiasm! And how charmingly she sings! Her voice, without being beautiful, is so full of feeling, and she enters so completely into the spirit of the music. Most refreshing of all is their relation to each other. They love each other so heartily, and indulge all the while in what they call their bearplay – touching and pushing and pulling and poking each other, and most especially when they are thrilled by something in one of your songs. One feels they are thoroughly good and kind people. They will leave a huge gap when they return to Leipzig.

But I will have plenty to keep me busy – packing our things to be sent to Frankfurt at the end of this month. We were there at Easter and found a nice house. We will settle as soon as we can, but I do not think we will be really comfortable until September or October. Still, I am sure we are doing the right thing. I will be glad to be back on the Rhine, with the Schwarzwald, Switzerland, and Bavaria within easy reach. The city too offers many artistic attractions, the orchestra, the museum, the theater – and unlike Berlin it is not too large, everything is more get-at-able, the neighborhood is beautiful, and the forest but an hour and a half by train. Of course, I would never have considered

it without the offer from the Conservatory. You were right to tell me to hold out for
everything I wanted. I never thought they would comply – but they did! You see how
much I still rely on you! They were so anxious to have me that I am allowed to give lessons
at my own house if I wish, and with Marie as my assistant who is also to be paid! I am
also allowed time for concerts. Not even Joachim was as forthcoming with his offer from
the Hochschule. He is not happy that I have chosen the Frankfurt Conservatory instead.

Frau Herzogenberg would like to take a few lines to send you her best wishes for your
birthday. So, here's luck, and continued delight on your journey.

Your Clara

THE HERZOGENBERGS TO BRAHMS

Dear Herr Brahms,

As you can see, Heinrich and I are celebrating your birthday here with dear Frau
Schumann. How your ears will burn when we drink your health! Let me tell you, you
dear man, that it is no less a red letter day for us, the day you so graciously condescended
to descend upon this planet.

It is so comfortable here with Frau Schumann, so very charming to see her in her
professional capacity, with flushed cheeks bringing forward her best pupils to play for us,
severe and lenient, teacher and mother in turn. I could not help thinking to myself: "How
very nice it would be to be born again as her pupil!"

Be kind to yourself on this your 46th and take the best care of yourself. We all have
selfish reasons for wishing you to live as long as possible.

The husband and wife Herzogenberg

BILLROTH TO HANSLICK   *Sicily, May*

My dear Hanslick,

Five hundred feet above murmuring waves! Dolphins playing under full moon!
Intoxicating scent of orange blossoms! Red cactus blooming as luxuriantly on the huge
picturesque rocks as moss in Germany! Forests of palms and lemons, Moorish castles,
well-preserved Greek theater!

The broad line of snowclad Etna, the pillar of fire! A wine called Monte Venene!
Above all, <u>Johannes in ecstasy!</u>

Yours

Th. Billroth

BRAHMS TO CLARA   *Rome, May*

My dearest Clara,

Billroth and Nottebohm left for home a few days ago, but I am in less of a hurry.
Why do I not stay until driven out by heat and insects? I enjoyed the first spring in Sicily,
the second here in Rome, and in Vienna I will have my third! In Sicily the strawberries
were almost over, here they are just beginning, in Vienna they are a delicacy yet to arrive.

In Italy it is a mistake to make inquiries about what one has not seen. One can easily
see too much, and fortunately music is not one of the attractions. On the contrary, it is
atrocious. Otherwise, one's brain would reel. One sense has a long rest. How far they have

strayed from Palestrina and Gabrielli and Rovetta. It is true that I listen to everything that interests me, but you would have derived little pleasure from it.

Cordiali saluti!

Johannes

BRAHMS'S ONLY LETTER FROM ITALY TO SIMROCK　　　　　　　*Rome, May*

My dear Simrock,

This is the last of my greetings. I hope you have kept, and read well, my earlier, better, and longer letters. I saw Venice, Florence, Rome, etc. in fullest spring. They were magic days. There was no music in the Sistine Chapel, and terrible music in St. Peter's.

J. Br.

BRAHMS TO CLARA　　　　　　　　　　　　　　　　*Portschach, June*

My dear Clara,

Well, here I am again in Portschach. I meant only to stay for a day on my way back, but the day was so beautiful I stayed for another – and another, and another – and so I am still here for my third consecutive summer and cannot say when I will be back.

It is such an unspoiled village, and the same might be said of the people though it has changed a little since last year. I am getting too well known for my own comfort. I have my "seven beds" again, and keep most of the rooms closed as usual. I prefer just two or three rooms, not much furniture, but plenty of windows, light and air and space in which to move about. I take my coffee at Werzer's hotel as before, where I read the newspapers at my regular table, overlooking the blue lake with the snowy white mountains and the trees a delicate green.

Werzer's daughter, the charming Fraulein Christine, is still here, and still my little postmistress, still ready to help me pack my manuscripts to send to Simrock – and she still thinks I am charming! Can you believe it? What a place this must be where even Brahms, with his splendid reputation for sarcasm, is thought to be charming!

You know I have been offered the post of Cantor at Leipzig, the same as Bach occupied in his time, and it is a temptation to accept for that reason alone – but when would I find time to do anything else? How did he manage, and with his huge family, creating such divine works in such crabbed quarters?

He was, of course, Bach, and I am, merely

Johannes Brahms

ii

Klaus Groth was disappointed, but Brahms had surprised him before, never more than when he had awakened him in the middle of the night, coins chinking in his pockets, buckled shoes clinking with his footfalls in the garden, when he had fled Copenhagen on the heels of his remark about the Thorwaldsen Museum more than ten years ago. "He will be here yet. You know he likes nothing better than a joke, and he will keep us waiting for the longest time before showing up."

He stood in a crowd with Henschel and Hanslick, all of them glum. Henschel recalled Brahms catching bullfrogs in Sassnitz, surprising them with their freedom when they least expected it. "I think Herr Groth might be right. Brahms is fond of jokes, indeed."

Hanslick shook his head. "I hate to say it, but I do not think this is a joke. I am afraid Brahms feels most grievously wounded."

It was fifty years since the Hamburg Philharmonic Society had been founded with Wilhelm Friedrich Grund as kapellmeister, to be succeeded in turn by two Juliuses, Stockhausen and Bernuth, each a stranger to Hamburg, each selected over Brahms. Stockhausen's appointment, shortly after Brahms's first visit to Vienna, had persuaded him to accept the appointment with the Vienna Singakademie. Bernuth's appointment, coupled with his pappa's death, had persuaded him to move permanently to Vienna. For its Golden Jubilee celebration the Society had written to Brahms in Pörtschach, inviting him to conduct his Symphony in D major. When they had failed to hear from him they had written to Hanslick in a panic, requesting him to persuade Brahms.

Brahms had replied to Hanslick: *I reply to your letter only to prevent you from preaching the doctrine of decorum to me again. If I do not appear at the festival it will be the concern of the Hamburgers and no one else. They give me no opportunity for showing them politeness and gratitude. On the contrary, some rudeness on my part would not be misplaced if I had the inclination to lose my temper over the matter. However, I do not wish to disturb your temperament with a detailed communication and will say only that the inquiry from Hamburg made no mention of an honorarium or any kind of remuneration. As for the symphony, it will be better received from Joachim than from myself.*

Five days of celebrations had been planned: three concerts of works by Bach, Handel, Haydn, Mozart, Beethoven, Mendelssohn, Schumann; a cruise up the Elbe to Blankenese; three rockets were to be launched from the deck, aligned with three shots from the shore, the signal for the waterfront villas to illuminate their houses and gardens; Clara was to play Mozart's Piano Concerto in D minor, and the festival to be attended by many friends, among them Hiller, Henschel, Hanslick, Grimm, Groth, Gradener, Gade, Kirchner, Reinecke, Reinthaler, Ave, Marxsen, Bargheer, Barth, members of the Hamburg Frauenchor, members of his family.

A stout man appeared from the crowd beside Henschel, a full grave beard trailing his face. Catching Henschel's eye he made a deep stiff bow and spoke in a cracked voice. "Herr Musik-Direktor Muller – at your service."

Henschel bowed deeply himself. "Georg Henschel, sir, at yours."

The man stood up straight, turning his eye next on Hanslick. Groth, imagining he meant to bow to each of them in turn, prepared himself, but Hanslick suddenly slapped the stranger's arm. "Brahms, man, I swear upon all that is holy, you are a clown! You are a clown, indeed!"

"Hahahah! Henschel, how very well you bow! Indeed, I had no idea you could be so respectful."

Henschel laughed. "Brahms! but why?"

Brahms stroked his beard. "Do you not like it, Henschel?"

"It is a magnificent beard, but why now?"

"After a certain age, a cleanshaven man is taken for either an actor or a priest," he grinned – "and in Italy, and then in Portschach, I had nothing better to do than to let it grow."

CLARA WAS NOW SIXTY YEARS OLD, whiter and thicker, but sat up straight playing the Mozart D minor with the mastery of age, but no less the fire of youth; Joachim and others conducted concert after concert to much aplomb and success; but Brahms's reception made the main attraction clear. He was greeted with a flourish from the orchestra when he ascended the podium, a huge laurel wreath, and a huge ovation, repeated after every movement of his symphony, the third movement of which had to be repeated by special demand. At the conclusion, ladies in the chorus and front rows rained flowers upon him until he was covered in carnations and smelling of roses. No one would have disputed it: the Hamburg Jubilee had become a Brahms Festival.

Later, at a banquet, someone made a speech: It could not be said of Hamburg that a prophet was without honor in his own home, not when the prophet was Brahms and Hamburg his home, not when the entire society united in its praise and love for their Johannes Brahms. Brahms nodded and smiled, but spoke under his breath to Groth seated next to him. "They have the gall to say this to me, after twice giving the post of kapellmeister to a stranger over me. Had it been offered to me at the proper time I could have become a good citizen, I could have married, I could have been like other men, but as it is I am still a vagabond!"

Groth recalled the folktale of the little red hen planting a grain of wheat, reaping, threshing, and grinding it to flour, who had been refused the help she had requested from the dog, cat, pig, and turkey – all of whom were ready to eat once she had baked the flour into a loaf of bread. The honor had come too late to Brahms: his presence was now a greater honor to the Jubilee than any honor the Jubilee could confer upon him.

Max Kalbeck left the Hotel Kaiserin Elisabet in Ischl shortly before sunrise, and Ischl itself shortly after, settling into a stroll along a country road. Ahead lay a meadow, damp from a shower the night before, a glittering sea in the early sun. Beyond the meadow lay woods, dark with conifers encroaching upon mountains, peaks lost to mist and cloud. He was a giant of a man, wearing a giant of a hat, later to write a giant of a biography of Brahms. His fair hair (curly and combed straight back), slender face, aquiline beard, and grey eyes, would have granted him entree to Asgard, so would his height – but not his hat, not its wide brim, the hat of a gambler in the Wild West of America. His face might have been called Mephistophelian for its narrowness and beard, but he had a child's propensity for joy. He had studied philosophy and law and gained a reputation as a writer, poet, and critic.

He had met Brahms in Breslau in 1874, but become friendlier after he had moved to Vienna himself, friendlier yet in Ischl, where Brahms had chosen to summer after three summers in Portschach. Elisabet had been surprised: half of Vienna disported itself in Ischl – which was precisely the attraction for Brahms. He had become too wellknown in Portschach; in Ischl, a society spa, patronized by royalty, he mattered less, but his response had surprised Elisabet further: *Half of Vienna does not spoil Ischl for me, nor would the whole of Vienna, as would half of Leipzig or Berlin – but half of Vienna is quite pretty and need not be ashamed of itself.* Ischl, a polite sneeze of a name, accounted finally for eight of his summers, his destination as much as Italy for holidays.

A man appeared on the meadow in the distance, out of the woods, approaching at great speed. As the man drew nearer, Kalbeck saw that it was Brahms, but running as he had never seen him before, almost undressed, sans waistcoat, sans collar, hat in one hand, coat in the other trailing the ground, hair like a rag on his head.

Soon he could hear him pant and groan, see his hair matted and pasted with sweat to his brow, beads of perspiration sliding down his cheeks. Kalbeck called his name, but the tiny man appeared not to see the giant, and stumbled past, close enough to touch, rumbling under his breath. Kalbeck noticed his eyes, unfocused, wild, wide open – and blind – very likely in the thrall of his muse. Kalbeck thought of calling again, thought again.

WHEN IN ISCHL, Brahms took his meals at the Post Restaurant, or the Cafe Walter on the Esplanade where he read the newspapers, or at the Cafe Ramsauer with Johann

Strauss, but lived in the Gruber House, double storeyed, lined with windows, high on a hillside overlooking the much traversed Salzburgerstrasse. Kalbeck ascended a flight of stairs etched into the side of the hill and walked around the house to the back entrance. He was about to ascend the stairs to Brahms's rooms when two massive chords from the music room fell like hammers and held him fast. An arch of notes followed developing into a melody until the two original chords fell again like hammers. The melody appeared in different guises, hammered continually by the chords until Kalbeck realized the Master was improvising, refining, finding the perfect shape for his inspiration. He sat on the stairs: to interrupt would have been rude, but to leave unthinkable.

As he listened, the texture of the work deepened, only to be accompanied by a whine. Kalbeck had once owned a dog who whined at certain pitches and imagined the house dog might be in the music room with the Master. The whine developed to a growl and he marveled that the Master's concentration never flagged. Gradually, as the growl rose to a howl, he became more concerned. Rising from the stairs, he took a step toward the music room, but halted, not wishing to interrupt, afraid to disturb the Master more than the dog.

After about thirty minutes, music and howling stopped simultaneously, and Kalbeck entered the room. Brahms sat at the piano, cheeks wet, drops beading their way through his beard. When he saw Kalbeck he wiped his eyes with the back of his hand, but too late. His face was flushed; he had been crying. Kalbeck said nothing, looking around the room instead for the dog.

"Have you lost something, Kalbeck?"

"No." He might have asked about the dog, but felt foolish seeing none, and embarrassed he had embarrassed the Master.

Brahms motioned him to a chair. "Sit. I want to show you something. I want to know what you think."

"A new composition?"

"Yes, but first something else." He pulled a letter from his pocket. "You know, the University of Breslau wishes to honor me with a doctorate?"

"Yes, I know! It is my university!"

Kalbeck had been born in Breslau and lived there almost thirty years before coming to Vienna. Brahms thrust forward his lower lip. "Ah, yes, your university. I had forgotten – but look at this. See how they have worded the address. Did you ever hear anything so ridiculous in your life?"

Kalbeck frowned: the Master paid respects too carelessly. He watched as Brahms clapped pincenez on his nose, held the letter to the light, and injected a pompous tone into his reading.

"Under the exalted auspices of the Most Serene and Mighty Prince Wilhelm, German Emperor, King of Prussia, etc., our most just and gracious sovereign, and in virtue of his royal authority, under the rectorship of His Magnificence Otto Spiegelberg, Rector of the University of Breslau, Doktor of Medicine and Surgery, regularly appointed professor and Direktor of the Gynecological Clinic, Medical Privy Councillor, Knight of the Order of the Red Eagle of the Fourth Class and of the Iron Cross, the name, title, and rights of an honorary Doktor of Philosophy are conferred upon the most illustrious Johannes Brahms of Holstein, now the First Master of the stricter style of the art of music in Germany, in accordance with the resolution of the Faculty of Philosophy, by Peter Joseph Elvenich, Doktor of Philosophy, Master of the Humane Arts, duly appointed professor, privy councillor, and Knight of the Order of the Red Eagle of the Second Class, dean of the Faculty of Philosophy during the current year, licensed by statute to confer this degree; as publicly attested by this diploma, given this day, 11 May, 1879."

Brahms chuckled, putting away his pincenez. "Is it not considerate of them to remind me of their own degrees and orders, and blue and green eagles, and iron crosses, and tin medals, and God knows what else – when I have so burdened them already with remembering my own?"

"It is a great honor, Master. I am glad my own university is the first to have granted it to you."

Brahms was less impressed. "Yes, a great honor, but it does not come without a price. I am expected to honor them in return with an overture that is to be performed during the ceremony."

"Do you mean the work I just heard?"

Brahms lost his smile, glaring at Kalbeck.

"I waited, Master, about five minutes. I did not wish to interrupt."

He held Kalbeck's eyes a few moments longer, shaking his head. "Na, not that work – that would not be appropriate."

"But it would be. From what I heard it had nobility, grandeur, beauty. It would be perfect."

Brahms chuckled again. "Na, I have a better overture for them. Sit, Kalbeck. Listen. You will have heard some of this already as a student."

Kalbeck frowned, but sat quietly on one of the red upholstered chairs, listening carefully, gradually understanding what Brahms meant. He had incorporated a number of student songs into the texture of the overture, the last, "Gaudeamus igitur," a drinking song – so unexpected that Kalbeck lost his frown against his will. Additionally, the mystery of the invisible dog was resolved: as he played a hum and howl escaped the lips of the Master, apparently inadvertently since he seemed unaware himself.

Brahms turned when he had finished. "That is what I intend to offer the university for my doctorate. Do you not think they will find the references appropriate?"

Kalbeck almost smiled. "It would be a good joke, but you are not serious."

Brahms picked up his music. "Ah, Kalbeck, you are hopeless!"

"You cannot be serious, Master – not about the Fuchslied."

"Tchhah, Kalbeck! Of course! Especially about the Fuchslied!"

Kalbeck groaned, shaking his head, holding his hands to his temples, afraid the Master would make a fool of himself. "I feel I must caution you against it, Master. They will say that you lack respect. I confess I do not understand how you can consider such a jest on so auspicious an occasion."

Brahms, leaving the music room, could not have been more dry. "Fortunately, my good Kalbeck, it is not necessary that you should."

ii

No sooner had the servant interrupted the Billroths at lunch to announce Brahms's arrival than Brahms brushed past the servant and burst into the diningroom. A saddle of roast beef in the center of the table was wedged by crisp brown roast potatoes and a side of cabbage. The entire family – Billroth, wife, three daughters – stared, as did the servants, but for Brahms there might have been no one in the room but Billroth. His face was flushed and damp, his hair wild, eyes no less; he panted as he spoke. He cupped his left ear tenderly with his hand as if it might fall off. "Billroth, you got my telegram?"

Billroth pushed his chair back in surprise. Brahms was shouting. "Yes, yes, I got your telegram. We have an appointment this afternoon with Herr Doktor Dressler. He is an aurist. In the meantime, come, sit, have lunch with us. You look well enough."

"What?" Still he shouted, turning his head, his uncupped ear to Billroth.

Billroth raised his voice. "I said you look well enough to have lunch with us. Will you not sit?"

"What?" Brahms widened the fan of his ear cupping it from behind with his hand.

Billroth raised his voice again. "I SAID, WILL YOU NOT SIT FOR LUNCH?"

Brahms shook his head. "Na, I want you to look at my ear at once. It is not something to waste time about."

"But I am not an aurist."

Brahms continued to stand with his head twisted, both hands to his ears. "You are a doctor. If something is wrong you will know. Just look, please – right away."

Billroth got up. "All right. Let us go to my study. I will look if it makes you feel better."

"Danke."

In the study, Billroth peered into Brahms's ear, held to the light. "Does it hurt at all?"

"Na, if it was just the hurt it would be nothing – but I cannot hear from that ear at all."

Billroth manipulated Brahms's ear gently, peering into it with an instrument. Brahms relaxed, receiving the attention for which he had clamored – until his attention was captured by a framed inscribed photograph of himself on the desk. He had not inscribed the photograph when he had mailed it to Billroth, but he shelved his puzzlement when Billroth spoke again. "Ischl is very wet, is it not, this time of the year?"

He had invited Billroth to visit him in Ischl and imagined he spoke conversationally as doctors did to calm patients. "Yes, but you know it well. I do not have to recommend it to you. The air is very soft and warm – but you are right, yes, there is also much rain."

"And you have been caught sometimes in the rain?"

"Yes – but on the other hand, the living places, the paths, the restaurants, they are all excellent. You must at least think about it – just to take a look."

"Yes, I know – but what I mean is you have been caught in the rain a lot, maybe early in the morning in the woods?" Billroth knew Brahms's habits, early morning sojourns in the country, often before sunrise, part of his schedule. The country provided themes, rambles provided development, ferment of creativity by night, deep woods silvered by moonlight, inclement weather, bubblings from the lake, susurration of leaves, mirrors of the soul. Beethoven had worked the same way, rambles in the rain, naps in damp hollows, slumbers in the woods. Neither cared much about his health and Brahms had so far been fortunate. "What I mean is that your carelessness of dress during precipitation might account for your trouble."

Brahms had always shied from comparisons with Beethoven, against such expectations you could not win; there was only one Beethoven; but in the matter of his ear he had no wish even to attempt a match. "Do you mean to say – like Beethoven?"

Billroth understood his fear, precedents induced superstitions. "That I cannot say, but I do not think so. The ear canal is very red. It might be no more than a catarrh. More than that I cannot say. We will know better this afternoon."

Brahms shook his head. "I am not Beethoven. I have never said so. It is always others who say it. I am Brahms! I have never wished to be Beethoven, not in that respect, never!"

Billroth's house on Alserstrasse was so large the garden in the back was far enough from the main road to create the illusion they were no longer in Vienna. He sat with Brahms in twilight, both with cigars and goblets of cognac. There was no sound but a twittering of sparrows and doves. "Is it not peaceful here?"

Brahms sipped the cognac, grunting his pleasure. Three days of observation had proven the ear trouble to be as Billroth had suspected, an aural catarrh, his ear had caught a cold, he could hear better already, but the newspapers had seized the story, making much of the parallel with Beethoven, and letters of condolence had begun to pour. He had heard from Elisabet: *Is it true what we hear in the newspaper, that you are not well? We can hardly believe it, for it is not at all like you – but I must ask, so as to be prepared to let loose all the flood of sympathy I hold ready at your disposal. I should grieve more for you when not very well than for others downright ill, for you are such a complete stranger to illness – lucky man! – and would certainly be a bad patient.*

He held the letter in his lap; there was more. "Frau Herzogenberg can be very outspoken when she pleases."

Billroth chuckled. "I can see that – a charming woman, but not one to put up with a donkey."

Brahms waved the letter. "In this case, I appear to be the donkey."

"You?"

Brahms explained. He was dedicating two rhapsodies to Elisabet and had asked how he ought to address her – Elsa or Elisabet, Freifrau or Baronin, nee or not. He grinned. "This is what she says. *I answer your question by signing my own name, such as it is, and such as you know it. Yours sincerely, Elisabet von Herzogenberg. You have always written it this way. What brings you to this idiotic question?*"

Billroth laughed. "Hah! You cannot buy off such a woman with a dedication – not even Brahms can buy off such a woman!"

In the confusion over his ear, Brahms had forgotten the inscribed photograph in Billroth's study, but mention of the dedication brought back the memory and clarified the mystery. He had given Billroth both photograph and inscription, but on separate occasions, the photograph in response to Billroth's request which he had never inscribed, the inscription on the autograph of his A minor String Quartet, dedicated to Billroth – from which Billroth must have cut the inscription to paste onto the photograph! He would never have expected a man of Billroth's breeding to mutilate an original manuscript, but could not confront him about the vandalism. He recalled also how Billroth had distanced himself when his pappa had visited Vienna; he wished he had said nothing about nights in the Hamburg bars for which he was certain Billroth blamed his pappa; but wishes were for young girls and regrets for old women. He turned his face away, but woman that he was he couldn't turn away his regret. "Brahms has no wish to buy off anyone with manuscripts. He expects only that once he has dedicated his manuscripts the dedicatees will treat them with respect – but even doctors, it seems, can behave like donkeys!"

Billroth's days were long. He was interrupted even at breakfast with his family by porters from hotels wanting appointments for their guests and secretaries of committees wanting his signature. He followed with visits to private patients, then to his clinic, then back home for a twenty minute lunch, then the operating chamber, then two quick glasses of cognac, then home for tea where the interruptions continued. It was not until seven o'clock in the evening that he found time for books, music, relaxation, during which time he refused to be baited into disagreements. He blamed Brahms's rudeness on his upbringing, remembering the stories about Zur schwarzen Katze, and ignored him at such times – which succeeded only in annoying him further. "It is as I said to Engelmann. These dedications of yours will keep our names longer in memory than the best work we have done."

Billroth was turning the other cheek. Brahms scowled; he had dedicated his third quartet to his host in Utrecht, also a doctor, Professor Engelmann. "Tchhah, enough! You flatter me to no purpose."

To his surprise, Billroth smiled. "I have some news I think you will find most interesting."

He recognized Billroth's manner, dispassionate tone, evasive eyes, his way of suggesting they change the subject. He yielded, but without grace. "What could be more interesting than doctors who are donkeys?"

Again Billroth ignored him. "Does the name Johann Peter Frank mean anything to you?"

"Should it?"

"He was a physician who once owned my house – though at that time it was on the Alser Brook, still surrounded by forest and bushes."

Billroth smiled; Brahms said nothing.

"Frank's daughter-in-law once sang under Haydn in his *Creation*. It is not inconceivable that Haydn has frequented this very house."

"Haydn has frequented many houses in Vienna. What does it signify?"

Billroth grinned. "Ah, but there is still more! Frank was also consulted in my house by Beethoven – about his ears!"

Brahms was finally silenced.

"Is that not an amazing coincidence?"

"Beethoven consulted Frank in this house – about his ears?"

"Let me put it another way. For me it is interesting in the extreme that Johann Peter Frank and Beethoven developed a friendship in my home, and that such a friendship – let us be arrogant for once – that such a friendship is carried on in this house between you and me almost a hundred years later. Haydn, Beethoven, and Brahms – now is that not a beautiful trio?"

"And what is it you wish to be when you grow up?"

Brahms could see in the face of Johannes Joachim, oldest son of Joseph and Amalie, that he was the son of his father. He wore his dignity like a skin, fifty years old at fifteen, the same dark hair tousled across his brow, the plump white cheeks – but no musician he, perhaps the only sign of revolt he would show, that one dissimilarity. "I would like to join one of the learned professions, Herr Brahms."

"Which one?"

"I do not know yet – maybe medicine."

"Aha, then you will be a real doctor, like Billroth, not like your pappa and myself."

Joachim smiled stroking his beard, not yet the length of Brahms's. "Herr Brahms is only joking, Johannes. We are, both of us, real doctors – at least, Herr Brahms, is soon to be. The universities do not hand out their degrees lightly."

Brahms was in Berlin at Joachim's invitation to rehearse his overtures with the Hochschule orchestra for the doctoral ceremony in Breslau early the next year. They were in the Joachim sittingroom, still laden with Turkish motifs, wall hangings, hookah, slippers. He was as thrilled with his titles and awards as Joachim, but less willing to admit it. He spoke without looking at Joachim. "All the more reason to wear them lightly, Joseph, would you not say?"

Amalie laughed, throwing her head back. "It is good to have a fresh voice among us, Herr Brahms. A family is apt to turn to stone without outside influences. Do you not think so, Joseph?"

Joachim grunted, looking away from his Ursi.

Brahms smiled, glad to have made Amalie laugh. He had been Joachim's friend first, but liked Amalie better for her temperament, admired her no less for her talent, and remained infatuated not a little by her beauty. Despite their best efforts, his friendship with Joachim had yet to regain the comfort of the days before the Schumann Festival. He turned to Hermann, the second son by two years, with Amalie's straight blond hair. "And what do you plan to be, Hermann, when you grow up?"

"I want to join the army, Herr Brahms."

"And why is that?"

"Because Onkel Rolfe says Germany will be a great country only as long as its army is great."

Brahms nodded. "That is a noble aspiration, to keep Germany great. Tomorrow I will show you more strategies with your wooden soldiers."

"I want to sing in the opera, Herr Brahms, like Mamma used to do, but Pappa does not wish it."

"And I wish to be in the theater, Herr Brahms, but Pappa does not wish it."

Brahms noted the difference: neither of the boys wished to follow in Joachim's steps, but Marie and Josepha, eleven and ten, both wished to follow in Amalie's.

Joachim continued to stroke his beard. "You are too young to know what you want. When you are older we will see."

There was a cry from an inner room – Paul, the youngest at two, though not for long: Amalie was pregnant again. Paul had achieved greatly already, Joachim liked to say: he had been born on Brahms's birthday. Amalie got up. "I will be back soon. Children, say goodnight to Herr Brahms. It is past your bedtime."

"But Mamma, I am not sleepy!"

"Hermann!"

"I have something to show Herr Brahms!"

"He will still be here tomorrow, Josepha. You can show him tomorrow."

Brahms opened his arms. "Come, Josepha, liebchen. Give your Onkel Brahms a kiss goodnight."

Amalie left the room; the children followed after they had kissed their pappa and Brahms.

The friends had recently toured together, Hungary, Romania, and Transylvania, their first tour in more than ten years, but both remained aware of the distance between them. "They are lovely children. Amalie has blessed you, indeed."

Joachim frowned, shaking his head, gripping his beard. "They are lovely children, indeed, but I fear for them – poor dear children to have a mamma such as Amalie."

"Tchhah, Joseph, I cannot see it your way. It only ruptures my brain. You must give it up."

"Give it up? Should I do as Bulow has done – become the laughingstock of the country? Is that what you advise?"

"Na, Jussuf, Bulow's case is different – entirely different. He suffers from real causes. Yours are all in your head. Come on, man, really! First Stockhausen – and now Simrock, of all people?"

"Johannes, you know what great stock I set in your judgment. You know I consider you upright and shrewd, but you do not know him as I do. You know him as a friend and as a businessman, but not as a man. At a time like this you are blessed, indeed, being wifeless. You cannot imagine the agony I suffer. Through the offices of this Simrock person, my days are turned to night. My days are night, Johannes – and all on account of him. He has behaved toward me as the basest scoundrel."

Brahms had imagined more than once the blessing of a wife like Amalie: artiste, mother, and a Helen of Troy to behold. "Joseph – Jussuf – old friend, I beg your pardon, but I must say that if your days are turned to night – and I do not see that they are – it is not on account of Simrock."

"What are you saying, Johannes? On whose account if not Simrock's?"

"Forgive me, old friend, but it is on your own account. If your days are turned to night it is the case only in your head. To the common eye you are blessed with a beautiful wife, lovely children. You are a stronghold in the community." He shrugged. "I only tell you what is plain to everyone."

Joachim frowned. "I wish it were as plain to me, Johannes, as you appear to believe it is to everyone else – but I do take it as a show of good faith that you have chosen to stay with us instead of Simrock. It shows more effectively where your sympathies lie, and it is good that the world should know."

When in Berlin, Brahms often stayed with Simrock, but he had chosen to stay with the Joachims hoping to bring an accord between them. "Tchhah, if it shows anything it shows that I care about your marriage. It matters little to me where I stay. The difference is to my hosts. They are the ones who polish the furniture and clean the windows. Simrock is perhaps thanking me this very moment for my consideration."

Joachim opened his mouth, but said nothing. Amalie had returned to sit beside Brahms. Both wondered what she might have heard. She looked first at Brahms before narrowing her eyes at her husband. "Danke, Herr Brahms. It is a comfort to know that you, at least, see how it is – oh, the poor dear children, for having a mamma such as myself."

"Ah, Frau Amalie, some cherries are sour in every tree – but what worries me most is that you will both forget the many that are so sweet. I see how it is, but I also see how it might become. You look well together, you have much in common, you are such fine musicians, which once presaged such a long and happy life together – and now with five children and another on the way ..." He shook his head. "I see how easy it is for two people to separate, but it is not so easy to come together again. I saw how it was with my own parents. Reason is more easily lost than regained."

Amalie looked at her hands clasped tightly around a handkerchief in her lap. "I thank you again, Herr Brahms, but I am very much afraid that much reason has already been lost – and that he has worked very hard to lose it." She took a deep breath. "If he spent less time touring and less time at the Hochschule, he would have more time to appreciate what he has instead of bemoaning what he imagines he has lost." Her voice trembled. "I am very much afraid he loses what he fears to lose simply by imagining it lost already. He loses the trust of his wife by taking it away from her. His thoughts were just as morbid when I took lessons from Stockhausen. I was forbidden for a while even to talk to him. Can you imagine the humiliation? And now I am forbidden Simrock's company – and for no reason other than that he commands me. He does my reputation more damage with his fears and suspicions than I might accomplish being seen with Simrock and Stockhausen together – yes, Herr Brahms, and with you as well to make a third."

One snowwhite hand dabbed her eyes with a white lace handkerchief. Brahms remained quiet. She spoke as if Joachim were not in the room. Joachim whispered to avoid disturbing the children, but angrily. "We know you are an actress, madam, but I will thank you not to stage this melodrama for Johannes's benefit. No one is deceived. You have been *seen* with him. This is not a matter of conjecture but of a bald and verified truth." He tugged on his beard now with both hands.

"It is a fine state of affairs, indeed, Joseph, when you can accuse me of melodrama while moaning that your days are turned to night. Of course, I have been *seen* with him. He is my friend. Are you not *seen* with Frau Schumann? and have I not always encouraged it? What does it signify to be *seen* with someone? If, tomorrow, I am *seen* – oh, at the zoo, let us say, with Herr Brahms, will we then become subjected to this same diseased examination?"

Brahms spoke before Joachim could reply. "Jussuf, please, listen to me. On this point I have to agree with your wife. You work much too hard. It is the English disease. Let me suggest different terms for our next tour."

They had planned next a tour of Poland. Joachim still frowned and stared at his weeping wife, but glanced at Brahms though he appeared hardly to hear him. "What terms would you have?"

"I have thought it over carefully. We have got different philosophies about touring. I prefer to travel at a leisurely pace and see new countries and people while earning enough to cover my expenses – but you prefer to give concerts everyday and it matters little to you if you see nothing. We arrive at a concert barely an hour before it starts and we are off an hour after it is over. You wish to make the most economic use of your time –"

Joachim flushed. "Of course, I do! I am not on holiday! I am not touring for my health! For me, it is a business, man! What would be the point if I merely covered expenses. I do not have royalties pouring in from publications. I have a family that depends on me, unlike –"

"Ah, but that is my point, exactly! I do not have a family, I do not need to make money at the same pace, and here is what I suggest – that I receive no more than a quarter of the receipts – but in return I ask that we travel more comfortably, that we spend more time in each town, and that we do not give as many concerts. Will you agree to my terms?"

Joachim shook his head. "This is madness. I cannot accept such terms. I would feel I was taking advantage of you."

"Then you will know how I have felt on every tour we have shared since your marriage."

"But it would not be fair to you!"

"But I am the one who suggests it!"

"I cannot do it."

"Then I can no more do what you wish. It is to be either as I say or not at all. We have always done it your way and I think we may have paid a price. I would like us, first of all, to enjoy ourselves as friends, as we once did, and only secondarily as colleagues."

Joachim left his beard alone finally. He felt sometimes Brahms cared about him only when it was to his advantage and was glad of proof to the contrary. "Would you consider a third of the receipts?"

Brahms shook his head. "I insist: no more than a quarter."

"Very well, then, since you insist, it will be as you say."

Amalie had ignored their conversation, and wiping her tears got up to leave.

"Frau Joachim, please believe me. I am going to do everything I can to convince him of the truth as I see it."

She spoke without conviction, "Danke, Herr Brahms," and left the room.

ii

There was a nimbus around Hans von Bulow as if he were vibrating, living simultaneously in more than one dimension – a small man, but in constant ferment, outlined in a thick white glow. "I trust everything is to your satisfaction, Brahms?"

As the guest of the Duke of Meiningen and the Baroness von Heldburg, Brahms had three large rooms on the ground floor of the castle, a fine Bechstein piano in the largest of the rooms, and direct access to the grounds. He was no stranger to castles, nor to royalty, had dealt with courts and their etiquette daily in Detmold and Hanover, but he had never lived in a castle. The luxury was gratifying – lavish supplies of candles and lamps, gilded chandeliers, paintings and statuary; doors, walls, and floors dressed in velvet, satin, and silk; meals sent to his rooms at all times, carriages always at his disposal, even chairs in which to be conducted around the castle – but more than anything he wished his mamma and pappa could see him.

During the summer, working on a new piano concerto in Pressbaum, near Vienna, he had received a letter from Bulow, now kapellmeister to the Duke, offering the services of his orchestra should he wish to rehearse anything. Brahms had known Bulow a long while. He had shared Bulow's rooms with Remenyi during their visit to Liszt's Altenburg almost three decades ago. Bulow had then been on tour, but they had been introduced by Joachim in Hanover shortly thereafter. Bulow had been the first to perform his music in public, before even Clara, his first opus, the C major Sonata, but his first loyalty had been to Liszt, and they had gone separate ways – until the scandal had broken. Liszt had sympathized with Bulow against his own daughter, but though they remained amicable a close friendship now with Bulow compromised Liszt's ties to Wagner and Cosima.

Brahms had replied to Bulow's invitation mentioning the concerto and Bulow had made it the centerpiece of the rehearsals for the season. Arriving in Meiningen, Brahms had noted the change in Bulow immediately, the expression of the hurt child all too ready to cast the first stone, eyes continually flung over his shoulder. He smiled to set him at ease. "It could not be more satisfactory, my friend."

Bulow's head appeared more skeletal for his thin glossy hair, large forehead, receding hairline, and imperial beard which brought it to a point, like an egg or lightbulb; a cigarette dangled as always from his mouth. He appeared to be thinking ten things at once and feeling a hundred slights where there were none, and Brahms was pleased to see him smile, the frogeyes recede, the haughty expression turn gracious. "Good! I have come to take you to dinner, after which we will rehearse the concerto again."

He appeared so eager to please that Brahms was almost embarrassed, but he knew what Bulow had suffered, all of Germany knew – all of Europe. He turned to a mirror, trying to fit his collar. "Sit! I am not ready yet. I am not accustomed to dressing for dinner. It takes me forever to adjust these damn collars and cuffs and ribbons and all the rest of this frippery."

Bulow chuckled; he found Brahms's impatience with dress refreshing; Wagner fussed like a princess over the smallest detail of his couture. "You do not have to dress up if you do not wish it. We are quite informal here, you know."

Learning of Brahms's preference for comfort over style, the Duke had permitted him to wear what he wished, shabby or otherwise, and Brahms had obliged, wearing his usual striped woollen shirt, sans collar, sans cravat, around the castle and grounds. "Yes, I know, but it would be a good way to show my appreciation, do you not think, to dress up at least for dinner?"

"The Duke will not care – but it is up to you."

"Hah! The Duke will not care if I do not wear his own decoration?"

Brahms had laid his decorations on the bed, the last of which, the Commander's Cross of the Order of the House of Meiningen, had been awarded by the Duke concluding two Brahms concerts during his summer visit, a silver medallion hanging from a red and yellow and black ribbon. Bulow nodded. "No, he will not care – but, yes, it would be a nice gesture."

Brahms grumbled, struggling with the collar. "It would be an even nicer gesture if he could see how much trouble I go to for him."

Bulow turned him from the mirror. "Let me help you."

Brahms grunted, submitting to Bulow's ministrations. "Ah, my sweet Fraulein Bulow, where would I be without you?"

Bulow stiffened, fastening the collar, and Brahms was afraid he was too sensitive even about jokes that questioned his manhood – but, to his relief, Bulow laughed. "Ah, *I* should be the one asking *you* the question."

Brahms grimaced, anticipating what was to come. "Bulow, enough – you have done enough."

"On the contrary, I have only just begun."

Brahms grunted again; there was no escape.

"Since you are so modest I have to be immodest in your behalf. Your works may be great, but they have received indifferent performances. Not even your own performances do them justice. It has fallen upon me to reveal to the public the fire that is hidden in your compositions. Do not argue with me, Brahms. I know whereof I speak. You are beginning to understand your own work better through my performances. Do not say it is not so."

Brahms only grunted again, but he had written to Elisabet about the Meiningen Orchestra: *These fellows play excellently. In Leipzig there is no conception of such rehearsals – nor anywhere else.* Elisabet had complained of Bulow's analytical approach, worshipping the workings of bone and muscle at the expense of a creamy complexion, emphasizing the fruitpicking machinery at the expense of the fruit. Brahms understood her objection, but Bulow also rendered the largest landscapes, formerly obscured by mist, visible to the smallest detail, displaying both fruit and the fruitpicking machinery to greater advantage. He scampered onstage like a weasel, but at the podium he became a god displaying the beauties of creation, playing the orchestra like a single instrument. He had learned the art from Wagner: to realize the composer's intent to the most insignificant detail, to respect every direction in the score, to disregard nothing – or, as he liked to say, "The word they shall leave untouched." His detractors accused him of premeditation, exaggerating effects, lacking spontaneity – but Bulow found spontaneity a euphemism for a sloppy performance. His orchestra was small, less than fifty players, but he accomplished miracles through innumerable practices, rehearsing single groups of the orchestra, and insisting that each member of the orchestra entirely memorize his part. His own memory was prodigious. "Again, please, from twelve bars before the F major entry of the cellos," he would say, conducting even rehearsals without a score, spurring his performers to still greater efforts. His dictum was simple: keep the book in your head, not your head in the book.

After adjusting Brahms's collar, Bulow busied himself with his cufflinks and necktie, talking all the while. "Every blow aimed at you, Brahms, stabs me to the heart – yes, to the heart – even when it barely touches you. I have made it my task to shield you from even the most negligible blows with the greatest performances possible."

Not many years previously Bulow had been Wagner's most faithful baton. Brahms was neither unaware of the irony, nor dissatisfied with the symmetry of the the exchange: he had lost Levi to Wagner only to have Wagner lose Bulow to him. Bulow had not only premiered Wagner's *Tristan* and *Meistersinger*, but memorized them, each opera more than four hours in length, the most dense difficult music written, during which time Cosima had borne Wagner two daughters – whom Bulow, believing Cosima against the world, had raised as his own, but the advent of a son shortly after their separation shattered all his illusions. His dilemma was unenviable: Cosima was his wife, Wagner's mistress, and Liszt's daughter – he loved Cosima, admired Wagner, and wished not to embarrass Liszt now taking orders for the priesthood in Rome. At first, he had acknowledged nothing, even become Court Kapellmeister in Munich for Wagner's patron, King Ludwig of Bavaria through Wagner's intervention, hoping the affair would fizzle. Instead, he had become famous as the favorite of the favorite of the King, cuckold of the world, subject to everyone's pity or contempt or ridicule, exchanging the favors of his wife for a place in the sun, or so it appeared.

Following his divorce he had succumbed to a row of depressions and breakdowns, but emerged from the chrysalis of his illness by escaping to Italy, concertizing in England, Russia, and America, making a name for himself as an interpreter of Beethoven, as pianist and conductor, returning to Germany the year after Brahms's First Symphony which he had dubbed the Tenth, dubbed his Second the following year the Eleventh, and provided the alliteration of the three B's. He knew how to get under Wagner's skin, but he could not have done it had he not believed what he said.

Brahms was finally ready, decorations blazing on his chest. "Shall we go?"

The two headed for the dining hall, heels clacking on the marble floor.

"IT IS SUCH A PRETTY BELL, is it not?" Brahms rang the little silver bell.

He and Bulow awaited the Duke and his wife in a long blue room sitting on the same side of the table. Portraits of members of the House of Meiningen lined one wall; a row of windows lined the other overlooking stands of oaks and beeches in the garden. The table was set with gold plates and crystal goblets. Gilded chandeliers hung overhead, gilded sconces lined the wall.

"Sir, you rang?"

Brahms looked around. A redhaired maid stood before him, her face brown with freckles. He grinned. "Yes, I rang." He said nothing more, but stared and smoothed his moustache.

The maid curtsied. "Did sir want something?"

Brahms continued to stare and smooth his moustache. "Only to look at a pretty young maid."

The maid blushed, staring at the floor. She had noticed the gentleman, of course, who dressed as cheaply as her brothers, but dined with the Duke.

Bulow shook his head, frowning, nudging Brahms. The Duke had arrived.

The Duke appeared always angry, a bald man with sharp narrow eyes, dark eyebrows arched like an owl's, and a beard bright and sweeping as the Milky Way – but his manner was always sweet and rational. He wore a tweed vest under a dark morning coat. "Herr Bulow, Doktor Brahms, the best of the morning to you." He raised his hand. "Please, remain seated."

The two kept their seats only to be asked to keep their seats again when the Baroness arrived. Formerly an actress, Ellen Franz, she was forbidden the title of Duchess when she had married the Duke. Her head, tilting to one side, made her appear attentive and kind, but her kindness was not to be abused: her eyes were too direct, her mouth too firm. Her hair was swept in braids around her head; the bodice and sleeves of her striped satin gown were embroidered in gold, the sleeves tiered in triplicate. She was Bulow's pupil; the Duke, sharing her interest in music, had brought Bulow into the Meiningen fold.

The Duke sat at the head of the table, the Baroness across from Bulow. Brahms pushed the bell on the table.

"Doktor Brahms?"

"Your Highness?"

"Perhaps Herr Bulow has told you, but that dinner bell you appear to covet so very much –"

"Hahahahah!" He liked the Duke's sense of humor, in particular for joking at his expense. "It is a very pretty little bell – it is a magic bell. If I ring it a very pretty maid appears." Brahms stared at the maid at the side of the hall who smiled into the ground.

Brahms's preoccupation did not bother the Duke. He had married an actress himself and Brahms's people had not been much higher in the social scale than his servants. He had noticed rings of admiring women around him during the Meiningen concerts in his honor, but though he reveled in their attention he seemed little interested in more than flirtation. "Indeed, Doktor Brahms, that is hardly the least of its charms, but it might interest you to know that it was once a possession of Mary, Queen of Scots."

"Indeed!"

They started with a champagne toast and oysters. The Baroness looked at Brahms. "What will you be rehearsing today, Doktor Brahms?"

Brahms spooned turtle soup into his mouth. "Oh, just a few small piano pieces."

"Ach!" Bulow put down his spoon. "I keep telling Brahms he is too modest. He needs me to be his trumpet. What he has composed is nothing less than one of the greatest piano concertos yet – maybe the greatest ever –"

Brahms interrupted, spooning more soup to his mouth, eyes on his spoon. "Tchah, Bulow! Don't talk rubbish!"

Bulow ignored him, looking at the Duke. "Beethoven would have been proud, Your Highness. Mozart would have laughed for joy."

Brahms wiped his mouth with the back of his hand. "For a great conductor, Bulow is an idiot. Beethoven and Mozart have nothing to fear. What else is there to eat?"

The hosts smiled; so did Bulow. Again Brahms showed himself different from Wagner who could never stop talking about the great importance of everything he wrote. There was trout au bleu to follow, quail stew, chicken a la francaise, compote, chestnut puree, ice, cheese, and fruit – more champagne, chablis, and sherry.

iii

Joachim plucked at his beard like a bird pecking at seed, his face a clenched muscle, pale and glistening, his forehead wrinkled like bark. "It is good to see you are doing so well, Johannes." His tone was ironic, which did not become him, but he soon lapsed into his more customary bitterness. "I daresay you deserve it, never having married. Mark my words, only a fool marries – only fools dare to be cuckolds."

Brahms screwed his eyes, shook his head, and raised his hands as if to restrain Joachim. He said nothing, but Bulow's face paled; he rose from his chair. The three were in Brahms's rooms. "I will take my leave, then, Joachim, since you go to such pains to show you have not come to see me."

It was not until Bulow got up that Joachim understood Brahms's gestures. The hand plucking his beard became yet more agitated. "Forgive me, Bulow. I meant no offence. I am not myself. I spoke for no one but myself. I must talk with Brahms on a personal matter, but I will look forward to talking with you later."

Bulow remained stiff, his face pale, but nodded politely. "I take no offence, but I will take my leave."

They remained silent after Bulow left. Joachim stood by a desk, resting on his knuckles, hanging his head, shaking it deliberately and slowly from side to side. "Ach, Johannes! Things have come to a pretty pass indeed if I must now listen to you play the diplomat."

Brahms laughed. "I see you have no qualms about offending me either."

Joachim looked up, anxiety scribbled anew on his face. "I am sorry, Johannes. I am truly not myself these days."

Their tour of Poland had been successful, but Joachim's problem had deteriorated since his return to Berlin. Brahms shook his head, waving the apology aside, patting his friend's shoulder, and leading him into the garden. "Is it not wonderful here, Joseph? I wake to birds at my window, squirrels at my door. The Duke has extended a standing invitation to me. These are to be my chambers whenever I wish – and the grounds too might as well be mine. I wander through them whenever I please. I have my own piano. I bother no one and no one bothers me. I do not even have to dress up – but I live like Wagner!"

Joachim stared at Brahms, face flaccid, hair lank, beard limp, eyes glazed. "Indeed, Johannes, for you things could not be better – but for me the heavens are falling."

Brahms winced. "Pull yourself together, man, Joseph. Tell me what is the matter."

"It is the same thing. My Ursi no longer listens to me. She defies my authority – in the home, in front of the children, in public. She no longer behaves like a dutiful wife. I do not know what is the matter with her." He buried his face in his hands. "I tell you, Johannes, the heavens are falling."

"What do you mean? How does she defy you?"

"It is the same thing. I tell her not to see Simrock, but she insists he is her friend. People are already beginning to talk. I want to nip it in the bud," he whispered – "before it grows the thorns of an affair like Bulow's – before I am horned like he is."

Brahms shook his head. "If people talk, they talk about you, Joseph, and how you are jealous about nothing. If you do not open your eyes and see your wife as she truly is, it is you who will be the loser, not she. If you insist on seeing dragons where there are only dragonflies, you have no one to blame but yourself."

Joachim clawed his hands through his hair, glaring at his friend. "Johannes, she is *seen* with Simrock – again and again and again she is seen. Am I to ignore the evidence of eyes and ears?"

"Joseph, what does it signify that she is seen with him? They are friends – and, as she has said herself, are you not seen with Frau Schumann? Does that not signify the same thing?"

"I am not the one asking for a divorce!"

"A divorce? What are you talking about a divorce?"

"She – my Ursi – wants a divorce – but I will not give it to her."

"A divorce? It has come to that?"

"I will not give it to her. I will not permit it. My reputation will stand me in good stead against hers. She cannot divorce me without my consent. The burden of proof will be upon her. I know I can count on you to vouch for my good character, Johannes, can I not?"

"Joseph, you are talking nonsense. It will not come to that."

"It *has* come to that. She wants a divorce – but I will not give it to her. It *has* come to that!"

Brahms could not say what he thought: like the dog in the manger, Joachim would neither divorce Amalie nor treat her with the respect due a wife.

"One more thing, Johannes. I have cut off all dealings with that Simrock person, and I must ask you not to talk to him either about me or my family. I cannot expect you to cease all business with him, but I will thank you to keep personal matters to yourself."

Brahms frowned, took a deep breath. He was working with Joachim on arrangements of his Hungarian Dances for violin and piano for Simrock to publish, but the work would have to come to a stop – or they would have to find another publisher – but he was well satisfied with Simrock who had published him when others had been unwilling, when he had been unknown. He trusted Simrock to manage even his financial affairs, but he had Joachim to thank for even more – but standing by Joachim he only encouraged him to make a greater fool of himself, and Amalie too was his friend, his champion no less for the *Alto Rhapsody* which she had made her own. "We do not talk about you – and you should know better than to ask that of me."

Joachim was immediately contrite. "You are right, Johannes. You are right, and I thank you. Forgive me. I should have known better than to ask, but I am not myself. I am constantly out of sorts with myself – and all on account of that Simrock person!"

Brahms shook his head. "Simrock has got nothing to do with it. If you are out of sorts it is on account of yourself."

Joachim's fingers, combing his hair, came to a sudden stop. His eyes fastened on Brahms. "Simrock has everything to do with it, but it does not seem to me that you speak as a friend! I would like to know if you mean to side with me or with my wife in this matter!"

Brahms shook his head again, but kept his eyes on the floor, saying nothing.

"I know it is difficult for you, Brahms, but you cannot know how it is. You have never been married, but a disobedient wife is a harridan and a gorgon – and if she is as beautiful as my wife she is ten times a harridan and a gorgon."

Joachim's head resembled a hive; he had picked the hair on his head no less than his beard. Brahms grinned to soften his words. "You must take better care of yourself, Joseph, or you will succeed only in making yourself crazy. You begin to look like a gorgon yourself."

Joachim stared a long while, still as a statue before speaking again. "I see how it is. The heavens crash around me, but my friend of so many decades sees fit only to make jokes. I have often thought that about you, Johannes, that you never cared about me, only about what I could do for you – and now that I have served my purpose I am to be discarded like an old newspaper. It seems you have more in common with Wagner than I thought!"

Brahms grimaced, shaking his head again, but this time he twisted his lip in a half smile. "Is that not strange? You say the heavens are crashing around you, but I see nothing – except a little boy who sees only what he wishes to see."

They stared for a moment into each other's eyes, Brahms with his lower lip thrust forward, Joachim with his jaw raised, hands clutching his beard. Joachim got up and left without another word. Brahms shrugged, and a week later wrote Amalie a letter.

Dear Frau Joachim,

As you perhaps know, your husband has been to see me about a matter of which you can easily guess. I have known about your problems as long as they have existed. Therefore, let me tell you, first of all, that I have never by word or thought adopted your husband's point of view. There was never any reason to do so. I have always thought of you with sympathy, but now I agree with you even more completely. How I wish I could do something!

Unfortunately, I can only relieve myself by sending you a word of sympathy. I believe no one else can understand your case as clearly as I. After all, my friendship with your husband is older than your marriage.

You may, however, have noticed that in spite of a friendship of thirty years' standing, in spite of my love and admiration for Joachim, in spite of all the mutual artistic interests which bind us together, I have always been careful to limit the length and intimacy of our intercourse. I have never even thought about living in the same town and working with him. Love and friendship should be breathed as easily as air; if not, they become morbid, and I become much alarmed. Unnecessary scenes brought about by imaginary causes fill me with dread. A partial separation is sad, even in friendship, but it is possible, and it is with just such caution that I have managed to save my friendship with Joachim. Without it, I should have lost it all a long time ago.

I therefore want to tell you, explicitly and plainly, as I have told Joachim innumerable times, that I believe he has done you and Simrock a grievous wrong. I can only hope that he will abandon his terrible delusions.

Your love, on the other hand, may be so great that you can forget what has passed, and Joachim's compliance and Simrock's generosity so great that tolerable relations between them may be possible, but for such a circumstance, so devoutly to be desired to come to pass, Joachim would first have to admit his mistake.

You see from this long letter how vainly I have tried to satisfy myself. If only you could feel the affection with which I think of you and write to you (I am not ashamed of my emotion!), and if only he could feel it, and if only I could write to him in the same way! But it is hardly possible not to feel bitter toward him or to imagine that he would not receive well-meant advice in a bitter and entirely mistaken spirit.

Believe, then, that you have a friend in me. Dispose of me where you think I can be of some use. Unfortunately, as you see, I have little hope of being of help.

With all my heart,
Your devoted
J. Br.

Clara smiled to herself: how easily Johannes filled his chair at her breakfast table. There was otherwise no trace of the slender boy who had played for her and Robert in Dusseldorf so very many years ago. The streaming mane and beard hid most of his face, but his eyes remained recognizable – more penetrating than before, but still as blue as icebergs. She stiffened for a moment, aware suddenly that he was watching her watching him. He exhaled a series of puffs like smoke signals, releasing each with a soft explosion of his lips, smiling ironically through the brown fog building between them. "What are you thinking, Clara, that you have the smile of a cat that has caught the pigeons?"

Clara lost her smile, but grew it back in a moment. Her face was so round the sharpness of her nose was lost. Her eyes remained blue as midnight; streaks of grey distinguished her coiffure pulled in a bun behind, secured by a blue ribbon. "I was thinking your face is so red that after your beard turns white you could be Father Christmas." She gave him a sly glance. "You would not even need a pillow."

To her relief, Johannes laughed. "Yes, and all those people who mistook me once for your son will mistake me for your pappa."

She, too, laughed as Marie joined them smiling, refilling his coffee cup. "That would mean, Herr Brahms –"

"Ah, Fraulein Marie, none of your cheekiness. I am a *Dok*tor now, do you not know?"

"Ach, sorry, I will *ne*ver get it right – *Dok*tor Brahms, *Dok*tor Brahms. Old habits die hard."

"What was it you wished to say?"

"Only that from being my brother you will have become my grandfather!"

Brahms twisted his lip. "Yes, yes. You are very clever, Fraulein Mariechen. Of that we are not unaware. Maybe we should give you a medal?"

Marie exchanged glances with Clara, shaking her head – as did Clara, accustomed to his irony.

Brahms was too comfortable even to catch the exchange, but recalled how full Clara's breakfast table had been in Lichtenthal, what he had called her Cabinet Meetings, her Court in Session, when the children had read their letters out loud and planned their day, Clara presiding – as she did now, looking through the day's letters, but with only Marie and Eugenie in attendance. Elise, married, was in America, and Ludwig incarcerated in the Colditz institution; Ferdinand, established with a bank in Berlin, treated by a less than scrupulous doctor for injuries during the Franco-Prussian War, was addicted to morphine; Julie and Felix had succumbed to consumption, as had her oldest grandson, Julie's firstborn. Much as Brahms begrudged his solitary existence, he wondered how she could lose so many without losing herself. She said the loss of Robert had inured her to the others; she lived for her living children, but after Felix's death she had written to Brahms more bitterly than he could remember: *One grows old only to bury one's children. Why a poor unfortunate fellow like Ludwig goes on living while my gifted son dies I will never understand.*

Her bitterness was not inappropriate, but Felix's death had made her sentimental. She had been less appreciative of Felix's giftedness before his death, more solicitous of the Schumann name, requesting him to publish what he wished but under a pseudonym to spare her unpleasantness should he prove unsuccessful.

During his last days, the twenty-four-year-old Felix had crept like an old man, losing his breath in half a flight of stairs, coughing every minute of the day, snatching a few hours rest at night with the help of medicine, Marie and Eugenie attending him by the hour. He had died one night in their Frankfurt home, gasping in Marie's arms, breath draining from his lungs in a rattle. Marie had not called Clara, wanting to spare her, knowing what she preferred: the only way she could deal with her tragedies was to look away. She had not visited Julie when she had been sick saying Julie needed peace and quiet, but she had sent Marie to see her in Italy – and when Julie had died she had played a concert the same day saying she had long been resigned to her death and needed no longer to mourn. Ludwig she had visited just once though he continued to live; it had drained her too much to see him relive his father's last years to visit him ever again.

Brahms found himself increasingly like her, uncomfortable around sickness, avoiding even the Herzogenbergs, both younger than himself by more than ten years, when they were ill, Elisabet with heart trouble, her husband with rheumatism – avoiding also Billroth sick with pneumonia. He wondered if Robert's illness, taking two and a half years from his own young life, might not have affected him as well – if not inuring him as it had Clara, then making him averse.

"Here is a letter for you – from Frau Herzogenberg."

His eyes opened wider, suddenly brighter. "Ah, then I have not lost them yet!"

Clara noted the glitter in his eyes. "They are the nicest people. Why would you think you had lost them?"

Brahms shrugged, holding out his hand for the letter.

"Why do you shrug your shoulders when I ask you a question?" When he remained quiet, opening and reading the letter, she drew a deep breath. "Johannes, do you not hear me? Do you not see me? Am I no more than air to you?"

Marie exchanged glances again with her mother, shaking her head in sympathy, saying nothing. Clara had long explained her huge debt to her children. When Robert had been incarcerated nothing had raised her from her doldrums like Brahms's music. She had played her husband's music without end, but his was now music of the past, and Brahms's of the future, and her interest in resolving the problems of the new music had been instrumental in saving her from her worst self. Brahms had sacrificed almost three years of his young life to her wellbeing, not only with music, but with his presence, minding the children, minding household accounts, minding business affairs – teacher, friend, brother, son, and steward all in one. For that early sacrifice Clara not only endured his moods and tempers, but insisted on the same from her daughters. She had read to them of her difficult time in a passage from her diary: *When I am with Brahms I never think of his youth, but feel myself finely inspired by his genius, and instructed as well. He is an astonishing person. I am grateful that heaven has sent me, in my great sorrow, a friend like this, who lifts up my mind, reveres my dearly beloved husband, and shares my suffering without reserve and without question.*

Brahms caught the second exchange of glances between mother and daughter, the shake of their heads. "You are right. They are everything you say."

Clara turned her attention quickly back. "Then, pray, what is the matter?"

He had criticized Herzogenberg's First Symphony at their request, found it too complicated, to which Elisabet had replied his own first was hardly less complicated – to which he had had no reply. It was one thing to be complicated following your own inspiration, but quite another following someone else's. "I thought I might have offended them in some way."

"Why would you think that?"

Brahms grimaced. "You know why. It is my way. I do not mean to offend, but I do, and I am the last to know it myself."

"That you do – indeed, you do – but how is it that you think you might have offended them?"

"He sends me his things, he wishes to know what I think, and if that were all it would be all right – but the wife is constantly by the husband's side and more offended than the husband by what I say."

Clara could imagine what he might have said. Even his compliments were ironic. She shook her head. "It is a pity, Johannes, but you really should think more about what you say – or write, as the case may be. You give your friends much reason to resent you – and your oldest friends the most reason."

Brahms said nothing.

"What might be but the expression of a moment for you is too often for others – for me – an impression to be carried for days. You give so little thought to how you might be misunderstood. Have I not written to you, when I send news that I think might upset you, that you are not to reply at once, but to give me your second and your third impressions rather than your first?"

Brahms shrugged. "I would be particularly sorry to offend them – but I am reminded only too often what a difficult person I am to get along with, and I leave the world to go as it likes. I am getting accustomed to bearing the consequences of my shortcomings." He looked up – "but do you not think they should stop sending me his things if they do not wish to know what I think?"

"Oh, but I am sure they *do* wish to know. It is not what you say that is so very upsetting, my dear Johannes. It is how you say it."

"You may be right, but that is how I am – and knowing it, do you not think they should stop asking me – and if they must ask, do you not think they should stop being offended? It is so difficult to turn them away. Here is a page from Herzogenberg. If you read it you will know what I mean."

Clara read the paragraph he indicated: *You know how much a word or two of recognition from you means to me. I can appreciate as a kindness even a well meant disapproval – but I know, too, how keen an interest this presupposes on your part, an interest which must be spontaneous, and is not to be had for the asking. If you knew how I turn over in my mind any casual remark of yours, you would understand why I come to you in spite of your lack of encouragement. You, as a great master, must indeed be hard put to respond to all the affection your mere existence inspires, your mere presence. Those with whom you stand on an equal footing are all dead. When you met Schumann you were twenty. I feel as if I will never be older than twenty with respect to you – so you must put up with something like a love letter once in a while from such a hobbledehoy as myself.*

"Oh, Johannes, this is a charming letter. You do not deserve it. You most certainly do not deserve such an appreciative man."

"On that point I will not disagree. I, too, wish he were less appreciative. Then, maybe, I would not be so hard put – as he puts it – to respond."

"There we are in agreement. He is, indeed, too good for you – and so is his wife."

Brahms was reading the letter again, smiling. "Hah, the wife! She has changed her opinion of Bulow."

Clara, like Elisabet and many others in Brahms's circle, found Bulow meticulous, his memory astounding, but his performances cold, studied, and soulless. "Has she?"

A small orchestra traveled more easily than a large, and Bulow had taken advantage of the size of the Meiningen Orchestra to take it on a whistlestop tour of Germany to promote Brahms's works. They had promoted the new piano concerto together, Brahms at the piano, Bulow conducting, occasionally reversing roles, playing also the first concerto to great acclaim. Bulow had promised Brahms he would bring even the Leipzigers to their knees and Elisabet's letter proved Bulow as good as his word. Brahms indicated the paragraph: *Do you know, the audience quite lost their heads at the end of the C minor! The din was so great we had to ask ourselves if we were really in the Gewandhaus – in short, the audience was so charming and sympathetic that one felt like kissing them. When the allegretto received relatively less applause, Bulow repeated it – and then came the deluge! Oh, how happy we were in our corner, like children, vindicated finally for our patience!*

Clara did not think it worthy of Brahms to have peddled his new concerto like a haberdasher's latest fashion. Within a month they had covered Kiel, Hamburg, Bremen, Utrecht, Munster, Frankfurt, Stuttgart, Zurich, Vienna, Breslau, Leipzig, Berlin, and innumerable points in between, Brahms and the "Battling Baron von Bulow," as they were billed, with the entire orchestra – like a circus. An artist behaved with more decorum, but they had been triumphant everywhere – and, however great a composer, success helped him surpass himself. She handed the letter back to Brahms. "I, too, would enjoy hearing a work perfectly performed as regards technique, even if it were only for once – and I must confess that Bulow is the man to do it."

Brahms raised his eyebrows, saying nothing, understanding her antipathy, not unrelated to her rivalry with Bulow as a pianist. She herself could no longer play his first concerto; it strained her muscles now beyond their capacity, her memory suffered, so did her hearing, and as much as she loved the second she knew she would never play it in public.

Clara was reading a letter of her own. "Hartel is in a hurry for the *Carnaval* and the *Fantasiestucke*. You were right, Johannes. It is tedious work just to get the metronome right – but I would not wish anyone else to do it."

Brahms had undertaken to help Clara edit the complete edition of Schumann's work. "There is no hurry. Do not let him hurry you. There are plenty of publishers waiting in line and he knows it – and you should know it, too – Simrock, for instance."

Marie frowned, nodding vehemently, looking at Clara. "Indeed, Mamma! I think it is ridiculous that you have any consideration for Hartel in this matter at all."

Clara looked at Brahms. "Mariechen has been reading some old letters from Hartel to Robert."

Marie turned to Brahms. "You would not believe it, Herr – I mean, Doktor Brahms, how he beat Pappa down over the details. I do not think we should do business with him ever again."

Clara's voice got smaller. "In this matter I am constantly hovering between duty and sentiment. Other publishers have certainly expressed interest in Robert's work, but he dealt with Hartel for so long I feel indebted to them. I feel they are almost friends – but it is also true, what Mariechen says. They treated him very badly."

Brahms clucked his tongue. "They are all the same, they will all treat you badly – if you let them. Hartel needs you more than you need him. Your name is valuable to him for his publication of your husband's work, and he can afford to pay for it. You must think only of what you want and you must demand it. It is to his advantage to keep you happy. Also, you must trust no one – and forget all this hovering between duty and sentiment. You must not hesitate to keep them waiting, even a month if necessary. They would not hurry for your benefit if it did not suit them, but they are always pressing others to hurry for them."

Clara was silent, nodding her head before finally speaking. "You are right, of course, Johannes, and it does me good to have everything outlined like that. It becomes too easy for me otherwise to lose my perspective – in my negotiations as much as in my editing."

Brahms grunted; Marie refilled his cup; Clara opened another letter, from Levi. She spoke nonchalantly, looking surreptitiously at Brahms as she read. "Levi writes that he is not well again. I cannot believe how foolish men can be, behaving forever as if they were twenty. I cannot think how many times I have told him to be careful, but he insists on smoking all day, staying up all night, taking no exercise – and then expecting always to be well."

Clara looked at Brahms, but he said nothing, looking away. She had tried to reconcile the two without success. She was no less happy than Brahms with Levi's interest in Wagner, but Levi had proven too good a friend during the difficult times with Ludwig and Felix – chaperoning them to doctors, institutes, and hospitals – to be dropped over a difference of opinion even in music. Besides, he continued to perform Robert's music though he appeared no longer interested in Brahms, in neither the man nor the music. Under his baton, Brahms's symphonies had been greeted with either silence or loud hissing, to be expected in Wagner's stronghold, but Brahms's mulishness had driven the final wedge between them.

"I give him my own example, how I walk every morning before breakfast, and again after my lessons, between one and two, when I pay calls and do my shopping, but will he listen? Of course not! He is no better than you. You are two of a kind."

Brahms raised his voice. "Clara, enough! Do not think I do not know what you are doing. It will not work."

Clara's eyes clouded. Marie stared, narrowing her eyes; whatever her mamma said about her debt to Brahms during the time of her pappa's sickness, she found it hard to forgive the way he sometimes addressed her.

"Johannes, will you never make it up with him? Do you care so very little about your friends that you can cast them aside with no more regret than if you had lost a groschen?"

He looked at her; for a moment she thought he might shout again, but his mouth drooped, a sad small arch hiding in his beard; his eyebrows made a larger arch, and she saw him more clearly than she had in a long while. "Sometimes, life ... robs us ... of more than death."

The pitch of his voice had risen; she thought he might cry, and knew he was thinking also of Joachim. The court had been disposed in Joachim's favor against Amalie – until she had produced Brahms's letter, turning the verdict against Joachim. At Amalie's request, Brahms had given her permission to use his letter as she wished, never dreaming she would have it read out loud in court. Clara still befriended both Joachim and Amalie, but Brahms spoke with neither.

"I have no friends. If anyone tells you he is my friend, do not believe him."

Clara could not imagine how he felt, alienated from his oldest friends, but understood easily how one by one they had been alienated. Shortly after the Hamburg Jubilee she had been honored herself by a three day festival at the Gewandhaus for her Golden Jubilee, fifty years since her first performance, when she had been nine, when the wrong coach had picked her up. The hall had been decorated with leaves of oak in wreaths and garlands of green and gold in the same room she had performed her first concert. She had been overwhelmed with presents, telegrams, speeches, buried under a shower of flowers, presented with a gold laurel wreath, its leaves imprinted with the names of all the composers she had ever played. Her own compositions had been performed, and Robert's; old friends had appeared who had attended that first performance, friends she had not seen in years, but not Johannes. True, he had been informed late; and true, he had prior commitments in Breslau and Dresden; and true again, she had written he need not come if he could not combine the journey with some other project since it was a long way and she did not wish to inconvenience him – but amid the hundreds of greetings she had received from strangers, he had sent not even a note of congratulation. Flesh had withered within her, but she had reconciled herself: the world was made of all kinds of people; she did not understand Johannes; but others would have been less forgiving. What he gave her was music, the chief joy of her life – but at one time he had sent her his work no sooner than the ink had dried; now he was less prompt. The day before he had mentioned a new symphony, but only incidentally.

The better he was known the more secretive he became – but he was no less secretive about his virtues. He had deposited a thousand thaler, his honorarium for the Violin Sonata in G major, into her account, making it an anonymous contribution to the Schumann Fund. She would never have known had Simrock not told her once, swearing her to secrecy, when she had complained of Johannes's coldness. He knew of her difficulties, expenses for the family, Ludwig in Colditz, and more recently Ferdinand's family since his addiction had become more severe, and he had done what he could – discreetly, knowing she would never accept money from him. No less was she aware of his kindness toward Dvorak, whose work he had discovered among the entries sent to the Gesellschaft scouting for scholarships. He had ensured not only that Dvorak received the money he needed, but proofed his work as well: Dvorak was not only poor, but a poor proofreader.

Footsteps descended the stairs. Brahms looked at his watch as Eugenie entered. "Hah! The Princess stirs." He blew a long plume of smoke. "You do not know, Fraulein Eugenie, what you are missing when you are not in the woods by five o'clock in the morning."

Eugenie poured herself coffee, brushing aside smoke with her hand. "I might not know what I am missing, Herr Brahms, but I am also less fond of aural catarrhs than you."

Clara smiled, Marie laughed, Brahms laughed loudest. At Clara's request, Eugenie had taken piano lessons from him one summer in Lichtenthal. She had found him always kind, always patient, his bearishness a pose, and understood better than most how to manage him.

Marie looked at her own watch. "Doktor Brahms, you really must practise now or you will not play at all properly at your concerts."

His itinerary for the month included Bonn, Krefeld, Cologne, Hanover, Schwerin, and Meiningen. Brahms blew a long plume in her direction. "You only say that because you wish to be rid of me – and I cannot say that I blame you." He got up, pushing his chair so roughly it almost toppled. "Here I go again, through the squirrel's wheel of the virtuosos."

The girls laughed as he left the room. Soon they heard the sound of arpeggios in contrary motion; it was his habit to attack the top and bottom of the keyboard simultaneously with his little fingers, galloping up and down, passing through one key after another. Eugenie shook her head. "There is such a struggle when he plays, is there not, as if he were accepting a challenge? I cannot believe he enjoys it very much."

Clara smiled, the pedagogue in her aroused. "It is no secret. The piano has always been for him a necessary evil."

Marie poured her mamma more coffee. "But not for you?"

When Clara practised the tones surged like waves in sixths, octaves, tenths, double thirds, arpeggios, scales, all at an accelerated pace without pause or hesitation, skipping from key to key in the freest of forms in a perennially new fantasia, drawing inspiration from an unfathomable source, followed by Bach fugues and partitas, Chopin etudes, Schumann's toccata, and music by Brahms. She shook her head vigorously. "Never! The piano is my dear and trusted friend."

Brahms was practising his B flat major Concerto. "He plays it so broadly, does he not?"

Clara nodded. "He does, indeed, Mariechen. What else strikes you about the way he plays?"

"It is very spirited, but more of a sketch than a portrait. He outlines the themes so broadly that the impression is very strong of light and shade – and he plays very passionately, like a tempest scattering clouds."

Eugenie said what Marie could not. "Yes, but when a passage becomes too much for him he simply slows it down – or he skips the notes altogether!"

Marie laughed. "Yes! Yes, he does, indeed, does he not?"

Clara smiled. "Indeed, much of his style is now thump, bang, and scrabble – but at one time ..."

The girls started to laugh, but stopped seeing their mamma's reverie. She could imagine him in the next room, cigar in his mouth, shirt dusted with ash, feet barely reaching the pedals. When he leaned back his hands barely reached the keys, but he did not seem to care. Even when it was necessary to cross his hands, his eyes were invariably closed. He played like a composer, not a performer, rocking and swaying, humming and rumbling, hitting notes apparently just in time. When he missed it no longer mattered, and she was not unaware of the irony: he had played beautifully once and been hissed, but now even his most disgraceful playing was applauded.

The vestibule of 4 Karlsgasse, now Brahms's permanent residence, enclosed a dark winding stone stairway wide enough for three, but he trudged slowly up the middle, grinning because he knew it made his guest impatient.

Behind him, Hermine Spiess skipped from side to side on each stair, taking three steps for one of his; Klaus Groth lagged far behind them both, the claw of his hand gripping the rail as he climbed. Hermine's eyes were large, her forehead was narrow, her mouth small, her jaw round; curlicues of light brown hair rose to a point on her head like a hill; a wide neckline revealed plump shoulders and a plump chest. When she pouted her tiny nose almost disappeared, but her plump cheeks got plumper. Her voice chirruped up and down the scale, seemingly mimicking her movement as she zigzagged behind Brahms, bouncing on her toes, fluttering her hands, almost pushing him ahead by the wide seat of his pants. "Doktor Brahms, why do you climb so slowly – like a snail?"

Brahms's eyebrows rose; his smile was effortless as he came to a stop, knowing what would happen next.

Hermine bumped into him, missing a step. "Ach, why do you have to stop like that – without giving a warning?"

Brahms took another step, careful not to let the grin in his face seep into his voice. "I am old, Hermine. I am fifty years old."

She replied quickly, too quickly; she had spoken without thinking. "That is not old! I am more than half that age myself."

He continued climbing slowly. "Hah! Yes, twenty-six years. That is just what I mean. I am at an age when a man must be twice as careful not to make a fool of himself – because it is twice as easy with a girl half his age."

"I am sure I do not understand what you mean at all. I am, maybe, too young to understand."

Brahms laughed. Hermine had studied with Stockhausen; the quality of her voice matched the best, so did her enthusiasm. Much was expected of her, many recommended her for the stage, but she wished only to sing lieder. They had met in the spring in Krefeld where she had sung a number of his songs at a recital. He had been drawn to her voice, a sonorous contralto, deep as indigo, also to her vivacity. They had spent time together that summer in Wiesbaden where Brahms had completed his Third Symphony. Already long intoxicated with his music, she had become his Rhinemaiden, liedersangerin, chief interpreter of his songs, and was to sing the *Alto Rhapsody* during the Viennese premiere of the new symphony. She had also been bold enough to admit her "Johannes-passion" to friends. What matter his age when his music was eternal? "I do wish you would hurry up, Doktor Brahms. I do believe you are trying to annoy me."

Brahms laughed again. "Ah, Hermione-ohne-O, I would not dare – but let me make it up to you. Let me tell you a riddle."

She liked it when he called her Hermione-ohne-O, Hermione without the O. "What is your riddle?"

"In what way is a girl like a piano?"

"I have heard this one. It is because they are both grand, is it not?"

"Yes, but not quite. They are both grand, yes – but only when they are not upright!"

She slapped his back. "Doktor Brahms, you are very naughty! That is a very naughty riddle – but maybe that is why I like it."

He stopped, staring at her over his shoulder, twirling his moustache, raising an eyebrow. "You are the naughty one, Herminchen. You bring out the naughty in me."

"You must not stare at me like that, Doktor Brahms. It makes me feel like – like a saddle of roast beef."

"I would say you are more like a peach."

Groth grinned from behind her. "I would say you are like a pear!"

Brahms unlocked his door, leading them into a narrow hallway lit by two windows on the left, the air humid from the kitchen on the right. "Hallo, Frau Vogl."

A woman replied from the open kitchen door. "Doktor Brahms, you are back, are you?"

"Yes." He glanced backward again to Hermine. "My landlady."

Hermine nodded, saying nothing, wrinkling her nose at the smell of cabbage, holding her elbows close, huddling her shoulders. Groth followed almost ten paces behind.

Brahms opened the door to his bedroom at the end of the hallway. Two windows lit the room. A tiled stove held a bust of Haydn. A narrow bed was flush with one corner, a couch at its foot, chest of drawers in the adjacent corner. A table and armchairs spread in a fantail from the couch. A painting of the "Conclusion of the Peace of Munster" hung over the couch, a portrait of Bach over the bed.

Curtained glass doors led into the sittingroom where a floor of polished woodblocks was partly carpeted. The far left of the room was occupied by a grand piano, the near left by a rocking chair, sofa, and table laden with a coffee machine and cups and saucers. A bust of Beethoven peered from a bracket over the piano flanked by a wreathed portrait of Bismarck, a copy of the Sistine Madonna, and a portrait of Cherubini by Ingres. The far right of the room held a desk bearing a framed photograph of Elisabet and an inscribed picture of the Schumanns: *To Johannes Brahms, from a couple sincerely attached to him, Robert and Clara.* Curtained glass doors by the desk led to his workroom, the library. Cane chairs were scattered around the room. The smell was strong of cigars and Hermine's hands fanned the air. "I beg your pardon, Doktor Brahms, but how you so-called gentlemen can constantly bear this smell I will never understand." She rushed to the windows, drew aside the lace curtains, threw open one casement, took a deep breath, and sighed.

Groth sat in the sofa, Hermine stared out of the window, Brahms went to his coffee machine. "You will not think of the smell if you try this – mocha coffee. It is my favorite."

Hermine shook her head from the window. "No, it is not good for my throat." They had come to rehearse songs, including a poem by Groth, "Komm bald," which Brahms had set to music.

"A little bit will not hurt your throat – besides, we have only ourselves to please today."

"Well, then, if *you* prepare it, Doktor Brahms, I will not be able to refuse."

An admirer sent him monthly shipments of the mocha from Marseilles. Groth grinned, pink skin of his scalp shining, chin balding, sparse white hairs of his goatee unsightly and long. He spoke breathlessly. "If you do not mind, Brahms, I too would like some coffee."

Hermine looked out of the window. "You have a beautiful view, Doktor Brahms. I can see as far as the river."

"Yes, but I took the flat for the view of the church." You could see the Wienfluss, a finger of the Danube, in the distance, spanned by the Elisabet Bridge, Brahms's route into the heart of Vienna; but the Karlskirche was closer at hand, its great copper dome, rococo columns like minarets, easily visible from his window. He had had many addresses in Vienna, on Novaragasse, Singerstrasse, Postrasse, Wohlzeile, Ungargasse, and in the homes of various friends, but felt himself increasingly settled at Karlsgasse. "Come, do not stand by the window all day. Take a chair – take the rocking chair."

Brahms glanced at Groth, warning him to say nothing. Groth raised his eyebrows and smiled.

Hermine spun on tiptoe from the window, bouncing as she spoke. "Why should I take the rocking chair? Do you think I am an old woman?"

"It is not a rocking chair for old women, but for young girls."

"Why? What do you mean?"

"You will see – if you will only sit down for once instead of flibbertigibbeting around like a butterfly."

"I am not flibbertigibbeting around – and I am not a butterfly!"

"Then sit down, will you not, please?"

Hermine skipped across the room. "All right, then, if it will please you." She dropped deep into the chair, but was unprepared for what happened next – and screamed. The chair rocked farther back than she had anticipated – and her legs, flung into the air, revealed white ankles, white calves, white frilly drawers. She jumped from the chair as if it were in flames. "Doktor Brahms, I swear I will never trust you again – never, as long as I live, I swear it!"

Brahms could not stop laughing. "What did I tell you? It is a rocking chair for young girls only."

Groth, too, was laughing. "An old woman might die in such a chair, might she not?"

"She might very well – and I, too, might have been hurt."

"Na, Herminche-Herma, that would be impossible. If you had sat forward instead of backward it would have dropped you to your knees – but it is designed not to tip over. Otherwise, what would be the fun?"

Hermine took a deep breath, her face still red. "I feel so embarrassed."

"Ah, but Hermine, my Hermine, you must forgive me," he indicated the grinning Groth – "us, I mean. We old men must get our fun where we can. Do you not see how much pleasure you have brought us today – and what did you have to do? Nothing!"

"I wish you would stop saying that, Doktor Brahms. You are but fifty."

He held a cup of coffee toward her. "I have made it not too strong – for your voice."

"Danke." She took the coffee and sat on one of the cane chairs, testing it first.

Soon they were ready for the rehearsal. Brahms wiped his hands in his beard. "Would you be so very good, Herminchen, as to fetch me a book, or a sheaf of manuscripts from the next room. My chair is too low."

His regular piano stool was being repaired; he had substituted one of the cane chairs. They watched her go, winking at each other. She knew they were watching and wagged her behind as she walked. The shelves of his library and cupboards overflowed onto armchairs and the floor. Among volumes of the Bible, Koran, Crusoe, Kleist, Novalis, Grillparzer, Grimm, Shakespeare, Fenimore Cooper, travel, and history, lay original manuscripts of Mozart's G minor Symphony, Haydn's six Sun Quartets, the conclusion of Wagner's *Tristan* Prelude, a sheet of music with Beethoven's writing on one side, Schubert's on the other, sketches by Beethoven. The room was otherwise empty except for armchairs, traveling bags by the window, and a lectern at which he worked standing during the winter. Hermine returned with a book of Beethoven symphonies.

Brahms frowned. "You expect me to sit upon that, do you?"

They watched again as she left the room, smiling as she wagged her behind again. Her own smile was no less sly when she returned. "Here are some books you may sit upon without shame." She had brought back volumes of his own works.

ii

An unusual aspect of Brahms's Third Symphony, in F major, something new in all symphony, was that each movement concluded on a diminuendo – but as Artur Faber settled to absorb the coda, elongated into an entity by itself, a hiss sounded from behind, not for the first time that evening. Glancing over his shoulder Faber locked eyes with a young man, blond, cleanshaven, broadshouldered, sullen. The man's lips widened in a humorless smile, revealing an army of gleaming teeth, a tongue which flicked and quivered in the dark red cavern of his mouth. Another man sat beside him, no less sullen, without a smile, young, handsome, darkhaired, broadshouldered.

Faber had long looked forward to the premiere. Following Brahms's progress had become his great satisfaction since Berta had introduced him to her Hamburg friend. Nothing could match the pleasure they got from his music, sometimes more personal than was immediately understood. The "Wiegenlied," composed for their firstborn, a cradlesong now famous the country over, had been sent with a note: *Frau Berta will realize that I wrote the Wiegenlied for her little one, but she will also realize that while she is singing Hans to sleep a love song is being sung to her.* He had incorporated into the harmony the melody of the song Berta had sung during their walk home to her aunt after the last meeting of the Frauenchor:

> You think perhaps, you dream perhaps,
> That love will yield to force.
> But love, the gentlest love, can bend
> The mightiest river's course.

Horns led the melody onstage, cushioned by strings, quietly coiling and uncoiling, perhaps the most delicate part of the symphony. Berta understood her husband's annoyance and took his hand, both of them ignoring the continuing hiss, not wishing to disrupt the music further.

Wagner had died early in the year, hardly unaware of Brahms's vaulting progress, masterwork by masterwork, in seven league steps, never looking back – but Wagner had been looking over his shoulder a long while, imagining the hot breath on his heels, stomping on the hands approaching his summit, unleashing his pen at every opportunity to discredit the only man who mounted a credible challenge to his supremacy.

His paranoia was unwarranted, his position secure, Brahms had composed no operas, Wagner almost nothing else, but the doctorate proclaiming Brahms First Master of the Stricter Style of the Art of Music in Germany had spurred his resentment and released his bile – and no less the bile of his followers. Brahms accepted the factions, though not without regret, his regard for Wagner the musician undiminished. He had professed his admiration to no less than Wagner himself when he had put himself forward as the best of Wagnerians, the one who understood him most clearly, unlike the Wagnerian factions who understood only special effects and spectacles, unlike his own factions who could not see beyond the special effects and spectacles.

After Wagner's death the Wagnerians had transferred their allegiance to Bruckner. Wagner had shown the way, walking past a welcoming committee at a train station once in Vienna to clap his acolyte on the back. Bruckner had dedicated his Third Symphony to Wagner and Wagner had returned the compliment with a comment, "Bruckner! He is my man!" setting in motion antipathy between Brahmsians and Brucknerians though Brahms had never wavered in his admiration. When news of Wagner's death had reached him in Meiningen he had cut short a rehearsal saying, "A master is dead, we shall rehearse no more today." He had sent a wreath to Bayreuth which had not been acknowledged. A witness had gossiped about Cosima's response: "Why should the wreath be acknowledged? The man was no friend to Our Art." Faber knew of Brahms's disappointment at the lack of comity, of his distaste for Wagnerians more than Wagner – of the kind sitting behind him, transmogrified now to Brucknerians.

As the gossamer chords faded, sustained by a roll of tympani like the last breath of a storm, the audience rose, swelling the applause with howls of appreciation – but the hissing swelled no less, mixing bravos with boos. Faber was a patient man, a small man with a narrow beard which made his narrow face narrower yet, smaller yet. He was not given to public demonstrations, but turned finally to the man behind him. "If you do not like good music, my good man, you should not have come."

The man bared again his army of teeth. "I have the right to express my opinion as much as you, old man."

Faber gripped his hat tightly in his hand. "You have not the right to ruin the enjoyment of others. You might have expressed your opinion better by leaving."

The man put his hands on his hips. "I have purchased a ticket. I have the right to express my opinion any way I wish."

Berta held her husband's elbow, but Faber hardly noticed. "It is one thing to express an honest opinion – but quite another to express a preconceived opinion."

The man narrowed his eyes, smiling yet more brilliantly. "Be careful what you say, old man – or I will have to teach you something about good music."

"To do that you would have to learn something first yourself."

The man suddenly grabbed Faber's beard and tugged.

Berta gasped and dropped her husband's elbow to obtain a firmer grip on her parasol. Artur Faber spoke firmly. "Unhand me, my man."

"I am not your man."

"Unhand me, I say."

The man still smiled. "Who is going to make me? You, old man?"

Berta brought her parasol down on the man's shoulder. The altercation had been lost to the audience amid the applause, but the focus suddenly changed. The man's friend wrenched the parasol from Berta's hand, but someone else wrenched it from his from behind. A third person struck the blond man still holding Faber's beard.

Order was soon restored; the Brucknerians were in a minority; and Faber able to laugh. He had lost more than his pride, a few hairs from his beard, but as he said to Berta, incidents such as these were the spice of life, the cement in relations between husbands and wives.

IN ANOTHER PART OF THE HALL a tall man with a squat face rose from his seat to survey the trouble. His hair was swept back without a part and gleamed – but it had thinned, retreating to the dome of his head, unlike the hair of his moustache and beard, dry and bristling, sticking out in all directions like straw, interlaced like the roots of a mangrove. He recognized the differences were political masquerading as musical and blamed the Brahmsian faction as much as the Wagnerian-turned-Brucknerian. All such masquerades implied a bigotry that had nothing to do with music. If you felt inferior to others you attacked them for traits over which they had no control, Jewishness or Bohemianism or the color of their skin – or, indeed, even height and weight among other intangibles. His own music was the richer for having absorbed both Wagner and Brahms. Those who insisted on choosing between the two only impoverished themselves.

In his estimate the Third Symphony surpassed the first two – if not in greatness and power, certainly in beauty. It showcased a mood the Master rarely revealed: the most splendid melodies, the most subtle harmonies, the most glowing orchestration – and love. There was no other way to describe it: it did one's heart good to hear it. The Master must have been in a good mood to have written so beautifully, showing a depth he otherwise rarely revealed, a depth he had known and come to love in the Master who had been responsible in part for his own success and fame. Wagner had flailed at the approach of Brahms, but Brahms had welcomed the rise of a man sometimes hailed his successor – not only welcomed but aided. Such generosity was not to be overlooked and was gloriously audible in the Third Symphony.

The Master's sense of humor was no less to be celebrated. Invited to dinner after the concert he had requested a second invitation from his host: *Would you have anything against my bringing along a friend to your house? I will give him something from my little plate and my little mug, and as far as I know he does not make speeches!* He had been unable to attend, after all, but the effort had touched him profoundly, so much so that he did not mind when the Master, ignorant of the Czech language, entertained himself with random diacritical marks ornamenting his name: Dvořák.

BRAHMS HAD APPROACHED JOACHIM that summer, expressing regret about his letter to Amalie, not for what he had written, but for the public knowledge of private affairs. He had never hidden his sympathy for Amalie, but the tawdriness of the affair was a matter apart. If Joachim could tolerate a friendship based on such an understanding, he wished to offer his hand – which Joachim had accepted.

Many cities had vied for the honor of presenting the second performance of the Third. All had been disappointed when he had sent the manuscript to Joachim who had continued to perform his work despite their differences, finding more comfort in the work than in its creator. Joachim wrote to say he loved the symphony, but Brahms made no response, and the next time he was in Berlin made no effort to meet Joachim – but their correspondence was gradually renewed though only about musical matters.

Bulow programmed the Third twice in the same evening in Meiningen. A new symphony was not to be absorbed in a single hearing. His audience had agreed applauding the second performance more vociferously than the first.

At the breakfast table in Frankfurt Clara's attenuated court was in session again, Brahms puffing on his cigar, Clara reading letters, Marie making coffee, while Eugenie still slept. Clara put down a letter she had been reading. "Johannes, the more I think about it the more I am convinced we should not dawdle. We have less time than we think."

Brahms knew what she meant. In going through Robert's letters for publication she had found many she never wanted published, mainly from the final years, all from Endenich – which had aroused her concern about her own letters.

"They are one long wail – and while they are justified by my fate they are no pleasure to read. I would prefer no one to read them at all."

Brahms felt as she did, but for different reasons. His letters, no less than hers, would have been of no interest if not for his celebrity. He was no Goethe, no Shakespeare. His genius, if such it was, and hers, lay in music, on which their letters shed little light, and even there he was no Beethoven, no Mozart, no Bach – but the public was prurient, and publishers were fed by the public. He had done well, but lived a small life, not like Liszt or Wagner, not in large splashes of color, not a play worthy of Schiller, but biographers were accumulating material already though he insisted his biography lay in his music. Still, he resented returning Clara's letters, representing the bulk of his private life, but she had offered his own in return – which he wanted.

"You see, the letters would be quite safe in my hands. If I were to die suddenly they would fall into the hands of my children."

He understood her implication: if he died anyone might get the letters in his possession. "But that is precisely why it is more urgent that I get my letters back from you."

Clara stared, not understanding what he meant.

"Ha! You imagine I am in a rush to despatch them to the printer, do you?"

Clara understood he meant to destroy them, but that was not what she wished either. "We must exchange the letters, Johannes, but maybe not right away."

"I thought you were the one who did not wish to dawdle."

"I do not, but I wish to read through yours again first. I am afraid you mean to destroy them immediately."

"What I do with my letters is my concern – but I will be ready when you are."

"Good! I am glad we have settled that." Clara put her letters to one side, but her voice remained suppliant – "but I have one more thing to ask."

He frowned, wishing she would not preface her requests as if to gain his promise before he knew what he promised. The years appeared to have made her more fearful rather than less. "With you, Clara, it is always one more thing. What is it? Just ask me."

She looked away. "If that is how you are going to be, maybe I should ask another time."

He softened his tone. "Ask – ask me now."

She smiled, surprisingly shy. "Well, then, everyone at the Conservatory has asked me to tell you that they would like to hear your Fourth Symphony again – soon."

"They will, in a month, when Bulow comes back."

"But they wish to hear it again by you – not by Bulow. They are not so fond of Bulow's baton – and neither am I. His baton is not so warm as yours."

No one had been more surprised than himself at the reception of his Fourth Symphony, his most serious work. He had written it over a period of two years and after the responses from his friends had lowered his expectations, but the public had received it the best of his symphonies. He imagined his celebrity contributed to its success, but remained no less surprised. On hearing the piano transcription for four hands, Hanslick had said he had felt browbeaten by two incredibly intelligent people; Kalbeck had begged him to substitute new movements for the third and fourth; Elisabet had been more precise, but no less baffled: the further she penetrated, the more impenetrable it became, a tiny world, designed too microscopically, meant only for the wise, the initiated; the rest would walk in darkness.

He had submitted the score to Bulow with his customary diffidence, "a few entr'actes – which, put together, might make a symphony," and Bulow had produced it as he had produced the last concerto and symphony, rehearsing the orchestra thoroughly for the premiere under Brahms in Meiningen. The success had been more overwhelming for being unexpected. They had taken the symphony on the rails: Frankfurt, Siegen, Dortmund, Essen, Elberfeld, Dusseldorf, Amsterdam, Utrecht, The Hague, Rotterdam, Krefeld, Cologne, Bonn, Wiesbaden. Reviewers had run out of words – powerful, profound, passionate, poetic, original, noble, compared him with Bach and Beethoven. Hanslick had revised his estimate, likening it to a dark well: the longer you stared into it the more brightly the stars shone back. Brahms had been so pleased he had conducted every performance and included it on every program. Bulow had submitted to his wishes under duress: Brahms left him nothing to do; worse, his own baton could have done more for the symphony than Brahms's, his beat was clearer – and Brahms had agreed to let him conclude another tour by himself in Frankfurt, to let the Frankfurters hear the difference for themselves.

"But I have agreed to let Bulow conduct it when he returns to Frankfurt."

"I do not say he should not conduct it – but what is to prevent you from conducting it again as well with the Frankfurt Symphony? Surely you cannot complain about too many performances?"

This Brahms knew: without Bulow the Fourth would not have secured its immediate success. And this: a second performance of the symphony by the composer in so short a while in the same city would diminish interest in a third performance by anyone else. But also this: whether or not it was true, he had resented Bulow's implication that he conducted the symphony better than its composer. "I will think about it."

ii

Bulow shook so hard with rage, with what he perceived to be yet another slight, that he appeared to be three people at once. His eyes dipped in a V, and together with the imperial beard and the deep V of his nose he appeared Satanic. "What the devil were you thinking, Brahms? Are you a goat or a donkey to have a head so full of shit? Are you a camel? Tell me, Brahms, who do you presume to be?"

Brahms's guilt, which had led him to Bulow's hotel in search of absolution, had also rendered him silent. He looked away.

"Will you not answer me or am I supposed to guess at your motives? Why did you bother to come if you had nothing to say."

Brahms's eyes wandered. "I came as a friend – to see how it had gone with you – on the tour."

"TCHHAHH!" Spit rained on Brahms's face, a large glob fell on his hand on the table. "I used to think Wagner was the most cowardly of great men, I used to think only he could aspire to such villainous heights – but you ascend – oh, how well, how swiftly you ascend those selfsame heights. Were you so very afraid to have your baton matched against mine? Hah? Was that why you did it?"

When Wagner had died Bulow had fallen again into a depression, taken almost a year to recover, hoping to the very end for a resolution of their differences – at the very least, an acknowledgment that he had been wronged – but it had not come, was never to come. He had recovered through his work, and through Brahms's work. He said repeatedly that he owed his life to Brahms, his sanity to Brahms's sanity, to his friendship, his solidity, solidarity, confidence; no one, not even Joachim, had absorbed Brahms's music as fully, as deeply; after Bach and Beethoven he was the greatest composer; the remainder of Bulow's life belonged to no other.

But despite his selfless efforts, his many successes in Brahms's behalf, he had yet to win the regard of the Brahmsians, among them Hiller, Joachim, Elisabet, Clara, all of whom begrudged Brahms's generosity to Bulow, who remained for them a Wagnerian, whom they called "imposter," "impious," "modernist," "anatomist." Bulow, in turn, called them "timebeaters" for their mindless adherence to the beat, but he had wished to redeem himself on their own turf with the Fourth, an opportunity Brahms had now scuttled.

Brahms shrugged, unable to explain, tired of the tantrum.

"Why do you shrug your shoulders? Do you not care? Is that what you are saying? Is that what you mean? I ask you again: What the devil were you thinking? It is obvious you do not think I am good enough to conduct your symphony. Not once did you allow me to conduct it in your presence. What are my men to think?

You have no respect for me, you need me only for my orchestra – but about me you care nothing."

"Bulow! It is nothing to do with you. It is true that I do not care, but that is nothing to do with you. It is the way I am. That is all. I do not care about concerts. I have never taken them seriously. You see how I perform my own concertos. They are a diversion. That is all. They have been written. That is the important thing. There will always be concerts." He shrugged again. "It is foolish to take it too seriously."

Bulow closed his eyes and drew a deep breath. "So now I am a fool!"

"I did not mean it like that."

"Of course, you did – otherwise, you would not have said it – but let me tell you something, Herr Doktor Brahms. I am done being your fool. If I attempt to convince people of the glory of your music I do not do it, God preserve me, with the object of offering you a diversion." He held up his hand to cut off Brahms's protest. "I do it for myself – only for myself. That I use your music is incidental – but that is now past. I have sent my letter of resignation to the Duke. I cannot command the orchestra, not after you have seen fit to humiliate me before my own men. You doubtless imagine I am offering you but another diversion," he held up his hand again – "but I assure you, my good Herr Doktor Brahms, I do no such thing. I do what I do out of the greatest respect for myself, and for no one else – because, you see, my dear Herr Doktor Brahms, my selfrespect is all that I have left, and if I give that up I give up everything. The Duke will have no choice but to accept my resignation." He got up from the table and walked to the door. "I will thank you now if you will do me the courtesy of leaving without further argument."

Brahms gripped his upper lip with his lower, only beginning to understand: Bulow had carried Wagner in his head, Cosima in his heart, Liszt in his soul, only to be betrayed by all three at once. He was sensitive to slights as no other man, and with more right than any other man. He got up. "I have chosen a bad time. You are not in a good frame of mind. We will talk again later."

Bulow yanked open the door, sputtering. "I think not. Your presumption only mocks me further. You wrong me by failing even to acknowledge that you have wronged me." His hand trembled on the knob. "Even a baboon would understand that – but the great Johannes Brahms is, of course, no baboon."

Brahms nodded, walking through the door. "We will talk again."

Bulow slammed the door so hard it swung open again, and he choked on his words slamming it again.

"Nineteen! Twenty! I win, Doktor Brahms! I win! I counted twenty bears first!"

They had just turned onto Kramgasse where stood the fountain of the armored and helmeted bear on its hind legs, spear in one paw, shield in the other, sword strapped to its waist, mail around its shoulder, cub dawdling at its feet. "I concede, Hannachen. You are too quick for me. You win."

High on his shoulders, Johanna Widmann held his gypsy hat by its wide brim on her own head. "Heeheeheehee! I win! I win!"

A black Scottish terrier trotted obediently behind them, but at Johanna's excitement scampered around Brahms's feet. "Argos! Heel!"

Argos paid no attention. Brahms stopped; he might otherwise have tripped or stepped on Argos. Old arcaded stone houses with oriel windows, corner turrets, and window boxes overflowing with red and blue geraniums abutted the street. Ahead lay the Clock Tower. He lowered Johanna to the ground and led her across the cobbles to a bench. "Shall we wait here for the pappa of my Johanna?"

Johanna giggled; Doktor Brahms never tired of his joke, nor she of hearing it; he said he was going to marry her when she grew up. "All right, Doktor Brahms – but I won! I won! Did I not?"

"I have conceded already, Hannachen, have I not? But to make it more interesting, shall we extend our game to twenty-five?"

The city of Berne had been named for the first animal to be killed on a hunt when the colony had been settled, a bear, and the symbol was everywhere in evidence: on flags, walls, mugs, steins, souvenirs. There was no shortage of bears to be counted. The six-year-old girl smiled, dimples forming in her cheeks and chin. She had known about the armored bear and its cub, and she knew that four minutes before the clock struck the hour a jester would come out of its tower ringing bells in his hat, followed by a crowing rooster, a knight in gold armor, Father Time with scepter and hourglass – and a troop of bears playing drums and fifes. She grinned, nodding vigorously, blond pigtails flying, but spoke calmly, imagining he would not suspect. "All right."

They sat on the bench, Johanna's eyes on the clock, Brahms appearing to look around, fumbling for something in his pocket. For his second summer in Thun he had rented an entire floor: large rooms, a long verandah, in a brown house with green shutters and a red roof, perched on a hillside garlanded by villas, villages, vineyards, and wooded hills overlooking the River Aare pouring out of the Thunersee. The ancient castle was within walking distance, the Hotel Bellevue convenient for visitors, and mountains gleamed like diamonds in the distance. Weekends he visited Joseph Viktor Widmann, poet, playwright, critic, and journalist, a friend from his first visit to Switzerland when he had been struggling with the *Requiem* – from whom he borrowed books and with whom he attended operettas in the summer theater on the Schanzli. The train from Thun to Berne took less than an hour. He spoke quickly and calmly. "Nineteen, twenty, twenty-one, twenty-two, twenty-three, twenty-four, twenty-five! I win!"

Johanna turned from the clock to see he had pulled chocolate bears from his pocket, enough to win. Her fists flew to her mouth in protest. "Doktor Brahms! Na! You cheated! You cannot bring your own bears! That is cheating!"

He laid the chocolate bears between them. "Heeheeheehee! I win, I win, I win, I win!"

"You do not! You do not win! You cheated!"

"I did not! I won fair and square!"

"You did not!"

Passersby stared, but Brahms was accustomed to stares. He had augmented his striped flannel shirt with a dull grey shawl secured around his shoulders with a large safety pin – to guard against rain he said while wearing it on the sunniest days – but rain or shine his hat remained in his hand. His overcoat, the color of coffee, reached past his knees; his pants barely reached his ankles, but when his tailor had lengthened them he had cropped them himself – with shears. However his circumstances improved, his origins remained the same. He had come a long way, proud of the distance traveled, and could not understand why he needed to conceal it – and if clothes bespoke the man what better way to trumpet the distance? He had once been reduced to repairing tears in his pants with sealing wax, and his clothes remained his fist in the air, his finger in the face of respectability. "Sorry, little Hannachen, but you lose." He patted her cheek, slipping one bear into her pocket, scooping the rest off the bench and into his own pocket again.

Their squabble had attracted others. Johanna looked up as her friends approached, but they focused on Brahms.

"Good morning, Doktor Brahms!"

"Good morning, Doktor Brahms!"

"Aha, Wilhelm and Wilhemina, is it not?"

Both nodded and smiled, twins, blond, a year older than Johanna. They knelt to play with Argos jumping around them.

"And where is Konrad?"

"He is with his mamma – but he is just coming."

Brahms saw Konrad approach, darkhaired, the oldest friend.

The twins spoke simultaneously. "We want to play the game again, Doktor Brahms."

He laughed at their synchronization. "What game?"

Again they spoke together. "With the chocolates."

Brahms shook his head and clucked. "Such greedy children you are, I fear for your lives. Did your mamma not tell you that if you eat too many chocolates you will turn into little chocolate children yourselves – and then the ogre will eat you up?" He cocked his head in the direction of the Kindlifresserbrunnen, the Ogre Fountain on the Kornhausplatz: an ugly man in a purple helmet, hunched and gnarled, a child captive under one arm, another strapped to his back, two more in a barrel tied around his waist – and the head of yet another in his mouth.

The twins shook their heads together. Konrad had joined them. "That is just a fountain, Doktor Brahms. There are no such things as ogres."

"Please, Doktor Brahms, let us play the game?"

"Hmmm, well, all right, but do not say I did not warn you."

Johanna had peeled her chocolate bear out of its wrap, bitten off its head and popped the rest of it into her mouth at once. Brahms got up, fished another chocolate from his pocket and held it above his head. Johanna, Wilhelm, Wilhemina, and Konrad, bobbed around him, under his arm, jumping for the chocolate which he snatched continually out of their reach, somehow avoiding Argos jumping around their feet. How simple were the appetites of children, how easy to comprehend. How complicated his dealings with adults: Levi, Joachim, Bulow, none of whom spoke with him now – and women were no easier.

The Clock Tower's mechanism began to whir. Johanna divided her attention between the moving figures and Doktor Brahms. Another of her friends, Richard, grinned as he watched them bob for the chocolate. "Ha, my pappa is rich. He gives me what I want. I do not have to jump around like a hamster for a chocolate."

Brahms lowered his hand allowing Konrad to get the chocolate, and turned his attention to the new voice. "It is Richard, is it not?"

"Yes."

"Well, then, since you are so rich, shall I give you what rich children deserve?"

"What is that?"

Brahms shrugged. "A reward for not taking away chocolates from poor children?" Richard did not move. "Is it money?"

"If you do not come to me you will never find out – but I can assure you that you have earned it."

Richard approached and Brahms gripped him firmly by the shoulders. "There, now, you are right. Your pappa will give you what you want. I can only give you a nice pat on the cheek for being such a good boy." Brahms's pat was as sudden and hard as a slap.

Richard raised his hand to his reddening cheek and jerked his shoulders away, but Brahms held him long enough to administer a pat as well to the other cheek, just as hard.

Johanna was just as surprised as Richard, but her attention was drawn to her pappa who, finished with his shopping, approached with a bag. "Brahms! Why do you do that? Has he been a naughty boy?"

Brahms turned to greet Widmann. "Na, but he is a rich man's son. He said it himself. I am only giving him what he deserves, a nice pat on the cheek – since chocolates and money mean nothing to him." He released the boy who no longer grinned and left without a word.

Everything about Widmann was trim (hair, beard, person); his spectacles made his scholarly face yet more scholarly; but he was grinning. "I am glad he was not too rich for his own good."

Brahms scowled. "Ja, not too rich for his own good, maybe, but too rich for mine. The cheeks of poor children refresh me – but the cheeks of rich children hurt my hand." He appeared to give Widmann his full attention as they walked home again, but coins, sweets, and chocolates dribbled continually from his hand and the line of children following in their wake widened proportionately, Johanna giggling with pride for her generous Onkel Brahms.

ii

Karl Goldmark had the large brown eyes of a deer; his black hair sat in clouds on his head; his chin was bald, but a bushy moustache with thin waxed tips sat on his upper lip. "Did you know that I, too, have composed a violin concerto?" He had come with Hanslick and Kalbeck from Vienna to visit Brahms and been invited with Brahms and Hermine Spiess (visiting Berne) to the Widmann home for dinner. He sat on Hermine's right at the Widmann table.

Brahms, on Hermine's left, sniffing the aroma of fried potatoes and pork and sausage mixed with sauerkraut, poked her with his elbow. "But mine is better."

Hermine was no longer sure of her Johannes-passion. Some assumed they were engaged for the time they spent together and the performances she gave of his songs, but he made no overtures except to seek her company, though less frequently now than before. "But how can I tell? I have not heard Herr Goldmark's concerto."

"Ah, Herminchen! You lucky thing! We others are not so fortunate!"

Goldmark's eyes widened. He had not meant to boast and was nervous in company, particularly of vivacious young women and smug old composers, and often said things he later regretted. Surely Brahms could not imagine he meant to compare concertos. "Oh, but mine is not so very bad. It is not so very bad at all."

"Oh, but it is! Why else do you suppose I am honored with so many more orders than you?" As pleased as Brahms was with the honors he received, for the recognition and publicity if nothing else, he preferred to give the impression it made no difference (which it didn't to his work), but he knew Goldmark wore his orders less lightly – and Brahms had been decorated recently with Austria's highest honor, the Order of Leopold, while Goldmark still carried only the lesser Order of Franz Joseph.

Frau Widmann, sitting across from Brahms, looked at her husband at the head of the table. Kalbeck and Hanslick sat across from Hermine and Goldmark, Johanna at the foot of the table to Brahms's left. Goldmark reddened, but Brahms spoke in a louder voice made louder yet by the silence. "But I have a solution for you, Goldmark. Now that the kreutzer is no good, why do you not write a Heller Sonata? That will surely earn you more honors yet." Austrian currency was changing from gulden and kreutzers to kronen and hellers. Brahms laughed. "But, of course, a Heller Sonata would only be worth half as much."

The others kept silence. Widmann had noticed the difference in Brahms among his Viennese friends, his delight in baiting them. "But, Brahms, if Herr Goldmark writes a sonata it will surely be the Goldmark Sonata – and then, of course, it will be worth much more."

Brahms joined in the laughter, wishing only that Goldmark himself might have returned the wit. He made himself too easy a target, too tempting. Kalbeck, for all his size, was no different. Not even Hermine appeared as independent as when they had first met. He proposed a toast: "To Herminchen's future father-in-law."

The company seemed puzzled, none more than Hermine raising her eyebrows. Such were the remarks with which he baffled her, saying little, implying much, but guarding his thoughts like gold.

Brahms laughed again. He was surer of her than he had ever been, and tired of her for the same reason. She had become less interested in her career and her voice had begun to pall for the same reason. Elisabet had put it best: *The more easily she attains applause the more careless she becomes until her singing becomes mere sightreading. You should warn her, nice and – at bottom – serious girl that she is, against resting too long on her oars; but you would have to be very plain, indeed, because she has become too spoiled to take hints easily.* Brahms agreed with Elisabet, but did not trust himself to say the right words. He smiled, baring too many teeth, staring into her face. "She is wondering now whether Brahms has still got a father."

Hermine said nothing, turning from his gaze. He was no longer the Johannes she had known and seemed almost to hate her. In her consternation she toppled her wineglass. She jumped from her chair, darting glances between her hosts, seeming ready to cry. "Ach, I am so sorry! I am so sorry!"

Frau Widmann was immediately by her side, giving Brahms a harsh look. "It is all right, my dear. It is quite all right. Anyone might have done it."

Vreneli, the servant, brought a sponge and cloth. When the wine had been soaked and the space cleared Goldmark attempted to inject new cheer into the dinner. "This reminds me of the time we were dining at Countess Lehmann's and she tipped over her bottle of red wine. Do you remember, Kalbeck?"

Kalbeck buttered a slice of bread. "Of course. I was just thinking the same thing myself."

Hanslick nodded, smiling, fatter with the years and balder, but his moustache remained as thick, and his chin as clean though it had multiplied. "I have heard about the incident. It is a priceless story – if it is true."

Goldmark grinned. "It is true all right. We were both present, Kalbeck and I."

Johanna thumped a tiny fist on the table. "But what happened? What happened? Please, Herr Goldmark, will you not tell me?"

Everyone laughed. Frau Widmann smiled. "Johanna is afraid that if everybody has heard the story she will not get to hear it."

Goldmark smiled at Johanna. "Well, when the wine was spilled she rushed from the table, the countess, and she came back with a funnel and a sponge. Can you guess what she did next?"

"What?"

"She soaked the sponge with the spilled wine and funneled it back into the bottle!"

The table laughed. Johanna giggled. "She did not!"

"She most certainly did!"

"A countess!"

"And that was not all! When she saw us all staring at her, she said: 'Do not worry. This is, of course, my face sponge!'"

A raucous laugh burst from the table. Widmann shook his head. "People are so strange."

Brahms nodded knowingly. "And the nobility are the strangest of all."

Frau Widmann took another deep breath, glad her table appeared to have found its legs again. "Fraulein Spiess, whose songs do you like to sing the most – after Doktor Brahms's, of course."

"Oh, there is no doubt about it. I like to sing Schumann's," she looked sideways at Brahms, "and sometimes I like to sing Schumann's even before Doktor Brahms's."

Brahms was the first to laugh and the company relaxed again. Frau Widmann drew a deep breath, and exchanged a look with her husband, but frowned again almost at once at Johanna who was still laughing. "What is so very funny, Johanna? Why do you not share the joke with everyone?"

Johanna said nothing, but continued to laugh, looking at Brahms.

"Why do you not answer your mamma, Hannachen?"

She giggled again. "Doktor Brahms is feeding a sausage to Argos – with his own fork!"

Frau Widmann got up from her chair and came around the table. The tiny black dog sat on his haunches, tiny pink tongue hanging from his mouth. "Oh, Doktor Brahms! This is surely not necessary! You will only spoil him and he is spoiled enough already in this house."

Brahms smiled, bending down to feed Argos another sausage. "He is a good little Argos. You can trust dogs better than you can trust people, do you not think?"

"THE PLUM CAKE WAS GOOD, was it not?" Brahms was walking Hermine back to her hotel.

"You should know. You had four slices."

"You had three!"

She laughed. "It was good, was it not?"

Brahms smiled, taking her hand, squeezing as they walked. "Yes, it was good. Frau Widmann is a good cook. I especially like her rosti, but I do not know how she makes it so special."

"She bakes little bits of bacon and mixes it with the potatoes before frying. I know how to do it."

He looked at her, the soft round smiling white face, soft white neck, soft rounded shoulders, white flesh of her chest, dark cleft of her decolletage. "You?"

"Yes, me. Why? Do you not believe me?" She returned his look, but he looked ahead, and again she was unsure what it meant. He might have been shy, but he might also have been uninterested. He was Johannes Brahms, famous composer, some said the first composer in the world – but she was young and vivacious and beautiful. There were others as young and vivacious and beautiful, but they were not singers – but she could never be sure what he thought. She had to find out, and if he would not help her she would have to do it alone. She took his hand in both of hers and lowered her voice. "Johannes, I like it when we walk like this. I feel so … tender."

His hand remained limp in hers. She might have been talking to the street.

"Do you not also like it?"

His hand remained limp, his eyes on the street ahead. "Yes, I like it."

"How does it make you feel?"

"The same as what you said – tender."

"Na! In your own words."

"But you have already put the words in my mouth – and taken them out again."

He laughed and the mood was broken. Her voice rose in exasperation. "Johannes, will you never give me a straight answer? I never know what you are thinking." She pulled his fingers apart.

"Ow-oochh! You will break my fingers!"

He was joking, but she pulled his fingers apart more earnestly. "Why do you not say what is in your heart? Why do you not tell me what you think? Do I not make it easier for you when I … when I tell you how tender you make me feel? Do you imagine it is easy for me to say everything when I know so little about how you feel?"

"What should I say?"

"You should not ask me what you should say! You should tell me of your own accord! What you feel! What you think! What you wish with me! I have my pride. I cannot dawdle forever waiting for you to make up your mind about me." She held his fingers firmly apart.

"OWCHHH! I will never play the piano again if you keep that up – but, Herminchen, seriously, I do not know what you mean. Do we not enjoy each other's company? Do we not make each other happy?"

"I do not know. Do I make you happy?"

He looked ahead again. "The other night – I had a dream about you."

She squeezed his hand again, massaging his fingers. "Did you, really? What did you dream?"

"I dreamed that you had missed a whole bar's rest at a concert – and that you sang quarter notes instead of eighth notes."

She held the back of his hand to her cheek. "Ah, it is so very kind of you to put it that way, Johannes. It is so very kind of you only to dream that I am not musical. I have known it for a long time, and not only in my dreams – but in the manner of our performances we are not unalike."

Her cheek was soft and cool against his hand. His breath got deeper. "What do you mean?"

"You do not care either about the specifics of the music, Johannes, not the way you play the piano, as long as you get the broad outlines – and I find that quite satisfying for myself as well."

"But that is because I am a composer. If I were not a composer I would not play the piano. If I did not compose I would not perform – but you are a singer. What is your excuse?"

"I have none. Maybe I am not a singer, after all. Maybe I only have a pretty voice and that is all. I prefer to sing just for myself. It is so tedious to have to be perfect all the time, knowing there are people just waiting for you to hit the wrong note. I do not like that at all. When I am married I will sing for my husband alone – and a few close friends. What is the point of concerts after one is married?"

Brahms said nothing. She dropped his hand and he put it in his pocket. Music was no more for her than an entertainment, a way to make money, to gain the admiration of others – but music, by itself, meant nothing. She had broken a singing engagement once for another which had offered more money, leaving the first in the lurch. She was not serious about art, and if she were not serious about art she could never be serious about him – not as Clara was, nor as Elisabet about his music, nor even Amalie whom he had ignored since Hermine had become his liedersangerin.

All of Berlin had ignored Amalie since her divorce from Joachim, even Elisabet after a single visit during which she had found her lonely and disconsolate. Brahms obtained concert engagements for her, but otherwise kept his distance. Their friends pledged loyalty to her husband because she had betrayed the bond of family, initiating and driving the divorce against his will, the women more than the men. Hermine was a member of that very tribe of women, interested in kinder, kuche, and kirche – and nothing else. It was a conflict Brahms could not resolve: he wanted the respectability of marriage, but not the humdrum, not the waste; the comfort of the bourgeois life, but not with a bourgeoise.

Perhaps she was only young and marriage would compensate for her inadequacies, but those were chances he was unwilling to take, that marriage would change her – or him. The sight of her white neck made him tremble, to think it might so easily be his to caress – but his own neck prickled again with all the old fears. "Speak to me, Johannes. Say something. I get nervous when you are so silent."

"What should I say?"

She took a deep breath and shook her head. "So we are back again, I see. We have come all this way only to go back."

Her voice was much smaller. He imagined she might cry and stepped a little farther from her as they walked.

"I think, Doktor Brahms, I would prefer to walk the rest of the way to my hotel alone. I am sure I will be quite safe. Thank you for your concern."

Brahms shrugged. "If that is what you wish."

She waited, hoping he would take her hand again, insist on walking her home, but he seemed not to know what to do, awaiting direction, showing a boy's face in the fierce frame of a man's wild hair and beard. She jerked her face from his and walked quickly away.

She was barely out of sight before a man on a bicycle brushed past him from behind. Brahms jumped at the sound of the bell, shaking his fist at the retreating bicyclist. "Why do you not look where you are going, you stupid donkey?" Some said bicycles would cut the traffic of horses on the street and that they were cleaner, but he hated them for whooshing suddenly by during his early morning walks, disrupting the flow of his ideas. He hated also the ugly trampling motion of the riders, but returning to the Widmanns he knew he had been angry at more than the bicyclist. He was sure he would see Hermine again, less sure he would see her alone.

iii

The guide pointed toward the village hidden in the valley. "You may say it was not very sensible to call Grindelwald the Glacier Village, like naming your child after his worst feature – but it would have been even less sensible to call it the Ocean Village or the Desert Village, would it not?"

He had made the speech hundreds of times and evoked polite laughter as always though the party, including Brahms and Widmann, was breathless from the climb. Brahms swore under his breath. "I must be crazy, Widmann, to listen to you. I am no longer the godling I once was."

Widmann grinned and put Argos down. Brahms never failed to complain, his weight was no doubt a handicap, but they had climbed the Niesen together, walked from Kandestag to the Oeschinensee at the foot of the Blumlisalp, and he had enjoyed himself thoroughly. They had followed the guide for more than two hours up a steep ascent. From the Grosse Scheidegg, a high saddle in the Swiss Alps three thousand feet above Grindelwald, the village appeared tinier than they had imagined. Someone suggested they should have called it the Toy Village and there was more polite laughter.

The guide nodded. "That, too, my friend, has been suggested – and since Grindelwald is nestled between two glaciers they are called the Upper and Lower Glaciers."

The laughter was more strained. "In 1779, Goethe stood on the Upper Glacier. At the time both glaciers were moving toward the village – but retreated before it was too late. The villagers still believe it was an exorcism that halted their progress."

Someone said they were too modern to believe such hocuspocus anymore; someone else was not so sure, the medieval was sometimes better than the modern – the glaciers, after all, had retreated.

The guide gave them time to explore, but warned they would be leaving in thirty minutes. Brahms and Widmann checked their watches and set off down a path, Argos at their heels, but were stopped by a man from the party. "Excuse, please, gentlemen."

Brahms silenced Widmann, touching his wrist. "Yes?"

"I beg your pardon for interrupting your holiday, but all through the climb I could not help wondering if you were he of whom I was thinking – until I heard your friend call your name. Can it be?"

Brahms shook his head. "Alas, my friend, but it is not. I know of whom you are thinking – but, alas, he is my brother, not me – and, alas, he is far away in Hamburg, in Germany. I am so sorry."

The man smiled. "It is, indeed, a great pity, but never mind. I am glad, at least, that I asked. I hope you are enjoying your holiday."

Brahms said nothing, bowing his head, leading Widmann quickly away. Widmann shook his head. "Alas, my good friend, but you are going straight to hell – or are you truly your brother?"

Brahms shook his head. "Autograph hunters are the same everywhere – everywhere, shameless."

"But surely it is not too much to ask?"

"Not too much to ask, to make of me no more than a notch on the butt of a rifle? Am I to have no more chance than the Sioux?"

They had been discussing Custer's defeat at Little Big Horn the night before, Brahms strongly on the side of the Sioux though not with much hope for their future. Widmann shook his head. "It is not the same thing at all. A gunman kills to win his notch. Autograph hounds – well, at least, they admire you."

"Only enough to harrass me. What can my little scribble mean to them, really? They only want it to gain the envy of their friends – though why anyone should envy such a trifle I cannot understand."

"Some would still call it a mark of admiration."

"And some would sell their mothers for a sack of peas."

Widmann shrugged, keeping silent.

"Do you know what Hannachen said to me when I asked if she collected autographs?"

"What?"

"She said she collects only stamps! I told her she was a sensible girl."

They had reached a promontory and stopped to survey the panorama, the village cradled in the valley, wide meadows alongside, fields of maples and fruit trees. Closer at hand were sprinkled splotches of blue and white and pink and red and yellow, carnations, lilies, columbines, narcissi, buttercups, edelweiss. Beyond the village coniferous forests, beyond the forests the Kleine Scheidegg, another saddle though lower than the Grosse, and beyond the saddle the Eiger, Monch, and Jungfrau, snowcapped giants, heads in the clouds.

For a long while neither spoke, but stared at the peaks. Widmann was the first to look at his watch. "It is almost thirty minutes. We should be going back."

Brahms looked around. "Where is Argos?"

Widmann called. "Argos!"

There was no answer. Brahms joined in the calling. "ARGOS! COME ALONG! WE ARE GOING! AAAARR-GOOOOSS!!!!"

THE COMPANY WAS MELANCHOLY all weekend, Johanna continually in tears; the guide had been sorry, so had members of the party, but staying longer they would have been trapped by darkness. That had been Friday; on Monday, as always, Brahms was the first to wake, back from his walk before most of the others were out of bed. Widmann sat at the table nursing coffee as Brahms checked his brown leather satchel, books he was borrowing for the week, Stanley's *Africa*, Fenimore Cooper, Nietzsche.

It was six o'clock. Frau Widmann prepared breakfast with Vreneli in the kitchen. Brahms was fully dressed, but the Widmanns remained in nightshirts and robes.

"Did you hear that?"

Widmann looked at Brahms who appeared to be listening for something. "What?"

"That – like somebody scratching!"

Brahms opened the door and immediately fell to his knees. Widmann watched in alarm as he lurched forward with a whoop to grab something, but then smiled as he rolled onto his back. He held Argos high in his hands, lowering him for a kiss, almost licking the dog who could not lick him back enough. "Argos, you little scamp! You little darling!"

Frau Widmann and Vreneli rushed from the kitchen. Widmann stood up suddenly at the table. "JOHANNA! COME QUICKLY!"

Widmann joined Brahms still on his back on the floor, playing with Argos; his wife and Vreneli stood beaming; Johanna rushed into the room and commandeered Argos for herself. Vreneli rushed from the room for water and dog biscuits. Widmann shook his head in wonder. "He must have crossed the Scheidegg, run all the way to Interlaken, alongside the lake to Thun, and then all the way again to Berne! How did he do it?"

Brahms shook his head, no less amazed. "They are true, all those stories about animal instinct!"

Frau Widmann laughed. "Or maybe he took the train – like you?"

Billroth rose slowly from his piano bench, breathing heavily, attempting a smile for his guests, some of whom, setting aside cigars and cognac, continued to applaud. "Bravo, Herr Doktor!" "Encore!" He raised his goblet, shaking his head. "From me no more. You will get no more from me tonight." His face was unsmiling, his eyes were sunk in his face, as if even an attempt at gaiety were beyond him. His clothes sat loosely on his frame since he had lost stature. Pneumonia had transformed the air itself into a weight and breathing into an exercise. He raised his chin at Brahms. "Come, Brahms, will you be next? I am afraid I have tired myself out already."

Brahms raised his head, looking down his nose, down his cigar, at his friend before turning away. "Am I your jester to play at your command? Am I your performing animal?"

Billroth found Brahms the least sympathetic of his friends and himself losing patience with his friend, but smiled again. "Of course not, Brahms. You need do no more than you wish – as always."

From the way Brahms glared they might have been enemies, but Billroth was too concerned with his health and accustomed to Brahms's manners, what Elisabet rightly called his Prater manners, to see anything unusual in his behavior. If he had given Brahms cause he could not have said what it was, but he appeared to wear his unpleasantness with greater pride of late.

Brahms spoke ironically. "Well, then, since you put it so forcefully, I will perform. What will you have me play?"

Dr. Giebeler, a bird of a man, raised a hand on a toothpick wrist, his smile fragile and brittle as china, voice resonant as tin. "We should all be much obliged, Herr Doktor, if you will play your Rhapsody in G minor."

Brahms's laugh was a cackle. "If it is rhapsody you desire, it is rhapsody I will deliver."

Billroth grimaced. "Danke, my friend. We are much obliged."

Brahms lost his laugh and said nothing, still glaring at his friend as he took the bench. He had learned from Hanslick that Billroth had critiqued every new work of his in letters which ran five to six pages, and had requested to see some of the letters. Hanslick had pulled four immediately from his desk, realizing only later he should have been less precipitate. One of the letters contained a passage Brahms should never have seen. Among paragraphs flooded with praise for the music Billroth had written: *It is amazing the number of parallels to be made between*

Brahms and Beethoven – unfortunately, not all of them to their credit. Beethoven was often inconsiderate and harsh to his friends and so is Brahms. Beethoven never rid himself of the pernicious effects of a neglectful upbringing and it appears neither will our friend.

That Billroth might blame him for his shortcomings he could understand, but that he would blame his mamma and pappa he found unforgivable. He recalled with regret his confession to Billroth so many years ago about the dockside bars, recalled with fury Billroth's reluctance to meet his pappa during his Viennese visit understanding finally the reason, and recalled with renewed fury Billroth's mutilation of his manuscript for its signature – might as well mutilate a Rembrandt as an original manuscript. Such was this man – cultured, educated, intelligent, respected – who had seen fit to call him the product of a "neglectful upbringing." Hanslick was in despair that he had acted so carelessly with two good friends and swore him to silence. He had comforted Hanslick with Goethe's dictum: *Blessed is the man who can withdraw from the world without hatred.* He might once have been dismayed, but no longer. Dismay was a luxury for youth and he was long past his youth.

Seating himself at the piano he began to play, cigar clamped between his teeth, ash dribbling on his shirt, smiling at the puzzled countenances of his listeners attempting to follow the rhapsody through the fugue he had chosen to play instead. When he was finished he turned, his smile twisted to a sneer, seeming to challenge his audience to contradict him. Herr Grassberger asked in a tone made of a dozen broken pieces: "Herr Brahms, was that not Bach you just played?"

Brahms shrugged. "Ah! Bach, Offenbach! What does it matter, eh? One is the expanded form of the other, is it not so? But why not something by myself?"

Herr Grassberger's smile was no less an amalgam of a dozen broken pieces. "Of course, Doktor Brahms. We would be delighted."

Brahms laughed. "Of course, you would!" He played his rhapsody then, but only a fragment, launching into another fragment, following with yet another, completing nothing, continuing in the same vein through the evening, neither playing well nor giving up the piano. Billroth resolved never again to invite him to such a gathering, but wondered how he might have offended his friend.

ii

The restaurant at the Wildpretmarkt faced a street paved diagonally with bricks. It was lodged on the ground floor of a three-storeyed tenement building – but its name, RESTAURANT ROTHER IGEL, the Red Hedgehog, was embossed across the facade between the first and second storeys as if it occupied the entire building. The building was topped with dormers, wide entrance doors with Romanesque arches and tall mullioned windows graced the facade. It had two diningrooms, one more elegant frequented by the military and high officials of the city, but Brahms preferred the other, a long room with a bar along one long wall, long tables in a row along the other, a cavernous room more cavernous for clouds of smoke. It had become part of his routine. He rose early for a breakfast of coffee and pastries, worked through the morning, ate his midday meal at the Igel, walked in the Stadtpark, returned home to work, prepared sometimes for an evening (a concert or opera), and ate again at the Igel or a beer hall with friends.

Seated at one of his favorite meals, a beef pilaf with a glass of Hungarian Tokay (stocked in the cellar for his private consumption), a newspaper spread before him, he awaited Billroth who had said nothing more than that he wished to talk with him, but Brahms guessed what he might wish to discuss. No one knew better than himself how miserably he behaved, and no one understood his reasons better. He could not point to failure to account for his behavior, only success, but his success as a musician so outstripped his success as a man that he felt ignored by those who professed to know him best. The success of the man had been handicapped by the success of the musician. It was the way of the world to pave your path with either gold or mud, whichever you needed least. A single honor brought a dozen in its wake, but if the first steps were withheld the chasm loomed ahead.

Many were kind, but all saw in him something to exalt their own status. The man alone, the man without the musician, meant nothing, and that was a failure he could confess to no one without appearing ungrateful for the greatness thrust on him from all quarters of the globe. Such a cosseting kept him closeted in a world of one – but if the man were alone the musician was surrounded by men content to bask in reflected glory. Speaking his mind was no more than a variation on the theme of shearing his pants, and the more gratuitously he spoke his mind the better when dealing with people who should have known better themselves. Walking into the Igel he had seen Max Bruch who had sent him the manuscript of his oratorio, *Arminius*, for an appraisal. A hurdy-gurdy played outside and Brahms had shouted: "Listen, Bruch! That fellow has got hold of your *Arminius*!"

"Doktor Brahms?"

Brahms looked up from his newspaper. "Yes?"

A cleanshaven middleaged man smiled, dressed in new clothes. "I am Otto von Graber. My wife is a great admirer of yours. We have been married for only a month. She is sitting at the next table. She would be much obliged for a moment of your time."

"Your wife?"

"Yes, Doktor Brahms – and so, indeed, would I."

Brahms stared through clouds of smoke to the next table. A much younger woman fanned smoke from her face, dark eyes (peering over the fan) topped by a white forehead and black hair, an expensive white silk-covered umbrella furled on the table. She wore a highwaisted street dress in the American style, the skirt secured to reveal the double flounce of her petticoat and smart brown shoes, her chair turned from the table to reveal her finery. Not even fifteen years ago only the wealthiest could afford brown shoes, not to mention the laughter of commoners less in the know, chained to the tradition of black footwear. Brahms stared back at the man. "You would, would you, even in the middle of my meal?"

The man's smile broadened. "We would – indeed, we would."

Brahms mouthed another spoonful of pilaf, grains of rice falling into his beard which he dusted with his hand. Not for nothing had Richard Strauss called him

Lentils in his Beard. "Perhaps it would make a difference if I were to tell you I was expecting company?"

"We would be only a moment, Doktor Brahms?"

"You wish to see the prickly in the prickly, then, do you?"

The pun was lost on the man who continued to smile, nodding vigorously.

"Very well, then – but it will be at your peril."

"Danke, Doktor Brahms. You have no idea what this means to me – to us." The man beckoned his wife to join them. Brahms lifted his stein, watching her closely. She closed her fan with a flick of her wrist and appeared no less able to stop smiling than her husband as she approached. "My wife, Doktor Brahms, my recent bride – Gertrude von Graber."

Brahms nodded; Gertrude curtsied. "This is an honor, indeed, Doktor Brahms. I cannot tell you how much pleasure we derive from your songs."

Still her husband smiled. "My wife plays the piano, Doktor Brahms – and she has the loveliest singing voice. May we sit with you for just a moment?"

The woman had tiny features; her mouth was small, bright red; her nose almost Japanese; her face was white and round. Brahms stared through narrowed eyes, licking his lips clean, lifting his stein again, wiping his mouth with the back of his hand, drying his hand on his beard. "You wish to sit? Yes, of course!" He smiled. "So, you are newlyweds, yes?"

The couple nodded together, still smiling.

He looked at Graber. "What a feeling it must be, eh-eh, for a newlywed husband to bring home his newlywed wife, to insert the newlywed key into the newlywed lock – behind which he is to be tied forevermore to a newlywed person!"

Still Frau Graber smiled and her husband laughed. "I am that man, Doktor Brahms. I have taken that risk – such as it is."

Brahms's eyes pierced Gertrude. "As for me, I must say that I would not have risked it." He looked again at Graber. "Who can know, after all, what he is marrying?"

Brahms noted, not without satisfaction, finally, the strain in the smiles glued to their faces. Graber nodded placatingly. "But that is life, is it not, Doktor Brahms? Who can know, after all, what lies in store – but face it we must."

"Yes, life we must face – but in marriage we have a choice, do we not?"

"But we have a choice in life as well, Doktor Brahms. We choose, do we not, at every moment, whether or not we wish to live or die?"

"Yes, indeed, Herr Graber, we have a choice – to be or not to be, and all that – but only in choosing to end it, not in choosing to begin. As for myself, you see, I have, unfortunately, never married – and, thank God, I am still single." He winked at Gertrude whose smile had turned to a thin red line.

Graber laughed, but his mouth stiffened. "My wife wished to be a concert pianist, Doktor Brahms – like yourself. She has given many concerts already – but she never meant to pursue a career once she was married. She is not one of those women who put themselves before their husbands."

"That is a blessing, indeed, is it not? I am reminded of a joke about a woman who came from a musical family. It was said her pappa played the tuba – and her mamma looked like one." He laughed, looking at Gertrude, leaning forward, forcing her to lean back. "You see, it is enough for the daughter to be pretty – that is how she hooks her husband – but sooner or later the daughter is bound to look like her mamma." He leaned back and looked at Graber. "Now, that is a good joke, is it not, if all that he has seen in her is her pretty face?"

Graber did not bother to laugh.

"Ah, here comes my friend." Billroth had appeared at the door, gazing without focus, lost as a child in a forest. Brahms felt a perverse satisfaction that Billroth no longer commanded a room with his entrance. "Billroth! Over here!"

Graber got up. "Unfortunately, Doktor Brahms, we must be leaving. We wished to bother you for but a moment."

"And now that you have bothered me for more than a moment, do you not wish to stay?"

Gertrude stood by her husband, their smiles reduced to dots, brows wrinkled like bark, eyes squinting, hands fluttering. "We have an engagement, Doktor Brahms. Thank you for your kindness, but we must go."

Billroth's smile as he joined Brahms was no more convincing than that of the Grabers.

BRAHMS SAT WITH BILLROTH on a bench alongside a walk in the Stadtpark amid hedgerows tall enough to ensure privacy. Lilacs scented the air; chestnut blossoms of pink and white festooned the trees. The clop of hooves and whirr of wheels was blanketed by the chirrup of birds and rustle of animals in the bushes. "Are you sure you do not want to keep on walking, Billroth? I know I would prefer it."

Billroth spoke slowly. "Yes, old friend, I am quite sure. I no longer walk as easily as I once did. I am no longer the man I once was."

Brahms burped, leaned back, and looked ahead. "As to that, which one of us can say he is. What we must do is look ahead, not back."

"Yes, of course, you are right – but … Brahms?"

"Yes?"

"I would like to tell you something?"

Billroth spoke deferentially, not the Billroth of old. "Yes?"

Billroth took a deep breath, gently rubbing his chest. "Do you know – when my illness struck I had the feeling I might not see you again. I sent my last greetings to you through Hanslick, as you know, since there was no direct communication with you at the time."

Brahms nodded. He had been in Thun, but not bothered with condolences even later.

"I thanked you for the great beauty you have brought into my life. My dear friend, without your creations my life would have been so very much the poorer, and I mean that from the bottom of my heart."

"Billroth, you must not get sentimental. There is no need. Our friendship has always been mutual. Otherwise, it would have been no friendship."

Billroth raised his hand. "Please, Brahms. Let me finish."

Brahms grunted.

"Now, those days are like a dream, all behind me – but during that time, in my not unpleasant halfsleep, like every physician observing himself, I noted how shallow was my breath, how my spirit wandered. I remember it clearly, I spoke the words of one of your songs: *It is to me as if I had died already.* I moved among the clouds, everything was mild and quite beautiful, and I saw my friends so quiet and friendly below me."

Brahms watched a squirrel, following its antics through the boughs of a chestnut.

"I beg of you, Brahms, whatever you think of this, to hear me out."

Brahms kept his eye on the squirrel. "I am listening."

"Danke. I am sorry if I am being presumptuous."

Brahms said nothing, but kept his eye on the squirrel.

"Very well, then. I was shaken suddenly and made to sit up. I was commanded, like a soldier, to breathe, and to swallow all kinds of liquids. I begged them to leave me alone, I had felt so good, I wanted to die, but it was no use. So many voices told me continually what to do – and finally the voice of my wife rose above the rest, begging me to do as I was told for the sake of the children." He paused, took a deeper breath again, and rubbed his chest. Brahms appeared still disinterested. "That is all I wished to say. The rest, you know."

Brahms burped again.

"I cannot say as yet I am fully alive. You know how it is, a life without doing something, without work, is no life – but for the present I can do nothing else. I still have a great compression on my chest, my lungs are still not in good condition – but I am confident that by the autumn I will be able to work again."

Still Brahms said nothing.

Billroth recalled the days when a new composition by Brahms would fill not only himself with joy, but everyone he met; even his surgery improved. He regarded the quartets, of which he had been the dedicatee, among the proudest moments of his life. "You may not believe this, my friend, but of late I have grown lonelier than usual. Work has always been my solace … and I do not have that at present. My wife … has never understood that … and my children … well, they are children. I do not expect them to understand. They cannot understand."

Brahms drew a deep breath. He understood loneliness better than anyone. He had been lonely since he had lost Clara long years ago, he could call it nothing else. Then he had lost Levi, then he had lost Joachim. Bulow was in Vienna again, performing the complete cycle of Beethoven sonatas, but neither had written nor spoken to the other during the year following their quarrel – and now Billroth. They were still friends, but without intimacy. "Billroth, you know that I am no stranger to loneliness myself, but neither is it a subject that bears discussion. It is just another thing that has to be borne."

Billroth had always pardoned his friend's shortcomings, related them to his upbringing, but for a long time now the old intimacy had slipped beyond reach – it seemed forever. His face shriveled; Brahms thought he might cry. "Tell me, then, my friend, how I have wounded you – for I have wounded you, of that I am sure. Can you not tell me?"

Brahms recalled Billroth's many kindnesses, his long friendship, unstinting loyalty, and considered unburdening himself of his anger regarding the mutilated autograph – but how unburden himself of the letter to Hanslick when he had promised Hanslick his silence, of the insult to his pappa for whom Billroth had never had a kind word in all their years of friendship, a simple goodhearted man whom he had emphatically avoided during his visit to Vienna blaming him for his son's "neglectful upbringing"? Forced to choose between two masters Brahms chose his pappa who had never thought ill of anyone and died a happier man than he and Billroth had become despite their many advantages. "You are getting old and foolish, Billroth. Your imagination is too morbid for a man of your *grand* upbringing. I am not such a child as to imagine wounds where there are none."

The words were resentful, but not without regret. If Billroth had looked he would have seen Brahms's eyes swelling with dampness, he would have seen him turn his head to hide his eyes, he would have seen him choking as if on air – but he had turned his own head, unable to hear the hateful sentiments, unable to look at his old friend, unable himself to say more.

LATER IN THE DAY, late into the night, Brahms and Bulow walked arm in arm through the Prater. Around them swirled the nightlife: music from the roundabout, explosions from the bowling alley and shooting range, laughter from the comic revue, hawkers selling wine, beer, lemonade, ices. It was too noisy for conversation, but they had talked for an hour already at the Igel. If the girl had not tapped Brahms on his shoulder he would not have heard her. "Herr Doktor?"

"Yes?" Brahms turned his head, still arm in arm with Bulow, and smiled when he recognized the girl. "Constanze?"

The girl smiled hearing her name, a tentative smile. She was barely twenty, but it was difficult to tell: her face was painted the color of paprika, her lips purplish, her hair a shade of pink, the bodice of her red dress cut low enough to reveal she wore nothing underneath. "Herr Doktor, I was wondering …"

Brahms disengaged his arm from Bulow's and dug into his pocket. "You were wondering – of course, of course! How much?"

"Two gulden?"

Brahms thrust coins into her hand, five gulden. "Take it. Take it. You deserve so much more – so much better."

Constanze looked at the money in her hand, her smile widening to that of a girl at Christmas. "Danke, Herr Doktor. Danke schon. I will remember this next time." She kissed his cheek, squeezed his arm, and was gone.

"She is your friend, yes?"

Brahms turned back to Bulow, his face redder than usual. He was tempted to defend himself: there was, at least, no hypocrisy about his relations with Constanze, unlike the hypocrisies that multiplied between married couples. Constanze and others like her, unlike wives, delivered what they promised making no demands, but he let it go. Bulow had remarried and long paid dues enough for a hundred bad marriages; more importantly, they had renewed their friendship and he had no wish to let it founder again. He spoke simply: "She is a good girl."

Bulow merely nodded, more suprised by Brahms's embarrassment than his acquaintance. "Of course, she is – and if she is not, it is not my business – it is no one's business."

The color remained in Brahms's face, his voice rose. He could not face his friend. "I want you to know something, Bulow. I have never made a married woman or a fraulein unhappy. I have never broken up a household nor treated girls from good families with disrespect. I just want you to know that." It was true: women from the best families offered themselves, some of them married, in letters and in person, throughout the country and beyond; girls half his age offered proposals, walks in the Prater, visits to his rooms, whatever he wished, and continued to do so; he accepted none of their offers, but could not explain it to Bulow, hardly understanding it himself.

Bulow remembered the maidservant in the palace of the Duke of Meiningen whom Brahms had summoned with the dinner bell. There was much he did not understand, a man of Brahms's stature consorting with servants and women like Constanze, but it mattered little. Wishing only to comfort his newfound friend he took his arm again. "That is to your credit, my friend. Were there more in the world like you, mine would have been a happier life. What is it to me what you do if it makes you happy?"

Brahms glanced quickly at Bulow who appeared already to have forgotten the incident. He noted also that Bulow stared ahead as if to change the subject, noted as well that Bulow was almost tearful again. He sighed, nodded, and fell back in step with his friend. He had left his card at Bulow's hotel on which he had scribbled a musical phrase from Mozart's *Zauberflote* and Bulow had rushed to Karlsgasse in tears, and from Karlsgasse to the Igel where he had found Brahms. He had recognized the phrase immediately and supplied the words from memory: *Dear One, shall I see you no more?*

"Madam?"

"Yes, Solange? What is it?"

"Madam, the tailor wishes to see you."

"What does he wish to see me about?"

"He did not say, madam."

"Did you not ask him?"

"I did, madam, but he would not say."

"Did you not give him the bread and soup?"

"I did, madam, but he still wishes to see you."

Maria Fellinger finally looked up from her painting. "Oh, very well, tell him I will be with him soon."

"Yes, madam." Solange left the room. Frau Fellinger added a few more strokes to an apple before setting down her brush and following Solange into the kitchen. The Fellingers had come to Vienna from Berlin more than a year ago, old friends of Clara, new friends of Brahms, Richard Fellinger a general manager at Siemens and Halske, Maria a painter and photographer, both large blond North Germans in their middle thirties. Maria's mother, a composer, had been admired by Mendelssohn; her father, a professor at Tubingen, had written poems which Brahms had set to music. They had two sons, Richard and Robert.

Frau Fellinger liked the tailor's work, but he was old, hard of hearing, and tried her patience though she did not show it – but a surprise greeted her in the kitchen. It was not the tailor she saw sitting in his customary chair, dipping a roll of dry bread in the hot soup. "Brahms!"

Brahms looked up, soggy bread in hand, beard stained with soup. "Frau Fellinger, how is it with you?"

"Is this one of your jokes, Doktor Brahms?"

"No."

"What are you doing here?"

Brahms cocked his head toward Solange. "You should ask her. She brought me here."

Solange's eyes widened, one hand flew to her mouth. "Madam, but you told me to bring him here."

"There! You see?"

Frau Fellinger laughed. "She is new. She does not know all our friends. I was expecting the old tailor and told her to take him to the kitchen. Let us go to the sittingroom."

"But I have not finished the soup."

"Bring it with you and let us go to the diningroom."

Brahms followed Frau Fellinger to the diningroom, bowl in one hand, breadroll in the other, pleased with his joke. During his first Christmas with the family they had piled his gift table with toilet accessories: candlesticks before a burnished mirror; a black silk necktie pinned to a pincushion; something labeled "Finest Perfume" wrapped in pink, tied with a blue ribbon, placed beside a covered breadbasket – and packets of writing paper. He had paced the room, stroking his beard in silence, watching the family open their gifts, hating to think of the false thanks he would soon have to profess, when Frau Fellinger had inquired: "Will you not look at your own gifts, Doktor Brahms?"

He had stood mute before his table, pouncing finally on the packets of writing paper. "Ha! This is mine! This is for me!"

"But they are all for you, Doktor Brahms – everything on the table."

"But surely these must be for you? Surely, these cannot be for me?"

"But why do you say that? Just look at your things. Do you not like perfume?"

He had picked up the perfume to find it contained bars of unscented soap, the only kind he used. Gift by gift the deception was uncovered: the candlesticks were milkjugs, the mirror was a nickelplated coffee tray, the pincushion a sugar basin, the breadbasket contained a clothesbrush and his favorite quills.

He often invited himself to Sunday dinner at the Fellingers, they knew what he liked, Frau Fellinger even knitted him socks and neckties. She sat in her usual chair, he across from her. "Now tell me. To what do I owe this unexpected pleasure?"

Brahms made one last sweep of the bowl with the bread and spoke with his mouth full. "In short, Frau Fellinger: you were right, I was wrong, I am ready to do what you say."

Frau Ludovika Vogl, the last member of the family subletting his rooms, subletting even his furniture, had died, leaving him with three options – finding new rooms, taking his chances with the new renter, or renting the whole flat directly from the landlord – none of which appealed to him. He had remained an itinerant, but made 4 Karlsgasse his base for fourteen years, and now he found himself the sole inhabitant of nine rooms, much the larger for being unfurnished. News of his predicament had spread not only through Vienna, but Europe. He had received offers from widows and spinsters all the way from Constantinople to be his housekeeper, happily to make his bed.

During his last summer in Thun, Frau Fellinger had put his things in order and tidied his drawers, listing the contents of each on a sheet of cardboard. Her husband had taken the opportunity to install electric lights. Brahms, insisting he needed no more than a bed and washstand, had consented finally to curtains – but only in the sittingroom.

Friends had contributed furniture since he refused to buy his own. The less a bachelor possessed, the less effort went into caring for possessions and the more time he had for himself. He wanted no one else in the flat, he could open the door to his own visitors – and the old Hausmeisterin, who occupied a room in the courtyard, who cleaned the staircases and lobbies, could manage his cleaning as well. Frau Fellinger had contested his wishes – in vain, until her last visit. She had lifted a cushion raising a cloud of dust, sat on the couch raising another, slapped the couch raising more clouds, and left without a word – but now she raised her eyebrows. "Do you mean about your situation?"

He nodded. "You were right. I was wrong. There, I have said it again. You know how I am. I do not like to be disturbed, I do not like my things to be disturbed – but I need my things clean, I need my things dusted."

Frau Fellinger nodded, knowing him better than he imagined. He was being pliant now only to justify the stubbornness she knew would follow when he rejected everyone she sent, proving her wrong, himself right, but she wished to help him despite himself, rescue him from his worse instincts. "I will see what I can do, Doktor Brahms."

He grinned. "Danke. Now, is there any more of the good soup?"

ii

Brahms answered his door on the third ring. It was the fifth time he had been disturbed that morning. A buxom woman stood before him, her face pale, paler for eyes of grey – and plain, plainer for her plain black dress, plain black hat – a serious face, plump but not fat, her hair drawn in a bun revealing tiny ears. "Yes?"

"I have come to see the flat."

"What?"

"I understand there is a flat to let. I have come to see it."

He gave no indication that she should enter, but continued to stare.

The woman remained calm. Frau Fellinger had warned her not to appear eager. Brahms worked in contrary motion. He would want her most if she seemed not to want the rooms at all. She spoke in a confident tone. "But perhaps it is not to let?"

Brahms said nothing until the woman appeared ready to turn around, then nodded. "Yes, this is the place."

The woman's face remained impassive. "My name is Celestine Truxa. Frau Fellinger has mentioned the circumstances. I thought the flat might suit me."

Brahms let her in and showed her the place.

"My husband was a journalist, Doktor Brahms. He died recently."

"I am sorry to hear it, madam."

She shook her head, she was not looking for pity, just telling him about herself. "I only mention it to let you know why I prefer to move to a new location. I have two boys and an old aunt who stay with me. I daresay the flat is just the right size for us with one boarder. Indeed, if you choose not to stay I will have to find another boarder – but that, of course, is up to you."

Brahms said nothing, but was glad she was considering other boarders, his celebrity appeared not to play a part in the choice.

"Perhaps you will consider the matter, Doktor Brahms, and send me a communication should you wish to pursue the matter further. I stay on the Schwarzpanierstrasse." She gave him her card. "If I hear nothing more from you, I will consider the matter closed."

A week later Frau Truxa's maid announced a gentleman awaiting her in the sittingroom. When she went to greet her visitor she found Brahms on his knees measuring her couch with a tape. He got up smiling. "It appears your things will fit."

FRAU TRUXA SOON LEARNED that Doktor Brahms expected others to read his mind and made his mind her study. Asked why he rearranged his things from the laundress after they had been placed in the drawer he had replied: "It is better, is it not, that the items sent last should be at the bottom so that they are all worn alike?" She had instructed the laundress to arrange the clothes as he liked, but realized he would never have told her himself. The maid had complained once in tears that Doktor Brahms was no longer friendly and refused to greet her when they met. Frau Truxa noticed that she left the waste basket shut after she had emptied it though it was always open on her arrival and suggested she leave it open. The next day the maid beamed: "Doktor Brahms greets me again!"

Frau Truxa came to understand him better even than Clara. He was pleased by the attentions of others when they gave it unasked, but he could not tell them what he wanted – and if they could not tell what he wanted without being told he grew sarcastic or silent. If a glove or sock needed mending he would leave it on top of a drawer apparently left open by accident; and Frau Truxa did what was needed without a word being said. She never had a more congenial boarder; he occupied his rooms only during winter, and preferred even then to be left alone.

Clara was miserable: it was difficult growing old, more so for traveling musicians than for most. Travel had grown progressively easier, heated trains were preferable to the cold carriages of yesteryear, rails smoother than the mudpaths which had passed for roads during her girlhood, but she could never be sure of the temperature of the rooms, the quality of the pianos, orchestras, and conductors, nor for that matter when her rheumatism would become inflamed, or her hearing undependable. The balm for the many ills of age were friends, the old more than the new for the comfort of long acquaintance, but for all the years she had known Johannes, practically since boyhood, he remained a mystery. She found him constantly in a temper, angry for no reason it seemed other than that he breathed – worse, he seemed almost to hate her. She knew it was not so, it was his temperament and she didn't take it personally, but it made friendship a trial, and she was miserable seeing the black moods that had developed from such golden beginnings.

She found him fiercer sitting than standing because they were the same height, and she sometimes taller depending on what shoes she wore, but seated his head dominated her perceptions, his tangled beard glimmering now with silver, moustaches winged again with silver, head larger for the beard, face smaller, eyes narrowing to slits, forehead wrinkling into a fist. They sat at a table in her hotel room at the Deutsches Haus in Baden-Baden, two boxes of their letters between them. He pushed his box almost toppling it into her lap, but she put a proprietary hand over her own. "You seem angry, Johannes. You must tell me what is troubling you if that is indeed the case."

"If you do not know, I cannot tell you." His voice, never deep, seemed more ominous for its pitch when he was angry, as if he were piqued at its pitch as much as anything else, a small man unable to get the attention of a larger – but getting attention was the least of his problems. He was now the lion of German music, in appearance as much as reputation, but his speech and actions proclaimed him the most petty of lions.

She sighed, shaking her head in exasperation. "I do not understand why it is always thus with you – why we cannot have more plainspeaking between us. If I do not know, there is all the more reason for you to tell me. Why can you not simply tell me?"

"I cannot."

"Why not?"

"Because yours would be an insulting question – if I chose to answer it."

In a different context she might have laughed, but it had been too long since she had laughed in his presence. She turned her attention instead to her box with a tender look. "Johannes, it was such a pleasure to read your old letters again – but such a melancholy pleasure. I felt as if I were taking my leave of you."

Brahms felt not unlike Clara, but he was not the one requesting his letters back. Taking her letters back she was not just taking her leave as she said, but taking back what meant more to him than it could possibly mean to anyone else, even to Clara, as if they were indiscretions to be hidden – but held against her wishes the letters meant nothing. He pushed his box forward again. "It was your idea, was it not, that we exchange them?"

She knew he wanted his own letters back no less than she wanted hers, guarding his privacy no less than she, but she was no less willing than he to admit what they both wanted. The recent deaths of Liszt and Jenny Lind, raising concerns about her own mortality, had persuaded her to remind him of their decision, years before, to exchange their letters. Death was unpredictable: Liszt had died during the second Bayreuth Festival, organized by Cosima, but she had not allowed her father's death to disrupt her dead husband's festival, neither canceling receptions at their home, nor lowering the flag at the theater, nor spending time with her dying father, nor allowing others to his bedside. Her father's dying word, so she said, had been *Tristan*. Her allegiance was clear: when Wagner had died in her arms, twitching and trembling from the last of his series of heart attacks, she had held his cooling stiffening body for a whole day, whispering endearments. Clara spoke with a tremor. "Yes, it was my idea, and I believe we are doing the right thing. There are some things in the letters which are no one's business but our own – as you very well know."

She meant the letters concerning Robert in Endenich, which he understood, but the same letters contained the full swollen orchid of their once undying love, and that he understood less. She had also wanted to keep her favorite letters to which he had agreed.

"Johannes, you need not take it so personally. You know Hartel has been pestering me for all the letters I can find about Robert, and you know how opposed I am to publishing any of the letters from that time. I certainly do not wish to provide the means for their publication. I am omitting one of Joachim's letters for the same reason."

He resented the implication that their correspondence was no different from her correspondence with Joachim, the implication that the letters regarding Robert had anything to do with the time of their great passion, their orgy of denial, but he said nothing.

"Unfortunately, many of these Endenich letters say exactly what I would wish to see published about you. You were so kind then, Johannes, so considerate of our needs, Robert's and mine – and the children's – but that is no less evident in Robert's letters to Joachim."

She had skirted entirely the points of difference between himself and Joachim, implied he was no longer considerate, but he did not argue. Clara suffered enough, most recently through Ferdinand, dying now of the morphine addiction induced by the doctors; she had accepted responsibility for the care of his wife and five children.

"It would be a shame, Johannes, if you were simply to destroy your letters. You should think about compiling a kind of diary from them. They contain the whole of your career – and there are so many remarks and opinions that a biographer would find invaluable."

Brahms's concern about his letters was not much different from Clara's: Fritz, his younger brother, was dead; Billroth remained a phantom of his former self; Ferdinand and Herzogenberg lay in the same hospital, both younger men, both ill, both with little hope.

Clara raised her eyebrows. "You are thinking about Herzogenberg, are you not?"

"Among other things."

"You should never have written such a letter, Johannes."

"What should I have written? I wrote as diplomatically as I could – that I approached his things with a great deal of care, that I was vastly entertained by his skill. Should I have said I loved his work when I did not?"

"Under the circumstances, would that have been such a terrible thing?"

Herzogenberg's sickness had begun with his wife's. Elisabet had developed a persistent cough, an inflammation in her throat, which the doctors said would affect her heart were it to become permanent, for which they had visited her sister in Florence for the spring – but the weather had been icy, the stone floors cold, the little alleys drafty, and Herzogenberg had developed an attack of rheumatism relegating him first to bed, then crutches.

Brahms had followed his critical letter with a letter of regret: *It would be such a consolation if you were to write just a line to say that you took my words for idle chatter and nothing else. We have all sinned and fallen short of the glory of God!*

Elisabet had replied: *We are glad to have either your grumblings or your flattery, and when you combine the two as you have sometimes done Heinrich is the first to say "God bless you!" Naturally, he would have been pleased, poor devil! had you been able to say of even one movement: "I like that!" But these are the remarks a wife makes, who alone has the right to make them. He sends you many thanks for your kind letter.*

Brahms shook his head. "They know how I feel. They should not continue to ask me what I think. If I am diplomatic they do not understand – but if I am direct they are upset."

"It seems to me, from Frau Herzogenberg's letter, that you are more upset than they."

For reply he shoved his box of letters forward again, but she hesitated to make the exchange, afraid he meant to destroy his letters without looking at them. She was excited about rereading her letters – but no less excited that Johannes was in Baden-Baden to meet Joachim again after so many years, and imagined him no less nervous himself, accounting for his prickliness – but Johannes no longer needed such an accounting: prickliness had become his nature.

"Johannes, I am so very afraid you mean to destroy the letters. Will you not promise me, at least, to look through them first?"

Clara was right to assume Brahms was concerned about the meeting with Joachim. He still believed he had been right about Amalie, but wished to patch up their quarrel. Joachim had continually performed his works during their time apart, praised his Fourth so perceptively that Brahms had written: *Praise and sympathy such as yours are not only gratifying, but necessary. It is as though one had to wait for them for permission to enjoy one's own work!* Next he had sent a draft of the Violin Sonata in A major, composed at Thun. He had incorporated the melody of his song, "Komm bald," Come Soon, into the harmony of the sonata, hoping to draw Joachim back as he had drawn Bulow with another reference at another time, but Joachim had not responded.

Finally, he had devised the Double Concerto, for violin and cello, and engaged again Joachim's technical expertise: *Be prepared for a shock. I tried to resist, but the impulse to write a concerto for violin and cello proved too strong. It is a matter of indifference to me, however, except regarding how you will react. Most of all, I ask you, in all friendship, to be frank. If you send me a postcard saying simply, "not for me," I will understand. Otherwise, however, I will proceed with further questions: Do you want to see a copy? Would you and Hausmann take the trouble of examining the playability of the solo parts? Would you consider trying the work somewhere with Hausmann and myself at the piano? Would you rehearse it in some city with an orchestra and ourselves? I would ask more – but, well, maybe you will write the above-mentioned postcard even after seeing the score. I will not say explicitly what I am hoping and wishing, but give my best to Hausmann.*

Brahms reached across the table and grabbed the box. "They are my letters to do with as I wish – and by your own wish. You have no right to make demands."

His tone was so hostile her breath caught in her throat and she sputtered as she spoke. "It is no demand I make, Johannes. God knows, I have never made demands of you. It is only a request – indeed, you may take it as no more than a suggestion – and I hope you will consider it when you are in a more peaceable frame of mind."

She turned aside her head and took the box he had brought to the bedroom, not without difficulty (she was now sixty-eight years), but not before he had seen that she was crying. He wished he had been less brusque, but pretended not to notice.

ii

Robert Hausmann was the cellist in Joachim's quartet. He and Joachim played as well as possible during the rehearsal with Brahms at the piano, but Clara could not understand how a composer could so maltreat his own work, reducing it to chaos. Joachim and Hausmann barely made up for his banging. Besides, her hearing had deteriorated almost as much as Johannes's playing. She could no longer distinguish harmonies which followed in quick succession unless she was familiar with the work. Worse, she sometimes heard notes different from the ones played. There were harsh passages in the work which could easily be altered, but she said nothing. Johannes no longer heeded what she said and seemed almost to delight in dampening the enjoyment of his listeners.

As always, Brahms solicited Joachim's advice, but kept his own counsel. He wished to be aware of alternatives, but found his own solutions best. Joachim proclaimed the Double Concerto not among his happier inspirations, but Clara was glad the friends were talking again. That had always been the greater purpose of the piece, and though their relations were barely more than cordial Brahms sent Joachim a copy of the printed score with an inscription: *to him, for whom it was written.* He said later to Clara: "I know, finally, what has been missing these past few years of my life – the sound of Joachim's violin." Clara breathed more easily; she could see the smile on his face; better yet, she could hear it in his voice.

CLARA READ HER LETTERS, feeding them one by one to the fire. The facts were already related in her diary – but Marie interrupted her, convincing her to save what yet remained. Brahms saved some letters, as Clara had suggested, and threw the rest, boxed and ribboned, into the Rhine.

PART EIGHT

CLARA AND BRAHMS

Piotr Ilyich Tchaikovsky had embarked on his first major tour as a conductor on 27 December, 1887, his first engagement to be at the Leipzig Gewandhaus, and he had taken the opportunity to visit Berlin to renew his acquaintance with Desiree Artot. He had been infatuated enough once with the Belgian soprano's voice to pursue a more personal commitment: his first serious effort to fend off homosexuality. Rumors had arisen, not without reason, of their impending marriage – but he had been dissuaded by friends. He was too young for her; he was unable to provide; marriage to a famous woman was humiliating for the husband. She had married a Spanish baritone within a month of the rumors, offering Tchaikovsky no explanation, making humiliation still his ration. He had been devastated, and on her return to the Moscow stage had cried through her performance in one of the stalls – but that had been twenty years ago. He had subsequently made his own name, and the affair had not been to his regret for they had become better friends than they might otherwise have been.

It was now 1 January, 1888, a new year and a new world, and he marveled as he headed for the Brodsky residence for dinner. He had agreed to talk with Brodsky in Leipzig over the telephone from Berlin. They had set a time for both parties in telephone offices in the two cities. Considering the distance Tchaikovsky's heart had thumped violently and he had excused himself almost at once. "Dear friend, please let me go. I feel so nervous."

Brodsky's wife, Anna, had said later that her husband had looked forward to a chat with his friend, and though Brodsky had put up no resistance Tchaikovsky had wondered about his choice of words. "I have not got you by the buttonhole. You can go when you please."

Looking back on the incident he found the telephone nothing short of miraculous, and if he had offended his friend he meant to make it up. He had stopped in Leipzig on Christmas Eve on his way to Berlin and could not have been more comfortable than at the Brodsky home, a Russian among Russians in a strange land, a home away from home. He had hugged and kissed everyone from the first greeting as if he had known them for years, and they had spoken unreservedly of intimate matters forgetting his celebrity, their trust padding his comfort.

Adolf Brodsky had championed his violin concerto in Vienna after the first dedicatees, Kotek and Auer, confessed themselves defeated by its difficulties, and he had acquitted himself splendidly, receiving deserved praise – but for his virility, not for the concerto. The difficulties were formidable, even Brodsky had protested, but he had mastered them and continued to perform the concerto, giving mightier wings yet to Tchaikovsky's reputation. He could forgive the critics, many of whom had been unforgiving, they had a job to do, but Eduard Hanslick's viciousness had been a matter apart. There were paintings so lewd, Hanslick had written, that you could see the stink – but never before had music been composed so lewd that you could *hear* the stink! He should not have been surprised: Hanslick recognized genius in Brahms, but he found Brahms dry, chaotic, meaningless – a selfconscious mediocrity. He had been consoled by friends: Hanslick didn't like nationalistic music, but the Five, the Russian nationalists (Balakirev, Cui, Mussorgsky, Rimsky, and Borodin) shunned him for his internationalism.

Turning the corner into Brodsky's street he saw a huge dog leashed to a lamppost. The leash seemed loosely wrapped and Tchaikovsky walked warily to the entrance, careful not to cross eyes with the animal, careful to stay out of range of the leash. Mounting the stairs he heard music, never a surprise in the Brodsky residence, but it sounded like something by Brahms, and though he knew Brodsky had championed the Brahms violin concerto no less than his own, though he knew they were friends, he would never understand his interest.

ANNA BRODSKY, a large woman with a pretty face, enjoyed the role of hausfrau catering to the needs of her artist husband – A. B. as she called him, but she had misgivings about the dinner. Everything about Piotr Ilyich (his eyes, his voice, his smile) was kind; his mere presence warmed a room – but knowing how Tchaikovsky felt about Brahms's music, A. B. had cautioned her to say nothing, hoping that if he heard Brahms play his own music he would come to recognize its merit. She sighed when she heard the bell ring, knowing it would be Piotr Ilyich, knowing it would be up to her to enlighten her guest finally of their deception.

Tchaikovsky's consternation was evident from the start, brow wrinkling, eyes contracting, hand trembling, uncertain what to expect. "Who is there? What are they playing?"

She ushered him into the vestibule, taking his hat and coat. "It is Brahms. A. B. is looking forward to introducing you."

Anna took his arm, but Tchaikovsky shrank against the wall, shaking his head, unable to say what he thought without appearing discourteous. Had they been less kind he would have demanded his hat and coat, but he remained paralyzed instead with indecision.

There was a pause in the music and Anna beseeched him with her eyes. "Please, enter, I beg you. It will be all right. I know it."

Again he shook his head. "I am sorry. I cannot. I am too nervous."

His arm was rigid in her hand and she opened the door to call her husband. Brodsky appeared with a smile, cleanshaven with a nest of thick black hair on his head, a man not yet forty who clearly liked his table, thick jaw complementing a thick waist, but he moved with the agility of a man half his size. "Come, Piotr Ilyich. Prepare yourself for a treat." He exerted more strength than his wife, pulling Tchaikovsky from the wall into the sittingroom.

Brahms presided from the piano. Julius Klengel, the cellist of the Brodsky Quartet, waved his bow in greeting. Some guests, including a pageturner, also turned and smiled. They were rehearsing for the next day's concert Brahms's new trio, a form Tchaikovsky loathed, preferring the colors of the orchestra though he had memorialized the death of his friend Nicolai Rubinstein with a trio as sumptuous as a symphony. The friends had made their peace a year after their altercation over his piano concerto. Rubinstein had not only championed the concerto despite its failure in St. Petersburg, but won its first successes, first as conductor, then as pianist – recognizing, however belatedly, its huge merit. He had died at just 46 years of tuberculosis and Tchaikovsky had written a trio for his friend's funeral, preferring the intimacy of a chamberwork to the sweep of a larger ensemble for the occasion.

The two composers could not have been more unalike: Tchaikovsky, a nobleman by birth, elegant and refined and softspoken; and Brahms, the son of a peasant, his short, square, energetic figure mounted by a head made more powerful by its mane. Brodsky could not stop smiling as he made introductions, amazed once more that a man as willowy as Piotr Ilyich had constructed so vigorous a concerto. He swayed on his feet as if he might swoon, but just as it seemed his knees might buckle he spoke, his voice so soft it might have been unheard had he not been the center of attention, so melodious it might have passed for music more than words. "Do I not disturb you?"

Brahms's voice was in sharp contrast, high and hoarse as always. "Not in the least – but why are you going to listen to this? It is not at all interesting."

Brodsky interrupted. "I disagree, but why don't we let Piotr Ilyich be the judge of that?" He was about to introduce the other guests, when Brahms's pageturner stepped forward, a trim and pretty Englishwoman of thirty who smiled as she offered him her hand – and he accepted it like a lifeline, stepping forward with the ghost of a smile.

Her name was Ethel Smyth and she saw in Tchaikovsky a similarity to the great friend of her life: Harry Brewster. Both men exhibited the shyness of a well-brought-up child – gentle, kind, and courteous until he became more confident of his place. Both were tall with faces that turned heads, each with a broad brow, perfect nose, and perfectly oval face though her Harry was cleanshaven and Tchaikovsky's beard was neat and trim, her Harry's eyes were brown and Tchaikovsky's blue, her Harry's hair was fair and fluffy and Tchaikovsky's prematurely grey and thinning – but Tchaikovsky's age added to his charm, the simplicity of a child in an older man. Both had the face of a dreamer, but her Harry was also an acute observer of men, a reader and thinker, witty, amusing, and companionable when he chose – all attributes she assumed in Tchaikovsky in the moment of their meeting. Even German musicians (who detected genius in brutish behavior) respected him as a master of orchestration and man of the world.

Tchaikovsky thawed visibly with the shake of their hands and she recognized something else in him she would not otherwise have guessed. She saw herself in him, a likeness at the core however different the surface. Despite her great friend Harry Brewster, and despite Tchaikovsky's marriage, she recognized that he (as much as she) shielded his true self from others by pretending to be like them. She saw in his smile that he had recognized her true self no less in that moment.

Brahms caught the moment of comity between Tchaikovsky and Ethel, but thought no more of it than the gratitude of an older man for the attention of a pretty young woman, neither more nor less than he had felt on many an occasion himself, not least the attention of his Hermione-ohne-O – whom he still missed, but whom he could not have treated otherwise. Ethel had first been brought to his attention by Elisabet (who had mothered the young girl in her first year through a sickness) when she had told him of a performance Ethel had organized in England of his Liebeslieder Waltzes. She had come alone from England to Leipzig, a girl of nineteen, to live and travel alone and study music at the Conservatory. On learning she knew nothing of counterpoint Herzogenberg had insisted on teaching her himself, inspiring Brahms's opening sally when they had been introduced: "So this is the young lady who writes sonatas and does not know counterpoint!"

Brahms's affection for the young woman had grown fatherly, impressed as he was by her athleticism and courage as much as her musicianship – as competent at lawn-tennis as the piano and as apt to jump over a fence or table or chair as walk around it, to the utter bewilderment of Germans, young and old alike, ladies and gentlemen, most of whom found the English more than a little mad.

Tchaikovsky listened as the rehearsal resumed, wishing he might turn to air. After Leipzig his itinerary swept through Berlin, Hamburg, Prague, Paris, and London. He followed in the footsteps of composers conducting their own works such as Wagner and Brahms, but fluent as he was in French and German he had never been entirely confident as a conductor and filled with cold comfort at the thought of Brahms attending his Leipzig performance. It was now twenty years since he had first mounted the podium, but he had never forgotten the terror of the evening. He had been unable to see the score in front of his eyes, his *Voyevoda* Dances had been wiped from his mind, and he had continually given the orchestra incorrect cues. Fortunately, the players had known the music well enough to laugh and ignore his direction. Worst of all, he had imagined his head would drop from his shoulders unless he held it firmly in place and had spent the entire evening with one hand gripping his jaw while the other waved the baton.

Ethel's handshake had helped him breathe more easily, but knowing he would be expected to pay compliments his terror returned hundredfold when they finished. He did not like the music, much as he might have wished differently, for his own comfort more than anyone else's, but his own trio was richer by far, more sumptuous in length and breadth. Fortunately, one terror was overshadowed by another. A howl grew in volume like the whistle of an approaching locomotive, accompanied by a thudding up the stairs he had just ascended, deflecting the eyes of the company from him toward the sound. The door was flung open, toppling a chair as it slammed into the wall. The hellish dog from the street burst like a cannonball into the room, upsetting the cello stand, sending sheet music flying as it launched itself at Ethel Smyth.

Ethel greeted the dog with open arms and the indulgent smile of a mother. Tchaikovsky watched in awe as the trim woman stood her ground against the shaggy dog, as tall on its hindlegs as herself, dwarfing her with its bulk. Embracing the dog, its forelegs on her shoulders, she might have been embracing a man. Tchaikovsky trembled as Ethel pushed it down on all fours to the floor. "SIT, Marco! SIT! Naughty,

naughty! How dare you leave your post!" The dog sat like a lion, revealing by its smile that it recognized the mayhem it had caused. Its coat was of a dark indeterminate color; a white ring around its muzzle arrowed into its forehead, matched by white socks on three paws; its floppy ears flapped like batwings as it bobbed its head, but its eyes seemed tiny in a head twice the size of Ethel's.

Amid general laughter the company gathered sheet music from the floor and righted the chair and cello stand. For want of something to do Tchaikovsky picked a page from the floor, careful to keep his distance from Marco, but seemed not to know what to do with it. Brodsky plucked it from his hand, thanking him for his trouble. He remained so focused on the dog that he was hardly aware that Brodsky spoke. "That is a magnificent animal, Fraulein Smyth. What kind is it?"

Ethel laughed. "Half St. Bernard and the rest what you please. He was given to me by a friend who bought him in Vienna. I am told they are used there for drawing washerwomen's carts – but I am afraid I have rather spoiled him. He does nothing for the pleasure of his upkeep – but I can begrudge him nothing, my little puppy, my little Marco."

Brahms admired her way with the dog. "He is not so little, your little Marco."

Ethel was on her knees, rubbing Marco's face. "I know, but he was just a little yellow and white thing when I first got him, and I still remember him that way – but you would not know it to look at him now, so dark and huge, like a bear – my best friend for lo these many years. I thought it best to leave him on the street, but he goes everywhere I go – and, well, you see what happens when I leave him."

So engrossed was everyone in tidying up and minding Marco that no one noticed two new guests, a man and woman, until they stood side by side in the room. They appeared the same age, in their late forties, the man small, one shoulder higher than the other, pale blue eyes, a receding jaw, and blond tousled head, the woman so like the man it came as no surprise that they were related, husband and wife, but also first cousins. Brodsky almost shouted when he saw them. "O mein Gott! Where are my manners? Everybody, here are Herr Grieg and his wife." He shrugged his shoulders with a smile for the Griegs. "You see we have had a little accident!"

A CURRENT MIGHT HAVE PASSED THROUGH NINA GRIEG for the way she quivered, seated between Brahms and Tchaikovsky at dinner. Marco, tall enough to lay his head on the table, his wagging tail strong enough to cause accidents, had been relegated to a backroom with a joint. The repast for the company included bread, butter, jam, fish soup, cabbage soup, fried sausages, wiener schnitzel, saddle of venison, sauerkraut, mixed vegetables, mashed potatoes, with cherry tarts and Christmas cake and cream to come. Anna sat with Ethel and Grieg across from Brahms and Nina and Tchaikovsky. Brodsky at the head of the table, aware of Tchaikovsky's continuing discomfort, wished to set him at ease. The man had important concerts ahead and needed to be at his best. "Did you know, Herr Tchaikovsky, you are younger than Brahms by seven years, but you have the same birthday?"

Tchaikovsky seemed startled to be addressed, but looked at Brahms, apparently glad to have found a point of harmony. "25 April?"

It was Brahms's turn to be startled, and he looked from Tchaikovsky to Brodsky. "But it is not so. My birthday is on 7 May."

Brodsky smiled. "Ah, yes, but in Russia we still follow the Julian calendar. We are twelve days behind the Gregorian calendar."

Brahms eyebrows rose in recollection. "Ah, yes, yes, I remember Clara saying something about it."

Grieg looked from Brahms to Tchaikovsky and back with a smile. "Ha, so that was my mistake! I was born too late, on 15 June – a matter of a few days. My parents were always so slow."

The company laughed, but Brahms frowned, looking at Brodsky, appearing to count in his head. "Did you say twelve days?"

Ethel's tone was as ironic as her words. "That depends, Doktor Brahms. In the eighteenth century it was eleven days, and in the twentieth it will be thirteen, but in the nineteenth it is exactly twelve days between the 25th of April and the 7th of May."

Brahms grimaced, replying no less ironically. "Ach, the girl thinks she has got a mind!"

As greatly as Ethel admired Brahms she was frustrated by his disinterest in her work, no less frustrated by the prevalence of German men who spoke as if their every word were infallible, and no less by German women who prefaced every remark with *mein Mann sagt*. She had satisfied herself against Brahms with a sarcastic poem expressing the sentiment that since Brahms proclaimed women of intelligence to be nothing, they had best cultivate their stupidity as diligently as they dared if they wished to court his attention. She had given him the poem only to learn he had annoyed everyone at a supper in his honor by showing it to all who approached him and insisting they read it out loud. She shook her head with a smile. "If the girl had no mind, would she recognize the greatness of Brahms?"

Unaccustomed to challenges, Brahms was openmouthed but silent. Tchaikovsky squirmed during the silence, too confused to think, let alone talk, admiring Ethel Smyth's courage, but appalled by her assessment. It was true that Brahms never strove for artificial effects, he was never banal, always serious, always elevated, even noble – but he missed the most important quality in music: beauty. Astonishingly, she seemed unaware of her audacity, bearing out his contention that no Englishwoman was without eccentricities, and Ethel Smyth's were her dog – and Brahms! He said nothing, wishing neither to lie nor concur with everyone's opinion of Brahms, growing more uncomfortable with each passing moment – until Nina Grieg leaped, without warning, from her seat. "I am sorry, but I cannot sit between these two! It makes me too nervous!"

Grieg could not have been more attentive. He had been aware of her discomfort from the start, but not of its intensity. It had been not quite five years since he had left her for Elise Schjelderup, but so dependent was he on the quality of Nina's vocals that she was his muse as much as his wife, the most natural singer he knew, able to convey the feeling of his words even to listeners who knew no Norwegian. He had not seen her for almost eight months and away from her his inspiration had dried. He had returned, wanting to make restitution for his desertion, but had written only three songs since. He got up as suddenly as his wife: "But I can! And I will!"

The company laughed as man and wife exchanged places and Ethel turned her attention to Tchaikovsky. "Herr Tchaikovsky, how do you like Leipzig?"

Tchaikovsky swallowed and spoke cautiously. "The Gewandhaus has a great reputation. So does your conservatory."

Ethel sat up straight. "Yes, but it is not always deserved. Some teachers are conscientious and some are merely dull – just like anywhere else."

Tchaikovsky's interest suddenly peaked. "I understand that they do not teach instrumentation. That is a pity."

It was something he deplored about the Germans, too prudish to exploit orchestral resources, too immersed in theory for sensuality, his very problem with Brahms. He would have preferred to say no more, but Ethel was persistent. "What would you suggest, Herr Tchaikovsky?" She glanced disdainfully at Brahms before returning her gaze to Tchaikovsky. "Even the rough diamonds of German music confess that you are a master of orchestral effects."

Tchaikovsky became more animated than he had been all day. "You must never be afraid to conduct experiments with the orchestra. You can learn so much from everyday conversations. Listen to the inflections in people's voices. There is instrumentation for you. It is everywhere, in everything you hear – birds, bicycles, trains – if you will only listen."

Ethel's brow furrowed. "How very interesting. I never thought of it like that – but I will. Danke, Herr Tchaikovsky, you have done me a great service." She turned her gaze to the other end of the table. "Why is it, Doktor Brahms, that you have never done me even half so great a service though you have known me more than twice as long?"

Brahms laughed. "Hah! Have I not always said you are an oboe?"

So he had, holding that everyone resembled one instrument or another, but she had ignored what he had said as just another of his witticisms. "The trouble is, Doktor Brahms, I never know when you are joking and when you are not."

Brahms shrugged, returning his attention to his schnitzel and potatoes. "That is not my problem. What Herr Tchaikovsky says has head and foot," he fixed Ethel with icy blue eyes – "but, then again, any selfrespecting musician would know that."

Tchaikovsky seemed to relax, gratified by Ethel's interest as much as Brahms's endorsement, but Brodsky knew how much he had been upset by Hanslick's review of his violin concerto, and he knew that Tchaikovsky knew Hanslick was Brahms's friend. He also knew what Tchaikovsky did not know, that while Brahms may have been Hanslick's friend he did not esteem his friend's musical pronouncements – and Brodsky, wishing for a deeper harmony between the two composers whose violin concertos he had done so much to promote, smiled at the table. "Also any selfrespecting violinist. Do you not know what Hanslick said about my performance? I did not play the violin, he said, but tore it to pieces. I tortured myself as much as I tortured the audience."

Brahms took the bait as Brodsky had hoped. "Hah, Hanslick! You know what I think of him!"

Brodsky nodded. "Yes, but Herr Tchaikovsky does not."

Brahms sighed. "Ah, Hanslick! It is all politics, you know. He is a good man and a good friend – but he does not understand music. He is a critic, but that is his misfortune more than anyone else's because he knows so very little about music. He is like critics everywhere. He does not write about music, only about what he *feels* about the music, what he *feels* about the composer. He knows what he likes, and he knows *who* he likes, but about music he knows nothing. He does not like Wagner's music, but that is a black mark against Hanslick, not against Wagner. He makes a fool only of himself."

Brodsky sat back satisfied. He had heard Brahms on the subject before and he was glad to hear him again for Tchaikovsky's benefit.

Brahms continued, still in his sighing mode, wishing it seemed that things might have been different. "He needed a counter to Wagner and he found it in me, but the best he has done is to provide Wagner with his model for Beckmesser. Everyone knows that Beckmesser was first called Hans Lich in *Meistersinger*. It is not the way he might want to be remembered, but it is the way he will be remembered best. My regard for Wagner is matched only by my lack of regard for Wagnerians – but Hanslick set me up as the antiWagner when I am only antiWagnerian. Indeed, the Wagnerians understand Wagner no better than Hanslick. As I said, it is all politics – but now on to more important matters. Fraulein Smyth, the jam, if you please?"

Brodsky found his reward in Tchaikovsky's smile. Brahms's tone, addressing Ethel, was ironic again, but even he seemed lighter in spirit for his ventilation, eating directly from the dish of strawberry jam, refusing to give it to anyone else.

Tchaikovsky's eyes narrowed, his view of Brahms changing with each moment. He was different from what he had expected, shorter and stockier, but hardly foreboding, his head that of an old man, reminiscent of an elderly Russian priest, handsome and benign, thick beard sprinkled with white. Best of all, his manner was simple, free from vanity, jovial even to childishness the way he had commandeered the jam.

Anna Brodsky was pleased with the developments though she shook her head in disbelief at the three composers. Grieg was telling a story from his boyhood. When he was ten years old his family lived in Landas, a short distance to Bergen where he walked each day to school. Often it rained, and if the boy was sufficiently wet on arriving he was sent home again. Grieg made sure he was sufficiently wet by standing under a drainpipe on the days it rained – until the day he aroused the suspicions of his teacher. The rain had been light, but the boy looked as if he had been washed ashore.

Her husband proved himself no less foolish than the others. The virtuoso violinist concluded dinner by producing her Christmas present to her nephew, a conjuring chest, and distracting the company with its miracles. Doktor Brahms, as she might have expected, demanded detailed explanations of each trick.

ii

Anton Bruckner sat at the head of a table in the long diningroom of Zum roten Igel, girded by two of his pupils, August Lamberg on his left, Cyrill Gollerich on his right.

He could not have said whom he feared more: the four pretty girls three tables away, none a day over thirty; or the arrival of the rest of his dinner party. He was sixty-five years old, but a pretty girl could still turn his will to water. The wisdom that came with age appeared to have passed him by. He understood his music, he understood his God, but nothing else, not what made the city Catholic, not even what made Catholics Catholic though he was a good Catholic in a good Catholic city. On one occasion he had presented a girl who had caught his fancy with a prayerbook, an intimation of his piety as much as his intentions, but she had laughed and flung the book down a stairwell. On another occasion, in the wake of a successful choral festival, members of his choir had coaxed him into a room, there to be joined by Olga, a waitress he had fancied, but dressed too seductively for his comfort she had scared him from the room, angry and confused, to resign from the choir, to lose both Olga and choir. On yet another occasion he had spoken affectionately to a girl in the college of St. Anna where he was a teacher, but she had complained that he had spoken too familiarly, upsetting him enough to request that he be relieved of his duties in the female section of the college though it meant losing part of his salary, even to request testimonials from friends confirming the rigor and discipline of his classes, the probity and piety of his character.

All of that was enough in the past to have become part of his myth, but it never ceased to be part of his neurosis. During the early days his lack of success with the fairer sex had been matched by his lack of success with music. He was years past fifty before time had erased his failures with music, but not before he had deposited himself in a sanatorium in Bad Kreuzen for a cold water cure, talking of impending madness, hinting at suicide, imagining himself forgotten by family and friends. What had sustained him then had been a compulsion to count anything and everything – leaves on a tree, stars in a nightsky, grains of sand on the beach. The cure had been successful, but traces of his numeromania remained in his insistence on numbering the bars in his scores.

He was also sustained by huge quantities of food, a plate of roast pork beside a mountain of cabbage and a mug of Pilsener second in his affection only to music. Arriving early, the three had taken the liberty of ordering while they waited for the rest of their company, eel soup for Bruckner, potato and leek for Lamberg, cabbage and sausage for Gollerich. Bruckner was eating his second order of soup when Lamberg, who was facing the door, looked up. "They are here at last." He put down the spoon and got up with a smile. "Joseph, Emil, how is it with you? Doktor Brahms, welcome."

Joseph Hynais and Emil Schalk were friends of Lamberg and Gollerich, all of them smiling, as much for one another as to inject a pleasant note in the proceedings. All admirers of Brahms and Bruckner, they had arranged the meeting, hoping for an accord. There was at least one irrefutable similarity between the two: both dressed for comfort, appearing to have borrowed clothes from a wellfed though unfashionable cousin – but even Bruckner stared as Brahms came into sight. He wore an overcoat with a removable cape and a feathered homburg, all of which he removed to reveal a brightly checkered scarf secured like a patch on his shirt by a large safety pin. He had heard of this affectation of Brahms and had it been anyone else he would have laughed, but he dared not laugh at Brahms (his junior by almost a decade). No one dared laugh at Brahms, most assuredly not with his forehead clenched like a fist and his eyes narrowed to slits – though he dressed apparently to dare the world to laugh.

Aside from their bulk and the puffy fit of their clothes the two composers could not have been more dissimilar, Bruckner bald as a baby, Brahms bearded as the old man of the sea. When Brahms ignored the extended hands of Lamberg and Gollerich, Bruckner chose not to offer his own. Brahms was a small man, everything about him was small including his vision of music – but he had powerful friends and Bruckner dared say nothing. Brahms had called him priest-ridden, his symphonies musical boa-constrictors – but he had also joined in the mammoth ovation awarded his Sixth Symphony while Hanslick had sat beside him still as stone. Bruckner had come to the lunch out of respect for his pupils and friends, but no less respect for Brahms when he learned the composer had agreed to the meeting. To his friends he had confessed Brahms's music soothed the nerves, but his own stirred the blood; Brahms designed to comfort, he to discomfort; one left you glowing in your skin, the other made you jump out.

Brahms had not known what to expect when he had learned Bruckner wished to meet him. He had said of him what he had said of Liszt, that his music was a swindle, that his death would spell the death as well of his music. He had gone further, declaring himself responsible for Bruckner's fame for the same reason that Nietzsche had declared Wagner responsible for Brahms's fame: Wagner's enemies, needing a counter to Wagner, had elevated Brahms to the role – and Brahms's enemies, needing a counter to Brahms, had elevated Bruckner to the role. Nietzsche had been wrong, and while Brahms felt justified declaring the same argument true of Bruckner there was something about Bruckner's boa-constrictors, amateurish, confused, and illogical abortions that they were, that he did not understand. Instead of following the path of exposition, development, and recapitulation he meandered far from the fields tilled by Haydn, Mozart, and Beethoven, simply repeating his exposition in increasingly grandiose terms – Wagnerian terms – but someone had compared the repetitions to the evolution from caterpillar to chrysalis to butterfly, and that was something he did not understand. If symphonies were animals, Bruckner's would be rhinos, hippos, elephants, but never butterflies. Fixing Bruckner with his narrowed eyes he spoke dismissively. "You must not feel hurt about this, Bruckner, but I really cannot make out what you are trying to get at with your compositions."

All the stories regarding Bruckner's softness as a man came to fruition in that moment in his face. Despite the hawknose and bulldog wrinkles it shrank like that of a boy who had been slapped. His lower lip trembled in an otherwise frozen face, but saddest of all were his eyes set in resignation as of one accustomed to slaps. His friends had led him on a fool's errand; any hopes he might have had of winning Brahms's approval faded; he would do what he did in all such occasions, make the best of a bad situation. "Never mind, Doktor, that is quite all right. You see, I feel just the same way about your things."

Brahms felt a twinge, recognizing something in Bruckner he had seen in his father, both of them villagers, brusque in dealings with townsmen to cover their outsider status, both touchingly childlike in their attempt to be other than what they were. He knew the stories that had made Bruckner a laughingstock in sophisticated quarters: when Richter had made a success of his Fourth Symphony he had pressed a thaler into the palm of the wealthy and cosmopolitan conductor, telling him to drink his health with a glass of beer; when the Emperor had conferred on him the Order of Franz Josef (which neither he nor Wagner had received) and asked what else he might do for him, Bruckner had asked him to forbid Hanslick from criticizing his music. He acknowledged their mutual lack of understanding with a nod and took his seat across the table from Bruckner. Hynais and Schalk seated themselves on his right and left. "Hmm, well, let us see what there is to eat."

Bruckner nodded his approval. "It is all good. We did not want to wait as you can see."

Brahms looked around the table. "We will have to order twice to catch up. I will have a turtle soup and a fish soup – to begin. Then, the smoked ham and dumplings. It is very good here."

Bruckner slapped the table, a huge smile cracking his face in two. "That is it, Doktor! Smoked ham and dumplings. That is the point on which we can understand each other!"

Brahms smiled, setting the rest of the party laughing. There was no more talk of music through the meal, but after Bruckner had left Brahms nodded approval to Hynais and Schalk. "I would not go through thick and thin with Bruckner, but he is a man whose intentions are damn serious – and that deserves respect."

CLARA TO BRAHMS   *Franzensbad, 11 July, 1888*

My dear Johannes,

Our Ferdinand is looking well, but unable to move about except with great difficulty on crutches. The doctor says it is hardly possible that he will ever be able to resume his old activities again. The addiction has taken too great a hold. I had always feared this, but it still came as a great blow and I cannot for the life of me see how the poor fellow is to end his days.

I am arranging for his wife and the two youngest children to move to a small town where living is cheap. He himself must yet remain for some time under medical supervision. His three boys in Schneeberg are lively and most lovable, but we are much preoccupied with their future. They must earn a living as soon as possible. I am now an old woman, no longer able to give concerts as easily as I once could. It is not merely my rheumatism that makes it so very difficult, but my hearing too is now very bad. It is blurred and I hear all the higher notes a semitone too high. It is not possible for me to afford an education for them all, nor for my children to do so after my death. I can barely afford what they cost me now. Their keep runs me into 2,000 marks a year for the three alone, and in addition I cannot reckon on less than 500 marks a month for Ferdinand. I have often wondered whether I should not sell my house and find a cheaper one, but I should hate to do this. I may have only a few years left to live and it would be dreadful to have to retrench now. The children are constantly begging me not to do it – but all this is quite between ourselves, of course, dear Johannes.

Herzogenberg's malady, as you know, is of an altogether more mysterious nature. They have imagined it to be an inflammation of his hip bone, but they have also called it muscular rheumatism! Thank heaven his pains have yielded to morphia injections. He, too, now relies on crutches for motion. They are convinced that it is a disease with which he was born which has chosen just this moment to erupt, and it appears an operation is necessary to realign his leg. I cannot help but feel sad at the sight of him, both him and his poor dear Elisabet whose worries on his account are quite wearing down her own health.

You must thank God for your own good health, dear Johannes – and forgive, for this miserable letter, your old Clara

BRAHMS TO CLARA

My dear Clara,

I delayed answering your dear letter because I had something in my heart and in my thoughts which I found difficult to tell you, but I find after all that I must let it out. So summon all your goodness and friendship and listen, and then please be kind enough just to say "Yes."

There is little I can do about your greater cares, but about your smaller cares, which are financial, it annoys me that you have such cares at all when I am rolling in money which is of no use to me and gives me no pleasure. This is what you must consider: I do not wish to live any differently than I do; it is quite useless to give my relations more than I give them already; and I find myself in a position to help without feeling a pinch myself. After my death I will have no obligations to fulfill, no particular wishes, no legal dependents.

In short, the position is simple. If you take me to be as good a man as I am, and if you are as fond of me as I should like to think, then you must allow me to unburden myself of some of my superfluous pelf in order to contribute toward the expenses of your grandchildren. I wish to lighten my load by about 10,000 marks and wish you would help me.

Simrock has again taken a heap of choral pieces, quartets, and songs, but I will not even see the handsome fee. It will slip quietly and uselessly into the Reichsbank. Now think how much pleasure these works and the fee would give me if you were to send a good clear "Yes!"

Now, to a totally unrelated matter. I think you will derive considerable pleasure from what I have enclosed – an exact score of the <u>original</u> concept of Schumann's D minor Symphony. He described it modestly, and I think unjustly, in his introduction, as a rough sketch. You gave it to me yourself, as you will no doubt remember, but it has not been included among his complete works and to my way of thinking it is high time that wrong was righted. You are, of course, familiar with the state of affairs that led to the revision. Schumann was so upset by a first rehearsal in Dusseldorf, where he commanded a bad and incomplete orchestra, that he orchestrated it afresh, doubling many of the instruments for the sake of safety, but thickening many of the textures in the process. The original scoring has always delighted me. It is a real pleasure to see a bright and spontaneous work expressed with corresponding ease and grace. In this respect it reminds me of Mozart's G minor. Everything is so natural that you cannot imagine it different. There are no harsh colors, no forced effects, and so on. You will no doubt agree that one's enjoyment of the revised form is not unmixed. Will you not also agree that the original score should be published? I will see to it myself if that is the case.

Your Johannes

CLARA TO BRAHMS

My dear Johannes,

What can I say to your friendly offer? I was deeply moved while reading your letter. Words are so inadequate compared with what one feels, and all I can do is press your hand affectionately and acknowledge that your offer gives me a sense of relief to which my heart has long been a stranger. But I cannot accept your dear offer at the moment. It would not be right unless my need were really urgent. Thanks to what I earned in England last year I still have a small sum available which will suffice for this year. In addition, I have Elise who is giving me substantial help by defraying the expenses of educating one of the boys. Moreover, I am still negotiating the sale of Robert's manuscripts and some settlement will be reached soon.

It is also a blessing to me, such as rarely befalls the wife of a great man, to see how the number of my husband's adherents has grown. At first I received royalties of about 300-400 francs per annum from his works performed in Paris. A few years ago the sum increased to about 1,000 francs. This year the sum is 1,500 francs – and this is commensurate with increases everywhere: England, Switzerland, Holland, Austria, Germany, a striking testimony to Robert's genius, in spite of whatever Wagner, Berlioz, and Liszt have said about him.

In any case, there is no need for me to break into my capital for the present. What chiefly troubles me is the future. My prospects of earning money through concerts must grow ever less, while my expenses for Ferdinand's children must go on increasing. So this is my conclusion: as I do take you to be as good a man as you are, and as I am as fond of you as you would like to think, I promise to appeal to you without hesitation as soon as my need becomes sufficiently pressing. Can you be satisfied with that? I hope so, and beg you to rely on this promise and take no further steps.

I have not had a chance yet to look properly through Robert's D minor, but Herr Muller of the Frankfurt Conservatory has very kindly offered to go through it with me, bar by bar. I will let you know what I think after we have read it through.

Marie and Eugenie have asked me to tell you how very much they appreciate your deep friendship for me, and so with the most affectionate greetings from three grateful hearts, I am

Your faithful old friend Clara

BRAHMS TO CLARA   *Thun, 7 Aug*
My dear Clara,

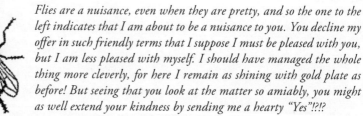

Flies are a nuisance, even when they are pretty, and so the one to the left indicates that I am about to be a nuisance to you. You decline my offer in such friendly terms that I suppose I must be pleased with you, but I am less pleased with myself. I should have managed the whole thing more cleverly, for here I remain as shining with gold plate as before! But seeing that you look at the matter so amiably, you might as well extend your kindness by sending me a hearty "Yes"!?!?

All this time I have been wanting to write to you in greater detail about the symphony, but I hope to be able to discuss it with you some time with the score in front of us. Wullner has better judgment than Muller, and he is in agreement with me about the symphony. He is also most anxious to produce it with his orchestra in Cologne and willing to edit the final manuscript at no benefit to himself. Of course, the final decision lies with you. So think it over and let me know what you think.

In anticipation,
Your Johannes

CLARA TO BRAHMS   *Frankfurt, 15 August, 1888*

My dear Johannes,

Thank you for your patience regarding Robert's D minor. I am afraid I am not so very sanguine as you. It is certainly interesting to compare the two versions side by side, but Muller is convinced that the rescored version is the more brilliant and the more effective. We found only a few passages in the andante and the scherzo more beautiful in the original. Muller is not in favor of publishing the first version, but if I had the instrumental parts he said he would gladly have the symphony played to me at a rehearsal. But the cost of copying all the parts would not justify the expense. I could not justify charging the orchestra with the expense for just one rehearsal. Besides, Robert authorized the revised version. Though Muller could not agree with your assessment, he has gone through the scores with the greatest interest, and would like very much to discuss them with you.

Your old Clara

BRAHMS TO CLARA   *Vienna, 22 Sept*

My dear Clara,

Do not be angry with me if I return to my old request. In the summer you refused my proffered assistance so kindly that, now that we are both back home, I venture to ask you again. I ought perhaps to have set about the whole business more cleverly, but I am still at a loss to discover how. So please consent, and let me lay 15,000 marks (this includes simple and compound interest!) most respectfully at your feet. All I most earnestly beg of you is to send me a card to say it is lying there, but nothing more.

With all due respect to Muller, Wullner has greater insight and judgment – but it is not just Wullner. Everyone who has seen it agrees that the score has not gained by being revised. It has certainly lost in charm, ease, and clarity.

With affectionate greetings to you all, and begging you not to be angry but to take the thing quite kindly, Yours ever,

Johannes

CLARA TO BRAHMS   *Frankfurt, 9 October, 1888*

My dear Johannes,

The money is here and I stand before it not knowing what to do! Give it back to you? How could I behave like that to such a magnanimous friend? Keep it? I cannot tell you what I feel about doing that except that by taking it I show a trust in you which I would certainly not show to anyone else in the world!

For the present I will put the money by and regard it as capital to be broken into and used for Ferdinand and his family without my having to feel that I am robbing the other children. This gives me a real sense of relief and I press your hand affectionately, but there is sadness in my gratitude. I cannot tell you all that stirs the soul of

Your old Clara

More than Clara, more than Billroth, more than all of his friends, the Herzogenbergs had both deteriorated in their health, and both were among his younger friends. Brahms was now almost sixty, they still in their forties, she in her early, he in his late, but the walk up three flights to his rooms had proven almost too much for both. Herzogenberg had limped up the stairs, clutching the rail, clutching his wife. She had rested at every third step, forbidden by her doctor to exert herself beyond what was absolutely necessary. Sitting together on Brahms's sofa each seemed more breathless than the other while he poured coffee and laughed. "You know, the two of you really must take better care of yourselves. One would visit you more often if one or the other of you were not always lying down."

Elisabet looked up suddenly, her mouth a straight line. They had gone to Nice for her husband's convalescence from his operation, from where she had entreated Brahms to visit them during his recent trip to Italy, but he had written to say Nice was too fashionable to count as part of Italy and did not feature in an Italian tour. She had described her day in Nice in a letter to show it was anything but fashionable, saying he might really take his share of inconvenience since they loved him so well, but he had remained unconvinced. His comment made her realize he had never understood the seriousness of their problems. "Doktor Brahms, if you knew what we have been through you would not see fit to make light of it."

Brahms raised his eyebrows, but kept his smile. "I do not mean to make light of anything, Frau Liesl, but to put you at your ease. You see, I know whereof I speak. I have never missed a meal in my life, never taken a drop of medicine, and never been ill a day of my life."

Herzogenberg appeared almost not to hear, shriveled to half his original size, moustache drooping, beard limp and dry, wrists scrawny as chickenlegs. He moved as little as necessary, legs splayed in front, hand held in his wife's.

Elisabet's lungs had long been unwell, her heart trouble exacerbated by her concerns, and her breath came more heavily than her husband's. "With respect, Doktor Brahms, if that is your counsel, then I am convinced you know not whereof you speak. You must thank the fates that have been so much kinder to you in that respect. We may not be as well as we might wish, but it is not because we have missed meals, nor because we have taken medicine. Your presence in Nice would have made two faithful Herzogenbergs much happier through a difficult time at little cost to yourself."

Brahms lost his smile, giving them each a cup of coffee. "Was it, then, really, so very bad?"

"I do not blame you for not understanding. We could scarcely understand what was happening ourselves – and we had lived with the disabilities for months before the operation."

Brahms sat down, sipping from his own cup. "Why did you not tell me about it?"

"I tried – but we, each one of us, have our own lives to live. There is only so much one can say about oneself before lapsing into selfishness. If an appeal becomes too direct it becomes a supplication, and between friends there should be no such thing."

Brahms seemed chastened and looked at the floor. "I do wish to know. Will you tell me now?"

Elisabet looked at her husband who merely nodded.

Brahms spoke without levity. "I understood it was a kind of rheumatism – very severe – of the muscles. Was it not so?"

"That was the diagnosis, but they kept changing it until his knee began to exude itself. By this time, of course, there was no question of walking without help – and even with help it was too painful. The leg needed to be straightened and Heinrich's wish was for energetic handling of the knee under chloroform, but our own doctor was afraid of the result. It is impossible to ascertain beforehand, you see, if the knee has lost all tendency to exudation – and even if the leg can be straightened it can hardly become supple again."

Brahms nodded sympathetically.

"Finally, we consulted Professor Angerer – he is the principal surgeon in Munich – and his verdict secured our decision. The knee could not be cured through splints and bandaging, nor through extensions. Only an operation would help. Angerer pronounced his views with such conviction that I was immediately encouraged to persuade my Heinz – but he needed no persuasion. He had suffered too long already."

Herzogenberg sipped coffee, nodding, saying nothing.

"They came on a Friday morning at eight-thirty – four strong – to butcher my poor lamb. The sittingroom was arranged as an operating room. I was there when they sent him to sleep, but then they carried him away and I was not allowed over the threshold of the torture chamber. The wife was left to bear it as well as she could." She stroked her husband's knee. "I was prepared to wait for two or three hours and the first forty-five minutes were so quiet I imagined they were still making preparations – when the door opened at nine-thirty and the doctors brought him back, all neatly bandaged. I was so scared. I thought something must have gone wrong for them to have brought him back so soon – but thank God it was all happily over and Heinz regained consciousness soon afterward. His first words were, 'What? Is it over already?'"

Herzogenberg smiled, the two gazed at each other. "When we learned everything had gone well we burst into tears. Angerer said the operation had established beyond all doubt the necessity of the action. It had shown the worst possible necrosis of the kneecap, part of which had to be removed since the joints did not fit properly. In short, the leg was doomed, but the resection could not have been more successful.

The leg will be stiff, of course, and shorter than the other, but an illness of this nature makes one humble in the extreme and grateful for even this much."

She kept her hand tenderly over her husband's knee. "After that it has been mainly a matter of rest and recuperation – much of which was aided by your music, dear friend. The new songs you sent, the dear violin sonata, the new string quintet, have all played their part, for which we are both much in your debt – but you might really consider letting us have them for a little longer before sending them off in such a hurry to Frau Schumann. She must be jealous of our having had the pleasure first – but my poor Heinz should really be allowed this special favor. If we contrive to be happy it is a hardearned happiness, and people who show us a little extra kindness will not find it wasted."

"Frau Schumann knows the sadder side of life as do few others, Frau Liesl. You know about her Ferdinand, but he is only the last in a long line of dear ones that she has lost. I do not know how she manages to stand it all."

Elisabet pursed her lip. "Yes, of course, you are right. Our pain makes us selfish. Is that not ever the case? We should just thank you for your gifts and keep our mouths shut. Your G major String Quintet is so lovely and lighthearted one would think the composer were celebrating his thirtieth birthday."

Brahms laughed. "More like his sixtieth, and it will perhaps be his last work. I am thinking of retiring."

"Retiring? Why?"

"The ideas do not come as easily anymore, and I do not wish to force them – and after all this time do you not imagine I have earned it?"

"Yes, of course, but what a loss for the rest of us."

"But perhaps not – if you saw the rubbish I throw away you would be obliged to agree with me."

"I do wish you would let us be the judge of that. I am sure your rubbish exceeds the pearls of lesser men."

Brahms laughed.

Elisabet shook her head. "You laugh, Doktor Brahms, and I am done with the subject. Let us talk about something else. What do you think will become of Germany now without Bismarck?"

Kaiser Wilhelm I had died, and three months later so had his son, Kaiser Frederick III long ill with cancer, leaving the throne to the grandson, Kaiser Wilhelm II. Bismarck had instituted Europe's first social welfare programs including insurance against sickness, accident, and age; he had established colonies in Africa and the South Pacific; he understood how to manipulate world events to his advantage – but the new Kaiser, unlike his grandfather, was vain, swaggering, autocratic, and saw in Bismarck no more than a tiresome old man. Imagining himself a populist, he had steered a New Course of supposedly Popular Policies, embarking on what he called Personal Rule, and finally dismissing Bismarck.

Brahms had been no less shocked than his friends, but defended the young Kaiser. Germans were first to criticize Germany, Nietzsche had castigated the German Empire as the triumph of the philistines, even Widmann had criticized the Kaiser in an article provoking an argument between the friends. The new Kaiser was young and entitled to the mistakes of youth, but his good will and moral purpose were unquestionable. "What will become of Germany is no more and no less than what becomes of any great country which loses its bearings for a moment – but all that comes from Germany is secretly criticized by Germans themselves in politics as in art. If the Bayreuth Theater had stood in France, it would not have required anything so great as the works of Wagner to make the Germans – not to mention the whole world – go there on a pilgrimage – but in Germany we are the first to tear ourselves down."

As with so many of Brahms's champions, the Herzogenbergs had little love for Wagner, and were no less bewildered than the rest when he showed his admiration. Elisabet was convinced he was prompted by patriotism, not musicianship, convinced that in defending Wagner he was defending Germany. Nietzsche had attacked Wagner in print, the Bayreuth Festival in particular. He had attacked Brahms no less, calling him the eunuch of music, his work the music of impotence, and his followers dissatisfied women. Elisabet was not wrong in imagining Nietzsche's remarks had disturbed Brahms and showed her solidarity. "You are thinking about Nietzsche and you are right, of course. I am always lamenting that such an intellect should have gone to the wrong man, and I would rather disagree with one of his caliber than agree with many others, but one has constantly to sift the wheat from the chaff in his work – and, really, his vanity will deposit him in the insane asylum yet."

Brahms was rarely disturbed anymore by what people said, reconciled as he was to his bachelor's life. Nietzsche was a man of consequence, but his words were colored by personal animosity. He had denounced Wagner's music after their friendship had terminated – and after Brahms, less enthusiastic about Nietsche's music than his words, had declined the dedication of *A Hymn to Life*, a musical work by the philosopher, he had also denounced Brahms's music.

During her last visit to England Clara was a tiny woman, some called her dumpy in her black cap and gown, but she was greeted onstage by prolonged applause, settling and unsettling herself at the piano, adjusting her cap, shaking her gown, rising just as the conductor raised his baton to go to the first oboe with instructions to follow her in a certain passage, returning to the piano, fussing again with cap and gown before settling again like a mother hen, nodding to the conductor that she was ready.

At seventy-two her face had lost some of the chubbiness of her middle years, turned angular again as in her teens, but her features were thicker, the hook of her nose, the hard line of her jaw, and the angularity was sharpened by thinning lips and a widening mouth, now a straight line lacking the resilient bow of baby lips. You would not have thought she was a patient lady to look at her, and she would have said that what with her lumbago, rheumatism, bad hearing, and inflamed lungs, patience was no longer her virtue; age was enough to suffer without suffering patience; it was no surprise that she cut Brahms short about his new works for the clarinet. "I thought you said you had given up composing. Did you not say you planned to retire?"

They were in her sittingroom in Frankfurt, on Myliusstrasse, home now to just Clara and Marie, Eugenie living in England on piano lessons and concerts. Brahms was on a quick visit, Marie out shopping. He looked now as he was to become best known, the man with the Moses beard, snowwhite sprigs and twigs jutting from the jungle on his jaw, swarming from the jungle on his head, blue eyes as pale as icebergs, forehead mounted like a fist on his face, cones of smoke spiraling ceilingward. A watch chain gleamed and pincenez hung from his vest pocket. He smiled, his upper lip still grey, contrasting with his snowy hair and beard. "That was before I met Fraulein von Muhlfeld, my primadonna."

That was his joke: Fraulein von Muhlfeld, his primadonna, also called Fraulein Klarinette, his nightingale, was no fraulein but Richard Muhlfeld, clarinetist of the Meiningen Orchestra, who had enchanted him with his tone, inspiring a trio and quintet for the clarinet; but Clara's expression did not change, she had never found his jokes funny, now less than ever. "Why is it, Johannes, that you did not send me your clarinet pieces to read? Why must I plead to be put in a queue – after Frau Herzogenberg and Billroth and who knows how many others."

As the number of his admirers had grown she had remained the most critical, the least struck by his celebrity. The Herzogenbergs and Billroth might preface every adverse criticism with a hundred compliments, but not she; she would say what she thought, good or bad, but Brahms knew what she would say before she said it. He sent his work for her pleasure, not her criticism, but received only her criticism. "I did not send you the clarinet pieces because there is so much transposition of the clarinet part that it would have spoiled your pleasure."

Clara was aware of her difficulty reading simultaneously in different keys, reading orchestral scores. He had sent the piano score of his Fourth Symphony first to Elisabet who had mastered the difficulties before he played it to her.

"Besides, I did not think you would have the time. You always take so much longer than the Herzogenbergs to tell me what you think."

He was being cheeky. Since she had retired from the Frankfurt Conservatory she had had more time than in a long while, but she remembered how he was. He had appeared for her birthday a few years ago saying he had meant to get her a bouquet, but the shop had been out of his way; he had meant to get her photographs of the Schumann Memorial, but he had been too lazy. He had brought nothing, which she did not mind, but he made light of it, which she did. She lost patience with his jokes and spoke without humor. "It is true that I once had too little time to spend day after day over a single piece like the Herzogenbergs, but that is no longer the case and you know it. In any case, it is not just the clarinet pieces. I could have read your last sonatas easily, and your trio, but I had to wait until they were published to see them. It was not always like this, Johannes."

Brahms wished to talk of something in particular, but was afraid from her bluntness that she had heard something already. "This is not it, is it, Clara? This is not what upsets you. There is something else, is there not?"

"This upsets me very much, indeed, but you are right. It is not the only thing."

He could see neither of them wanted to be the first to mention the subject. "What is it, then, Clara? What is it that upsets you so very much?"

"Everything! Everything upsets me! What I could once bear so easily becomes impossible as I get older. I expect more from my friends, especially from my old friends, but I get less. They take me increasingly for granted and I am no longer as patient as I used to be."

"If you include myself among those old friends, Clara, as I hope you do, then you must be more explicit. How have I taken you for granted?"

"Very well, then, since you force the issue –"

"I do."

"Then tell me if it is true, what I have read in the *Signale*, that Robert's D minor Symphony is to be published in its original form edited by Wullner?"

"It is true."

"After my express indications to the contrary?"

"You never said no."

"I never said yes!"

Brahms had anticipated her objections, but resented her for accepting Muller's recommendations over his own. He was convinced the original version of the D minor Symphony had to be published, and was proud of the new edition with both versions printed side by side on opposite pages for easy comparison, but he was afraid she would have refused if asked directly and had kept his mouth shut until it had been too late. "If you meant to say no, you should have said No! I am not a mind reader!"

Clara responded not only to the new hurt, but the accumulated hurts of years. He had missed the celebrations for both her golden and diamond jubilees, whereas she had not only attended his celebrations but performed in them. Her pleasure was now always contingent upon his convenience. He was generous with money, but not with himself, not even with the Herzogenbergs when they had been recuperating in Nice. She recalled the thousand and one slights Joachim had suffered, most recently the premiere of Brahms's second string quintet by the Rose Quartet instead of Joachim's though it had risen from a request by Joachim for a companion to his first. He proved as no one else that you bit the hand that fed you. "You did not have to read my mind to know what I meant. You had only to read my letters."

"I read your letters – very carefully indeed. I wanted most particularly not to contradict you, not on any point, but nowhere in your letters did you say that we were not to publish the symphony."

"Let me say it again: Nowhere in my letters did I say that you *were* to publish the symphony. Re*pea*tedly in my letters did I say that Muller had advised against it. Re*pea*tedly in my letters did I say that Robert had not authorized it. How low will you have me stoop to make my point? How vulgar will you have me be? Must I spell everything out as to a village idiot? Am I to maintain no vestige of the subtlety required of a lady? Am I to countermand what you say so very directly like a fisherwoman in the marketplace? Is that what you would reduce me to? You knew what I wanted, did you not? I dare you to say, as an honest man, that you did not!"

Brahms was momentarily silent; he could not answer her directly. "I did what I thought best. I will not argue anymore for the superiority of the original, but you always pursued your argument on Muller's authority, not on your own. Had you argued the case yourself, instead of through Muller, I might have been better obliged to listen, but that you did not do."

"Aha, I thought not. You cannot say that you did not know what I wanted."

"I can say that I knew what you wanted against your own judgment. I can say that I knew what you wanted when you did not know it yourself. *That* I can say with the greatest confidence."

"We are back, then, to our original point, are we not? You insist that you know my mind better than I myself. You insist on treating me like a child, do you not?"

"Yes, indeed, if you insist on behaving like a child."

"Ah, that was not warranted. You are in the wrong and you will not own up to it. It is true that I gave you the manuscript and have thus lost any legal right in the matter, but I had at least the right to expect that no person of sensibility would have published the symphony without first obtaining my express consent. Even if, in the course of conversation, I might have remarked that I should have no objection to the publication, this could by no means have been construed as permission – and why Wullner, of all people, with whom I have less in common than with any other musician, should have been entrusted with this is entirely beyond my comprehension. It would have been quite another matter if you, who were nearer and dearer to Robert than anyone else, had published it – but I am beginning to understand that I must count you, too, as just another unhappy experience in my life."

Brahms understood her objection, but found her objection objectionable. Wagner had spoken badly of Schumann, and Wullner had conducted the premieres of *Rheingold* and *Walkure*, also programmed Wagner's work once in a concert during which Clara had played the Schumann Concerto – but he respected Wullner's musicianship. When he had been offered the directorship of the Cologne Symphony Orchestra he had recommended Wullner in his place. "I alone am responsible for the publication, but as I had no orchestra at my disposal to test the work, and as I am a bad editor, I gave it to Wullner. He admires the work, he has an excellent orchestra, and he has long proven himself an excellent editor with some of the most difficult volumes of the Bach editions – but you seem to regard him, and by association myself, not as two upright men and musicians who are perhaps misguided, but as a couple of thorough scoundrels – though I even paid for the copying myself and Wullner will receive only a nominal sum for his pains. You fail entirely to consider that we have been guided only by our love for the work and a zeal to fulfill what we consider a sacred task."

He was being disingenuous; any orchestra in Germany would have provided him with rehearsals, and he was a fine enough editor himself; but she wanted only to vent her own hurt. "I do not care what you say anymore, Johannes. I only know what I feel, and I feel that I have been stabbed in the back. I understand now why so many of your friendships turn to ashes."

"I have made up the friendships that were worth making up. Levi gave up on me, not I on him. He showed no interest in my work – and Joachim behaved through his entire divorce like an idiot – but I still made up with him – and when I was in the wrong, as I was with Bulow, I made up with him as well."

"Then how is it that I have been able to maintain friendships with both Levi and yourself, and with Joachim and his wife, but you have not?"

"That is because you are you and I am me. You have not lived my life. You do not know what I have endured."

"Ah, and can you even begin to fathom my losses? You know of them, sure, but can you feel them as I feel them?"

She meant the many deaths in her family, last of all Ferdinand, just months past. He said nothing.

"You must not blame others, Johannes, for that which you should seek within yourself. It matters little whether *I* know what you have endured. It matters much more how *you* choose to continue to endure. The choice is yours, always, but it seems to me that you have given it up. You expect others to bow to your every wish because of what *you* have endured without giving any concern to what *they* have endured. Unfortunately, you have become more selfish than you have any right to be, and you have been much spoiled because of your genius. I am afraid it has been good for no one – least of all, for you. People treat you like a child because you give them so much in your music, but in submitting to you they do you no favors. They shield you from your own nature, they flatter the worst part of it when instead they might improve it by treating you as you deserve – that is, without any special favors, like everyone else."

Brahms's eyes narrowed, the fist thickened on his brow; otherwise, he made no movement. They were no longer talking about the symphony – if, indeed, they ever had been – but he could answer her no other way and raised his voice as if to distract her from his sidestep. "I will not enlarge upon my reasons for preferring the original version – but I am in no doubt that you are in agreement with me even now, if only tacitly. As for the rest, you are the only person who may speak thus to me – but be warned, I will not bear it, not even from you, not for long."

His raised voice always swallowed her arguments; when reason failed you shouted; but she did not flinch, considered it a victory that she had said what she had said at all. "You still do not understand, Johannes, but maybe you will yet. I speak for you as much as for myself. A friendship so onesided is no friendship at all."

Brahms turned from her in silence. The front door was opening. Marie had returned.

ii

"Doktor Brahms, how good to see you. Tell me, will your next work take us to heaven or to hell?"

Hugo Conrat had transcribed Hungarian folksongs into German verses for Brahms to set in his Gypsy Songs. He grinned, welcoming Brahms to his home, one among a dozen guests for supper. It was a joke, but Brahms was sick of the same stupid jokes, the same stupid questions, the same gowns and jewelry on the women, dinner jackets and decorations on the men, detritus in the homes – bibelots, paintings, upholstery, wall hangings. There was even a portrait of himself on the desk next to a silver inkstand. He glowered at his host. "If I may say so, Conrat, it is all the same to me where you go."

Conrat laughed goodnaturedly, joined by the Friedlanders and Miller von Aichholzes. Professor Max Friedlander, almost twenty years younger than Brahms, a singer and once a student of Stockhausen, gave Brahms a shallow bow. "Brahms, may I present to you my wife?"

Frau Professor Friedlander bounced beside her husband, white face wide as the moon with her smile. "I cannot say what an honor it is, Herr Doktor Brahms, finally to be making your acquaintance. Is it not strange that you have known my husband for so long and yet we have never met?"

Brahms smiled, giving Frau Friedlander a deep bow. "Alas, but the misfortune is mine. I wish it might have been the other way around – that I might have known you for so long and never met your husband."

Again the company laughed, including Frau Friedlander though with a crimsoning face.

Victor von Miller zu Aichholz, a Viennese industrialist, grinned – a trim small man, sporting a Vandyke beard and a full head of slick chestnut hair combed straight back. "You must not be embarrassed, Frau Friedlander. It is ever thus with Doktor Brahms –"

"No, Victor, you are not to tell that story again." His wife, Olga von Miller, black hair piled in a bun on her head, almost shouted across the company, but her eyes smiled on her unlined face.

Brahms shouted louder still. "Why not? If he does not, I will!"

"Oh, very well, then – but I must say, Doktor Brahms, that it is not very chivalrous of you to make the ladies blush for your pleasure."

Brahms laughed. "I can assure you that I do it for their pleasure as much as mine."

Miller shook his head. "Unfortunately, after all this fuss you will be expecting more than the story delivers. All I meant to say was that Brahms met me at the station a while ago with the warmest embrace, a kiss on both cheeks – the wettest kisses, I might add. I had not realized I inspired such deep emotion, until he held me at armslength and said: 'Oh, it is you, is it, Miller? I took you for your better half!'"

The company laughed. Frau Friedlander turned to Frau Miller. "Well, then, am I to assume that Doktor Brahms says that to all the ladies?"

Brahms spoke with authority. "Indeed, you are, Frau Friedlander. It is the reason I have never married. Why tie myself to one woman when I might have them all?"

Friedlander laughed. "Why, indeed?"

Frau Ilse Conrat shook her head. "I think that might just be the Herr Doktor's way of saying that he very much wishes – as he puts it himself – to be tied to just one woman. We will see what we can do about that, Doktor Brahms."

Brahms laughed. "I am afraid you are too late by about sixty years."

Frau von Miller turned to Frau Friedlander. "Chivalry is not Doktor Brahms's strong suit, but he makes up for it in other ways." She turned again to Brahms. "Will you be playing for us again later tonight, Doktor Brahms?"

Brahms shook his head. "I am very much afraid I no longer practise cruelty to dumb animals."

Again the company laughed, but Frau Conrat noted that Brahms was not smiling, his brow more knotted with wrinkles than she could remember.

MORE CARRIAGES DROVE UP TO THE HOUSE, more guests were introduced, among them Baroness Gisela Bachrich, a divorced woman of forty years; her hair was black, also her eyes and gown; a diamond barette held her hair, a diamond pendant drew attention to her decolletage. She leaned forward when she spoke, enveloping Brahms in a fragrance of jasmine and myrrh, touching his sleeve, laughing at everything he said. He noted her expanses of rich white skin not without a pang, bare shoulders, tendrils of fashionably escaped hair. He had met her before, but however inviting, however accessible she appeared, he always found himself hopeless. Flirtations were easy, followups impossible.

The Baroness sipped champagne. "I am often told, Doktor Brahms, that I resemble Emilia Rontgen. Do you not find that it is so?"

Emilia Rontgen was an actress, renowned for her roles onstage and off, also for her beauty. Brahms gripped his champagne glass in his left hand, his third refill, a cigar wedged between the fingers of his right. "Hah! Yes, I find it so – indeed, I do."

The Baroness smiled, standing closer. "Do you really?"

Brahms laughed again. "Yes, really. I simply cannot tell the two of you apart. When I am next to one of you, I invariably wish it were the other."

The smiles around them became more strained, the Baroness's most of all. "Ah, Doktor Brahms, I know you are joking, but you are cruel to say it."

"Well, well, it must be as you say. I am joking and I am cruel."

Professor von Ehrenstein, another of the guests in the circle, nodded at the Baroness. "It is said, you know, that you always hurt the one you love."

The Baroness smiled more comfortably. "Then I wish that Doktor Brahms would not love me quite so very much."

Laughter spread spontaneously through the company, including Brahms.

FRAU CONRAT absented herself from her friends to mind the preparations, but Brahms followed her into the diningroom. "Frau Conrat, why has the cloth been laid in the diningroom and not in the verandah?"

"It is October, Doktor Brahms. I thought it might be too cold."

"But it is not cold yet, Frau Conrat – and I always dine outdoors in October."

Frau Conrat stared at him, but only for a moment. He had always been a difficult guest, but seemed recently to have become impossible. "Very well, it will be as you wish, but we will have to eat a little later. I will send instructions to the kitchen that dinner is to be delayed by twenty minutes."

Brahms bowed, still frowning, and returned to the drawingroom. It was true what Clara said, his friends treated him like a child. They had continued to correspond, but Clara's letters were now starchy with decorum, hiding all the wrinkles of her personality. No one dared talk to him anymore as she had, not Billroth, not the Herzogenbergs, never Joachim. He had managed to offend them all, reducing all conversations to externals, forcing their friendships into retreat, isolating himself in the process.

Frau Conrat reentered the drawingroom. "Friends, since the weather is holding up so well this year we will be dining, by Doktor Brahms's special request, in the verandah, after all – but since dinner will be a few minutes later than expected, let me entreat you to take advantage as well in the meantime of a walk in the garden – and to thank you for your patience."

Brahms nodded, apparently approving what he heard, but his forehead seemed almost to pulse.

THE CONRAT VILLA LAY ON THE OUTSKIRTS of Vienna. The chestnut trees were yellow and red, statuary dotted the landscaped garden, quilted meadows rolled into hillocks of firs, pines, and beeches; the setting sun turned the hills to a haze, the green to gold.

Brahms was seated at dinner between the Baroness and Frau Ottilie von Grotze, a widow, not unlike many with whom he was seated at such dinners, young, wealthy, attractive, hanging on his every word, smiling, laughing, flattering him. They all meant well, but understood not a word he said. He could not explain it, but even when he said exactly the same thing as Conrat or Faber or Fellinger or Friedlander, they meant different things. The same words meant different things because he was different, and this was the difference everyone ignored, the difference he wished he could ignore himself. When Frau Conrat had asked him to escort the Baroness to the verandah for dinner he had given his arm instead to the governess, Frau Hilda Schoenberg. He was saying one thing, but the others heard something else. He was treated as everyone's equal, but felt equal only to the governess. He wished to be like the rest, but was proud of his difference, and rude to emphasize the difference. Without his celebrity he faded, meant nothing to anyone in the room, however loudly they would protest to the contrary. He seemed as unable to accept company which accepted him as to marry a woman who might wish to marry him.

Red wine and champagne accompanied each plate, servants hovered in the doorway, jewelry glittered in the electric light, conversation bubbled like music. The meal was the best part of the evening for Brahms: four kinds of bread; a cold elderberry soup with apple slices and liver dumplings; a stew of peas, carrots, cauliflower, asparagus, mushrooms, crayfish tails, medallions of veal, and dumplings; steaming wiener schnitzels with fried potatoes and beans; a saddle of venison simmering in a sauce of red wine with sauteed pears and potato croquettes – and the promise of plumcake, pastries, and schnapps to come.

The guests congratulated Frau Conrat on her table; she apologized for the simplicity of the meal. Brahms, who had become quieter, suddenly slapped the table with his palm, shaking the glasses, spilling some wine, glaring at his hostess. "It is not so very simple a meal, Frau Conrat – and even if it were, why bother to apologize?"

For a moment there was silence, all eyes turned toward him, but Frau Conrat recovered quickly. "I am sorry, Doktor Brahms. I seem to have upset you. May I apologize for my apology?"

Some of the guests laughed; what he said was again different from what was heard; but Brahms smiled himself. It was no one's fault, Frau Conrat's least of all, that he was different, only perhaps his own for being among them – but he had nowhere else to go. He had changed too much to remain a Hamburger, but not enough (never enough) to become a Viennese – the consummate bourgeois Viennese. He would always be Johannes Kreisler, Jr. among the haut monde, cocooned in a loneliness no one could understand, not even Clara who had made the greatest effort. He raised his wineglass again. "The wine is very good, indeed, Frau Conrat. You must give me the recipe."

The laughter that followed was tinged with more relief than mirth, but allowed the dinner to proceed as before. Brahms said little as he ate, heard even less, but found himself suddenly the focus of the table. Friedlander narrowed his eyes as he spoke. "I believe you know the lady, Doktor Brahms. Pray, what is your opinion of her?"

Brahms looked up from his plate. "Which lady do you mean?"

"Why, the lady of whom we have just been speaking."

"I am afraid you will have to be more specific. I find it very hard to concentrate when a lady on my right chatters constantly in E major and a lady on my left in E minor."

No one laughed. Friedlander spoke seriously. "I mean the Countess von Zellner. I believe you are acquainted with her?"

"Ah, the Countess! What is my opinion of the Countess? Well, let me put it thus: I have seen the many portraits she has commissioned of herself – and I can honestly say that the portraits are all flatteringly *un*like her."

Again, there was silence, broken finally by Frau von Grotze on his left. "Herr Doktor, perhaps I should say something. Perhaps I should have said it before. The Countess is a good friend of mine. I do not find that funny."

Brahms spoke without turning. "Well, then, since she is a such a good friend of yours, let me say something complimentary about her. She played for me some of her compositions once, for my opinion, and I must say," he smiled, turning to Frau von Grotze – "her writing paper was quite exceptional. Not even Beethoven could have improved upon it."

The silence began to descend like a shroud. Brahms put down his fork and knife and looked around the table. "Why do you ask me these things? She is a purse and a cutpurse – like all the others of her tribe. On her arm she carries the cowskin purse in which she accepts a man's money – and then there is the other skin," he raised one eyebrow, "in which she accepts the man – like a Venus flytrap." He snapped his left hand twice like the jaws of a crocodile. "Why do you suppose it was named after Venus? And what are men if not reduced to flies in such circumstances?" He raised the middle finger of his right hand. "And what happens when the fly gets near the flytrap?" Both eyebrows rose. The fly of his middle finger zigged and zagged, but the maw of his left hand rose suddenly and snapped shut around the finger. "Purse or pussy, where is the difference? A man who succumbs loses everything – and he deserves it."

There was a collective gasp from the women, the men looked from their host to Brahms, Hugo Conrat addressed Brahms directly. "Doktor Brahms, perhaps you would care for some coffee?"

Brahms understood the implication; the company had consumed seven bottles of champagne before embarking on a strong red wine. His eyes were bloodshot. "Keep your bloody coffee for those who need it, Conrat!" He swallowed the rest of his wine in a gulp, the rest of his champagne in another, wiping his mouth with the back of his hand, wiping his hand in his beard, brown with gravy, red with wine, glistening in the electric light, and looked around the table. The group stared, still as statues, as did the servants. He wanted to get up but could barely move. He had eaten too much, drunk too much. He looked around the table again more slowly, still the focus of everyone's gaze. "It would appear that I owe everyone here an apology."

He waited for a protest from one of the Conrats, but there was none forthcoming. Perhaps he had said too much, but could not stop himself. "Very well, then, I apologize." He laughed, but cut himself short, glaring around the table. "If there is anyone here tonight whom I have not insulted, I humbly apologize." He filled the ensuing silence again with his solitary laugh.

"FRIEDLANDER, thank you for coming with me."

Brahms sat in the carriage with Max Friedlander. The dinner had not lasted much longer. He was aware he had behaved badly, but not apologized. Instead, he had drunk two cups of strong black coffee, and ridden back to Vienna in silence with the Friedlanders, but as the carriage had reached Karlsgasse, and the full horror of the evening sunk into consciousness, he had asked Friedlander if he would mind staying with him for a while. His wife's expression had remained stiff since they had left the Conrat villa. She had sat across from Brahms, an arm crossed with her husband's, but said nothing to the suggestion. They had driven her home first and Brahms had given the driver directions. Alone in the carriage with Friedlander he gave the first indication that he was sorry. "Was it, after all, so very bad?"

Friedlander nodded, but spoke gently. "Yes, it was. It was very bad."

Brahms pursed his lips, thrusting forward his lower. "Look here, can you tell me a little something about your childhood?"

Friedlander did not understand but complied without question, speaking sentimentally of a large family in Silesia, poor but happy, protected from everything ugly.

The veins in Brahms's forehead throbbed as he spoke, his beard bristled. "Tchhah! You have been raised in cotton. You have known nothing about how coarse women can be – yes, women. You would not have so very exalted a view of women if you had known them as I did at a very early age."

"Why, Brahms? Whatever can you mean?"

The carriage stopped. "You will see very soon. You may remove your cravat and your collar, if you wish. You will not need them where we are going."

"But where are we going?"

"You must trust me. This is not easy for me, but there is something I *must* show you."

"But can we not take the carriage to where we are going?"

"Believe me, it will be less conspicuous this way."

Friedlander left his cravat and collar on the seat, followed Brahms out of the carriage, found himself on a narrow winding cobbled street of the inner city, and left instructions with his driver to wait where he was. Brahms walked ahead, bowler in hand. Men in the street walked alone; women exhibited themselves in the windows. The smell of beer and urine hung in the air like a living thing. They were on one of Vienna's oldest streets, houses from the fifteenth century built with thick stone walls for protection against the Turkish invasion.

Friedlander recognized the place from his student days, taverns where you could get a pint and a piece of sausage for less than a florin, women for the same price. The people on the street were silent, moving like zombies, but women and barkers called from doorways, shouting their rates, promising Parisian postcards, Turkish bellydancers, oriental massages, an African and her snake, a Brazilian and her monkey, a gypsy and her dog. From the taverns there was piano music, loud voices, laughter. The places appeared no less rowdy than when Friedlander had been a student, no less lascivious, but they no longer appealed.

Had he not kept close behind Brahms he might have missed entering one of the narrow stone doorways, but as he followed him in he noted the thick walls, some still pocked with bullets from the 1848 revolution. The room was dark, dense with smoke, pungent with sweat, the ceiling low. Brahms chose a table, ordered two beers without asking Friedlander, nursed his stein, and stared at the people in silence. A small space had been cleared for dancing, an upright piano stood against the wall.

Friedlander sipped his beer, saying nothing; he would have had to shout to be heard. He could not understand what Brahms meant to show him and was about to ask when a woman shouted from the next table. "Professor, play us some dance music. We would like to dance."

To Friedlander's astonishment, Brahms left his table without a word, crossed the dance floor, seated himself at the piano, and began to play, resembling for all his bulk and beard nothing more than a scared schoolboy. The woman and two men from her table followed him to the dance floor. Friedlander's eyes, accustomed now to the dark, made her out clearly. She wore a single garment, more like an undergarment, a chemise, blue, filmy, barely covering her knees, barely even opaque, trimmed with lace, and held by straps thin as tendrils, a woman long past her fortieth year.

Both men wore long loose coats with wide sleeves, top hats, riding boots, but as they danced, the three of them together, Friedlander noted to his dismay that one of them wore a pink leotard underneath his coat, apparently nothing else, and the other was barechested with a bright red scarf around his waist for a belt. Both were young, muscular, barely thirty.

No one astonished him more than Brahms. The man who had been awarded the Freedom of the City of Hamburg, the Order of Leopold in Vienna, the highest honors the cities could bestow, who had consorted with royalty, and was recognized as the foremost composer in the country – on the continent – was playing the cheapest dance music – waltzes, quadrilles, czardas, popular music – at the command of the commonest people.

Others joined the trio on the floor. Brahms played for more than an hour before rejoining Friedlander at his table. His eyes were bright with defiance, but he said nothing as he sat down.

Friedlander spoke as one hypnotized. "Do you know that woman?"

"What do you think?"

"But she is a prostitute."

"There you are mistaken. Her prostitution days are long behind her, but she runs a house on Komptegasse. I have known her a long time and women like her all my life. I used to play dance music for women like her a long time ago."

Friedlander remained silent.

Brahms nodded, twisting his lip, holding Friedlander's gaze. "Yes, we, too, were poor when I was growing up in Hamburg – but I used to play in places very much like this one by the Hamburg docks, all through the night, for the sailors and their girls – and I never left them behind. Now, do you understand?"

"My dear Brahms, I am so sorry."

Brahms screwed his face into a knot. "Tchhah! Do not be sorry. If you are sorry you have understood nothing. I do not want your pity. I want you to understand. People think they know Johannes Brahms – the great Johannes Brahms. They know nothing."

Brahms glared across the table; Friedlander merely nodded.

SLEEP WAS DIFFICULT THAT NIGHT: if he had married and lived a regular life he might have given up composition like Joachim, burdened by the cares of a family, overcome by the money madness, or done worse, like Schumann – but he had begun to question his own motives. Perhaps the reverse was true: he had dedicated himself to music because a regular life was beyond his capacity – at least, with women he found worthy. Nietzsche had been right to call him a eunuch: music was his substitute for passion, his yearning for love, his cure for everything. Clara, too, was right: he sought in others what he needed to seek in himself – but he could not imagine how he might have done anything differently.

Lying on his back he found himself shaking, tears creeping into his ears, onto the pillow. As his sobbing got louder he clamped the pillow over his face, afraid the noise might reach Frau Truxa and her family. He still imagined Clara, Agathe, Julie, Elisabet, Hermine, and others beside him in bed. Was it merely a price paid for special gifts? a deal made? an exchange? Beethoven never married, nor Schubert, nor so many others – but Bach had married, and Mozart, and Wagner – but perhaps they had paid a different price, he was not to know. There was always a choice, always a price. It was the worm in the harmony. Change came from changing oneself, not forcing change on others, and at some point he had isolated himself from everyone: Joachim, Bulow, Billroth, the Herzogenbergs – worst of all, from Clara.

A week later he returned to the Conrat villa with a bouquet. Frau Conrat was twice surprised: first, she had not invited him, and second it was known he had never given flowers to anyone, not even to Clara Schumann. His voice was gruff, his gaze remained on the floor. "Maybe we can have another outing – in the country – as we did last year – as we talked about?"

Frau Conrat smiled, touching his arm. "But, Doktor Brahms, do you not realize that it has already been arranged? We have even engaged your room just as we agreed."

Brahms looked up from the floor, smiling, almost shy. "Hmmm! Well, then, it is all right."

iii

BRAHMS TO HEINRICH VON HERZOGENBERG   *Vienna, Jan. 1892*

My very dear Friend,

I am too much with you in thought to write much. It is vain to attempt any expression of the feelings that absorb me so completely – and you will be sitting alone in your dumb misery, speechless yourself, not desirous of speech from others.

I am full of sorrow and profoundest sympathy when I think of you. I could ask questions without end, but to no avail. You know how unutterably I myself suffer the loss of your beloved wife, and can gauge accordingly my emotions in thinking of you, who were associated with her by the closest possible human ties.

As soon as you feel at all inclined to think of yourself and others, let me know how you are, and how and where you intend to carry on your own life. It would do me so much good just to sit beside you quietly, press your hand, and share your thoughts of the dear marvelous woman.

Your friend,

J. Brahms

BRAHMS TO CLARA *Vienna, 13 September, 1892*

My dearest Clara,

On this, your 73rd birthday, after a friendship that has lasted forty years, I find myself more distant from you than on the day we met. Please allow a poor pariah to tell you today that he always thinks of you with the same respect, and out of the fullness of his heart wishes you, whom he holds dearer than anything else on earth, all that is good, desirable, and beautiful.

Alas, to you more than to any other, I am a pariah. In my dealings with my friends I am aware of only one fault: my lack of tact. For years now you have been kind enough to treat this leniently. If only you could have done so for a few years more! It is very difficult after all this time to be called merely "another unhappy experience." This, too, can be borne, but let me repeat to you one more time that you and your husband constitute the most beautiful experience of my life, and represent all that is richest and most noble in it.

Of your interest in my music I feel I can always rest assured, but the artist cannot and should not be separated from the man – and in me it happens that the artist is not so sensitive as the man, and the man has but small consolation if the work of the artist cannot expiate his sins. But today I am not thinking of myself and still less of my music, but am hoping with the most heartfelt sincerity that everything will go ever better and better with you.

I feel that owing to my peculiar ways – and not to anything else – that I may have deserved the great pain of seeing you turn away from me, but loving and reverent thoughts of you and him will always shine warmly and brightly in the heart of Your devoted
J. B.

CLARA TO BRAHMS *Frankfurt, 27 September, 1892*

My dear Johannes,

Your good wishes for my birthday reached me in Interlaken just as we were about to leave. Meanwhile we have been traveling about a little and have only just settled down here with the peace and quiet necessary for answering your momentous letter. It made me very sad, but I am glad you have spoken out so frankly, for now I can do the same.

You are certainly right in saying that personal intercourse with you is often difficult, and yet my friendship for you has always helped me to rise above your vagaries. Unfortunately, on the occasion of your last visit, I was unable to rid my heart of the bitter feelings it harbored against you.

But enough of this! Nothing makes me more miserable than these disputes and explanations. Am I not the most peaceable person on earth? So, my dear Johannes, let us strike a more friendly note. Greeting you, the man as well as the artist, with the same old affection, I am still
Your Clara

BRAHMS TO CLARA *Vienna, October*

My Dear Clara,

From the bottom of my heart I thank you for your kind and comforting letter. The subject of our altercation I do not even remember, but I infinitely regret not having kept a sharper guard over my tongue.

As you wish to have them, I am sending you a volume of pieces for the piano. You can let me have the whole lot back at your convenience. In the short C minor piece you will probably do well to take the six-eight time as it is given in brackets at the upbeat.

Your Johannes

"Johannes!" Clara wore a lace cap and black taffeta gown which rustled when she moved. "All I need now is a treasure chest for all the pearls you have sent me these past few months. I cannot tell you how happy they have made me. They are like cordials to my soul."

Brahms sat smiling in his red flannel shirt by her side on the sofa, holding her hand in silence.

Clara smiled no less. "When I play your things I quite forget where I am. I feel only rapture. They account for my happiest hour everyday – you, Johannes, you account for my happiest hour!"

Still he smiled, saying nothing, squeezing her hand. Herzogenberg had found short piano pieces composed by his wife among her effects, prompting Brahms's efforts though he had written nothing for solo piano in almost twenty-five years. He recalled similar remarks by Elisabet (How happy! How happy this sonata makes me!), by Herzogenberg (They made me so happy for a couple of days I almost felt again that life was worth living), by Billroth (They have given me the happiest hours of my life), by Bulow (They have returned me to my life). He recalled as well the comfort he had derived himself from playing Bach's Goldberg Variations on hearing his mamma had died, never imagining his own music could bring such comfort, such joy, but he no longer questioned it, no longer separated the musician from the man, merely smiled.

Clara marveled at how the work poured from him, how full were his ideas of imagination, grandeur, depth, how he combined tenderness and passion in the smallest spaces – and how quickly she forgot the tribulations he caused. Since their quarrel he had made up everything, sent not only his new pieces for the piano still drying on the page, but also Richard Muhlfeld, his Fraulein Klarinette of the Meiningen Orchestra, and other musicians, to perform his works for the clarinet in her sittingroom – even an emissary from Thomas Edison with his phonograph and a recording of himself squeaking greetings to the inventor, playing a few bars from his first Hungarian dance.

He had also sent Alice Barbi, an Italian contralto, thirty years younger, with whom he was said to be in love, to perform his new songs for her. She could understand the attraction (Barbi had risen to fame overnight, known for her programs of songs by Schubert, Schumann, and Brahms; she had large black eyes, wore her luxurious dark hair loosely knotted behind her, and combined Italian songfulness with German seriousness), but she no longer asked Johannes about such matters and was glad she had said nothing. Nothing had come of his dalliance with Hermine Spiess who had died at just thirty-six years, and nothing had come of his dalliance with Alice Barbi who had married an Austrian nobleman and retired from the stage – but not before a final concert in which Johannes had surprised everyone by appearing as her accompanist, lumbering onstage it was said with the awkwardness of a great Newfoundland dog following its mistress.

He tended to her now as no one else could, as he never had before, not even in his youth when he had been prompted in part by infatuation. Now he cared only for her comfort, asking nothing in return, and all thoughts of him always found her smiling. "These piano pieces are perfect, not only of themselves but also for me at this time. My hearing is now so poor I can no longer endure the music of orchestras, nor even of quartets. I feel as if each musician were playing something different. I can enjoy music now only on the piano."

His smile faded, his face expressed concern. "Is it so very bad, then, your hearing?"

"It is not painful, but I simply do not hear correctly. Even on the piano, I sometimes have to play the bass in the treble before I can follow the harmonies for works with which I am unfamiliar. Otherwise, they all blur together."

He grinned. "The sounds that are blurred to you would sound pleasurable to so many today. They make symphonies now out of what you find insupportable, and they study the blurs and write long essays about them."

Clara did not smile, understanding him literally as always; he needed a microscope to locate her sense of humor and she a club to deflect his; but she squeezed his hand. After Robert's death there had been no one else to withstand Wagner, no one else to continue the tradition of Bach and Beethoven, no one else to preserve her faith in the future of music. "You do not mean it, surely, Johannes, what you have said about retiring again?"

Brahms sighed. "I am afraid it is so, Clara. The tale is told. The snake bites its tail."

"Oh, Johannes, please, do not speak in riddles. My poor brain simply cannot take it. Whatever do you mean? What is this snake?"

He had recently arranged forty-nine German folksongs, seven sets of seven, to be sung with the piano. "It is no great riddle. The last of the folksongs, 'The Moon Steals Up,' is the very song upon which I based the slow movement of my very first sonata, my Opus 1. The circle is closed. That is all I meant to say."

"Ah, I see. That is poetic. Did you plan it that way?"

"No – at least, not at first. That is what I like best about it."

"So this is really the end?"

"We are now in the front line, Clara, you and I."

She knew what he meant. His sister, Elise, had died the same year as Elisabet; Hermine the following year just one year married; Billroth and Bulow the next, just six days apart. True to Elisabet's prediction, Nietzsche had been institutionalized, but his influence was only beginning. It was still a while before his work was bowdlerized by his sister to appeal to the Nazis – as were Wagner's political writings, still later, to appeal to everyone else, after they had become Hitler's favorite reading. "That is not what I meant."

"I know – but I meant it both ways."

They continued to hold hands. Brahms was visiting for just a day. His train left within an hour. When Marie came to remind them of the time the two had risen but held each other tightly, Clara's cap askew against Brahms's shoulder, her face wedged against his beard but lit by an inner brilliance as they swayed gently together, seeming to dance– in three-four time and prestissimo though they hardly moved – and Marie said nothing, shuffling softly backward out of the room.

Marie sat with Clara in their garden, Clara in her wheelchair. "Mamma, do you know it is Doktor Brahms's birthday today?"

Clara raised her eyebrows, surprised, opening her mouth, her lips trembling, but no sound issued, and she raised her hand, writing in the air.

"Shall I get you pen and paper?"

"P'ease."

Marie went into the house. It had been more than a month now, her mamma had given a piano lesson in the morning, in the afternoon they had gone for a drive, when her face had undergone a change midconversation. She had refused to own she felt ill, insisted on a walk when they reached home, but she had suffered a stroke. Since then she had had difficulty speaking, difficulty writing, and wishing to write her name under a picture she had taken up her pen, begun with the wrong letter, shaken her head at Marie, put down the pen – but she had improved subsequently, well enough for them to plan the summer again in Interlaken.

Marie had written to Brahms who had canceled a trip until he had been assured there was no immediate danger. He had offered to come to Frankfurt on the subterfuge that it was on his way to Berlin for the Academy Festivals, but Marie had not wished unnecessarily to alarm her mamma and persuaded him there was no need. Brahms had written: *If you think the worst is to be expected be so good as to let me know. I would like to come while those dear eyes are still open, for when they close so much will end for me. Forgive me, I sincerely hope my anxiety is unfounded.*

The pen was unsteady in Clara's hand, but she seemed not to mind from her smile. Marie smiled herself at the smile, but asked not why, preferring her mamma to have her joy without the difficulty of explaining it. The pen continued to wiggle in Clara's hand, but her smile remained steady. Johannes had been so funny during his last visit. Seeing a large quantity of tobacco in his traveling bag she had asked the obvious question. "What are you going to do with all that tobacco?"

His answer had been so short, so guileless, it made her smile all over again. "Smuggle it."

She had said nothing, only shaking her head and smiling at the antic. It was the last thing he had said before leaving – his smile, despite the heavy white beard, that of a child bent on his prank. He often asked foreign friends to smuggle tobacco across the frontier when they visited Austria, and had once turned contrabandist himself, hiding his favorite Turkish mixture in a stocking, imagining none would be the wiser – only to have the customs officers gravitate unerringly to what looked like an amputated leg. He had lost the leg, his temper, and seventy gulden to a fine – but not his resolve to have the last laugh.

Clara wrote, not without difficulty, not legibly, on the paper Marie had brought:

> *Dearest Johannes,*
> *Heartiest good wishes from your affectionate and devoted CLARA SCHUMANN.*
> *I cannot very well do anymore yet, but or soon Your* _____

ii

Everything that could have gone wrong went wrong. Brahms did not get Marie's telegram, *Our mamma fell gently asleep today,* until he was in Ischl. Frau Truxa had forwarded it by regular mail imagining it was from just another of his myriad admirers. A guard forgot to wake him on the train and he woke to find himself traveling away from Frankfurt. Arriving finally in Frankfurt he read in a newspaper that a memorial service had been held in the city, attended by the mayor, directors of the conservatory, playrights, actors, artistes, a Bach chorale had been sung, the funeral chant from the *Peri* – but the funeral was to be in Bonn since Clara had wished to be buried with Robert.

She had received his letter of thanks for her birthday wishes: *The last was the best! Never has this maxim been brought home to me more beautifully than today when the dearest thing of all, your wishes for the 7th, arrived.* She had felt better yet again, but two days later suffered a more severe stroke than the last, Marie had called Eugenie who had arrived from England four days before the end – but said nothing to Brahms until it was too late. He did not blame her: in matters of consequence he remained a child; he would have been only an inconvenience. When Joachim had written to him the year before that he feared their friend's days were numbered he had replied with bravado: *The thought of losing her can no longer frighten us, not even me, the lonely one, for whom all too little lives in this world – and when she has left us, will not our faces shine when we think of her, of that glorious woman whom we have been happy enough to know during the course of a long life, loving and admiring her ever more and more. Thus, and only thus, shall we mourn her.* He had been too foolish, a man in his sixties, to recognize his insincerity, his false hope. He wished now she might have lived forever – at least, until he had died himself. Not surprisingly, he had proven more prescient again in his music, come out of retirement a second time to set four passages from the Bible to music. He had written the songs before he had known of Clara's stroke:

> The condition of mankind is the condition of the beast;
> As the beast dies, so dies the man.
> All have but one breath,
> The man no more than the beast,
> For all is vanity.

When he arrived finally in Bonn he had been traveling continually for almost forty hours, an old man, sixty-three years, tired, dirty, smelly, his shirt sticking to his back, hair on his head lank with sweat, beard stiff, askew for the way he had slept on the train. He was too late for the service in the chapel, but in time to join the funeral procession to the grave. It was 23 May, 1896; he had walked the same path almost forty years ago, following Robert's casket with Joachim and Dietrich and the mayors of Bonn and Dusseldorf, Clara straggling behind, adding his clods of earth after the casket had been lowered.

The grave was covered with wreaths, more than two hundred, from all over the continent. Joachim had attended the service in Frankfurt, but left then for commitments long delayed in Italy. A choir sang, "When the Time Has Come for Me to Go," the pastor spoke, "Eye hath not seen, ear hath not heard, neither hath entered into the heart of man the things God hath prepared for them that love him."

Brahms crept away. Thick ivy framed the chapel door, nightingales sang in the bushes, churchbells rang for the Whitsunday Festival, but he stopped before he reached the gate, blinded by tears, rocking on his feet, fists clenched, shoulders shaking, face fallen, nose sunk like an egg in his beard, sobs popping in tiny bursts snatched back in long wheezing breaths.

Herzogenberg followed him out and stood silently with his friend, head bowed.

Dr. Grunberger was still making the last entry in his ledger when Brahms erupted through the door. "Herr Doktor, I am Johannes Brahms."

Grunberger, a round man with a round face, stroked his Vandyke beard, looking up from his ledger, adjusting his round spectacles. Dr. Hertzka of Ischl had written to him about Doktor Brahms, the famous composer, a case of jaundice, sent to Karlsbad for the waters, for Grunberger to prescribe a regimen. Brahms's appearance spoke for itself, yellow face, dry skin, dull eyes, brittle white mane, seeming to shrink as he stood in the doorway, hat in hand, clothes too large by a size or two. The receptionist was close behind the intruder, frowning to indicate the patient had rushed past him, ready it seemed to launch into a tirade, but Grunberger held up a finger for silence. "Doktor Brahms, I am indeed pleased to meet you, but did we not arrange for me to examine you tomorrow morning in your home?"

Brahms spoke sharply. "I am here now. Examine me at once!"

The voice surprised Grunberger, forceful despite its pitch, despite his appearance, but he noted as well the whites of his eyes, yellow as mustard, panic in his voice. "Very well, then." He turned to the receptionist. "Herr Boll, please see that we are not disturbed."

The young man still frowned; an anteroomful of patients awaited the doctor; but he nodded, shutting the door behind him.

Having won his battle Brahms relaxed, his shoulders slumped, and his clothes seemed yet another size too large. "All of my life I have avoided Karlsbad like the plague." He laughed. "I have never been ill a day in my life. I have never had much faith in spas and water cures. It is all in the mind, is it not, Herr Doktor, whether a man is ill or not?"

"Sometimes, it is, yes."

"Most of the time – but I am glad finally to have come. I have my bourgeois illness to thank for bringing me here – and I see that Karlsbad's reputation for sunshine, at least, is not undeserved."

The doctor smiled. "Sunshine is, indeed, something we can guarantee." He could see his patient talked to comfort himself. "Well, Doktor Brahms, shall we get on with it?"

"At once."

"Will you sit here?"

Brahms sat where he indicated, shy as he smiled. "Now remember, Herr Doktor, it is your responsibility only to cure me – and not to tell me anything unpleasant."

The doctor entered into the spirit of the game. "Of course – but if you say A, you must also say B. It is your responsibility, Doktor Brahms, is it not, to allow me to cure you? You must follow my instructions to the letter, must you not?"

Brahms grinned weakly. "Of course."

"Tell me, then, when did you first think something was the matter?"

He had caught a severe chill on the night of Clara's funeral, succumbing to the exhaustion of his long journey, his sorrow without end. Marie had offered him mementos from Clara's treasures, a brooch of Beethoven's hair, an amulet once owned by Mozart, Robert's cigar case, the seal with which he had signed letters and articles, but he had wanted nothing, the most beautiful mementos had long been locked in his head. He had left Bonn only to roam the Rhineland, revive old memories, revisit old friends, the path he had taken more than forty years ago when he had first visited the Schumanns. He had appeared next, unannounced, in Vienna for the silver anniversary of the Fellingers, before returning to Ischl. "It was more than a month ago, Herr Doktor, on a very hot day, when I set out to walk from Ischl to Lauffen – but I was so deep in thought that I just walked and walked and walked, without looking much around me – until, to my astonishment, I was in Steg – eight miles from Ischl. Then I walked all the way back. That night I thought I was going to die. I went from one swoon into another – but the next day I was convinced it was only because I had exerted myself beyond my limit. After a while I realized something was wrong and I visited Doktor Hertzka. The rest you know." He did not mention that he had completed the last of a set of eleven preludes for the organ while in Ischl and a fantasia on the chorale: "Oh, world, I must leave thee." It seemed too ominous.

The doctor nodded, asked him to unbutton his shirt, and began his examination at the head, frowning when he reached the abdomen, much swollen, the liver seeming twice its normal size. He knew what the matter was at once, but said nothing. Brahms wished to hear nothing unpleasant, and though patients joked about such things they meant what they said, each had his own way of coping. "When did you eat last?"

"About two hours ago."

"Then I must make another examination in the morning when your stomach is empty." The examination was merely to confirm his finding, but there was another complication. If he allowed his patient to take the cure for jaundice, for which he had come to Karlsbad he would be dead within a fortnight – but neither did he wish to alarm him. He persuaded Brahms that he was too weak for the big cure and prescribed a preparatory cure instead – half a mug of a prepared water, morning and evening, to stimulate his appetite, and strengthen him for the big cure for which he would be ready the following year. His earnest manner convinced Brahms. "Herr Doktor, what you say has head and foot. I pledge you my word of honor I will follow your instructions."

The doctor remained serious, successful at least in relieving Brahms temporarily though he knew his cause was lost. It would make no difference how carefully he followed instructions: his liver was greatly enlarged, his gall ducts obstructed. The entry he made in his ledger left no doubt of his finding:

3 September, 1896
No. 1033: Hr. Brahms – Vienna. hep. hyp. m.

1033 indicated the number of the patient for the year, the abbreviations "hepatis hypertrophia maligna" – malignant swelling of the liver, cancer of the liver, which had also killed his father.

ii

Brahms's Fourth Symphony glides so smoothly into its first theme that the listener finds himself deep in its wake before he realizes it has even been launched. The large generous melody comprises groupings of two notes, rising and falling, is borne by violins, lapped by winds, and buoyed by violas and cellos as it rocks with the gentleness of a cradle into its development – toward the first squall.

Brahms heard it for the last time under the baton of Hans Richter, in Vienna, on 7 March, 1897, but his mind was elsewhere, combing the past as it now did incessantly. The good, earnest, impressive Dr. Grunberger had lied – for his own good, and perhaps it was his own fault asking for the deception, but his rage had been bottomless when his deterioration revealed the lie. His strength continued to ebb, his color to deepen, his body to shrivel. He had refused even to accept mail bearing the hated postmark of Karlsbad.

His doctor in Vienna had set him on a special diet, but like Grunberger said nothing to Brahms about his malady. Brahms had not asked for specifics, but began slowly to accept the nature of his illness. He had dined with the Fellingers as was his habit for Christmas, but invited himself back for the next three days as well, offering a toast to seeing them again in the New Year, hesitating before adding in a smaller voice, pointing to the ground, "but I will soon be there," and no one had contradicted him. At a party at the Fabers he had downed several helpings of peppercarp, large quantities of burgundy, coffee drowned in rum, and when cautioned about his carelessness he had said it made no difference in the end.

The end came to everyone. Tchaikovsky was dead, younger by seven years, but he was glad for the evening they had spent drinking in Hamburg, Tchaikovsky thrilled to know Brahms had delayed his departure to hear his Fifth Symphony. Bruckner was dead not even six months, innocent still as a babe. When Brahms had applauded his F minor Mass, Bruckner had surprised him, coming to his box to thank him. He had suggested a performance of Bruckner's *Te Deum* the year before (more than Wagner had ever done for his acolyte), the last concert Bruckner was to attend, so ill he had been carried into the concert hall. He had purchased a ticket for Bruckner's funeral, but arrived late, finding the Karlskirche filled to bursting. When invited to enter he had shaken his head, unable to keep from weeping – as much for Bruckner as himself. "Never mind ... my coffin next."

The first movement concluded, he joined the applause, not realizing at first that Richter was applauding as well, beating his baton on the podium, directing the gaze of the audience with his own toward his box. He rose finally, realizing the second movement would not commence until he acknowledged the ovation. All eyes were turned on him, a tiny man shrinking as he stood trembling with tears, the auditorium awash with light and color in his blurry eyes. The last of the songs he had set from the Bible came to mind: "Faith, love, hope; all three abide; but the greatest of these is love."

It had been the same earlier in the year: Joachim, visiting Vienna on an Austrian tour, had invited him to share the applause onstage for his G major Quintet. Brahms marveled at Jussuf's activity, still roaming the country like a twenty-year-old – and still, apparently, as naive. Brahms had explained his appearance saying he had exchanged his romanesque figure for one more gothic for a while, his jaundice was taking longer than usual to leave, and Joachim had been convinced by little more than a smile and a pat on the back, noting only that Brahms had never appeared more warm, more gentle in his ways. Brahms had smiled and kissed his friend's cheek. "I have given up being rude to people."

The following month Joachim had invited Brahms to perform his Piano Quintet, but Brahms had confessed he was now too feeble, he had stayed home every evening since he had last seen his friend, playing the piano, but even that tired him within thirty minutes and he was good for nothing but gazing from his window at the Karlskirche and Elisabet Bridge among other familiar sights until after dark.

The second movement, an andante, displays a plaintive melody hovering around a single note like a hopeless lover. The young Richard Strauss had been reminded of a funeral procession moving in silence across moonlit heights, but Elisabet had expressed the most poetic sentiment of all: Only Brahms could have written it, but even Brahms had had recourse to certain locked chambers of his soul for the first time. It was the movement she would have chosen for her companion through life and in death.

He had finally run out of locked chambers, and the future of music gave him little cause for hope. Walking along the Traun river in Ischl with Gustav Mahler he had talked about the decline of integrity in music – but Mahler, recently turned thirty-three, true to the optimism of youth, had gripped his arm and pointed to the water. "Look, Master! Look down there!" He had looked, seen nothing, and when he had asked what he was looking for Mahler had laughed. "The last wave! There it goes! There goes the last wave!" He had shaken off Mahler's hand with a growl. "Very nice, but will it go into the ocean or into a swamp?"

He no longer made predictions: composers he admired had come to nothing, and composers from whom he expected nothing had surprised him. He was applauded again at the conclusion of the second movement, and stood again before his Viennese, eyes awash as before, a shrunken old man, hollows in the back of his neck, skin discolored to bronze. He had never paid attention to his appearance, rarely consulted a mirror, but his friends left nothing to chance. At their last dinner party the Conrats had drawn all curtains and illuminated all rooms with red electric globes the better to hide his color. He had seen Frau Truxa altering his pants so they would appear less baggy, but affecting not to notice he had paraded the pants for her later. "Look, Frau Truxa! I have become a little fatter at last." Even the state had been considerate, allowing the railway to heat his carriage during the return from Karlsbad though regulations forbade it for another month.

The third movement, a scherzo, was the most humorous he had written, Tweedledum and Tweedledee of the orchestra, bouncing in many directions at once, making liberal use of the triangle. Kalbeck had advised against publishing it, fearing it would make him a laughingstock, but the effect had been just as he had wished, raising smiles or eyebrows – but no longer, not smiles, not eyebrows, not for him. His days remained filled with visitors, he went for walks, and when he was too tired for walks his friends called in carriages for drives, called just to sit with him, but he had also suffered a stroke, apoplectic rheumatism, so the doctors called it, and fell asleep at parties – even at home, in his sofa, midconversation. It was all he could do to bring his affairs to an end, write his will, destroy old letters, other papers, ash in the stove, in his mouth, in his soul.

Again, the applause, acknowledgment, tears, as the third movement ended. He had recognized three peaks in his life: the time he had spent with Schumann; Bismarck and the birth of Germany; and publication of the complete works of Bach, begun in 1851, completed in 1896, just the year before. He had written to Clara long ago about Bach's Chaconne in D minor for violin, among the most incomprehensible pieces of music he had heard. Adapting the technique for a small instrument Bach had created an entire world, encompassed the deepest thoughts, the most powerful feelings. He was sure the tension and excitement of creating such a work would drive him mad – but in the fourth movement of the Fourth Symphony he had attempted something similar: thirty variations on a series of eight ascending notes. He had feared it would be too monotonous, but Elisabet had wished it three times as long. It stands alone in the symphonic literature, without peer, without precedent, some call it Brahms's greatest single symphonic movement, certainly among the greatest symphonic movements composed – and, no less without precedent, it provided the first ever tragic conclusion to a symphony.

His state was so fragile as the variations unrolled that his emotions changed with each fine modulation. He was to be envied; he was immune to pain; there was no one left whose death could affect him as had Clara's, no one left whom he had loved so bottomlessly though so badly – but he did not want to think about such things. For all he had accomplished, he remained fundamentally ignorant. Was life worth living when you lived alone? Were children not the only true immortality? What did the rest matter or mean?

His world was coming to an end in more ways than one. The liberalization of the country, coinciding with his own advent to the city almost forty years ago, had fed the monster rising now to bite its hand. Educational reforms had alienated the Roman Catholic Church, secularism had been opposed to popism, the music of Wagner had stoked PanGerman fires, the music of Smetana and Dvorak nationalistic fires, all had risen to merge with the freefloating antiSemitic winds of the century to manifest themselves in the form of the unashamedly antiSemitic mayor, Karl Lueger, despite opposition from the Emperor. Had the matter been of less consequence it would have been hilarious: a Jew, Theodor Herzl, had published an article arguing for a new Jewish State in their ancestral homeland of Palestine. It was all madness, but he could not understand how Mendelssohn and Joachim among so many others had persevered, anathematized even after conversion for the supposed stain under which they had been born.

The world spun like hundreds of thousands of wheels, wheels within wheels; the wheel of his life spun within the wheel of his country's life, and the wheel of the country within the wheel of the world, but the world went the way of the world, and a man the way of a man – if he were a man of consequence. When he had learned that Mahler's Jewish descent was an obstacle to the conductorship of the Vienna Opera he had wielded the cudgels himself to get him instated: not even his disaffection with Mahler's pen could overwhelm his admiration for Mahler's baton after he had heard his *Don Giovanni* – and after hearing Mahler's Second Symphony he had transferred to him the title hitherto reserved for Richard Strauss: Chief of the Insurrectionists. When someone had asked what they should do about the Jewish question he had answered only half in jest: "I am going to get myself circumcised next week." Small though they were, such were the victories that mattered, the seeds that inoculated the body politic. If enough men changed themselves they changed the body politic.

He had expected the final ovation, but not the downpour. He stood once more to acknowledge the applause, but fifteen minutes later he still stood, they still applauded, the downpour swollen to a monsoon. He was tired, wished to sit, but wished no more to leave than they wished to let him go, his lovely Viennese, eyes no less damp than his own. All knew it was to be the last time. What did anything mean? What did it matter what anything meant? That was not the question. He had done what he had to do. Bismarck had done it with blood and iron, Goethe with ink and scribbles, he with sounds snatched from the sky. Clara had said that when she performed she had no more tears. It was the same for him when he composed. He understood finally what she had been telling him all those years, bringing forth ironically more tears but touched with a tenderness that now touched everything left of his life. He remained standing, supported by the applause, the love, clinging to the rail, tears streaming in bright sheets down his cheeks, glistening like diamonds in his beard.

iii

HEINRICH VON HERZOGENBERG TO BRAHMS   *Berlin, 26 March, 1897*
My very dear Friend,

I have two habits which refuse to be shaken: one is that I still compose; the other that I still ask as I did thirty-four years ago: "What will He say to it?"

"He," I may say, is you. It is true you have had nothing to say about it for some years – a fact I am at liberty to explain in my own way. It has certainly not affected my devotion to you, to which I propose to give expression with another dedication, my second quartet for piano, for which I claim your indulgence.

My thoughts are more than ever with you, dear friend, now that you are ill. Let us hope spring will make a change of air possible. Even if the direct medicinal effect is not

apparent, it refreshes and enlivens one mentally and physically, and no doctor will deny
that that may lead to a cure.
    Your old friend and admirer,
    H. Herzogenberg

Brahms had written to his landlady in Ischl to prepare his rooms earlier than usual for the summer, but a couple of weeks before Herzogenberg's letter had arrived he had had to leave a performance of Strauss's new operetta, *The Goddess of Reason*, after the first act. He had since attended a concert rehearsal at the home of a friend, but fainted the same week ascending a staircase. He had subsequently been increasingly obliged to interrupt dinners with friends, too racked with pain to sit long, battling the alien presence in his chest, armies of worms gnawing his liver, bacteria foraging through his entrails. Friends continued to visit, paying last respects, but he spoke little himself, too weak even to notice who came.

The day the letter had arrived he had taken to his bed, written to his stepmother: *D. M. For the sake of a change, I am lying down a little to see how my jaundice responds, and cannot, therefore, write comfortably. Otherwise, there is no alteration, and, as always, I only need patience. Affectionately, your Joh.*

He also dictated to Frau Truxa a letter of thanks to Herzogenberg for his dedication.

Dr. Josef Breuer was Vienna's preeminent specialist for internal complaints, but better known for his theory of hysteria which he had developed with Dr. Sigmund Freud into a book: *Studies in Hysteria*. He had realized from the moment he had taken over Brahms's treatment that it was strictly a matter of alleviating pain. He had been delirious more than once, hemorrhaging from his stomach and intestines. On the night of 2 April he had said to his son, also a physician, "Brahms is nearly finished. Will you stay with him for the night?"

Dr. Robert Breuer had found Brahms weak, but hospitable, concerned about finding the doctor the most comfortable rest for the night. The doctor had pulled the closest chair, announcing himself comfortable.

Frau Truxa left shortly after the doctor arrived, saying she would stay within calling distance. Brahms thanked her, he could never thank her enough, she was now constantly by his side.

Dr. Breuer pulled his chair close to the bed. "Doktor Brahms, do you feel any pain?"

"A little, but it is not unbearable."

"Will you try, then, to sleep?"

"Yes."

At first he lay still, but around midnight he twisted in bed, unable to get comfortable, and around two o'clock in the morning he almost fell out of bed, delirious: "But she is not here! She is not here!"

The doctor was immediately beside him, holding him until he woke. "Where do you feel the pain?"

"In my stomach, there is tension, a constriction."

"Shall I give you something for it?"

"Perhaps it would be better?"

The doctor gave him an injection of morphine, a glass of wine. The Duke of Meiningen had sent a case from his cellar, the Baroness warm slippers, Simrock champagne, and the Frauen Miller and Conrat his favorite meals. Brahms quaffed the wine in a single swallow. "That was lovely. Danke."

After that he appeared to sleep peacefully, but the smell got stronger of blood and feces: he was hemorrhaging again. Until very recently he had not allowed anyone even to wash him, walking instead with Frau Truxa's support through two rooms, "washing up with police escort" he had said of her presence outside the door – but the doctor cleaned him as well as he could without disturbing him and took his leave the next morning at seven, telling Frau Truxa he would return in a couple of hours.

Frau Truxa continued the vigil in the doctor's chair, shock registering in her face, remembering how Doktor Brahms had been, seeing him now no larger than a child, his skin greenish bronze, his face a mask of life. Her eyes blurred, but she shook off her tears, determining instead to be useful, freshen the air with eau de cologne, fluff the pillows, clean the room. She wiped her eyes, but saw his own eyes were open. He had been watching.

Brahms felt little pain, little of anything, and imagined his chest sunken, his body drained, himself a tadpole, a comma, a crotchet, head like a hammer, tail for a torso. He wished to see the doctor, to thank Frau Truxa again for her kindness, but everytime he opened his mouth his plate of artificial teeth fell, getting in the way of his tongue.

In the hour of Beethoven's death a storm had thundered; Beethoven had scowled and raised his fist before collapsing; the fools who compared them so ceaselessly would see again how different they were from their deaths. Beethoven had been defiant to the end, but not he. Seeing him, Frau Truxa could not hold her tears, and seeing her tears Brahms could not hold his own. She was by his side, stroking his face. He tried to raise himself on one elbow, sighed when he could not, sank back in bed, and shut his eyes for the last time.

iv

If Brahms could have attended his own funeral, he would have laughed. Sketched, photographed, a mask made of his face, he was dressed in death as he had always hated in life: he might have been going to a ball or to meet the Kaiser. The room was draped in black velvet, hung with silver crosses, a huge brass candelabra, wax candles burning, par for the course in Catholic Vienna though Brahms was Protestant and nonpractising. Admirers filled the room with flowers rising so high they hid the coffin from view. His Honors and Orders were displayed on crimson cushions. Flags flew at halfmast in Hamburg, also on the ships in the dock. Vienna offered a plot in the Central Cemetery next to Beethoven and Schubert.

He had died on Saturday, 3 April, 1897, between eight and nine o'clock in the morning. The funeral followed three days later. Friends and admirers and deputations holding wreaths and palms and flowers filled the streets, three flights of stairs, all the way to the bedroom. All major German cities had sent representatives, as had London, Cambridge, Paris, Prague, St. Petersburg, Basel, Zurich, and Amsterdam among others.

All heads were uncovered, all sound hushed, when the coffin was brought from the doorway to the open hearse. Two enormous wreaths from the cities of Hamburg and Vienna were fastened to its lid. The procession was led by a column of seven riders, each on a black horse, each in a cutaway coat, jodhpurs, bicorne hat, each carrying a lit taper on a long pole, followed by six open funeral cars, flooded with wreaths and laurels and flowers sent by friends including sundry kings, queens, princesses, dukes, trailing with ribbons of many colors, appearing like gardens in motion.

The procession stopped before the Gesellschaft where doors and pillars had been draped with black cloth. Blue flames ignited by wine flickered in metal bowls perched on high candelabra on either side of the portal. His partsong, "Fahr Wohl," was sung. His friends carried funeral torches, among them Dvorak, Hanslick, Henschel, Kalbeck, Faber, Fellinger, Simrock, Herzogenberg. Joachim was in London, trapped by engagements. An address was delivered: "There have been great artists who have been little men, and great men who have accomplished little in art. Here was the ideal. In Brahms, both were great and noble, the man and the artist." The ceremony closed with the text from the close of the *Requiem*: "Blessed are those who die in the Lord, for they may rest from their labor, and be followed by their works."

EPILOGUE

Brahms was seated again at the piano in my apartment, but fading with the night, growing dimmer as the day grew brighter – and the more he dimmed the more the room swelled with his music.

It is said that the spin of the planets on their axes and around the sun creates harmonic vibrations, that the universe hums with this music of the spheres, and that we are so infused with the music that we are no more aware of it than of the movement of the earth. It is said further that the laws governing this celestial harmony are echoed in the laws governing harmony in music, explaining perhaps why a third harmonizes with a fifth but not with a seventh. It is an article of faith with many that these laws have been revealed by Bach in his Well Tempered Klavier, a harmony maintained by the Classicists, but ripped and clawed by the Romantics and decimated by the Modernists.

Brahms was discredited for approaching composition too mathematically and credited with discovering a calculus for rhapsody; of speaking in the tongue of angels, the language of the seraphim, while stuffing them into boxes – but, as Joachim said two years later at one of the many dedications to follow: "For the man who dominates all its resources, form is no binding fetter, but a spur and an incentive to new and free designs that are preeminently his own." Brahms might equally be called the last of the Caesars as the first of the Moderns. No one else had summed the past as successfully – but, as Elisabet had said of his Fourth Symphony, many passages were to be enjoyed with the eye on the score rather than the ear in the concert hall, illuminating for the first time the eye versus ear controversy so prevalent in twentieth century music, developed by Schoenberg, Berg, and Webern, later by Boulez and Babbitt, but his influence is felt no less in the works of Dvorak, Reger, Elgar, Sibelius, Nielsen, and Ives among others.

Wagner proclaimed himself a musician of the future rather than a modern, but Debussy was closer to the mark calling him a glorious sunset rather than a dawn – but Richard Strauss was no less further from the mark when he said the same about Brahms, though less poetically, that after Brahms no one should write as he did. He had tried it himself, found he was no Brahms, and proceeded to become Richard Strauss. He had discovered the maxim true of all great composers: each was a beginning and an end in himself.

Brahms was playing the intermezzo again, lullaby of his sorrows, but now appeared so spectral I could see through him; the piano might have been playing itself, keys moving of their own volition. The opus sounded now like a waltz, now a slow march, now a lullaby, now a dirge, depending on the listener's mood, all in the space of a few minutes, a bundle of contradictions, as was much of his music, symphonies criticized for being inflated chamberworks, chamberworks for being symphonies in the egg – as was the man, criticized for taking no chances and for deviating from the models, for being unprogressive and modern, for being too much like Beethoven and not enough – but the contradictions clarify rather than confuse our understanding: he looked constantly to the future, never forgetting the past, fashioning holograms from palimpsests.

What remained – the residue, the essence, distillate of his life, gold from straw – remains impervious to fang and claw, at once the heart of the riddle of life and medicine for the heart.

THE END

AFTERWORD

I said something about my approach to *TRIO* in the Foreword, but considering the hybrid nature of the book it would not hurt to say it again. *TRIO* is a novel biography: a biography for people who hate biographies (for the footnotes and other such intrusions) and a novel for people who hate novels (who read only about "real" things). I wrote what I knew, I researched what I did not know, and I imagined what I could not research. The bibliography comprises more than a hundred books; I was sometimes too anal for my own good, reading three biographies of Bruckner (for instance) to get a single scene right – but Clara's diaries were easily the most plundered sources. Correspondences also played their part, namely Brahms's with Clara, Joachim, the Herzogenbergs, and Billroth among others, not to mention numberless biographies of both Schumanns and Brahms and other composers – but, as I said in the Foreword, nothing happens in the book that might not have happened historically.

My most egregious invention was easily Chapter 49: "Their Wedding Night." There is no evidence to suggest that Brahms and Clara's relations developed beyond the high romance of the early years or the friendship of the later, but I was faced with a technical choice. Brahms was victim to the Freudian conundrum: "Where he loves he feels no passion, and where he feels passion he cannot love." I could have invented a character for the singular purpose of dramatizing Brahms's impotence with a woman of Clara's stature, but (1) Clara was available, (2) their correspondence at the time was more affectionate and friendly, (3) the point was made more dramatically with Clara than with a fictional character, and (4) there may have been evidence supporting just such an invention among the letters Brahms tossed into the Rhine later in life.

On the other hand, Jeffrey Pulver mentions in his biography of Brahms that during this visit Clara and one of her daughters stayed at the Halliers household (a prominent Hamburg family, two of whose girls sang in Brahms's Hamburg Frauenchor), not at zur Stadt St. Petersburg (as I have it) – and Nancy Reich mentions in her book on Clara that the daughter in question was Julie. Julie, then on the cusp of sixteen, was the only one of the Schumann children to receive a dedication from Brahms (Opus 23, "Variations on a Theme by Schumann"), and the visit may have provided the seed for Brahms's affection, later to culminate in the inspiration for his "Alto Rhapsody" – but I made the choice because: (1) It is conceivable that something similar happened at another time. (A grandson of Clara published an account of a fullblown affair between Brahms and Clara during the time of Schumann's incarceration, very likely the product of a mind irate at being shut out of Clara's will for reasons that need not concern us. Brahms was also suspected of being the father of Felix, Clara's lastborn, but Felix was born eight months and eleven days after Brahms and Clara met – not impossible, but not likely considering their characters and situation.) (2) I lost sleep over the matter, realizing that a biographer was at liberty to say we do not know what happened, but not a novelist. *If* their relations ever vaulted the platonic and romantic stages it is unlikely to have occurred except *after* Robert's death, and *if* I have gratuitously strayed into the truth something along the lines I have described may have come to pass, maybe with one or two more attempts at concupiscence, but no more. The final outcome would not have changed. (3) The fact of Brahms's debility seemed more important to the story than the fact of his absolute relations with Clara, an example of the novelist trumping the biographer, my most egregious example as I have owned – but I have provided reasons for my choices and the reader is free to make his own.

Unfortunately, there was no such character handy to illustrate Brahms's potency with women of the stature of Helga and Lena and Frau Grummer (Chapter 28: "Zur schwarzen Katze"), or Rina (Chapter 60: "The Schumann Festival"), or the redhaired maid of Meiningen (Chapter 69: "The Joachims"), and it seemed necessary to invent them for the dramatic purpose they served. Constanze, who appears during the reunion with Bulow (Chapter 74: "Zum roten Igel"), is not fictitious; the incident is apocryphal, if not factual. I can say unequivocally that the incidents as I have related them (Chapter 28: "Zur Schwarzen Katze") are inaccurate. I can say no less unequivocally that something of this nature MUST have occurred, and I have supported my claim with arguments in "The Boy Brahms," the article mentioned in the Foreword.

The dinner (Chapter 80: "Purse and Cutpurse") is a factual event, Brahms attended many such dinners, but this one collects a number of his bon mots (some factual, some apocryphal, all part of the legend) into a single scene. I wanted to be true to his character rather than to his exact words and thoughts that evening (an impossibility in any case, whatever I might have wanted). The dinner with Bruckner (Chapter 77: "A Clutch of Composers") is again a factual event, but since we do not know the names of the actual attendees I took the liberty of mixing up the names of some of Bruckner's pupils (in one instance, the son of an admirer). The description of Grieg earlier in the same chapter comes from Tchaikovsky, as does the analogy of his presentation to Rubinstein of his Piano Concerto in B flat major as a dish cooked with his own hands to be ignored by his so-called friend. Schumann's idiot babble (Chapter 43: "A Release") is lifted from a letter of Brahms to Joachim. I could mention other such choices, but I have mentioned enough to clarify what I mean by fact versus fiction for the purpose of the narrative.

Sometimes, the sources contradicted one another. For instance, Robert Haven Schauffler contends it was Viktor Widmann's daughter who said she collected stamps when Brahms asked whether she collected autographs, but Anna Brodsky's memoir credits her nephew with the same quote. It does not matter who it was, only that Brahms asked the question and was pleased with the answer, hating autograph hounds as he did. In the same vein, Wilson Strutte mentions in his biography of Tchaikovsky that Nicolai Rubinstein and Nicolai Hubert were both present at the Conservatory when he played his Piano Concerto in B flat major (Chapter 62: "Discomposed Composers") before heading for Constantine Albrecht's 1874 Christmas Eve party, but Simon Mundy says he played at the party itself before many others as well. It seems more credible that he played the work in private rather than in public since he was looking for criticism, but I chose as well to eliminate Nicolai Hubert from the room as he was little more than a toady to Rubinstein and only cluttered the scene. Again, it mattered less where the scene took place and who was present than that it did in fact take place and that Rubinstein did in fact excoriate Tchaikovsky regarding the concerto.

There are some personages I left out altogether: Bettina von Arnim for one (grande dame of German letters and a friend of Beethoven, who in her twenties had chased Goethe in his fifties saying: "I have got to have a child by Goethe at all costs – why, it will be a demigod!"), who visited Robert in the asylum and made a strong case to Clara for having him removed, but her remonstrance carried no weight and she made no difference in the long run; Jenny Lind for another, whom I mentioned regarding her relations with the Schumanns, but not with Brahms (Brahms could not sympathize with Lind's lust for money, nor she with what she called his "mistaken [musical] tendencies"), but she too made no difference in the long run; Johann Strauss for a third, often Brahms's host in Ischl where Brahms signed Strauss's daughter's fan, quoting the opening bars from "The Blue Danube," writing below, "Unfortunately not by Johannes Brahms," again, making no difference in the long run. It may be argued that neither did Tchaikovsky and Grieg and Bruckner and Dvorak make a difference to Brahms in the long run, but I chose to include them, however briefly, for their place in the history of music, more relevant in that respect to Brahms than Arnim or Lind or Strauss, meritworthy though the last trio may be in their own right. There were many others, among them Ole Bull, Johann Verhulst, Julius Allgeyer, Anselm Feuerbach, Julius Spitta, Max Klinger, Eusebius Mandyczewski, Siegfried Ochs, and Gustav Jenner to mention a few, each of whom might have merited a mention or two in a biography, but whom I left out of the narrative in the interest of streamlining the work (an admittedly unscientific process).

I also decided against all accents, all umlauts, cedillas, tildas, circumflexes, et cetera (except for the one time that Brahms exaggerated them for Dvorak's name), on the grounds that I was writing in English and English eschews accents.

Finally, I would like to make a request: I was told by one publisher too many that there was no call for so very large a book about classical music in the US. I was also told they wouldn't know whether to market it as a novel, biography, history, or music. My recourse in this brave new world of DIY publications was to publish the novel myself. I published it initially in two volumes because the publisher could not accommodate the entire manuscript in a single volume, but now that obstacle has been happily hurdled and I have published it again in a single volume. I am happy with the publication, but there is no way I can match the iron bones of the publicity

CHRONOLOGY

This is at once not an exhaustive chronology and too exhaustive for its own good. An exhaustive chronology would be impossible, and as tedious to compile as to read. More than anything, I wanted to provide an impression of the times. Dates of tours, among other things, provide a credible snapshot of how itinerant the lives of musicians have always been, even of the most exalted, traveling as they did in early days by horse and buggy through field and stream, later by road and train. Dates of compositions, unless otherwise indicated, refer to the year of composition, not publication. When composition took longer than a year, I indicated only the year of completion. When the month of composition was unavailable, I indicated just the year. When sources contradicted one another, I used my best judgment on the consideration that a perfect chronology was, again, impossible, not to mention unnecessary. I also added details from Clara's diaries that I left out of *TRIO* in an attempt to tame the mammoth manuscript as much as I could. Her pronouncements on Liszt, Wagner, and Brahms among others are of interest for who she was as much as for what she says. She arguably revealed more about herself than about the composers, but she was also arguably more credible regarding comments on technique than on composition. I also inserted chapter headings from *TRIO* to indicate their places in the narrative.

1685
February 23: Birth of George Frederick Handel (Halle).
March 31: Birth of Johann Sebastian Bach (Eisenach, Saxony).

1732
March 31: Birth of Franz Joseph Haydn (Rohrau, Austro/Hungarian border).

1750
July 28: Death of Bach (Leipzig).

1756
January 27: Birth of Wolfgang Amadeus Mozart (Salzburg).

1759
April 14: Death of Handel (London).

1769
Birth of Johann Brahms, innkeeper, Johannes Brahms's paternal grandfather, son of Peter Brahms (carpenter, joiner, wheelwright, of Brunsbuttel, where he had migrated from Hanoverian country in 1750) and Sophie Uhl (of a peasant family).
Birth of Christiana Magdalena Asmus (Heide), Brahms's paternal grandmother.
August 15: Birth of Napoleon Bonaparte.

1770
December 16: Birth of Ludwig van Beethoven (Bonn).

1771
Birth of Johanna Christiane Schnabel (Robert Schumann's mother).

1773
Birth of Gottlob Schumann (Robert Schumann's father).

1774
Birth of Carl E. Carus, merchant and manufacturer, born in Bautzen, moved to Zwickau where he and his wife familiarized young Robert Schumann with Mozart, Haydn, and Beethoven.
Publication of Goethe's *Sorrows of Young Werther.*

1775
Birth of Johann Gottfried Kuntsch, Robert's first music teacher.

1782
October 17: Birth of Niccolo Paganini (Genoa).

1785
August 18: Birth of Friedrich Wieck (Pretzsch).

1787
July 17: Death of Maria Magdalena (Beethoven's mother).

1789
July 4: Birth of Johanna Henrika Christiane Nissen, Johannes Brahms's mother (Hamburg).

1791
December 5: Death of Mozart (Vienna).

1792
Johann Brahms, Johannes Brahms's paternal grandfather (23 years) moves to Heide, marries Christiana Magdalena Asmus (also 23 years), daughter of Jurg Asmus of Heide.

1793
Birth of Peter Hoeft Hinrich Brahms, Johannes Brahms's uncle, Johann Jakob's older brother, an innkeeper like his father, also a pawnbroker and an antique dealer.

1797
Birth of Eduard Schumann (Robert's eldest brother), later to marry Therese.
January 31: Birth of Franz Peter Schubert (Himmelpfortgrund, Viennese suburb).
May 17: Birth of Marianne Tromlitz (Clara Schumann's mother).

1801
Birth of Karl Schumann (Robert's second brother), later to marry Rosalie.
Beethoven composes his C sharp minor Piano Sonata (#14/*Moonlight).*
October 6-10: Beethoven writes the "Heiligenstadt Testament."

1802
Birth of Agnes Carus (who, with her husband, introduced Robert Schumann to Haydn, Mozart, and Beethoven).

1803
December 11: Birth of Heitor Berlioz (La Côte-Saint-André, France).

1804
Beethoven composes his A major Violin Sonata (#9/*Kreutzer).*
August: Beethoven composes his E flat Symphony (#3/*Eroica).*

1805
Birth of Julius Schumann (Robert's third brother).
Birth of Marie Catherine Sophie de Flavigny Frankfurt-on-Main, later to become Marie d'Agoult, mother of the three children acknowledged by Franz Liszt).
Beethoven composes his Piano Sonatas in C major (#21/*Waldstein),* F minor (#23/ *Appassionata),* and the Triple Concerto in C major.
November: Beethoven premieres *Fidelio.*
November 15: Birth of Fanny Mendelssohn.

1806
Beethoven composes his F major, E minor, and C major quartets (#s 7/8/9), the *Razumovskys.*
June 1: Birth of Johann Jakob Brahms, Johannes Brahms's father (between Hanover and Holstein in Lower Saxony).

July 23: Birth of Eduard Marxsen (Brahms's teacher to whom he dedicated his second Piano Concerto).

December 23: Beethoven premieres his D major Violin Concerto (Vienna).

1807
Birth of Emilie Schumann (Robert Schumann's only sister).

1809
February 3: Birth of Felix Mendelssohn-Bartholdy (Hamburg).

May 31: Death of Haydn (Vienna).

May-November: Occupation of Vienna by Napoleon's troops.

October: The Treaty of Vienna.

Beethoven composes his E flat major Piano Concerto (#5/the *Emperor*, never performed by him, he's no longer a performer), E flat major Quartet (#10/ *Harp*), and C minor Symphony (#5).

1810
Beethoven composes his F minor String Quartet (#11), his only composition of the year.

February 22 or March 1: Birth of Frederic Chopin (Żelazowa Wola, Poland).

June 8: Birth of ROBERT ALEXANDER SCHUMANN (Zwickau).

1811
Beethoven composes his B flat major Piano Trio (#6/*Archduke*).

April 11: Birth of Rebecka Mendelssohn (Mendelssohn's youngest sister).

October 22: Birth of Franz Liszt (Raiding, Hungary).

October 24: Birth of Ferdinand Hiller (Frankfurt).

December 3: Birth of Eduard Julius Friedrich Bendemann (Berlin).

1813
Birth of Paul Mendelssohn.

Beethoven meets Goethe; writes Immortal Beloved letter.

Peter Hoeft Hinrich Brahms (innkeeper), Johannes Brahms's uncle, marries Christine Ruge of Bennewohl; they have five children, Johannes Brahms's cousins.

May 13: Beethoven completes his A major Symphony (#7).

May 22: Birth of Richard Wagner (Leipzig).

October 10: Birth of Giuseppe Verdi (Le Roncole, Italy).

1815
Downfall of Napoleon, Congress of Vienna.

1816
Robert in private school.

June 23: Marriage of Friedrich Wieck and Marianne Tromlitz (Clara Schumann's parents).

<u>1817</u>
Robert Schumann begins piano lessons, first compositions (dances).
August 10: Birth of Adelheid Wieck (Clara Schumann's brother).

<u>1818</u>
February 24: Chopin's first recital (eight years old).
May 12: Death of Adelheid Wieck.

<u>1819</u>
September 13: Birth of CLARA JOSEPHINE WIECK (Leipzig).

<u>1820</u>
Robert starts at the Lyceum (Zwickau).
Autumn: Beethoven composes his E major Piano Sonata (#30).
October: Liszt's first recital (nine years old) in Oedenburg, near Raiding.
October 6: Birth of Jenny Lind (Stockholm).

<u>1821</u>
Liszt's father takes him to Vienna to meet Beethoven and Schubert and study under
    Salieri and Czerny.
Easter: The Wiecks move to a house in the Salzgasschen.
May 5: Death of Napoleon at 51 (St. Helena).
August 27: Birth of Alwin Wieck (Clara Schumann's brother).
December 25: Beethoven completes his A flat major Piano Sonata (#31).

<u>1822</u>
January 13: Beethoven completes his C minor Piano Sonata (#32).

<u>1823</u>
Beethoven composes his *Missa Solemnis* and *Diabelli Variations*.
January 31: Birth of Gustav Wieck (Clara Schumann's second brother).
December 11: Liszt moves to Paris with his family.

<u>1824</u>
Beethoven completes his D minor Symphony (#9/*Choral*).
Liszt conquers Paris, performs for George IV at Carlton House.
February 22: Birth of Victor Wieck (Clara's brother).
May 12: Mariane Tromlitz leaves Friederich Wieck, goes to Plauen with Victor to
    arrange a legal separation. Clara, Alwin, and Gustav stay in Leipzig with
    their father.
Summer: Clara stays with her mother.
September 17: Clara returns to her father.
September 18: Clara begins piano lessons.
September 24: Birth of Anton Bruckner (Ansfelden, Austria).

1825

Liszt performs for George IV (second time) at Windsor Castle, gives a concert in
    Manchester.
January 22: Friedrich and Marianne (Clara Schumann's parents) divorce.
August: Marianne marries a music teacher named Adolf Bargiel, a friend of Wieck,
    returns with him to Leipzig for a year during which Clara frequently visits
    bringing notes stiff with injunctions from her father.
December 16: Johann Jakob (Johannes Brahms's father) receives his certificate of
    music from the Stadt Pfeiferei.

1826

February 2: Birth of Louise Japha (Hamburg).
Johann Jakob (Johannes Brahms's father) arrives in Hamburg.
Robert's sister, Emilie, commits suicide by drowning.
August 10: Death of Gottlob Schumann (Robert Schumann's father).

1827

Marriage of Marie de Flavigny (later to be the mother of Liszt's three acknowledged
    children) and Comte Charles d'Agoult.
January 2: Death of Victor Wieck (Clara Schumann's brother).
March 27: Death of Beethoven (Vienna).
May 7: Friedrich Wieck begins writing Clara's diary.
August: Death of Liszt's father.
October 27: Clara starts piano lessons with her father.

1828

Robert composes early lieder (WoO 10, 19, 21).
Birth of Woldemar Bargiel, Clara's half-brother from her mother's side.
Robert Schumann leaves the Lyceum, tours Bavaria with Rosen.
January 17: Birth of Eduard Remenyi (Miskolc, Hungary).
March 25: Robert comes to Leipzig, ostensibly to study law.
March 31: Robert meets Clara at the home of Ernst and Agnes Carus.
May: Robert enrolls as a student of law at the University of Leipzig.
July 3: Friedrich Wieck marries Clementine Fechner, daughter of Pastor Samuel
    Traugott Fechner of Grossfarichen in the Niederlausitz attended by Clara,
    Alwin, and Gustav.
August 28: Robert begins piano lessons with Wieck.
October 20: Clara Schumann's first concert at the Gewandhaus.

[Chapter 1: To the Gewandhaus]

October 29: Wieck writes in Clara's diary saying, among other things, that she's lazy.
November 19: Death of Schubert (Vienna).

1829

Brahms's father becomes a lodger in his mother's home at Ulricusstrasse 37.
May 11: Robert begins his Rhine journey.

July 4: Robert leaves Leipzig for Heidelberg to study law.

August 11: Chopin's Viennese debut at the Karnthnerthor Theater. Performs *La ci darem Variations* and *Krakowiak* (both for piano and orchestra).

August 18: Chopin's second appearance in Vienna, again at the Karnthnerthor, again with the *La ci darem Variations* and *Krakowiak*.

August 28: Birth of Albert Dietrich (Meissen).

September-October 20: Robert visits Italy (Vicenza, Verona, Padua, Venice, Milan), Switzerland, the Adriatic, before returning to Heidelberg.

October: Clara performs for Paganini.

October 20: Robert returns to board and study with Wieck.

1830

Robert composes his *ABEGG Variations* and Toccata in C major.

Birth of Klemens Wieck (Clara's half-brother).

January 8: Birth of Hans Guido Freiherr von Bulow (Dresden).

March 6-April 7: Clara gives private concerts in Dresden.

Easter: Robert hears Paganini and is so overwhelmed he gives up law for music.

May 21: Johann Jakob (Johannes Brahms's father) becomes a citizen of Hamburg.

June 9: Marriage of Johann Jakob and Johanna Christiane Nissen (Johannes Brahms's parents).

July: Robert tells his family he intends to switch from law to music.

[*Chapter 2: Mozart – But!*]

Wieck writes a reassuring letter to Robert's mother about the "breadless art."

[*Chapter 3: Doppelgangers*]

October 20: Robert moves again into the Wieck household.

November 8: Clara's first solo Gewandhaus concert.

December 25: Clara and Wieck travel to Dresden for a series of concerts.

1831

Robert composes *Papillons*.

January: Clara and Wieck return from concerts.

Brahms's father is employed at the Alster Pavilion.

Robert's affair with Christel.

[*Chapter 4: Frau Geyer's Son*]

January 10: Clara performs with the royal band in the Hotel d'Pologne.

January 25: Clara performs solo before and after the presentation, *Doktor und Apotheker*. Also a second concert at the Hotel d'Pologne.

February: Birth of Elisabeth "Elise" Wilhemine Louise (Brahms's sister).

March 9: Paganini's first Paris concert, attended by Liszt.

June 28: Birth of Joseph Joachim (Kittsee, village near Pressburg, Hungary).

September 25: Clara and Wieck leave Leipzig for concert tour of Paris.

September 26: Clara and Wieck arrive in Weimar.

October 1, 12 noon: Clara has an audience with Goethe, plays Herz's La Violetta, also Herz's Bravura-Variations.

October 7: Clara performs at the town hall in Weimar.

October 9: Clara performs again for Goethe, a duet with Herr Gotze, Hunten's Rondo for Four Hands with Wieck, and her variations.

October 12: Clara and Wieck leave Weimar with a medal and testimonial from Goethe for Erfurt.

November 3: Clara and Wieck arrive in Kassel where Clara performs for Spohr after stopping days in Gotha, Arnstadt, and again in Gotha.

November 29: Clara performs in Kassel at the opera house.

December 7: Clara is prevented from playing again in Kassel by revolts.

December 7: Robert (reviewing Chopin's *La ci darem Variations* in the *Leipzig Allgemeine musicalische Zeitung*): "Hats off, gentlemen – a genius!"

December 13: Clara plays a private concert at the Stadthaussaal in Kassel, a success despite the continued unrest. Spohr provides a testimonial when they leave.

<u>1832</u>

Robert composes Paganini Caprices and *Intermezzi*.

January 11: Robert writes to congratulate Wieck on Clara's tour and another letter flirting with Clara.

January 17: Birth of Marie Wieck (Clara's half-sister).

January 25: Clara's concert in Frankfurt-am-Main.

February 3: Clara and Wieck arrive in Darmstadt.

February 4: Clara's rehearsal in Darmstadt.

February 5: Clara's performance in Darmstadt is not as good as in Frankfurt according to Wieck, but receives greater applause.

February 11: Clara and Wieck leave Mainz for Paris.

February 15: Clara and Wieck arrive in Paris. Eduard Fechner has rooms for them at the Hotel de Bergere, rue de Bergere, Faubourg Montmartre.

February 26: Chopin plays his F minor Piano Concerto and B flat Variations for his Paris debut to an enthusiastic Mendelssohn among others.

March 2: Clara plays at a soiree at Princess Vandamore's where Kalkbrenner cheers her on and the crowd follows.

Mid-March: Paganini gives a series of concerts in Paris.

March 14: Clara and Wieck hear Chopin play his E minor Piano Concerto at Abbe Bertin's. Mendelssohn's Octet is also played. Mendelssohn, Hiller, and Chopin amuse themselves bear-fighting.

March 18: Mendelssohn plays Beethoven's G major Piano Concerto in Paris, the first time it's heard in the city.

March 19: Clara plays at a soiree at Franz Stopel's music school.

Spring: Robert cripples his hand.

April 9: Clara's concert at the Hotel de Ville is moved to Franz Stopel's music school again because the vast numbers are reduced on account of cholera and revolution.

April 13: Clara and Wieck leave Paris, pass through Metz, Saarbruck where they spend days in quarantine, Frankfurt where Clara falls ill, Hanau, and Fulda.

May 1, 11:30a: Wieck and Clara return to Leipzig.

[Chapter 5: The First Paris Tour]
[Chapter 6: On the Road to Connewitz]

May 20: Chopin's second concert in Paris.
July: Clara gives solo concerts in Leipzig.
September: Clara gives solo concerts in Leipzig.
November: Local concert tours for Clara with Wieck in Altenburg, Zwickau, Schneeberg.
November 18: Robert joins them in Zwickau, Clara meets the Schumanns.

1833

Robert composes *Impromptus on a Theme by Clara Wieck* and a second set of Paganini Caprices.
Liszt meets the Comtesse d'Agoult, transcribes Berlioz's *Fantastique*.
January/February/April: Concerts for Clara in Leipzig, and local tours to Chemnitz, Karlsbad, and Schneeberg.
February 5: Clara's half-brother, Klemens, three years old, dies, after an illness of four hours.
May 7: Birth of JOHANNES BRAHMS.
June 28: Robert writes to his mother about plans for the *Neue Zeitschrift fur Musik*.
Death of Rosalie, wife of Robert's brother Karl.
October 17-18: Robert imagines at night that he's "losing his reason," his first nervous breakdown, visits the doctor who advises him to seek a woman. He turns to Ernestine because Clara's too young.
[Chapter 7: The Sickness of the Schumanns]
November 18: Death of Julius, Robert's third brother.

1834

Robert composes the *Symphonic Etudes*.
January 1: Establishment of customs union in Germany.
April 3: First issue of the *Neue Zeitschrift fur Musik* published.
April 21: Ernestine von Fricken comes to stay with the Wiecks. She and Robert fall in love.
July: Birth of Cacilie Wieck (Clara's younger half-sister).
August: Robert and Ernestine are engaged.
September 1: Baron von Fricken comes to Leipzig.
September 5: Ernestine and the Baron leave Leipzig for Asch and visit Zwickau to meet Robert's mother.
October 25: Robert flees to Zwickau to escape Schunke's illness.
Last Days of October: Robert visits Ernestine at her home in Asch and meets her family.
November 11: Clara leaves to tour Northern Germany (Hamburg, Hanover, Magdeburg) with Wieck and Carl Banck.
[Chapter 8: Clara's Gentlemen]
December 4: Robert visits Ernestine again in Asch with his sister-in-law Therese.

December 7: Death by consumption of Ludwig Schunke, Robert's close friend, a promising composer and pianist, cofounder and editor of the *Neue Zeitschrift*.
December 13: Ernestine is formally adopted by the Baron.
December 15: Robert returns to Leipzig.

1835

Robert composes his *Carnaval* and Piano Sonatas in F sharp minor (#1) and F minor (#3).
Robert becomes sole editor and publisher of the *Neue Zeitschrift fur Musik*.
January 14: Clara's concert (Hanover) with Wieck and Banck.
March 26: Birth of Fritz Friedrich (Brahms's brother).
April 4: Clara returns from her tour of northern Germany with Wieck and Banck via Berlin.
August: Mendelssohn arrives in Leipzig as conductor of the Gewandhaus.
August: Robert learns of Ernestine's background.
August: Liszt and Marie d'Agoult fly to Geneva.
September 13: Clara's 16th birthday (with Mendelssohn), she plays his capriccios for two pianos with him, Bach's C sharp major fugue, and (at Mendelssohn's request) Robert's F sharp minor Sonata (just the scherzo). Mendelssohn plays a Bach fugue and impersonates Liszt and Chopin at the piano.
[Chapter 9: Mendelssohn Comes to Dinner]
Early October: Chopin visits the Wiecks to hear Clara.
[Chapter 10: A Visit from Chopin]
November 8: Thalberg's arrival is announced in the *Gazette musicale*, first to be heard at M. Zimmermann's soiree alongside Pauline Viardot-Garcia, Duprez, and De Beriot.
November 9: Clara performs her own concerto at the Gewandhaus, Mendelssohn's Capriccio Brilliant, Herz's variations on the Greek chorus from the Siege of Corinth, and Bach's concerto for three pianos with Mendelssohn and Rackeman of Bremen.
November 25: Robert and Clara's first kiss.
[Chapter 11: Ernestine's Secret]
November 26: Clara tours Zwickau, Plauen, Glauchau, and Chemnitz.
December 4: Clara in Zwickau where Robert joins them.
December 6: Clara's concert in Zwickau.
December 7: Opening of the Nurnberg-Furth railway.
December 15: Clara plays Beethoven's Choral Fantasy at the Gewandhaus.
December 18: Birth of Blandine Rachel (Geneva), first daughter of Liszt and Marie d'Agoult.

1836

January 1: Robert breaks his engagement to Ernestine in a letter.
January 14: Wieck takes Clara to Dresden to remove her from Robert's influence.
February 4: Robert's mother dies.
February 7: Wieck leaves Clara in Dresden with friends to attend to business.

February 7-11: Robert meets Clara secretly in Dresden.

[*Chapter 12: Dresden Rendezvous*]

February 28-April 3: Clara tours Breslau with Wieck, passing through Gorlitz from Dresden.

May 8: Clara returns to Leipzig from Breslau through Dresden.

June: Clara returns Robert's letters.

Summer: Robert composes his Fantasie in C major, his lament for Clara, dedicated to Liszt.

September 12: Chopin visits Robert, they spend a happy day together during which Chopin plays his Ballade in G minor.

September 13: Robert continues to celebrate Chopin's visit on Clara's seventeenth birthday, the first he hasn't attended in a while. Clara's carriage overturns on her way to a performance, but she performs admirably though her hand swells the next day.

November: Clara tours Naumburg, Jena, and Weimar with her father.

December: Liszt returns to Paris looking for Thalberg.

1837

Robert composes *Davidsbundlertanze* and *Fantasiestucke*.

Chopin meets George Sand.

February 7-May 3: Clara tours with Wieck (Berlin, Hamburg, Bremen), meeting her mother again in Berlin.

March 27: Clara arrives in Hamburg.

March 28: Mendelssohn marries Cecile Jeanrenaud.

March 29: Piano duel between Thalberg and Liszt.

[*Chapter 13: A Duel*]

April 17-27: Clara and Wieck tour Bremen.

May 3: Clara and Wieck return to Leipzig.

July 11-22: Chopin in London.

August 14: Clara and Robert secretly engaged. Robert asks for her "yes," she gives it.

[*Chapter 14: A Simple "Yes"*]

August 24: Mendelssohn arrives in London.

September: Robert leaves for Vienna.

September 1: Mendelssohn writes to Hiller about Chopin's incognito visit earlier in the year to London.

September 13: Robert requests Clara's hand on her 18th birthday, but is rejected by Wieck.

October 15: Clara leaves on tour with Wieck for Vienna.

November 13: Liszt praises three Schumann compositions in a review in the *Parisian Gazette musicale*.

December 24: Birth of Cosima Liszt (Como).

1838

Schumann composes his G minor Piano Sonata (#2).

Brahms concocts his own musical notation.

The Brahmses moves to Ulricusstrasse 38.
March 15: Clara receives Austria's highest honor: Royal and Imperial Virtuosa.
March 21: Emperor Ferdinand dubs Clara Wundermadchen.
April 11-20: Liszt arrives in Vienna, flings his card through Clara's window.
May 15: Clara and Wieck return from Vienna. Robert is to be granted "friend of the family" status. Clara says it's Robert or nobody.

[*Chapter 15: The Vienna Letters*]
[*Chapter 16: A Plan*]

July: Clara visits Dresden.
September 27: Robert leaves Leipzig for Vienna (for half a year), discovers Schubert's Great C Major, publishes *Kinderszenen, Kreisleriana* (dedicated to Chopin, who in turn dedicates his Ballade in F major to Robert), *Humoreske, Novelletten.*
November: Chopin and George Sand set off separately for Majorca, meet in Perpignan, and travel on together.
December 15: Chopin and George Sand move to the monastery in Valdamosa.

<u>1839</u>
Robert composes *Arabesque, Blumenstuck, Humoreske, Nachtstucke,* and *Faschingsschwanke aus Wien (Carnival of Vienna).*
Death of Agnes Carus.
Death of Johann Brahms, Brahms's paternal grandfather (age 70).
Brahms begins music lessons with his father, attends the Privatschule of Heinrich Voss, Dammthorwall.
Clara announces her intention to marry Robert.
Ernestine von Fricken marries Count von Zedwitz, an old man, who dies eight months later.
January 8: Clara leaves for her second tour of Paris (without Wieck).
February 6: Clara arrives in Paris.
March 17: Joachim's debut.

[*Chapter 17: Robert in Vienna*]

April 6: Death of Eduard (Robert's oldest brother).
April 16: Clara gives a concert during which she plays Chopin's Etude #5, opus 10.
May 9: Birth of Daniel Liszt (Rome).
Summer: Joachim moves to Vienna.
June 15: Robert petitions the Court of Appeals for permission to marry without Wieck's consent.
August 14: Clara returns to Germany from Paris.

[*Chapter 18: The Second Paris Tour*]

August 20: Wagner arrives by steamship in Boulogne with Minna, meets Mrs. Manson, a Jewess, who gives him an introduction to Meyerbeer.
September 3: Clara goes to live with her mother in Berlin.
September 13: Robert surprises Clara at her mother's place in Berlin on her birthday.
September 16: Wagner and Minna arrive in Paris.
Autumn: Death of Henriette Voigt (Robert's friend). Robert depressed again.

November: Liszt separates temporarily from Madame d'Agoult, returns to Vienna, later to Hungary, the start of his career as a virtuoso.

[*Chapter 19: A Girl Demoralized*]

December: Wieck defames Robert in court.

December: Clara comes to Leipzig for the second Court attempt at reconciliation, Wieck accuses Robert of alcoholism.

December 25: Robert and Clara in Berlin.

<u>1840</u>

Robert composes *Liederkreis, Myrthen, Dichterliebe*.

Liszt plays for Queen Victoria at Buckingham Palace.

Johann Jakob succeeds the old contrabassist of the Sextet at the Alster Pavilion.

February 28: Robert receives an honorary degree for his work as a composer, critic, and editor, from the University of Jena.

March 18: Liszt in Leipzig with Robert, Clara accepts an invitation to a concert on March 30 (for the poor). Liszt makes his remark about a lack of countesses in Leipzig. Clara decides she's less enthralled with Liszt's work than she was in Vienna.

March 17-30: Liszt gives three concerts and a private musical soiree at Mendelssohn's home.

[*Chapter 20: Liszt in Leipzig*]

April 17-30: Robert visits Clara in Berlin.

May 7: Birth of Tchaikovsky (Kamsko-Votkinsk).

May 27: Death of Paganini (Nice).

June 5: Clara returns to Leipzig.

July 11-12: Robert composes *Frauenliebe und leben*.

August 12: The Court consents to Robert and Clara's marriage.

August 13: Pauline Garcia-Viardot performs in Paris.

August 16: Wedding banns posted for Robert and Clara.

September 5: Clara's last concert as Clara Wieck in Weimar.

September: Clara in Berlin with her mother until she marries Robert.

September 12: Marriage of Robert and Clara in village church of Schonefeld, one day short of her 21st birthday.

[*Chapter 21: A New Life*]

Clara performs concerts in Berlin and tours with her mother and Robert through North Germany.

Brahms starts lessons with Otto Friedrich Willibald Cossel.

[*Chapter 22: A Tune in a Thimble*]

<u>1841</u>

Brahms family moves to Dammthorwall 29.

Robert composes his B flat major Symphony (#1/*Spring*) and his D minor Symphony (#2, later to be reorchestrated as #4).

February 4: Death of Adolf Bargiel (Clara's stepfather).

February 27: Clara gets her piano back from her father.

March 31: First concert as Clara Schumann (Gewandhaus), also premiere of Robert's *Spring* Symphony, both unqualified successes.

June: Meyerbeer recommends Wagner's *Rienzi* to Baron von Luttichau, director of the Dresden Hoftheater, where it's premiered.

September 1: Birth of Marie Schumann.

September 8: Birth of Dvorak (Nelahozeves, near Prague).

September 13: Christening of Marie Schumann (on Clara's 22nd birthday).

November 21: Clara plays in Weimar, her first invitation since marriage (coincidentally, her last engagement before marriage had also been in Weimar), in aid of the pension fund for the musicians of the chapel royal. Robert's First Symphony is also on the program.

November 25: Clara plays at the palace for the Grand Duchess. Robert's songs are sung to much appreciation.

December 6: Robert's Symphony in D minor is premiered in a concert featuring Clara and Liszt. Liszt's bravura performance overshadows everything, annoying Clara, the beginning of her differences with Liszt, "as a composer I could almost hate him." Robert's unsatisfied with his symphony and recalls it to be much revised and published finally as his Fourth.

1842

Brahms attends *Burgerschule*.

Wagner meets Liszt in Paris.

[*Chapter 23: The Man in the Blue Beret*]

February 14: Clara tours Hamburg with Robert, who returns to Leipzig when Clara goes on to Copenhagen.

March: The Berlin Opera accepts Wagner's *Flying Dutchman* at Meyerbeer's recommendation.

[*Chapter 24: First Discord*]

March 20-April 18: Clara tours Copenhagen.

April 18: Clara leaves Copenhagen. Richard Wagner returns to Leipzig from Paris.

April 20: Clara concertizes in Kiel.

April 25: Robert goes to Magdeburg to meet Clara from Hamburg.

April 26: Clara and Robert return to Leipzig.

May 8: Fire destroys much of Hamburg.

Summer: Robert composes three string quartets in A minor, F major, and A major.

July 19: Mendelssohn visits Queen Victoria and Prince Albert.

[*Chapter 25: A Pleasant Afternoon*]

Autumn/Winter: Robert composes his E flat major Piano Quintet and E flat major Piano Quartet.

October 20: Wagner's *Rienzi* premiered in Dresden.

1843

Robert composes his oratorio, *Paradise and the Peri*.

Brahms performs in a Beethoven Piano and Wind Quintet and a Mozart Piano Quartet. An American impresario is impressed and wants to take him to

America, but Cossel won't stand for it. Brahms plays a study by Herz at a charity concert.

Brahms starts lessons with Eduard Marxsen who discourages composition at first in favor of technique, but when composition remains a strong urge he provides structures based on Beethoven, Schubert, Mozart, and most of all Bach.

[*Chapter 26: Marxsen of Altona*]

January: Robert begins teaching at the Leipzig Conservatory founded by Mendelssohn. His fame spreads, Wieck makes reconciliatory overtures.

February: Clara visits her father for a reconciliation in Dresden.

Spring: Joachim moves to Leipzig.

April 2: Leipzig Conservatory opens.

April 25: Birth of Elise Schumann.

June 10: Birth of Heinrich von Herzogenberg (Graz, Austria).

August 18: Concert by Clara, Mendelssohn, and Pauline Viardot during which Joseph Joachim (12 years old) also performs.

November 24: Robert's debut as a conductor during rehearsal for the *Peri*.

December 4: Premiere of the *Peri* (Gewandhaus) a success.

1844

Ernestine von Fricken dies of typhoid.

Robert resigns from editorship of the *Neue Zeitschrift*.

January 25: The Schumanns leave for tour of Russia (children left with relatives in Schneeberg with Robert's brother, Carl).

March: Joachim's first visit to London.

March 1: The Schumanns leave Dorpat (where they arrived via Berlin, Konigsberg, Tauroggen, Riga) for St. Petersburg.

March 4: The Schumanns arrive in St. Petersburg.

March 5: Clara is named honorary member of the St. Petersburg Philharmonic Society.

April 2: The Schumanns leave St. Petersburg.

Easter: The Schumanns stay with Robert's uncle in Tver.

April 10: The Schumanns arrive in Moscow.

May 8: The Schumanns begin their return journey from Moscow to St. Petersburg.

May 27: Joachim plays the Beethoven Violin Concerto in London.

May 30: The Schumanns return to Leipzig from Russia.

August: Robert suffers a nervous breakdown.

September: The Schumanns visit the Harz mountains for a cure, also Karlsbad for the salts, but in vain.

October 3: The Schumanns visit Dresden.

October 17: The Schumanns take a flat on the ground floor of Waisenhausstrasse 35 in Dresden.

November: Farewell party for the Schumanns by Hartel in Leipzig at which they meet and hear Joseph Joachim (13 years).

[*Chapter 27: Russian Winter*]

December 13: The Schumanns settle in Dresden.

1845

Brahms gives badly paid lessons.

Robert composes his A minor Piano Concerto and Studies and Sketches for Pedal Piano.

Paul Brendel assumes editorship of the *Neue Zeitschrift fur Musik*.

March 11: Birth of Julie Schumann.

March 13: Premiere of the Mendelssohn E minor Violin Concerto (Gewandhaus).

Winter: Clara composes her G minor Piano Trio.

Robert composes his C major Symphony (#2).

1846

Brahms plays dance music in bars in the Gangviertel (Lane Quarter; Adulterer's Walk), reading Eichendorff, Novalis, Heine, or Holderlin as he plays.

[*Chapter 28: Zur schwarzen Katze*]

New Years Day: Clara premieres the A minor Piano Concerto at the Gewandhaus, Hiller (the dedicatee) conducting.

February: A continual roaring/ringing in Robert's ears.

February 8: Birth of Emil Schumann.

July 6: Robert and Clara in Norderney (miscarriage).

August 25: The Schumanns return from Norderney.

November 23: The Schumanns (Clara, Robert, Marie, and Elise) leave for Vienna.

[*Chapter 29: Discontent in Dresden*]

1847

Birth of Elisabet von Stockhausen (later von Herzogenberg).

Robert composes his Piano Trios in D minor (#1) and F major (#2).

Chopin breaks with George Sand.

February 4: The Schumanns return from Vienna.

February 11: The Schumanns go to Berlin for performances of the *Peri* and concerts for Clara.

February 20: Robert conducts the *Peri* in Berlin.

April 1-5: Robert sketches the overture to *Genoveva*.

April 13: Mendelssohn suffers dizziness in England near where he had dined with Dickens by the Thames.

May 14: Death of Fanny Hensel (Mendelssohn's sister).

Spring: Brahms lodges at Winsen, a village on the Rhine, with Adolph Giesemann, his father's acquaintance, gives piano lessons to Leischen (Giesemann's 13-year old daughter), and becomes friendly with Herr Blume, a bailiff, also a good amateur musician, who familiarizes him with folk-songs which influence the composition of first two piano sonatas.

[*Chapter 30: Winsen*]

June 22: Death of Emil Schumann.

July: Robert and Clara attend the Schumann music festival in Zwickau.

September 17: The Schumanns move from the Seegasse to the Reitbahngasse 20.

October: Liszt's last public concert, in Elizabetgrad, Russia, before moving to the Altenburg with Princess Jeanne Elisabeth Carolyn von Sayn-Wittgenstein.

November 1: Mendelssohn collapses.

November 4: Death of Mendelssohn. Marxsen says, "A master of the art has gone; a greater arises in Brahms."

November 20: Brahms (14 years old) performs in the Apollo Concert-room (Thalberg's Fantasia on airs from Norma).

November 27: Brahms assists Frau Meyer-David in a duet for two pianos by Thalberg.

1848

Robert composes Scenes from the East, Album for the Young, and *Genoveva*.

January 20: Birth of Ludwig Schumann (named for Ludwig Schunke).

February: Princess Wittgenstein arrives in Weimar to live in the Villa Altenburg. Liszt joins her shortly.

February 16: Chopin's last Paris recital.

February 22: Revolution in Paris.

March 11: Brahms hears Joachim perform the Beethoven Violin Concerto with the Hamburg Philharmonic, imagines Joachim had composed it since he didn't have a program.

June 9: The Schumanns break with Liszt.

[Chapter 31: Liszt Comes to Dinner]

Summer: Brahms revisits Winsen, returning to Hamburg once a week for his lesson with Marxsen, sometimes Leischen goes with and stays with his family, Herr Giesemann pays for the Hamburg Opera where Brahms hears Mozart's *Marriage of Figaro*. Forty years later he repays the kindness by arranging a scholarship in Vienna for Leischen's daughter (Agnes). Brahms continues playing bars and private parties.

August 4: Robert completes *Genoveva*.

September 21: Brahms gives a concert: Dohler's William Tell Fantasy (from Rossini), Bach fugue, one of his own compositions, two movements from a Rosenhain Concerto, a Bach Fugue, and a Serenade for the left hand by Marxsen, also a study by Herz.

November: Bulow attends Wagner's reading of "Siegfried's Death" in Dresden.

1849

Robert composes For Children Little and Big, F major Concertstuck for Four Horns and Orchestra, *Manfred* Overture and Incidental Music, and G major Introduction and Allegro Appassionato for Piano and Orchestra.

March 1: Brahms's (second) public concert with Theodor Wachtel, a droshky-driver turned singer, plays Thalberg's Fantasie on Motifs from Don Juan.

April: Death of Karl (Robert's brother), the last of the relatives of his generation.

April 14: Another concert for Brahms, plays Thalberg's Don Juan Fantasy, his own Fantasy on a Favorite Waltz, Beethoven's *Waldstein*, Mayer's Air Italien.

May 3-10: The Dresden uprising which affects Wagner and Remenyi. Liszt rescues Wagner.

May 5: Schumanns move temporarily to Maxen (suburb) owing to the Dresden uprising.

[*Chapter 32: The Fires of Dresden*]

June 12: Schumanns return to Dresden.

July 16: Birth of Ferdinand Schumann.

August 28: Premiere of Robert's *Faust* (Dresden, Weimar, and Leipzig, on Goethe's centenary).

October 17: Death of Chopin (Paris).

1850

February 5: Clara and Robert leave for a tour of Leipzig, Hamburg, and Bremen. Jenny Lind joins Clara for one concert.

[*Chapter 33: A Package for Doktor Schumann*]

March 17: Robert conducts *Genoveva* Overture in Hamburg, Clara plays his Piano Concerto.

March 29: Schumanns return from tour.

March 31: Schumanns decide to leave Dresden for Dusseldorf.

May 9: Wagner in flight.

May 18-July 10: *Genoveva*'s Leipzig premiere.

August 28: *Lohengrin* premiered by Liszt in Weimar (on Goethe's birthday).

September 1: The Schumanns arrive in Dusseldorf.

Late September: The Schumanns take a Rhine tour, capped by the Cologne Cathedral.

October: Joachim arrives in Weimar as Liszt's concertmaster for 500 thaler. Liszt makes 1,600, other musicians 100-300.

October: Robert composes his Cello Concerto in A minor.

October 15: Josef Wilhelm von Wasielewski arrives in Dusseldorf as concertmaster.

October 24: Robert's debut in Dusseldorf.

November 2-December 9: Robert composes his E flat major Symphony (#3/*Rhenish*).

November 9: Musical soiree in which Clara performs in every number, Robert's second public event in Dusseldorf.

December 29: Robert completes his Overture to *The Bride of Messina*.

1851

Robert composes his G minor Piano Trio (#3), A minor (#1) and D minor (#2) Violin Sonatas, and Overtures to *Julius Caesar, Hermann and Dorothea*, and *Bride of Messina*.

Brahms composes his Scherzo in E flat minor, also songs.

Brahms meets Remenyi (seeking asylum in Hamburg from revolutionary activities), engaged to provide party music at the house of a rich Hamburg merchant.

Brahms plays with Remenyi at private functions for several months.

[*Chapter 34: Remenyi*]

Bulow becomes Liszt's pupil in Weimar.

January 11: Robert conducts his fourth subscription concert.

Late January: Robert composes his *Julius Caesar Overture*.

February 6: Robert conducts the first performance of the *Rhenish* Symphony (Dusseldorf).

February 20: Robert conducts another concert (Dusseldorf).

February 25: Robert conducts the *Rhenish* (Cologne).

March: Audience refuses to applaud Robert's *The Bride of Messina Overture*.

March 13: Robert repeats the *Rhenish* in Dusseldorf, his eighth and last concert of the season, after which an article appears in the Dusseldorf *Zeitung* criticizing his abilities as a conductor.

March 17: Robert debates whether to stay in Dusseldorf.

March 26: Clara discovers she's pregnant again.

April 13: Robert conducts Bach's *St. John*.

August 16: Robert judges competition of male choruses in Belgium.

September: First dissatisfaction with Robert from the Music Society.

October: Albert Dietrich befriends the Schumanns.

October 16: Clara tries Robert's A minor Violin Sonata with Wasielewski.

October 27: Performance of Robert's G minor Piano Trio.

December 1: Birth of Eugenie Schumann.

December: Robert composes *Hermann and Dorothea Overture*.

<u>1852</u>

Joachim appointed violinist to King George V at Hanover.

March 4: Robert's sixth subscription concert. Clara (first concert since Eugenie's birth) plays Chopin's F minor Piano Concerto, Robert conducts Beethoven's *Pastoral*.

March 15-22: "Schumann Week" in Leipzig, many Gewandhaus concerts, also in neighboring cities, Liszt attends. Robert says goodbye to his friend, Dr. Reuter, for the last time (he dies the next year).

March 18: Julius Tausch conducts the seventh subscription concert in the absence of the Schumanns, setting people wondering why he doesn't conduct more.

Late March: Returning to Dusseldorf, the Schumanns find their house has been sold, they're forced to move to Herzogstrasse (noisy from new construction work).

April 27-May 8: Robert composes his *Requiem for Mignon*.

May: Louise Japha becomes a student of the Schumanns.

May 6: Robert's ninth subscription concert. He conducts the *Spring* Symphony (enthusiastically applauded), Clara performs Beethoven's *Emperor* Concerto.

June 10: Robert conducts Beethoven's *Mass in C minor*.

Summer: Robert faints after strenuous hike during a 10-day Rhineland vacation.

July 8: Robert undertakes the first of 18 riverbath treatments at the recommendation of Dr. Muller, who blames Clara for shielding her husband too much.

July 20: Robert feels better until Clara informs him of "frightening hopes" of another pregnancy.

July 30: Against Dr. Muller's advice, Robert assumes the baton from Tausch to conduct the *Julius Caesar Overture* during rehearsal.

August 3: Assumes the baton again from Tausch for the concert which Tausch was to lead. Clara performs Beethoven's *Emperor*.

August 11-September 17: The Schumanns vacation with Marie (11 years old) in Scheveningen, Holland where Clara miscarries.

October 28: Tausch conducts opening concert, Clara plays a Henselt Concerto and Beethoven Sonata.

November: Brahms composes his Piano Sonata in F sharp minor.

November 18: Tausch conducts the second concert, Ruppert Becker, son of Ernst Adolph Becker (who replaces Wasielewski as concertmaster), solos the Mendelssohn Concerto.

November 21: Robert hears an A (auditory problems from anxiety about conducting again).

December 2: Tausch conducts the first half of the third concert before handing the baton to Robert (anonymous admirer presents Robert with a laurel wreath).

December 11: Music Society convenes again to discuss Robert.

December 14: An "impudent letter" arrives from three officials asking for Robert's resignation, also the formation of the "Anti-Music Society" to protest bad and badly played music. Dr. Hasenclever from the Music Society arrives to soothe matters.

[*Chapter 35: Debacle in Dusseldorf*]

December 30: Robert conducts Beethoven's A major Symphony, Gade's *Spring Fantasy*, Clara solos.

1853

Robert composes his C major Fantasy for Violin, D minor Violin Concerto, and D minor Introduction and Allegro for Piano and Orchestra.

Brahms composes his Piano Sonata in C major.

February 17: Robert conducts Haydn's *Seasons* in Dusseldorf.

April 19: Brahms sets off with Remenyi on tour, beginning at Winsen.

April 24-29: Robert is interested in table-tapping.

May 2: Brahms and Remenyi perform in Celle (Brahms transposes Beethoven's C minor Violin Sonata to C sharp minor on sight).

May 3: Brahms and Remenyi leave Celle for Luneburg.

May 9: Brahms and Remenyi perform in Luneburg.

May 11: Brahms and Remenyi are so popular they perform again in Luneburg.

May 12: Brahms and Remenyi perform again in Celle.

May 15-17: Dusseldorf Rhine Festival [Neider-Rheinische Festival].

May 15: Robert conducts his D minor Symphony, Clara plays his Piano Concerto.

May 17: Joachm plays the Beethoven Violin Concerto with Robert. Robert gains respect again as a composer, but is deemed inferior to Hiller as a conductor in the papers.

May 18: Joachim leaves Dusseldorf to spend a week in Weimar with Liszt before returning to Hanover.

Brahms and Remenyi arrive in Hanover where Remenyi wishes to reestablish his friendship with Joachim, once a fellow-student, now leading the King of Hanover's orchestra, but police discover Remenyi's a revolutionary and he and Brahms are expelled. Joachim gives them an introduction to Liszt in Weimar.

June 15: Brahms and Remenyi arrive at the Altenburg.

June 24: Brahms leaves Remenyi and the Altenburg.

Late June: Brahms returns to Joachim now in Gottingen attending university lectures on philosophy and history. When Brahms's parents imagine he's obliging himself to Joachim, Joachim writes back in Brahms's defense. They give a concert and Brahms leaves for a walking tour of the Rhine country to mull things over with introductions from Joachim to many of his friends, especially to Robert, but he's wary of Robert after the rejection in Hamburg and unaware of much of Robert's work.

[*Chapter 36: A Visit to Weimar*]

Late July: Clara organizes a series of concerts in Bonn with Wasielewski's help unknown to Robert.

July 30: Robert has a stroke in Bonn, momentarily paralyzed. Dr. Domenicus Kalt suggests sciatica.

August 28: Joachim appears on Robert's doorstep on his way to the Karlsruhe festival to meet Liszt.

Autumn: Liszt and Wagner meet in Basel (Joachim travels with Liszt), they travel together to Paris.

September: Thanks to Joachim, Brahms meets the conductor Wasielewski in Bonn, who also encourages him to visit Robert, as do the Diechmanns in Mehlem (also Schumann enthusiasts whose collection of the composer's works Brahms discovers with delight), and Carl Reinecke and Ferdinand Hiller in Cologne.

September 12-13: The Schumanns 13th wedding anniversary and Clara's 34th birthday. Robert presents Clara with a new grand piano, songs, work for piano and orchestra.

September 30: Brahms meets the Schumanns, stays at their insistence, meets Albert Dietrich.

Robert is dismissed as music director of the Dusseldorf orchestra.

[Chapter 37: *Trio*]

October 13: Robert writes to Joachim asking for his perspective on his essay, "Neue Bahnen" (New Paths, or New Tendencies).

October 27: Joachim is expected in Dusseldorf to partake in the Rhine Musical Festival. Robert conducts his last concert in Dusseldorf.

October 28: Clara and Joachim play through FAE in Dusseldorf, Joachim guessing each movement correctly. "Neue Bahnen" published in *Neue Zeitschrift*.

[*Chapter 38: New Paths*]

November 2: Brahms follows Joachim to Gottingen.

November 3: Brahms follows Joachim to Hanover.

November 7: Illing and Herz arrive to let Clara know Robert's to conduct only his own work.

November 9: Robert says he will conduct no more.

November 16: Brahms writes to Robert with thanks.

November 24-December 22: Clara tours Holland with Robert.

Late November: Brahms arrives in Leipzig, meets Heinrich von Sahr (Schumannian), also Breitkopf and Hartel on Robert's recommendation who agree to publish his opuses 1-6; also among others Julius Rietz/conductor, Ignaz Moscheles (who'd known Beethoven), and Ferdinand David (leader of the Gewandhaus), also Berlioz. He stays initially at a hotel, but von Sahr invites him to stay with him and later in November he spends a few days on the estate of Ida von Hohenthal.

December 17: Brahms plays his C major Piano Sonata and E flat Scherzo at the small hall of the Gewandhaus, Berlioz hugs him, Liszt says to Bulow he's "genuinely interested" in Brahms.

December 20: Brahms leaves Leipzig with Otto Grimm, originally for Hanover, but Joachim's in Cologne so he's home in Hamburg by evening.

December 20, 22: Joachim performs in Cologne.

Christmas: Brahms returns to his family in triumph, even defiantly banging out the dance tunes he had played at the Gangviertel.

<u>1854</u>

Brahms hears Beethoven's Ninth for the first time in Cologne.

January 4: Brahms arrives in Hanover from Hamburg, lodges with Joachim (Bulow's also a lodger, so's Grimm), and composes most of his B flat major Piano Trio (#1).

January 19-30: The Schumanns visit Joachim in Hanover.

January 21-30: The Schumanns arrive for Clara's concerts in Hanover including Robert's *Peri*, D minor Symphony, Violin Fantasy (with Joachim), and Beethoven's E flat Piano Concerto.

February 10-12: Onset of Robert's breakdown. He can't sleep for hearing a note, sometimes chords, indescribably exquisite music.

February 27: Robert throws himself into the Rhine.

March 1: Bulow performs the first movement of Brahms's C major Sonata at a concert in Hamburg, the first pianist to perform Brahms in public.

March 3: Brahms leaves for Dusseldorf, summons Joachim.

March 4: Robert is admitted to the asylum in Endenich near Bonn.

[*Chapter 39: The Lure of the Lorelei*]

March 31: Clara leaves the house in Bilkerstrasse, Dusseldorf.

April: Brahms sketches a sonata for two pianos (later to become the D minor Piano Concerto).

June: Brahms writes to Joachim that even two pianos are not enough for his ideas.

June 11: Birth of Felix Schumann (Dusseldorf).

June 19: Brahms's letter to Joachim, "seems so natural putting my arm around Clara."

July: Brahms attempts to transform the first movement of his sonata for two pianos to a symphony, but his knowledge of orchestration is too limited.

July 19: Clara travels with Joachim to Berlin to leave Julie with her mother.

August: Clara leaves on tour after recuperating in Ostend. Brahms composes *Variations on a Theme by Schumann, Variation on a Hungarian Theme*, Ballades, and walks in the Black Forest taking stock and moping over Clara.

September 14: Robert (in the asylum) begins to correspond with Clara.

[*Chapter 40: Consecration*]

October: Brahms stays a few days at Gisela von Arnim's house which prompts her letter to Joachim about his lack of social graces, which prompts Joachim's letter back in agreement, but both are at pains to balance them with his good qualities.

October–December: Clara begins concert tours.

October 14: Brahms and Grimm accompany Clara and her companion Fraulein Agnes Schonerstedt to Hanover where they meet Joachim.

October 16: Clara performs for the Hanover court.

October 17: Clara leaves Hanover for Leipzig.

October 19: Clara is warmly received at the Gewandhaus where she performs Beethoven's G major Piano Concerto among other things, but bursts into tears in her box during a performance of Gade's C minor Symphony.

October 23: Another concert at the Gewandhaus is packed, all Schumann program (except for the Andante and Scherzo from Brahms's F minor Sonata), after which Clara concertizes in Frankfurt where she realizes she remains subject to personal grudges and petty jealousies despite her circumstances. Liszt is kind, but she sees too much distance between his music and hers. After Frankfurt she meets Joachim and Grimm again in Hanover.

November 7: Clara meets Brahms in Harburg and the two head for Hamburg.

November 13: Clara performs in Hamburg and meets Brahms's family.

November 19: Clara leaves Hamburg for Bremen where she plays Brahms's Scherzo and spends time with Brahms, Joachim, and a friend of Robert in the Rathskeller after the concert.

November 23: Clara and Brahms part, she for concerts in Berlin with Joachim, he for Hamburg. She promises to address him with "du" in her letters. She accepts an invitation from Breslau and plays to packed houses before returning to Berlin.

December: Joachim visits Robert who asks to be moved to another asylum.

December 4: Clara performs in Berlin, spends a pleasant evening with Paul Mendelssohn.

December 10: Clara appears at a soiree with Joachim.

December 11: Clara is invited to the home of the Brothers Grimm (of the fairytales).

December 15: Brahms declares his love for Clara in a letter, rushes to a concert by her in Hamburg, but he's absent for Christmas with his family for the first time rushing back to Dusseldorf with Clara. Robert requests, energetically, to see Brahms.

December 16: A second soiree for Clara with Joachim.

December 20: A third soiree during which they play Bach, Beethoven, and Robert.

December 21: Clara takes a train to Leipzig in the morning for a concert at the Gewandhaus in the evening with Joachim.

1855
Death of Robert's teacher, Kuntsch.

Liszt's daughters come to Weimar to live with Bulow and his mother, Cosima throws herself at Bulow in six weeks.

January: Brahms has a dream in which he sees the solution to his problems with orchestration, to make a piano concerto of his "symphony which came to grief."

January 3: Clara and Brahms visit Joachim in Hanover to hear his *Henry IV Overture*.

January 11: Brahms visits Robert in Endenich.

January 15: Brahms sees Clara off at Ems for Holland (for concerts in Rotterdam, Leyden, Utrecht, Amsterdam, the Hague), but to her surprise follows her two days later to Rotterdam.

January 23: Brahms returns to Dusseldorf.

February 24: Brahms visits Robert who is anxious to leave the asylum.

March 8: Clara performs Beethoven's Fantasia for Piano, Chorus, and Orchestra in Berlin.

March 10-20: Clara tours Pomerania, Stralsund, Bergen, before returning to Berlin.

March 22: Clara returns to Dusseldorf.

April 13-24: Visits Hamburg with Brahms, staying with him at his parents home, to hear Otten conduct Robert's *Manfred* and *Bride of Messina* on the 21st.

Spring: Brahms attends the Lower Rhine Festival in Dusseldorf featuring Jenny Lind-Goldschmidt, also meeting Eduard Hanslick, critic, later to become his friend.

May: Clara plays at Detmold.

May: Bettina von Arnim visits Robert and tries to get him released.

May 1: Robert writes his last letter to Clara.

[*Chapter 41: The Solution to the Problem*]

July: Clara meets Richarz, agrees to Robert staying in Endenich.

July: Robert abandons all correspondence, resigning himself to his fate.

July 15: Clara plays at Ems where Brahms is rude to Jenny Lind-Goldschmidt. Clara quarrels with Jenny over Brahms, whose music Jenny says has "mistaken tendencies."

September 10: Letter from Richarz depriving her "of all hope of a complete recovery."

September 15: Joachim performs Robert's Violin Concerto for Clara. She claims it has a "defect, showing definite traces of Robert's illness."

October-December: Concert tours for Clara in Danzig and Berlin.

The Brahmses now live at Lilienstrasse.

November: Brahms joins Joachim and Clara on a concert tour, visiting Danzig. The tour is so successful that Brahms continues on his own, playing Beethoven and Mozart concertos in Leipzig, Hamburg, and Bremen, appearing as soloist with orchestra for the first time, living in Hanover, visiting Liszt, but fritters away much of the year over Clara, and returns to Dusseldorf.

November 20: Brahms performs Robert's C major Fantasia and Beethoven's G major Piano Concerto in Bremen.

November 24: Brahms performs at one of Otten's concerts in Hamburg, Beethoven's *Emperor*, also pieces by Schubert and Robert.

November 27: Brahms's B major Piano Trio is premiered in New York (by William Mason who met Brahms during his stay at the Altenburg), making America the first country to premier Brahms's chamber music.

[Chapter 42: Time and Clockwork]

December 3: Clara and Joachim give a concert in Leipzig before she returns to Dusseldorf in time for Christmas with Brahms.

December: Joachim attends a concert of Liszt conducting his own work and writes to Clara of his disillusionment.

1856

Bruckner moves to Linz as church organist, goes to Vienna once a week to study counterpoint with Simon Schechter (with whom Schubert began studying in the last year of his life).

January 3: Joachim writes that Robert is better.

January 10: Brahms performs Beethoven's G major Piano Concerto, also a couple of short pieces by Robert, at a Gewandhaus concert.

January 26: Brahms plays Mozart's D minor Piano Concerto with Otten for Mozart's birthday (the next day).

January-March: Clara tours Prague, Vienna, Budapest, giving five concerts in Vienna, all enthusiastically received, recalled fifteen times at her first concert on January 7, refuses to perform with Liszt (who's conducting) at the Mozart Centenary Festival in Vienna.

February 2: Anton Rubinstein writes to Liszt denigrating Brahms.

February 26: Brahms writes to Joachim suggesting weekly contrapuntal exercises via the mail.

April: Brahms visits Robert who is abjectly psychotic.

April 8-July 6: Clara's first tour of England.

May: Brahms still in Dusseldorf, moves to Bonn to be near Robert whose condition has worsened, meets Dietrich again.

May 11-13: Brahms attends the Lower Rhine Music Festival, renews acquaintance of Klaus Groth, the poet, meets Stockhausen, Hanslick again, Otto Jahn, and Theodor Kirchner.

May 27: Brahms performs with Stockhausen at Cologne.

May 29: Brahms performs with Stockhausen at Bonn.

June 8: Brahms visits Robert on his birthday with an atlas.

June 23: The *Peri* is conducted by William Sterndale Bennett (London).

July 4: Brahms meets Clara (returning from London) at Antwerp, but they go to Ostend together first so Brahms might see the sea for the first time instead of to Robert, uncertain as they still are whether Clara should see Robert.

July 6: Return to Dusseldorf.

July 23: Clara is summoned to Endenich, but still not allowed to see Robert.

July 27: Clara finally sees Robert for the first time in two and a half years.

July 29, 4p: Death of Robert.

July 31: Robert's funeral.

[*Chapter 43: A Release*]
August 14: Clara and Brahms take a rest in Switzerland (Gersau, on Lake Lucerne) with Ludwig and Ferdinand and Brahms's sister, Elise.

September 13: They return to Dusseldorf.

October 21: Brahms leaves Dusseldorf for Hamburg.

[*Chapter 44: Another Release*]
Autumn: Ludwig and Ferdinand are sent to boarding school.

October: Brahms sends Joachim the first movement of his D minor Piano Concerto.

October 28-December 25: Clara begins concert tours, including Denmark.

October 25: Brahms performs Beethoven's G major Piano Concerto with great success.

November 22: Brahms performs Robert's Piano Concerto at the Philharmonic Concert with less success.

1857

January 1: Clara performs Mozart's D minor at the Gewandhaus.

February: Clara gives concerts with Joachim and Brahms in Gottingen and Hanover.

March: Clara tours Barmen, Cologne, Elberfeld.

April 21-July 2: Clara's second tour of England.

Whitsuntide: Brahms makes a preliminary visit to Detmold.

July-September 5: Clara and Brahms on the Rhine with her younger children, joined on July 27 by Joachim. Grimm, Otten, Fraulein Leser are also with them at different times.

August 14: Cosima marries Bulow in Berlin.

August 27: Joachim writes his letter of regret to Liszt.

September: Brahms, in Detmold, lives at zur Stadt Frankfurt.

[*Chapter 45: Detmold*]
October: Clara leaves Dusseldorf with her children for a teaching position in Berlin.

October 22: Blandine Liszt marries Emile Olliviere, a French statesman and minister of Napoleon III, in Florence [on Liszt's birthday].

October 27: Clara and Joachim tour Dresden, Leipzig, Augsburg, reaching Munich on November 12.

December 6-22: Clara tours Switzerland (Zurich, Basel, Berne), returning to Munich.

1858

January 1: Brahms is back in Hamburg, his family now lives at Fuhlenwiethe 74, but he moves to nearby Hamm, boarding at the house of Frau Dr. Rosing (to whom he dedicates the A major Piano Quartet/#2). She is also the aunt of Marie and Betty Volckers who live next door for whom Brahms starts a quartet of singing girls after he hears them in their garden.

January 27-March 11: Clara sets out on another tour of Switzerland (Basel, Guebweiler, Geneva, Lausanne, Vevey, Zoringen, St. Gallen, Schaffhausen, Winterthur), returning to Stuttgart and Berlin.

March: Brahms visits Berlin, ostensibly to see the picture-galleries, but actually to see Clara whom he imagines he deserted in her hour of need and who, in turn, regrets taking two years of his young life.

March: Brahms completes his D minor Piano Concerto.

April 23: Birth of Ethel Mary Smyth (London).

May 9: Clara goes from Berlin to Lockwitz to Leipzig to Hamburg (stays with Brahms's parents) to Wiesbaden to Gottingen.

July 26-September 14: Clara holidays with her girls in Gottingen with Grimm, Joachim, Brahms and others. Brahms conceives his Serenade in D major as a nonet and meets Agathe von Siebold. Clara, seeing Brahms with his arm around Agathe, leaves suddenly.

Early Autumn: Joachim plays his (Hungarian) Violin Concerto for the first time.

September: Back in Detmold, Brahms composes his "Ave Maria."

September-October 26: Clara sends her children back to Berlin, visits Dusseldorf, tours Cologne, Aix, and Crefeld before returning to Berlin.

November 9: Clara tours Vienna and Budapest with Marie by way of Dresden and Prague.

December 18: Liszt conducts Peter Cornelius's *Barber of Baghdad* in Weimar to hisses, marking the beginning of his determination to leave Weimar.

1859

Early January: Brahms leaves Detmold, visits Gottingen on the way to Hanover to see Agathe.

January 22: Premiere of Brahms's D minor Piano Concerto at Hanover with Brahms and Joachim (received enthusiastically).

January 27: Brahms's performance of the D minor Piano Concerto with Rietz is hissed at the Gewandhaus.

January 31: Brahms goes to Hamburg.

[*Chapter 46: Gathe*]

March 24: Joachim and Brahms perform the D minor Piano Concerto in Hamburg, Stockhausen also on program.

March 28: Brahms, Joachim, and Stockhausen perform jointly again, including the Serenade in D (first performance).

January-April 25: Clara tours Vienna, Dresden, and Berlin.

April 16-23: Brahms with Clara and her children for Easter in Berlin.

April 25-July 2: Clara tours England with her half-sister, Marie Wieck while Stockhausen and Joachim are also touring England.

Summer: Berta Porubsky, on a visit from Vienna, introduces Brahms to the Viennese style.

July-September: Clara in Dusseldorf, Kreuzenach, and Wildbad.

September 1-20: Clara in Honnef.

September 20-October 15: Clara in Mehlem.

September 19: Brahms's vocal quartet expands from four to forty, calling themselves the Hamburg Frauenchor for whom he composes songs.

Autumn: Brahms again in Detmold where he sketches his Serenade in A and *Handel Variations*. His G minor Piano Quartet (#1) is tried in Detmold by Karl Bargheer with Schulze and Schmidt, and he begins composing his B flat major Sextet (#1), F minor Piano Quintet, and G major Sextet (#2).

October-November: Clara gives concerts in Aix la Chapelle, Cologne, Bonn, and Bremen, concluding with a concert in Dusseldorf on November 22.

December 3: Death of Liszt's son, Daniel, studying law in Berlin.

December 19: Clara and Joachim give a concert in Celle, returning to Berlin for Christmas with her family.

End of year: Clara, Joachim, and Brahms are not invited to the 25th anniversary of the *Neue Zeitschrift fur Musik*.

[*Chapter 47: The Hamburg Frauenchor*]

Albert Dietrich marries.

1860

Early: Brahms visits Joachim in Hanover on his way to Hamburg from Detmold for a private performance of the Serenade in A, also a concert with Joachim playing Beethoven's Violin Concerto and Brahms playing Robert's Piano Concerto. They stay briefly with Clara in Berlin.

January 21-February: Clara tours with Elise (Hanover, Kassel, Braunschweig, Dusseldorf, Utrecht, Amsterdam, Rotterdam, the Hague).

February 18: Clara stops at Hanover, returning to Berlin to hear Joachim conduct the *Eroica*.

February 19: The Serenade in A is premiered at a Philharmonic Concert in Hamburg conducted by Joachim, Brahms also performs Robert's Concerto with great success.

March-April 12: Clara touring Vienna with Marie.

March 3: The Serenade in A is performed at Hanover for which Joachim gets an ugly anonymous letter calling it a monstrosity, a caricature, a freak, filth, while the D minor Piano Concerto from the year before still sticks in their throats.

March 21: Joachim writes to Robert Franz, a songwriter, urging him to sign the Manifesto with the others.

April 13: Clara performs in Leipzig "Where father was very nice to me."

April 14: Clara returns to Berlin.

April 28: Clara visits Brahms in Hamburg for a few weeks.

May 4: The Manifesto is published prematurely in the Berlin *Echo*, signed by Brahms, Joachim, Julius Otto Grimm, Bernhard Scholz.

May 24: Clara returns to Dusseldorf with Brahms and Joachim, going from Dusseldorf to Bonn.

[*Chapter 48: The Manifesto*]

May 27-29: Brahms visits Dusseldorf for the Rhine Festival with Clara, Joachim, Stockhausen, Dietrich (newly married), Ferdinand Hiller, Schnorr von Carolsfeld (Wagner's first Tristan), Heinrich von Sahr, Rudolf von der Leyen, also the Frauleins Volckers and Garbe of the Frauenchor.

June 15: Clara goes to Kreuzenach with Stockhausen where she stays until July, gathering her children around her.

Brahms visits the Dietrichs in Bonn (their first house-guest) and meets the publisher, Friedrich "Fritz" August Simrock, who publishes the Serenade in A and Sextet in B flat. He works on his G major Sextet in Bonn.

Brahms visits Theodor Kirchner, pupil of Robert, now the resident organist of the small town of Winterthur, Switzerland.

Early August: Brahms returns to Hamm, near Hamburg, and busies himself again with the Frauenchor, the Avertimento, their motto "Fix oder nix" (all/ thoroughness or nothing).

September 22: Clara leaves Kreuzenach for Coblenz, Bonn, Godesberg, Dusseldorf, reaching Hanover on October 19.

October 20: The G major Sextet is played for the first time in public by Joachim and colleages at Hanover.

Late October-November: Clara goes from Leipzig to Dresden, gives three concerts with Joachim.

November 8-yearend: Clara goes from Dresden to Berlin to Leipzig to Dusseldorf.

November 26: Joachim and Brahms perform at a Gewandhaus concert, Brahms performing his Serenade in A (Clara present), Joachim his Hungarian Concerto, each conducting the other's work; the press is cool.

Christmas: Brahms is back in Hamburg, but the family is quarreling.

<u>1861</u>

January 6-February 3: Clara tours Barmen (6th), Cologne (8th), Hamburg (11th/14th with Joachim and Brahms who also conducts the Frauenchor), Altona (16th), Hanover (20th), Osnabruck (24th), and Detmold (26th/3rd) before returning to Dusseldorf.

[Chapter 49: Their Wedding Night]

February 25: Clara leaves to tour Belgium.

Brahms's D minor Piano Concerto is published by Rieter-Biedermann.

Early March: Brahms performs Beethoven's Triple Concerto in a Philharmonic Concert with Ferdinand David (violin) and Carl Davidov (cello).

April: Stockhausen visits Hamburg, performs with Brahms.

April 29: Clara returns to Berlin from Dusseldorf.

April 30: Brahms produces Serenade in A as part of Stockhausen's concert.

May 6: Clara goes to Hamburg to spend a few days with Brahms.

June: Clara visits Spa.

July 3: Clara leaves Spa for Kreuzenach.

Summer: Brahms stays again at Frau Dr. Rosing's in Hamm.

August 11-September 13: Clara (with Marie) visits Switzerland.

September: Dietrich, now music director to the court of the Duke of Oldenburg, visits Brahms, stays with his parents in Hamburg while Brahms stays in Hamm. They spend much time together, Brahms shows him his tin soldiers, kept locked in a drawer.

Brahms takes a short walking tour in the Harz mountains, returning in time to greet Clara arriving in Hamburg from Switzerland, Marie returning to Berlin.

October 21: Clara (with Julie) sets out on another tour.

November 16: Clara premieres Brahms's G minor Piano Quartet in Hamburg and sixteen ladies from the Fraunchor sing six songs at her invitation.

November 17-30: Clara gives concerts in Bremen, Hanover, and Oldenburg.

December 3: Back in Hamburg, Clara performs the D minor Piano Concerto.

December 7: Also in Hamburg, Clara premieres the *Handel Variations* (which she had seen no earlier than November 1).

December 9: Clara leaves Hamburg for Leipzig playing Mozart's C minor Piano Concerto (12th), *Handel Variations* (14th).

December 20: Clara returns to Berlin, spending Christmas with her children and Joachim, Brahms joining them in the last week of the year to stay until January 3.

1862

January 9: Clara goes to Dusseldorf and Cologne (concert with Stockhausen), then Bonn and Frankfurt and back to Dusseldorf.

January 20: Brahms and Joachim perform at Munster, Grimm conducts.

February: Clara gives concerts in Karlsruhe, Basel, Guebweiler, and Zurich returning to Dusseldorf on the 28th.

February 14: Brahms and Joachim perform at Celle.

March 7-May 30: Clara visits Paris.

March 14: Brahms appears with Dietrich in Oldenburg as soloist in Beethoven's Piano Concerto in G, also performs Bach's Chromatic Fantasia. Dietrich conducts the Serenade in D. Brahms performs the *Handel Variations* for the orchestra during the rehearsal.

March 18: Brahms gives a recital with Leopold Auer (Joachim's student), still 17 years old, of the *Kreutzer*, Brahms also performs Robert's *Symphonic Etudes*, after which they tour. Rossini calls on Clara in Paris, she finds him wellbred and friendly.

March 25: Clara (with Marie) calls on Rossini, but is uncomfortable among other callers, all sitting in highbacked chairs, Rossini taking snuff, pressing lozenges into her hand from time to time, but also finds him amusing and a man of the world, his wife something of a vixen.

Spring and Summer: Brahms lives at Frau Dr. Rosing's in Hamm.

May 30: Clara visits her father in Dresden.

June 1: Birth of Alice Barbi (Modena, Italy).

June 2: Clara visits Kreuzenach.

June 8-10: Brahms goes to Cologne for the Rhine Music Festival where he renews old acquaintances and makes new ones, among them Frau Luise Dustmann-Mayer (from Vienna, who, vivacious as Berta Porubsky, also sparks his desire to visit the city).

June 29: Brahms, Dietrich, and Heinrich von Sahr take a walking tour in the Palatinate.

July 1-August 3: Clara in Munster and Baden-Baden.

Summer: Brahms and Dietrich set off to nearby Munster-am-Stein to be with Clara and kids taking a health cure in the spa town. He shows Dietrich the first movement of the C minor Symphony, mails it to Clara after leaving Munster.

July 1: Clara writes to Joachim about the first movement of a symphony sent by Brahms.

July 10: Brahms, back in Hamm, completes his F minor Piano Quintet and announces his intention to visit Vienna.

August 3: Clara leaves for Switzerland (Basel, Lucerne, Guebweiler).

Autumn: Clara buys a house in Lichtenthal (near Baden-Baden) for 14,000 florins.

September: Bismarck becomes Prime Minister of Prussia.

September 8: Brahms leaves Hamburg for Vienna, lives at the Hotel Kronprinz until he finds private lodgings in the Novaragasse.

At Julius Epstein's house, where Mozart had composed *The Marriage of Figaro*, Joseph Hellmesberger performs the G minor and A major piano quartets with his quartet and dubs Brahms Beethoven's heir.

November 16: The Hellmesberger Quartet introduces the G minor Piano Quartet in Vienna, Brahms at the piano.

November 18: Brahms writes to Clara about disappointment over the Hamburg Philharmonic Orchestra appointment going to Stockhausen.

November 29: The Hellmesberger quartet performs the A major Piano Quartet at the Vienna Philharmonic Society, Brahms also performs the *Handel Variations*, Bach Organ Toccata in F, and Robert's Fantasie in C.

November-December: Clara gives concerts in Frankfurt, Hamburg, Leipzig, Dresden, Breslau, and returns to Berlin for Christmas with her children.

December 3: Hanslick hedges about Brahms, says it's too early to pronounce judgment.

December 18: Brahms performs in aid of Heinrich Wilhelm Ernst, aged and once celebrated violinist and rival of Paganini, Four Duets for Alto and Baritone, Wechselleid zum Tanze, and is joined by Julie von Asten in Robert's Variations for Two Pianos.

December 20: Brahms performs again some Robert solos and a Sonata with Hellmesberger at a concert given by Frau Passy-Cornet.

December 28: Clara concertizes in Dresden.

[*Chapter 50: Vienna*]

1863

Brahms revises his F minor Piano Quintet from String Quintet to a Sonata for Two Pianos.

January 1: Wagner conducts, Brahms attends.

January 3: Clara (with Marie) begins another tour of Holland (the Hague, Amsterdam, Utrecht, Arnheim).

January 6: Brahms performs his F minor Piano Sonata and accompanies Marie Wilt on some of his songs at a concert attended by Wagner and Hanslick, but the composers don't meet face to face for another year. Hanslick's guarded, admits enjoying second movement of the piano sonata, Wagner's silent despite Brahms's help copying *Die Meistersinger*.

January 11: Wagner conducts, Brahms attends again, remarking to Wendelin Weissheimer that he should take care not to tear his brand new white kid gloves with applause.

January 31: Joachim writes to Ave-Lallemant castigating him for the committee's choice of Stockhausen over Brahms for the Hamburg Philharmonic.

February, second week: Brahms hears of Joachim's engagement to Amalie Schneeweiss.

February 21: Hanslick commences a series of lectures on musical subjects, Brahms provides illustrations on the piano for a lecture on Beethoven, playing the C minor Piano Sonata.

March 8: The Serenade in A is performed in Vienna, Hanslick says the composer is rapidly developing into a true master – but the orchestra, deciding it's too difficult, refuses to continue until Dessoff (conductor) resigns, Hellmesberger follows, and the players return to the fold.

March 8: Brahms composes the Paganini Variations.

March 25: Brahms performs Beethoven's Piano Concerto in G with Dessoff at a charity concert.

April 10: Brahms conducts his choruses for female voices at a concert of Julie von Asten, after which it's suggested that Brahms be offered the directorship of the Singakademie.

April 12: Brahms performs another charity concert.

May 1: Brahms leaves for Hanover to congratulate Joachim, engaged to Amalie Schneeweiss. Invited to return to Vienna as director of the Singakademie for its winter season, he accepts.

[Chapter 51: Snowwhite]

May 4: Clara arrives at the new house in Lichtenthal after concertizing in France, Hanover (to meet Joachim's fiancee, Amalie Schneeweiss), Trier, Luxemburg, and Saarbrucken.

[Chapter 52: Lichtenthal]

May 12: Wagner moves to Penzing, Viennese suburb.

May: Brahms returns to Hamburg, but his parents are at war and he lodges at nearby Blankenese. He spends his birthday under the rancorous circumstances, eventually escaping to Oldenburg and the Dietrichs.

August: Brahms moves from Oldenburg to Clara's new holiday home in Lichtenthal.

September 28: Brahms takes up his new appointment in Vienna.

October-December: Clara tours Aix-la-Chapelle, Frankfurt, Hamburg, Lubeck, Hanover, Braunschweig, and Leipzig among other cities, and returns to Dusseldorf for Christmas.

November 15: Brahms's first concert as director, Bach and Beethoven cantatas, Robert's *Requiem for Mignon*, folk-song arrangements by himself. Later concerts include works by Gabrielli, Schutz, Bach's Christmas Oratorio, even English Elizabethan madrigals.

Christmas: Brahms proposes to Ottilie Hauer, but she's just accepted someone else's proposal.

1864

Brahms composes his F minor Piano Quintet (in its third and final form following string quintet and two-piano versions); also his Sextet in G major.

January: Brahms is infatuated with Elisabet von Stockhausen.

January 6: Brahms's first concert of the Singakademie.

January 14: Clara sets out for her second Russian tour passing through Hanover and Hamburg.

January 21: Clara leaves Hamburg for Berlin, then further to concertize in Konigsberg, Riga, and Mitau.

February 6: Cornelius and Tausig take Brahms to meet Wagner at his residence in nearby Penzing where Brahms performs the *Handel Variations* to Wagner's approval.

[Chapter 53: Viennese Acquaintances]

February 8: Clara in St. Petersburg.

March 20: Brahms's third concert of the Singakademie.

April 17: Brahms's fourth and final Singakademie concert of solely his choral works. Clara in Moscow.

May 14: Clara returns to Berlin.

June 1: Clara returns to Dusseldorf and shortly to Baden-Baden.

June 11: Birth of Richard Strauss (Munich).

Second week of June: Brahms returns to Hamburg, but there is uneasiness on two fronts: national and domestic. On the national front, Austria and Prussia are at war with Denmark. On the domestic front, Brahms's father has been promoted, but is forced to practice the bass in the attic because his wife's unwell. Brahms removes his father to Grosse Bleiche 80, moves mother and sister to the Lange Reihe, and continues to live himself at the now-deserted dwelling on the Fuhlentwiethe. Brother Fritz, more successful as a teacher, lives elegantly in the Theater-strasse, but contributes nothing for his parents.

Late July: Brahms visits Joachim in Hanover, Grimm arrives, and the three go to Gottingen.

July 30: Brahms surprises Clara in Lichtenthal, lives in Rubinstein's villa when Rubinstein's absent, otherwise at the Bar Inn. Brahms meets Johann Strauss II in Baden-Baden, also Anselm Feuerbach and Turgenev who's traveling through Europe with his friend and lover, the singer Pauline Viardot.

August 22-25: Brahms meets Hermann Levi at a festival arranged by Liszt in Karlsruhe where Levi's the court conductor.

September 12: Joachim writes to Clara announcing the birth of his first child.

Mid-October: Brahms returns to Vienna.

October 30: Schleswig-Holstein is ceded to Austria and Prussia during the German-Danish war.

November-December: Brahms hears his mother and sister have moved to an apartment with a garden where they have kept a room for him, Clara tours Karlsruhe, Manheim, Hamburg, Kiel (staying with the Litzmanns), before returning to Dusseldorf.

1865

January: Brahms composes the Sixteen Waltzes for Four Hands dedicated to Hanslick.

January 12: Clara has plans to tour Hanover, Berlin, Oldenburg, Vienna, but slips and falls on her right hand, incapacitating her for performances until the end of February.

February 2: Fritz Brahms sends a telegram to his brother at Singerstrasse 7, Vienna: "Come at once if you want to see mother again." Brahms leaves immediately.

February 4: Brahms arrives, but his mother is dead of a stroke.

February 5: Brahms's mother is buried, his sister Elise lodges with Cossel and his family, and he sees his father settled before returning to Vienna.

March 3-13: Clara visits friends and her father in Dresden before heading for Leipzig to perform, also for a concert in Zwickau attended by Pauline Schumann (her sister-in-law, whom she hasn't seen since Robert's death) and her daughter Anna.

April 3: Clara concertizes in Prague, returning to Dusseldorf on the 13th.

April 10: Birth of Isolde to Cosima/Wagner/Bulow.

April 19-June 22: Clara, daughter Marie, and half-sister Marie Wieck leave Germany to tour England, the Joachims are also touring England.

June 10: *Tristan und Isolde* premiered by Bulow (Munich).

July-September: Brahms and Dietrich visit Clara in Baden-Baden.

Summer: Brahms composes his E flat Horn Trio in Baden-Baden (slow movement an elegy for his mother) alongside the *Requiem* and E minor Cello Sonata.

[*Chapter 54: Over Pancakes and Salads and Baked Pork*]

September 10: Elise Schumann leaves the household to teach music in Frankfurt.

October: Brahms and Joachim (no longer with a sinecure in Hanover) set off on a recital tour of Switzerland (Winterthur, Zurich). Brahms renews acquaintance with Hegar, meets Christian Albert Theodor Billroth, also Julius Allgeyer (photographer) and Mathilde Wesendonck at whose house he is impressed with the scores of *Rheingold* and *Walkure*, neither of which has yet been performed. He also meets Joseph Viktor Widmann who first sees Brahms in concert at the piano in Berne.

October: Brahms hears from his father that he's to marry again.

October 31: Clara and Elise perform Robert's Andante and Variations for Two Pianos among other pieces, Joachim also on the program.

November 9: Brahms performs his D minor Piano Concerto at Mannheim, Levi conducting, finally acclaimed a masterpiece.

[*Chapter 55: Dedication and Consultation*]

November-December: Clara tours Frankfurt, Karlsruhe, Berlin, Breslau, and Konigsberg before returning to Dusseldorf where she's joined by Brahms from Detmold.

December 7: Brahms premieres the Horn Trio (Karlsruhe).

December 12: Brahms appears at the fifth Gurzenich concert at Cologne, performing the Serenade in D and Beethoven's *Emperor*.

December 19: Brahms has a chamber music success with *Variations on a Theme by Schumann* and the G minor Piano Quartet and returns to Hamburg for just a day to meet his father's new wife.

December 20: Brahms leaves Hamburg for Detmold, performs the Horn Trio at the prince's chamber concert, also performs Beethoven's *Emperor*, but almost misses performing the *Kreutzer* at the palace with Bargheer after walking, eating, and sleeping it off at an inn.

December 24: Brahms leaves Detmold for Dusseldorf in time to see Clara light the Christmas tree and hand out presents.

December 30: Brahms visits Joachim and Amalie in Hanover for a day.

1866

January: Clara concertizes in Dusseldorf, Coblenz, Braunschweig, Dresden, and Vienna.

January 5, 10: Brahms's concert tour which opened in Karlsruhe in 1865 comes to a brilliant close at Oldenburg with the D minor Piano Concerto, A major Piano Quartet, Horn Trio, Schumann's B flat Variations for Two Pianos, and solos by Bach, Schubert, and Schumann.

February-March: Clara concertizes in Vienna, Budapest, Linz, and Pressburg.

Spring: Brahms appears for the first time with a beard, but his friends laugh it off of him.

March 17: Clara leaves Vienna to perform in Salzburg the next day, followed by ten days in Munich where she picks up Julie and comes to Lichtenthal.

March 22: Johann Jakob marries Caroline Schnack, sets up house at Anschar-platz 5 – and his wife, having closed her restaurant, augments his income by catering for a few paying-guests; a room is constantly reserved for Brahms, his library's moved as well.

April 16: Brahms leaves Karlsruhe for Zurich for the summer, occupies rooms in a well-situated house on the Zurichberg.

April-May: Brahms stays in Winterthur with his publisher, Jakob Melchior Rieter-Biedermann.

Late May: Clara (with Julie) attends the Music Festival in Dusseldorf.

Summer: In Zurich with his new friends, Brahms composes the bulk of his C minor String Quartet, not to be published for another seven years. Bismarck invades Hanover, Hesse, and Saxony.

June 27: Prussian forces occupy Holstein, defeat the Hanoverins at Langensalza.

July 3: Bismarck defeats the imperial army of Austria at Koniggratz.

August 17: Brahms arrives in Baden-Baden to stay near Clara.

Autumn: They visit the Dietrichs at Oldenburg where he and Clara play the first set of Hungarian Dances.

October: Joachim, at a loose end now that the court of Hanover no longer exists, joins Brahms on a tour of Switzerland until December when he returns to Hanover and Brahms to Vienna to join Billroth now Director of the Surgical Institute.

October 24: Their first concert (Brahms and Joachim) at Schaffhausen.

October 29: Their next concert at Winterthur.

October 30: Their next at Zurich.

November 1: Their next at Aarau, followed by dinner at the Stork Inn where they stage a fight over doubloons.

November 7: Clara leaves Lichtenthal for concerts in Frankfurt, Bremen, and Oldenburg. Then to Berlin for a rest.

December 9: Clara goes to Leipzig to play at the Gewandhaus.

December 16: Clara returns to Dusseldorf to concertize, also in Cologne, Bonn, and Coblenz.

Christmas: Clara in Dusseldorf with Fraulein Leser, Brahms with Berta Faber and her family. He stays in Vienna until Spring.

December 30: Clara is in despair about Ludwig who cannot settle down and writes to Levi with gratitude for all he is doing for her boy.

<u>1867</u>

January 12: Clara (with Marie) tours England with Joachim (including Edinburgh and Glasgow).

February: Brahms needs money, performs three concerts in Graz and Klangenfurt, two more in Vienna.

February 3: Premiere of the Sextet in G at the Hellmesberger concert.

February 17: Birth of Eva to Cosima/Wagner/Bulow.

February 18: Joachim writes again to Ave-Lallemant regarding Brahms's appointment to the Hamburg Philharmonic.

March 17: At a piano recital, Brahms surprises his audience by performing the finale of Beethoven's third Razumovsky quartet as an encore.

March-April: Brahms performs the *Handel* and *Paganini Variations* in concert and is rejoined by Joachim for concerts in Vienna, Graz, Klagenfurth, and Pesth.

April 10: First of three concerts in Hungary (Pressburg) with Joachim.

April 20: Clara returns from England to Dusseldorf to visit Julie in Mannheim. Ludwig comes from Karlsruhe saying he's left his place in bookselling for which he's trained and wants a place in music.

April 22: Second of Brahms and Joachim's three concerts in Pesth.

April 26: Third of Brahms and Joachim's three concerts in Pesth.

May: Clara, in Karlsbad with Julie for her health, writes to son Felix who wishes to become a violinist that he must audition for Joachim first to see if he's suited.

June 17: Clara arrives in Baden-Baden from Karlsbad via Dresden and Berlin (to see Ferdinand and Felix).

Summer: Brahms invites his father (who's not been outside Hamburg in 40 years) to visit him in Vienna for a summer holiday, also goes to Styria with Gannsbacher.

Late July: Brahms sends the *Requiem* manuscript to Dietrich with the suggestion that he would be pleased if it were performed at the Bremen Cathedral. Dietrich shows it to Carl Martin Reinthaler, organist and conductor of the choir, who prepares the *Requiem* for Brahms to conduct.

July 31/August 1: Brahms and his father leave Vienna.

August 13: Brahms coaxes his father to the summit of the Schafberg, walking beside the old man, who rides on a donkey.

Autumn: Brahms decides to settle in Vienna. Billroth also moves to Vienna (Alsergrund suburb) as University professor and Director of Operations.

October 12: Clara concertizes with Stockhausen in Hamburg, Kiel, Lubeck, and Schwerin among others cities.

November 13: Clara and Stockhausen again in Hamburg after concertizing in Dresden and Leipzig among other cities.

November 22: Joachim writes to Amalie that he and Brahms were going to Brunn – "it will only take up one day and probably bring in about two hundred florins for each of us."

December 1: First three movements of the *Requiem* are performed in Vienna, but the tympanist drowns the choir and orchestra during the third movement conducted by Herbeck (Brahms's rival when he was director of the Singakademie).

[*Chapter 56: In the Shadow of Bismarck*]

Christmas: Marie goes to Julie who's not well in Divonne.

1868

Bruckner settles permanently in Vienna.

January 3: Clara visits Karlsruhe for a performance of *Genoveva*.

January 6: Marie returns alone because Julie's not well enough to travel.

January 7: Clara begins a tour of Belgium.

Mid-January: Brahms visits Hamburg, lives with his father, his sister to marry a sixty-year-old watchmaker. Stockhausen resigns, but Brahms is passed over a second time by the Hamburg Philharmonic. Brahms composes *Schicksalslied*.

January 24: Clara leaves Brussels for a tour of England. She hears that Felix's lungs are weak and Ludwig has lost his post through unpunctuality, but a friend has found him another post with Rieter-Biedermann in Leipzig.

February 14: Brahms performs the Beethoven G major with his own cadenzas with the Hamburg Philharmonic. Stockhausen sings Schubert to orchestral accompaniment arranged by Brahms.

March 4: Brahms performs at one of Dietrich's concerts in Oldenburg.

March 7: Brahms appears for the first time in Berlin, performing Robert's Sonata in F sharp minor. Stockhausen sings *Magelone* songs.

March 11: Brahms and Stockhausen back in Hamburg.

March 13: Brahms and Stockhausen perform in Kiel.

March: Concert tour with Stockhausen of Brahms songs of Berlin, Dresden, and Kiel – finally Copenhagen, where Brahms says it's too bad the Thorwaldsen Museum is not in Berlin and is expelled from the city by Danes still smarting under the loss of Schleswig-Holstein to Bismarck.

April 1: Brahms returns to Bremen.

April 9: Clara arrives in Bremen against her will (Brahms has repeatedly, even rudely, said she's past her prime and should retire) at the persuasion of Rosalie and Marie for the *Requiem*.

April 10: Two weeks after expulsion, Brahms conducts his *Requiem* in Bremen Cathedral where it's received well enough to generate a second performance, also in April in Bremen, though Brahms returns to Hamburg to write one more section for soprano solo.

[*Chapter 57: A German Requiem*]

April: Clara goes from Bremen to Hanover for the christening of Joachim's daughter Marie (Clara's her godmother).

April 21: Clara sees Julie (still unwell) in Frankfurt and goes later with Felix (spending time with his grandfather in Dresden) and Marie to Karlsbad.

May 24: Brahms composes the soprano solo for the *Requiem*.

May 30: Clara hears Ludwig has not only lost his job, but his mind isn't well. She sends him to his grandfather in Dresden.

June 1-2: Rhine Music Festival in Cologne (Brahms attends).

June 9-30: Clara returns to Baden-Baden before heading for St. Moritz.

June 21: Bulow premieres *Die Meistersinger* (Munich).

July 25: Brahms and Stockhausen perform at Neuenahr.

Summer: Brahms polishes *Rinaldo* in Bonn.

Summer: Brahms, again with his father, travels down the Rhine to Switzerland, but Johann Jakob's growing old and feels his age.

Autumn: Brahms tours Hamburg, Bremen, Oldenburg.

September 4: First exchange of letters between Clara and Brahms expressing animosity about his boorishness.

September 12: Brahms sends Clara the horn call (from his Symphony in C minor) in a letter.

Third week of September: Brahms and his father return to Hamburg, Johann Jakob promising his wife that no amount of coaxing by Brahms will entice him from the comforts of home again.

Last week of October: Brahms visits Dietrich. Clara's also there with daughter Marie. Clara and Brahms perform the Hungarian Dances for Four Hands for the first time.

October 30: Clara performs in Oldenburg.

October 31: Clara hears from Divonne that Count Marmorito has asked Julie to marry him. Clara is anxious on account of differences in position and creed, but "love is not to be frightened."

November: Brahms and Stockhausen perform again in Hamburg. Brahms also performs his Hungarian Dances.

November 3: Clara plays Beethoven's C minor Piano Concerto in Bremen, improvising her own cadenza.

November 4: Clara leaves Oldenburg for Berlin, picking up Eugenie at Wolfenbuttel.

November 9: Clara (with Marie) goes to Breslau for a concert by Rubinstein which she calls "a perfectly wild noise or else a whispering with the soft pedal down."

November 16: Cosima moves in with Wagner (Tribschen).

November 17: Clara (with Marie) arrives in Vienna to concertize.

November 20: Brahms arrives in Vienna, to perform with her on one of her dates. After a short stay in a hotel, he finds temporary lodgings and composes his second set of waltzes.

November 23: Clara is called by the King of Hanover, now deposed in Hietzing, for a conversation of two hours which she enjoys, except that she keeps Brahms (who had accompanied her so she wouldn't have to go alone) waiting for her in a restaurant.

November 30: Brahms performs in the Piano Quartet in A.

December 4: Clara meets and befriends the Billroths.

December 20: Another concert by Clara in Vienna.

1869

January: Joachim becomes director of the *Hochschule fur Musik* (Berlin). Brahms stays at the Hotel Kronprinz in Vienna, but eventually moves to the house zur Goldspinnerin near the municipal park.

January 20: Clara begins another English tour with Joachim.

February 18: The first performance of the complete *Requiem* (with the soprano solo) in Leipzig is conducted by Carl Reinecke.

February 20: First of a series of concerts for Brahms and Stockhausen in the small Redoutensaal (Vienna).

February 28: First performance of *Rinaldo* in Vienna.

March 8: Death of Berlioz (Paris).

March 26: *Requiem* performed at the Zurich Town Hall.

April 10: Clara returns from England to stay with friends in Dusseldorf, Cologne, and Coblenz.

April 24: The sixth of Brahms's concerts with Stockhausen, the second, third, and fourth given in Pesth, the fifth on Easter Monday in Vienna again.

May 3: Clara returns to Lichtenthal.

May 8: Julie arrives in Lichtenthal with Ludwig who finds great satisfaction in music though "His music is something dreadful.... He has no ear and no sense of rhythm.... His compositions are terrible ... and yet he works so hard at them that I am quite anxious about him."

May 9: Brahms (with Allgeyer) visits Clara.

May 12: Clara visits Karlsruhe to hear Brahms conduct the *Requiem*.

June 6: Birth of Siegfried to Cosima/Wagner/Bulow (Lucerne).

July 10: Clara receives Count Marmorito's formal proposal for Julie's hand.

July 11: Clara consents to the marriage though her heart bleeds.

July 16: Clara notes that Brahms is different, speaks only in monosyllables, even to Julie to whom he was always especially nice – but he never thought about marrying and Julie never showed any inclination toward him.

July 26: Julie is engaged to Count Vittorio Radicati di Marmorito, and afterward known to her friends as The Countess. Brahms, Allgeyer, and Levi present the bride with a bronze plaque as a souvenir of the occasion. Brahms stays in Baden-Baden till the wedding.

September 14: Count Marmorito arrives.

September 21: Pleasant evening with the Count, Levi, Brahms and others, Clara playing among other things Hungarian Dances with Brahms. Allgeyer gives Julie a large portrait of Clara, Brahms gives her a daguerreotype of Clara.

September 22: The wedding takes place in the Lichtenthaler Catholic Church, followed by breakfast in the house, after which the bridal couple leaves. The wedding had originally been planned for September 8, but was postponed owing to a death in the Count's family.

Late September: Brahms arrives at Clara's house with a new work, bitterly calling it his Bridal Song, *Alto Rhapsody*. He returns to Vienna, to the Prater pleasure gardens, soon on a first-name basis with ladies of the night.

[*Chapter 58: Alto Rhapsody*]

October: Clara visits friends in Dusseldorf, Coblenz, and Bonn instead of concertizing because she hurt her hand in Lichtenthal.

October 5: Brahms writes to Simrock hoping to receive 40 Friedrichs d'Or for the enclosed manuscript of *Schicksalslied*.

November: The Suez Canal opens.

November 10: Clara returns to Berlin.

November 28: Clara performs for the first time since she hurt her hand.

December 7: Clara performs with Joachim.

December 8: Clara leaves for Vienna.

December: Clara performs in Vienna (Brahms joins her in the four-hand piano part for the Liebeslieder waltzes). She also performs many other Brahms works.

<u>1870</u>

January: Clara's second concert in Vienna, again performing many of Brahms's works.

January 6: New premises of the Gesellschaft der Musikfreunde open, two large concert halls, conservatory, offices, meeting place. Brahms's library is now on the second floor among many other archives.

January 21: Clara leaves Vienna to spend two days in Dresden where she's horrified that Ludwig looks "so white."

January-February: Clara plays in Cologne and Dusseldorf.

February 10: Clara leaves for London.

March: Pauline Viardot premieres *Alto Rhapsody* in Jena.

April: Ludwig is diagnosed with an incurable disease of the spine which affects his brain.

May 3: Clara leaves London

June: Ludwig is institutionalized in Colditz and Clara back in Baden-Baden – but Brahms, offered the conductorship of the Gesellschaft, cannot come to her as planned.

Summer: Brahms visits Munich, attends performances of *Rheingold* and *Walkure*.

July 14: Clara concertizes in Kreuzenach, and returning to Baden-Baden by way of Frankfurt and Heidelberg sees everywhere preparations for war.

July 15: Franco-Prussian War begins.

July 18: Cosima and Bulow divorce. Ferdinand Schumann is called to serve in the War.

Late July: Clara prepares to greet Brahms in Lichtenthal, but he doesn't come because the trains are all being used for the War.

August 25: Cosima and Wagner marry.

September 2: Napoleon III surrenders at Sedan.

[*Chapter 59: A German Strasbourg*]

November: Clara in Berlin receives a letter of thanks from the "Society for the Support of the Families of Those Called to Serve the Flag."

Christmas: Clara (with Felix and Eugenie) is grateful Ferdinand is well though he's been through terrible experiences.

1871

January 2: Clara performs in Breslau.

January 4: Clara returns to Berlin.

January 6: Clara departs for a tour of West Germany, Holland, and England.

January 18: Bismarck unifies Germany, the Prussian King Wilhelm IV is declared emperor with the title Kaiser Wilhelm IV. Brahms composes *Triumphlied* and dedicates it to the Kaiser because protocol prevents a dual dedication to Bismarck as well.

January 22: Brahms performs his Piano Concerto under Dessoff with the Vienna Philharmonic.

February 5: The first complete performance in Vienna of the *Requiem* (including the soprano solo) is conducted by Brahms.

February 22: Clara hears Jenny Lind-Goldschmidt sing again in a private home. "Her voice has almost gone, but many of her notes still have that veiled sound, a charm, a power of moving the heart, that is indescribable."

March 20: The *Alto Rhapsody* is premiered in Vienna by the Academic Choral Union of Vienna under Ernst Frank. Brahms travels after the *Alto Rhapsody* in Vienna to spend a night in Berlin with Tausig (who dies four months later).

April 3: Brahms performs the Piano Quartet in G minor in Oldenburg.

April 7: Brahms conducts the complete *Requiem* again in Bremen, again on Good Friday.

April 17: Clara is robbed in London. "The thieves climbed in at the window, bolted the doors inside, lighted the candles, and broke open everything in my room, though they took nothing but jewelry and money ... throwing all the other things about in the room and leaving them there."

April 18: Jenny Lind to Clara: "It is horrible, it is shameful, that you should be robbed of your keepsakes. It cuts one to the heart. There must certainly be a hell in store for the wicked, wicked men. At least they must be far from God – and that is hell enough. I cannot refrain, dear friend, from begging you to accept the accompanying little brooch with my love, and to wear it on Thursday. The old Queen of Sweden gave it to me, years ago, and as I have a bracelet and several other things as well from her, you need feel no qualms, and it would give me real and great pleasure to know that you had something of mine."

April 25: Brahms performs the D minor Piano Concerto in Bremen.

April 30: Brahms meets Allgeyer and Levi in Karlsruhe at midnight on his way to Baden-Baden.

Spring: Florence May (Brahms's first English biographer) comes to Baden-Baden for lessons from Clara – who directs her to Brahms.

May 10: The Treaty of Frankfurt expands the borders of the new German Empire to include Alsace and Lorraine. The first section of the *Triumphlied* and *Requiem* are performed in a benefit concert for the German dead in Bremen.

Summer: Brahms visits Berlin, then Baden-Baden, where he finishes *Schicksalslied*.

August: Brahms and Stockhausen perform in Baden-Baden and Stuttgart where Stockhausen's living. Brahms and Levi in Stuttgart witness the triumphal entry of troops from France.

August 14: Clara returns to Baden-Baden from Switzerland.

August 22: Clara's second grandchild (Robert) is born to Julie and the Count.

September: Ferdinand Schumann returns from the war.

October 18: *Schicksalslied* is premiered (Karlsruhe) conducted by Levi, also two Schubert songs orchestrated by Brahms sung by Stockhausen, also extracts from Robert's *Faust*, after which Brahms returns to Vienna.

Late October: Brahms stays at the Hotel Kronprinz at the Aspern Bridge, Leopoldstadt, Vienna.

November: Clara concertizes in Bremen and Munster. Amalie makes the *Alto Rhapsody* her own when she sings it in Bremen.

December 6: Clara is in Frankfurt, but cannot play until the 16th owing to severe rheumatism.

December 20: Clara plays in Dusseldorf and spends Christmas there with Fraulein Leser.

December (after Christmas): Brahms undertakes the sub-tenancy of two furnished rooms on the third floor of Karlsgasse 4 where he stays for the rest of his life.

1872

January: Clara concertizes in Kassel, Frankfurt, and Barmen before heading again for England (joined by Felix for three weeks).

January: Brahms's stepmother writes to summon Brahms to Hamburg, his father's ill from cancer of the liver.

February 11: Brahms's father dies. Brahms reconciles with his brother, Fritz, who's been in Venezuela for a couple of years.

March 10: Death of Marianne Bargiel (Clara's mother).

Late April: Clara plays for Queen Victoria, the Duchess of Cambridge, and Princess Louise at Buckingham Palace.

Late April: Brahms travels from Vienna to Karlsruhe stopping at various cities en route to see friends, among them Stockhausen in Stuttgart.

May 1: Brahms attends a concert by Stockhausen.

May: Clara is back in Baden-Baden.

Spring: Brahms is offered the directorship of the Philharmonic Society in Vienna at a salary of 3,000 gulden per annum.

June 5: Levi's farewell performance at Karlsruhe before he takes his appointment in Munich, attended by Clara, Marie, Eugenie, Felix, and among others Brahms who makes his way from the second row to take a bow for the *Triumphlied* when Levi calls him up.

June 16: Brahms is deeply moved by Bruckner's F minor Mass conducted by the composer. Hanslick gives it some praise in the *Neue Freie Presse*. Liszt thinks highly of the piece.

Summer: Brahms visits Baden-Baden, Lichtenstein.

July 13: Clara leaves Baden-Baden with the Lazaruses for Interlaken.

August 16: Clara returns to Baden-Baden to be met by Julie (looking as if she were recovering from a severe illness) and her oldest child.

August 29: Brahms performs Robert's Piano Concerto, also conducts his Serenade in A.

September 27: Julie returns to the South via Paris though her health appears to worsen from day to day.

Autumn: Brahms begins his appointment in Vienna as the artistic director of the Gesellshaft der Musikfreund.

October 1: Rehearsals begin for the Philharmonic Society.

November 10: Death of Julie Schumann.

November 10: Brahms begins music season with Handel's Dettingen *Te Deum* among other choices, Luise Dustmann among his performers.

November 13: Clara heads from Heidelberg to Munich to Vienna where she performs with Amalie (Marie, Eugenie, and Ferdinand also present).

Early December: Brahms conducts a triumphant performance of the *Triumphlied*.

December 16: Clara goes from Vienna to Berlin where she stays with the Simrocks.

December 28: Clara performs with Amalie.

1873

January: Clara takes rooms in Berlin at 11 In den Zelten, but remains undecided whether to sell her house in Lichtenthal.

January 5: Clara performs with Amalie.

January 13-20: Clara in Leipzig (living with the Freges) performs at the Gewandhaus. During a concert on the 16th, a friend (Voigt) hands her the sum of 3,500 thaler. Robert's friends had given him an amount for Robert's illness, and after his death he had invested the money which had now collected interest.

January 20-25: Clara in Dusseldorf (living with the Bendemanns).

January 25: Clara leaves for London.

April 6: Last concert of Brahms's first season. Brahms can do no wrong, lionized now like never before, never again not to be lionized.

April 28: Bulow's English debut.

May: Currency Law of May 1873 establishes uniform metric currency (the mark) in place of the thaler, gulden, etc.

May: Clara returns to Baden-Baden.

Mid-May: Brahms leaves Vienna for Tutzing on the Starnberg lake in Bavaria.

Summer: In Tutzing (a village near Munich), Brahms is visited by Luise Dustmann among others, and composes his first two quartets and the *Haydn Variations*. He often visits Levi in Munich to escape from Tutzing when necessary.

August 13: Marriage of Ferdinand Schumann and Antonie Deutsch in Bonn at the Schumann Festival for their honeymoon.

August 14: Clara, Marie, and Felix head for the Festival in Bonn. They are met by Eugenie at Coblenz on her way from Ems. The Lind-Goldschmidts, Freges, Reinthalers, Hiller, Grimm, and Dietrich are among many others (including Brahms) also present.

August 15: Elise arrives to join the family and they visit Schumann's grave.

August 17: First day of the Festival: the D minor Symphony (Joachim conducting) and the *Peri*.

August 18: Second day of the Festival: *Manfred Overture*, *Faust* (Stockhausen singing alone), Piano Concerto in A minor, and the *Nachtlied*.

August 19: Third day of the Festival: the E flat Piano Quintet (with Clara), *Andante and Variations for Two Pianos* (Clara and Rudorff), A major Quartet (with Joachim).

August 20: Ferdinand and Antonie leave the Festival.

August 21: Clara and Brahms play the *Haydn Variations* on which he's been working through the summer.

[Chapter 60: The Schumann Festival]

September 3: Felix, attacked by an inflammation of the lungs, is in bed for weeks.

September 17: Clara sends Brahms poems by Felix for his appraisal.

October 15: Brahms provides no appraisal, but sets three of the poems to music.

October 6: Death of Friedrich Wieck (88). Clara's diary shows she loved him at least as much as she loved Robert and without the dissonance that might have been expected: "He was on a grand scale, there was nothing petty about him." Learns later that he left behind a fortune (60,000 thaler) "and has remembered me more kindly than I ever thought he would."

November 2: The *Haydn Variations* are performed by Dessoff opening the winter season in Vienna.

November: Clara hears Brahms's quartets in Munich, also *Manfred* under Levi, heads next for Hamburg, then home to Berlin.

December: Clara performs the D minor Piano Concerto in Berlin.

1874

January 25: Gesellschaft opens its post-Christmas season.

January: Brahms visits Leipzig for a Festival of his own music organized by Heinrich von Herzogenberg to find him married to Elisabet von Stockhausen.

January 29: The Leipzig branch of the Allgemeine Deutscher Musik Verein welcomes Brahms with his *Variations on a Theme by Schumann*, Ballades, Horn Trio, and Marienlieder.

February 1: Brahms performs the *Handel Variations*, also the Piano Quartet in G minor at the Gewandhaus.

February 3: *Rinaldo* is performed, also at the Gewandhaus.

February 5: Fourth Leipzig concert in aid of the Pension Fund, *Alto Rhapsody* (Amalie Joachim), *Haydn Variations*, Liebeslieder Waltzes, three Hungarian Dances.

February 7: Back in Vienna, Brahms is busy with remaining Gesellschaft concerts.

[Chapter 61: Elisabet and Amalie]

March 2: Brahms performs Robert's *Manfred*, Kyrie and Credo by Schubert, with the Gesellschaft.

March 13: The *Haydn Variations* are performed in Munich and the D minor Piano Concerto (Brahms and Levi). Brahms is awarded the Order of Maximilian by King Ludwig of Bavaria (Wagner's patron).

March 14: Josef Walter (Munich violinist) produces Brahms's Piano Quartet in A major and Sextet in G major.

March 19: Brahms writes a comforting letter to Clara who has learned that Felix has an infected lung.

March 31: Excerpts from Handel's Solomon, Bach's Christmas Oratorio, Haydn's E flat Symphony, *Schicksalslied* at the Gesellschaft.

April 28: The *Triumphlied* is performed in Bremen with the *Haydn Variations*; Brahms also performs Beethoven's *Emperor*.

May: Brahms meets George Henschel at the Lower Rhenish Musical Festival in Cologne.

May 24: The *Triumphlied* is performed at the Rhenish Festival in Cologne.

May 21-June 30: Clara in Teplitz where she goes (with Marie by way of a treatment center in Budesheim, Elise's home) instead of the Cologne Music Festival on account of pain to her arm.

Late Spring/Early Summer: Brahms partakes in many concerts in various parts of Germany and Switzerland.

June 9: The *Triumphlied* is performed in Basel, part of a two-day music festival with Brahms also performing in his Piano Quartet in A.

July: Clara is invited to perform 100 concerts in America, but says she would have refused even without the pain in her arm: "why should I try to earn more than I need?"

July 6: Clara and Marie reach Baden-Baden.

July 11: Brahms meets Widmann (poet) again at a music festival and visits the Widmanns in Berne.

July 11-14: Zurich Music Festival.

July 12: The *Triumphlied* is performed attended by Brahms with Kirchner among others.

Summer: Brahms visits Ruschlikon, near Zurich, for a performance of his liebeslieder and stays in Switzerland until mid-September, living near the Nidelbad of Ruschlikon, high above the Lake of Zurich.

August: Nietzsche leaves Brahms's *Triumphlied* on Wagner's piano in Bayreuth.

September: Clara spends a few days with Count Marmorito by Lake Geneva before returning to Baden-Baden.

On his return to Vienna, Billroth housewarms his new residence at Alserstrasse 20, including the new music room where much of Brahms's work is first aired.

Late in the year: Death of Elise Junge, companion of Rosalie Leser (their blind friend from years ago in Dusseldorf before Robert's death).

November 8: Gesellschaft concert-season opens, songs for mixed choir by Brahms, Berlioz's *Harold in Italy*. Brahms also performs Beethoven's *Emperor*.

November 18: Joachim conducts Handel's *Hercules* with Amalie singing Dejanira and Henschel in the title role (Clara attends).

Winter: Brahms's last season with the Philharmonic Society. His *Requiem* upstages Wagner's *Ring* Excerpts.

December 24: Clara is visited by Ferdinand and Antonie – and Marie Fillunger, Eugenie's friend, with whom she stayed the rest of her life, who is buried alongside Marie Schumann (who never married) and Eugenie (who also never married). She was also to become Clara's secretary.

December 24: Tchaikovsky performs his B flat minor Piano Concerto for Nikolas Rubinstein and Hubert to their disapproval, prompting him to change the dedication from Rubinstein to Hans von Bulow.

Christmas Holidays: Brahms visits Breslau where Bernhard Scholz conducts the Orchestral Society.

December 29: Brahms performs his D minor Piano Concerto under Scholz's baton in Breslau.

1875

January 10: The Gesellschaft season opens with Amalie and Joachim performing the *Alto Rhapsody*, Schumann Fantasia for Violin and Orchestra, Joachim's Hungarian Concerto, orchestrally accompanied songs, and more.

January 16: Clara goes to Dusseldorf to stay with the Bendemanns and console Rosalie Leser for the death of Elise Junge, her friend and nurse for 36 years, missing the Cologne Festival on her account.

January 25: Clara goes to Hamburg where she's met by Marie coming from Berlin.

January 26-March 24: Clara and Marie go to the Baaschs' nursing home in Kiel to remedy her pain. The doctor (Esmarch) insists, alongside massages and douches, that she play everyday despite what other doctors may have said, and she does, practising at the Litzmanns since she could not have a piano in the nursing home. Pleasant meetings throughout with the Litzmanns and Groths.

March 18: Clara performs after an interval of almost eighteen months at the insistence of the doctor, is joined onstage by Marie Fillunger (also well received), and receives a magnificent anonymous bouquet later discovered to be from Franz Mendelssohn.

March 23: Brahms conducts Bach's *St. Matthew Passion* with Dustmann, Bettelheim, Henschel, Gustav Walter.

March 24: Clara returns to Berlin from Kiel.

March 26: Brahms, with Henschel and others, visits the room of Beethoven's death on the 48th anniversary.

March 30: Clara with Marie and Eugenie in Leipzig for a performance of *Genoveva*.

April 15: Letter from Ludwig to Clara wishing very much to see her.

April 18: Max Bruch's *Odysseus* performed with Georg Henschel. Brahms resigns Directorship of the Philharmonic Society, never again to take a permanent or semi-permanent post.

April: Brahms breaks with Levi over Levi's adoration of Wagner.

May 4: Clara experiences pain in her arm (neuralgia) which lasts three weeks.

May 8: New Liebeslieder performed by Brahms and Dessoff in the hall of the Museum of Karlsruhe.

May 24: *Haydn Variations* first heard in London.

Whitsuntide: Brahms meets Joachim who conducts *Schicksalslied* at the Rhine Music Festival in Dusseldorf.

June 8: Clara returns to Kiel with Eugenie for more treatment, spends more mornings with the Litzmanns on her way to Baasch's nursing home.

June 24: Joachim arrives for the First Schleswig-Holstein Music Festival.

Summer: Brahms visits Ziegelhausen, near Heidelberg, composes his B flat major Quartet and C minor Piano Quartet (#3).

July 15: Clara leaves Kiel to visit Brahms in Ziegelhausen. From Ziegelhausen she goes to Klosters where Felix awaits her.

August 20: Clara, in Klosters, receives a telegram from Marmorito wishing to visit for a week with Duaddo (her grandson) and two daughters from his first marriage. Clara writes that Marmorito is delightful with her grandson.

August 30: Marmorito leaves with his children.

September 6: Clara arrives in Munich to be met by Levi who takes her to her hotel.

September 7: Levi conducts *Manfred*.

September 8: Levi conducts *Tristan und Isolde*. Clara writes: "It is the most repulsive thing I ever saw or heard in my life. To have to sit through a whole evening watching and listening to such love-lunacy till every feeling of decency was outraged, and to see not only the audience but the musicians delighted with it was – I may well say – the saddest experience of my whole artistic career. I held out till the end as I wished to have heard it all. Neither of them does anything but sleep and sing during the 2nd act, and the whole of act 3 – quite 40 minutes – Tristan occupies in dying – and they call that dramatic!!!"

October: Brahms becomes commissioner to the Austrian Ministry of Education, awarding grants to promising composers. Brahms nominates Dvorak for his Symphony in E flat major, later persuading Simrock to publish his work.
[*Chapter 62: Discomposed Composers*]

October 25: Bulow premieres Tchaikovsky's B flat minor Piano Concerto (Boston), dedicated to him.

November 18: The Hellmesberger Quartet premieres the C minor Piano Quartet (Vienna), Brahms at the piano.

Winter: Brahms works on his symphony, visits Holland as a pianist of his own work, stays with Professor Engelmann and his pianist wife (in Utrecht) whom he had met in Zurich, and dedicates his Quartet in B flat to them.

1876

January 18: Brahms conducts his *Requiem* in Amsterdam.

January 19: Brahms performs his D minor Piano Concerto in The Hague.

January 21: Brahms appears again in Amsterdam.

January 22: Brahms repeats his D minor Piano Concerto in Utrecht.

January-February: Clara concertizes in Chemnitz and Dresden.

February 2: Brahms leaves Holland, calls on the Grimms at Munster.

February 5: Brahms performs the D minor Piano Concerto at Munster, Westphalia, also the *Triumphlied* with Henschel, and the *Requiem* with Frau Kiesekamp.

February 13: Brahms assists in a charity concert (Baden-Baden).

February 18: Brahms performs the D minor Piano Concerto (Frankfurt-am-Main).

February 21: Brahms performs the Piano Quartet in A (Mannheim).

February 24: Brahms appears with Henschel (Coblenz).

February 25: Brahms appears with Henschel (Wiesbaden).

March 4: Clara and Marie head for London from Dresden, stopping at Dusseldorf and Utrecht (where she performs) on the way.

March 5: Death of Marie d'Agoult (Paris).

March 21: Brahms performs the D minor Piano Concerto with Bernhard Scholz (Breslau).

March 23: Brahms performs Beethoven's C minor Piano Sonata, also his own C minor Piano Quartet (Breslau).

April: Cambridge wishes to confer a degree on Brahms, but he won't go to England.

Mid-April: Clara leaves London for Berlin again and on the way hears Liszt: "I was quite carried away by some things of Schubert's which he played exquisitely, but not by his own works – a duet for two pianos on B.A.C.H. was horrible, and the only enjoyable thing was when he tore up and down over the whole piano. He masters the instrument as no one else does – it is a pity that one can get so little calm enjoyment out of it, it is always a demonic force which sweeps one along. I have observed him a great deal, his delicate coquetry, his distinguished affability, etc. etc."

May-June: Clara in Berlin.

May 22: Joachim and his quartet play Brahms's B flat Quartet for Clara.

June 7: Brahms leaves Vienna for Berlin to visit Clara before leaving for his holiday proper.

June 8: Brahms arrives in Berlin. Clara writes: "Brahms took us by surprise. This time he was very pleasant throughout his whole visit ... so that we really enjoyed having him."

June 8: Death of George Sand (Nohant-Vic, France).

June 12: Brahms leaves Berlin for Sassnitz on the Baltic island of Rugen.

June 12: Clara leaves Berlin for Kiel after a couple of days in Hamburg.

June 15: Clara reaches Kiel, staying for a 3-week cure and more pleasant evenings with the Litzmanns.

July: Clara in Berlin and Budesheim (with Elise).

July 7: George Henschel joins Brahms in Sassnitz to catch frogs and have his songs critiqued.

August: Clara in Klosters.

August: Brahms returns to Hamburg, then goes to Lichtenthal.

[*Chapter 63: The Bullfrog Pond*]

August 13-30: First Bayreuth Festival. *Ring* premiered by Hans Richter.

[*Chapter 64: Bayreuth*]

Autumn: Brahms completes his C minor Symphony (#1).

September: Clara, in Hertenstein, is visited by the Herzogenbergs, later the Kufferaths, and still later returns to Baden-Baden as the guest of Frau Kann, her neighbor in Lichtenthal for many years (now that she's sold her own home in Lichtenthal). Felix goes to Meran for his health for the winter.

September 25: Brahms plays two movements of the C minor Symphony for Clara: "These two (the first and the last) are grand, full of life and of thought from end to end; only certain of the melodies seem to me rather thin – but I must hear the whole."

October 10: Brahms plays the whole symphony for Clara: "I cannot deny that I was grieved and depressed, for it does not seem to me to compare with other of his works, such as the F minor Quintet, the sextets, and the piano quartets. I miss the sweeping melodies, in spite of its general interest. I debated with myself for a long time whether to tell him or not, but I must first hear it properly given by the orchestra."

October 30: Premiere of the B flat String Quartet.

November 4: C minor Symphony premiered (Karlsruhe), conducted by Otto Dessof, then in Mannheim.

November 7: Brahms conducts the C minor Symphony in Mannheim.

November 11: Joachim conducts the C minor Symphony in Berlin.

November 15: Brahms conducts the C minor Symphony in Munich.

November 16: Julius von Bernuth conducts the C minor Symphony in Hamburg.

November 30: The B flat String Quartet is performed by the Hellmesberger Quartet.

December 11: Clara performs Beethoven's G major Concerto in Breslau with Scholz.

December 17: The C minor Symphony is conducted by Brahms in Vienna (Gesellschaft).

[Chapter 65: The C minor Symphony]

1877

January 8: Clara performs Beethoven's G major Concerto in Berlin.

January 16: Clara and Marie visit Leipzig for a performance of Brahms's C minor Symphony.

January 17: Clara attends a rehearsal: "The symphony was grand, quite overwhelming: the last movement, with its inspired introduction, made an extraordinary impression on me; the introduction is so gloomy, and then it gradually brightens in the most marvellous manner until it breaks into the sunny motif of the last movement, which makes one's heart expand like a breath of spring air after the long dreary days of winter. In the first movment I do not think the 2nd subject rich enough – I feel it lacks swing. I will not trust myself to give an opinion of the adagio until I have heard it again once or twice. The third movement is a little jewel, tender and gay, except for one passage in the middle, which seems to me dull."

January 18: Brahms conducts the C minor Symphony at the Gewandhaus alongside the *Haydn Variations* and songs sung by Henschel.

January 23: Brahms conducts the C minor Symphony in Breslau.

February 8: Clara leaves Dusseldorf with Marie for Utrecht staying with the Engelmanns.

February 10: Clara performs Beethoven's G major Concerto, receives an invitation from the Queen to go to the Hague. "The Queen was more gracious than almost any other royalty I have met. She spoke of Brahms and Wagner. She is very fond of the former, but cannot bear the latter, etc. As a rule I attach little weight to royal opinions except when, as in the case of the Landgrafin Anna von Hessen they are the result of a sound musical education."

February 12: Clara (in Utrecht) writes to Brahms about his C minor: "I cannot trust myself to say in writing exactly what I think of the symphony, there is such a difference between writing and speaking. In one respect you have unconsciously met my wishes, and that is in the alteration you have made in the adagio. To my mind one needs some rest between the first and the last movements – some broad melody, which, particularly at the beginning, should be less elaborate in form and which would not obscure the actual melody itself. I was never quite satisfied with the end of the 3rd movement, it is so abrupt. And may I say a word about the last movement, or rather about the very end of it (presto)? It seems to me that from a musical point of view the presto shows a sudden falling away when compared with the splendid climax which precedes it. The tempo increases, but not the actual feeling, and the whole thing seems not so much a natural outcome of what has gone before, as added in order that there may be a brilliant ending."

February 15: Clara plays in Rotterdam before heading again for England.

March 8: Joachim conducts the C minor Symphony in Cambridge.

March 30: Clara returns from England.

April 18: Clara is back in Berlin.

May 2: Clara writes to Brahms at his request critiquing a number of songs he has sent.

May 3-8: The Herzogenbergs visit Clara and they play on two pianos almost every morning.

June: Brahms summers in Portschach on the Worthersee in South Austria (first of three summers in Portschach), starts composing the D major Symphony (#2). "The Worthersee is virgin soil," he writes to Hanslick, "the air is so full of melodies that one must take care not to tread on them." Writes to Clara about basing a movement on a chaconne that Bach used in his Cantata No. 150, also to Bulow about the same subject, which later provides the structure for the fourth movement of his Symphony in E minor (#4).

July: Clara, in Kiel, hears from Marmorito of the death of his eldest son (her grandson).

July: Clara, in Baden-Baden, visits Elise in Budesheim to find her engaged to an American businessman, Louis Sommerhoff, with excellent prospects.

July 6: Brahms sends Bach's *Chaconne* to Clara arranged for the left hand.

July 26: Ethel Smyth (19 years) arrives in Leipzig (her dream of the last seven years).

September 17: Brahms goes to Baden-Baden to see Clara.

September 30: Brahms visits Mannheim to see friends on his way to Vienna.

October 3: Felix leaves for Sicily for his health.

October: Brahms plays his Symphony in D major for Clara: "[The first movement] delighted me. It seems to me more deeply conceived than the first movement of the First Symphony. I also heard part of the last movement and am full of joy over it."

October: Clara visits Hamburg and Schwerin.

November 11: The C minor Symphony is a success conducted by Joachim (Berlin).

November 27: Elise Schumann marries Louis Sommerhoff.

December 23: Clara, in Berlin, hears Elise and her husband have arrived safely in New York.

December 30: Richter premieres the D major Symphony in Vienna with the Philharmonic Society.

December 30: Clara, in Berlin, gives a party with a performance of Brahms's Horn Trio (horn part played by a cello), receives a telegram from Billroth saying Brahms's D major met with great success in Vienna.

1878

January 1: Brahms performs the D minor Piano Concerto at the Gewandhaus.

January 10: Brahms conducts his D major Symphony at the Gewandhaus (heard by Ethel Smyth who later stays with the Herzogenbergs).

January 18: Brahms conducts the C minor Symphony (Hamburg).

January 22: Brahms conducts the C minor Symphony (Bremen), also *Schicksalslied* with Amalie singing songs by Brahms.

January 26: Brahms conducts the C minor Symphony (in Utrecht where he stays with the Engelmanns) and is joined by van der Wurff in the new Liebeslieder waltzes.

February 4: Brahms conducts the D major Symphony in Amsterdam.

February 6: Brahms conducts the D major Symphony in The Hague.

February 8: Brahms conducts the D major Symphony again in Amsterdam.

February 9: Clara goes to Cologne, stays with Marie Fillunger at the Deichmanns.

February 11: Brahms visits Clara in Cologne on his way from Amsterdam. "He was very pleasant and, to my great joy, thought I played better than I have ever done before. He could not well have said anything that would have given me more pleasure."

February-March: Clara decides to move to Frankfurt because it's centrally located (for Germany, Switzerland, and Vienna), has much culture, and is offered a position on her own terms with the Frankfurt Conservatory. Brahms advises her to accept.

March 6: The D major Symphony in Dresden (Royal Opera House).

March: Brahms places two of Dvorak's string quartets with Simrock, one of which, the D minor, is dedicated to Brahms.

April 14-20: Brahms visits Naples with Billroth and Karl Goldmark on the way to Rome (Brahms's first of eight holidays in Italy). Goldmark stays in Rome where he'd gone to hear rehearsals for his *Queen of Sheba*. They also visit Florence, Venice, Sicily.

Easter: Clara househunting in Frankfurt.

First week of May: Brahms, back in Portschach, writes to the Fabers to send him his clothes because the clothes for Italy are unsuitable for Portschach. He declines invitations to visit the Lower Rhine Festival to conduct the D major Symphony saying he hasn't good clothes.

May 21: Clara (with Marie) sets out for a performance in Wiesbaden.

Late May: Clara moves from Berlin to Frankfurt.

June: Clara visits Dusseldorf.

Summer: Brahms grows his famous beard in Italy, working on short piano pieces which become his opus 76, also composes his Violin Concerto in D.

Summer: Clara resettles in Frankfurt, begins work at the faculty of the Hoch Conservatory.

July: Clara, in Wildbad-Gastein, critiques Brahms's songs.

August 12: Clara, in Munich, hears from Marmorito that Felix is very ill. Clara: "One grows old only to bury one's children."

August 24: Felix arrives in Munich, very ill.

September: Clara goes to Budesheim while Marie prepares the house in Frankfurt and joins her on her birthday (13th) while Eugenie takes Felix to a consumptive hospital in Falkenstein.

September 29: Brahms conducts the D major Symphony with the Hamburg Philharmonic, making his first public appearance with the famous beard, and is showered with roses, then to Leipzig to work on the Violin Concerto with Joachim.

Late September-early October: Clara in Hamburg for performances (Brahms also present), climaxing the Festival with his D major Symphony. Brahms shows her the first movement of the Violin Concerto, Joachim plays it through.

October 20: Clara's 50th Jubilee as concert artist celebrated at the Museum (Frankfurt Conservatory) and Leipzig.

October 22: Clara heads for Leipzig for the celebration of her Jubilee.

October 22: Brahms conducts the D major Symphony and *Alto Rhapsody* (Breslau).

October 23: Clara plays solos for the benefit of the Leipzig Conservatory students.

October 24: Only works by Robert are performed at the Gewandhaus, including the A minor Concerto by Clara, who then retires to the Freges for more celebration.

November: Brahms eliminates the middle movements of the Violin Concerto, "of course they were the best," and substitutes a "poor adagio" in their place.

November 1: Felix and Eugenie come home to Frankfurt from Falkenstein.

December: Brahms meets and greets Dvorak for whom he has procured artist's stipends among other things with open arms.

December 12: Joachim receives only the violin part of the Violin Concerto to be performed on New Year's Day less than a month away.

1879

January 1: Brahm premieres the Violin Concerto with Joachim (Leipzig).

January 14: The Violin Concerto is performed in Vienna.

January 31: Clara returns to Frankfurt after four engagements in Switzerland.

February 16: Death of Felix Schumann of tuberculosis (in the arms of his sister Marie, who doesn't call Clara because she wished to spare her the sight of Felix's death-struggle).

March 11: Brahms returns to Vienna, Breslau offers an honorary doctorate, Leipzig offers Bach's old post, cantor of St. Thomas.

[*Chapter 66: The Violin Concerto in Leipzig*]

April: Clara receives the piano score of the Violin Concerto: "I am particularly charmed with the first and third movements. The adagio is clever, but it does not warm my heart as the others do."

Mid-May: Brahms visits Clara, now settled as professor of the piano at the Hoch Conservatory in Frankfurt.

Late May: Brahms visits Portschach for the third and last time, composes the Violin Sonata in G major (#1) and the two Rhapsodies.

June: Clara, back in Kiel for treatment, spends time with the Litzmanns.

July 10: Clara writes to Brahms about how well she likes his G major Violin Sonata.

August: Brahms visits Aigen where he plays the Violin Concerto and the new Violin Sonata with Joachim for Clara and the Herzogenbergs.

[*Chapter 67: The Italy Letters*]

Brahms meets Marie Soldat (19 year old) a violinist whom he teaches the Violin Concerto.

September 21: Clara receives a telegram from Baden-Baden saying her Lichtenthal house has finally been sold. She has been renting it since 1873 when she moved to Berlin and 1878 when she moved to Frankfurt.

October: Brahms requests Simrock to deposit his entire honorarium for the Violin Sonata (1,000 thaler) into Clara's account as if from an anonymous donor.

October 10: Clara performs Mozart's D minor Concerto (sadly because she imagines each public appearance will be her last). She realizes she can no longer play Brahms's D minor Concerto because it strains her muscles too much.

November: Dvorak's Third Slavonic Rhapsody is performed in Vienna. Dvorak sits next to Brahms and is invited afterward to the home of the Court Opera Director Franz Jauner, to whom Brahms warmly recommends Dvorak.

November 20: Brahms and Hellmesberger premiere the Violin Sonata in G at the quartet concert.

December 4: Joachim visits Clara in Frankfurt and they play Brahms's G major Sonata at the home of friends.

December 5: Clara hears the Violin Concerto with an orchestra for the first time which "has carried me off my feet."

December 8: Brahms performs in the Quartet in C minor (Budapest).

December 10: Brahms conducts the D major Symphony with the Budapest Philharmonic, also performs the D minor Piano Concerto with Alexander Erkel.

December 11: Clara (with Marie and Eugenie) visit friends in Karlsruhe.

Christmas: Brahms is back in Vienna with the Fabers.

December 27: Brahms visits Clara in her house on Myliusstrasse (Frankfurt).

December 28: Clara discusses the Hartel edition of Schumann's works with Brahms who says there is no need to hurry, but she can't see dragging on for six or seven years what might be accomplished in two.

<u>1880</u>
January 3: Brahms conducts the *Requiem* (Hanover).
January 13: Brahms conducts the *Requiem* and D major Symphony (Cologne).
January 20: Brahms conducts the D major Symphony, also performs the Rhapsodies (Krefeld).
January 21: Brahms conducts the D major Symphony and plays the D minor Piano Concerto (Bonn).
January 24: Brahms repeats the Bonn program in Hanover.
February 2: The G major Violin Sonata is premiered in England by Bulow and Madame Norman-Neruda.
February 3: Brahms conducts the Violin Concerto in Vienna with Joachim. They tour Poland and Galicia, performing concerts in Lemberg, Cracaw, Prague (where they visit Dvorak).
February 25: The G major Violin Sonata is performed in Cambridge by C. Villiers Stanford and Richard Gompertz.
April 10: Brahms repeats the January 21 program in Schwerin.
April 13: Brahms repeats the January 21 program in Konigsberg.
Rest of the Month: Brahms divides his time between Hanover (where he performs the Violin Concerto again with Joachim), Bremen, and Hamburg.
May 2-4: A monument is dedicated to Schumann over his grave in Bonn for which Brahms conducts the *Rhenish*, *Requiem for Mignon*, and his own Violin Concerto (with Joachim) among other works. Clara: "Unfortunately the end, with the E flat major Quartet, was disappointing. Brahms was not at his best, so that I felt as if I were sitting on thorns and so did Joachim, who kept on casting despairing glances at me. I was deeply distressed that I had not undertaken the quartet myself."
May 7: Brahms visits Clara (Frankfurt) for his 47th birthday.
May 8: Brahms returns to Vienna.
Summer: Brahms's first holiday in Ischl (he dines at the Hotel Kaiserin Elizabeth or the Post restaurant, drinks his coffee at a cafe on the Esplanade where he reads the newspapers, excursions to Gmunden to see the Victor von Millers, or to Berchtesgaden to visit Clara), composes two overtures and the Piano Trio in C major (#2).
July: Brahms imagines he's going deaf and returns to Vienna to consult Billroth, but it's just an aural catarrh. Talks to Joachim to set his mind at ease regarding Amalie's fidelity.
July 5: Clara writes to Brahms: "I am much alarmed by the trouble in your ears. Does it affect your hearing, or is it external? I have just heard that you had been lying in a meadow and had caught this cold in consequence. Do be a little more careful. One cannot always be young, but gets little reminders.

Tell me how you are, nothing more. I feel anxious, very likely more anxious than you do."

[*Chapter 68: Beethoven's Ear*]

July 11: Joachim writes to Brahms that he has cut off all relations with Simrock and requests Brahms to avoid speaking to Simrock about himself and his family.

July 27: Brahms replies to Joachim that he is sorry to get the news because he's sure there is no foundation to Joachim's suspicion.

Autumn: Bulow is appointed Musical Director to the Duke of Saxe-Meiningen.

September 6: Clara visits Brahms for three days, Brahms returns with her to Berchtesgaden.

September: Brahms writes to Amalie the letter which she uses in court to get her divorce from Joachim, fraying his friendship with Joachim.

September 13: Brahms and Joachim celebrate Clara's 62nd birthday in Berchtesgaden, Professor Engelmann (from Utrecht) and the Herzogenbergs also present. Brahms and Clara play the new overtures in piano transcriptions. "Johannes was in a particularly nice and friendly mood, so that I was able really to enjoy his visit. He played me the first movements of two new trios, of which I liked the one in E flat major best [this trio was never published]." Brahms tries again to persuade Joachim that his suspicions regarding Amalie are groundless.

September 23: Brahms returns to Vienna.

October 8: Clara performs the Beethoven E flat Concerto at the Museum.

October 13: *Fidelio* is conducted by Dessoff, much admired by Clara though she can't help hearing Schroder-Devrient in the role of Leonora, apparently unmatchable though Clara had declined to perform with her in her later years because she was no longer at her peak.

November: Dvorak comes to Vienna to show his new symphony (the Sixth) to Brahms and deliver it to the Vienna Philharmonic for performance.

November 25: Clara sees *Aida*: "It is curious to see the old composer venturing along new paths. Many parts of it pleased me very much, but many others I did not like. But I must say it filled me with respect for Verdi. It is extraordinary to see a composer striking out a new path in his old age, and what talent he shows in it!"

December 4: Brahms visits Berlin to hear Joachim conduct the *Requiem*.

December 14: Joachim performs the Violin Concerto at the Gewandhaus.

December 26: Richter premieres the *Tragic Overture* (Vienna).

<u>1881</u>

January 4: Brahms receives a degree from Breslau where he conducts his D major Symphony and *Tragic Overture* and premieres his *Academic Festival Overture*.

January 6: Brahms performs his two Rhapsodies and the Horn Trio.

January 13: Brahms visits the Herzogenbergs in Leipzig and conducts both overtures at the Gewandhaus.

January 22: Brahms conducts the overtures in Munster, Richard Barth joins him, adding the Violin Concerto and Hungarian Dances (arranged for violin by Joachim).

January 25: They repeat the Munster program in Krefeld.

January 29: Clara performs at the Gewandhaus, shines with Schumann's *Symphonic Etudes*.

February 3: Clara performs again at the Gewandhaus.

February 5: Clara receives a letter and 3,000 marks from a publisher who has accrued the profit from Schumann's compositions, but been unable to say anything earlier owing to matters of a private nature. She should expect to receive amounts in the same way until 1887 when the copyright comes to an end. Clara accepts with gratitude.

February: Brahms visits Holland, conducts at The Hague, Amsterdam, Haarlem, and visits the Engelmanns at Utrecht.

Second Week of February: Brahms visits Budapest.

February-April: Clara in London again and performs eleven times at the Popular concerts.

April 1: Clara is made an honorary member of the Royal Academy of Music.

April 12: Elise, her husband, and children reach London.

April 15: Clara, Marie, Elise (and her brood) return together to the continent.

March 20: Richter conducts the *Academic Festival Overture* in Vienna.

Spring: Brahms cements his friendship with Bulow who begins propagandizing for Brahms with talk of the three B's: Bach, Beethoven, and Brahms.

March 25: Brahms leaves for another trip to Italy (for which he studies some Italian) with Billroth, also Nottebohm and Prof. Adolf Exner, a more leisurely tour than before: Venice, Florence, Sienna, Orvieto, Rome. Nottebohm leaves them in Rome, then on to Naples and Sicily. Billroth delivers a baby on the steamer back from Sicily and leaves Brahms in Rome for Vienna. Brahms lingers, but returns to Vienna in time for his birthday.

April 10: Richter conducts the *Academic Festival Overture* again in Vienna.

Summer: Brahms rents a villa at Pressbaum in the Vienna Woods and sketches his B flat major Piano Concerto (#2).

July: Composes the Piano Concerto in B flat, also composes *Nanie*.

July 7: Brahms writes to Elizabet von Herzogenberg about "a tiny little piano concerto, with a tiny little scherzo."

July 11: Brahms sends the score for the new piano concerto to Billroth. Friends visit Brahms in Pressbaum, including Henschel (now married), Widmann, the Herzogenbergs, Simrock, and Joachim.

September 11: Joachim seeks Brahms's advice about Amalie, but leaves in a bad temper when Brahms is more sympathetic with Amalie.

[*Chapter 69: The Joachims*]

October 17: Brahms rehearses his B flat major Piano Concerto at Meiningen with Bulow. Duke George II and his Duchess (a former actress) are sympathetic hosts, not hidebound aristocrats as in Detmold. The Duke curtails a hunting expedition to meet Brahms.

November 9: Brahms solos, Bulow conducts, the premiere of the B flat Piano Concerto (in Budapest, with Budapest Philharmonic), also performing the *Academic Overture* and C minor Symphony.

November 12: Chamber concert in Budapest, Brahms performs the Rhapsodies, and (with Krancesevic) the Violin Sonata in G.

November 22: Concert in Stuttgart, the B flat Piano Concerto, Hungarian Dances, Rhapsodies, *Academic Overture*, the C minor Symphony, and songs.

November 27: The B flat Piano Concerto is performed in Meiningen; also the two Overtures, *Haydn Variations*, and the C minor Symphony.

December 10: Clara and Eugenie go to Munich to be greeted by Levi and the Fiedlers at whose home they stay.

December 14: Clara performs Robert's A minor Concerto among other things to be received enthusiastically.

Christmas: Back in Frankfurt, Eugenie dresses up like Santa Claus and gives out presents with doggerel rhymes to Clara's pupils to much merriment.

December-February: Brahms and Bulow join the orchestra on a whistle-stop tour through Europe by train, playing the B flat Piano Concerto and the other recent works in Stuttgart, Zurich, Breslau, Leipzig, Hamburg, Bremen, Munster, Utrecht, Frankfurt (visiting Clara), Kiel, Vienna, Berlin (where they perform both piano concertos). Florence May, seeing Brahms for the first time with his beard, almost doesn't recognize him.

<u>1882</u>

January 1: The Herzogenbergs hear the B flat Piano Concerto in Leipzig, Brahms at the piano.

January 6: Brahms performs the B flat Piano Concerto in Hamburg.

January 8: Brahms performs the B flat Piano Concerto with the Meiningen Orchestra at a Berlin Singakademie concert, conducting when Bulow plays the D minor Piano Concerto the following evening. Also the *Tragic Overture* and the C minor Symphony.

January 13: Brahms performs in Kiel with the Meiningen Orchestra.

January 14-15: Brahms performs in Hamburg with the Meiningen Orchestra.

January 16: Brahms reaches Munster for rehearsal, having said farewell to Bulow and the Meiningers in Hamburg.

January 18: Brahms leaves Munster where he is assisted in a benefit for Grimm.

January 20: Brahms stays with Professor Engelmann in Utrecht.

January 21: Brahms performs the B flat, Amalie sings the *Alto Rhapsody*.

January 25: Clara hears Saint-Saens in concert: "great technical skill."

January 26: The program is repeated in Rotterdam.

January 27: The program is repeated in Amsterdam.

January 30: Again in Arnheim.

February: Brahms travels with Dvorak to Prague from Dresden, where Dvorak had gone to hear Brahms play his new piano concerto.

February 2: Bulow performs an all-Brahms concert attended by Liszt. Bulow plays the Piano Sonata in F sharp minor and *Handel Variations* (when the applause seemed unstoppable, Bulow threatened to play the fugue again).

February 3: Brahms writes to Simrock to send Liszt two copies of the B flat Piano Concerto at Liszt's request.

February 3: Clara hears a concert of Tchaikovsky's *Suite*: "a good deal of talent and ability. The national tone which runs through it often makes it interesting, but only in places. The first movement – introduction and fugue – interested me most, it seemed the most finished."

February 17: Brahms performs the B flat Piano Concerto in Frankfurt.

February 22: Brahms arrives at Wullner's in Dresden (the B flat Piano Concerto and *Nanie* performed).

February 24: A choral concert is performed, including the motet "Warum," also the Serenade in A and Violin Sonata in G. After the concert Brahms performs both Rhapsodies and boards the 1 a.m. train to Vienna.

March 14: Bulow performs the D minor Piano Concerto in Leipzig, directing his orchestra from the piano, also the C minor Symphony and *Haydn Variations*.

April 7: Good Friday, *Requiem* is performed again in Hamburg. Brahms spends time with his stepmother before returning to Vienna.

April 26: Clara attends *Rheingold*: "I felt as if I were wading about in a swamp. The boredom one has to endure is dreadful. Every scene leaves the people on the stage in a condition of catalepsy in which they remain until one cannot bear to look at them any longer. The women have hardly a bar to sing in the whole opera, they simply stand about, and the gods altogether are a flabby and villainous set."

Early May: Brahms visits Ischl, composes his *Gesang der Parzen* dedicated to the Duke of Meiningen, F major String Quintet (#1), and C major Piano Trio (#2).

May 9: Clara attends *Walkure*: "Many things interested me, but boredom predominated. The gods are quite uninteresting, they are such a rabble and Wotan is the štupidest fellow. Musicians say so much about the interesting orchestration – I will make an effort and hear the operas once more and pay more special attention to that side of it."

May 16: Clara attends *Rheingold* again: "There are some fine orchestral effects, but they keep on recurring."

May 18: Clara attends *Walkure* again: "I wanted to pay more close attention to the music and in the 1st act found some well sounding passages but many reminiscences of Mendelssohn – Schumann – Marschner. Otherwise, my opinion has not changed."

May 25: Clara attends Mendelssohn's *Antigone*: "I was disappointed in the music, which I had not heard for many years and had quite forgotten. It does not suit the greatness of the subject. It puzzles me how Mendelssohn could make such a mistake."

July: Bulow marries Marie Schanzer (who becomes his biographer and editor).

July 13: Brahms sends the F major String Quintet, and C major Piano Trio to Simrock.

July 26: Levi premieres *Parsifal* (Bayreuth).

September 15-October 1: Brahms, Billroth, Brull, and Simrock visit Italy. Clara, Eugenie, Marie, and the Herzogenbergs are also in Italy.

October: The Piano Trio in C and Quintet in F are performed in Billroth's house.

October 10: Clara about mistakes in an article by Liszt: "[The mistakes] have reference chiefly to my father, who, because he himself took art seriously and trained me to do the same, has unfortunately been placed before the world in quite a false light. People do not understand that, if anything of importance is to be achieved in art, one's whole education and course of life must differ from that of ordinary people. My father always kept physical as well as artistic development in view: in my childhood I never practised for more than 2 hours, and in later years for 3 hours a day, and every day I had to walk with him for an equal number of hours in order to strengthen my nerves, and until I was grown-up he always took me away from any party at 10 o'clock as he considered it necessary for me to have sleep before midnight. He did not let me go to balls because he said I needed my strength for other things than dancing, but he always let me go to good operas, and even in my earliest days I had constant intercourse with the most distinguished artists. Such were the pleasures of my childhood, not dolls, which indeed I never missed. It is absolutely false to say that I was kept at the piano as long as my strength held out. Further, Liszt says that in spite of all this playing I never found music a burden. I can only reply that of my own free will I spent many hours of my free time over operas, piano-scores and other music, as it is impossible to do when one is over-tired."

October 29: Death of Nottebohm. Brahms visits Graz, arranges funeral, undertakes expenses.

December 10: *Gesang der Parzen* is premiered in Basel, the D major Symphony also performed.

December 17: *Gesang der Parzen* is repeated in Zurich with *Nanie*.

December 20: Repeated with *Nanie* in Strasbourg.

December 21: Brahms surprises Clara at home in Frankfurt as she's playing his new Piano Trio (in C) with friends.

Christmas: Brahms with Clara in Frankfurt. Clara on the F major String Quintet: "The 1st and 2nd movements are magnificent, but the 3rd does not appeal to me so much. We also tried over the trio [in C major], but although I am delighted with some things in it, I am not really satisfied with it as a whole, except for the andante which is wonderful. In the evening when my pupils came and we lit up the tree I was quite carried out of myself. They were all very merry. Brahms was in the best of humors."

December 29: The Quintet in F and Piano Trio in C are performed (Frankfurt). Clara: "Brahms's quintet was enthusiastically received – it really is a magnificent work. The trio did not take so well. The pity is that Brahms plays more and more abominably. It is now nothing but thump, bang, and scrabble."

[*Chapter 70: Her Cabinet Meeting*]

December 30: Brahms leaves for Vienna. Clara: "We felt certain that he had enjoyed this week with us, but we felt too that our intercourse had been purely superficial."

1883

Early January: Stays only a fortnight at Karlsgasse.

January 2: Clara on the piano-score of *Carmen* (brought to her by Brahms): "I am delighted with the charming music and skilful instrumentation."

January 15: Brahms visits Clara, but on his departure she's sorry for him. "How lonely one must feel when one is no longer really in touch with one's best and oldest friends." (Brahms has alienated himself from Levi and Joachim.)

January 17: Piano Trio in C (Berlin).

January 18: Brahms visits Clara again in Frankfurt on his way to Bonn where he plays the B flat Piano Concerto, Wasielewski conducting, and conducts *Nanie* himself.

January 19: Brahms hears Hermine Spiess sing *Gesang der Parzen* (Krefeld).

January 22: Piano Trio in C (London).

January 23: Brahms repeats the B flat Piano Concerto, meets Hermine Spies (26 years old).

January 26: Concert in Coblenz.

January 28: Performance of the *Peri* at the Museum, Marie Fillunger as the *Peri*. Clara is happy with "Fillu," Muller, and Fraulein Spiess.

January 30: Concert in Cologne.

February: Brahms tours Hanover, Schwerin, Meiningen, and Oldenburg.

February: Clara in Berlin is impressed with Marie Soldat's performance of Mendelssohn's Violin Concerto.

February: After the performance (of the two middle movements of Bruckner's 6th) there was a colossal ovation, and while Hanslick remains silent and still Brahms joins in the general applause.

February 10: Brahms in Schwerin.

February 13: Death of Wagner (Venice). Brahms closes his rehearsal (in Meiningen) saying "A master is dead, we shall rehearse no more today." He sends a wreath to Bayreuth which is not acknowledged by Cosima, reputed to have said: "Why should the wreath be acknowledged? The man was no friend to Our Art."

February 15: Quintet in F organized by Hellmesberger (Vienna).

February 17: Brahms goes to Nuremberg, then by night train to Vienna.

February 18: Dvorak's Symphony in D minor (#7) is performed in Vienna (*Schicksalslied* also on the program) attended by Brahms and Simrock, neither aware of the other at the concert.

February 18: Clara's anxious about a concert because she's fallen and injured herself enough to forego the first concert, but the rest, including Beethoven's *Choral Fantasy*, goes well.

February 19: Clara leaves Berlin to return home to Frankfurt again.

March 15: Piano Trio in C organized by Hellmesberger (Vienna).

April 1: Brahms, in Meiningen, conducts *Schicksalslied* in anticipation of the Duke's birthday the next day (Bulow's convalescing).

April 6: Brahms in Hamburg.

April 8: Brahms visits Schwerin where his *Requiem*'s performed for the first time.

April 13: Brahms performs again in Wiesbaden.

May 7: Brahms's 50th is celebrated with friends for dinner in Vienna (Billroth, Faber, Hanslick).

May 9: Brahms attends the Sixtieth Lower Rhine Festival (Cologne), playing the B flat Piano Concerto, conducting the D major Symphony.

Mid-May: Brahms stays briefly with the Beckerath family at Godesberg, but settles in Wiesbaden where he composes his Symphony in F major (#3).

July: Conducts the *Alto Rhapsody* in Coblenz with Hermine Spiess.

September 13: Brahms comes to Baden-Baden from Wiesbaden for Clara's birthday bringing excuses for no present (the flower shop was out of his way, wanted to get photographs but was too lazy). He's in good humor, but they haven't even a minute alone and mention of his Symphony in F slips out just incidentally before he returns to Wiesbaden.

Early October: Brahms leaves the Rhineland for Vienna.

October: Vienna. Dvorak's letter to Simrock of October 10: "Quite lovely days with Dr. Brahms. We were together every noon and evening." Brahms performs for Dvorak the first and last movements of his Symphony in F.

October 10: Dvorak writes to Simrock, "I say without exaggeration that this work [the F major Symphony] surpasses his first two symphonies, if perhaps not in greatness and powerful conception then certainly in – beauty!"

October 13: Brahms writes to Simrock: "Dvorak was here for several days and was very nice."

October 30: Brahms asks Joachim (who had left in a bad temper when last they had met in Pressbaum) if he would like to conduct the first performance in Berlin. Joachim, always more enthusiastic about the music than the man, accepts.

December 2: Richter premieres the F major Symphony (Vienna). Dvorak is present, in Vienna to hear Franz Ondricek perform his own Violin Concerto on the same bill. Brahms takes Dvorak to dinner at Faber's, a guest along with Goldmark, Hellmesberger, Hanslick, Richter, Simrock, and others – including also a lady friend from Marseilles who keeps Brahms supplied with the Mocha coffee he loves so well. The F major Symphony is hissed by Wagnerians. Faber almost comes to blows with one such.

1884

January 4: Joachim conducts the F major Symphony in Berlin, then twice more.

January 18: Brahms visits Wiesbaden with the F major Symphony and the B flat Piano Concerto where Clara hears the symphony for the first time: "In my opinion it comes between the 1st and the 2nd, a sort of Forest-Idyll, the tone is elegiac from beginning to end. The workmanship is wonderful, as it always is with Brahms, that is his chief strength. Its melodies and motifs are less distinctly original than in his earlier symphonies, but I must hear it frequently before I can form an opinion as I lost too much of the soft passages. It was unfortunate that I did not know it before."

January 21: Brahms performs the Piano Quartet in G minor, the Piano Trio in C, and songs by Hermine Spiess in Wiesbaden.

January 29: Clara gets to try Brahms's F major Symphony with Elise on two pianos. "If I had made acquaintance with the symphony beforehand, what a difference it would have made to me."

Late January: Berlin. Brahms conducts his F major Symphony (Dvorak present), but pleads too much correspondence to see Joachim.

February 3: Bulow conducts the F major Symphony in Meiningen for its greatest triumph yet, performing it twice on the same evening, printing it twice on the program. The second performance is applauded more than the first, sandwiching between the two performances Beethoven's *Grosse Fugue.*

February 9: Elisabet von Herzogenberg writes to Clara to let her know how much pleasure Brahms derived from Clara's appreciation of his F major when she showed him her letter. He had not expected such appreciation from her.

February 11: Clara writes to Brahms about his F major: "What a work! What a poem! What a harmonious mood pervades the whole! All the movements seem to be of one piece, one beat of the heart, each one a jewel! From start to finish one is wrapped about with the mysterious charm of the woods and forests. I could not tell you which movement I loved most."

February 16: Brahms performs the Violin Sonata in G with Adolf Brodsky.

February 17: Brahms conducts the F major Symphony in Leipzig, with songs by Hermine Spiess.

February 27: A program is devoted entirely to Brahms in Amsterdam (*Tragic Overture,* B flat Concerto, Symphony in F, and songs).

Brahms conducts the F major Symphony in Cologne, also *Gesang der Parzen,* continues performing *Gesang der Parzen, Alto Rhapsody, Academic Overture,* songs, the B flat Concerto, in Elberfeld, Barmen, Dusseldorf, Essen (part of the *Requiem,* but the rehearsals go so well he presents the whole), and Dresden (the F major Symphony conducted by Wullner with the Royal Orchestra of Saxony so Brahms can hear it, also the *Alto Rhapsody,* D minor Concerto, and F minor Sonata by Bulow).

March-April: Clara again in England.

March 3: Clara performs Beethoven's *Les Adieux* and Robert's F major novellette to huge applause.

March 14: Brahms conducts the F major Symphony in Frankfurt (Clara is on her sixteenth tour of England).

March 16: at a Museum Gesellschaft concert, Hugo Heermann and colleagues perform the Piano Quartet in C minor and String Quintet in F.

[*Chapter 71: Hermione-ohne-O*]

March 17: Clara performs Robert's F sharp minor Sonata.

April: Hiller resigns as Head of the Conservatorium of Cologne. Brahms, offered the post, recommends Wullner.

April 16: Clara returns to Frankfurt from London.

May 8: Brahms leaves Vienna for Lake Como (guest of the Duke of Meiningen at his Villa Carlotta), then Murzzuschlag (a village near Vienna where he and his father had stopped on their walking tour through Styria) with the industrialist, Dr. Richard Fellinger (manager for Austria of the firm of

Siemens and Halske) and his sculptress wife, Maria, at whose house in Vienna Brahms was often a guest.

Later in May: Brahms conducts the F major Symphony and *Schicksalslied* at the Whitsun Lower Rhine Music Festival.

June 19: Clara reads through her correspondence with Kirchner: "If only I could wipe this old friendship quite out of my life! I gave my heart's best to a man who I hoped it might save. I wished to make one so highly gifted into a worthy man and artist, to enoble his character which had suffered so much from being spoiled, and through friendship to give him new joy in the happiness of life: in short, I dreamed of an ideal and never thought that I had a fully matured man before me. It was a sad experience. I suffered much and found comfort only in the thought that I had meant all for the best."

Late June: Brahms stays in Murzzuschlag, close to Vienna, where Clara, Billroth, and Hanslick visit, to learn he's working on another symphony, even through October.

October 16: Brahms returns to Vienna from Murzzuschlag.

October 24: Brahms visits Hamburg for the F major Symphony under Julius von Bernuth. It is so successful that a second performance is scheduled immediately for early December to be conducted by Brahms.

November 14: Clara performs Robert's F sharp minor Sonata at the Museum.

November 25: Bulow and the Meiningen Orchestra play the D minor Piano Concerto in Vienna.

December 2: Brahms performs the B flat Concerto, Bulow conducts the F major Symphony, also the *Haydn Variations*.

December 11: Brahms asks Simrock to send four-handed arrangements of the three symphonies to Maria Cossel (daughter of Otto Cossel, his first piano teacher).

December: Dietrich organizes a Brahms Festival in Oldenburg (the F major Symphony, the B flat Concerto, and Liebeslieder Waltzes with Hermine Spiess).

December 24: Brahms visits the Herzogenbergs in their new (still barely habitable according to Elisabet) abode.

Christmas: Clara invites her pupils as usual, but they're made to earn their presents from Eugenie (Santa Claus) by playing something on the piano, which they do to the enjoyment of all.

December 26: Brahms asks Simrock to send Amalie a song, opus 91/2 for contralto and viola to patch things between her and Joachim, but in vain.

1885

Brahms spends the beginning of the year in Vienna editing the first four Schubert symphonies.

Late January: Brahms in Krefeld organizes a performance of the six-part *Tafellied*, also the first performances of the Two Songs with Viola and Piano.

February 15: Clara's house in Frankfurt is burglarized. The thieves spend the night stealing from the dining and adjoining rooms, taking among other things the gold and silver tops of glass decanters, but not from the bedrooms where she had most of her jewelry and money. She's more upset about the loss of personal security than financial security.

February 22: Clara begins playing again, but is much disturbed by the hammering and iron bars being set up wherever thieves might find an entrance. She is full of ugly thoughts, would like to die if not for the children and her piano.

March 13: Clara performs for the first time in the year, Robert's Quintet.

March 16: Clara is invited to play once more at the Gewandhaus on the 26th before they rebuild it. She accepts thinking it might be the last time she will play in public, providing symmetry with the first time she played in public, also at the Gewandhaus.

April 1: Brahms is overwhelmed by a performance of Bach's B minor Mass conducted by Richter.

April 24: Clara performs in Berlin, Brahms Rhapsody alongside Joachim performing his own Violin Concerto.

May 11: Death of Hiller (Cologne).

May 12-19: Herzogenberg arrives to help Clara sort Robert's letters, they work daily for 3-4 hours.

June 12: Queen Elisabeth of Romania writes to Clara, asking her to come. "I have so much respect for your time that I am afraid of worrying you by my wish but I am so seldom in Germany, and I never know how long it may be before I come back again, that I want to do all I can to gather my friends round me, if only to prove to each other that we have not altered! I do not count a gray hair or two, or a wrinkle under the eye, the soul shines through in eternal youth in its power of loving and giving happiness. It is in love and happiness that youth consists, that life should consist, unless it has been something very different from what it should have been, and we have let it get warped and twisted. I come from a death-bed, by which I have once more learned that life in itself is a costly gift, with which one finds it hard to part. For how many years have I despised it and thought it of no value!" Unfortunately, Clara does not feel well enough to accept the invitation.

Summer: Brahms returns to Murzzuschlag to complete his E minor Symphony (#4).

September: Returning from Murzzuschlag, Brahms performs a two-piano version of the E minor Symphony with Ignaz Brull for Kalbeck and Hanslick. The Fellingers are also in attendance.

September 4: Brahms sends Elisabet the first movement and part of the second of the E minor Symphony, asking her to send it on to Clara.

September 17-26: Clara sits for Adolf von Hildebrand who sculpts a bust with which she's well pleased though she found it tiring to sit such lengths of time.

Autumn: Herzogenbergs move from Leipzig to Berlin where Heinrich is appointed Professor of Composition at Joachim's Hochschule.

October 10: Brahms sends Elisabet the entire E minor Symphony for two pianos, asking her to send it on to Clara no later than November 1.

October 17: Brahms premieres the E minor Symphony (Meiningen).

October 21: Death of Alwin Wieck.

October 25: Brahms premieres the E minor Symphony in Meiningen. Richard Strauss, twenty-one years old, just appointed Bulow's assistant conductor, is deeply impressed, particularly with the second movement, "a funeral procession moving in silence across moonlit heights."

November 1: Bulow conducts the E minor Symphony in Meiningen.

November 3: Bulow conducts the E minor Symphony in Frankfurt, but the post had delayed Clara's receipt of the symphony from Elisabet causing friction between her and Brahms and embarrassment to Elisabet who had held on to it till the last minute so Joachim might see it.

November: Brahms and Bulow tour nine towns in Germany and Holland with the E minor Symphony and the Meiningen Orchestra, so triumphant that Brahms cannot help conducting it in Frankfurt during Bulow's absence though Bulow's scheduled to conduct it there again in a few days. Bulow resigns as a consequence feeling not only upstaged by Brahms, but shamed before his own orchestra.

November 3-25: The E minor Symphony is taken to Essen, Elberfeld, Utrecht, Amsterdam, The Hague, Krefeld, Cologne, Wiesbaden, and many other places.

[Chapter 72: A Difference with Bulow]

November 26: Clara performs in the hall of the new Gewandhaus, wonderful acoustics, Chopin's F minor Concerto, last played by her in 1852, also in Leipzig, but neuralgia had prevented her from performing it just recently in Frankfurt.

Late December: Clara receives many letters, including one from Brahms, expressing delight and appreciation for the publication of Robert's early letters.

<u>1886</u>

January 4: Clara's knees are so inflamed by neuralgia she is forced to stay in bed for days, foregoing a concert she was to perform at the Museum on January 22.

January 17: Richter conducts the E minor Symphony in Vienna.

February 1: Joachim conducts the E minor Symphony in Berlin.

February 9: Brahms conducts the E minor Symphony in Cologne, also *Schicksalslied*, also plays the D minor Concerto.

February 18: Brahms conducts the E minor Symphony at the Gewandhaus, also the Violin Concerto performed by Adolf Brodsky (professor at the Leipzig Conservatory).

February 19: Clara performs Chopin's F minor Concerto painlessly and "magnificently."

February-April: Brahms tours with the E minor Symphony, covering Cologne, Mannheim, Berlin, Dresden, Frankfurt, Meiningen.

March 2: Brahms arrives in Frankfurt to rehearse his E minor Symphony.

March 3: Clara attends the second rehearsal of the E minor Symphony, much affected in particular by the 2nd and 4th movements.

March 5: Clara on the E minor Symphony: "I was much struck by the influence of Wagner in the method of orchestration. There were often the same peculiar shades of tone, only with this difference, that in the one they serve to express beauty and dignity, and in the other, ugliness and triviality."

March-April: Clara again in London.

March 29: Clara performs, among other things, the *Waldstein* and Schumann's *Arabeske* at the Popular concert.

April 3: Liszt arrives in London, performs for Queen Victoria, spends Holy Week in Antwerp.

April 5: Clara performs her *F sharp minor Variations* composed for Robert then in Endenich.

April 9: Brahms in Hamburg (with *Schicksaslied*, a capella choruses, songs for alto and viola with Hermine Spiess and Bargheer, *Triumphlied*, plus other songs and choruses).

April 13: A Vicountess asks Clara to play for a dying woman who had often come to hear her and wishes to hear her just once more.

April 14: Clara plays for the dying woman slow movements from Beethoven sonatas.

April 25: Clara: "I have once more been struck by the fine perception with which so many people here express themselves with regard to my art. This is seldom the case in Frankfurt, for example. The English are wonderfully responsive, though their stiff manners often conceal it, but if once they let themselves go, their feelings break out with greater energy than is the case with us Germans."

May 10: Richter conducts the E minor Symphony in London.

May 14: Clara, back in Frankfurt, suggests she and Brahms return each other's letters.

May: First of Brahms's three summers in Thun, near Berne, recommended by Widmann, where he composes his Cello Sonata in F (#2), Violin Sonata in A (#2), Piano Trio in C minor (#3), and songs, visiting the Widmanns on weekends, the Schanzli summer theater nearby for the latest Strauss operettas, and where he is visited by Klaus Groth and Hermine Spiess.

Mid-June: Wullner conducts the E minor Symphony in Cologne.

Summer: King Ludwig II of Bavaria, Wagner's patron, drowns himself.

July 20: Liszt attends Bayreuth performance of *Tristan*, catches a chill, develops pneumonia.

July 31: Death of Liszt (Bayreuth).

Autumn: Brahms burns many manuscripts, letters, private papers, returns Clara's letters, requests his own back, also requests the return of old manuscripts from friends.

Early October: Brahms leaves Thun, serenaded by the town orchestra, a gypsy band performing Hungarian Dances.

[*Chapter 73: Thun Summer*]

November 5: Death of Fritz Brahms (leaves his brother 10,000 marks).

November 24: The Cello Sonata in F is premiered with Robert Hausmann of Joachim's quartet.

December 2: The Violin Sonata in A is performed by Brahms and Hellmesberger at one of Hellmesberger's quartet soirees.

[*Chapter 74: Zum roten Igel*]

December 20: The C minor Trio is played in Budapest by Hubay, Popper, and Brahms.

December 22: Brahms conducts the E minor Symphony in Budapest.

<u>1887</u>

January: Prussia confers the order Pour le Merite on Brahms.

January 7: Clara is impressed by Richard Strauss's Symphony/*Aus Italien* (he's just 22).

January 13: Clara's angry with Brahms because, among other things, he provides feeble excuses for not sending her his sonatas and for curtailing a Brahms evening he had suggested himself.

February 1: Wullner conducts the C minor Symphony in Cologne.

February 6: Bulow, performing the complete cycle of Beethoven sonatas in Vienna, receives a note from Brahms bearing a phrase from Mozart's *Magic Flute* to which Brahms knew he would know the words: "Dear one, shall I see you no more?" They not only become friends again but travel together to Budapest where Brahms thanks him in a public speech for his performance in the F minor Piano Quintet.

February 25: Brahms performs the C minor Piano Trio in Vienna.

March-April: Clara in England.

March 9: Death of Princess Carolyne Sayn-Wittgenstein, a fortnight after she completes the twenty-fourth and last volume of her enormous work which no one will read.

April 4: The thousandth Popular concert in London. Clara performs Robert's Quintet among other pieces, walks from the hall to her carriage through an audience which waves handkerchiefs and shouts: "Come back again, Frau Schumann."

April 25: Brahms visits Italy with Simrock and Theodore Kirchner, impecunious Kirchner as their guest.

April 30: Clara goes to Ems with Marie for an audience she had requested with the Crown Princess of Prussia, playing for them in return for a place in a girls' school in Berlin for her granddaughter, Julie.

April 30: Clara receives some of her letters which she had requested back from Brahms.

May 15: Brahms arrives for his second summer in Thun (weekends with the Widmanns in Berne). Hanslick and Kalbeck visit. Brahms also visits Widmann's mountain house in Meiligen despite the cold.

Summer: Brahms entrusts Maria Fellinger with the task of finding him a new housekeeper since his old housekeeper, Ludovica Vogl, has died. She finds him Celestina Truxa who could not have been more suitable (also the only person with him when he died).

[Chapter 75: Frau Celestine Truxa]

June: Clara reads through and nearly tears up her letters to Brahms because she finds "them very monotonous in tone, one wail of sorrow, though this was justified by my hard fate," but Marie saves most of them.

June 24: Brahms stays with Clara in Frankfurt on his way to Cologne, during which he plays the A major Violin Sonata, F major Cello Sonata, and C minor Piano Trio.

June 26-29: Brahms visits Cologne for the Rhine Festival at Wullner's invitation for the C minor Piano Trio (Brahms at the piano), *Triumphlied*, and Violin Concerto (with Brodsky).

July 23: Clara suggests Brahms make a diary from his early letters which she returns, covering so much of his career.

Early August: Brahms visits the Beckeraths in Rudesheim before heading back to Thun, there to see Hermine again with her sister, but nothing comes of the Beckeraths hope for the two.

September 4: Clara goes with Marie from Obersalzberg to Munich.

September 16: Clara and Marie go to Baden-Baden.

September 21: Brahms and Joachim and Hausman rehearse the Double Concerto, Brahms's olive branch to Joachim, Clara also present. The *Zigeunerlieder* stem from the same period.

September 23: The Double Concerto is rehearsed with the Baden-Baden Municipal Orchestra.

October 6: Marie Soldat performs the Brahms Violin Concerto at the Museum.

October 16: Brahms visits Clara to exchange their respective letters. Clara begs him to let her cull his letters for matters relating to his artistic or private life for his biographers, if she were to die the letters (his and hers) would fall into the conscientious hands of her children, if he were to die they might fall into unsuitable hands, but Brahms does not wish it and she hands him back his letters in tears.

October 18: The Double Concerto is premiered in Cologne conducted by Wullner.

[*Chapter 76: A Double Concerto*]

October 28: Clara performs in the Brahms Trio in C minor.

November 2: Death of Jenny Lind-Goldschmidt (Malvern, UK).

November 17: The Double Concerto in Wiesbaden.

November 18: Death of Marxsen (Nienstadten, near Altona).

November 18: The Double Concerto in Frankfurt.

November 20: The Double Concerto at Basel.

December 9: Brahms writes to Simrock: "Very agreeable and nice were the hours with [Dvorak]."

December 22: Tchaikovsky arrives in Berlin, soon to be touring as a conductor of his own work.

Christmas: Brahms goes to Meiningen (accepting an invitation left at Karlsgasse by the Duke in person). The concert program includes the *Haydn Variations*, the F major Symphony, and the B flat Concerto (with Eugene d'Albert).

December 31: Tchaikovsky arrives in Leipzig, meets Brahms and Grieg among others at the Brodsky home during a rehearsal of Brahms's C minor Piano Trio.

[*Chapter 77: A Clutch of Composers*]

<u>1888</u>

January: Brahms dumps his letters from Clara unopened into the Rhine.

January: The Herzogenbergs moved to Munich from Berlin because the dankness is no good for Heinrich's deformed leg which later requires surgery. In her letter to Brahms, Elisabet says: "Sometimes I think it never will be the same again, and down goes my head into my hands, while the tears – which I can generally control – trickle down."

January 1: Brahms conducts the Double Concerto with Joachim and Hausmann at the Gewandhaus.

January 2: The C minor Piano Trio is performed in concert in Leipzig.

January: Nietszche, fallen out with Wagner since 1878 when he had defended Brahms, wishes to dedicate his own composition, *A Hymn to Life*, to Brahms – but embarrassed by the banal music Brahms declines acknowledgement on a postcard.

January 2: Brahms attends Tchaikovsky's concert at the Gewandhaus, conducting his First Suite for Orchestra.

January 3: Tchaikovsky notes that though Brahms made no encouraging remarks, he learned later that he was very pleased by the first movement, but did not praise the rest.

February 6: The Double Concerto is conducted by Bulow (Berlin).

February 15: The Double Concerto is conducted by Henschel (London).

February 20-March 31: Clara in England for her final tour.

February 21: The Double Concerto conducted by Henschel again (London).

March 9: Death of Kaiser Wilhelm I. The new Kaiser Frederick III dies of cancer three months later. Wilhelm II, unbalanced military autocrat, takes control. Brahms worries about the fledgling German Empire, but does not live to see his downfall and Germany's in 1918.

March 26: Clara performs *Carnaval* at the Popular concerts, sad because she had determined it would be the last time she performed in England.

May: Nietszche publishes *The Case of Wagner* in which he insults Brahms as "the eunuch of music," whose compositions enshrine "the melancholy of impotence." Brahms is depressed because he respects Nietzsche the philosopher if not the musician, but Elisabet writes prophetically, "Really, this man's vanity will bring him to a lunatic asylum yet."

May 7: Brahms meets Widmann on his 55th birthday in Verona to travel to Bologna, passing through Rossini's home town, Pesaro, on their way to Loreto and Rome (each sings an aria from the *Barber of Seville* as they pass), before returning to Thun via Milan, Turin, and the St. Gothard Pass.

May 18: Clara performs in a Dvorak quintet which greatly interests her.

May 29: Brahms reaches Thun for his third and last summer in the town.

June 28: Clara leaves with Marie and Eugenie for Franzensbad through Weimar, Kostritz, and Schneeberg. In Weimar she visits Goethe's house to find the same piano she had played in 1831 in the same place in the same room. Ferdinand is undergoing treatment in Kostritz, walking on two sticks, but it is unlikely he will ever work again.

Summer: Brahms composes the D minor Violin Sonata (#3) and dedicates it to Bulow in another gesture of reconciliation. Hermine stays with the Widmanns in

Berne and is shocked by Brahms's suddenly-white hair, writing to Maria Fellinger: "Were it not for his youthful blue eyes he would be an old man."

July 24: Brahms writes kindly to Clara from Thun about Ferdinand, requesting to send her 10,000 marks as his share of expenses for her grandchildren, to which she replies with thanks, saying she will not hesitate to turn to him should she need to do so.

August: Brahms quarrels with Widmann over an article published by Widmann the same summer regarding German nationalism. Widmann appeals to Gottfried Keller, a novelist and mutual friend, to mediate, Keller faults both and the friends reconcile – after which Brahms leaves Thun to stay with Clara at Baden-Baden.

October 3: Brahms sends 15,000 marks to Clara, wishing to hear only that she's received it. She's in a dither, but replies with thanks.

October 26: During her 60th jubilee celebration in Frankfurt, Clara is overwhelmed by a shower of love and affection from as far as England.

[*Chapter 78: Flies Are a Nuisance*]

October 31: The premiere of the *Zigeunerlieder* (Berlin Singakademie).

November 22: Clara receives Brahms's D minor Piano Sonata, but is sad her arm's not good enough to play it.

December 8: Clara plays the D minor Sonata with great enjoyment which she's been working at a quarter of an hour at a time.

December 21: Brahms premieres the D minor Violin Sonata with Jeno Hubay (Budapest).

December 23: Brahms conducts the Viennese premiere of the Double Concerto with Joachim and Hausmann.

Christmas: The first of the annual rituals in which Frau Truxa's tree is trimmed in Brahms's library and he gives presents to her two sons who now call him Onkel Bahms.

1889

January 3: Brahms visits Meiningen, belatedly accepting the Duke's invitation to Christmas, conducting the Double Concerto with Joachim and Hausmann, after which he returns to Vienna. Eugen d'Albert performs the D minor Piano Concerto. During rehearsal Joachim also plays both Beethoven and Brahms Violin Concertos, also the D minor Violin Sonata and C minor Piano Trio (with Brahms and Hausmann).

January 7-12: Brahms in Frankfurt with Clara, plays the D minor Sonata, also the Hungarian Dances and *Schumann Variations for Four Hands* with her for her students, on his way back to Vienna, everyone in great humor.

January 18: *Zigeunerlieder* performed in Vienna.

January 19-February 3: Clara goes to Berlin with Marie for a concert on the 25th with Joachim, visits the Litzmanns, Spittas, Bargiels, Rudorffs, Franz Mendelssohn (whose wife died on January 5, who dies himself the same month, February 20), and returns via Dusseldorf.

February 13: Joachim performs the D minor Violin Sonata (Vienna).

March 4: Brahms and Bulow perform at a Berlin Philharmonic concert, Brahms conducting the *Academic Festival Overture*, Bulow performing the D minor Piano Concerto.

March 4: Clara goes to Leipzig to perform on the 8th, spends time with old friends (Livia Frege and Emma Preusser).

March 9: Brahms visits Hamburg to see his stepmother, stepbrother, and sister (now married to a much older man), a clockmaker.

March 11: Tchaikovsky arrives in Hamburg to stay at the same hotel as Brahms, who extends his own stay to attend the rehearsal for Tchaikovsky's E minor Symphony (#5). At lunch he gives his opinion (likes the first three movements best), which Tchaikovsky appreciates.

March 15: The concert featuring Tchaikovsky's E minor Symphony is a success.

March 17: Brahms joins Joachim in Berlin for his Jubilee concert (50 years since his first performance).

April: Brahms at the Villa Carlotta on Lake Como.

Mid-April-mid-May: Clara visits Italy (Nice and Florence) with Marie and Eugenie, staying with the Herzogenbergs in Florence, returning by way of Baden-Baden.

May: Brahms goes to Ischl.

May 7: The D minor Violin Sonata (London).

May 23: Brahms is awarded the Freedom of the City of Hamburg.

Summer: Brahms summers in Ischl because a new promenade near his house in Thun keeps him away (tourists gather to listen to him practise). Ischl remains his summer resort for the rest of his life. There is no direct train to Berne so he misses the Widmanns, but visits Billroth (an hour by boat or train) in his lakeside villa in St. Gilgen. He also visits Gmunden staying with Victor von Miller zu Aichholz and his family, who establish a Brahms museum after his death at Gmunden containing mementos set in an exact replica of Brahms's rooms at Ischl down to the windowframes. He also visits the Strauss villa where he autographs a fan with bars from the Danube saying, unfortunately not by Johannes Brahms. He composes *Fest und Gedenkspruche* for the Hamburg honor, also composes Three Motets and revises his B major Piano Trio (opus 8), which could now be opus 108.

June 6: Brahms is awarded the Knight's Cross of the Imperial Austrian Order of Leopold, for which he's persuaded (with great difficulty) by Frau Truxa to go through the ordeal of being decorated at the palace later in the year in clean (or nearly clean) white gloves and clean boots and after much grumbling he arrives by carriage.

Autumn: Friends organize dinner for Brahms with Bruckner in Zum roten Igel, they're cool toward each other until they agree on the quality of the smoked ham and dumplings.

September 9-13: Brahms returns to Hamburg to accept the Freedom of the City of Hamburg. The Cecilia Society of Hamburg arranges a festival featuring the *Alto Rhapsody*, the Violin Concerto (with Brodsky), and the *Fest und Gedenkspruche* premiere.

September 13: Clara's 70th, much remembrance from friends, but her age and ailments make for "a melancholy joy."

September 14: Official ceremony awarding Brahms the Freedom of the City of Hamburg at the Town Hall.

September 20: Brahms arrives in Baden-Baden to celebrate Clara's 70th birthday (a week late) and plays the revised B major Piano Trio (the next day). Widmann, in Baden-Baden at the time, goes to Karlsruhe with Brahms for a couple of days before Brahms returns to Vienna.

October 30: Clara, back in Frankfurt, revels in Brahms's C minor Sonata, despairing that the playing tires her: "Ah! How can I go on living if I have to give it up entirely!"

November: Brahms records his voice (in German and in English) and a minute of the First Hungarian Dance for Theodore Wangemann, a European agent for Thomas Edison. "Grusse an Herrn Doktor Edison. I am Dr. Brahms. Johannes Brahms."

December: Brahms and Dvorak have an audience with Emperor Franz Josef I in Vienna to thank him for honors they have received.

Christmas: With the Fellingers where his table is heaped with gifts wrapped as pranks.

December 28: Death of Bendemann (Dusseldorf).

1890

January: Brahms is much impressed by Mahler conducting *Don Giovanni*. Later in the year, with Brahms venting about the decline of music, they cross a bridge over a stream during a walk. Mahler points to the water: "Look, Herr Doktor, look!" Brahms: "What is it?" Mahler: "Look – there goes the last wave." Brahms: "Maybe, but the point is whether the wave flows into a lake or a swamp."

January: Clara, with a bad attack of influenza, is nursed by Marie and Eugenie.

January 8: Brahms sends Bulow an autograph of the Symphony in F for his 60th birthday with an inscription: To his dearly beloved Hans von Bulow in loyal friendship. Vienna, 8 January, 1890. Johannes Brahms.

January 10: The revised B major Piano Trio is premiered in Budapest (Brahms, Hubay, Popper).

January 19-23: The Joachim Quartet gives a series of concerts in Vienna, including the Quartet in B flat major (Brahms's favorite of the three).

February: Brahms writes to Clara that many things could not be sung more beautifully than by Alice Barbi.

February 22: Second performance of the revised B major Piano Trio (Vienna).

March 13: Wullner performs the Mottoes and Motets, opuses 109 and 110. Brahms is also present and performs the B major Piano Trio again.

March 17: Brahms arrives in Frankfurt to rehearse and perform the revised Trio, in good humor, but Clara writes that what with visits and rehearsals and the theater they see little of him except for a little pleasant time at breakfast.

March 21: The B major Trio is performed in Frankfurt where Clara hears the rehearsals and performance.

March 26: Clara attends *Figaro*, but she is embittered in general because she no longer hears as she once did, not only music but even words can be a problem.

March: The Kaiser engineers Bismarck's resignation.

April: Brahms makes another Italian journey with Widmann who meets him at Riva and they visit Parma, Cremona, Padua, and Verona before Brahms returns to Vienna.

April 27: Clara enjoys Saint-Saens's Concerto in G minor: "It is a clever work, and in places shows warm feeling. The 1st movement in particular, pleased me extremely, and so did the scherzo. The instrumentation is very interesting throughout and that of the scherzo piquant – certainly the best of the modern virtuoso-concertos."

April 28: Clara performs Brahms's D minor Sonata at an afternoon musical party, also Robert's F sharp minor Sonata, but gets confused. "Eugenie is always scolding me because I never practise, but there is so little here to incite me, and why should I wish to practise old things? And then I always consider that my day is over. This may be wrong, but it arises partly from physical conditions."

May-early October: Brahms in Ischl, composes the String Quintet in G major (#2), imagining it will be his last composition because his best work is behind him.

June 9: The Schumanns invite forty persons to a party at their home, Joachim performs the A minor Quartet with Heermann, Koning, and Robi Mendelssohn (arrived with Joachim from Berlin). Clara performs Robert's E flat major Quartet surprising herself how well she plays.

November 11: The G major String Quintet is premiered (Vienna).

December 10: The G major String Quintet is performed by Joachim and colleagues (Berlin).

Christmas: Brahms with the Fellingers.

1891

January 19: Brahms, in Budapest, performs the revised B major Piano Trio.

February: Victor von Miller zu Aichholz persuades Brahms to sit for a portrait by a painter and a sculptor about which Brahms writes to Simrock that one is doing me from the front, the other from the back, where incidentally the most brilliant parts reside. This is the only portrait for which Brahms sat.

March 12: Clara's final public concert in Frankfurt.

March: Brahms visits Meiningen, guest of the Duke (Widmann is invited in deference to Brahms's wishes) for performances of his symphonies in C minor and E minor. He hears Richard Muhlfeld (originally a violinist, then a selftaught clarinetist) perform the Weber Clarinet Concerto and Mozart Clarinet Quintet, and is inspired by the tone of the clarinet to an "Indian summer" of composition.

March 20-27: Brahms visits Clara in Frankfurt, but they quarrel over a misunderstanding about the Viennese reception of Borwick, one of Clara's students.

April 6: Death of Arthur Burnand (Clara's host in London): "I have lost my 'home' in England."

Mid-May: Brahms writes to Simrock what's to pass for his will providing for his sister, his landlady Frau Truxa, his Ischl landlord, and donations to various musical associations in Hamburg and Vienna, but it's later invalidated for imprecision. He requests cremation and all correspondence and unfinished work destroyed, but he's buried instead, destroys his own unfinished work, and his correspondence is saved by his executor, Dr. Joseph Reitze of Vienna, with the approval of just about everyone. To the Gesellschaft der Musikfreunde he leaves his books, music, and original manuscripts, among them the scores of Mozart's Symphony in G minor, Haydn's Sun Quartets, a sheet with Beethoven's writing on one side, Schubert's on the other, songs and dances by Schubert, sketches by Beethoven, the conclusion of Wagner's Prelude to *Tristan.*

June 6: Death of Ferdinand Schumann (Gera).

[Chapter 79: The Herzogenbergs]

Summer: Brahms in Ischl, composes the Clarinet Trio and Clarinet Quintet.

October: Brahms and Clara quarrel in correspondence over the publication of Robert's D minor Symphony, Brahms wanting to publish the original version side by side with the more heavily orchestrated, Clara only the more heavily orchestrated, Brahms insisting Robert thickened the orchestration because he didn't trust the Dusseldorf orchestra, Clara that he wanted only the last version published.

[Chapter 80: Purse and Cutpurse]

November: Brahms invites himself to Meiningen, meets Joachim and Hausmann and they rehearse the clarinet works with Muhlfeld. Widmann's tragedy, *Oenone,* is staged.

November 24: The Clarinet Trio and Clarinet Quintet are premiered for the Duke and his Court.

Late November: Back in Hamburg, Brahms remonstrates successfully with his sister Elise, through letter and word of mouth, to change the beneficiaries of her will from some lady friends to her six stepchildren.

December 12: Brahms visits Berlin as Simrock's guest for performances of the Clarinet Trio (with Joachim and Muhlfield) and Clarinet Quintet.

December 17: Back in Vienna, Brahms performs the Clarinet Trio.

1892

January 1: Clara falls and sprains her right arm.

January 5: First Viennese performance of the Clarinet Quintet.

January 7: Death of Elisabet von Herzogenberg (San Remo, Italy) of heart disease.

January 19: Muhlfeld and the Joachim Quartet perform the Clarinet Quintet in Vienna, Brahms in the audience.

January 21: Brahms performs the Clarinet Trio.

February 1: Clara, lungs inflamed, sends her resignation to the Frankfurt Conservatory. Also suffers from rheumatism and a buzzing in her ears.

March 28: Muhlfeld performs the Clarinet Quintet in London at a Monday Popular Concert.

March Eugenie is dangerously ill, doesn't recover until April.

April 2, 4: Two more clarinet evenings (Trio and Quintet) in London for Joachim and Muhlfeld, Fanny Davies at the piano.

Early April: Electric lights installed in Brahms's flat by the Fellingers over his protestations.

May 8: Clara and Eugenie meet in Locarno.

May 21: Brahms goes to Ischl for the summer.

June: Clara recuperates in Interlaken attended by Marie.

June 11: Death of Elise, Brahms's sister, in Hamburg, Brahms at her side. Brahms composes intermezzos and cappricios for the piano, seeing Elisabet's piano pieces for the first time.

September 4: Eugenie, who had not been with Clara and Marie in Interlaken, finally joins them.

September 13: Brahms's mea culpa to Clara: "Please allow a poor pariah to tell you today that he always thinks of you with the same respect, and out of the fullness of his heart wishes you, whom he holds dearer than anything else on earth, all that is good, desirable, and beautiful."

September 27: Clara responds conciliatorily and they make up, after which he becomes sweeter to her than ever, sending her his new short piano pieces as he writes them, singers to perform his new songs for her, even Muhlfeld to perform the new clarinet pieces.

October: Eugenie leaves to settle permanently in England to teach music.

October 3: Brahms, as Simrock's guest in Berlin, assists at the opening of the new Bechstein Hall.

October 4: Bulow performs at the new Bechstein Hall.

October 5: Brahms and Joachim perform the D minor Violin Sonata at the new Bechstein Hall; the B flat Sextet and Clarinet Quintet are also performed.

November: The first ten piano pieces, opuses 116/117, are published by Simrock.

1893

The complete edition of Robert's works, begun in 1881, is published, Clara as editor.

January: Brahms visits Widmann in Meiningen where they stage Widmann's dramatic parody of Nietzsche's *Beyond Good and Evil*, also a performance of the Clarinet Quintet.

January 23: Clara on the state of music: "I hardly ever go to concerts now as orchestral music has become more than I can bear, and I hear everything wrong. But with the present tendency and the manner in which our present conductors study classical works with all the tricks – tremendous fortissimos and pianissimos and ritardandos, etc. – it is almost fortunate that I cannot hear anything, otherwise I should be forced out of politeness occasionally to listen to performances of this kind."

January 31: Brahms visits Clara in Frankfurt. She's nervous, but it goes well for them both.

February: Brahms visits Hamburg to settle his sister's estate.

February 26: Death of Hermine Spiess (Wiesbaden).

March 16: Clara hears a rehearsal of the Brahms Clarinet Quintet.

April 15-May 10: Brahms escapes to Italy in time to avoid celebrations for his 60th, setting off for Genoa with Robert Freund (pianist), Friedrich Hegar of Zurich, and Widmann to embark on a ship for Naples, but arriving on April 16 they find the only ship available is Hungarian and Brahms persuades everyone to take the train. They visit Hanslick in Sorrento, spending an afternoon in his orange grove drinking Chianti and watching dolphins play in the Bay of Naples below. Brahms is finally persuaded to board a steamer for Sicily. Widmann breaks his foot when it catches in an iron ring. Brahms spends his 60th birthday by his bedside, sending Hegar and Freund off to the ruins of Pompeii. Seeing Widmann off to Berne, Brahms returns with Freund and Hegar, stopping at Rome and Venice. Visited Genoa, Palermo, Catnia, Syracuse, Taormina, Messina, and Naples before returning to Vienna. On the way he loses his purse containing all his traveling expenses, but remains unperturbed knowing Simrock can send him a few thousand florins.

May: Brahms sends Clara a piano piece, possibly 118/6, "full of delightful discords," which gives her great pleasure.

May 7: His 60th is celebrated in Vienna in his absence, the Gesellschaft der Musikfreunde striking a gold medal (by Anton Scharff) in commemoration of the event.

May 10: Brahms returns to Vienna from Italy.

May 18: Brahms summers in Ischl (easy strolls, dinners at the Empress Elizabeth Hotel, coffee at Walter's), composes more intermezzos/cappricios to be published as opuses 118/119, and begins annotating the folksongs he has collected throughout his life, the first set ready for publication by the end of the year.

June: Brahms sends a cast of the Scharff medal to his stepmother, asking if she needs money.

September 2: Clara from Interlaken writes to Brahms to thank him for the pieces he continually sends: "It is wonderful how he combines passion and tenderness in the smallest of spaces."

October 19: Clara: "I play some of Brahms's new works everyday. How grateful I am to him for the comfort which he gives me in the midst of my sorrow!"

November 3: Clara goes to the Museum to hear Brahms's Symphony in D, but hears nothing except one forte, everything sounds wrong, and the soft parts are inaudible.

November 6: Death of Tchaikovsky (St. Petersburg).

December: Brahms's last collection of folksongs is issued.

December 6: *Genoveva* is performed in London, rehearsals attended by Eugenie.

December 21: Alice Barbi's farewell concert (marries), Brahms unexpectedly accompanies her on the piano.

December 27: Death of Clementine Wieck.

1894

January 17: Joachim visits Clara, they run through Brahms's D minor Sonata in which she revels. Joachim's quartet also plays her Robert's Quartet in F major.

February: Grieg sends Clara an article he has written for an American review in a letter. She can see he's sincere, but she's vexed by the article which says (among other things) that only Robert's opuses from 1-50 should be considered after which his strength was broken.

February 6: Death of Billroth (Abbazia).

February 12: Death of Bulow (Cairo). Brahms sends a wreath and honors his memory with a thousand marks each to pension funds of two orchestras associated with Bulow. He is incensed when the gifts become public, "Now I look like any vulgar benefactor," but his instructions to Simrock had been unclear.

March 20: Brahms hears his *Requiem* conducted for the last time by Wilhelm Gericke in Vienna.

March 24-April 3: Clara and Marie visit Frau Bendemann and Fraulein Leser in Dusseldorf.

April: The Hamburg Philharmonic finally offers Brahms the directorship, but too late.

April 21: Eugenie visits Clara and Marie in Frankfurt.

April 28: Brahms writes to Simrock that the seven books of folksongs are ready for publication, 49 songs, seven books of seven songs each (the last for solo and small chorus).

April 23: Henschel (visiting Vienna with his wife) finds Brahms joking with young contraltos in a lokale, finds him next morning content in his apartment.

April 24: Henschel and his wife visit Brahms in his flat where he meets them dressed almost too casually as was his habit and reads to them Wagner's Putzmacherin letters (to his milliner with elaborate specifications regarding tailoring).

July: Brahms composes the clarinet sonatas in Ischl, specifies they might also be played with the violin or viola, also completes the seven books of seven folksongs each, finishing with "The Moon Steals Up" which had provided the theme for the set of variations in his Sonata in C (his very first opus), writing to Clara that it represents the snake biting its own tail (the circle is complete).

July: Clara and Marie visit Basel.

July 29-September 27: Clara and Marie in Interlaken before returning to Frankfurt. Clara writes to Rosalie Leser that she has been receiving ever-increasing royalties from Paris for Robert's works, beginning with 300-400 francs to 1,000 francs, and in 1894 1,500 francs ... "in spite of Wagner, Berlioz, Liszt, etc."

September 17: In a letter to Simrock, Brahms talks about putting together several piano pieces to make a larger rhapsody of sorts for the orchestra.

September 19: Brahms meets Muhlfield in Berchtesgaden as the guest of Princess Marie of Meiningen, the Duke and his consort coming from Bad Gastein to hear the music.

September 25: Brahms returns to Vienna.

October 12-29: Brahms attends the Golden Jubilee celebrations for Johann Strauss's first public appearance.

November 9: Brahms meets Joachim at Clara's house in Frankfurt. Directors of the Museum-Gesellschaft hear of Brahms's arrival and change their program to the *Tragic, Haydn Variations,* Violin Concerto, and C minor Symphony. Brahms is seated by Clara's side, Joachim on the platform (the last occasion the three are together). Joachim drags Brahms onstage to acknowledge the applause.

[*Chapter 81: Comfort and Joy*]

November 10: Muhlfield arrives in Frankfurt from Meiningen so Clara can hear the Clarinet Sonatas which had been Brahms's rationale for coming to Frankfurt.

November 11: Joachim performs in the B flat Quartet.

November 12: Stockhausen joins Clara, Joachim, Brahms, and Muhlfield. Brahms and Muhlfeld play the two sonatas at a party given by the Sommerhoffs. Clara, Joachim, and Mulhfeld play Mozart's Clarinet Trio.

November 13: Brahms and Mulhfeld perform the sonatas for the third time in Frankfurt at a music party in Clara's house. Clara and Mulhfeld also play Schumann's *Fantasiestucke for Piano and Clarinet.*

November 14: Brahms leaves Frankfurt.

November 21: Brahms returns to Vienna after a sojourn with Muhlfeld in Meiningen including walks through the woods accompanied by pheasants and deer.

December 9: Brahms enjoys Dvorak's *Carnival Overture* by the Vienna Philharmonic.

Christmas: The first year of a tradition: never leaving Karlsgasse until he's witnessed the lighting of the Christmas-tree candles at Frau Truxa's.

1895

January 7: The two Clarinet Sonatas are performed by Brahms and Muhlfield at the Tonkunstler Verein (Vienna).

January 8: Brahms and Muhlfield play the E flat Clarinet Sonata at Rose's Quartet Concerts of Vienna.

January 11: Brahms and Muhlfield play the F minor Clarinet Sonata at Rose's Quartet Concerts of Vienna. The G major String Quintet is also performed.

January 11: Clara attends Moliere's *Malade Imaginaire,* but cannot laugh thinking of Eugenie leaving Frankfurt again for London the next day.

January 20: The F major Symphony conducted by Richter in Vienna is attended by Brahms.

January 24: Both Clarinet Sonatas are performed at one of Joachim's Quartet Concerts in Berlin.

January 27: Brahms and Muhlfield play the clarinet sonatas in Leipzig. The G major String Quintet is also performed.

January 31: d'Albert performs both piano concertos at the Gewandhaus, Brahms conducting there for the last time, the D minor is enthusiastically received as he had predicted since its failure in 1859. Still, in Leipzig, hearing a young American girl perform ragtime on a banjo he remarks he knows now where Dvorak got his American tunes from, adding that he thought he might use the interesting rhythms of ragtime, but didn't know if he would ever get around to it because the ideas didn't flow as easily anymore.

February 8: Clara receives a letter from Brahms asking if they might rehearse the Clarinet Quintet for Mannheim at her place. She's happy to oblige.

February 13: Brahms arrives in Frankfurt, flush with his Leipzig success.

February 14: Brahms produces the Clarinet Quintet in Mannheim.

February 15: Brahms produces the clarinet sonatas in Frankfurt.

February 17: Brahms plays the piano for the G minor Piano Quartet at the Museum and conducts his D major Symphony and *Academic Overture*, Clara in attendance. It proves Brahms's last public appearance in the city.

February 18: Brahms visits the Beckeraths in Rudesheim.

February 19: Brahms returns to Frankfurt to be with Clara.

February 20: Brahms goes to Meiningen for more celebrations in his honor, also a performance of *Fidelio* which he enjoys well enough to attend all three performances.

February 21: The clarinet sonatas in Merseberg (Brahms and Muhlfeld).

February 25: The clarinet sonatas again in Meiningen after which Muhlfeld leaves for tours of Switzerland, the Netherlands, and England. Brahms gives him the original autographs.

March 18: Brahms conducts the *Academic Festival Overture* at the Jubilee concert of the Gesellschaft der Musikfreunde Conservatoire. It is the last time he conducts in Vienna.

April 2: The Berlin Philharmonic gives the first of three concerts in Vienna, Richard Strauss conducts Beethoven's Symphony in A major.

April 4: Felix Weingartner conducts the Berlin Philharmonic in Brahms's Symphony in D major.

April 6: Felix Mottl conducts the Berlin Philharmonic in the *Eroica*.

Mid-May: Brahms goes to Ischl.

June: Clara and Marie visit Dusseldorf, staying with Frau Bendemann, seeing Rosalie Leser for the last time.

June 24: Both clarinet sonatas are performed in London by Fanny Davies and Muhlfield (who was specifically called from Meiningen for the performance).

Summer: Brahms in Ischl and Gmunden.

August 4: Death of Frau Bendemann (Dusseldorf), Clara is in Interlaken.

September 11: Hanslick's 70th birthday, hosted by Viktor von Miller zu Aichholz at Gmunden, large circle of friends, the Waltzes performed while the party's at table.

September 13: Clara's 76th, receives "masses of letters."

September 27-29: Festival in Meiningen which takes Bulow's 3 B's of music as its theme, Bach's St. Matthew, Beethoven's *Missa Solemnis*, Brahms's C minor Symphony (also the B flat Concerto, E minor Symphony, *Triumphlied*, clarinet sonatas, and some vocal quartets), Fritz Steinbach at the podium, d'Albert and Muhlfield among the performers.

September 27-29: Brahms hears several of his works performed by d'Albert and Muhlfeld in Meiningen as well as choral and instrumental compositions, Steinbach at the podium.

September 28: Clara and Marie leave Basel returning home to Frankfurt.

October 3: Brahms visits Frankfurt, performs for the last time for Clara, frail and ill, the last time the friends meet. The last recorded dialogue between Clara and Brahms. Clara: What are you going to do with all that tobacco? Brahms: Smuggle it.

October 4: Brahms returns to Vienna.

October 15: Brahms stays with Hegar in Zurich for a festival celebrating the opening of the new concert hall.

October 19-22: Brahms conducts the *Triumphlied* at the Zurich Festival as a prelude to Hegar conducting Beethoven's Ninth. The F minor Quintet is also performed by the Joachim Quartet and Freund. Brahms sees his portrait painted on the ceiling of the concert hall alongside Beethoven and Mozart among others. It is his last visit to Switzerland, the last time he sees Widmann.

November 6-7: Clara gives lessons in Marie's place, but she's unwell herself.

November 15: Joachim performs at the Museum and visits Clara.

November 25: Joachim passes through again. Clara's too unwell to play, but they have a cosy chat before he heads for Berlin.

December 7: Marie's better.

December: Dvorak visits Brahms in Vienna. The two are together almost constantly.

December 16: Brahms writes to Simrock that Dvorak's visit was a great joy.

1896

January: Henschel dines with Brahms and Grieg, finds Brahms in the "merriest of moods," consuming an "astounding quantity of Munich beer."

January 10: Brahms conducts the *Academic Festival Overture* and both piano concertos (with d'Albert) in Berlin, the last time Brahms conducts, 43 years since his first appearance as a professional musician with Remenyi. During the following celebration, Brahms interrupts Joachim's toast with "Ganz recht; auf Mozart's Wohl" (Quite right; here's Mozart's health).

January 12: Bruckner attends his last concert, a performance of his *Te Deum* suggested by Brahms.

January 23: Clara plays for the first time that winter, too unwell before.

February 16: At the Viennese premiere of Dvorak's *New World Symphony*, Dvorak and Brahms sit next to each other.

March: Grieg visits Brahms in Vienna and invites him to Norway whose mountains will inspire his Fifth Symphony, but Brahms prefers Italy. He suggests another Italian trip to Widmann, but Widmann's too sick.

March 19: Dvorak's Cello Concerto is premiered in London.

March 26: Clara suffers a stroke.

March 28: Clara wishes to write her name under a picture, picks up a pen, begins with the wrong letter, looks at Marie, shakes her head, puts down the pen.

March 30: Clara feels so much better that they begin to make plans for the summer to be in Baden-Baden.

Late March: Simrock is allowed to publish the clarinet sonatas which Brahms had held for Muhlfeld's monopoly until then.

April 3: Clara takes another turn for the better which lasts five weeks (but for one short interval).

April: Brahms receives a legacy of 1,000 pounds from Mr. Alfred Behrens of London of which he donates half to the Gesellschaft der Musikfreunde.

May 1-7: Brahms composes *Four Serious Songs*.

May 7: Brahms receives numerous calls from friends for his 63rd birthday, including inarticulate lines from Clara (semi-paralyzed), shows Kalbeck the *Four Serious Songs*.

May 8: Clara comes downstairs for the first time in a while, visits their garden with Marie.

May 9: Ferdinand (her grandson, now staying with them) plays for her Schumann's Intermezzos and Romance in F sharp, the last music she hears.

May 10: Clara suffers a second stroke, but Brahms is not informed, Marie afraid his presence might do more harm than good.

May 14: Brahms leaves for Ischl, convinced Clara's on the mend, hearing she had planned to be in Baden-Baden for the summer.

May 17: Eugenie arrives from London.

May 18: Death of Rosalie Leser (Dusseldorf).

May 20 (Wednesday afternoon, 4:21p): Death of Clara. Brahms sets forth immediately from Ischl, but owing to a series of misunderstandings arrives exhausted in Bonn almost three days later, barely in time to toss clods of earth onto her coffin as it's lowered into the grave next to Robert.

May 23: Members of the musical and artistic circles in Frankfurt bid a last farewell at Myliusstrasse 32, friends arrive from Berlin (including Joachim, Herzogenberg, Mendelssohn). Stockhausen's choir sings "Wenn ich einmal soll scheiden" (When the time has come for me to go), and the ceremony concludes with the funeral chorus from the *Peri*.

May 24: Clara's buried. Brahms accompanies Rudolf von der Leyen to spend a few days at Leyen's relative's house across the Rhine at Honnef. Much music in honor of Clara during which many of the party leave the room overcome by remembrance. The *Four Serious Songs* are performed.

[*Chapter 82: Ecclesiastes*]

Summer: Brahms composes the eleven Choral Preludes, his final opus.

June: Muhlfeld plays the clarinet sonatas at St. James's Hall with Fanny Davies in London.

June 15: Brahms visits Vienna for the Fellingers' silver wedding anniversary and returns immediately to Ischl to pick up his habitual way of life, but Clara's death and his feverish subsequent activity have taken their toll. He's sallow, losing weight, continually exhausted.

June 24: Brahms plays seven of the Choral Preludes for Richard Heuberger (composer, organist at Ischl, once a student of Brahms), who suggests that he see a doctor.

July: Dr. Hertzka of Ischl diagnoses jaundice, advises using Karlsbad salts, also a second opinion from Professor Schrotter.

August 31: Brahms returns to Vienna.

September 3: Brahms leaves for Karlsbad itself when the Karlsbad salts fail, accompanied by Fellinger, but though Professor Schrotter reassures Brahms he has observed a swelling of the liver and complete blockage of the gall-ducts.

September 13: Professor Engelmann visits from Utrecht as do many of his friends.

October 2: Brahms returns to Vienna in a heated compartment (especially maintained by the railway for his benefit). Cancer of the liver is confirmed on his return to Vienna, the same disease that had killed his father.

October 11: Death of Bruckner (Vienna).

Late October: Brahms is considerably weaker, his clothes loosely flapping, his pallor turning yellow.

November 9: Brahms hears a concert of the *Four Serious Songs*.

November: Hausmann visits, they play through Dvorak's Cello Concerto. Grieg arrives in Vienna with his wife to partake in concerts of his own works of which Brahms attends at least one, following with a late supper with the Griegs.

Early December: The Joachim Quartet visits Vienna with whom Brahms spends as much time as he can, convincing Joachim he's on the mend.

December 24-27: Invites himself to dine with the Fellingers every night.

1897

January 1: The Joachim Quartet performs in Vienna attended by Brahms.

January 2: The Joachim Quartet performs the G major String Quintet in Vienna. Brahms attends not only the performance but also the rehearsal in Joachim's hotel rooms.

January 17: Brahms is given an ovation when he appears, sunken and emaciated, in his box at a Gesellschaft concert.

February 7: Brahms lunches with the Fellingers, asks for time with them alone after the meal to say he wishes to make a new will, but hated to think of the formalities required. They work together from two to six, the Fellingers discussing his affairs in minute detail, Dr. Fellinger to be his curator.

February 8: Fellinger brings the copy of the will to Brahms the next morning to his rooms saying he will need to write it out himself, date it, sign his name, and it will be valid according to Austrian law. Brahms, about to leave for dinner, places the paper in a drawer of his writing table, and forgets all about it, relieved as he is to think everything is as he wishes. Brahms says nothing about the subject again, and neither do the Fellingers imagining the matter has been settled.

February 13: Kalbeck hears Brahms playing the piano.

February 18: Brahms suffers a slight stroke, paralyzing the left side of his face, but recovers by early March.

March 7: Dvorak's Cello Concerto precedes Brahms's E minor Symphony conducted by Richter at the Vienna Philharmonic Society, Brahms in attendance, standing for ovations after every movement.

March: Brahms writes to his Ischl landlady saying he will be arriving earlier than usual so his rooms might be ready for him. The last opera he attends is Goldmark's *The Cricket on the Hearth*.

March 13: Brahms's last public appearance is at Strauss's *The Goddess of Reason*, but he leaves midway.

March: Tries to read Busch's book on Bismarck, but cannot remember what he reads.

Dr. Viktor von Miller zu Aichholz calls everyday in his carriage to take Brahms for a drive in the Prater.

Brahms attends the rehearsal of Weber's Clarinet Quintet which he had requested earlier.

Brahms pays the Fabers a visit, but faints ascending the staircase.

March 19: Brahms calls on the Fellingers (Maria was ill).

Brahms plays the piano for a half hour every evening, sitting by the window when he's too tired to continue.

March 24: Brahms writes to Joachim that every word, spoken or written, is a strain.

March 25: Conrat visits for a quiet talk, but Brahms, sitting on the sofa smoking, drops his head saying "There must be something in it" and falls asleep.

March 26: Brahms retires to bed to rest a little, never again to rise, after which he visits the Millers for his last lunch outside his home.

March 29: Brahms scribbles a few words to his stepmother, dictates to Frau Truxa a note of thanks to Herzogenberg for a dedication.

April 2: Frau Truxa brings him a glass of the Duke of Meiningen's wine.

April 3 (8:30 in the morning): Death of Brahms.

April 6: The funeral. Many, including Dvorak, Alice Barbi, and Henschel, accompany the hearse drawn by six horses and footmen in ancient Spanish dress preceding six cars laden with flowers from friends and admirers. Dvorak is among the pallbearers. "Fahr Wohl" is sung, and Brahms buried next to Beethoven and Schubert.

> [*Chapter 83: hep. hyp. m.*]

The Duke of Meiningen erects a memorial in the "English Garden" of the Residenz containing a portrait bust of Brahms by Professor Adolf Hildebrand.

1899
January 9: Death of Ludwig Schumann (Colditz).

1900
October 9: Death of Herzogenberg (Wiesbaden).

1901
January 27: Death of Verdi (Milan).

1902
Spring: Death of Frau Karoline Brahms.

1903
May 7: 70ᵗʰ birthday, a memorial is unveiled at the Central Cemetery where Brahms is buried, designed by Ilse Conrat.

1907
August 15: Death of Joachim (Berlin).

1908
A monument is erected in the Ressel Park, Karlsplatz, near Karlsgasse, sculpted by Rudolf Weyr, full-length, seated, with Muses at his feet.
November 20: Death of Dietrich (Berlin).

1909
May 7: Max Klinger's monument is unveiled at Hamburg, close to the "Neue Musik-Halle."
A bust by Marie Fellinger is placed in the garden where Brahms worked in Murzzuschlag, now to be found in the pavilion used by the band since the garden was purchased by the municipality.
A small bust of Brahms is commissioned in Pressbaum, several other such memorials are scattered around.
Victor von Miller zu Aichholz conceives the "Brahms House" at Gmunden containing a replica of the suite of rooms occupied by the composer at Ischl, together with a valuable collection of manuscripts, prints, portraits, and other souvenirs.

1916
November 2: Death of Marie Wieck (Clara's half-sister).

1928
July 1: Death of Elise Schumann.

1929
November 14: Death of Marie Schumann (Interlaken).

1930
April 1: Death of Cosima Wagner (Bayreuth).

1938
September 25: Death of Eugenie Schumann (Matten).

1948
September 4: Death of Alice Barbi (Rome).

1949
September 8: Death of Richard Strauss (Garmisch-Partenkirchen, Germany).

ABOUT THE AUTHOR

Boman Desai was born and raised in Bombay (now Mumbai), but has lived his adult life in Chicago. After studying Architecture and Philosophy, and getting degrees in Psychology and English, he was set to become a market analyst when a chance encounter with Sir Edmund Hillary, his earliest hero, brought him back to his vocation: writing novels. He took a number of parttime jobs ranging from bartending to auditing to teaching to find time to write. He got his first break when an elegant elderly woman personally submitted a number of his stories to the editor-in-chief of *Debonair* magazine in Bombay. The stories were all published, but the woman disappeared and her identity remains a mystery to this day. He has published fiction and non in the US, UK, and India. His work has won awards from the Illinois Arts Council, Stand Magazine, Dana, Noemi, War Poems, and New Millennium (among others). He has taught fiction at Truman College, Roosevelt University, and the University of Southern Maine. He is an amateur musician and may be reached at boman@core.com.

Printed in the United States
By Bookmasters